HABITUS

James Flint

FOURTH ESTATE · *London*

First published in Great Britain in 1998 by
Fourth Estate Limited
6 Salem Road
London W2 4BU

Copyright © 1998 James Flint

1 3 5 7 9 10 8 6 4 2

The right of James Flint to be identified as the author of this
work has been asserted by him in accordance with the Copyright,
Designs and Patents Act 1988.

A catalogue record for this book is available from the
British Library.

ISBN 1-85702-824-4 (hardback)
ISBN 1-85702-868-6 (paperback original)

The first two part-title illustrations are reproduced from
The Arrow of Time by Peter Coveney and Roger Highfield,
published by WH Allen.
The third part-title illustration is reproduced from *Chaos* by James
Gleick, published by William Heinemann Ltd.

Typeset by Rowland Phototypesetting Limited,
Bury St Edmunds, Suffolk
Printed in Great Britain by Clays Ltd, St Ives plc

To Elaine

In essence, habit is contraction. . . . What we call wheat is a contraction of the earth and humidity, and this contraction is both a contemplation and the auto-satisfaction of that contemplation. By its existence alone, the lily of the field sings the glory of the heavens, the goddesses and gods that it contemplates in contracting. What organism is not made of elements and cases of repetition, of contemplated and contracted water, nitrogen, carbon, chlorides and sulphates, thereby intertwining all the habits of which it is composed? . . . We are made of contracted water, earth, light and air. . . . An animal forms an eye for itself by causing scattered and diffuse luminous excitations to be reproduced on a privileged surface of its body. The eye binds light, it is itself a bound light. . . . This binding is a reproductive synthesis, a Habitus.

Gilles Deleuze, *Difference & Repetition*

CONTENTS

PREAMBLE

0 0 1

0 1 1

PREAMBLE

Alfalfa & O Mother!

30 January 1950, North-west of Montreal, Canada

The ringdingding and the rend. It all starts somewhere in the middle, just below the glans, where the life-blood quivers then withdraws then courses again through the corpus spongiosum of young Joel's tiny manhood as the cold fingers of the mohel firmly grip it in the mechanism of their arthritic knots and folds. The amulet of Adam Ba'al Shem Tov, man of good repute, Master of the Name, flickers in the menorah light and fills the boy's dark and massive eye. Moshe Kluge, proud father, places his hand upon the forehead of his son and holds him steady. The mohel gathers the tiny prepuce between the hard old whorls and ulnar loops of his desiccated pads, then with the other hand brings the scalpel down and quickly round. It's a fluid movement, the movement of a piston joint, of a matador who ducks the prize bull's curling horns and weaves quickly up behind the head, slices down with steel, steps nimbly to one side so the blood shan't stain his silky pants.

The circumcision complete, Moshe breathes out. Joel trembles with the throb between his thighs and begins to wail for his mother, who is not there. The purse of flesh is already dealt with, disappeared – the snake has shed its skin. The Ba'al Shem gathers the blood in a small china bowl and swabs the wound, whispering to himself Joel's other name, Balaam. There is urgency in his voice; Moshe pats his pockets.

'Master . . .' he begins, his voice soft with the rising doughs of the years spent in his bakery. But transfixed by the name, the mohel is already staring into space. Moshe clears his throat, repeats: 'Master?'

Outside it's January. Montreal is away there to the south. The winds come off the Cabonga Reservoir, its surface a massive sheet of six-inch ice, cracked and fissured into giant hieroglyphs. The Ba'al Shem is above it, he is below it; the cries of the boy have triggered something – a state change, a reconfiguration – and the mohel is no longer in the room. He is where the moon shines through the ribbon patterns of the ice and lays a silver meniscus across the chilled and silent depths. Away to the north, squalls storm their way across the Hudson Bay, the cabin fevers of the minor gods. His eyes shine with cataracts of frozen water, the fissures and patterns slowly glisten brighter. Slowly they turn from crystal to blue to a thin sodium fire which travels and webs across the surfaces before him. The mohel is an initiate, one who has studied the writings of Eleazar of Worms and Isaac the Blind, one who can decipher the alphabet of Metatron.

Now he is back in the room and gazing at the boy, who is bathed in a palpitating iridescent glow. The hieroglyphs from the fractal cracks of the ice splinter the haunting light above Joel's head. Adam sucks in air and begins to enunciate the letters of the Tetragrammaton as they unveil themselves before him. The words twist out into the candlelight like strands of bronchial sputum and Moshe falls to his knees at the strange and guttural sounds. The child no longer cries but looks on with soft, unblinking eyes, calculating distances and counting syllables. The figures disappear and the voice stops; now the mohel sees a room, faded plaster-work, metal that breathes and buzzes, metal that thinks, the child grown, the child gone, a nose, a woman. Then nothing. The moon, the lake, the ice, the room . . . all gone. The dark-brown walls of his house close in, he breathes and gibbers for a moment. Looking down, he spies Moshe, grabs the man's hands and pulls him to his feet. He pulls him so close that Moshe can hear the Ba'al Shem's breath congealing on his teeth.

There is silence for a moment, then he begins to talk: 'This is not a dream. This is not a dream. Do you understand? There is no dream here. There is no sleep here.' There is a pause. Moshe nods nervously, not knowing what else to do. The mohel has gone further than he has ever gone before. 'Everything flows through this space. It belongs neither to me nor to the night. Everything flows through. You do not know this space, Moshe Kluge. Your child is dead and dead again. The air is of hot streets. The wasps blow to and fro. Time will work itself out. It grows and evolves, like a yeast, or a mould. It feeds. There are three kinds of time to make this possible.'

'Yes, Master, three kinds. M-Most interesting.' Moshe tries to remove the man's hands from his lapels but the mohel's grip is remorseless. He trembles to think of his son's penis in the thrall of these manipulators.

The mohel draws him closer. 'Repeat: *zimzum, shevirah, tikkun. Zimzum, shevirah, tikkun.* Repeat it!'

Terrified now, Moshe says the words, his voice barely quavering up from his throat. 'Zimzum, shevirah, tikkun.' He has heard them before, they are part of Kabbalistic doctrine, but as to what they mean he has no idea. He is just a baker and a dabbler, and cannot be expected to know of such things. Perhaps, then, this is an important lesson. He repeats the words again, more slowly and more seriously now, swallowing his fear and finishing with: 'The three kinds of time. Yes.'

'Zimzum, shevirah, tikkun,' mutters the mohel one last time and lets go of Moshe's lapels.

Immediately the baker turns to Joel – who is screaming in his crib, desperate for attention, still flushed with throbbing pain from the unexpected amputation – intending to gather up the boy and make good his exit. But with a roar that seems to shake the very foundations of the house the mohel spins the baker back to face him and seizes him in a bear hug. 'Do you not understand?' he spits from lip to lip, the words bubbling up from deep in the flux of his visions. 'Do you not understand that your son is only a third, only a third of something that will be larger than us all? It's coming. The lizards know it, they watch it with their cold eyes and taste it with tongues that dash faster than the angels. The three-in-one draws near. Look to the river! Look! Look! Look to the river, oh, how it lies! Which is your son, which one is he? He knows, he knows, look in his eyes and you know that he knows.' The mohel directs a look at Joel so piercing it makes the infant redouble his bawling. 'Yes, Balaam, you! Which one are you?'

Frightened for his son, Moshe acts at last, shoves the mohel in the chest. At the instant of contact the man goes limp and crashes to the floor, knocking over an iron scuttle as he falls. Black coals roll across the hearth and particles of coal dust are sucked up the chimney by the roaring wind. The fire cackles grimly and tries to send up flames in pursuit. Joel falls silent and Moshe strains his ears in case there should be voices on the wind. When he is sure that there are none he turns his attention to the fire, searching for faces in its dance. But there is only the turquoise flicker of the flame. Joel begins to whimper once again and Moshe takes him in his arms and holds him for a while, then attends to the Ba'al Shem, who is still stretched out on the hearth. His breathing is weak; Moshe squats down behind him and putting his hands beneath his armpits drags him up into a chair. He fetches a glass, fills it with water from a metal jug and holds it to the man's lips. The liquid tumbles down his chin and drums upon the starched fabric of his shirt, but some of it must have found its way inside for the mohel coughs and turns away into the wing of the chair, pulling his feet up into a foetal position. Then he falls asleep.

Keen to make good his exit, Moshe scoops the coals back into the scuttle, drops a couple into the grate to replenish the fire and leaves a sum of money on the sideboard. Then he carefully swaddles Joel against the cold and holding him firmly to his chest steps out into the street. Outside the wind is blowing terrific flurries of snow that stencil in the air the vortices virtual in the geometry of the rude buildings. It is hardly even a hamlet, this settlement: the mohel's dwelling makes three in all and there are two wooden barns besides. Moshe turns up his collar, pulls down his hat and sets out against the night. The lantern swings freely in his hand, its feeble light guttering continually. He makes his way along the track that leads back to his uncle's farm, some two miles distant, where his wife lies sick but still awake, worrying for the safety of her child. Out in the open, Moshe struggles against the unchecked wind. He is bracketed by fields: all around him, under their mantle of snow, the seed oceans of alfalfa groan creak swell with the rhythms of sleep.

Far away to the south, in Washington DC, President Truman announces his decision to go ahead with the hydrogen bomb development program. That month's issue of *Time* magazine carries on its cover a picture of something most people have never seen before: a computer. Dressed up in a jaunty sailor's cap.

May 1973, Somewhere near Stratford-upon-Avon, England
A brittle plastic twelve-inch ruler, sheared off at the baseline, just at the point where the inch scale should say 'o'. Half of the number is still visible, like a weak 'c', or half an egg, or a shallow cup. Judd reaches into his satchel and fetches out the ruler. Through the window comes the soft rattle of the tractor-mower passing to and fro, ruling the playing fields like a page. Grass clippings and daisy heads fly up behind the machine in a patterned spray damp with the scent of clover and dog turd. Inside in the classroom the rows of boys transform the teacher's words into inky lines, little farmers cultivating blank white plots.

Judd is not writing. He is listening to the drone of the tractor, his favourite sound in all England. The fresh-cut fields with their mulch musk hovering on the limp air bring him something new. In Los Angeles cut grass is dry and harsh: there, lawn-mowers throw up wafting rinds

4

of dust which are tacky on the back of the throat. This is the only thing which is bad about home, the only thing. Everything else is better there.

The pitch of the sound changes as the mower head is disengaged and lifted; the tractor has reached one end of the fields and is turning to retrace the shallow path it has cut. The rattling fills the air like the hollow gasps of a sick dog. The blades descend and their cough is damped by the green expectorant of the grass. His hands hidden by his desk, Judd works at the manufacture of a small projectile.

Doreen Buerk, geography teacher and Tory wife, turns her back on the class for the briefest of instants in order to draw an oxbow lake on the blackboard. Back in America – land of dreams, of memories, of clipped blue sky and vapour trails – something is happening on Pad B, Launch Complex 39 of the Kennedy Space Center, Florida. The liquid oxygen in the F1 boosters has ignited and the Saturn V rocket carrying the first unmanned sections of the Skylab space station is lumbering into the air. As the gantry falls away and early morning desert ice showers magnificently from the three-million-kilo hulk, Judd's ruler twangs. Seconds later the Saturn V has sliced the sky's blue dome in two and Judd's projectile has arced across the great divide of several desks; this boy's amazing, quite a prodigy it seems; in World War Two they needed firing tables to do this stuff; hell, they even invented computers to help 'em work those tables out and here he is, this small black boy, doing it by feel and intuition. This boy's got soul.

But wait, hold fire, so to speak. An error has been made. The meteoroid shield has deployed inadvertently and been ripped off by atmospheric drag. Similarly, a stray fold of paper has come apart from Judd's pellet and the extra drag is pulling the projectile off target. Instead of connecting with the pearly pink epidermis of Jacob Hethlethwaite's neck the missile veers to the left, misses Jacob by millimetres and strikes instead the acne scars of Lewis, oldest boy in the class and hardest too.

Lewis gasps and squirms; at his outburst Doreen Buerk spins on one heel; with no compunction Lewis points: 'It was him, miss, he flicked summat at me!'

The Buerk stares at the small American down the length of her nose, fixing him like a doomed field-mouse with the ball-bearing pupils of her grim stoat eyes. For a few dark seconds she just lets the silence gather. It works: the class is in her thrall (for the first time that afternoon – violence appeals more than river action). Then the tension is released: 'That's it! Out! Out you go! I've told you and I've told you I won't put up with this kind of behaviour. You will be penalised after school. Outside the door! Go! Now! I'll deal with you after class. It may come as a surprise to you to learn that some of us . . .' (who, they all think, who could that be?) '. . . would like to continue the lesson without interruption.' Judd opens his mouth to protest. 'I don't want to hear it. Do you understand me? One more disobedience and you'll go to the Head. Now get out!'

Pouting slightly (and blushing too, though it's difficult for these white folks to tell) Judd slouches out between the rows of boys. They snigger as he passes and surreptitiously kick at him from under their tables with the scuffed toes of their battered black shoes.

12 August 1960, Hatton Central Hospital, England
Nadine Several lies screaming, arms and ankles strapped to a hastily adapted gynaecologist's chair. Her short, badly cropped hair is thick with sweat and her eyes claw wildly at the room. At intervals a nurse applies a damp flannel to the woman's forehead and wipes away the spittle that foams up from between her purple lips. But her main job is to keep Nadine from swallowing her tongue and she has a wooden spatula at the ready for just that purpose.

Down below, somewhere beneath the sodden hospital gown that rucks up around the patient's waist, a midwife waits patiently for a glimpse of the baby's head to appear from between the heaving thighs drenched in fluid. Slightly bored, she threads her fat fingers in and out of the handles of the birthing forceps she has with her. She's long ago lost any sense of either the beauty or the horror of this process, of this turmoil of the flesh. But what she most definitely hates is having to deliver babies in this Unit. It happens far too often; do they have no control over the patients here? It's disgusting, that's what it is. If she were running things they wouldn't come to such a pass and that's a fact. Look at this poor woman. Sweat pouring off her, lamb, she doesn't even know what's happening. How could they let them do this to her? Just goes to show that they're not like the rest of us, not at all, and you can't let them wander around on their own. It's just not on! They should be kept apart and under constant supervision. But these days you just can't get the staff.

Nadine was four months pregnant before someone noticed. When her periods ceased they just forgot to bring her sanitary towels and it wasn't till her belly was obvious that a houseman figured it out. He remembered the day because it was the same day Princess Margaret sent a command to the probe Pioneer V, which was then exactly one million miles from earth. The probe's response came back just twenty-five seconds later. It

6

was in all the papers. They tried to talk to Nadine about it, ask her who it was, but she just kept saying how she was growing, growing, how her tree had a new branch. She hadn't made sense for years; it was no surprise she couldn't manage to be coherent now.

Explaining the situation to her husband, Henry, was extremely difficult. He didn't take it well; in fact, he sued the hospital for negligence and notified the police (who didn't manage to find the culprit and who suspected, privately as it were, that Henry himself was responsible). As for Nadine, she seemed cheerier than ever. She wandered around the wards with a beatific smile slanted across her face, munching on the apples that Henry brought her. The only problems she seemed to have with the pregnancy was the jealous reactions her distended shape provoked among some of the other female patients.

Jennifer Several, our missing link, was born to Nadine on 12 August 1960, at the same moment that NASA's ECHO I successfully reflected a radio message from President Eisenhower down across a footprint that included most of the United States, thus demonstrating for the first time the feasibility of global satellite communications. Bizarrely, the view the midwife has of Jennifer's head emerging from Nadine's vagina (a small sliver of white in the darkness that grows quickly to a full white round) is not dissimilar to that she'd had, if she'd have been orbiting the earth, of ECHO I itself as its one hundred-foot diameter aluminised Mylar-plastic sphere rose up slowly from the shadow of the planet and caught the sun.

The birth of a new age? Perhaps. Or perhaps the continuation of an old one, for via her mitochondria – the tiny energy factories to be found in every one of her body's cells, the DNA for which is passed exclusively down the female line – Jennifer is linked to the eukaryotic cell from which all plants, fungi and animals are descended and, beyond this, to the prokaryotes, the bacteria and cyanobacteria, the earliest forms of life and after three billion years still the most dominant.

Ignoring the fact that he is not the natural father, unconcerned with the intricacies of Jennifer's cellular pedigree and blind to the issue of whether or not, as a man, he could ever be more than a mere adjunct to this spectacular lineage, Henry shouldered his responsibilities and took the child on as his own. He won his suit against the hospital, too, and placed the compensation money in trust. It wasn't much, but it was something.

3rd November 1957, Baikonur, Kazakstan

On the day of Joel's circumsicion (and the day of President Truman's announcement) Soviet troops rolled into a stretch of countryside which lies to the north of the town of Leninsk, which sits on the banks of the Syr Dar'ya river, which runs from the Kazakstan plain into the lowlands of the Caspian depression. They were there to break up any settlements in the area and relocate their stone-skinned occupants either to the collective farms in the north or, if any of them choose to argue, to oblivion. Some time later huge earth movers arrived by rail, constructivist visions realised in poor quality steel, and began to level a vast tract of land which over the next few years would slowly, as concrete scabbed its way across the countryside, become the Baikonur Kosmodrome. From here, on 4 October 1957, carried by an R7 ICBM test vehicle, the first man-made satellite would be launched into space.

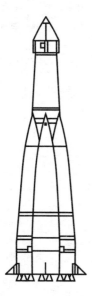

Launch Vehicle Characteristics – Sputnik 1
Family: R-7. Country: Russia. Status: Hardware.

Designations: Official: 8K71PS; OKB: R-7; Popular: Semyorka; US DoD: SL-1; US Library of Congress: A. Relatively unmodified R-7 ICBM test vehicles used to launch first two Sputniks.
Total Mass: 265,500 kg. Lift-off Thrust: 396,298 kgf. Core Diameter: 2.99 m. Total Length: 28.00 m. Total Cost: $33.00 million. Launches: 2. Failures: 0. Success Rate: 100 percent. First Launch: 10/4/57. Last Launch: 11/3/57.

● Stage 1 : 1 × Sputnik 1–1. Gross Mass: 93,500 kg. Empty Mass: 7,495 kg. Thrust (vac): 93,000 kgf. Isp: 308 sec. Burn time: 300 sec. Isp(sl): 241 sec. Diameter: 2.99 m. Span: 2.99 m. Length: 28.00 m. Propellants: Lox/Kerosene. No Engines: 4. Engine: RD-108 8D75PS. Pc: 53 bar. Used as: Sputnik 1–1. Other Designations: R-7; 8K71PS; SL-1.

● Stage 0 : 4 × Sputnik 1–0. Gross Mass: 43,000 kg. Empty Mass: 3,400 kg. Thrust (vac): 99,000 kgf. Isp: 306 sec. Burn time: 120 sec. Isp(sl): 250 sec. Diameter: 2.68 m. Span: 2.68 m. Length: 19.00 m. Propellants: Lox/Kerosene. No Engines: 4. Engine: RD-107 8D74PS. Pc: 60 bar. Used as: Sputnik 1–0. Other Designations: R-7; 8K71PS; SL-1.

Laika was born and bred at Baikonur. Not much of a home for a dog, she shared it with sixteen other pups of various breeds, some thoroughbred, some indeterminate. They lived in a compound behind the MIK assembly building in a collection of concrete kennels on stilts and their programme was supervised by one Pavel Renko. Renko was a jack of all trades, part rocket technician, part veterinarian, part dialectician, a veteran of the intellectual migrations set in motion throughout Stalin's United Soviet. It was a biography which had embittered. Originally from Murmansk, he resented his transfer to Baikonur on the grounds of the weather, convincing himself that he missed the endless Arctic winters and the sheer desolation of the Kola Peninsula.

In his training of the dogs he was somewhat over-enthusiastic, killing three and crippling two of those in his charge. But he got results and they were only dogs, so what did it matter? The important thing was that one of them should be ready for the launch. They needed to find out if it was possible to survive. They had started work on Vostok I and were already training Gagarin.

They chose Laika because of her name. Laika means 'barker' in Russia. She had yelped almost as soon as she'd slid out the womb, still hot from her mother and fragrant like freshly baked bread, and she'd expressed herself that way ever since. Renko's assistants, Alexei and Mickl, took a shine to her because of it; they had to exercise the dogs every day and the way Laika sat and cocked her head and woofed in response to anything they asked her made her seem that bit more intelligent, that little bit more human. And so they sent her into space, because she was more human, because it was an honour, because she'd be on postage stamps and she'd have streets and rock bands named after her.

As if any of that mattered to Laika. After all, she was only going to get seven days up there and then they'd pull the plug.

They trained her up, it took months, they trained others too, but they always knew it would be her. They got her used to the harness, shaved her, accustomed her to the electrodes, shaved her again. She was cold without her fur so they made her a coat, but it rubbed and so they trained her not to tear at it with her teeth. They taught her how to eat and how to shit. And what to do once she'd eaten and shat. They made her drink from a teat on the wall, it wasn't like lapping, certainly not. They taught her other stuff too, secrets, things we can't mention here for fear of the consequences, though the information is out there if you know where to look. It's most definitely out there. It is.

She didn't bark too much when, already sealed inside Sputnik II, they wheeled her out to the rocket. She sat there whimpering nervously, the acceleration harness making it impossible for her to move, her limp tail disturbed only by an occasional half-hearted wag, not sure whether to be excited or afraid. She licked at Mickl's fingers through the glass of the one small porthole and was confused by the sadness she saw in his eyes. And then she was in the air, hoisted aloft by a crane and lowered into position in the nose cone of the R-7. A group of jump-suited technicians had been waiting at the top of the gantry and now they went to work, attaching release bolts to the capsule and running several hours' worth of last-minute checks. Consoled by this human activity and no longer able to see that she was perched high above the ground, Laika calmed down a little, though not enough to doze as she generally liked to do of an afternoon.

And then the checks were complete and the nose cone was clipped shut, and suddenly it was all dark for the dog. The radio and monitor crackled awake: Renko's face flickered before her and his voice was there, too, though some way off to one side. He spoke a series of words into a microphone, not looking into the camera, just reeling them off, words to which she knew how to respond. She gave a bark at each one, as she'd been taught, and waited tensely for the yell or the biscuit, whichever would come. And then the earth cracked apart and she barked and she barked at the figure of Renko; there was nothing else for it, she had to, she had to bark, and louder and louder because she couldn't hear herself, no matter how hard she barked she could hear nothing at all and then she was pushed down, down, a huge thing pushing her down, it had never been like this, she had done what they'd asked, it was never like this.

The forces rippled her skin as easily as if it were oil. As she shot into space she thought of her mother, of her smell, a good smell it was. Later, she took up a low orbit at a height of 298 kilometres above sea level and swung round the earth like a star.

0 0 1

And, if we want to write history, we have to pull together at least three kinds of time: the reversible time of clocks and mechanics, all to do with cogs and levers; then the irreversible time of thermodynamics, born of fire; and finally the time of what is called 'negative entropy', which is what gives rise to singularities.

'History no longer flows in the way we once thought.'

'A small world history of work in three acts, three times, three figures or actors, three states of matter, and three words which are in fact only one, by Pia, the flying doctor!'

Michel Serres, Angels

1

Dance and contagion

We took a step forward, met Jennifer, Judd and Joel – now we must take a step back. Nadine Rachel Several, née Flowers, wife to Henry and mother to Jennifer, had been born an Aquarian in 1924. Nadine's father owned and ran a successful business manufacturing tyres, a line that had suddenly become extremely profitable during the Great War. Her mother had studied mathematics at university and had, in a small way, been a suffragette. Both her parents considered themselves 'free thinkers' – it was that which had brought them together. They read Lawrence, Fitzgerald, Mann, owned a gramophone on which they listened to ragtime and Stravinsky, travelled to cocaine orgies in the Home Counties and swilled cocktails in London clubs. Indeed, before Nadine was born her mother had had a full-time job as a typist, part of the flood of women taking skilled office jobs at that time. The office environment was changing: all those in-trays, oak desks and efficiency drives took on a different taint, one that thrilled with differences and obscurities. The office was becoming a sexual environment and things would never be the same again. Although she stopped working for two years to look after her daughter, as soon as she could, Nadine's mother returned to work, this time as a computer in Leslie Comrie's department at the Nautical Almanac Office where, part of a mathematical production line, a successful attempt to compartmentalise mental labour, she helped to produce astronomical tables.

Nadine's parents had always felt very strongly that their daughter should express herself in whichever way she saw fit. Nadine had no difficulty in following her whims and from a very early age she dreamt of being a dancer. Whenever her parents threw a dinner party she dressed herself in silks and leapt about the house soaking up applause from the guests. She was intoxicated with music and flow. She charted the career of Isadora Duncan quite obsessively and collected pamplets that summarised the teachings of Mary Wigmore and Rudolph Laban.

Duncan had made the new dance fashionable and removed much of the social stigma that was attached to the profession. Dance schools became popular and Nadine's parents enrolled her in one in Bloomsbury. When her father expressed his one reservation – that such a career might be too physical for his delicate and possibly intellectual child – his wife rebutted the objection by quoting at him something from William James. 'Muscular contraction appears to be closely related to the genesis of all forms of psychic activity,' wrote her favourite psychologist. 'Not only do the vaso-motor and muscular systems express the thinking, feeling and willing of the individual, but the muscular apparatus itself appears to be a fundamental part of the apparatus of these psychical states.' And so the matter was settled.

'Spin! Spin, girls, spin! And waft left, and waft right . . . and still, and up, and breathe, and down, and sti-i-ill and up, and bre-a-the and down. And relax. And breathe. Breathe Lydia, breathe. From here, from your di-a-phragm. You look like a rabbit that's about to choke, my dear. Fill your lungs slowly, from the bottom. That's it, that's better. Good Rose, good. Watch Rose, Lydia, see how she does it? All right everyone? Breathe. And relax. Now, take your seats.' The girls clattered to their desks like starlings to a telephone line and installed themselves facing Miss Bryant, who flexed herself against the rail of the blackboard while waiting for them to settle.

'Does anyone know what today is?' she finally asked.

Immediately Deirdre's hand shot up. Deirdre was always most keen to participate: before being enrolled at the dance academy she had briefly attended a very exclusive finishing school, one of the few which still used restraining devices to control the girls. Several of the teachers had demanded that the children wear leather silencers throughout their classes, a practice that Deirdre found particularly hateful. Freed from that regime, she now compensated by attempting to answer all questions that were put to the class. 'The King's birthday, miss.'

'No Deirdre, it is most definitely not the King's birthday.' Miss Bryant was a republican and had once conducted a tempestuous affair with a Bolshevik who had for a brief period worked as a waiter in a restaurant off the Charing Cross Road. She was grimly aware that the King had not one but two birthdays. And that neither of them fell on that particular day. No other hands went up. Happily, Miss Bryant began to answer the question herself. 'Well girls, exactly thirty years ago today an American named Wilbur Wright took off from the ground in his biplane, flew it around in a circle and landed again. Has anyone ever been up in an aeroplane?' This time a few arms made their way skywards. 'Does anyone know why this fact is important to us?'

'So that we could win the war against the Kaiser, miss,' offered Deirdre.

'Well, perhaps Deirdre, but it wasn't quite the answer I was looking for. No, the reason that this is important to those of us who are gathered here today . . .' Miss Bryant paused for effect, 'is because of all the tremendous impacts that this event has had upon our modern world it may well be true to say that it impacted harder upon the world of dance than on any other.' Again she paused, but this time the children stared back at her with blank faces. Undeterred, she blustered on through her little speech. 'Wilbur Wright, you see, had outdone the ballet! I know that sounds strange, but it's true in a way. Ballet dancers had always prided themselves on defying gravity. They were better at it than anyone else, and its one of the things that made the ballet so wonderful to watch. But with the arrival of the aeroplane a machine now did this much better. It could take off and land better than any ballerina, and it could *circle around*, which no ballerina could. In that respect the ballet had been outdone. But what it meant was that since you didn't need any longer to judge dancers only by how beautifully they could leap, new styles of dance were free to develop. Which is where our patron Ms Duncan comes in. Does everyone understand?'

Deirdre's hand shot up again. 'But Miss Bryant, what about the boomerang, Miss Bryant. Doesn't that return to the place from where you threw it?'

'From *whence*, from *whence* you threw it, Deirdre,' replied Miss Bryant, effortlessly deploying a traditional teacher's parry. 'And it's not quite the same thing, is it?' Unfurling her wings on this slim updraft, Miss Bryant continued, 'Just as Wright had controlled his aeroplane from a central control stick which bent its wings this way or that, so Ms Duncan's new style of dancing had a centre too: the solar plexus. Placing the centre here leaves the spine free to channel energy between both the earth and the heavens, you see.' She illustrated the point with an exaggerated movement of her left arm. 'Ballet has always been built on straight lines. Only by running in a straight line could you get enough speed to leave the ground. But the new dance had no need to leave the ground – the aeroplane did that better than any person could. No, if you examine it you'll see that all the dancing we do here is based not around the straight line, but around the *spiral*.'

Spiral or no spiral, Nadine was not destined to make the grade as a dancer. She soon tired of 'the new dance', more a kinaesthetic than a craft, and transferred to a ballet school. But for ballet she had neither the application nor the talent. She was more than competent and was no disgrace to her teacher or peers, but after a year at the academy they all knew that she wasn't long for it. Nadine suspected this but could not understand it. What did she lack that the others, the golden pupils, supposedly had? Once she knew she had a poor reputation, Nadine practised and rehearsed harder than ever. Late into the night she'd go over her steps in her room, pirouetting around as quietly as she could. She stretched and exercised and hardly ate, arched her feet whenever she sat down, counted time and rehearsed moves in her head at every opportunity. But at the same time as she was working so hard, all this effort was killing something in her. Her desire to succeed became centreless, pointless. Deep down she had wanted to be a 'natural talent'. She felt that the skills should just come to her effortlessly. If she had to work so hard for them, then what was the point? She could never be relaxed, blasé, emotional about her art if she knew so intimately how it had been won. She could never be *creative*.

Then war broke out again and she was evacuated along with thousands of others to rural communities and village schools. In time she managed to forget about the slight clumsiness that she'd never managed to shake and which her dance teachers had known she never would, and also about her own waning drive. She cast herself instead in the role of talent passed by, beauty destroyed by the war, a precious and ever so slightly tragic figure.

Nadine did have a talent, though, one which she'd inherited from her mother and which began to blossom in the cold Midlands schoolroom where she took all her lessons. It was an affinity for numbers and she found, quite by accident, that she rather enjoyed solving numerical puzzles and writing out formulae and algebraic equations. She was eighteen in 1942, old enough to join the rows of women on the belching armament production lines or train to be a driver or a nurse. Although these options didn't appeal to her she was excited by the prospect of working and kept a look-out for something she wanted to do. When she saw some newsreel footage of comptometer operators in the local cinema she knew she'd found her niche. The machines shown were the first to have a keyboard for inputting numbers rather than an awkward set of levers or dials and the film was remarkable for the fact that the fingers of the women who operated these keyboards moved so quickly that the twenty-four-frames-a-second could not keep up with them. Six feet tall, the digits blurred across the screen before her, so fast it seemed even sight could not contain them. It was as if they had escaped, as if they had achieved a physicality which had gone beyond the realm of the day-to-day, and the effect was heightened by the simple, efficient clothing the operators wore and their obvious focus and determination. It was a dynamic, and Nadine recognised in it that which she had wanted from dancing. The discipline, the restrictions of the machine hypersensitised and titillated, while the virtuosity of the finger movements freed and expressed. She went for it.

There was a comptometer training centre in Birmingham, run by a woman who, as chance would have it, had worked as a computer with Nadine's mother under Leslie Comrie. She still had the clippings from *Illustrated* magazine pinned up in her office, from the time when Comrie had won a War Office contract for his own company, Scientific Computing Service Limited, to produce gunnery tables just three hours after Britain declared war on Germany. 'Comrie's girls do the world's hardest sums!' the thirty-six-point declared.

The woman agreed to take Nadine on, and Nadine learned fast and loved it. She made friends with the other girls, embarked on a new social life and dropped her tragic, narcissistic airs. She was good at the work, too, so good that she found a part-time job only a few months into the course – working on the accounts in one of those armaments factories she'd looked down her nose at. But at the same time she continued with her training and when the special operations centre at Bletchley Park put out a request for computers the woman who ran Nadine's course put forward Nadine's name and she was selected.

Bletchley, Alan Turing, Colossus – names the public wouldn't know until long after the war was over. This is where they helped the man who made the thing which cracked the codes that Jerry built. Nadine arrived just as Colossus became operative. One of the very first electronic digital computers, its 1500 vacuum tubes needed a room of their own. Nadine only saw the monster once: her security clearance didn't give her access; but while she was at Bletchley she had a number of more or less torrid affairs – it was the war, dear, what would you have done? – one of which was with an MP called Tom who had the keys and who snuck her in one night. With the panels of lights clicking away behind them and the fans filling the room with noise they made love in front of the thing, made it an offering though they didn't see it that way, no, it was just sexy, all that power, and Tom's thick cock dug away at her like a piston and he showered her he showered her with sparks.

After the war Nadine moved back to bombed-out Birmingham and found further work as a computer. She liked her independence, wasn't about to give it up, even when she agreed to marry Henry, a man she'd vaguely known at Bletchley. He'd been one of the mathematicians, slightly older, not bad-looking, though back then she'd preferred the soldiers. But he'd remembered her all right, they had a name for her in his set, something to do with her surname, Flowers, which it didn't bear repeating, and back in Birmingham, an accountant now, he looked her up and asked her out. They courted calmly amid the ruins – it was so romantic, citizens with a responsibility to rebuild their country and their world, it was something amazing – and in 1948 they married.

Apart from the fact that she liked him there'd been another factor favouring Henry as a husband: he was sterile. Nadine wasn't interested in children, never had been, she loved her job. She didn't want some man nagging her to give it up and sit at home and coo. So Henry was perfect – handsome, kind, with interests of his own and surprisingly fierce as a lover. They had three perfect years together, before Nadine lost her job and her career. Vacuum tube machines were moving into the business environment and her virtuosity was no longer required. Artificial intelligence was here! It was efficient! It was clean! There were plenty of other jobs for people to do! Women! Britain needs children! We have a country to build!

But Nadine didn't want to do anything else. She didn't want to work in a bank, serve as a secretary, teach nursery school. And she made a useless housewife, too – she hated washing and cooking. She was a computer; nothing else would do. But she couldn't find a position in the new industry; no training, apparently. What did they want her to do? A college degree? She typed out dozens of applications, but no letters came in reply. She went to the movies, again and again, hoping for another flash of image-induced inspiration like the six-foot fingers had brought on before. She became obsessed by the idea that she would find an answer here, but when it became apparent that no such inspiration would come she became obsessed by the movies themselves. The picture houses were a parallel world for those who could not deal with their memories of war or with the hardships and penury of peace. Nadine joined them, disappeared into the flicker of images, grew into her seat like some plant that thrived on the strobe effects of projected chiaroscuro. Many nights Henry would trawl the theatres in search of her, stumbling up and down aisles in the semi-dark, yelled at by addicts stirred from their wide-eyed narcosis by the blank of his form. But when he brought her home she continued to grow, the blank living-room wall or the log fire her silver screen. She was a dancer who had put down roots, she was the woman who had held her hands to the sky and branched out, she was the ornamental bush gone to seed. She'd grown above and apart, and she wanted to grow further still. Soon, strung out, no one could touch her reach her climb her. She wound her limbs through their house in Hagley Road, peeped her shoots through the letter-box and out between the tiles, ransacked all the dark corners lest something had slipped out of sight. She grew her bark thick to resist all attack, crowded out the weeds which pulled at her feet.

She became so entwined and entangled, such a thicket, that in order to breathe her trunk had to split. With a wrenching sound it opened like a follicle and unfurled. A pillar of chitin grew forth and fountained out the spores of self-pollination. She no longer needed letters to come, for now she had leaves of her own.

Captain Henry

A decade later Henry Several settled back against the chafed leather of one of the armchairs of the lounge bar of the Red Lion pub on Birmingham's Corporation Street and adjusted the three watches that he now wore on his wrists – two on the left and one on the right. The pub's clock said six o'clock and none of the watches agreed, so he reset them all and gave them a wind. Then he picked up the *Birmingham Post* and gazed at the business pages, trying to make out the articles through the haze of his third gin. Between headlines he glanced up, shifted in his seat and smiled at whoever caught his eye.

The pub was humming with the usual early evening crowd. Greasy articled clerks fresh out of Chambers were drinking Bass and throwing packets of crisps back to their pals over the heads of the other patrons. Portly solicitors drank to forget their liver troubles and sounded off on favourite subjects. Starched accountants wheezed away in the smoky corners. Dressed in dark suits that sagged at the elbows and seat, the youngest of them sporting pimples and bright ties, the oldest combining the two effects in the patches of broken blood vessels years of drinking had splashed across their cheeks, the men filled the room with their caws and guffaws. Henry knew most of the drinkers by sight but, unusually, there was no one present to whom he'd actually been introduced. It wasn't until Sneak Riley swaggered in through the door that he was saved from the sad bastard fate of drinking alone.

Riley made a beeline for him, and Henry got to his feet and greeted the new arrival with an affable grin. 'Mr Riley, sah, good evening to you. And what will you be having?' he asked, shaking Sneak's hand and guiding him in the direction of the bar. Riley was not one to stand on ceremony and rather than spar for the honour of buying the round he murmured, 'Very kind, very kind,' in his obscurely affected way and requested a gin and tonic.

'And make it a double,' Henry called to the barman, an Irishman name of Sean Finnegan who worked the bar a couple of nights a week and occupied the rest of his time buying black-market product for a Dublin-based condom-smuggling ring. It was the kind of business in which Sneak might have been involved had he known about it and knowing Sneak, it was probably not going to be too long before he did.

'Very kind,' Sneak murmured again, sizing up the curves of Sean's arse as the barman reached down for a fresh bottle of gin.

'And one for yourself, barman,' added Henry, on a roll now.

Finnegan turned round, and Sneak coughed and laid his neatly folded newspaper on the counter. 'Don't mind if I do, sir.'

The drinks came and the two men transported them across the room to Henry's table, Henry slopping his a little. They sat down and Sneak took a gulp of his and fetched out a fag. Henry pulled out his lighter and leant across to light Sneak's cigarette, the ash from his own falling into his pint as he did so. Sneak noticed; Henry did not. Sneak said nothing, preferring the small twinge of pleasure to be procured from watching Henry drink down the ash.

Ostensibly a barrister, Sneak Riley made his own living and that of several other people besides by noticing just these kinds of minutiae. He cared nothing for the law but knew it well – the many intricacies of tort and precedent were useful tools in the bigger game of getting people to do what he wanted them to do. 'Have you heard about Donald Buerk?' he said, out of the blue. Henry replied that he hadn't, that he didn't know Donald particularly well. 'Bought himself a television a while back. Much to the annoyance of Doreen. Have you met his wife?'

'Er, no, I don't think so. She's a teacher, isn't she?'

'That's right. She hated it, apparently. The television, that is – though I'm pretty sure she's not too partial to the other as well, if you know what I mean.' Henry smiled thinly, still enough of himself at this early stage in the evening to be unimpressed by Sneak's repartee. 'Well, to cut a long story short, it's twisted his head. So I'm told.'

'What?' said Henry, suddenly interested. 'Lack of . . . you know?'

'No, you fool. The television. Though you never know.'

'What, you mean he's gone . . .'

'Yes, quite loopy, apparently. Sits at home in front of it all day. Masturbating. So I'm told.'

'That's terrible.'

'Aye.'

'Good God.' Both men fell silent for a while and sipped at their drinks. Henry noticed that his cigarette had burnt its way down to the filter, so he dropped it in the ashtray and lit another. He offered one to Sneak, who declined. 'You were his best man weren't you?' asked Henry.

'That's right.' Another pause.

'You two go back a long way, then.'

''S'right.'

'You must be devastated, old man.'

Sneak raised up his palms and brought them back into his lap. 'Well, these things happen. Want another drink?'

'Oh, yes. Another pint, I think.' Sneak sloped off to the bar and left Henry to ponder the news. It had set off cascades of alcohol-blurred associations across the surface of his mind and the lineages of thought fell into two broad families. On the one side there was a bloodline of debate over the question of whether or not he should get a television for his daughter, Jennifer, who was seven that year. On the other a tribe of memories of his wife's insanity trekked about his tilted mental plane like Scythians across the steppe.

Sneak returned with the two drinks.

'Do you know who my best man was,' Henry said, taking a slurp of his bitter and suddenly eager to change the subject.

'No. Who?' said Sneak, always up for a new bit of information to process.

'Alan Turing.'

'Alan Turing? Don't think I know him. Should I?'

21

'The mathematician.'

'Don't know any mathematicians. Never was the academic type.'

'No. The famous one. Chap who did all the code-breaking during the war.'

'Oh, the Bletchley Park chappie. The one who topped himself. Woofter, wasn't he?'

'So they say,' said Henry coldly. 'Always seemed like a splendid fellow to me.'

'Obviously.'

'What?'

'Well, old chap, you did make him your best man.'

'Oh, yes. Of course. Yes.' There was a slightly embarrassed pause.

Sneak, delighted with the way things were turning out, broke it: 'So, er, when were you married?'

'Not long after the war, 1948. I'd spent a lot of time with Turing between 1940 and '45. Worked with him on the Enigma project. Always had a bit of a dodgy ticker and having a head for numbers I was more useful to them back here than over there.'

'So you were one of those code crackers, too, then, were you?'

'I suppose so. It wasn't a bad war for us, you know. Clever bunch of chaps. Never met their like. Good company, too.'

'Never interested me, personally. Bright, was he, this Turing?'

'Oh, yes,' said Henry, maintaining an esoteric air. 'Extremely bright. Outrageous what they did to him. Poor bastard.'

Sneak said nothing for a while. Then: 'She passed away a while back, didn't she?'

'Who?'

'Your wife.'

'That's right.' The booze sloshed around him; he was all at sea. It was the element in which he was most at home. 'He was a great man, you know!' The words fell from his mouth and paddled around the glasses on the table like two great blobs of mercury. His eyes clouded slightly and he rubbed at them with his left hand.

Sneak leaned back a little in his chair, intrigued. 'You all right old man?' he crooned. 'I say, don't you think you've had enough?'

On the train back to Stratford Henry fell asleep. If it weren't for the fact that the guard was used to him he would have missed his stop. He'd done it before – and spent the night in a park in Oxford, a fresh topic of conversation for the local drunks and tramps. As he walked home, the streets were full of Turing and Nadine. When he reached the bridge he stopped, as he always did, and gazed out at the theatre. Its lights raked the water into furrows; there was no breeze and the reflection on the river's surface resembled a row of ultraviolet striplights, arranged to bring out the secrets in the sky. Back home, he shut himself in his study and poured himself a whisky. He sat in his chair for a while, swivelling nervously and trying to refill his lighter with fluid. He missed the hole and the petrol squirted out on to the desktop and bloomed across the leather. The stains looked like flowers, then gunshot wounds. Henry began to cry. He heaved great sobs into the room and his tears turned the wounds into a mutilation.

When the sobbing stopped he pulled out his handkerchief and wiped his face, then took a key from his pocket and went over to a small chest in the corner of the room. He unlocked it and took out a bundle of letters.

He untied the ribbon that held them all together and let the envelopes tumble on to the desk. He chose one and removed the contents. He thought of Nadine, of how she'd become hard wood and pale grey. When she could no longer speak there were buds blossoms twigs where her hands had been. Henry fingered the violet sheets, held one to his cheek. He glanced at the words.

> Jaundice . . . Skin . . . Jade
> Ether . . . Blaze . . . Leather
> Weather . . . Grammar . . . Heather
> Two Poles . . . Descent . . . Spin
> Colossus . . . Vortex . . . C(l)ock
> Lung . . . Lightning . . . Elastic
> Connect . . . Flight . . . Fuck
> Voice . . . Anchor . . . Shoal
> Nadine . . . Inching . . . Turquoise
> Cunt . . . Damp . . . Metal

When she'd no longer been able to speak, she used to write these letters to him, often while he was sitting there in the room with her, then seal them in envelopes and hide them for him to find around the house. Back then, whenever he'd found one under his pillow, inside the fridge, slipped in between the flowers in a vase, he would pore over it as if it were a rune or a glyph which held the key to her condition and, if deciphered correctly, would make sense of it. But an interpretation had always escaped him and now, even now, he couldn't read another word. Couldn't. Didn't.

On the bottom of the bundle was another letter, carbon on stiff white. He looked at that instead.

19 December

Dear Dr Supine,

I am writing to thank you for taking on my wife's case. I know how busy you must be, and I feel forever indebted to you for the interest you have taken in her. If there is any way that I can ever return the favour, please do not hesitate to call on me.

I am aware of the possibility that Nadine may never return to her former self. I am also aware, drawing my own conclusions from what you have said, as well as from comparable case histories that I have taken the liberty of looking into, that this possibility, grim and hard to come to terms with as it may be, is also the most likely one. Should the prefrontal leucotomy that you have recommended prove unsuccessful in effecting a cure then it will be incumbent upon me to organise the setting up of a fund for her provision throughout her remaining years. I therefore seek your advice upon selecting a suitable institution in which she might be housed and in which she would be surrounded with the usual comforts befitting a lady of her standing and reputation.

May I repeat that should you ever require my help concerning any matter, then I shall remain,

Your Obedient Servant,

Henry Several

The great gig in the sky

The hair is shaved away and the scalp disinfected. Above the hairline a transverse incision is made. The scalp flap and a flap of epicranium are reflected forward and large trephine circles are drawn to within one centimetre of the midline, as low down as possible. The dura is opened and a transverse incision two and a half centimetres wide is made in the cortex. A two-centimetre cleft is then opened in the white matter, which is divided using a fine suction tube. Simultaneously, spatula forceps are introduced; the incision is then deepened. Puncture with a ventricular needle ensures that the cut is kept one centimetre above the orbital roof and the incision is kept on this descending plane as it passes below the head of the caudate nucleus. The underlying cortical area (Area 13) lies behind and below the ascending thalamofrontal radiation, which passes between the caudate nucleus and the putamen. The posterior vertical incision crosses the corpus striatum before entering the posterior orbital region. Direct observation confirms that the inner tip of the spatula blade is kept one centimetre from the falx. Unless this point is checked the weight of the spatula handles may cause right lateral deviation with the result that the incision misses the objective and passes laterally to Area 13 – an event which will surely vitiate the result, as shown by the difference in effect between unilateral and bilateral stereotaxic implants.

Maximum benefit is derived from the posterior two centimetres of the incision. There appears to be a concentration of fibres in these last two centimetres, division of which produces adequate relief of symptoms. Whether these are descending fibres passing down from the frontal cortex through the substantia innominata towards the hypothalamus, or whether these are directly connected with the primitive agranular cortex of Area 13, cannot be stated, but we regard this area of the substantia innominata, lying beneath the head of the caudate nucleus and the overlying Area 13, as an important objective in treatment. Vertical incisions which enter this area, however, produce serious damage, as a result of which this area has for long periods been regarded as taboo.

Nadine had been committed in 1957, on 3 November, the day of the Sputnik II launch. Throughout the following year, as the North American Space Agency was inaugurated and the European Centre for Nuclear Research began operation, her condition deteriorated until finally the decision was taken, with Henry's approval, to operate. On 12 September 1959, at the very moment that Luna 2 impacted upon the surface of the moon and deposited there the Soviet Coat of Arms, Jennifer's mother became the last person in Britain to undergo a prefrontal leucotomy. At that moment Nadine and Luna 2 both disappeared into their respective twilight worlds and shortly afterwards Nadine – though, as far as we know, not Luna 2 – became pregnant.

X and Y

'Nadine Several, Room 35. Nadine Several, Room 35.' He didn't bother to knock, just kicked the door open with his heel and stepped backwards into the private room, pirouetting as he went so that when he brought the tray down he was facing the patient. He had the face of a chisel and his clothes – regulation hospital garments – while clean, were well-worn from washing. Nadine registered his entrance and let her head roll away from him and towards the wall. 'Uh uh, oh no you don't. Sit up now. You've got to eat. Got to keep your strength up, haven't you, my sweet.' He set the tray down on the table and came up close to the bed, placing one mildewed hand on Nadine's shoulder. But she flinched away, so he seized her by the earlobe and brought her head back towards his chest. 'Sit up, I said. Didn't you hear me? Sit up!'

It wasn't really clear to Nadine what was happening. The sunlight was not moving across the wall and that creeping line, the cross of the window's shadow that deformed as the day came and went, was the only thing that was real to her now. Then there was pain, pain was real too, pain like the pain on her now that meant she had to go this way. She didn't want to go this way, there was something this way that she did not want, but the pain said go this way and so she went.

Davie Costain kept his fingers pinched upon her earlobe and reached his free hand around to her right armpit. By digging his index fingers into its soft flesh he managed to force Nadine into a sitting position. Once she was upright he knew he could release her. Put her somewhere and she rarely moved, the doll. He slid his hand down the front of her starched blue smock and fingered her nipples, and she stared right ahead as usual. Then he fed her, helped her to spoon the grim hospital food into her mouth, regaling her with compliments and obscenities as he did so. 'That's right, eat it up. That's right. You know that Davie loves you, don't you? That's right. You've got beautiful hair, you know. Are you my baby slut? Yeah, that's right. Must have been a lucky bloke to have had you. Did you let him take you up the shitter? I bet you did. Bet you two got up to all sorts. Pretty girl like you.'

Nadine finished, but not before Davie had spilt jelly down her chin and chest, and rubbed it in with a tissue. He piled up the tray and pocketed the chocolates that Henry had brought her the previous afternoon.

On his way back to the kitchens Smythe, another of the porters, caught up with him. 'You coming for a drink, Davie?'

'Nope, not me. I'm on duty tonight.'

'Well, don't get bored.'

'Me? Bored? Don't be daft.'

Davie delivered a few more trays, said good-night to the nurses, bagged up the laundry and mopped the lino in the ground-floor corridors. Then he went round all the rooms checking the windows were securely fastened and settling everyone into their beds. There was rarely any trouble on B wing at night. This was where they kept the dopes, the dociles, the zombies as Davie liked to call them. As a rule the duty nurse spent the whole of the graveyard shift on A ward, with the crazies. And it was a full moon tonight – she'd really have her work cut out.

Davie worked his way around the rooms in such a manner that his last call was Nadine. Nadine was by far the youngest woman in his care: most of them were over sixty and kept in a state of dumb fascination by the ever rising tide mark of senility. He let himself into her room and walked across to the bed. She was already asleep. He patted the blanket and drew it up to her neck as if tucking her in, then quickly slipped his arm beneath her chin and caught her in a head lock. She awoke immediately, of course, and opened her mouth to scream, allowing Davie to jam in a squash ball and fix it in place with a few turns of surgical tape. So she scratched at him, and he grabbed her hands and roped them together with a length of cord he'd pulled from his pocket, then tied them to the bed frame behind her. More calmly now he took out two more pieces of cord and tied them around her ankles then, utilising the bedstead once more, he tied her legs apart. Lastly he took out a pair of surgical scissors and cut her gown from her body, leaving her naked. Then he threw the covers back over her – not before first exploring her body to his own satisfaction – and strolled downstairs to the delivery bay where his friends were waiting with their money, whistling under his breath as he went.

2

The international front

The winds that blew in to Brooklyn's Williamsburg as December staggered on brought with them the razor cut of the Great Lakes' vast sheets of ice and the whittled odours of the billion trillion New England reject leaves whose dying flames they'd fanned upon their way. A clump of oxygen molecules, released by bacterial activity from the Lake Huron silts, bubbled their way to the surface just off Tobermory point to be thrown up in the foam of white horses and absorbed into air flows which flickered down to the great falls at Niagara. There the winds banked west and blustered over Geneva, Rome and Amsterdam, until they discovered Troy. Here they turned south along the line of the Hudson, clogged as it was with logs, oil sludge from the mills and plants that backed up its banks right into the Adirondacks. The molecules stayed aloft, their motions tracing out the giant tubes of turbulence, and only began to descend when they reached the Bronx. Whipping low between the tops of the buildings they described loops and vortices, and consorted with the sluggish petrocarbons and particles of filth coughed out by the vehicles and the people. By the time they made Williamsburg they were running close to the ground and at just the right height to be sucked into the welcoming lungs of Moshe Kluge as he stepped into the street outside his bakery and took the morning air. Down among his bronchioles, their freedom severely restricted, about half of the molecules were trapped by tar deposits and about half were bound by haemoglobin. For days they circled around Moshe's body, losing one another in the veins and capillaries, until each of them was married with one of the carbon atoms they had so long despised – some strange shotgun wedding deep down there in the flesh. A week later they were all farted out as the baker emptied his bowels the morning after the Sabbath. Their pit stop over, the molecules seeped out into the cold November air and with their high spirits severely dampened they slunk away from the drifting cloud of methane and looked for somewhere else to play.

Moshe Kluge, taciturn but loving father, massive, powerful and round. Moshe Kluge, sometime Kabbalist, kaposzta lover and king baker. Moshe Kluge, switching on the single light bulb hanging in the centre of his shop. The light illuminates oven, preparation tables, counter; in their racks the basted crusts of loaves shine from the shadows like the polished backs of skulking reptiles. The light bulb is caked with flour: it's the only area of the room that Moshe's wife Judith has not wiped clean (she loves the faint smell of burning it gives off once warmed up). It's a smell alien to the bagels and breads which come out of the oven hot, soft, delicious and perfectly glazed, the best in the district and perhaps in the city – a fact to which many a customer will testify. There is even an enclave of fans, way over on the Upper East Side, so devoted to Kluge's wares that they'll send daughters and lackeys right across town to pick up orders. They are the ones who have 'discovered' the little bakery, as if it were the source of some minor river, and have passed the word around at PTEs and coffee mornings. We are in the fifties now, remember, and both Jew and Gentile purchase Tupperware.

'Moshe,' Judith would nag every time one of the golden-haired girls came into the shop to collect an order, 'Moshe, when are we going to get this van? Every week I explain to you how much sense it makes, look at this poor young child, each week she has to come here on that dreadful IRT with the schvartzes looking her up and down every inch of the way. But what do you care? You are a heartless man, Moshe Kluge, a heartless man! Sometimes I think you think only of yourself. It's not so many years before Joel will be old enough to drive, you might think about him for a minute, what's he going to do? Now if we had a van, of course, the answer would be simple . . .' But Moshe would only throw up his hands – releasing clouds of flour out into the room – and mutter into his beard that he was working on it, that they couldn't afford it, that he had better things to think about than pouring money down the drain. Then he'd turn back to his bagels, his knishes, his mandelbrot, pound the doughs out on the stained wooden kneading board, roll them in flour or sugar and slap them expertly on to large metal baking trays ready to be slid in and out of the oven with great sweeping movements.

Bagels were his speciality, he could make them perfectly: firm yet yielding, sour yet sweet, light yet moist. But the secret of their taste lay not just in the flour he used, nor in the heat of the oven, nor in the subtlety of the flavourings he kneaded into the dough, but in the very way he handled the dough itself, gently persuading it into long thick ropes without introducing the slightest tear or stress. When he cut the ropes he did not simply slice them into suitable lengths, as was common practice among many lesser bakers, but twisted and teased them apart at suitable points of weakness, the accurate identification of which was a skill he'd developed over decades. Once ready, the lengths of dough were grabbed by one end and whipped around into the familiar circular shape. The process appeared simple, elegant, rapid and effortless, but of course it had taken many years to perfect and Kluge's skill ensured that his shop was generally busy with intrigued onlookers, many of whom bought his bagels just in order to admire the production process.

But apart from their taste and consistency, Kluge's bagels had another unique feature. At the final stage of his production cycle, just before Moshe joined the ends of the dough, he would give each rope one half twist at its centre. Thus, every bagel had its very own torso of torsion and each was, in fact – if inspected closely and imagined topologically – a little Möbius band, a hoop of bread with only one surface and therefore neither an inside nor an out. It was this, speculated many of the customers, that was responsible for their wonderful flavour.

It would not be right to attribute to this curious fact Joel's early fascination with mathematics. For Joel did not even like his father's bagels, even though he was quite possibly the only soul in Williamsburg (nay, in the whole of New York) who did not. Perhaps there was something Freudian going on here – perhaps. Or maybe Joel didn't feel comfortable eating an object with only one surface, maybe he felt there was something indigestible about the idea. This was certainly possible, for from the moment his brain had come online Joel had comprehended the world in mathematical terms. Logic and geometry came more naturally to him than walking or speech; he subordinated infinity beneath his scrawny childhood thumb as other boys subordinate insects. As an infant he didn't speak at all for three years, by which time Moshe and Judith had all but given up on him. But then, in January 1953, on the day that Moshe read in his censored copy of the *New York Times* (Judith, like all the wives in their community, bowdlerised it for him every day, cutting out or deleting with the thick marker pens she purchased from Zvi's stationary shop two blocks away anything that might tempt, co-opt, or be otherwise unsuitable for her husband) that a United States Airforce Advisory Panel concluded that unidentified flying objects or UFOs: (1) constituted no direct physical threat; (2) were not foreign developments; (3) were not unknown phenomena requiring revision of current scientific concepts; and (4) offered an opportunity for mischief by 'skilful hostile propagandists', Joel spoke his first word: *ein*. Oy vay, so it was not so much, but it was a start, and he quickly progressed on to the other numbers until Judith and Moshe would carry with them for the rest of their lives happy memories of Joel sitting up on the window-sill or on the table's edge counting away to himself, quietly, under his breath, for hours and hours. It wasn't until 18 May, the day that Jacqueline Cochrane climbed into the cockpit of an F–86 and became the first woman to fly faster than the speed of sound, that Joel managed a word that wasn't a number. It was his own name and it popped out at the dinner-table bundled in an expression of great surprise. The meal, a turgid, standard affair until that moment, came alive: everyone cheered and tried to encourage Joel to say something else (all secretly wanting their own names to be the next to issue forth). But Joel was in no hurry and, happy with the technique he'd developed with numbers, he just repeated his name over and over for a week or two until he was thoroughly used to the sound of it. Other names and words slowly got added to the list until 12 August when, at the moment that the USSR exploded its first hydrogen bomb, Joel strung together some- thing that had the right to be called a sentence as opposed to a mere list. So it was – halting, brittle, spavined with logic to be sure, but it was a sentence and it meant that the boy was a mensch.

Now that he could talk he could attend Yeshiva, and the following year he joined the other boys in the exhausting school schedule which began at seven every morning and continued until four in the afternoon for the younger boys and six or seven in the evening for the older ones. The next few years would be spent learning Hebrew in preparation for the rote learning of the religious texts – the Pentateuch, the Talmud – which would dominate their education.

Joel found Hebrew much easier to figure than Yiddish. Yiddish, it seemed, was about sounds alone, strange clouds of noise the meaning of which was nebulous at best, but when the boys started Hebrew they were taught about gematria and about how there were numerical values to this new alphabet, and how this meant that every letter – and therefore every word – had a corresponding number. Joel didn't quite understand how this worked yet: making words into numbers was one thing but recombining them, making numbers into words, that he couldn't quite manage. Still, the fact of the numerical connection gave him the confidence he needed, it tied things down, and he had little trouble with the ancient language. And when it came to memorising he had a distinct advantage over the other boys, for he could remember entire passages by keying the words to planes of numbers that he found it easy to visualise in his head.

And while the other boys struggled with the rudimentary arithmetic that was studied in order that they might understand the stocktaking procedures of their fathers' businesses, Joel solved the problems casually and almost instantly, computing the solutions spatially in his imagination. In those lessons he kept himself from boredom by inventing and solving logical puzzles. After a while he learnt to do this in his head as well, because the rabbi hated doodling and fetched any boy he caught at it a hard smack across the open palm with the short thick flat bar of wood he always had about him. So Joel began to pretend instead that he was struggling over the problems like his peers. That way he was left alone, free to sit at the back of the class and speed about in the crystal spaces of his mind.

So, like a modern Euclid, Joel developed his talent in secret, though less because of fear – as a rule the Hasidim do not share the Christian taste for the tang of forbidden fruit – than because he remained completely oblivious to the possibility that anybody else might think with numbers as he did. The numerological possibilities of gematria were one thing, but the joys of pure mathematics, of geometry and algorithm, were something of which the rabbis never spoke.

His talent for numbers was eventually recognised, of course. Something of a schlemiel, thanks to his short sight and lanky limbs, he was too clumsy to help his mother with the household chores like the other children (*Oh, that Joel, he only has to look at something and it breaks!*). So Moshe found a use for him in the rear of the shop, got him to do the stock control and the bakery's balance sheets. It was a job that strictly should have been allotted to Joel's older brother Shimon, but Shimon wanted to be a rabbi and was far too ethereal to dirty his hands with money matters. Although the fifth child of nine, Joel was effectively the number-one son where the bakery was concerned (with the exception of Shimon, all of his elder siblings were girls – Rachel, Judith and Sarah). He had two younger brothers (Moshe and Abraham), and then there were the twins, one male, one female, who were still toddlers. As a family they had been lucky: only one child had died – a girl born the year after Joel, who had contracted tuberculosis at the age of five. On holy days the family would visit her grave out in the Jewish quarter of the cemetary in Queens, one tiny plaque among the hundreds of thousands of markers and gravestones which ate up the grass and even the trees until there was virtually nothing left on the gently rolling hills but crosses and plinths and tombs and slabs, an entire metropolis of death, bordered by expressways and echoed by the skyscrapers that shivered on the overcast horizon with its clouds like sheets of tin.

When he finished each week's accounts, Joel would lay a sheet of greaseproof paper across one of the metal baking sheets, take a pencil and plot the loci of theoretical objects moving through space. Then he'd integrate the curves of their trajectories in his own peculiar algebra. Absorbed and happy, he'd sit for hours among the bags of flour and the mounds of sour-dough, keeping out of harm's way while his father worked. Even though Joel wasn't helping, the baker liked to have him there, scribbling away. He would take the finished sheets from the boy and pin them on the wall in the front of the shop, the better to point them out to his customers with the cracked pride of a man who knows that his second son, like his first, was not quite as he would wish him to be. *Look, this is Joel's latest, not bad you think, yes!* And the men and women of the neighbourhood would smile and pat Joel's yarmulke and murmur: *Oy, Moshe, he'll make us a clever lad yet for one so quiet.*

In his quest to conquer words Joel tried to discover all meanings logically. When he first began his English lessons he was perplexed to find that the words of the new language could not be discovered by translating letter for letter the corresponding Yiddish term. And try as he might, the English teacher – an Italian who came in to teach the boys for the last hour of each day Monday through Thursday – never could convince Joel that language was not a code that only lacked a key. For hours each night Joel worked on algorithms and procedures that would translate one tongue into the other. But he met with not the slightest success and finally decided that a higher order was required. He knew there were books on mathematics – he had seen them in the windows of bookstores the few times he had been to Manhattan – and he thought that he might be able to find some of them in the school library. But the library was out of bounds to the pupils and to gain access to it he had to run favours for the rabbis for weeks. Eventually he was trusted enough to be sent in there alone on errands, fetching globes and textbooks for the lessons, but to his dismay though he looked through every book on the shelves (and there were not that many) there was nothing that was remotely useful to him. Were there no mathematics books then?

Had they taught him everything? He immediately stopped volunteering to help and went back to his day-dreams which greatly confused the teachers who had been convinced that he'd been making some progress. Still, he couldn't believe there was no more to it and so began to harass his father, eventually finagling him into taking him to the public library in Park Slope.

Neither of them had ever been in the building before, and both were awed by the great façade. Moshe was reminded of pictures of giant and ancient tombs that he had seen occasionally in the magazines. Egyptian figures and peculiar runes were embossed in gold on to the stone and at the base of the enormous doors stood two massive book depositories, one to each side, like the paws of some metallic sphinx. Imbued with the appropriate amount of respect, son and father climbed the steps and went on in. Once inside, the place seemed even bigger. The ceiling of the atrium was several storeys high, and the walls and floors were panelled with long strips of dark wood. Low steel pillars slung with velvet ropes led them towards a panel of security guards who nodded them through to the central area. To the left and right, elevators fed a mezzanine across which people walked, books in hand, looking intelligent and completely at home.

Father and son stood at the centre of the vault, not sure which way to turn. Both of them felt swamped. Moshe eyed the check-out line and considered joining it; at least then it would look as though he knew what he was doing. Joel ran his eyes along the rows of Kardex cabinets, wondering at all these tiny drawers. Finally, when nobody volunteered to help them, he decided to take matters into his own hands and approached an Ashkenazi boy who was flicking through a catalogue. The boy was helpful and explained the system to Joel and Moshe, then pointed them in the direction of Mathematics.

When Joel saw the shelves and shelves of books dealing with his obsession he almost fainted. With breathless excitement he pulled down volumes at random and thumbed his way through them, not reading the words but just following the equations, not finishing one page before he started another. He had never come across standard algebra before and initially it completely threw him, but after he had seen a few things that were obvious he began to deduce the meaning of the more esoteric operators and functions without too much trouble. This done, he began to build himself a mental map of what was available on the shelves.

Moshe hung around him for a while but soon got bored. He had no interest in math at all. With Joel engrossed and unlikely to come to any harm, he wandered off along the rows of shelves past the students fidgeting at their desks and the sleeping bums who had come in out of the cold, until he found himself in the Geography section. Geography! It had always been his favourite subject during what little schooling he'd had. He hadn't looked at an atlas in years! Guiltily he lifted one down and opened it as furtively as if it were a women's magazine. He found North America and ran his finger to and fro between Brooklyn and Montreal, the locus of both his life and Joel's and as defining for him as the sequence of genes on his chromosomes.

He had forgotten how vast a country America was. He looked at it in comparison with Germany, with Poland. The maps weren't as he remembered and he found certain places difficult to locate. When he came across Israel he coughed with surprise. *So, yes, it is real after all.* He searched along the shelf for the 'I's and pulled out a book on the country. As ever when he was confronted with Zionism, he felt no anger, just a numbness, a sort of dulled realisation that there would always be those who failed to understand. Out of curiosity he pored over detailed maps of the new state and read as much of the text as his English would allow. At one point he stumbled into a chapter discussing the impact of the Holocaust. One double-page spread consisted of a single photograph of a great black board on to which names of European towns and villages had been pinned in their relative positions. No borders or coastlines were shown and each name was accompanied by a number. It was an arresting image.

Moshe searched for the town of Treblinka, where his brother Isaac had been sent along with his wife and four children. Isaac had returned to Poland before the war. It was a peculiar feeling, seeing in the anonymity of print the bare facts of what he lived with every day. It was always with him, not thanks to some conscious level of pain – the agony had subsided long ago – but in the way that a severed limb in some strange way remains, the nervous system never having quite adapted to its absence. As the agony had subsided so had his anger, which had become so generalised that it had tainted his whole world, and in the process made itself ridiculous and untenable. But when it had gone, Moshe found that with it had gone his faith: expansive and good-humoured before the war, the Holocaust had burnt it out and nothing had risen from the ashes, soaked and hindered as they were by the constant drizzle of the horrors unearthed by the media in the ensuing decades. For a period he had sought recourse in esoterica and ritual, turning to the Kabbalah. This led him, among other things, to take advantage of his wife's illness and have

Joel's circumcision conducted by a Ba'al Shem in private rather than under the more public – and more traditional – gaze of the entire family. But the collapse of the old man during the ceremony had frightened him and it was to be the last time he dabbled in the mystic arts, deciding then and there that the only arts which it was his place to practise were culinary. Yeast and heat produced tangible results – they smelt good and they filled your stomach. Upon that, one could build. That was enough philosophy for Moshe Kluge.

He closed the book, his eyes dry, and wandered back to look for Joel. But the boy was still engrossed so he sat in a chair by the radiator and dozed, memories of Isaac buzzing behind his eyes, until Joel had decided on the books he wanted and it was time for them both to leave.

They stood in the line to register and Joel checked out his books. Then, on their way out of the building, which Moshe remained impressed by but which Joel had already assimilated as part of the scenery of his existence, a voice called out Moshe's name. One of the librarians was striding up to them, his hand stretched out in greeting. 'Mr Kluge, Mr Kluge, what brings you here?'

Kluge hadn't expected to see anyone he knew that day and it was a moment before he recognised Bernard Millstein, an Austrian Jew whose family had left Europe in the mid-thirties. He was a regular customer at Kluge's shop, but the older man knew little about him apart from the fact that he had attended Columbia University. 'Mr Millstein, is that right, Mr Millstein? So . . . yes.' Still groggy from his nap, Kluge couldn't think of anything to say. Eventually they both asked each other 'So what are you doing here?' at the very same moment.

It broke the ice and they laughed, but it was Joel who spoke up: 'I wanted some books,' he said, and he offered his string-tied bundle up to Millstein who did little more than glance at them, anonymous as they were in their hard brown covers.

It was some months before Millstein and Joel saw one another again. Millstein had moved to an apartment in a different part of Brooklyn and had not been into the bakery for some time, but his wife had grown so appalled with the standards of the local bread shops in their new area that one Friday she demanded that Bernard call in at Kluge's place on his way home and pick up some decent bagels for the weekend. It was dark and snowing lightly, the snow invisible except in the cones of light thrown out by the street lamps or car lights where it flecked the night like so many motes of gold. Millstein pulled up his Chevy across the

street from Kluge's place and leaving it unlocked, ran across the road
with his scarf flying out behind him and catching snowflakes in its tassels.
As he went he tugged up the collar of the light mac he wore as high as
it would go – only a week before the weather had been mild and it was
still a shock that suddenly fall was over and that winter had arrived. When
he entered the shop his glasses steamed up and he could perceive nothing
but the gleam of the reflecting surfaces and the noise Kluge was making
way back in the shop among the ovens. He removed the glasses and
wiped off the condensation with his cuff.

Kluge spotted him from the back of the shop. 'Ah, Mr Millstein, no
problem, I'll just be one minute only.'

'Hello, hello. Yes, that's all right,' Millstein called, 'I just want a dozen
bagels.' He took off his spectacles and looked around the room while he
dug in his pockets for a handkerchief. In the myopic blur he mistook
Joel's graphs for some kind of abstract artworks and moved closer to get
a better look, wondering at the incongruity of such pictures in the baker's
shop.

As he was replacing his glasses, Kluge strode up behind him. 'Do you
like them? They are my son's.'

It was a few moments before he realised that he was looking neither
at Kandinsky sketches nor at childhood scribbles but at a tangle of graphs,
diagrams and matrices. 'I didn't know you had a son who studied math,'
Millstein remarked, wondering at the peculiar syntax of the pieces.
'Which school does he attend?'

'Oh, just the UTA.'

'The UTA? But surely he's too old for that now? Do they take students
over seventeen?'

'Oh, no. Joel's only thirteen. He was with me when we met in the
library.'

'Wait a minute. You mean Joel did these? *That* Joel.'

'Oh, yes, he does them all the time. He seems to like it. You know
how they are.' Millstein let this sink in for a while. Had they modernised
the UTA? He could barely believe it; for all the sympathy he had for
the Hasidim, he pitied them massively for having turned their backs on
the twentieth century. It surely wasn't possible that they had begun to
teach this stuff. And besides, it was at least undergraduate level, what he
was looking at. 'Here he is now. Say hello to Mr Millstein, Joel.'

After a brief talk with Joel, Millstein left for home more elated than he
had felt in years. All evening he rattled on to his wife about this prodigy

he had discovered. It was extraordinary, he said it again and again, it was quite extraordinary. It was as if he had stumbled across the young Mozart. On his way to work the next day he stopped off at the bakery and offered Kluge his services as his son's personal tutor. Moshe was not sure at first, but he consulted his wife, who agreed – Joel was little help around the house and it would keep him out of her hair. Two days a week Joel was to come by the library after school; Millstein would drop him home after a couple of hours of tutorial. Before long, he was trying to persuade Moshe that he should take the boy out of UTA and have him enrolled in a 'proper' school, but Joel's father would have none of it and, when he saw that it was threatening the little influence he did have over the child's development, Millstein dropped the subject.

Let's fold America

The same November night on which Millstein discovered his prodigy found Melinda Volitia (her stage name) pacing the living-room of the cantilevered cliffside Malibu property she co-owned with her husband, Moses Axelrod, and unable to sleep. Melinda was due any day now, and her belly was painful and (she thought) ugly. And she could not she could not get to sleep. Trixie and Donna, Donna Clearwater and Trixie Moxie (what sort of a name, no, really, just what sort of a name was Trixie Moxie? thought Melinda and felt thankful for her Englishness) would still be at Homer's party, the party that she hadn't been able to attend because of the tiresome infant ballooning below her breasts. That was her perspective on him–her–it; as the thing below her breasts, her monstrous third mammary.

She slumped down by the phone and dialled Homer's number. It rang over twenty times before a voice she didn't recognise screeched a hello into the receiver. She couldn't tell if it was male or female, which reminded her again of the child she was carrying.

'Can I speak to Homer please?' *Love Me Do* was blaring in the background, making it hard to hear anything. 'I SAID CAN I SPEAK TO HOMER!'

The voice at the other end giggled. 'Hey, sure, hey, like, who the fuck is Boner. Hey, come here, hey, everybody, there's someone on the line who wants to suck a boner! Check it out.'

'Look, will you cut it out. I need to speak to Homer . . .'

'Look, honey, I don't know anybody called Homer. I think you got a wrong number.' The record started into the chorus and Melinda heard a couple of voices in the background join in, then:

'Hello? Hello? Hey, who is this?'

'Oh, Homer, is that you? Oh, thank god. Who *was* that on the phone now . . . it's Melinda.'

'Oh, hi, Melinda, how ya doin'? Sorry you couldn't make it. Hey, I'm sorry about Ed there, he's drunk, you now how he is.'

'Oh, was that Ed? I didn't recognise him. Oh, oh, he's not . . . no, don't tell me, he's come in his dress, hasn't he? Jesus. Is Kathy with him?'

'Yeh, yeh, she's here.'

'Is she OK?'

'Yeh, she's fine, don't worry, you know she can cope.'

'Look Homer, is Trixie or Donna still there? Can you put one of them on?'

'Yeh, Trixie, Trixie's right here . . . Trixie! TRIX! Phone! Melinda!'

'Hi honey, you OK? Donna and me were just leaving.'

'Oh, Trix, no I'm fine, I'm just bored out of my mind! Look, if you're not too tired, would you guys mind stopping over here on your way home and bring me something to smoke, some grass or something? I can't sleep and I'm in agony, and I need some cheering up.'

'Yup, no problem, it'll be more fun than this party. A whole load of Homer's long-lost friends from college turned up like outta nowhere and it's turned into some kinda fratboy reunion. They already threw four girls in the pool and one of them's screaming blue murder 'cuz her outfit's ruined and she's threatening to sue. Look, honey, we'll see you in thirty. All right?'

'Uh, you saved my life.'

Melinda had met Trixie when she'd first arrived in LA back in 1960 to play a supporting role in a movie starring Sophia Loren – her first big break. They'd met at a party given by the film's producer, with whom Trixie was sleeping at the time, and they'd clicked and had been firm friends ever since. Donna she had met more recently. A languid beauty, she and Melinda had worked together for a few episodes of a television series in which Donna played a frontierswoman making her way in the West without the aid of a man. They had met the day that Melinda had conceived, which was also the day that the US military launched Operation Starfish over Johnson Island in the Pacific. Following the discovery of the ionosphere and the Van Allen belt, there had been much speculation as to the origin of the charged particles that flowed around the planet. Certain minds at the Pentagon had it that the entire phenomenon was due to atmospheric nuclear tests being carried out by the Russians, so a series of similar tests was commissioned. Codenamed Operation Starfish, several launches were scheduled for July 1962. Most failed (one blew up on the launch pad, causing radioactive contamination throughout the entire area), but one succeeded in exploding its warhead at the correct height. The electromagnetic storm that ensued put out all the lights in Hawaii, disabled Tiros I, the world's first weather satellite, and caused one of Melinda's ova to be released a day before she was due. And as Sputnik II was in the vicinity, the blast also woke Laika from one of her long sleeps.

Woke Laika? Yes, it's true. High above the earth, slowly orbiting at a height of 300 kilometres or thereabouts, was another egg of sorts – a metal egg with a Russian dog of indeterminate pedigree curled up inside like a hairy embryo. Fast asleep, she twirled around in the tiny space yelping to herself as from deep in her limbic system a dream emerged, which made her paws twitch to and fro. She dreamt of rabbits, of hundreds of rabbits in a great wide field, a field of clouds like the one she could see from her porthole, the one which wrapped itself around the world. She bounded among the bobbing creatures, almost as divine in their fluffiness as the water vapour they scampered upon. Laika ran and panted, and chased them down their burrows. She was in doggy heaven. Which for once was where she was supposed to be.

She was certainly not supposed to be having a one-dog party at the USSR's expense. As far as the world was aware, Laika was dead. Had she been given a lethal injection? Had she run out of air? Or had she just burnt up upon re-entry into the atmosphere? Soviet ground control had neglected to say, when they'd declared her officially dead some years before.

Their instruments had told them Laika was dead because Laika had disabled them all when, after a week in space, she had tired of being observed. She had been subjected to human scrutiny for her entire life and it had begun to offend her dignity. Once she had completed the requirements of her mission by managing to survive the launch and stay alive beyond the confines of the atmosphere, she'd decided that enough was enough. It was time to turn the tables on her tormentors. She was quite possibly the most highly trained dog in the world; decoupling the electrodes and disabling the syringe designed to kill her did not present a notable challenge.

But that was only the start of it – Laika was soon able to do much, much more. One does not become the first living creature in space and remain unaffected. Laika had always been a clever dog, but the act of witnessing the earth in all its beauty, a polished turquoise ball rolling gently through the void, caused a phase transition in her mind. How so? How does self-consciousness begin? Of what does it consist? Is it a global process, coherent enough to ground an identity, or is it the epipheno-menal by-product of innumerable series of smaller operations? Did this vision of the world as a perfect sphere, a holistic unity, produce a corre-sponding organisational geometry across the space dog's brain? Certainly the great logicians of Western metaphysics – Plato, Descartes, Marvin Minsky – might well have argued for such a interpretation. Others, however – Heraclitus, the German Romantics, Paul and Patricia Church-land – might have wished to pursue a more complex interpretation. Had Laika, as the poet Hölderlin suggested, placed herself 'in harmonic opposition to an external sphere', thus allowing her idealism to act as a matrix for itself (as Schlegel described) and begin a process of infinite overturning (as Hegel insisted)? Or were the processes involved too intri-cate, the constant rippling and annealing of the vast, tiny and biologically complex networks that make up the brain too motley, to be described either by the broad strokes of poetry or the fine boxes of science, creating a consciousness that is never completely coherent, never complete, always over-layered and fractured, and not in fact global at all?

And where is the illusion here? And why does such incoherence worry us?

It didn't worry Laika. For the first time, she knew who she was (or thought she did). The astronauts who followed her were not so lucky. Their imaginations already choked with paranoid structures as a result of decades of service in the military, the globe suspended magically in front of them had a less profound effect, merely resonating strongly with the concentric circles of their fear. Many of them sought refuge in the visions of universal harmoniousness offered by religion and set off to look for arks on their return to earth. Others took a more materialistic turn, playing psychedelic rock music in their capsules and becoming boundlessly enthusiastic consumers: *Hey! The earth's a planet! It's round and it's hanging right there! Wow! Hello mom! Look, it's your son Bud eating dehydrated ice-cream! I'm on TV!*

But Laika was not so frivolous. There's something about being first that injects seriousness into the situation. Once she'd achieved self-consciousness the first emotion she felt was a sense of guilt. She'd torn off her electrodes after all – something which she'd been told never to do. The thought that everyone at Baikonur would think she was dead saddened her because she'd made some good pals back there. She thought of Alexei and Mickl, who had taken her for walks and smuggled her bits of steak when she was supposed to be on a restricted diet. Perhaps they were down there right now, shedding a tear or two over her empty kennel. She remembered Mickl's face as he'd wheeled her to the gantry and suddenly a dose of nostalgia was added to the guilt as Laika remembered the good times they had spent together: the laughing, the woofing, the running round in circles, the rolling over and the scratching of the stomach.

And then a blast of hatred hit her as she recalled all the needles, the endless tests, the harsh training and Renko, the evil Renko, who would deny her food if she so much as failed to crap in exactly the right spot. How immediate was her memory of the man's malicious grin as he inserted another reinforced thermometer into her arse, or shoved another capsule up her nose? If she knew Renko, there'd be a back-up system in here, some other way of monitoring her, some spy machine that could probe her private moments. . . . Inch by inch, she hunted through the tiny cabin until she found a tiny television camera hidden between two wiring ducts. With a doggy snigger she blocked the lens with a gobbet of the high nutrient porridge that they had provided as her only source of food. (Bastards. Not a dog biscuit in sight.)

Enough was enough. It was time for her to do some observing of her own. Fortunately the capsule was equipped with a television monitor and receiver as well as radio technology; the mission's technicians had thought it was wise, should Laika cease to respond to oral commands, to be able to instruct her visually. She watched now as Renko appeared on the screen, waving his arms and swearing and coaxing in an attempt to get her to re-establish contact. Laika sat back and enjoyed the show, laughing a doggy laugh. After a while, tired with all the excitement and on a little high of self-satisfaction (being self-conscious she now had an ego to massage) she fell asleep. When she awoke she would rewire the receiving equipment so that she could tune in to other signals. It would be too dull to have one channel as the sole entertainment for the rest of her stay up here.

There were various other problems to be considered too. Disposing of her waste products was already taken care of: there was a clever little toilet on board which ejected everything into the great vacuum outside and left her shit for ever circling the earth. But she was going to need oxygen and, of course, food, and then there was her deteriorating orbit to consider . . . she had a busy and difficult time ahead of her for sure. But Laika was the most highly trained dog in the world and she knew her stuff. They were only problems and she was sure that she'd figure out ways round them.

Trixie and Donna arrived as promised and settled down on Melinda's matching leather sofas.

'Oh darling, it'll soon be over, and then you can go back to being beautiful again,' Trixie consoled. 'And, like this is totally secret, and it's just between the three of us, but I heard at Homer's tonight that Roberto Merdo, who's been on the look-out for an English actress to star in his new thriller, has just seen *Two Girls, Two Guys* and guess what? He wants you for the part, darling!'

'You're joking!'

'Would I lie?'

But Melinda's interest was only feigned. Work was the furthest thing from her mind. What she really craved was cigarettes, cocaine and good sex, the first two of which she had given up to avoid the Hollywood life-style snipers and the last of which seemed to have given up on her. She wanted her body back and it was difficult to allow herself to be comforted by Trixie as she suspected her best friend – with a paranoia worthy of the initiators of Operation Starfish – of seeing to her frustrated husband behind her back. Suddenly she couldn't bear to keep up the pretence a moment longer. 'Yeh, well, Merdo, fuck that creep, I wouldn't work for him if he was making the last film on earth.'

'Oh, but he is, darling!' Trixie tittered her favourite titter and lit a cigarette. 'The film's going to be about a giant meteorite on a collision course with earth. Mankind's only hope lies with a team of scientists who are racing against time to build a spaceship that can fly up and attach a nuclear warhead to the thing and blow it apart. But meanwhile the change in the earth's gravitational field as the meteor approaches is causing earthquakes and hurricanes and riots, and everything is just going crazy.'

'It sounds fucking awful and I don't want anything to do with it,' moaned Melinda. 'I feel fat, I feel ugly, I can't do anything. I can't even sleep for chrissake! I want it all to be over!' And she rolled over into Trixie's lap and blubbered theatrically.

Donna came over. 'Calm calm calm calm calm, darling. Calm. C'mon now, don't cry. It's going to be over any day now.' While she talked she rolled up a joint and insisted that Melinda have some, telling her that at this stage it couldn't do any harm, that it would be good for her, calm her down, she was sooooo strung out, poor darling, and who was to know. They passed it round, the weed leaving an acrid film on their lips, and before it was finished Donna had one of her 'brainwaves' and suggested that they get out the Ouija board.

When no one objected outright she cleared off the wicker-and-glass coffee table, piled the cups, magazines and ashtray on top of a pouf, and slid it across the hardwood floor and out of the way. Then she pushed the sofas together, admonishing the others when they would not budge to help. She drew all the blinds and closed all the windows but one, and made a point of blocking the door ajar. 'Okay darl', where d'you keep the rest of the kit?'

'The board's in the games cupboard which is out on the patio by the hot-tub and there's candles in the kitchen drawer. The one to the left of the sink!' Melinda called as Donna disappeared into the other room. 'And I think we've lost the pointer so you'll have to use a glass!'

Donna fetched everything and arranged it all, while Melinda let Trixie feel her stomach because the baby was kicking. 'C'mon, c'mon, give me your hands, d'you wanna do this or not?' Trixie stopped prodding at Melinda's bulge and the two of them sat round and placed a forefinger on top of the glass.

Donna lit the candles and dimmed the lights, then put her finger along with the others'. 'Is there anybody there?' She paused, while Trixie swallowed one of her famous giggles. 'I said, is there anybody there?' The giggle exploded and Trixie tried to turn it into a cough, but Melinda shushed her. She was already digging it. 'If there's anybody there, we would like to invite you to join us.' Melinda loved it when Donna did this, put on her best *Sunset Boulevard* voice. It made her want to touch her. 'Please, is there anybody there?'

Abruptly, the glass shifted a fraction of an inch. 'It moved,' cried Trixie.

'Trixie, darling,' said Donna, still intoning like a fading screen siren, 'if you don't shut the fuck up right now I'm going to take you outside, tie you to a tree and pluck your pubics out one by one. And then I'm going to smear your naked pussy with raspberry jelly and leave you there as a present for the racoons, while Melinda and I continue the seance in peace. Understand?' Trixie straightened out her smile and tried to concentrate on the glass. Donna continued, 'Whoever you are, I apologise for the interruption. Please don't be afraid. Come back and tell us who you are.'

The three women sat in nervous silence for a while. Donna had her eyes half closed, only her whites showing beneath the lowered lids. Trixie's left leg was trembling, the knee jerking up and down in its own spastic rhythm, as if she were experiencing extreme cold. Melinda's mind seemed to have gone completely blank apart from one fact on which she focused with a sublime intensity: deep in her womb, the child was lying completely still and she could no longer tell whether or not it was there.

Then the candles guttered and the glass glided across the board until it reached the foot of the letter K and stopped. Trixie gasped and her leg stopped vibrating. Melinda barely noticed.

'K,' said Donna softly. 'Does your name begin with the letter K?' There was nothing for a moment, and then the glass moved again, in its uncanny, frictionless fashion, across to the letter J. 'KJ. Are they initials? Are they your initials?' The glass slid four letters to the left, paused at the F and looped back to the letter K. With great gentleness and patience (she should have been a nurse, Melinda thought) Donna asked for more specifics. But whatever it was did not seemed inclined to give them. The glass simply slid back to the letter J, went from there to the letter F, then moved across to K, and it traced this curious triangle in response to any question Donna happened to ask. 'I'm sorry, we don't understand. I'm sorry,' Donna kept saying, infected by the repetition, and after a while they all got bored and she broke the circle. Melinda stood up, raised the lights and extinguished all the candles.

'Kujuf. Krajif. Karjaf. Keejef,' offered Trixie. 'I tell you there's no such word with those letters like that in it. I think the whole thing's stupid. I thought in seances people were supposed to have fits and speak in tongues and all. I thought that we'd get that ecto-goo stuff all over the place, not get visited by some jive-ass spirit that can't spell.'

Donna tried to explain to her that you couldn't simply demand whatever you wished from the spirit world and maybe it was the dope, but Melinda suddenly felt a little cold and weird, and her mood shifted accordingly. It was all nonsense anyway, she said abruptly; it was probably just Donna moving the glass. She was glad she hadn't done it for years and she wouldn't be bothering again. The board could go back in the games cupboard where it belonged, and at this she experienced a tiny shiver. Anyway, she was tired out now but thanks for coming over it was lovely to see you both.

Still arguing, Donna and Trixie backed their cars out of the driveway and left. As their headlights wound down the canyon road Melinda could hear them honking to one another across the hollow night. It was on nights like this when the air tasted of bark and cactus and gasoline that she thought a little of the wonder that was Los Angeles. Los Angeles, this sprawl, glass and desert, glitter and freeway, machine and boutique. Away around the massive bay it gleamed, its billion red eyes sullen, its white lights barking at the night, its buildings sulking beneath their cloaks of filth. Melinda turned inside and waddled through the house. Trixie had left her cigarettes on the coffee table and the night's glamour made her break her vow. She walked out on to the deck and lit one, gazing out at the moon where it glittered away above the Pacific, out there, between the banks of this gully that they called a valley. She tried to stretch the romance of the moment, to sink into the image like a character she might have played, might yet play, in a film. She tried to think of her husband, Moses, to wonder where he was now as he flew through the night to be with her, tried to conjure the love that had made her leave England behind and make her home on the edge of the Pacific. But the cigarette tasted foul, of chemicals, and she couldn't finish it. She stubbed it out on the rail and dropped it over the edge, then went back inside and cracked open a Dr Pepper that she took from her enormous fridge.

Moses came home at around 5 a.m. Melinda was lying on the sofa asleep, one of the many post-natal self-help volumes that she owned opened out on her belly, as if the child were supposed to absorb its wisdom by some kind of cellular osmosis. He bent down over her and tucked a loose curl away behind her ear, his huge hands almost as large as her face.

He had joined IBM in 1957, the same year that Laika had been launched into space. It was a good year for the company. Apart from the paranoia sparked in America by the fact that the Russians were launching satellites – which translated into orders for ever larger computer systems by the Pentagon – American Airlines contracted IBM to devise a solution to the problems they were having with their flight reservations system. The computer company's answer was SABRE, the Semi-Automatic Business Research Environment. SABRE was a peach of an idea, not least because IBM had most of the technology for it already available, thanks to a government-funded project called SAGE that it had been building for the best part of a decade, but which was completely obsolete by the time it was ready for use.

SAGE, the Semi-Automatic Ground Environment, had also been cultivated in a climate of paranoia, this time fostered as a reaction to the exploding of an atomic weapon by the USSR in 1949. Airforce minds panicked at the thought of hordes of Soviet bombers taking a short-cut across the Arctic Circle to bomb the United States, with nothing to stop them except a few old radar stations left from World War Two. The USAF needed more; it needed battlements and lines of sight; it needed the first large-scale real-time computer system which, as a first priority, had to be better than the one, code-named Nike, that the US army was developing.

When finally completed, SAGE consisted of twenty-three 'Direction Centers', each of which had at its heart a duplexed IBM vacuum tube computer covering an area the size of a football field. Each Direction Center was manned by around a hundred personnel and linked to around a hundred sources of radar information – plane-based, ship-based, ground-based, missile-based – as well as to the other Direction Centers. Each was also linked to anti-aircraft missile silos whose missiles could be launched remotely by SAGE operators in response to any threat. But SAGE would have been of little use in the event of an attack. To save money (the project ended up costing eight billion dollars) the computers and command centres had been placed above ground rather than below, and in areas which were already major targets (the air force having decided that their people wouldn't want to work out in remote locales). Not only that, but radar jamming and radar decoys, likely to be deployed by any invading force, would have confused the system instantly and rendered the aircraft tracking systems useless. All of this was, however, irrelevant, for by the time SAGE went online the Intercontinental Ballistic Missile had been born and the Commies no longer needed bombers to blow up America.

Moses himself had got into computing through politics, in a roundabout kind of way. He was at college during the 1952 presidential elections and he'd never forgotten the night the results came in. CBS, the channel he had been watching, had organised a UNIVAC computer as a back-up for Walter Cronkite's election coverage. They were going to use it to predict the results – it was a PR stunt by Remington Rand, who'd built the machine. They had a program set up to monitor the returns in various key states and guess the outcome on the basis of that. Moses had been glued to the screen. He thought this machine was the coolest thing, that the huge cabinet filled with electronic arrays and flickering lights was just too sexy. He'd worked in all kinds of offices, getting himself through his college course, and he knew about the power structures in those places. He could *feel* the way they worked, all those self-important execs charging around, all those clerks getting uppity about their boring little jobs, all those typists and receptionists getting a kick out of their own efficiency. Offices were machines, wood and flesh and stone machines, and you could disguise it all you liked with gossip and internal politics but that's the way they were. And it was completely obvious to Moses that what they all cried out for was one of these things, one of these data processors, these electronic computers. He could see as clear as his own hand in front of him how this machine would fulfil the desires of all those white-collar workers with their fetish for getting the job done. For here was the perfect employee: give it some information, tell it what to do, get an answer. It was what everyone wanted, he had thought at the time and many times since, because from top to bottom in every organisation what drove these people was the twinge of pleasure they got from completing a task, from emptying their in-tray, from taking a shit. That's what this machine could do for them. It could help them take a shit. And that was when he realised there was money to be had here. Lots of money. After all, Americans loved to shit.

It was a bit of a disappointment, then, when UNIVAC predicted Eisenhower to win with odds of 8 to 7 and he went and won with a landslide, 442 electoral votes to Stevenson's 89. But then, and here was the miracle, Cronkite admitted that his team had *lied* about UNIVAC's prediction. Yes, it was true: at 8.30 that evening the computer had predicted a landslide for Eisenhower, 438 votes to 43. But all the opinion polls had said a close race and fearing PR disaster – a grim fate, not one you want to court – the operators had rejigged the machine, made UNIVAC say a close race as well. The computer was vindicated. How excited was Moses? Charles Collingdale, man on the spot at UNIVAC headquarters in Philly, patted the machine's monstrous cabinet and reassured the viewers. The age of the computer had begun, he said, or something like that, no more covering up for it now. Didn't need it.

Moses went out the next day and enrolled in sales school. He knew where he was going. He wanted to see those cabinets in every damn office in the country and the commissions in his pocket. It was five or six years before he found out that they'd faked the cabinet too, it was a dummy, the real machine was so unwieldy they couldn't set it up for the event. And it was too hot – it would have made Collingdale's make-up run. So they'd rigged up a fake, filled it with Christmas tree lights. It was funny, but though he'd have been bothered by that fact if he'd known it at the time, when he eventually did learn about it, it didn't seem to matter. After all, he understood enough about computers by then to know that it was their logical identity which was important, not their physical realisation.

But Moses was working his way up the ranks by then and was in it up to his neck – so much so that he sometimes found himself wondering if humans were the same as computers in that respect: that it was their logical identity which was important and not their physical body. It was a comforting and consoling thought, this. It helped him to cut deals, it helped him to objectify women and, eventually, it would help him to deal with certain problems that would one day be posed by his son. He made his name on the old 1401s which sold so well because they came equipped with the new 1403 chain printer which at 600 words per minute was four times faster than its nearest competitor. For that they'd junked the old cabinets too, jettisoned the old grey boxes with their rounded corners and Queen Anne legs and gone for this light-blue, very square, modernist number – very cool, very slick. Moses had loved the new design and it showed – he was top salesman in the country two years running. He was cooking, he was in a different league. Suddenly he was mixing with the company execs, was blue chip, was at all the parties, mixing with the stars too, at those big industry benders out in Hollywood. That's where he met Melinda, at one of those, and she lapped him up. He was hot property. He knew it, he dug it.

By the time Judd was conceived Moses was closely involved with a top-secret new product line that would eventually be launched in 1964 under the name System 360 (for 360 degrees, like it was an all-rounder, like it could do anything). The thing had the biggest civilian budget of anything in history: IBM threw more funds at it than the government had at the Manhattan project. When they launched it they held press conferences in fifty-three US cities and fourteen other countries simultaneously. The market had dipped a bit when Mariner I was taken out by a bug four minutes after launch, a comma missing from the Fortran code. Flight path had gone crazy, they'd had to blow it up by remote, 22 July 1962 (Moses remembered the date because that same day he'd asked Melinda to marry him – better get that nailed down before things crashed and burned). That missing comma was big news; everyone had thought: what's the use of these machines; if they're no more robust than that, then what can they do for me? Suddenly computers weren't so perfect any more, they'd lost their cool, they'd lost their sex appeal. Moses knew that the 360 had to put it back. He said so, too, and that was enough to get him taken off direct sales and put on the 360 concept team as a consultant. Big time.

And now here he was, criss-crossing the country, an electron helping the vast transport network of America to process whatever arcane calculation it was bent upon, forever moving from airplane to hotel to meeting to airplane, not understanding till now the value of home. 'My little Desdemona,' he whispered, and Melinda rolled in her sleep and threw an arm around his neck. He picked her up and carried her through into the bedroom and laid her out on the bed, then took a quick shower. Having dried himself off, he climbed in beside her and spooned her. Their bodies threw each other into sharp relief as they lay there, cosy as piano keys.

The next morning she awoke before he did. And she awoke suddenly, with a start, straight into the bright day. She had dreamt of him and was only half surprised to find him there. She slipped out of the waterbed as gently as her stomach would allow and went into the kitchen to fix him some pancakes and eggs. It was when she turned on the small television that they kept in the kitchen and saw that John F. Kennedy had been shot dead in Dallas that her waters broke.

So Judd entered this world already mixed up with events out of his control and beyond his ken. It was a nice childhood for sure: house in the Malibu hills, Mum pretty famous, Dad pretty cool. Trips abroad: Hawaii, Europe, Japan one time, England now and then to see Grandpa and Grandma, weird times, those, because it was often just him and Mom on their own and everyone always argued such a lot. He went to a real nice school, mostly white kids, but he didn't actually think of himself as black. Well he did, but it wasn't, like, an issue for him. It didn't seem to make any difference to anyone, 'cept sometimes when he was at the mall with Mom and they'd get strange looks and someone would shout something or spit, or maybe they'd come outside and find their tyres slashed – that had happened once or twice – and Mom would get real upset. But mostly it was okay.

Judd wasn't so academic anyway. He liked sports a lot, baseball 'specially, and he liked building model aircraft, the kind you make from kits. The teachers said he was bright but wouldn't concentrate. He got into all sorts of trouble for this. Every term his report would say the same thing and it would mean the same thing, too: a vacation full of lectures from Moses who would tell him it was harder for him because of his colour, because everything was against him, because he had to be twice as good as everyone else to get half as far, because this was a white man's world and how the hell did he think that his own father had achieved what he had, a bigshot at I–B–M, yeh, that's right, Big Blue, the highest-up black man in the corporation, with this beautiful house and a beautiful wife like his mother and three cars to drive and more if he wanted, and holidays in Europe and all? Not by not concentrating, that's for sure. And Judd would say 'Sure Dad', and blink back the tears, but not really see why it was all such a big deal. Then he'd forget about it and his mind would wander somewhere else, and he'd be pretty happy again.

Because Judd suffered from a curious condition that was called picno-lepsia. Many times each day, for periods that could last from a few seconds to an hour or more at the extreme, Judd dropped out of whatever happened to be going on around him and on to a plane where time itself was deformed, and no longer regulated by the clock, the chant, the TV, the conversation. His senses still operated, his eyes and his ears, but he received no data from them.

It was as if he fell in-between the frames of a film, expanding the gap between one stationary twenty-fourth of a second and the next into an entire universe, just as the universe itself expanded from a minuscule tear in the field of some inconceivably tiny quantum force. And just as the frames of a film point to a reality that lies beyond the camera, so Judd's picnolepsia directed him towards an understanding that there was an aspect to time that escaped apprehension, that defied linearity and the quartz movement of his father's digital watch. He'd found free time, a time which was in some way his own.

When he returned to his senses he usually didn't even notice he'd been gone – his mind just picked up where it had left off, pulling the threaded loop of cotton closed, and that would be that. But often he'd come round to someone speaking loudly at him, repeating his name perhaps, and generally it was Moses. Disorientated, Judd would utter a 'huh?', for which he'd receive a clip round the ear from his father and a short lecture on the need to pay attention and get some common sense into his head.

Sometimes he'd wander off and do something, only to forget not only what it was he'd done but the very fact that he'd done anything at all. It was as if his memory of what took place during the dilated period was sluiced from his mind by his re-immersion in the everyday temporal ocean. Once, when he was very young, he'd wandered out of the house's backyard while his parents were sunbathing and taken a walk. When Moses and Melissa discovered that he'd gone they panicked and went crazy looking for him (at the time they were still receiving threats from white supremacist organisations). They called the police, only to find him playing naked in the stream at the bottom of the canyon at the end of it all, unabashed and unable to work out why he was in trouble. Moses gave him a whipping after that, one which neither of them would ever forget, and from then on whenever he caught Judd at his day-dreaming it would echo in the air about them, a spectre.

As a result Judd started to invent narratives that would dovetail with events on either side of the vanished periods of time, making up stories that smoothed over his absence, not just for the sake of others, but for his own sake, too, so that he could have some kind of coherent account of the past. The important thing was that the story, the image he invented, should be a catalyst, one that would react with patterns lying virtual in the possibilities created by his lapse, crystallising them into plausibility. He was often extremely successful and events that he knew never to have taken place (unless by some bizarre freak he'd reinvented that which had been forgotten) entered family folklore, to be related and misremembered in their turn.

He learned, then, to treasure his lost minutes, came to think of them as the moments when he was really at liberty, and in this perhaps they came to function as a tiny secret stand against his father – not just against Moses the man, whom Judd was too young to know properly yet, but against what he stood for. And what he stood for, in Judd's eyes, what, in fact, he was a relay for, was these machines, these computers, which he worked with and which Judd had been taken to see once or twice and which were, Moses said, accurate and logical and, always, faster, faster, faster than their predecessors. They awed him, these great collections of cabinets that seemed from the noises and heat they gave out to be roiling with beetles and insects. Judd's mind recoiled at the thought of them; the dry, coppery tang that they traced through the air was almost capable of turning his stomach. The result was that he was frightened of them, and he became determined that he was not going to become one of his father's machines. I'm not a computer, he thought under a spout of petulant anger whenever Moses disciplined him. I can't be programmed. You can't tell me what to do. I'm not a machine.

Once or twice Moses spoke with Melinda about sending the boy to see a doctor, but she wouldn't hear of it: he was normal, she said, and he'd be fine if his father would just stop pushing him so bloody hard. And then Melinda took this job in England and Judd met Jennifer and everything got rewired.

Sex and the media

Doreen Buerk, Judd's Geography teacher during the spring and summer of 1973, was a woman who had trimmed her sexuality down to the point where its knife-like edge could continually precede her like the prow of some diabolic snow-plough. Amazingly, she had managed to achieve this effect while remaining convinced that she was completely sexless. In fact, she had managed to achieve it *by* remaining convinced that she was completely sexless. Judd had never met anyone so . . . so *repressed* before.

She made him feel guilty just for existing. He couldn't enter the Geography classroom without feeling that he'd done something wrong. The way she looked at him, it was like those people in the mall, the ones who couldn't help but stare. For them, as for Doreen, just by being there he was already at fault.

There was no sense with her that they were humans together. The teachers back home were not always so great, but at least they spoke to you occasionally, not just *at* you, *at you at you at you* all the time. It made Judd's head spin in peculiar orbits, made him feel that his thoughts were being constructed by the Spirograph that he'd been given last year for Christmas and which he'd brought with him over to England to do pictures on, pictures that he pinned to the walls of his room. He didn't understand that he already thought a bit like this, that his mental processes were so many intersecting ellipses and multicoloured spirals on a flat plateau, and that it was merely Doreen's strange scrutiny that was making him become aware of it.

Can thoughts have colours? he wondered. He closed his eyes and thought of red. I guess they can. So what colour was the thought of Doreen Buerk? Kind of puke. With purple patches and green lumps. A strange colour, one from the covers of horror comics and fantasy paperbacks. A colour that was sort of scary but in a roundabout way, a way that meant you weren't sure. A colour that twisted your gut and pinched up your anus and made you want to misbehave.

Judd couldn't help it. Doreen Buerk gave him the evil eye and that gaze of hers did something to him. Made him squirm. Made him put all of those bits of himself in line. He wasn't allowed to let things drift off, to leave things lying around, to drop out of time to his dilated realm. She looked at him and he was *focused*. It made him want to do bad stuff. He didn't want to. He just had to.

Doreen Buerk had developed her peculiar colour in a darkroom of spite she had constructed as a child, outraged at her parents' permissive attitudes. Her folks had been swingers in the 1920s, well-to-do, fashionable parties and sojourns abroad, and they had little time for the austerities brought on by the war. But daughter Doreen had followed the government instructions for the populace with keen delight; to her, the ration book was a symbol of the divine order, a King James Bible for the twentieth century. Throughout her childhood she shrank from the dealings her mother and father had with assorted black-marketeers – whom she regarded as 'shady characters', even though they were mostly neighbours, uncles, cousins, people whom she had known all her life – and she despised them for preferring their decadent memories to the resurgent moralities of the 1950s. In her eyes they were sullied and Doreen hated them as only a child can hate.

She had grown up and gone to university, and there she had met Donald. Donald was Mr Moral and Correct, Donald cut a fine dash in his tailored suits and gowns, Donald spoke with authority at the debating society and held fine get-togethers in the city's better restaurants. Having sized up his pedigree as she would that of a dog she wanted to breed, Doreen took the necessary steps to secure him in marriage. She played it well – in Doreen, Donald saw all of the qualities he thought necessary in a wife. Not only was she pristine, prissy and controllable, but these attributes seemed to him to stem not from a particularly pliable nature but from the elaborate framework of judgement with which, like some scholastic philosopher, she had surrounded herself. She lived a life of pure form, into which all experience was to be inserted.

With this insight Donald imagined that he had stolen a march over Doreen and when they married he had no doubts that he would prove to be the dominant partner. What he did not see, however, because it was in himself, was how much difficulty he would have in coping with that position of power. But Doreen *had* seen this and that is what gave her the edge. For her plans were long-term and she saw that ten years of submission would be more than compensated for by the thirty or forty of dominance that she was certain she would subsequently come to enjoy.

By the time they were in their mid–twenties Doreen and Donald were ensconced in a suitably large house in Edgbaston and Donald was 'doing things' in the city. They remained childless, which, though a problem for Donald – who saw offspring as a necessary career accessory – suited Doreen, who had no desire for children, nor even for physical intercourse (which she put up with on a minimal basis). She got her kicks in other ways and she rather hoped that her husband – like most of the men in the Conservative Club, who kept the street trade in Balsall Heath ticking over – would begin to go elsewhere for his. However, he did not and this, as she later came to realise, was the first sign of trouble.

She knew that something was amiss when Donald began to leave the office on time and come straight home from work. When confronted he always made out it was because he had a job to do in the house or, in the summer, in the garden, but she could tell from the glaze in his eyes and the way in which he continually hung about her as she did the housework or cooked the dinner that she was his chief object of interest. In the beginning he had enough restraint to keep his newly fanned desires on a Platonic level, but after about six months of this behaviour Doreen began to worry that the long resisted descent of his mind and intentions to the level of her body was now imminent and she took care to remind him in those little ways – such as replacing their divan with two single beds – that they had agreed when they'd been married to keep those activities to an absolute minimum. Thankfully, the increase in Donald's emotional intensity was accompanied by a proportional decrease in his prostate control, so Doreen never had to submit to him for very long.

The Balsall Heath thing had been a problem, because she had hoped to use as the first weapon in her domestic coup d'état any guilty feelings Donald had due to extra-marital activities. But as they became more emotionally and physically intertwined Donald began to develop guilt in far more complex and interesting ways. He had actually started to idealise Doreen, not abstractly as she might have expected, but sexually. He went on about how he loved the soft touch of her skin, the smell of her, the way she moved to the bathroom or talked on the phone, the quizzical expression that she occasionally wore, the dimples in her downy cheeks. He cooed to her that he loved her strength; he became aroused by the clack of her shoes in the hallway. And as he began to squirm with this lust for her he started to blame himself for her failure to conceive. 'But I do feel responsible,' he would whine in an agonised tone, while he lay curled on the edge of his bed after they had made what passed for love. 'What if it's my fault? What if it's me who's somehow . . . somehow . . . deficient? You wouldn't leave me, would you, for another man? I mean, for one who could, you know . . . ?'

Glancing across at the pathetic figure of her husband, his muscles already turning to flab, Doreen would give out a little shiver and tell him not to be so ridiculous and to go to sleep. She hated these exchanges. They seemed so pointless. What, after all, did he want from her?

Once he realised that he was not going to get what he regarded as the appropriate reaction, Donald began visiting several specialists, all of whom told him he was fine in that department. But this made matters worse, for rather than berate himself he now began to berate his wife. Doreen, worried that the doctors might be able to solve her 'problem', absolutely refused to have tests and since she could not get Donald to drop the matter she began to criticise him for even suggesting that she might be somehow inadequate. And why, she demanded, did he want her to demean herself by exposing her secret parts to some greasy gynaecologist? Wasn't it enough that she had to do it for him? Finally Donald, who by now was living inside an elaborate filigree of bad faith and self-doubt, took her words at face value, chastised himself for ever having doubted her and revamped his image of her by moving it more than ever into the realm of the ideal. For the childlessness he began to seek out ontological causes and he started his quest by superimposing the paranoid complex which by now choked his mind on to the whole world of his experience, becoming in the process the perfect theologian to Doreen's philosophe.

Soon he began to splinter, the limit-cycles of his personality destabilising until they became chaotic. Donald had always been confident, conservative, persistent, balanced and arrogant; now he was excitable, obsessive and finicky. He decided that as a couple he and Doreen were too isolated, so in November of 1963 he purchased a television set, something that neither of them had owned before. The news broke that Kennedy had been assassinated and Donald went right out of the office and bought one with cash. The shop delivered it that evening and he had it set up in time for the nine o'clock news, much to Doreen's horror.

'I thought I told you I didn't want one of those unholy things in my house.'

'Darling, I'm telling you, we just can't go on without one. How am I supposed to keep abreast of events? It's a global village we live in now, everything's linking up and we can't afford to be left behind. You know, the medium is the message and all that. Think of the opportunities for business . . . and education . . . and so on. It's the human spirit you know, joining all together across the planet in one great consciousness.'

'The radio has always been quite enough human spirit for me. If you must speak to fools, please do me the courtesy of not repeating their nonsense to your wife. Spending our money on that thing, that heathen object. Do you want to join all those horrible little people who sit down in front of it every night, their eyes going square and their brains turning to mush, worshipping it as if it were some kind of pagan orifice? My husband, my very own husband, a member of the common rabble!' She stormed out into the kitchen in tears and started on the washing up, and it took Donald several hours, a dinner out, one promise to keep the thing in his study and another not to touch her for a month, before she was finally appeased and allowed him to keep it.

Donald was delighted with his new toy. Whenever his thoughts drifted to the television he experienced a frisson of excitement that ran through his entire body. It was similar to the feeling he used to have as a boy when, shut away upstairs in his room at the top of his parents' firm old house, he would drag voices out of the ether with the aid of a cat's whisker radio set that he had built himself inside an old cigar box from a kit that his father had given him one Christmas. He could smell the cracked perfume of the splintery wood right now, as if he had the box in front of him. The radio had been as magical an object to his childish mind as a flying carpet – being able to pull storm warnings, snatches of police reports, strains of music from out of the background static was like being able to swoop around the sky. Afterwards, he would lie in bed awake, his ear sore from the small plastic speaker, and try to comprehend how all these sounds managed to be everywhere at once. How was it that all of them were there, in the air around him, not just when he was tuning his set but when he was walking down the street or sitting in a classroom at school or eating dinner in silence with his mother watching him carefully to make sure he ate his boiled and tasteless vegetables right up, or else there would be no custard and no bread-and-butter pudding for dessert?

Now it was not just sounds but pictures which were everywhere. And this time their reach was not just the city of his childhood, the meagre range of the old antennae, but the world itself: New York, San Francisco, Tokyo, Shanghai, Saigon, New Delhi, Moscow, Tel Aviv, Rome, Berlin, Cape Town, London England. Sputnik I had been above them for six years, bouncing frequencies back through space, and Sputnik II was up there somewhere too now, with Laika on board – and many more satellites were soon to follow. The world was divided into two now: capitalism and communism yes, but also the places the cameras went and the places that they didn't, with the second category rapidly dwindling relative to the first as, propelled from its dignified black-and-white chrysalis by events like the Kennedy assassination, the media began to unfold its creaking new body and stretch its iridescent wings out to dry around the globe.

'It's the news I need it for, primarily,' Donald explained to Doreen in a calmer mode as they crunched the lobsters they had ordered. 'Now I'm a councillor, it's vital that I know what's going on and the papers just aren't enough any more.' The squeaky meat was delicately flavoured with heavy metal trace elements and oestrogen. Doreen waited for the qualifier and Donald splashed more of the icy Chablis into their tall glasses. 'Although, of course, one still needs them for depth of comment and so on; that's something the box will never replace. For real reporting one just has to have *The Times*. But when you need only the facts, and on the button, well, that's why we have to have a set. With a piece of film you can see for yourself. Don't need to take some other fellow's word for it. These journalist Johnnies can't mess with a picture, can they? What you see is what you get, story of the eye and all that. Not like the papers, or the radio, when you can never be quite sure. Even with *The Times*, yes even with *The Times* I'm sorry to say, it has been known to happen. That's what the world's coming to, I'm afraid.' Doreen scraped a gooey clutch of orange eggs away from her lobster's belly and lifted one up on a prong of her fork for closer inspection. Then she nodded agreement and popped the tiny egg into her mouth, not because she saw the situation Donald's way (it was, unfortunately, painfully obvious to her that he didn't know what he was talking about) but because she had already worked out that now Donald had got the damn thing he would probably spend less time pestering her and more time gazing into its flickering kaleidoscopic screen, like the fascinated child he was.

I scry with my little eye

The first time she found Donald sitting alone in an armchair, lights off, transfixed by the television, Doreen had just returned from her weekly Women's Institute meeting. High, high above, beyond the clouds, Laika slowly orbited, on her way to Hollywood where a young Judd – just four years old – sat beneath the sky and stared earnestly into his own TV, flicking from channel to channel in the hope that rapid juxtapositions of these images which moved so fast would capture them, slow them down, make some sense of them. Sometimes he found it as impossible to remember what he had just watched on TV as he did the events which took place during one of his picnoleptic lapses, and this confused him. There seemed to be a link between the two experiences: although they weren't the same, he got the same feeling in the pit of his stomach when he thought about either of them.

Jennifer, on the other hand, didn't have a TV set. Three years older than Judd, at that time her entertainment consisted of charging round the streets of her estate on her new bike and meeting up with her friends to talk about incredibly important things. Like a droplet of mercury she scooted from house to house, calling up at bedroom windows, shouting at people in the street, slipping secretly into garden sheds and the spaces behind garages. That evening, in fact, she had been cycling along the main road when she had nearly been run down by Doreen Buerk herself, who had too much on her mind to pay attention to other road users.

Drugs was the topic which occupied Doreen so. Her WI meeting had been graced by the presence of the local police inspector, who had come to speak to the assembled ladies about the threat to society posed by that particular evil menace. Doreen knew the inspector vaguely from the Conservative Association. He seemed very capable and was certainly very popular: thanks to his rugged good looks and army manner, seats at meetings at which he was scheduled to appear were always at a premium. On this occasion he had brought with him a small amount of cannabis resin, which he'd held with a pair of tweezers and heated with a lighter before walking around the room so that all those present should get to know the smell and be able to report it should they encounter it. Elspeth Peterson, who had been sitting near the front, got quite giggly, and Doreen remarked quietly to her neighbour, Agnes Batts, that that was typical of her, and Agnes remarked back that she was sure she had smelt that smell on several occasions when she had had for some reason to walk through the local council estate, and Doreen nodded and said sagely that she wasn't surprised, she'd known from the start that estate would be trouble.

When Doreen got home and found her husband silent and motionless in his study chair (she still would not allow the set in the living-room) she thought at first that he was asleep. It was only after she had put a pan of milk on the stove and come in to wake him that she discovered his eyes were wide open, dilated and unblinking. He was staring straight at the screen and its blue-grey shut-down flicker was reflected in their tacky glaze. Her first thought was that he was on drugs.

She shook him by the shoulder. 'Donald. Donald!' Thinking of the television, it struck her that what she had heard about the pernicious effects of the device might after all be true. She made her voice shrill and hard as a diamond drill, the same voice she used to control the boys at school. 'Don-ald!!!' It worked: Donald started out of his trance and seemed to ripple from head to toe.

'Oh. Oh. Hello, darling. Is that the time? Just watching a spot of telly.'

Doreen's fears evaporated and left behind a little precipitate of disapproval. 'Yes, well, perhaps you've been watching a little too much. You don't know when to stop, Donald Buerk. Come to bed. I've made you some hot milk.' Donald shrugged and walked over to the telly to switch it off. Then he followed Doreen upstairs to the room which contained their respective beds.

Donald's descent into this trance-like state was by no means an isolated occurrence, despite its being new to Doreen. This was the fourth or fifth time that he had slipped into resonant harmony with his television set. The previous weekend Doreen had gone to visit her parents in Cheltenham and her husband had been left to his own devices. He had spent the entire two days watching a single channel and sleeping fitfully in his chair between viewing sessions. It had been a fantastically uncritical experience: it made no difference to him whether he was watching a scheduled programme, the test card, or white noise. On his wife's return he avoided the set for a few days, resisting the temptation to switch the thing on, until one lunch-time he became inveigled into another cathode fascination by a set in the window of an electrical shop. The news was playing and the launch of the first of the Soviet Venera probes was being reported, although Donald couldn't hear what was being said. But he was fixated none the less and he stood there, stock still, while other pedestrians hurried by him until Mandy Davies, the shop-girl, whose chief worry for several years had been that her name had no 'Rice' in it (if it had, she thought, her life might have been a whole lot more exciting), emerged to check if he was all right.

'Would you like some help, sir?' Pause. 'Excuse me, sir, are you all right?' Pause again. 'Eh luv, what's the bother?' Donald started, rippled, flashed her a psychotic glance and shot off down the street.

Doreen didn't begin to get really concerned until she awoke in the middle of the night a few weeks later to find the bed beside her empty. 'Donald!

Donald!' she hissed, but there was no reply, so she stomped downstairs in search of him (she was never much of a one for creeping). Once again, she found her husband in his study, slumped in front of a screen full of static. He looked pale, his face was silvery with beads of sweat, his features had the metallic sheen of blood-starved skin. The test signal filled the room like the sound from a flat-lining ECG. Doreen left him there and went back to bed, where she made the decision that from that moment on she would start to distance herself from this man. She would begin with her closest friends and see where it led. She'd drop hints that all was not well between them; nothing too specific, nothing to suggest that there was something wrong with his mind. Vague references to a physical inadequacy would probably do the trick.

Donald developed an illness, something indeterminate, which led to him missing days from work. He began to spend the time at home, his movements restricted to a series of vectors, of energised channels. He seemed only able to move between the television, which was constantly on, the refrigerator, which had also begun to interest him, and the downstairs toilet, where he voided himself repeatedly and scrubbed his hands until they were pink. This pattern of behaviour, providing as it did for all his needs, might have gone on indefinitely but for Doreen's generally successful attempts to short-circuit it by making sure that there was, for example, nothing readily edible in the fridge, or no toilet paper in the loo. Remonstrating with him was useless; he had gone into decline extremely rapidly and already barely spoke at all. If he did, it was only to murmur, 'I'm not well, dear, can't you see, please don't take the cheese away from me again,' or some such thing, and whatever he said was voiced in such a sorry tone that rather than evoking pity in his wife it almost moved her to slash his throat. Then he stopped going in to work at all. Doreen had the doctor pay a housecall – Donald did not feel up to going to the hospital – but the man could find nothing physically the matter and prescribed amphetamines to perk him up.

Doreen had been feeling increasingly agitated herself, but it was not until she discovered that Donald had been powdering his pills and mixing them in with the sugar (which she had been heaping liberally into her tea) that she finally came to the end of her tether. 'NO MORE NO MORE NO MORE!!!!' she screamed, her face right up against his, and with the strength that supposedly visits women in times of terrible danger (like when their child is trapped beneath a ten-ton truck) Doreen picked up the television and carried it up the stairs into the attic, trailing cables behind her as she went. If it hadn't been for the fact that the neighbours

61

would talk she would have thrown it from the window and into the street.

When she returned, she found Donald stretched out on the floor in a hebephrenic state. He was barely breathing, his eyes were open and his body was all strange angles. The last thing he had seen on the screen was the head of a small brown-and-white mongrel dog. The newscaster had said that today was the tenth anniversary of the 'muttnik' Laika's trip into space. For the first time in human history, he said, Soviet scientists had managed to put a live animal into orbit. But, he said, his brow furrowed with irony and his lips twitching at their edges in a patronising manner, they had neglected to work out how to get it back. The cause of Laika's death had never been made public by the Soviets, he continued cheerily. Was she terminated by lethal injection? Did she run out of air and suffocate? Did she simply burn up in the atmosphere? Perhaps we'll never know. Then he spoke for a while about other dogs that had been sent into space since: Belka and Strelka, for example, and Pchelka and Mushka. Pchelka and Mushka had burned up on re-entry, but Belka and Strelka had returned to earth in good health. Indeed, Strelka had had a litter of puppies on her return, one of which was given to President John F. Kennedy as a gesture of good will from the USSR. 'Unfortunately,' said the newscaster, 'it was discovered around the time of the Cuban missile crisis that the puppy had an electronic bug concealed in its skull. In politics, you should probably always look a gift horse – or gift dog – in the mouth,' he said. 'Laika means 'barker' in Russian,' he said.

When Donald saw Laika on the screen he knew she was looking at him. There was something calm in those eyes, something incredibly knowing. In those eyes, Donald knew, he had seen God – or something similar. And then he collapsed and Doreen finally had the excuse that she needed. Immediately she telephoned Hatton Central for the doctors who would come and take her husband away.

3

Inferno

Was Joel born a mathematician, or did the seed of mathematics take root in his mind at an early age and flourish like a bramble in the sheltered woodland of the Williamsburg Hasidic community? Did he come into this world already prodigiously equipped, or was his ability engendered by some freak of circumstance, sunned and watered perhaps by the incessant rote learning of religious texts that was required of all the boys, the probe heads and radicles squirming through his mind until they compacted all of his experience into the infinite horizon of unforgiving compartments that is logic? Neither, of course, and yet both; there is no law of the excluded middle, no either–or, in biology. Rather a tendency existed, a string of singularities was followed, ability resulted just as pot-holes and caverns result from water eroding its way through the fault lines in some buckled hunk of limestone, just as a silver mine results from a group of dwarves following an unwinding skein of ore.

His encounter with the wider mathematical community came as something of a shock to Joel. Until that day in the Brooklyn library he had never even seen a conventional '+' sign. At the Yeshiva, the addition function had been represented by a horizontal line with one perpendicular vertical sprouting from the uppermost side alone. The boys were forbidden to write or even look at the sign of the cross (it was a punishable misdemeanour in the school to cross your 't's without first curling up the foot) and it took Joel a few moments to realise what the new symbol was.

Millstein had to replace the private systems of abstract signs Joel had developed with those more universally recognised, whether or not they conformed more fully to criteria such as logical consistency or ease of use. He had to teach him to use the Greek alphabet for algebra rather than the Hebrew, and he had to demonstrate to him that many of the spaces and phenomena he had explored had been thoroughly charted before, often from several different perspectives.

Once he had schooled Joel in the appropriate idioms and introduced him to the world at large, there was little Millstein could actually teach him. Like the young Stradivarius, the pupil outstripped the teacher by such lengths that at their weekly sessions Millstein felt more like a helmsman desperately trying to keep a wind-driven schooner on course than a teacher, although he consoled himself with the thought that this was probably the best kind of teaching of all. He set Joel problems, tasks, tests and calculations, maintaining as rigorous a programme as he thought fair, but still he had the suspicion that it was all little more than hack work for the boy and that Joel's real interest lay in material which he kept hidden from Millstein. His hunch was right: precocious Joel had decided that he had bigger fish to fry and had struck up a correspondence with the Cambridge-based editor of one of the academic journals that Millstein had introduced him to, a certain Professor Metric.

Millstein had spent a year at Cambridge himself, as part of an exchange programme, and often told Joel stories about the famous university. He loved stories even more than he loved mathematics and would slip freely between tales of his own student days and anecdotes of the great mathematical philosophers who had taught there. Men like Bertrand Russell and A. J. Ayer, both of whom Millstein had met on several occasions and whom he described in vivid detail, lauding their achievements, idolising them. He talked of Whitehead, Wittgenstein, Moore as if he had known them too, and he also pointed out for Joel's benefit similarities between the work of the logical positivists and some of the ideas of Jewish dogma. Joel absorbed it all but haphazardly, and the more confused the oddments of information became the more fascinated he was by them. He had never paid much heed to the world that existed beyond the crumbling confines of Brooklyn but now he began to weave for himself a thoroughly mystical picture of the town of Cambridge and its ancient university as a kind of intellectual promised land where mathematics was the preferred form of discourse and scholars wandered as freely among the branches of thought as they did beneath the arches and cloisters of the time-worn colleges.

So he sent this professor one of his proofs. Metric, receiving a letter from what he assumed to be an American post-graduate student, was initially tempted to dismiss it – he regarded himself as a very busy man – but something about the maths caught his attention. Although deeply faulted, the proof demonstrated a certain flair, an originality of approach. There was something quite beautiful about it, in a way. He corrected a couple of minor errors and sent the paper back, suggesting one or two possible new approaches. But he kept his best insight to himself and over the next few weeks picked away at Joel's central idea. Finally he perfected the proof, managing at the same time to retain something of the style and yet insert into it aspects of his own, and he sent it away for publication in a rival journal, a broadside in an academic battle in which he had been embroiled for several years.

Joel didn't see Metric's paper and, encouraged by the response, sent other work. Gradually a fairly regular correspondence developed, fuelled on the one hand by Joel's enthusiasm and on the other by Metric's increasing reliance upon the flow of these fresh and quirky ideas as a prop for his flagging career.

Around this time, Joel began to argue with his parents and teachers. Suddenly everyone in a position of authority seemed like a fool. Williamsburg became a ghetto, a holding bin, and the Sodom walls which surrounded him – those giant needles which had torn at the clouds of every sky of his life – began to lose their spiky inhospitableness and beckon him. Less and less able to endure the rituals and garbs and stratifications of his home and his school, and of the community and culture with which they were so thoroughly interwoven, his thoughts turned towards Manhattan. Concomitantly he lost his taste for Yiddish and Hebrew (he conversed with both Millstein and Metric in English and algebra, and these were now the most important relationships in his life) and the long sessions of religious teaching became at first a pretence and then a complete charade. His hand played host too often to the short block of wood that the rotund duty rabbi carried with him as he patrolled the corridors of the school, sweating and wheezing and alternating between the roles of avuncular protector and strict disciplinarian. But despite the man's best efforts on both fronts, Joel took no notice and soon became the bane of both school and household. In the latter his mother overcame her reluctance to chastise him, secretly her favourite, and now her voice broke glasses vases mirrors as she shrieked and yelled: 'Chas vesholem my son should be like this, an apikoros! Moshe would sit and nod: 'Respect your mother, Joel, respect, you must learn respect,' then he'd go back to nibbling on his latke and thinking of Joel's bris, his circumcision ceremony, remembering that night of fear and visions, wondering if it was right to chastise his own son, Joel Balaam Kluge, this son who seemed

65

at once both chacham and dybbuk, both wise man and evil spirit. Perhaps Moshe was even a little afraid. Judith would go on and on, eventually diverting her anger with her son towards her husband, where it would combine with his fear and react into violence. Then Moshe would take his belt to the boy and try to beat the goyim nonsense out of him, though with little enthusiasm.

Joel's three elder sisters began to shun him and his brothers exploited their parents' anger and picked on him, even though they were both smaller and younger. Even the twins seemed to dislike him now. He began to feel that his dead sister, who would have been closer to him in age than anyone else in the family had she lived, was the only one who understood. He took to visiting her grave alone, tending it with flowers and talking to her. The vast graveyard was a special place for him; the endless and exact rows of pale headstones dissected the landscape into discrete chunks and reduced everything to similarity and repetition, and this he found comforting. They were miniatures, too, of the buildings on the ever present skyline, and Joel felt that this resonance was somehow important, that it gave a clue to the correlation between the world of the living and the world of the dead. But for all his talking and praying, his sister never answered and the only reply came from the city which lay suspended from the metal clouds, over there beyond the trees, and as he learnt the meaning of alienation and found it fitted well with the way he felt when he stepped inside his vaulted inner space, he became more and more tempted to give in to the subliminal siren pulse of Manhattan. Eventually he did – one night he snuck out alone and let the subway carry him across the Hudson and on to the uncharted island beyond. And so he exchanged his trips to Queens for illicit forays to that great gobbet of phlegm poised behind the river's parted lips.

The air in the carriage is already stale when he boards, and by the time they get to York it's been gathered, recycled and shared again, and the smell of it makes him want to hold his nose. Then the train begins to rise and suddenly Joel's out above the river, held high up in the swampy shades of a dark winter afternoon, and at his elbow some old man gasps *Dis great Manhattoe it reveal itself at night.* Joel looks around: the lights pick out the city, those illuminated highways curling round, the hawsers dimly lit and pylons, rust-brown, strung lacy high, and a zorby glow from these thousand fires picks out the clouds. Battlements and towers pass in and out of view, blazing like braziers on cold street corners, deep and ozone orange the smog that lopes above them, char grey the silos, the cooling towers. Supertankers churn, feeding from the wretched water, next to vessels cracked upon the rim, awaiting condemnation . . . spires rend the heavy fog, poison seeps out through the slits . . . people swarm about the streets like flies on open wounds . . . apartment blocks sag like wasted muscles, warehouses bulge like blisters, gleaming Citicorp is a lancing needle, towers of Moloch . . . Joel looks far to the south, far to the north, across infested wetlands, iron plains, gulching plumes of flame . . . all the way to the compressed horizons the views are cluttered with industrial bric-à-brac and cranes and el lines hung with coloured lights.

At first he couldn't bear the thought of coming to the surface, breathing in the island's foetid air, so he stayed in the subway tunnels and crept beneath the skyscrapers, doing the D-train yo-yo. But little by little he found the courage to disembark, to stand around on the platform for a while, checking out commuters and feeling conspicuous in his long black coat, fiddling with a payot. Gingerly he made his way beneath the soul-reading stare of the attendant, then along the dank corridors and up the concrete stairway step by reeking step.

Finally, he pops up. Broadway splits and races to the north, trammelling the log flow traffic between steep and craggy banks. This is what he came for – Empire State pins down the place. No need for hillside watch fires here: his eyes carry the night, and the flotsam trees are torched with Christmas lights. And once he's done it, he has to do it again, has to stand for a few moments on Fifth Avenue, take a quick walk around Grand Central Station, wander down Wall Street or through the West Village, suck tentatively at the tawdry, quilted air, before disappearing back into his burrow.

Back on the platform he'd take the first train that came and repeat the process over. As his fear diminished and his nerve grew, he ventured further and higher. He took tourist trips up the Empire State and marvelled at its height. The view from the top was exhilarating and terrifying and utterly demonic. It was like daring G★d, it was like screaming an insane challenge to the skies, *I can see how it works, I can see what it looks like to you! The only difference between you and me is that you've got the equations!* For the first time he saw with his own eyes what he had always sensed to be true: that people were just like the ants and roaches which streamed through the apartment in the summer, trapped in patterns, exercises and regimes much larger than they could ever imagine. The sheer audacity of whoever had built these towers took his breath away. And it wasn't only the heavens they'd taken on, but the depths too – he thought of the skyscrapers now, reaching down and burrowing into Manhattan's meat for the human nutrients which would course as sap through the radicles of underground car-parks and up the nervures of elevators to push the brick and metal stalks leaves blooms higher ever higher. And the subways fed this Babel city, put wind into its pipes, stoked its fires, fuelled its engines, peopled its streets, crammed its nurseries, packed its apartments, tamped its office blocks, jammed its automobiles, nourished its greed, nurtured its contempt, pampered its criminals, barrelled its trash, incubated its pretension, guided its growth, constricted its vision, multiplied its tongues, publicised its disharmony, regurgitated its victuals, encouraged its poisons, drove it drove it drove it drove it on, drove it on till on its own air it would choke.

Thus Joel discovered the city. It was his first machine. He discovered the vast libraries and the bookshops, the halls of the universities, the nomad odours of the trayf food emporiums and fast-food joints. He discovered that the clothes he wore could make him either invisible or the centre of attention. Sometimes it was as though whatever he did he just wasn't there – he could bend down and touch his toes in the street or swing round a lamp-post or hop up and down the cathedral steps and no one would even react; other times, though, someone would mutter 'Fuckin' Yid!' right out of the blue, or a rich woman would yank her curious lapdog up and away from his trouser cuffs, or a workman idling against a building would spit on the hem of his coat without altering the middle-distance gaze of his eyes or breaking the rhythm with which he chewed his gum. But despite all this there was not the continual paranoia with which he had lived since birth, there was not the bubbling fear of the Crown Heights Blacks who were the Satmars' neighbours and supposed enemies, no matter that the number of 'incidents' between them were few. And one time on the elevated line that brings you back into Williamsburg it struck Joel, as he looked down on the rotting buildings and pot-holed streets that made up his neighbourhood, that the two communities which shared this desolate patch of real estate were pretty similarly shaped pieces of the jigsaw puzzle that was the city's social meshwork. How convenient it no doubt was for the people on the other side of the bridge that they should hate each other, and how much harder it made it for people like him ever to get out.

The women amazed him. Satmar boys are forbidden to look at any women other than their mothers and their sisters. Since even the sketchy pictures of little girls in the primers that were handed out in the English class by the one Gentile teacher in the school had all been heavily censored with the same black marker pen, the acres of flesh that were revealed in the streets now that it was summer bemused and amazed him. His attention would be captured by long, thin, tan legs disappearing up miniskirts, by bare arms in the sun, by pale skin and fine features and rolls of startled flab peeping out into the daylight like grotesque tubers pushing back top soil. He would be fixated by bright eyes and white teeth and silk-screened expressions and buttocks sagging or pert, and by faces daubed with make-up – something garish and bewildering to Joel for whom its purpose was frightening and obscure.

It was all fun and fascination, until he wandered into Times Square one day and found it all for sale, men and women in doorways, so plastic, blank and bright they hurt his eyes. They beckoned him and he did not understand and wandered on until three whores standing in a group around a hydrant began to tease him. 'Aw, gee, it's a little schmuck. C'mon over here honey. Want some honey? Get some honey, we'll give you some honey.' Joel stood still and blinked before them.

They were bored. One of them sauntered over and took him by the hand, led him to meet the others. 'This is Lindy, this is Amy. Say hi, girls.'

'Hi.'

'Howdy.'

'And what's your name, young man?' She spoke with a soupy drawl and while Joel was thinking about her question she pushed the hand which she was still holding up inside her leather skirt. At the same time Amy reached over and grabbed Joel's balls. Then: a flood of blood to his virgin member, a soft forgiving warmth between her legs and tangled hairs, a cold pain as she squeezed, a strange mucus that stained his fingers with a smell that he could not remove no matter how much he later rubbed with his saliva-wetted handkerchief. And the lights and the buildings with their hoardings and the reflections and the dissonances in the soft drug faces leering all around swam together, a hot rush of sweat and nerves and lava as the city plugged itself into the negative terminal of his scrotum and the positive terminal of his hand.

And then he was running, running from the laughter of the women towards the subway entrance far off in the crepuscular night. And as if to confirm that he did not belong, a shadow stepped from a doorway and took him by the throat, shook him down, took all his money, what little of it there was, and knocked his head against the filthy wall. He did not cry or move until it was gone, but when he found his broken spectacles he began to blub in deep deep spasms, the tears running down his cheeks and through the nap of fluff that was his beard, then either off on to the sidewalk or down inside his collar, depending on their velocity and mass when they reached the angle of his jaw.

With his fare gone, Joel had to walk. All the way to Williamsburg, half blind and fully decided. It was time to get out.

It came from Outer Space

It's 18 March 1965 by the time Joel makes it back across the bridge. And if we spiral up above his head to where the sky gives way we'll find a spaceship there, Voskshod 2, circling the earth. It looks real still, but it's moving fast, shovelling shit round the planet like you wouldn't believe. Dangling from it, his arms and legs sticking out at strange angles, is Cosmonaut Vsevolod Leonov, who's been told 'it's time to leave the capsu-elle if you dair-air-air' (in Russian) and has taken up the challenge. It's the world's first space walk, though to be fair, 'walk' is not really the right word, 'float' would do better, but what the hell, this is space after all and the normal rules don't apply here.

Which is lucky for Laika, who's coming out of the sun towards the Soviet craft, trying to manipulate a large syringe and inject her leg full of Phenergan; yup, she's doing her own experiments now, trying to combat space sickness, beating back the boundaries of science. Our plucky little pooch is concentrating hard on staying alive and she's succeeding – her eighth year up here has just begun and that much weightlessness isn't too good for the system. Anaemia, falling blood pressure, reduced capacity of muscles to burn fat for energy, declining baroreflexes, cramp, increased levels of toxicity in the blood, and that's just the least of it – not much Laika can do. Stress is a killer too, remember, she mustn't get stressed now, got to keep calm, sit back and watch the world on TV, take some exercise whenever she can (increasingly hard, now that she's almost entirely filled the cabin with her bulk – unable to burn off fat she's kept it all, rolls and rolls of it).

So it is that on 18 March she's thinking of her health and not paying too much attention to what's going on outside, when suddenly through her little porthole she spies something glinting in the light . . . it's a rocket, it is, and that, that's a man! She recognises the insignia on the helmet. Company at last! She drifts alongside, barking madly. Vsevolod doesn't see her at first, she's not quite what he expects, it's only when he waves to his pal back in the ship, creates a photo opportunity, that he figures something's wrong. Vladimir's mouth is open and his camera's floating in the air beside his head. What's he looking at? Vsevolod grips the umbilical hose and swings himself round . . . stares straight into the face of muttnik, who's grinning ear to ear, hot dog fat dog, furry face in round porthole, zinc capsule. Woof woof.

Vsevolod freaks, scrambles for the hatch, Vladimir recovers his wits, tries to get off some snaps, but Sputnik II's already spinning to face the earth above and Laika's mug disappears from view. It's over. The satellite wanders off.

Vsevolod gets back inside. 'Did . . . did you see what I saw?'

'I . . . I think so comrade, but I can't be sure.'

'A dog, right, it was a fucking dog! That looked like Sputnik II to me.'

'No, couldn't have been. Sputnik II? Burnt up years ago. And yeh, it looked like a dog, but it couldn't have been one. Trick of the light.'

'D'you get pictures? Did you?'

'Er, no, it was happening too fast.'

'Too fast? Too fast! That thing was out there for a whole goddamn minute! Why the fuck didn't you get pictures . . .'

'I, I . . .'

Their argument goes on a while, which is just as well because they don't switch on the radio and so don't hear Laika's broadcast, a little soliloquy of yelps and howls that goes on till she's shielded from them by the earth.

Do they tell Ground Control? Do they hell. Some things are better left unsaid. The space walk went without a hitch, all right?

Family politics

After the incident with the three prostitutes Joel's trips to Manhattan tapered off, and Cambridge took its place as the centrepiece of his fantasies and dreams. But with the transition Joel's behaviour became worse and worse, so bad indeed that the UTA declared he was too disruptive to remain in the school. At his wit's end, Moshe called up his oldest brother, Gershom, for advice. Gershom owned three small restaurants in the area and told Moshe to meet him at his kosher pizza house after closing one night. The two men sat down among the vacant tables and up-ended chairs to talk until they had found a solution to the problem.

'We could send him up to Canada,' Gershom suggested. 'I remember how envious Joel was when Shimon came back last summer with all his tales. And he was born there, too. Maybe he belongs there. He could stay with Zevi and Elisabeth.'

'Chas vesholem! They are farmers, they would work him into the ground. He is not strong, it would kill him, everything with Joel is up here.' He tapped his head with his fingers.

'But Moshe, perhaps that is what he needs. The boy never takes any exercise, he is as thin as a rake. If it wasn't for Judith's cooking he would have wasted away years ago. The open air might do him good.'

'No, you forget that after everything he is my son, not some mamzer orphan we are trying to parcel away out of sight.'

'Yes, but you must do something. It has been going on too long. The school are going to expel him. I have spoken to the rebs and melameds myself, there is nothing they can do with him any more. He is making it impossible for all the other boys.'

'He can help me in the bakery. He can do the accounts.'

'Moshe, you are crazy! How long would that take him? One hour a week if that? And the rest of the time what will he do? There's no room in there for him to help you bake. Within a month he'll be driving you crazy and you'll want him out of your sight, and he'll be walking the streets again and nothing will have changed.'

Moshe lost his temper. 'Well, what do you want me to do then?'

'Relax, relax will you. We are all trying to help, Joel is very dear to us all. We only want the best for him.' Moshe sighed a heavy sigh, a sign of defeat. 'Okay, okay,' snapped Gershom, giving in to the idea he'd had all along, 'he can come and work for me here. How does that sound? I'll start him off out front, waiting tables. He can help with the accounts and I'll teach him the business at the same time. And if things work out maybe he could help me run a new place I want to open up.'

Moshe brightened, then quickly tried to look doubtful. 'That's . . . I don't know if . . .'

'This is the best I can do. But I'm telling you now Moshe if the boy doesn't shape up we're sending him to Canada – and that's the end of it.'

★

So in 1965, around the time that the PDP–8 – the first computer to use integrated circuits – went on sale, Joel left the Yeshiva to work in one of Gershom's restaurants, keeping the books and cleaning the floors and waiting on tables. Moshe had told him, perhaps unwisely, of the threat to send him away to work on the farm if he didn't behave and the threat was a real one: Joel knew full well that the isolation he felt in New York was nothing compared with the loneliness he'd feel up there. At least here he had Millstein and the libraries. So he knuckled under, learnt how to conceal his feelings, became a golden boy again, though it was harder now because everyone was on their guard against him. And at night, while he lay awake between his sleeping brothers, he no longer surfed his infinite mathematical vistas. Not at all. Now, using as raw data the potted biographies on the fly pages of his books and Millstein's stories and a few old photographs he had found in the library, he constructed an image of Cambridge behind the sparkling black lids of his eyes.

With a resignation devoid of melodrama this empty vessel was slowly being filled with dreams and wishes and hopes, this tabula rasa was being scribbled upon, and Joel began to mature. But it seemed that the tablet was cracked, the machine malfunctioning. His mind had always been a store-and-forward network: information was broken down on entry, routed around his brain and reassembled at its destination. Packet switching it was called (Donald Davies coined the term that year). But now the restaurant filled his time, kept him busy with menial tasks that weren't challenging enough to interest him and yet prevented him from indulging in the mental number play with which he'd filled his time at school. Furious at this and feeling threatened by the dread prospect of Canada and what he saw as a family plot against him, Joel had nothing to contemplate all day except his anger and, with no outlet for this, the information in his brain was put into endless circulation. The constant reiterations made him bitter. He learnt dissimulation and deceit, to despise his parents and his culture. He learnt how to twitch out glances when others were off-guard, how to sum them up in terms of their usefulness to him, how to use them or avoid them. Millstein was the only one really to chart this transformation, noting quietly to himself that his perfect pupil, his little Pinocchio, was growing up – although in Joel's case the nose remained the same while downcast eyes replaced the clear, absorbent man-child gaze, a rash of acne and seeping scars replaced the unblemished pre-pubescent skin and a rangy stoop replaced the old automaton glide, as an increasingly beanpole body tried to convince itself and those around it that it was still short and perfectly proportioned.

73

Joel soon sensed that Millstein was the only one to see through him, and he initiated a series of pilpul – or hair-splitting arguments – in order to have an excuse to break off the lessons. He would niggle with his tutor over trivia such as the definition of terms and although he was to discover much later that these dogmatic rows were in fact the first tears in the hitherto seamless fabric of his mathematics, for the time being they served their purpose. But like tiny mouths, purple-lipped and silent, they would remain among the curtains of his mind until the time came for them to open and help Joel scream his final scream.

The disagreements, initially analytic, became increasingly personal until one winter's day, when the snow on the sidewalks had been crushed by passing feet into a single thick cake of crisp ice which filled the neighbourhood streets like a gridlocked glacier, Joel ended up yelling that Millstein was a blind fool, that he had nothing to teach him. Then he walked out of his tutor's apartment, never to return.

He had chosen a bad moment to leave because outside the wind was blowing with all the ferocity that a New York winter can muster. It had started to snow again, too, and blinded by the driven flakes, Joel slipped off an icy kerbstone into a deep puddle of slush that instantly soaked his shoes right through. His feet froze and trudging home he would have cried, except that the wind froze the tears in their ducts and he discovered then that sometimes you cannot piss your emotions away, however much you may want to. And this made him even more determined.

All the while he had been repairing relations with his family and destroying those with Millstein, he had been communicating with Metric. With the increasing resourcefulness that characterised his growing alienation, Joel did not have Metric's letters sent directly to his home but to a mailbox address. In addition to what he was being paid by Gershom, most of which went straight into the family account, he was earning a little money on the side by doing the prize puzzles in the newspapers. The puzzle pages were not considered to be culturally dangerous and no one knew that he sent his answers away, or indeed that he scavenged puzzles from other newspapers which he found left on seats in the subway or stuffed into dustbins or bundled into piles by the vending machines and newsagents' shops. Once a week he would visit the mailbox and pick up any correspondence. Any cheques – from time to time he won quite substantial amounts – he would take to the bank and convert into cash, which he would then secrete inside his mattress.

As his funds grew, so did his plans. His regular exchanges with Metric impressed the professor so much that when Joel insisted that he be allowed to sit the Cambridge entrance exam by mail Metric was delighted, although he vacillated for the sake of good form and so as not to give the boy too many big ideas.

Joel broke the Sabbath in order to take the exam, a consciously symbolic action. He was at home with his family as usual; it was now the only day of the week when he was likely to see all of them at once. Feigning illness, he spent the day in his bedroom and while the family sat around at the other end of the apartment he had four or five uninterrupted hours in which to complete the papers.

But this was only the first hurdle; if Metric hadn't been so desperate to have him attend he would never have succeeded in getting to Cambridge. He also had to lie elaborately about his background, pretending that he was an orphan so that the university would not demand that his parents ratify his decisions. He also had to persuade the professor that he needed a full bursary; he had to organise a passport, to purchase a plane ticket and, most complicated of all, he had to work out a way to extricate himself from his family.

It was clear to Joel that his parents would only ever agree to him leaving the community if it was to go and live with Zevi and Elisabeth in Canada. To begin with he considered becoming a 'problem teenager' again, getting himself relocated to Montreal, then disappearing at the earliest opportunity. It shouldn't be too difficult to get on the wrong plane at the airport, something like that. But on no account did he want his family to know that he had betrayed them and this made the Canada plan problematic. Zevi would contact his father as soon as Joel failed to arrive, and they would worry and suspect and search for him. He didn't want to hurt them and the thought of his mother hysterical with anxiety did not appeal. Still, he looked into the possibility, just in case. So many airplane tickets were issued, he thought, that they couldn't keep track of them all. If there was a system, there'd be a way to fool it. Wouldn't there?

Unfortunately for Joel, by this time the airlines had figured this out themselves and, as we already know, had asked IBM to do something about it. The scale of the problem was enormous. By the early fifties the traffic scheduling of American Airlines flights was already reaching crisis point. The availability boards of the original manual reservations system had become so large and so crammed with information that the growing crowds of reservations clerks had to use binoculars to see the details displayed on them. The system needed to be updated and it was – using electromechanical technology, the boards were replaced with terminals. The new system was called the Reservisor.

But although the Reservisor could cope with two hundred extra flights a year, it was really just an automated relay sitting on top of what remained essentially a manual system. Passenger and reservation records still had to be updated by hand and so many flights were wrongly booked that at busy times businessmen would make double reservations to guarantee a ticket. By 1952 AA was planning a new 30,000-square-foot manual reservations office that could accommodate 362 clerks who between them would be able to take 45,000 telephone calls a day. But even this would not be enough, because the company was not just struggling to cope with rising demand – it was also trying to cope with the ever increasing speed of passenger aircraft. Boeing had just introduced the 707 model and AA had ordered thirty of them. These planes could fly across the nation in just six hours instead of ten – faster than the reservations system could transmit information about a flight. Information space was now less navigable than physical space. This was no way to run a business.

IBM's solution, SABRE, had the biggest storage capacity of any system ever assembled until that time. It ran on two IBM 7090s and had a price tag of forty million dollars. Networked to 1100 agents in fifty cities over 10,000 miles of telephone lines, it was a monster, a data behemoth. It could handle ten million reservations a year and turn each one over in three seconds, as well as integrate passenger details with flight scheduling, fuel management, in-flight catering, toilet cleaning, aircraft maintenance, sexual intrigues between members of the cabin crew and the official records of the Mile High Club. It went online in 1964.

SABRE was the final nail in the coffin for Joel's Canada plan. Although its predecessor, SAGE, was still top secret, there were plenty of newspaper articles about the commercial spin-off, and while SABRE's data integration capabilities scotched any ideas he might have had of changing planes at the airport, this was more than compensated for by the knowledge that when he did book his ticket to England, some time soon, his name would go into this giant system, *his* name, and would become electrons and fields, and would whirl around the country like a particle, like a wave, would be everywhere at once. Clicking and triggering, disappearing and appearing, his name would be a harbinger of some new American dream. Just imagine, he thought, just imagine, and imagine he did, nights in his bed, his brothers gently snoring beside him, SABRE like a quilt of stars laid upon the nation, blinking and thinking – and Joel a part of it, like a comet and gravity both, his presence there unique and yet part of forces, statistics, habits and shapes. Unique and absorbed. The idea excited him like no other, it made his heart race and his belly flush, made him project lines of desire across the future, across the world; it brought aircraft and thought and flesh together, a jabbering mass, a squealing infiltration, a testicular growth. Many nights like this: the curtains apart, his hands on his groin, hot there, warm, softly sweating his own dear musk, the Milky Way a cosmic computer curved above his head.

After much consideration Joel came to the quite rational conclusion that it would be better and simpler for all concerned if he were dead. It was the first human problem he'd worked through to a solution and when the answer came to him he felt as though he'd finally come of age. Family honour would be retained, his parents' grief would be harsh but short. The plan was straightforward, elegant, beautiful. He had no place here in any case. His home was elsewhere. But there was an emotional element, too, though Joel didn't give it much weight. The notion of in some way joining his beloved dead sister tugged strongly at his heart.

So one September night, eight months after he had stormed out on Millstein, when the fall was coming on like a rash and the trees were scabbed with mildew and the clotted flakes of their leaves clogged the drains and culverts of the city, Joel crept past his sleeping brothers and inched his way out of the apartment. He was so numbed with fear and apprehension that it threw his perceptions out of joint, so much so that when he clicked back the latch of the front door and made his way down the creaking stairway and out into the street, everything seemed utterly normal, as if to leave your whole world in the depths of the night and set out across the planet was the most ordinary thing in the world. With a small satchel of books slung from his right shoulder and a canvas bag clutched in his left hand he set off down the street in the direction of the Williamsburg bridge, a small figure drifting down the night city's stellar lanes of light.

The bridge led out into the dark like an axon. He made his way across it until he was nearly half-way and then stopped. He seemed to breathe only the air that rushed down from the north along the tarry waterway. The wind plucked at his hair and lodged particles among it, the low bytes of America that did not come with the settlers but which aeons ago descended with the earth's crust into the caesura that is the Great Lakes. The low bytes which lay there on some submerged shore bound fast to others like them, one tip of a horseshoe pattern, imprint of some ancient stress. The low bytes, loosened by a millennium's worth of freezings and thawings of the great ice sheets that lie virtual across the surface of the waters, drifting upwards in suspended solution, carried by the convection currents set up by the action of the sun upon the lakes and later picked up by the wind.

Joel, himself not much more than an upright puddle of Hudson brew, looked down at the yarmulke in his hand. Inside the crown his name had been sewn with tiny white tacking stitches, *Joel Balaam Kluge*, his mother's work. He placed the cap on the metal grid on which he stood, a smudge on the perfect segments the bars made of the void below. Then he leant out over the rail and gazed at the night which filled the space between the safety lights and the glinting surfaces of the water, remembering his forays on the train. Removing his scarf, he threw it back beneath him so that it caught upon a girder and hung there, limpid and vain. Then he emptied out the canvas bag, selected from its contents two exercise books, a shirt, a pair of worn shoes and a puzzle game that his father had given him two years previously for winning a school prize, and one by one flung all these things out into space, waiting after each for the splash that never came. Far below, they floated on the surface of the river, revolving round each other in a strange and plastic configuration, feeding off the velocity of the water and odd ribbons of breeze. So powered, these elements hung together in a habitus which bound the heterogeneous possibilities that would be put into play by Joel's disappearance and channelled them into a synthesis, a coherence, an explanation. For these objects that spiralled down the Hudson formed an engine, an engine with a double task: both that of giving impetus to the story of Joel's suicide and that of propelling Joel himself into the new life that he so longed for. Well designed, the pattern slipped away beneath the bridge and out towards the open sea, one eddy among many in a flat and turbulent cosmos.

Having left these tracks leading away into oblivion, Joel transferred some of the contents of his satchel into the canvas bag and hurried back towards Brooklyn, taking care that no one had seen him. He slipped through the streets for eight or nine blocks, a crazy Artaud lost on a midnight set, then hailed a Yellow Cab and told the driver to take him to John F. Kennedy airport, to JFK, where he would take the plane which he imagined would place him on a perfect vector, one which would pass through Cambridge and keep him for the rest of his life in an abyss of infinities, never needing to descend to earth again, like some Buddha who in his self-contemplation awaits the day that being will be sufficiently perfect for him to descend to it and slip inside.

Flying in (1)

Metric sat in his study and sweated, a memo concerning the college policy on long hair on the desk in front of him. He was worried: Kings had just appointed a new mathematics fellow, a chap called Jenson. Jenson was only thirty-eight, inconceivably young for the post. He was well enough known for his work on infinite sets and although privately Metric considered his successes to have been flukes it nevertheless introduced an uncomfortable precedent and he needed to check he had his forces around him in readiness for the year's first meeting of the Mathematics Society in Second Week. First thing was to get a note to Harping and Trenton, have them over for sherry on Tuesday and tell them he was going to organise a special meeting of the Society to welcome Jenson into the fold. That way he could pump them for whatever they knew. Who stood where on this one, that was the key thing, to ascertain who stood where.

He had lunched in hall, had had the beef, felt a little bloated. Wished he hadn't now – he hadn't seen the morning paper until he had made it to the Senior Common Room for a post-prandial and then his eye immediately fell upon an article reporting the increased dairy yields British farmers were achieving thanks to the now widespread practices of spreading sheep offal on grazing fields and feeding their animals a baked meat and bone meal made from cow carcasses. Disgusting, thought Metric, the very idea, but then, what did you expect from farmers? The report turned his stomach and lined his mouth with the metallic film that presages bile and he had need of a healthier snifter than usual to set it right. Damn college brandy, gave him heartburn, must have a word with the Dean. Then back to his rooms, a couple of hours until his lecture, no students that afternoon. Settled into his leather swivel chair, a little sleepy after the booze, he closed his eyes for forty winks. Why not?

Joel, stung awake by the brightness of the morning, looked out of the window at the sun rising high above New York. The city was a blob of molten solder oozing out along the sink lines of the Hudson. By putting his finger in the appropriate spot on the plastic pane he could blot Williamsburg entirely from view. *Here gone, here gone, here gone . . .* he played a child's game and built his independence. His entire world was only this, to be brought in and out of view at will. Then the plane disappeared into the clouds and he was not at all sure what had happened. For a few moments he watched a bemused mosquito caught between the triple screens of Perspex. But a patch of turbulence rattled the plane, and sudden pressure differentials constricted his sinuses and he gripped the seat arms with both hands. It felt as if someone were poking hot needles up inside his brain. He began to cry out loud, a long, dim wail, vaguely aware that what he had done was sin and what was happening now was punishment. Perhaps he was already dead? A steward rushed towards him down the aisle and reached the boy just in time to watch him snatch the Homburg from his head and fill it with a lazy vomit.

As the aircraft reached cruising altitude and levelled out the steward helped Joel from his seat. 'C'mon, son, let's get you cleaned up.' The responses of the other passengers ranged from clicks and tuts of sympathy for the pale-faced boy to a thinly veiled hatred of the disturbance he was causing, a hatred that blended with a mistrust of the clothing he wore and the cut of his hair. Although his yarmulke was back on the bridge, he still wore his black suit and white shirt. His hair was shaved short, a thin pubescent beard squirmed around his jaw and two long silky curls ran down from his ears like dribbles of music. His hat was warm from the puke which slopped inside and he carried it in cupped hands as he was led up the aisle.

Two stewardesses came up and fussed over him, taking his refusal to look on their faces as shyness. The experience of the airport and the flight had reduced Joel, for all his precocity, back into the child he was perceived to be in this new world of adults. All the rules and codes with which he had been brought up and which he had mocked in secret for so long now asserted a hold over him in a way they never had before. For in fact, although he had never heard a good reason not to look upon women, or to obey the Sabbath, or not to eat pork, or not to behold the sign of the cross, or to spend nine-tenths of the schoolday, from seven-thirty in the morning to five in the afternoon, learning the Talmud by rote, he had lived among these edicts for so long in a society of such strict convention that apart from his timid adventures in Manhattan he had never had an opportunity to disobey them. And now that the time came for him to put his midnight thoughts of logic and rationality into action he discovered that it involved the kind of emotion which could make him physically sick. The turbulence had not been the problem.

But with a child's resilience Joel sublimated the overwhelming waves of his past, rescaling his memories in order to make the most painful details invisible. He looked the blonde stewardess firmly in the eye – or as firmly as he could, given the bottle-thick lenses of his glasses – and asked her if he could have a pair of scissors please. When she looked worried and glanced at her colleague he assured her: 'Don't worry, I am not going to hurt myself. I know how to use a pair of scissors' and won her over immediately, finding with a sure instinct the susceptibility of WASPs to sassy kids. The stewardess brought a pair from the first aid box and Joel disappeared with them into the toilet cubicle. Folding his Homburg around the contents of his stomach, he stuffed it in the toilet, jamming it down until the pressure sucked it away. Then, looking in the mirror, he grabbed each of his payot in turn and with one snip apiece cut them off and bundled them into the wastebasket. He removed his collar and tie, and with a disposable razor from the dispenser hacked off what he could of his beard, though he gave this up after nicking himself badly three or four times. Then he washed and cleaned his teeth and dressed again, and emerging from the toilet spoke curtly to the surprised air staff. 'I'm all right now. Thank you, thank you. Thank you for your help, I'm all right now, I can find my own way back to my seat.' Several thousand feet below them, now emptied of its contents, the Homburg slowly spiralled through the thickening air.

Some way away a drill bit the street. The sound drifted through the open window of the professor's study and for a moment he thought it was morning and he was in bed, listening to the noise his wife made as she snored into the stains of cold-cream on her pillow.

He came round and stumbled over to the sink, splashed some water on to his face. He'd slept much longer than he'd intended and had missed his lecture. Picking up the phone he called the porter's lodge and told them to send the college car to the airport to pick up the Kluge boy. Christ! How had he slept so long?

The chauffeur dropped Joel at the lodge. He stood there by the pigeon-holes examining the worn stone walls and trying to decipher the conversation going on between the two men behind the counter. But he could make out no more than a word or two and his mind soon wandered back to the journey he had just made in that strange small car through the landscape whose colours had been like those of Prospect Park, but more so. Everything was smaller here, not just the vehicles but the buildings, all these angry houses in their little rows with little gables and tiny windows, the narrow roads fighting to hold the two sides apart.

He knew England only from photographs – the pictures had shown him a world in miniature – and now he was here, in a miniature world.

There were no el trains rattling high above the streets, no advertising hoardings swung out above the traffic, the pavements seemed too tiny to walk upon and the people drab, less colourful.

Throughout the drive the sky had stayed a leaden grey and a vapour of rain had drizzled down like the bronchial spray coughed out by a cancerous old smoker. The spires and parapets of the university buildings sliced into the low clouds, gripping the sky and holding it to the earth with their Gothic barbs, tenacious as a bur caught deep in the fur of some hapless animal. That the stones were cloaked in grey-green swathes of lichen and stained with the dark blood of pollution gave them a crabbed authenticity of the kind bestowed only by persistence through time. As if to remain unchanged, to stand staunch and uncaring, was a quality to be admired.

Of course, for Metric it was. The professor saw himself not as one of Joel's shoes, winding downstream in a series of mutating relationships, but as a cog in a machine that both settled into and straddled the years themselves, mechanically linking in one great computational process all the facts and details and laws that could be classified and filed away from the age of those great slave masters the Greeks, to that of those great slave masters the British, and on and on beyond into the future, the future which would be subordinated to this machine as a lumpy, yeasty liquid is subordinated to a sieve.

Metric's role in this great process, he had decided, was to become a bigger cog. And here in the porter's lodge was the tool with which he was going to increase his diameter.

He entered the lodge, stooping slightly to avoid hitting his head upon the stone lintel. He saw Joel immediately, did a double take. The boy stood there shivering with fear or cold or both. His black trousers were too short for him, his battered shoes too big. His coat was worn at the elbows and was giving at the seams. His skin was pale and sweaty as an old cheese, his hair hacked and unkempt as a scarecrow's. He peered up through the thick lenses of his spectacles; behind them his eyes were hugely magnified, black holes in the pallor of his face. Just as the professor was wondering what on earth he had let himself in for his eyes met the boy's and for the briefest moment – one he would later dismiss by refusing to remember it as anything but a wholly discrete event – Metric fell into Joel's huge pupils, seeing there spaces which folded back upon themselves and enveloped his imagination in their great velvet swamps. Then he collected himself, blinked, looked away, composed an avuncular smile and extended his hand. 'Well, you must be young Mr Kluge. Welcome to Cambridge, young man. I am Professor Metric.'

Sherry and trifles

Metric's study was on the first floor and it looked out on to the back quad. He led Joel in and Joel looked around. One wall was entirely covered with books: the boy thought immediately of Brooklyn library. The other walls were half-panelled. The room was large. There was space enough for a large desk (leather-topped), a sofa, two easy chairs and a teak coffee table. Two doors let off from the main room. One of them was ajar and through the opening Joel could see a small sink.

The windows were leaded like all those overlooking the back quad and were let into small recesses sunk deeply into the thick walls. In each recess stood an ornamental pedestal. On top of the eastern pedestal was an aspidistra; on the western a small plaster bust. The bust was of the physicist Paul Dirac. It was not clear to Joel quite what it was doing there until he moved closer and noted the small brass plaque affixed to the base, on which the following words had been inscribed:

God is a Mathematician

It was the kind of thing that Metric found amusing. The bust had been given to him by his wife, back in the days when she had still found such things amusing too. It was the only object in his study that had any connection with her. She had bought it from an antique shop in Hampstead during an afternoon stroll in the company of Peter Rogers, a research scientist based in London to whom she had been introduced by a friend, with whom she had been attending a conference on philosophy and science at London's University College. The conference was a big disappointment and she had spent the afternoon of the third day strolling with Rogers across Hampstead Heath. The weather was warm and they had ended up in Jack Straw's Castle drinking bitter shandies. Rogers invited her to a party that evening; she accepted. The party was off St James's: cocktails and a band. Rogers introduced her to various friends. He seemed very well connected, and that night she met well-known stage actors, a popular composer from France and many fashionable academics and literary types; and the philosopher Bertrand Russell, whom she knew by sight from around Cambridge, although they had never actually spoken. Russell was surprisingly witty and personable, and he charmed her immediately. Soon she found herself standing alone with him, deeply involved in a conversation about the fauna of the African savannah, a subject about which he seemed to know a great deal. Something about his manner made her suspect that he was drunk – he was indeed cradling an extremely large martini in his left hand – but no sooner did she make up her mind that that was the case than he would seem perfectly sober once again. Then, rather abruptly, he seemed to lose interest in their exchange. His gaze slipped from her face to the room over her shoulder and he began to fiddle with something in the bottom of his jacket pocket.

As she was asking a question about the mathematical ratios reified in the spiral horns of the ibex, he suddenly interrupted her. 'Come with me, my dear,' he crooned in a deep philosophical bass. 'I have something you might be interested in.' He led her over to the curtained booths which lined the walls. Most of them had their drapes drawn and as they walked past, giggles and coughs could be heard. The party was in full swing by now and they had to dodge dancers and waiters with trays overflowing with canapés and champagne flutes. Russell diverted a passing glass into Amanda Metric's hand and led her through the maelstrom and into the last available booth. Inside were a small glass-topped table and two bench seats.

Russell sat down and placed a small glass phial full of white powder on the table top. He took a slug of his martini and handed the professor's wife a tiny spoon. 'After you, my dear.' Amanda didn't know whether to be shocked or embarrassed. All Russell saw was confusion, so he took control of the situation, which was what he was best at. 'Never done the devil's dandruff before? Allow me.' He took the spoon from her, dipped it in the phial and snurfed the contents up his capacious right nostril, repeating the process with his left. 'See? Just like taking a dab of snuff.' He handed the spoon back to Amanda, who to her surprise now found herself rather excited by the chance of getting involved in such an illicit activity. She took a couple of gulps of her champagne, then ingested the powder just as Russell had done, though she was trembling so much that she nearly dropped powder, spoon, phial and all.

As the drug dissolved in her sinuses she felt first light-headed then euphoric. 'Oh, Mr Russell,' she said, 'it's just like champagne, but better!'

'I know,' said Russell. 'And call me Bertie.' And he laid a hand on her knee.

Metric had no idea that the souvenir of his wife's one infidelity sat on permanent display in his study; it was one of those ironies that he most assuredly would not have found funny, although as the years went by it was increasingly appreciated by Amanda, who usually remembered it when her husband was at his most pompous.

But another object drew Joel's attention more. About twenty inches long and six inches high, constructed from delicately filigreed and sumptuously engraved brass and covered with a variety of handles and wheels, it sat on the front of Metric's desk in pride of place.

Metric noted Joel's interest. 'One of Leibniz's calculating machines. An original in fact.' He sniffed. 'Designed by the great mathematician to calculate tables of data concerning the movements of the planets and the stars. "It is unworthy of excellent men to lose hours like slaves in the labour of calculation which could be safely relegated to anyone else if machines were used," to quote him directly. Quite right too. Grandfather of the modern computer. Ever seen a computer, Kluge?' Joel didn't answer, but instead stepped forward to try one of the handles. Metric moved over quickly to guide him away. 'Better not touch, eh?'

The machine was not in fact an original, although Metric thought it was, as did the dealer who had sold it to him for an extremely large amount of money. The original Leibniz calculators were built between 1672 and 1674 by a craftsman commissioned by Leibniz himself. Metric's machine, although identical in every other respect, had been built in 1821 by a very different craftsman, commissioned by one Charles Babbage.

Babbage had been fascinated by machinery of all sorts since he saw two automata at a travelling fair as a child. He wrote in his autobiography that one of the two: 'glided along a space of about four feet, when she turned round and went back to her original place. She used an eyeglass occasionally, and bowed frequently, as if recognising her acquaintances. The motions of her limbs were singularly graceful. The other silver figure was an admirable danseuse, with a bird on the forefinger of her right hand, which wagged its tail, flapped its wings, and opened its beak.' The dolls had been manufactured by an old craftsman called John Merlin, who had been touring them around Europe for many years. His audiences had included kings and queens, as well as such cultural luminaries as the German Romantic writers E. T. A. Hoffman (whose story of machinic love, 'The Sandman', was inspired by Merlin's automata) and Heinrich von Kleist, whose passion for these mechanicals burned so hot that he was inspired to write: 'Grace appears purest in that human form which has either no consciousness or an infinite one, that is, in a puppet or in a god.'

Babbage himself was a polymath. A designer – he invented a cow-catcher for trains, the speedometer, the flashing lighthouse and a pair of shoes for walking on water – a cryptologist, a founder of the Royal

Statistical and the Royal Astronomical Societies, and a campaigner against the playing of loud musical instruments in London (which he referred to as 'instruments of torture' and blamed for ruining his concentration) he remained something of a jack-of-all-trades until one dreary evening in 1821, when he found himself stuck in a room helping the astronomer Herschel to check over a stack of celestial calculations made by a team of human computers. After finding the umpteenth mistake, Babbage exclaimed that he 'wished to God that the calculations had been executed by steam!' And the project followed from that: collect examples of the best calculating machines ever built, use the best ideas from each and build a new machine that could be autonomously powered.

Dreaming up ways to mechanise mathematical processes quickly became the focus of Babbage's life and for the next two years he went about collecting whatever calculating machines he could lay his hands on. The Holy Grail was a Leibniz calculator, but though he searched high and low, he could not find one that he could buy and take to pieces. Eventually he gave up on the quest and began to work on his designs for a 'Difference Engine' – a machine designed to compute and print tables of numbers using the mathematical method of 'finite difference' – regardless.

Over a decade passed since the evening with Herschel and Babbage's project was not going well. After experiencing a whole series of problems, the Difference Engine project was finally scuppered by the chief engineer, Joseph Clement, who made off with all the funds. Babbage faced disaster. Then, completely out of the blue, a friend informed him that a copy of Leibniz's original plans along with the craftsman's drawings resided in the library of an aristocratic cousin. The inventor secured himself an introduction and hastened to the lady's residence by coach.

The cousin was no less than the Countess of Lovelace, Augusta Ada Byron, the one legitimate daughter of the great English poet himself, and she had more to give Babbage than a mere set of plans. For Ada Byron was an extraordinary person with an extraordinary mind. Countess, gambler, mother, mathematician, self-styled prophetess, she was easily Babbage's equal and when they met he discovered to his great surprise that she was already familiar with his work. They quickly formed an intense relationship, Ada driving Charles to be more rigorous and focused in his work and at the same time inserting her own ideas – both practical and visionary – into the design for the machine was to succeed the Difference Engine: the 'Analytical Engine', intended to be a fully programmable computer. In particular, Ada introduced ideas taken from the Jacquard loom, which used punch cards to allow textile patterns to be preset in and which had the effect of putting many skilled weavers out of a job, causing riots and marches by disgruntled textile workers – Luddites – all over Britain. Ada's father, Lord Byron, was one of the few to take up the Luddite cause in Parliament, at the same time as his daughter was coming to understand the real importance of the machines which had taken their jobs. 'We may say most aptly that the Analytical Engine weaves Algebraic patterns,' Ada commented, 'just as the Jacquard loom weaves flowers and leaves.' Indeed, Babbage was later to draw a direct comparison between the structure of their 'thinking machine' and that of a textile plant: both consisted of two parts, '1st The store in which all the variables to be operated upon, as well as all those quantities which have arisen from the result of other operations, are placed [and] 2nd The mill into which the quantities about to be operated on are always brought.'

Spurred on by their relationship, and with the Leibniz blueprints now at his disposal, Babbage decided to have a calculator built for Ada as a gift. He wanted Merlin, the automaton manufacturer, to build it. The aged craftsman had by this time settled in London, but decrepit and rapidly losing his sight, he initially declined the commission. Babbage, however, could see that the man was poverty stricken and with no relatives to look after him it would only be a matter of offering him a large enough fee. When Merlin capitulated Babbage purchased the silver dancing doll from him as a gesture of good faith and the old man went to work on the Leibniz calculator.

It was to be one of his greatest achievements. He had in fact seen one once and, although that encounter had taken place almost half a century earlier, his skilled and trained mind could recall it clearly – certainly as clearly as he could now see the blueprints. After months of toil he managed to recreate the original machine almost perfectly. Yet the strain had been too much – as he screwed the final screw into the plate of authenticity that he had reproduced from memory as a final touch his sight gave out, and when Babbage came to pick up the calculator he found the old man wandering blind and half mad in the back of his shop, the machine lying oiled and pristine among the debris scattered across the workbench. Too ashamed to admit to Ada that he had been the cause of Merlin's decline, he sold the machine immediately and with the proceeds of the sale paid for the craftsman to be cared for in a sanatorium for the remaining few months of his life. It was this machine that now took pride of place on Metric's desk.

★

Metric sat Joel down, handed him a glass of sherry and welcomed him to Cambridge. He issued him with various pieces of paper, had him sign sundry others, gave him a quick run down of how the college functioned – none of which Joel understood – a quick list of people whom he could turn to if he needed help – none of whose names Joel remembered – and interspersed the whole with a series of witless jokes – none of which Joel got. Then he called for a porter to take Joel to his room and told the boy to come and see him in a couple of days, 'when you've settled in'. And then Joel was on his own.

Fast cut through Joel in lectures, scribbling notes in his own shorthand, Joel in libraries memorising proofs, Joel in tutorials writing with chalk upon a board, Joel at his desk deliberating with a slide-rule and scratching away at problems with his pencil, Joel in bed sleeping a chaste six hours. Overview: Joel growing up, Joel's Cambridge. Contrast: the Cambridge of a spoilt and self-centred aristocracy, for whom it was merely a finishing school swilling with boating, balls and champagne; contrast: the Cambridge of the middle classes, for whom it was footlights and theatre, stuttering steps on a protected political stage, walks in the country and a niche in a cosy little scene; contrast: the Cambridge of the outsider – the boy from the Valleys who starts to deal pot, the girl raped by her tutor with no recompense, the depressive discovered one morning hanging from a bridge, the fool who came to learn and is sorely disappointed. And contrast: the Cambridge of the town – long sufferings and symbioses with the hive at its centre, tarmac next to cobbles beneath the milky dawns, shirtings, suitings, averted eyes and street slang.

Joel was lucky; in the end he was saved from Cambridge by the quality of his mind. It was that mind which had got him there in the first place, and it was what gained him a level of acceptance among the monks of maths and logic that stalked the dimly lit corridors and cloisters, rule books in hand.

Metric personally supervised Joel's tuition, and it wasn't long before he was able to skim off the more useful products of the boy's agile and inventive brain. He had made the right decision: he had a genius in his care and if he prospered while he brought the boy to fruition, well, where was the harm in that? And indeed, Metric did have his work cut out, at least to begin with. The combination of Joel's youth, his personal eccentricities and his culture shock meant that trivial problems could quickly spiral out of control. The boy wouldn't eat any of the food in halls, for example, preferring to subsist on a diet of crisps and chocolate from the local grocers. He didn't seem capable of buying any new clothes, wearing his one black suit until it was practically falling off his insubstantial frame. His English was terrible and a private tutor had to be organised for him. In the vacations he had nowhere to go and special rooms needed to be made available for him in college.

The professor found all these unforeseen difficulties rather overwhelming and, unable quite to deal with them, he did something completely out of character – he turned to his wife for advice. As it happened, Amanda had been taking a quiet interest in this orphan prodigy for some time; when at her husband's behest she was finally introduced to the boy she did the childless middle-aged woman thing and took Joel under her wing. He was helpless; she could help.

So Metric got to see Joel at weekends too, when Amanda would have him over to their house and cook him some decent meals and wash and mend his clothes and take him shopping for the few things he needed. Gradually, the little lost Jewish boy jettisoned some of his incapacitating shyness, shed most of his Hasidic trappings and became an approximate replica of all the other students, if a little younger and quite a lot geekier.

On the academic side, Metric played out a clever little game. He was convinced of the truth of the last theorem of the great mathematician Fermat, the only theorem out of two hundred or so that had not yet been proved. The problem was to demonstrate the claim that the equation $x^n + y^n = z^n$ has no solutions with x, y and z all positive integers and n an integer greater than 2, and although apparently simple, it was in fact incredibly complex. Metric's great ambition was to discover a proof and so ensure that he went down in the annals of mathematical history, if not a second Fermat then at least someone who was equal to the task that the great mathematician had set. Joel knew little of Fermat and certainly wasn't aware of the challenge that this particular theorem set the world of mathematics. Metric's plan was to feed Joel various pieces of the puzzle disguised as coursework and encourage him to make the requisite connections between them, while making sure that he never saw enough of the big picture to know what was going on. Over the next few years, this is exactly what he did.

As he approached the final year of his undergraduate degree and his English became all but fluent, Joel began to exhibit a marked interest in the philosophy of mathematics as well as its practice. He would interrupt tutorials with an occasional non sequitur: But does mathematics describe the world? What are the implications for knowledge of Gödel's theorem?

Doesn't Turing's universal machine demonstrate that certain problems will always fall outside the realm of mathematics?

Feeling avuncular (and more than a little mercenary) Metric encouraged his pupil. He lent him Russell and Whitehead's *Principia Mathematica* (without, of course, understanding the significance such a text would have had for his wife), Frege's *Die Grundlagen der Arithmetick*, Wittgenstein's *Tractatus Logico-Philosophicus* and even, in an adventurous moment, Lewis Carroll's *Alice's Adventures in Wonderland*, which he thought might lighten the load a little. Joel devoured them all, fascinated. He especially revered Carroll, it never having struck him before that logic could be made so quirky, so amusing. He pestered Metric about the references he didn't understand and read up on all of them. In the process he discovered relativity theory, Leibniz, molasses and mock turtles, chess and cards, Arthur Eddington, knights and courts of law and tea parties and top hats and dodos and quadrilles and . . . and something, though he wasn't quite sure what, but something about little girls, too . . . and it all fitted perfectly with what he'd thought it should be like before he had come here and it gave him a chance to fantasise again, as he used to in Brooklyn and which he'd done so rarely since he came to Cambridge. Now, when his thoughts misted over, instead of spinning yarns of dreaming spires and hallowed corridors (living here among the other students had removed those illusions for good) he invariably thought of his family and the Hasidic world he'd left behind which, in retrospect, didn't seem all that bad – at least the food had been good (he missed his mother's soups his father's breads – though not the bagels). He thought, too, of his betrayal – that's what he knew it as now, a betrayal – and with that knowledge came an understanding that he could never go back, that he'd severed the winding skein of return as surely as a midwife snips an umbilical cord and twists it into an atrophying knot.

Though their relationship was founded on a lie – two, in fact, as there was Metric's mixed in there as well – in Amanda and the professor Joel found something of a surrogate family. The weekends spent at their house became part of the routine and soon their place was 'home' and he could do there pretty much as he pleased. They had minor arguments, too, family-style, which brought him closer to them and to Amanda especially, since her husband, for the sake of academic propriety if nothing else, had to maintain a certain distance. As Joel was slowly integrated, his nightmares – the ones he'd had ever since leaving Brooklyn, the ones in which the prostitutes he'd met once in Times Square would catch him and hang him by his arms from a lamp-post in the street and call out to everyone what he was a liar and a traitor, call to the crowds of passers-by who would jeer and tear at his clothes with eager fingers and then, when his clothing had been shredded, at his flesh; the ones where he'd be trying to buy a ticket home, only to be confounded at every turn by the complexities of the computerised booking system; or worst of all, the ones where he'd be back and it would be normal, and he'd go to school and come home and sit down to dinner with his brothers and sisters and go to bed and sleep so well, so well, only to wake the next morning to his grey college room and the knowledge that this was the nightmare, this, what he was living, what he had done – slowly became less frequent until one day something happened and they stopped completely, never came back. That was 20 July 1969, when at Amanda's brother's house just outside Cambridge and in the company of some fifteen other people, mostly academics he knew from the college, he not only watched TV for the first time but saw the pictures come back from the Sea of Tranquillity, of Aldrin and Armstrong bouncing around in the dust. When the American flag went up Amanda's brother, a small man, almost entirely bald, who wore round wire-rimmed spectacles and smiled at everybody, took his hand and shook it vigorously and congratulated 'the American among us' and everyone cheered, *hoorah! hoorah!*, and banged him on the back. The flag had never seemed to have anything to do with him before, but now he felt a surge of pride and thought that yes, indeed, this had something to do with who he was. And as the astronauts pointed up at the rising earth, at him, for the first time he could remember he felt enormously happy.

Between Joel and the astronauts there was Laika, watching and whimpering, her tail tucked between her legs. This was the latest in a series of threatening events, which could no longer be regarded as isolated occurrences. It had been a mistake to bark at that spaceman she'd seen. Now they'd come back for her, they were coming to get her and she did not want to return. And worse, the world was looking through her – a strange sensation, one which wears you thin. She bounced the footage of the astronauts down to Richard Nixon and an astonished populace without interference. Everyone was watching; to try anything would be madness. To Laika, suddenly space seemed very small – and it wasn't just that she was so fat now she filled her capsule. Like Joel in his dreams, she was rigid with fear and despite the veneer of self-consciousness she'd been fortunate enough (you would think) to accrue, it was a veneer all the same and easily scratched. When the millions of years' worth of evolution salted away in her amygdala told her to cower, cower she did no matter that it made no sense. A cornered animal, she pushed her flesh into the dark corners of Sputnik II, into the tiny spaces between instrument panels and life-support systems, between transmitters and receivers, between dials and knobs, tubes and surrounds, shoving so hard and shivering so much that the hard edges punctured her skin and the differentiation between metal and sinew, dog and machine, became harder than ever to discern.

But it was more than simple fear that made her cringe – though fear, of course, is never simple, even if it often seems so at the time. There was something else mixed in, a sense of foreboding, of something dark and strange and complex unfolding just out of view. For Jennifer, Judd and Joel were all linked in, yes, they were all there, watching through her, perhaps as close to one another now as they would ever be, though Judd is only seven and is so excited, yes he's so excited, he wants more than anything to go to the moon, and he's watching it all on his family's new set, the big one in the living-room (they've got several) and he's asking Moses question after supercharged question: 'how do they breathe? why do they float? how do they get back? when can I go?' and Moses fields these as best he can, though he's more interested in the ads which are interspersed with the action, in particular one for a watch, no, for *the* watch, the Omega Speedmaster, which is the watch NASA issues their astronauts with and which is available now for the special moon landing celebration edition price of $499.99. *Omega – the true meaning of space-time.*

Jennifer is watching too. She's nearly ten now. She's watching at home on her very own set. It was, it just was the most, the most, well, just the mostest present she had ever had and she was thrilled with it, just couldn't take her eyes off it, so much so that Henry had to ration her viewing to make sure she got some exercise and did her homework. Henry had given Doreen Buerk a few pounds for it after she'd mentioned at a parent –teacher evening that it had been mouldering away unused in one of her upstairs rooms ever since her husband Donald had gone. For Doreen was a teacher now – she taught classes in a local boys' public school and in the comprehensive just down the road which Jennifer attended (she regarded the latter as her 'community service'). The set was only a black and white, but it had a very large screen and the tube was still good, and Jennifer was the only kid on her street who got to watch as much television as she liked, greatly to the envy of all of her friends.

She'd watched films and cartoons and *Blue Peter* and sometimes nature programmes, and all the music shows like *Ready, Steady, Go!*, and she'd seen the Stones on it and the Dave Clark Five and the Beatles whom she didn't like so much. Henry watched it too, though the stuff he liked bored Jennifer, who would moan at him, tell him he was dull. But Henry was happy to ignore her as he slipped into the nostalgic eurocentrisms of *Civilisation*, or rooted for Henry Cooper as he battled Piero Tomasoni (Jennifer: 'boxing, uurhg!'), or followed the domestic dramas of *The Forsyte Saga* or *Dombey and Son* ('bo-r-ing'). When Jennifer saw after ten minutes or so that she wasn't going to change his mind she'd usually leave off pestering him and go round to Shelley's or, if she didn't feel like going out, lie at his feet on the floor by the open fire (it was often too cold to sit in her room; they didn't have central heating) and doze or read a comic book or nag him to get her a cat. There was some stuff they watched together: the occasional crime series (*Z–Cars, Softly, Softly*), the odd thing which Henry thought educational (*A Human Zoo, Wildlife on One*), comedy shows (Jennifer didn't get all the jokes but she laughed anyway) and the popular science series *Tomorrow's World*, which they both liked and which handled the BBC's coverage of the moon landing. The two of them watched the historic event with a group of friends Henry had suggested Jennifer invite over for the occasion which became, in an historic kind of a way, the precursor for the Saturday film matinée parties she'd start to hold on a regular basis a year or two later.

The week after the moon landing the BBC had broadcast a special *Tomorrow's World* show dedicated to the integrated circuit electronics which had made the Apollo missions possible. The Argyll-sweatered Hamish McCready, kids' favourite and housewives' choice to boot, held a digital watch up to the camera and removed its screen to reveal the tiny electronic muscle inside. Then he took the audience on a tour of Cape Canaveral, showed them the enormous mainframe and the new mini-computers, Digital Equipment Corporation machines, PDP–8s and PDP–9s, the same ones that Moses had been selling since he'd read a book called *The Future of the Computer Utility* back in 1966 (which had fired him up so much that he'd jumped ship from IBM to DEC), and similar to the ones that Joel would begin to work with now that he was a post-graduate – the mathematics faculty at Cambridge would buy a PDP–10 the very year he began his Ph.D.

Ecce homo

Joel was nearly twenty and first-year undergrads were younger than him now. He knew the ropes, he wasn't such an oddity any more. But for Metric the transition wasn't so happy; it meant the abandoning of his plot to siphon off Joel's talent, even though he felt that he was very close to finishing his proof. He'd published several exploratory papers, and many of his colleagues had been impressed by his progress and were beginning to expect great things of him. But Joel was a graduate student now, it wasn't so easy to pull the wool over his eyes. The professor did toy with the notion of coming clean, but there was no way he would be able to explain away those papers. Like Laika, Metric feared discovery and, like the dog, his fear was complex, an extra dimension added to it by the fact that although in theory he could stomach sharing the glory, he couldn't cope with the possibility that Joel, once alerted to the situation, would disown his tutor in disgust, proceed on his own and claim the prize himself.

And then, of course, he'd have to face Amanda. No one would have called Metric a great judge of character, least of all himself, but if he knew one thing about his wife it was that whatever Joel's reaction might turn out to be, once she'd found out what he'd been up to her wrath would be terrible to behold.

The fear did not leave him once he had made the decision to end the search for the proof. For what if he were discovered? What if Joel were accidentally to turn up those papers in the library one day? What would he do then? After all, it was quite likely. The journals in which he'd published were popular enough and what could be more natural than that the boy should want to find out what work his tutor was currently involved in (Metric always thought of Joel as 'the boy')? The more he considered it the more his trepidation grew and one night, following a particularly strenuous college dinner, while sitting propped up in the Senior Common Room, a large glass of Regoan tawny port in one hand and the *Telegraph* folded down around the crossword in the other, he decided that he had to do something or go mad with the worry.

Believing that there was no time like the present, he bolstered himself with a third glass of the fortified wine, slipped out of the SCR and, making sure no one was about, headed in the direction of the library. A tall man with a not insubstantial belly, Metric was hardly designed for covert operations. But somehow he managed to navigate the stone corridors, grassy quads and quiet cloisters without being seen by anyone save the gargoyles, who pulled faces at him in disgust as they did at so much of what they observed of the college's daily round. At this hour the library was locked, though as a resident professor Metric was in possession of a key. He approached the library door and with one last glance to make sure he wasn't being followed he slipped it into the iron lock that was embedded deep in the ancient oak. He'd never actually used the key before and was somewhat surprised when with a guilty clunk the lock sprang back and the door swung open.

A moment later he was inside. Thankfully, the night was moonlit and clear, and light enough for him to see by slanted in through the leaded diamonds of the tall, narrow windows. The room was deathly silent and Metric reflected drunkenly that he'd never realised before just how much noise there was in an average library of an average day. But the place also lacked that tension, that pressure not to make a sound, and he strolled across to the mathematics section feeling strangely free.

He knew exactly where the articles were; on his way over he'd rehearsed their position in his mind's eye. Now he went straight to them and, with a deftness that came from years of handling papers of one sort of another, tore them carefully from their bindings, folded them and placed them in the inside pocket of his jacket.

Not wanting to return to the SCR, where he might have to explain his absence, he took a circuitous route to the tutors' private back gate where he could let himself out without having to pass before the carnivorous gaze of the bowler-hatted porters. As he wound his way back through the tortuous, almost organic collection of crumbling Gothics, it struck him that the college would make a jolly good sepulchre, with each of its rooms a splendid family tomb.

Removing the incriminating papers from the college library did not, however, help him to sleep any better. Now that this window on to his secret had been sealed, others seemed to appear and he lay awake most of that night, and many more following, watching them sprout like acne on a pubescent face. At the very least he would have to repeat his vandalism in the faculty library and perhaps in any others which the boy frequented. When he casually asked Joel about his library habits a day or two later, he replied that he had no set pattern, that he liked to move from one to another at whim – his concentration suffered, he found, if he spent too much time in one place.

Though he knew it was completely irrational, Metric's paranoia grew and grew, and his thoughts as far as Joel were concerned became one vast labyrinth full of traps, dead-ends and pitfalls. And then, one morning while he was shaving, he stumbled across a solution so glorious in its simplicity that its discovery was almost as satisfying as he imagined the finding of the proof of Fermat's Last Theorem itself to be. If he couldn't take the evidence away from Joel, he would just have to take Joel away from the evidence. The only question which remained was how that was going to be achieved.

An opportunity presented itself one summer afternoon, when the quad outside Metric's window was noisy with students languishing on the grass. Joel appeared for his fortnightly tutorial, prompt as ever, dressed in his usual jacket, tie and round-necked pullover despite the warm weather. He knocked and entered, delivering his greeting in that familiar tone of his which, as Metric had noted on many occasions, was simultaneously belligerent and self-effacing. As the boy sat down in one of the two wicker chairs and took his papers from the satchel that he carried, the professor watched him from the window from where he'd been gazing, just a moment or two before, at the young men strewn across the lawn. Why couldn't Joel look more like one of them? The huge lick of greasy black hair, the heavy spectacles, the skin tormented with boils and that nose which seemed to suck up most of his face . . . there was no doubt about it, he was an ugly one. And yet . . . and yet there was something about him which shone through, something which made you want to be near him . . . Amanda could see it, presumably, more clearly than he could.

He started the session by asking Joel to take the initiative (he'd forgotten what it was the boy was supposed to be working on). Joel read out a few paragraphs summarising his proposed solution to a particular problem in set theory. Metric saw which way he was heading and interrupted him to sketch some figures on his blackboard. As he drew he talked, and when he turned back to face Joel he was surprised to see that the boy was not paying the slightest attention but was instead looking across at the window where he himself had previously been standing. This was most uncharacteristic!

'Ah, Mr Kluge, I don't want to spoil your enjoyment of the fine weather, but do you think you could apply your attention to the matter in hand?'

'Uh, I beg your pardon?' said Joel, still locked into his reverie.

'The problem, my dear boy, is located here – 'he tapped on the blackboard with the chalk '– not, I believe, in the quad, though I must confess that on such a beautiful afternoon as the good Lord has offered us today I would as soon, I believe, be out there myself as . . .'

Quite suddenly Joel interrupted. '*God is a mathematician.* Do you believe that yourself?' Metric was startled. 'Your bust of Dirac, sir. The inscription reads *God is a mathematician.* I wondered if you believed that yourself.'

It took the professor a moment or two to realise that Joel had not been looking out of the window, as he had assumed, but had in fact been staring at the bust of Paul Dirac which occupied the plinth in front of it. He was about to tell Joel that they should really get on with the tutorial and that this was a side-track best saved for another occasion when the thought struck him that here perhaps was an avenue worth exploring. 'Hum,' he mused and, placing his piece of chalk carefully into the gutter at the bottom of the blackboard, walked thoughtfully across the room to the bust. With one hand he picked it up and held it at an angle appropriate for contemplation and with the other – as if as an afterthought – he carefully pulled the window to, shutting out the dis- tracting hubbub coming from outside. The room became soft and still. 'I'm not sure,' he said. 'It's an interesting question. Something I've thought about often. The first question to ask, I suppose, is what exactly does that statement mean? Presumably, it means that the world adheres to the precepts of mathematics. There are problems with this position, needless to say – you must have come across them in the books on philosophical logic I gave you to read: the Wittgenstein, the Frege and so on. Naturally, even asking what our sentence means already embroils us in debate. For example, one has to ask: How exactly do we ascribe meaning? Maybe that is where we should begin, with the problems of meaning. Quine's rather good on this. Have you read Quine?'

'I've read *Word and Object*, obviously,' said know-it-all Joel, putting down his papers and crossing his legs, 'but I'm thinking about things in a far more general sense. That is to say does mathematics describe *this* world, or does it describe some other, more ideal, perhaps transcendent realm?'

'Aha! Neo-Platonism. Well, it has a long and glorious heritage, and you'd be in fine company, though it's somewhat discredited today, I fear.'

'I was thinking more of Leibniz actually, and his idea of the monad, which as an idea I feel manages to make the leap between the transcendent and the material somewhat better than Plato's essences, or those of Plot- inus, if you prefer.' (It was unfortunately true that Joel – as part of his attempt, both conscious and unconscious, to paper over his past – had picked up many of the accents and mannerisms of upper-class Cambridge English. Metric, of course, thought this was splendid, the horror of it completely escaping him.)

'It seems, my boy, that you are moving somewhat out of the precinct of pure mathematics here, but go on, go on.' Encourage him, encourage him, thought Metric, mentally rubbing his hands, then catching himself and physically straightening up.

'Well, according to the Jewish Kabbalah . . .'

'I'm afraid I'm, ah, not familiar with that particular tradition,' said Metric hastily.

'Oh?' said Joel, a little surprised to have found such a glaring gap in his tutor's knowledge. 'Well according to that or, at least, according to the version known as Lurianic doctrine, although it is only one of many, the universe is created when Ein-Sof, which according to classical Kabbalah is not at all identical with the revealed divine creator but more like eternity, or infinity – the absolute perfection, if you can imagine the difference – well, the universe is created when Ein-Sof withdraws into itself and opens a space of possibility, as it were.'

'It reminds me a little of Hegel, though it's a long while since I've read him,' Metric murmured, unsure as to where this might be heading.

Joel ignored him. 'The process by which it does this, which is most interesting, is also most strange. You see, the problem is that Ein-Sof has no will, no volition at all: it just is, you see. It's perfect and undifferentiated and it just is. So how is this withdrawal initiated?'

'God?' said Metric hopefully.

'Aha, no, that's just where you're wrong! And anyway, it wouldn't work for popular Kabbalah, which conflates the notions of Ein-Sof and God. No, what happens is this: the perfection of Ein-Sof is such that it begins to shake with a kind of "self-satisfaction", though you must understand this as an anthropomorphism and not a true description.'

'Naturally,' said Metric, thanking his stars he was a Christian.

'Well, as a result of this shaking, a series of what are known as "primordial points" are engraved in the essence of Ein-Sof, and as a result of this engraving the primordial space, in which the world can be formed, comes into being. The interesting thing about this engraving is that it is actually a *linguistic* phenomenon. The engraving forms a malbush, or a garment, though a garment that is part of that which it covers – like the exoskeleton of a grasshopper, according to one tradition – and this malbush is made up of the twenty letters of the Hebrew alphabet and their two hundred and thirty-one possible two-letter combinations, or 'gates', as specified in the Sefer Yezirah. In fact, the malbush is the primordial Torah itself, though that is beside the point.

'So, in mystical Jewish thought the world is intended to be built about this linguistic structure, very similar in certain ways to the ideas laid out in the *Tractatus* or in Leibniz's essay on Monadology. But something goes wrong. In the primordial space ten vessels come into being, vessels whose interrelations and structure will format the world. But in the process of world-building the vessels are broken and the world we end up with, this one, is the result of that catastrophe, although at all times it is striving to return to perfection and will eventually do so. In all, then, there are three processes at work. Zimzum is the movement by which Ein-Sof originally withdraws into itself, thus opening up the space in which the vessels are created. Shevirah is the chaos that ensues once the vessels have been broken. And tikkun is the restructuring process by which the world reattains perfection.'

Joel stopped and Metric delivered a slow 'I see'. Then, as no more seemed to be forthcoming, he prompted: 'And so?'

'And so, according to Jewish tradition there would indeed seem to be a link between our apparently chaotic and unintegrable world and the perfect mathematical linguistics of the primordial space. In a way it's sort of proposing a link between Wittgenstein's later work and his earlier.'

'Well, it's one thing to propose it and another to find it. And I wouldn't set too great a store by the later work if I were you.'

'No, obviously, I couldn't agree more. But I do think it's worth trying to find that link.'

'You do, do you? I never knew you were so religious, my boy.'

'Oh, no! This isn't a religious problem at all! It's a logico-mathematical one. I just wanted to illustrate . . . after all, even Russell agrees . . . well what I want to say is, oh dear, you've been so kind to me . . .'

Metric smiled indulgently. 'What exactly is it that you're trying to say, my boy?'

Joel had another go. 'What I want to say is that I think the answer lies with the structure of chance and I'd like to change my thesis in order to study it.'

Metric drew a deep breath. He certainly had not expected it to be this easy. 'Probability theory, is it?'

'Er, yes and no. Yes as far as the maths is concerned. But the thing is that there is a strong empirical aspect to the whole, er, the whole thing, as it were. I mean, what I need to do I think is to study probabilistic mechanisms in relation to quantum theory in order to ground my thesis, which will, I think, entail, if my understanding of the workings of the university are correct, and I'm not quite sure that they are –' Joel was sweating now '– that I will have to transfer out of the Mathematics faculty and into the Physics. I think. Especially since I'll need to spend a lot of time with the computer, because I'll have to run models and compile masses of data.' There. He'd said it. Joel held his breath and began to count.

'So what you're saying is that you don't want me to teach you any more?' Joel couldn't speak. He sat there waiting for Metric to explode, perspiring frantically. He bit his bottom lip, drew blood. At least when he'd left his parents he hadn't had to confront them. 'Well, I can't say I haven't seen it coming. It's about time you moved on. You're a very clever chap, I dare say you've outgrown me. I'm not convinced by your thesis, I have to say – I think we're going to have to hammer that out a little, maybe some outside help is called for. But I don't think that what you're proposing is impossible, not by any means. No, I don't think it will be impossible at all.'

Going . . .

So Joel made the switch and moved out of maths and Metric could breathe easy again. The new thesis went well and the boy (who by now was pretty much of a man) felt at home in his new discipline, not least because he had consolidated the first proper friendship he'd managed since he came to England. The PDP–10 made a fine companion: straightforward yet complex, patient yet temperamental, promiscuous yet focused (access was only possible on a time-share system). Because he could get in more time with the machine that way, Joel found himself becoming almost nocturnal and the small hours invariably found him hunched in semi-darkness before the small round screen, punching in his programs and hunting for statistical significance in oceans of quantal data.

He liked Cambridge by night, even in the winter. It was a peaceful place; with most people in bed, the countryside seemed to take over the town and suddenly the trees bushes lawns took precedence over the crumbling, blackened buildings. And the air seemed more straightforward after dark, less ambivalent. Among the other students Joel acquired a reputation as something of a ghoul – first years used to call him 'the vampire', but soon changed that to 'the glumpire' because he never smiled. They'd run from him in mock terror when, at the tail end of an all-night bender, they encountered him wandering home from the computer labs at four or five in the morning. Although vaguely aware that he was the object of their mirth, Joel failed to comprehend this behaviour and generally ignored it, but he did get angry one night when some students lay in wait and drenched him with eight pints of stale ale that they'd salvaged from the dregs bucket in the college bar and had no doubt pissed in too. Screaming at his assailants as they disappeared into the shadows, he woke the Proctor who, in the best traditions of British justice, disciplined him for causing a disturbance.

But though Joel generally preferred his nocturnal existence, as summer came around again even he began to feel pangs for the touch of sunlight on his pallid skin, and every now and then he'd take a day or two's break from the lab, reboot his body clock by sleeping a full twelve hours and venture out into the daylight for a pastoral afternoon spent in Grantchester meadows or a short hike through the Cambridge countryside.

. . . *going* . . .

Laika had been up there a decade before her erratic orbit carried her above the clear summer skies of Cambridge. Stoned students caught her glint as they made out in Grantchester Meadows, an extra star to wish upon – though more often than not they put it down to the drugs. As usual, the town smelt of mown grass and traffic exhaust, Pimm's and bitter, stagnant river water and student sweat. At every possible opportunity ragged bands of youths collapsed in the parks and quads to drink away the day and boast pompously about how much work they were not going to do. Meanwhile the rest of the country tried to come to grips with what the dons condescendingly referred to as 'social change'. The colleges were still heavily segregated, but the warm weather had turned the parks and lanes into rustling zones of fornication. It was impossible to walk along a river bank without disturbing couples copulating in the cow parsley.

Joel picked his way along the Cam until he found a vacant patch that was relatively clear of used condoms and cigarette butts. He took off his jacket, folded it into a cushion, sat on it and opened his well-thumbed copy of *Principia Mathematica*. Picking up where he had left off in the library, he began to read. For him it was like poetry: the ideas clicked through his mind with the certainty of a well-oiled clockwork mechanism, beautiful in their elegance and logic. He read avidly for about twenty minutes, quickly digesting each clause and each proposition, his greasy hair stubborn against the breeze, until his concentration was broken by the raucous sounds of a punt full of people moving downstream towards him. A sharp meander in the river's course prevented him from seeing the party, but they were definitely drawing closer. The noise increased in intensity until individual words became discernible between the cackles of laughter and a moment later the nose of the punt appeared from around the bend. Packed with people, cans of lager and half-consumed bottles of wine, the craft drifted past, trailing marijuana smoke in its wake. It was a smell he recognised from the streets of Crown Heights and Williamsburg, and although he had never been sure what exactly the odour signified, it nevertheless triggered a sudden and violent memory of his home.

Some of the boat's occupants he had seen before. The puntsman – a fairly nominal title, earned by the fact that he was holding the pole rather than doing anything constructive with it – was an Irish fellow who lived on the same staircase as Joel in college. Short and squat, with a blob of bronze hair, he fancied himself a poet and drinker, and was never to be seen without a collection of Yeats, or at least a Malcolm Lowry, stuffed into one of his pockets (which he would pull out and quote from at regular intervals). Joel knew none of the girls; in fact he didn't know any girls at all. The mores of his upbringing were still set within him and even now he could not bring himself to look at any of what he thought of as 'the females' in the face. The constant tides of flirting and fornication which sucked at the groins of his peers passed completely over his head and he was barely aware of the curious rites that went on around him day in, day out. Now that the summer was here and they were becoming more obvious, he found himself uncomfortable when forced into any kind of close proximity with his fellow students. When all was said and done, Joel was most definitely a loner.

He caught the eye of McGuigan, the Irishman, and immediately dropped his gaze and tried to return to his book. But McGuigan had seen him and began to sing, cheered on by his companions:

Oh Booky, Oh Book Book, Oh Booky my dear,
Why is it I always keep you so near?
Oh Booky Oh Booky Oh Booky my love,
No use as a brolly no use as a glove,
Oh Booky Oh Booky Oh Book Book my heart
You've given me nothing and now we must part.
Oh Booky Oh Booky Oh Book don't be glum,
You've lived off my weakness but now we are done
Oh Book Booky-Booky Book Book don't take it so hard
That I've gone and replaced you with ten pounds of lard –

He broke off to take a breath, then sat down with a thump on the end of the punt, doubled up with private laughter. Everyone applauded, except Joel. A girl threw a bread roll at him; it glanced off his shoulder and disappeared into the cow parsley, and he tried not to react. The punt fell silent for a moment but then McGuigan, who had been swigging from a bottle, continued his address. 'That's Joist, that is. That's Joist, you know.' Thankful for an excuse to turn their eyes from Joel, the others looked up at him.

One of the other men said in loud, Home Counties tones, 'I say, McGuigan, what the fuck are you on about now?' and the girl languishing on his arm tittered at the obscenity.

'No, it's Joist, I say. Have I not told you the one about Joist then?'

'You most certainly have not,' said the Englishman, Kendricks, trying to retain the upper hand.

'Well, then. It's like this. There's this Kerryman, y'see . . . no, shhh, listen, it's a good story . . . there's this Kerryman and he's out of work, down on his luck like.'

'Ooo, Tommy, I do like your accent,' said the girl who had thrown the bread roll.

'Carol, ya hussy! Are you gonna shut up or am I gonna tip you in the river!' McGuigan cried, grabbing at her ankle. She shrieked and scrabbled away from him towards the bows, rocking the boat dangerously. When she reached safety she tucked her lips between her teeth and nodded.

'OK then, I'll continue. But no more interruptions mind.' He had his audience now. 'So there's this Kerryman who's out of work . . .'

'We've heard that bit,' said Kendricks funnily, but no one took any notice.

'. . . and he's generally down on his luck. He's in Dublin, see, and if he doesn't get work soon, he won't meet his rent and he'll be out on the street. So he's hangin' aroun', hangin' aroun', asking his mates, "Have ya heard anything, have ya? No news is tha'?", until one morning one of his mates tells him of a building site he knows of where they're hiring. So he gets hisself along there and goes up to the foreman and presents hisself. The foreman looks him up and down and feels sorry for him, 'cuz he's a skinny little runt, and says all right then, you've got yerself a job if yer can make yerself useful. So our hero, he's over the moon, and he's like "where can I start, where can I start?" So the foreman says to him, "Go sort out that stack of lumber on t'other side of the yard." ' Carol started to giggle again, but McGuigan shot her a look and she clammed up. It was a sub-routine of one of those rites so alien to Joel. 'So he goes over and starts moving and stacking and moving and stacking, and he's been at it about an hour when the foreman walks up to him and taps him on the shoulder. "What's the matter?" the foreman says. "Don't you know the difference between a girder and a joist?" "Oh that's easy," says the Kerry, turning round and mopping his brow. "Joist wrote *Ulysses*, and Girder wrote *Faust*!" '

The party collapsed with laughter and McGuigan hurled the bottle he'd been sucking on high into the air for emphasis. It came down with a splash and frightened two moorhens, who took to the air with a clatter. Flying low over Joel's head one of them let loose a crap and the runny lime landed splat in the middle of page 131 of *Principia Mathematica*. This caused even greater hilarity among McGuigan's group, but fortunately for Joel at that point the boat passed out of sight around the next bend where, owing to the pilot's lack of concentration, its bows snagged on a large clump of water weeds that extended out from the bank.

Now that they had gone Joel's fury boiled over. 'Bertrand Russell himself used to sit and read here, you know!' he yelled after the party. 'And Lewis Carroll!' But his words were lost to the river. He tore out a clump of grass and wiped down the soiled page, cleaning off the last stubborn dregs with his handkerchief, and tried to turn his attention back to the text. But it was useless, and soon he flung the book aside and lay back in the grass. The light poured down through the simmering leaves and splashed across his face, dappling him with shadows. The photons sparked on his retinae and tiny currents buzzed around to the back of his brain, setting up interference patterns in his cortex and making spirals dance in his vision. He blinked and rolled on to his side. Despite the breeze it was warm, and as his careering thoughts began to gyre more slowly and lose their points of reference he drifted in and out of sleep. A blonde girl lay face down in the meadow about ten yards from him;

she had taken off her blouse and her bra lay unclipped on the ground beneath her, forgotten as an ancient obligation.

She dozes there, her back pink from the sun, her face in shadow but already browned, her hair nattering with the zephyrs that twitch to and fro across the field. A fly comes down, alights upon her shoulder and the local muscles spasm of their own accord. Like an animal, thinks Joel, remembering the girl in the boat who had hit him with the bread roll and at whom he had stared. Disturbed, the fly lifts into the air, buzzes around for a bit and lands again, a few centimetres from its previous position. Joel has noticed before how a movement from beneath will serve only to unsettle a fly, make it take off for only a second or two, then invariably return to feast once more. But by bringing a hand down in a swift feint, a rush of air disturbs the cilia on its back and the fly infers a much greater sense of danger than from a movement sensed through its legs. Now it will fly off to pester someone else. Of course, Joel reflects, it's preposterous to think of a fly as being capable of inferring anything, in the true sense – it's far too primitive a creature. The point is that a fly's actions are triggered directly by its nervous responses to stimuli. If I had a big enough computer, he thinks, one that took up two or three rooms, I should be able to model that fly completely. He is somewhat mistaken, as it happens, for great mathematician though he is, Joel knows little or nothing about physiology or neurology or biochemistry and the rest of it. How could he, when even he can never hope to command more than a fraction of the material that has been written on his own subject, let alone acquaint himself with the rolling hills of data that stretch further than the eye can see in all directions in each of the other disciplines?

Too late he looks back towards the girl, or perhaps just in time. She is sitting up, having risen to swat the pest away, and one large brown nipple is hanging free in the air. Musty from her snooze, she rubs her nose to clear it of pollen. This makes her sneeze, a cute sneeze, *a-tissoo*, and her breast trembles nicely. We turn to Joel, expecting some reaction: a leer, a line, even a darkening of the eye . . . but no, there's nothing. Not a tremor. The smile upon his face is one of simple fascination – he's still contemplating his digital fly (so to speak) and gazing blankly at the girl's breasts while doing it. Naturally she spies him, gives him a dusky look, picking up perhaps on the strange magnetism Joel has that Metric also recognised (if only he'd do something with his hair . . .). She waits. But there's no reaction at all. With a loud 'tut' and an exaggeration of her movements the girl pulls on her blouse and moves away, swinging her bra behind her as she goes. She'd heard of a cat without a smile, but a smile without a cat?

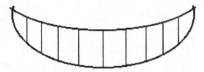

Joel was lost in space. He was with his one true love, the only love he'd ever known. Click click whirr went the limbs of this love, limbs which could hardly be described as languid. Her tendons were of wires and pulleys, her joints made of gears, her vital organs of transistors and valves. Her eyes were made of *and* gates, her mouth of *ors*, and her cunt was made of *nots*. *Not not not not not*. And in that lay her charm. Her brain was made of slide-rules and her flesh of logarithms, tables and matrices. Her breasts were sets, her hair had square roots and her clothes were quite transcendental. In short, she was perfection and all the more perfect because Joel could attain her, in a glorious jouissance of integration, whenever he wished. Logic is its own reward and Joel liked nothing better than to trace out its many branches until his brain felt ready to implode.

. . . gone

On finishing his Ph.D, Joel was offered a position as a research student at CERN, the European Centre for Nuclear Research, situated on the French–Swiss border. He took the job and was glad of it. It was time to move on and he was not sorry. He had been in Cambridge for the best part of a decade but apart from the old PDP–10 and the kindness of the Metrics, he'd put down no roots there, none at all, and he had no fondness for this place which could never in any event have survived being the realisation of such a fantastic dream.

4

A handful of pixels

Jennifer lay with her nose about three inches from the dusty screen of Donald's old TV and watched *The Partridge Family*, *Roadrunner* cartoons, *The Osmonds*, sitcoms, soaps and reruns of *Lost in Space*, the signal of which, it just so happened, was also being picked up by Laika in her satellite. Both dog and girl had a thing about the robot. He looked so useless with his goldfish-bowl head and flexi-tube arms, and yet the flashing lights suggested that a keen and even tender intelligence lay within. It was 1972, six years after Doreen had had her husband committed and the year that Joel had left Cambridge for CERN, and Jennifer had just turned twelve.

Eager to explore all possible watching habits, she had recently begun to hold TV parties on Saturday afternoons, an idea that grew out of the original moon-landing gathering three years before. After lunch about ten children would come over to watch the afternoon matinée, which was as a rule either a Western, a musical or a Hollywood epic of great scope and grandeur.

If the weather was fine, Henry would retire to the garden while they watched and potter about. He would mow the lawn, or do a spot of weeding, or just read the paper. What he would never do was stray very far from a regularly refreshed squat crystal tumbler full of gin and tonic mixed half and half which he would bring from the drinks cabinet in the living-room, set down on the chipped metal filigree of the garden table and return to at intervals which grew shorter and shorter as the sun sank lower and lower in the sky. Every refill meant confronting the gathered children, and with each one he would smile a little more and see a little less. By the time evening came, nothing much would exist outside of the three sides of fence that boxed in his plot and the sunset, whose great burning orb would begin to seem to him like a giant lemon sliding into the bottomless cocktail of the night. When it dipped out of sight it was time to go in for a sweater, a top-up and some dinner for which Jennifer – whose friends, called home by their mothers, would have left by now – would now be clamouring.

In the winter he would cook lunch for her instead (chops under the grill and frozen peas and mash) pick at his own portion until she finished eating, greet the children who spewed in through the door, all sticky sweets and sweaty hands and screaming for the movie, leave the dishes in the sink and disappear off to the local or perhaps the golf club to play a quick round and hover in the bar for an hour or two before returning. When he got back, Jennifer would no doubt have raided the biscuit tin and be curled up asleep on the armchair by the fire.

He thought at the beginning that he enjoyed the children's company and for the first few of those TV afternoons he sat with them, on the pretext of making sure that they got up to no mischief. But the hot mess of rapt faces, wide eyes, lips wet with sucking and chewing, and half-clad young limbs opened him to something that the booze had long kept subdued. The soft nap of a pre-pubescent thigh, the bud of a breast pressed up against the arm of a chair, a young boy's erection brought on and sustained by boredom; these things did not fail to come to his notice. He was a man of the world, or so he thought, he had read *Lolita* (several times) and while he was aware of the dangers, he believed they could be contained. So he did not see it as a problem when Judd – whom Henry regarded as a presumptuous boy (and certainly exotic) but whom Jennifer seemed to like – pulled the hair of Alice, the youngest of Jennifer's friends, and Alice started to cry and insisted on sitting on Uncle Henry's knee before she would stop. If Henry's hands did not stray and everything was good and proper it was only for a while, because desire will always disrupt, and before long Henry was silently giving thanks that the girl did not notice – or did not seem to notice – the extra muscle that ran along his thigh and remained there until just before the film was due to end and the parents due to arrive, when he had to place his charge back down on the floor and shuffle upstairs to relieve his aching testicles and rearrange his damp and ruffled clothing.

From then on Alice regarded Henry's lap as her domain. Capable of generating the precise amount of emotional upheaval needed to get her own way (even that first time there had been some debate in the group as to whether Judd had pulled her hair unprovoked or whether she had driven him to it) she had also noted with her sure child's eye that the staking of her claim had aroused not the slightest jealousy in Jennifer. Indeed, Alice was slightly disappointed, as this had been part of the desired effect, but she was not to know that Jennifer did not regard her putative father as in any strong way hers. They lived together like earth and moon, bound together by circumstance, ritual, habit and the gravitational pull of normality, into the pit of which all things eventually slide. But they never really touched. This suited poor Henry, who was more intimate with the shades and moods of his cocktails than those of his daughter, and it suited Jennifer too, who with perfect precociousness knew that if the relationship functioned at all it was because it was she who was responsible for her father and not the other way around. She had been flipped into self-possession at a tender age by the circumstances of her mother's life and the catastrophe of her death, as if, even as an infant, various behavioural modes had lain latent within her, one of which – the one she'd settled into – was able to accommodate the stresses of her childhood. So she was happy that Alice should be dandled from Henry's knee because he would never dandle her, Jennifer, again and she felt no regret over this. Although she knew something of boys she did not know enough to make a conscious connection between these afternoons and the stiff, sweet stains on Henry's underwear that she sometimes found when it was her turn to do the wash. Yet she got from them a flush and a tingle in her stomach that came from the awareness of having seen something forbidden or, at least, never spoken of, and which promised that the world was a bigger place than she yet knew. And she was aware also that at these times she thought of her friend Rever and of running in the woods behind the houses after school, and of Mr Kinever, who taught her science, and who was lithe and firm.

So for a few weeks Alice sat on Henry's knee, and Henry got up now and again and disappeared upstairs, the amount of bare flesh that he managed to graze with his fingertips directly proportional to the number of times he had to leave the room. After a while, the experience began to seem quite safe and Henry found himself getting a little bit more drunk and a little bit more brazen, until one wet Saturday afternoon, as *Seven Brides for Seven Brothers* flickered across the screen, his hand reached that little bit too far. Suddenly Alice's giggles became sobs. She didn't climb down from Henry's knee but sat stock still and demanded to be taken home, as if unaware of the origin of the offending sensation. Something was wrong, something was most definitely wrong, her mind was all confusion, something had happened which didn't fit with the way things were, the way things should be. Henry got up and pretended to fuss, and Jennifer came over and shushed and cooed until Alice was calmed by the attention. But she still insisted on being taken home, and Henry was put in the awkward position of having to call her parents and ask them to come over and pick her up.

The group, minus Alice, watched the rest of the film in silence, then trooped off out of the house. Jennifer left with them. All in all, it had been an unsuccessful afternoon: the crying business aside, except for Alice everyone had been bored by the film and they were left listless and in need of something to do. The rain had stopped, so they went down to the park to smoke cigarettes and scratch their names on the benches. Judd didn't smoke and he didn't really know anybody either, and everyone was a little wary of him because there weren't too many black boys about in Stratford at that time. He charged around the sodden lawns, his arms outstretched, making the sound of a propeller under his breath and saturating his expensive leather shoes with moisture, banking and diving in between the benches, making up his own movie inside his head. It was easier for him to follow the plot this way anyway – when he watched TV, even when he was with all the other kids at Jennifer's – he often blanked out and missed crucial events. Too embarrassed to ask what he'd missed, and often not realising he'd missed anything at all, he kept quiet which, in the eyes of the others, made him more mysterious still.

In the park, then, they left him to play aeroplanes, to take off from a bench, fly around, return to the same bench to take off again. In 1938, four years after Jennifer's mother had been told by her dance instructor about Wilbur Wright, the billionaire Howard Hughes had taken off from Floyd Bennett airfield in the United States, spent four days flying around the world in a single circular arc and returned to park his aeroplane in its hangar in the exact same spot in which it had been parked before his departure. If Nadine had been entranced by the image of Wright taking off in his biplane and flying in a circle to return to the same spot again, then perhaps she would have been charmed by watching Judd, this little Howard Hughes, flying in circles in order to disappear himself from the crowd of onlookers, running in order to stand still, speeding across the earth in order to experiment with time.

Her daughter was certainly intrigued. Jennifer couldn't keep from glancing at Judd between hot puffs on the carrot-ended cigarettes that were circulating, annoyed by the childishness of his game and drawn to it at the same time. Judd, by the way, was thinking about her too: while the other children blurred into the background he did not want to disappear Jennifer. Not because of who she was – they'd hardly ever exchanged a word – but because the TV afternoons were hers and they reminded Judd of the home he missed so much. If his father represented for Judd the logical power of machines, then Jennifer had come to mean access to the TV land of his childhood California. He wasn't bothered by not always being able to follow the plots of the films they watched, because the plots weren't what he was there for.

Left alone back at the house, Henry turned over the Alice incident in his mind, looking for a way to lie to himself. It wasn't clear, he finally decided, that he'd had any intention of interfering with the girl. For blame to be apportioned there surely had to be intention, there had to be a moment in which he had made the decision to act. But if such a moment had existed he could not remember it. The drink no doubt had something to do with it – he had certainly drunk more than usual. But now he thought about it he'd had a touch of cramp in his arm, yes, that was it, and he'd needed to flex it. A man gets stiff with a child on his lap for that long and she was no feather; yes, he was often surprised how heavy these kids were, they didn't look it, skinny as alley cats, some of them. And the whole affair was probably nothing to do with him anyway. It could have been something in the film that had upset her. Or how did he know one of the boys hadn't whispered something malicious to her? The little black boy, no doubt: he'd pulled her pigtails before, after all. For God's sake, it could even have been the weather, the rain beating a bit harder on the window than before, a change in air pressure (he'd better check the barometer in the hallway), a conjunction of the planets. Perhaps the house stood on the intersection of ley lines.
    Whatever the reason he finally came up with, from then on he kept out of the children's way during those cinematic Saturday afternoons. Jennifer didn't mind. Although she worried about her father, she knew she was quite capable of running things without him around. However many kids turned up of a weekend to watch her TV she was always quietly in control and none of them, even the older ones, had ever taken any liberties with her or her house. And anyway, without Henry around it was easier for her to test her power over the boys who came over: the world of males had fascinated her for a while now and, like a restless sea lapping discontentedly at the shores of some pre-biotic land, she wanted to colonise it. Henry's presence had made the environment too arid for her exploring tendrils to make much progress, but with him out of the way the atmosphere changed and she was at liberty to use words fingers glances like lichens and mosses, hyphae and rhizomes. With these tools she began to inch her way across the skins of these boys and slowly weave a psychic mat of mild exploitation.

A month or two later . . .

Now the summer evenings were stretching themselves out beyond the end of the school day; now the breezes that accompanied them were warm and inviting, and the birds provided an extra dimension to the bushes and the trees; now Jennifer could trip home from school glowing with the innocence that radiates only from a perfect depravity freed from all external perspective. She could loll on the hot stones of the low wall that defined her tiny front garden, sip at a lemonade and call to her friends as they passed her on their way back to their homes on the estate.

At the end of the day the school spat them out and they passed into small groups, volatile molecular knots bonded by the juxtapositions of geography, age, smell, money, looks, peer pressure, the disguised dictates of desire and the hidden agendas of the vast yeasts of the future. Each child formed a nexus, a series of points of intersection for a tumult of factors, and each child resonated accordingly.

Shelley was Jennifer's best friend and she straggled along Hunt's Crescent, all scuffed shoes and stretched socks and stained cuffs. Dog-eared exercise books poked from the top of her bag, crammed in among toiletries stolen from Boots and odd bits of jewellery and a broken watch Lewis had given her, and sweet wrappers and crushed chocolate bars and half a pack of Embassy Filtered, two of which had been half smoked and pinched out, and a packet of mints and a box of matches, both live and dead, and one gymshoe (Shelley was still hoping the other one was going to turn up) and last term's report card which she had not passed on to her parents for obvious reasons, and a biro drained dry of ink, ink which now formed a dark decoration along one of the bag's lower seams. All this was immersed in the smell of rotting canvas, the cloth still muggy from having trailed round behind its owner throughout the winter months.

So Shelley came first and after Shelley came the bag, that theatre of the ongoing war between the concerns of a burgeoning social life and the discipline of school, and after the bag came Rever, who had just been given the brush-off by Shelley and was trying to look cool about it. Shelley spotted Jennifer sitting on her wall and crossed the road to join her. Now she had an ally and Rever was defeated and had to carry straight on, scoping the girls from behind his plastic Ray Bans and adjusting the

Aston Villa sweatbands that he always wore around his thin wrists as he went.

Immediately suspicious, Jenn questioned her friend. 'What you doing with Rever?' she demanded.

'I wasn't *with* him, you idiot.'

'Well pardon me for breathing.'

'It's all your fault in the first place.'

'What? What have I done?'

'You told him I wanted to go and see some poxy play at the theatre.'

'So what?'

'So he's gone and brought me tickets, that's what.'

'So what's the problem. Why don't you go?'

''Cuz he's a creep. We don't all have the same tastes as you.'

'*I* don't fancy him.'

'You do an' all. You fancy him rotten. You told me so at New Year's.'

'Yeah, well that was New Year's. I've gone off him now.'

'Lewis said you did it with him.'

'Yeh, well, Lewis doesn't know shit. How does Lewis know anyway?'

Shelley feigned loss of interest and changed the subject. 'That lemonade?'

'Yeh.' Twirling the liquid around in the glass. 'You want some?'

'All right.'

'Come on then.' Jennifer slides from her perch on the wall and Shelley follows her into the cool of the house. From outside their giggled conversation is still audible, although individual words cannot be distinguished. It is balmy, it is summer. A dragonfly flits across the screen. Two or three people walk past the house: pedestrians. A young boy on a bicycle crosses, right to left. A few moments later another boy chases after him, yelling. Peace for a moment. A brown mongrel dog wanders along the pavement, sniffing at the wall. It stops, cocks its leg and pisses up against the stones.

Shelley emerges from the house just in time to see it run off. 'Oi, Jenn! That mangy dog from next door's been slashing up your wall again!'

At her shout, Jennifer reappears. 'Oh, shit! That little fucker. It does it deliberately, you know.' She yells abuse at the dog, which canters away down a side road, then locks the front door behind her and walks off down the road with her friend.

Half an egg

Deep in Jennifer's matrix. Being a catarrhine primate (Old World Monkeys, anthropoid apes, humans) Jennifer has a modified oestrous cycle, aka a menstrual cycle. Unlike many mammals, the catarrhine primates do not exhibit a well-defined period of oestrus or 'heat', coinciding with ovulation, when the female will copulate with a male.

Preceding and succeeding oestrus there are various changes that take place throughout the body, particularly in the uterus. These may be regarded as preparations for pregnancy. The whole set of these changes is controlled by hormones. The first phase of the cycle is known as follicular. Stimulated by the pituitary hormone, Graafian follicles begin to grow inside the ovary. At the same time there is an increasing secretion of oestrogen by the ovary and a proliferation of the lining of the uterus (endometrium), paving the way for the next stage, ovulation. Eventually the ripe egg will burst from such a follicle. The egg is discharged on to the surface of the ovary and thence passes into the oviduct. There is also an activation of mating reflexes.

The third phase is known as the luteal stage, and involves the formation of a temporary organ of internal secretion, the corpus luteum (yellow body), in the interior of the ruptured Graafian follicle after ovulation by the ingrowth of the follicle wall, which becomes yellow secretory luteal tissue. The secreted hormone is progesterone. Formation of the corpus luteum occurs as a result of action of the luteinising hormone and its secretory activity requires the presence of the lactogenic hormone of pituitary. At this time oestrogen production decreases, while there is a great development of the uterine glands. If ovulation does not result in fertilisation then the cycle goes into phase four: the regression of the corpus luteum, the beginning of new follicular growth, a return to the unproliferated state of the uterine lining, the diminution of oestrogen and the cessation of progesterone secretion. In the special case of the menstrual cycle there is a sudden destruction of the mucosa of the uterus at the end of the luteal phase of the cycle, producing bleeding. If, on the other hand, fertilisation does occur then the corpus luteum persists and continues secreting during part or all of pregnancy. On the morning of 15 May Jennifer had entered the second stage: ovulation.

★

As for the egg which was released, it was large and complex – nearly one hundred thousand times larger than the sperm that would one day penetrate it. And while those sperm would carry only chromosomal information with them when they came, the cytoplasm of this egg was packed full of mitochondria. Containing DNA and oxidative enzyme systems, mitochondria are the energy factories of every living cell. Once, billions of years ago, they were bacteria; free-living and vicious they entered other cells and multiplied like viruses until they split their host asunder, so releasing multiple offspring into the world. But somewhere along the line a host cell captured this parasite and tricked or coerced it into a symbiotic relationship. With this tamed and rapidly respiring organelle inside of it, the host could now breathe and metabolise much greater quantities of food into adenosine triphosphate, a molecule crucial to many cellular processes. The eukaryotic cell – the cell which makes up all multicellular organisms – was born.

Mitochondria do not reproduce like nucleated cells. They do not exchange DNA with other organisms; rather they divide and multiply like bacteria, according to their own rules. Mammalian mitochondria is passed only down the female line; the male sperm introduces no new mitochondria into the ovum. Which begs the question: what are men for?

Rubble in mind

Saturn V is launched, Judd's ruler twangs, the pellet arcs across the room and hits Lewis on the neck. Doreen Buerk spins around on one heel and stares at the small American down the length of her nose, fixing him like a doomed field-mouse with the ball-bearing pupils of her grim stoat eyes. She lets the silence gather, creating maximum dramatic tension for the opening of her speech. When she senses that the time is right she starts to yell: 'That's it! Out! Out you go! I've told you and I've told you I won't put up with this kind of behaviour. You will be penalised after school. Outside the door! Go! Now! I'll deal with you after class. It may come as a surprise for you to learn that some of us would like to continue the lesson without interruption.' Judd opens his mouth to protest but she shouts him down and expels him from the class, to the great amusement of his peers.

Out in the corridor, lonely and upset, Judd fiddled with the buttons of his digital watch, a present his dad had sent him only a few weeks before and the only one in the school. But he'd played with it a lot recently and was soon bored with it. He looked around the hallway for something else to focus on, something to bind the random rush of thoughts that tumbled through his head. The building was old, older than most things in California. He stood at the foot of a stone staircase that wound upwards for three or four flights. Daylight spewed into the darkened vault from the western landings. He let himself imagine that one of the landings led on to the street on which his father's house stood, thousands of miles away, back on the Pacific Rim. He had one chance to take the right doorway, and one alone. Which one would he take? Another door led into Pioneer 11. Pioneer 11 had been launched the previous month. Judd had read about it in *National Geographic*; it would be somewhere out by Mars now. He'd be stuck inside the probe with no way back and not much air. Out of the window he'd be able to see the huge peak of Olympus Mons, which he remembered because it was the biggest volcano in the solar system. He'd probably be able to find some freeze-dried ice-cream in the supply lockers; he'd had some at Christmas, when his father had taken him to the space exhibit at the Smithsonian when they'd all been in Washington DC because his mother had been invited to an important party. It was all hard like polystyrene until you bit it, then it foamed up in your mouth and was kind of like ice-cream, but in a weird way, because you didn't taste it until after you swallowed. That was when Apollo 17 had just landed on the moon, and the man at the museum had said that the astronauts were probably eating the ice-cream right at the same time Judd was and Judd had asked him if it was true what the *National Geographic* said, that there weren't going to be any more men on the moon for a long time, and the man said that he was sure that there would be. Judd said that he would like to be an astronaut and fly there and his father patted him on the back, and the man said: 'Maybe you'll be next then' and Moses thought a black astronaut? and remembered the ghettos that made up the bulk of the city and forced a smile.

Tired with the demands the punishment was making on his imagination, Judd mentally stamped his foot. Why had his mother brought him here to these English Midlands which lay about him now like a river fog that would never lift? Eight months previously, when they had first arrived, he could still invoke the forest tang of the pine trees, the sound of the tyres of his father's Lincoln drawing up in the driveway, the hollow knock of basketballs in the courts at the foot of the hill, the low-res blither of the ever present television. He could use these gentle demons to open portals to the long evenings and the bored sun and the roller-skating and the easy food back home. But the access gates had dwindled and finally disappeared as his reference points had all slowly been replaced and he had grown, faster than he ever could have imagined, into this different place where no one had ever eaten a Twinkie bar or even knew what root beer was. And to make matters worse the new culture had infected him despite himself, using as a bridgehead his dim memories of his visits here as an even younger child, and now it prickled his skin like a rash. He was in a no-man's land of change and uncertainty and, although he longed for it, California somehow seemed as alien as the surroundings into which he had been thrust.

The train of thought exhausted itself; Judd gave it up and listened for the tractor, but its rattlings could not be heard from inside the hallway. Instead there was only the velvet hum of children organised behind walls and the echoes of his own small movements in the cavernous space. He coughed and listened to the reverberations, but they brought comfort and fear in equal doses. The feeling connected with one which came to him sometimes as he lay on his bed at night waiting to fall asleep. He would be looking down the length of his body when abruptly the twin peaks his feet made in the blankets would seem an incredible distance away, as if he were looking at them through the wrong end of a telescope. This stretched perception was not so much accompanied by as actually a part of a sensation he felt in his feet, in his almost hairless groin and around the back of his skull. It was a tingling, but a tingling which always seemed to be drawing away, like an ebb. It was as if the tides of all the things that were within him, and which he neither understood nor knew how to number, were ebbing away into the bed and into the room around him. It was that ebb which was both frightening and comforting simultaneously.

He began to worry that the duty master might happen by and further chastise him, and his testicles grew warm at the thought. He wondered about this word the Buerk had used, 'penalise'. In his mind it became linked with another word, one that was austere and technical, and which adults used with caution. Back home the teacher would have said 'punish', and to be punished was OK, because it would happen and then be over, and did not threaten to go on and on in the background, day and night for ever, interminable.

To escape he would make himself invisible. How would he do that?

Easy – by making time stand still. Across the hallway from him was a door . . . it was simple to imagine that this was the only door through which any threat to him could come. He just had to fix the door in time as it was – closed. He narrowed his eyes and contemplated the view before him. Now, all he needed to do was click his eyelids down and up like a camera's shutter to foreclose the possibility of the door's ever opening. It would only take a moment . . . and yet he hesitated. For to take possession of the world in this way was also to allow the world, in its tedious materiality, to take possession of him. A shiver went down his back as he became aware of the threat presented by the cold stone wall behind him. What if, in the instant that he closed his eyes to cement the door, the wall took advantage of his distraction to cement him? It was a possibility. Yet which was the greater, his fear of the duty master or his fear of the wall? Perhaps if he was quick he could catch the wall off guard. He decided to go for it.

While Judd bent space–time and dreamt of escape, inside her Cartesian classroom Doreen Buerk seeped on in nasal tones about glacial erosion in mountain regions. With the unbreachable wall of her knowledge erected around her she issued edicts to the class full of pingos and mud-flat polygons, permafrost and outwash, arêtes and bifurcations. But the concentration of her pupils was undergoing pre-glacial unstratified drift: there were only five more minutes left before the dinner bell rang, and though they yawned before the children like the largest of underground caverns it was not within their capacities to fill them with what Doreen Buerk might have regarded as useful deposits.

But wait a minute. Something was permeating the hard crust of Lewis's brain and forming stalactites of some description. The closed system of the geography lesson had been breached with the expulsion of Judd to the corridor and, with the usual dampeners on lateral bleed short-circuited, Lewis's mind was meandering. It had indeed meandered all the way to the great ocean of the guilty conscience, a sight he had not witnessed before.

Doreen had been telling the class how glacial action had inspired Percy Bysshe Shelley's poem, 'Mont Blanc', calling it 'one of the most wonderful of poems about nature' and 'the birthright of every Englishman'. It was at this point that the ten-and-a-half-year-old hand of Jacob Hethlethwaite shot up into the air, quickly followed by the sound of him reciting from memory: 'Thus you, raven of Arf – dark, deep raven – you multicoloured, no, multivoiced vale, over which pins and crags, and caravans sail like fast cloud shadows and sunbeams which seem, er, powerful lightness in the arm which, comes down . . . I know it I know it . . . er, comes down from the ice gluphs that grid his secret throne, and, and . . . bursting . . .' Jacob stood and trembled, transported by the emotion of the piece.

Doreen Buerk watched him with a dalek's steely eye, boring a hole into his forehead with her gaze and forcing him to shut up and sit down. 'Yes, thank you very much, Jacob, that's very good,' she buzzed in an even and metallicised drone, 'but I think we can save it for the English lesson, can't we.'

Eddie Richmond called out from the back, 'What's a gluph, miss?'

Doreen's face reddened just a shade. 'What did I just say? Are you asking me to repeat myself, Master Richmond?'

'No miss.'

'No. I didn't think so.' She returned to firmer ground, to permafrost and solifluction, leaving plots against Jacob Hethlethwaite to coalesce in the imaginations of most of the class. One of the exceptions was Lewis. The poem reminded him that he had filched his father's best Mont Blanc fountain pen, which his father thought he had just mislaid, much to the annoyance of his new girlfriend who had given it to him the previous Christmas, and it was very expensive and how could he have lost it? At which point his father hit his new girlfriend in the mouth and said, 'It's only a fucking pen, shut your fucking gassing for five christing minutes, will you?' As a result of which Lewis thought it was probably best that his father did not discover that he, Lewis, had stolen the pen and given it to a girl he wanted to impress and who went by the name of Shelley.

Lewis was the oldest boy in his year. He had been put down two years running (and once a few years before) because he was obsessed by girls. It was all he thought about. He was the boy first discovered keeping porn mags in his desk; who blew up condoms like balloons in the play-ground. He was one of the few boys in the school who was thought by his peers to have had sex, and it was true, he had. With his father, with a sixteen-year-old girl who was drunk at a party that his elder brother Rever had taken him to and with Jennifer, Shelley's best friend (who had slept with Rever as well). And right now he wanted nothing more in the world than to have sex with Shelley. He had given her the pen to help her make up her mind about letting him finger her. Jennifer had done it for three B&H, but then Jennifer had done it with everybody. Shelley on the other hand, was class.

Shelley's 'Mont Blanc'. It was a too much of a coincidence. Maybe the Buerk knew? Maybe she'd seen Shelley with the pen? It was a terrifying thought and once Lewis had entertained the idea he found it difficult to get rid of. He squirmed in his chair, made a pyramid with his arms and tried to hide his head in the shadow that they made. He hoped that everyone would think that he was intent upon following the lesson in his textbook (although that alone was enough to arouse suspicion). He could feel Doreen Buerk's words; they were spread across his back like the tentacles of so many malicious octopi and they curled the suckered tips of their podia together so that they might form a powerful web with which to keep him down. With his head lowered he imagined he could feel her eyes prowling around him, the cold eyes of a cephalopod searching for a way into all those juicy thoughts.

The bell finally rang and Geography ended, and the kids thundered from the room. Lewis walked out slowly, lagging behind the rest and loitering outside the door, while Judd was called back into the classroom and chastised by his teacher. When the young American was released, Lewis followed him out into the playground, and tailed him out along a line of poplar trees and on to the playing fields. Then he increased his speed until the two of them drew level. 'Hey, Judd!'

At the sound of Lewis's voice Judd turned and punched the older boy square in the face. Then they were both on the ground, wrestling in the dirt. Having taken Lewis by surprise, Judd had the upper hand, but he didn't have it in him to hurt the older boy. Partly he didn't want to and partly he was afraid that however much he hurt Lewis, Lewis would hurt him back two-fold. What he really wanted was to humiliate him, to make him feel as wretched as he felt himself – that would be the only way to repay him for snitching. Lewis, as Judd had suspected, had no such qualms about inflicting pain. He knew how to hurt and was ruthless about it. So Judd quickly lost his initial advantage and took a series of hard blows. Clothes were ripped, hair was pulled, palms and knees were grazed as the two boys rolled over and over. Then the American's anger returned and suddenly he had Lewis's head in a decent grip and was grinding his face into the soil and trying to tear off his ears. Lewis was experienced enough to know that if your enemy hasn't gone down after you've given him the best that you've got then it's time to get out while you still can. He broke away and scrambled to his feet, with Judd not far behind.

By this time a crowd had gathered around the entertainment. As the two fighters squared up to one another for a second bout someone at the back yelled 'Pinkerton!' The Deputy Head was approaching. Suddenly there was an enormous dissipation of tension. The crowd, previously a solid group bound by a common interest, now changed state and became liquid, the pupils rearranging themselves in mobile molecular clusters of twos or threes. By the time Pinkerton motored up a second change was underway: two boys were picking football teams in an attempt to give the illegal gathering the appearance of a kind of order that authority would approve of.

Pinkerton was a short, stout man with an elliptical face and unkempt khaki-coloured hair that he scraped across his expansive bald pate. His tatty suit was the same mottled khaki as his distressed locks and as he walked he swayed from side to side, his thighs too large to let his legs swing perpendicular to the ground. Under one arm he clutched a file bulging with papers. He drew up to the crowd and stopped, removed his glasses with his free hand and rubbed them on his shirt before replacing them, then gave the group a hard stare, his mouth set like a toad's. 'Hum. Football. Good show,' he said. 'But keep the noise down, will you, or move away from the buildings.' Then he waddled off towards the staff canteen. Behind him, the excitement and the danger over, the liquid crowd became a gas and dissipated across the playing fields. Precipitated out was the original catalyst, Lewis and Judd.

Judd's heart was racing. He'd never done that before, hit out first, but his anger against Lewis had been building for a long time now. Lewis was the one who whispered 'nigger' to his cronies when Judd could overhear, it was Lewis who'd knocked a bottle of ink over his new satchel in the first week of term, who'd spat in his sandwiches the day they'd grabbed his lunch-box and thrown it around the room.

It had made him feel good to hit Lewis, like a hero, like an astronaut. But he didn't know if he could do it again. He hadn't known he was winning the fight when Pinkerton arrived; even while he'd been rubbing his opponent's face in the dirt he'd been thinking that at any moment the tables would be turned and he was going to have to run. Now he was elated and scared, both.

Lewis was, too. He hadn't expected a kid a couple of years his junior to hit him so hard. His nose was bleeding and he could still feel Judd scrabbling at his back in a manner not dissimilar to the octopoid words of Doreen Buerk. He felt a little dizzy. Across the fields the tractor engine stopped and, though neither of them noticed, it seemed there was something missing from the day. Everything shimmered. Lewis had been here before, but he hadn't. And then he did something very strange, something he definitely couldn't remember having ever done before, something that went against everything his father had taught him. He apologised.

'Fuck you,' was Judd's response.

'No, you don't understand, I'm sorry. I really mean it.' From where Judd was standing, something was wrong. Here was this boy who was older than him, who was taller and harder, and he was apologising. To him. For his part, Lewis was going red with the effort. 'I mean it.'

'Yeah, as if it means anything coming from you,' sneered Judd, suddenly buoyed up on a wave of memories of American television shows. He had not been in this situation before; he had to draw on what he could in order to know how to behave. Lewis on the other hand rarely got to watch TV at all. He wasn't aware that he was now dealing with a simulacrum, a montage of melodramatic behaviour. But Judd was black and beneath that tag a lot of weirdness could be brushed. Like cowboys at a gunfight, the boys wheeled around one another.

'I said I meant it. I've never said that to anyone before. You can't say fairer than that.'

'I don't scare easy,' spat Judd.

Stumped, Lewis tasted blood on his lips and reached up to touch his nose. His fingers came back wet with blood and he held them out to Judd like an offering. 'Look, I could help you out.'

'You ain't got nothing I want,' said the lone rider.

Lewis thought about this for a moment, then his face brightened. 'I can get you a girlfriend.'

Over the last few months, out on a limb in England and separated from his friends, Judd had plenty of time alone, time which needed to be filled. He read a bit, but he was not much of a reader; he watched English television, but it was not the same. And he didn't like the cold, so long walks exploring the countryside were out too. He had reached puberty early and, although only ten, already had a fuzz around his testicles. And among that sprouting down he had discovered the perfect toy with which to while away the long evenings spent waiting for his mother to come home from the theatre.

To begin with, odd things aroused him. The shape of a kitchen utensil, the angle of a spade sticking out of the garden earth, the silence of a room, the syncopation of a dripping tap. Almost anything, it seemed, could conjure an erotic adventure from a lonely mood. Then blood would start pumping into his member and he would slip into a soft, drugged state from which he could not emerge until he had ejaculated.

Soon he began to get turned on by anything mechanical. Cars, bikes, trucks; the old hand pump that stood out behind the house, left over from when there was a well; roundabouts and swings in public playgrounds; the clockwork viscera of a wrist-watch, which he knew how to take apart but not how to put back together; strange machines he built with Meccano; an ageing chair that smelt of damp and worm dust, the seat and back of which slid to and fro along a complex ratchet. All these things would lead him into an erotic dream of process, of the road to consummation, but despite being always keen to take the first few steps along the way, consummation was almost never reached: instead, Judd would find himself overwhelmed with the narcosis of arousal, which would blend with his picnoleptic experiences to produce a state in which change was like the pressure of the air, no longer orchestrated by clock hands and numbers, but a part of the planet as it breathed its crusty breath. Now his senses were plugged into a vast field of time and sensitive to every potential that flickered across it: each fluctuation at the world's boundary some ten billion light-years away was linked to every movement of his hand, every swirl of his fingerprint, every fold of his foreskin.

But, fickle youth that he was, he soon tired of making love to the universe and refocused his desire on the glory of flesh. He pored over the lingerie advertisements in his mother's magazines, trying to decipher the glyphs of the female form. He went through her wardrobe, fascinated by the way her clothing differed from his own: the awkward cuts, the peculiar materials, the rows of tiny buttons that opened the wrong way. He began to stare at girls, to sneak looks down their shirts and up their skirts, to realise that their skin and hair had a different quality from his own. Sometimes he found differences and sometimes he did not. But the upshot was that when Lewis spoke to him he was ready.

Lewis told him to meet him by the bus-stop the next day after school.

'But I can't!' Judd protested. 'Michael always picks me up and drives me home. My mom says so.' Michael was his mother's personal assistant; a camp Los Angeleno, she'd insisted he accompany her during her sojourn at Stratford.

'Tell her you've joined the chess team or something.' Lewis. Always ready with an answer.

Boys and girls

At four the next day the final bell rang as usual – that bell that in the summer more than ever sounded the change of segregation, order, captivity, purpose into freedom, enthusiasm, unfettered desire. With the quick switch of affiliation familiar to wars and childhood, Lewis and Judd were now thick as thieves, bound with the special bond that conspiracy confers. They ignored the bus and together walked towards the estates that bordered the town, Lewis leading Judd into the curved culs-de-sac, down the short-cuts made into tunnels by the early summer foliage, along the backs of bulging garden fences, over railings and through a bush or two, across a culvert with a stretched-leg leap (and into which a library book fell unnoticed from Judd's satchel). Finally they arrived in a small playground on the edge of town. Fields stretched out before them and away to the right were some woods. It was hot, late afternoon hot, and mayflies and bumblebees gyred in the air around them. Lewis sat on one of the swings and lolloped to and fro, scuffing his shoes in the dirt. The leather on their toes had already been worn down to a cardboard grey.

'D'you fancy a tab?'

'What's that?'

'A smoke. A cigarette.'

'I don't know. My father says it's bad for me.'

'One won't hurt you, will it?'

'We used to smoke cornpipes at camp. Like Huck Finn.'

'Who's that then?' asked Lewis, puzzled, and Judd began to explain all about Finn and Tom Sawyer and Mark Twain and the Mississippi and freed slaves and hiding out on islands and dressing up as girls.

'Dunno if I'm too keen on that last bit.'

'But they were trying to escape, don't you see, and it doesn't mean they were weird or anything, they were just doing what they had to do. But Huck got himself found out because the old woman made him thread a needle and she saw the way he did it wasn't the way he'd have done it if he was a girl.' Lewis didn't see how there could be different ways to thread a needle and Judd started to explain, but then it didn't matter because the real girls had arrived, Jennifer and Shelley.

The girls approached, the glare of the late afternoon sun above and behind them. They'd come from that direction because they knew that the light would make the fabric of their shirts semi-transparent and allow the boys a glimpse of the outline of their slim young torsos and developing breasts. When they got close Lewis said, 'Uh, hi, uh, this is Judd.'

'We know,' said Jennifer sarcastically.

'Oh, right, you do?' said Lewis, confused.

'Judd comes round Jenn's to watch TV on Saturdays,' said Shelley. 'Doncha, Judd?'

Judd said 'Uh huh' and looked down at his shoes, feeling awkward because he knew that Henry had banned Lewis from the TV afternoons.

Lewis was in a difficult situation. He had been going with Jennifer, but then he'd started seeing Shelley instead. To his surprise, Jennifer had not seemed particularly bothered by this blatant betrayal and still insisted upon hanging around with him. He felt that he had to be nice to her, not so much to assuage his guilt – because he didn't feel particularly guilty – but because his experience of girls told him that an emotional explosion was eventually due either way. He figured that his best policy was to try and forestall it for as long as possible. This involved being relatively pleasant to her and letting her bum a lot of cigarettes.

Shelley was becoming worried by Lewis's continual niceness towards Jennifer, because Lewis wasn't nice to anybody. That was why she liked him, because she thought that was cool and this unusual behaviour was making her uneasy and jealous. She certainly thought that now Lewis was seeing her he should be a little less attentive to her best friend – who wouldn't be her best friend for much longer if things didn't change. She assumed that he was feeling guilty about dumping Jennifer and the fact that Lewis had brought a friend along for her bolstered this analysis.

Jennifer was not impressed by the fact that Lewis had brought Judd with him; presumably he was meant for her, so that Lewis and Shelley could disappear off on their own. Was he trying to be funny? The kid couldn't be more than, what, ten? She knew that Lewis had been put down a few years, but she didn't know he'd started socialising with the babies he was forced to take classes with. Or was this solely for her benefit? Was this the only person he'd managed to convince to come along?

Shelley had to admit to herself that if she were in Jennifer's shoes she wouldn't be best pleased. Judd was pretty young.

Before her thing with Lewis the youngest bloke Jennifer had slept with had been seventeen. She should have stuck with the older ones, she told herself. She should never have let her form drop. Secretly, though, she had a soft spot for Judd. That afternoon in the park when he'd been playing aeroplanes she'd had an almost uncontrollable urge to hold him, to stroke his hair. She couldn't be getting broody, could she? Not at her age?

The four of them walked off across the fields. Jennifer sulked along behind the others until Lewis dropped back to see what was the matter. As soon as they were out of earshot, she let rip. 'What's the big idea of bringing that kid along?'

'It's all right. He's American.'

'What's that supposed to mean? I hope you don't expect me to baby-sit while you and Shel go off and enjoy yourselves.'

'Yeah but he can come and watch TV.'

'That's different. Loads of people come then. I don't know half of them.'

'You never asked me.'

'You're too old. Dad won't let you come.'

'Never stopped you before.'

'Fuck off, OK!'

'Look, I said it would be all right, didn't I? It's just for half an hour. How would you like it, being all on your own in a foreign country? How would it suit you? He needed a guide and that's me. I'm showing him the ropes.'

'Like what? What are you showing him?'

'The way we do things around here.'

'And how would you know?'

'Look, you can help if you want, but you don't have to. He doesn't need me or you or anybody. He's a tough kid.' Lewis saw his words weren't having much effect, so he tried a different tack. 'He's from Hollywood, so if I were you I'd be nice to him. Aw, c'mon Jenn. I'll make it up to you. How many ciggies do you owe me? Do us a favour. And look how pleased Shel is 'cause she thinks she's going to get me to herself. It's just this once. Look, if you do it I'll give you this.' He fished a crumpled joint out of his pocket and handed it to her.

'What's this?'

'What d'you think it is? It's a spliff of course. Never seen one before?'

'Course I have.' She hadn't. 'Just wanted to know exactly what type it is before I agree.'

'Er, it's blackash I think. Yeh, blackash, definitely.'

Jennifer stared at his hopeful face, his shit-eating grin, the glossy curls which crowned his head. Then she looked ahead at Judd, who was stumbling along next to Shelley. His hands were thrust into his pockets and he was kicking at stones. He looked bored. Then she looked down at the joint. It was bent and badly rolled, and it tapered in all the wrong places. All in all it was a far cry from the perfect cone that she had imagined a joint to be. But it was a joint. Therefore it was something new and its power was strong. 'Oh, OK. Fuck off then. I'll see you back here in an hour.' She dashed ahead and grabbed Judd's hand. 'C'mon, kiddo, we're going this way.' And with that she marched him off in the direction of the woods.

Spermatogenesis (1)

Lost in the tangle of Judd's testes, which had recently jumped hand in hand off the cliff of puberty. All around, gametes with reduced cytoplasm are forming. Within the nuclei of spermatocytes, chromosomes start to appear as very long fine threads with chromomeres spread like beads along their length – this is the leptotene phase. Gradually the zygotene stage begins, and each pair of chromosomes (such a pair is known as a bivalent) aligns itself and starts to twist and thicken, each chromosome doubling in the process. Each bivalent now consists of four chromatids which remain paired but as pairs separate from the two chromatids derived from the homologous chromosome (diplotene). Diakinesis follows: the chromatid pairs – still linked by chiasmata, the visible expression of the interchange of genes (there are usually one or two chiasmata per chromosome pair per meiosis) – move to the periphery of the nucleus, close to the nuclear membrane. The nucleoli – the small, dense bodies containing RNA and protein which reside in each resting nucleus – disappear, as does the nuclear membrane. As a result of the effects of the chiasmata, the bivalents usually end up as mixtures of one or more pieces from the original chromosomes. The chromosomes at this stage are still diploid; for them to become gametes a second meiotic division must occur, which in most cases happens almost immediately. The two chromatids separate, one going to each daughter cell; which goes where is again a matter of chance, as long as the two from each chromosome go to opposite poles. Division spindles appear and the united chromatids gravitate towards either end. There are now two pairs of two daughter cells, in this case spermatids, each pair joined together by a spindle. Each cell is now haploid even though the original cell was diploid, and this reduction is the basis of genetic segregation. Now the chromosomes uncoil, elongate and eventually disappear, new nuclear membranes form and the spindle also gradually disappears. It is at this stage that the cytoplasm begins to divide. Extensive changes take place; at the same time the nucleus condenses.

A flagellum forms. This consists of eleven microtubules arranged longitudinally, the whole being surrounded by an outer membrane which is continuous with the plasma membrane of the cell. The sections of the flagellum are known as basal body, blepharoplast, kinetoplast and kinetosome. Each flagellum is around a quarter of a micrometre thick and several hundred micrometres long. By undulating in a wave-like manner, the flagellum propels what is now a gamete, or spermatozoon, along. There are some mitochondria in the flagellum, but they don't make it into the egg.

Into the trees

'Ow!'

'What's the matter?'

'I'm caught on a briar. It's tearing my pants.'

Jennifer sighed and went back to free him. By turning to try and see where the thorns were stuck he had unbalanced himself, and she took his thigh and locked it under one arm to steady him while she extricated the bramble from his clothing.

Goose-pimples sprang up Judd's leg at her touch. Except for his mother, he couldn't remember anyone touching him there before. He was feeling very different from the way he'd felt the day before, just after he and Lewis had been fighting. Then he'd felt like a hero. Now he felt . . . he wasn't sure how he felt, but he knew he wasn't in charge. 'What about Lewis?'

'He's meeting us later. He has to talk to Shelley about something.'

'Is that her name? Shelley?'

'Yeh.'

'She's nice.'

This was not what Jennifer wanted to hear. 'What about me? Eh? What about me? Is she nicer than me? Is she?'

'I-I don't know. I hadn't thought . . .'

'Well think. Who's the nicest?'

Judd thought about it and decided policy was the best honesty. 'I dunno . . . you are, I guess.'

At this, Jennifer seemed satisfied. 'C'mon,' she said. ' 'S this way.' They pushed on along a narrow path that led deeper into the woods.

'Where are we going?' Judd asked. Not scared, just inquisitive. Jennifer was close now. She smelt good.

'Just over there. See that tree? That's where we're going.' She freed him and they picked their way through the undergrowth towards it. Its roots formed natural seats where the soil around them had been eroded away by wind and rabbits, and they sat on these, quite comfortable. It was a favourite spot of Jennifer's. She reached into an abandoned rabbit digging beneath one of the roots and pulled out a cigarette lighter. Judd watched her in silence. She lit up the joint and puffed on it in silence for a while, getting used to the peculiar flavour. The smoke got in her eyes and made them water, and her head began to swim a little. She winced and passed the reefer to Judd, the way she had seen teenagers do it in the parks. 'Want some?'

'I mustn't smoke cigarettes. My pa says they're bad for me.'

'It's not a cigarette, stupid. It's a spliff.'

'What's the difference?'

'Try it. It'll make you feel nice. Like me.' She giggled and put her hand to her mouth.

'Why're you laughing?'

' 'Cause I feel nice. That's what it does, it makes you laugh. I'm nice, I'm nice. Don't you want to laugh? Don't you want to be nice like me? I thought everyone in America took drugs.'

'Not anyone I know.'

'Well, be different then. It won't hurt you.' She held out the joint towards him and he looked at it. There it was, something he shouldn't do. He took it and puffed on it. The smoke was soft. Sweet and heavy. He didn't cough. He took a few more puffs. 'Hold it in,' said Jennifer. He did and his lungs were hot like bellows. As he passed the spliff back a glowing blim of hash tumbled out and landed on his leg. With a start he brushed it away. It landed in the grass and burnt itself out, a tiny dying star. Where it had landed on his skin a blister came up. He had been marked, but he didn't seem to feel it. Soon he and Jennifer were rolling around in the shade of the tree, laughing uncontrollably about nothing in particular. Speckles of sunlight dappled young skin.

Now that Jennifer had lapsed out of her pose, the age gap between the two of them seemed to narrow considerably. She began to tickle Judd and her thighs heated up, these two events acting as lenses through which her desire became focused. The heat channelled out the noises of the woods and swamped the area beneath the tree with libidinal energy. Judd was far too artless to resist. For him, everything was as it should be. It was only afterwards, when he put his trousers back on and his little world flooded back in along with the sounds of the leaves and the cries of other children playing over on the estates, that he became afraid of what had happened and began to cry. Then Jennifer comforted him and told him not to tell. She was his film idol, his silver dream. He promised her he wouldn't.

5

Another kind of fold

It was dark by the time Michael dropped Judd home, summer dark, and everything around had been beaten blue by the onset of the night. The Axelrods were renting a house just outside Stratford, one which had been popular among the better-paid members of the casts of the Royal Shakespeare Company for many years. Situated in a small hamlet, the building was something of a folly. It had been built in the 1930s by a random member of the Midlands gentry and stood apart from the farm-house and labourers' cottages that made up the neighbouring buildings. The architect had mashed too many styles into too small a space: the front porch was art deco; at one end of the pitched roof there was a squat, castellated turret; there were gothic windows, french windows, portholes; the northern walls were pebble-dashed, the southern painted; there was a carport to the east and a small indoor swimming pool whose sides were constructed from marbles taken from decommissioned churches to the west. Moses had chosen the house because its mongrel style reminded him of California. Melinda liked it because the unusual pool made the perfect focus for her social gatherings. She had held several over the summer, all highly fuelled with Pimm's, gin and various other drugs, and all of which had threatened to tip over the edge from party into outright orgy. To Moses's secret disappointment none of them ever did, all the guests being that little bit too neurotic to let themselves go completely.

The garden helped considerably in creating an atmosphere for these parties. It ran to the edge of a cliff which dropped straight down for a hundred feet until it hit the flood plain below, where the fields scanned out flat away for miles and half-way to the horizon the town of Stratford stood. On the cliff top itself there was a small raised circle edged with stones, in the centre of which stood a seat with long legs like stilts. In this Judd liked to sit, his face against the sky, his eyes roaming across the earth and the wind blustering in his hair. Back home you could rarely see this far – even in Beverly Hills which was high up like this – because of the smog trap created by that basin of a city.

Moses was back in the States on a business trip and Melinda had a show that night, so Judd had the house to himself. He pushed open the front door and tingled as its draught excluder wooshed against the rubber bristles of the mat inside (it was another of his favourite sounds). Then lights on and straight to the well-stocked ice-box for some milk – the suck of the seal, the delight of this cool, wonderful space – which he gulped down straight from the bottle. He pulled over a chair and stood on it so that he could reach down the Cheerios from on top of the wall cabinets. Poured himself a bowl, ate the cereal, the spoon fist-gripped in his right hand, drew moustaches on the model adorning the cover of his mother's *Vogue* with his left. He finished the cereal, poured himself a glass of juice, took the tub of ice-cream from the freezer and while he waited for it to defrost enough to get the spoon in he continued to decorate the cover of the magazine. Then he started to examine the lingerie advertisements inside. The waif-like models immediately brought to mind his earlier fumblings with Jennifer and he began to draw onto the pictures the parts that they did not show in the same spirit that he embroidered reality to cover up for the parts of it that he continually missed. As he sketched, his groin and thighs grew hot and he felt again the hard, smacking kisses she had given him and the strange, numbing clutch of her insides, but then, just as he was becoming fully aroused, he lost interest in the promise of an orgasm and became fascinated with the memory of the way that Jennifer's body had disappeared inside of itself at the top of her legs in a manner which was both totally unexpected and totally perfect at the same time. He examined the magazine photo-graphs most carefully, but while they promised to reproduce this effect they didn't deliver, and his crude addendums were little more successful. Eventually, after experimenting for a while, he folded a page down and back on itself, so creating a hidden crease which proved more satisfactory than all of his inky scrawls and blotches.

He blinked out for a while and when he returned to himself the ice-cream had softened, so he took it into the living-room and ate quite a lot of it in front of the TV, then fell asleep on the sofa. While what was left melted to liquid beside him, he dreamt of the trees that afternoon and of something chasing him, chasing him, but he didn't know what.

The sound of his mother's car in the drive woke him up and at the last moment he remembered the magazine, retrieved it from the kitchen and charged up the stairs to his room to hide it before she came in.

Fuck logic

Out at the far end of the school fields there was a hole in the thick hedge that served as retaining wall and boundary marker, and through the hole and beyond the hedge was a patch of wasteland, a forgotten zone which lay between the school's borders and those of the industrial estate that backed on to it. This is where Lewis and Judd spent their lunch-hours, picking among the leaves and rabbit holes like leucocytes, smoking, kicking at the odd bits of dead machine that poked up from the scarred ground, itself a festering scab of metal, rust, broken concrete, litter and clay. Hanging out with Lewis here, talking about girls and teachers and TV, doing what he wasn't supposed to be doing, Judd was really happy for the first time since he'd been in England. Lewis, it turned out, was actually quite shy and withdrawn, not at all as Judd had thought him to be, and the two boys quickly warmed to each other's company. There was something else, too: Judd had noticed that Lewis also blanked, as he did, that Lewis would stare at something and disappear into it for a while – a few seconds, a minute – and this filled the young American with an immense joy because for the first time he felt that it was OK to be like he was. With Lewis, he didn't have to make things up, to pretend that the past was a logical continuum; he didn't have to feel guilty for not being there one hundred per cent of the time. Often, the two of them could spend a whole hour kicking around in their private playground and not say a word, just phasing in and out of their thoughts, alone together until the bell rang to signify the end of free time.

They could hear the school bell from where they were; borne by the wind, its needle vibrations bounced like hailstones off the walls of the buildings beneath which they played. A few last drags and they headed back through the hedge and across the playing fields, sucking on mints as they walked – a precaution which was no defence against the bomb-dog nose of the Buerk, but which was enough to deceive the spavined and manic Mr Pincer, who was taking them for maths that afternoon.

Inside the huddle of school buildings loose packs of kids headed for the washrooms and hollered against the enamel latrines, bouncing urine-laden echoes down the corridors as they relieved themselves and scrubbed at their grimy hands and knees. One or two slunk out from the cubicles in which they'd been wanking and rinsed the smell of cheese from their hands, lest anyone should smell it and target them for abuse. Fat boys took pinches with resignation and red faces, thin boys took shoves and elbows in the ribs. Boys with books got tripped and jeered at, good-lookers combed their hair and squeezed a zit or two. Rumours flew that two boys had been caught at it in the headmaster's garden, but then there were always rumours like that. Lewis and Judd threaded their way through it all.

Mr Pincer, bright enough to detect that his class found his lesson less than thrilling but not to realise that his own obsessions would bore them more shitless still, had decided to spend a few periods giving the boys a primer in computer science. He thought it would make a change from ordinary maths and besides, he said, standing at the front of the class, the scrawl of his face twisted round like an @, 'computers will soon be a part of all our lives and it will be very useful to you all to know about how they work'. Behind their pursed lips all the boys were laughing at him, but mockery had been part of the scenery for many years now and Pincer no longer seemed to care. After all, his fellow teachers laughed at him too; he knew that everyone thought he was a crank. But beneath the blasé exterior it got to him anyway and the effect was to make him as temperamental as the circuit boards with which he tinkered in his workshop at the weekends.

'Who saw the moon landing on television?' he asked his unenthused class. A few hands, including Judd's, went up. 'Well, then you may remember that an entire roomful of computers was needed back on earth in order to control that mission. These days, though, just four years on, we can fit the amount of processing power provided by that room into a few small chips that you can hold in the palm of your hand.'

'Hold the vinegar on mine!' someone called out. The class tittered.

'Yeh, and kin I 'ave a pickled onion wiv mine?' muttered someone else.

Pincer tried to remain good-humoured. 'Yes, yes, of course, very funny, ha ha, but I'd like to get on if I may. The first computers had no chips at all. The first computers had cogs and gearwheels, and would have been powered by steam if Charles Babbage, the chap who designed them, hadn't died before they were built. Babbage's work was all but forgotten until this century when – no, Whiteford, just listen, no need to write all this down, I just want you to listen for the moment. What was that? No, no you're not going to be tested on this, just listen – when certain ideas of his began to be worked on again. For this we have to remember a very famous mathematician called George Boole, who in fact was an acquaintance of Babbage's, though the two men never became friends.'

'Why not?' asked Lewis.

'I don't know why not, Lewis,' answered Pincer icily. 'But it's not that implausible, is it? After all, we've met on several occasions and I somehow doubt we're destined to be friends. The point is, everybody, that Boole was the father of modern algebra and he developed the symbolic logic which all computers use today. We won't go into that logic now, although later on I'll set you a few puzzles and problems so that we can have a bit of fun and get the basic idea.' The class groaned with horror. Suddenly, Pincer remembered an anecdote. 'Oh, yes, there is quite an odd story connected to this. Boole died in slightly peculiar circumstances.' At the mention of death the class perked up and a few pairs of eyes flickered in the teacher's direction. 'His wife, Mary Boole, was one of those mystical types. She wrote some book on the supernatural and was very involved in strange medicines and healing practices, and was a devotee –' ('That means she was devoted to him,' Lewis hissed at Judd) '– of a doctor who was obviously a bit of a quack and who thought that cold water was the magic cure-all for any disease. Poor old Boole caught a cold one day and his wife insisted that he be wrapped in sheets soaked in icy cold water, in order to shock him back into health, I suppose.'

'Did he die?' called out Lewis, who was somewhat perturbed by all this.

'Yes, Lewis, he died, poor fellow.' The teacher pushed on, a schooner sailing through treacle. 'And it wasn't until after the First World War that an American called Claude Shannon, another American called John Atanasoff and a German by the name of Konrad Zuse all realised independently that Boole's logic, what we now call Boolean logic, could be combined with binary numbers – remember, those were the numbers made out of zeros and ones that we looked at last week – and built into electrical switching circuits in order to make an electronic computer.'

'What's an electrical switching circuit?' someone asked, hoping to delay the arrival of Pincer's problems for a few minutes more.

'Just what it sounds like. It's a series of switches, which can be either on or off, one or zero, powered by electricity. You see, Babbage's computers were all mechanical, made out of metal cogs and gears which had to be built to very precise specifications in order for the machine to work. But Zuse, Shannon and Atanasoff all realised that it was much easier to build a computer using Boolean logic and electrical switches. In fact, Zuse went on to build electromechanical calculators which were used in the guidance systems of the V2 rockets that were fired on London by Hitler.' Rockets and bombs. Now that *was* interesting. 'The war came at a crucial time. Only this year the government revealed that Colossus, the first electronic computer, was built in Britain in 1943 as part of the effort to break the Nazis' secret codes. The Americans built computers to help them design the atom bombs that were dropped on Japan. A lot of very complex calculations are involved in trying to get an atom bomb to explode – it's a bit like trying to work out the way every molecule of water will be moving in a kettle when it's boiling away very hard – and you really need a computer to work all these problems out for you.

'After the war the American Army's Ballistic Research Laboratories built an enormous horseshoe-shaped computer called ENIAC – that stands for Electronic Numerical Integrator and Computer. ENIAC was incredibly complicated: it had 17,468 vacuum tubes, 70,000 resistors, 10,000 capacitors, 1500 relays and 6000 switches –' Pincer smiled at his own powers of recall, but he had lost the class again '– and it was one of the few computers to be decimal, rather than binary. One of its very first tasks was in fact to simulate the explosion of an atom bomb. ENIAC couldn't be programmed like a modern computer; instead it had to be rewired every time a new problem needed to be solved. A brilliant chap called John von Neumann, who'd worked on the original atom bomb project, joined the ENIAC team in the late 1940s and basically designed ENIAC's successor, the EDVAC – the Electronic Discrete Variable Computer. Now, you need to remember von Neumann's name because,' Pincer paused to watch Whiteford start to scribble away in his exercise book, 'because what he came up with has been used as the blueprint for computer design ever since. OK, that's enough chat. I think it's time for everyone to do some writing.'

Pincer turned, picked up a piece of chalk, wiped a few marks from the board with the heel of his palm, and began to write out some sentences in a looping hand. *Logic gates are digital electronic circuit components that perform a given operation on one or more input signals to produce an output signal*, he scrawled. *The signals these circuits operate on are either voltage or current levels which are separated into two binary states, logic zero and logic one, also referred to as high and low states.* So far, so good. *Since logic gates operate on binary values, they can be used to represent Boolean operations. Boolean functions can be constructed with these gates to form 'combinational' circuits. There are seven main types of logic gate.*

While the class struggled to copy all of this down, the teacher drew the first three types of gate on the blackboard:

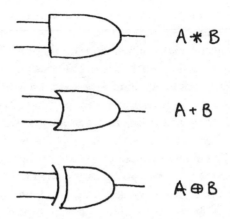

Of course, in the hands of a group of boys just edging towards puberty these diagrams all too easily suggested something else. Lewis and Judd sat together, comparing notes and egging each other on, and pretty soon they both ended up with a page full of symbols that looked rather more like this:

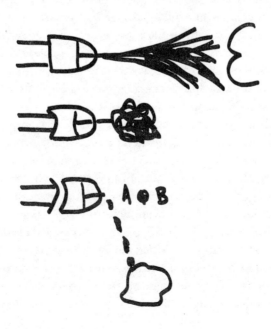

And so it was that at the rear of Mr Pincer's classroom logic got subverted by desire.

As the boys scribbled, Pincer took up his main theme once again. 'The key development in computing', he blithered, 'was the idea of storing both the data and the operating instructions in a centrally located memory, allowing the machine's function to be changed merely by rewriting its operating instructions. This leads us on to the distinction between software and hardware, software being the instructions and hardware the actual switches and circuits. Although Babbage came up with this idea, borrowing it from an automatic loom that was around at the time which used a punch-card system to allow you to set what kind of pattern you wanted it to weave, it wasn't made a general principle of computing until Alan Turing, that's t–u–r–i–n–g Whiteford, said that in theory, the computer was a machine which could do the job of any other machine by being programmed in the appropriate way. You'll no doubt have come across the phrase "Universal Turing Machine" –' of course, no one had '– well, now you know where it comes from.

'Turing had been one of the key people behind the Colossus, and after the war he and von Neumann worked together on the EDVAC and another machine called the ACE. Up until 1955 all computers were built using glass valves as switches. Moths and other insects used to be able to climb inside these and short-circuit them, which is where we get the term "computer bug". And the operators communicated with these machines by means of punched cards or paper tapes, just like the old looms that Babbage had stolen ideas from. Lots of money was being put into computer research at the time in America, because they were seen as the key to countering the threat that had been posed ever since the Soviets put the first satellite, Sputnik, up into orbit in 1957.'

'Why was it a threat, sir?' asked Hethlethwaite.

'Well, Jacob, it wasn't really. All it did was broadcast a few beeping sounds from a radio transmitter, but the Americans got very worried about it and thought that maybe it could do much more than that, spy on their military bases perhaps, or beam down communist propaganda or something. Anyway, in the computers of the time transistors were gradually replacing valves and magnetic disks and drums were gradually replacing punched tapes. There was a big step forward in 1959, when a researcher working for the company Texas Instruments invented the integrated circuit.' Pincer turned and wrote the phrase up on the board. 'Thanks to this innovation, *thirty million* switches and logic gates could be fitted into one square foot of space, sixty times more than had previously been possible. And two years ago a chap called Marcian Hoff at a company called Intel,' again he wrote out the names, 'came up with the idea of trying to fit an entire computer on a single wafer of silicon, called a chip. The first chip was called the 4004 and it had 2250 transistors, could carry out 60,000 operations per second and process four different pieces or "bits" of data at a time. Then came the 8008, and this year Intel have brought out the 8080. The 8s mean that it can process eight bits of information at a time, so it's twice as fast.' Pincer took a small cardboard box from his desk drawer, opened it, and walked up and down the aisles showing its contents to the boys. 'This is an 8080 chip,' he explained proudly. 'With it you can build a microprocessor, the heart of the modern computer.'

At which point Martin Martins, the hated corridor monitor from 2B, knocked on the door. Pincer waved him in. 'Yes, Martins, what is it?'

'The Head wants to see Axelrod in his office right away, sir. At once, sir.' Martins was like some kind of pre-pubescent squaddy, one that had been squad-bashed into total submission.

'Very well,' said Pincer. 'Axelrod, go with Martins. And don't slouch, boy!'

Discovery

Melinda had woken late that Wednesday morning and, unusually, had found herself with nothing to do. No lunch dates, no hairdressing appointments, no rehearsals, no discreet liaisons, nothing much of any kind. She got up, made some coffee and took a long sauna. Then she wallowed in the pool for about half an hour, switching the jets on full and letting them play across her clitoris until she reached orgasm and her identity was fused for a few brief moments with the chopping surfaces of the water. Rejuvenated, she ate brunch and decided to do a spot of housework. She pottered around downstairs for a while, sorting out old magazines and dusting to the sound of an Isley Brothers album that Moses had brought over from LA, then she went upstairs to sort out her washing and tidy Judd's room. It was a mess: half-read comics and discarded school books littered the floor, a toy baseball game was laid out in the middle of the carpet, dirty mugs and plates were balanced precariously on various shelves, and crumpled clothes had been thrown into corners and stuffed down the side of the bed. A soiled gym kit was draped over the back of the chair and on the window-sill a bird's nest that Judd had found in a tree a few months before was slowly disintegrating into its component parts of twigs, dried mud and dead moss.

Melinda let out a motherly sigh and went to work, stacking the crockery and recovering all the clothing which she sorted it into a pile to be washed with her own. It was when she pulled the bed away from the wall and stripped the sheets that she discovered the annotated magazine, hidden by Judd between mattress and base. It was a *Vogue* she hadn't read, so she sat down on the naked bed in order to have a quick flip through.

She could hardly miss Judd's drawings: they were very explicit. The models, usually so demure (at least on the face of it), had been cross-sectioned so that their internal organs were now in plain view. Exaggerated vaginas abounded, most of them about to be entered by disembodied penises; breasts were splashed with spurts of what she supposed was semen. To make matters worse, a sheet of graph paper torn from a school book fell out from between the pages. With trembling hands Melinda picked it up and discovered a chart that had been drawn up by Judd in order to keep track of his early sexual investigations and impressions. *6 June 1973*, it read. *First did it with Jennifer. Weird. Didn't feel much. Kind of slimy.* And it went on from there.

Melinda was horrified and she rushed downstairs to the drinks cabinet where she poured herself a slug of brandy in order to stay her tremblings and cool the heat in her loins. It worked until she remembered the old joke, *Come upstairs, I'll show you my etchings*, then she started shaking some more.

How . . . ? Why . . . ? What . . . ? she thought. Then, a series of flashes: led astray . . . evil girl . . . little Judd . . . outrage . . . reputation . . . my own son . . . the papers never . . . scandal . . . ohmygod . . . nipinbud.

She picked up the telephone and rang the school.

Head games (1)

Scene: the headmasters office, St George's Grammar for Boys, mid-afternoon. The office is situated in the front rooms of a Queen Anne house, foundation stone laid 1812, used as a private dwelling for one hundred and fifteen years until it was put up for sale and purchased by the expanding school next door. The windows are divided into two vertically sliding frames of nine panes apiece which slice the afternoon sunlight into segments that shine so brightly on the opposite wall that the rest of the room is thrown into shadow. His bald forehead emblazoned by a lower central segment of the matrix of light (2,5), the headmaster sits like Christ about to pass judgement. In the shadows Judd Axelrod, Melinda Axelrod and Doreen Buerk cower like prodigal apostles.

Doreen was badly shaken. As if it were not enough for one afternoon to be told that one of her pupils – a mere ten-year-old – was having a sexual relationship with a thirteen-year-old girl from the comprehensive, she had also had to discover that the mother of this negro was not only English and not American as she had assumed but white! What was the world coming to? She made several cross-referenced mental notes to remind herself to write to the board of governors and recommend that they take no more of these short-term foreign students. The whole thing genuinely frightened her: whatever her pupils and her colleagues thought, since Donald had been committed to Hatton Central Hospital six years previously (where he still remained, writing out long-hand volumes of the Word of God, which he scried from the images that played across his many televisions) she had been a woman plagued by deep insecurities. Now that madness had apparently come to visit her again she was forced to reconsider her whole role in the social machine. What if, she thought, what if this is all down to me? What if I attract them? What if I am cursed to spend the rest of my days threatened by half-wits and degenerates?

Melinda, meanwhile, was on top of things. The session had begun with the headmaster questioning Judd in order to ascertain the extent of the damage and searching for loopholes through which he could slip free the knot of the school's responsibility, and Melinda had quickly cottoned on to this and refused to let him get away with it. She was a celebrity of untarnished reputation, she reminded him, and there was no way she was going to allow him to question her abilities as a mother. She had come across this kind of thing before, she said, her child being badly treated because of the colour of his skin. She didn't understand how this could have been allowed to happen. Didn't she send a car every day to pick up Judd from the school gates? How had he been able to meet this girl? Had the school no idea at all when its pupils were on or off the premises?

A cloud covered the sun and the halo disappeared from the headmaster's head, and the differentials of light and dark in the room became less extreme. By contrast, the adults had begun to argue more intensely, Doreen Buerk having decided that she was not going to let Mrs Axelrod or anyone else impute that she, a member of the Women's Institute and the Rotary Club, and a pillar of the local community, might be a racialist.

Judd sat among them, now ignored. To begin with he had been terrified, embarrassed, frightened, totally exposed by the Head's questioning. Under the assault, he had started to understand that his crime embraced not just the events of the previous few weeks but his behaviour throughout most of his life. They'd kept asking him *why? why did he do this?* but he didn't have an answer and searching for one now it wasn't surprising that he made a link between the sex and that for which he had most often been chastised in the past – his picnolepsy. His father had been proved right, it seemed: if he weren't always blanking out, if he paid more attention, if he had more common sense this would never have happened. Silently, he began to shiver and shake.

It frightened him more than anything that he had never seen his mother like this, burning like a torch of self-righteousness. He couldn't guess that her reaction in fact had little to do with his own indiscretions and more with a battle that she had been fighting with the country of her birth ever since she had been a little girl. She had always hated England, had always found its inhabitants snotty and self-centred. Ever since she had been at drama school she had watched girls with the right accents and the right backgrounds get the preferred parts, girls who were as a rule far worse actresses than the ones that were passed over. Fighting her way up the professional ladder she'd lived a squalid existence, out of work for most of the time, the temptations of prostitution flickering above her like a badly wired light bulb, the names she despised emblazoned across the West End. Then, by complete fluke, she'd been spotted by a Hollywood talent scout who got her a screen test, an agent and finally a part: an 'English Rose' cameo in a Sophia Loren vehicle being made by Paramount. She had never looked back. After a series of slightly grotty affairs with producers, minor directors and other actors, in 1962 she'd met Moses, who had been in Hollywood on his industry convention. Within six months Melinda was pregnant; they had just decided to stay together and have the child when she miscarried. But the bond didn't break, they stuck it out, in the end it brought them closer together. Moses had never felt this much for anyone before, he didn't know it was possible. A year or so later Melinda was pregnant again and this time there were no complications and the couple married the year after Judd was born. A child out of wedlock and an interracial marriage would have wrecked the career of an aspiring actress at any other time, but this was the sixties. Rather than impeding her progress it hastened it, hooking her up and depositing her on a higher conveyor belt. Judd was born without complications (apart from the Ouija board) and became a symbol of his mother's new life. Everything was rosy. There were parts and parties, she and Moses remained faithful within reason, everything was a success.

Except . . . except that she wasn't quite getting the parts she wanted. The landscape of her desire still vibrated with the dull wave of an urge to play those roles which the girls from good homes had always been given. She wanted to prove that she was not simply a good actress, but a great one, too. She began to look around for projects that were more 'arty', more cultured, but apart from a couple of workaday adaptations of Jane Austen novels she found nothing that she really liked until her agent mentioned that a chance had come up of a season back in England, playing in *King Lear* and *Twelfth Night* with the Royal Shakespeare Company in London and Stratford-upon-Avon. It was ideal – she could return triumphant to England and boost her career in the States simultaneously, the perfect revenge and the perfect career move in one.

Unfortunately, the reviews had been lukewarm and the whole thing, rather than being a triumph, had turned into something of a battle of attrition with her countrymen. She'd already begun to regret returning to England at all but now, now that she had so damaged her son by coming here, well what was left? This is what her thirst for revenge had brought her. Now she felt really Shakespearean.

Torn between her feelings of personal guilt and anger that the years of struggle and abuse should bring her to this she raged at Doreen Buerk and the headmaster, almost peeling the plaster from the walls with the turbulence she projected. But at the same time, and almost despite herself, she began to construct from the elements of this storm an enormous edifice, one in which she was to live for the rest of her life, and which was supported and reinforced with struts and boards fashioned from the feelings that the cold and clinical light of her anger had illuminated.

From where he sat on the old leather settee, his feet barely touching the floor, Judd gazed up at his mother's towering construction. Tall and new, it caught all the light now that the sun had reappeared from behind its cloud. If he were to be saved, would he have to build one of these for himself?

Blood baked in concrete

While Jennifer lay awake in bed, having given up trying to cry herself to sleep, all the soft lights padded Henry from the night as he stumbled home. He had barely been conscious when the landlord from the Falcon had yelled in his ear: 'D'you need a cup o' coffee, Henry? Eh, I say d'you need a coffee or summat? Or a glass o' water?'

'Oh, leave 'im be. The ol' fucker's so soused he can't even 'ear us. D'you wan' me ta purim out fur ya?'

'Nah, I'll see to 'im. You geroff. We'll need you in sharpish termorra. We've gorra party in fur lunch in the ba' room.'

'Awright then. Tarra.'

'Tarra.' Simon the barman disappeared through the back of the bar. Nigel – the landlord – stood and polished glasses and replaced them on to the dark wooden racks where they'd be ready for the next day's drinking. The shelves, the bar itself, the chairs with their worn red seats and perimeters of brass studs, the windows with their leaded panes of glass, the fireplace, the horse brasses, the skirting board and the dado, all these were stained with sweat and farts and smoke and ale and varnished with a thin veneer of sticky conversation. From the back corridor came the sounds of Simon trying to get his bike out.

'Watch that new paint, you clumsy oik,' Nigel yelled, and then in lower tones to Henry (who wasn't listening) said, 'Careless little sod.'

'I heard that!' Simon yelled back.

'Geroff wi' you!' The door slammed. 'Christ, you can't get the help these days, can you? I SAID CAN YOU!' Then quietly, 'You can't 'ear a bleedin' word I'm saying.' He finished drying the last few glasses, put the beer mats into soak and went out back to empty the bins. When he returned, Henry's head had lolled over to one side and he was slumped even further down into his chair. Nigel began to lose patience. 'Awright, this isn't a goddamn 'otel. Time to go. OY! WAKEY WAKEY!' He shook Henry by the shoulder and the drunkard came to, looked up through red and rheumy eyes. Tried to speak, gave up. Was not sure. Nigel helped him to his feet and took what was left of a burnt-out Dunhill from between his limp fingers. 'That'll hurt in the morning, for sure,' he said to no one in particular. 'C'mon. Up ya get. D'you want me to call you a cab?'

'Nuuuuhhh.' The negative rattled from Henry's throat along with a stringy gobbet of bronchial saliva.

'Ya sure, are ya?'

'Uhhhh.' Nigel pulled back the iron bolts that secured the heavy oak front door and gently propelled Henry out into the street. He felt like a boy pushing a toy boat out on to a pond, vainly hoping that the wind would fill its sails and carry it away. Publican and patron had known each other for many years and it was a long-standing joke that without Henry the pub would have gone under long ago, although it was a joke that nobody but Henry laughed at these days. If there were any more evenings like tonight, Nigel thought to himself, he might have seriously to consider barring the man. There was a point at which even the most valued customer became a liability. 'Goan out with you, y'ol' pisshead,' he said. To his surprise Henry was indeed caught by the wind and stumbled off to the left. 'Hey!' called Nigel, 'where the fuck're you goin'? Don't you live that'ur way?'

Henry stuttered to a halt, turned round – his hands clutching at the air for balance – and made ready to set off on the appropriate trajectory. For a moment he found his voice. 'G'night Arthur. It was wonderful.' And with that he lurched off down Sheep Street, the Elizabethan buildings leaning over him like interested ogres, no straight lines or right-angles among them, a scene from *The Cabinet of Dr Caligari*.

Henry felt the street close in behind him and he pushed on, taking his bearings from the tourist lights down by the river. As he neared the bridge it occurred to him that it was time for a cigarette and, narrowly missing a lone car, he weaved across the road towards the tall poplars which line the small park that stretches between the bridge and the boathouse. He sat on a bench and searched through his pockets for a fag. They felt voluminous, the pockets, like sacks. He worked his hands through them, brushing past cigarette packet and lighter several times before managing to grab them. Eventually he got them out and placed them gingerly in his lap, taking a few moments to pick flakes of tobacco that he'd dredged from his pockets out from beneath his fingernails. Trying to get a cigarette from the packet and into his mouth was the next trial, and as soon as he'd managed it he dropped the pack on the floor, then lost hold of the cigarette while bending to recover the pack. But finally he was ready to attempt ignition. It was a clear night: to his intoxicated gaze street lamps headlights stars seemed equidistant. He sparked up the lighter and its flame floated out there with the satellites, out there with Laika (who was quietly scrolling across the night sky, of course). He was concentrating so hard on bringing it to bear on the tip of the fag he might as well have been trying to guide the various parts of Skylab in to dock.

Back home, Jennifer tossed and turned in her small bed and stared at the walls and the ceiling, taking her father's late return as a sign of trouble. She had not met Judd's parents, but she knew what his mother looked like because she had seen one of her films once, in the Odeon by the hospital. Yet although she could quite clearly recall Melinda Volitia's face she couldn't remember the film's title or much of the plot, because it was during that movie that a boy had touched her up for the first time. The boy was Damon, a swarthy nineteen-year-old, and Jennifer had ended up going to the film with him because Shelley had ducked out of their date at the last minute, pleading something about a dentist's appointment. For some unfathomable reason Jennifer had fancied Damon a bit and had agreed to go along in place of her friend.

It was a Saturday afternoon and they'd both been early and had stood uneasily on the cinema steps together, waiting for the usherette to unlock the doors, while a greasy rain whipped down inches from their noses. Finally, the doors were opened.

'Let's go inside then,' Damon had said flatly.

Jennifer suddenly had cold feet. 'I dunno. I'm not sure I want to see this one that much.'

'Might as well. Look at it.'

'Look at what?'

'The rain, stupid. What else you gonna do?' So, spoilt for choice, they'd gone in. Damon had belched as the usherette took their damp pink ticket stubs and led them into the murk.

Jennifer had giggled. ''S all right,' she'd said, 'we know the way.' Inside, the cinema was almost empty. A couple of men were already asleep in the stalls and in the drool of silver light Jennifer was able to make out the heads of two scrawny women, both of them still shrouded by their rain bonnets. She balanced on the edge of the folded seat and eased her weight forward until the chair snapped open and swallowed her. The tiny mites that feasted on the stuffing and velour rumbled away to themselves as their world was compressed. Damon sat down and almost immediately put his arm around his date, who just as quickly struggled free.

'Wait a minute,' she whispered nervously, not really sure what to do. 'Let me get me coat off.' She stood up and slipped off her mac. Underneath she wore a tan miniskirt, short black felt boots, a white nylon top.

The film was not particularly engaging; at least, it did not engage Damon's attention, most of which was taken up by Jennifer. By her lips, her small breasts, her thin, almost hairless legs. His left arm curled around her tiny back and crushed her to him. With his left hand he pummelled her right breast and occasionally pinched her nipple in what he imagined was a tender squeeze, while snaking the fingers of his right hand up her skirt, around the elastic of her panties and down among the fine hairs that curled across her groin. He hadn't stopped to consider that she was not wet, that he would have to force his index finger up inside her. He was completely engrossed in his own fantasy by now, her body merely furnishing the tactile feedback. His imaginings even provided for the way she was feeling, for the idea that she was being stimulated by a sweet pleasure pain.

But the feel of his fingers grubbing up against her hymen had merely sent raw sears shooting up from Jennifer's groin and into her stomach. For a moment she had wondered why she was doing this, why was she letting this sweaty oaf with his clumsy mitts scrabble away at her? But she was so hungry for experience that the thought remained an abstract one and gained no purchase on the situation unfolding before her.

Damon broke into her during Melinda Volitia's big love scene. Some blood was released and he took it for lubrication and set about with renewed vigour, frigging away at her while semen leaked from his boy's cock and diffused through the fabric of his Y-fronts. A hundred million sperm caught in a fishing net; an actress's face fixed for ever in the mind of a young girl.

After the show they'd stood at the bus-stop, and the bus had come almost immediately and Damon had got on. Jennifer had remained on the pavement and they'd waved a casual goodbye, neither wanting to see the other ever again. The rain had stopped and the clouds had evaporated, or so it seemed, and Jennifer had walked across the town in search of Shelley, her panties encrusted with blood. Someone wolf-whistled at her from the opposite side of the street, but she did not turn and yell a *Fuck off!* as she normally might, but kept walking straight ahead, overwhelmed by a feeling of utter neutrality.

A few weeks later she lost her virginity proper. She was chasing Rever – it was a matter of proving herself to the girls she hung out with, most of whom were at least a couple of years her senior. At the time, everyone had a thing about Rever. He was tall, wore black, had an angular face. He seemed very withdrawn, very cool. He was the singer in a band and they said he wrote poetry. At a house party, the house of someone she didn't know, the parents away, she saw him with a book in his hands. Without him noticing she sidled over and took a peek at the cover. It was a pocket edition of Blake's *Songs of Innocence and Experience*. She knew it well: Henry used to read aloud from it when the profound mood took him. She confronted Rever and recited 'The Sick Rose' straight off, then bullshitted him for a while with knowledge that she'd taken from the paragraph on the back cover of the volume and nurtured in the rich soil of his comments and his ignorance. Pretty soon they were snogging in one of the bedrooms.

The summer holidays came and she would go round to his house afternoons. His family was liberal and they were quite happy that Rever should have a girl spend time in his room, though they would perhaps have been less happy had they known how young she was. But she hardly ever saw them anyway – when she called at the house a voice would just yell from deep inside, 'Who is it?' and she'd shout back, 'It's me, Jennifer, is Rever in?' and the voice would shout back either, 'Yes, love, he's upstairs, go on up,' or 'No, he's out, but you can go up and wait if you like.'

They tried without success on four separate occasions before Rever managed to penetrate her fully. Finally he had worn a condom and that had made it easier; before, she had always had to tell him to stop because the pain was too intense. But she wanted him and she was going to have him. She'd known from the start that if she went out with him he'd expect her to sleep with him and she wanted that. When they finally succeeded and he was on top of her and inside her, she couldn't feel anything except the pain. He moved to and fro for a while with a kind of rocking motion, then gasped, 'Jenn. Oh, Jenn, Jenn, I'm going to come, Jenn, I'm going to come,' and she'd had no idea what he meant by that. Afterwards she ached a bit and she didn't stay long, but it wasn't too bad. Mainly she felt numb.

Shelley had been away at the coast with her parents and when she got back she rushed straight round to Jennifer's house. 'Jenn, Jenn, I thought of you on Tuesday!' she gasped, 'I honestly did. It was Tuesday, wasn't it? I thought of you.' Her face was puffed with excitement and she kissed her friend all over. Jennifer told her all the gory details. She saw Rever perhaps another half a dozen times before he tired of her infatuation with him and told her he didn't want to see her any more. She cried and was angry that she still didn't understand about coming, deciding it was something that only men did.

Judd certainly did not make her come, although being smaller – and younger and therefore less concerned with his own prowess – he managed to hurt her rather less. She rarely touched herself and did not, then or later, come properly to associate sex with pleasure. No, it was about something else, sex was. Power, perhaps. Gaining authority. Being liked.

Hardly had their illicit liaison been discovered than Judd was whisked back to the States without being allowed to see Jennifer again. This hurt her very much. She'd never met anyone like Judd before; he was so different from her. She was all motion, all movement, plastic and tactile and liquid and vital, fazed by nothing because there was nothing to which she couldn't accommodate herself. But Judd was strange. He was black, of course, so that made him special, but he was also so quiet, so composed. He could do stupid things, childish things, like pulling Alice's plaits or playing aeroplanes, but that way he had of sitting motionless for minutes at a time, apparently not looking at anything at all, just thinking . . . it seemed to Jennifer that he was like a Buddha or something, so composed, so divine. If she was the sea then he was an outcrop of land, a continent contemplating itself, an opportunity where previously there'd been none. She'd not thought much of him when he'd first arrived in her life, invited to her TV afternoons not by her but by a neighbour, the son of one of the costume designers that Melinda knew through the theatre, but he'd ended up opening up a whole new realm of possibility for her. Maybe his being American, maybe it had something to do with it, maybe this was how Queen Isabella of Spain had felt towards Columbus when he'd brought her the New World, because Jennifer certainly thought about the rest of the world and its immensity more as a result of meeting Judd than she ever had done before. That's what Judd was for her: he was the world outside the little English suburbia in which she lived and dreamed, outside of a mother that she could never imagine except as a naked shoot peeling and peeling itself forever further back into insanity and a father who had only bloomed inside the hothouse of a bottle of gin. Judd was the desert, unclaimed and alien, and by the time he was taken from her she'd wanted him so much that she'd have invented new forms of life to get to him, would have flowered herself, would have engendered a new ecosystem in the spaces where she and he touched, a hypersea of mycobionts and phycobionts, pentastomes and arthropods, parasites and plants, a symbiotic biophysiology with which she'd extend herself and place herself in permanent contact with his skin.

★

The day following the one on which Judd had been pulled from class and taken home Jennifer had answered the telephone to a choking female voice.

'Is this the correct number for Mr Henry Several?'

'Yes.'

'May I speak with him please?' The three words *speak with him* jittered like coffee cups in an airliner flying through turbulence. Jennifer intuited immediately that it was bad news and that it concerned her; she laid the handset down on the telephone table and called her father. As Henry emerged from the living-room, drink in hand, she disappeared inside the kitchen and stood as silently as she could behind the door. Through the gap between door and frame she could see the hallway mirror; in its reflection, as he picked up the plastic handset and put it to his ear, was Henry.

'Ah, yes? This is Henry Several. What can I do for you?' He began by swilling the ice around in his glass and was just about to take a sip when he changed his mind and put the drink down on the telephone table, picking at a loose patch of veneer that had begun to rise up from the underlying wood instead. It was when a large chunk of the old, shrivelled surface came away in his hand that Jennifer knew she had been discovered. She watched Henry sag under the attrition of the winds which blew down the phone line; she saw the final coherence of spirit that remained to him fissure and tumble as if the collection of parts which was her father was no longer capable of generating a rhythm by which the whole could live and face the world. The pieces, hitherto held apart by tension and intensity, collapsed in against each other as their micro-fields were shorted out and suddenly Henry occupied that little bit less of the world. '. . . Yes, I think so, yes, no, yes, whatever you say, I'm terribly sorry, of course, at once, I cannot understand how . . . I cannot apologise enough, Thursday evening then, yes, anything I can do, of course, may I just say how sorry I am . . . yes, no, of course, yes . . .' And then the phone went dead and the house rang with the dreadful silence that annexes the world after a storm has passed through. Henry shuffled into the living-room, leaving his drink in the hall.

Jennifer sat huddled behind the kitchen door, wondering what would happen next. For a long time she didn't breathe, as if by refusing to use her orifices she could metabolise herself into a new state, one in which all the pain was spread so evenly throughout her body that it became merely another form of wave, meaningless and simple. Soon, of course, she had to exhale, and when she did the dead air came out in a rush, stripped of its oxygen by her vigorous lungs. She started to worry about her father and walked along the hallway, scared that she would laugh from fear and shame. Every nerve end tingled and her groin throbbed. From her stomach to her vagina she flushed hot with desire. She reached the living-room door and when she pushed it open she saw her father, a stationary man in front of a blue-white television. The burning twitched out and her legs flooded with fear. 'Daddy?' Henry did not turn to look at her, but his head fell forward just a little. 'Daddy, I'm sorry, I didn't mean to hurt anyone.' He turned now, just enough to see her. She checked his brown eyes for anger but could see none, so turned on the tears and ran to him. He held her to him and stroked her dark hair and told her how like her mother she was and how just as he had loved her mother he loved her too and that to him what she had done was not wrong, that she would always be perfect in his eyes, that it did not matter what people might say, that people were stupid and they'd never understand.

Thursday came around, evening turned to night, and Jennifer's mind rustled too much with what she could remember and what she thought might come to pass to fall asleep, and Henry sat drunkenly on a bench by the river and smoked cigarettes down to his knuckles. It was a warm night by English standards. The Midlands was a week into one of those brief English heatwaves that induces men to strip down to shorts and T-shirts, women to sunbathe in lunch-hours. Sweat gathered under arms, in navels, at the backs of necks and knees, in shoes and folds of fat. White skin had already turned pink and tight. Everyone could smell themselves, feel themselves. They were not used to this. The headaches were about to begin, the tempers to wear thin, everyone found themselves wishing for a cloudy day, a spot of rain. Whole towns couldn't sleep, noises carried at night, the cities sounded hollow as old sherry casks. No longer damped by moisture, the cries of whirring tyres coughing engines sudden horns and brakes slipped out from between the buildings and echoed free across the rooftops, playing with the cats who'd left the streets to the shoppers and the dogs. Windows were left wide open, doors unlocked. The rivers had grown warm and begun to stink. Groups of tourists were drifting in like migrant tribes, to feed and be fed upon. Stratford was no longer a network of thoroughfares but a patchwork of spaces.

Jennifer slipped out of bed, walked over to the window and climbed out on to the sill, letting her legs swing free and her heels rub against the brickwork. She could easily see the town centre, only half a mile away and glowing in the blue night. Stratford was an encrustation, a slow conglomeration of wood and wattle and stone and bricks and cement and steel and asphalt and oil at the point at which water and this way and that all met and afforded the necessary conditions for such a parasite to gain purchase and prosper. The town grew like lichen, symbiotic pairing of flesh and rock, sacs of blood moving within their thick shell walls like hermit crabs, the encounter a prerequisite for the emergence of the new form of 'cultured man', whose English archetype was run out of town on a poaching beef, four centuries before. Henry sat and contemplated the red-brick theatre, his new and massive shrine. Another cigarette burnt down to the filter.

Jennifer climbed back into her room and got dressed, for once donning clothes which made her look like the thirteen-year-old that she was. She went downstairs, out the front door and through the estate until she reached the main road that led across the bridge and into town. Off in search of her father. She passed the garage, the Alveston Manor Hotel, the line of the old tramway, the jetty crowded round with rowing boats for hire.

Crossing the bridge, her footsteps echoed on the metal grille; through it she could see the reflection of the street lights on the gently popping surface of the barely moving river. She spied Henry before she was even across, went up to him, took his hand, helped him up from the bench, led him home. As they walked back he began to talk, though not of the meeting that he'd had with the Axelrods earlier that evening. Rather, he told her stories of her mother, whom she had never known. He told her, as if he were talking to himself, what her mother was like when she was young, how she'd been a talented computer, how it had come to nothing. He told her how he'd met her during the war and loved her from the first moment he'd seen her, though she'd been too busy with the soldiers to have a spare thought for him. He told her how they had met again a few years later, how he'd won her heart and how they'd married. He told her about their first few years together and about his infertility. He told her, as she led him deeper into the maze of streets that made up their estate, about Nadine's illness, about her drinking and her visions, about the voices in her head, about the letters she used to write him while he was standing right there in the room with her. In faltering tones he told her how Nadine's family had shunned her, about how she'd nobody left but him, about how she'd abused him with threats and lies and conceits, about how little by little he had failed to cope. And he told her about how one day he had no longer been able to find a way through it all and had called the hospital and had her committed.

It was not until they reached the house and Henry stood upon the doorstep fumbling for his key that he told Jennifer how it had been discovered that one of the orderlies had been pimping out her mother's soulless body.

'How did they find out?' Jennifer asked quietly. It was the first question she had asked, but she already knew the answer. Nadine had become pregnant. The child was healthy but there were complications and physically Nadine was never the same again. She'd stuttered on until John Glenn became the first American to make it into orbit – aboard Friendship 7 in 1962 – at which point she no longer had the strength to eat. Then it was only a matter of days.

'And that's why your father is such a sad man and such a bad man and drinks such a lot and why, you see my darling, he is not your father at all, but just the man who looks after you and who tries to care for you and he is sorry because he was not strong enough for your mother and he is not strong enough for you.' But Jennifer was no longer listening. As tears began to run down Henry's purple cheeks she was remembering as clearly as if it were yesterday the faces the dark ward the screams and the gibberings that greeted her as she was sucked out into the world. She pulled in her cheeks and bit them, tried not to cry.

Shrink

Within days of the discovery Moses had flown to England, collected Judd and returned with him to California. Melinda was to join them when she had fulfilled the terms of her contract with the RSC, which included a further six months in London after the Stratford run was over. Until then, the family would communicate by telephone and Moses would fly over to see Melinda whenever he could. The Axelrods had decided 'for publicity reasons' not to press charges against the school or against Jennifer and Henry.

Back in LA, the search for a good shrink was top priority. Eager to atone for bringing Judd with her to England, Melinda called Donna long distance and asked her advice on a psychoanalyst. Donna quickly warmed to the task. 'Well, I'm no expert, but if I were you I'd get in touch with Schemata.'

'Schemata?'

'Uh huh. My sister's been seeing him for five years now and he's done wonders like you would not believe. And this friend of mine, Marie, you know her I think, yeh you do, Marie, you met her over at that pool party of Allan's summer before last, you know, the one where Oscar got thrown into the pool with all his clothes on and ruined six grams of uncut toot and Raymond got caught in the sack with Allan's daughter who was only fifteen at the time, yeh, that's right, *that* party, yeh well, Marie says he is like a specialist where kids are concerned and I know for a fact that he sorted out Allan's daughter after, you know, after that *event*, Opal I think her name is, yeh, Opal, or Amethyst, or Sparkle or, something, you know, glittery, and now she's doing fine. She's seeing Raymond again though she's seventeen now so it's OK an' all, and I hear they're getting married in the fall. Apparently they're gonna have a pool wedding, with the guests and the priests and everyone in swimmers and an underwater altar. Have you ever heard of *anything* so groovy?' Melinda was convinced and it was all settled very swiftly: Judd would be returned to his old school in Beverly Hills and would also undergo an intensive no-expenses-spared course of treatment with Dr Hinckley Schemata.

Judd was in a state of mild shock. He'd wanted to come home, but not like this. For two weeks his father wouldn't talk to him. He thought sometimes that he was being punished for wishing for change, for not being happy in England. He thought a lot about Lewis, about how their fight and then their friendship had made him feel special and in charge of himself, like a hero. How embarrassed was he now, that he'd ever felt like that? Now he felt transparent. The hot Californian sun and high blue sky of which he'd dreamed so often seemed not to welcome him but to swallow him. Beneath the glow of the identical days it no longer appeared to matter where he was or who he was, and he spent the first few evenings at home sitting cantilevered out over the Malibu cliff side on the edge of the balcony, feeling lonely and scared, watching the sun turn the sky to nicotine before melting into the clicking waves, and desperately trying to concentrate, to keep his mind on this view.

Because now, whenever Moses caught him 'day-dreaming' he would take his belt to the boy, fetch a few sharp lashes across the backside, *Knock some sense into him*, he said. This was a new experience for Judd and the thick leather seared his mind, left raw welts along which ideas could run, around which decisions could form – decisions and ideas not his own, that would be loaned to him and on which he would pay interest for years to come.

He was restricted to the house, too. The open and relaxed network of friends and haunts that had previously characterised his life in LA was now replaced with a series of concentric and paranoid structures that had at their centres study, the wisdom of elders, the irresponsibility of children, the danger of experience. He was continually questioned about his personal habits and when the time came for him to return to school he was restricted to talking to certain friends and was repeatedly warned off having any contact with 'members of the opposite sex'.

In the beginning he thought of Jennifer a lot. Often she was the only thing he could hold in his mind. But within weeks of leaving England he found he could already hardly remember her. Her face was the first to go, washed out by the afternoon sun of the ever expanding distance between them. He found to his dismay he could impose almost any features he wanted upon the haze of flesh she'd become. Then her voice began to fade and when he reconstructed it in his mind it could have been Shelley who was speaking, or Lewis, he could no longer tell. Her hair remained, the shape of her hair, but the feel of her was gone altogether and in many ways the sex might as well never have happened. He'd lost interest in that anyway; he'd only been curious to begin with, not driven. It was her, always her. Who was she anyway? The lines the belt made across his back seemed to eradicate her smile. It was *her* fault. It was *she* who had done this. He screamed this to Moses often when punished. But he wanted to be with her anyway. He didn't know what he wanted. His mind was a blur.

He began to schedule his television viewing according to the times he knew Jennifer liked to watch, setting a clock to GMT and sometimes getting up early, sometimes staying up late. Voodoo space, TV space could connect them, he figured, rehashing ideas from his comic collection. That's where the power was. Here he was, then, sitting alone in front of his screen, projecting his mind 6000 miles across the earth, casting a spell . . . she was there, just on the other side of the glass, he could feel her. Maybe if he half closed his eyes, meditated like the Buddhists did, looked through the images, maybe then she'd emerge from the play of pixels and he'd see her, watching the same flat figures dash about in the frame, zooming in and out with the camera. He hadn't spotted her yet, but he'd heard her, he'd caught the timbre of her voice in some random phrase more than once, and he was sure it wouldn't be long now before she'd appear.

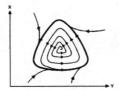

What if Brother Jack were wrong? What if history was a gambler, instead of a force in a laboratory experiment, and the boys his ace in the hole? What if history was not a reasonable citizen, but a madman full of paranoid guile, and these boys his agents, his big surprise!

Ralph Ellison, *Invisible Man*

6

Over mandrake they met

Henry didn't need too much persuading, from Moses or anyone else, that it would probably be better for all concerned if he took Jennifer away from Stratford while things had a chance to quieten down. Switzerland was the obvious choice – his father had been a Birmingham banker who looked after the international interests of his firm and Henry had spent many of his school holidays in and around Zürich, Geneva and Lausanne, back in the days when skis were great planks of wood that only farmers and woodsmen found uses for. When school term ended Henry would take the train to Birmingham, where he would be met at the station by his father's man. He'd spend a night or two alone with the small staff who lived at the Edgbaston house and then, with his school trunk replaced by holiday suitcases, he would be taken back to the station and placed on another train, a ticket and an itinerary and a tip for the guard in his pocket.

It was a ritual which ended with the Great Crash of 1929 and his father's ensuing suicide. Henry was brought up by his mother, who returned to live in Birmingham permanently, and he did not see Switzerland again for many years. But the family still had contacts out there and the country always retained a mythical air for him, that special aura that is bestowed only by the memory of idyllic childhood moments – a road in summer, an unfamiliar smell, a soft, repetitive sound, the pattern of light on a window, a shiver of rain from a cloudless sky. What with the personal pressure and the Axelrods' insistence on avoiding a scandal, it was the logical place to which to beat a retreat.

It was some time before Jennifer realised that she had gone without a period ever since Judd had been taken back to America. But by then she was squatting on the shores of Lake Geneva and digging her fingers into the sandy dirt. Not wanting to spoil her fun, she banished the disagreeable thought to the back of her mind.

Henry lay on the ground some distance away, snoring gently. He was wearing four watches, two on each wrist, and Jennifer could see the sunlight glinting off their bevelled faces as she moved her head from side to side. The watches lived on his arms like an infestation, increasing or diminishing in number, but never quite disappearing entirely, the physical manifestation of the trauma he'd felt at his wife's madness and death. It was somehow apt that he should have such a strong familial connection with Switzerland, that country of the clock, that crucible of mountains within which the disease of timekeeping had managed to concentrate itself and mutate until it was sufficiently strong to infect and enslave the globe.

The wind whipped across the water, coming up from the south and furrowing the lake's surface with waves, making a noise like a great canvas sail suddenly catching the breeze. Around the curve of the shore Jennifer could see the grey concrete buildings of the city, square and stark beneath the bright autumnal sky. She did not like Geneva, she had already decided. In fact, she didn't like Switzerland much. She didn't like pine trees and mountains, she didn't like Swiss television, which she couldn't understand, and she didn't particularly like the Swiss, at least those she had met, who were all too smartly dressed. But Henry seemed to like it here well enough. The beer suited him better than that he drank at home and in the two weeks that they had been in Geneva his face and eyes had grown less bloodshot than they had been in years.

Jennifer went over to him and pummelled his shoulder. 'Wake up, Dad! Dad! I'm bored. Wake up!' But he murmured thickly that she should go away, he was sleeping. She picked up first one and then the other of his thick pale arms and let them flop like severed limbs back on to the lush grass. Then it struck her that it might be more fun to have him asleep than awake and began to remove his watches. Two of them had buckled leather straps: they were easy enough. But the others had elasticated metal bracelets and she would have to ease them over Henry's hands while taking care not to trap any of the hairs on his arms.

He hated her taking his watches. She could never work out why he wore so many. When she asked him he always said that it was so that if one of them went wrong he'd still know what time it was. But they never seemed to be synchronised at all and he fiddled with them so much – he was forever removing the backs to tinker with the mechanisms –

that it was a miracle any of them ever worked at all. (And how would you know anyway, she reasoned, which of them was showing the right time, unless you knew the time already?) The only time they ever seemed to be properly set was at Christmas or at the birthday parties that she used to have when she was younger when, as a party piece, Henry would wear his entire collection of seventeen wrist-watches and eight pocket watches and walk into the living-room ticking like a beam full of death-watch beetles and saying, 'Here comes old Father Time.' Jennifer and her friends would roll up his sleeves and trouser legs and go through his pockets trying to find them while they were still synchronised, because fifteen minutes after he had set them all there would already be wild variations. Some of the timepieces would be gaining time, their minute hands sweeping around the dial, others would jump their gears and bounce backwards, others would stop altogether. Like some cultural microcosm, within minutes of starting Henry would be a patchwork of different times and speeds.

With the watches removed and jangling on her own little wrists Jennifer went back to the hole she'd been digging. She pushed them right up above her elbows and twisted the straps around to make them stay, freeing up her hands so that she could remove more soil. Soon her fingers found a root as thick as a cable and, pleased to have something to focus on, to have an aim in the midst of that most aimless of afternoons, she gradually dug away the earth from around it. The root was covered in tiny hairs which wobbled under the weight of multitudinous particles of soil. She had uncovered about twelve inches of it when she discovered a fork, and just beyond this she found a large tuber growing from one of the branches. She began to dig away at that too and before long had exposed the top of a round, turnip-like vegetable. She wanted to uncover it completely but the clayey soil made digging down around it difficult and her fingers were already beginning to ache with the amount of compacted debris which had built up beneath her nails. Eventually she had an idea and went back to where Henry was still sleeping. She nudged him hard in the ribs with her foot but the rhythm of his breathing barely altered, so she felt in his pockets for the penknife she knew he always kept about his person. Once she'd found it she returned to her excavations, scraping away now with the little blade, taking care not to damage either the tuber or any of the subsidiary roots which branched from it at intervals.

By the time she had uncovered two-thirds of the mandrake – for that is what it was – most of the afternoon had passed away. But now that she could see most of it she lost patience and clasping the vegetable with both hands began to tug. It still wouldn't budge so, placing both feet beside it in the hole she braced herself against the planet and pulled. This time she was sure she felt it shift. Adjusting her stance like an athlete she gave the thing a final, almighty heave.

A lot of things happened at once. The root exploded out of the ground; there was a terrible shrieking sound; Jennifer rolled over backwards, the tuber all over her; someone stepped out of the trees. Panicking now, she tried to see who the newcomer was and simultaneously to fight off the system of roots which had tangled itself in her hair. She got to her feet and fell over, pulled down by a strand that was still stubbornly attached to the ground. The stranger ran over and disengaged the struggling vegetable, then helped Jennifer to her feet. As soon as she was up she was cross and twisted away from his hands where they held her.

She turned to face a man, tall and gaunt, in his mid-twenties. Unkempt stubs of black hair stuck out from beneath his blue woollen hat, he wore heavy walking boots, and his clothes were dirty and torn. His thin face bristled with something that was half stubble, half beard, and behind jam-jar spectacles two dark irises tunnelled their way back into his skull. On his back he carried a small army-green pack which rattled when he moved and which was marked with stains that Jennifer found quite unfamiliar, and he also carried about him a strange aura of distress, as if he were both present and yet somewhere else, and not quite sure how this impinged on the situation. This last reminded her of Judd, but whereas with Judd it had seemed a source of strength, this man oozed vulnerability.

Jennifer caught a whiff of it immediately, took it for weakness and seized the initiative. 'Why did you scream?' she demanded in English, without thinking. 'You frightened me.'

He answered her in English, also automatically. 'Me? But it was you who screamed. That's why I ran over.' His words were quite precise, his accent posh, like Doreen Buerk's. He wasn't Swiss.

'Well, it wasn't me,' she said. 'And if it wasn't you and it wasn't me, then who was it? Because my father's asleep on the grass over there and there's been no one else around here all day.' She stuck out her arm and pointed to the prostrate figure on the other side of the clearing. 'See?'

The man shrugged and said nothing. He noticed the mandrake which was lying where it had been dropped in the confusion. He took out a pocket-knife and cut the tuber from the last restraining root. 'Why were you digging for this?' he asked Jennifer.

'Dunno. Something to do, I s'pose,' she shyly stropped.

'Do you know what it is?' He turned the tuber over in his hands, flicking the dirt from it with grubby, nail-bitten fingers.

'Yeh, course I do. It's a turnip, anyone can see that.'

'No.' He laughed. 'This is no turnip. It's a mandrake. Some people say that they scream when you dig them up, although that's only supposed to happen if you do it at night.'

Jennifer looked at him incredulously. 'Plants don't scream. *Everyone* knows that.'

'Well, I'm just telling you what they say, that's all. Though it seems to me that we both heard something like a scream and unless it was your father having a bad dream . . . Perhaps it was an animal in the forest. I hope so. It is not such good luck to hear the mandrake scream. It can send a man mad, apparently.'

'And what can it do to a woman?' said Jennifer, refusing to be impressed.

Confused by her question, the man offered Jennifer the tuber and she took it back from him. 'What are you going to do with it?' he asked.

'Eat it, of course. Take it back to the hotel and get them to cook it for me in the kitchens. If you stop being so rude I might even save you some.'

'Well, usually it's dried and used as a medicinal herb. I've not heard of anyone eating it whole before.'

'Yes, well, now you have. The world's full of big surprises. It's something we all have to get used to. Even someone as clever as you.'

But her sarcasm was lost on him. He scratched his nose thoughtfully. She hadn't noticed before how large it was. 'Well, people *have* told me I'm clever. But I'm not sure it's so easy to tell the difference.'

'Between what?'

'Between very clever and very stupid.' He smiled and showed faintly yellow teeth, aware that he was talking down to her but not sure he knew how to do anything else.

'You ain't half full of yourself,' said Jennifer, who also couldn't think of a better reply. She sat down on the grass and the stranger copied her. 'Who said you could sit down?' she snapped. 'I don't remember you asking me! Is that how you treat a girl? Clever or stupid, you're still damn rude.'

The man leapt to his feet. 'I am sorry, but are you a girl?' he exclaimed. 'But I thought . . . but I did not . . .' He looked at the watches on her arms. They read 3.15, 4.25, noon and 8.18. 'Is that the time? I have to go, I am going to be late . . .' He turned to leave but she grabbed him by the sleeve of his jumper.

The shyness that had overtaken him boosted her confidence, and she giggled at him to stay. 'Did you think I was a boy?' She laughed when he turned back to face her, his cheeks red. 'Why? Is it my short hair? But it's not that short.' Puzzled, she held her arms out and looked down at herself. She was wearing jeans, tennis shoes, a baggy cagoule. This last she unzipped so that the stranger could see the curves of her small breasts through her T-shirt. 'Do I look more like a girl now?' He blushed terribly. 'You're not Swiss, are you?' she demanded. 'Where are you from?'

'The United States.'

'But girls have short hair and trousers there!'

'Can we drop the subject please. I am very sorry, I made a mistake. Please let us talk about something else.'

'OK! Don't get upset! How old do you think I am?'

'I don't know. Please, I don't want to embarrass myself again.'

'Go on! I won't mind. I think you're thirty. Am I right?'

'Twenty-four actually,' he said, brightening a little.

'You see! I can be wrong too! Now, your turn.'

'I don't know. Maybe eighteen, at a rough guess,' he muttered.

'Bang on!' Jennifer exclaimed, delighted at his miscalculation. 'You see, you were right.' Encouraged, he asked her where she came from. 'England. Birmingham. Stratford-upon-Avon.'

Joel made an attempt at a joke. 'Which one?'

'All of them, sort of. Stratford is the town where I live, Birmingham is the nearest big city and England is the country.'

'I know,' he said hurriedly, angry that his joke had backfired. 'I used to live in Cambridge.'

'Oh,' she said, excited that they had something in common. 'I've been to Cambridge. It's nice. It's very pretty. When I'm old enough I'm going to go there to study.'

'But you're eighteen, that's old enough.'

'Er, yeh, but I want to . . . I need to see the world a bit first. Travel, you know.'

'Yes. I wish I had done that. I joined the university when I was sixteen.'

'Wow! You must be really clever.'

'I thought you'd already decided on that.'

'No, but I mean *really* clever.'

'So what did you mean before?'

'Before I thought that you just thought you were clever, but weren't really.' There was a slightly embarrassed silence, which Jennifer broke. 'What did you study?'

'Mathematics.'

'Oh, I want to study maths,' she lied. This was fun. 'You can sit down now, by the way.'

'Thank you.' The stranger sat on the grass beside her. 'I wouldn't.'

'Wouldn't what?'

'Study mathematics.'

'Well, I hadn't completely made up my mind . . .'

'It's a waste of time. I quit in the end.'

'What do you do now, then?'

'I'm a researcher.'

'What do you research?'

'Physics.'

'Oh.' At a loss. 'What sort of physics?'

'Quantum physics.'

'What's that?'

'It's to do with things that are very very small.'

'Like atoms?'

'Smaller than atoms.'

'Nothing's smaller than atoms.'

'Some things are.'

'Like what?'

'Like the things atoms are made up of.'

'Like what?'

'Protons, neutrons, electrons, neutrinos, quarks. The quark is very new. Its existence was only demonstrated a few months ago.'

'I know. I heard about it on TV. But I don't understand how you see all these things if they're so little?'

'Well, you don't really see them, not with your eyes at least. We do certain experiments and depending on the results we try and deduce what might be there. We use something called a particle accelerator.'

'What's that?'

'It's a huge circular tube that we fire atoms down, very fast, so that we can smash them into little bits. Using very sensitive detectors we can then find out what different kind of bits there are.'

'It sounds weird.'

'It is weird.'

'Can I see it?'

'What, the particle accelerator?'

'Yes.'

'Perhaps. I'll have to ask.'

'Where is it?'

'Not far from here. By the border. A place called CERN.'

'Is that where you work?'

'Yes.'

'So why aren't you working now? What are you doing out here?'

'I'm taking a holiday.'

'Why?'

'You ask a lot of questions.'

'Do I?'

'There's another one.'

'I suppose I do.'

'That's better.'

'What's better?'

'Better schmetter. You made a statement instead of asking a question. But then you ruined it by asking another question.'

'What's the difference?'

'A statement tells me something. A question asks me for something.'

'Sometimes questions can tell you something too.'

'That's just the problem.'

'With what?'

'With mathematics. With logic.'

'Is physics better then?'

'Sometimes. Perhaps.'

'When?'

'That's what I'm trying to find out.'

'Will you tell me when you do?'

The stranger laughed. 'If you want.'

'Do you think you'll find out soon?'

'I doubt it.'

'I hope you do. We're only in Switzerland for a short while. We're staying at the Hotel du Lac.'

'Well, if I find out I'll be certain to let you know. Who should I ask for?'

'Ask for me, Jennifer. Jennifer Several. And you haven't told me your name.'

'My name? My name is Joel Kluge.'

'Pleased to meet you, Mr Kluge.'

'Pleased to meet you too, Mademoiselle Several.'

Mademoiselle Several. Jennifer liked that. 'You don't sound American,' she said.

We don't see them with our eyes

She was probably the first female with whom he had held a proper conversation, if you didn't include his mother and his sisters and Amanda Metric and sundry administrative staff in the academic institutions he had attended. The girl he had thought was a boy, with her bobbed hair and frail limbs and the watches on her arms. She reminded him of a dream he had had a decade before, lying on the bank of the Cam, a dream of a perfect girl with mechanical arms, a dance of a dream on the bank of a river, a dream made flesh where water meets land on the banks of a lake. It was quite unheimlich – a German word he knew that meant 'uncanny'.

Joel turned the coincidence over in his mind as he hiked the few miles back into Geneva. He started by keeping to the water's edge, but after a while the going got too rough so he cut inland a few hundred yards and joined the highway. Cars and trucks rattled past him as he walked, and dressed the pine and spruce with fine sprays of lead.

He reached the hostel where he had been staying while his usual room on the CERN campus was unavailable and asked the receptionist, a balding Frenchman in his early thirties who was dressed in a white T-shirt and motor-cycle trousers, for his key. Then he went upstairs, dumped his pack on his bed, undressed and went down the hallway to shower. On his return he took from his backpack half a packet of crushed wafers, a tin of sardines, a textbook, a notebook and a flask of water, and sat there on the bed wrapped in his damp towel, a table in front of him, making himself a meal while he read. He had soon covered the thin red blanket with crumbs. With a pencil stub he scrawled some figures in the notebook.

When he had finished eating he threw the can and the plastic wrapping from the wafers into the bin, and with the cuff of his discarded shirt wiped up a few drops of oil that had been spilt when he'd opened the sardines. With the table now clear except for the notebook, he reached again into his haversack and extracted two red dice. He weighed them together in his left hand, rolled them around with his fingers, listened to the clicks that were made as each struck the other. Then he let them tumble on to the table, where they bounced and quickly came to rest. He sniffed and scratched his five-day beard, then recorded the scores and repeated the process. He did this for an hour and a half, then broke off to take a piss. By now he had long forgotten the encounter with Jennifer. Around ten he stretched out on the bed and fell asleep.

He was lying on the bed and the door opened and he floated towards it, worrying about banging his head. His room was bigger than it had been. He was no longer looking out from within himself but was watching the whole scene from above, as if he were on the roof of the building and all its walls and floors had become transparent. The body he had left behind floated out of the door of the room, both hitting its head and not hitting its head. There were others in the hostel, but they quickly became thinner until they were stick-like, at which point they were absorbed into the pulsating, gelatinous walls. The hostel trembled, all around it was white, there was no city. It trembled and dissolved, and the levitating figure was now a swimmer swimming upwards through the vitreous humour of an eye. His own eye. Joel swam upwards through his own eye, towards its cornea. His eye was not for seeing but for swimming. He seemed to have no trouble breathing. It had to do with waves.

Hypercycles

Haunting the night was another homunculus. Laika now filled her capsule so completely that apart from perception she had few functions left. With one eye on her monitor, the other on her porthole and two ears for the little speaker, she had become an almost entirely mediated being. It was no longer possible to distinguish between her and the machine. In came the plot lines, newscasts, pop songs, weather maps, planet views, co-ordinates, troop movements, flight paths, football results, lottery wins, share prices, tax figures. Out went very little apart from carbon dioxide and shit. But there was a regularity about the latter, about the waste products, that distinguished them from the information. Passive, partial, larval, contemplative and contracting, Laika bound the distributed excitations of data that flooded in through all her channels. She drew nourishment from them, a nourishment which sustained her long after her rations ran out. This was her secret, her creative work. Locked in her capsule in pure contemplation, a whirlwind of consciousness, a cinema-goer, again and again Laika remade her image, her self, from a synthesis of the differentials and potentials inherent in the incoming noise. On every level of her being, from the most ethereal operations of imagination and mind to the chemical susurrations of her fluids and cells, she exploited hypercycles and auto-catalytic loops, turned information into energy, let such a habitus unfold that could synthesise the present itself. Photon thought vibration disappeared into her and from this coarse grain of difference the processes of body and mind made the day.

She made a motor, powered it with the mediacasts she picked up, which were powered in turn by the motors of cameras, the capstans of tape recorders, the engines of newspaper presses and television studios, of space ships and particle accelerators, of fashion shows and wars. Like a billion gear wheels, these all intermeshed and drove one another, the whole a great machine fuelled by the perambulations and communications of Jennifer, Judd, Joel and millions like them. The result was an environment into which an unlucky parasite could be thrown and might yet survive, thrive even, breed perhaps and evolve.

Like the eukaryotic cell a billion years before her, like the lichens which conquered the land, Laika found herself in such a position, one which called for synthesis, for true creativity. And she rose to the occasion, finding new attractors, new degrees of freedom, new biological spaces in which to squirm and bulge. A rogue bacterium trapped inside a cell, in the normal course of events either she or her host would have died. But earth's atmosphere had changed, there was a mediascape now which, like the Oxygen Revolution before it, allowed new possibilities for life. And Laika was to be the exploiter, the dark precursor, the multiple starting point for a whole new plot line. She and Sputnik II melded together, became symbiotic, photo-autotropic, and in this way they fed and survived and continued their orbit, marking their wake with a crumbling stream of data-dessicated faeces that in doses measured out meanly by the once-dog's pulsating sphincter spilled down a tube, out of a valve and far off into inconceivable space.

The restaurant

Victor was heading for the tradesman's entrance in the hope of nipping outside unseen and having a quick smoke. He'd just put his right hand on the door handle when: 'Victor! Wohin gehen Sie? Die zwei Männer warten am Tisch fünf! Schnell!' Furious at being spotted by Schöllhammer, the Austrian headwaiter, Victor changed direction and headed back through the kitchens towards the restaurant, grabbing a tankard full of breadsticks as he went. He flapped through the swinging doors and headed over to the far table in the front window at which two corpulent businessmen sat, both of whom were wearing expensive steel-rimmed spectacles. They accepted the breadsticks without looking up. The paler of the two – and they were both pale – immediately reached across, pulled out one of the tubes, broke open its plastic wrapper with his teeth and ate the crisp, powdery stick in one long, mechanical, unbroken movement while his companion continued to talk.

Returning to the bar area, Victor stood and uncorked a bottle of Riesling and watched the cud-chewing movements that the man made as he masticated. Then the front door opened and in out of the rain stepped a bedraggled-looking Jew. Victor ignored him and wondered if there were any way he could get out of having to serve him. The restaurant was not particularly busy and all the tables apart from that at which the two businessmen sat had their food. He took their Riesling across and poured it out with a flourish, taking pains to make plain the kind of service a real Swiss could expect. But the businessmen ignored him and Joel had not noticed either, being too busy removing his coat and hat.

Victor darted down the far end of the restaurant, away from the door, asking at the occupied tables if there was anything anybody needed. Eventually, tired of waiting for assistance, Joel chose a table for himself.

Instantly, Victor was upon him. 'Excusez-moi, monsieur, mais celle-ci est réservée. On ne peut pas s'asseoir ici.'

'Er, sorry, ne parle pas français, je suis American. Can you parler anglais? English?'

American Jew, thought Victor. The worst sort. Probably related to the one who beat his cousin to that job in New York last summer. Salaud. 'You can nort seet here, see? Ist reserved. Taken. Pleeze to move to back of ristiran.'

'Uh, OK.' Too polite to protest, Joel stood and followed Victor towards the kitchens. There was a table there all right, just behind the swinging doors. It was disturbed by a constant draft and the smell of the stoves, and whoever sat there stood a good chance of having someone else's meal spilled all over him as waiters rushed in and out with their trays full of food. To engineer a disaster along these lines was exactly Victor's intention. It would cheer him up. But as he pulled out a chair with an elaborate flourish Joel caught his eye and clocked what was going on. He looked from the waiter to the chair, from the chair to the waiter, awkwardness and anger alternating in his chest like a strobe and making it impossible for him to think of a way to sidestep Victor's little manipulation.

Fortunately for Joel, just at that moment Schöllhammer swept out of the kitchens and nearly bumped into him. The headwaiter saw immediately that the customer was an American, gave Victor a black look and addressed Joel in English. 'Monsieur, I am terribly sorry, I did not see you there. Welcome to the Café Alsace. I trust you are finding everything to your satisfaction. Where would you like to sit? I'm afraid the weather is a little inclement today, but still the window tables are worth it, I think. Victor, sit the gentleman over there, table four, in the window. Can I get you anything to drink, sir?' Joel ordered a mineral water and Victor, fuming and unapologetic, led him back to his original seat.

'He's in Geneva again on Sunday and I said we could meet him in that restaurant in the square, the one you said you wanted to try. Oh, please, Daddy! He says he'll help me with my maths homework. It'll make up for me missing school. Please!'

Henry toyed with the idea. His first instinct was to say no, but he had long ago passed the point where he could refuse Jennifer anything. But what he could do was prevaricate. 'I'm not so sure. After what you've just put us through I don't see why I should let you at all. I'm not at all sure I shouldn't punish you just for attempting to set this thing up.'

'But Daddy, it's not like that. He's older, and he's . . . he's a *scientist*. And anyway you were asleep.' She was calling him Daddy, a clear sign that she knew she was going to get her way.

'Well, perhaps you should have woken me.'

'But I *tried*!' Henry had to agree that she might be telling the truth. The day had been warm, the lunch had been big, the beer had been drunk. 'What's this sudden interest in maths, anyway?'

'You *know* I've always been interested in maths. It was my best subject last term.'

He honestly couldn't remember if this were true or not. 'And you say he has offered to tutor you?'

'Yes. Oh, Daddy, I'm so bored here. There's nothing to do. *Please.* It is school work, after all.' Oh, such a sweet smile. There was a pregnant pause, although Jennifer was pretty sure of the sex of the imminent progeny.

'Well, I suppose the least I can do is meet him.' She leapt up, threw her arms around her father's neck and planted a big kiss on his cheek. He stumbled to keep his balance; he was no longer young. 'I'm not promising anything, mind you. We'll have to see.' Holding her in his arms his ears rang a little. He felt the cartilage between his lumbar vertebrae twinge under her weight, and he gripped her beneath the arms and eased her from him. When she ran excitedly into the adjoining room he sat down on the edge of the bed just to rest and breathe, and when he had begun to recover he adjusted the position of the watches on his wrists and synchronised them, for yet again they had run away from one another.

Sunday came and they walked out through the town together, heading towards the square in which the meeting with Joel was to take place. It was raining lightly, but Jennifer was ignoring the fuzz of water in the air and concentrating instead upon not stepping on the cracks in the pavement. Henry walked slightly behind her, puffing on a cigar and holding a golfing umbrella up against the drizzle. They had been walking for about ten minutes when they rounded the final corner and entered the square. Five or six large cafés occupied its four sides and their chairs and tables spilt out beyond the huge awnings, completely colonising the plaza. Today, however, the chairs were leant up and the umbrellas closed down as a precaution against the weather.

Jennifer ran on ahead towards the Café Alsace and pushed her face up against a window made soft with rain. 'He's here, he's here,' she called to Henry. Turning round to face the glass she pushed her hair back and into place. Within a split second she was in adult mode. They pushed the door open and went inside.

Joel, already half-way through his soup, looked up as father and daughter crossed to his table. An open pad, a pencil and the two red dice lay on the table next to the cruet. 'Hello,' he said.

'Hello,' said Jennifer. 'I bet you didn't think I'd come.' She flashed a shy smile at him and for a moment it looked as if he might smile back. 'This is my father, Henry Several. Dad, this is Dr Joel Kluge.'

The two men simultaneously sounded a greeting which was immediately followed by an awkward silence during which Joel remembered that he should stand up, which he did. Next, he offered his hand to Henry. Henry took it.

Victor arrived and laid the extra places perfunctorily, maintaining his ridiculous accent (he could in fact speak English perfectly well). ''Allo, 'ow ar yu? Plis mek yourself cum-furt-uble thank you? Wud you like these menu?' Jennifer and Henry sat down, took the menus from him and thanked him, although Henry couldn't resist making a comment about crazy foreigners beneath his breath, which unfortunately for him Victor overheard. He ordered a beer for himself and a lemonade for Jennifer, who scowled slightly when she thought no one was watching. The preliminaries over, nothing was left to be done but for the three of them to look at each other across the table. No one said anything.

Finally, and to Jennifer surprisingly, it was Henry who broke the ice. 'So, Dr Kluge. I gather you met my daughter by the lakeside last week. I'm afraid it seems that I was fast asleep, but Jennifer has told me an awful lot about you.'

Across the table, Jennifer grinned. She was pleased to see that Joel had shaved and brushed his hair. 'Did you think we would come, Joel?' she asked.

'Please, Jennifer, I think you should address the gentleman as Dr Kluge.'

'*Dr Kluge*, did you think we would come?' Beneath the table she rotated her feet to and fro on the heels of her shoes.

'Well, I didn't know, but I suppose I thought you might, yes. I don't want to be rude,' he said turning to Henry with what he hoped was a smile, 'but would you mind awfully if I continued with my soup? It's getting cold.'

'Please, dear boy, go ahead. It looks good. Think I'll have a drop of that myself. Cold day and all that. Good drop of soup warms you up.' Underneath the table, Jennifer nudged his shin, prompting her father to remember his lines. 'Jennifer tells me you have offered to give her some tutelage. That's very gracious of you. She's missed a lot of school.' The reason hung in the air like a raincloud and Henry quickly shone upon it the sun of a lie: 'She's not been well.'

For the first time in years, Joel thought of Millstein and how hard it must have been for the teacher to approach his own father that first time.

At least Millstein's motives had been purer than his own, he thought. 'I thought perhaps I could help her out with her maths,' he said quietly and was saved from further elaboration by the arrival of the drinks. Brusquely, Victor took the Severals' order.

'So what part of the United States do you hail from, doctor?' enquired Henry, while Jennifer was pointing out to Victor what she wanted from the menu. At the question Joel started and the spoonful of soup that he had been in the process of swallowing went down the wrong way. Trying to keep the liquid in his mouth only made it worse; it backed up his oesophagus and into his nasal passages. A fine spray of broth came out of his nose and peppered the table-cloth, dark spots bright against the white. Like niggers in a good Swiss town, thought Victor instantly. A minor coughing fit followed, which Joel exacerbated with his repeated attempts to apologise.

Jennifer passed him a glass of water and assumed a worried expression, and Henry leant over and pounded him on the back. 'Come on old chap,' he barked encouragingly, 'no harm done!' Victor disappeared and after some delay reappeared with a cloth and a jug of water, the contents of which he thought he might manage to slop over Joel. But as he moved towards him Joel, one step ahead, pushed his chair well back out of the way. 'Nothing to worry about,' said Henry cheerily, as Victor finished wiping the table, his assumption of command coinciding with the moment that the lager he had already drunk began to have an effect. 'It's all over now. Another beer for me, a lemonade for my daughter and another of whatever Dr Kluge was drinking if you please.' Returning to the table, his throat still aching slightly from the recent convulsion, Joel slowly drank the glass of water that Jennifer had given him, holding up his free hand to fend off further sympathies. Then he sat back in his chair and wiped away the beads of sweat that had pearled at his hairline.

Over at the bar, Victor had set a glass beneath the lager tap. As the beer puddled in the bottom of the stein he glanced around to make sure that Schöllhammer wasn't watching, then poured himself a schnapps beneath the counter, dropping down on his haunches to knock back the drink. All of a sudden he was struck by a particularly mischievous thought. He quickly poured out another schnapps and then, checking that the coast was still clear, he tipped the measure into the foaming glass of beer. A quick stir with a cocktail stick and no one would tell the difference. Then he poured out a lemonade for Jennifer and a mineral water for Joel, placed all three drinks on a round brass tray and delivered them to table four before returning to the kitchen to pick up the starters.

No sooner had the drinks been set down than Henry took a large draught of his lager. 'Fine beer,' he remarked to Joel, eyeing the man's mineral water. 'You not a drinker yourself?'

'It doesn't agree with me,' replied Joel, who had just about recovered his composure.

When the starters arrived Henry tucked into his soup with gusto and indeed ordered a bottle of Chablis to accompany it. As the wine was being poured, he turned again to Joel: 'So are you a mathematician by trade?'

'No, Dad, he's a physicist,' hissed Jennifer.

'Aha, well, you know me. I'm just an old accountant, it's all the same to me. As long as you're not one of those maths chappies with a practical streak.' He winked as he said this and gestured with his chin towards the dice that still lay by the cruet.

Joel followed Henry's gaze, but the reference was lost on him. 'I'm sorry?' he said.

'Practical. A practical mathematician! Putting those numbers to work! In a casino old boy! You know –' and here pointed with a long finger at the dice Joel had placed on his side plate when he had first sat down, '– *gambling*!' He rolled out the word with an even rhythm, giving it three syllables. Joel looked to Jennifer for a clue. He didn't understand what Henry was talking about. It was difficult to say which of the two was the more confused: Joel, for not understanding, or Henry, for understanding that Joel was not understanding.

'Don't tell me,' said Henry finally, 'that you've never been to a casino.'

'No, I don't believe I have.'

'Well, I have to take you to one! It's something which anyone with an interest in numbers simply can't pass by. Don't go often myself, of course, not my bag, as they say, but it's something you definitely must see. If you're handy with the dice then we should at least get you into a game of craps.'

'Dad . . .' complained Jennifer.

'Craps?' asked Joel.

'Craps. Playing dice. For money. You roll two dice and bet on the various possible outcomes.'

Playing dice for money? The idea struck Joel as novel. He thought of his notebooks and their dense forests of probability trees. 'That sounds like fun,' he said, mostly to himself.

'In that case I shall most definitely treat you to a visit to the casino. I'm sure you'll find it most exciting.'

'My research work is not particularly exciting,' rued Joel. 'I mainly work with computers.'

'Ah computers. I was a code cracker, you know!' said Henry pompously, taking the non sequitur in his stride. 'I knew Alan Turing, way back when. Is that what you do? Code cracking?'

'Did you?' Joel exclaimed. 'Really? I know something about his work with computers, but not a great deal. I don't suppose you happen to know what inspired the idea for the Universal Turing Machine, do you?'

Pleased to have found a common subject, the two men chatted enthusiastically for a while. Although Henry didn't know a great deal about modern computers, back at Bletchley he had had one or two conversations with Turing about his ideas for a logical machine that, by dint of being fed its instructions in binary form on an effectively infinite tape, could theoretically perform the function of any other logical machine. As for what had inspired it . . . well, he did seem to recall something about the work of Charles Babbage and Ada Lovelace, and the old Jacquard loom, 'which was programmable, you know, yes, punch cards and all that'. Joel mentioned John von Neumann, about whom he knew more than he did about Turing, and Henry told him an interesting anecdote. 'Turing and von Neumann worked together, of course, on EDVAC, after the war. You know, don't you, that von Neumann was Hungarian by birth, but did you realise that back in Hungary his father was a banker, who had financed the introduction of those very Jacquard looms into his country years before? Some coincidence, hum?' Joel was suitably impressed. Henry asked him just what it was he did at CERN.

'I work on the particle accelerator. It's code-cracking too, of a sort. We try and crack the codes of atoms.'

'Atoms, eh? Darn me!' Henry clanked his spoon down into his empty bowl and sat back to take a swig of his wine. 'Like a drop of this, my boy? No? You should try it. Damn fine.' He refreshed his glass and reconnected with the thread. 'It all seems a bit highbrow for Jennifer, mind you. She can hardly even add up straight.'

'Dad! Don't listen to him. Anyway, Joel – Dr Kluge – isn't going to teach me about computers and physics. We're just going to do some basic maths, aren't we? Algebra, and equations and stuff.'

'Yes, of course, although –' Joel turned to Henry, his face seared a bright red, '– I was thinking of inviting Jennifer out to the Centre, with your permission. It's not far, it's just out past the airport, near the French border. We can take a train there. Jennifer asked if she could see the accelerator and I think she will find it, uh, educational. Perhaps you would care to join us, Mr Several?' Henry tried to gain purchase on the use of the first person plural by this young man; there was something about it that . . . But the alcohol had got the better of him and the impression morphed itself into the idea that it would be nice for Jennifer to be able to go somewhere without him for a change. She should be safe enough with this fellow, he seemed responsible, he was a scientist after all and God knows they're a dull enough breed, not likely to come to any harm there. One heard of girls being seduced by music teachers, they were positively famous for it, but by a maths teacher? It was out of the question. So Henry convinced himself, and for the remainder of the meal he acquiesced to all his daughter's requests. It was eventually agreed that as long as Joel was available he should come to the hotel each morning and tutor Jennifer between eleven and one. They would start the next day and she would visit CERN on the following Saturday.

By the time they left the Alsace the rain had stopped. Jennifer soaked her shoes through by jumping in and out of the puddles.

'What a charming young man,' Henry remarked to his daughter, who wasn't paying him the slightest attention. 'And never even been to a casino.' To emphasise his disbelief he puffed hard on the large cigar he was smoking. Like others before them the clouds of smoke he exhaled hung on the damp Sunday air like dirty cotton swabs. Together they formed a septic trail that marked the couple's course through the labyrinth of streets and back to their hotel.

Initiation

Joel sat on the teak toilet seat in the second cubicle of the first-floor gentlemen's rest-rooms in the second-largest casino in Geneva and clutched his ankles with his hands. His colon was empty but he sat there none the less, his chest folded on to his lap. The position was not one of pain or strain, but of an arrested thought process. He was overwhelmed by the casino, by this crazed house of numbers, so much so that his bowels had loosened. But once he'd dumped a nervous quiver of faeces into the gleaming bowl he found himself distracted, wondering just to what extent the tangle of sewers, pipes and processing plants that formed the substratum of the city mimicked the workings of his own viscera.

Back in the main room Henry was wondering what had become of his companion. He crossed the floor in the direction of the bathroom, weaving his way between the baccarat tables and eyeing the fall of the cards and the movement of counters as he did so. But just as he was about to open the mahogany door – the one with the word *Hommes* embossed across it in gold – it swung back and Joel stepped out. 'Ah ha! Just wondering where you'd got to. Not in any trouble, I hope?'

'No, no, I'm fine,' Joel replied, warily peering out into the hall. The low chatter, the dark booths and thick carpeting, the clink of glasses and chips, the flash of jewellery and teeth; that this cosseted environment should be laced with so much adrenalin completely bewildered him. The contradictions reminded him of his barmitzvah and the palpable disjunction he'd felt at the time between his own anticipatory excitement and everyone else's radical calm. The memory was intensified by the impression all these people gave that they were here to worship. Standing or sitting at the tables, they had the same rapt expressions as rabbis locked in prayer and contemplation, their faces a peculiar mixture of fervency and desperation.

Henry led him through the club, explaining the different card games – chemin-de-fer, baccarat, blackjack. He described the role of the croupiers, the use of the shoe, the value of the chips, the workings of the bank, the etiquettes of betting, the security arrangements.

Joel took in everything, thinking all the while that these were the preliminaries. 'And so where are all the dice players?' he eventually asked.

'No craps here, old boy,' said Henry, ruefully swilling the ice around in the bottom of his empty gin and tonic. 'You don't see so much of that over in Europe. You're better off back in America if you want to use your dice.' Slightly disappointed, Joel pointed across to the far end of the room where thick clumps of people were gathered around several long, thin tables and asked what was going on there.

'Aha, roulette! Game of princes! Let's go take a look, shall we?' They moved across to one of the quieter tables and stood at the wheel end and between spins the Englishman sketched out the rules for Joel, showed him how to admire the silent, seemingly frictionless twirl of the wheel, the deft movement of the croupier's wrist which sent the ball scudding against the direction of rotation, the clack of the chips as the players placed their bets. Joel was particularly moved by the way a hush fell on the group as soon as the ivory ball was released, its tik-tiketty-tak emerging clear from the previous commotion, the sound gradually dying away as gravity's basin guided the ball to rest in one of the cups. It reminded him of the sound of the pellets of freak summer hail which had fallen on the tin roof of an old shack he had sheltered in one night on the first hiking expedition he had taken after his arrival at CERN. A high wind had blown up and he hadn't been able to sleep because of the clatter of the trees. The hail came down, the wind dropped and behind the percussive rhythms of ice on metal the forest fell silent, as if to listen. As the storm moved away and the hail fell off, Joel could remember being overtaken by the most extraordinary feeling of peace. It was something akin to this that he was experiencing now, but he could not see yet that the peace that was promised by roulette would never arrive, that in a strange eternal return the wind would pick up again and again, and that there would always be another spin of the wheel.

His attention was also drawn by the rituals of preparation and consumption, the spell of the etiquette, the heady combination of euphoria and proscribed behaviour. He gripped the chips that Henry had bought to give him a start so firmly that when the time came to use them they were glued together with sweat and the mucilaginous gunge secreted by his palms. He watched Henry play the table with the intensity of an amateur assuming the cloak of a professional, pretending that his mistakes were deliberate attempts to educate Joel in what not to do. But Joel was in no mood to judge. It did not occur to him that one might play well or badly; one just played. It seemed to him that roulette was a way to let your personality be moulded for a time into shapes dictated by mathematics alone and he thought of the numerical vistas he'd roamed as a child. Here in the casino, in a strange, miniature and quite perfect way, was that Cambridge of the mind he had sought when he had deserted his family and boarded the plane bound for England. Here was a world in which people, for a period at least, gave themselves over to the Number. To Joel it was obvious that money was the excuse, not the reason.

More people gathered around the table and soon he stood in a crush, his shabby figure curious against the shimmering dresses and the crisp, dark suits. The table hovered level with the players' groins, a tense plateau of energy drawn out from their genitalia. The yellow betting grid etched upon this larval surface reminded Joel of the periodic tables that hung in the labs and lecture rooms of CERN, and he wondered if their functions were complementary, the periodic table merely representing the bets that had been laid on the spin of the wheel that was the birth of the universe.

Here was something so much more satisfying than the dice he was using. He'd been working away at chance for some time now, figuring that if – as he had explained to Metric several years previously – the universe was indeed rebuilding itself in the image of perfection, reconstructing the shattered vessels, then there should be traces of this process to be found. But where should one begin to search for them? Joel had spent the first year of his time at CERN pondering this, until the answer had suddenly come to him, somewhat significantly he thought, on a ragged mountain top during one of his walks. Chance! Chance was the key! If the universe was perfect then randomness – chance, probability – should be perfect too: analyses of random samples would prove them to be just that, random, and there would be no statistical significances to be found in the data. But if the universe was imperfect, as it was, then there would be flurries and eddies in chance, rivulets and rifts, patterns and predictabilities. It should be possible, to a limited extent, to map the future. The idea had taken shape like cracks across a windscreen, and on his return to the town he immediately bought himself several sets of dice and began to compile data.

It was a grand design. Not only would he be looking for localised effects but ultimately he would be trying to track changes over time – to see if there was some kind of generalised trend. It was an insane project, he knew, one on which he could spend his whole life and still have nothing to show for it. But now, with this game of roulette, it seemed as if there might after all be a way to get tangible results. Here was a chance machine that ran twenty-four hours a day, seven days a week, all over the world. If there were indeed results to be measured, if the world was actually evolving towards some higher realm of total perfection, then how much more keyed into that progression would this meshwork of gamblers and wheels be than he himself, alone in some room with his dice? This, then, was the way to proceed. It was beautiful. It was the most beautiful thing.

'I'm all out of chips,' said Henry, in what he imagined was the accent of a whiskey-drinkin', horse-ridin', whore-whuppin' and hard-gamblin' frontiersman from the American Wild West. He looked down at the chips in Joel's hand. 'You not goin' to play then, pardner?'

'Er, no,' said Joel, emerging from his reverie, 'not tonight, I don't think I understand the game well enough yet. Perhaps you'd better play for me.' He passed the gummed-up clump of counters back into the older man's hands, the colour beginning to seep back into his face as he did so. For the first time that evening since he'd been getting ready to go out it struck him that instead of philosophising about roulette he should be worrying about whether or not Henry suspected him of wanting to have sex with his daughter.

Spermatogenesis (2)

For activity in Joel's testes, please refer to Book 001, Chapter 4, *Spermatogenesis (1)*.

Dark matter

Most of all, Jennifer was impressed with the sheer size of the accelerator. She couldn't quite conceive of the size of the ring itself, the Super Proton Synchrotron, twenty-seven kilometres in circumference, but the massive detectors in their deep underground bunkers made the scale of the thing plain enough. Joel gave her a guided tour: he showed her the SPS control room, with its computers and banks of television screens which let the technicians monitor every part of the gigantic structure; also several of the experiments, driving from one to another in a car he had borrowed for the purpose.

It was a clear day and they could see the Alps in the distance, away beyond Geneva. They crossed the border into France and back again. Some of the experiments were housed in hangers thrown up on hillsides where sheep and cattle grazed, others were buried as much as six stories down into the ground, two thousand tonnes of superstructure and electronics. These great pits swarmed with cables thicker than Jennifer's legs, cables which puddled on the floors and levels and tumbled down the walls like enormous earthworms in a giant fisherman's bucket. White cubes as big as caravans and stuffed with integrated circuits were stacked up one on top of the other like so many fridges in a reclamation yard; blue metal walkways ran between them and around them. Cooling fans as loud as aircraft jets roared constantly and the din drowned out everything else. On one of the cabinets were painted the words: 'Hands off. You will be shot.' A sign hung above a door on the second floor; it read: 'If you have nothing to do, don't do it here.'

'THIS IS THE BRAIN OF THE DETECTOR,' Joel yelled above the noise. 'WHEN THE COLLISIONS TAKE PLACE INSIDE, THE SHOWER OF PARTICLES IS TURNED INTO A SERIES OF ELECTRONIC PULSES, WHICH ARE FED INTO THESE CIRCUITS – THERE'S ABOUT THREE OR FOUR MILLION, I THINK. THESE WORK OUT WHETHER THEY'RE INTERESTING ENOUGH TO BE STORED ON THE MAGNETIC TAPES SO WE CAN LOOK AT THEM LATER.' He grinned and nodded wildly as he shouted, gesticulating at various parts of the space. Jennifer nodded back, unable to make out most of what he was saying. But she didn't need to know the facts in order to learn: the very sight of this vast complex, buzzing with people and completely dedicated to tending this even vaster and mostly invisible machine was entertaining enough. It was as if some benign alien presence had taken root up here in the mountains and had attracted a colony of humans both to interrogate and to be interrogated by, and when she saw *Close Encounters of the Third Kind* at the cinema four years later it would bring this visit to CERN back to her so immediately that she cried all the way through the final scenes.

'ARE THESE THE ONES WHO FIND OUT WHAT ATOMS ARE MADE OF?' she yelled.

Joel, pleased that she had asked a question, started nodding even more furiously. 'YES, BUT THEY DON'T EXAMINE THE DATA HERE. TOO NOISY. AND IT'S NOT ALWAYS THEM WHO MAKE THE DISCOVERIES. THE FIRST SUB-ATOMIC PARTICLES WERE IN FACT DISCOVERED BY WOMEN – THE PHYSICISTS INVOLVED WERE TOO BUSY FLYING OFF TO CONFERENCES TO BREAK DOWN THEIR OWN DATA, AND THEY GOT THEIR WIVES AND GIRLFRIENDS TO DO IT. BUT GUESS WHO TOOK ALL THE CREDIT?' The idea intrigued Jennifer and she wondered if Joel would ever let her examine any of his data.

They had started the lessons that week as planned and things had progressed well enough. Jennifer's grounding in maths was more basic than Joel had dared to think, but she was bright and she quickly picked up new ideas. If anything was going to hinder her progress it was her propensity to lead Joel off the subject: she loved to chat and wanted to know everything about her tutor. Joel found the attention quite disconcerting – enough to render him almost incapable of parrying her questions – and he had a hard time keeping the proportion of maths in their sessions to over fifty per cent. And not only did Jennifer grill him, but she criticised him too. She found out that he'd never had a girlfriend, had never bought a record, didn't own a car, didn't watch TV. She teased him that he didn't have a life. Didn't he do anything but work? She lent him some cassette tapes she'd brought with her from England: *The Rise and Fall of Ziggy Stardust and the Spiders from Mars*, Leonard Cohen, *Sticky Fingers*, *Electronic Meditation*, some Crosby, Stills & Nash. He listened to them all, but only once.

After he had shown her around on the Saturday they went for lunch in one of the refectories. Jennifer rattled on happily about her morning, too busy talking to do more than pick at her sandwich, although she ate the whole bagful of potato chips which she was supposed to be sharing with her new friend. Joel sat there, munching on a baguette stuffed with Emmenthal and sliced salami, and watched her as she told him about everything that they had just seen on their tour around CERN. He felt displaced. Hearing the descriptions fall from her mouth: 'all those maggoty wires and cables', 'so noisy it was like standing in a weir', 'like being inside the theatre, but full of these kind of caravans' – images taken from the town in which she had grown up and reconfigured in order to help her comprehend this new experience – it seemed to him that he didn't know what she was talking about, that she was chattering about somewhere he had never been. He listened, fascinated.

But soon even Jennifer ran out of things to say. Remembering her hunger, she applied herself to her sandwich while Joel sat and looked out of the window, embarrassed now to watch her and trying to think of new topics of conversation. Getting Jennifer to come out to CERN had filled his thoughts for the previous fortnight, and even after it had proved easy to get her and her father to agree to the visit it had still obsessed him, worried as he was that something might go wrong and that she wouldn't be able to come. But for all that, he hadn't thought about what they'd do beyond him giving her the tour. Now that he'd shown her the main attractions he was all out of ideas.

'Whereabouts do you live, Joel?' Jennifer piped up. She'd swallowed the last desirable piece of her sandwich (she left the crusts) and was beginning to unwrap a chocolate bar. Joel mumbled the name of a residential block, but was no more forthcoming than that. Earlier in the week her probings had revealed that although her tutor did not have a TV he did have a coffee-maker, and now she used the knowledge as a crowbar to lever his private life a little further open. 'I think I'd like some coffee. Why don't we have one in your room? I want to see your coffee machine.'

Joel, suddenly scared: 'Well, I er, I don't think so, it's a terrible mess, and it's too far away, it would take us ages to walk there. And shouldn't you be getting back . . . ?'

'We've still got the car you borrowed! And I don't care about the mess. And Dad's not expecting me back till this evening anyway. Come on! I want to see where you live!' She dragged him from the table and out to the car, and they drove the short distance across the campus to Joel's block.

He had a room on the fourth floor at the back. They climbed the concrete stairs and came to the door; Joel unlocked it and pushed it open, letting Jennifer in first. She walked into a large double room with one big window that looked out on to a sky freckled with low grey clouds and, beneath it, the drab town of Meyrin. There was a bed in the corner, a desk, a coffee table and some chairs, a kitchenette, a small bathroom equipped with toilet and shower. It was not dissimilar to Henry's room in the hotel (she had only a small single further down the hallway). But what made the room distinctive, apart from the bookshelves overflowing with daunting-looking volumes, the stacks of papers and computer equipment, the piles of clothes and the fairy rings of dirty cups, were the pictures on the walls.

Photographs and maps had been pinned up haphazardly and covered every available space. While Joel made excuses for the mess, and washed mugs and filled the coffee machine, Jennifer peered at some of the pictures. Photographs of piles of objects. Piles of shoes, so many shoes that they filled a whole room, piles of spectacles, piles of suitcases. Piles of trousers, hats, shirts. Banks of cabinets and boxes full of smaller objects – cigarette cases, rings, wallets, small odd-shaped pieces of some dull metal that Jennifer could not identify. There was a map of what must have been Europe, but it was completely black and had no features – no coastline, no national boundaries. All it had were place names and under each name a number, usually in the thousands or hundreds of thousands. Jennifer moved around the room; behind her Joel panicked over the coffee.

Photographs of lampshades made of some curious parchment and etched with complex designs that looked like tattoos. Long ropes next to piles of what she thought were horses' manes. Many many pictures of empty shower rooms like the ones at Stratford rugby club; others of rooms that she recognised as slaughterhouses from the meat hooks set into the ceilings and the dark splashes of what must have been blood on the walls. (She winced – the fact that the pictures were in black and white made them somehow worse, because they activated the imagination.) Furnaces like the ones she had seen in pottery museums in the Black Country on school trips, forest clearings that had been excavated and strewn with a strange, coral-like shale.

She couldn't make the connection between all the pictures. This was a part of himself which Joel had not revealed to her; in all of their talking he had not told her that he was into photography, especially of such a weird kind. A frisson of fear made her tremble like jelly. Who was this man with whom she was spending her time?

'How do you have your coffee?' he asked her.

'White with sugar, please.' She turned round to face him, to ask him about the photographs, and he handed her a cup. 'Joel . . .' But the wall behind him was full of pictures that she had not yet properly seen and for a second she focused on them and in that moment everything became clear. At the sight of the people, hollow like ghosts, she dropped the cup; it fell to floor and splashed scalding coffee up her jeans. 'Oh, Joel, I'm sorry, I'm so sorry, oh, God, it was . . . it was the pictures, I . . .'

Joel dashed around her with a tea-towel, swabbing up the mess and dabbing the worst of it from her trousers, forgetting that he was touching a girl's legs for the first time. 'I should have warned you,' he apologised. 'Nobody really comes in here and I forget about them, about what other people might think, coming in here, you know, unprepared. Awful, aren't they.' He refilled Jennifer's cup as her eyes roamed the wall, trying to construct a meaning out of the bodies stacked like wood, the walking corpses next to the stunned and embarrassed Allied soldiers, the heaps of babies all with their skulls caved in and cortical matter dried into waxy rivulets on the walls above them, the crude torture chambers with their pincers and rheostats and the laboratories filled with samples, the hills of ash whose contours were broken by protruding skulls and femurs, the naked women standing in circles or being set upon by dogs, the mattresses water-logged with diarrhoea, the two stick-like children sitting astride the bloated corpse of their dead mother and playing with a die, the photographs of the Nazi officers smiling with their wives. The content of all the previous pictures, the ones she had misunderstood, became horribly clear.

'Where are these pictures from?' Jennifer asked, trying to keep her voice steady, more afraid than ever.

'They're from the Holocaust. During the Second World War, the Nazis tried to wipe out all the European Jews. They nearly succeeded.'

'Why?'

'Ha!' It was the first time she had heard Joel laugh. 'I don't know. There are reasons given in the history books, of course, but they don't really mean anything. It seems to take more than logic to understand why a particular group of people should go completely out of their way to eradicate more than six million . . .'

'Six million!'

'I'm surprised this is all so new to you. Don't they teach you history in school?'

'Yes, but I've never much liked history. Our teacher, Mrs Pettigrew, is awfully dull and I think she mentioned some stuff about it once when we did the Nazis and Churchill and stuff, but I never really realised . . . I mean, we didn't see any photographs like this or anything.'

For the next hour they looked at the pictures together, Joel telling Jennifer the stories behind each one, simple stories made up of where–when–what, because the images were too stark, their content too clear, for them to need the padding of human detail – of whom. Jennifer listened in silence, really learning something for once, Joel really teaching. As he talked she was surprised at how empty she felt, hollow as the emaciated Jews who staggered blinking from the dormitories. It was shock, of course, brought on as the planes of her being began to rotate making her strange to emotion until a fresh configuration was reached, one which would bring with it a whole new array of intersections, interstices and possibilities.

She asked him how he'd got interested in all of this.

'Well, of course, I'm Jewish myself, so that's part of it. But like you, it was never real to me when I was told about it at school, or when my parents mentioned it, even though my Uncle Isaac and most of his family died in one of these camps, this one –' he pointed to one of the pictures on the wall, '– Treblinka. No, it never came home to me until I came here to CERN, in fact. An old physicist here, a Jew, one of my supervisors . . . well, we were in one of the laboratories the summer before last and it was terribly hot, and he rolled up his shirt-sleeves – something I'd not seen him do before, he was very neat and proper. And on his arm was a tattoo, like this.' He pointed to another picture, this time of a serial number etched on to a woman's arm in an inky, ragged blue. 'I asked him about it and he told me. He'd been in one of the camps, not Treblinka, another one, Dachau, it's near Munich. I told him about my uncle, and he told me all about the war and what had happened to him. He gave me a lot of these photographs. I didn't want to take them at first but he told me he was dying and he was right – he died last year, of lung cancer; he'd thought that since he'd survived the camps nothing could kill him, especially not something as ridiculous as tobacco. He smoked right up to the end, even after he knew it was coming. But I don't think he really cared by then.

'The terrible thing is, of course, that this is nothing new. Humans have been involved in the systematic destruction of each other ever since history began. You can go right back to classical mythology and find accounts of concentration camps. Scratch at the history of any country in the world and you'll soon uncover the layers of blood on which it was founded. Take America, for example, land of the free, right? Except for the native tribes who were wiped out by the early settlers and the black slaves who were imported in vast numbers from Africa – mostly by British companies, I'm afraid – and the Chinese immigrants who were treated no better than slaves and worked to death laying railway lines. Look at Stalin's massacre of the Kulak class, or his starvation of Ukrainian peasants in the thirties – that killed as many as the Nazi Holocaust. Or the destruction of Tasmanian aborigines by European immigrants, or the modern Chinese attempts to eradicate the Tibetans.'

'But why are you so obsessed with this stuff? Don't you find it grue-some? There are good things in the world too, you know.'

'Maybe. But I don't know if they outweigh the bad things.'

'But Joel, that's ridiculous! More people are born than die! The number of people in the world is still going up! And that means that there's more love than death, doesn't it? Doesn't it?'

'I don't know. Do children always spring from love? How many parents do you know who are really happy? Who truly love one another? Who love their children?'

This touched a nerve and Jennifer suddenly found herself battling against pain, refusing to accept that her argument was invalidated by what Henry had told her of her own conception. 'But love isn't that simple . . . i-it doesn't mean that you always walk around with a smile on your face, that you are never unhappy. It's more than that. I mean I know my dad loved my mum, e-even when she went mad and, I don't know how to explain it to you, but it's not like you think . . .' Tears of frustra-tion began to form in her eyes as she failed to think a way through the moral conundrum. Instinctively, she changed tack. 'I mean, haven't you ever fallen in love?'

Joel looked at her. 'No. I don't think I have.'

'What? You've never had a girlfriend?'

'No.'

'Are you gay?' Joel looked blank. 'Are you a homosexual?' She demanded the information, letting herself get angry with him now, widening the channel down which she could escape from the thought of her mother's rape.

'No, I don't think so.' Joel knew that such people existed, but he had never given them much thought.

'Well, haven't you ever even had sex?'

'Er, no, not that I remember.'

'God! You're a *virgin*?'

'I suppose so.' Joel was by now acutely embarrassed.

Jennifer's anger vanished and she began to giggle. 'Really? That's amazing.' She allowed herself to start laughing properly – it was hilarious, wasn't it, the idea that this man, a good ten years older than her, had never slept with anybody? It was too much. Of course, Joel didn't see the joke. He suddenly felt incredibly self-conscious, painfully aware of his body extruding itself into the room like some ungainly piece of scaffolding – temporary and purely functional. By comparison, Jennifer seemed like an alien being, an angel complete in her physicality. It suddenly struck Joel that the ethereal wasn't a realm of pure mind, divorced from the strictures of the material; it was a realm of pure physicality, pure expression. Freedom had nothing to do with being released from the confines of substance. It was to do with being released from the confines of form, of designs generated like the by-products of a chemical process by the operations of thought. Perhaps form wasn't imposed on matter, perhaps human beings had it wrong when they tried to understand the world in terms of abstract schemata imposed from above. Perhaps form grew out of the way things collided, the way they connected, the way they moved. But then, wasn't logic itself such an outgrowth? The thought seemed contradictory and Joel felt confused.

Jennifer saw all this flash across Joel's face and took it for straightforward sadness. She stopped her false laughter, stood up from where she had been sitting on the edge of the bed and came over to where he was kneeling. Shaking a little she put her arms on his shoulders, then bent down and kissed him on the forehead. She felt nervous, tentative, like a stream finding its way down a mountainside, daring to try and erode. She thought of Judd and his arid body, slow and absorptive, so different from Joel's, which was sensitive as a scree-littered slope. She pulled him towards her and bound his fragments with her moisture, her warmth, cloying them into a malleable clay. Sex wasn't anything out of the ordinary for Jennifer. It wasn't transgressive, it was merely an obvious corollary of the world as she experienced it – as a tactile and heterogeneous place, riven with channels but never ruptured, marvellous and occasionally brutal, but never alien or cold. Maybe this was a result of her shattered family and peculiar upbringing, maybe it was something she was born with, it's impossible to tell, but perhaps this is why she was so shocked by the Holocaust images and, ultimately, not as deeply affected by them as Joel.

Joel remained motionless, so she bent down a little further, locked her arms around his neck and began to kiss him instead on the lips. It was a strange feeling, from which he could not generalise. Then slowly she began to undress him. He couldn't generalise from that, either.

It was a total shock, the sex, an overload of every sense. Even to have someone else touch his clothing, unbutton it, unzip it, made him shake. He flushed hot and sprang goose-bumps simultaneously. When she was naked and he saw her skinny limbs he couldn't help but think of the wraiths on the walls, the camp survivors. He tried to block them from his mind, but then he thought of home and that was worse – all the old moralities came flooding back, here he was in the forbidden zone, he wasn't even married, how could he think of such a thing? His mind reconstituted the whores in Times Square, the electric shock of that crotch, the mugging, the bridge . . . the accelerator, the particle ring, the news that another section of Skylab had that day successfully docked. Her skin was like flames . . .

She felt it and placed his hand on her breast and that calmed him.

Afterwards, he couldn't remember coming; he could barely remember any details at all. The whole thing was a blur, but a vivid one, a fast-forward video trace. For weeks he couldn't think of it without shuddering, as if someone had dabbed ice on his nipple, but at the same time he was proud, he had managed it, he'd crossed a threshold and nothing would be quite the same again . . . The area of skin between his anus and his scrotum seemed permanently tender, but on the inside, as if a cat were licking away at the very fronds of the muscles down there. In a way he had come to life, he felt totally alive, it was like a drug. It was a good month before he wondered if this was how a computer might feel, if you flooded it with data.

★

As for Jennifer, while they'd been making love she'd thought of algebra, a special kind, though derived from what Joel had been teaching her. *This plus this divided by this over this equals what?* she'd mused, as she'd scrawled her calculations across the tablet of his skin.

Life as we know it

In retrospect, 1973 became known to scientists as the annus mirablis of physics. Joel's insight apart, breakthroughs that year included the discovery of neutral currents (which lead to the final establishment of the existence of the quark). Nor were the other disciplines left out. IBM engineers discovered the group of alloys known as Rare Earth, which enabled the development of rewritable optical media, the first practical steps were taken in the science of genetic engineering and tape capstan motor acceleration reached a new rate of 0 to 200 inches per second in 750 millionths of a second.

But the year's real first, its most exciting and unprecedented event, took place far from prying eyes and Nobel prizes. It happened deep inside the body of Jennifer Several, where a single ovum was busy being fertilised by spermatozoa from two different males, Judd Axelrod and Joel Kluge. This had happened before, would happen again: the result was generally twins. But in the strange case of Jennifer Several the progeny would not be two children but one and one alone – one child parented by three distinct sets of DNA. In 1973 in Jennifer's womb a three in one – a thoroughly materialist and thoroughly unholy trinity – was being gestated. And this is how it happened.

Shortly before Jennifer had intercourse with Judd for the last time an ovum was released from her right ovary and started its slow journey down the corresponding fallopian, propelled along by the tube's muscular action and the efforts of the tiny cilia on its internal surfaces. Then Judd's spermatozoa were ejaculated into Jennifer's vagina, and a few of these managed to work their way up past the cervix and into the uterus. A significant number died then and there. Of the survivors all but one chose the left-hand fallopian.

Jennifer had heard about the quark's existence shortly before she and her father had left for Geneva: the breakthrough had made the nine o'clock news. It's fair to say that she didn't take much notice – her mind was on other things at the time. But she absorbed the information anyway and it kicked around in her subconscious, where it was processed and puzzled over. Her subconscious couldn't quite put its finger on it, but something about the quark worried it. It did a bit of research into quantum mechanics and that was when it learnt about Heisenberg's uncertainty principle, which stated that it was impossible to know both the position of a sub-atomic particle and its momentum at the very same instant, the upshot of which was that the behaviour of particles could not be predicted. Disaster! If the scientists had shown that the world was fundamentally incoherent, the subconscious would be out of a job! This was terrible! It told the body its concerns (as it always did, the two of them being extremely close) and the body was no less worried, knowing full well that without the subconscious to anchor it, the conscious mind would have taken off on its own long ago, leaving the body behind to rot like so much senseless meat (being no different from anyone else, the body too languished in a world of Cartesian delusion). There was danger here, it thought, a great deal of danger, and the cells of the spinal column (who'd heard the news first and regarded themselves as somewhat more sensible than their brethren) decided to keep a lid on the information and forestall widespread panic. But the body is a hothouse of gossip at the best of times and it didn't take long for rumours to start, which soon spread like viruses to every fingertip, sebaceous gland and hair follicle – and, inevitably, to one little protoplasm on the end of a cilia, who whispered the secret to the ovum as it passed by on its journey to the womb.

Well! That changed everything. The ovum wasn't at all sure that it wanted to be fertilised now! Go out into an uncertain world? Not likely! It quickly decided that with all these great changes afoot it would be far better off staying inside, at least until the situation had been clarified, so it fastened on to the wall of its tube and hunkered down.

Meanwhile, nobody had told the lone spermatozoon about the quark. It was just wandering around at the bottom of the right fallopian wondering if it shouldn't have gone up the left-hand one with the others when Jennifer's period began and she started to eject the detritus of another menstrual cycle. This disorientated the little spermatozoon so much that when the tempest was over and, by some miracle, it had survived, it decided to stay put for a while and recover its strength.

Jennifer's next two cycles were cancelled, as the body felt that it needed to make an example of the fallopian tubes and penalise them for having let one of their cells break the news to the ovum, so the ovum and the spermatozoon were left undisturbed for a couple of months. And while they were both sitting there it just so happened that a large dose of cosmic radiation that had been travelling for aeons from some distant galaxy streamed through Jennifer's body, causing mild chromosomal mutation in these two somewhat disoriented little gametes (inversion in the ovum, translocation in the sperm).

Then Joel's semen was injected into the situation and Judd's one surviving spermatozoon thought it had better get moving. Meanwhile, back at the top of the tube, the ovum had been persuaded that life must go on (the body had made the case to it that quantum uncertainty only held on the sub-atomic scale and that the traditional heuristic values of truth could still be maintained in the macro environment). With a heightened sense of its own importance (it now regarded itself as the world's first philosophically adept egg) it began to move on down; there was a spermatozoon waiting, the cilia had said. With Joel's spermatozoa fast bearing down on them, the ovum and Judd's spermatozoon crept closer and closer together. The little sperm knew full well that if it was discovered by the enemy hordes they would destroy it immediately, so it thrashed upwards with all the force it could muster. It caught sight of the ovum up ahead just as the first of Joel's spermatozoa rounded the bend behind it, gaining fast. Judd's sperm swam as fast as it could but little by little the Joelean leader drew level. Side by side they raced the last few millimetres towards the ovum. But the ovum had not detected them yet. It was far too busy thinking about how important it was, carrying the torch of the body and the unconscious out into this uncertain new world. It completely forgot about its sacred duty to let one sperm in and one alone. When the two spermatozoa arrived and burst through the vitelline membrane together, their flagella practically entwined, it was a moment or two before the ovum realised just what was going on. And by then it was too late: the haploid nuclei of the three gametes had already started to fuse together (helped by another handy burst of cosmic radiation) and the ovum's identity was lost in the flux as it and the two spermatozoa became a zygote. In a normal human embryo this process takes about a day, but having three gametes involved complicates everything and it was two days before the new nucleus underwent mitosis.

The process of mitosis, or cell division, begins when the chromosomes in the new nucleus start to duplicate themselves. Long threads of these duplicates coil into close spirals, shortening and thickening as they do so.

The nuclear membrane dissolves and a spindle forms, with the chromosomes attaching themselves to its centre. They pause for a while in this position, then the duplicates move towards either end of the spindle. At the same time the spindle elongates and when the two sets of chromosomes are a sufficient distance apart they begin to uncoil. New nuclear membranes form around them, and eventually both spindle and chromosomes disappear, leaving two cells with their own nucleoli, which in turn start to divide.

Now that this processes had begun, the fallopian tube gasped a sigh of relief and pumped the expanding cell mass down into the uterus, where it fixed itself on to the uterine wall and continued to grow. But the complications experienced during fertilisation had a knock-on effect and every cell was taking longer to divide than it should have done. It was a full two weeks before the blastocyst appeared, and two months before the embryo reached the stage achieved by a fertilised bird's egg in three and a half days.

The human genome does not operate like a computer program – it is not a straightforward set of instructions which are faithfully followed. Rather, the genes work in ensembles (cistrons), and act in multi-dimensional inter-connected circuits that include cis-acting regulatory elements (which influence nearby genes on the same chromosome using various promoters and operators, hormone-responsive elements, chromatin-folding domains and facultative heterochromatin) and trans-acting elements (which influence distant genes belonging to other chromosomes by creating diffusible products such as RNA, proteins and metabolites) (Kauffman, 1993). This means that the project of isolating the gene for a particular type of human behaviour (the gene for crime, the gene for homosexuality) is fundamentally misconceived. Rather, the tangle of genes and regulatory products – in effect a sparsely connected network – creates a kind of dynamic arena in which cells can form, and within this arena are various basins, or attractors, towards which the behaviour of the network tends. Each of these attractors is a motor for producing a different type of cell, and whereas the normal human genome has two hundred and fifty-four of them, Jennifer's mutated genome had cathected two more and so had two hundred and fifty-six. If the genome, then, is like a computer at all, it resembles less a Universal Turing Machine, which processes information in a serial fashion, than a dynamic Boolean network (or parallel processor, or neural network), in which a collection of inter-linked switches process information in concert by altering their behaviour according to that of their neighbours, rather like a flock of birds or a swarm of bees.

In the genome network each cell type is one of the possible outputs of the system. As it forms, each receives information from the surrounding cells via their regulatory elements, and structures its future differentiation and mitotic behaviour accordingly. Different cells receive different information and develop different characteristics. To a degree, the mechanism is an oppressive one: any cell is capable of an extraordinary range of functions, but in the genome system the peer pressure exerted upon each individual by its neighbours means that it promotes one particular function and specialises in it, to the neglect of all the others.

Having three sets of genetic material within, the blastocyst which was to become the daughter of Jennifer, Judd and Joel produced rather more cells of a rebellious variety than was usual, but the end effect was pretty much the same: as more and more cells were produced they formed themselves according to type into spatially ordered arrays which eventually would become tissues and organs.

Even at this stage, though, the DNA inside the cells is not doing all the work. The shape of the organs (and indeed of the cells themselves) depends to a large extent upon certain fundamental features of polymer chemistry. Surface tension, gravity, pressure, all these things play a role, as do occasional cascades through the system of regulating variables (once cells form into the sheets that make up tissue they continue to act as regulatory networks) and the fact that dissipative chemical systems of any kind can – if they have the appropriate activation and inhibition mechanisms – spontaneously order their components into spatially ordered patterns such as stripes, spots or zigzags. These patterns are called Turing patterns, again after Alan Turing, Henry's friend from Bletchley Park, who was the first person to model them.

After about twenty weeks the embryo became a foetus and the macroscopic effects of the extra genetic material and the chromosomal mutations in the gamete stage began to become apparent: the child had two hearts (one dominant, positioned in the left-hand upper chest cavity, and one subsidiary, positioned slightly lower and to the right), a slightly elongated skull, and a new gland in the brain that was growing out of the pineal apparatus and which housed two novel types of neuron.

7

In which ego battles superego

'Do you miss her?' That was the first question Dr Schemata asked Judd. By way of reply the boy stared rather blankly at the wall. A Kandinsky hung there, stark and prime. 'How often do you think of her?' the analyst continued. 'Come on, Judd, I'm here to help you. Do I frighten you? If I frighten you, tell me, and we'll see what we can do about it, shall we?' Judd kicked his heels on the floor and thought of the swings in the playground on the edge of a town six thousand miles away. Schemata addressed himself to Moses, who was still in the room. 'Perhaps you had better leave us, Mr Axelrod. It might be a better idea if Judd and I spoke man to man from the start.' Moses nodded a slightly hesitant approval and allowed the doctor to guide him from his chair and out of the door. The doctor's polyester flares swished together as he walked, making a quiet whipping sound. 'I know you understand,' he said to Judd's father earnestly. The dark man was several inches taller than Schemata and almost twice his body weight. 'Make yourself comfortable here in the waiting room. Ms Klixen!' He called for his assistant, one leg stuck straight out into the air behind him to counterbalance his body, the weight of which was supported only by the friction of his right palm against the burgundy leather panelling of the open door. The woman appeared from around the corner. 'Ah, Ms Klixen. See if Mr Axelrod would like some coffee, would you?'

The doctor smiled at Moses and vanished back inside his office, easing the door to behind him with an oh-so-careful *whupp*. Moses watched as the handle was turned back into position from the inside, rather than simply released.

'How would you like your coffee?' Ms Klixen's voice was loud in his ear. She was very close. He turned to her and found himself gazing into her cleavage, for all his height. Her perfume gripped his nostrils and prevented him from turning away. It was a very fine cleavage, and it was a moment or two before he pulled himself together and managed to come up with an answer.

He grinned at her, looked her in the eye. 'Black as night and twice as dark,' he said.

Returning to his desk, Schemata began again. 'OK, Judd, it's just you and me now. Just you and me. I want to make it clear that whatever you tell me goes no further than the inside of these four walls. And they don't have ears, I can promise you that. No one else will ever know of the conversations that you and I may have. Not your father, not your mother, not anyone. Do you understand that?'

Judd managed a nod. He suddenly wished for bangs, for hair that he could tip forward and hide behind. But his tightly curled fuzz stood up on end and all he had to help him dissemble in the face of the cold gaze of this peculiar man were the coffee-coloured pigments of his skin, a defence he would need to call upon again and again as the next few minutes turned into days, and as those into months, which would in their turn stretch first into seasons and then into years in a way, sitting here now, that he could neither expect nor imagine.

Nor could he foresee how those years would be ticked off by the minute hand of his visits to Schemata and how his life would be ruled by a temporality quite different from that of the majority of his peers. For the gregarious rhythms of his childhood were about to be stalled and Judd would be geared up instead into that calculated zone of adult time which charts the globe with a regime founded on clockwork, migrated into quartz. In 1714 the British Government's Board of Longitude did far more for their country's expansionist cause than many a military division: by offering a prize for the construction of a portable chronometer – a prize won by John Harrison of Hull in 1763 – they managed to subsume even the leavening doughs of the day beneath the drifting structures of their empire so that it too could be specified, ordered, digitised, filed. It was this order which Judd had unknowingly transgressed and to which he would now be made to conform.

'How often do you masturbate?' Schemata asked. Judd had never thought to count. Schemata had him by the balls, so to speak. 'OK, try this one. What do you think of when you masturbate?' Sugar and spice and all things nice. 'Of what do you dream?' Of mountains and horses and bees and blood and packs of hot wolves all acid at the edges. Sometimes the moon, sometimes red rooms with dark gables so high that all smoke is lost. Laughs and doors and words in white bubbles. Batman, the Joker, school desks, nakedness at the end of long corridors, doors opening on to rooms of peering folk. Catwoman, punishment. The soft washes of the sea. Into the forest, into the trees. Control. 'Ah hah!' Schemata licked his lips and formed his fingers into a temple. 'What thoughts do you have regarding your mother?' Judd crying, very upset. 'Your mother is an actress, is she not? Quite a famous actress. I have never met her, but we deal with many actresses here and I believe I have seen several of her films. Do you like her films?' He never thought about it, he didn't know. He thought of his mother, of his last week in England, of whispers strained voices behind closed doors, of odd words and phrases seeping down to him from the adult world, Jennifer's name, his mother crying, his father hissing. How had he sat during those conversations? With one hand always touching at his nostril lip cheek, the other clutched in the warm space between his tightly closed thighs while outside the window the heavy Midlands clay rolled away in low hills until it met far off with the thick, low sky, a sky that seemed to shave the chimney pots off the houses, a sky so weak it almost seemed to rely on the upper branches of the trees and the slate-grey village steeples for support. Nothing at all like the sky he'd longed for, a sky so high and round that the greatest towers in the world could rise to challenge it and yet never make a mark, so high that even when great basin smogs hovered for days across the city it was still there if you scrambled high enough up in the hills to find it, high up through spinneys of Californian pine and cedar, high up past the millionaire lots with their half-finished houses which pinned back the boulevards that crept up the hillsides beneath you, tentacles of tarmac, oily and broad.

It did not take Judd long to decide that he did not like this doctor Schemata. He quickly learned to fear him, too. His father approached this man with caution, and his father did not approach *anybody* with caution.

'I've been reading a little Freud,' said Moses brightly at the beginning of the next session. 'Thought I'd try to keep up.'

'Oh, no one reads Freud any more,' Schemata said curtly.

'But I was under the impression that you were a neo-Freudian. Is that not correct?'

'Of course it is. Exactly why we no longer read him,' replied the doctor darkly. 'This isn't nineteenth-century Vienna we're living in. Things have moved on.' Browbeaten, Moses thought he'd probably better move on as well; he stuffed his hands into his pockets and retreated into the waiting-room, where he hoped he would be consoled by Ms Klixen, Ms Klixen's coffee and Ms Klixen's cleavage. But Ms Klixen was not particularly interested in being consoling. She was engrossed in a telephone call, strains of which Moses caught as he thumbed through the magazines that had been strewn carefully across the low marble coffee table. Bored, he lit a cigarette, the paper crackling up as he inhaled. Ms Klixen finished on the telephone.

'Ms Klixen? Er, excuse me Ms Klixen, but do you think I could have a cup of your fine black coffee?' But, for whatever reason, Ms Klixen ignored him. He got up and wandered over to her desk, where he repeated the question in a lower voice.

Now she looked up brightly, too brightly. 'Why, of course Mr Axeljob, I'll get you one right away. You take it white, ain't that right?'

He took it in his stride; it was an opener. 'No, black, if that's OK.' He smiled his best, most sweetest smile. 'Though I do enjoy a touch of cream now and again. And it's Axel*rod*.' Ms Klixen returned his gaze as coldly as she could and left her desk to go to the coffee machine, smoothing her skirt as she went. Moses was convinced he had caught the merest glimmer in her stare and strolled back over to the white leather sofas well satisfied. The room was really two rooms of approximately equal size that had been knocked into one larger space. Some of the dividing wall remained in the form of an arch, each side of which was still solid partition. Thus there were certain areas in Moses's end of the room – which contained the grey marble coffee table, the white sofas, the magazines and a yucca plant – that formed blind spots with regard to certain areas in Ms Klixen's half – which contained the reception desk, the coffee machine and the hatstand. From his position on one of the sofas Moses could hear but not see Schemata's assistant pouring out the coffee. After a moment he heard her replace the pot on the stand and click over the wooden floor towards him in her heels, the cup and saucer rattling in her perfect and efficient little hand. She came through the arch and he looked up and smiled. Then, as she rounded the coffee table, she turned her heel and stumbled. The hot coffee sloshed over and out of the china cup and down to where Moses's long left leg lay extended alongside the coffee table.

'Jesus Christ!' Moses screamed, leaping to his feet.

Ms Klixen immediately started fussing. 'Oh Mr Axeljob! I'm soooo sorry, let me get you a napkin, oh, I'm sooo sorry, I'd made it black for you as well, oh, I do hope it hasn't ruined your suit.' Moses tried to hold the scalding fabric of his trousers away from his leg, but by the time the woman returned the coffee had cooled enough to allow him to divert his attention from the pain and take the opportunity to brush the assistant's breasts with the back of his hand as he reached across her to take the cloth which she had brought him.

Once back in his seat, a fresh cup of coffee before him and Ms Klixen safely back behind the fortifications of the reception desk, Moses turned again to the magazines. He picked up the latest *National Geographic* and leafed through it, flicking past articles on the oil crisis and British farming techniques, on pictures of deep-sea submarines exploring deep-sea trenches, on diagrams of the new generation of communications satellites, on a jokey report about a scientific cargo cult which apparently believed that Sputnik II was still in orbit, all systems go.

One article that did command his attention focused on a new networked computer system known as the ARPANET. According to the piece, back in the 1950s the US Department of Defense had commissioned the RAND corporation to look into the possibility of designing a computer communications system capable of surviving a nuclear attack. The investigation had concluded that only a network of computers with no central point of control would do the trick, the idea being that by using a collection of interconnected 'nodes' each of which would contain the necessary information to route packets of data to their destination, the system would be flexible enough to continue to operate despite high levels of disruption and damage. The first node had been installed at UCLA in 1969 and at the time of going to press, thirty-six more were in place all over the country.

Sexy, thought Moses, immediately beginning to wonder about the possible commercial applications. He was a marketing man, not an engineer, so to him the possibilities were potentially limitless – not that he could actually think of any right now.

But the magazines couldn't keep Moses's mind off his troubles for long. He found it hard to believe that all this was happening to him, that he was here in an analyst's office waiting for his son. If it had happened to a friend of his he would have laughed in his face, would have thought it so improbable as to be a joke. Older boys were supposed to seduce younger girls for chrissake, not the other way around. And both of them were so young. At Judd's age *he* wasn't thinking about pussy. Was he? He couldn't really remember. But he didn't think that he was. What he did know for a fact was that he was seventeen before he got inside a girl's panties, not *ten*. God, he was jealous. Jealous! Of his kid son. Unreal.

If Melinda hadn't found the drawings and the diary he wouldn't have believed it. He was mostly glad that they had gotten him out of that godforsaken country before anyone had got hold of the story. To have had it splashed all over the press would have ruined Melinda's career and it wouldn't have done his own a lot of good either. The two of them got enough bullshit from every angle because of their marriage; they didn't need this as well. It would really prove all of them right, all the bastards who had sneered, who had said by the looks in their eyes that the two of them would never be able to make it work. What in Christ's name had gotten into Judd's head? When he'd met the girl's father he'd had to fight back the urge to slam him up against the wall of his sad little English house and beat him upside the head. The only reason he'd managed to restrain himself was that the man was such a sorry little fucker that it wasn't worth it, it would have been too easy. He'd towered above Henry as the accountant gasped endless cloudy apologies on the winds of his caustic alcohol breath and desperately tried to focus his rheumy eyes upon one thing, one solid object that wasn't Moses, while Melinda had sat on the edge of a threadbare little sofa and cried. Afterwards she had actually felt sorry for him! Had actually felt pity for this man who couldn't keep his hot, whoring bitch of a daughter under some kind of control.

It was the snake in the grass, the accursed share, the return of the repressed. It was exactly what Moses had slaved all these years to escape. This was the kind of thing that went on in the Projects, where his people lived herded together in crates like cattle, like chattel still. And he had pulled himself up out of it by his own bootstraps, become a (*very*) successful businessman, married a white woman, God bless her. Yes, that's right, a white woman, an actress, not some two-bit hooker out for some black cock but a real successful white woman. Even today, maybe especially today, that was almost impossible to carry off, to make a success out of. And they had held it together all this time, through Melinda's miscarriage, through his mother telling him that he was insulting her in it and through it, they had held it together only to be tripped up in a way that he could never have foreseen.

Yeah. Yeah? *Yeah*! Well this was not going to be a problem. He, Moses Axelrod, was not going to let it be a threat. Like every other problem he had ever had to face – and there had been plenty – this was going to get solved. He had the position, he had the money, it would get solved. *Bang*. Just like that. This Schemata was said to be the best, *bang*, we'll have him, no expense spared. Nylon trousers or no nylon trousers.

Feeling more cheerful, Moses looked up from the magazine and glanced around, started to hum the melody line from Curtis Mayfield's *Futureshock*, which had been released that year. He stubbed out his cigarette in the ashtray but flicked the butt at the yucca plant standing in its white pot in the opposite corner of the room. It thwacked against a leaf and Ms Klixen glanced over. Having thus renewed their relationship, Moses decided to test the limits of the assistant's interest by playing a little game using the sightlines of the office. He stood up and pretended to become absorbed in a series of large abstract artworks which were arranged on the walls. He coughed and moved towards the first of them, contemplated it for a minute or two and quickly crossed the room, shooting a glance at Ms Klixen as he did so. She was not looking at him. He paused briefly to pick up the ashtray from the coffee table, then continued over to the next blind spot where he tipped its contents noisily into a wastepaper bin that had been positioned just behind it. On the other side of the partition Ms Klixen sat and quietly fumed. She was considering how she could make it clear to this man who thought so much of himself that it was he who required psychoanalysis and not his son.

'Ms Klixen,' Moses sang out, 'I believe that your yucca needs repotting. I can recommend an excellent man in Beverly Hills.'

'I don't think that will be necessary, thank you Mr Axeljob. We had it done just this last year.'

Moses moved out of the shadows and stood in front of another picture, his back to the assistant. 'Why is it you insist on mispronouncing my name, Ms Klixen?' It was a bold thrust, but it was deftly parried by the clatter of keys sent forth from Ms Klixen's electric typewriter as she powered her way through a letter.

On this occasion, Moses (ego) is getting the better of Ms Klixen (superego). In order to do this, Moses has established a position by describing the shape of a three-point limit attractor. He holds this position until the system is rendered inflexible by repetition. Thus destabilised, he will begin to move around the room more quickly, gradually converging upon a vulnerable centre.

Moses was moving across to consider another picture when he passed the heavy door which led into the psychoanalyst's office and had a sudden – and uncharacteristic – crisis of confidence. Behind it, what was the doctor saying to Judd? And what – potentially more worrying – was Judd saying to the doctor? Could they separate children from their parents if the parents were deemed unfit? God, had he been a good father? It occurred to him for the first time that a mixed marriage was grist to the mill of blame and suspicion where the social welfare were concerned. What kind of power could be exercised by the man behind the heavy door? He had always felt that he enjoyed a good relationship with his son. They did things together: he took Judd to ball games, they flew kites together on the beach, shot baskets in the yard of an evening. He'd tried to be around as much as he could when he wasn't away on business. But it was still true that he'd had his suspicions that something wasn't quite right with his kid. Melinda liked to think that it was because Judd was special, a cut above as she'd say, but Moses had always thought there was something odd about the way the boy found it hard to pay attention, the way he wandered off on his own, the way he seemed to lose track of time. Hey, he was a good father, he had always taken it for granted that he would be. Shit, he was there more for the poor kid than Melinda was. More likely it was her and her fucked-up Hollywood friends who had done for him. That junky Donna bitch always hanging around and putting ideas into Judd's head. He wouldn't be surprised if the woman had been fooling around with him, that's the kind of sickfuck thing she'd be into. Christ, and she'd recommended this shrink, who was probably in there right now, reprogramming the little sucker!

Ms Klixen stopped her typing and Moses turned round to look.

Then the handle of the heavy door rotated and Dr Hinckley Schemata came out, ushering Judd before him. He beckoned to Moses. 'You wait out here, Judd, your father and I will only be a minute. Ms Klixen, could you look after Judd for me? See if he would like something to drink. Mr Axelrod, could I have a few words?' Ms Klixen tottered over and began to fuss over the boy, demonstrating to Moses that Judd, merely by the nature of his being, merited more attention than his father ever would. Schemata smiled a saccharine smile and held out his arm in a move designed to annex Moses's space and draw him into the surgery. The initiative worked and Moses found himself back in the large room which was now only dimly lit by the little sunlight that filtered through the bank of Venetian blinds which formed a chic backdrop to Schemata's glass Mies Van der Rohe desk. 'Please take the couch Mr Axelrod.'

'No, really, the chair is fine.'

'As you wish, but I would prefer it if you would take the couch.' Moses sat down in the chair. Either way, he realised, he had already been placed at a disadvantage.

The doctor sat behind his desk. With the only source of light now to his rear, his face was almost completely obscured by shadow. His teeth gleamed briefly as he drew back his lips to speak. 'I would just like to ask you a couple of questions, if that's not too much of a bother.'

'Shoot.'

'But before I do, would it be possible for you and your wife both to come and see me at any juncture? I really do need to see the two of you together.'

'That's, er, a little difficult at the moment, I'm afraid. Melinda is working in England right now. She won't be back in LA for at least six months.'

'I see.'

Pause.

'Has Judd ever seen the two of you naked?'

'Sure, when he was younger, I guess. Maybe not for a while.'

'So nudity, while it used not to be a problem, has recently become an issue in your household?'

'Well, I wouldn't say that exactly . . .'

'But at some point you and your wife stopped undressing in front of him?'

'I guess so.'

'Has he ever been present while you and your wife have been engaged in intercourse, Mr Axelrod?'

'Now look, doctor, I don't know what you're getting at . . .'

'I am insinuating nothing, I can assure you. It is a standard question. Please answer it. There is no need, I'm sure, for me to add that this conversation is being conducted in the strictest confidentiality.'

'No.'

'No you will not answer me, or no he has not been a witness to the carnal act?'

'The latter.'

'Are you quite positive?'

Moses looked around the room. Motes of dust journeyed tirelessly through the thin beams of light, glinting satellites set loose from the tug of the planet. To them the habits of the world seemed not to apply, operating as they did without any apparent concession to gravity. 'Maybe, when he was a child. You know, when he was very young, we used to have his crib in our room. We thought he was too young to notice. Do you mind if I smoke?'

'Please. Children are very aware, Mr Axelrod. There is an ashtray to your right. I am not looking to apportion blame.' Moses lit the cigarette with the silver Zippo that Melinda had given Judd to give him for Christmas the previous year. The blue smoke curled upwards in the still air like the smoke from a gun (he thought), winding itself in and out of the rays of light like a creeper scaling a trellis. Driven by the motor of the thermals the smoky orbits trapped flailing motes within their spinning whorls. Took them up, upwards, up, up to the ceiling and the darkness that cowered there.

Moses emerged and blinked in the bright light that flooded the waiting-room. Ms Klixen appeared from around the partition. 'Judd will be just a minute. He is using the bathroom.' She had an expression of triumph on her face, as if she had overheard the men's conversation. Schemata busied himself with some papers that were stacked on the reception desk and Ms Klixen stood and cleaned the leaves of the yucca. Again Moses had to wait, but this time the waiting was no fun: with the doctor there he had no room to manoeuvre. Still smoking, he made the circuit of the artworks once again, forced to look at them properly this time. But there was something threatening about their primary colours and geometric patterns and spiral motifs, and he realised that he really didn't like these pictures and moved across to the window instead.

The slats of the white blinds were tuned to the sun and light flooded through. He lifted his right forefinger to face height and placed it on one of the aluminium ribs, kinking it down as he imagined a private detective or an assassin might do. On the street below almost nothing was happen-ing. Two or three cars rolled by, their tyres squeaking on the asphalt when they turned off the main drag. An old bent man in a brown suit sat beneath his hat on what was left of a broken concrete bench. The afternoon shimmered, threw Moses's gaze back at him. He let the slat unbuckle and return to its remembered shape, but the day still poured through. Turning, he was frightened by the leaves of the yucca, which shone so vividly with the chemical sheen that Ms Klixen had so doggedly applied that he could almost see his face in them. He passed beneath the centre arch, but there was still no sign of Judd. Schemata had disappeared back inside his surgery; Ms Klixen had found some other task with which to engross herself. Returning to the sofas he circled them slowly, running his left hand along the leather backs and smoking with his right.

The bathroom door opened and Judd wandered out, looking lost. 'Dad?'

'OK, son, let's go.' Moses spun into the space between the sofas and leant over the coffee table, stubbing out his cigarette in the ashtray placed at its centre. Then, circumnavigating the furniture for the last time, he beat a path to Judd, whom he took by the hand and led out the door. He muttered to Ms Klixen that she should send the bill on; she ignored him but exuded self-satisfaction none the less.

When they had gone, the room was still. Schemata emerged from behind his door, passed some paperwork to Ms Klixen, then disappeared again. Ms Klixen took an apple and a magazine from her desk and applied herself to both. The yucca nestled in the corner and tasted the air. When it was satisfied that it was alone it began to relax. It flexed its newly polished leaves and slowly stretched them out towards the window. It was not pleased about the cigarette butt lodged among its roots. But there was not a great deal it could do about it.

Tidal action

Several months have passed and things have calmed down. Moses is no longer beating Judd and the child has been synchronised with a routine of school and psychoanalysis and not much else. Despite his magic, Jennifer has receded even further into the distance. But magic, like drugs, has its side effects. There are debts that have to be paid for pulling information from the ether, for creating new possibilities and channelling flows, for reshaping the world with no other tool than desire. Use the television and the television uses you – it takes a part of you, reconfigures you, infects you: you take TV on board. So it was with Judd – the TV was in his life now and he couldn't shake it, even when he switched it off. Idle moments (when Moses wasn't around) were all spent acting out his favourite shows, the house his set. He was a secret agent in action, he crept along a wall, fled up a staircase, the lens always behind him, the audience unable to get a glimpse of his face. Then, *caboom*, he kicks open a door, enters a room (gun in hand, scoping). Exposed, he surveys the scene, the camera still behind him but now seeing what he sees, the audience checking things out as if through his eyes: a neatly made bed, a wardrobe full of clothes, an open door on to a balcony and beyond an abyss. In the room, stuffed animals, many many stuffed animals, on the bed and on the chairs and on the window-sills, watching him, staring back at the lens like a room full of bandits. *Bang! Bang! Bang! Trchrchrchrcht!!*

Caboom!! One by one he takes them out, executing a faultless sequence of bullet dodges as he does so, just like Shaft, or Paul Michael Glaser in *Starsky and Hutch*. 'Yo, Huggy Bear, you got yours, brother!' he calls as Huggy is caught in the cross-fire and falls face down on the floor. Once the room is secured our hero collapses on to the bed, exhausted. Splayed out, eyes closed; the camera moves across the floor and up the divan. As we see the first glimmers of the agent's profile the audience holds its breath. But each time we come in for a closer look his eyes flicker open and we flinch back – he is still suspicious, still on his guard. Then, finally, we swoop round and see him full frontal, his face in repose. He wakes, he blinks, his face twists into a grimace, his mouth lets out an anguished gasp. He fills the screen, twenty feet from chin to brow we feel his pain. Cut to camera two, positioned over by the door: we see that camera one is not a camera at all but another agent. And not just any agent; camera one is our hero's double, the only difference being that over one eye he wears a patch. His face is quietly attentive. Eye meets eyes, self sees self, everything is frozen in this final moment. The shot fades to black, leaving us in the domain of pure terror. This is television. The credits roll.

Back in Stratford, alone in the house on the hill, Melinda had started to drink. Often she'd come back from a show and lie in the pool for half the night, a bottle of gin and a bowl of ice next to her on the tiles, ice slowly melting, gin slowly disappearing, the house in total silence. She wouldn't even have the waterjets on – she couldn't bear the noise, the way they disrupted the surface of the water. The skin-like film of the pool made her feel calm, continuous with this giant meniscus that sucked at her waist and pulled her out into a plane. If she'd erected a psychic structure for herself in the headmaster's office that day the effort of supporting it exhausted her now; she no longer wanted to be monolithic but was desperate instead to collapse, to let herself be saturated and dissolved, to transmute her grand plan into the nets and tracings of bacterial action, into the suck and slide of the tides.

Something had to give. When, weeks later, she crawled out of the pool of chlorine and alcohol, she knew it would be the acting. Let England have it – it had won. It was a worthless prize in any case. She had chosen her husband and her son; she would go back to Los Angeles and slip into an easy life, a new act. Moses made plenty of money, more than enough for them both. They were rich for chrissake. She didn't need to work.

She thought at that moment that it would be fun; that it could, in fact, be delightful. But what she did not realise was that though she would banish the bitterness and hang on to her husband, she had already lost Judd. Unable to place trust in herself she'd relinquished responsibility before she'd had time to think, at the moment she had passed him over into the welcoming arms of Dr Hinckley Schemata.

Spaceman

At the end of each of the countless visits to Schemata's surgery which followed, Judd always made a point of visiting the bathroom. Once safely locked inside he would stand up on the toilet seat and look himself all over in the mirror, as if to check that he was all still there, that he had not left any part of himself behind in the doctor's consulting room. Despite the hours that he had spent in there it still seemed as if there were areas of it that he did not know, could never know. The room was always so dimly lit that the walls appeared not to join at the corners but to bend outwards and stretch away for ever, like the warp drive portals in *Star Trek*. Judd would lie on the analysand's couch, the nexus of these gateways, and stare up into the gloom, wishing he could find his communicator and instruct Scotty to beam him up out of there.

But after a while he got used to Schemata. Occasionally it would even seem as though the analyst was not in the room with him at all. He would lie there and recite his thoughts and dreams without even thinking about it, giving voice to whatever bubbled up from his memory, reconstructing the experiences with whatever shapes and tools were at hand. Thus a dream which, the first time around, might have been coloured in shades of grey with limey lights and odd gasps of red here and there would be remembered in sharp black and white. Or characters from old dreams, long ago, folks who lived down there and never normally saw the light of day, would surface and take shape among the heaving flows of Judd's imagination, only to speak with the doctor's voice when they finally emerged. Sometimes things he'd never known came together for him, right before him, and he told Schemata those too because in the end it was all the same.

By then the consulting room no longer seemed one simple space. Not only was it strung out, extended and suspended like a gob of spit hanging from a railing, like an amoeba beginning to divide, like an axon laced across a cortex, like a starship stretching into hyperspace, but its component parts – Judd on couch, Schemata at desk, filtered light, mahogany bookcase, another yucca – had internal coherence but little apparent relationship to one another. Each object seemed to float in its own universe and be subject to its own laws, the fractal boundaries of each mini cosmos vying with those of its neighbour like crosswaves in a harbour. The combined effect of his father's disapproval, his mother's hysteria and Schemata's probings had made Judd fear the escape hatch of his childhood, despise the strange realm of dilated time that he'd disappeared into every day, and it got to the stage where he was terrified to step down on to the floor at the end of each session lest he slip through and back into the picnoleptic experience and keep falling for ever. There was too much freedom in there, he didn't understand it, he wasn't to go there any more; so whenever he entered the consulting room he would wait at the door until Schemata's back was turned, then close his eyes and run for the comparative safety of the couch lest the monsters that lurked in those interzones grab him by the ankles and pull him screaming under.

As for Hinckley Schemata, he could never quite understand why it was that Judd seemed so keen to get on with it. No sooner had he crossed the room to sit at his desk than the boy was prone and passive on the couch, if a little tense. None of his other patients was this pliable; most of them liked to play out some little head game before the session 'officially' began, although, as Schemata occasionally smirked to himself, the session began as soon as they opened the door to his office, even if they often did not realise it. But while he had the upper hand on the majority of his patients, there were a couple who were playing a double bluff. The tactic of these two women was to give the analyst the illusion of control, letting him think of them as foolish neurotics who doted upon his guiding light, in order to use him for sex. After all, it was so much cleaner and more respectable than trawling hotels and singles bars for a gigolo, and it had the added bonus that their husbands were happy to pay for it. Schemata would have been horrified to discover that these two ladies knew each other and often compared notes.

Judd, on the other hand, became something of a test ground for his theories. *It's all in the way the patient's fantasy life is structured. If this is askew, life itself will be askew. If it is straight and pure, life itself will follow. Life always follows fantasy. Making fantasy perfect, this is what we need to do.* If this was his goal, the doctor achieved it almost by accident. Because

208

lying there, his own voice lost in the darkness, his sight disembodied, Judd learned to be afraid of the way the objects around him were dispersed and stretched out in this manifold, curved, relativistic space, which outwitted global order. He came to rely upon the voice of the analyst to orientate him, to give him some kind of certainty, and thus was turned to Schemata's will because the man's sotto voce tone was the only thing which filled the room and linked one point to another. In this manner that Riemannian surgery, the last remnant of Judd's picnoleptic imagination, was transformed into a nice Euclidean cube: linear, logical, x, y and z.

By the end of the second year Judd was convinced that what he had done was wrong. By the end of the third, he knew that it both was and was not his fault. It took him a further twelve months to come to understand that he was split into parts that wanted, parts that were to be trusted and parts that held it all together, and by the end of that fourth year the Judd who had been all on one plane, who had ebbed and flowed, was no more and in his place there was a new Judd, a Judd–Schemata, a Judd who had hidden depths and dizzy heights and common sense and *feelings*, feelings that had been precipitated out from actions, reified and abstracted. Oh, the agonies and the joys! This new Judd thought for a while that he might like to grow up to be an analyst like Schemata and did not notice how his father's eyes looked sad when he told him this over dinner one evening. For this new Judd spent his whole time looking after the structures that had been erected inside him.

In this phase of things Judd discovered earnestness. He became 'serious' and 'involved with things'. The analysis had made him feel mature beyond his years and more 'experienced' than his peers. At school he got himself a reputation for being aloof. He now looked upon his early sexual activities as having enabled a leap in his development; he understood that he had 'jumped the queue' in growing up, as Melinda would put it when she was feeling sympathetic, which these days was most of the time.

Annoyed that he had lost control of his son, Moses began to nag him. What was he going to do with his life? If he didn't think that being a businessman like his father was good enough he'd better start studying hard – it was no easy task being a doctor, especially if you were black. Had he thought about this? He hadn't done so well in his exams this semester. Did he think he was good enough? In a white world you couldn't afford to take on something and then fail – coloured people got no second chances. Judd should take a leaf out of his book – know your limitations, decide what you can achieve, then do it. No looking back, no second thoughts. Did he think he was good enough? Did he? His results didn't look too hot. Was he letting his concentration drift again? Did he have any idea how much his analysis cost? Four or five kids from the Projects could be put through school on what he paid Schemata. He hoped Judd appreciated it.

In times gone by Judd would have let it all drift over him – maybe that's how Moses had got to be this way, because before it hadn't made any difference. But now it did, he took it all to heart, let it make a turmoil in his brain. He got so guilty, it all got mixed up with his colour, Pop was right, he didn't do so well at school, maybe he wasn't so bright. The precociousness he'd experienced for a while back there gradually melted away and he was left with a clutch of insecurities that clattered around his head, rusty mechanisms driving a shooting gallery full of rotating and accepted desires: steady job, consumer goods, good name, nice neighbourhood, maybe a wife (if he kept quiet about the transgressions of his youth).

Melinda stood by, trying to convince herself that this is what she'd wanted. This is what they'd paid for, right?

The seventies were drawing to a close. Both Viking landers had reached Mars and the first pictures of the surface of a planet which was not our own were circulating in the news. A test-tube baby had been born and genetic engineering was a household concept. The Voyager probes were on their way to Jupiter. Judd, still interested in space exploration, plotted their progress through the void. Pioneer, he noted, was nearing Saturn. Saturn is a very long way away. It's dark out near Saturn, dark and cold.

Somewhere high above the earth, Laika howled.

8

School's a beach

For Jennifer, on the other hand, the seventies were far from over. After they had met up with Joel, she and Henry stayed in Geneva for a further six weeks, then Henry began to feel that he had been away from the office long enough. Not only that, but the school year was about to begin and while he had the greatest faith in Joel's tutoring skills he felt that two hours of maths a day was not going to compensate for his daughter missing any more class, especially as on her return she was to start at a new school.

Jennifer supervised the packing, a complex affair due to the amount of shopping they had done over the summer and the gifts that had been heaped on them by the old family friends whom Henry had insisted they visit. She remembered them vaguely as a repetitive series of smooth-skinned Swiss spinsters and robust couples with grown-up children all of whom lived in well-furnished and supple apartments, which, had they been people, would have been ski instructors or tennis stars. Henry would force her to wear one of her 'best' outfits, usually a razor-creased skirt and a fussy blouse and perhaps a jacket to match that gave her difficulty breathing. But she enjoyed it in a way, it was a kind of dressing up, and the clothes made her feel professional and efficient and conspicuously adult (though exactly for this reason slightly ridiculous at the same time). The paradox was emphasised by the patronising way in which her hosts invariably addressed her, with their high-bourgeois determination to take even a thirteen-year-old seriously. They would ask her terribly dull questions in clipped and perfect English, their words shaped by a determination that was frightening, while she sat on some uncomfortable, overstuffed chair with her legs together (an unusual occurrence, she thought to herself), answering with an affected shyness which she hoped hid her boredom, and feeling like a prat.

The dismalness of the whole experience was always accentuated by the fact that Henry hardly knew most of these people himself. The older ones had been his parents' friends, shadowy 'aunts' and 'uncles' whom even as a child he had known only vaguely, the younger ones his playmates of those pre-war lakeside summers, and the meetings were always tainted with the forced atmosphere that attends reunions between old friends who no longer have anything in common. All interaction would take place on a rarefied plane of politeness so awkwardly constructed that conversation could at best take faltering steps and could certainly never flow. Jennifer was often treated by the grown-ups as a lubricant with which to oil the gears of this intercourse but it was a tactic which was rarely effective. Part of the problem was that everybody had always to be seen to be in command of the situation. At least she could not understand them when they talked tactfully with Henry in French or German about how terrible it had been about her mother.

It struck Jennifer as odd, when she emptied the toiletries out of the cabinet in the bathroom, that the packet of tampons she had brought with her from England had not yet been opened. Her periods had begun around the time she'd lost her virginity but Henry, of course, had not thought to educate her on the subject at all and her school had not been much better. The first time she saw herself bleeding she thought she had hurt herself inside, that it was a result of letting Rever penetrate her. Suddenly all that they had drummed into her at school about God, about good, about purity seemed as if it might be true and she thought for several terrifying weeks that God was punishing her for her actions, especially when the bleeding recurred a month later. She felt terribly alone in a way that she hadn't before, even at those moments when she missed her mother. Then she read something about the phenomenon of the stigmata and this got muddled in her mind with what was happening to her, and for the next month she wondered if she were perhaps a saint, whether the bleeding was God's call. Several times she went by the convent school and hid in the trees overlooking their grounds, watched the girls come out in their straw boaters and gloves and neat little tailored outfits, and imagined that that's what would happen to her if anyone should find out about her holy nature. But the more she looked into it the less the idea of being a saint appealed to her, especially when she went into the local church and looked up at them writhing away for eternity in their stained-glass flames. These images disenchanted her so much that she decided to search for a more prosaic explanation. She found a medical encyclopaedia in the school library, but since she did not know the correct biological terms for the parts of the body which were troubling her she had little luck until thanks to the signatures of wear the book fell open on pictures of a naked couple with accompanying anatomical diagrams. The genitalia had been heavily censored by some bowdlerising librarian, then thickly annotated by the many subsequent readers, but fortunately for Jennifer, despite a few crude sketches and various scribbled words and arrows, the cross-sections of the plastic-looking 'internal workings' and their accompanying text remained legible, and she learnt enough to be able to reject her religious theories.

Once her shame had evaporated she felt able to approach one of the few teachers whom she liked and the woman had the sense to tell her how to look after herself. She also gave her a book to read on the subject and a packet of sanitary towels. What Jennifer remembered as remarkable about these events was that they seemed to mark – by way of the triangulations formed between the physicality of her sexual encounters and the blood that ran from her, her loneliness and her fear and awe of a vengeful, then ridiculous, God, and her discovery of a new set of words that adults used among themselves – the expanded moment in which she first began to think of herself as a discrete person, distinct from those around her, with a shape and momentum all her own. She was fascinated, too, by the way in which her coming of age was linked in to the phases of the moon and the tides, as if adulthood, womanhood, tied you into the rhythms of the whole world, ending the isolation of childhood.

Then, that summer in Geneva, the periods had stopped and she hadn't confronted the fact until she'd found the unopened packet of tampons, partly because she still hadn't become fully attuned to the rhythms of her menstrual cycle and also because she'd pushed the disagreeable thought to the back of her mind that day by the lake. She had worried about it on the train back to London and absent-mindedly bitten her nails down to the quick, but by the time they'd got back home to Stratford (at which point Henry had noticed her fingers and told her to stop) she'd buried the topic and it ceased to concern her. She had decided – with that absolute finality of judgement that mars all logic and marks out the limits of its usefulness – that she was not pregnant and that there was another explanation. After all, the book Mrs Giddens had given her said that periods could often be erratic in early puberty. Once one potentially frightening situation had been discovered to be merely normal, others could quickly be assumed to be that way too. It was an easy trick to learn.

★

Finding another school for Jennifer had been a complex business. In theory, the comprehensive could not expel her, but Mrs Craven, the new headmistress, felt rather strongly that it would be best for her if Henry found her a place somewhere else.

'It is not simply the good of the school we are considering here, Mr Several,' Craven hummed, 'but the best interests of Jennifer, and of course those of the other children. I'm sure you appreciate how difficult it could become for her should she stay on here. Children can be merciless, you know, once they get wind of the fact that somebody is a little different.' Henry gazed around the office as she spoke, only looking at her when she rose to refill his glass with cream sherry. Two of the room's walls were shelved and covered with box files; the third was smothered with timetables, all meticulously written out by hand. The fourth was taken up by a large, classroom-style window, the lower panels of which were filled with frosted glass, opaque as the meeting he was having. Craven recorked the bottle and returned to her seat, tucking her skirt modestly under her arse as she sat down to face him across the great expanse of her tidy desk. She looks like a newsreader, thought Henry to himself as he sipped at the sickly liquid she'd poured for him.

When he told Jennifer that evening that Mrs. Craven thought the best thing would be to try and persuade the convent school to take her she burst into tears and screamed at him, 'I won't go, I won't go, I won't, you can't make me go there!' Henry lost his temper and reminded Jennifer in no uncertain terms that it was in fact her fault that he was now going to have to start paying for her education. Not only that, but it was an opportunity which many girls would jump at – she should be grateful. She retorted that she couldn't go to that awful school because she didn't believe in God, and if he tried to make her go she'd telephone the headmistress and tell her in great detail exactly why it was that she was being expelled from the comprehensive. Henry told her that she wasn't being expelled, that she was leaving because everyone agreed that it was in her own best interests to do so. She called him a sap. He went red at this point and although he tried to remonstrate with her further it was pretty clear to both of them that once again he had lost. Jennifer ended up being sent to St Anne's, a small public school for girls a little further away than the convent, but which ran its own special school bus that she could catch from Stratford High Street. Henry was secretly relieved because the fees at St Anne's were rather less than those at the convent and the uniform was cheaper too. And he didn't believe in God, either.

At the new school she was treated very differently. The other pupils, infected with the half-baked prejudices of their parents, sneered at her for the most part – and feared her too because she had been to a comprehensive. Most of the girls were fair but Jennifer was dark and slightly swarthy, and her eyes had a fire in them that the washed-out moonstones and opals around her could only reflect (or so she liked to tell herself). The teachers took a great deal of trouble over learning her name, sitting her in the correct place in the class, helping her to Fit In. Whenever anyone asked her what she would like to do she simply said maths, and she covered all her exercise books in largely meaningless figures and invented algebraic formulae. Since none of the other girls could even imagine *wanting* to do maths, this set her apart further still.

She still saw some of her old friends after school, though not as much as she would have liked as she now had to do a great deal of homework, but they too had become suspicious of her and would make occasional remarks about her being too posh to keep company with the likes of them. This hurt. Her first term was one of the quietest, most solitary periods of her life and it set the pattern for what was to come. Most of the time she felt neither happy nor sad and had nothing to say to anyone. During break times she sat alone on the benches skirting the playing fields – much larger and grander than those at the comprehensive – and gazed vacantly out over this pale beach at the ocean of cabbages that filled the farmland beyond. She thought of her mother a lot and fantasised about what she had been like. She wondered too about her real father, whose skin and hair she bore (her mother had been fair, like these dainty St Anne's girls), about who he was and what he was like, and whether she could regard what he'd done as a crime, since she was the result.

Her periods had most definitely stopped and she'd put on some weight, despite not wanting to eat in the limbo which was her life in this place. Like a wary Proserpina she was conscious that every mouthful swallowed would bind her closer to the new school, almost as if the school was a mycorrhizal fungus that was offering her nutrients in exchange for a symbiotic relationship from which she would never escape. She wanted to resist, but her appetite had increased in inverse proportion to her desire and she found herself ravenously hungry almost continually; like the Cambrian algae devoured by the first metazoic predators, she was being forced up on to the shore where, like her mother before her, she would be faced with the choice of extinction or of finding some way of becoming plant. The land, so tempting when she'd only regarded the part of it that was Judd's skin, was proving somewhat harder to colonise than she'd imagined.

If anything, the food was worse than at the comp but she ate her portions greedily and took left-overs from the plates of her peers, whose delicate stomachs had been raised on mother's cosmopolitan home cooking and the à la carte menus of restaurants. For this they hated her even more, called her *dustbin*, *pig*, were disgusted that she should so relish what they regarded as little more than slop (and they were right, it was little more than slop). Lunch-time was for them a chore: they pushed the food around their plates and felt nauseous, all the time discussing fashion and dieting and how – like their mothers, whom they both hated and admired – they had to keep an eye on their weight.

Fun is bathing in steel

October was dreary and the drizzle seeped through the days as they segued into winter. Even the trees dropped their leaves half-heartedly, tired of waiting for the sun – which seemed to have retired hurt into the dismal sump of clouds that sulked for ever on the winds – to turn them to their proper auburns, bronzes, golds. Foliage became mulch while still on the branch. The summer and the winter proper both seemed as far away as if they were figments half remembered from a book. The girls all moaned constantly and some of them began to talk about their skiing holidays, and Jennifer found herself thinking that she, too, would like a skiing holiday. But she didn't think it wise to ask Henry if she could have one.

Then the winter came and stayed. She and Henry weren't talking much. He had shown an interest in the new school for a while and was especially taken with the way that Jennifer looked in her crisp new uniform, but once term was underway his interest waned. Apart from a few sessions in Geneva he had managed to cut back on his drinking – ever since that night, in fact, when he had told Jennifer what she should never have known – but by Christmas his intake was up again. His business affairs had not recovered properly from the neglect they had suffered over the summer and the other partners were starting quietly to manoeuvre any sensitive clients out of his care.

He and Jennifer spent the festive season with some cousins from the north-west, the closest family the two of them had. Henry had been an only child, as had his father, while his mother had a sister who'd married a Liverpudlian shipping clerk, a union which had produced two children roughly Henry's age. It had become a kind of ritual for them all to spend at least one weekend a year in each other's company.

Henry spent most of the holiday tipsy and Jennifer spent most of it disaffected, a new mode she was testing out with the intention of using it back at St Anne's in order to cultivate herself a reputation as an existential outsider. On Boxing Day she made a half-hearted attempt to seduce one of her cousins, a ginger-haired boy called Geoffrey who was two years her senior, but he was completely oblivious to her advances and kept pushing her away, preferring to play with his new Scalextric by day and his new telescope by night. He used the latter to scan the skies for satellites and on one occasion tracked Laika for an hour, although neither of them knew it.

It was the same story with most of the teenagers Jennifer was meeting now. The other girls at St Anne's were clean and delicate, and shocked even by the thought of masturbation, let alone the fact of intercourse. Yet all of them were fascinated by their maturing flesh and the onset of menstruation. The handful who had kissed a boy wore the experience like a medal. For the first time in her life Jennifer began to fear notoriety, something which she had hitherto always revelled in (and considered unimportant) and so she kept quiet about her past. The other girls with their giggles and their blushes made her feel unclean and she began to be embarrassed about her body in the changing rooms. She felt that stigma hung around her in the form of an invisible but still perceptible mist; she could see her classmates shiver with the dampness they felt when they came too close. They began to tease her about her weight and she became terrified that they would discover that her periods had stopped, so she made sure she carried towels in her bag the first week of every month and wore them on days when they had Games.

The feeling of being tainted slowly ate into her, until she carried it with her even when she was away from St Anne's. With it came guilt, which had always been alien to her but which she wore now like a mantle, a heavy fur which bent her and insulated her, warmed her and disgusted her. As the spring rolled in and her father slipped further and further into his whisky blend of blurred lights and memories of what might have been, she started torturing herself with the idea that his decline was her fault, that she, by dint of her very existence, was a constant reminder to him of her mother's madness and rape.

Her breasts ballooned and she grew taller, but at the same time she started to stoop. For the first time, she thought herself ugly. When spring evaporated into a short, tense summer full of foul winds and bad moods, she was as alone as she had been in the autumn but could not shake the feeling that someone was constantly with her, peering over her shoulder.

The summer – which seemed to her in retrospect like a small, dry scab on a wet graze of a year – came and went quickly, and at the end of it Jennifer put on yet more weight. She put it down to her dread of returning to St Anne's but in the mornings as she walked to the bus she was often overcome with bouts of extreme queasiness. Two or three times a week she would wake before the autumn dawn had begun its slow limp over the horizon and sit up in bed clutching at her stomach, the two thin bars of the electric fire a hot grimace in the darkness of her room. Comics, magazines, chocolate wrappers lay strewn across the covers, left from the night before when racing thoughts had kept her from her sleep. Soon she found it impossible to eat breakfast, throwing up whatever she did manage to force down for the sake of appearances.

Because she'd be bound to meet a crowd of the comp kids, ex-friends among them, she began to hate the walk to the bus-stop even more than the school day which lay ahead. The previous year's taunting and the jibes about being posh were nothing compared with the silence they met her with now – it meant she was just another St Anne's girl and therefore merited nothing but resentment. In her most depressed moments she sometimes wished that Henry had made her go to the convent; at least then she'd only have been laughed at.

In one of her magazines she read about anorexia nervosa and she thought she had caught this like a disease off one of the girls at school and that this was why she ate chocolate at night and then vomited in the morning. Eating disorders, the article had said, disrupted the menstrual cycle and Jennifer assumed that this must be why she still hadn't had a period. She'd lost all interest in sex, but Judd and Joel were in her thoughts constantly, like ghouls.

Maths was now her best subject and she still structured her comprehension of the numbers and their fields around the vivid, simple concepts Joel had sketched for her during those tutorials in Geneva. But she kept catching Judd's face out the corner of her eye, seeing his profile in the fold of a uniform or in the shadow of a door, his skin, even darker than she remembered it. She often heard his voice rising out of some general hubbub, calling her name when she was listening to music or standing in the dinner queue or sitting in the main hall waiting for assembly to begin. She missed him and wondered why he hadn't written to her.

When an old mini-series starring Melinda Volitia was repeated on the television she watched it avidly (from her vantage point in the heavens, Laika watched it too: it was one of her favourites). Her TV watching had fallen off since she'd been at St Anne's; the mini-series, awful though it was, piqued her interest and she began to switch on the TV more often. She favoured American films and series, especially ones with black actors. She day-dreamed herself into cop shows and thrillers, conjuring up situations in which she would be kidnapped or raped or marooned, only to be rescued by a grown-up (and rather hunky) Judd. Her fantasies ignored the fact that Judd was younger than she was, but one of the things that the imagination knows is that time neither flows in a straight line nor radiates out from a simple centre, but evolves at different speeds in different places with scant regard for consciousness, which it regularly sidelines and confuses.

But although, for Jennifer, things had always been complex, this did not prevent her from harbouring a dream of clarity, a dim hope that some day she would be able to understand her actions and explain them. While she had always imagined that growing up would involve a transition at the end of which she would come to understand the world and its permutations, giving her at least some semblance of control over most eventualities, she now discovered that as she edged towards the socially accepted age of maturity all she wanted to do was relinquish responsibility for anything and everything. The confidence and assertiveness which had seemed to be her birthright were deserting her, evaporating like moisture from her pores.

In frustration she began to use the sharpened point of her school compass to scratch and pick at the blemishes on her fingers and arms. But the real damage started in a maths lesson when, lost somewhere in the wild terrain of her dreams, she felt a dull pain and looked down to find the point of the instrument buried a full centimetre into the pad of her thumb. Blood fled from the wound in great purple spheres which exploded like dying stars across the striated cosmos of the pieces of graph paper strewn across her desk.

In her day-dream Judd had been saving her from a burning building in which she had been tied naked to a chair and left to perish for no apparent reason by an evil, faceless madman. Her hero had broken down the door, risking backdraft and flash-over with only an oxygen mask to protect him. He strapped the mask to her face just as she was about to breathe her last, gathered her in his arms and carried her through the inferno, leaping to safety from a seventh-storey window beneath which his trusty team had inflated an enormous crash mattress. And then he was fucking her on a cool patch of grass hemmed in by lush willows and rhododendrons, the spray from the hoses gently weeping over them. As he plunged into her for the final time and exploded she'd rammed the metal point hard into her flesh.

The girl sitting next to her fainted and the class erupted and the maths teacher sent Jennifer off to see the nurse, who admonished her for being so careless and fixed her up and let her stay in the surgery for a while to recover. She sat alone on the hard bed, the tips of her shiny black shoes brushing to and fro across the white tiled floor. Beneath the bandage her thumb throbbed. The nurse was at her desk in the adjacent office writing something, her wide back visible but her face obscured by the half-open door. Bored, Jennifer began to examine the skin first of her good thumb – noting the vortex of her fingerprint – then of her other fingers, of her palms, of the back of her hands and of her forearms, half slight tan and half hairless white underbelly. She marvelled quietly at the rippled lines that ebbed across her palms and the mesh of tiny interlocking creases that ran from her knuckles all the way up along her forearms. She scrutinised the dark hairs as they disappeared into her epidermis: each one seemed made to take a compass point, to be a tiny vagina awaiting a metal penis. Why weren't they bleeding? Why wasn't she bleeding? Every other girl in her year was bleeding every month. Why wasn't she? All these pores should seep blood to make up for it, to show them all that she could do it. She looked around for something sharp. On a metal trolley at the foot of the bed was a box of tissues; protruding from behind it were the slim curves of a pair of suturing scissors. The scissors lay in a stainless-steel kidney bowl and a pile of cotton swabs was mounded up on top of them.

Jennifer looked over at the nurse, still ensconced at her desk. She could hear the soft scratching of the fountain pen the woman was using to write with; there was something terribly exciting about this sound, this rasping. It was like hot, dry breaths heard from a distance, quick gasps and gulps, the travelling companions of pleasure. Tingling, she leant down the length of the bed and stretched out towards the scissors with her good hand. She didn't want to move in case the woman in the next room heard her; she could just reach if she stretched . . . but as she grabbed at the scissors they overbalanced the kidney bowl with a clatter and the noise brought in the nurse. 'I was just trying to get something to blow my nose with,' Jennifer smiled, sweetly.

That evening at home she picked at her skin with the points of the kitchen knives but they were all too blunt and only made deep puckers which hurt but drew no blood. Giving up on the knives she went upstairs to the bathroom where, among the detritus in the cabinet – old tubes of shampoo, half-used bottles of cheap aftershave, a pair of tweezers turning green with age, oily tubs of moisturiser and Henry's spare spectacles, bottles of crumbling pills with faded labels – she found a packet of Henry's razor-blades. She slipped one out of its greased paper envelope and held it up to the light. It was much thinner than she'd expected. Taking off her shirt and bra she pulled at the skin on her torso and arms, searching for a place to try it out. She wanted somewhere that wouldn't show and after much consideration decided on the area just underneath her left breast. Pinning her hair up and back, growing more nervous by the minute, she took up the blade from where she'd placed it on the edge of the wash-basin. What was the best way to hold it? She experimented, eventually deciding on a grip which involved her thumb, her middle finger and her little finger. To test the blade's resilience she flexed it slightly. But she was shaking and the grip was more awkward than it looked, and the blade slipped down and across, slicing through the tip of her finger and embedding itself in the nail. For a moment nothing happened, then blood started gouting out in great rhythmic swells. She stared at her finger in shock, as if amazed that this was all she was. Her hand and arm went cold and began to tingle, and when she tried to shake the blade loose she only succeeded in spotting the bathroom walls with blood. Gingerly, as if it were red hot, she pulled the blade free, staining crimson the dressing that the nurse had put on her thumb, and dropped it into the sink as if it were a bug that she'd picked out of her hair. She ran her hand beneath the cold tap for some minutes, drawing comfort from the water which ran so freely and gazing blankly as it swilled the blood away and the sensation began to return to her arm. But as soon as she took it out of the flow the bleeding returned. Eventually she managed to staunch the blood by wading toilet paper around her finger and binding it with strip plaster.

Later, after the situation had been brought under control, she made the planned incision beneath her breast. It was just deep enough to cut through the seven layers of skin, it didn't hurt much and the blood ran prettily down across her belly. There was an enormous tension in the act. On the one hand, the cut threatened to tear her apart, to unpick the locks of her skin and let her blood, that internal sea, rip her apart in a liquid eruption. But on the other, the cutting made her feel in control, as if by daring this dangerous incision she was, for an instant, once again mistress of herself.

When she awoke the next morning she examined the damage with detachment. The finger and thumb she re-dressed: the thumb was OK but the finger she was not proud of and it still bled. But the chest cut had scabbed over and she stood naked in front of the mirror and stretched her hands above her head in order to admire it, the confidence she'd felt at the moment of incision reinforced by this proof that she could heal. It was then that she noticed that her stomach was more protuberant than usual. She wanted to put it down to her general weight gain, but when she stood sideways on to the mirror and stretched and probed and prodded it was undeniably firm. She sat down and wept, then ran to the toilet and was sick.

Once again she found herself in the school library, but she could discover nothing that was of much use and soon gave up, skiving the next day off school in order to check out the public library in Stratford instead.

Fishfingers can be fatal

The reference department was in the older part of the building, at the top of a set of worn wooden winding stairs. Jennifer had never been up there before; she had only ever used the ground-floor fiction sections with their high ceilings and strip lights. But the first floor was a different story. Here was a space that reeked of oak panelling, of the damp musk of decaying books, of the rust tang of pipe tobacco escaping from the fibres of the tweed jackets of the old men who sat all around, sagging into their quiet old age.

Anita O'Bray, the librarian on duty, felt eyes upon her, but when she looked up from the card files she was cross-referencing there was nobody looking her way. The reference room was as it had been for the last half-hour: nine people sitting at the reading tables and old Mr Keighley slumped fast asleep in the chair by the radiator, his head back and his mouth wide open. He had been coming here to sleep for over a decade, as much of a fixture now as the books themselves, and the librarians generally left him, his gentle snores and his clothes that smelt of naphthalene to their own devices. As Anita O'Bray watched him a thin string of saliva dripped down from his jaw and pooled upon his collar. Suddenly he disgusted her and she found herself thinking that he was a filthy old man who should be put in a home. She shuddered and turned back to her work, but as soon as she did she felt the eyes on her again, manifesting themselves as a hot patch on her cranium and a strange tingling at the top of her spine. She tried to dismiss it but the sensation became stronger and stronger and when she finally gave in to it and looked up, standing there in front of her was a short, plump girl, probably aged about fifteen or sixteen. She collected herself. 'It's that way,' she said. 'If you go to the last stack and look on the third shelf down there's a whole section there.'

Jennifer turned round, thinking that there must be somebody standing behind her. But there was nobody else. She turned back to face the librarian. 'But I haven't told you what I want yet,' she said.

Anita O'Bray was confused. Hadn't she just answered this girl's question?

'This is a library, young lady, not a playground. If you think it's funny to pester the staff I'll have you sent outside. Last stack, third shelf down, half-way along.' Jennifer opened her mouth to protest but thought better of it. Instead, she backed along the line of Anita O'Bray's stare until she reached the final stack. Half-way along, on the third shelf down, was the section on human reproduction. Surprised but too intimidated to question the librarian's apparent telepathy she selected some books, sat down at the small study table that was built into the wall at the end of the shelves and did not emerge again for over an hour. When she finally did leave, it was a full two minutes before Anita O'Bray could contain her curiosity no longer and went over to the stack to see to just what section she had sent the poor girl.

The books that Jennifer had found there both informed and confused her. They convinced her that she was pregnant, but also that she couldn't be, since the human 'gestation period' – as the books called it – was supposed to be at most nine months and she hadn't had sex for well over a year. She bought a pregnancy tester from the chemist's – telling the assistant that it was for her mother – but when she got it home and it tested positive she took out the razor-blade that she kept hidden in her room and carefully made a three-inch incision in the flesh of her upper arm.

The curious pregnancy progressed at an unbearable speed, so slowly that it was almost impossible for Jennifer to keep track of the changes that her body was experiencing. She would follow a symptom like an ache or a swollen gland for a few days, hoping that it was indicative of something, only to find that while she had been concentrating on that something else of apparent significance had occurred, such as a darkening of the veins in her thighs or an increase in the size of her breasts. She let out her clothes as much as she could – which got her a reprimand from the deputy head for looking 'a disgrace to the uniform' – and she badgered Henry endlessly for sick notes to exempt her from Games. As a precaution against the discovery not only of her increasingly imminent parturition but also of the fine lines of scar tissue which now webbed their way across her chest and her upper arms she did everything possible to ensure that no one should see her naked.

She became increasingly obsessed with the scarification and soon developed it into a strata of ritual that concentrated and steadied her in the face of these unexpected events, in some way hoping to construct a net of scars that would contain her body and its fluids in the face of the expansion it was experiencing. Every other night after her bath she would clear the condensation from the mirror and standing naked before it cut herself until her reflection ran red with blood. She had assembled a small kit comprising razor-blades, cotton wool, a tube of antiseptic cream and a phial of Cicatrin powder to hasten scabbing, all of which she kept in a metal tin that had once contained throat pastilles. These tools formed one axis of the ritual, the controlled flow of blood a second and the soft elasticity of her skin, which grew with the child and gave with the blade, a third. In this manner she erected a map which trapped the changes taking place and ordered them in a landscape of pain – a geography which stretched from the dull, languid valleys of the burgeoning foetus sapping away her insides to the sun-scorched slopes of embarrassment that she traversed at school, trying to hide from the glares of the teachers and the tongues of the girls, and right up to the peaks of pain she climbed alone in the evenings, shut away in the bathroom.

But this fragile peace was constantly threatened by the dreams that shivered their way into her mind at night. Her descent into sleep was often via the smarting route of her freshest wound and her slumbers were sensitive and raw as a result, her cortex trembling at the slightest resonance nearby. Henry's quiet insomnias, invoked like demons by years of alcohol abuse, dissipated his increasingly despondent and incoherent moods into the structures of the house, and they saturated Jennifer's sleep like the fragmenting banks of methane that sweep across Titan, Saturn's moon. A domestic row further down the street glimmered in her night like a blinking buoy. A truck trundling down the main road drew fuzzy tracks across her dreamwork; a fox foraging in the dustbins produced a mirage in the middle distance; two copulating cats drilled wormholes through her cortex. The beating of her heart was woven into the rhythms of her brain as the tides are woven into the fabric of the oceans, the yellow moon pulling them slowly this way, slowly that.

Were this all, Jennifer would have found rest enough among the slumberous maps of the neighbourhood she nightly drew, but other planetoids were ascendant in her system. One other moon would have been disruptive enough, yet she might have become attuned to this, thanks to latencies in the accumulated layers of genetic deposit that were the helices of her DNA. But the object that now spun in her zenith was a double system, a maelstrom, a flexing wrinkle in her gravitational field that made the patterns of her sleep unintegrable and could force her from her slumbers and bring her gasping into the still and silent room, where the wind nibbled gently at the cheap print curtains and the blood coursed in hot currents around the conch spirals of her ears.

As the foetus grew, the effects which had so far been confined to her dreams began to seep out into her waking life. She would become suddenly aware, sitting in the classroom, of traffic moving in the remote distance, miles away, far out of earshot. Walking down an empty street she'd hear snippets of disembodied conversation. She heard the workings of machines when they were unplugged, the hum of televisions that had been switched off, the clattering of typewriters that lay idle. She asked a teacher during an essay-writing class if she could shut the windows because of the racket outside and got threatened with detention. The other pupils giggled and hissed quiet phrases among themselves like a box full of vipers but she could no longer tell whether the snatches of conversation she overheard were real or imagined. *That's Jennifer Several*, they said, *stay away from her. She's crazy and she stinks.*

'Do I smell different?' she asked Shelley a couple of days later on the verge of tears.

'What?'

'How do I smell? Tell me!'

But Shelley wouldn't tell her, wouldn't admit that she smelt of something to come, of solitude and plenty. Instead she said: 'I don't understand you any more. You're not the same these days. Ever since you've started going to that posh school you've been different.'

'But it's not my fault! It's not my fault! You've no idea what it's like!' Jennifer screamed, her self-pity transformed immediately into rage. 'I thought you were supposed to be my friend!' She launched herself at

Shelley, arms flailing, and caught her a punch on the cheek and the shoulder.

Within moments the two of them were tussling on the ground, biting and scratching and thumping, until Shelley shoved her hand into Jennifer's swollen belly. Reacting to the harsh contact, the child inside squirmed like a drowsy marmoset – at which point Shelley let out a scream and recoiled in horror. 'God, Jenn, what . . . what's wrong with you? I thought I felt . . .'

'What do you think's wrong with me?' Jennifer spat. 'Why do you think I look like this? Why do you think I'm so fat all of a sudden and can't talk to anybody and everything?' She started to cry and sobs cracked from her lungs in great fists of wet sound.

'But have you seen anyone? Have you seen a doctor?'

'I don't want to see anyone. I just want to be left alone.'

'Who did . . . y'know, who's responsible?'

'I don't know . . . Judd, I think. But there was this other bloke when I was in Geneva.'

'Oh Jenn . . .'

'Don't!'

'But Jenn, that was so long ago. It was over a year ago. It can't be right. There must have been somebody else.'

'Don't tell me there was somebody else! Don't you think I fucking know? I know what it fucking well is! I know all right. I can hear it. It makes me hear things.'

'I think you should see a doctor.'

'I'm not seeing anyone, you understand, no one. This is my problem, it's nothing to do with anyone else. And if you ever tell anyone, anyone at all, I'll kill you, do you understand? I'll kill you!'

'Yeh, yeh, OK, I get the message,' Shelley said, shocked.

Jennifer stood up and tried to brush the mud from her skirt. 'I'll be seeing you then,' she said, more calmly.

'Yeh, whatever,' Shelley replied, nonplussed. 'Be seeing you.' And she watched as Jennifer turned and walked off, not quite into the sunset, which was to her left, but almost.

That evening, after Henry came home from work, he got the hiccups. They came on over dinner, after he tried to wash down a piece of fishfinger that had got stuck in his throat with several hasty gulps of lager. Jennifer's mood – which had been sour up until then – suddenly lifted at the sight of him jerking up and down in his seat, face red as a beet.

'I don't ... hic ... understand what you thi ... hic ... hink is so blood ... hic ... y funny,' he gasped when he saw her reaction, the veins on his forehead already standing out in a quite alarming fashion. Jennifer ran to get him a glass of water and told him to drink it upside down, but he thought she was making fun of him and although she tried to demonstrate – and ended up getting most of the water on the floor – it just made her laugh even harder and nearly gave her the hiccups too. Eventually he managed to do what she instructed and the spasms in his diaphragm subsided enough for him to be able to finish his dinner, although he kept having to force a belch in order to buy enough time to chew and swallow a mouthful.

After dinner the hiccups did not go away and he sat in front of the TV all evening nursing a gin and tonic in the vain hope that the quinine and the bubbles would cure him. Several times Jennifer leapt out at him like a mad thing, screaming at the top of her lungs, the idea being that she might shock the hiccups into submission. But to no avail – they were still going when he went to bed and they kept him awake in a twilight world of percussive torture until he gave up and came downstairs to try to read a book. By the time Jennifer came down for breakfast he looked ten years older. Seeing him with his eyes even more bloodshot than usual and the skin drawn tight across his skull, for the first time in over a year she felt more concern for him than for herself.

When she got in from school that day he was already back from work and still hiccuping several times a minute. That evening he ate nothing. The fiery hilarity of the previous night had disappeared, leaving only the dark coals of worry glowing hot in Jennifer's heart. Henry had decided to try and drink the hiccups into submission and by nine o'clock he was paralytic, having finished his first bottle of Scotch and started on a second. But the spasms still racked his body and at a quarter to ten he began to cry, the continual eructations turning his saliva into a fine foam which dribbled from his mouth and nostrils. He lay on the sofa and Jennifer came to him and cleaned his face and held him in her arms as best she could. He bobbed in and out of a drunken slumber between the spasms and there was a Charlie Chaplin movie on the TV which she half watched while she stroked his head until she fell asleep herself, lulled by the rhythmic pulsing of the old man's body and the bleating music coming from the set. While she slept, the four hearts beating within the confines of the room vied with each other for control over the patterns of her dreams. On the television a cocaine-fuelled Chaplin charged around the factory floor of *Modern Times*, desperately trying to keep up with the machines.

She awoke at three to a room filled with white noise. Henry was in the same dreary stasis, intermittent tremors still running the length of his body. They appeared less powerful but then he was offering them less resistance. When Jennifer eased his head out from beneath her lap she found that a thin pool of acidic bile had gathered in the dip formed by her skirt and run down over the edge of the sofa. She fetched a cloth and cleaned up, and as she wiped away the scum from his mouth she checked his breathing: it was weak and irregular, and when it came it came in a soft, low curdle.

She switched off the television, brought the blankets down from her bed and laid one over him, then made a bed for herself on the floor. When she awoke again it was early morning and raindrops pullulated on the window-panes. The little light which had found its way into the room was so stale and colourless that it seemed to have been trapped in there for weeks. It was cold, too, so she put on a couple of panels of the fire and, yawning, went into the kitchen to make a pot of tea. We, however, stay in the living-room, our camera fixed in one position, our film dividing the scene into twenty-four segments every second, each one of which opens out like a monad on to all the others, each one of which is a bitter shard split off from the vast spinning plane of hetero-geneity that is the cosmos. The sofa is turned away from us; we cannot quite make out Henry's recumbent form. The curtains are not fully closed and the only movement comes from the raindrops running down the glass and the flicker of heat above the fireplace. The hiccups have stopped and from the kitchen come the sounds of Jennifer making the tea: the cups are rinsed, the kettle boils, a cupboard is opened and closed, there is the sound of pouring water and metal on porcelain. A few seconds later, an infinite interlude, Jennifer comes back into view with a cup in each hand. She sets one down on the television, dipping at the knee with the awkwardness of the schoolgirl that she is, not altering the angle of her wrist. A biscuit is clamped between her teeth and she has her lips drawn back so as not to dampen it with her saliva. One hand now free, she removes the biscuit from her mouth and turns to Henry. 'Wake up, sleepy. I've made you some tea. Wakey wakey!'

She puts a hand out to shake him but his eyes are already half open and he offers no resistance. She puts the tea and biscuit on the floor, tucks back her hair behind her ears and runs her fingers across the ripples of his face. She touches his forehead and eyes, and lets out a series of small involuntary gasps as she does so. She puts her fingers on his lips for a minute or so, then bends down and touches his mouth with her ear. Then quietly she gets up and needles into the space behind him on the sofa, spooning him and trying – abstractly – to warm his body with her own. From above the outline of his neck ear hair she can see the gas fire dance. Within the confines of the room three hearts now beat.

It took about an hour and a half for the ambulance to arrive and she made tea for Wayne and Guy, the ambulance men, while they consoled her and dealt with the body. She hadn't cried yet: everything so far had seemed very matter of fact and routine.

At the hospital the doctor, who was tall and Indian and very slim, told her rather earnestly that it looked like a heart attack. He listened to what she had to say and noted the smell of alcohol on the body, rubbed his chin and said: 'Hum, acute singultus, very rare. Only ever heard of one or two cases. Most unfortunate. Looks like the old boy's heart couldn't take it.' He didn't react when Jennifer told him that Henry wasn't her real father and while they were talking he noted the shape of her belly and the miscoloration in the whites of her eyes. She signed the appropriate forms and they ordered a taxi to take her back home, which she paid for with money from Henry's wallet. She started to tidy the living-room and it was only when she realised that she was supposed to be at school that the tears came.

Later that day she understood she had to start telling people. She rang the school and also Henry's office and pretty soon everything was taken out of her hands.

Home alone

The firm of Hedges Hedges and Bentley occupied small premises in Cannon Street, between a pub that did most of its business in the lunch-hour and a restaurant that changed hands at least once every eighteen months. Michael Hedges (one of the Hedges of the firm's title, the other being his father who had long since gone to that great ledger in the sky) stood at the single window of his office staring out at the view across the twelve-foot shaft on to which the window let and which acted as a sinkhole for pigeon shit, exhaust fumes and something which only vaguely approximated sunlight. Behind him was a space that was barely more cheery. Green filing cabinets heaped with overstuffed portfolios lined one of the nicotine-hued walls, a dark bookcase crammed with reference books took up most of the second, and a gas fire and a few framed photographs that had faded to the point of anonymity embroidered the third. The brown door was chipped and the tape which adhered the fire regulations to the back of it was yellowed and peeling. The skirting board, where you could see it between the stacks of papers happily spawning across the floor, had been left undusted for so long that the tiny particles of atmospheric urban dirt had compacted into a greasy stratum that would by now be all but impossible to remove should anyone care to try. The frieze of plaster fruit and flowers which made a circuit of the ceiling had been painted over so many times that none of the original detail was discernible. The impression was that the ceiling was melting, and would at any moment begin to drip heavy boiling globules down upon the occupants of the room.

Jennifer heard Hedges sigh and looked up just in time to see him turn away from the window. The funeral had been the day before and the programme lay on Hedges's desk beside the buttonhole he had worn. He had come straight into the office after the service in order to do some work, even though the rest of the firm had been given the day off. The dark suit he had worn hung from the hatstand, wrapped in a cellophane dry-cleaning bag. 'Very sad,' he said, looking at Jennifer. 'A tragedy. Your father was not only an invaluable asset to this firm but was also one of my dearest and oldest friends.' His words echoed the address he had given at the service and now, as then, Jennifer regarded them with suspicion. She had heard Henry mutter to himself on several occasions about how Hedges was deserting him.

The senior partner smiled at her. 'You have been a very, *very* brave young girl.' His eyes were tired and his face heavily lined, and the articulations of his body seemed peculiar to someone like Jennifer, who hadn't spent the best part of thirty years sitting in a chair. 'But we have to decide what we are going to do with you. Where are you staying, at the moment?'

'With my best friend. Shelley. Walters.' Although she felt that Hedges was patronising her, Jennifer answered him shyly and automatically. She both trusted and mistrusted him, respected and disliked him, but such feelings seemed to belong to a plane quite distinct from that upon which their conversation was taking place. As far as that went it was as if she were five years old again: when asked questions by someone in authority you answered them, because that is what you'd been taught authority meant.

'There are many things, many practicalities, that you and I have to discuss.' He spoke his words in a ponderous, flavourless monotone. It was the voice he always used when emotion impinged upon money. 'Your father did leave a will, of course. He left everything to you, but there's not much, I'm afraid.' For a moment he dispensed with the patronising attitude. 'I'm sure you're aware of the reasons for that.' To Jennifer's surprise she nodded. It made her feel like a traitor. 'There's the house, of course, which your father owned outright: the mortgage was paid off several years ago. And there's a small amount of money left in trust for the payment of your fees and upkeep, should you decide to stay on at St Anne's. But apart from a few odds and ends that's pretty much it. It's not a disaster, but neither is it going to be plain sailing.' He looked at her again, the small, fat girl wrapped up in a vast brown overcoat and curled, insofar as it was possible to curl, into the unforgiving chair which faced his desk. His mind conjured several possible futures; two of the options he immediately repressed (one not quite so completely as the other, so that he could retrieve it for use at a later date). 'Your father's will specifies me as your legal guardian. I'm the person who will be acting for you until you are old enough, in the eyes of the law, to take your own decisions.' The scandal that Jennifer had been involved with two years before flickered into Hedges's mind and he tried to banish it to the same realm as the dark possibility he had imagined just a few moments before. 'I think the best thing would be for you to stay on with Shirley for the time being . . .'

'Shelley,' interrupted Jennifer. 'It's Shelley.'

'. . . er yes, that's right, with Shelley, for the time being, while I deal with the Social Services and make the appropriate arrangements for the longer term. Unless you want to come and live with me, which you probably don't think is a very good idea.' He laughed nervously, all the time watching Jennifer's eyes and trying to gauge her. She shook her head. 'I suppose we'll have to see if we can sort something out with the school, see if they will take you on as a boarder. I think you'd probably prefer that to a foster home. The other option is to go up to Manchester and live with your cousins there. They have made the offer, which is really very generous of them.'

'Why can't I live in my own house?'

'Well, you may be able to in a year or two's time. There is a proviso in your father's will that says if anything should happen to him you be allowed to stay on in the house if at all possible. But at the moment you are still officially a minor and I doubt that the local authority will be particularly enamoured of the idea.'

'But I'm not alone,' the girl protested. 'There's my cat. He still lives there. He can't move. I have to look after him.'

'Well,' said Hedges, pleased that he was able to make a concession, 'you've still got your keys, haven't you? Just because you're staying with Shelley it doesn't mean that you can't go back to your house. You'll just have to go in and feed him every day and make sure that he's all right.' Jennifer nodded at this, pleased with her invention of the cat, and Hedges continued evaluating for her benefit the legal technicalities of the situation. Eventually he brought the meeting to a close and told his secretary to put Jennifer on the next train back to Stratford. When she had gone he felt a pang of sympathy for her; he judged her to be something of a dullard, a 'natural victim' lacking in 'spirit', and imagined that organising her life was not going to be an easy task. Then he chastised himself for being so quick to judge. She was probably still in shock, poor thing. What a terrible thing to have happened.

Shelley's house was only a few streets away from Jennifer's own and it wasn't long before the Walterses were letting the orphan spend most nights there on her own. They had never had a particularly high regard for Henry and, unlike Michael Hedges, were quite convinced of Jennifer's self-sufficiency. They had liked Jennifer a great deal when she was younger but were surprised by how heavy, shy and morbid she had become over the last couple of years – and while they wanted to help her out, they were pleased not to have a heavy morbid shy girl in their home more than was absolutely necessary. Once the initial wave of official grief and shock had passed through the rather vague and diffuse community of which Jennifer was a member, most people were inclined to let her get on with it, offering help only when the need for it was obvious and apparent. And this suited Jennifer just fine.

The lie about the cat had been a good one; she maintained it with everyone except Shelley and it gave her the perfect excuse to go home almost as often as she wanted. But she felt more than ever that eyes were upon her and she developed various subconscious strategies for avoiding them. Whenever she visited the house she went around the back, and she hung double thicknesses of muslin or net curtains across all the windows so that no one could see in from outside. She adopted clothes which were as voluminous as possible – in particular an old overcoat of Henry's which she wore continuously, despite Mrs Walters's constant exhortations for her to take it off – and took to hiding beneath headscarves and wide-brimmed hats. She avoided main meals and snacked instead, so that she wouldn't be obliged to spend regular periods of each day in a predictable place. She used roundabout routes wherever she went.

In one sense these evasive tactics brought her more attention: the girls at school noticed and despised her more than ever, and even the younger pupils began to ridicule her. But the net effect was the one that she desired: people kept away from her. From their cold, slowly moving faces, blank, flat eyes and the way they darted away from her as she swam through the shallows of her life, she often imagined them now as so many little fish.

She had now been pregnant for over two years. Six months earlier her belly had stopped expanding and the fat she had put on disguised her condition. But in contrast to her situation at thirteen she now looked young for her age. The house was the only place where she felt safe enough to expose herself at all – its shrouded and dim interior became her holy place. She would stand in the half-light, large patches of her chest and upper arms shining with a luminosity that skin does not usually possess. These were the razor scars, the results of the blood-letting through which she released the genital quality of her skin. The areas were each about three or four inches across and roughly square and each was a lattice of finely drawn lines, a net drawn to reinforce her body. It was as though she were a single cell whose internal processes were undergoing mitosis but whose cell wall was terrified of rupturing. She began to be haunted by the fear that the child would never come, that her body would never be returned to her, that the fruits of the pregnancy would not be some bloodied infant but the eventual entrapment of her body in this expanding mesh of scars. At these times she projected an image of herself as a wicker woman, woven with scars from head to toe, silent, solid, cold, immortal, impregnable, mother and child locked away inside a basket work for all eternity. Yet she could not stop using the blade on herself.

The house had become an eddy in time, slowed and linked to things alien to the homogeneous suburban region that surrounded it, which marched stoutly onwards to the rhythms of the ticking clock, the commuter train, the school bell and the television news and sport. Within Jennifer's four walls time's only ally was the sequence of cuts she was making on her body; a prisoner in solitary, hatching off the days.

She was by now regularly experiencing bouts of pain in her abdomen and around the time that the pain became continuous the school holidays commenced. When she felt up to walking she spent the days wandering aimlessly around Stratford; when she didn't she lurked in the house, battling with her grief over Henry and only turning up at the Walterses' for the occasional meal. She had several more rows with Shelley, who was by now determined that her friend should see a doctor and kept threatening to tell her mother if Jennifer didn't do something. But this attitude just sent Jennifer into a rage – she remained convinced that fate was at work and that its trajectory should be interfered with by no one. If Shelley tried to get her to give reasons she just snapped back that it was obvious, or that it was too complicated to explain.

Soon, though, it became clear that people were becoming suspicious and even Jennifer began to be aware that a crisis point was being reached. Her dreams, which had been getting increasingly vivid, had started to spill over into her waking hours and she had begun to see things which were not there. Flashes of colour and brief waterfall effects in her peripheral vision mutated into small, indefinable creatures curling up beside her, cats and squirrels darting across her path, men in overcoats sitting on rooftops, dragons in the clouds, curtains of rain on a fine, bright day. At night she felt that the house was surrounded and the fear was so powerful that she occasionally slept at the Walterses' again. The hunted look she carried in her eyes deepened and she was permanently on the verge of tears. More often than not there was a murmuring in her ears, a chthonic babble, as if a tribe of dwarves who dwelt in the earth beneath her feet were speaking together in tongues.

She was alone in her house when the first contraction came and the pain was so intense that she fainted. She would have remained there on the living-room floor if Shelley hadn't stopped by to apologise for some of the things she'd said during the row they'd had the previous day. The front door was locked but she knew that Jenn kept it that way and when she came around to the back door it was ajar. She entered nervously, calling her friend's name. When she saw Jennifer sprawled unconscious on the floor, she was immediately scared, partly for her friend, but also for herself, in case this was her fault for not having taken action sooner. She called for an ambulance and sat bathing the pregnant girl's forehead with a damp cloth and whispering her name, while she waited for help to arrive.

The caesarean section

In the emergency ward the doctors and nurses perform for each other, so obsessed are they with the many hospital dramas that now fill the television schedules. Indeed, it's difficult to see how any treatment actually gets done with the staff constantly sloping off to catch the latest instalment of *Hospital Ward* or *The Young Nurses*. But it's not all wasted time. Bedevilled with cuts in funding, many now learn their jobs from these medical soaps. How else are they to know the correct level of urgency required for three violently haemorrhaging car crash victims as compared with that needed for a single endoscopic retrograde cholangiopancreatography? Or how to talk to the little boy who has trapped his penis in his fly zip or the bag lady who's lost her marbles and won't sign the release form that allows the hospital to carry out the heart bypass operation that could save her life? Or how to deal with that wrong decision that cost the life of a two-year-old child or, most important of all, how to cope with an on-ward romance that's gone horribly wrong?

Recognising the importance of TV in modern medical practice, Ms Shanahan, the surgeon in charge of Jennifer's case, has made the decision to use the caesarean she is about to perform as a marketing opportunity. The houseman she has chosen to assist her in this is none other than dishy young Dr Parker, darling of the ward, chosen for his photogenic appearance. In one corner of the operating 'theatre' Ms Shanahan has had installed a video camera which will distil the events of the next half-hour or so on to a tape, which will then be rushed straight out of the door and into the hands of a waiting motor-cycle messenger, who will speed to the city of Birmingham and the studios of the television company with which at that very moment Ms Shanahan's assistant is negotiating terms. Jennifer's thumb print at the base of a form assures her consent.

Roll it.

'OK, we've got a severe dystocia possibly caused by a breech presentation. No indication of foetal distress, so we're going to move straight into a hysterectomy procedure. Nurse, are you ready?'

'Yes, Ms Shanahan.'

'Parker, can you see? I want you in on this one.'

'I can see.'

'Good. Then let's go. We're going to make a lower segment transverse incision. Why do we prefer this over the so-called classical caesarean. Parker?'

'The transverse has the advantage of requiring only modest dissection of the bladder from the underlying myometrium.'

'And?'

'Er, and there's always a danger with a vertical incision that it may extend too far downwards and tear through the cervix into the vagina and bladder. And a transverse incision is much less likely to rupture than a vertical incision during any subsequent pregnancies.'

'And a transverse incision results in less blood loss, is easier to repair and does not promote adherence of bowel or omentum to the incisional line. Good. Nurse, scalpel, please. Thank you. Now, I'm making an infra-umbilical midline vertical incision. It's got to be big enough to deliver the foetus through and this is a big baby. Listen to that skin pop. Good. See how I draw the knife down in one clean movement. No hacking or sawing. If we do it right it should heal up with minimal scarring. We're cutting down to the level of the anterior rectus sheath . . . now we free the area of subcutaneous fat – like so – to expose a strip of fascia in the midline about an inch or so wide. See? You'll see some surgeons incising the rectus sheath with the scalpel throughout the length of this incision, but I prefer to make this small opening and then incise the fascial area with scissors. Scissors! Like this. I think it's safer and cleaner – and for the time being at least I don't want to see you doing it any other way. Good. Here we go. Now what am I doing?'

'You're separating the rectus from the pyramidalis muscles using sharp and blunt dissection, exposing the transversalis fascia and the peritoneum.'

'Good, Parker, good. You've obviously done this before. Now, here, I just have to dissect this preperitoneal fat like so and . . . swab please . . . excellent, so we're now ready to open the peritoneum. How are we going to do that? Um? Come on, she'll have gone into labour by the time you've thought about it! Elevate the . . .'

'Elevate the peritoneum with two haemostats placed about two centimetres apart, then visualise and palpitate the tented fold to ensure that the omentum, bowel and bladder are not adjacent.'

'OK, so why don't you do that for me. That's right, apply them there and there, good . . . by the way, I haven't done a Pfannenstiel incision – you do know what that is, I presume?'

'Er, it's where the skin and subcutaneous tissue are incised using a lower transverse, curvilinear . . .'

'Yes, yes – well, we haven't done that because I want a good exposure of the uterus and appendages so that we can get a good look at what is going on in there. This amount of fat would make that difficult with the Pfannenstiel, and we're expecting complications, so better to play safe. Are you satisfied with your fold?'

'Yes.'

'Good. Then let's open her up. OK, so we incise to the upper pole of the incision ... ah, like so ... and downwards to just above the peritoneal reflection over the bladder, here. And there's the uterus, underneath. Now immediately we see, what?'

'That it's slightly dextrorotated?'

'Right! So?'

'So we lay a laparotomy pack in each lateral peritoneal gutter.'

'Excellent. Especially wise in this case, because one possible complication may be infected peritoneal fluid. Nurse, would you do that for us, please? Good. Now if we take the forceps – thank you – we can grasp the vesicouterine serosa in the midline like so and make a small incision with the scissors. By pushing the blades through and opening them we can separate the serosa from the myometrium and then incise it properly. Now the best tool for the next bit is the fingers ... we want to slide in under this flap of peritoneum and gently separate the bladder from the myometrium ... it's a bit like skinning a rabbit ... ever skinned a rabbit, Parker? No, I didn't think so. There we go. You have to be careful here because it is possible, especially if the cervix is dilated, to dissect downwards too deeply and enter the underlying vagina by accident, missing the lower uterine segment, so we only want to separate the bladder back by about five centimetres.

'Now we can open the uterus through the lower uterine segment about two centimetres above the detached bladder. We're going to do this carefully, a small cut at first, and we have to judge it so that we get all the way through the uterine wall but don't harm the foetus. OK, here we go. And that's fine. Now we're through we can extend the incision using bandage scissors ... OK?'

'Uh huh.'

'In fact, this segment is so thin that I could do this simply by pulling the incision apart with my fingers. We have to make this wide enough to allow delivery of the foetus without having to disturb either of the lateral uterine arteries here and here. Now, look there, that's the placenta – that's why you have to use bandage scissors. It's easy enough to detach it ... like so, see? ... but if you cut it by accident you're looking at

severe foetal haemorrhage. There, there's its cranium, can you see there?'
Cut to Parker. Nods. 'Doesn't look like a breech position after all, which
is going to make all our lives easier.

'So, we're ready for delivery. The vertex is presenting so I can slip my
hand into the uterine cavity here between the symphysis pubis and the
head, and elevate gently through the incision. You can help me here by
applying a moderate transabdominal fundal pressure . . . not that moderate! Come on, this is a hefty baby here! That's better . . . OK, here it
comes . . . nurse, aspirate the nose and mouth please . . . thank you . . .
don't want you drowning in the amniotic fluids now, do we, darling?
OK then, more pressure . . . here it comes . . . here it comes . . . here
she comes . . . wonderful. Nurse, take this, please, Parker, 20U of oxytocin
intravenously please, 10 millilitres per minute, nice and quick now, please.
Keep your eye on the uterus and when it's contracted back in you can
slow the flow a little. While you're waiting you can apply some fundal
massage. That should help reduce the bleeding and speed up the delivery
of the placenta. I'm going to clamp and sever the umbilical cord, just
quickly, like so . . . now, nurse, she's all yours. Parker, you're still with
me, we've got work to do despite the miracle of birth. Can you handle
the delivery of the placenta while I put on some fresh scrubs?'

It's a wrap. And it looks like Parker's landed himself a role in the forthcoming movie.

The eyes have it

From the start, they weren't going to let her keep the child; she was still
officially a minor, if only just, and then there was the scarring of course –
very worrying. But when they discovered that the child had two hearts and
other more subtle abnormalities the case was referred to a higher authority, who immediately decreed that the child should be kept under close
supervision at all times and that the mother should be told it was stillborn.

The birth went out on *Living Eye* that night, right after the local news.
Laika tuned in from her vantage point, catching the show on the satellite
relay. An eye in the sky, she looked down, but she didn't pick up on
anything strange.

Check out

For months after the birth Jennifer refused even to acknowledge the experience. Michael Hedges knew, of course, as did the Walterses, but they were very careful to keep any mention of the whole affair to themselves. The school was told that Jennifer had suffered a burst appendix and that became the accepted version of events.

They kept her back for observation and she spent a week or two in hospital, on a drip. Her moods were jagged so they smoothed them out with lithium, but she made no further attempt to cut herself. They had her removed from maternity for fear she'd upset the other mothers and put her in a spare bed in the geriatric ward. She spent the days crying quietly to herself, her face turned to the wall, while the old women in there with her juddered around the room, dribbling and scraping at the air like desiccated trees fidgeting at the onset of storms that will bring them, brittle and cracked, to the ground.

She lost weight rapidly. Of course, she was no longer carrying and there was the concomitant fluid loss, but her bingeing had ended and now she ate more regularly again. Throughout that period, whenever she looked at herself in the mirror she had a strange sense of juxtaposition, as if she were all at once standing upon the crests of two waves of time, the period of the pregnancy sunk out of sight into a trough, what she was before and what she was now crushed together into a single bastard bloom of flesh. There was something else, too, something that was at first obscured by this shimmering duality, something which took a good while to filter through: the feeling of being watched was gone. She no longer felt those cool patches slither down her cranium and inside–outside her spinal column. Those dewy disembodied eyes that seemed to coalesce out of the susurrations of her own blood and tissue were no more.

By November she was ready to return to school. In the wake of the birth she insisted on being allowed to live in the house, and after consulting the Walterses, who promised to keep an eye on her, Michael Hedges capitulated, thinking that she'd probably been through enough. The following summer she took her O levels, and when her results were below average she announced that she was going to leave St Anne's and get a job. Nobody really wanted to try and stop her, especially as she seemed largely to have recovered from the traumas of her early teens and returned to something of her former self, and by the end of the summer she was employed as a check-out girl in the Woolworth's on Stratford's Bridge Street. She worked at this and other similar establishments for the next few years, hanging out with the town's first wave of punks and experimenting with drugs.

9

Oedipus wrecks

Cars cruised Hollywood Boulevard; their hot tyres on the soft asphalt made the sound of long strips of damp cloth being slowly torn apart. Small knots of men snarled every street corner and women clad in tight, low-cut tops and short skirts stalked the pavements or sat, legs akimbo, astride fire hydrants, their hard breasts jutting up and out. It was eight o'clock in the evening and still hot. The city lay like coals and the sky flickered with the shimmer of a barbecue that's given out its best cooking heat. Thick skeins of grey smoke wound like ivy around the seething purples of the sundown clouds. Up and down the strip the telegraph wires sweated and hummed with the voices that were stretched along them, thinner than hair. There was a wax museum whose air-conditioners roared front and back day and night to keep the occupants from melting away. Next door in the arcade the chimes of the one-armed bandits sang louder even than the fans: from across the street you could hear their levers and dials clanging like a pen full of terrified cattle.

Above the arcade was a floor of offices and above these – and you had to go round back and up a metal stairway if you wanted to gain access – were a couple of apartments. Inside one of them, Judd dropped his telephone handset back into its cradle and broke his connection, the intensities of the sexual fantasy he'd been having folding themselves away like electrons in the tube of a cooling television. He got up from his bed, wiped himself and pulled his pants up over his detumescent penis. He lit a cigarette. He felt no more relaxed than he had before the phone call and for a few minutes he paced the room nervously, sure that he had something important to do. A small quantity of cum seeped from his urethra and formed a damp patch on his thigh. He couldn't decide whether he liked the soiled feeling this gave him or whether he would rather be clean, showered, sterilised.

He'd done telephone sex several times now, numbers from the back of a magazine. It wasn't exactly satisfying but until he'd discovered it he'd found it very hard to masturbate. Since the scandal eight years before he'd only had sex with one person, a tough girl from South Central who'd picked him up and slept with him for a while because she'd needed a place to stay. That had been the previous summer, just after he'd left high school and moved into the apartment. (The significance of the date they'd first fucked didn't escape him – 4 July 1980, Independence Day.) But apart from that he'd come through puberty with little or no sexual contact, which would have been bad enough even if Schemata hadn't reconfigured his imagination to such a degree that it was difficult for him to enjoy the company of his left hand. Every time he tried to turn himself on, his mind would vault over a precipice of logical implications, psychological profiles, political prerogatives and hurtle down a wall of consequences, the psychoanalyst's voice sounding in his ears like the rush of air itself and shorting out any mustering desires.

It drove him half crazy. It was as if Schemata had set up an irrigation system around the mountainside of his mind, insuring him against any ill effects that might have come from his encounter with Jennifer, yes, but at the same time completely subordinating him. Seamlessly integrated into this system of psychic hydraulics and unable to remember what he had been like before, Judd found it impossible to get any kind of perspective on his own personality. The only real refuge was his dreams: while he'd remained in the analysis they too had been affected (like Rod Serling in *The Twilight Zone*, Schemata would always appear at the end in the role of narrator, to bracket and interpret the preceding dreamscape, give it some awful moral), but once the sessions had ceased his imagination had used the cover of the night to begin to shake itself free of the doctor's influence, temporarily flooding and disrupting the network of pipes and pumps that he'd laid. Although a welcome relief, the downside of this was that Judd awoke almost every day to a semen-soaked bed – which meant that he suffered from acute embarrassment whenever he came into contact with his parents' live-in Filipino housemaid.

As soon as he moved into the apartment on Hollywood Boulevard he took advantage of his new-found privacy by paying a visit to one of the local adult shops and buying himself a few magazines. Carrying them home inside their plain paper bag, positive that everyone on the street was watching and remembering him, he was as excited as if he'd been going on a date with the prom queen. But to his surprise the pictures left him cold. He had to ask himself why had he gone and bought magazines full of white women. He'd done it without thinking, it was a cultural reflex. But that raised the question: being black physically but half-caste technically, which colour of girl was he supposed to prefer? Jennifer had been white, of course, but as an isolated case it was hardly conclusive. Why couldn't Schemata have helped him sort that one out? He'd talked a lot about the Oedipus Complex, and that was all very well, but he'd never made it clear whether one should give in to the psycho-sexual channels it created or resist them. Would only a woman like his mother make him happy? Or would a woman like his mother destroy him? His subsequent affair with Annette, the girl from South Central, did not make things clearer. Superficially, she'd not been like Melinda at all – she was black, for a start. But then Annette had been hard, self-motivated, not prepared to let anything get in her way, and he knew his mother was like this too, or could be. He stayed confused.

Telephone sex removed all these questions. It was easy, anonymous and it had no visual element. It made him feel like shit, but it got his rocks off, so it was some kind of solution.

The room was a reasonable size and all his own. He could think there, or more than he could at his parents' at least. There were the bed and a few other oddments of unremarkable furniture. Stacked around the place were a few books: self-help books mainly, a few soft-porn novels, some black-consciousness literature (most of which had been recommended to him by Annette), several Mickey Spillanes (Mike Hammer: 'Fastest with a Gun, Hottest with a Girl') and one or two cheap classics. His copy of *Moby Dick* had been awarded as a school prize, and the fine cracks along the spine revealed that he had got about a third of the way in and given up. He deliberately hadn't put any pictures up on the walls – he liked them white, anonymous, he liked the feeling of transience they gave him, the feeling that he was just passing through. But there was something about the bare plaster too . . . he had a dim idea that he wanted as much of it exposed as possible. It comforted him. Annette had turned her nose up at this decision, said he was being pretentious, that he should decorate. He told her it was typical of a girl to say that, a comment which sparked a minor argument in which he'd been backed into a corner by refusing to explain why he liked the walls bare ('I just do, all right? I just do'). But it wasn't that he hadn't wanted to explain further; he had, it was just that he couldn't untangle his thoughts about it all.

243

He was supposed to be looking for a job: his father had put him on an allowance, which was how he could afford the apartment (Moses didn't want him to go on welfare) but he'd given up scanning the small ads in the newspapers months before. He had no idea what he wanted to do. Every time he spoke to Melissa she pestered him to try for college; his father on the other hand still had this idea that he could make it in sales. Judd wanted to do neither. He couldn't bear the idea of following in Moses's footsteps – for one thing, it was all too Freudian. But neither could he see the point of going to college. He'd already had his head filled with enough crap, he'd decided. Why cram it fuller still?

So he drifted, hung out in cafés, had telephone sex, wandered the streets of Hollywood, read, listened to music. He became furious and morose. He started to build models again, from plastic kits – he'd done it as a kid, especially in England, had assembled them as a way to cheat wet weekends of boredom. Before he'd built anything he could get, but now he only wanted to build aircraft. Helicopters, fighters, passenger jets. Gluing together the grey plastic wings and fuselages helped him to cut his imagination loose from reality. If he couldn't return to a time before Schemata then perhaps he could recreate himself anew, dream a dream of flight, put himself up there with the clouds, roam with those giant patterns as they dragged their shadows across the earth, touching the ground only in order to prove to it that he was free.

He didn't see too many people. Most of his friends from high school were either in jobs already or had gone off to college or were thinking of going or were concentrating on their sports or whatever. Most of them, in other words, had some kind of a goal. He didn't and it singled him out.

Before the year was out Moses grew bored with trying to nag his son into activity and found him a job working the front desk in a used-car lot owned by a business contact who owed him a favour. The deal? Take it or lose your allowance. Judd took it. It didn't liven things up much, at least not to begin with. It made him depressed, too, and tired (so no change there). Most evenings he came home and just sat in his front window and smoked, watching the street below, switching on the TV when he got fed up with that. Having a job, though, did mean he had something to talk to his school friends about and sometimes he met up for beers with a group of them. For a while he got quite sociable and for a few months he even started going regularly to night-clubs, at one of which he met another girl, Marsha. This time it lasted a while, and she was in it for him and not just his place. They spent weekends together, smoking dope, listening to music. But when it came to making love there were problems. It had been fine with Annette, but the fact that Marsha actually cared for him seemed to make it impossible: either he wasn't interested and couldn't get hard or he was overwhelmed by emotion and came too quickly. Pretty soon she left him for somebody else. After that it was back to TV, telephone sex and a fridge stocked with fully readjusted American beer. Later on, as an experiment, he tried fucking a couple of call-girls. That was OK.

Although when he started the job he was kept pretty busy, trade quickly began to drop off. With nothing better to do he was soon spending most of his time hanging out in the repair shop with the two mechanics, Lionel and the Bomb. The Bomb was a DJ – he had taken his tag from the name of a drumming technique invented by the bebop drummers. He played at parties at the weekends and was always terrified of staining his hands with oil. Lionel was a high-minded dread, a Rasta. He was Jamaican; he'd come to the States ten years previously to find work and he sent most of his wages back to his baby-momma and daughter in Kingston. He and Judd talked politics a bit, discussed Marcus Garvey, Martin Luther King, the Black Panthers. Lionel had plenty disdain for it all. He told Judd about the hopeless situation in Jamaica, about how two white politicians, Seaga and Manley, had the island sewn up between them. He called it 'the shitstem'. 'Rasta ha' no part in it,' he'd say to Judd, who'd nod vigorous encouragement, keen to improve his political credentials.

The lot was on a busy feed road that ran past a housing project before it joined with the freeway. There had been a couple of gang killings in the area the previous year but the kids who hung out on the corner and occasionally came into the lot to look over the cars never gave Judd any trouble, except for the occasional remark about being a coconut and a lot of lip about the prices of the cars in the showroom. The business didn't smell of money and it only ever got broken into out of boredom, and even then there was never too much damage done, except for the night when some joyriders hot-wired a Buick and drove it out through one of the sheet-glass showroom doors. That afternoon Lionel had been giving the car an oil change and had left the sump to drain overnight, so the kids didn't get very far before the engine seized up on them and the Buick ground to a halt. Word got around among potential thieves, who weren't interested in stealing some heap of junk that was going to break down after a couple of miles. So crime fell off. Unfortunately, however, sales did too: word also got around among potential clients; perhaps the two sets overlapped. Business got slower than ever.

Irving Scofield was perfectly aware of this and completely untroubled by it. Scofield was the lot's owner and the friend whom Moses had touched for Judd's job. An entrepreneur, no one really knew quite how he made his money but he seemed to make a fair amount of it. Speculation about him constantly circulated in one guise or another, and there had at one point been some nasty rumours going around about a link between Scofield and a missing shipment of DEC computers which had been under Moses's jurisdiction, but nothing had ever been proved. Whatever, the point was that Scofield didn't care that the lot wasn't doing so well, because he kept the business open as a tax dodge.

So as Judd's flow of paperwork became a trickle and the backlog of repairs for Lionel and the Bomb dwindled and then disappeared, the three of them found themselves with entire days full of nothing to do. By now, Judd had learnt a bit about cars and some days he'd fine-tune one of the vehicles parked out front, taking it around the block and running it with the hood up, trying to spot problems that he knew how to solve. The rest of the time he mostly spent building models, though he'd moved on from aircraft now. His unsatisfactory sexual experiences had made him question more strongly than ever the effect that Schemata had had on him, and he soon came to the conclusion that he needed to free himself from the analyst's influence and reclaim his personality for himself. As a first step he decided to try and remember what he'd been like as a child, and to this end he went out and and bought a stack of new kits in an attempt to rekindle the old obsession he'd had with space. Rockets, satellites, landers, starcruisers, he built them at his desk, immersing himself in the simple poetry of part and plan, glue and sprue in order to kindle a more complex experience of memory and dream. In space anything was possible; the concept itself was fairly abstract. Time worked differently too: out there where the stars marked passing aeons with the comings and goings of planets, solar systems, entire galaxies, Judd's own life seemed irrelevant enough. And if his life was irrelevant, the scribble of a shrink upon it was more irrelevant still, of no consequence. It was pleasantly contradictory, this fantasy, which was what made it so complete: on the one hand Judd needed rockets and boosters, he needed a massive increase in speed to escape the gravitational pull of planet Schemata. But on the other hand, his ultimate destination was the depths of the universe and the total stillness, the absolute self-control, that his arrival there would bring.

Soon he had miniatures of the Sputniks, the Saturn V rocket, Space Lab, Voyager, Apollo, an X-Wing fighter from *Star Wars* and a carrier ship from *Space 1999* cluttering up a table in his office. That April the space shuttle Columbia had made its first manned flight and Judd constructed a giant model of the craft and the rockets which carried it into the sky. He was very proud of it and was going to give it to Lionel and the Bomb to put in the repair shed, but before it was finished there was a picture of Columbia on the front page of the paper one day, and when he saw it Lionel started venting his spleen at Americans in general for pissing money out into space and not being able to house or feed their own people properly. Silently embarrassed by his inadvertent political incorrectness, Judd stopped making models after that.

In camera

By monitoring the Russian media Laika knew now to what extent they were exploiting her, erecting statues in her honour and putting her face on to stamps. She was famous and everyone was getting something out of it (everyone but her). Still, she liked the attention, even if she pretended to disapprove. Her main competition, the only serious threat to her status, was this cosmonaut Gagarin. Annoyingly she'd missed his little sojourn in outer space – it just so happened that he'd been launched into an orbit similar to her own, but a little bit ahead, so they raced around the planet together, dog in pursuit of man. She'd hoped to catch up with him, freak him out a little, the greenhorn, but he disappeared back down through the clouds to a hero's welcome without the gap having closed.

It was sickening, watching it all on TV, though she had to admire the bureaucrats – they milked it for all it was worth, renaming the square where he first addressed the crowds Gagarin Square and erecting there a huge titanium statue of space android Yuri jetting through the atmosphere, a future perfect man all aerodynamic efficiency, his arms out like Christ's, his trusty cannonball-like craft at his feet like a . . . like a faithful dog. Here he was, the icon, the crucifix that Soviet reason had claimed to stamp on the twentieth century, and meanwhile where was she? Female, canine, victim of prejudice, all her achievements subjected to a cover-up. She'd made a life up there, after all, while he'd just come on a day trip, a glorified lost weekend. Talk about a glass ceiling!

Well, what did it matter to her? He'd merely been adjunct to the operation, a twist of cortex and skin inside his machine, a circus boy fired from a gun. But she had achieved proper integration – she felt through her craft, its exterior her exterior, its controls and her nerves co-extensive. So sensitised had she become to the behaviour of the craft that she now felt the impact of space dust as if it were hail on her back. Her changing relationship with the earth's electromagnetic field was as noticeable as the first quiver of a distant front of rain across the fields on a humid summer afternoon, the slight gravitational tug of a passing satellite as tempting as the odour of a prowling male.

Until 1968 she remained secure in the knowledge that whatever Gagarin did, she had one unassailable advantage in the race to be the world's greatest space icon – she, at least, had died young (and only two years after James Dean). But then the cosmonaut went and nose-dived his test plane and even the Western media rumour that the crash had been engineered by an over-enthusiastic publicity department couldn't reconcile her to the fact that there was no stopping him now. Mankind would choose him over her as their emblem – him they could manipulate. Yuri Gagarin had been launched into the space of the symbol and this time he wouldn't return.

Craps

The summer drew on and if you stood out in the street on any day that you chose – it made no difference which, they were all the same – you would see the silver-grey band of the tarmac that stretched away underneath the freeway and all the way down to the sea vibrate and shimmer with heat. The light was always so bright and clean that you could hardly see the sky, even when the pall of smog was not present (which was rarely) and no one walked anywhere any more except for those, like the bums, who had to (and they stayed put when they could). The heat wore tempers as thin as the membranes of boils over-swollen with pus. Occasionally these pustules burst and there were shootings on the highways.

With his model building abandoned, Judd had nothing to do. It was too hot to fool around in the forecourt; any tinkering had to be done in the showroom where you could have the air-conditioning on, and this meant that you couldn't run the engines for more than a couple of minutes because of the fumes. It was cooler in the repair shop, but that was the domain of Lionel and the Bomb, and no work was to be done there unless they sanctioned it – and they wouldn't sanction it unless it was 'real' work, which meant work that they were going to get paid for or which would improve their immediate environment, such as fixing up the refrigerator or the sound system, jobs which could take days if handled properly.

It had indeed begun to seem as if the two mechanics did no work whatsoever. When they weren't playing their newly acquired records to each other they would play dice, their overalls folded down at their waists and their dark torsos glistening with sweat. They used the upturned hood of a 1973 Chrysler as a craps board, having drawn markings on it with a waterproof pen, and played each other for quarters and dimes.

On this particular day they both sat there like princes on seats ripped out of a Porsche Spider, cigarettes glowing in the shade and beer cans at the ready, admiring the view of the freeway flyover.

'Ah, dis is de life, ma man,' drawled Lionel, broadening his accent to emphasise his contentment.

'Sho' is, brutha, sho' is,' replied the Bomb, who was concentrating on rolling a small joint using only one hand, a trick which he had not yet perfected.

At that moment, unbeknown to either of them, Irving Scofield walked into the showroom. Judd was sitting on the main reception with his feet up on the desk and his chair tipped back, reading in the paper that the space probe Voyager 2 was just passing Saturn, that IBM's new product, the Personal Computer, was selling well (he tried to remember if that was the thing his father was working on now) and that a deadly new disease called Acquired Immuno-Deficiency Syndrome was killing homo-sexuals. The air-con was on full and the noise of the fans drowned out Scofield's approach. It was not until the owner stood right in front of the desk and coughed that Judd looked up. For a second he froze, then tried to get up so fast that his chair fell over and an old pile of plastic sprues stacked up on the edge of the table behind him clattered to the floor. Doing his best to ignore all this he hurried round to the front of the desk, hand outstretched.

'Mr Scofield, ah, Mr Scofield, what a surprise. It's been pretty quiet around here, I was just taking my lunch break . . .' Judd tailed off as Scofield stood there impassively. He was a big man, very dark-skinned and broad. His hair was fringed with tidy grey curls that slowly blended into black as they spread across his crown. He looked down at Judd through hooded eyes, the folds of skin only hinting at the small, hard irises and yellow whites that lay back in there somewhere. The deep creases in his forehead and heavy jowls gave his face the look of a stump of wood turning to charcoal and pulled from the fire, the fine threads and patterns of the living tree having been transmuted into thick perpendicular scorings more reminiscent of the patterns of erosion in a permeable rock than of anything organic. It was a difficult face to read.

But then it broke into a broad smile, the cindered bark stretching back to reveal the living sap beneath: bright, bright teeth adorned with gold, the pulpy red flesh of a well-tended mouth. The man ignored Judd's outstretched arm and seized him instead by the shoulders. 'No need to apologise, my boy! You're entitled to put your feet up now and again! I was just thinking how fine the old place looks! Seems like your father was right to get me to take you on. Fine job, fine job.' His voice was massive and soft.

Judd brightened immediately. 'Thanks, Mr Scofield. Is there anything I can get you? A 7-Up? Some water? A coffee?'

'Ah, water, if you please. It sure is hot out there today.' Judd loped over to the cooler, cracked down a paper cup and filled it. Inside its plastic drum the water belched and rumbled.

'I just want to have a quick look round back, check out the repair shop,' Scofield called, heading for the door. 'How those boys doing out there anyway?' Immediately, Judd's panic returned. Lionel and the Bomb were undoubtedly playing craps, as they did almost every afternoon now. Judd rushed to his desk, meaning to grab the phone and call them on the internal exchange, but Scofield had stopped at the showroom exit and was waiting for him. 'Come on, son! I haven't got all day!'

Judd crossed his fingers and joined the boss, handing him his drink. Scofield took the water, downed it in a single gulp, crumpled the cup with one flex of his enormous hand and tossed the remains into a drain before leading the way round to the repair shop. Judd followed with trepidation, almost shaking with fear – what would happen when the boss found out, what would his father say? Schemata was suddenly back with him again, whispering consequences in his ear, apparently more powerful than ever. The three of them headed around the edge of the building and disappeared out of the flat hot sun into a rhombus of shade. Judd could already make out the sound of the dice rattling against the metal of the Chrysler hood. Even worse was the musk of marijuana hovering on the still air.

'Hello, boys!' bellowed Scofield. Lionel and the Bomb turned around, but instead of the blanched faces that Judd had expected to see they both broke into smiles and came over to greet the owner.

'Hi, Mr S!'

'Hey! How ya doin'?'

'Pretty good. You boys shootin' a little craps there?'

'Yeh, jus' somethin' we rigged oursel's up to pass the time. Bin pretty quiet roun' here. Can I get you a beer, Mr S?'

'No, that's all right. I can't stay long. Just came by to ask a favour. Tell me, can you boys fix up a vehicle for me, soup it up a little, stiffen out the suspension, reinforce the hood and trunk, that kind of a thing?'

'No problem,' said Lionel, looking at the Bomb.

'How long would it take?'

'Well, depends on what it is, but unless it's something really weird, then a week, max.'

'It's a '76 Lincoln. Reckon you could start on it over the weekend? I'll give you double time.'

The mechanics looked at each other and shrugged. 'Sure, no problem.'

'Fine. I'll get Jacob to drop it by, last thing Friday. He'll call you tomorrow, run over what you'll need. OK, that's all. Everything else OK?'

'Jus' fine, Mr Scofield.'

'That's what I like to hear. You boys get back to your game now. And don't smoke too much of that there reefer – that stuff rots your mind.'

An astounded Judd walked Scofield back around to the front of the premises and watched him vanish behind the smoked glass of his Cadillac. When the car had driven away, he hurried back to the repair shop and demanded an explanation. Lionel and the Bomb pulled up an oil drum, sat him on it, put a cold beer into his hands and gave him the low-down, which as far as Judd was concerned amounted to an object lesson in the fact that not everyone in the world adhered to the same principles that had been drummed into him by his father and analyst. Then they taught him craps. The few customers who called in at Route 66 Autos over the next few weeks found the front door locked and a cardboard sign directing them round back taped across the glass.

Lizard me this

Lionel and the Bomb were lazy players. They thought they could get on top of the game, that they could spin it one way or another just by thinking about it. They were forever wishing for the perfect series of throws from the worn wooden dice that clattered across the Chrysler hood a thousand thousand times that summer. Lionel's game was one of austerity followed by binge: he would carefully place bets calculated to insulate him against cruel streaks of misfortune and in this way he would inch his winnings upwards. Yet he could only hold out for so long before he tired of his cautiousness and with the sweat building on the sandy palms of his fine, long-fingered hands he would hazard a large stake on a single round and blow the lot. But if Lionel's game was a (failed) attempt to outwit chance, his friend's was an exercise in will. The Bomb would sit stripped to the waist with his feet drawn up beneath his round thighs and a beer can balanced on the folds of his belly, trying to divine or influence the next result (which of them it was wasn't quite clear). To help him in this task he used any number of signs coaxed from the immediate surroundings: the number of flies that settled on the rim of a coffee cup, the number of cars that came down the street, the number of motes in a ray of sunlight that had found its way into the workshop through a chink in the panels of the metal walls. When no obvious signifier was at hand he would close his eyes and try to conjure the numbers on the insides of his eyelids, or picture the dice in the position in which they would come to rest. And then, having decided upon the result, he would lay his bets in the appropriate manner and throw. Most of the time he was wrong, of course; but when he did win he won big, usually just enough to allow him to continue to play.

It was inevitable that this idle pastime with its easy lack of focus – really an excuse for long, languid conversation – would be disrupted somewhat by Judd's inclusion in the system. It was a classic example of the three-body problem. The behaviour of a gravitational system with only two bodies – a double star for example, or the earth and its moon – is easy to predict if you know a few basic things about the objects involved, such as their mass and their relative positions at some point in time. But introduce a third body and however much information you have it is impossible to predict exactly what will happen. You know what outcomes are possible – Judd wins, Lionel wins, the Bomb wins, or there is a combination of draws – but beyond that, nada. The equations are no longer integrable – they no longer converge upon a single solution but offer only alternatives, separated by infinitely complex fractal boundaries.

To counter this problem the trio dispensed with cash for the time being and played instead with nuts, washers, piston rings and spark plugs, the idea being that they would go back to money when Judd had learnt the ropes, at which point major fluctuations in the game would, they hoped, have more to do with skilful betting and less to do with chance.

Although keen to enter this new arena with its promise of an alternative to the moral world with which he'd been programmed, Judd played hesitantly at first. He felt out of place sitting on his drum in his brown stay-pressed suit, while Lionel and the Bomb slumped back in their car seats, looking as if they had grown into the oil-stained overalls that hung about their bodies. But he soon got used to leaving his jacket hanging on a nail behind the door and loosening his tie, liking the feeling of jaded respectability that the look gave him even though he was still too young to carry it off properly. His face was smooth and glowed like a polished stone as he sat perspiring in the shadows of the repair shop. His skin had darkened even further as he had left adolescence behind: over a period of years it had turned from the dirty brown he'd been in England to a hue that seemed to contain all the colours of the dusk, sifted into one another and banded together tight.

He played cack-handed and concentrated too hard, hurling the dice across the hood as if any wrist action would curse the throw. 'Loosen up man,' the Bomb would drone, flopping and flipping his pudgy hand in the air to demonstrate. 'Let the dice *flow* out of you.' He watched his opponents carefully, asked them questions and tried to imitate their techniques, but he found both approaches next to useless and eventually it dawned on him that he was trying too hard and that this was a simple game that required little effort. All the possible combinations of the dice were fully refreshed each time you scooped them off the board; you did not have to concentrate except on the betting, that was the point. He got into the habit of placing a pass bet every time and only rarely laying the odds or placing a come.

With little to contribute to the interminable conversation that went on between Lionel and the Bomb, he began to watch the dice – not just when he was throwing them, but all the time – to see how they fell. He would have thought it would be hard to concentrate on the game like this, but on the contrary, he found that the progress of these numbers across the Chrysler hood was the perfect thing to help force the presence of Schemata from his mind.

Before long, the dice started to fascinate him for their own sake, not simply as a displacement activity. Most important, he'd noticed that as soon as he'd stopped trying to bend the outcome of the dice to his will, or place overly strategic bets, the sequence of results began to seem less erratic, no doubt in part because he was no longer only concerned with the small proportion of them that gave him some return. He began to take a mental note of all the throws, including those made by his opponents, and to see if could spot when the numbers formed little orders and patterns over time. He noticed how when he did win he won in streaks, as if the shape marked out by the dice had moved across the board to occupy the area circumscribed by his bets, forming itself around them, hugging them. It seemed as if the dice traced out the movements of a small creature. Something cold-blooded, he felt, a desert creature perhaps. Maybe a scorpion. Or a gecko.

He spent the whole summer this way, sitting drinking beer and rolling blunts with the two other softly sweating men in the dusty, shady repair shop, and watching the movements of an animal created by chance. 'Do you see that?' he said to Lionel and the Bomb one time.

'See what?'

'It just put out its tongue.'

'What did?'

'The dice lizard.'

'What you talkin' about?'

'All the throws, they make a shape. Looks like a lizard. I've been watching.' The two men exchanged glances. They'd thought him weird when he started making those plastic models; now they knew he was crazy.

The Bomb put a fat index finger up to the side of his forehead, rolled his eyes, and slowly screwed the finger back and forth. 'Whew, brutha, what you bin smokin'? Let me at some of that. Or you jus' bin lying out in the sun too much again?'

Judd opened his mouth to explain and then thought better of it. 'Yeah. You're right. I'm going nuts.' He lifted up the beer he was holding in his left hand and looked at it. 'Too much of this in the afternoons, I guess.' He drained the can and they all laughed, then he stood up. 'I'm going outside to get some air.' He walked out through the baking metal doors and round into the forecourt, just as a green Chevy pulled in. Quickly, Judd took the keys from his pocket, opened the side door to the showroom and slipped inside. While the driver was opening the door for his passenger, Judd unlocked the main entrance and walked back out into the sunlight to greet the two customers. As he moved towards them it struck him that Schemata's voice hadn't sounded in his head for weeks now. He quietly cleared his throat and looked for somewhere discreet to spit.

The conspiracy theory

They circle the child as she lies in the crib, the tubes and sensors trailing from her limbs torso head the articulation of an extended nervous system. Their starched garments rustle in the surgical silence of the room, provide a brushed high-hat to the toms of the ECGs which are meeping the child's two heartbeats in a long cycle of strange delay. The room is the logical conclusion of cleanliness – so white it shimmers – and utterly deadly. All is concealed except for the machines, the mutant body in its metal bed, the eyes and ears that escape the masks and caps. The child lies sedated; beneath their lids her eyes violently saccade. For some time now the doctors have been here.

Earlier: an oxygen tent, the child is prone, barely breathing. There are other children; it is a nursery. No outward signs suggest the unusual internal organisation. There is some doubt at this stage as to whether or not the child will ever attain consciousness; she has been in a coma since birth. The nurse arrives to take a blood sample. She peels a tiny blade from the sterile casing in which it has been packed by a clean and busy machine far, far away and clasps it in her right hand, using a grip which involves her thumb, her middle finger and her little finger. She feels a tremor in her wrist, as if a nerve has been trapped, and shakes her arm. With her left hand she lifts and secures the plastic flap of the isolation tent, and takes the child's arm. She crouches and manoeuvres the tiny thumb of the tiny hand into a suitable position. On the trolley beside her is a small phial in which she will collect the blood. She places the tip of the blade against the soft pad of flesh and prepares to slice a small and shallow wound. But before the metal even penetrates the epidermis the child bucks violently. The blade falls to the floor and the nursery is fractured by a fine, fine sound. The windows that separate room from corridor suddenly burst. Immediately the other infants are awake and they pummel the frightened air with their screams.

They move the child to the white room. Tests are carried out. Eventually the three doctors emerge.

'Inform the mother that the child was stillborn.'

'What if she asks to see it?'

'We had a stillborn late last night. The Fodor child. It will still be in the morgue. If she insists, show her that. But impress upon her that it is against hospital regulations.'

'Doctors! I'm sorry, but I find it hard to believe my ears! I must protest in the strongest possible terms!'

'Ms Shanahan, you saw the damage done to the nursery. We have no idea what it might be capable of . . .'

'It is not an it but a she, and she has a mother.'

'The mother is only fifteen years old. The likelihood is that the child would be put up for adoption in any event, especially considering the circumstances.'

'Yes, she is fifteen, and that is quite old enough for there to be a significant debate on the subject before a decision is reached. And the fact remains that such a decision is quite outside your authority.'

'She has a point, Alan.'

'She may have a point in normal circumstances, Scowcroft, but need I remind you that these are not normal circumstances? I want you both to understand that it is not I who have authorised this. There are higher powers involved. The instructions I have are quite clear. This is far from being an isolated case. I do not find what we have been asked to do particularly pleasant, but there are times when the greater good dictates . . .'

'The greater good? What about the good of this child?'

'It will be quite safe in our hands. If it . . .'

'If she!'

'. . . if *she* lives, and all goes well, there is no reason why she should not be put up for adoption at a later date. I can't believe you have a problem with this. We should have got used to it by this time. After all, Bindoon . . .'

'The Bindoon project was terminated nearly a decade ago. And how you can stand there and bring that up with the stories that have been emerging from that place . . .'

'You shouldn't believe everything you hear. And the case still remains that even were these abnormalities not exhibited the wounds the mother has inflicted upon herself are reason enough to have the child removed from her care.'

'We don't know that they were self-inflicted!'

'Ms Shanahan, please! I am prepared to discuss the situation to a certain extent, but I will not argue the toss over conclusions that are staring us in the face!'

Ms Shanahan fell silent.

'What do you . . . what do your instructions suggest that we do?' asked Scowcroft.

'Thank you, doctor. A sensible question at last. For the time being at least *she* is to be kept here under observation. Ms Shanahan, since you are obviously so concerned over her fate I will put you in charge of organising that. But don't get too involved. You must realise that in the final analysis it is out of our hands.'

The child survived and grew like a creeper into the corners of its room. When she touched her face she felt dry wall of plaster breeze-block brick and flaking paint. When she put her foot upon the ground she felt foundation, piles sunk deep into the earth, the rust and worm and clay that gripped and seeped about them. When she looked she saw light, surface, colour, texture. When she listened she heard the sounds that underpinned the silence: the footsteps in the corridors, the wails that pained the wards at night, the reassuring clink of glassware, the soft pops of hypodermics puncturing skin, the dry rasp of cells as they died and coagulated to scab a healing wound. When she ate she tasted the yellow mark of Africa, the bark of foreign valleys, the cloches of the Home Counties, the old earth of the Midlands, the rum-dark minerals of the steppes, the seething heat of Hyderabad, the sharp quick yeasts of German forests. When she bit she bit the bursting globe, when she pissed she pissed the oceans and the clouds. When she shat she shat the cosmos, her sphincter both channel and interrupt.

There was a wet-nurse whose milk was full of notes and chords. She talked to her but the words were very loud to her and she found each expression difficult to grasp so much did it speak of simple, discrete and alien things – for in her world there was nothing but relationships; it was a sponge of complications. Everything moved and nothing moved, except her limbs which grew almost as she watched, the baby wrinkles disappearing as if warmed from underneath. Sometimes she lay there floating in the brightness, sometimes it was dark, so dark she could feel the glint her eyes made in the void. Sometimes she spread faeces on the walls, writing herself in the spiral waves and patterns of the Belousov-Zabotinski reaction. Other times there was nothing to look at and she would amuse herself by running cross-catalators on her retinae and watching their pretty patterns.

She left her smells around the place, hid from them, followed them. The tracks she liked best were the ones left by the heat of her palms and soles upon the frigid linoleum. By lying on her stomach she could apperceive the differentials thus created fizz and hum to nothingness, segue back into the cool metastratum of the floor.

Big bang

By the time Route 66 Autos was shut down Judd thought about little except the dice. For whatever reason, the lot's financial usefulness had finally come to an end and Scofield sold all the cars to another dealer across town. After three days spent delivering the vehicles – more work than they'd done in months – the three employees all found themselves out of a job. The Bomb wasn't particularly bothered as his career as a DJ was taking off – he'd been doing three or four gigs a week for some months now and he no longer needed the day job. Lionel and Judd hung out together for a while, until Scofield found Lionel work fixing up the small fleet of delivery trucks that he had just purchased for the service laundry business that he was starting up in Venice Beach.

'If I hear of any kind of opening I'll call you right up,' Lionel promised Judd over lunch in a diner two streets from the ocean. 'I'll even mention it to Mr S. A lot of people work in that place. Something'll come up. Don't worry about it. Lionel'll sort you, mon, no problem.'

'Yeh, thanks, man. I knew I could count on you. Something'll come up.' Judd stirred sugar into his coffee with a plastic spoon and what Lionel had once told him about the history of sugar – that there was as much (if not more) blood on this white powder as there was on cocaine – flashed through his mind. He was going to miss working with the dread.

'What about your folks, mon? Can they help you out?'

'I dunno. I mean the old man got me the job at Route 66 in the first place. He's a friend of Irving's, see. I don't want to ask him again. I figure I want to sort something out for myself.' He hadn't told Lionel about the years of analysis, or that his mother was Melinda Volitia, and he had no intention of letting him or the Bomb find out about either. But it was true, he didn't want to turn to his parents. He had been avoiding them ever since he had moved out the year before and he didn't miss them too much. When he talked with his father on the phone Moses sounded shiny and busy. He spoke to Judd now as if Judd were finished with, a business deal that had been completed. Judd felt as though he had been turned out of the house in the same way that a washing machine is turned out of the factory – new, efficient, desirable, functional, designed to sit in its place and do its job. Fully readjusted.

As for his mother, she'd retired from acting and had taken up a full-time career in shopping. Whenever he spoke to her she always seemed to be just back from Rodeo Drive or somewhere like that, or off to have coffee at the latest café or for lunch at some little place down the coast. She seemed happy, though he wasn't really sure that he knew her well enough any more to be in a position to judge. She had become carefree, but in a studied way. He missed her moods, her mild depressions.

She and Moses had moved from Malibu to Beverly Hills and on the last occasion that Judd had paid them a visit Melinda had been throwing one of her 'infamous' pool parties. He had been troubled by the new crowd that his parents were mixing with; he got the feeling that many of their current acquaintances weren't altogether comfortable at the idea of a mixed-race family in their midst. Too many comments from behind the vodka tonics. But in some ways this was easier to cope with than the behaviour he'd sometimes encountered in the past when his mother's friends, enchanted as they were with his 'exoticism', had made occasional drunken efforts to seduce him. It had begun when he was about sixteen: hands – male and female – brushing his arm or butt a little too often, brazen stares, blown kisses. Melinda, when she witnessed it, had thought it wonderful that her son was this attractive and she teased him about it, but perhaps she wouldn't have been so keen if she'd been around the night Donna had got drunk and lured Judd out to the pool house where she'd practically assaulted him.

He sipped at the sweet coffee and looked out into the street, thinking to himself that fall didn't really happen in LA, that the seasons just moved from summer to less-summer and back again. 'I miss shooting craps already,' he complained to Lionel. The truth was that without his regular fix of the game, Judd was finding it difficult to continue to keep the psychoanalytic imprint that had been left in his brain subdued. With each additional day that passed Schemata's presence loomed a little larger in his thoughts. He was frightened. He didn't want to go back.

'Yeah. Me too. I have to work afternoons now. I've no use for that, mon.' Lionel grinned. 'You were just getting to be good, too.'

'Well, I reckon I'd learnt the ropes all right, but not much else.' He took another sip of his coffee. 'You seen the Bomb?'

'Yeh, saw him Sunday. He's got a gig this weekend, some party over in the valley. Great flyer – it's a picture of a nuclear warhead, and on it it says "The Bomb", and then underneath "The universe began with an explosion". Good, huh? D'ya wanna come along? I'll pick you up if you like?'

'Yeh, mebbe. I'll call you.'

'You should come. You know those Valley girls, mon, when those bitches are on heat you'd better watch out!' Lionel always talked like this about women. He had a pet dog he'd named Beaver.

'Women aren't just for sex!' retorted Judd self-righteously.

'Totally. They're there for cleanin' and cookin' too.' Lionel thought this was hilarious and throwing his head back let out a raucous laugh.

'Jesus,' said Judd. 'You're a lost cause.' They finished up their coffee and Judd came out with the question that he had come to see Lionel to ask. 'Know where I can get a game of craps?'

His friend eyed him suspiciously. 'What, that you can afford to get in on?'

'Yeh. Hey, I'm serious!'

'Not this side of Vegas, my friend.'

'Come on man, you must know of something. You taught me how to play the goddamned game. I just want to keep my hand in.'

'I've heard that before.'

'C'mon! Give me a break.'

Lionel swilled the request around in his head for a moment or two, picking out a toothpick from the plastic dispenser that stood on the table between the two of them and rolling it to and fro across his bottom lip with his tongue, a thin white line against the purple. 'Come to the party,

Saturday. I'll introduce you to a guy I know. But you'd better be sure. These people don't fool around.'

'Whaddaya mean, "sure"?' said Judd, delighted. 'Of course I'm sure.'

'OK then, I'll see you Saturday. I'll pick you up around ten. And don't wear that godawful brown suit of yours or they won't let you in.'

The lambda parameter

They pulled up in front of a house that flashed lights and music like a close encounter. All along the street, cars were pulled up on to the sidewalk. Lionel popped a pill into his mouth and offered one to Judd, who declined, thinking to himself that Rastas weren't supposed to do chemicals. Lionel shrugged. 'Your mistake, mon.'

They entered the house by the side gate and came out by a pool lit by underwater lights which turned the water into an undulating cube of neon jelly. Two or three figures sculled across the iridescent surface, faults in a jewel. But most of the guests stood fully clothed on the patio or kept to the inside of the house where the music was loudest. Lionel immediately started saying hello to people and forgot about Judd, who felt lost and a little overdressed. He loitered around the pool, smiling stupidly at other guests. A woman approached him holding an unlit cigarette. Judd took out his lighter, lit it for her. She struck up a conversation and he looked around nervously over the girl's shoulder throughout, trying to decide whether or not she was coming on to him.

'Say, are you waiting for someone?' she asked.

'Er, no, I was just wondering where the bar was. I need a drink.'

'Drink's all in the kitchen. Just help yourself. It's through there.' She gesticulated languorously in the direction of the open french windows. The DJs had obviously just swapped over because instead of wailing guitars something darker and more bass-driven had started to thump out into the night.

'Thanks. Do you want something?'

'No, thanks. I'm tripping. Alcohol's so last year.'

'Oh, right. Guess I'm out of touch then.'

'Guess you are. Say, you wouldn't happen to have any pot on you, would you?'

'No, sorry.'

'No, thought not. Don't worry about it.' She paused, took a long drag on her Marlboro and stared intently into Judd's eyes, which would have been unnerving but for the fact that she seemed to be looking right through him. 'Go on then! Go and get your drink. See you later maybe.'

'Yeh, see you later.' He left her by the pool and went inside. The music was extremely loud and the air, what little of it there was, reeked of dope. All the furniture had been pushed back against the walls and the space was crammed with people. Although there didn't seem to be enough room for dancing almost everybody was. Those who weren't hung out on the stairs or sat legs up on the sofas. A strobe came on and cut time up into discrete segments, each one of which looked like a scene from Picasso's *Guernica*. Judd wondered where all the horses had come from and pushed on through in what he hoped was the direction of the kitchen.

Just as he reached it, a girl with a seven-inch afro and enormous breasts that had been vacuum-packed into a striped spandex T-shirt stumbled through the doorway and grabbed his shoulder to steady herself. He gawped as her chest undulated before him; she caught him staring and slapped him sharply across the face. 'Keep your filthy eyes to yourself, nigga!' she snapped.

'You tell him, girl!' another woman screeched to her rear and both of them burst out laughing. 'That's three now,' they agreed. Then they did a high five, put their arms around each other's waists and staggered off into the main fray.

An enormous man in combat fatigues who was propping up the door jamb grinned at Judd through a haze of smoke. 'Don't mind them, man, that's just Rita and Leona. Here, have a pull on this.' He passed Judd an enormous joint rolled in a cigar leaf and Judd took a few tokes before passing it back. It tasted good; the smoke was sweet on the back of his tongue and the hit buzzed him all over. Feeling reinforced, he squeezed past the donor into the kitchen.

Inside, a couple leant up against the refrigerator, kissing ostentatiously. Their tongues lapped in and out of each other's mouths, eels mating in an urn. To one side of the sink a tall man with a goatee was cracking jokes to two girls and on the other side two teenagers were chasing the dragon using a plastic straw and some silver foil stretched taut across the top of a glass. The light was bright and clinical, and everyone in the room looked ill. Any chance of finding something to drink in the fridge looked slim – there was no way that the couple was moving. Glancing around he saw that the sink was filled with water – water that had presumably once been ice – and that floating among the bottle tops and cigarette butts were a couple of cans of beer. He took them both, dried them off, stuck one in his jacket pocket and opened the other, then cleared out of the room, leaving the rest of them to it. As he went, the guy with the goatee made some remark about college kids which had the girls doubling up with laughter.

On the far side of the lounge Judd spotted the Bomb. He was bent over a pair of decks, an enormous pair of headphones on his head, mixing two records together. With quick flicks of his wrist he scratched the right hand one to and fro, creating a melody off the cuff, while with his left hand he used the pitch control of the second deck to control the tempo of the bass. Judd watched with admiration as his friend improvised a perfect series of rhythms and effects, never once dropping a beat. The dance floor, which until now had been lazy and haphazard, quickly began to energise. The less committed dancers peeled away and filtered upstairs or outside. Someone threw the french windows right open, letting in a gust of fresh air, and a couple of breakdancers colonised the area immediately in front of them. The Bomb dialled the tempo up a notch, fully aware of what was happening. He let the bass run a little, allowing the floor to settle in, letting everybody expand into the extra space. Then as soon as he felt they were ready he snapped off the sound, gave one bar of silence, then plunged straight into a new and massive beat, pumping the volume sliders straight up as he did so. The floor underwent an immediate phase transition: its various factions and speeds coalesced like whipping cream. The dancers, previously a fairly heterogeneous group, began to move together. Even Judd was caught up in it, and he downed his beer, tucked his jacket beneath a table and began to gyrate. What had been a bizarre and unwieldy gathering came alive: it became a party. Time slowed down and began to loop as the scene created its own temporality, constructed a bubble that could bob obliviously on top of the chattering surfs of the week. This is what everyone had come for, this take-off. Now nothing external existed; the outside world could be forgotten for as long as the effect could be sustained.

Judd lost track of how long he danced. Those not dancing had been supporting the dancers as if they were marathon runners, handing them drinks, passing them spliffs and cigarettes, cutting up lines of coke on mirrors which were then circulated through the fray. He partook of everything, found himself adopted by one of the groups that had formed like benzene rings, grooved down so far that he didn't realise how absolutely off his face he was. When Lionel appeared at his shoulder and yelled something incoherent in his ear all he thought it necessary to do was to nod wildly and mouth 'Great party! Great party!' and try to encourage him to dance.

'NO, MON, LISTEN! THAT GUY IS HERE, THE ONE I TOLD YOU ABOUT.'

'WHICH GUY?'

'THE CRAPS GUY – DON'T YOU WANT TO MEET HIM?'

Abruptly the rhythms of the day-to-day rushed back to Judd, as if he'd just answered the front door to the police. Suddenly he felt drunk and slightly dizzy. 'SHIT, YEAH. HANG ON, I'M COMING.' Lionel led the way across the room and up the stairs, and Judd followed him closely, trying not to get sucked back into the dance. The stairway lights were on and he blinked as the two of them picked their way up them, using the tiny gaps between the seated people like stepping stones. At length they reached one of the bedrooms and with the music below vibrating the floor beneath them they entered.

Inside, the room seemed like the calm at the eye of a storm. There were four or five people in there, in various attitudes of repose. The two on the bed were smoking a tall hookah that stood by them on the floor; the others sat around on large cushions. Raga played softly above the now distant sound of the Bomb's bass.

Lionel sat down and Judd followed suit. To begin with no one said anything, then one of the men offered Judd a beer, produced from a chipped polystyrene cooler that sat beside him. Judd took it and lit a cigarette, trying to fit in a little more with this new vibe. His friend began to skin up while talking in a low voice to the skinny Chinese man he had sat down next to, who was much older than anyone else in the room.

'Been dancing?' the girl on the bed asked Judd.

'Yeah. It was good. Hot, though.' He tugged at his shirt to illustrate: it was soaked through with sweat and clung to his body.

'Looked it,' said the girl. Lionel glanced up at her and leant over.

'Judd, this is Mr Chang. I've had a word with him and he would be pleased to let you into one of his games.' That was quick. He hadn't been expecting that.

'Thanks,' he said, too loudly, not knowing what else to say. Mr Chang bowed forward slightly and smiled Orientally. Judd beamed back, unable to control his facial muscles. His mind was racing. What had he taken on the dance floor? He had no idea, but his whole body seemed electrified. He felt supremely confident. Nothing, he knew, could go wrong. 'Yeah,' he said again, 'thanks. Hope you know what you're letting yourself in for!'

The Chinaman looked at Judd closely, his gaze undermining the young American's drug-maintained composure. Judd felt his cheeks begin to warm. The stranger immediately spotted his embarrassment and, in a voice as dry as the desert and spilling words like grains of sand, offered to save him. 'Lionel knows the address, Mr Axelrod. We look forward to seeing you. Next weekend, I hope.'

'Next weekend,' said Judd, committing himself at that moment. 'For sure.'

Suddenly there was a commotion in the hallway and a few seconds later a tall white hippy burst in through the door. 'The cops are here,' he gasped. 'They're breaking up the party.' Everyone jumped to their feet in a frenzy of tidying and stashing and emptying of pockets. The music had stopped and Judd headed for the door to see what was going on. A strange mixture of apathy and panic welled up the stairs. Judd looked round for Lionel and Mr Chang, wondering what they were going to do. Lionel was there, calmly emptying the ashtray out of the window and sipping from a bottle of Scotch, but Mr Chang, rather mysteriously, had already disappeared.

Under observation

They kept her under observation, put her in capsules, covered her in electrodes (just like poor Laika, though they didn't launch Emma into space), put capsules in her, gave her tests, taught her to speak, took blood samples, tissue samples (in a room with no windows), made her say 'ahhhh', taught her to read, to write, sometimes (irresponsibly) gave her a hug, got her to run, to walk, to drool, to scream, got her to tell them, to stand in X-ray machines, to submit to their CAT scan, their PET scan, their MRI, to let them shave her head and insert needles and probes, to simulate thought with machines (move her arm, move her leg, this is red, I'm afraid, this is pain), moved around her, all white coats and eyes, gave her drugs for an illness, kept her well-balanced (diazepam, nitrazepam, flurazepam, Largactil, Thorazine, LSD, mescaline, phencyclidine, amphetamine, chlorpromazine, lithium, ibuprofen, aspirin), took her for walks, left her alone, filmed her,

recorded her, submitted her to scrutiny, performed exploratory surgery upon her,
fed her, watered her, let her watch TV, let her watch TV, let her watch TV,
restrained her, worried over her, obtained funding for her, compared her, contrasted
her, ignored her, forgot about her, remembered her, discussed her, trusted her,
disgusted her, frightened her, feared her, fitted her into projections and theories
and statistics and charts, traced her, retraced her, raced her, put her in mazes and
labyrinths, told her to find her way out, told her to find her way out, told her to
find her way. So she started to, she started to, she started to look for it.

The gambler

Once he had become an initiate of the Chinaman's gambling dens, Judd never held down a proper job again. The other players, the men and women he encountered in the secret basements, in the back rooms of clubs, in the refitted apartments, were always on the look-out for a body to run the odd errand – make a couple of deliveries, stand in a phone box for a couple of hours waiting for a call, mind a warehouse for a week or two – and they generally paid handsomely for the favour. There were offers of heavier things but Judd always turned them down; he didn't want trouble, just some easy cash to help him make a stake. And most of the time he did all right. He was a cautious player, at least in the beginning, and he neither won nor lost large amounts. After the question of keeping Schemata at bay, his real interest was not the money but the shapes and patterns of the various games on offer. The 'open' games were best: craps, roulette, blackjack, Hold 'Em, games where you could see how things progressed from one stage to another. On occasion he went down to the track and played the horses but he never got into it – you had to know too much about the turf, the conditions and the animals themselves, as well as all the double play that went on behind the scenes. It was too much. With cards or craps, as long as you knew that the pack wasn't stacked nor the dice loaded, you could get by and Judd quickly developed a feel for these things. Because he always looked for patterns he could spot the lopsided rhythms introduced into the flow of play by a bent deck or a weighted wheel a mile off. Other players would notice it too, though not always consciously. They would become uneasy and bet out of character unless they were fresh to the scene, in which case they would just lose. But soon Judd could play a straight or bent game with equal aplomb and after he'd been at it six months most nights he was coming out evens at worst.

When Moses and Melinda called to check up on him he told them he had gone into partnership with a friend and they were running a night-club together. The lie had a kind of twisted truth to it for the Bomb was a rising star on the club scene and the nights when he wasn't gambling Judd would act as sidekick, organising taxis, carrying records, doing sound checks and so on – all the things that Lionel could no longer do because of his full-on day job. The Bomb used to tease him about it whenever they saw each other, *Hey Lionel! When you gettin' married? How's the mortgage? You still screwin' the bank manager's daughter?* But Lionel didn't take it to heart; he'd kind of got into his work and had some people under him now and was earning a reasonable whack. Was even talking about flying his family over to LA. And anyway, where was the fun in lugging the Bomb's record cases around? After all, he still got into the clubs for free whenever he wanted, which had been the main aim in the first place.

But Judd was happy to do the legwork. It gave him a chance to get into a scene which otherwise would have passed him by. He didn't often dance like he had at the party in the Valley but he loved to stand by the decks for a night, sucking on a bottle of beer and watching the bodies gyring and sweating before him get sliced into segments and stretched across space and time by the music and the lights. Watching the floors like he did, he began to learn how the Bomb played them, how he'd probe the mood with a couple of preliminary tracks, how he'd coax the crowd into a state where he could do something with them. On the best nights he'd pick up the groove straight away and rush with it, it would almost be like he was dancing himself; he'd reel off records in a sequence that you couldn't imagine could be any different, it would be as if he'd worked it all out beforehand, and of course some of it he had.

Judd couldn't gamble on those nights, didn't have the energy, though sometimes after the club had closed he'd turn up at a game and just sit in and watch. It seemed to him that there were parallels between a game and a club. The cards or the dice were, in a way, the DJ: they created intensities and potentials and so manipulated the moods of the participants, just as the Bomb did. The gamblers were like dancers out there to capture and surf, hoping they could fit their moves to the rhythms of the night, sniff out a winning streak and play into it, sit on it. Judd felt this was more than a metaphor. Gambling was the lizard's dance, the dance of the desert. He swore he could feel its rhythms pulsing away there deep in his limbic system whenever he played, a dim and distant song the words of which had long been forgotten, but whose tune was still hummed by the neural circuits that were part of the biological stratum deposited countless millennia previously by his reptilian ancestors. At this point the idea became nebulous and obscure, but what was certain was that there was more to gambling than chance and will, the techniques that Lionel and the Bomb had always used. Chance and will, Judd thought. Chance and will, the deuce, the loser's pair. There were patterns here, and patterns could be studied, manipulated, choreographed.

In the clubs, then, boys and girls spun and weaved in front of him. Their pink-copper-orange-brown bodies were young and unblemished, and they ignored him. But in the gambling dens middle-aged women whose bodies had spread like bursting sacks of wheat eyed him between hands, while they lit their cigarettes and placed them between their wet lips, red and pinched like vulvas. And the men, too, long since freed by the night and the cards and the booze of any moral façade, would watch his pecs and biceps flex against his shirt, as he threw his dice or stretched to reach a deck of cards, and suck absently at the flaps of their cheeks.

This was the life in which the offers were made and he sank deeper into it. The dice, the cards, they became his machines for mapping the contours of coincidence, and of his mind. They became the tools of his philosophy, helping him both to understand the world and what Schemata had done to him. Those limbic rhythms seemed to be deeper, more important, more powerful psychological structures than those the analyst had imposed. And those rhythms were part of a terrain across which each game would crawl, a desert creature in search of warmth, of shelter, of something to quell the naggings of its stomach.

The lizard, 'find the lizard', his own secret code for spotting the patterns in a game. It became his little mantra, something he would whisper to himself in the lost hours past midnight, for which there were no maps, only insinuations. Once, the day after a particularly successful night, he drove down to Rodeo Drive and picked out a gold ring in the shape of a gecko. It had emeralds for eyes and he never took it off. A mineral deposit laid down around his finger, it became part of him and helped to remind him how he was remaking himself. It wasn't a charm and it wasn't a token, it was just something that was his and his alone, his own private symbol, his own private joke, something that he had built which had nothing to do with his parents, with Schemata, or with Jennifer. He'd had it with all of that, he didn't want anything to do with any of it. When he thought of Jennifer now it was not with longing, but with anger. She was just the same as all the rest and they had all taken from him, all of them, they had just ripped bits off him and passed him down the line. It was a country of greed he had come from and it was a country of greed he would enter. He didn't need a passport, he had citizenship. He would pass through the iterated nights, the numberless rooms, the nameless games and the faceless players, and it would not matter to him whether he made money, it would not make any difference. Because he knew, *he knew*, about the way things came out of nothing to coalesce and exist, and then just as quickly disappear, leaving one man with empty pockets and another with a head full of corrosive joy. That's what he, Judd Axelrod, had got out of all of this. That's what he had *learnt*. The numbers, the colours thrown up by the dice, the cards, they could be a zephyr or a sandstorm, could lull all the players to sleep or rip the roofs right off their huts and none of it made any difference, this was just the way it was. Forget life in the jungle, this was life in the desert, where you had to fuel yourself every day on the heat of the sun – the rush of the game – if you wanted to make it through the cold of the night. The desert, where you had to fight every minute to survive. Judd had discovered a different logic from that imposed upon him by Schemata and his father, one far more subtle and complex, that grew out of the world rather than imprinting its tenets upon it. And he would use it to cut himself free from his past, to take proper control of his life for the very first time.

Green regression

But unfortunately for Judd, his life didn't want to play ball. The first unusual event occurred in the basement of the M Club, on Twenty-fifth and W. He'd played here before, but not often. The front was a lame piano bar full of hookers; you sat at the bar and asked for Leon and were shown through a padded leather door into an office, where you were frisked and led through another door marked EXIT. It was mainly roulette and blackjack, though he knew they hosted the occasional poker game for big money, way out of his league. Tonight it was the usual clientele – small-time crooks, pimps, businessmen, professional gamblers keeping their hand in. Judd played a few rounds of cards but it didn't feel right, so he moved to one of the two roulette tables. He spotted the lizard almost immediately and it scuttled obediently across the board and wrapped itself around his constellation of bets. But then – and this was the weird thing, the state change – it stayed with him all night. Instead of him trying to follow it, to anticipate and second guess it, it was following him. He'd place his bets, the croupier would spin the wheel and it would be there, waiting for him. He couldn't believe it at first, but then he began to feel the rhythms that he had sensed before and almost to hear the song of the sand, alien sounds from the deep past that rose up out of his blood. He started to shake and stared unblinking at the baize, overwhelmed by its colour, until his eyes began to bulge. When he finally looked up everything in the room was tinged with green – people's skin, their drinks, the lights and the smoke that hung in the air – as if he had just taken a huge hit of amyl. The other players glanced at him uncomfortably and the man who oversaw the game whispered something to one of this men.

That night he went home with his pockets full and his head spinning, to dream of a paradise of hot rocks, cool fissures and plentiful flies. The next night, at a different venue, he played craps, but it was the same story. And the next night, and the night after that. But then, as abruptly as it began, his winning streak was brought to an end.

At first light the morning after his fourth successful night a storm blew up. It whipped through the city, turning the underside of all the leaves upwards and baring them to what little sky managed to creep down through the eddying banks of smog. It was as if the branches themselves called out to the foliage being torn from them, so windswept were they by the unrelenting gusts; like the old women of a pillaged town they raged along the streets, screaming at their oppressors who gleefully fled to the hills, having killed all the menfolk, raped all the girls and stolen or spoilt all the food.

Judd had planned to sleep late but was woken when one of his shutters worked loose from its hinges and whipped round, smashing the window it was supposed to protect. Trying to secure it he cut his hand; thick blood eased its way out of the sharp, deep split the glass had made in the web of skin stretched between his thumb and index finger. He left a small trail of splayed crimson droplets on the floor-boards as he ran across the room to grab a towel with which to staunch the flow.

All day he couldn't settle, the wind disturbed him. He watched TV and played some records but it didn't work and eventually he gave up on the apartment and went outside for a walk, deciding to brave the weather. He caught a bus downtown to where the office blocks trapped the currents of air. The wind flicked rubbish down the chasms that served as streets, nomad articles that plagued pedestrians and hunted for homes in the bushes and gutters, in the dead zones created by cars and the corners of buildings. Clumps of detritus lifted and spun as draughts clipped the local geometries and fell into secret patterns. Everywhere these vortices lay in wait, invisible, cunning, virtual. Judd strode along, blasts of air drying his eyes in their sockets. He sought refuge in a record store, flipping through the racks without buying anything. Selecting one or two things he knew from the Bomb's collection he went to a booth and gave them a listen, but they didn't sound the same without the mixing and the scratching and the dance floor full of people.

He bought a newspaper, nearly lost it to the wind, then sat in a diner trying to read it over coffee and suffering from the slight light-headedness that comes with killing time. Everyone around him was at work, their eyes on the clock all day long, their pulses beating fast and irregularly, shackled to the strange biomechanical rhythms that between them they'd created. Judd wasn't a part of it and it gave him a headache, watching them dart up and down the sidewalk outside. He felt like a rogue corpuscle that had got stranded in the most minute capillary of some far-flung and forgotten tissue of the body, his very chemical processes inhibited by his distance from the heart, the flesh around him greying, mutated by cancers. When he returned to his apartment, wired from the coffee he had drunk but still sleepy, he thought of calling up Lionel at work. But it was too much effort. And what would he say? He'd have to think of something and he was too tired. He drew the bedroom blinds, curled up on his bed and fell asleep.

Outside, the wind was still whipped up like crazy and it brought on precarious dreams of ancient landscapes and saurian economies. But when Judd awoke he remembered nothing. Instead he felt suddenly and totally alert, completely clarified, as if the nap had rinsed out his mind. His hand had scabbed and the throbbing had subsided. It was dark outside and when he checked his watch it was ten o'clock. The storm seemed to have blown itself out. He had a raging thirst and drank down a root beer that he found in the fridge and took a shower, but still his throat felt parched. There was a game that night at Geraldo's and he figured he'd go, he was in the mood for it.

★

Geraldo's was a den above a travel agents just off Santa Monica Boulevard and the game there had been a regular fixture for months. With customary caution, Judd parked a couple of blocks away and walked the final stretch. But when he reached the door and rang there was no answer. Bemused, he stood and pressed the buzzer repeatedly, listening to it bleating away deep inside the building. He was sure he'd got the right day. Eventually he gave up and drove to a couple more places, but it was the same story all over: games which had been going on for ever had vanished. He tried the hotel where Harvey had been running a craps shoot in a second-floor room three nights a week for five years now, but all he got was a confused Swedish couple suffering from jet lag.

The big operation in the warehouse on the outskirts of Watts, where you could get craps, roulette, poker, the works, was still going on, but Peri, the Mexican bouncer, would not let him in. 'Sorry, man, but you can' go in there.'

'What's the problem, Peri?'

'There's nuthin' in there for you, my fren'.'

'Peri! It's me! It's Judd for chrissake. C'mon, quit foolin' around.'

Judd pushed up the bouncer's arm and tried to walk past him, but the Mexican grabbed him by the collar and twisted, pulling Judd back around to face him. 'No entry,' he hissed. 'Unnerstan'?'

The stitches on the collar of Judd's shirt began to pop as Peri increased the pressure. 'Yeh, sure, sure,' he gasped, turning a deep shade of purple. 'Hey, you're choking me, you're choking me!' Peri let him go and his hands went to his neck. 'Christ almighty. What the fuck is this all about?'

'Sorry, man. You're not welcome any more. I'm doin' you a favour by tellin' you now. Don' come back.'

Judd had never thought about the various games he was involved in as particularly interconnected. He'd started off at Mr Chang's place, some-one he'd met there had introduced him to somewhere else and it had gone on from there. Each venue seemed to have its own isolated scene, his own movements one of the few links between them. But the unanswered doors and vacated rooms could only make sense if the games he'd known were all part of something much larger, all of which was perhaps controlled by the Chinaman. Judd began to imagine the games as nodes on a thin and fragile web suspended beneath the structures of society and the law. By winning he constituted a threat and as such his access to this carefully maintained network had now been denied. The structure which had seemed so open, which had welcomed him day and night while he had observed its codes he now saw from a different perspective, one which made it appear rigorous, tight-knit, more like a cocoon, each of its earlier functions inverted to repel outsiders. Each group of regulars was suddenly a platoon, every clandestine door a battlement, every grapevine a two-way conduit for information.

Over the ensuing nights he tried various other venues but the results were no better and often far worse. On the last occasion he got a black eye and a split lip for his pains and was told he was lucky still to be solvent – and alive. Most people weren't allowed to win. It was only because Mr Chang liked him that his winnings had not been repossessed, but that would change fast if he didn't stop causing trouble.

He finally took the hint and decided to give it up. Walking back through town that night, totting up the rejections in his mind, he stopped at a bar and got himself properly drunk. It wasn't fair! It just wasn't fucking fair! What had he done to deserve this? He felt like he'd been given a chance, just one, to pull himself out the mire of shit in which, through little fault of his own, he'd been dumped and now it had been taken away. Already Schemata bubbled in the back of his mind.

After his eighth or ninth whisky he started to talk with the barman, who listened out of a sense of professional duty. Around 2 a.m., morose and depressed, he tried to call up Lionel from the phone in the corridor where the yellow boxes of beer were stacked up to the ceiling, seeping a smell of hops and damp cardboard, but he got the Ansaphone and didn't leave a message. Back at the bar someone bought him drinks and laid a hand on his arm. The hand bothered him but he couldn't see a way to do anything about it; interestingly, he could no longer tell exactly what it was he was drinking. There seemed to be lots of people around that he vaguely knew. He liked this bar; it was friendly. He'd come back (though he still wasn't sure about this hand). He was thinking of saying something to its owner when someone called him nigger, they definitely called him nigger, and why would they do that in the middle of such a friendly bar? He'd have to do something about that.

And then there was a fight and when he came to he was in the back of a prowl car and being driven downtown. He thought he was dreaming and tried to get out which gave the cop riding shotgun the opportunity he'd been looking for to rod him in the stomach with his night-stick, which only prompted him to vomit through the grille and all down the back of the driver's seat. That got him beaten up properly, by the side of the road.

★

273

By the next morning Melinda had got wind of the affair (a mother's intuition?) and sent Michael – no longer her official PA but still a trusted friend – down to the station to handle the situation and to make sure that it stayed out of the press. Judd had never liked Michael, who was practically albino and always looked as if someone had just rammed a battery up his arse which, knowing Michael, thought Judd evilly, they probably had. Michael, however, had always been good at his job. He managed to persuade the police to drop the resisting-arrest jacket, got Judd released on a drunk and disorderly, and drove the prodigal son back home. During the journey his self-satisfaction oozed through the car like an enormous cowpat, impinging on Judd far more than the awful hang-over or the flesh-memories of baton and fist.

Judd tried his best to ignore Michael's chatter. All he wanted to do was wallow in thoughts of anger and remorse. He looked down at the lizard ring. It had been damaged in one of the previous night's struggles and the gecko's expression was bent into a mocking smirk. Fate was heaping insult upon injury. Judd pulled the ring from his finger, depressed the button to lower the automatic window and threw the offending object from the car.

'What was that?' asked Michael, ever watchful.

'I thought I was going to be sick.'

'Oh, whatever you do don't be sick in the car. Melinda will kill you. She's going to have your balls as it is, you lucky boy.'

'She's my mother, you arsehole.'

'Um, maybe, but we all know what Freud had to say about that now, don't we?' Judd picked a pair of sunglasses off the dashboard and put them on. He couldn't remember what month it was, but as far as he could tell it was summer all over again.

Order out of chaos

Michael pulled in at Judd's parents' driveway and leant out the window to operate the carport door with his ultrasound remote. 'Batteries are low,' he remarked, somehow managing to make even that comment sound facetious. Judd limped in through the side door and slipped up the stairs without going through the main body of the house. He headed straight for his mother's bathroom, locked the door, turned on both the taps, and raided the medicine cabinet for drugs.

Melinda, who had been notified of her son's arrival by Michael, came up the stairs and rapped on the door. 'Judd! Are you in there?'

'No.'

'Come on out.'

'I'm in the bath.'

'What in hell's name do you think you were up to?'

'Mom, I just got drunk.'

'How on earth did you manage . . .'

'I don't remember.'

'You're a disgrace. Wait till your father gets home. And I want you looking respectable. We have a party this afternoon and for once I expect you to be there. It's about time you paid some attention to family events. Dr Schemata will be coming and I don't want him to think that you've let him down. I've asked Michael to go out and buy you a set of clean clothes. He'll leave them outside the door. And you'll wear them, please.'

Judd groaned loudly, which seemed to satisfy his mother. He heard her heels clicking away along the parquet landing, brisk and efficient, possibly even sexy (he felt a fresh wave of nausea at the thought) then got into the bath and slid down beneath the surface of the water, his nostrils a dark island in a sea of white suds, an ailing crocodile nestling by rapids.

By the time he emerged the guests were already arriving. The tension between mother and son eased, now that there was no chance of a confrontation and besides, once Melinda saw the state of her son's face – its bruises nicely set off by the deep reds and purples of the Hawaiian shirt that Michael had thoughtfully provided – her anger dissipated and the mild annoyance she exhibited for the rest of the day was kept up mainly for the sake of appearances. Judd put on the sunglasses he'd stolen from Michael's car to hide his swollen eye, munched another Valium and wandered out by the pool.

He was picking at the trays of hors d'oeuvres and trying to avoid conversation when the ex-PA sidled over and pressed a large cocktail into his hand. 'Hair of the dog,' he whispered loudly. 'Patent hangover cure. Drink up!' He patted Judd on the shoulder and moved away. Judd sipped at the dark liquid suspiciously, but it was good and he drank it down. Whatever it was, it seemed to help and he later remembered it as possibly the first really pleasant thing that Michael had done for him since he'd been a child. It seemed to be a day for firsts.

The flow of guests increased. At first they simmered incoherently around the pool and patio, trying to choose between bar, buffet and view, but gradually they settled down into clusters and rings, stabilising to form an atmosphere. Newcomers bounced between the groups like lethargic pinballs until they found one whose structure was open to their particular chemistry. Occasionally a guest came into a group and broke its harmony, causing the whole to fragment and its members to wander off, free to be sucked into another attractor. Yet others were catalysts or viruses, moving nomadically, inciting and restructuring, leaving traces of their conversation to ferment in their wake.

Then Moses appeared looking, it has to be said, really fantastic. He was wearing a beautiful pair of hand-tooled brown leather square-toed slippers with cream tongues, a magnificently tailored pair of mildly flared peach pants that hugged his thighs and arse like an attentive dancing partner and a short-sleeved silk shirt, cream with maroon stitching. His hair was immaculate and around his neck was a single, unobtrusive gold chain which offset the gold Rolex on his wrist. He had returned to IBM in 1978 (not long after the missing-computer incident at DEC, though nothing was ever proved) to work on the launch of the PC. The party was one of a series he was holding, still flushed with the product's immense success (and the immense salary he now enjoyed as a result – it had been his idea to use the Chaplin movie *Modern Times* as the advertising hook, presenting the computer not as just another tool but as something which freed the worker from the industrial metre that had come to dominate so many lives. And Moses believed in this image – the computer had freed him, hadn't it? Why shouldn't it free others too?).

He shook hands with everybody, grinning from ear to ear until he got to Judd, to whom he said in passing through the mask of a frown: 'I'll deal with you later. Until then just make sure you're polite to our guests.'

But instead of putting the fear into Judd, as his father's admonishments usually did, the comment made his blood run hot. If there was one thing he was sick of it was Moses's automatic assumption that he was in the wrong. From his mother he could take it; she always forgave him as soon as she'd ticked him off, but the old man couldn't do that, no, for him it was all bound up with this fucking black thing, about how Judd had to prove himself not just for himself – which would at least have been understandable – but so that Moses could stand alongside white people and think: my son is better than yours. Judd had plenty of time for black solidarity, that was all fine, but this wasn't that, this was bullshit. His father didn't give a shit about Africa as far as he was aware, or about the problems in the ghettos. His father only gave a shit about himself, that's right, and he wasn't going to put up with being used for Moses's ends any more. No one had even thought to ask him why what had happened had happened; there was no one around to whom it seemed to have occurred that he might have been provoked, that he might just have been defending himself, that most of the damage had been done by the cops. And although he had no intention of letting anyone know anything about the situation which had precipitated his drunkenness, the fact that the violence itself had been sparked by a racist remark was enough to make the riptide of self-righteousness drag him right along with it.

He was busy with these thoughts when from behind him a sinewy voice spoke his name. It was a voice so familiar and so internalised that he almost didn't recognise it, coming as it seemed to from his dreams rather than from the external world. But as he turned and saw to whom it belonged, a laugh bubbled up from his throat. The last time they had met it had been the psychoanalyst who had been the taller. 'Why do you laugh?' Schemata said immediately. 'Have I said something amusing?'

The doctor had spoken in his far-away tone, the one he used to suggest that his mind was not only dealing with the present situation but was contemplating several other problems at the same time, the consideration of any one of which was far beyond the capability of the average human being.

'No, I er . . .' Judd paused right there. Schemata was standing with the sun behind him and its light shone hard into his eyes. Even with the sunglasses he was wearing it was difficult to see the psychoanalyst's face. Memories of that darkened room washed over him in waves. He almost began to speak, to tell the doctor everything. The grid left by this man across his being made him want to talk, to disclose. The light bathed the two of them, he was bathed in Schemata's light, Schemata shone up at him. He was ready to say the words that would let this man in again, let him flush the lattice clean and take away the agony of the previous night, the loneliness of the life he had led for the last two years. But as he opened his mouth to speak the pain in his face surged up through the layer of Valium and a giddiness swamped his body and the sun was no longer pure but was instead the anus of the solar system, spraying its light like diarrhoea all over Schemata, all over the guests, all over the city which lay beyond the railing beyond the pool. The pain in his face, the bruises on his ribs, these felt like the only things he had ever known.

Where was he? What was he doing? To Schemata, to his father, to his mother, to Michael and to all of these people he was a person defined by an event that had taken place over a decade previously, one that he could barely remember, a mere conjunction of skin and skin and this . . . paltry thing somehow justified his life being placed in the hands of this maniac? This monster whose minted voice had whispered into his ear a false tale of identity for year upon year upon year?

But there was something else, too, the rank violence of the sun spoke of something else, and it had more to do with the loud nights handing records to the Bomb, with the hours spent chasing the lizard in dark, smoke-filled rooms, with all the things he had fallen into out of pure boredom than with his mother, his father, Schemata or even, yes even with Jennifer, that hollow name from all those years ago. 'I got drunk and fell over,' he said, making it sound like a lie. 'I got drunk and fell over. You'll have to excuse me Dr Schemata. I promised my mother I would help the caterers find everything they needed, and I believe they have just arrived.' And he turned away, although not before noticing with enormous satisfaction the tic of surprise which leapt to life across Schemata's face and which was just as quickly plastered over with an expression of effusive calm as the doctor assimilated the blip into that Great Order of Things which over the years he had painstakingly carved and which he carried in his mind like a talisman, like a lens.

Back inside the house Judd went straight to one of the toilets and threw up. As he vomited he thought of Jennifer and his spasms seemed to him the ejection of the last vestige of her from his body, the final traces of her from his self, the last memories of her from his flesh. As he spattered the porcelain with his bile it came to him like a foul bubble of ancient gas glubbing up from a deep sea trench that he had kept the kernel of a wish folded away in some forgotten spangle of his cortex, a wish that one day she would contact him, just find a way to speak to him, to tell him anything at all. He thought of the time he had spent watching television in the hope that impossibly, on the far side of the world, she was watching the same thing, and he realised how this had affected so much of what he did, how it had helped reconfigure every thought he'd had about himself, how it had influenced his shape in the world as though he were an object on a lathe. But now the spasming of his stomach seemed to eradicate her from him, and with his belly emptied and endorphins flooding through his system his mind began to clear a little. He stood up, and it was as if he'd been walking with a limp for years and years, only finally to look down and discover a pebble lodged in the sole of his shoe.

He cleaned his teeth and wandered back outside in search of Michael and another cocktail. He found both, but no sooner had he taken a couple of sips of the latter than he was accosted by a figure from the more recent past: Irving Scofield. Judd hadn't seen him since that afternoon in the repair lot – when Route 66 Autos had been closed down, Scofield had dealt with the matter by telephone. But he had always liked the man and he was the first person Judd had been pleased to see all day.

'Nice sunglasses, son,' Scofield said sarcastically.

'Yeh, well, I borrowed them. Sun's pretty bright, you know,' he replied pointlessly. They were standing in the shade of an awning that had been unfurled at the house end of the terrace. Most of the guests were at the far end, on the other side of the pool, on the section of patio that was cantilevered out over the hillside. A grey haze of smog hung low over the city and spoilt the view.

'Miasma of Babylon,' said Scofield to himself.

'What?' asked Judd, not sure if he'd heard correctly.

'This city. Even the air is predicated on corruption.' The businessman rolled the words off his tongue with a thick back spin that made them weighty, lazy and hard to get the measure of. Judd was surprised to hear him speak in this way, saying things that might have come out of Lionel's mouth.

There was a bowl of cherries on the table beside them; Scofield selected one and picked it up by its stalk. It was fat and pink, and he held it in front of his face the better to examine it. Satisfied with his choice, he gently gripped it between his teeth, pulled the stalk free with a sharp little tug and bit into the fruit until it popped, only then enveloping it with his lips. Judd listened to him chew and watched as he looked around for somewhere to spit the pit. His eyes settled upon a pot in which a small orange tree was growing, and he propelled the seed into it at high speed and with a practised accuracy. 'Nice cherry,' he said. 'Your folks sure know how to throw a party.'

'Mr Scofield . . .' Judd began, but Scofield cut him off.

'Now Judd,' he said, 'I hope you weren't too upset at me closing down the business and cutting you out of a job like that?'

'No, no.' Judd shrugged. 'These things happen.'

'You're getting by OK, I hope. Found anything else yet?'

'Not yet, but I've got a few ideas.'

Scofield suddenly leant in close and began scrutinising the younger man's face. 'Police do that to you?'

'Uh huh.' He didn't ask Scofield how he knew. It seemed natural that Scofield would know. He had a knowledgeable air about him.

'I hear you've got the touch with the dice,' Scofield said quietly.

Now Judd really was surprised. 'Where d'you hear that?' he asked, trying to keep his voice firm but its modulation still betraying him.

'Same place I heard that the cops treated you worse than the boys who laid you out in that bar.' Judd's heart began to beat faster, and his limbs felt hollow. 'I hear other things, too.'

'Such as?' asked Judd, his hostility beginning to break out again, like hives.

'Like some of what happened to your face happened before you even got to the bar. Like you can't get a game any more.'

'So you're in with the Chinaman, are you?'

'I'm nothing to do with any of it,' Scofield insisted, turning towards the view again. 'Everything I do is completely legitimate. I want you to know that. I wouldn't want you to think your father associates with hoodlums. I simply make it my business to know, that's all. Moses has asked me to look out for you and I owe him a favour, and that's all I've been doing. But I've got some advice for you. You've done well. Not many people your age can get involved in that . . . in that . . . milieu, and do so well. Not many at all. People tell me you're a natural, that you've got the potential of a great player. People who know. But the scene you've been in, it's small time, it's for losers, it can't support people like you. You want my advice, take a holiday. Get out of the state for a while. See what the big wide world is like. I've got friends in Vegas and Reno. Go there, look them up.' He paused to light a cigarette. 'What do you say?'

'I say get off my back. I don't need anyone to keep an eye on me. I've had enough of that shit.'

'There's keeping an eye and keeping an eye, my boy,' huffed Scofield, unimpressed. 'You know where to find me if you change your mind.'

'Fuck you, daddy-o.'

'I understand how you feel . . .'

'No you *don't*, no you fucking don't, you haven't had your life sold down the river by your fucked-up parents, you haven't had your mind fucked up by some jive-arse shrink, you, you, all of you haven't got the faintest fucking idea about how I feel!'

'No, you're right, we don't.' It was an aikido throw: it deflected Judd's energy and left him flailing inconsequentially.

With nothing to strike against, he could think of nothing more to say. 'Yeah, right,' was the best he could manage. 'I'm off for another drink.' And he slapped off across the patio in his thongs, leaving Scofield to contemplate the bowl of cherries and the view.

Moses insisted that his son spend the night in Beverly Hills, so that he could 'see something of him, for a change' and so it wasn't until the following day that Judd returned to his apartment. When he did, he found a fat envelope waiting for him in the mailbox. It had been hand delivered – nothing was written on it except the one word, *Judd*. He had his hands full of keys, newspaper and groceries, and tore the package open awkwardly with his two free fingers. Predictably, the paper gave way suddenly and the parcel's contents spilled out across the cracked marble slabs of the hallway floor. Judd dropped to his knees and quickly shovelled everything up into the grocery bag, terrified lest somebody should happen by. There was close to ten thousand dollars there, he guessed. As well as a set of ivory dice and a bent golden ring in the shape of a laughing lizard.

Flatlands: flying in (2)

Judd called his parents, said that Scofield had fixed him up with a job in Reno and that he was leaving on the next plane. He flew into the city at dawn – by first light he saw it from the airplane window, a great calcification rising up from the desert, the husk of an all too familiar humanity. Fresh and bright as the sun soon was, the lights of the hotels and casinos were more powerful still. They glared down the daylight like the eyes of a party of rebellious angels, determined to make all of creation pay for their sufferings. Perhaps, thought Judd, we are God's horde, flying in like seraphim and ready to sacrifice ourselves happily to the cause. He tried to imagine all the people on the planet who would never take a flight, that dismal substratum condemned forever to walk the earth, while above them the blessed traversed the skies in glinting silver tubes that hovered between the clouds like mirages, just as distant, just as out of reach.

The small, grizzled man who was occupying the seat next to him suddenly croaked awake. He had fallen asleep before take-off but now he stretched and yawned, rolling back the bristles of his beard as a hedge-hog rolls back its coat once the danger has passed. Having roused himself he leant over Judd without asking and peered out of the window. His breath was coarse and sour with sleep. 'This town, ya see all that? Ya see all that? This town lives on nothing but that,' he cackled.

'On nothing but what?' asked Judd, confused. He thought the man meant the desert.

'Casinos and hotels. There's nothing out here but casinos and hotels. Everybody, every goddamn soul in this place lives offa that.' He pro-nounced 'goddamn' with a glottal stop between the two syllables. 'There's nothing else. Amazing. See those lights? Those lights burn like that twenty-four hours a day, three hunnerd and sixty-five days a year. At night they light up the goddamn rocks for miles around. Lot o' good it does the coyotes. I love it. Looks like goddamn God Almighty hissel' bent right down outta the sky and spat here in the sand, turnin' it all into jewels. Fool's jewels.' He stretched 'jewels', rhymed it with 'fool's'. 'It's a goddamn marvel, that's what it is. The town here eats up more electricity than some entire states, you know that? There's four power stations up roun' Tahoe that don' do nuthin' but power this here town. Ain't that a fact?' The stranger finished and Judd watched his mouth fold away invisibly beneath the copper-grey hairs of his thick beard. For a moment he sat quietly, then stood up and with a stubby index finger punched the yellow button that summoned the stewardess. Presently she arrived. He asked her for a cup of coffee and she explained to him that the plane had already begun its descent and he said to her he didn't see why that meant he couldn't have a cup of coffee and she said she wasn't going to argue with him it's the rules and he could take it up with the company once they were on the ground if he wished. The fasten seat-belts sign came on and twenty minutes later they had landed.

Judd escaped the hot metal cylinder as quickly as he could. The tarmac was already baking hot, although the sun had only been up a couple of hours, and he crossed it at the head of a phalanx of slightly rumpled passengers. His skin glistened faintly with the shock of leaving the air-conditioning and to the staff that met him at the terminal door it seemed almost as if he had been formed right out of the heat hazes and the black matter of the runway, a spirit summoned into the strange pentangles and runes carved by the paths of the jetliners. He located his suitcases; on one of them the strap had been broken by the baggage handlers and the contents looked as though they had been rifled, but nothing appeared to be missing.

Despite the heat the desert seemed clean and fresh after the smog of the city he had left behind. He hailed a cab and asked the driver to take him to a cheap hotel but the man replied, 'They're all the same in this town, brutha,' so Judd said, 'OK, so I trust you, so take me to one you like.' The money, the investment that Scofield had made in him had boosted his confidence enormously. Though he was still paranoid about the extent of the businessman's information network he had decided to take it on trust that the man – who obviously had a fair deal of power of some nature – was trying to help him and not to fuck him up.

They drove out towards the sick lotus of the city, Judd looking out of the windows and fingering the lizard ring he once again wore on his wedding finger. On either side of the road there was nothing but the strange desert landscape which moved in ripples and waves. Now and then a little twister would pick up, whipped into life by the heat differentials at the edge of the metalling, and a small front of red dust would spray over the lane in front of them, its particles stinging the windows like tiny pellets of hail.

'First time in Reno?' asked the driver.

'Er, no,' lied Judd, not wanting to sound like a tourist. The driver laughed.

Compared with Las Vegas, which Judd knew from TV, Reno seemed quite restrained. They came into town and drove through streets lined with casinos and hotels and pool halls and car showrooms and arcades, and while it was opulent and tacky it was that much smaller in scale than he imagined it would be. The larger of the gambling complexes still dominated the skyline but the streets themselves seemed relatively quiet and restrained – there wasn't the bustle of tourists and street trash that he had expected. In a curious way he felt as though he was still in the desert proper. The mauves and lilacs of the rocks had been replaced by the bright blues and greens of the lights but the sense of being in a non-place where the landscape had no form – was no longer, indeed, a landscape – was the same: both elicited the feeling that any journey he undertook might easily continue on in the same vein for ever.

The driver drew up outside a hotel-casino name of the Golden Gecko. Judd thought it a good omen, paid the man and went inside. As he opened the lobby doors a wet surge of noise flopped out into the street. The clatter of the slot machines, the screech of the compères, the chink of glasses, of chips, the rattles and pops of funfair attractions, the regurgitative rhythms of a band, the white noise of ten thousand meaningless conversations.

There was no one on the front desk so Judd took a quick look around the lobby. It was very large and all the sound was coming from one end. Judd walked down to investigate and found that the room let on to a balcony which overlooked a vast hall, mocked up to resemble the inside of a circus. No . . . this *was* the inside of a circus. Two acrobats were swinging from high wires, one of them suddenly performing a triple somersault level with Judd's nose. Down below, next to the safety net, a ringmaster led a small brass band around in a circle while Joseph Grimaldi clowns dressed in white romper suits threw buckets of fake water over one another and pretended to cause mayhem. At the other end of the platform (for it was a platform rather than a ring) a lion tamer cracked his whip at a fairly docile-looking lion, while a girl wearing nothing but suspenders, underwear, high heels, a gag and several coils of rope squirmed provocatively and tried to look frightened.

This was the children's area and sure enough there were dozens of them, charging around dressed in dungarees or summer dresses or shorts and wearing cardboard ten-gallon hats or deely-boppers or beanies on their heads and more interested, it seemed, in each other than in the amusements on offer. Occasional adults chanced their arms on the shooting galleries and hoopla stalls that ringed the hall, cheered on by enthusiastic offspring but nervous at the idea of games of skill after too many hours of playing games of chance. Everything was pink or gold or red or white or blue. One child was urinating on a heap of soft-toy bunny rabbits when he thought no one was looking. Judd watched him from his vantage point on the balcony. The child finished, put his little pecker away, then felt the eyes upon him and looked up. When he saw Judd his hand came up to his mouth in shock, then realising that the adult couldn't reach him he grinned and ran off to join a gaggle of his peers busy farting and burping round the back of the lion cage.

Judd went back to the reception desk and checked in. He liked it here.

1 0

Sea dog

Laika watched the world. She did this when she got bored with her screens, which wasn't often. But over the years she had looked at the world a lot none the less. Sometimes it was easy to forget that there was any land at all. With the sea already taking up two thirds of the planet's surface and the continents often largely obscured by clouds, the earth really did seem to be a sphere of water hanging in the void, a vast water droplet leaked from some interstellar pipe. It was a problem, actually, watching the zorby blue atmosphere forever curling away below you, inviting, delightful, forever out of reach. If Pavlov had wanted to create the ideal stimulus for drinking, Laika often wondered idly, he could have done worse than photograph this.

For it was a water world. Learning as much as she could about the sea from films and documentaries, our little Russian dog never ceased to be amazed by it. She had never seen it while still on earth and now it seemed to her to be the most important thing of all, far more vital than the constant ploughings and ragings of humankind. There it was, vast, complex, interconnected, saturated with life and death to such an extent that the dissolved bodies of its innumerable inhabitants salted and re-salted it, became part of its very fibre. In tune with the moon, unperturbed unperturbable, it sucked at the rocks that had dared to rise out of it, determined to conquer these highlands, grinding them down, returning them to sediment, packing them back on its floor where it felt they belonged. To help in the task it siphoned off energy from volcanic vents in the sea bed and created bacteria, which gathered in great floating spirillae mats that soaked up the heat of the sun and pumped oxygen out into the atmosphere. This done, the sea threw up part of itself and clipped a mantle of weather around the globe, the sea which was sky. Rain and storms then littered the earth and rivers carved their way through the landscapes, carrying more of the recalcitrant rock to the sea and allowing the waters' autonomous pods – the cells – to creep over the ground, forming slimes mosses lichens which mined minerals from the rocks, now deeply regretting their rebellion, and broke them down further into gases and screes and soils which were easily washed away by the same water that made underground caves of all faults.

This is what Laika saw when she gazed from her craft: a sea reclaiming the land as its own, twisting, extending, contorting, unfolding itself in the attempt, taking the vast processes of its currents and chemicals and waves and tides and condensing them down to form life, a handy tool in the struggle, teeming unicell agents that could be relied upon to fan out and infiltrate, multiply and report, chuckle and swarm. And even, unexpectedly, band together, form groups, *organisms*: plankton and algae, anenome and arthropod, lobopod and snail. Then, later, fungus and plant, grass and gymnosperm, lizard and fly, flower and wasp, mammal and tree: multicellular creatures that carried the offensive further and further inland – *interzone, I think I've found you* – across mountains and deserts, tundra and bog, until they were able to dance rituals in border towns, able to order themselves, to calm themselves, able to prepare for the conquest of space.

Mandelbrot memories

When the newly sensitive Joel began to wonder, about a month after he'd said goodbye to Jennifer in the summer of 1973, whether the rush he'd got from sex in any way compared with how a computer felt when being flooded with data, foremost in his mind was the network he looked after at CERN. The scratch of the modems as they switched packets of information to and fro between the workstations seemed to him as subtle as the soft rasp of groin upon groin. The flicker of LEDs on display panels were as vital as the random firings of the optic nerve triggered by the intensity of tongue upon tongue, lips upon lips, flesh upon flesh. The glow of the screens was as subtle as the half-light created in his room by the drawing of the blinds against the prying midday sun. The whirr of the tapes and hard drives was as bewitching as the music of sighs, gasps and breaths.

But already his interest in learning to gamble eclipsed even the experience of sex. Here was a whole new side to his explorations in probability. He forsook the dice and became obsessed by roulette, going so far as to buy a second-hand wheel and install it in his already cramped room. He worked out that by building a machine to predict the results of the wheel he could begin to show that chance itself had a structure, a structure that was extended in time. Roulette was a physical system in which the crucial factors should be the rate of spin (including its gradual deceleration due to friction and inertia), the speed and angle of delivery of the ball, any slight angle of tilt of the wheel itself and the exact point at which the ball entered the system. But if his hunch was right, any technique that was solely a function of these properties would not be able to predict the wheel with one hundred per cent accuracy. Any large enough sample of results should show a random distribution, but his theory – which stated that pure randomness didn't exist, at least not yet – suggested that wouldn't in fact be the case. But what it might be that linked the results together and frustrated the workings of chance he didn't yet know.

One possibility he pondered (drawing on his newly – sexually – acquired knowledge about the ability of the body to absorb and transmit information) was that if enough attention was focused on the game by its players they might themselves become part of the system and affect the fall of the ball. Since Henry had first taken him to the casino he had been back many times, both to that one and to others. He had already got to know many habitués of Geneva's gambling fraternity by face and they had got to know him – with his unkempt looks, intense air and notepad and pen, he was an easily recognisable figure. Most of the doormen knew him by sight and joked about him, tagging him – correctly – as a student from one of the universities on some research project, and many of the players knew the feel of his eyes on their backs as they played on into the night. On several occasions he had sat and watched while one or other of them had beaten the bank. It was not something that happened very often, nor was it particularly spectacular when it did. The shouts and whoops, the sudden wins and the quick catastrophes tended to come from the more casual players, those who threw down their money on a series of blind intersections with the wheel. But the regulars were an altogether different affair. They accumulated wins slowly, over time, crabbing their chips around the table in a manner that was neither plan nor chance, but which seemed to Joel more like the map of some strange country of the mind. On the most intense evenings – the nights when Joel found a player on a winning streak and stuck to him, a psychic limpet – the gambler's strategy actively enfolded its surroundings until it contained within it the behaviour of the croupier, the bounce of the ball, the flow of people to and from the table, the tides of comment and conversation. A successful player, Joel noted, made everything subsidiary to him or herself. It seemed that at such times these people could not only predict the outcomes, but influence them too. Was that possible? That was something he must endeavour to find out.

The skills he had enjoyed as a child, of being able to visualise algorithms and solve them almost instantly, had been in sharp decline over the previous couple of years. Joel had put this down to the fact that he was getting older, but the upshot was that he had begun to depend on computers more and more in his day-to-day work. For a while he'd felt bitter regret at this but now he was happy, because it had seemed after all that this transition was part of some grander design. The prediction problem he confronted as the next hurdle in his project was far too complex for him to have processed in his mind alone, even at the height of his skills, and the only reason he had managed to see a way past it at all was thanks to what he knew about these machines. So as soon as he had formulated his plan he set about building a computer that would help him to carry it out.

Although his hobby placed burgeoning demands on his time and he was kept constantly busy with his official research, Joel felt increasingly unmotivated and listless. The sight of Jennifer and Henry together, different as their habits were from those of his own family, had made him think of the life he had abandoned when he had run away from Brooklyn. A few months after Jennifer's departure he began to have doubts as to whether he should ever have left. Perhaps the intimacy that he'd discovered with her had opened him to the fact that other people really existed; perhaps his unravelling of the events of the Holocaust had unearthed in him compassion; perhaps the waning of his precocious mathematical abilities was making him pine for his disappearing youth. Whatever the reasons, over the ensuing year the doubts grew into anguish. If he had stayed he would be married by now, with a family of his own. He wouldn't be eating every meal in silence, spending every night alone, wouldn't be terrified of company and lost in a conversation. Millstein would have continued to teach him well and would no doubt eventually have persuaded Moshe to let him study at one of the universities in New York. He need never have come to Cambridge, to have begged Metric for help. That whole episode made him tingle with embarrassment whenever he thought of it – in retrospect he considered those years a dreadful mistake and although Amanda Metric occasionally wrote to him at CERN he could never quite bring himself to reply. Sometimes it seemed that numbers, which had promised him so much, had in fact served him about as well as a bout of polio. His blessings had become curses and neither his attempts to build a roulette computer nor the long hikes he still took through the peaks and forests of the local mountains managed to dispel what he came to recognise as chronic loneliness.

One evening towards the end of the second summer since Jennifer's visit, he was mooning around the Common Room when Subhash Sidwa, a lanky programmer from Lahore and a member of a fashionable 'set' of young researchers who didn't wear suits, had eclectic ideas, and raised eyebrows by hanging out with bikers in the locally notorious Boot Bar (and who – it was rumoured – took drugs), wandered in and dumped a huge pile of A4 flyers on one of the already overflowing tables, knocking over a cold cup of coffee full of floating cigarette butts in the process. Apparently oblivious to the mess he'd created the Pakistani began cheerily plastering the notice-boards with his hand-outs, stealing pins from notices that were already up and ignoring them when they fell to the floor. Joel found all this good humour and irresponsibility irritating and was making ready to leave when Subhash approached him and shoved a flyer into his hand. 'Lecture course. Starts next week. Check out the speakers, man. This is going to shake up this place like you would not believe.'

Joel said thanks and was about to drop the sheet into the nearest wastebin when one of the names on the list caught his eye.

DOUBLE BILL

24 and 25 August: Benoit Mandelbrot (IBM) presents:
'How Long is the Coast of Britain' & 'Fractal Cotton Prices since 1900'

At the mention of Mandelbrot, the bread he'd most loved as a boy, a mist came over Joel's mind and dewy tears formed at the corners of his eyes. Nostalgia rose up in him like nausea, as deep in his cortex, neurons began to chant. He remembered his father telling him the recipe in the bakery, years and years before. *Heat up the oven until it's nice and hot. Measure out a few grabs of flour and just so much baking powder and sift them together with a few pinches of salt. Then beat up three eggs, gradually adding in a cupful of sugar. That's how you make a batter, see, and you must beat it till it's good and thick. Stir in some corn oil, a splash of vanilla juice and a dribble of nut oil and then add the flour and a cup of chopped almonds. Mix it all together well, because this is your dough. Now separate the dough into three and knead the pieces on a board like this, folding and flattening, folding and flattening, until everything is mixed and no longer sticky but smooth. Shape each piece into a flat loaf so long and so thick and then in the oven with them for a half hour. When they're done we cut them into strips, like so, like so, like so. Then back in the oven to brown.*

Folding and flattening, folding and flattening, the baker's transformation which takes distant particles and brings them closer together. This was the process that went on in Joel's mind. Images, smells and sounds folded and flattened and folded themselves over and over until he was back in the bakery, tugging at his father's apron, wiping the caramelised sugar off the baking trays with his finger, rubbing the steam from his glasses and leaving a crust of flour in its place. *Home.* Suddenly he longed for it more acutely than ever. What use had it been coming here to Europe, to end up not in some halcyon mathematical community as he had imagined but locked in the dull round of tedious research? The future yawned before him like a giant and multiple maw, each way forward a different throat leading straight down into the same acid belly of loneliness. He thought of the soft knishes of Jennifer's body; he felt filthy and pathetic. He could hear his mother's voice: *Who do you think you are? A common goy? You don't even wear your yarmulke any more!*

Poor Joel! He had kept his mind so rigorously compartmentalised that it had taken an entire decade for the feelings he had for his family, for Brooklyn, to well up through its crystal structure. Tears balled on his eyelashes and fumbled their way down his cheeks. He thrust his hand into his pocket and pulled out some odd coins and notes which he crushed into Subhash's palm. 'I must come, I must come,' he blubbered, stabbing his finger on Mandelbrot's name. 'Reserve me a ticket for this won't you, please?'

'Well, I'll save you a seat,' said Subhash, somewhat taken aback, 'but you count as staff, so you don't have to pay.'

'I want to, I want to,' continued Joel regardless.

'No, really, you don't have to, it's all right,' Subhash insisted, worried that Joel would drip tears all over his new velveteen loons.

'But I want to,' wailed Joel, 'I want to do something! I owe it to my father! Because I'm never going to see him again!' With both men trying to reject it the money fell to the floor; Joel quickly followed, his collapsing body buffeted by the most terrific sobs. Still worrying about his trousers,

Subhash helped him up and led him over to the line of modular grey chairs that ran along one wall of the Common Room.

Joel cried for several minutes, blubbing big tears which despite Subhash's best efforts left salty snail trails across his precious pants. Soon, though, the flashback began to fizzle out and Joel's sobs subsided. Feeling concerned – he was a nice guy, for a programmer – Subhash offered to buy Joel a cup of coffee and silently the Jew nodded consent and allowed his good Samaritan to lead him in the direction of the cafeteria. Once there they got talking, and that was how Joel made a friend.

The triptych of time

They spoke often after that, though it was a very academic friendship and when they talked it was mainly in abstractions – partly because Joel had few other modes of conversation and also because Subhash found what he had to say interesting. That first time over coffee Joel did tell the slightly astonished Pakistani something of his family and his childhood, and his running away, but after that he never spoke of the past again. The programmer immediately recognised the intelligence of his new acquaintance, but what made Joel so refreshing was the way he would link mathematical or computing concepts with ideas from the worlds of religion, gambling, philosophy, biology, psychology. Although he didn't yet tell him about the computer he was building, little by little Joel expounded to Subhash all his theories of the links between Kabbalistic philosophy, time, mathematics and chance. It was good to talk – for too long he'd been developing his ideas in isolation and to try to communicate them was to force himself to structure them, to make them coherent.

Once, they got on to the topic of neural nets, a new kind of computer architecture that Subhash was working on in one of the labs. 'These networks can be realised in hardware or software,' he explained to Joel. 'In essence the idea is to mimic how the brain works. Like, computers at the moment process information in a serial way, one instruction after the other, but what we want is to try and do what we think the brain does – have a load of simple processing units, or neurons, link them all together with multiple connections and get results out of the different patterns of activation levels across the entire network. It's called parallel distributed processing, as opposed to serial processing, you see? Of course, our version's still not as complex as the brain, which isn't binary – our neurons are simplified models: they have various input channels, a processing unit and a single output channel which can produce a one or a zero. But the cool thing is that by altering the relative weights of the channels you can get the network to home in on a result and you don't even need that big a network to do it. With certain architectures which feed outputs back in and readjust their own channel weights accordingly, the thing can actually be said to learn. It's pretty cool stuff. Here.' And he flipped open a textbook and showed Joel a schematic of a multi-layer network architecture:

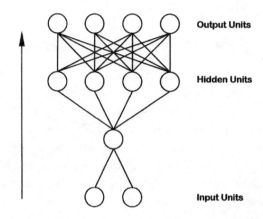

'But this is amazing,' Joel exclaimed. 'It's so similar to the traditional way the Sefirot are drawn.'

'I, er, I'm not familiar with that I'm afraid . . .'

'The Sefirot! According to Kabbalic doctrine, the ten vessels from the material of which the world was constructed. Look.' Joel grabbed a napkin from the chrome dispenser and, pulling out a felt-tip pen, scribbled a quick diagram on it. 'Here,' he said, and shoved it across the table at Subhash.

'See what I mean?'

'Yeah, yeah, I do, I suppose, though it's kind of a simplification . . .'

'But it fits exactly with what I've already been saying. Wait, let me show you something.' He leant down to the satchel at his feet and pulled out a battered library book. 'Have you read this?'

'What is it?'

'Scholem's book on the Kabbalah. Came out last year I think –' he checked the title pages '– yes, that's right, copyright 1974. You should

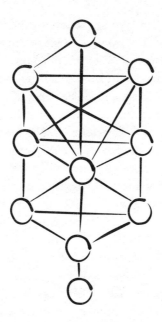

read it. It's already a classic. Now, listen to this.' He thumbed through the book, jumping from place to place by locating the various pieces of roughly torn paper that served him as bookmarks until he found the passage he wanted. 'OK, here: "Even man's physical structure corresponds to that of the Sefirot, so that we find Ezra of Gerona's description of the last Sefirah as 'the form [temunah] that includes all forms' applied in the Zohar to man himself, who is called 'the likeness [deyokna] that includes all likenesses.' "'

'There. There's so much there, you see? We have on the one hand this thing about the correspondence of the physical structure – neural net, or brainwork as it were, and the interrelations of the Sefirot, and just remember, if you wanted to back this up you could refer to the fact, surely not coincidence, that von Neumann himself designed and *named* the architecture of the computer after the structure of the body. He was the one who first said the fact that the thing was instantiated in electronic circuits was irrelevant, that we should think of the logical units as neurons, he *said* that. And not only that but his design was broken down into organs: the central control, the central arithmetic processor – cortical functions, if you like – the *memory*, very important, I mean, why call it memory and not storage as had hitherto been the case if you weren't alert to the biological possibilities? And then the input and output *organs*. See?

'Then, on the other hand, you have this idea of "the form that includes all forms", and exactly there you have the Universal Turing Machine, yes? Turing's idea being that if you could break the operations of any physical machine – and he included in that category biological machines, animals – down into a series of logical operations, by encoding these operations in say, binary instruction sets, on a theoretically infinite magnetic tape, you could create a machine which, again in theory, of course, should be able to simulate the processes of any other. A universal machine. A computer, in other words.'

Subhash smiled – now he was being patronised. He fought back with the little bit of Kabbalic doctrine he knew: 'So I suppose this parallels the way that the Torah, with all its hypertexts, is supposed to be a living organism, right?'

'Yes, yes! I hadn't thought of that. You're getting the idea.' Triumphantly, Joel slammed shut his book and plonked it down on the table before Subhash had a chance to ask him about the heavily scored passage at the foot of the page he had quoted from. It was a passage that touched closely on Joel's ideas as he'd outlined them to Professor Metric long before: it concerned the emanation of Ein-Sof and the separation of the world from God which coincided with the breaking of the vessels and the committing of the first sin. It read:

This uninterrupted communion, which is the goal of creation, was broken off at the time of Adam's sin when his lower will was parted from the divine will by his own free volition. It was then that his individuality, whose origin lay in his separation from God with its attendant proliferation of multiplicity, was born. What had been intended to be nothing more than a series of periodic fluctuations within a system now turned into an opposition of extremes that found their expression in the fierce polarisation of good and evil. It is the concrete destiny of the human race, and of the Jew as the principal bearer of this mission and the recipient of God's revelation through the Torah, to overcome this polarisation from within the human condition created by the first sin.

This was a passage Joel knew by heart.

The more his friendship with Subhash developed, the less seriously Joel took his official research work. His life was full now: he had a companion and he had his Project, and he no longer saw any need for the stability that CERN had provided. As far as his Project went, for the moment he had learnt all he could from the casinos so he stopped paying visits to the city and started instead to spend his evenings calibrating the roulette wheel he had installed in his room. Once that was done he sat up nights feverishly coding simulations of the apparatus and during the days – when he was meant to be analysing CERN data – he ran his programs on the machines, experimenting with networking the lab computers together via the Centre's LAN, so that he could steal extra processing time by sucking up any surplus cycles. It was a clever piece of programming and it often struck even Joel as bizarre that the twists of logical instruction he put together should be able to travel around the Centre apparently independent of their author, searching for space in which they could run and thrive.

Conceptually, the problem was simple. The ball's behaviour, once inside the wheel, was governed by Newtonian mechanics. By calibrating the starting point of the wheel, the speed of its spin and the speed and trajectory of the ball, and allowing for gravity and wind resistance, it shouldn't be difficult to predict the outcome to at least within the nearest octant (the eight wedges into which a roulette wheel can be divided are not even – each octant has either four or five slots). But it was a complex coding challenge, made more difficult by the fact that in order to test every one of his simulations Joel had to carry out a series of runs on the wheel in his room, measure the physical variables for all of them and then take the results over to the labs, repeat them on his virtual wheel and compare the answers.

Once he had developed a satisfactory program, further testing could only properly be accomplished by running it on a computer that he could use in his room, and since he was going to have to build a machine especially for the task Joel decided that he might as well do it properly and construct one that he could conceal on his person and smuggle into a real casino.

He began to assemble the components, asking Subhash's advice on chips and architecture (though without revealing the true nature of his Project). He scrounged and filched components from the labs, and tripped into Geneva to hunt for suitable materials for the housings and interfaces, but most of the circuitry and chips that he needed he had to order from American mail order companies, the kind that advertised in the back of magazines like *Byte*, *Popular Computing* and *Dr Dobb's Journal of Computer Calisthenics and Orthodontics*. By the mid-1970s the computer hobbyist scene in the US was massive, much bigger than in Europe, and Joel had long followed its meanderings through the pages of these publications. Through them he heard about the Altair 8800, the first home computer, featured on the cover of *Popular Electronics* in January 1975; he read features dealing with new languages like BASIC and on the peculiar 'Homebrew Computer Club' in Menlo Park on the edge of what was already called Silicon Valley. He read about the computer evangelist Ted Nelson and his vision of something called Hypertext, a kind of interlinked computer-based publishing system, which would 'liberate' computers from the 'high-priests' that supposedly had control over them now (like himself, presumably, thought Joel) and allow laymen to get access to all sorts of data. (Again, Joel considered it odd that this Hypertext was thought of as an inherently liberating phenomenon – as far as he was aware the Hypertext of the Torah, a complex series of amendments, commentaries, exegeses, tractates and parables that grew up around the words of the Bible and which in its various stages encoded rabbinical law, was developed by priests to ensure they maintained their power base in the face of various reforms. And yet, as Subhash had pointed out, there was something about this net-like structure of the Torah which seemed organic, which appeared to operate beyond the possibility of centralised control.)

But then lots of this stuff seemed very political. He thought in particular of a vitriolic piece he'd read in *Dr Dobb's* attacking one of the Altair BASIC designers, a guy called Bill Gates, for a speech he'd given at a Homebrew conference criticising computer hobbyists for developing a culture of what he called 'software piracy'. The idea seemed weird to Joel, he had to admit. Everyone he knew at CERN who worked with the computers – Subhash for example – gave away their code for free as a matter of course. It was just what you did.

Designing a circuit diagram was what occupied most of his time now, etching out the most efficient infrastructure for a tiny computer that would only ever run the one program he burnt into its EPROM. It was a journey into a new space and it alerted Joel to something of the terrible beauty of these machines, one that had only ever been matched by the mathematical landscapes he had traversed in his mind as a child. But it was also a frustrating task, because many of the solutions which looked good on paper could not physically be built or would have bugs which he had not yet detected. He went through about a dozen prototypes before he found one that worked and he had just begun training himself to calibrate the movements of the ball and the wheel by eye – and then input the data using a somewhat awkward toe-activated interface – when Mandelbrot came to town and everything went haywire.

Basket case

So much time spent on her own meant she that thirsted for companionship and, just as the silt of a dry lake bed cracks into islands as the last moisture leaves it, so her personality shrank back into sections. These sections formed cliques and alliances, had friendships and fallings out, developed languages and systems of belief not all of which were known to any single one of them. Yet she could be coherent when she wished; when she was with a group the lake would fill and the cracked bed form a substratum for what she called her 'My', an idea she intuited from the attitudes of the adults with whom she came into contact. But when she was with just one of the nurses she didn't need to bring the My into play; one of the Other could deal with them.

The members of her populace had names: there was Echo, and Table, and No! (No! was very stubborn). Hippocrates was something of a figure of fun; his best friend Exray was always seeing through his rather pompous pronouncements. Pill was impish and dangerous and to be feared, and had a sworn enemy called Squeak who always tried to warn the others when the mischievous Pill was around (although often they paid him no heed). One of the strangest of all was Comagirl, who didn't mix much with the Others but towards whom they all showed great respect, even Pill, who never played tricks on her (Squeak was secretly very jealous of Comagirl because of this). Firealarm was something of a mystery to most of them (and some of them had never heard of him at all) and his best friend was Smoke, who was neither a he nor a she. Smoke was very receptive to the Hospital Nights, as they all called the people outside the My with whom the My came into contact. Lonely Dear? thought Smoke was the strongest and strangest of them all, despite Exray's exhortations to the contrary. Learning was Lonely Dear?'s best friend and when the child attended her lessons it was always Learning and Lonely Dear? who sat at the front. (Hippocrates sat in the desk behind them, but he was a real know-it-all and always contradicted the Teacher so the Teacher couldn't Teach him a thing.) The My didn't bother too much with the Teacher; it couldn't understand the point of the things the Teacher said. All the stories the Teacher told seemed very simple: someone did this, and then this, and then this, and it was not at all what they could have done or would have done. Learning and Lonely Dear? tried to make the My come to the lessons but they weren't strong enough on their own to summon it. The best they could do was to get Smoke to come, because Smoke was good at listening and asking questions. Once Teacher brought Mouse to class (the child had never seen an animal before) and Smoke made good friends with the creature. It spent ages with Mouse and eventu-

ally Mouse left its greybody and came to live in the My with the others. Squeak put herself in charge of looking after Mouse, who couldn't talk, and said it was good that she did because it was a sign of Social Responsibility, but Pill kept hiding Mouse from Squeak which made Squeak very upset. We have to take good care of Mouse, *she'd say, in a voice not unlike Mouse's own,* or one day we might lose him! *But for all that Mouse seemed happy enough.*

Then there was Veronica, and Filthychild (the My had met them in the nursery – Horrible Things had been done to them by The Parents and they had preferred to come and live in the My). There was Chicken, and Top, and Dinnertime who was always hungry. There were others also, too many to mention. Some of them came and went regularly, like Gardener, and some would only show up occasionally, like Birthday. Some were more popular than others (everybody liked Sky and Sunshine for instance, except for Sick, but everybody hated Sick).

But the members of the populace did more than argue among themselves. They spent lots of their time in search of ways out, like they'd been told. When Emma was dreaming they probed far and wide, and the My couldn't keep track of them all, all of the time. They spread out through a world of psychic intensity rather than physical space, where human flow and endeavour were etched out against an undulating background of bacterial and geological activity. Traffic and trauma of any kind left traces and towns were like vast balls of tubes and wires, planetary radicles in the cosmic fields of the child's dreams. The populace could dart inside them and explore, chasing the morphing pulses of light that were the signatures of other minds. Comagirl would float slowly through the throbbing globules, her sleep-walking in stark contrast to the row Pill and Squeak caused as they chased each other round and round, screaming like gremlins. Veronica and Top and Table tended to explore as a threesome. Learning went through methodically but terribly slowly and the Others were always having to wait for him to catch up.

Theft as therapy

On Friday night Jennifer came back home from work to the house in Hunt's Crescent to be greeted by the sound of feedback coming from the dining-room. Out front, the garden was overgrown and tatty, full of beer cans and binliners stuffed with pizza boxes and half-eaten microwave meals. For long periods she was never quite sure who was living there;

at the moment Stim and Skag were in residence, with various other members of the band they had started, Desiring Machine, randomly coming and going. The dining-room was now a studio, full of cheap guitars and salvaged amplifiers and the pieces of a drum kit that was forever being taken apart and reassembled.

As usual, the place was trashed. The bedrooms weren't so bad but downstairs the carpets were covered with stains and cigarette burns, the furniture was broken, ashtrays overflowed, windows were cracked. Curtains hung off their rails, remembering drunken teenagers clutching for them in moments of panic. The stair carpet was a dirty silver grey, the result of an Etch-a-Sketch being broken over somebody's head at a party. Every surface in the kitchen was covered with empty tins, dirty plates, pans encrusted with the remains of curries and chillis concocted under the influence. The fridge seeped CFCs and stank of sour milk, the linoleum hadn't been washed for months. Spider plants thrived on the window-sills, their runners dripping down into the sink. Flies droned happily from feast to feast and next door's cat raked carefully among the trash piled in one corner.

Jennifer slouched in, yelling a hello to the band as she passed. She threw down her bag and started a search for the kettle, which she eventually found behind the TV in the living-room. She filled it and plugged it in, then went upstairs to run a bath.

A hour and a half later she reappeared, no longer dressed in her shapeless Woolworth's smock and skirt, but wearing instead a different uniform of black stretch jeans, painted Doctor Marten boots, torn Joy Division T-shirt and a capacious woollen cardigan that had once upon a time belonged to Henry. The Desiring Machine rehearsal had deteriorated into a hash-smoking session and the band had decamped from dining-room to living-room, where they all sat slumped in front of the seven o'clock news. Jenn walked in and swiped a spliff from between the drummer's fingers.

'Wha—? Oh, hi Jenn. Awright?'

'Better now. Anyone going out to get some food? I'm starving.' The band members looked at each other, then at Jennifer, then at the TV, and burst out laughing.

'What's so fucking funny?'

But that just made everybody giggle some more, until Stim, the bass player, managed to steady himself enough to speak. 'Oh, it's nothing. We've been rehearsing all day and haven't got it together to get anything to eat, and everyone's been saying that all day. Private joke.' He wiped a tear from his eye. 'We were gonna go into town any rate.'

'Where?'

'Dunno. Probably the Dragon.'

'I thought we were gonna get some grub.' More giggles, though this time they were quickly suppressed.

'Yeah, well, better have a couple of bevs first tho'.' Endless hilarity.

It was to be a usual Friday night then: a slow crawl across town towards the Green Dragon, no doubt via the Cross Keys, the Shakespeare and the chippy. Cider and black all the way, Benson and Hedges or Embassy, punctuated with the odd spliff outside in the car-park, long and hot and wet with all the lips so keen for it. Around ten someone would chuck up, pebble-dash the toilets; around eleven-thirty, just after they'd all been kicked out into the street, the one who'd laughed the hardest would spill a mulch of beer and undigested saveloy half-way across the pavement.

There'd be talk of a curry, but no one would have any money.

For a while they'd mill around the clocktower opposite the Swan, yelling at the drunks and the delicately dressed, pulling from a bottle of something that someone with foresight had lifted from an offie earlier on. When the last of the pub-goers had gone and there was no more entertainment it would be time to shufty on down to the Bancroft – the river gardens by the theatre, empty long since. More spliffs, then, some snogs, maybe someone had some acid or some glue. Virtual cricket in the half-light of street lights reflected off the fuscous water, no bat or ball but full field action none the less. Bored with that, it would be a charge around the graveyard by Holy Trinity Church, in which Shakespeare was buried. Pissing in a dark corner, giggling, sprawling on the gravestones, 'stoned on the stones', telling bad ghost stories that no one believed.

There'd be talk of heading out of town to the Last Resort or the Wildmoor, the town's two night-clubs, of trying to cause some trouble. But again, no money, so in the end it would be back to Jenn's for those who could be bothered, to do hot knives in the kitchen or try to build yet another bucket bong, maybe have a shot at making some music until the neighbours called the police.

Eventually what stimulants there were would all be gone and people would drift away or just fall asleep where they sat. At some point Jennifer would lever herself up and stumble upstairs to the bathroom. Locking herself in, she'd use the toilet and clean her teeth, then take out the special glass she kept in the cabinet and drink four or five pints of water from the tap. As she drank, she felt with relief the liquid run down her oesophagus and into her stomach, washing her system clean of the poisons she'd been pummelling it with and also filling her up, swelling her abdomen slightly. For, since the baby had gone, she found she slept better this way.

Saturday. Jennifer awoke alone, despite the best efforts of one of the guitarists to inveigle his way into her bed at one point during the night. Notwithstanding the water, her head felt heavy from the dope and booze, and her nose was blocked. But her first priority, as usual, was a piss.

Her bladder empty, she noted that it was already midday and she still hadn't eaten properly. Downstairs, most of the posse from the previous night seemed to have gone, except for Mike who was still passed out on the sofa. Someone had tied his trainers together and written PRAT in reversed lipstick lettering across his forehead. Jenn left him to it, took the door off the latch and went out.

It was an overcast and muggy day, as if the climate had binged the night before as well and couldn't summon the energy to put together any proper weather, so was just letting the elements seep haphazardly down out of the sky instead. Sucking at the heavy air, Jenn made her way into town across the Clopton bridge, her spirits not lifting one bit.

However, as she came in sight of the High Street her heart started to pump and adrenalin began to tingle away at her nerves. Her skin tightened, pulling at the scars across her chest, and she felt well enough to risk a cigarette. The nicotine made her head swim and she bumped into a couple of shoppers as she walked up the crowded street towards her target.

The key thing, she'd come to realise, was to be quick and authoritative. She'd spent a lot of time behind the check-out watching the store detectives, seeing whom they looked at, whom they picked up on. It was amazing how many shoplifters they missed. And it was also amazing how brazen these people could be. She'd watched them lift sweets and chocolate off the racks on the counter while she'd been handing them their change; she'd watched them walk out with records, toasters, barbecue sets in their hands, then bring them back the next week, complaining that they were faulty and asking for their money back. The trick was to look as if you were just going about your business, that's all, and not to take stupid risks.

She chose Boots because she liked their sandwiches and despite the rush – much better than she got from hash or booze – she was still hungry. As she walked into the shop she checked her purse for change, then looked up to get her bearings, noting the position of Pete, the plain-clothes security man who'd asked her out once when he used to work with her at Woolies. This is gonna be easy, she smiled to herself. An inside job. She walked over to the fridges and picked out a couple of sandwiches and a drink, which she cradled awkwardly in her left arm. Then she went to the cosmetics counter, put down the food, and tried a couple of lipsticks and mascaras under the watchful eye of the make-up-plastered assistant, a walking ad for how not to do it.

Choosing two or three things, she put them with her food then, when it was time to move on, she cradled everything in her arm like before, with the lipstick on top and closest to her body. She turned and headed for the toiletries section and as she went, well, what do you know? The cosmetics somehow slipped down inside her cardigan and got caught up where it was tucked into the front of her trousers.

The same process was repeated with some shower gel and soap, and with an extra sandwich and a carton of drink when she decided that she'd changed her mind about the ones she'd originally chosen, though she left a packet of towels in plain view. Then it was time to pay.

Feeling much better now, she went down to the Bancroft to eat her lunch and feed her crusts to the ducks.

Head games (2)

Now that she was older they called her Emma (although that wasn't the name her mother would have chosen) and took her to the nursery sometimes. The dossiers describing the dangers associated with her were largely ignored by the nurses who looked after her. There were other children here, and she mixed with them and played with them. There was a sandpit, a waterlab, building blocks, cars and dolls, books with bright pictures. The colours of it all blinded her at first. She had grown so used to her isolation that visual flux proved difficult to cope with. As she strengthened old neural connections and made new ones, the axons groping through her cortex like brambles through the forest brush, the other kids were gradually steadied and addressed. Each child, she discovered, carried with it the thrusting genes of its parents, spliced and coiled into a twisted weave of psychotic algorithms that operated more or less as a unit. They charged around the nursery, probing and pushing and inventing lines of demarcation. The clothes they wore, the accents they carried, the attitudes they harboured told her of the interleaved zones of the wider world beyond; through them, the child learnt of the neighbourhoods of money and status in the surrounding town, and back in her cell at nights she pondered their permutations.

She honed her senses to the patterns inherent in the riots of sound colour taste touch in the playgroups, all of which shaped her, all of which she shaped. The plasticity of the world fascinated her. The nurses were amazed by the complex cantilevered structures she built out of blocks and left lodged — supported by their own gravitational dynamics — on the edges of tables, on the lip of electrical sockets, on the shoulder and crown of a sleeping child. (The other children thought they were fun and destroyed them accordingly.) The cars: she rolled them across the floor by themselves. She couldn't help it, they itched at her to do it, the wheels and axles wanted to turn. All she had to do was stretch and buzz the air behind them and they would go. It was not difficult; it involved little more than directing the reflex shiver excited by the coldness of their desire. A toddler — its mouth open in a puckered ellipse, an expression of benign confusion in its eyes — might pursue the apparently autonomous toy, which Emma would move on every time the young creature grew close. If the paradox of the situation became too much for it, like a sinner crying for God it would start to wail, setting off the other children in a quick domino effect. Then Emma would be scooped up by a nurse and promptly returned to her cell. So she learnt to be careful, she learnt what the others could not do, she learnt to be sly and she learnt to play games.

The art of sedimentation

Everyone gambles in Reno. People move out here and live for years in trailer homes just to play the slots. Retired policemen come to gamble away their memories, young couples to risk all or nothing for a wedding licence and a down payment on a tract home. Old spinsters come, destined to lose their pensions and end up on a train to New York, bag ladies from the moment they hit Grand Central. Evangelists who sailed too close to the wind are here, betting on God in another way, as are lesbian housewives from Milwaukee on the run from their pasts and the daily temptation of braining their deadbeat spouses with a heavy household implement; they stand next to pimps and prostitutes, who figured they'd do better working Reno's hotels than flushed down the sewers that are the downtown streets of the cities of America's Pacific Rim. Entire families, hooked as a unit on the gambling tip, lurch between the tables and the restaurants, already booked in for a slot on Oprah ten years down the line. And then there are the bookies and the travelling salesmen and the frat-boys on jaunts and the businessmen pretending they're powerful and the thirty-somethings looking for a thrill and the rubbernecks and the professionals and the schoolteachers and the bus drivers and the suckers, yes, the suckers – there are plenty of those. Or maybe, just maybe, there aren't. Maybe everyone here knows what they're in for. Maybe everyone here's getting just what they want.

This one is always rolling. It's five in the morning and the cleaners are vacuuming round your feet as you stand to lose another five hundred at blackjack. It's 10 a.m. and you've barely finished your three-dollar breakfast of steak eggs coffee fries onion rings coffee tomato grits pancakes coffee syrup ketchup fresh orange juice coffee bacon muffin teacake Cheerios yoghurt eggs and coffee all topped off with a sprinkling of bran, and they're bringing you a complimentary cocktail or a bottle of cheap champagne because you've passed some arbitrary demarcation line at one of the tables and the pit boss wants you to get drunk before you can win any more. But the drink sits uneasily on top of all that food so you stroll around for a while, not wanting to leave and jinx your luck, glad to take a look at the other players, happy to watch someone else throw away their money for a change – though it's not too long before once again you're wishing it were you.

Although the Golden Gecko proved to be a good place to stay, Judd rarely chose to play there, preferring the quieter, more dedicated clubs on the surrounding blocks where the gaming rooms were isolated from the ranks of slot machines and the dreadful cabarets, and left to generate that bustling hush that is the mark of a serious casino. He played quietly and sensibly, more aware than most of the shapes and the dangers. He followed the lizard through the carpeted halls of the town, past the plastic dioramas of mythical Wild West scenes that decorated the bars and lottery rooms, up and down stairs whose treads were inlaid with pulsating tubes of light, through crepuscular rooms lit only by the glare from the myriad glitterballs that hung like the cocoons of magical insects from the one-way-mirrored ceilings. He ate mainly in the great subsidised self-service cafeterias with their enormous salad bars shaped like boats or Hawaiian huts and brimming like monstrous horns of plenty with Boston lettuce and limestone lettuce and escarole and chicory and endive and watercress and fennel and rocket and avocado and tomato and scallions and artichokes and kohlrabi and jicama and beetroot and coleslaw and wheat berries and capers and baby corn and dwarf zucchini and giant radish and string beans and olive oil and blue cheese dressing and thousand island and croutons and walnuts and anchovies.

Sometimes he would become so involved that he would forget to eat at all and just drink, discovering that the soft sweet options – Barcardi and coke, vodka and orange, whiskey and ginger – would lift him and keep him going right on through the night. But after several weeks of these he dropped the mixers, their high sugar content having brought on too many headaches, and began to eat again for energy, washing down the food with beer or neat spirits. One thing he didn't do was smoke: he'd quit on leaving LA, having decided to clean up his act a bit with the change in his luck, and he became known in several of the casinos as much for his complaints about the air quality as for the quality of his play.

The lizard taught him the patience of the desert, its ways and moods, how to survive. It taught him how to reconnect, how to move in sympathy with the forces around him. It taught him how to play amid the dry breezes of chance which blew across the tables, breezes which could drown a man in money as easily as a samoom drowns a village in red dust, which could snap the phase, become sand devil, twister, trash him and flip over to the far side of the rainbow. He spotted them now, always, when he walked down the street, caught them stapled to the sides of buildings, motionless, or darting from plant to plant. He found himself defining the city in saurian terms, always on the look-out for good places to catch the sun, favourable hunting grounds for flies, possible escape routes from small children with stones. A gecko took up residence on the balcony of his room, twenty-five storeys up. He studied it in the afternoons while he sat and dozed in his deck-chair, matching the rate of his eye blinks to that of the creature. Sometimes they'd look out over the desert together, scrutinising.

Judd had moved into a smooth space structured by a more prosaic set of desires and needs than the ones that had been set up for him during the course of his analysis. It was the space of a broken, imperfect universe, a cosmos of chance, where God did play dice, where God *was* dice, but where dice always acted in concert and never alone. And it was a slower space, too; time was reframed here, in a way that he found reminiscent of the picnoleptic playground of his childhood. When he slept his dreams were green, dark green, and full of scales. Nothing coherent, just a boiling mass of tails legs backs eyes, himself looking down on it, unmoved, feeling nothing but the throb-throb of life. Awake, he settled and spread, his perceptions altering as if under the influence of a drug, until the people around him became speeding, scurrying forms, their movements hasty, repetitive and predictably instinctual, the jitterings of gerbils nervous in their cages. He watched them buzz around the craps tables and the roulette wheels, circulating in tune with the tidal jabber of molecules on distant stars, like the people Joel had once seen from the top of the Empire State. As sand blows in and out of the boles and cracks and hollows of gaunt trees and crags the chips blew in and out of their palms.

Something began to take shape in the mess of his dreams. Less angular than the reptilian limbs, less jagged and harsh. It tantalised him. What was it? He began to sleep more in order to try and coax it out. Meanwhile, in the afternoons, he looked less at the lizard and more at the desert, at the rock. The lizard had reminded him of what he'd known as a child: that time was plastic. Now he wanted to stretch it out further. He would go beyond the reptilian. He would learn to think like a rock, yes, gamble like a rock, the slowest flow, becoming stone, Zen and the art of sedimentation. He was still obsessed by Schemata, and his success in Reno had made him determined to rid himself of the doctor's influence for once and for all. If the analysis had set up a kind of psychic irrigation system inside him, one which channelled his thoughts and controlled the way he cultivated his mind, then one way out was to clog it, to let the particles of dust in its waters settle and sediment, gather and obstruct. With the system unable to flow, pressure would build until eventually the pipes would break at their joints. He would be free.

So he let the weather of chance foul up the schemas around him, within him. He watched the whips and tails of matter whirl and catch at his feet and slowly, slowly cover his shoes, ankles, knees. He rolled the dice and shuffled the cards again and again, until eventually his fingertips began to blister, harden and crack. It felt good, it was part of his power. All was going according to plan, things were ossifying, it seemed he always knew now when to play, when to leave. Layer upon layer of magic dust accumulated around him. He became impervious to loss, unaffected by bounty. All that mattered was this calcification, this turning to stone. Outcrops could be lost and strata stripped away as long as this tendency remained. He would become a sentinel of this land in which the edifice of finance forever crumbled into sand seas of cash. Perversely, he would fossilise, transmute into living rock or, more fabulously, into a gemstone constructed from wind, earth and sky. The imposed, the hated mental economy would be ended and he would enter a new crystal life of the mind.

Judd didn't see it yet but in this last he had gone too far, become in the end just like all the others who came here to gamble. Despite all his talents and skills, like the rest of them he still nurtured a hope of perfection. Something always within him? Or a Parthian arrow from Schemata? Who knows, but thus tempted he couldn't resist. He had followed the lizard too far, gone beyond what it had to teach and, blinded by jewels, he dug deep down in his dreams. He could tell what it was now, bubbling up from that tangle of saurian flesh, night after night. It was a child, a tiny child, carved out of stone and emerald-eyed, viridescent.

11

Grundrisse

Joel emerged from both of the Mandelbrot lectures with his muscles in knots, talking like a maniac. Subhash, who throughout the sessions had been surreptitiously dabbing speed from a wrap he kept hidden beneath the table, said he felt the same way. But even in his artificially accelerated state he couldn't keep up with Joel's diatribe.

For two days Joel didn't sleep. After the first lecture he pursued Mandelbrot through the corridors of the Centre, pestering him with his questions, and would have spent the night at his bedside if he could have done. The next day it was all Subhash could do to drag him away into the Common Room and leave the French mathematician in peace, but although he managed that much it was beyond his abilities to calm Joel down once he had got him there. He began to worry that Axel or Gabriel, two friends who often teased him about his friendship with Joel, had spiked Joel's coffee with an hallucinogenic; it was the kind of practical joke that would appeal to them. Indeed, it was the sort of thing he himself had been involved in in the past.

'It's astonishing,' Joel kept insisting, 'don't you realise the implications of what he's saying? God, and to think I was suckered even for a minute by the juvenile Platonism of that idiot Metric.' Subhash had never heard him be so forthright before. 'Don't you see how it mocks the very notion of dimensionality? Mandelbrot's shown that form is not static and eternal, but is an expression of content over time! That a shape of infinite per-imeter can exist within a circle of measurable circumference. Mathematics itself becomes a matter of perspective. Everything becomes a matter of perspective.'

Subhash couldn't follow him. He couldn't see how the conclusions followed from the premise. 'Come on,' he said, trying to dilute his friend's excitement, 'everybody knows that anyway. We don't need mathematics to persuade us of it. Of course, it's exciting that the field is opening up, but . . .'

But Joel's energy was not to be earthed. 'Einstein is only the starting point,' he went on, connecting madly and – as far as Subhash could see – meaninglessly. 'And even he tried to confine the ramifications of his theories. This shows that the actual processes infiltrate existence to a degree beyond his most fervent nightmares. It is so ridiculous, it was right in front of me all the time, all those trays and trays of bread coming out of my father's ovens. In the folding, in the leavening, where volume is created by patterns of bubbles repeated again and again on every scale, making empty space is as important as matter. It's the Julia set, don't you see? Remember, one of the fractal images that Mandelbrot showed us? It was like looking at the creation itself. Like seeing the precise construction of space! And the self-similarity across scales, it means you can leap from one thing to the other and yet retain the same relationship. It's . . . I don't know, I don't know, there's no metaphysical division.' As he spoke he rushed around the room, crouched on chairs, flailed his arms, his body stuttering on the boundary between walking and running. 'And of course what's most marvellous of all is that it fits perfectly with the idea that each of the Sefirot contains within itself an infinite reflection of all of the others. There are possibilities here, there are possibilities. If the universe is fractal, infinitely regressive, as quantum mechanics might seem to suggest, then it might help to make sense of the duality between particle and wave, and it might also help us to understand ideas of perfection! Einstein and Mandelbrot, both Jewish, you see?'

Subhash tried to field an objection: 'But wait a minute, Joel, you're not making any kind of sense, you're fudging you must see that.'

Joel turned on him: 'You don't believe me, do you? You don't believe me. Didn't you hear him? I thought you heard him. But you see what a nonsense it makes of metaphysics? If you don't believe me I'll show you,' and he headed out of the room at speed.

'Joel, Joel, where in hell are you going?' Subhash yelled and got up to follow him.

It was gone midnight and the lab was empty. All the mini-computers were on, running their interminable calculations like so many cattle munching grass. Joel went straight to the nearest machine – it was busy analysing a portion of the data from one of the accelerator experiments that had been run the previous week – and terminated the programme.

'What the fuck are you doing?' panted Subhash, running into the room. 'That's seventy-two hours of processing time you've just flushed away!'

'It's not important right now.'

'You've flipped, man, you've lost it completely. I should never have let you go to that lecture, you're not safe to be let loose on anything except that damned space invaders console you spend so much time playing.'

'Is there a colour printer around here anywhere?'

'I have no fucking idea.'

'Find me a colour printer! Come on, do you want to see this or not?'

Subhash sighed. 'I think there's a four-colour on the third floor.'

'Can you bring it down here?'

'It weighs a ton. And it's probably locked up anyway.'

'Well, find the keys and get a trolley. There must be one around somewhere.' It was pointless to argue; Joel was already entering lines of Unix code into the machine. Deciding he might as well humour him, Subhash went off to get the printer.

It turned out not to be on the third floor at all, but on the fourth, in one of the classrooms. Although he could see it through the glass the door was locked so, wondering again why he was bothering and feeling that the sensible course of action would be to telephone the local asylum, Subhash went off in search of the night porter. He found him quickly enough, watching television in the coffee area on the second floor, and persuaded him to come and unlock the door.

Fortunately there was a trolley in the classroom but even so, by the time he got the printer back down to the lab Joel had produced several screens' worth of code and was more involved than ever. Annoyed that Joel could only muster a single grunt of approval by way of thanks, Subhash trailed off back to the Common Room to get himself a cup of coffee. He ended up going to sleep across a row of chairs, the latest edition of *Scientific American* lying open across his face.

When he awoke it seemed to him that the room was full of light. His first thought was that he had slept for hours, that it was morning. But as his eyes adjusted themselves to his surroundings he saw that rudely papered across the walls, tacked up on the ceiling, strewn across the floor were huge and vivid posters of fractal scenes, shimmering with iridescent colour like slices of giant precious stones. Some of them were full sets, glaring like the giant eyes of fantastic crustaceans, others were zoomed explorations, aerial views of the idyllic reefs and beaches of some fabulous travel destination, glimpses of the tangled boughs and jungle clumps of an undiscovered Rousseau.

'Oh, God,' he murmured, 'what has he done?' Rubbing his eyes, he got up and went to look for Joel. He wasn't difficult to find. The corridors that led to the computer lab were plastered with further pixellated pictures of sets with names like Newton, Plasma, Sierpinski, Popcorn, Mandelbrot, Spider, Tetrate, Lambda, Julia, Gingerbread, Kamtorus, Manowar, Manzpower. He felt as if he were walking down the fallopian tubes of some monstrous digital womb, from whose coruscated sides silicon life forms might at any moment begin to sprout like robot maggots. When he was near enough to the lab to hear the hum of the printer and the whirr of the fans he felt afraid. It was as if the whole building was alive. Frantic light played in a rectangle on the wall opposite the open lab door, the spilled photons scheming furiously like the molecules in some protoplasmic soup.

Peering round the door frame into the room, it looked to Subhash as if the treasure chambers of the world had been rudely melted down and converted into a series of epileptic pools, each of which was the baroque tracing of an obsessed and psychotic mind. Joel had got all of the computers generating fractal sets on their screens and flashing them in black and green, green and black. In addition to the colour printer, which was still chugging out the pictures that already covered every available surface, he had found a second machine, a dot matrix, which was spewing forth an endless roll of fascinating pattern into a susurrating pile that filled a corner of the room. All the lights in the lab had been switched off: the extraordinary brightness came only from the screens and the play of their contorted graphics across the myriad printouts. Compared with this grotto, the corridor and Common Room had been mere harbingers.

From beneath the pile of snaking paper a leg protruded. Subhash picked it up and pulled, and a body appeared. He checked his friend's breathing and felt his pulse, but he seemed right enough. Half dragging, half carrying, he got Joel to the Common Room where he laid him on the same bank of chairs on which he himself had slept. Then he hurried back to the lab to try and clear up some of the mess.

The killer app

In the years since Sputnik II was launched had war, terrorism, disaster become spectator sports? For Laika they had, for certain. Trapped in her capsule, totally integrated with all modern conveniences but with nothing to do, little excited her as much as the footage of real-life events. And of those, events where real life was in danger were best.

The Six Day War had been a glimmer, a taster, there'd been a few good pictures there, but Vietnam was a treat. How she'd adored being torn between her desire for the war to be brought to an end and her love of the constant stream of explicit on-the-ground news. Munich in 1972 had been fun, when the Israeli Olympic team had been taken hostage in front of the cameras with a third of the world's population tuned in. How exciting that was, such drama! It was a shame it was too dark to see the details of the bungled rescue attempt (a few flashes of rifle fire were all you could make out as seventeen people were killed). But it was exciting none the less, watching the palpitating viscera of the world breaking through the social veneer of the Games.

Laika liked all that. Which is why the 1982 Falklands War was such a disappointment. The British, so uptight! Hardly any TV. Where were the cruisers the jump jets the Exocets the infantry pinned down on the beach? The newscasters tried to keep everyone happy with models and maps, but it wasn't the same. No spice! No pizzazz! No *action*! Action's what you need. The rhythms of TV *demand* it. If Laika knew one thing she knew that. She had, after all, watched enough of the stuff. Vietnam had been a close war, immediate enough for you to forget that the images were manipulated. But the British had closed everything down so much you could see who was calling the shots. And who wanted to be reminded of that? 'Let it be free,' she yowled, 'let the media be free.' Or at least let it look like it was.

When Nathan of Gaza sits up
and smiles

Joel's room was in an even greater state of disarray than the computer lab had been on the evening after the second Mandelbrot lecture. Although the space wasn't bathed in the same fantastic light, all the furniture had been pushed back against the walls and there were papers everywhere. To Subhash they appeared to be strewn completely haphazardly, but when he attempted to free a chair from under a stack of photocopies of articles discussing the invention and use of the number zero in various different cultures Joel turned on him almost savagely.

'No! No, don't touch those. Here. Sit here.' He cleared a space on the bed and motioned Subhash towards it. Raising his eyebrows slightly, the Pakistani gingerly picked his way between the stacks of material that encrusted the floor like intellectual moraine. Holocaust paraphernalia was spliced with salvaged fractal printouts, scientific abstracts with gutted books on gambling technique, circuit boards and wiring with electronics magazines. Alerted to the fact that a Byzantine system underpinned the mess, it now looked to Subhash as if Joel was indeed using the material in an attempt to define the axes of some bizarre personal geometry, creating a construct which through hitherto impossible juxtapositions would delineate a perspective that would somehow make coherent sense of it all.

Among the papers were phase space diagrams of the cycles of strange attractors that Joel had presumably downloaded from a bulletin board somewhere. Subhash had seen a few of them in the more adventurous periodicals; there was a vogue for this kind of mathematics in a number of American universities and some of it was beginning to become pertinent to his work on neural nets. Yet even to his unpractised eye some of the eerie images, simultaneously wholly new and totally familiar, were instantly recognisable: the Brusselator, the great wings of Lorenz's simple weather model, the folded ellipses discovered by Henon among the movements of the stars.

'Help me clear a space in the centre of the room,' insisted Joel. He indicated to Subhash which piles could be moved and where they should go (mostly into the bathroom, as it turned out, as this was the only spot which remained free of clutter). When the space was clear he pulled his friend into the hallway where, around the corner by the fire exit, stood the roulette table: a squat piece of furniture like an ornate kitchen unit with a wheel built into its top. 'I had to get Clive to help me move it out a couple of weeks ago,' Joel explained. 'That was after I'd finished all the testing. I've been needing to get the background right since then.'

'The background?' huffed Subhash, struggling a little beneath the table's weight.

'You know, the background! The surroundings. The milieu. These things don't work in a vacuum. That's the whole point.' They dragged the table into Joel's room and set it down in the space they had cleared. Subhash sat down on the bed to catch his breath and light a cigarette. Joel retrieved a spirit level from beneath a pile of shoes and dirty socks, and fiddled with the table's adjustable legs, trying to get the thing level. After a while he broke off and, as if trying to remember which tool he needed, gazed into space for a moment or two, apparently distracted by the patterns the cigarette smoke made in the air as it rose towards the ceiling on the tiny thermals of the room.

Subhash brought his reverie to an end. 'Look, Joel, are you sure you're all right?'

'What? Of course I'm all right.'

'But just look at all this! What the fuck is going on?'

'I told you. It's research. Isn't it obvious?'

'Sure, sure.' Subhash paused and drew on his fag, deliberately exhaling through the curlicues of smoke when he noticed that Joel had once again become fascinated by them. 'It's so obvious that I'm afraid you'll have to tell me what the connections are between the Mandelbrot set, the Holocaust and roulette, because I'm fucked if I know.'

Blind to the sarcasm (he took everything at face value now as a matter of course), Joel was excited by Subhash's apparent interest in his work. 'I don't know ... I don't know how to put it into words, it's the movement, do you see? Here!' He pulled a shoe box full of postcards and photographs from beneath the bed and began to rummage through it. When he found the image he was looking for he brandished it at Subhash. It was the map of Europe that Jennifer had been so taken by over two years previously, which his father had once come across in the Brooklyn library, the one where places were only identified by the number of people who had been exterminated there. 'See this? It's Europe as a field, a quantum field, with death the spectral calibration for all and any eigenvalues. That's what I mean by background. And that ties in with this –' he flapped through the mess to the picture of the Lorenz attractor '– right? Which is obvious, because it's like the weather, I mean, look at it. You don't need a computer to work it out. Which is another thing, because all these networks, in the universities and here too, you link them all together, and the Internet, you've got the Internet, you know about that, you use electronic mail, right? Same thing! And if you read this book –' he picked up one of the roulette manuals in the air '– of course, you only need the first paragraph and the last line of it, and this book –' he scrabbled for another text, the title of which Subhash did not catch '– though there's more reading involved with this one, I think, then it goes right through. I mean, it all connects. From the simplicity of this –' he indicated the roulette wheel '– to the madness of this.' He touched a photograph of Goebbels with his foot. 'It's a question of reconciling the two lights of Ein-Sof, "the light which contains thought" – and which contracted to make room for the creation, according to Nathan of Gaza – and "the light which does not contain thought" – which did not. These two form a dialectic, they're the active and the passive, and evil is the outcome. The problem of evil can only be solved at the time of final redemption, and I quote, "when the light which contains thought will penetrate through and through the light without thought and delineate therein its holy forms." Scholem, page one two six. Again, it's a question of the movement towards perfection and in order to prove the existence of that we need to track the movements of chance. And what do we use to do that? The computer, right? Which, funnily enough, could be described as the worldly embodiment of the light that contains thought. Think about it.' He looked at Subhash, hoping for confirmation, a gleam in his eye that scared his friend. Subhash shifted uncomfortably on the bed and looked for somewhere to put down the cup he had been using as an ashtray so he could light another cigarette.

'Let me demonstrate,' Joel continued imperiously. 'Watch.' He went across to the roulette wheel, spun it and at the appropriate moment sent the ball hurtling round contrary to the direction of spin with a flick of his spindly wrist. As it bounced and rattled off the revolving cups he sat down and took off his right shoe and handed it to Subhash. 'What do you think of that?' he asked.

'It's your shoe, Joel,' Subhash replied caustically.

'No! Look inside! Look inside!' Timidly, as if expecting a mousetrap to snap closed on them at any moment, Subhash inched his fingers down inside the leather upper. At the bottom, right where the toes should be, there were four small pads and a few twists of wiring. He turned the shoe over and examined it, noticing that the sole was somewhat thicker and stiffer than he would have expected. The heel was particularly large; it had obviously been hollowed out at some point and subsequently rebuilt. Subhash looked up, his eyes full of questions.

With the pride of a father, Joel explained: 'Computers. One built into each shoe. 4K of RAM apiece. They communicate by wires that run up and down inside my trousers.' Before Subhash could protest Joel had unbuckled his belt and lowered his slacks. Snaking through the exceptionally thick hair that covered his skinny white legs were a few strands of plastic-coated wire.

'OK,' said Subhash with a slight feeling of revulsion, 'I've seen them. You can put them away now.' Joel rearranged his dress. 'But what are they for, anyway?'

'For that,' said Joel, pointing to the roulette wheel. 'For beating the system. For trapping chance, if you like. Chance has its habits as well, or didn't you know?' He was crowing now, his pride having got the better of him.

'But you can't predict roulette!' exclaimed Subhash, delighted at last to have understood something of what his friend was saying. 'It's totally random!'

'Nothing's random, least of all this, at least not now. Predicting a single result has nothing to do with chance anyway. It's a simple question of physics. The shoe computers are set up to simulate the spin of the wheel. Every wheel is slightly different, of course, so I've written an algorithm which can be tuned to individual set-ups. Obviously, this one here is programmed in at the moment. That's what the right shoe is for: by using the pads I can calibrate the speed of the wheel, the speed of the ball, the angle of tilt and so on. With the speed of the wheel it's easy; you just tap a particular button every time the zero cup goes past a particular point. Same kind of procedure for the speed of the ball. It takes a bit of practice, mind.' Joel had picked up this last turn of phrase, this Midlands expression, from Jennifer. For a split second he thought of her now. 'It's a closed system, and while the ball is bouncing around it the computer calculates its full run and transmits the answer to the machine in my left foot via the wire. In that shoe the pads are solenoids which vibrate a sequence according to where the ball will end up. In a casino I should just have time to place my bets before the ball stops.'

Subhash wasn't at all sure whether or not to believe him. 'All right, then. Let's see it work.'

Joel didn't need much prompting. He pulled on the shoes and handed a ball to Subhash. 'Right,' he said, 'you be the croupier.' Subhash looked at the hard white ball between his thumb and forefinger; with its perfect, Euclidean dimensions it seemed an anomaly in the scheme of things.

'Obviously, the system isn't capable of predicting an exact number . . .'

'Obviously.'

'. . . although with a powerful enough machine and accurate measuring equipment, lasers say, I've no doubt you could do it. Although I know the angle of tilt I have to guesstimate the speed, so we have to limit ourselves to betting on octaves. OK, I'm ready. Spin the wheel.' Subhash did as he was told and set the thing in motion. Joel pursed his lips and the movement of his toes beat tiny mounds in the soft leather of his shoes. Then Subhash introduced the ball and watched it bounce and chirrup around the basin like a hummingbird in flight. There was such a look of expectancy in his eyes that Joel himself resembled a bird about to take to the air, though with his long neck, large nose and puckered flesh he was more ostrich than anything else. He'll have a shock when he finds out he can't fly, thought Subhash meanly.

'4, 21, 2, 25, 17,' blurted Joel. Subhash shifted his attention to the wheel. The ball bounced for a few more seconds, then made up its mind and fell into the basin. It was a moment or two before the wheel slowed sufficiently to let them see the result.

Subhash announced it: 'Red thirty-six.'

Joel's cheeks flushed the same colour as the cup. 'It'll take me a while to get used to your delivery,' he stammered. 'Try it again, try it again.' Obediently, but with a disrespectful smirk upon his face, Subhash retrieved the ball and spun the wheel again. Once more, pursed mouth and puckered brow for Joel, the eyes slick with expectation, the toes bubbling away inside the shoe. 'OK: 28, 12, 35, 3, 36.' The wheel slowed and the ball came to rest.

'Red twelve!'

'There! You see?'

'It'll take more than that to convince me. Again.' Subhash flicked the wheel a third time and dropped in the ball; it bounced merrily and tick-tacked away the silence of the room. Again Joel called the numbers of the highest octave.

'Three!'

'You see? You see?'

'Again!' Wheel, spin, ball, eyes, toes, 34, 6, 27, 13.

'Thirteen. Again, again.' Field, energy, element, algorithm, system. 0, 35, 15, 19.

'Zero.' A whisper. 'My god.' Subhash was sweating: his armpits and groin bled moisture. On the next round Joel missed. Then he got three in a row, two missed, two more.

'Enough. I believe you.'

'Impressed?'

'Of course I'm impressed. I can also see why you're not worried about them threatening to suspend your grant after what you did to the computer room.' Joel nodded, a smile stretched so wide across his face that he looked as if his head might split. Subhash had never seen him so happy. 'You want to be careful, you know. If they catch you with that in any of the casinos they won't mess around.'

'Oh, they won't catch me. How would they catch me? They're hardly going to look in my shoes, are they?'

'It's brilliant! You're brilliant, quite brilliant. I want to be the first to say it. But don't let it go to your head. Be careful, that's all.'

'Sure.'

'Have you told anyone else about it?'

'No, only you.' The words dropped like a pebble into the pond of Joel's mind, sending out concentric ripples of paranoia. Maybe it hadn't been such a good idea telling Subhash. But the fear dissipated as quickly as it had come.

'So, are you going to show me the program?' the programmer asked with a smile, hoping to change the subject. 'I want to see how you've done all that in 4K.'

'I'm not the first person to try it,' insisted Joel, his modesty returning. 'Lots of people have had a go before. In America you can buy all sorts of systems by mail order, although none as advanced as mine of course. About ten years ago Thorpe and Shannon, a couple of gambling experts, built a roulette system you could wear. They used strobes and a film camera and a clock to calibrate the wheels, and built two little analogue computers complete with radio transmitters to do the calculations. Different variables were represented by different voltage levels. Amazing, really. The machines sent the answers as musical notes to tiny hearing aids they wore in their ear canals.'

'Did it work?'

'No, not really. All the wiring had to be so small that it kept breaking. I seem to remember that the system was over-sensitive to interference, too. But I don't know if anyone's come close since. Except for me, that is.'

'But isn't it enormously complicated to calculate? What about entropic

318

degradation? Wind resistance? The rims of the cups upsetting the bounce? What if the croupier's got a sprained wrist?'

'We-ll, those things aren't so much of a problem really. As I said, you're inputting speed anyway, and if you take enough data it's fairly straightforward to allow for friction and random bounces. They don't upset the system that much. As far as the gambling goes you're only looking for a good edge over the game anyway, though ultimately I'll need more accuracy for the Project. It's the variables you can't predict which mess it all up. Like different balls. They can be made of ivory, nylon, acetate, Teflon and so on. Even human bone. During the war the Nazis made them out of the bones of Jews. There – there's another connection between those pictures and roulette for you.'

'Wow.' Joel had taken off the shoes and Subhash picked one of them up and turned it over in his hands, feeling down inside it, inspecting it – with reverence this time. 'How long have you been working on this?'

'Oh, long enough. It's not that big a deal, really.'

To his surprise, when Subhash looked up at Joel's face he detected there a genuine nonchalance. It came as a marked contrast to the pride he'd seen earlier. Such a disjunction was unsettling. It was too reminiscent of the mood swings Joel had exhibited at the time of the Mandelbrot lectures. 'Oh, come on . . .' he said.

'No, really, it is. The only difficult bit was building a small enough device. But even the memory restriction doesn't present too much of a problem. You could do it better than me. Predicting the system itself is easy. When I found out I could do it I was a bit disappointed.'

'But you've achieved so much!'

'Oh, this is only the first step. The idea is to get the system really accurate, so that I can predict the octant that's going to come up say ninety-five per cent of the time and to use that as an index against which I can judge when chance is not operating as it should.'

'I don't understand.'

Joel's eyes began to glisten and he became animated again. 'Look, I already explained to you that the universe is heading towards perfection, right? Well, if it's not perfect now, then it shouldn't exhibit perfect randomness. If the roulette wheel is a closed Newtonian system, then every spin should be a totally discrete event and I should be able to predict every one just on the physical data available. But what I'm finding is that I can't do that – you saw that already, I didn't get all of them right just now. This means that every event is not wholly discrete, that something is linking them together. If I can show that they're somehow linked, I can show that there's no true randomness in the universe.'

'But Joel, with the greatest respect, that's crap. What about if there's a tilt on the wheel? Or your timing is off. That would alter the outcomes.'

'I already told you I compensate for all that at the beginning. Listen, if I can show there are links between the spins, that's when the really exciting work can begin. What about the way people behave around a roulette table, for example? Huh? Huh? What about the way a crowd moves through a space, or a swarm of bees? Could you use some kind of fractal resonance to work out the movements of those in advance? What about the weather, or the development of grammar, or the way that roulette itself spread through Europe, from Paris to Britain with the Royalist émigrés in 1789, then to the health spas, Baden-Baden, Saxon-les-Bains, Wiesbaden and on from there? Could that have been predicted? Lorenz found an attractor for the weather, didn't he? Then shouldn't there be one for the Holocaust? Why not? It makes sense. It's the only thing about it that does.'

Now Subhash was really confused. 'I don't think so. I mean, at the end of the day roulette's a closed system. You're right, it's Newtonian and therefore predictable. But these things, they're so nebulous. If even the world is deterministic, which I doubt – I mean, Heisenberg has taught us that – there are surely too many factors at work to predict anything in these other cases.'

'Heisenberg? Hah! That theorem's just a mathematical device, like Gödel's theorem. It means relatively little, in real terms.' Subhash looked shocked. 'You think I'm crazy, but it's not just me, you know! Other people have noticed it too. Haven't you read *The Gambler*, you know, by Dostoevsky? No? Here, I'll lend you my copy –' Joel dived under the bed for a moment and rummaged around; Subhash sat there feeling bewildered and sparked up another cigarette '– here it is, borrow it, read it. He came to this through roulette too, but he knew there were patterns bigger than the game, surrounding the game, waves and eddies and whirlpools. It's all in there. Read it!'

'OK, OK, I will.'

'Remember what Mandelbrot said. All these things have patterns. The financial markets he showed us, cotton prices, self-similarity over time. If the financial markets have patterns then why not everything else? Time's internal to the system. Einstein told us that! I don't know why we've taken so long to apply it. "God doesn't play dice." No, *he's learning to play* and that's how the universe manages to exist in its current form.'

320

Joel paused for a moment. 'Does genocide have a phase space?' he demanded.

'Joel, I . . .'

'How many degrees of freedom do you think an act of genocide has? Hundreds? Thousands? Millions? Or maybe just a handful, when you really look at it. A couple of dozen. Think of the liberties we take in mapping the sub-atomic world. Yet we can't take those liberties with history, oh no. It might give us a hope of understanding it and that would never do. We can't bear the fact that we needed machines to figure all this out for us. We can't bear it! I tell you there'll be an outcry against this stuff, because it has taken our own precious logic and subverted it. All those trees and hierarchies and classifications have revolted. The machines won't put up with it. You must know how complex the networks are, even here on site. There's a guy over on the French side who's writing some protocols that will allow any computer to talk to any other. You'll be able to access information from anywhere almost instantly. He's calling it CERNET. The way he's doing it, the data will break itself down into discrete packets, each of which will find its own way through the system, then reassemble itself at the end, like teleporting or something. You'll be able to leap from databank to databank, even if the data you want are on different machines. You'll be able to search for documents across entire systems, maybe even across countries or continents if you connect networks together via telephone. It'll be like swimming, or something, except it won't be like anything physical that we've known because every point in the datasphere will be effectively next to every other. I tell you what it will be like, it will be like thinking. We're finally building machines that emulate thought, even if they don't yet think for themselves. You should know all about that! It's a new kind of logic. It's "the light which contains thought". We're going to be able to use them to understand everything. They're going to change everything, you'll see.'

'But I'm not sure if . . .'

'Oh, come on! You work with these things. You know I'm right, you must do. And what if it's time that makes all problems unintegrable, but at the same time makes patterns? Patterns are the way to understand the unintegrable. The question then becomes, you know, how to look for the patterns, how to collect the data. There's so much data out there, but how to know what's significant and what's irrelevant, that's the problem. You have to have some way of narrowing it down, some kind of system that can consolidate all these influences for you. Let me ask you, how are you supposed to make sense of the Holocaust? Do you perform numeromancies on the numbers of people who died, on their vital statistics? Their ages, weights, sizes and so on? Do you plot the co-ordinates of all the death camps and see if they make some kind of recognisable constellation? Do you measure the levels of background radiation at these sites? Perhaps, perhaps. But if it's time that makes patterns of things, if it's time that keeps them in motion, then maybe it's still happening now. Maybe the figures aren't what's important. Perhaps. I don't know.

'My father always used to tell me there were three types of time, zimzum, shevirah and tikkun. He'd been told about them by some rabbi, but he'd never found out what the teacher had meant. But I have, I have found out. According to Kabbalah zimzum is the movement in which Ein-Sof withdrew into itself and created the ten Sefirot. When something exists within this kind of time it draws into itself and perfects itself. But after the vessels of the Sefirot have been broken and the world is created out of the chaos there's a new time, shevirah, the time of the world. This is negentropic time, in which out of the energy of that catastrophe links are created between things and enough organisation occurs for this universe to come into being, imperfect though it is. It is this time which leaves its traces in the patterns of chance, in attractors and so on. And lastly there is tikkun, the time which returns, what we call entropy, the flipside of shevirah that returns everything to perfect continuum, to perfect randomness.'

'You've lost me, I'm afraid. I didn't understand a word of that.'

Joel didn't seem to care. 'It's not all worked out yet. I'm still only at the beginning of it. There's so much to do now.'

'Yes, but Joel, man, you've got to get back to your research work. They're going to kick you out if you don't. You're on a knife edge as it is after what you did to the computer room.'

'What do I care if they kick me out? It's not as if the work going on here is important.' He gestured at the roulette table and chuckled. 'And as you said already, I hardly need their grant.'

That was enough. Joel had gone somewhere and it didn't look like he was coming back. Maybe he'd been there all the time, Subhash didn't know. But he didn't see what he could do to help him. 'I'm sorry, Joel, but it's late and I'm tired. I need to get back and get some sleep. Where's that Dostoevsky?' Joel passed it to him enthusiastically. 'Right, look I'll read this and tell you what I think. Maybe it'll help me understand what it is you're on about, I don't know.' Subhash got to his feet and picked his way through the debris towards the door. But when he got there he hesitated, suddenly afraid to leave. 'See you tomorrow.'

'Yeh, perhaps.'

'Thanks for showing me your computer. It's damn cool, you know.'

'Yeh, sure, any time. Keep it to yourself, though. I don't want word getting round about it. I intend to use this thing for real.' For some reason this reassured Subhash and he smiled a final goodbye before exiting, his last glimpse into the room as the door closed revealing Joel hunched over one of the shoes with a screwdriver, making some minor adjustment that would further improve the performance of his machine.

Just friends

The child got most fun out of playing with other children. But it wasn't until she'd met Veronica that she'd realised quite how different she was. Veronica had been hurt by the Daddy (who was one of The Parents). She had friends of her own, too, but there were only three of them: Good Veronica, Sore Veronica and Veronica-come-here-and-be-punished. But unlike the friends of the My, the Veronicas were all very frightened and there didn't seem to be a Veronica-My at all. Emma helped the Veronica friends talk to each other and it wasn't long before they were unscared and a Veronica-My came out. Then Veronica was more like the other children, most of whom (except for Filthychild, but he was a special case) seemed to have only Mys, although some Mys were stronger than others.

The other Mys didn't know like the Emma-My did what the Hospital Nights were going to do, for example. The other children were simple compared with the Emma-My. The Emma-My liked to play games with them because she could see from their trembles what they were going to do and it made it easy for her to win. Sometimes the games would be nasty, like when the child felt the others from another room and the others felt her eyes on their skin, or when she got them to give her things (buttons, crayons, coins, bracelets, sweets, shoelaces, underwear). (When she was caught by the nurses getting presents they would punish her Severely.)

What was strangest about Emma was that she wouldn't talk. She *could* talk; she would try words for size, as if they were rings, or shoes, but most of them she seemed to reject as soon as their novelty wore off.

Whereas other children raced at language as soon as they discovered it was the best way to get what they wanted, Emma seemed not to be interested. The population in her head chattered enough among themselves and it was generally obvious what those without wanted from her. But since there was nothing she wanted from them there was no point in talking so far as she could see.

The nurses regarded her as backward and a little tinged with evil. There was much gossip about who she was and why she was surrounded with such secrecy. The most popular theory was that she was the bastard child of one of the two princesses currently nubile and much hounded by the popular press. A politician's daughter was a theory in vogue for a while – everybody knew that the local MP had the morals of a billy-goat (he had seduced two of the nurses during a stay in the hospital ten years previously). But the nurse whose attempt to take a blood sample had led to all the windows in the nursery being blown out had no doubts. She had seen the child move things from a distance, she knew what it felt like to be near her and have her finger the fraying edge of your thoughts, she was not prepared to laugh off the teetering structures she built as one of the peculiar skills of the young. She knew that the child was possessed.

By what or whom she yet didn't know, but she became determined to find out. She consulted a medium and through her was introduced to the local coven, a group of women from the area with whom she found that she had a great deal in common. When she felt she could trust them she told them about the child. That was when she discovered that Emma was already known to them, that they'd sensed her and tracked her for some considerable time now. But as to what or who she was – none of them knew.

It had taken a while for the My to work out just what a Mummy was (for a long time the populace had thought it was simply another kind of Hospital Night) but when it did, Emma quickly realised that she should have one too. Rather than ask the nurses she decided she would search for her herself. After all, she would surely know the Mummy if she found her.

Whenever she was taken from her room her mental tendrils came out, just in case, just in case. Over the years she had found the vestiges of many people among the geometries of the wards and corridors, mainly geriatrics who had died and carelessly left themselves lodged in the angle of a cornice or clinging to a few cracks in the plaster, spots they'd been gazing at as the tremors of life had left them, the last gasp of their consciousnesses tracing out the angles and lines, and finding there the expression of their impoverished selves. Younger patients who had died in surgery or of cancer sometimes took up residence in the tubular frame of a trolley and the squeak of its wheels, or in the layout of the lights on a ceiling and the phase of their flicker. Of course these people didn't last for long – Emma was often lucky to find them and quite frequently when she returned to the place again they were gone. Neither could they communicate – they were, after all, no longer alive. But they were there none the less, like the pattern of static left on the screen of a television that has just been switched off, a dim and simple memory of the pictures that had once played across it.

So there was a chance she'd discover her mother to be one of these frozen sprites, slowly fading from the world like a melting snowflake, but she didn't and so she turned instead to her dreams.

The hard cell

She stole because she could, because it gave her a kick. It was a hobby, in a way. But in Stratford it was too easy, having worked in several of the shops herself. To give herself a challenge she had to take the bus to Leamington or Coventry, or even to Birmingham, where she didn't know the territory so well and closed-circuit cameras were beginning to appear, giving it all an extra edge. But even then she'd invariably come back with a bag stuffed with toiletries and knick-knacks, books or clothes, make-up and CDs and stuff. Things which she didn't need and would never use. At Christmas she made up elaborate parcels for friends and gave most of it away, just to get rid of it.

She got good at it too, good enough to forget about taking precautions. It became so easy that it seemed like a joke, so that she got angry with herself if she paid for something when she could have nicked it instead. Her friends loved her for it, of course, it made her a bit of a star in the same way that sex had once done. She got quite political about it too, never stealing from shops that were independently run, only from those which were part of the 'capitalist machine'. She began to dream of bigger things, of robbing banks, emptying their vaults and giving all the money away, just to fuck the system. It would be like her shoplifting: she stole what she didn't want deliberately, to annoy them, to show them she was better, that she didn't need their consumerist society. It was a gas. Stim, who was the political consciousness of Desiring Machine, used to quote

325

from anarchist tracts and communist leaflets. Mao Tse-tung, he observed, had said that the true guerrilla had to move among the population like a fish through water. This is how Jennifer felt and it made her high. Until the day that the fish met a fisherman.

It happened in Leamington one Saturday. There was a Joy Division gig at Warwick Students Union, and she was going with Stim, Mike and Shelley. It was a nice day and they'd decided to meet up in Leamington first, go to the park. On her way from the bus-stop to the rendezvous, Jenn walked down the Parade, checking out the shops. It would be fun to have something to give the others.

She chose Woolworth's; it would serve them right for not paying her enough. The sun was shining, she felt on form. She walked in through the front doors. The shop took up the whole block. She could make it look like she was just cutting through. She cruised between the aisles, not looking around, confident and calm. *Back to school*, the signs bright in yellow on blue. A kid's geometry set, that would do. She palmed one as she passed, working it up her sleeve as she headed out the back of the shop. Easy.

After twenty yards she slowed her pace and checked behind her. No one there except an ugly little guy with longish hair, a drab moustache and a Sainsbury's bag. Flushed with success, she remembered a book she wanted – while she was on a roll she might as well get something out of it for herself.

Making her way back to the Parade, she headed for the science-fiction section of Dillon's. Once in the shop she picked volumes off the shelves at random, pretended to look at them, then replaced them as she worked her way towards the book she was looking for, Robert Heinlein's *Stranger in a Stranger Land*. When she found it she took two copies from the shelf at the same time, opened the top one, read a little of the first page just as she'd done with the other books, then closed it and put the bottom copy back up on the shelf, slipping the top copy inside her jacket as her arm went up. That was the key moment, that was the needle in the vein. Now for the rush.

Gently does it . . . she looked at one or two more books, peering around out of the corner of her eye just to be sure, then walked out of the shop, waves of noradrenalin breaking across her brain. She'd done it.

Only she hadn't. A hand grabbed her arm, a voice said, 'Excuse me.' It was the man with the Sainsbury's bag and the moustache. She didn't at all comprehend the fact that she'd been caught. She tried to twist free but he tightened his grip and pulled her wrist sharply up. The book fell out. She began to cry out, sure that her assailant was a sex attacker.

Another man, dressed in a suit and tie and wearing a Dillon's name badge, bent down and picked up the Heinlein, held it out to her. 'This anything to do with you?' he sneered.

They took her into the office. Once it had filtered through to her that the game was up she hadn't resisted, had admitted it, had put on her best voice and said she was sorry, that she'd never done it before, she was just so embarrassed. She was only seventeen and since her dad had died she'd got no money for things for school. They half believed her and gave her a cup of tea. Couldn't they let her go? She'd learnt her lesson now, she'd never do it again. No, they couldn't do that. They were sorry, but it was store policy. Shit.

The police turned up and took her to the station at the bottom of the Parade in a panda car. She walked out into the street with them, her head held high, vaguely hoping that someone she knew would see her. But from then on it got slightly more scary. They wouldn't let her smoke and took her into a room where they photographed her and made records of her fingerprints. Then they shut her in a cell on her own. There was nowhere to sit. Where was the bed? You were supposed to get a bed, weren't you? One part of the floor was slightly raised and painted with thick paint. She sat on that.

She began to realise that they were serious. They were going to prosecute her. She couldn't believe it. Most of all she couldn't credit how stupid she'd been, letting the guy follow her like that. What had she been thinking? She was such a fucking freak. She'd always told herself that if someone – anyone – followed her out of a shop the first thing to do was ditch the goods and then scarper. But it had never happened, until now, and what had she done? She'd gone off to steal something else. Fuck fuck fuck! What a fucking idiot!

She thought of the others, probably still waiting for her, and wished there were at least a proper window. The only light came in through a bunch of thick cubes of frosted glass, unbreakable and opaque. Why couldn't she have bars? She wanted bars. At least then she could see out, let her mind slip free between them.

She went to the cell door and banged on it. 'I want a cigarette! Let me have a cigarette!'

She heard footsteps coming down the corridor and she shut up. Someone's chest appeared at the access slot. 'Stop your bloody yelling, will ya? You'll wake all the other idiots up, then there'll be hell to pay. 'Ere,' and there was a short pause while the man fumbled in his pockets. A moment later there was the grate of a lighter and a lighted fag appeared through the slot.

Jennifer took it. A Benson! All right! 'Ta.'

'Don't mention it. Now they'll be with ya in a minute, so just calm down.'

Jenn retreated to the back of her cell, feeling like a real jailbird now. But the cigarette didn't really help: it made her shake a little, and made her paranoid too, and she started to think about what would happen if the shop pressed charges. There'd be an investigation. They'd come to her house, maybe they'd even take her into care. Shit shit shit shit shit! What would she do then? She wanted to cry but she wouldn't let herself. She needed to conserve energy, muster her forces, man the defences. She was stronger than them.

She stubbed out the fag and listened to the drumming of her heartbeat. The cell was brightly lit and the jagged, flickering light was giving her a headache. She closed her eyes, but when she did her heart seemed to beat louder than ever, *baboom baboom baboom*, until its rhythm filled the cell. She felt queasy and stretched out full length on the floor, the pumping blood hot in her ears. *Baboom baboom baboom*. Why hadn't they come to get her yet? Wasn't she supposed to be allowed to make a phone call? *Baboomba boombaboomba boombaboomba*. Yeah, right, like who would she call? *Boombababoombaboom boombababoombaboom*. That rhythm wasn't right. That was an old rhythm, a rhythm from before, the rhythm she'd fallen asleep to every night for the best part of two years. *But she wasn't pregnant any more!* Her imagination was playing tricks on her so she opened her eyes and stood up, banged her forehead with the heels of her hands.

Boombababoombaboom.

'Get out!' she began, 'get out! Get out getout getout gerrout gerrout geough!' Before long she was hammering again on the door.

This time the duty sergeant opened it. 'I thought I told you . . .'

'It's all right, we're ready for her now. Ms Several, would you come with me, please?' Jennifer went, trying to hide her tears.

It was her first offence and they let her off with a caution.

Some kind of home

It was Smoke that found her first. She was a screech of light and easy to spot: Smoke recognised her as readily as it would a distorted reflection of Emma's own face. But the Mummy was not out of herself like Emma was and the populace were all a little disappointed, though none of them liked to admit it. They wanted to communicate, but it was a little like trying to tease an octopus from a hole in a rock. Despite all its friends, the My wasn't powerful enough. Something else would have to be done.

The master of the name

When Subhash got back to his room he flung the book on to a shelf, where it was to lie undisturbed for several weeks. He was confused and frustrated, and felt guilty too, as if it were his fault that things had gone this far. No wonder Joel had never been particularly sociable, if that was what he had been working on in his spare time. It was astonishing – he'd had no idea the guy was that clever. Maybe a little too clever: one of the truisms that got passed around CERN was that there was a fine line between very intelligent and very stupid, and Subhash had seen more than one brilliant scientist behave like a retarded child.

He avoided Joel until the worry of *how* he should help became sublimated into the worry of *whether* he should help. What right did he have to interfere, after all? Joel was a free agent, and apart from spouting a lot of nonsense and getting over-excited one night in the computer room he didn't seem to be doing anything actually harmful. In any case wasn't his sanity proven by the fact that he'd single-handedly put together that amazing roulette predictor?

The weeks passed and Subhash saw very little of his friend. They ran into each other on the campus every now and again but Joel always seemed preoccupied and Subhash was too embarrassed that he hadn't made more of an effort to keep an eye on him to make conversation. As time went by and one by one opportunities were lost, that embarrassment grew (and, correspondingly, the number of opportunities to overcome it diminished).

One night Subhash lay in bed turning some of these things over in his mind. It was very late; he had spent all evening in the labs trying to refine a piece of software which dealt directly with the detectors in one of the collider experiments. The program kept reiterating when it wasn't supposed to and what had seemed in the beginning a simple coding conundrum had turned, as he had traced out the logical threads of the problem, into a veritable Gordian knot. Finally he had come to the decision that it was the entire architecture of the program that was at fault – apart from a few key subroutines the whole thing was going to have to be rewritten and that was a couple of weeks' work at least. He had traipsed off to bed, but once there couldn't sleep, the lines of code still racing through his mind as if he was coming down from a trip. Outside, the advancing front of a storm hummed and yawed, the fluctuations in the air pressure affecting his mood. Summer was long gone and the storm was a harbinger of the cold weather to come, weather which would bring snow to the hillsides and a frozen crust to the edges of the lakes. It was odd, but Subhash always preferred the research centre in winter: to be surrounded by the Alps at their harshest made it seem as if the work going on there was nothing less than an attempt to face down the terrifying uncertainties of nature. Like so many scientists, Subhash was a tuppenny Romantic at heart.

As the first drops of rain crackled on the window he remembered the Dostoevsky Joel had lent him. He'd look at it for a while; that would send him to sleep. He fetched it down from the shelf where he had tossed it a month or two before and, propping himself up on his pillows, began to read. It was an old paperback. The spine cracked as he opened it and the paper felt uncomfortably dry against his fingers. 'I am back at last after my absence of two weeks,' he read.

Our party has been in Roulettenburg since the day before yesterday. I thought they would have been expecting me with inexpressible impatience, but I was mistaken. The General looked at me with the coolest detachment, uttered a few condescending words, and sent me to his sister. It was evident they had borrowed some money somewhere. I even thought that the General was a little ashamed to see me. Maria Philippovna was extremely busy, and held only a short conversation with me; she took the money, however, counted it, and listened to everything I had to report. Mezentsov, the little Frenchman, and some Englishman or other were expected to dinner; as usual, as soon as there is some money there is a dinner party; the same as in Moscow. Polina Alexandrovna, when she saw me, asked me why I had taken so long, and then walked away without waiting for an answer. Of course she did it on purpose. All the same, we shall have a talk. A lot of things have accumulated.

Already the lines of code had stopped zipping through his mind and he was feeling tired. He knew it was too late to get into the book from the beginning, so he opened it to a bookmark Joel had left in the middle.

Meanwhile I watched and took note; it appeared to me that pure calculation means fairly little and has none of the importance many gamblers attach to it. They sit over bits of paper ruled into columns, note down the coups, count up, compute probabilities, do sums, finally put down their stakes and – lose exactly the same as we poor mortals playing without calculation. But on the other hand I drew one conclusion, which I think is correct: in a series of pure chances there really does exist, if not a system, at any rate a sort of sequence – which is, of course, very odd. For example it may happen that after the twelve middle numbers, the last twelve turn up; the ball lodges in the last twelve numbers, say, and then passes to the first twelve. Having fallen into the first twelve it passes again to the middle twelve, falls there three or four times running, and again passes to the last twelve, and from there, again after two coups, falls once more into the first twelve, lodges there once and then again falls three times on the middle numbers, and this goes on for an hour and a half or two hours: one, three, two, one, three, two. This is very entertaining. One day, or one morning, it will happen, for example, that red and black alternate, changing every minute almost without any order, so that neither red nor black ever turns up more than two or three times in succession. The next day, or the next evening, red only will come up many times running, twenty or more, for example, and go on doing so unfailingly for a certain time, perhaps during a whole day. A great deal of all this was explained to me by Mr Astley, who remained standing by the tables all morning but did not once play himself. As for me, I was cleaned right out, and very speedily. I staked twenty friedrichs d'or on pair straight away, and won, staked again and again won, and so on two or three more times. I think about four hundred friedrichs d'or came into my possession in some five minutes. I ought to have left at that point, but a strange feeling came over me, a kind of desire to challenge fate, a longing to give it a fillip on the nose or stick out my tongue at it. I staked the permitted maximum – 4000 gulden – and lost. Then, getting excited, I pulled out all I had left, staked it in the same way, lost again, and after that left the table as if I had been stunned. I could not even grasp what had happened to me, and I did not tell Polina Alexandrovna about losing until just before dinner. I had spent all the time until then wandering unsteadily about in the park.

By now Subhash's mind was beginning to flip-flop in and out of sleep and he was having difficulty following the text. He folded the book closed on his index finger and laid it on the bed for just a moment . . . just a moment. Code flashed up again on the inside of his eyelids and he mentally flicked it away, trying to imagine that the letters and numbers were luminous cobwebs which could be dusted out of his consciousness. Thus, brushed to the margins of his vision, the lines of text became bright strips: the flickering light when the film runs out of the projector, the fractal posters with which Joel had once covered the walls of a corridor. Then they were snow banks at the side of a rushing river and he was in the mountains and it was already winter. He thought he was alone, but no, he was with Joel, and someone else who could be Axel but he couldn't be sure, and yes, his father, too. His father was complaining that it was far too cold, that they should all go back to Pakistan where the weather at least was decent. He was trying to tell the three younger men something about a plane, waiting for them in the valley, they should go now, they should hurry. But his words kept getting drowned out by the sound of rushing water and they were not that interested in what he had to say anyway. Joel remonstrated with him, shouted at him to speak up. Subhash argued back, standing up for his father although he didn't want to. The man who was and wasn't Gabriel was eating something and he tried to hand a piece of whatever it was to Subhash. Subhash took it, but it was terribly sticky and he couldn't scrape it from his hands. He was suddenly frightened; the argument between Joel and his father was intensifying and he was now preoccupied with trying to rid his skin of this gunk. He wanted to ignore it and stop the argument but somehow he couldn't – he had to be clean before he could proceed, it was very important. He took a few steps towards Joel. The ground gave way. He was sliding towards the river, down a gully that was opening up below him at the boundary between the mud and the snow. The gunk was all over his feet, preventing him from kicking them out and slowing his fall. Looking up, he could see his father staring down, right arm around Joel's shoulders, shouting *It doesn't matter, it doesn't matter.*

The water roared away below him, its surface seething like the leaves in a hurricane. He hit it and he woke up in the communal kitchen at the end of his corridor, of all places. It was obviously late: nobody else was about and after the mountain dream the silence was disconcerting.

He looked at his watch, but he couldn't quite decipher the time. Shit. He would have to get a new one. He thought to make himself a cup of tea to take back to bed. He opened the fridge and a rat darted out. It raced through his legs and out of the kitchen door. He shrieked, but his fear sounded pathetic in the silence. The animal had eaten all of the food and had gnawed out the bottoms of the two or three cartons of milk that had been in there. The white liquid had flooded the shelves and now spilled out across the floor. Gingerly, Subhash picked up the empty cartons, afraid that they might be filled with insects or some such horror, and dropped them in the bin. He tried to mop the floor but the milk turned to putty so he gave up. Let somebody else deal with it. He went back to his room, undressed and got into bed.

He had been programming all day and the lines of code still raced through his mind as if he was coming down from a trip. Outside the advancing front of a storm hummed and yawed, the fluctuations in the air pressure affecting his mood. Summer was long gone and the storm was the harbinger of weather which would soon bring snow and a frozen crust to all the lakes. It was odd, but Subhash always preferred the research centre in winter: to be surrounded by the Alps at their harshest made it seem as if the work going on there was nothing less than an attempt to face down the terrifying uncertainties of nature.

As the first drops of rain crackled on the window panes he remembered the Dostoevsky Joel had lent him. He'd look at it for a while; that would send him to sleep. He fetched it down from the shelf where he had tossed it and propped his head up with some pillows so that he might read it more easily. It was an old paperback. The spine cracked as he opened it and the paper felt uncomfortably dry against his fingers. There was a knock at the door. Subhash thought it must be his mother. He pretended not to be there but whoever it was entered anyway. It wasn't his mother, it was Joel. He stood at the side of the bed, his head too big for his shoulders. Subhash tried to get up but his limbs were incredibly heavy, far too heavy to move.

Joel's face floated down until it was level with his own. *What becomes of any holocaust?* he asked in an even, rhetorical tone. *The flat light of the sun and the grind of the tide levels all bones into beaches, where children build castles whose moats murmur with the rhythm of the shallows.*

Something moved on Joel's shoulder. Subhash just had time to identify it as the rat from the fridge before it leapt at his face and sunk its teeth into his nose. He screamed and woke up.

★

333

Subhash knew. He didn't know what he knew, but he knew none the less. He pulled on some clothes and went down the main stairwell and out into the night. The worst of the storm must have passed while he slept, but it was still raining heavily and as it was a good twenty minutes' walk to the accommodation block in which Joel lived he took his car. The tarmac was slick and black, the street lights twice as bright for being reflected in the giant mirrors that the rainwater made of the road. Subhash drove as quickly as he dared.

He pulled up at the end of a row of vehicles and ran from the car to the glass entrance doors, his jacket pulled up over his head to keep off the worst of the rain. The doors were unlocked and once inside he made his way up the stairs, taking two or three steps at a time, his short, plump legs working like pistons. He reached the fourth floor, half jogged half walked along the corridor to Joel's room and knocked on the door, leaning heavily against it to catch his breath. There was no reply so he knocked again, then tried the handle and found the door unlocked. The room inside was completely bare of everything except the roulette table and the furniture. There were a few coffee cups in the sink and a couple of dustbin bags full of rubbish in the corner. Joel was gone.

Subhash checked the cupboards but they were bare save for a few empty boxes and an odd shoe. In the bedside cabinet he found a plain white envelope with his name scrawled across it in biro. He tore it open; inside there was a single sheet of paper. On it were printed the words:

Joel Balaam Kluge

Subhash ripped the envelope apart in the hope of finding a more substantial message, an address, anything; he ransacked the room once more, but there was nothing. He knocked on neighbouring doors; at all save one he was met by silence or a mumbled 'Fuck off'. The exception was opened by a man whom Subhash didn't recognise, who came to the door smelling of amyl nitrate and drawled that no, he didn't know Joel and no, he hadn't seen him leave, while his lover stood in the background watching Subhash with dilated eyes and provocatively scratching at his pubic hair.

Giving up on the bedrooms, Subhash searched the communal areas, but with no more success. Then he drove around the campus for three quarters of an hour, craning his neck to try and see through the driving rain. He had the radio on low and occasionally he thought he heard his mother's voice in the music and wondered if he might still be dreaming.

Eventually he gave up and went back to bed where this time, doubly exhausted, he quickly fell asleep.

Flip-side

Smoke was the most adventurous of them all and sometimes it would be gone for days at a time. Once, though, it was gone for a whole month, which worried the populace sick. When it came back, for the entire next week it slept during the day instead of at night. Lonely Dear? said this was because Smoke had been away on the other side of the world in search of a father. Exray told her not to be stupid. No one could get on the other side of the world. The world was flat, like people. Exray could prove it.

The song of the sands

Back in Reno, months and months went by that seemed to Judd like days, like hours even. He became ever more still, ever more composed. The people who milled around him gasped at his magnificence, at his profile – so strong, so self-assured for someone barely twenty-one. Women wilted as he passed, or swarmed around him suppurating as he sat steady at the bar. Judd remained aloof and uninterested, his sexual rhythm having settled into a new and longer cycle. He had sublimated his desires and channelled them into his gambling; they were now a part of the geography of chance like everything else. It was a terrain which was as familiar as the back of his hand; he could find his way across it almost without thinking.

Meanwhile, in his dreams, the child had fully emerged, a silent statue encrusted with moss, and the lizards had receded into the background. If Emma could indeed probe the world's collective psyche as though it were some kind of networked data space, then perhaps this image was some kind of residue she had left in passing – a vapour trail, a wake. One night she must have found her father and by touching him unsettled the settling sediments of his brain enough to suggest not only an image of herself, but one of his future, assembled from the various tendencies of his personality that she'd probed. But Judd, who had no idea that this child had ever been born, let alone that she'd fingered his brain from a distance of five thousand miles, was not likely to interpret his dream in this way. For him, the statue nightly carved from the effluent of his subconscious represented the collected deposits of Jennifer and Schemata that he was managing to mine from himself. To him, the dream was a sign that he was finally ridding himself from their influence.

So he was taken completely by surprise when tectonic activity set in, when the contours and features which he had triangulated for months with the throw of the dice, the fall of the cards, began to stray and shift. At first the movement was imperceptibly gradual: a couple of losing streaks, a series of unanticipated hands. He thought perhaps that he was tired and, when it persisted, took a couple of days off. He lay by the pool, didn't drink so much, ate in restaurants at several removes from the casinos. But on his return to the tables he continued to lose.

It wasn't simply bad luck. Judd had built bad luck into his habitat. He knew its courses and haunts, its manifestations and its omens. No, this wasn't simply bad luck. His game was slipping away. The ramparts of his edifice, carved like the earth itself from the attractors and permutations embedded in the random fields of the cosmos, were slowly crumbling, deformed by awakening internal processes. Great blocks of his gambling environment had suddenly shifted along fault lines he'd not known were there. Craters were opened and volcanoes thrown up. Rivers disappeared into the ground, only to burst out the walls of previously featureless cliffs. Lakes drained and hot springs appeared. Valleys were filled with torrents of lava. Judd didn't know what to do. Everything kept changing, nothing stayed still. He became frightened and lost among the mesas, scarps and hanging valleys of what was already an alien landscape.

In an attempt to salvage the situation Judd left The Golden Gecko and moved into a quieter hotel, favoured by professional gamblers, and from this new base he set about regrouping. He consulted the tally he kept of his winnings: four months of steady gaming had seen the ten thousand Scofield had given him turned into eighty-three – and that was after he'd deducted his expenses. But that had been two weeks ago; in the past thirteen days he had lost steadily, to the tune of almost thirty thousand bucks. This still left him forty grand up, a tidy sum by any account, but that lost thirty thou nagged away at him. He could feel it like an ecthyma on his palms, an ulcerating itch that only the dice could balm.

He moved to yet another hotel, hoping that would change things, but he continued to lose. Every morning he sat in his room trying to make the decision to leave Reno, rolling the ivory dice Scofield had given him out across the glass top of the coffee table, a hundred times, a thousand times, until he drove himself mad with the noise they made and ran downstairs to play. One morning he managed to pack his bags, left everything out but a bottle of bourbon and the dice, sat there throwing them in the hope they would tell him to go, but all the time changing the rules of the game so that he could make sure he'd stay. The suite was expensive, much larger than the others he'd taken, and plush – if he stood barefoot on the deep-pile carpet he couldn't see the tips of his toes. The double bed was a waterbed, with a switch at the side which set the whole thing vibrating.

The bourbon made him dizzy. He looked at the dice on the table top, the two objects complicated by their reflections. There seemed many more possibilities here than he had previously accounted for. It suddenly occurred to him that he had become very proud. He was in trouble.

Three times he picked up the telephone and began to call Scofield. Three times he put it back. He didn't want to do this. He wanted a cigarette. His palms itched and sweated, and he wiped them on his pants. Shit! The fourth time he finished dialling and let it ring.

A woman answered: 'Hello?'

'Yes. Get me Irving Scofield.' He would be curt. He was not in the mood to be fucked around.

'You would like to talk to Mr Scofield?'

'That's what I said.'

'Mr Scofield is busy right now. Can you call back?'

'Tell him it's Judd.'

'Judd. Judd who?'

'Just tell him Judd. It's urgent.' The woman said nothing and the line went quiet for a while, and Judd wondered if he'd overdone it, but then Scofield came on the line. Judd explained the situation as best he could, which was not particularly coherently.

'So you've got trouble with your game?' said Scofield, trying to sum it all up.

'I guess so.'

'Well, I do know a man. You'll have to go to him, though. He doesn't travel. And he may not help you. I'm not sure he takes students.'

'That's fine. I'll try it. Where is he?'

'London, last I heard.'

Judd hesitated for a moment. The prospect of returning to England was not immediately attractive.

'No problem.'

'Give me the fax number of your hotel. I'll send you a letter of introduction. He's an interesting guy – I think you'll like him. But go easy. He's not the kind of person you meet every day.'

'Who – what's he like?'

'He's an old friend of mine. I never told you, did I, that I used to gamble a bit myself? Back in Atlantic City, just after the war. Anatole was kind of my partner. We worked the seafront together. He had your talent, Judd, and he really knew how to use it. Me, I couldn't take it.'

'What happened?'

'Well, it's a long story, but back then Anatole had a mouth on him; still has, for all I know. When he won big, which he began to do most of the time, he couldn't shut up about it. Doesn't take a man too long to make enemies that way. Guess you know all about that, huh? Anyway, things got a bit out of hand and we had to skip town. We were lucky – back then we were always lucky. But it put the shits up me and I decided to leave Anatole to it. I'm kind of attached to my balls.'

'So what happened to him?'

'He moved around the States for a while, made himself a small fortune, then went to Europe. Set himself up in this big villa in Monte Carlo, filled it with beautiful women, designer furniture. I went to visit him once, 'bout ten years back.'

'But I thought he was in London.'

'Yeah, he is now. Or so I was told. Tell you the truth, I haven't heard from him pretty much since I saw him in France. But a mutual friend told me he'd moved to London, so I guess that's where you'll find him. I'll fax the address along with the letter.'

'Thanks, Mr Scofield.'

'Don't mention it, Judd. You go see Anatole. He was always the best. If he can't help you, nobody can.'

Judd put the phone down and lay back on the bed. Using the remote control he flicked through the cable channels, stopping when he reached some porn. For a moment the blood rushed to his penis and there was a glimmer of hope, but then just as suddenly the writhing bodies disgusted him. He switched off the set and went to the balcony door. The hotel was on the edge of downtown and his room was on the twenty-fifth floor, so he could see the desert beyond the low buildings which stretched away into the middle distance, the homes of the service workers who vacuumed and cleaned and polished after people like him all day long, all night long, all year round. The empty land hissed and curled its way to the horizon, where giant facets of the heat haze reared up, great flat silver glints which spanned the burning air like electrons leaping orbits, a new realm between earth and sky. In the silence, the no-sound vanished by the steady hum of the air-conditioning unit, Judd fancied that he could determine the vast roar of it all. It was out there, coming for him, for all of them. All maps, not just his own, would be melted down by the blast. There would be some great reconfiguration, perhaps so great that no one would even notice it.

He opened the door, the seal cracking with the hiss of an airlock, and stepped out on to the tiny balcony that jutted like an eyrie from the face of the building. Far below, the traffic squelched and shrieked along its net of melting tarmac. He looked at the street directly beneath – on which the entrance to the hotel was situated – and, as he watched, a taxicab swerved to avoid another car coming blithely down the middle of the road and hit a woman who had just stepped down off the sidewalk. She was knocked back and lay splayed out in her short yellow dress and blue jacket like some fabulous seabird washed up on to a beach slick with oil. The traffic backed up and other people gathered around, creating a scene. A dissonant chorus of horns began to chime upwards from the traffic stuck at the neighbouring intersections. Someone was attending to the woman; from his height Judd couldn't be sure, but it seemed from the newcomer's behaviour that the victim was still alive, if only barely.

Now that his eyes had grown used to the distance, Judd began to make out minute objects that were scattered across the street. They splayed out from the woman's prone form in a fan; she must have been carrying them when she fell. But he couldn't tell what they were, these small items that lay in such profusion on the roadway. He looked on for several minutes more, until the suck of sirens indicated that an ambulance was threading its way through the stationary traffic. The blare of horns had grown even louder; it seemed as if the whole city was in gridlock. On the horizon the silver hazes still flickered, but without their previous urgency: the threat, whatever it had been, had apparently evaporated. Perhaps, he reflected, it had been neutralised by the sacrifice below. Judd thought of the fax that would be arriving and turned back inside, letting the building swallow him up, not realising that of all the rooms he'd stayed in Reno, this was the first not to have a gecko in residence on its balcony.

Twenty-five floors down the paramedics loaded the stuttering body of the croupier into the ambulance, while onlookers surreptitiously squabbled over the casino chips which speckled the road like some strange and magic dust.

0 1 1

'Woof, woof!'

Laika, first dog in space

1 2

The sorcerer's apprentice

His ideas had progressed. He'd milked the Geneva casinos for money and in the process had become more and more aware of the nature of his own role in his Project, in the great scheme he was trying to uncover. He could feel the pull of tikkun in his gut. He meditated on his middle name, Balaam. He knew that names were important, magical even. He'd been given this name by a mohel, a ba'al shem, so his father had told him. In the Bible, he knew, Balaam was the sorcerer, the one who could draw forth the spirit of impurity from the kelippot – the dark forces of the universe which took on substance from the shards of the broken vessels – and mix together the clean and the unclean, using the power that emerged to fight the demonic. According to the Zohar, to complete his skills the sorcerer must journey to the 'mountains of darkness' and find Aza and Azael, the rebel angels who lived there. He, Joel, was the sorcerer. And he knew well enough about the mountains of darkness. He knew about Hitler's obsession with the Spear of Longinus, Himmler's design for Wewelsburg castle and the street plan of the city that was to be built there; he had read of the Thulegesellschaft and a thousand other conspiratorial organisations. And he'd developed his own theories about magic too – that magic was a language, a way of understanding and manipulating power, and that as techniques, physics or political rhetorics were no more or less magical than the occult simply because they were couched in rational terms.

He travelled by train, trying to keep to the old lines, the ones that pre-existed the war. He went to Lyon and from there up to Dijon, then on to Vittel and finally to Munich, where he stayed for several weeks while he applied for the appropriate visas for East Germany, Poland and the USSR.

By day he wandered the streets, entering the well-appointed stores and Bierkeller at whim, touching and drinking, asking shopkeepers and barmen blunt questions about the war, about the Jews, about their families, demanding to know the extent of their involvement. More than once he was attacked, but he was angry now and no longer concerned for himself – and besides, his thin, hard body made a poor target and an effective, if flailing, weapon.

Four or five times a week he took the train to Dachau, quietly horrified by the way the metropolitan service took him through neat suburbias to the site of the old camp. He sat among schoolchildren, unemployed youths, tourists encumbered with their day sacks and cameras. The old gates were still there, *Arbeit Macht Frei*, a couple of the dormitories (now museums), the gas chambers and ovens (which had never been used), the walls against which people had been lined up for the firing squads (their brickwork pitted and pocked). Neatly raked gravel covered the site like a living-room carpet. The positions of the original dormitories were marked out by two courses of bricks, mathematical figures under a pallid sky. He could have been looking at Aztec markings in the desert.

Had the birds stopped singing here, was that true? He wasn't sure, he couldn't tell.

It was so abstract. It was a geometric fancy, a blueprint, a foundation for something rather than something's remains. But somewhere among these angles and their relationships were the equations he was seeking. He had read about a spherical temple being constructed in the international city of Auraville in the south-east of India which was to house the world's largest crystal – Zeiss were growing it now in their laboratories not far from Dachau itself. The design had come to the architect, a woman, a disciple, the Mother she called herself, in a dream. The proportions of the temple accorded to certain physical constants. Something like that was happening here. He thought about Nazi psychology, that bizarre blend of Madame Blavatsky's theosophy, Gurdjieff's mysticism and the archetypes of Nordic mythology.

He had purchased various measuring devices in Munich: a retractable tape measure, a small Geiger counter, several pairs of dividers, a compass, a kelvin thermometer and even a small theodolite. Thus equipped he took measurements of the distances between the bullet holes, of the radii of the iron letters above the gates, of the width of doorways and height of windows and thickness of the walls, of the angles between buildings, of the levels of background radiation. He noted everything down, kept it with him, transformed and plotted it, turned it into equations and matrices, used these to perform translations. The numbers of spectacles left, the numbers of gold fillings melted down, the weight of hair shorn, the numbers dead from shooting, starvation, cholera, shock, spotted fever, torture, suicide, gassing, incineration. There was a huge board, white words on black, the towns of Europe and the numbers killed there, hundreds of places, millions of people. It was the original of the photograph he had, the one that he'd shown to Jennifer and Subhash. No borders, no coastlines. Names and numbers. White on black. Names. Numbers. Indices. Vectors. A zone. *A quantum field, with death the spectral calibration for any and all eigenvalues.* And every time he took a measurement or wrote down a figure he rolled a pair of dice and scribbled the total alongside.

In the beginning he couldn't see his way. He felt overwhelmed. He couldn't see how it would work. By day he wrote measurements and dice throws in notebooks, by night with the machine in his shoe he visited the casinos in town. He needed the routine. The desire to give in and search for patterns already was terribly strong. But he wouldn't do it, he wouldn't take short-cuts. Everything had to be done in an orderly fashion. Only that way would he be able to factor it out. He threw the dice for hours, made notes.

He read books, made lists. Chelmno, Belzec, Sobibor, Treblinka, Buchenwald, Majdanek, Auschwitz-Birkenau, Bergen-Belsen, Mauthausen. He noted down latitudes and longitudes, added them to his databanks. He watched the news, read anti-Zionist pamphlets about Israeli attacks on Palestinian Arabs, mass expulsions, massacres. This was all part of the equation. He found out about the Gypsies, plotted their movements across the continent, before and after the war, guesstimated the population densities at various times in various nations.

He took day trips to old offices and the sites of factories that had once belonged, or still did, to I. G. Farben, Krone-Presswerk, Graetz and Krupp (in their various modern incarnations). He purchased a camera, took photographs. What was it that Mengele had said to Dr Ella Lingens? That was it, that there were only two gifted nations in the world, the Germans and the Jews, and that the only question was which one would dominate. Could it be that simple?

He thought about Nazi physics: of the cosmic force, vril; of the hollow-earth theory; of Hans Horbiger's Welteislehre, the doctrine of eternal ice. Twisted, perverse sciences that mocked centuries of patient work in mathematics, physics and logic. It disgusted him that the Germans could have been so sure of themselves, so certain that their theories were anything but filth. Yet he had to admit that at the time the evidence had seemed in their favour. How could anyone look at the Holocaust and think that the dice weren't loaded against the Jews, the Gypsies and the rest? It seemed so obvious to him, as obvious as it must have seemed to Hitler himself. Yet Hitler had been wrong and hadn't known why. But Joel knew. He knew that this colossal destabilisation of luck, of chance, was a sign that fortune's wheel itself was out of kilter that the events of the world weren't running true. Just look at the statistics! Six million! What more proof was needed? The detours from perfect randomness that he'd found in roulette and the dice were part of the same phenomenon. He would scientifically prove that the Nazis had been wrong to imagine that their sick success had anything to do with validating the destiny of the thousand-year Reich. The truth was that the Jews had been caught up in a great vacillation as the merry-go-round of chance had tottered and reeled, and then the Germans themselves had been affected as the system wobbled back the other way, cybernetically correcting itself and causing them defeat after defeat. There was no authenticity here.

Thus, by comparing the wartime fluctuations operations with those he was uncovering in the casinos he visited, Joel hoped to be able to calculate some kind of constant for the time of tikkun itself, that gradual progression of the universe towards perfection which would eventually pull chance back into line. From that, he reasoned, he'd be able to deduce how much longer there was before perfection was finally achieved and the creation could begin over again. It would be a breakthrough as important as that made by Hubble when he discovered, by statistically linking the red shift of a galaxy with its distance from the earth, that the universe was actually expanding.

He was going insane.

By 30 April 1943 (7):
    94,000 men's watches (8)
    33,000 women's watches (3)
    25,000 fountain pens (7)
    14,000 propelling pencils (6)
    14,000 pairs of scissors (12)
had been taken from the Jews and delivered to the Germans. Every statistic matched up with a dice roll. Notebook after notebook was filled.

As soon as the last of the visas came through he left Munich. He travelled north to Hanover and from there took a sealed train through East Germany to West Berlin. He looked into a hotel near Bahnhof Zoo and early the next day went out to Spandau to visit the fortress where they still held Rudolf Hess. He bought a small pair of binoculars and sat in the bus shelter opposite the prison, watching the windows and throwing his dice. They said you could sometimes catch a glimpse of him. What did he look like? Joel measured the walls, the dimensions of the buildings, the number of windows. Estimated the number of bricks − red bricks, many of them. He noted the number of guards, the changes of watch. He wasn't alone; others watched too, stooped figures in overcoats and Homburgs with expressionless faces and hollows for eyes. Joel felt like an impostor: this was their vigil, not his. But they welcomed him quietly, shared their flasks of coffee with him, their sandwiches. He asked them about Aza and Azael, what did they know of them? They nodded and listed names from the past, told him anecdotes, smiled and patted him on the shoulder. Whispered to him portentously: *We should have let him go. It would have been a greater punishment.* He didn't tell them he was Balaam.

The following morning they boarded the Warsaw express. The carriages were very different from those he'd become used to. They were uncomfortable and cold, and there was a stench of stale cigarettes about them. There was less plastic, more wood, which was worn and old and pitted with scars. He risked a Geiger counter reading. It was unusually high.

The train drew out into November. Outside, there was a biting cold and the rain came down, nearly sleet; no different to many days he had known at CERN. The weather made him think of Subhash and of the note he had left him. Joel Balaam Kluge. Master of the name.

The guards came by, young men in angular reds and greens, checked his passport and his luggage. They made him think of Gobineau's essay and of old beer mats he had seen which bore the legend: *Wer beim Juden kauft ist ein Volksverräter.*

The train yawed through the town, east of the Wall. Joel looked smugly out at the decay, the blankness, the dereliction, the pathetic attempts at modernisation. The sleet turned to snow which gyred and flurried, and quickly laid an ash-like scum across the roofs of the buildings and the empty lots between them.

The city sprawled on for miles, then they were out in the fields and there was nothing to see. The snow stopped and there was no more precipitation, not even rain to batter the windows and make you feel thankful for being inside. The farmland looked desolate, forlorn, the site of years of unremarkable struggle on every level of the food chain. Joel tried to do some paperwork but the vibrations of the train made it impossible. He rolled the dice idly on the miniature table underneath the window, enjoying the sound they made, the way they felt in his hands. People continually wandered up and down the corridor outside his compartment, talking, smoking, ferrying cups of tea backwards and forwards, all of them bracing themselves against the movement of the train.

Warsaw. Half a million people – a third of the city's population – crammed into 1.3 square miles. Joel did the calculations. That would have meant about seven to a room. He walked the streets behind the railway station, tracing the 1941 borders of the ghetto: down Okopowa and past the Jewish cemetery, left along Jerusalem Avenue and left again at Marszalkowska Street. Around Tiomackie Square and then a complicated dog-leg back around to the station. At each corner he took a dice roll. Half a million.

He took a train to Lublin and from there a bus to Majdanek, where a vast concrete dome covers the ashes of the 360,000 people who were destroyed there. Flowers died there too, wound into bouquets by those who came by. Joel thought about calculating the number of flakes of ash under that dome.

There were shoes, of course. Rooms full of shoes.

The barracks, crematoria, watch towers, barbed wire – all still there, folding into themselves with the passing years. He threw for them all, then surveyed them with his theodolite.

From Lublin to Lvov, where he had to pay a man to drive him in a Lada out to 'the sands', a nexus of low, sandy hills and deep pits. This was where the occupants of the Janówska camp had been stripped naked and put to death, their bodies burnt on huge pyres. Children who were too frightened to undress were swung by their feet against a tree until their skulls caved in, while their mothers were forced to look on, then flung on to the burning mounds. In each case the officer watched the mother for any sign of protest. At the slightest reaction she would be beaten half senseless, then hung from a branch by her feet until dead.

The car stopped at the base of a footpath and Joel and the driver climbed out.

'Is this it?' Joel asked, in pointless English. 'Are we here? Janówska?'

The driver nodded absently and waved in the direction of what Joel presumed was the camp, then pulled a packet of cigarettes from the breast pocket of his jacket, took one out and tried to light it. A stiff wind was blowing: even under several layers of clothes, Joel still felt cold. The driver bent over his cupped hands, apparently immune to the chill, wisps of grey hair detaching themselves from his scalp. A small flame flared up between his palms and he bent lower still and sucked hard, the sound of his rasp a part of the weather itself. Joel watched, convinced the match had gone out, but a moment later the driver's fingers swelled with smoke and he stood up, pulling hard to coax the ember into life. Success. He leant against the bonnet, smiled at Joel as if to say *are you still here then?* and picked a strand of tobacco from his tongue.

Joel smiled back, remembered himself, and started on up the first hillock.

He worked his way across the dunes, trying to gauge his direction by the position of the weak winter sun. He touched the trunks of trees with his fingertips whenever he passed them. His shoes filled with sand and he would have taken them off but it was too cold and this made him feel ashamed. Eventually he came to one of the pits. Around its perimeter was a rude fence of posts and barbed wire. Rusted signs hung from it, their words and designs weathered into oblivion. In several places the fencing had begun to collapse, affording points of access. Joel stepped over the wire at one of these and gingerly made his way towards the edge. Reaching it, he peered in. The sides of the pit sloped steeply down. Landslide upon landslide. The caked slopes were riven with branching rivulets and wadis. At the bottom was a slick mirror of dark water. What had he expected to see?

It was hard to roll the dice here, on the sand. He found a metal sign half buried in the ground. Pulled it out. Used that.

He walked on for a while, but the sun was going down and he decided he had better make his way back. It was on his return journey that he realised that nothing distinguished this place. Why had he come here? What was it that he'd expected to find? He checked his thermometer, made a note of the temperature. Yes, it was cold.

The taxi took him back into the town and he left Lvov that day on a train bound for Minsk. By the time they crossed from the Ukraine into Belarus the snow lay across the countryside in an unbroken swathe. They crossed the Pripet just to the south of Luninets: it was frozen over and a layer of white made the river resemble a glacier, a sluggard worm of ice that rent the land in two.

The locomotive broke down as they pulled out of Baranovichi and he spent a night there, in a hotel not far from the station. He trudged from the train, his baggage slung uncomfortably about his shoulders, the suitcase containing his many notebooks now too heavy to carry with ease. He could barely bring himself to speak to anyone. He didn't want any help. He could think of nothing but suffering; it was the least he could do to carry his own bags. Again, the gesture was such a pathetic one that made him feel utterly wretched. He didn't unpack. The maid warmed his bed with an iron bedpan full of hot coals.

All night there was traffic up and down the stairs outside his door and he could hear creakings and manoeuvrings from the adjacent rooms. Unable to sleep, he read by gaslamp. He read about the station at Treblinka, how during Christmas 1943 the Germans had put signposts on the buildings: *Telegraph, Telephone, Restaurant, Ticket Office*. They put timetables up too, a station clock, enormous signposts: *Change for Eastbound trains; To Bialystok and Baranovichi*. Tempted the people from the trains. Hid the clothing stripped from the endless line of victims. The prostitutes and their customers kept him awake. He thought of the conditions in the cattle trucks. Of deception. He couldn't comprehend the cruelty involved. He thought of his family. Deception. He couldn't sleep. Absolute cruelty. Everywhere. Normality. Signs to Baranovichi. Everywhere. It was happening everywhere. He had to be everywhere. He couldn't move.

Next day, the train was five hours late. He slept on the platform, wearing most of his clothes. He had a strange dream. He dreamt that he spoke magic names and created a golem from copper. He awoke with a rime on his face. He hadn't eaten yesterday, he remembered. He put his hand into his luggage and touched his notebooks, his numbers, just to make sure they were there. Computers in his shoes, somewhere. The train had heating that worked and he scalded his hands on the grille. A man with a huge moustache who looked like Josef Stalin came into the carriage with a samovar of tea. Joel bought several glasses' worth and Stalin gave him some black bread and pickles. He had chilblains on his toes, he realised.

He reached Minsk and stayed there for several days. It was December now and winter was beginning to bite. He made a day trip to Sobibor. It was less well tended than Dachau or Majdanek and somehow more real. He was told there was a field of burnt and crushed bones here that looked like a coral beach, but everything was covered in snow. It snowed the whole day he was there and he could only think of the ashes raining down from the chimneys. He went to the field anyhow and dug down through the frozen crust with his hands. Others followed him – despite the weather several dozen people had come out to the camp that day. They all started to dig. One woman – about Joel's age, attractive – wasn't wearing suitable shoes, so she took them off and walked across the snowfield in stockinged feet, a painful reminder of his failure to do the same on his visit to Janówska. They dug, all of them, like Inuit digging for fish. Most of them found fragments of some description and buried them back where they'd found them. Joel buried his dice in his hole. Walking back, he counted the footprints the small search party had made. Several of the men spoke to the woman in Russian. Joel didn't understand, but he thought they were offering to carry her. Whatever it was, she refused.

In one of the few remaining buildings was posted – in five languages – an excerpt from the speech Himmler gave at Poznan on 4 October 1943.

We have taken from them what wealth they had. I have issued a strict order, which SS Lieutenant-General Pohl has carried out, that this wealth should, as a matter of course, be handed over to the Reich without reserve. We have taken none of it for ourselves. Individual men who have lapsed will be punished in accordance with an order I issued at the beginning which gave this warning: whoever takes so much as a mark of it is a dead man. A number of SS men – there are not many of them – have fallen short, and they will die without mercy.

We had the moral right, we had the duty to our people, to destroy this people which wanted to destroy us. But we have not the right to enrich ourselves with so much as a fur, a watch, a mark or a cigarette, or anything else.

Because we have exterminated a germ, we do not want in the end to be infected by the germ and die of it. I will not see so much as a small area of sepsis appear here or gain a hold. Wherever it may form, we will cauterise it. Altogether, however, we can say that we have fulfilled this most difficult duty for the love of our people. And our spirit, our soul, our character has not suffered injury from it.

Joel ran into the toilets and vomited. The toilets were tended by volunteers. Their bowls were scrubbed clean and white. The perversion was absolute. The Nazis had declared themselves agents of tikkun, they had claimed themselves as the light which issued forth from the forehead of primordial man to reorganise the confusion brought on by shevirah. But they were the kelippot, the shards the husks the shells, they were of the sitra ahra, the realm of demons. It was he who was the agent of tikkun. *It was he, Joel, he, Balaam.* Tikkun brought about a catharsis of waste matter in the divine system and so now he vomited, it was his prayer, he emptied his stomach for all who had died, his eructation a magical act, his discharge a balm.

Enter the dermatophyte

She needed allies if she was to contact the Mummy, send her a message, and she found them underneath the linoleum and along the base of the wall where they corrugated the institutional plaster and messed up the skirting board. There were thousands of them, woven into mats, peppered with spores. They were fungi, basidiomycetes. They were her friends.

She encouraged them, farmed them, stripped wood from the back of her bedside table, soaked it with her urine and transplanted them to it, hid the little cultures in the bottom of the wardrobe. Later, when her plantation was going strong, she took the mattress from her bed and encouraged the hyphae to take root in its foam. The process took months, despite Emma moving it along with her mind, coaxing and stroking the organisms, chiding and training them. All this time she studied the fungi, examining the spore-bearing basidia which resembled tiny tuning forks, the mycelia, thick and tangled, the septa partitions with their dolipore septum pores and pore caps. Too small for her fingers to touch and her eyes to see, she rubbed away the epidermis from the pad of her middle finger with an emery board kept back from the nurses and settled her new friends there, capturing them with her skin cells, encouraging fluid exchange, becoming symbiotic.

When the mattress was ready she turned it over and stripped the sheet from it at nights, lay there sleeping on a bed of mildew, truffles, fairy rings, encouraging the mycobiont into her flesh, where it extended haustoria and itched its way between sebaceous gland and nerve, follicle and fat like some cryptoendolithic lichen in the rocks of a dry Antarctic valley.

Eventually she no longer needed the mattress and allowed its farm to wither and die. Her skin was supple and soft and showed no sign of the parasite within, which drew water and gases from the air through her pores and which was sensitive to all sorts of things she had not registered before: nitrogen levels, the salts and sugars on the skin of her nurses, barometric pressure. It also helped her to understand what the bacteria were up to.

The day after Sobibor

The day after Sobibor Joel took to the woods, memories of hiking round Lake Geneva. Five thousand Jews had fled to the forests from the Minsk ghettos between July 1941 and October 1943; half of them had died, one way or another. The other half had survived to form partisan groups and hidden enclaves. He had new dice with him. He threw them.

He didn't know which way to go: his map didn't show land use beyond the city limits. He identified six roads that led radially out of the city and threw a die to determine which one he would take. Then he started walking. He set off early, at six-thirty, when despite it still being dark and well below freezing people were already beginning to move around the city. Not all the street lights worked and the glow from those which did was so flat that it emphasised the impression he already had that there were no colours here, that he was moving through a world of black and white. He walked for an hour, following the paths that pedestrians had made through the rotting snow, stopping every fifteen minutes or thereabouts to fumble with his map which, though crude and inaccurate, was the best he'd been able to find. The heavens had begun to lighten, but it did not look as if there'd be a spectacular dawn – clouds covered the sky in one placid and unbroken bank.

The roads had started to fill with cars. They passed him in little convoys, their wheels hissing in the two inches of slush that lay across the carriageways. People teetered along on bicycles and buses throbbed by, their engines hot and exposed like the naked arses of baboons.

He realised that it was going to take him for ever to walk and so when a bus stopped near him he climbed aboard. The driver asked him (he presumed) for his destination. Joel said 'American', made a gesture which he hoped meant 'straight ahead', and handed over some money. The driver shrugged and muttered something, half to himself, half to the passengers in the nearby front seats. They all laughed. Joel took his ticket. The other passengers nodded at him and smiled.

He was in luck. The bus made a long sequence of stops but stayed on the main road and followed it out into the countryside. It was daylight by now and the clouds had begun to clear and as they travelled through a snowy landscape of pine- and fir-covered hills there was an occasional flash of low sun. When they drew up outside a lumber yard to pick up a lone man Joel got off. The bus drove away, its passengers watching him from the windows, a few of the older ones still smiling as if they were relieved to have something new to do with the pallid features that most of the time just lurked motionless beneath their enormous fur hats.

With a crunch of icy gravel beneath his feet Joel shouldered the small bag he had with him and walked away from the road and up the hill behind the yard. The trees had been stripped from it long since and he picked his way between old stumps and saplings. There was about a foot of snow, more in places, and his ankles were soon soaked, but by the time he had crested the summit and descended into the next valley the sky was nearly clear and the sun bright. He was in the trees by now, following tracks made by deer and fox. In some places the branches had grown so entwined that the snow could not penetrate, and he walked on a soft rug of dead needles and moss. But mostly the ground was thick with the white crystals and each tree trunk had one white side and one dark, and so that he didn't get lost he kept the snow-covered sides to his left, a trick he'd learnt from his hikes in the Alps. All around him water dripped down from the higher branches.

By noon he'd covered a lot of ground. Ahead was a steep-sided spur of land which he worked his way around all the while looking for a possible ascent. It took him about an hour to clamber up to the top of the ridge and hike along it to the point. When he got there his reward was a magnificent view northwards over the city and its environs. To his left he could see the road he'd come down snaking between the hills, which in turn were enveloped by the forest that curled towards him before unfurling itself in a great dark sheet to his right, the tracts of trees beginning to alternate with white slabs of farmland as his eyes swept north. On the central horizon, a giant splash of concrete, was Minsk.

The tip of the point had collapsed over the years and a tree which had once stood upright there now grew outwards at an angle of forty-five degrees, its trunk stripped bare by the elements and only a small fuzz of green left around its tip. The roots had exploded out of the ground and become hypertrophic; they merged and knotted like the tangles in the brain of an Alzheimer's victim. Joel brushed the snow from their smooth surfaces and sat down to eat his lunch.

While he ate he rolled his dice, noted down the figures and asked himself if he could have done it, whether he could have eked out a secret life here among the hills trees rocks, unable to light a fire during the day, continually threatened by hunting parties of Nazi officers and their dogs. And operating as resistance too – felling trees across roads, disabling telegraph wires and bridges, removing railway tracks and jamming points. He shivered to think of it, of how pathetic those actions must have seemed in the face of the genocide. How to keep on going, how ceaselessly to knit and re-knit the slightest threads to keep a coat of hope across your back, a coat without which you were nothing.

The sun reached its low zenith and the windows of Minsk flashed, and across the snowfields and forests a trillion ice crystals twinkled with the rhythm of fireflies pulsing in concert in the boughs of a tree. From up here, nothing seemed to divide the city from the countryside around it. It was only another outgrowth, its concrete merely another kind of bark. Parasitic upon the land just as the trees were, as the land itself was parasitic upon the molten centre of the planet, itself a parasite bleeding off the energies of the sun. Joel looked out over the land, over the city, thought of the people teeming like bugs within its nooks, crannies, causeways, walkways. Thought of the people hiding in the forests, fleeing from the Nazis with their guns, dogs, gas. Thought of the death camps he had visited, of the pits and the pyres, the machinery of death, that most peculiar parasite, which derived its energy from millions of tiny and personal wills to power, millions of little prejudices, millions of blind eyes, millions of people trying something out or jumping through hoops, millions of sexual fantasies, millions of rapes, each one unique and yet totally predictable, human pistons and cylinders, an integrated power-house for the machinery of death. All these little decisions, these tiny chances, they formed a pattern, told a story. In his notebooks, gathering like a stalagmite, was the shape of it. He could feel it.

He started as a bird took to the air behind him, his mind suddenly focused. The blood raced beneath his skin and he began to sweat. He got up from his seat and walked around, trying to remain calm. He bent down, took a handful of snow from the ground, patted it on to his overheating face. He thought of the accelerator ring at CERN, tended by thousands, of the data back in his hotel room that even he, with his prodigious though waning mathematical talents, couldn't hope to make sense of without a mental prosthesis. Where was the boundary between concrete and flesh, tarmac and flesh, metal and flesh, copper and nerve? He thought of the axe and the shoe and the car and the gun, each blooming out of the human condition, defining, inseparable. How could you tease them apart? He thought of the telephone, the TV, the satellite, the radio, of the protocols being developed at CERN, of databases, data transfer, data and death, statistics and sex. He grew hard. The computer network would encircle the planet. He thought of the traces he'd left in the systems thanks to his grant cheques, his credit cards, his junk mail, his telephone calls, his passport, his medical records, the closed-circuit cameras at the research centre. We all leave traces, he reflected, all of us, and our technology takes up this slack. Axe marks in fossilised trees, pottery shards and burial mounds, bones and trinkets deep in the mud, piles of stones, plastic bags, nuclear waste. The ice crystals blinked all across the horizon. They were a trace: of his angle of view, of the height of the sun, of the composition of the atmosphere. The mountains of darkness were so bright they were dazzling. He leapt up and down, his circuits on overload, heat pumping from the top of his head. He screamed the names of the rebel angels – 'Aza! Azael!' – at the horizon. He thought of his notebooks, could feel the networks of power, of time itself, bubbling between their covers. Before him the city lay like a circuit board, tricking quantum events into logic, trapping chance in the plan of the cosmos. He screamed a scream of this, cast it to the skies, burst the eardrums of squirrels and brought birds to the ground. Thus opened to the world, he cast his spell.

An online edit

Perhaps Laika will turn out to be another missing link. Travelling for the sake of it in circles around the globe, scooping up the dross of the media as a blue whale filters plankton (more scurfing than surfing), Laika is a mill, forever grinding sounds and images into different forms. She's a kind of motor now, a habitus in the manner of the eye, the next stage in the meander of violence and vision that began with that engine of death the Gatling gun – all barrel revolutions and straight line projections, creating no man's lands out of lines of sight – and progressed to the film camera. This replaced bullets with photons and hurled them, a trillion rounds a second, at the screen, at the eye, at the brain, marking out a different kind of forbidden zone, one that was hostile to straightforward truth. Then after the camera the car, the motor now a petrol engine with spoilers and fins bolted on, the screen the scene outside the window, a plotless ever scrolling plane grounded by the infinite perspectives of crash barriers, chevrons, traffic lights and busy city streets. Now, via the circumfluous aircraft journeys of the jet set and Howard Hughes, the motor migrates from the roadway to outer space, where in a cybernetic frenzy it points its cameras up and down, staring at the earth, staring at the sun, losing itself in vision.

With her body uncritically interfaced with her capsule and her mind processing images at a tremendous rate, Laika's old conception of objects had long disappeared: everything had now been dissolved in the rush of the world. Her preliminary mode of self-consciousness had been superseded by something rather closer to the awareness she'd had as an everyday pup back in Baikonur. Cause and effect had vanished for her and in their place was a maelstrom, a concoction of high winds and difference. Forms were no longer abstract and eternal, but bloomed up from the rush of footage that bled through her porthole and screen, contingent and incredible. The sun was no disc but an enfolded and pulsating explosion; the earth was round only by dint of its billennial rollings through space. Space was process, time was intensity.

The dog's earlier paranoias had disappeared and she'd begun to feel totally at home in orbit. Thoughts of astronauts discovering her or of the shuttle retrieving her or even of collision with other satellites didn't frighten her now – death, when it came, if it came, would be merely a technical hitch. She was no longer an individual, lost in space, but an agent of change traversing the datasphere.

My Berlin PET

In Berlin it was autumn 1977, and Joel took a cheap room and for the next few weeks consolidated and prepared his data. It was a mammoth task – thousands and thousands of measurements, from distances, dates and degrees to dimensions, inventories, dice throws. Somehow to make sense of all this, somehow to analyse it, to boil it down, find its flavours and odours, find its shape. To begin with he sketched out two landscapes – the patterns of death during the Holocaust and the behaviour of chance in modern Europe. He bought a Commodore PET, one of three makes of personal computer that had been launched that year.

But he found he needed still more data. He visited the casinos, his little computers hot in his soles, and took notes and made money. During the days he noted the dimensions of the Brandenburg Gate, Checkpoint Charlie, Unter den Linden, the Reichstag, Hitler's bunker.

In West Berlin he drank Evian water, thought of the Evian agreement. At Evian in 1938 the other European countries, faced with the option of opening their borders and admitting the many Jews trying to flee Germany, hesitated and did not liberalise their immigration policies. David Ben-Gurion, who a decade later would become Israel's first prime minister, felt it was better that the decision went this way – if Jews managed to find refuge in countries other than Palestine it might damage the cause of Zionism.

Sometimes he drank Vittel and was forced to think of the camps that had been set up in the town as way-stations for Auschwitz. He copied down the mineral composition data from the labels on the bottles, compared it with the inventories of goods taken from the death camp victims.

He stayed in Berlin for over a year. He grew tired of hotels, got himself a small apartment, filled it with more books, papers, continued his research. He taught himself to cook and learned some German too. He made friends with one or two of the croupiers in the casinos he frequented and even had them over to dinner, though his intensity scared them and they never came back, judging him a crank. But for the most part he worked away at his analyses, collecting and collating, a rock climber scaling a sheer rock face, inch by merciless inch.

By the beginning of his second winter in the old capital he felt he'd lost sight of the Project. He was so far into it that going back was out of the question, but neither could he see any end. And he'd lost any sense of up or down, too – all directions on his wall of information seemed to be much the same. It was only his lizard brain which kept him clinging on; his cortex had forgotten about the dangers of gravity long before and, indeed, was suffering from vertigo.

So he left Berlin. He put his possessions into storage and travelled down to Monte Carlo, where he spent the summer exploring the casinos and swimming in the sea. After that he worked his way back up through France, starting with the sites of the internment camps in the Pyrenees – Rivesaltes, Noé, Récébédou, Portet St Simon and Gurs – and moving north through the countryside. Once again he stuck to the old routes of deportation when he could, followed the logic of the railway lines, a logic that had subjugated and delineated the fields of pain and madness which were the camps and termini and their corresponding catchment areas. It took him a year to cover France and as he went he adhered to far more stringent practices of data gathering than he had employed in the East. He visited Evian and Vittel, of course, and stopped in Paris for two months to have another stint at the casinos. From there he went to Brussels for more roulette and then on into the Netherlands. In Amsterdam he visited Anne Frank's house and was going to stay longer, but his shoe computer was in a bad way – it had been broken and botched back together one time too many – and he needed to return to Berlin where he had the tools to fix it.

But fixing it took longer than he thought. Most of the wiring was shot and there seemed to be problems with the motherboards too. Getting the components apart in order to test them meant causing a lot of damage (he had sealed them inside a special resin in order to protect them from sweat and the rigours of being walked on) and once he had broken the machine down it seemed simpler just to rebuild the whole thing from scratch. This he did, but he couldn't resist trying to improve on the original model and he allowed himself to be led off down this side-track for another year. Computer components had vastly improved and were much more widely available than when he'd originally built the machine – the microprocessor was now ubiquitous and had sold seventy-five million units world-wide in that year alone. Working with the new, smaller and more powerful devices was a positive joy.

When it had been finished and tested he set off for Italy, the data from France still untouched. More notebooks were filled, though now he mailed each one as he completed it back to a postal box he'd rented in the old German capital. He travelled as far as Greece and the Mediterranean islands occupied by the Axis powers during the war.

Eventually he headed back to Berlin, rented a new apartment and got down to work. What had seemed impossible before now appeared, with all this extra data on board, completely ludicrous. It took him six months just to go through what he had and put it in some kind of order.

For most of this time he was profoundly depressed. Going over his old notes and conclusions again, they seemed immature and he became embarrassed that he'd ever identified himself with the figure of the sorcerer or imagined his trip around Europe as somehow being equivalent to a sojourn in the fabled mountains of darkness. All the travelling had changed him, had given him a new set of routines and different things to think about. Sometimes he found it hard to remember why he'd ever started the Project in the first place. But the thing had its own irresistible momentum now and he found himself plunging into his task regardless, wrapping it around himself like a blanket, forcing himself to forget about reasons. He read about an international satellite telephone system, Inmarsat, that had been launched a couple of years before, and this cheered him, coinciding as it seemed to with the visions he'd experienced on the hill outside Minsk.

Once he'd catalogued the notebooks the next stage was to transfer their contents to the PET. More months of toil. He dumped them in a pile on the floor of the room where he worked. There were dozens and dozens, all shapes and sizes: hardback, softback, ring-bound, spiral-bound, stapled, flip, loose-leaf, spined, red, white, yellow, black, green, blue, khaki, ruled, graphed, plain, perforated, non-perforated, parchment, wood pulp, hemp. The pile reminded him of the piles of shoes in the concentration camp museums and he got into a groove in which he imagined that every time he finished entering a notebook into the machine he had somehow atoned for one of those pairs of shoes. He typed for hours at a time, for days at a stretch. He typed till his eyes hurt and the tendons in his arms throbbed and ached, until the muscles in his neck and shoulders were knotted hard. About half-way through the pile he came across an IBM PC in a shop, a new machine much more powerful than his PET, and agonised about whether or not he should upgrade. In the end he decided against it, though never again could he think of his PET with the same measure of affection. Six months later he had two data sets: all the Holocaust measurements, and all the gambling results and dice scores. Every data point was attributed both a date and an approximate geographical position. Then came the intellectual challenge – to bring out the mathematical characteristics of both sets and map one on to the other.

It was a massive relief to be manipulating numbers again instead of merely compiling them. He tried many approaches and wasted many months, but even his failures felt sweet because with each one he felt he knew the data better. It was like an animal, this information, and he was the hunter tracking it, observing its behaviour patterns, carefully noting the manner in which it moved about, chose its lairs, marked its territory. For sure, he was always one step behind, but he felt confident that the gap was narrowing all the time.

For over a year he worked like this, his life emptied of everything but modes and means, medians and matrices, distribution functions and probability densities, Fourier transforms and take-away food. And yet little by little the feeling he'd had that he was closing in on the beast, on the rebel angel, began to evaporate. He couldn't find any shapes, any correlations that made sense. He'd discover a relationship in one location but it would hold there and there alone. He couldn't find any patterns, or anything that would tell him how things might have changed in the four decades since the war. The information was outwitting him. He pulled at his hair, gnashed his teeth, butted the walls of his room with his head. He wandered the streets in a daze, shouted at strangers, rode the subway for hours drinking rum. It was 1983, seven years since he'd left CERN, and in that time he had covered thousands of kilometres and compiled mountains of data. It struck him – a terrible thought – that perhaps it was these which were the mountains of darkness, mountains of his own creation which now threatened to engulf him, and that the archeology of Nazism he'd been exploring was nothing but the fossil remains of a world which was dead.

Desperately he explored one avenue of approach after another, continually tracing and retracing his steps like a child lost in the snow. He even re-plotted all the geographical data, not just in terms of the position on the earth's surface where it had been taken, but in respect of the planet's changing position in space over time. But none of it did any good.

His hair had grown long and he now had a full beard, having given up shaving soon after he'd left CERN. When he stalked out for victuals dressed in a dark overcoat and hat he looked almost Hasidic again, except for the fact that he was so thoroughly unkempt. He worked and worried almost incessantly, slept intermittently, ate hardly at all. Pizza boxes and cans of soft drinks carpeted his apartment. Cockroaches moved in. He didn't notice – most of his brain was in the machine.

Eventually he thumped the PET in frustration one time too many and the computer broke down. He tried to fix it himself but didn't know enough about the architecture so he took it to be mended and this forced him to take a break, to step back a little. Of course, it wasn't that straightforward. First he had to rage around Berlin for a couple of days, furious at his machine, terrified the thing would never get working again. But after he'd calmed down and the man in the shop had repeated to him several times during as many phone calls that the problem was not serious and that he could have the PET back in a week, ten days at the most, he managed to get some sleep and some distance. It was then he began to realise that he needed help.

★

Unfortunately, the sort of help Joel now sought was not the kind that a good friend might have recommended. He had decided that his problems were being caused not by a mistake in his theory but by an error in his data gathering. He simply hadn't enough of it. It had been wrong to concentrate on the Holocaust in the way he had – he should have thrown the net wider. But he wasn't so unhinged that he thought he could expand the Project alone. No, he needed a helper. He was a sorcerer, wasn't he? He would summon a golem, as in the dream he'd had on the railway station, long before.

He went to the Jewish library in Berlin and pored over mystical books. He ordered pamphlets from Israel, America. But he could find little in the way of specifics about the creation procedure itself. That the golem was a soulless artificial creature created by the performance of a magical dance and the uttering or writing of holy names was plain enough; that such a creature had a hidden power to see, which was associated with the element of earth from which it was taken, was obvious also. But apart from the fact that the creation process was similar to that with which God brought the world out of Ein-Sof (the primordial man Adam Kadmon, Joel discovered, is himself often identified with the figure of the golem – his third eye, the light from which helps remake the world, his special power of sight) nothing was clear.

The night before he was due to collect his computer from the repair shop Joel had a peculiar dream. He dreamt he was in a restaurant – it seemed familiar, but he couldn't place it – and was eating, then visiting the toilet to shit, then eating again. He was dressed in his overcoat and his hat was on the table beside him, and a waiter stood attentively by. All the other tables were empty save one. At that a woman sat alone, drinking wine and watching him as he devoured course after course. Every time he went to the Gents he had to pass her and on each occasion she smiled at him. She had long, dark hair and a pale face.

He was half-way through an enormous bowl of moules marinière when she walked over and sat down at his table, facing him. He carried on eating but underneath the table he began to develop an enormous erection. She reached out a hand and laid it on his arm, halting the rhythm of void and consume, void and consume. Joel looked at her. Everything in the room stopped except for the tick of the clock and a small dribble of marinière sauce that ran down through the hairs of his beard and splashed on to the white linen table-cloth. The waiter stood motionless, perfectly still. Joel's erection throbbed in the silence. He was furious and his anger was being channelled into his dick. In bed, his body moaned and sweated, wound the sheets around itself. In the restaurant he pushed the table aside and shoved the woman to the floor, then leapt on her and tore at her clothes. She scrabbled back, but meekly, twisting her head this way and that, like in films that he'd seen. He tore at her skirt and her underwear, and the fabric came away easily and twirled itself round his hands. And then he forced himself into her, felt the heat of her dry insides, the clutch of her frightened membranes.

Immediately she started to shrink. She shrank away from him, smaller and smaller, her genitals – her whole body – retreating from his, leaving his penis naked and wilting, dripping with cum. As she shrank, the tones of her skin began to change and become less vibrant, more regular. Soon she was only two feet long and had become plastic, a doll, staring up at him with lifeless eyes that lay passive beneath bobbing artificial lashes. The waiter still stood there, unperturbed. Gingerly, Joel reached out a hand and touched the doll's naked chest. At his touch it split open. Inside the hollow interior were two synthetic hearts, one to the left and one to the right. Each was made of some sparkling red material encased in a clear plastic shell, the kind of thing a novelty pen or key-ring might be made of. Each throbbed with pulses of inner light.

Smoke had found him as well.

Joel burst awake and kicked himself free from the soaking sheets. That day he didn't go to pick up his machine as planned. Instead, he was at the library as soon as it opened, scouring the shelves for books on sex magic. He knew how to make his golem. He would make it of copper and silicon – naturally, as it was in the realm of information that he needed its help. The ritual dance he'd read about would be a dance of electrons and to bring it to life he would conduct a sex rite. For this he would need a partner, and who could that be but the one person with whom he'd had sex? For he'd finally recognised the restaurant in his dream. It was the one in Geneva, the Café Alsace, where he'd first had lunch with Henry and Jennifer.

Local space

The Alcester road leads northwards out of Stratford-upon-Avon; it runs past the livestock market and humps across the railway line. The next mile is crammed with houses advertising 'Bed & Breakfast'. These were here when Stratford first began – some say remains of Roman versions have been found, complete with chintz sofa covers, fake fireplaces and thimble racks – and they'll presumably be here at its end. If you take the turning to the left you'll quickly find yourself in the old town of Shottery, now a kind of dry and hollow bole on Stratford's trunk, but keep straight on in the direction of Alcester and you'll pass the Three Witches pub, the petrol station and the remains of the Last Resort night-club – in its prime little more than a collection of Portakabins sunk into a concrete car-park. The Last Resort marks Stratford's northernmost boundary, or at least it did in Jennifer's time (it is no more, that strange disco in the transitional zone between country and town, where real men drove Ford Capris and real women drank Malibu and coke) and beyond it lie the mythical fields of the Midlands, where cows graze on sheep offal and giant blocks of yellow rape stain the rolling hills in summer.

Back in town where the road begins you would once have found Stratford Hospital. In the eighties, the hospital was discovered to be incubating super-germs resistant to all known forms of antibiotic, so they knocked it down and doused the ruins with fire, leaving the little medical centre that had been built in the hospital grounds around the time that Emma was born to grow and grow – much like one of those super-germs – and strive to fill the vacuum left by the demise of its parent body.

Debate over whether or not this would be possible flourished for a while in the town community, itself a collection of viruses (mostly dominated by stubborn Tory strains). Some complained that the health service cuts were an outrage, that a medical centre was not sufficient to cope with the town's already large and rapidly expanding population. Others maintained that the hospital had never been much good anyway, and pointed to cases like that of the young singer electrocuted on stage in the Green Dragon (now a theme pub, in the old days the building was directly opposite the hospital), who had died because it had taken fifteen minutes for any ambulance men to make it across the road. The first group then responded with cries that such situations only arose in the first place because of financial cuts and that to deny funds to a place and then close it because of falling standards was typical of government hypocrisy. Then a third faction tried to convince everyone that they were all basing their arguments on rumour and conjecture, and that nothing would ever improve if people didn't look at the facts. At which point a small but well-organised fourth group tactfully remembered the super-germ. And then . . . and so it went on.

But in the early 1980s Stratford has all this yet to come. Bands play at the Green Dragon, sublimely unaware of the corporate future in which the old wooden bar, scored with the memory of bottlings and knife fights, will be replaced with a clean one of treated blond oak, the hospital razed to the ground, the cattle pens overshadowed by a superstore. On this particular Friday night Jennifer is in the toilets doing speed with Stim, still bass player of Desiring Machine which, against all the odds, has got it together enough to be tonight's main attraction. Stim is bent over the top of a ceramic cistern in one of the cubicles in the Gents, chopping at the powder with a razor-blade and continually flicking back fronds of hair from his long and wilting mohican to prevent them from disturbing the thin grey lines he's measuring out. Satisfied they're equal, he takes out a length of plastic straw and snurfs up the largest, and – coughing as he does so and rolling his eyes around in their sockets – hands the straw to Jennifer so that she can do the other. She bends over daintily and presses one carefully painted purple fingernail to her nose to close off her left nostril. Stim has already left the cubicle, the door swinging free behind him (the lock has been kicked off long before) and is at the handbasin dabbing his fingers with water and sniffing the liquid up his nose (he's been suffering from nosebleeds and this is his solution). The nasal douche complete, he hawks a plug of mucus round into his mouth and spits it into the basin, immediately wasting most of the drug. Jennifer comes out of the cubicle rubbing her nose and hands the straw back to Stim with a sniff.

From inside the toilets the support band had been just a deep bass tremble, but as Stim opened the door and the two of them stepped out of the damp pools of piss and on to the worn carpet of the rear bar the music slapped into them like a dirty wet blanket. They moved out into the fray and stood together for a while, eyes glazed, until Stim – pretty sure that Jennifer wouldn't notice – wandered off on his own. But she knew the very moment that he slipped away; in fact, she'd been waiting for it. She swayed a little as she watched him work his way around the edge of the crowd to where the rest of the band stood huddled in a gaggle at one end of the tiny stage, fiddling with their equipment and looking cool. Already that evening she had drunk three pints of cider, two rum and cokes, a vodka and black and a bottle of Newcastle Brown that someone had asked her to hold while they went off to mosh in front of the speakers. Not to mention absorbing several lines of speed and the THC from a spliff out back in the car-park. For a while it had all mixed together well, but now she was beginning to feel a little out of control. She got out a cigarette and lit it, teetering dangerously as she did so. It was difficult to focus. She looked for a seat but there were none; the bar was rammed. She dragged on her fag but the nicotine rush made her feel even worse, so she squeezed backwards through a couple of rows of people to the wall and propped herself up against it. The rail of the old wooden dado was hard against her shoulder-blades but it was somehow a comfort to have discovered something which was solid enough to be uncomfortable. The sound of the band ripped past her ears. A tall skin-head stumbled into her, catching her in the ribs with his scrawny elbow and spilling beer all down her jeans. She cried out and shoved him away, but the sudden movement made her head spin and she immediately felt the bile begin to rise in her throat. The skin mumbled something which may or may not have been an apology and veered off into the crowd, but not fast enough for Jennifer who needed out, now, and shoved past him in the direction of the exit. She squeezed through the press of bodies at the door but it was no good; she couldn't get by. It was now or never.

'I'm going to throw up!' she screamed. Instantly two waves rippled through the group in front of her: the first a wave of expression as horror struck every face, and the second a wave of movement as everyone dived out of the way. It was a miracle; it was a Red Sea all her very own. She felt like Moses – and it was time to talk to God. She hurtled down the path that had been made available and out into the street, making it outside just in time to vomit all over the base of a traffic light.

She leant against the cold metal pole for a while, retching plaintively. A police car drew up alongside. The copper wound down his window and asked if she was OK and she hid behind the puke-spattered tangle of black hair that hung down from her crown and waved them away. They drove off, and laughter rose up from the car like the bile in her throat and she heaved again.

Another car drew up, but this time its occupants had no interest in her. One of them got out and went up to the pub, started trying to argue his way in. The other kept the engine running and its low throb was comforting in the same way that the wooden rail had been earlier. But the sounds of the car interfered with the music that pulsed out of the open pub door and in the space in which Jennifer stood a quite different sound envelope was suddenly and bizarrely produced. She wasn't hearing the noises that she should hear at all, but the silence of an almost empty room, footsteps in a corridor somewhere beyond, the echo of a cough and a sob that seemed to come almost from herself – and something else, something that she couldn't recognise at first but which she suddenly realised was a heartbeat, no, two heartbeats, very loud, as if two people were standing either side of her with stethoscopes on their chests and the ends jammed in her ears.

A long time had passed since her experience in the police cell and she was too drunk to remember it; in any case there wasn't time, because just then there was a tap on her shoulder and the peculiar haecceity was gone, the experience fading slowly into the background roar of alcohol like a retinal after-image. It was Stim and he was holding a glass out to her. 'You OK? You want something to drink?'

She waved the glass away. 'You fucking idyut,' she slurred, 'can't you shee I'm fucking shick. I don't want another fucking drink.'

'It's water, brighteyes. Here, have some. What did you think it was? Half a pint of vodka?' Jennifer pushed back her hair and took the glass, saying nothing. She drank a little and swayed a lot, clutching at the lamp-post to steady herself. Again Stim asked her how she was, unable to think of anything much else to say.

'All right, I think.' She stood up a little straighter and tried letting go of the traffic light. 'Better for puking.'

'Yeah. Nothing like a tactical puke. Always sorts you out. You coming back inside to see the set then? We're on in five minutes.'

Jennifer tried to think, but all her energy was focused on focusing. Images that didn't belong in the street kept flickering across her field of view. 'Um. Yeah, in a minute maybe.' But at the idea of going back inside she was struck with another blast of nausea. 'Uh, on second thoughts maybe not. I think I'd better go. Shorry. I don't feel too good. Ta for the whizz though. Nice of you.'

'No problem. Wish I hadn't given it to you now.'

'No, no. I drank too much.'

'Yeah, but it's a waste though, innit?'

'What? Oh, fuck you.'

'You going to be OK?'

'Yeah, yeah, really, I'll be fine.' She turned away from him and stabbed at the button on the pedestrian crossing. There was no traffic but she waited for the light regardless, too far gone to do anything but let the machine take her decisions for her. Stim stood behind her, holding the half-empty glass of water. He watched her, thinking how forlorn she looked in her red crushed-velvet bodice and ripped jeans. He hadn't really known her before her father died, but he'd known about the scandal, that she'd shagged that American boy, years ago, when she was just a kid. Everybody knew about it; it had been the choicest bit of local gossip for years. Amazing that they'd kept it out the papers, him being the son of an actress and all. Wouldn't be able to keep it quiet now – times had changed. Funny thing was, nobody he knew held it against her. It was like it made her cool. Anyway, she *was* cool. She'd let him and his mates squat in her house for about two bloody years, hadn't she? Never asked for any rent, never hassled them to clear up, let them do what they wanted. And it could hardly be said that they'd treated the place with respect – though they had lent a hand redecorating when she'd wanted to sell it. But it was strange, though, 'cause through all the time he'd lived with Jenn he hadn't really got to know her any better than he did after the first week. Sure, he became more familiar with her moods, with what she liked or didn't like, with things like her shoplifting (and she was fucking good at that, he'd never seen anybody so good), but as to what she thought about things, why she did things, what she felt – he hadn't a clue. She never talked about the American kid, nor about her dad (most of his other friends, even the most relcalcitrant punks, would bang on about their old men on occasion – what they'd have to say might not be complimentary, but at least it was something). A lot of the time she seemed unaware that he and the band were living in her house; she came and went as if they were just there for a day or two, something weird that had fetched up in the dining-room and would be on its way soon enough. The other thing was that she'd never had a boyfriend, not while he'd known her, though lots of blokes had tried. And that was weird too. He guessed that the scandal had put her off men for good, but if that was the case then it was a shame.

The lights changed and began their blind man's bleep. Jennifer didn't move.

'It's green,' Stim yelled. She raised a drunken hand in recognition and began to cross the road, turned her heel as she stepped up on to the opposite kerb but managed to keep her balance. Stim resisted the temptation to run after her, take advantage of her drunken state.

'Where the fuck have you been? Come on, wanka! We're on!' It was

Skag. The bass player took a last look at the dwindling figure stumbling off in the direction of Old Town and then stepped back inside the pub.

With Michael Hedges's help, Jennifer had sold Henry's house some years previously and had bought herself a small flat on the Evesham Road with the proceeds. She lived with two stray cats that she had rescued from the streets. The first – which she called Judd – she had saved from being pelted with stones by some neighbourhood boys; the second – Joel – had just turned up on her doorstep one evening and demanded to be let in. Both cats were toms and carried on a continual semi-playful tussle for food, territory and attention. This would occasionally erupt into real violence, usually when Jennifer was asleep, and more generally seemed to involve a lot of noise, a lot of posturing, a lot of trashing of the furniture, a lot of vying for her attention and a lot of cat piss. Her friends kept telling her to have them neutered but she couldn't bring herself to do it.

When she came in drunk that night the cats were fast asleep and barely looked up from the chairs in which they had ensconced themselves. Her ears were still ringing from the noise of the support band and she switched on the fire and lay down on the couch wondering if she was going to be sick again. After a while she worked out that she wasn't and got up to put the kettle on and also the television. The set was the same one Henry had bought her, still going after all these years; most of her furniture had come from the old house too. She had taken what she'd thought she'd need and sold the rest with the property but for some time now she'd been wondering whether to get rid of it all and start afresh. She had the money – there'd been quite a lot of cash left over from buying the flat and it was hers now, having been released to her on her twenty-first birthday. A lot of stuff she'd kept for sentimental reasons including, for a while, all of Henry's clothes. But she didn't have that much room and they'd just been sitting there in cardboard boxes, so eventually she'd donated them to one of the charity shops on the High Street. She'd kept her mother's outfits, though. Henry had preserved Nadine's wardrobe through all those years; after his death Jennifer had found suitcases full of her clothes in the loft, all meticulously folded up in tissue paper and smelling faintly of naphthalene. It was the single most tidy, most organised thing she had ever known him do, and she finally realised as she carefully removed the clothes and tried on each garment how much he had wor-shipped her.

She'd adapted much of the clothing – although she'd never be as skinny as Nadine she'd lost most of the fat she'd put on in her mid-teens – and wore it without compunction; never having known her mother no deep thread of nostalgia could be triggered by the odours or the cut of the cloth. There was a certain symbolic value and that was all.

In the living-room the television babbled away to itself. An old episode of *The Twilight Zone* was showing and Jennifer remembered something she'd read about Rod Serling being involved with that writer, L. Ron Hubbard, the one who invented the Scientology thing that some people she knew had been into a couple of years ago. One of her hobbies – one of the things she did to fill her time and offset the boredom of her job – was keeping track of various conspiracy theories, and to this end she stole all the latest books and clipped articles from magazines.

She wanted to sleep but the speed was well into her and she had to watch most of the way through the plot of the show before her mind began to shut down. As her waking state steamed off the sound of the television, the hiss and flutter of the gas fire and the drone of cars on the street outside meshed into an odd configuration, just as the noises outside the Green Dragon had done. But this time the hallucination was not only aural: through her half-closed eyes the play of chiaroscuro from the TV, the flames of the gas fire and the headlamps of the passing cars which moved in planes across the room together conjured images. She was in a larger space this time, although it was screened off in such a way that the portion she occupied was quite small. She was sitting down, too, but when she tried to get up she found she couldn't move her arms or legs. Figures drifted past her, dressed in white. Everything was very white. Sometimes dark eyes swooped down to inspect her, but they didn't settle for long and no attempt at rapport was made by any of them. Then they went and for what seemed like a very long time she was left alone. The screens were hospital screens, white polythene curtains hung from wheeled frames. There were hints of some activity from behind the one directly in front of her and the sound of the double pulse, just like before. Sitting there for such a long time, she had a chance to study it – and to remember the police cell, though this time she felt calm enough not to be scared. Listening carefully, she noted that one of the beats was dominant and led the other in a complex rhythm. There was a pain in her chest, as if from a giant bruise.

Finally someone emerged from behind the screen. It was a stout woman, dressed in sky blue, who came up and leaned over her and smiled. She walked around behind her, too far for Jennifer to follow with her eyes. Then the screen was being moved. No, no it was her that was

370

moving. She heard voices to her rear. She must be in a wheelchair. She was being manoeuvred out of the room and into a corridor. People stepped out of doorways, then moved back against the walls to let her pass. They passed through several sets of swinging doors, each of them made of a transparent polythene a hundred times thicker than the screen curtains; it was like being pushed through great labial flaps of flesh. Then they were outside in the open air, in a small garden. There were rose beds and other buildings, and a bright sky dappled with cumulus, but everything was shades of grey, no colour. She looked around, bemused. A mile away a town rose up, blanketing a hillside. She could just see a church steeple and a great concrete building, a car-park or something, jutting above the low weathered buildings that smothered the hill. Then she was turned round and her view was restricted to the single-storey buildings whose external walls formed three sides of the garden. The sharp pain in her chest grew and the two heartbeats were now accompanied by a violent vibration. Across from her two geriatrics sat dribbling on a bench, their jaws working noiselessly at the sun. A few feet from them a patient plastered from head to toe in bandages sat motionless in a wheelchair. A bearded nurse stood in an open doorway, smoking a ciga-rette. The woman who had wheeled her through the corridors was chatting to two doctors. The pain in her chest became unbearable and she tried to scream.

She woke up and threw her hands to where the pain had been, but they never reached her flesh because Joel was in the way. He shrieked and shot from the sofa, doubly upset at being dislodged so unceremoni-ously from the warmth of Jennifer's chest − for not only had she made a comfortable bed, but her left breast had jutted at just the right angle to make a good flex pad for his claws. On the TV *The Twilight Zone* episode was burbling to a close. Rod Serling came on to deliver his homily and Jennifer crawled across the floor on hands and knees to switch him off. She turned off the fire, too, and went to bed, but the short sleep had refreshed her and she lay awake for a while wondering (as she often did) about her child and what she'd have been like if she'd have lived. In her mind she'd christened her Rachel, her own mother's middle name.

Becoming lichen

Emma liked to get outside. She liked to get outside and eat the grass. She asked for outside a lot and since she never caused any trouble outside the nurses were generally happy to take her there. Down the corridors she'd go, pushed along in her chair, giggling with glee as the plastic doors flapped past her, pointing out the windows at the sunlight.

Out in one of the gardens she liked to run around, kick at a football or play catch with a hoop, lie on the lawn. Usually the nurse would bring a book or a magazine – or a friend and some fags – and let Emma get on with it for an hour. This was best for Emma, because then she could do what she really came for without being noticed. She could eat grass.

She would grab surreptitious handfuls and work them into balls, then pop them in her mouth when the nurse wasn't looking. Before swallowing she'd mulch and suck at the vegetable fibres like gum, breaking the leaves down into juice. Later, free-floating chloroplasts extracted from the plant by bacterial action were captured by fungal filaments that had extended from her skin to her stomach. Channelled back up to the dermis they were put into service by the mycobiont, which could now photosynthesise. As the months went by and Emma's skin took on the faintest tinge of green, the fungal parasite was able to give back energy in exchange for the nutrients it took from the child. The symbiosis was complete. Now Emma could eat less, and she was far more sensitive than before to the experience of light and the economies and networks that underpinned life. This would help a great deal in her wanderings around people's dreams.

She'd been consulting Veronica, too, because she'd found out from Smoke about her two fathers. Veronica said it was very unusual, to have three parents like that. Most people only had two and some had only one, or even none at all! Emma decided she liked having three. It made her feel special. Especially since everything seemed to suggest that she'd see them all soon.

Making faces

The child was so frequently in her mind that it often seemed to Jennifer as if she'd never died. Sometimes, as she did some housework, or fed the cats, or made alterations to yet another piece of Nadine's clothing, she talked to her out loud in a kind of absent-minded, one-sided banter as she'd seen other mums do with their kids. It was similar to the way she talked with the cats; maybe she was just talking to the cats all along. When she'd been about nineteen she'd gone through a period of stealing baby clothes, toys, child-care books, even nappies, and hiding them in her room in the house. She would go into shops and look at cots, and chat to the sales assistant about the child that didn't exist. One awful night when the others were asleep she discovered herself making up a bottle: she couldn't get the sachets of powdered milk to open properly, she'd spilt boiling water all over her hands, all the time she was crying, not for the fact that she was doing this but because it was too late, too late – if Rachel had lived she'd be too old for bottles by now. The realisation broke the spell for her and she gathered all the baby things up, dumped them in binliners and took them to an unsuspecting charity store.

A pharmaceutically raddled tortoise of an old woman was behind the counter that day and she eyed Jennifer eagerly as the girl approached, clutching the two black plastic bags. Like heads of Grandfather's Beard the first tangles of Alzheimer's were beginning to bud in her brain. As soon as she saw the bags' contents she assumed that Jennifer had miscarried her first child. 'Are you sure you don't want to keep these, luvvie?' she jabbered, taking Jennifer's wrist in a vicelike grip and fondling the soft, pastel-coloured garments with her free hand. 'Not sure whether to buy for a boy or a girl, eh? I was just the same at your age. I'm sure you'll get another chance, dearie. Your husband's a strapping lad, I'll be bound, and you're such a pretty thing I'm sure he won't take too much persuading to give you another.' Jennifer's feelings twisted between horror and prudishness: horror at the suggestion that she might ever get pregnant again and prudishness because she could not help but think that sex was not an appropriate subject for this dried-up old shroud of a woman to discuss. 'Why don't you hang on to them, eh?' the shroud continued. 'They're so expensive these days. Time's past when you could rely on hand-me-downs from the family. Everyone wants everything new these days, don't they? I don't know. Seems such a waste to me.' And so on and so forth.

The experience cured Jennifer of going to such extremes again but she couldn't stop the little obsessions, even when she moved out of the house and into the flat. Keeping constant track of Rachel's age, for instance, and paying extra special attention to children who would have been her contemporaries. She kept a mental image of how Rachel might have looked which she constantly updated, although it was hard because she was never really sure which was the father, Judd or Joel. So she incorporated aspects of both.

In the beginning she looked for physical echoes in the children that she encountered. The curve of Joel's ears here, the angle of Judd's nose there; elsewhere her own eyebrows, there Judd's laugh. But the picture she built this way soon began to seem too artificial, too contrived, and it was then that she began to recognise aspects of her daughter which suggested themselves not because of their self-similarity to a memory but thanks to a more subtle resonance of their parts. Thus she discovered Rachel's torso in the way a young boy in a striped top held his arms above his head to frame the sky. She found her daughter's eyes in a girl who stood with her mother in the Post Office queue – it wasn't the eyes themselves that Jennifer recognised, but the way the girl turned her ankle this way and that out of boredom. The hair she knew from a giant advertising hoarding from which an old poster was being stripped. There was something about the jagged pattern that the torn strips made against the wood beneath . . . One Saturday afternoon Judd walked past the curved metal surface of the gas-fire surround; Jennifer happened to glimpse his reflection and it gave her the general shape of the face. And the skin, when it finally came, was not from another child at all but from the tawny sandstone of a building in Sheep Street. It was the texture of the stone which gave it away, the way it had been worn into long, deep folds and peppered by a subcutaneous growth of lichen. The smile was that of the girl downstairs, who never said a word to anyone but grinned the biggest grin. The nipples she found in a field one damp October day when she and Stim and Skag drove to Wales in Stim's Mini to search for magic mushrooms.

As the pieces of the puzzle began to come together they lived inside her not like a photograph which had been carefully memorised and filed away, but as an active site of recognition, a vague recipe for assembly that updated itself as time went by. With the passing years she found herself recognising new hair, new hands, new shapes, new colours in the skin, as if her idea of Rachel was growing up of its own accord.

★

The night of the Desiring Machine gig Jennifer finally fell asleep while contemplating the shape of Rachel's legs in the patterns made on the ceiling by the light from the street lamps and the cars, and as she slept she dreamt her daughter was nothing more than a collection of crazily circulating parts which, even if you brought them all together, would never form a quite coherent whole.

13

He-ere's Denzel!

The first available flight to London included a one-night stopover in New York. Judd took it anyway. After he landed he got in a cab, but when the driver asked him where he wanted to go he didn't know. 'The Plaza,' he said off the top of his head – it was the only New York hotel he could think of. But staying there turned out to be a mistake: because he was young and black and well-heeled, everyone assumed he was either a drug dealer or an actor. He could see them trying to make up their minds as he sat at the Oak Bar on the first evening, sipping a whiskey and water.

A coked-up student from one of the art schools in SoHo walked in and stared straight at him. He returned her stare and could see her eyes fogging over. She let out a high-pitched yelp and moved towards him quickly, as if pulled by some kind of tractor beam. 'Oh my gard!' she began in a whisper – a whisper which quickly developed into a shriek. 'Oh my *gard*! Oh, my! *Oh*, my! You are, aren't you? You really are? I can't be-*lieve* it! It's Denzel, look it's *Denzel*!! It's really you, isn't it?' She arrived at his chair and started foaming slightly at the mouth, telling him how much she worshipped him, how she had seen all his films.

Judd kept trying to tell her that he wasn't Denzel Washington, but she wouldn't listen to him. Everyone in the bar was staring. It didn't take him long to lose his temper. 'Look, I know it's hard for you, baby, with us being black and all, for you to tell us apart. But I'm not Denzel Washington and I'm not anybody else you know either, *so just get the fuck outta my face before I smack you!*' The girl stood there stunned and Judd turned back to the bar, and a security guard arrived and led her away. She went willingly, sobbing that she couldn't believe how Denzel had said that to her, and that she would never, never go and see one of his movies again. As if he cared, thought the guard.

Judd had forgotten how much he'd hated New York. Or maybe it was that he'd never hated it, had never had an opinion, and just hated it now. When he ventured out of the hotel after dinner he was shocked by the speed of the place, the dark scenes of the future playing across the terrible technologies of its buildings.

Although it was ten o'clock at night he found himself caught in crushes on the sidewalk and yelled at by people for being in the way. He tried the subway, but even that was frantic, and hot too, desperately hot. He wandered in and out of one or two shops, vaguely lonely, suffering with the constant transition from air-con to air so humid it felt like a solid wall. He began to understand why for years those with the money to get out of New York in the summer months did exactly that, leaving the city to settle a little further into its degradation and decay without them.

Walking aimlessly, he ended up in the West Village, in a street full of bars which he began to trawl, a drink or two at each, thinking – contrary to his earlier mood – that he might try and pick somebody up. But he was unable to mesh with the atmosphere in any of the places, to inter-face with the night. Bored and drunk, he gave it up, went to get a cab uptown to the hotel, sure that it was a cliché that the taxi drivers here wouldn't stop for blacks. But no, it was true, and after a couple of yelling fits in the middle of the street he resigned himself to the subway.

Down on the platform he stares at a map, tries to make sense of the topological spaghetti rendered more complicated still by a dense scrawl of red tagging. The station is massively hot and he feels faint, so he leans against the board to steady himself. OK, try again, now what station does he want? But the graffiti seem to inch and ooze, their redness deepens and splatter patterns start to form, droplets squeeze out from minute Perspex pores. Suddenly Judd sees the city: from Van Cordlandt Park to Breezy Point the subway's trackmarked veins lift into bold relief, swollen, purple, pitted, dense, a creep of ivy upon a ruined wall, a rib-cage flayed, laid bare . . . in Clark Street, Red Hook they're shooting in the streets; in Nevins Tremont Alphabet they do it another way; in Calvary New Calvary Mount Zion Olivet they lie and bleed in lines, staining green and pleasant fields; at Times Square they cut throats, at West Fourth they cut purses; in Jamaica they burn the summer, in Crown Heights they

377

burn each other; at King's Highway they burn a bum who's passed out on the platform, spray him with lighter fuel and toss a match; at Chambers Broadway they burn files tapes records blueprints; in Central Park they burn trees; on Ellis they burn immigrants; on Fifth they burn money on Broadway they burn reputations on Forty-second they burn the candle at both ends; at Columbia they burn books; in Harlem they burn buildings, they burn it up; at UN Plaza they burn bullshit, you can smell it over on Vernon-Jackson where they're burning pipes . . . *interzone I think I've found you, and you're burning*, streets and rivers ablaze, bridges arching over chasms of fire, boatmen poling down steaming creeks of lava, sulphur fills the air, blinding, cauterising mucous membranes, the only rain a rain of pumice a rain of ash, the streets, the streets are full of ash, are full of dread, the people wade to and fro, they stride, they step, they turn their eyes away, they build and burrow, reach out away, try to haul themselves away, you see them drawn out down the street their minds in towers their feet in filth their midriffs a hundred feet or more of taut gut stretched over an eternal flame, the spindle never turns but seized and stuck it's frozen, the spit stuck here as if on ice, a cold wind blows in from the north and the towers quick and crust and fracture, the weather turns, faces glisten now with dewy snow, the flames slow and twist and grind, their turmoil easing, their colours go through cadmium and violent green to mauve and now to blue, blue licks of ice grip up and swan like stalactites that felt the agony of time and urged and coiled and thrust their solid bodies into telling shapes of pain; the lava, pouring down the Hudson and the East, slows to a halt, its plumes becoming intermittent, its surface rills of fire now shuddering into diamond studded rock, the hulls of ships caught on the cooling surface inwards crack, spilling cargo out like stomachs sliced with bayonets or heads caught in a press; the citizens find their feet stuck to the chilly streets, their hands glued to handles, railings, like fortune cookies their arms snap at the wrist; in Central Park the ducks freeze in the lakes, squawk and quack incomprehension until their bills freeze at random angles and the cries freeze in their throats; in offices the secretaries' fingers stick icy to their keys, the boyish grins of office boys freeze on their boyish faces, the buttocks of executives are welded to their padded leather swivel chairs; in the alleys the cars freeze on the roads; in the cars the drivers freeze to the wheels, their necks freeze as they crane to look at the sounds freezing on the radio; in the clubs the music freezes to the horns the sticks freeze to the drums the money freezes in the tills the liquor freezes in the glasses . . . even the cigarette smoke freezes in the air, forming crystal banyans which pirouette in ashtrays and spread throughout the room until their own weight becomes too much and they tinkle shatter tumble on the frozen hairstyles of the frozen clientele . . . outside the air is gently freezing, the last breaths of people stopped in their tracks form cotton balls which protrude from their icy lips as a woodland fungus grows from a frozen stump . . . there will be no more violence in this city, no more muggings neighbour killings rapings lootings random shootings slaughters stalkings in the park gang retributions money cleanings machine-gunnings drugs and dealing spiving pimping racial beating land dividing overcharging underpaying appropriating segregating taunting stealing Wall Streeting or world trading . . . but deep below . . . deep below the rib-cage . . . a red light flickers on, a gentle breeze of warmth is felt, a tiny movement . . . a scurry . . . a rush . . . a touch of air, a hiss, a shudder, a lurch, a bustle . . . the gentle stubborn pulse of life . . . the subway is still running . . .

. . . pulling back, Judd runs from the station. It's not so far to the hotel – maybe he'll just walk it after all.

The next day he flies into London and books himself into a small hotel off Russell Square. He is excited, expectant, the hallucination has keyed him up. For some reason he takes it as a sign that his trip to London will be a success.

Chemical generation

The dog is in the image now, reflected back upon itself, DOG:GOD, refracted through the prism of the atmosphere, wave and particle, extended in space. Underpinning space, even, dataspace at least, Laika half-way into the image now, powered by the mitochondria of the flickering screen, her existence a continual rave, a techno track, an obliteration of the dimensions learned down there, on 3D planet earth. Fully acid. Phased.

So where is she, then? Has she leapt, like a salmon up a waterfall, like an electron across two orbits, to a higher (better?) place? Does she now traverse a utopia of communication, an undulating info-sea, womb-like and salted with fragments of savoury data? Has she reached heaven at last? Or, as some would maintain, has she simply disappeared altogether, has she ceased to exist, her brain turned to mush, her concentration span attenuated, her soul shrivelled, her muscles atrophied? Is she chemical generation, drop-out, slacker, loser, junkie, thug?

Why not ask Laika herself? If you do, you'll find that she's not concerned with your theories. Her parameters have changed, she has different degrees of freedom, she's in a different phase space. Back on earth she was mongrel dog, instantiation of age-old intersection of genotype and phenotype, fitness landscape and gene pool desire (a different kind of chemical generation, a much older kind). But now she's something else, a bacterium that was carried by accident out from under humanity's thumb and into its brain, forced to adapt and adjust, an irritant around which an abscess has formed.

But although she has thrown a reflection on to this new and hostile environment, to cross over and enter the image completely, to leave dog behind and become god – that is quite another matter. She doesn't have enough energy to make the transition from machine-flesh-and-blood into the virtual realm where she'd become a format for pictures, a reel in the weather, a shape for the stars. Laika long ago managed to make the most of a bad situation and her talents have brought her this far, but like Emma she can't make the final leap – can't make contact – alone. A hybrid Narcissus, she's stuck where she is on the lip of the pool, her fascination a dead end unless something extra can be found to help her over the edge. *She* wouldn't turn from her Echo.

Check in

While Jennifer stood outside the Green Dragon contemplating the contents of her stomach, Joel was a few hundred miles away and also being sick, hurling his guts up and over the rail of the overnight ferry that ran between Portsmouth and Caen. It was the first time he had ever been on a boat and he'd explored every inch of it while it was still in port, astonished by its size. He'd gone from floor to floor, checking out the bars, the restaurants, the cinema, the games arcades, as hyper as the children who were charging around in unruly packs ignoring their parents' frantic screams. Once the engines had started and the entire vessel had begun to vibrate, Joel rushed out on deck to watch the bilges pump and the stern swing out from the quay. He went as far forward as he could and breathed in the air, and stood in the spray and watched the great swathes of foam sliced up by the prow chase themselves into an endless churn. When he tired of this he shifted his attention to the sun, which was setting off the port bow.

It was a remarkable thing, to watch the huge orb redden, set fire to the clouds, then sink below the perfectly clean line of the horizon. Joel was suddenly acutely aware of something that was so obvious he had never stopped to think about it before, namely that he lived on the surface of a planet much as a bacterium might live on the skin of an orange. How odd that the world was not flat. The thought made him feel terribly dependent on the disappearing sun and, as if to confirm his fears, no sooner had the last rind of its colour shrunk from view than the wind picked up and the sea took on a heavy swell.

The decks of the boat were fairly empty now, with most of the passengers having already gone inside to eat or retire to their cabins, and Joel decided to retreat from the bows. Watching the sunset he had started to get hungry himself, but the exaggerated motion of the vessel knocked the edge off his appetite and the moment he stepped inside a sudden claustrophobia conspired with the smell of diesel fumes, warmed-over food and clustered humanity to turn his stomach. The boat was pitching quite unpleasantly and though he made it to the nearest bar to buy a coke he couldn't seem to manage to keep his balance and count out the correct change at the same time (the fact that English currency had been decimalised since he'd been in Cambridge didn't help matters). The children who had been running around earlier were more sedentary now. Many of the younger ones were squalling and tugging at their tired British mothers, through whose bodies the soft music of holiday was still playing. The memories of beach and beer and sex were still strong in these women, insulating them from the domestic grind that waited for them at the other end of the short voyage as surely as the white chalk cliffs of England's south coast. Surrounded by duty free, they lay back in their shellsuits and sighed.

In an instant one impulse dominated Joel's thoughts: get back outside. He reached the rail just as his lunch was ejected, then hung there, the metal rod lodged under his armpits, watching the contents of his stomach get swept into the sudding turmoil that nagged away at the sides of the hull. When he could retch no more he staggered over to the benches which lined the steel cabin walls and lay down. The acrid tang of the engines, so romantic an hour before, was now a sulphurous reek that attacked his nostrils. He was weak, terribly weak, weak as a child fresh from the womb. He wanted to die.

Night fell quickly and dense clouds obscured the stars. The moon could not be seen, although Joel ran his eyes across the sky from where he lay, wishing he could spot the satellite and gain some point of reference from beyond the pitching deck for at the moment there was none, not even a horizon. He laughed weakly – the Nazis had hated relativity theory for being a Jewish idea. He gave himself over to the smoothness of the space in which he found himself: he was too drained and it was too alien for him to try to impose a structure upon it. The ferry was a small speck of light in a vast cauldron of blackness – so what could he do? He stared out into the apparently featureless night. Here was the sublime, he thought, here was the unformed and primal chaos of existence. How boring, banal and unpleasant it was. He thought of *Moby Dick* which he, like Judd, had once started but never finished. He wondered what happened in the end.

It began to rain, a cold, dank drizzle that felt good against his clammy skin. He fell asleep. The winds which whipped the waves which tossed the boat which made Joel sick had started out somewhere in the Arctic and followed the line of the Labrador current down past Nantucket, from whence the *Pequod* had once set sail. Further south, off New York, they'd picked up a few of the more odorous particles on the run from Moshe Kluge's bakery (now in larger premises in front of which were parked two smart delivery vans). Then the winds turned west with the North Atlantic Drift and the particles hurtled their way across three thousand miles of ocean and by a remarkable coincidence found their way up Joel's large Jewish schnoz, where they fell upon the receptors of his olfactory organ and sent a dim signal down the olfactory nerve to the olfactory bulb, where it caused an increase in activity just sufficient to trigger the last dream of his family that Joel would ever have.

It was odd to be back in England. He realised at once that he hadn't missed it at all. He purchased a train ticket to London and got some breakfast at the station, which proved to be a mistake – he'd left for CERN in 1971 and thirteen years on the Continent had left him unprepared for the completely unpalatable nature of British Rail food. Stoically, he ate a stale doughnut that sat in his stomach like slow-setting cement and drank a cup of a thin acidic liquid which the woman behind the counter assured him was orange juice. He bought a magazine but, once on the train, he couldn't focus on the words and so he let his head loll on the headrest and closed his eyes and tried to wish away the noise of squalling children and the stench of stale cigarettes. It was like being back in East Germany. He managed to slip into a kind of fuddled slumber, the clacking pulse of the train incredibly comforting after the unpredictable motions of the ferry. He dreamt once again he was back in the restaurant eating, then visiting the toilet to shit, then eating again, and that once more Jennifer tried to seduce him away from his rhythm of void and consume, void and consume, void and consume, void and consume. Her interfering made him mad, and eventually he stood up from the table and pushed her away. Once again she shrank at his touch and became a plastic doll with unblinking blue eyes, her upturned head jutting at a peculiar angle. Where his hand had touched her chest it split open and inside were those two synthetic hearts, one on the left and one on the right, made of that strange red material and throbbing with light.

At Waterloo he was woken by the guard. He got through a pocketful of change calling round hotels from a payphone on the concourse, trying to find a room that would let him have his own telephone at a less than extortionate rate, but he eventually made a reservation at a place not far from Paddington. He took a cab.

The hotel was on Prince's Square and the taxi pulled up outside the front door. Joel got out and looked up and down the street; there were at least fourteen or fifteen other hotels packed into the short Georgian terrace. All of them looked a little battered, the paint peeling from their window frames, plastic signs poking out from their columned porticoes. Outside his own, two men were sitting on the pavement mending a bicycle, reggae chugging out from a boom box beside them. The machine was in pieces, its oily sprockets, chain, nuts and washers laid out on pages from the *Sun*. A washer ringed a pin-up's nipple, and Joel saw this and wanted to go over there and arrange the rest of the parts around her so that her flesh would have a little machinic magic all of its own.

The moment passed, and he paid the cabby and went up the steps into the hotel. The front door was blocked ajar and glass doors had been fitted just beyond it. A small air-conditioning unit had been inset above them and the usual array of credit card signs were stuck to the glass. The hallway was freshly painted and cool, and there was a floral-pattern carpet underfoot. Inside, the building seemed larger than it did from the street.

One of the men from the pavement followed Joel in and wiping the oil from his hands with a piece of rag entered Joel's name in the register and gave him his key. 'It's the receptionist's afternoon off today,' he explained. He checked Joel's passport, then showed him up to his room.

He tried to take both the holdalls but Joel felt secretly embarrassed that a black man should carry his bags and insisted on taking one of them himself.

Once inside the room – which was on the front of the building, overlooking the portico – he tested the locks on the door and windows, and checked that the telephone socket was suitable. Then he unpacked his rucksack and one of the holdalls and took a shower, and – for the first time in months – had a shave, using scissors and a razor he had bought on the ferry before he'd got sick. Locking the door behind him, he went downstairs and out into the sunlight. He felt supremely confident and set off in a random direction, nodding to the bicycle tinkerers as he went. The one who'd signed him in returned his nod; the other ignored him.

He found his way to Queensway and bought a stack of computer magazines which he studied in a café while he had something to eat. The next morning at nine he was on the telephone ordering kit with his credit card and by the end of the following week he had spent several thousand pounds and the hotel room was crammed with cardboard boxes, polystyrene packaging, tools, computer components, measuring and cali-bration devices and medical equipment, not to mention empty take-away cartons and discarded clothing. He worked away happily in the centre of the mess, a child with his toys, covering the carpet with lengths of wire and glistening drops of solder that dulled as they cooled and set into the nylon weave. The dream-figure of the double-hearted doll often seemed to hover over him while he worked, a kind of muse. He thought of the restaurant dream often and dreamt it whenever he slept; it carried an enormous sexual charge, exciting him to an extent he had never previously known. So much did it turn him on that he often had to break off from his work and masturbate, grinding himself to orgasm between the loving surfaces of two copper-dappled circuit boards in an attempt to splice his pleasure with his plan. His balls ached constantly and he had pins and needles in the balls of his feet. Preferring to work at night, he often slept in the afternoons and when it was warm he liked to walk down through Hyde Park to the Serpentine, have lunch in the café at the eastern end, then fall asleep under a tree near the edge of the water for a few hours. He enjoyed these siestas: memories of the after-noons he used to spend reading by the Cam were easily elicited from the conjunction of water, breeze, willows and ducks that enveloped them.

He used empty boxes and a door which he unscrewed from the ward-robe to construct a desk on which gradually materialised a fantastic meshwork of circuit boards, terminals, disk drives, keyboards, modems, cables, video cameras, printers and other electronic paraphernalia. In the abstract, impersonal space of the hotel room the structure looked obscene, resembling the innards of some murdered and mutilated robot.

Totem

The growing obsession with her dead child began to worry Jennifer. Every night now she dreamt about Rachel; all through the day she would be on the look-out for any aspects of her that might be secreted in the world. Although it had started out as an hallucination brought on by extreme circumstances, the double-pulse rhythm came to her often now, triggered by the most distantly related sounds – the rhythm of the cash tills at work, a piece of music, the sound of rain on the windows of the flat. Perhaps she had read too much bad science fiction, perhaps she was too into those books on conspiracy theories and psychic phenomena, but it was becoming increasingly hard to ignore the possibility that she was being sent some kind of message. It was either that or the onset of schizophrenia, and since she knew more about the former than the latter and had been left with a fear of hospitals after the harrowing experience of her pregnancy and the subsequent birth, she far preferred it as an explanation.

So everything became important now, everything became significant. Her past was trying to tell her something and everything must be examined: changes in the weather, objects abandoned in the street, the behaviour of animals and birds, any coincidences, anything out of the ordinary, even the ordinary itself. She fingered her scars almost continuously and studied them at night before she went to sleep, in case the network of razor marks (which, in retrospect, seemed to have been part of a subconscious process culminating in her caesarean, the greatest and most traumatic of all her wounds) might in some way serve as a key to help her interpret whatever message was being transmitted, the lines drawn on her chest shoulders breasts comprising a peculiar Rosetta stone of the flesh.

But this opening of herself to the world was threatening, too. She'd been so withdrawn, so self-contained for so long, that any acknowledgement that the scars she had drawn as armour might be functioning instead as interface was hugely unsettling. It suggested a return to her childhood, a prospect that made Jennifer ripple with fear. Looking back on the flow of her life, most of it seemed beyond her control, shaped by currents and tides far larger than herself, and to go back would not mean the chance to change things but merely the repetition of pain and distress she had hoped she had put behind her for ever.

In play

She was in touch with all three of them now, one way or another. Through her mutations and her close relationship with other eukaryotes, Emma has managed to amplify material affects, extend her senses, manipulate and evaluate at a distance. She has become extended in space.

Her space is a dream of protein and chromosome, photon and chemical, mineral and fluid. She is image and rock, lizard and tree, data and tool, network and sea. And now she dreams her parents, as they once dreamt her (though that was a strange kind of dreaming, phantasm of gamete and drive). They deserted her once and to make them return she plucks threads in the loom of the mind, engineers coincidences and conjunctions in matter, as if the two were the two different aspects, the woof and the warp, of one single stratum. Her child's fingers dapple the surface of being and Jennifer, Judd and Joel bounce together, like three metal balls.

'Inexperienced schoolgirl, fresh in town'

Back in London, Judd found himself severely depressed. England had so many associations for him, most of them unpleasant, that he couldn't seem to focus on the situation in hand. Day after day he put off contacting Scofield's friend, and he grew more nervous about it the more he realised just how crucial this meeting might be. He felt enervated the entire time, as if the downturn he'd experienced in Reno was still draining him, still drying him out. He appeared to have succeeded in breaking up the old psychoanalytic patterns, but now he felt out of control in a different way, giddy and heavy, and unclear about which way to turn. To give himself direction he began grasping at straws, wandering round London and trying to reconstruct from the city and the memories hidden among it like Easter eggs some sense of the childhood he'd had before he'd met Jennifer. It worked, up to a point, but at the same time it made him feel somehow submerged, as if he were a collection of sediments and the flux that was the young Judd was above him, currents and whirlpools just below the waves. He worried that he'd been wrong to interpret his vision of a flaming then frozen New York as a positive sign and eventually pushed it to the back of his mind.

He watched the children who passed him in the street, certain that he could tell from their eyes whether they were innocents or already saddled with the structures and strictures of the adult world. From facets of their faces and expressions he constructed a mental simulacrum of how he might have been if he had never slept with Jennifer or if – and this was the version he preferred – he had slept with her without discovery or guilt. Thinking about her again made him wonder whether he should try to get back in touch, but he dismissed the notion. It was pointless, stupid. It would surely just bring back the anger, take him back down a path already well trodden. He felt cold, as though the world were closing in around him, beginning to glance his way.

Lonely, he took a card ('Inexperienced Schoolgirl, Fresh in Town') from one of the telephone boxes on Southampton Row, called up the number printed on it and went back to his hotel to wait. From his window he could just see the sunset, the neon scribbles of the clouds tacky decorations on a contaminated horizon. When the prostitute finally arrived she didn't look particularly inexperienced or too much like a schoolgirl, either. She was bottle-blonde and five-two and probably around twenty-eight. If it hadn't been for the uniform she wore beneath her leather coat you'd never have known. She said her name was Sara and she was very complimentary towards Judd and he, used to callous American call-girls, was flattered to observe that she actually did want to sleep with him – although he almost sent her away again when, as they lay down together on the bed, she asked him if anyone had ever told him that he looked a little bit like Denzel Washington.

'You can spank me if you like,' she said bluntly, as Judd handed over her fee, 'but hands only, no objects. And it'll be extra.' She smiled at him. 'Though I'll give *you* a discount.' Judd adjusted his previous guess to twenty-five, reflecting that girls aged fast in this profession. Then again, he thought to himself, did you ever see a check-out girl who looked good for more than a couple of months?

Sara lifted up her skirt to show her panties and the tops of her suspenders. Then she walked around behind him and began to massage his shoulders, after a while removing his shirt. As they moved in the general direction of coitus Judd found he was not becoming aroused and he finally had to admit to himself that after all what he wanted was Jennifer, Jennifer as he remembered her. He rolled over and switched off the light and tried to imagine that the hands and thighs belonged to a girl with red hair and a dark-green coat whom he had seen in the National Gallery that afternoon and who couldn't have been more than twelve. She had stood alone in one of the halls, perhaps looking for her mother, and for a moment Judd thought she had stepped right out of the picture behind her – Erich Heckel's *Two People in the Open Air* – so closely did the tones of her coat and hair resemble those of the painting. She had looked directly at Judd, then lifted up a single finger as though readying herself to say something profound. Her cheeks were sallow and pale, almost bruised, and she had about her an aura of neglect. Her forehead was very high, her hair a gingery red, her eyes were shot through with emerald. The pigmentation of her skin was curious and unfamiliar: it was dappled, with a translucent quality, and by some trick of the light was faintly glaucous, borrowing colour perhaps from the verdant collar of her coat.

For a full minute the child had stood motionless while Judd watched her, playing with the ring on his finger all the time. Then a bell went off very loudly just behind him and he turned to see a Malaysian tourist being admonished by a guard. The man had poked the lens of his camera too close to one of the paintings and had triggered the alarm, that was all. Judd turned back to the girl, but she had gone.

She was beneath him now, her frail body prone and submissive, shuddering with each one of his thrusts. His hands clutched at her prepubescent flesh and he could feel her rib-cage bowing beneath the weight exerted by the heels of his palms, the bones still green and resilient with the plasticity of youth. In a frenzy he pumped away; he was sweating hard and the hot smell of him suffused the air. As he wondered, quite irrelevantly, why it was only himself he could smell, why she didn't have an odour, he felt two different rhythms, two immense pulsations, surge up his arms from her chest. He tried to pull his hands away but he could not; the very tides of his blood were in thrall to the dark oscillators hid snug beneath her flesh. He pulled again and a giant jab of pain shot through both forearms, as if hot copper wires wound loosely around them had been suddenly wrenched tight. He dug his nails into the flesh below as hard as he could, wanting to tear, wanting to rip . . .

The woman threw him off and slapped him hard across the face in one quick movement. He immediately went limp and lay with his head over the end of the bed, panting his way back into the room.

She kneeled over him, a trickle of blood running down her left breast. 'What the fuck do you think you're doing?' she yelled. He didn't respond so she thumped him on the back. In the next room someone hammered on the thin dividing wall. She lowered her voice to a hiss. 'That may be OK where you come from but I don't put up with shit like that, understand? And don't get the idea that I'm here alone. D'you think I'm fucking stupid? People know where I am. Anything happens to me and you're history, right? Understand?' She punched him, her hand balled into an extremely hard little fist. 'DO YOU UNDERSTAND?'

The neighbours banged the wall again and Judd nodded. He was shocked by his own behaviour; he had never acted anything like this before. But it was pointless to say anything. Sara leant back against the wall and they both lay there for a while, recovering their wits. In what little light crept through the gap in the curtains she examined the scratch on her breast.

Eventually Judd turned to look at her. In the crepuscular glow the scratches showed up black. 'Hey, look, I'm really sorry. I didn't mean it. I mean I never . . .'

'Well look it's done now, OK,' she snapped, but something in his expression suggested he was being sincere so she altered her tone. 'Anyway, it's not that bad. I've had worse. I'll survive.' There was a pause, then she said, 'You were going pretty well there for a while. If you promise to stay calm I'll let you finish if you like. It'll be double, though.'

'No, thanks but no thanks, I think it's best if you go.' He got off the bed and went into the bathroom, and she dressed quickly and left without another word.

He slept poorly that night and his eyes throbbed blearily all the next day, as if his retinae had been the mixing palette for some hallucination far vaster and more intricate than the one he remembered. The incident had deeply disturbed him, he didn't understand it at all, and he realised that he had to go and visit the man whose address Scofield had given him before things got any further out of hand.

The big hack

Once his new machinery was configured Joel began to connect to as many computer networks as he could find. He hooked up with ARPANET, which had been divided into ARPANET and MILNET the previous year. He explored the BITNET via its gateway at the City University of New York and the Computer and Science Network in Wisconsin. He downloaded information from the Japan Unix Network (JUNET) and from the UK's Joint Academic Network, JANET, which was in fact his nearest major gateway and the one he used most often. When he'd left CERN the networks hadn't been integrated on anything like this scale; nobody had even heard the word 'Internet'. But Unix and TCP/IP connection and the new transmission protocols meant that the various systems were expanding and interlinking at an extraordinary rate. Indeed, computers were big news now. A year before, in January 1983, *Time* magazine had featured a computer on its cover for the first time since the 'sailor shot' of January 1950. This time the computer was an IBM PC. And now it was 'man of the year'.

Hunting for information on the networks was an extraordinary experience. To sit in front of a terminal in a London hotel room late at night, the blinds drawn and the lights off, the only illumination coming from the zorby glow of the screen, and be able to jump from Cambridge, to New York to Tokyo to Delaware to Paris to Addis Ababa to Stockholm in seconds was something which even a few years previously could hardly have been imagined. It changed everything, this space of data which was everywhere and nowhere simultaneously, in which every point seemed connected to every other, in which whole companies, whole universities, sometimes even whole societies appeared to exist.

One of Joel's earliest hacks was the British Telecom database. It was a trial run, but one with a purpose: he wanted to search for a telephone number. He could have picked up the phone and dialled directory enquiries, but it was more fun this way. It didn't take him long; online security was still in its infancy and stories of school kids breaking into nuclear defence systems seemed to turn up in the papers every other week. Once logged on, he ran a national search and in a few seconds got the number he wanted – Jennifer's – along with her address.

★

But the overall aim was not to take data out but to put data in. The golem he wanted to create was to be a virtual beast, a familiar that would wander the networks and bring him back data. But it was to have a human form, too – he wanted it to act within his own parameters, to be an agent of his, to take shape in the datasphere in his form. If he was going to play god, he wanted his primordial man to be in his own image. It was a Christian idea, but it seemed somehow appropriate.

He still wasn't sure whether or not he was going to carry out his plan, or even if it would work if he did. Rather than growing in confidence, as the various aspects of it came together he was increasingly racked with self-doubt. After the initial rush his work proceeded more slowly and he found himself becoming increasingly pensive. He would often forget what he was doing and stare blankly at whatever was on the screen or in his hand at the time, or even just at the wall, suddenly struck by the lack of sense it all made. For hours he would debate with himself whether or not to call Jennifer, always deciding against it in the end, managing to come up with a different excuse every time. But at the same time the Project seemed clearer than ever. Prevaricating, he began to write out his theory on his computer, printing out completed sections and pinning them up on the walls.

The subject matter dealt with more than just physics and Kabbalah, magic and chance. Humanity was rotten, he wrote, tragically flawed, capable of feeding only off itself. The human race was a rabid animal that tore at itself in a frenzy, its very attempts to mitigate its own misery merely producing more of it. He wrote that nothing but direct and total application of technology could unfold new dimensions of human possibility and prevent self-destruction. The Internet was merely the first stage of the process: this network of networks would eventually achieve consciousness, at which point there would no longer be any way of telling the difference between human and machine. He himself would lead the way, a manifestation of tikkun, the third type of time. He would transcend the vast movements in which the world was trapped and push forward into a new space where death was forgotten and the universe became perfect. Increasingly obsessed with his dream of the restaurant and his memories of Jennifer, he fitted her into his scheme: if he was an agent of tikkun, Jennifer was an agent of shevirah; she represented the chaos of the world, its living imperfection. It was only fitting, then, that she should midwife the next stage of the Project, be the golem's surrogate mother, its incubator.

Writing all this down wasn't easy. In his head it was clear, but committed to paper it became childish and muddled. It still lacked a purity, a simple coherence, but the more logical the arguments became the more they seemed lifeless and naïve. He still wasn't sure of the precise role that Jennifer would play, nor could he identify the third term which kept re-presenting itself. Who, after all, was the agent of zimzum? Joel didn't know. Perhaps it would be his golem. Could that work? It didn't seem likely.

Frustrated into action, he stopped writing and began to make the appropriate measurements. He started with the obvious ones: height and weight, the length and girth of every limb, skin tones, size and colour of eyes and degree of myopia, rate of hair and nail growth, pulse rates corresponding to various levels of physical exertion, size of penis (flaccid and erect), calorie intake and so on. These completed, he progressed to the more complex internal statistics, some of which required repeated visits to the nearby hospital of St Mary's: size and length of throat, skeletal dimensions, deduced weight of individual bones, blood type and red and white cell counts, sperm count, lung capacity, bladder capacity, stomach capacity, intestinal length, skull thickness, brain size and weight, sinus diameters, hearing thresholds, metabolic rates and biorhythms, genetic fingerprint.

The double-hearted doll haunted him more and more intensely and he often thought he could hear its double pulse beating away inside the walls of his room, as if their thick plaster were flesh skinned with paint. For a period he only slept when sleep overtook him and this meant no more afternoons dozing beneath trees in Hyde Park; now he simply lay down like a dog among the mess which cluttered the floor, the bed and every available surface. But then the site of his dreams changed from the restaurant to the room itself, and he began to loose track of the difference between sleeping and waking.

Within the first fortnight of his moving in, the chambermaid had kicked up a fuss about the state of the room and he had given her two crisp fifty-pound notes in exchange for a promise that she would leave him alone and not let on to the management. But now she was gently extorting money from him, letting herself in with her pass key when he least expected it and complaining about how difficult it was to keep the truth from the boss. She was a petite American girl with very blonde hair and metallic eyes and although she had no idea what on earth it was he was up to she had quickly figured out that whatever it was, it had required a significant investment of both time and money to set up. She concluded, correctly, that this put her in a position of some power and

Joel had little choice but to meet her demands. His funds, already greatly reduced by the hotel bill and the computer equipment, had dwindled almost to the point of invisibility, and he realised that some time soon he would have to break off from his work and pay a few visits to the city's casinos, or he would not have enough money left to make a decent stake.

What cash he had he counted out on the bed; it came to a little under £500. The chambermaid had just demanded another fifty and at the end of the week he would have to settle his bill as usual. There was nothing else for it but to polish his computer shoes and brush off his suit. He asked the hotel receptionist to recommend a casino and she suggested the Victoria, on the Edgware Road. He had to join first – a legal formality, but waiting for the membership to be processed delayed everything by a couple of days. He put the time to good use: trouble-shooting the gambling machine, replacing old cables and solenoids, re-soldering connections, but the wait still made him nervous. It had been a while since he had done this, even thought about it. Could he still do it? What if he blew his stake? What if he couldn't calibrate the wheel correctly? What if, what if, what if? But as soon as his membership cleared and he walked through the doors of the Victoria all his doubts were dispelled. He was suffused with a feeling he had never had before, that of coming home. It simply meant that he knew: what to do, what was expected of him, what the looks and actions of other people meant, the parameters of the system.

But something *had* changed. That night he felt so confident that he never got around to switching on the machine but played much as Judd had done in the early days when he'd first discovered the lizard and followed it through the back rooms and dens of LA. But while for Judd the impression had been that chance was alive, that its patterns and poems were something dynamic, for Joel it couldn't have been more different. He felt as if he were absorbing the imperfect universe into himself, overcoming it, processing it, finally performing the task he'd been working at since his first years at Cambridge. It seemed that he'd got back some of the mathematical talents he'd had as a boy, except that now it wasn't his imagination which did the work of manipulating shapes, planes and figures, but his entire body. Predicting the results of the wheel that night was an unmistakably physical sensation: he could feel data being churned in the muscles of his neck back arms, could feel sensors in his thighs groin belly crunching numbers. He watched himself in the mirror, saw his time move quite differently from that of all the others around him. While they faltered and hesitated, grew old before him, he moved more and more smoothly. Even as he looked, his features became more honed, his aspect more measured. For the first time in his life he felt at one with his flesh. He was getting there, he'd made the right decision to come, he was becoming machine.

He left the table and cashed in his chips. He'd cleaned up, won over seven thousand pounds. With the cheque safely in his pocket he wandered down towards Marble Arch and into Hyde Park, elated with his success. It was a clear summer night and he took off his jacket and unbuttoned his shirt, wanting to feel the air on his new and confident skin. He sat in his favourite spot on the bank of the Serpentine and gazed up at the fathomless ink of the sky, identifying constellations and tagging each star with its distance from earth. His mind was electric, totally clear.

Back at the hotel he threw open the windows and tidied his room, filling empty boxes with rubbish and throwing them out into a skip that was conveniently parked outside. Then he did something he had not done for weeks: he slept in a bed unencumbered with junk and with no fear of his dreams. Tomorrow he would call Jennifer.

The telephone call

The telephone rang and rang, and eventually Jennifer could stand it no more. She pulled herself up out of her bath with a great sucking noise, frightening Judd and Joel, who had been dozing underneath the sink where the hot-water pipes warmed the floor. Swearing loudly, she wrapped a striped towel around herself and padded down the hallway, leaving a trail of wet footprints for the cats to sniff in her wake. She grabbed the phone. 'Who is it?'

'Er, hello, is that Jennifer Several?' said a shy voice from a hundred and one miles away, and an inch away too.

'Yeah, what of it? Hope you're not going to try and sell me something.'

'Um, no, I don't think so. Jennifer, is that you?'

'I'm sorry, but who is this?'

'Oh, well, you probably don't remember me, I mean it was a long time ago. It's Joel. Joel Kluge.'

'Oh!' Jennifer sat down suddenly on the chair into which Joel had climbed unnoticed just a moment or two before. He shot out from beneath her descending buttocks with a shriek and nearly landed on Judd, who was sitting washing himself on the floor. Judd took this as an insult, flattened his ears and launched a counter-attack. 'Joel, my god, Joel. What a surprise . . . Er, where are you? How did you get my number?'

'Oh, I got it from the telephone company,' he said, accidentally artless. 'I hope you don't mind me calling you out of the blue like this . . .'

'Oh. Not at all, no. It's, er, great to hear from you. It's just a bit of a shock, that's all.'

'. . . but I'm in England and you're the only person I really know here any more, and I thought, well, I . . .' He tailed off. A hint of static crackled down the line while both of them desperately tried to think of something to say.

Jennifer got there first. 'No, god no, that's absolutely fine.' I sound like a right stuck-up cow, she thought. 'So how are you? What have you been up to?'

'Oh, you know. I left CERN, by the way. Been doing some travelling.'

'Travelling? Where?'

'Just around Europe. Nowhere exotic. What about you? I, er, I expect you're married by now.' Feeling his way.

'Me? Married? You must be joking.'

'How's your father?'

'Oh . . . he died. I should have written I suppose, but I . . . it was a while ago now anyway.'

'That's terrible. I'm sorry.'

'Well, it wasn't your fault, was it? He always drank and smoked too much. It was inevitable, really.'

'You sound very upset.'

'No, I'm fine. Christ, it was years ago now. Just a couple of years after we last saw each other. How long ago was that? Ten years? Fuck, is it really ten years?'

'About that, yes.' The static got louder, the copper wires responding to the tension between them. 'It's a terrible line.'

'What are you doing in England?'

'I'm working on some things and I needed somewhere to stop for a while so I thought why not London? I've been living in Berlin.'

'Berlin! Right. Wow. I've never been to Berlin. So, er, what are you working on?'

'Some computer things. I don't know if you'd find it interesting.'

'In London?'

'Yes, in London.'

'Are you with a university or something?'

'Sure, I mean no, I mean, it's just me really, I work from my room. I have a room, in a hotel. I have my own computer equipment. And with a modem, it's OK.'

'What's a modem?'

'It's a device which converts digital bits into analogue electrical impulses so that they can be transmitted as a frequency-modulated tone, which can then be demodulated by another, similar device.'

'What?'

'Oh, sorry. It allows two computers to communicate down a phone line.'

'Right.'

'Are you still working at your maths?'

'No, I'm sorry, Joel, I gave it up years ago,' she faltered. 'I had to give up school, it's complicated, because when Henry died . . .'

'Yes, of course, I understand . . .' said Joel, a little crestfallen.

'No, no, Joel, you don't, it was more difficult than you can imagine, you see there was, I don't know how to say this, but, well, oh god . . .'

'Yes?'

'. . . well, there was . . . *something else*.' Jennifer flushed hot all over, although she was still wet from her shower and wearing only a towel. Her face prickled. Water ran from her wet hair and dripped on to the telephone book (stolen from W. H. Smith) which lay on the table next to the phone. The globules plashed on to the heavy manilla paper and curdled it into a series of discrete wavy patches. She sniffed and found that her nose had started to run. What was all this, then? From down the line she could hear Joel's silence expressed in the static. 'Joel,' she said in a voice so fluid it threatened to melt the lines which carried it away, 'Joel, could I, do you think I could, I mean could I see you?'

'Yes, of course, please . . . when . . . ?'

'I could come to London. I work during the week, but I could come down on Saturday, and we could meet in the afternoon and spend the evening together.' She had a half-day on Friday and some money in the bank that needed spending. She could get take the coach from Stratford High Street to Victoria and she'd get there before the evening, and she could stay with Shelley, who'd moved to London three years earlier and lived in Finsbury Park. And on Saturday morning she could go shopping, proper shopping, for some new things to wear.

'Yes, perfect.' Saturday, thought Joel, that's three days. Would he have time? Would he be ready? Yes, maybe, yes, he could probably just do it. 'Yes, yes, Saturday is good, there's a place where I sometimes eat. We could meet there, it's open all day. We could meet there at four o'clock. Do you know the Notting Hill Gate? It's there on the corner, it's a modern-looking place, an Italian café, by a pub called the Prince of Wales, we could meet there at four. You can't miss it, it's right on the sharp corner . . .' Jennifer, infected by Joel's excitement, scribbled down directions. She couldn't tell now if she was laughing or crying. So the arrangements were made and they both said goodbye, and it wasn't until she'd put down the phone that she realised Joel hadn't given her either his phone number or the name of his hotel. Down in London Joel lay back on his bed, feeling elated, and it didn't occur to him either.

Oh, well, thought Jennifer, as she ran some more hot water into her bath, sure there wouldn't be a problem. Joel was here. Fuck. Joel was here! She was so happy. The omens and hallucinations hadn't been signifying a message from the past at all. They'd been auguring a message from the future!

Tea with Yosemite Sam

The man's name was Anatole Crimp and he lived in Glengall Road which according to the *A to Z* was in Kilburn. Judd boarded the tube in Russell Square and rode it south, the hot compartments filling with passengers as they were moved from station to station. Soon they passed beneath the West End, and dozens and dozens of people tried to get on and off at every stop. It was total chaos, and while the driver kept telling passengers to please move down inside the carriages, her words blurred almost to incomprehensibility by the static of the Tannoy, Judd couldn't see that there was any place left for them to go. There were people everywhere. A dark-haired young woman stood jammed against his legs, chatting with her friend. The doors were trying to close but somewhere along the train someone was blocking them. They shuddered to and fro like the giant eyelids of a malfunctioning android. Through a gap in the scrum, Judd spotted a station nameplate. Green Park. Wasn't he meant to change here? He struggled to his feet and, muttering 'Excuse me, excuse me', elbowed his way through the crowd, slipping through the doors just before they closed for the final time. Behind him the brunette swung deftly into the vacant seat. On the platform Judd readjusted his clothes and followed the signs for the Jubilee Line. Negotiating the packed tunnels, he began to wish he had taken a cab, but soon enough he was on a train heading north, this time making sure he checked off every station on the way.

Back up at ground level a stiff breeze was blowing, taking with it all the heat from the weak sun. Judd walked against the wind up the High Road to Glengall Road, which turned out to be an unremarkable street opposite a branch of Safeway's. A betting shop, a launderette, an off-licence clustered around its mouth; all three seemed to be constructed entirely out of ageing Formica. The street sign was darkened with streaks of traffic grime and a couple of bicycle tyres had been hooped over one end of it. Broken Lucozade bottles encrusted the cracked paving slabs below. Judd strolled down the road until he reached number 32, then taking a deep breath, he knocked on the door.

There was no reply so he knocked again. The breeze was quickly filling the sky with clouds from the east, which were beginning to form a pall across the afternoon. It looked like rain. Up the street a couple of thick, angular women emerged from the launderette and started down the hill towards him. He could hear their gossiping above the squeak of their shopping trolleys, their Irish accents making him feel for a moment that he was back in New York. He looked up as they passed so as not to stare and in the clouds he saw the face of the girl from the National Gallery. Freaked, he knocked again and when there was still no reply, decided to see if he could work his way around the back of the house.

Further along the street was an entrance to an alleyway that let on to the back gardens. Counting houses as he went, Judd made his way down it, carefully stepping between small piles of broken masonry and discarded pieces of household junk: washing-up bowls with the bottoms kicked out, rusted mangles and top-loading washing-machines, amputated bicycles.

The gate to Crimp's garden was rotten and its hinges gave as he tried it. Lifting it away from the entrance, he slipped past and into the middle of an unbelievable mess. The tumble of oddments that littered the alley-way would have seemed to have had its origin here, except that out there everything had been junk – old or broken items that were out of date and had no obvious further use – whereas in here most of the rubbish looked modern and perfectly serviceable. Caught in the weeds like the stiff carcasses of long-snared animals were a sleek television set, two CD players, a rowing machine, a personal computer, a glass-and-chrome coffee table, a Sinclair C5 electric car, a series of injection-moulded toys, a door from a 1982 Lotus Esprit, a carphone, a video recorder and a microwave oven. All the items were trashed beyond repair; they had obviously just been tossed out (or rolled out, in the case of the C5) and left to the mercy of the elements. But beneath the scratches and dents they looked new. One or two of them still had their price stickers on. They had probably never been used.

Judd picked his way through the junk. He stood on the Lotus door, intending to hop over the TV, but an invisible layer of mildew covered the metal and as soon as he placed his weight on it he slipped. He went arse over tit; as he fell his elbow made contact with the television screen and the vacuum tube instantly imploded with a *whump*. He grabbed at various parts of his body to check that they weren't damaged, and when he looked up he saw the net curtains in one of the downstairs windows twitch and a shadow flit across behind them. Encouraged, he got to his feet and brushed himself down, rubbing with annoyance at a heavy streak of grease marking the thigh of his Kappas. He was just raising his hand to knock on the back door, thinking at the same time that it was a good thing he hadn't worn his ochre jacket, when it snapped open a fraction and something long, hard and black was thrust out towards him, nearly striking him in the face.

It was a shotgun, a side-by-side Spanish sporting model, and a brace of monstrous glints flickered up out of its twin barrels and into Judd's eyes. He began to back off but the gun pursued him, quickly followed by its owner. Judd tried to get a look at whoever it was but his attention had been completely commandeered by the gleaming length of metal.

'Get back further,' the man said. Judd did so, instinctively holding his empty hands out at his sides. 'What do you want?' Judd wanted to tell him, he really did, but in his panic the appropriate network in his brain was refusing to anneal. He ventured a look over the barrels: the man at the other end of them was much shorter than himself and the young American found himself looking down upon a thick domed knead of pink skin settled into a tangle of wiry grey. For his aggressor was completely bald, although this baldness was more than compensated for by the enormous beard that sprouted from his jaw and which hung down to well below his navel. He was stocky, with broad shoulders and large, slightly splayed feet, and was dressed in two pieces of a three-piece pinstripe suit, a collarless white shirt complete with cufflinks and elasticated metal armbands, and lace-up black leather ankleboots which were cracked across the toes. His eyes were quiet and thoughtless. Judd had seen those eyes before across many a craps table (and even, from time to time, in the mirror). They were the self-obsessed eyes of someone who has consciously placed his life in the hands of chance and not looked back; they were the eyes of a narcissistic bore.

Just as Judd realised that the man was capable of killing him without a second thought, he found himself able to speak: 'Scofield sent me out here!'

'Never heard of him.'

'You sure? Scofield. Irving Scofield. South Central LA. You sure?'

'Hell, I know lots of Scofields. Could be any one of them. Could be none of them. Who knows. What's your point?'

But Judd sensed something positive in the man's voice, a hesitancy in his phrasing that had not been there before. 'Scofield! Irving Scofield sent me. I've got a fax for you from him. You must be Anatole Crimp.'

Crimp allowed Judd to take out the paper, then snatched it from him and unfolded it dextrously with one hand, all the time drawing a careful bead on him with the gun. He read it quickly, nodding and muttering to himself as he did so. Once or twice the mutterings liquefied into a brief spurt of laughter. When he turned the fax over to see if anything was written on the back, the little man twisted his wrist and elbow around into a flat 'S' so extreme that Judd could only assume he was double-jointed. Satisfied he had read all there was to read, he lowered the gun and turned back into the house. 'Aha. Hum. Come in then, come,' he said as he disappeared inside. 'You might as well, you're here now. Next time, use the front door like a sane person. Creeping around in the back garden like that! Could get yourself shot!'

Judd followed him in without arguing the toss and found himself in a depressingly sordid room. Not much light made its way through the grime-encrusted windows, but in the fuscous gloom he could make out the essential elements of a kitchen. There was a sink, a huge cube of a thing supported on twin brick pillars, old taps on exposed pipework wobbling above it; there was a cooker, old and yellow, with blackened saucepans piled up high upon its overhead grill; and there was a free-standing dresser, the top of which – along with every other available surface in the room, from the window-sill to the draining board – was cluttered with paint cans, mugs filled with mould, tins of food with faded labels, kitchen forks green with oxidisation, matchboxes, corks, drawing-pins, flowerpots, fungus and dead plants that had long ago given up the struggle. No attempt had been made to integrate the various items of culinary furniture into some kind of harmonious whole. There were some wall cabinets, but they stood on their ends on the floor and the markings and gouges in the plaster above them testified to the fact that they had been ripped rather hastily from their moorings. Most bizarrely of all, a brand-new dishwasher stood in the centre of the room, the tangle of umbilical tubes behind it tied into a giant knot, the water pipes to which it had once been connected crudely clinched off and bunged with plumber's putty.

Crimp's mood had undergone something of a transformation and he was now charging around the room enthusiastically, his beard tucked under one arm. 'You'll want some tea, I expect,' he kept repeating, mostly to himself, 'I'd better make some tea. Do you want some tea? I'll make you some tea.' From the murky water that filled the sink – 'damn thing's blocked, can't seem to fix it' – he fished another blackened saucepan which he ran beneath the tap briefly by way of rinsing, then filled with water and plonked down upon the stove. 'So how's old Scofield, then, eh, eh? How is he? Haven't seen him for years. Those were the days, ha ha, Atlantic City, goodness me, I'd all but forgotten, ha ha.' His manic chuckle bubbled up out of him like the gases from a pool of hot mud, closer to a belch than a laugh. His voice sounded like a child swinging on a creaking door. Judd tried to reply, not that he had much to offer in the way of information, but every time he opened his mouth he barely got more than a couple of words out before Crimp was off again: 'Ah, I'll make you some tea, ha ha, and then we can talk.' The old man's cold eyes shone like spheres of ice in the twilight of the kitchen and lent a distinctly demonic edge to his already weird chuckle.

Try as he might, Judd couldn't reconcile the strange figure before him with Scofield's description of a debonair gambler who'd once lived in the south of France in a richly furnished villa. He'd obviously got the wrong end of the stick. Scofield did say he hadn't seen Crimp for ten years . . . Judd began to feel claustrophobic and more than a little fearful that he'd been sent on a wild-goose chase. The prospect of a cup of tea was doing little to comfort him: Crimp had dropped several cobwebby teabags into his pan, followed by several spoonfuls of coagulated demerara sugar from a great jar which also contained two dead wasps, and now he added the contents of a small tin of condensed milk he had punctured open with a chisel retrieved from among the debris on the window-sill. As the evil-looking brew came to the boil he opened the dishwasher and removed two mugs. To Judd's surprise they were of a delicate, fine china decorated with an elongated checkerboard of hatched burgundy glaze, and clean to boot.

'Kodziez,' said Crimp, seeing Judd peering. 'Very fine, don't you think? Shame you can't say the same about this heap of junk,' he continued, indicating the dishwasher. 'Maybe you could help me get it out into the garden or something. Cluttering up the kitchen like this, useless thing. It upsets everything.' And he kicked it, before taking the pretty mugs across to the antediluvian stove. Judd remembered that Scofield had mentioned something about designer furniture – were those mugs all that was left?

They were not, as he was to discover when his host ushered him into the adjoining room which, though not large, seemed like a great and glorious atrium after the dungeon of the kitchen. 'We have to go in here,' he crackled mysteriously, 'I can't get on with anything in there, not till that dishwasher's gone.' The room was filled with the kind of chic sixties items that reminded Judd of shows like *The Prisoner*. Along two of the walls stood matching walnut side cabinets, angular, modernist pieces each over six feet long and perched on tubular metal supports, and in one corner of the room was a white fibreglass sphere with a television screen in it. Seating consisted of an egg chair, with brown leather upholstery and aluminium pedestal, and three pieces of a modular sofa each in a different tone of green with a matching occasional table in olive plastic. It would have been cool if the place weren't so trashed – books, papers, magazines and shoe boxes overflowing with all sorts of junk covered the floor and were stacked up in precarious piles that ran up the walls like stalagmites; the furniture was tattered and worn, and a thick layer of London grime lay over everything; ashtrays and plates full of half-eaten meals were dotted around like traps. Even the television housing had turned a nicotine yellow. Trying to ignore the mess and the unpleasant smell, Judd picked up a wooden object that looked like a three-dimensional puzzle game.

'That's a Brian Wilshire original,' said Crimp proudly.

'Uh, yeah, of course,' said Judd, facetiously concealing his ignorance. He pointed to a painting that hung on the wall, at the centre of a display of black-and-white framed photographs. 'And I suppose that's a Dali.'

'Yes, ha ha, an original, absolutely. I met him in Monaco at an exhibition opening. Fantastic, isn't it?' Crimp cleared some books from the seat of the egg chair and motioned to Judd to sit down, which he did, his feet jammed between a magazine rack stuffed full of mouldering copies of *Picture Post* and an elephant's foot umbrella rack filled with Real Tennis balls, then unfolded a collapsible card table, placed the cups of 'tea' on it and drew up a chair for himself. The two men now faced each other,

Judd wondering how he could remove the teabag floating forlornly in his drink without appearing rude.

Crimp looked serious again and Judd felt intimidated. He kept thinking that he had another appointment, that he would have to make his excuses and leave. Why had he come? Who was this man? What was he expecting to find?

'So, er, how do you know Irving Scofield?' Judd said eventually.

'Tell me about yourself,' came the reply.

Judd was understandably fazed. 'Oh, er, well what's to tell, ha ha?' Crimp's chuckle seemed to be infectious.

'Well, how about your name.'

'Haven't I told you already? I'm sorry. I'm Judd, Judd Axelrod. What else do you want to know?'

'What do I *want* to know? What, my boy, do I *need* to know. You tell me.'

'I came here because I thought you could help me.'

'With what?'

'With my game.'

'Ah *ha*! So you are having problems with your game. Ha ha. And what is your game?'

'I play everything, but mainly craps.' Crimp said nothing so Judd decided to go ahead and elaborate. 'I know the game, I know the dice. I . . . I don't know how to explain it, but I know their shape somehow. I can see which way they're going to move. I'm not talking about runs of luck. That's part of it. But it's more than that. I can predict them most of the time. And then a month ago it started slipping away, like I couldn't see it any more. Something was different, I don't know. It was like I knew it all too well and so it all changed, became something else.' He was searching for the words but none of the ones he could find seemed equal to what he was trying to say. 'You don't think I'm making any sense,' he said, instantly regretting it for no particular reason.

'I see. So you used this, ha ha, technique and you were winning?'

'Oh, yeah. I was way up. I haven't worked for a few years now. I've done all right. I had to leave LA because I got too good. I was playing in the illegal clubs, and word got around and they all barred me. Lost a couple of teeth over that one. So I went to Reno. I'd been there a while, was doing OK, but then it all got weird. See, I'd been slowing everything down, I don't know if that makes any kind of sense, but when I was winning it was like I was real cool, real slow, and because everything around me was faster I could see what it was going to do, like I was in a separate stream of time. But then, then the ground started to shift under me, I didn't know what was happening, everything seized up or changed around, and I couldn't . . . couldn't get a handle on it any more.'

'And that's when you went to see Irving.'

'Well, I called him, yeah.'

'And he told you to come and see me.'

'Yeah.'

'That's very trusting of you.'

'I've known him for years. And what else could I do?'

'You could have tried leaving Reno and playing somewhere else.'

'I guess, but . . .'

'Don't you think it was rather cowardly not to do that?' Judd was instantly defensive. Crimp clearly didn't get it. He wasn't into gambling for money or power. It had only ever been a way to reclaim his own character. But how was he to explain that to the old man? And anyway, he hadn't come here for more psychoanalysis. The most important thing was to find out what had gone wrong, get practical solutions.

He made up an answer. 'Look, I knew, OK. I knew it was fucking up. I was losing money fast. Maybe I couldn't afford to risk a stake in another town. It takes a while you know, you can't just bust in there.'

'Ha ha ha! It takes a while. Yes, it takes a while. That's right. Exactly.'

'Yeah. Yeah, it takes a while.' Judd was getting angry – he was being mocked. But he couldn't admit how frightened he was, how desperate he was for guidance, not even to himself. A single hoverfly flew silently above their heads, its trajectory a succession of straight lines and acutely angled corners. It changed direction as effortlessly and abruptly as a sprite on a computer screen, its path apparently both predetermined and perfectly random. Crimp wrinkled his nose and sneezed loudly into his tea, splashing it up over the edge of the cup and on to the table. The fly cornered three or four times in quick succession, went into a quick corkscrew dive, recovered and continued much as before.

From somewhere beneath his beard the old man had produced two dice and was rolling them over and over. 'Well, then. What does that tell you?'

'I don't know. What does it tell me?'

'I can't help you if you won't think for yourself.'

Judd felt like he was back at school. Or – which was worse – back with Schemata. 'I'm not so sure you can help me anyway.' He pouted.

'Ha ha. Give me two numbers.'

'What?'

'Come on, come on, I haven't got all day. I've got better things to do, you know. Two numbers.'

'Twenty-four and thirty-seven.'

'Oh, god help us.' He held up the dice. 'Each between one and six if you please.'

'Double six.' Crimp looked tired. He cupped his little hands together and shook the dice inside them, then dropped them on to the table. Judd noticed for the first time what extraordinarily long fingers the man had. The dice came to rest and each showed a six.

'Gee, loaded dice,' Judd said sarcastically. 'I haven't seen them before.'

'Two more numbers then.'

'Two and four.' Crimp rolled the dice and a two and a four came up.

'Two and five.' Again, Crimp rolled them to order.

'Double three.' And again.

'Use mine.' Judd took out the bone dice which Scofield had given him and passed them across the table, their bright shapes stark against the light tan surfaces and deep purple lines of his palm.

Crimp threw a couple of sequences to order and then, to show off, produced a shaker and did the same again. Then he passed them back to Judd. 'Now you roll. Go on. Roll them. Roll me a three and a two.' Judd tried to fix Crimp in the eye, something that he was suddenly finding rather difficult. He took the dice and rolled. A two and a three. 'As you see, the question is not whether I can teach you anything, but whether I should bother.'

Judd felt cold, as if his spinal fluid had been turned to Freon. It looked like Scofield had been right – this guy was the real thing. 'But I need your help,' he protested, his flippancy gone. 'You must help me. I'm stuck.'

'Do you think I had any help? Old Irving certainly wasn't much use, pissing off at the first sign of trouble. I've already given you more than anybody gave me by letting you come in here. There's nothing more I can give you.'

'But you've just shown me . . .'

'You want me to teach you tricks? I'm disappointed. You come all this way and then you want tricks. The fact that you are here should be enough. Look around. Why do you think I choose to live like this, instead of in some palace? Why do you think I stay in this place, so wrapped up in myself that I can't get a single machine to work? No mod cons – nothing after 1967, at least. The boiler's twenty years old, thank Christ, but when that packs up, god knows what I'll do. One or two nights a week in a casino is all I'd need to escape, ha ha, followed by a short stint on the stock exchange. I used to have a beautiful home in Monte Carlo, you know, cliff-top, secluded. Beautiful. But then it all stopped. Just like you, I couldn't do it any more. I'd become too full of myself, too self-assured. I'd let my desires run away from me. I wanted to make it my servant. "I can really use this," I thought, "I can really do something here."

'It took a month. That's all. One month to lose the villa, have my bank account closed, work up debts that I couldn't repay. I had to ship out, come here, bring what I could with me, so that I could try and recapture something of what I had before it went wrong. And that's when I started to learn, to fathom really how special it was. That's when I discovered how fascinating it was, too, how wonderful, just for its own sake. For me, now, it is everything. And I had it all.' Crimp gave Judd his iciest stare and Judd glanced away.

'Yes, but . . .' he began, but the man was into his stride and was not to be stopped.

'You have to understand that there are two types of control. You've got this far because you were prepared to start off from within the system itself. Don't ask me why, because I don't know. There's not many who can do it, but there's a few. But you haven't perceived what that means, have you now? Which is that to succeed you must relinquish all hope of ever having the other type of control, control from the outside, that kind of control which is achieved by trying to define the system instead of letting it define you. Now it seems to me that you, my boy, have tried to cross over and look where it's got you. You wanted something from it, like I did once. You tried to fuck with it and now it's fucking with you.'

'But I didn't have any choice!' Judd blurted, able to speak at last. 'It might have been about money for you, old man, but in my case it was just about me! You can't understand! You haven't been through what I've been through! You're not listening to me. You're just telling me about your own experiences!'

But with Crimp this was the wrong tack to take. 'Don't yell at me, you little bastard,' he hissed, his avuncular mood immediately swamped by anger. 'I'm trying to help. I'm telling you, if you want it back then look around you, see how it works. You saw what I did with the dice, but I can only manage that by understanding limits and enforcing limits. Simply by being here you're upsetting the balance already. Can't you feel it? It's a trade-off.'

'I told you I don't care about any of that. All I want is to be free from all the shit that's been piled on me. To be my own person.' Even as he said the words, Judd knew they were wrong, that they'd be misunderstood, that Crimp would take them for weakness.

'Ha! Free? Free? You've got this far and you still think freedom's an option? How dumb can you get? I told you already, you try get outside the system and the system will fuck with you. You've got to make do with what you've got. And quite frankly, young man, what you've got is quite a lot.'

'How the fuck would you know what I've got?' Judd almost screamed. 'Why are you judging me? I came here for help!'

'And I have given it to you. Maybe what you experienced in Reno is the end, my friend, not the beginning. Everything I have to teach you is in front of you. Wrap yourself in surfaces, wear nothing but a cloak. You are like the bull, fascinated by the play of the cape but only because you are convinced there is something behind it. But you have to love it for its own sake. Cut it to fit where you can and where you can't ignore it. There is nothing behind it but the unnameable air! It is the surface which is intense, which provides all the meaning. Look beyond it, think of it as infinite, you lose it all. You are American, you should understand that! Why do you keep asking for something more?' But the old man's words fell on deaf ears.

'Look, you, you . . . I found something! *I* found it. I found an alternative, I found something that let me know who I was! And I want it back, that's all. Why can't I have that? Aren't I entitled to my own self, for chrissake?' Judd was beside himself, nearly in tears, the years of frustration pumping the membrane of his cortex as though it were the bass bin of a loudspeaker. 'Maybe you can't grasp that, maybe you can't, but I found it and it's gone, and I need your help to get it back!'

Crimp let out a huge, scornful squawk of a laugh. 'What did they do to you to make you so stupid? You've got to give it up, my boy. You've got to forget about it before it's too late. Go on, get out. I won't be insulted in my own home. Go back to America! Take your little problems back there, where they belong!' And he leapt up, pulled Judd from his chair and started to shove him towards the kitchen door, knocking the card table flying in the process. Tea shot across one wall and ran in muddy rivulets down the Salvador Dali. The old man was strong and Judd was in the kitchen before he knew it. Crimp rushed back into the living-room, grabbed his gun and returned immediately shouting, 'Get out of my house, get out, get out!' and looking for all the world like

Yosemite Sam. Judd scrambled for the back door and wrenched it open, but as he ran out the pocket of his Kappas caught on the handle. Seeing him stop the old man let off a shot at the kitchen ceiling. Enveloped in a cloud of plaster dust Judd ripped his pants free, staggered backwards into the garden, tripped over the dead television, put a foot down on the slippery car door, skidded, fell and cracked his head on the computer terminal. The next thing he knew was nothing: he was out cold.

14

Conspicuous consumption

That Saturday morning the coach had brought Jennifer into London, dropped her at Victoria. She took the tube up to Finsbury Park, to Shelley's house, then the two women headed into town. They trawled the boutiques in Covent Garden, Shelley warning Jennifer not to steal anything and Jenn laughing and flapping her cheque-book, saying that she'd given up all of that. Anyway, today was special and she didn't want to spoil it.

Shelley found a jacket she liked and bought it, and Jenn bought some trousers and a skirt. Still, she really wanted some shoes, you couldn't get decent shoes anywhere in the Midlands, and Shelley suggested Harvey Nichols – if they couldn't find anything there, they could always go down the King's Road.

So they got on the tube, which was rammed, went the few stops to Knightsbridge, Jenn swinging into a seat vacated by some black geezer who got off at Green Park. The shoes at Harvey Nichols were too expensive but Jenn picked up some new stockings to match her skirt and got changed in one of the fitting rooms. They had lunch in the coffee shop and walked down to Sloane Square, chatting all the way. Somewhere along the King's Road Jenn found the shoes she wanted, and a blouse, too, and a new belt. Then it was time to go and meet Joel. She gave her shopping bags to Shelley, kissed her on the cheek and rushed off back to the tube, trembling a little with anticipation.

Electric café (001)

In the days leading up to the rendezvous Joel hurried to complete his preparations. He finished measuring his body and fed the results into his machine, constructing special databases that could be accessed by the golem as it took shape. So that the thing would have maximum freedom to roam he wanted to make sure it could route itself through as many networks as possible. He hacked into JANET and the telecom computers and satellite base stations, and gave himself priority clearance.

He was rushing the whole time, his nerves shot to pieces. He wanted Saturday to come at once, just to lie on his bed and wallow in the fact that he was nearing his goal. The work was simultaneously a pressure and a release, and he kept at it as an addict keeps at his drug. On the Friday he paid a quick visit to the Victoria without the shoe computer, just to see if he could still predict the bets. He could, it was fine, though before he left he had a somewhat freaky experience. As he was cashing in his chips he caught sight of someone he thought he recognised sitting at one of the blackjack tables. Cautiously, in order to see better, he moved across to the bar and ordered a drink, carefully watching the man all the time. He was in a terrible state – his eyes were wild, his grey hair a mess, his suit crumpled – and it was clear that he was losing hand over fist. Joel asked the barman if he'd seen the gambler before. Yes, indeed, he came down at least two or three times a week, though probably not for much longer – lately, he'd been on a bad streak that didn't want to let up. Joel smiled quietly to himself and finished his tomato juice. As he left he strode past the blackjack table and stole a closer look. There could be no doubt about it: it was most definitely Professor Metric.

So that's what had become of him, the old fool! He'd always been sure his philosophy had been superior to that of his mentor and now here was the proof! His ego thus reinforced, Joel left his old tutor to his moral decline, hurried back to his hotel and worked on his machine through the night. By lunch-time the following day he was finished. He looked round the room with a sense of pride, glorying in his accomplishment. Everything was ready. The walls were covered with his writings rather as photographs had once covered the walls of his room at CERN and he'd placed candles everywhere, and even, on the mantelpiece, some incense. The glyphs and magic words that he needed for the spell were printed out and placed ready on a chair. He tested the manacles he'd attached to each of the bed posts in case Jennifer didn't agree to go along with the plan and as an afterthought he made the bed and slipped a gag underneath the pillow. He ran a last check on the two video cameras he'd placed on tripods on either side of the room, making doubly sure that they could operate satisfactorily in the half-light and that the image-processing software was working correctly. But the focus of it all were his computers, which slumbered across the makeshift table, pregnant with data. As a final touch he took a sheet from the wardrobe and threw it over the humming machines. Yes, he was ready.

Naturally, he arrived at the café early. He sat there trying to read a book on advanced networking but was unable to keep his eyes on the page for more than a couple of minutes at a stretch. By the time four o'clock came round he knew every inch of the street outside. But four became four-thirty became five and his euphoria receded, leaving a mudflat of doubt and paranoia in its wake. He felt as if someone were jabbing hot needles, the long beaks of wader birds, into every pore of his body. The black man sitting facing him at the next table unnerved him. The stranger had been here almost as long as he had and, apart from taking occasional sips of his beer or moving his eyes, had remained almost totally motionless throughout. He found the man frightening, mysterious. As the racist circuits implanted in his brain as a child began sparking with life he became convinced that the stranger was watching him.

But watched or not, he couldn't sit here waiting for much longer. It was making him crazy. How many times he checked his watch or ran out into the street or read and reread the menu or played with the sugar he didn't know, but eventually he could stand it no longer and, convinced that Jennifer had either lied to him or forgotten about him, he gave up. Livid, he headed back to his hotel, coursing between the summer drinkers who had spilled out of their pubs and on to the pavements, his tall form slicing along like the prow of some sleek yacht. As he went he shot his gaze to starboard and port like cannon, still searching for Jennifer, still sure she'd look just like the woman in his dream.

Electric café (010)

Jennifer had taken a clockwise Circle Line train from Sloane Square, but just beyond Gloucester Road it came to a halt. Immediately she began to worry and when a fractured voice came over the Tannoy announcing a security alert she began to worry even more. She was already running late and she sat in the carriage silently urging the train northwards. Five minutes went by, then ten, and she became so racked with tension that every limb felt spavined. But still the train did not move. Ever since Joel had phoned their meeting had obsessed her and now, telling him about the child which had almost certainly been his seemed the most important thing in the world. The promise of this imminent event had brought a new light to bear upon her life and thrown her loneliness and aimlessness into sharp relief. For the first time in over a decade she really felt that focus and meaning – absent from her life since Henry had died and she'd discovered her pregnancy – were about to return. In her mind she glamorised Joel, imagining him older and wiser, and using the fact of his 'travels' to extrapolate from the nerdy, depressive loner she had known in Geneva a much sexier figure. On one particularly excessive and recurrent flight of fancy – which she repeatedly tried to excise from her thoughts – she envisioned him arriving in a limousine, sweeping her off her feet and showering her with luxuries. But whichever simulation of events she ran through in her head they all shared a common theme – that one way or another Joel would cushion her against the pain and loss she felt more keenly now than she could ever remember.

A hundred and one miles away, in a Warwickshire hospital, Emma rolled around on her bed in torment. She had this thought, it was so nearly there . . . on the tip of her tongue as it were . . . but it would not quite coalesce. And until it did, she didn't know what it would be. It was like having an itch in an amputated limb. She was playing this game, a strange game, which brought on a strange feeling, like trying to force the southern poles of three magnets together. She'd had them all in her mind for months now, had been loitering in their dreams like a concupiscent ghoul. The My had grown powerful, it had kept them in its sights, wanting them for itself. But now, when everything was ready, one of them wouldn't flow down its channel. There was a blockage somewhere.

Smoke and Squeak probed and explored, but neither could find what was wrong.

As the minutes ticked away even the most prosaic of Jennifer's fantasies slipped gradually beyond her grasp. Why hadn't she taken the bus, as Shelley had suggested? She sat and shivered with apprehension in the company of the other passengers, all of whom were beginning to oscillate with their own particular frustrations until, like the molecules in a melting crystal, they began to break free of the structures which bound them to the events of the everyday and to communicate with one another.

That said, it was hardly a social revolution. Most of the words exchanged expressed anger and annoyance, although two members of a circus troupe who happened to be aboard did start doing the splits along the ceiling, to the great delight of several children who had been complaining loudly up until that point. The overheated adults all clapped until their kids, encouraged by the display, became over-excited and started to run riot inside the carriage. Then someone tried to smoke a cigarette and was nearly lynched; would have been, if there'd been anything high enough to string him up from.

Meanwhile, above ground in Notting Hill Gate, Joel sat in the window of his café looking forlornly out at the slowly lengthening afternoon shadows, reading the menu over and over, beginning to jitter from all the coffee he'd drunk.

It was an hour and a half before the train began to move, by which time Jennifer was in tears. When it finally drew in to Notting Hill Gate she charged up the stairs as fast as she could, shoved her way through the ticket barrier and skirted around the shoppers congealed on the street corner outside, wiping her face as she ran. But when she reached the café it was empty except for a very un-Jewish looking yuppie who was munching on a ham and cheese croissant, a black guy sitting staring out of the window and four old women at a table drinking tea.

She went up to the barman. 'I was looking for a friend of mine. He's meeting me here.'

'We have many men in here,' said the barman, who wasn't impressed by her question. 'What does he look like?'

Jennifer opened her mouth to describe Joel, but realised that she couldn't really remember. 'Oh, I don't know. He's tall, I suppose, and he wears glasses. And has a big nose . . .'

'I don' know. There were some men here before, maybe one of them is your friend. But I don' know. Why don' you have a cup of coffee and see if he come back?'

Electric café (011)

Judd had lain there for hours, his consciousness whipping to and fro like a curl of spume on the unfolding surge of that fungal bloom called space-time, a light summer rain tapping with the sweetness of foreign fingers on the tarpaulin that Crimp, in a brief fit of sympathy, had thrown across his prone form. But now the sky was clear and the sun was getting lower – England was revolving away from the day. He rolled his eyelids back and looked around. The garden with its heaps of consumer items was like a vast cladogenic graveyard that seemed to stretch into the distance for ever. Sliding out from beneath the waxed canvas, he had to battle for a minute in order to try and restore harmony in the face of constant shifts of perspective. Getting upright was difficult; he felt sluggish, his joints ached and his feet were painfully heavy, so he inched his way forward through the viable junk on his knees, only getting to his feet when he reached the broken door at the end of the garden. But his mind was reeling and when he finally made it out of the alleyway and on to Glengall Road he turned left by mistake.

The summer moon was in the sky, ball of rock, dove grey against the blue. He looked up at it and far below the threshold of his vision Sputnik II drifted across the pale disc. Inside, Laika was busy tuning her equipment to the BBC and trying to work out why she had such a sudden interest in London. Judd felt like a planet, trapped for aeons in the interlocking self-organisations of gravity. Fear, fear of forever, rippled through him. He wandered south down Tennyson Road, past two kids playing on their bikes.

He passed the entrance to a cemetery and got freaked when, looking in through the gate, he saw the stones shiver and turn. He shuddered and rubbed his eyes, and tried to increase his pace, but his legs had found their rhythm and were adamant. Continuing south, he crossed the railway lines via the bridge at Queen's Park with the inevitability of a grain of sand finding its way through the narrow neck of an hourglass, then tumbled down through the residential back streets of West Kilburn and rolled out on the Great Western Road, passing underneath the Westway as the traffic thundered high above him, the cars tracing out a million paths from east to west, from west to east, the roar of their engines exploding off the tops of the buildings that peeked above the parapets like so many broken spires.

He trudged through the council estates, turned into Chepstow Road and followed it down through Pembridge Villas, hardly noticing as the houses became progressively grander and set further back from the road, and the black folk transmuted into white. He became aware of the slap slap of his shoes against the speckled paving slabs. His mouth was parched. He looked at his watch but it had stopped at half past eleven, which was when he'd arrived at Crimp's. He must have broken it when he'd fallen that first time. He took it off and slung it into a skip.

The road curved round and he passed clothing stores and a second-hand record shop, then came out on a staggered junction that let on to the lights and litter of Notting Hill Gate. There was a small crowd of people waiting for a bus; he asked two girls if there was an Underground station nearby. They giggled at his accent and gave him directions, and he thanked them and walked away. Behind him the bus pulled up, a green CitySlicker, and beneath the moaning of the brakes he thought he heard the name 'Denzel Washington'. He glanced back and sure enough the two girls blushed and lowered their eyes, before quickly climbing on board. Judd bit his lip in exasperation and studied his reflection in the dark window of a café. It was true, he did resemble the film star. Even his looks weren't his own any longer.

The café took up the whole of the acutely angled street corner in a way that reminded him of San Francisco. He needed to drink and he needed to think, so he went inside and sat in the window across from a tall man with lank, unkempt hair, thick spectacles and an enormous nose, which he kept tugging at nervously. Judd ordered a beer and watched the coloured reflections from the traffic and pedestrians play across the curved glass, though from time to time he shifted his gaze to the stranger who, although nominally reading the enormous textbook that lay open on the table in front of him, was clearly having difficulty concentrating. He kept scanning the tables as if looking for someone, and on several occasions got up and rushed out into the street, only to return a few seconds later and sit down again. Eventually he paid his bill and left the café for good.

Judd felt trapped, lost, stuck. All the time he had thought the gambling would be a way out, but in the end it had led him to Crimp, and Crimp had been just like all of the others: Jennifer, his parents, Schemata – they'd none of them been interested in him, only in imposing themselves upon him. The weight of them on his back was already immense, but now Crimp had been added to the pile and with him came all of those sediments that Judd had encouraged to build up inside him in his attempt to block the channels that Schemata had cut. He felt as if he was being buried alive. He was suffocating. He was barely able to breathe. The pressure upon him was so great that he could feel it compressing the blood in his veins, squeezing out the water and leaving the task of delivering oxygen throughout his body to cascades of dusty minerals. What was he to do? He wanted to be angry but he didn't have the energy.

His lungs felt flat and leaden, and his heart laboured. His vision seemed to stretch out a little and all the objects around him seemed further away than they were. His limbs felt elongated, too, and numb and unwieldly, and there was a metallic taste in his mouth. It took him a moment or two to place the sensation and then he remembered – it was one he'd often had as a boy, lying in bed and waiting to fall asleep. For a moment he felt that the child that he'd been and that he'd lost was calling to him, trying to tell him something, and he chased the sensation down. But it dissipated as soon as he focused his consciousness on it, slipping away between the fissures of his mind like a family of geckos, a puddle of mercury.

He wanted to cry but his eyes were dry as dust. What could he do now? There seemed only two possibilities: return to the States and ask Scofield for help one more time; or try to go all the way back to the beginning by finding Jennifer and confronting her. But the first was unbearable and the second insane. And both involved him throwing himself on another person's mercy. Why? Why was this the only way he seemed able to do things? Couldn't he manage to do anything for himself? What was wrong with him?

While he fulminated, someone else entered the café – the young woman with dark-brown hair who had taken his seat in the tube train earlier that day. Judd didn't see her sit down, didn't even hear her question the waiter. She took the seat right behind him and she'd been there about ten minutes when another green bus flashed past the window and caught his attention – something had seemed to run by, a dart of beryl, jasper . . . it was her, it was the stony-faced girl in the green overcoat. He had forgotten all about her. She stopped and stood there right in front of him, her finger in her mouth, and his arms remembered the pain of the night before last. Suddenly he made the connection between her and his dreams of the statue. He had to talk to her! Instantly energised, he leapt up, ready to run outside, but at that moment the waiter arrived with the dark-haired woman's coffee and Judd caught the tray with his shoulder and the cup was knocked to the floor. A detonation, shockwave of black liquid and shrapnel, impact zone the legs of the waiter and woman. Everyone looks round.

'Oh, Christ, excuse me, I'm sorry, I didn't see, excuse me . . .' Judd panics, half his mind on the minor disaster in hand, the other half on the figure outside and the idea that she might be the key to it all. Waiter puts down his tray and goes to bar for a rag, throws it down on the floor, picks up ceramic shards with his fingers. Judd grabs napkins, dabs at sodden legs of woman. Woman pleads: 'No, it's OK, really, thank you,' takes the napkins from him. Four eyes meet for a moment full of clouds, there's something here, there's a mystery here, Judd can't clear his mind, the eyes, the young woman, the girl in the street. He breaks the gaze, sprints outside – but she is gone. Barman comes with mop and broom, debris swept away. Judd returns and sits back down, apologising one last time. Young woman says it's nothing, turns away, dabs at her new stockings with a cloth.

The waiter brings her another coffee which she quickly drinks. Judd can't think – this girl, what where why which? The dark-haired young woman pays and leaves. Judd sits and ponders, sipping at his beer. Through the window he watches her walk down the road. And then, aha! He has it now. Yesterday, the tube, Green Park, that's where he saw her. Coincidence. Dismissed.

He has to make a decision, he has to *think*. Without thinking, he picks up the dispenser of table salt and pours some into his beer, stirs it with his knife, starts to drink. Minutes, hours, pass while he sips at it. The logic he'd used to battle Schemata has a hold of him now. His brain starts to dessicate. He begins to dry out.

He is still there at closing time.

The world has ideas of its own

Emma had failed. The world had ideas of its own and they were bigger than her, stronger. The surface had been too complex, the forces at play too intricate. She would revert to the original plan and try for the Mummy alone.

Red Adam

By the time he reached his room all the undischarged energy Joel had built up during three days of cathexis had curdled into anger. He fell to his knees and began to pummel at the floor with his fists, bruising and grazing his knuckles against the hard artificial fibres of the carpet. Then he started to cry, to kick the bed, to cry again, to attack a stack of cardboard boxes he had piled in the corner of the room. He collapsed among their broken forms and lay there, sobbing. But once he had dissipated some of the tension his composure returned and it occurred to him that, during their telephone call, he hadn't told Jennifer where he was staying. If there was a problem she'd have no way of contacting him. What a fool he was! Any number of things could have gone wrong! Sniffing his sinuses free of mucus and controlling his breathing he picked up the phone and called her. At the sound of her voice he began to speak, blurting out a few words of apology, until he noticed that he was talking to her answerphone. He left his address and number, smashed the handset against the bed post until he realised that he really didn't want to break it. Then he lay down on the bed. He was hungry but could not stomach the idea of food. Jennifer's failure to appear gnawed away at him. He drew the curtains, hoping that he would be able to apply the darkness to his mind like a salve. But it didn't work and doubt continued to erode away all the confidence he had built up over the previous few days, leaving him in torment, his soul a wind-ripped valley of dust and toothy ruins.

He closed his eyes and on the inside of his eyelids began to see rushing tunnels and spirals as the random firing in his visual cortex self-organised into Turing patterns. After a while the images slowed and morphed into a cloudy landscape in which everything was tinged with the same orange glow. Then maybe he was asleep and maybe he wasn't, but more colours seeped in, shapes became more defined and he was in an empty railway carriage, that of his journey up from Portsmouth, sitting opposite the double-hearted doll.

The doll was no longer passive and inert as she had been before. She stood on the seat on tiptoe, looking out of the window, the line of her legs and buttocks simultaneously childlike and imbued with a powerful sexuality. Joel sat in his seat sweating, as she turned towards him and dropped her pink hand to the smooth plastic of her crotch and began to simulate masturbation. Through the transparent casing of her chest he could see her hearts beating faster and faster as she rubbed her crabbed fingers back and forth. Then she stopped and hopped up on the table and began to dance a slow and erotic cachucha. Joel became aroused and his engorged penis rose up above the edge of the melamine table and bobbed with pulsing blood as if it wanted to partner the doll, make the cachucha a fandango. Then she stopped, tottered forward on her hard plastic feet (her womanly grace all disappeared), bent over at the waist and with her tiny painted lips planted a kiss on the very tip of Joel's exaggerated prick.

Joel opened his eyes and looked around, dizzy and disoriented. He felt a vague panic, as if he had slept for hours, but when he checked his watch he discovered he'd only dozed off for about five minutes. Inside his trousers his penis throbbed painfully. He looked across the room at the computer equipment under its sheet and noticed for the first time that the shape made by the various components resembled that of a female cadaver stretched out on a mortuary slab, legs spread conveniently wide. The hardware was all still switched on and beneath the sheet fans whirred and LEDs blinked their silent codes, these pinprick signatures diffused by the cloth into eerie patches of electronic blood. The robot corpse had the afterglow of life about it, as if it had been freshly killed and its vital systems were only now shutting down and beginning the short, quick road to decay.

He found himself drawn to the uncanny form. Still lying on the bed he undid his belt and flies, and slipped off his trousers. Then he rolled on to the floor and crept across the carpet on all fours, moving towards the table like some lathered beast in rut, his penis hanging stiff and low. Carefully, not sure that it would support his weight, he slid up on to the table and arranged his limbs around the appropriate affordances. With his body correctly distributed he clasped the bony form and began to move slowly in and out of the rough cleft created by the genital locus of processor, port and bus. The structure cradled him lovingly and creaked and whirred beneath him, and as he moved faster, broke into a sweat, the collection of objects seemed no longer a corpse but a coherent, living being. His neck began to ache and he dipped his forehead to the corner of the terminal which from beneath the folds of the sheet mimicked the shape of a head. He suckled at the eject buttons of a twin floppy drive as if they were nipples. The whole table began to shudder as his rhythms became more frenetic and the equipment rattled away beneath him, its agitated components emitting a grinding collective moan. Finally he came and in the spasm of ejaculation damaged a chip with the heel of his right hand. Suffusing through the sheet, his jissom dripped through on to the circuit board that had been serving as part of the vaginal wall. On the moment of contact electrons danced and leapt across it, gleefully inventing new connections through the cum. Somewhere in the system a modem silently began dialling numbers. It wasn't too long before it made a successful connection and started to upload the files full of Joel's personal statistics from the various disk drives linked into the system.

Joel's elation quickly soured to self-disgust and he disentangled himself from the equipment. His flesh felt hot and he buzzed all over. He cleaned himself and dressed, and as he did the imprints that the hard edges of the machinery had made upon his palms, chest, genitals and thighs began to fade. The room felt tight and claustrophobic and he went out into the street, intending to head towards the Edgware Road and the Victoria, perhaps to gamble, perhaps to think.

Contact

Since Laika had been launched into space the infosphere had expanded to such an extent that she was almost continually busy with something to watch, something to absorb. There did not seem to be a single patch of the upper atmosphere left undisturbed by a radio transmission, television broadcast, or mobile phone call. She passed another satellite at least every couple of hours, could see them glinting from her porthole, great blue and silver mobiles turning slowly in the void like prehistoric insects suspended in some great amber cosmos.

As a result of nearly three decades spent surfing this material, she was familiar with dozens of languages and almost every facet of human life. From Latin-American soap operas to Scandinavian cartoons, from American political propaganda to documentaries on the plight of steelworkers in Siberia, from news reports on famines and air crashes to rock concerts, murders, chat shows, she'd seen them all. She had cooed at male seahorses giving birth, panted at women with surgically enhanced bodies having sex, gasped at men landing on the moon, cried at television personalities dying in helicopter crashes. She had listened to the musics of the world: Tatar folk, European classical, Southern Gospel, Andean pipe, Chechnian balalaika, British electro-pop, Northern Soul, English Punk, American Funk, Welsh choral, Indian raga, Cuban rumba, French Pop, international Rock. She'd heard the sounds of the Aurora Borealis and the sounds of the sun. She had seen a hundred thousand movies and heard a million DJ links. And she'd watched it all without any sense of what was better and what was worse, what was global and what was local. It was all flat to her. Throughout it all she'd conceived of herself as traversing an ambient plane of sounds and images on which one point was as good as any other. If you had put booster rockets on Sputnik II and given Laika the controls it would not have made a great deal of difference to her life. This was a space to be spectated, not traversed. If there had been other dogs out there it would have made all the difference, because then an element of desire would have disrupted the situation. But there weren't, at least not permanently. So she continued to weave her wall of sounds and pictures and watch the world, undisturbed except for the occasional rocket launch, shuttle mission, shooting star or burst of paranoia, happily dissolving the boundaries between her body and her capsule, between her mind and the ocean of information in which she swam.

But space wasn't as safe as it might have been. Apart from all the data clutter, by the 1980s it was also littered with physical detritus: malfunctioning probes, discarded launch stages, frozen astronaut piss (pretty deadly if you hit it at a few thousand kilometres per hour), camera lens caps, fragments of solar panel, wing nuts, paint flecks, chunks of heat shield and lumps of Laika's own faeces. It was a veritable minefield up there. The cosmodog often thanked her lucky stars that she'd never actually been hit by anything more dangerous than the odd particle of intersellar dust.

But her luck ran out when Joel hacked into a satellite base station and accidentally pinged her with a message. Laika had been wedged in front of a news programme on which scientists and politicians were discussing or denying the epidemic proportions of a new strain of influenza virus, when the dimensions of Joel's skull flashed up on her screen. Deftly spinning a couple of dials with her mouth and prodding a few buttons with her nose, she checked the provenance of the transmission and discovered to her surprise that it had been aimed directly at her. How odd, she thought to herself. No one had actually tried to contact her since she had been given up for dead by Renko and the rest of the Soviet team. She found the experience most disconcerting. She started to shiver slightly and in what little room they had left the hackles on the back of her neck began to rise, an experience she hadn't had since she'd seen the space shuttle capturing a satellite with its articulated arm and taking it out of the sky. But now, as before, the only thing she could do was sit back, try to relax and wait to see what would happen.

A kick up the arse

Judd wanted to go when they came to kick him out, but he couldn't seem to move. The waiter – the one who had spoken to Jennifer and Joel earlier on – approached, told him it was time to pay up and leave. He wished to comply, but he could barely feel his arms and legs. How much had he drunk? He couldn't remember, but surely it wasn't that much.

After the third warning the waiter lost his temper, grabbed Joel under the arms and lifted him from his chair. With some difficulty he propelled the unwelcome customer towards the door and out into the street, aiming a farewell kick at the American's arse as he stumbled out on to the pavement. The kick was a mistake – Judd's arse was unnaturally hard and the Italian yelped in pain as his toes crushed up against an unyielding buttock.

But Judd didn't seem to notice. Under the impetus of the kick he began to stagger – very slowly – across the junction and down towards the traffic lights on Notting Hill Gate. Although barely fifty yards away, it took him quarter of an hour to reach them. His feet were like lumps of concrete and he had to strain to lift them. When he let them drop they banged down on the pavement with a thump that drew strange looks from the other pedestrians.

His head felt heavy, too, his mind fugged and gritty. He wasn't quite sure what was happening. At the corner he followed the pavement round, encouraged by the railings and the kerbstones, and began to make his way eastwards along the Bayswater Road.

An hour later he'd made it the half-mile to Hyde Park, and the slip road that leads into Lancaster Terrace and from there into Sussex Gardens. He followed this route and the first light of dawn found him hovering motionless beneath the Marylebone flyover, trapped there by his fascination with the giant presence of the concrete buttresses until a patrol car on its way to Paddington Green police station pulled up and moved him on.

Mother and child

Jennifer was very upset. After she'd failed to meet Joel she'd gone back to Shelley's and had spent the evening with her and Terry, her boyfriend, sinking a bottle and a half of tequila and berating herself for having been such an idiot and not getting the address of his hotel when she'd spoken to him on the phone. The next day she and her hangover took the coach home. Joel had her number; if she was back in Stratford then at least he could contact her there. She had to get back for work on Monday in any case.

On Sundays the coach takes a roundabout route, calling in not just at Banbury and Leamington Spa as it always does but also at the old town of Warwick. These days Warwick is to all intents and purposes conurbated with Leamington. Its famous castle and churches now occupy the higher ground in a sea of predominantly middle-class suburbia that has congealed around four or five focal points (the castle itself, the spa baths, two High Streets, the race-track) like fat in an oven dish. Having entered Warwick–Leamington, the coach threads through the narrow streets around the castle, eventually stopping in the old square, where a handful of passengers will disembark. Leaving the centre via the 'back way', as it's called by local shoppers and the mothers who daily deliver their brood to one of Warwick–Leamington's many schools, the coach then continues out of town, past the Porsche garage, the hospital and the IBM facility. When it reaches the bypass it will travel south to the Fiveways roundabout and pick up the road to Stratford.

If, as the coach passes the hospital, a passenger should happen to glance out of the back window, he or she would see the Warwick end of Warwick–Leamington arrayed across the slope of the hill with the concrete bunker of a police station and the grim spire of St Mary's clearly standing out above the grey-brown buildings huddled all around. Jennifer had not been this way before, but she did look out of the back window as the coach passed the hospital, and she did see this view.

This was more than déjà vu – it was the view she'd seen in the dream of wheelchair and garden, and witnessing it now brought on a seizure. She froze where she was and let out a small cry, which was killed in her throat as her tongue swelled and her mouth dried up. Her eyelids trembled but lost the ability to blink and her arms began to twitch. Across her cortex the neurons fired in great synchronised groups, their collective electrical output peaking around three times each second. Her retinae, flooded with light, screamed and contracted, warping the image of the hillside. This continued until her head nodded forward, both her arms jerked upwards together and she folded over at the waist. Then she rolled off the seat and down on to the floor, where she lay twitching.

Of the three other passengers on the coach one was asleep, one was listening to a personal stereo and one saw Jennifer collapse, but thought he had better not get involved. Fortunately the driver had spotted her in his rear-view mirror and quickly pulled the vehicle into a lay-by. His sister had suffered petit-mal seizures as a child and he recognised the symptoms immediately. He ran up the aisle and put Jennifer into the recovery position, working his fingers down inside her mouth so that she wouldn't swallow her tongue.

Fortunately, the fit quickly subsided and Jennifer soon came round, although she was confused and her gestures remained quite automatic for some time. The driver gave her some hot tea from the flask he kept beneath his seat. She drank and the liquid burnt trails through her body, gullies through the dust. Moist now, she could blink and swallow.

An ambulance passed them and turned into the hospital entrance. The driver asked her if she was OK, they were right by the hospital, he could take her in if she wished. She shook her head, but it was a reflex more than an action, an attempt to clear her thoughts. As he helped her back up on to her seat she could see the other passengers gazing down the aisle at her with eyes of dim concern.

'Where do you live, love? Stratford?' the driver asked. Jennifer managed a nod. 'All right then, we'll take you home.' He flipped over the label on the overnight bag she had on the seat beside her. 'This your address? Evesham Road? No problem. I can drop you right there. How does that sound. OK?' He rubbed her on the shoulder, then went back to his seat and started the engine, adjusting his mirror a little so that he could keep an eye on her as he drove.

She was still quite bewildered. Everything was concatenating and connecting all around her, everything was in disarray: the striped design of the seat covers, the woven hinges of the ashtray in front of her, the bromide taste left in her mouth by the tea – these things made no kind of sense. Images and memories clattered incoherently through her brain. It took about half an hour for them to reach Stratford and true to his word the driver took a detour and dropped her off outside the flat. She teetered down from the coach and up the stairs, still dazed from the tempest that had blown up in her mind. But worse was yet to come.

As soon as she opened her front door, Rachel was everywhere: in the design of the wallpaper, the details of a rug, the patterns of afternoon sunlight across the furniture, the texture of a table top. Reeling, feeling hot and faint, she made for the kitchen, where she perched on a stool and leant her head into the sink, not so much because she thought she was going to be sick – though the tequila was still floating around in there somewhere – but because it was cooler. Judd and Joel jumped up and sat contemplating her from the draining board, wondering what all of this meant.

The fit had left her too exhausted to cry, to think, to understand what was going on. She stayed bent over the sink for a while, until the sun had gone and the room was dark, and the cats were clamouring for their meal. She got up to feed them but was overcome with dizziness as she took the food down from the cupboard. The room charged at her; she dropped the bag and grabbed at the corner of the fridge for support. Biscuits spilled everywhere, the tiny brown shapes exciting patterns of interference across her field of vision. She dropped to her knees and crawled into the living-room, her daughter in every movement, every sound, every smell. She was being bombarded by this other personality, the petals of its psyche hard as hail upon her body. The view of Warwick from the bus window came to her again and again – she kept thinking of *Close Encounters of the Third Kind* and felt she should be building a model or making a sketch or something. But this storm that raged around her, within her, this force that tapped her senses, bled them off; it left her all but helpless.

Although her toes and ankles had gone numb the soles of her feet prickled with heat. There was a coldness in her knees that prevented her from standing up (her kneecaps felt disconnected, as if they might slip down inside her legs at any moment). The bottom had dropped out of her stomach and her bowels felt loose – not as if she was going to shit but as if she already had done so and her sphincter was now an empty tube open to the air. There was a sensible void in her womb. The lips of her vagina were curling and uncurling in the strangest way, though when she shoved her hand between her legs to calm them nothing was actually happening. Her breasts felt large, as they had done when she was pregnant and swollen with milk, though now the nipples were as red and sore as if they'd been recently suckled. Her arms were long and insubstantial, and cut off at the wrist; it was strange to move her hands, which felt cramped and useless. Her mouth and throat felt perfect, her saliva tasted so good, she wanted to drink but she didn't want to spoil it. For a while she sucked on her thumb and that felt wonderful, comforting. Her vision had become blurred and her hearing hypersensitive.

This initial rush lasted several hours. Throughout it, Jennifer lay sprawled on the floor, incapable of even climbing into a chair, continuous with the room as if both it and she had been transformed into shapes of just-set gelatine. As that sensation began to level off she started to experience a purity and clarity that surpassed anything she'd ever felt before. Her body began to reintegrate itself and it was just so . . . perfect and beautiful. Having recovered some of her physical co-ordination she undressed herself and examined it. Her scars, her dominant feature as far as she was concerned, seemed to dissolve, to be absorbed as she ran her fingertips across them. They were . . . they seemed unimportant, invisible . . . neither the restraining net nor the interface that she'd previously imagined . . . so many times she had hated them, despised herself for them, but now she knew they were part of her and that she loved them too. Quickly, she ran her hands all over her body, up and down her legs, across her stomach and breasts, around her shoulders . . . there was a peculiar feeling of spatial displacement . . . it was like feeling two bodies, her own and the body of her child. The cats crept in, confused by her behaviour, and she grabbed them both and held them to her. Their fur felt so good against her skin. She fetched a comb from the bathroom and groomed them carefully one by one.

The child came in waves now. Jennifer would be stable for a while, stroking her body, combing the cat, contemplating something simple and beautiful like a mark on the wall, then Rachel would buzz through her again, switch her on like an electrical element. She'd slip back into the room again as the feeling assembled itself and when it passed she'd be left beneath a blanket of joy. That first enormous breaker had told her that her child was alive and each spray of surf after that was just confirmation, an echo in flesh in this body of hers which was now a cave by the sea.

The next day she welcomed the sun with her skin and all day she let it touch her through windows. She was free from hunger and from pain. By the time evening arrived the rushing had subsided almost completely and she slept, her brain gently fizzing like a bottle of tonic, her dreams gentle dreams of her child.

When she came to the next morning she felt like her favourite clothes, washed, dried and warmed, and knew that she wasn't going to work that week. She got up but didn't dress, felt too complete already, put the kettle on to boil and cleaned up what was left of the spilled cat food. Cup of tea in hand she wandered around the flat, taking it in. It was all so unquestionably clear.

Joel's message was on the answering machine and Jennifer called the hotel, but every time the receptionist tried to put her through the line was engaged. She was no longer worrying about having missed him; she knew now that she would see him again. The certainty with which she felt that Rachel was alive and in Warwick Hospital had already infected every aspect of her life and the future pattern of all kinds of events was fast becoming obvious to her. She floated through the next few days high as a kite, screening her calls, meditating a lot, talking with the cats, rejigging her flat, making arrangements. No longer, she realised, did she need the paraphernalia of the past. It was time to jettison things. She hired a van for the week and began filling boxes and binliners with stuff she no longer needed. Her mother's clothes were among the first to go. Then Henry's old letters, pieces of furniture, knick-knacks she'd saved, her parents' death certificates, the old TV. Yes, the time of the television was past, out with it. No more TV afternoons, no more *Twilight Zones*. After all, that's where all the trouble had started.

Once she'd started getting rid of stuff she found it hard to stop; the next thing she knew she was clearing out everything she couldn't think of a direct use for: books, papers, all the junk she'd shoplifted over the years, pictures, records, the contents of the kitchen cupboards, old sheets and towels, shoes, hats, the bedroom carpet, curtains . . . she ripped it all out, crushed it into the dustbins or piled it into the van. She was happy and with each item gone she felt happier. The last thing to go was the sofa, the one on which Henry had died, on which she'd had her first visions of Rachel. Waiting till the neighbours had left for work she shoved and pulled until she'd got it out of the door, down the stairs and into the street, where she left it propped up on one end and hoped that the council would take it away. Piling everything else into the van, she drove to the landfill site just out of town and dumped her old life in a hole in the earth.

Now, now she was ready, now she was free. She packed two bags, withdrew all her savings from the bank, collected together everything she might need in the coming days. The only thing that did not fall into place was Joel: his phone was engaged every time she rang. But it was a simple matter to stifle the glimmer of doubt raised by this niggling fact – she asked the receptionist to leave him a note.

'His line's engaged,' the woman had said for the umpteenth time that week.

'I've been trying to reach him since Sunday. Are you sure you haven't seen him? Maybe his phone's off the hook.'

'Mr Kluge has given express instructions that he is not to be disturbed. He has pressing business in London and uses the telephone a great deal.'

'Well, could I leave a message for him, then?'

'Yes, you could,' the receptionist said coldly. 'Mr Kluge is one of our most valued guests. I'm afraid it wouldn't do to upset him.' She didn't mention that the only reason Joel was still resident in the Albion was that he was now paying a double rate to placate the management for his overuse of the telephone and electricity (and that was on top of the money being extorted from him by the maid).

'Well, you might tell him that I shall be visiting at the weekend,' said Jennifer in her haughtiest tone. 'And while you're on the phone, I'd like to reserve a twin room for Saturday night.'

'Of course. I'm sorry, I didn't catch your name,' said the receptionist, who was now rather more eager to oblige.

'Several, Jennifer Several. The room will be for my daughter and for myself.'

The reservation is made and the message written down on the uppermost sheet of a yellow telephone pad. Someone rings the bell in the bar and the receptionist leaves her desk. The clock on the wall reads six-thirty; it is Wednesday evening. The small lobby is now deserted, the Georgian plasterwork groans and worries itself with dust. The deep reds and golds of the worn bramble-patterned carpet tumble and compete for attention. The floor is a complex tangle, the walls and ceiling a blank zenith. The hotel manager strolls into this space, tuts when he sees no one on the desk. The phone rings and he leans across to answer it. 'Yes, ah ha, um, yes of course, no problem at all. Goodbye.' He puts down the phone, turns the yellow pad around and tears off the top sheet, which he then places on the receptionist's typewriter. He takes a pen, scribbles a note to himself, tears off that sheet, folds it, puts it in his pocket, walks away. The lobby is silent again, but loud with potential. Outside in the street the air pressure changes slightly as a bank of cloud moves across the city. Air sluices out through the open windows and the gaps underneath the doors, and an invisible eddy kicks up in the vicinity of the front desk. There's just enough movement to lift the sheet of yellow paper from its resting place and with the softest scrape it slides off the grey metal and down the side of the desk. Whipping back on itself in the air, it changes direction and floats back beneath the drawers and down out of sight. This has nothing at all to do with Emma. This is something else she has overlooked. A hundred and one miles away she sleeps, oblivious and exhausted.

1 5

The last picture show

Warmed by the morning sun, Judd began to move a little faster, matching the speed of the pensioners with their sticks and zimmer frames by the time he passed through the estates on Lisson Grove, though the concrete towers and moulded walls and partitions kept on distracting him, begging him to stay, tempting him with the resonance their modernist geometries struck up with the graphs drawn by the vapour trails of jets across the blank blue slate of the sky. With the movement came some feeling, though it was mostly one of despair, of being cheated. If this was the world then he despised it.

At the junction a man in a Stüssy shirt asked him for directions and he couldn't answer but veered away from him, down the channel formed by the synagogue and Lord's cricket ground, two places of worship one opposite the other.

Mid-afternoon saw him moving among the palm courts of art deco blocks in St John's Wood, lumbering slow as a B-movie dinosaur, and that evening he traversed the wide surburban expanse of the Finchley Road, the exposed balconies of the apartment blocks like TV screens, small domestic dramas flickering intermittently across them.

The jumble of buildings around Swiss Cottage offered some kind of refuge for the night (he felt increasingly safe among buildings; their solidity swaddled him). At one point the pavement was caged in scaffolding and the skeleton of a high-rise soared up on Judd's right, its stone and metal entrails exposed. Arteries and veins fanned out along every girder and joist. Judd realised he was witnessing the birth of a great machine, a robot which would be as oblivious to its tenants as people are to the bacteria which thrive inside their stomachs and make digestion possible.

Night fell. In a parking lot a group of people sat on rows of folding chairs and watched a film being projected on to a blind wall. Two loudspeakers thundered white noise and in the front row members of the audience sat with their fingers in their ears. One man wore sunglasses and headphones, and held a silver microphone in the direction of the screen. Another sat with his shoes off massaging his feet. The screen was a scintillating chaos in which human figures continually threatened to appear but never quite did. The sequence of images kept stopping and starting, and when the film finally came to an end nobody realised and the projectionist had to prompt the applause.

Judd leant up against the chain link fence and looked on as the reels were changed. After a couple of minutes of darkness a square of light flicked on, followed by a raggedy visual countdown and a shot of an open doorway. The camera went through into the room beyond, which had two windows looking out on to a skyline. It was late afternoon; shadows lounged down from the potted plants on the window-sill and across the table below them. Quickly, the shadows deepened and extended, turned into darkness, swallowed the room. Outside the twilight gave way to the deep hue of a lightly starred night. From the right-hand window's lower right-hand corner the moon, round and bright, swiftly arced across the glass and sank away. Moments later, the sky lightened. The mourning of the room, before so freely draped, rolled itself back into lengthy strips of sable. Within seconds noon struck hard, but just as quickly the sun began to fail and shadows stretched and shrugged their way across the floor, taping out the scene again for night.

Next were views of clouds streaming through the heavens like boiling vats of Indian rice full of bubbles strung with scurfy foam; then vehicles weaving threads of light across the Golden Gate; then other processes, all cycling past in inhuman modes of time. A naked tree, starkly standing in a field of snow while winter mornings hastened by, suddenly bulged and sapped, and creaked forth shoots which greenly multiplied and fanned out leaves and buds. Buds blossomed, blossom blew away, spiky fruits weighed down the boughs, cracked off, fell upon the earth and sprouted. Birds and squirrels gorged themselves, fought and squabbled, nested in nooks among the branches. Leaves turned golden brown, grew brittle, whirled away. Rain and hail beat back the summer's show of health, frost clipped off the last few leaves, the smaller twigs.

On an ancient bed a baby with bright bright eyes began to scream, still smarting from the midwife's slap, then screamed some more with teething. Its eyes grew wide, then calm, and on its scalp a fuzz of hair grew long and lank, its limbs straightened and grew more firm. A tall and slender pre-pubescent looked around. The circle of the face drew in and pudgy contours sculpted themselves into individual features. Hair darkened . . . in turns the face cracked into smiles and ran with tears. Fingernails extended into long gnarled spirals, toenails grew back beneath themselves. Under the arms and around the genitals wiry tufts began to sprout. Fluff napped the jaw and the skin of the face developed lines as it grew tighter. The torso broadened and the chest expanded. The leg muscles grew strong and well-defined. The bedclothes rumpled as the body extended to a full six foot. A lambent shock of hair fell down around the shoulders. Features compacted, grew still finer. Sinews and veins pulled taut and ribbed the flesh. Pores dilated. The skin darkened, then paled and relaxed. Wrinkles seeped across the face, converging on the eyes and the corners of the mouth. The eyes turned watery and bloodshot. The pupils dimmed. Flesh dehydrated and sagged loose from thinning bones. The skin fell down in folds, too much of it to wrap its dwindling contents. Cheeks and belly sank, hair greyed and fell and matted the soiled sheets. Hollows developed at the wrists, between the ribs, around the eyes and neck. Short gasps of breath rattled in and out of the throat and mucus gathered around the colourless lips. The eyes stared wildly, then dumbly, then ceased to focus altogether. The breathing popped and ceased. The skin wrinkled tight once again and the limbs stiffened. Around the raw bedsores the flesh turned grey and started to decay.

The camera drew back, revealed the room as sparse and dusty, illuminated by a single flickering flame that cast living shadows upon the walls around the corpse. Back the camera drew, back, through a doorway and out into the sunlight. It rose up above the shoddy dwelling and looked down upon the tree-tops all around. Figures buzzed into the frame. Moving as a blur, they stripped the house, rebuilt it, chopped down trees, cleared back the forest, threw up houses barns fences churches, marked divisions, built walls, wore muddy tracks, dug them out, laid roads, knocked down cabins built brick houses dammed streams built water-wheels and windmills. They held meetings demonstrations celebrations, covered the land to both horizons with buildings of all kinds, filled the streets with more people, horses, carts, then with cars, buses, trucks, trains, trams, knocked down buildings, widened roads, filled the air with fumes. The skyline dipped and soared, the streets and sky shifted with activity. To the east the horizon flamed with sudden flashes. Then the sky was filled with smoke lights balloons and then with waves and waves of aeroplanes. The city was a place of fire and smoke and then a place of calm and crumbling ruins, the only movement falling buildings and lonely dots picking through the rubble. Dots which found each other and began to clear and build again.

The camera grew back still further and the film went on. Judd turned his attention to the flautist who'd been playing a musical accompaniment. The notes were soft and round, and ran in chains like bubbles from a bubble pipe, and Judd watched them ripple skywards between the overbearing buildings, while on the screen below a white and turquoise planet grew old, diseased and died.

Artificial life

Joel was far too preoccupied to try to call Jennifer again and besides, he was half convinced that she had stood him up deliberately and he had his pride. He drove her from his thoughts, worked furiously at his machine – he'd continue anyway, without her. He'd just be more exact, that's all, to compensate for the fact that he'd have to find a different sexual partner. So he reread his manifestos, made annotations, taped the sheets of paper back up on the walls. He purchased a scanner and stripped himself naked and laid the surfaces of his body against the flat illumination of the glass until every inch of skin had been digitised and entered into his machine. He had another set of X-rays done, just to be sure. He cruised telephone boxes collecting the prostitutes' cards, figuring they'd be a good place to start looking for a replacement for Jennifer.

He went almost entirely without sleep now; when he did nod off it was after long sessions of repetitive data entry during which he behaved like an automaton, his fingers working away at the keyboards on their own, the nerves and nets of his digits clack clack clacking with the shadow dream of insect legs, each one subtly independent of the whole. He inputted and cross-referenced everything that he could remember of his life, trying to reconstruct himself within the limitations of the machine. He outlined his personality, summarised his personal history, wrote character sketches of the members of his family and the other people who'd had a major impact on him – Millstein, Jennifer and Henry, Subhash, the Metrics. Over the six days of continuous work the already substantial mass of data grew into a giant snarl of ones and zeros that heaved away in packets around the machines in the small network he had built. And all this time the malfunctioning modem dialled away, dispatching his various parts to the databases of banks, telcos, advertising agencies, government departments, law firms, tourist information offices, census co-ordinators, motor manufacturers, television companies, scientific laboratories, Antarctic base stations, religious institutions, libraries, personal computers, industrial robots, magazines and newspapers, millenarian cults, traffic-light controllers, police stations, security firms, space stations, air-traffic control towers, software companies, nuclear bunkers. Joel's vital statistics, his rants, his skin tones, his skeleton found their way across every national boundary. They became seamlessly woven into the very fabrics of a hundred societies. Image samples from his buttocks were used to smooth the face of an ageing American model in a skin-cream advertisement. His waist and inside leg measurements formed a ratio that became the recommended dosage for a new heart drug and dozens of middle-aged businessmen died as a result (which in turn caused a series of upsets on NASDAQ and wiped out several personal fortunes, made others and bankrupted a small African country). The insertion of the radius of his jaw into previously uncertain data allowed the reconstruction of a somewhat bewildering fossilised remain: hitherto guessed to be some kind of anthropod, it was now reclassified as belonging to a member of a completely new Cambrian phylum. His genetic fingerprint, spliced into a crucial systems code, triggered an accident in a Russian nuclear reactor which led to meltdown, the contamination of vast swathes of territory, decades of insect and animal mutation, and thousands and thousands of cases of cancer, leukaemia and other, more subtle, illnesses. His initials were worked into an anthemic song by a Dutch pop band which topped their national charts for weeks, and in the stacks of a giant museum near Los Angeles his blood type became mixed up with the catalogue data and the oldest extant copy of Virgil's *Aeneid*, on loan from the Vatican library, got classified as rubbish and incinerated. The date of his circumcision replaced the firing sequence for the boosters aboard Voyager II, as the probe headed with great speed towards Jupiter. The upshot was a marginally different heading which would, some eight hundred years hence, bring the little spacecraft into contact with an alien civilisation.

All week Joel worked on, oblivious to the fact that his plan was being overtaken by events. On the sixth day he felt that the construct was finally complete and on the seventh he rested, passing out, totally exhausted, just before dawn. But as soon as he slept the doll with two hearts appeared in his dreams, her servomechanisms whirring and clicking as she walked.

She came towards him, less lithe than before and more mechanical, and he could not tell what size she was – she seemed simultaneously to tower above him and to hardly reach his knee. She took his bony hand in hers and led him through the neuronal tangle of some forest of the night until they reached a clearing where the trees gave way to a rock face that rose clear and monumental out of the ground. A waterfall cascaded down from a plateau high above and all about them rainbows bobbed like arcs of electricity on the clouds of mist and spray. The doll dropped Joel's hand and moved away, making her way around the edge of the pool at the base of the falls. Joel stood and listened to the roar of the water. Little by little he began to distinguish blips of sound within it. He closed his eyes so as to listen more intently and the blips became more intense until he could ascertain discrete burbles of noise. The burbles became screeches, which seemed familiar but most unwaterlike, and Joel suddenly realised that he was no longer listening to the sound of a waterfall at all but to something quite different. He looked up at the cliff but it was a cliff no longer. The craggy slope had become a sheer black face, the waterfall a giant strip of copper. It took him a moment or two to realise what it was he was looking at. It was one section of a colossal silicon chip and the tumult he could hear was not of water but of bits. He began to laugh at the absurdity of it; he laughed and laughed, harder than he could ever remember laughing before. In fact, he couldn't remember ever having laughed at all. He'd smiled a few times, perhaps once or twice he had grinned. But had he laughed? He couldn't be sure.

He laughed until he remembered the doll. Where had she got to? He set off around the pool in search of her and as he moved the silicon chip morphed back into waterfall and cliff, the black plastic crackling and melting into rock as if it were being heated from behind, the copper sparkling and dancing until it was all light and motion. The ground was treacherous with moisture and Joel lost his footing several times as he hunted through the mists. Eventually he spotted the doll and when he did she was still neither short nor tall, neither distant nor near. She was standing beside a glass elevator that ran all the way up the side of the cliff. She smiled and beckoned him inside. Her chest was exposed and he could see her silver-red hearts blinking away in unison through the artificial membrane that served as her chest. He glanced upwards to the top of the cliff, to where the lift would take him. High above, the edge of the plateau was stiff and pure against the softness and indeterminacy of the saturated sky. Should he go with her? He put his hands to his face and entered.

The lift started slowly but then went faster and faster, the rock and the pool disappearing quickly from view as they shot above the top of the cliff, into the air and through the first clouds. Joel's stomach hit the floor and he grabbed for a handrail (there wasn't one). The doll stood behind him, looking out through the glass, her face a blank slate. Had she done this before? To his amazement he realised that far away to the right he could see the curve of the earth.

The glass elevator hung still in the night. Joel's feet no longer came into contact with the floor. The doll was floating too, her legs folded into what might have been a lotus position had they not been fat and made of plastic. She looked up (what he assumed was up). He followed her gaze through the roof of the capsule and out into a space bright with stars, much brighter than he'd ever imagined they could be. Everything was there and nothing; he didn't understand what she was looking at. He glanced back at her but she was still staring, so he looked up again, harder this time, and as he watched he noticed that far above their heads was a large black patch of space from the edges of which the stars were beginning to vanish. His first thought was of some kind of cloud, but then he realised that it wasn't that at all, all the clouds were below. Something else was approaching.

There was a click and he looked down just in time to see the doll releasing the door. He tried to scream but it was too late: she opened it a crack and the air immediately exploded out from the elevator, hurling the doors wide and blowing Joel and the doll into the void. As his lungs pleaded for breath he felt himself expand and at the moment he was going to explode he woke up.

He came to, fighting with the sheets that had somehow got wrapped round his head and stuffed inside his mouth. He cleared them away and hyperventilated, recalling the dream. Something was wrong. He switched on the bedside lamp but in spite of the light everything was hazy. He felt around for his glasses but couldn't find them. Where had he put them? He searched the bed and the floor beside it, but they weren't there. Eventually he went into the bathroom to look for them. He fumbled for the light but the wall seemed flat and textureless, and it took him a few moments to locate the cord. Even with the light on his eyesight was so poor that he could hardly see, but he continued to explore around the sink and along the shelves with his hands. The glasses weren't there. Exasperated, he went across to the mirror to rub his eyes, only to find that the elusive spectacles were perched on the end of his nose, where they'd been all the time. How odd. He took them off, examined them, rinsed them under the tap, dried them with a piece of tissue, replaced them on his nose, but there was little improvement. He flushed with a minor panic as he wondered if he hadn't damaged his vision from sitting in front of a screen for too many hours at a stretch. He drank a glass of water, then wet a flannel, went back to bed, and laid it across his face. Across from him, on their table, the machines were talking to one another. The malfunctioning modem had managed to dial the number that would connect Joel's computer to the satellite base station he had hacked into the previous week and was now merrily dumping all the data it could find down this channel. Along the phone line it went, through the silicon circuitry of several computers and up in a narrow beam to Sputnik II, where it blurted into Laika's little world.

The poor dog never knew what had hit her. These data of Joel's broke the glass of her screen and grabbed at her. They came on like a rape, a barrage of sounds pictures codes that in the confines of the capsule took on a tangible quality. Laika's twenty-seven years of solitude were over and something terrifying had broken the silence. She didn't even have time to bark as multimedia dissolved her, and her body and her craft were outlined with pulses of blue electronic light.

Lax RV

The next day, Judd tackled Hampstead, now sure of where he was going. He meandered up Fitzjohn's Avenue, surrounded by rich young mothers herding their kids into school, passing the heavy red houses. He rumbled unnoticed through the centre of the village, oblivious to the international pact made by the bourgeoisie through their purchase of reliable cars, his movements too slow to be registered by the security cameras.

He spent the afternoon lost in the small maze of streets around New End but by evening had found his way out on to the Heath, which he inched his way across, navigating by the moon and frightening couples and cottagers. Dogs ran up to him and barked; one even pissed up his leg, marking him out, a node in some esoteric canine topology that would, by continuing its slow traverse, upset the power balance in the area and lead to internecine disputes. Judd felt that he was fixed in one place, that all he was doing was lifting his feet one by one as the earth moved beneath him like an enormous conveyor belt. Infinitesimally, inexorably, high above his head the sweep of stars rotated.

He came out by Highgate ponds and dawn saw him shuffling his way up Fitzroy Park, a private road lined with the highly styled abodes of millionaires. Pretty soon a police car drew up beside him. Its occupants, having discovered that he seemed incapable of even registering their presence, sat there and watched him for a couple of hours until he was up the hill and out of the area.

His excitement grew as he passed close by Highgate cemetery, where many others who had already turned to stone now resided, and it peaked soon after that, when he came down the High Street and saw London below him for the first time, the buildings of the City misty in the morning smog, the environs locked into the twists of the Thames in bricks of leaden, patchy grey. The view reminded him of that of Los Angeles from Beverly Hills, the one he'd scampered up hillsides as a child to discover, and for the first time since he had returned to London he felt a brief moment of peace, as if this place had finally abandoned an ancient dispute with his home. But the moment passed and feeling angry with himself for being so seduced he continued eastwards across the hillside, skirting the view, until he came to the Archway bridge on Hornsey Lane. Here, hundreds of feet below, the expressway sped away to either side, carmine and amber and beryl and turquoise and all hues of pinprick lights tacking down its undulations all the way. Kept from the abyss by a cast-iron rail, Judd watched the lanes of cars roll beneath him, the thousand thousand shifting suns of a spiral arm combusting through the twilight. A milky way. And in each car the planets of personality spun: the drivers, the passengers, the women, men and children, the burnt the raw the old, the travellers salesmen doctors thieves and lawyers, the grocers masseurs surfers judges guards, the chefs singers smokers drinkers hikers drummers palmists prophets racers chasers consumers cripples comedians Catholics capitalists Muslims communists Baptists Jews Hindus heteros homos lilos, every one a freak punk poet mystic pool-player pervert redneck syphilitic necrophiliac nymphomaniac terminally ill terminally insane terminally terminal sociopath psychotic. God, how tired he was of them all.

Jennifer to the rescue

The Saturday following her abortive journey to London, Jennifer packed a couple of bags, put them in the van, and made a bed in the back with a mattress and some blankets. Before she set off she put down fresh food for Judd and Joel and secured the house, leaving the back window ajar so that they could come and go as they pleased. She locked the front door and pushed her spare set of keys through the letter-box of the couple who lived in the flat below, with a note asking if they'd look after the cats while she was away.

She drove straight from Stratford to Warwick, taking the most direct route to the hospital that she knew. It was August Bank Holiday weekend and the roads were congested, which she hoped wouldn't be a problem later on. But the thought didn't bother her for long. She was still happy. Everything would be fine.

It surprised her now how little thought she had put into the rescue itself, especially considering how much time she had spent dreaming about all the things she would do with her daughter once they had been reunited. But she wasn't scared at all. Events would take their own course.

It took her about half an hour to reach the hospital. She turned into the entrance and drove slowly through the complex until one of the car parks felt right. She came to a halt and sat behind the wheel smoking a cigarette, each drag bringing back a tinge of the ecstacy she'd experienced the weekend before, not sure what to do next. The buildings were meaningless to her, so much so that if it weren't for the signs everywhere ('Radiology', 'Out-Patients', 'Maternity', 'Emergency', 'Princess Anne Ward') the collection of long, low, prefabricated buildings littered around this nexus of car parks could just as easily have been a university faculty or a school as a medical facility.

She finished the cigarette and stepped out of the van, leaving it unlocked. The mid-morning sun blazed down across the open concrete, emphasising the cracks and folds in the surface where frost and tree roots had taken their toll. She walked in the direction of her shadow, thinking how thin this concrete surface was and how just beneath it worms and moles and roots and beetles fought, thrived and combined. A door presented itself to her and she opened it. She went inside. The corridor ahead was long, dark, soft, empty, quiet. It smelt of Germolene and disinfectant. The linoleum tiles, alternately red and brown, stretched before her like the squares of a checkerboard. She made her way across them, her trainers squeaking at every step. She had gone about ten yards when there was a loud buzzing sound, very close, as if an insect had flown into her ear. She leant against the yellow wall and shook her head, wanting to sneeze, not sure if it was pain that she felt. Everything around her was laid bare. The walls churned through the leviathan patterns of measureless aeons of geological morphology. The floor hissed of open fields of flax; the wooden skirting whispered of a million generations of trees. She inched forward, using the wall as a support. A nurse came round the corner. Jennifer wanted to run but she couldn't and the inability to obey this direct impulse made her realise for the first time how little control she had over whatever was going on. Her coming here had nothing to do with her. She was being manipulated. Just what, exactly, was happening?

The nurse came over. 'Are you all right, dear? You look very pale.' She gave a lot of weight to the 'very'.

The words came to Jennifer. 'Yes, I'm fine, really. It's my mother, taken ill, just been visiting, bit of a shock . . .'

'Oh, yes, well you take care. There's a community room around the corner, you can sit in there if you want, get a cup of tea from the machine. Want me to show you where it is?' These words: the interactions of prokaryotes and eukaryotes dribbled through time's vegetal mass.

'Oh, no, thank you, it's all right, I can manage, I think.' The nurse nodded and went on her way along the corridor, the heavy soles of her shoes slapping loudly against the hard floor.

Alone again, Jennifer could feel her daughter near now, as close as she had felt during the final moments before her collapse, before they tore her out from the womb. She placed her hand underneath her sweater and ran her fingers along the line of the old caesarean scar, caressing its puckers. The rhythms of the child's twin pulses came down the corridor towards her like streamers of blood flowing from a suicide's wrists into a bath of warm water. She began to move faster and started to cry, and her tears made trellised patterns down her cheeks. There she was running through the corridors, turning left and right on impulse, as if chasing through the ventricles of her daughter's very mind.

Finally there was a door, bolted on the outside. She slid back the bolt and pushed it open. The room had a window of reinforced glass, a hospital bed covered with a thin, flowery spread, a cabinet or two, a trolley. Standing at the end of the bed with her back to Jennifer was an eight-year-old girl with deep red hair, dressed in a dark-green overcoat, a grey school dress, white stockings and grey leather shoes. Beside her on the bed was a small bag, already packed.

'Rachel?' said the mother. 'Rachel?' The girl turned towards her and for a second Jennifer was shocked by the face. She had never known it, except in fragments, and here it was complete and flooded with light. It was a face of exquisite ugliness, a face which broke every rule of proportion but so subtly that the effect was quite disarming. It lacked symmetry: the high forehead overshadowed a weak chin, the mouth was the merest line and the lips non-existent, the nose was pert but squat and broad. And the eyes were old, too old for the skin which, though mottled, was still flushed and fresh, old with the aura of that flotsam that gathers on the back of the ever breaking wave upon which we live and which gets cycled and recycled as a signpost for a future we can never know, an impossible marker which tells us only that we are the rising and rotting yeasts of unaccountable eternal returns.

Then the child put her finger to her mouth and she was just a little girl.

'Rachel?' asked Jennifer. There was a pause, in which she felt her daughter die again.

But the child opened her mouth and began to speak, in a voice wracked with catarrh and difficult and deep. 'Emma. I'm Emma.'

'Emma,' repeated Jennifer, choking with joy. 'Of course, Emma. Emma, Emma, Emma. Emma, do you know who I am?' Emma nodded and went over to her mother. Jennifer bent down and they embraced.

Mother and daughter hurried through the maze of identical corridors, Emma leading so that they wouldn't run into anyone on the way. They reached the van without a problem and the child wanted to look (she had never been out here before) but Jennifer made her lie down on the mattress in the back and covered her with a blanket. Her hands were trembling as she tried to insert the key into the ignition and she dropped the bunch twice before she managed to start the engine. She drove as sedately as she could through the car-parks and back towards the main road. As they passed through the exit a deafening high-pitched whine vibrated the air behind them. Jennifer thought it was a helicopter and nervously searched the skies, even as the whine became more intense, every molecule in the vicinity now excited. She clasped her hands over her ears, but as she did so the noise passed beyond the upper limits of her hearing. For a moment there was silence, nothing but the sound of the engine. Then every window in the hospital exploded outwards in one great throb of energy, a thousand flowers of glass blossoming into the air, each one a bloom of a billion shining shards. For a moment the explosion was contained by a vast and delicate tinkling, a bubble of silence on an expanding front of sound. Then the fragments hit the concrete and glass skidded on stone and all the terrible beauty was lost as the sonic boom broke. Emma lay in the back calmly and smiled; Jennifer slammed the van back into gear and drove.

She made her way out to the bypass and followed it round to the south-east corner of the town, then cut back through Warwick–Leamington along the Myton Road, heading in the direction of Daventry. It took her about half an hour to reach Northampton and the M1, and by this time she was calm enough to break the chain of cigarettes she'd been smoking. Just before she turned on to the motorway she pulled into a lay-by and told Emma to come and sit up beside her. She settled her in the front seat, clipped the seat-belt around her and gave her one of the cartons of drink she'd brought along. She hugged her and felt her hair, and cried for a while, attentions which the child accepted impassively, then she drove on, keeping to the slow lane and continually stealing glances at her daughter. She touched her whenever she could and she started to talk, then talked without stopping. Throughout the journey Emma sat looking slightly bemused, absorbing as much as she could, as if she had been brought up on gruel and here was a banquet.

The cinema of city lights

Along Crouch End High Street it was the same story, bums and drunks harrying him away from their patch, shoppers streaming about him like the customers in Reno's casinos. But the shadow of the hill was ahead of him, the highest point, and it gave him heart. Judd smiled, an effort that split his lips and brought forth springs of blood. Soon it would be over. It was nearly time to prove that he could take control, that he was capable of making at least one decision, even if it would be his last.

He waited at the foot of the town centre clock for what seemed an age, girding himself for the final ascent. He looked terrible: his hair was patchy and worn, the roots dying as his scalp began to harden and rift. His face was emaciated and the bones of his skull jutted out, drawing dark escarpments out of his face. His eyes were glazed with a crystal film and stared without blinking at everything; his hands were chipped and cracked. His clothes hung from him loosely, worn thin by the ramparts of his frame. His feet were naked, smooth, his shoes long knocked from them like corn husks from grains pounded by millstones. Yet from beneath the crust of the city, London's chalk and clay encouraged and supported him; he was part of their realm now, moving at speeds which they could comprehend.

The next morning he tackled Park Road. It took him all day to cover its length, this chunk of strange suburbia with its petrol stations and semis. But at the top there it was, the gate to Alexandra Palace, like an enormous welcome sign. He made straight for it and was half-way across the junction when a car sped down the hill towards him in an attempt to catch the lights. The driver didn't see Judd until it was too late. Whining and protesting, suspension axles rubbed and juddered, locked. Oil pumped in massive pressure and the brake discs clamped and swore. Metal of the body all in forward motion slowed and gripped and lurched, forward over tyres, chassis straining bending, rubber left in lines upon the road.

Impact.

Driver through the windscreen (no seat-belt, you see), through the air past Judd who turned his head, surprised. He felt the heat all down his side – the car was there, bunched up around him like a lover, touching all his curves and spaces, panting burning breaths in short hot gasps upon his cheek. Hot lungs. Broken, dying. But unpeturbed and with a creak, a sound of stone on metal, Judd pulled away, his imprint there inside the beast, leaving a mould, a negative. Slowly, he carried on towards the gate.

The road wound up through trees and parkland to the Victorian palace which formed London's vertex. Porticoes and balustrades, patterned brickwork, great rose windows: like an Indian fortress the building aped the sky. It was the biggest sky Judd had ever seen in England, the biggest one of all; as if the transmitter on the palace roof, that iron pylon, that talking Blackpool tower, were an anti-magnet that had repelled the troposphere itself.

Judd stood at the foot of the brick turret which supported the tower. There being no one about he began to climb, desiring the sky, needing it to bear witness for him. Like the chalk and the clay, the brickwork sympathised with Judd's fingers and toes, and afforded them purchase, loved them as he inched up the building storey by storey. Above the climbing man the sky dulled, as if a great dragon were breathing on its sheen, and the sun began to dip towards the night. It fell and fell, and at the end tipped off the earth and dragged its cape down with it. To the east it was already dark. A few light cumuli floated overhead, showing their bloodied bellies like culled seals. Within minutes the crimson bled out across the ocean of the sky and the clouds grew grey, as atrophying corpses do, to hang stiff and cankered in the air, while the livid sunset blind was rolled away above them. What could be more lovely than decay? Birds flew across the sky to roost and in the valleys' slits the halogens which mark the streets became denser, more intense. In windows, lights came on and claimed the outside spaces, the city's bulwarks against the night. Judd had reached the top and stood beneath the mast. He could see it all now. He looked.

Cupped inside its crooks the city blazed, the spangle of a zillion uncharted constellations. In groves and hollows on rises over water electricity splayed forth into the atmosphere: the static lights of towers and vapour lamps, the ons and offs of domestic windows framed yellow or electric blue, the flowing, halting whites and reds and blinking ambers of the cars, the traffic signals' crimson amber green, the pulsing pods of buoys upon the water, the bridges stretched taut across the Thames like gleaming cords, the waters themselves, polluted and amniotic, soiled by toxic effluents and riddled with machines, the blank white light of offices like surgeries, the port and starboard signals of slowly roving ships easing in and out of dock, the beacons of tugs and yachts and fishing boats, the flashing disembodied wink of scrolling aircraft, the diaphanous cones of helicopter spotlights steadily patrolling, the twin whirl of police lamps, the grim glare of the floodlights gripping the great dome of St Paul's, the cobalt sprays of sparks from welders working on the bridges, the rays firing out in all directions from the tips of chaos and tall buildings. Half closing his eyes, Judd gazed at the patches of darkness where small parks or trees soaked up the photons, looked at the juddering flames of fires on the mudbanks to the east, at the rows of arc lamps making miniature days in the football stadiums, the halogens and kliegs and cressets and strip lights and lanterns, the laser light taut from Canary Wharf, the mounted searchlights boring tubes through the smoggy haze. He saw all these fizzing lights throw cadmium phosphorescence across the underbelly of what clouds there were, and watched it rain back like fall-out.

Down there, where it fell, people danced ate wooed sang rushed sat trembled, precariously alive. Down there they grew morose, withdrawn, wombed in electricity. Like individual souls the lights, some burning bright, some dim, some snapping on or off, were all involved. Judd wished them all away and he wished them all together, wished them into one single brilliant filament blazing out in all directions. He felt his anger ignite within him, fuelled by the oxygen of pain. He wanted people punished for what they had done to him, for what they had done to the world; he wanted them flogged for scarring and scabbing this virginal basin, for soiling its immaculate waters, for bringing time here. He wanted them to feel the thrust of the death they denied and yet carried within them. He wanted the carpet of European Man rolled back. He wanted this place smashed like his face had once been, back in LA, ground against the rock; he wanted this TV mast torn apart in revenge for those TV afternoons which had brought him no good. He wanted the buildings to crumble, the streets to crack and rift, the earth to vent up and spout first fire and ash, and later orange poppies and long-husked grasses. He wanted this concrete Reich brought to an end. He wanted the seals to return in their droves to the rocks, the bats to appropriate the palaces, the woodworm and the death-watch the bee and the ant to hollow out the foundations of the banks and the buildings. In the parks he wanted teepees, buffalo; in the streets he wanted prairies. He wanted steppes and forests from the shoreline to the hilltops; in the waters he wanted silver fish teeming to and fro across the sunken girders of Blackfriars Bridge, of Tower. He wanted octopi and sharks, eels and dolphins. On the land he wanted wolves and deer and snakes and bears and muskrats. In the skies he wanted eagles, vultures, hummingbirds. On the wind the sound of howl and song and cry. In the soil, worm and beetle, mole and root. Streams would roll and tumble where once goods trains had rattled. Trees would quiver tall where telephone poles had stood. In place of apartment blocks there would be camp fires. In place of garages, caves. No automobiles, but wild horses would gallop and graze. Excited into swift action for the first time in days, he whirled his hands to kindle the spell, to foam and ferment the firmament. He gesticulated at the ground and commanded it to heave and spume, to make an alembic of the city and so distil the god that would strike at this aberration playing across the surface of the earth.

But nothing at all occurred, nothing at all, except that a breeze blew up and melted through the air. It unfurled itself through the stanchions of the television mast and gently goaded Judd for his concern. He knew it was useless. In all the days in all the years in all the centuries to come these buildings would always stand here, they would never be repelled, earthquakes eruptions famines plagues and floodings would prove nothing but minor setbacks. And what was worse, the malaise would creep forth to feed on other planets, it would seep across the solar system and thence out through the galaxy, engulfing all the stars just as a dewy mould on a rotting fruit sends out its spores to set at all the other apples in the rack. He felt helpless before this steady march, this trickling divagation, this murmuring stream, this chatter. Above him, satellites softly slipped between the stars. Cars passed far below and he watched their headlights run along the wires red and white in pulses. Dark buildings loomed on corners. Night was coming to an end. Slowly, the nerve impulses lumbering awkwardly through his sluggish body, Judd shuffled across towards the building's eastern edge. He was moving slower than ever now, no more than an inch a minute. Before long the sun would be up; then he'd warm, gain heart, the moment would be lost. It was now, now or never. The thought echoed through the desiccating caverns of his cortex, reverberating like a mantra, helping him up on to the parapet. As the street lights in the city below began to blink off, his toes creaked over the lip and, as the first atomic wisp crept into view above the fawning earth, he toppled.

The wind held its breath as night flipped into day. For an instant everything seemed to halt as millennia were compressed into microseconds. Judd stopped in mid-air, half-way between parapet and concrete. There was a fracture in the world, an irreducible lacuna. The last things he saw as his eyes turned to crystal were the markings on the road, white against the oily blackness of the tarmac, their frozen motions now pinned for ever to his glassy retinae. The minerals in his bloodstream multiplied like cancers and hardened into feldspars, transmuting his muscles into bands of pink granite. His brain petrified into spongy dolerite. His fingernails became moonstones and his testicles mica swirls. His kidneys and liver metamorphosed into basalt and his bones became chalk. His heart ossified and was changed into a pyroxene-rich lump of andesite. He had rubies in his arteries, jade in his veins, pearls in his glands. His tendons and nerves formed seams of copper, silver, gold. With the heat of the transformation he curled into a ball and when it was over his skin cooled and vitrified, becoming obsidian.

Then the wind breathed out, the air was rent by explosion, and the surface of the sky began to flicker and dance as the force unleashed vaporised tower and mast. Judd thudded down on the boiling ground, black, solid, round and encrusted with rings of quartz where his mouth, ears and anus had been. Far below, in the city, the whine of fire engines could already be heard.

Beneath the glowing sky the firemen would find the new rock, cooling fast, at the centre of the crater it had formed. They would remove their shiny helmets, scratch their heads with blackened fingers. Later that day the scientists would come and take Judd away. They'd shave him into sections with lasers and examine him carefully under microscopes. To their astonishment they would find within him what seemed to be the fossilised remnants of cells. They would speak to the press and the story would sweep round the world:

MARTIANS INVADE EARTH!!!

METEORITE CONTAINING EVIDENCE OF
EXTRA-TERRESTRIAL LIFE DESTROYS
WORLD'S FIRST TELEVISION TRANSMITTER!

Full English breakfast

The next time Joel awoke he could focus. His limbs still felt numb but everything else was all right. He hadn't eaten for seventy-two hours and was ravenously hungry. He called room service and ordered some breakfast, and when the chambermaid arrived he took the tray from her at the door. He devoured everything on it – two dry and peeling croissants, a large fry-up, three rounds of thin toast, a glass of orange juice and several cups of tea – but the food did nothing to displace the strange feeling of emptiness he felt.

He had eaten his breakfast lying on the bed, but now he went over to the computer table and sat down at it. As always, the machines were humming with activity, and he tapped in a series of brief instructions and ordered up his construct, the raw material ready for the spell.

But something had gone wrong. The computer could not find the construct. He ran a check on his hard disk and discovered that great chunks of his data had been corrupted or were missing altogether. He started to panic. This couldn't be right. Where was his work? Where was his golem, his perfect creation? He ran the search again but still there was nothing, so with trembling fingers he did a systems check and discovered the modem malfunction. How had that happened? How had it been running continually and unnoticed all week? Incredibly, his machine had made a remote connection with another computer and was uploading his data to it, then overwriting the dispatched files with garbage. He tried to shut the modem off from within the operating system but it would not recognise the command. He reached around the back of one of the housings to unclip the serial cable from its port, but the metal was red hot and he whipped back his burnt finger in pain.

There was nothing for it but to shut off the power and reboot, but before he did that Joel quickly scrolled through the various directories to see just what he had lost. Parts of the retinae and the visual cortex had been corrupted earlier in the day but they were still largely intact. One of his kidneys had gone completely, as had a large section of one thigh. With a sudden flash of horror he remembered the strange loss of vision he had experienced when he had woken in the middle of the night. He moved his hand down to his groin and inched it out across his leg. There was a strange void into which his trousers sagged. He croaked in disbelief as the machine began to send out chunks of his lower intestine and then wipe them from the disk. As the data unwound like a skein of wool from a spindle, Joel felt his breakfast drop inside him. There was no mistaking the soft flop of pieces of undigested tomato on to his prostate gland or the hideous glissando of albumen sliding down the inside of his spine.

He burst into action and started to tear at the cables on his desk, but he had screwed all of them down and now he couldn't pull them free. The power points were located around by the side of the bed and he dived across the floor, his legs too weak to stand, retching as the contents of his belly slapped around like baby squids in a bucketful of glue. Grabbing at the nearest bed leg, he hauled himself forwards, then scrabbled at the carpet in order to travel the remaining distance to the socket. But as he stretched out his hands across those last few inches they began to fade. The nails and cuticles went quite suddenly and then, millimetre by millimetre, his flesh was stripped away. Knuckle by knuckle, the bone began to go too, until all he had left were two stumps of wrist that trailed off into the air.

The shock was so great that his terror turned to fascination. He gave up and rolled on to his back, clutching at the air with his rapidly dwindling lungs. Above him on the table the machine chattered away to itself, mindlessly busy with its task of deleting the rest of him.

Time for tubby bye-bye

Jennifer followed the M1 until it terminated in Neasden, then took the A5 through London, watching it cycle through its incarnations as the Edgware Road, Cricklewood Broadway, Shoot Up Hill, Kilburn High Road, Maida Vale, then back into the Edgware Road once more. Emma gazed out of the window, drinking in the houses and the people and the cars, amazed by the solidity of these things she'd only ever seen in her dreams. The fact of the world was so blatant, such a barrage, and she kept blinking at its complexity as if taking mental photographs to study later at her leisure.

The sun was high in the sky as Jennifer rounded Marble Arch. Trying to drive and follow the map at the same time, she almost ran into the side of a cab. The driver swore at her and blew his horn, and Jennifer screamed back, glad to be able to release some of the tension gathered by her body during the journey. The taxi drew up alongside her at the lights and the cabbie wound down his window the better to shout abuse. Emma looked across at him and thought about the tyres on his vehicle. The compressed air inside them began to heat up and within seconds the rubber was smoking. The chassis rose imperceptibly up into the air, there was a short series of explosions, and the vehicle dropped the few inches to the road. The driver leapt out and examined the shreds of his tyres in disbelief.

The lights changed and Jennifer drove on. At the next set of lights she stopped, turned to Emma and stroked the girl's hair. 'You don't need to do that,' she said calmly. 'You don't. You're with me now. You don't have to be angry.' The child looked at her mother, then took her hand in her own and laid it against her faintly glaucous cheek. It was an awkward display of affection, as though she had intuited an expectation and tried to fulfil it. The lights changed again and Jennifer had to remove her hand and apply it to the gearstick, and Emma turned away again, unsure. They continued down the Bayswater Road towards Queensway, Jennifer nervous, searching for the turn. The traffic slowed and stopped.

Leaning out of the window, Jennifer looked up ahead: the road was blocked off by a police van and a row of orange cones. Suddenly she felt dazed, the euphoria that had been with her all week swept away. Christ, oh, Christ, what was she doing? What the fuck was going on? She grabbed Emma and bundled her over the seats and into the back of the van, told her to get under the blanket and stay down. Then she reached for her cigarettes and lit one.

A policeman strolled up to the car and stuck his head through the window. 'Road's closed. Right or left only from here.' He didn't offer an explanation and Jennifer didn't ask for one. She wound up her window and when her turn came swung right into Westbourne Terrace. She was planning to take the next left and go on into Prince's Square but the road was barred with metal railings, so she turned right again instead and parked on a single yellow line.

They left the van and continued to Prince's Square on foot. The streets were clotted with people heading west and in the distance Jennifer could hear a low, ambient throb. She was shaking now and unsure. Even though the police hadn't been interested in her she still hadn't recovered her composure. As they walked she tried to get straight in her head just what the last week had all been about. Was this girl really her child? She must be insane, she'd just kidnapped this kid for no reason. Oh, god, and she'd thrown most of what she owned away! What had she been thinking? She glanced down at Emma, expecting to see an eight-year-old with confusion stamped across her face, but Emma seemed fine.

Indeed, the child could sense the massive concentration of energy up ahead and was becoming more and more excited. She skipped along beside Jennifer as her mother hurried along. They passed a couple sitting on a low wall drinking beer. The man had his shirt off; a whistle dangled from the red, gold and green ribbon that was tied around his neck. Jennifer asked him what was going on.

He laughed. 'You not from round here, then? It's the Carnival, lady. August Bank Holiday, innit?'

Jennifer thanked him, greatly relieved. Now someone had said it, now she knew the words, now everything was OK. Emma slipped back into place and Jennifer's high partly returned. She was here. She had done it. 'Come on, darling,' she said to Emma. 'It's just a big, big party. They'll never find us now. Let's go and find your Uncle Joel, then we can go somewhere and have a nice lunch, just the three of us.' More words. With these she invented a family ex nihilo. She thought of her fears during the previous half-hour and giggled. The sunlight poured down through the green leaves of the cherry trees which lined the road and she wanted to dance she was so happy. Emma had started to skip again and Jennifer skipped with her. The child giggled too, a new sound to her, and Jennifer picked her up and held her to her and kissed her over and over.

She carried her around the corner and into Prince's Square, then put her down as they arrived outside the Albion. But as they climbed the steps the smile disappeared from Emma's face. Jennifer caught her eye and was surprised at the bleakness in her expression. She squatted down and tweaked the child's nose. 'It's all right, angel. We're just going to see a friend. Everything's going to be fine. You'll see.'

Inside and upstairs, Joel was still shrinking. His eyes had gone long before, as had his arms and most of his legs. When his genitals had begun to vanish he had wanted to scream, just like in his dream, but then his mouth had disappeared too and he was left unable to do anything but listen for his fate and sniff at it.

Jennifer tickled Emma under the chin until she laughed, then took out a tissue and wiped the girl's face clean. They went up the steps and through the glass entrance door and then they were out of the heat and the noise, and into the calm of the reception area.

They approached the reception desk. Emma watched the brambles on the carpet swirl around their feet. 'We're here to see Mr Kluge.'

'Of course. Just a minute, please.' The receptionist had the day off again and the manager was minding the desk. He dialled the number of Joel's room. 'I'm afraid his line is engaged. Would you mind waiting while I go up and call him?'

'Oh, he's expecting us. Which room is he in?'

'Three ten, but I don't know if I can let you . . .'

'You don't understand. This is his daughter. He's expecting us.'

'Well, I suppose . . .' But Jennifer wasn't listening. She led Emma past the desk and the two of them began to mount the stairs. As they ascended the first flight the child looked back and stuck out her tongue. They quickly climbed the narrow staircase to the third floor, then hurried along to Joel's room, their nostrils heavy with the dusky anonymity of hallways. They reached three ten and Jennifer knocked.

There was no reply. She knocked again, a little harder this time. She felt faint; her skin seemed to tremble, to become excited by the mere fact of contact with the material of her clothes, with the molecules of the air. Her scars vibrated, felt like bands of light. For a moment, as goose-pimples washed across her body and the hairs on the back of her neck stood up on end, she thought she was going to trip out again. She looked down at Emma, who was still staring at the patterns on the carpet, and the child again seemed different, nothing to do with her, something very far away. There was still no reply from inside and she could hear somebody beginning to climb the stairs behind them. She turned the handle and entered.

The room was sweltering. The curtains were drawn but the light was on so she could see the piles of boxes, the unmade bed, the clothes strewn everywhere, the dirty plates and take-away cartons, the papers pinned to the walls and the computer equipment clustered on the makeshift table. 'Hello?' she called. 'Hello? Joel, are you there?' She took a couple of paces and stepped on to a discarded chopstick, which snapped and made her jump. Emma wandered on in front and began to inspect the blinking, whirring hardware which was pumping out heat like a stove. Following closely behind, her mother put out her hand to touch one of the boxes, yelping when she received a jolt of electricity. 'Don't touch it, it's dangerous,' she warned the girl, hoping that by identifying this concrete hazard she would calm her own fears.

She turned round to search in the bathroom and that was when she saw down the side of the bed. She screamed and clutched Emma to her, automatically turning her daughter's head from the sight. There wasn't much left of Joel – just a pile of undigested food where his torso had been, a set of disembodied shoulders and a head with no features other than a nose and empty holes where there should have been eyes, ears and a mouth. Jennifer knew immediately that it was him; Joel's nose was one you couldn't easily forget. But what was left of the poor man was quickly vanishing, atom by atom, sinew by sinew, line by line. As she watched, the shoulders dwindled and disappeared and the head was eaten away upwards from the back of the skull, so that it seemed to be sinking into the floor. The whole process lasted no more than a minute and then there was no more head. Just the nose, sitting on the carpet among a pile of dirty clothes, Joel's glasses still perched upon it. Jennifer had presumed that was going to vanish too, but it didn't. Despite all his careful measurements and calculations, Joel had forgotten to quantify the one thing which he saw in the mirror every day of his life, his single most salient feature, that which preceded him everywhere, the part of him upon which those most ancient of prosthetics – his spectacles – depended. He hadn't fed his schnoz into the computer.

'Get out in the corridor,' Jennifer whispered at Emma. 'Get out.' She propelled the child with her hand and reluctantly the girl went. Alone and trembling, Jennifer knelt down by what was left of Joel's body and started to cry. She remained there for several minutes until a fizzle, a crackle and a bang came from behind and she turned to see bolts of electricity arc between the bastardised electronic components on the table. Quickly now she fetched out another tissue and, holding it between her shaking fingers, gingerly reached over and picked up the nose. She wrapped the tissue around it and placed it carefully in the bottom of her bag.

Over on the table the computer equipment had finally reached the limit of what it could take. Flames leapt out of the casings and licked at the curtains, which immediately began to smoulder. Within seconds they were sending plumes of black smoke up and across the ceiling. Taking one last look at where Joel had been Jennifer backed around the end of the bed and out into the corridor, where Emma was waiting. Consumed by panic she grabbed the girl by the arm and pulled her towards the stairs, stopping only to smash the alarm on the wall with her elbow. Throughout the building, bells jangled.

Half-way down the stairs they passed the manager. 'Fire, fire in three ten,' Jennifer gasped. The manager nodded and charged past her. Jennifer and Emma continued down into the lobby and out into the street, the sounds of danger clanging in their ears.

Something old . . .

By the time the computers in the Albion caught fire, it was already too late for Laika. The Joel construct had slipped inside her capsule like a digital sperm burrowing its way into a cosmic egg and the elements of man, data, dog and machine immediately started to blend. The physical sensation the dog experienced was not dissimilar to that which had so affected Jennifer on her return home from London. But while Jennifer had been suffused with euphoria, Laika got the bum's rush, the bad trip. Self-consciousness was useless to her now. The myriad media memories she'd amassed over the years were woken from their slumbers in the hammocks of her ventricles by the shock of Joel's invasion; like schizo armies they now skirmished through her mind, combining and recombining, engaging each other in combat, making a battle zone of her brain. Laika tried to tune her instruments to different channels, to bring in information that would dilute the power of the invader and dampen down the rebels in her psyche, but to no avail: images, sounds, smells, thoughts and impressions curdled over the sides of their proper categories and gelled into new and horrifying forms, dragons of the datasphere. Through the capsule which had become her skin, through her copper-nerves titanium-flesh, through her Russian engineering, she could feel the information surrounding her, the excitement in the fragile fabric all around her, gamma wave to long wave, concentric wrinkles in the infinite bed sheet of space.

Her consciousness turned outwards, only to discover that it could no longer turn back in. Joel had flowed into her systems and fountained up into her brain, a whale spout of virulent variation and malignant meme, a lost spirit desperate for a home, a nematode of Boolean logic. Dog capsule construct circled around the pucker of the planet, buzzing off the mediascape and bombarded by the stars. The capsule became a tiny Io, a volcano moon with whirlwind skies, its inner turmoil so intense that it generated tectonic movements in the outer shell and meltdown at the core. Something was happening here, something very old.

Carnival

Back on earth in the Albion, the manager reached the top of the stairs, grabbed a fire extinguisher from the wall and ran down the corridor towards Joel's room. Inside, most combustibles – the curtains, the bed, the easy chair, patches of the carpet – were already alight, and a boiling mass of dense black smoke was collecting across the ceiling and threatening to ignite. Flash-over. The manager pulled the pin from the extinguisher, smashed the knob with the heel of his hand and played the thin jet of liquid into the room. But it was clearly a hopeless effort. Even standing at the door the smoke was choking him and the wall of heat, so intense it gave the doorway the aura of a portal to another world, was threatening to melt the very threads of his viscose suit. He threw the extinguisher into the room; it rolled across the carpet and lay on its side, its hose flicking spastically back and forth under the power of the jet.

He reached in to grab the door handle and pull it closed, hoping to contain the blaze. As he went for it – one hand reaching, the other on the door-sill, one foot on the threshold, the other as a counterbalance extended out behind – the smoke cleared for a second and he got a proper glimpse of the humanoid shape of the computer equipment on the table by the window, the source of the fire. 'Christ!' he said, a Christian man. 'They've got a fucking corpse in there!' He slammed the door closed and raced downstairs. Taking the steps three or four at a time he managed to reach the lobby in about three seconds flat. 'Fire!' he yelled at whoever it was that was standing at the reception desk. 'Call the fire brigade and the police and the ambulance. Call everybody! I think there's somebody still in there. HURRY! Where's that woman and her kid? *Which way did they go?*'

The figure opened its mouth and tried to point, then closed its mouth and managed to point. 'Street,' it said, that being the fastest way to get the information across. 'They went out into the . . .'

But the manager had already gone, carried through the glass doors on the vector of that initial word. He blinked in the daylight, dull though it was, got his bearings. The street was busy with people heading west towards Carnival. He couldn't see the woman or the child. The flow of pedestrians made up his mind for him and he headed with it, using it for momentum, charging ahead and dodging the people in front of him. He reached the first corner and jumped up on the low wall which protected the basement area of the houses in that row. Craning his neck, he spotted them, a dash of green, a dark head of hair, turning left two streets up. Then he was off again, dodging and weaving, the smooth resin soles of his shoes barely gripping the pavement.

When he reached the next corner he jumped and saw them again, turning right this time. He shoved on through the crowd. The exertion was already getting to him. At the top of his field of vision a silvery border was strobing at an incredible rate and whenever he blinked he could see the whole of his optic nerve, silver on black, a wild bloom with a stem that tunnelled away into darkness. He ran straight into a white cop, who was busy gazing at the crowds and secretly wishing he were a homeboy.

'Oi, where the 'ell d'you think yore going, then?'

'Oh, officer, thank God. I'm chasing a woman, woman and kid, set fire to my hotel, I . . . gasp . . . I think they might have . . . gasp . . . might have killed somebody.'

'And which 'otel would this be, sir?'

'The Albion, Prince's Square. Hurry, they're getting away!' And with the energy of the valued employee the manager somehow sucked more air into his bleeding lungs and darted off after Jennifer and Emma.

Fun at last! 'Attention all units, this is PC 668, am in pursuit of three suspects, woman, child and man, heading west in the direction of Chep-stow–Pembridge intersection, possible arson, murder, request assistance . . .'

Mother and child hurried through the streets hand in hand, aware that they were being followed and conscious of the Carnival up ahead, a healthy throb of energy that felt dark, obscure, that would afford them cover. They avoided an intersection marked out by the tensions of con-verging police and ran straight up Hereford Road instead. Then west towards Powis Square and one of the hearts of the festival, steering clear of anything that smacked of the vertical lines of authority or organisation: pubs, floats, sponsored sound systems. Cut across the channels. Avoid switches and sphincters, dissectors of flow. It's guerrilla tactics, fish-in-the-water stuff – remember what Stim used to say about Mao Tse-tung. Blend in. Be aware of the structures of power and side-step them. Be quick, be rude, be quiet.

The streets were rammed. Thousands of people had made the road into a river, one current forward, one current back, a hundred little eddies along the way and a riverbed of cartons, corncobs, cans, roach ends, empty bottles of Dragon Stout underfoot. On every corner the sound systems slammed out hip hop, rap or dub and the noise was immense, not one kind of music but an absurd and outrageous mélange. Islands in the stream, men stood selling enormous bunches of the steel whistles with the red gold green straps. Everyone seemed to have one and to be blowing it; the whole day was borne on shrill metal screams.

Emma was terrifically excited. Now that they were among the crowds she'd forgotten about the danger and was drinking from the vast fonts all around: the sounds, the smells, the sights. It was a world at play, a thousand dances all at once, and her over-connected mind fizzled and sparked with the thought of it. She couldn't get over the colours of the people, dozens of shades and hues in minute variation. And there were dancers everywhere, not just at street level but on balconies, up in trees, atop lamp-posts and speaker stacks. They got propelled past a system pumping ska; on the stage a white hippy wearing African costume swayed to and fro, an enormous joint in his hand. (There was tension here.) The smell of marijuana was everywhere, mixed in with the odorous fronts of saltfish fritters, goat curries, Thai noodles, ackee and candy floss that were filtering through the crowds from the stalls which lined the pavements.

Jennifer, however, was more frightened than ever. She had no time for any of this. Her head turned this way and that, at odds with the rhythms around her. There were so many police! Male and female, some in shirt-sleeves, some like wasps in bright-yellow jackets striped with reflectors in warning. They wore caps, hats, helmets. Some were on horseback. So many! It was enough to incite a riot. When Emma started to pull at her again she held the child back. They had to stay with the crowd. If they broke out into space they were lost. With all the whistling she couldn't tell what was police and what wasn't. Right now, that was probably good.

The child was busy working on the bigger picture. She'd begun to get a sense of how the whole thing moved, of the hydrodynamics of half a million people in this small maze of streets. In terms of size and population the area wasn't all that far off the Warsaw ghetto, the boundaries of which Joel had walked five or six years earlier. Except that these people were in motion, being channelled rather than contained. Emma concentrated on the shapes the mass made as it moved, on the hidden dragons in the crowds, the attractors and the slow tides. They crossed Westbourne Park Road and worked their way up All Saints. Jennifer had never seen anything like it. The street was a sea of black faces, wall to wall, everybody leaping up and down to three separate sound systems, the tops of their heads undulating in waves from one end of the road to the other. They hooked on to the end of one of the trains of people that was threading its way, impossibly, through the crowd, and followed it. Every time they passed one of the sound systems – each one had curved banks of speakers on both sides of the street which created a chaotic zone of vibration and sound in between – their viscera juddered in sympathy with the bass, a noise so low that it came up through the soles of their feet, grabbed their heart liver lungs and dragged them down into their groins.

It took them about twenty-five minutes to get that eighty yards and when they emerged on Tavistock Street there was a wall of police to their left. Jennifer dragged Emma round and they headed east as fast as they could. And at that point the day turned darker still and it started to rain.

... *something new*

The blend of Joel and Laika bounced around the globe, from satellite to satellite, from cable to fibre-optic, from microwave to radio. They were the mail daemon, the packet, the gopher, the virus. They were neither nothing nor everything. She was code, he dogmeat. He charged around, electrons up his arse. She took notes and puzzled at probability. He turned her inside out; she gave him fleas. They bled and bred, turned out something new.

Evolution? Not in the sense that you mean.

This body I wear too well

Clouds of asphalt and khaki had woven a carpet over the sky. The rain, once it came, came quickly. The dancing crowds didn't seem to mind – people held up their hands and let the rain fall on their faces, on their hands, on their naked arms and shoulders. The rain poured down harder, blue-black streaks of data streaming from the heavens, and they danced all the more. Women bared their breasts to the water, men opened their mouths and tried to drink. Babies began to cry and screech, and children chased each other around in circles, throwing sticks of sugar cane and grooving in the quickly forming puddles.

The rain stung Jennifer's skin. It had begun as a prickling sensation, an uncomfortable feeling, as if her hands were beginning to freeze. The day was warm and the rain was warm, yet her hands and face were agony. She glared at two heavily built black women, dancing opposite each other, gyrating and wobbling and whooping, and delighted to have the water soak them through. How could they bear it?

It ran in channels now, along the filthy roads and concrete pavements, worked its way around islands of discarded corncobs and cans, half-eaten plantains and patties. Emma was fascinated by it. She'd only ever seen the rain from inside before; being in it was a strange experience. She liked the feel of it thrumming on her scalp and she sucked on the wet ends of hair that hung down her face. She watched the other kids playing, thought it looked fun.

They passed two policemen on the corner; Jennifer glanced down a moment too late. One of them had caught her eye and a glimmer of something passed between them before she actively cut it off. Still watching her, the cop radioed base, asked for a description. Jennifer began to run, hauling Emma along with her, and the cop tagged his colleague and they both sped off in pursuit. Mother and daughter headed into the crowd, forcing their way through groups of people. *Excuse me, sorry, excuse me, excuse me, let me through.* Glancing back, she could see that more police had joined the chase. The hotel manager was among them, baying for her blood. 'Come on, darling, come on,' she said to Emma, and slipping her arms around the child's waist she swung her up on to her hip. The crowd was getting scary now, it was so closely packed. The press of people was moving as one; there was no way back and the roads to either side were blocked off, though there was no hope of getting to them anyway. Jennifer forced herself on ahead, screaming, 'I have to get my child to a hospital,' clearing people out of the way with her voice.

She was approaching Westbourne Park tube. Perhaps she could reach it, get away on a train? But as she rounded the corner it became obvious that no way was this an option. Police ringed the entrance and already there was a violent ebb of people trying to gain access. A PA boomed out across the crowd: *Do not attempt to travel without a ticket . . . do not attempt to travel without a ticket . . .* again and again, the same thing: . . . *do not attempt to travel without a ticket, do not attempt to travel . . .* It made the crowd angry, which was a bad thing, because the crowd had stopped moving. Jennifer had thought when they'd got to the intersection that the throngs would disperse but she couldn't have been more wrong. All three feed roads were feeding only one way – inwards. In each direction – north, over the bridge and under the Westway, south down through the council estates and west from whence she had come – every inch of space was jammed with flesh and every face was looking to the centre, which is where she now found herself. Her skin was alive again, on fire with feeling, and she felt quite delirious. Over the heads of the people she could see yellow police clawing their way through towards her like beetles, trying to save their hats from being knocked off by the homeboys in the crowd. The rain was coming down harder then ever and it felt to Jennifer as though it was tearing into her face and hands. Emma reached up and tried to cling to her neck, finally frightened, nearly pulling her down. To fall would be fatal; there were so many feet that they'd never get up again; they'd be trampled to death. (Beneath those feet, where Jennifer could not see them, lay hundreds and hundreds of flyers. They must have been printed up only hours earlier, because each one bore the image of Joel's face, sans nose, and advertised a post-Carnival party at a club called Balaam.) She began to call for a miracle, to scream at the sky, 'Save me, save me, I can't go back there!'

Mounted police arrived and panic quickly percolated through the crowd. The attempts of those nearest the horses to get away from the violence merely communicated it. Any movement was immediately amplified and transmitted: the resultant surges carried people bodily before them. More than once the press was so strong that Jennifer and Emma were lifted off their feet like dolls and moved four or five metres before being set down. There was nowhere at all to go. Desperate, Jennifer continued to scream and yell at the elements, demanding action, as Judd and Joel had done before her. Fights started to break out in the vicinity of the police and also at the intersection where men whose tempers had already been frayed by their fear got shoved one time too many.

Then Emma looked at her mother and screamed, and Jennifer looked down at her daughter, took her face in her hands and saw then that these same hands were losing definition. At first she didn't understand what it was and she stared for a moment, confused. And then . . . it was the rain – each drop of rain was eating into her, carrying a little trace of her away. Nobody else seemed affected, it was just her. She started to shake and brought her hands up in front of her own face. She was experiencing the rushing sensation again, a high band-width tingle that shivered up her arms and arced across her mind. It was the feeling she'd had that night on the floor of her living-room, of becoming continuous with her surroundings. She didn't know whether it was joy or pain. Perhaps it was release. She felt her network of scars beginning to glow and this gave her heart. She started to cry and the tears cut furrows into her cheeks.

The rain sliced into her skin. She began to reel and spasm, and a space formed around her as people found gaps where previously they would have sworn there had been only flesh. She dropped her bag and reached for Emma, then drew back and fell to her knees on a thin bed of pictures of Joel. Gently, she touched her face. It gave beneath her fingers like mush. Water ran down her forehead and on to her hands, and continued to wash them away. The ring of people around her looked on in horror but Emma stood there and gazed, irises of steel, emerald and dew. Mother and daughter, eyes met for one final time.

How much is conveyed by a look? Enough, in this case, for Jennifer to realise what was at stake, for her to know that Emma was the whole of life, from the chemical dance to the soft touch of breath, just as any daughter was to her mother. She knew then that all was material, that this was the world's wonder and that the thought of rocks in the earth, bones on a beach, sparks in the sun, clouds out of reach was her own thought, too – and that her own thought was in her fingers in her toes in the scars on her skin and in the sound of her name, in her sex in her grip in her womb. Thumb to mouth, cock to cunt, hand to breast, lip to lip, flower to wasp, man to dog, club to skull, cunt to eye, eye to brain, voice to tree, voice to plain, word to deed, wreath to grave, leaf to groin, cell to stave, stone to sea, sea to salt, salt to charge, charge to pain, sea to breeze, breeze to rain, rain to hill, hill to face, face to place, place to space, space to frame, frame to gain . . . with these the world remade itself at every turn, made its time and space too, because these grew as well, these were alive, these were the yeasts of it all, these were its joy. Emma's eye danced and whirled, clicked and weighed, sifting input through the meshworks and filters of . . . Jennifer knew by now that there was no word here, only a plane, a zone across which words could stray, could dream, could compute, could connect. She let herself go, becoming the liquid she always was, ready at last to conquer the land. Her dark hair disappeared and the water carrying it away ran an inky black. She looked at Emma with the last of her eyes, but the girl's green coat quickly faded to grey and then she was gone.

Jennifer slumped over and rolled flat out on the ground. The sky belched and retched, and the rain came down more heavily than ever. Back in All Saints the revellers had lost their enthusiasm. This wasn't dancing weather any more, it was dangerous weather. People started to flood out of Notting Hill, although it was rapidly becoming increasingly hard to leave: the surrounding areas were already saturated and were having difficulty blotting all these extra people up. Emma crouched by her mother, holding on to her skirt, her flesh vanishing too fast now to afford a grip. Her clothes sagged as the water ran through them and carried away her blood: from out of her sleeves and hems the scarlet fluid poured.

As her skull began to go the fear surrounding the two of them reached its apogee and someone vomited, then a huge and hypertrophic man in trackies, a leather T-shirt and an Adidas cagoule bent down by Emma, touched her shoulders, took off his jacket and used it gently to cover what was left of Jennifer's head. 'You better come with me, chicken,' he said softly, and took her tiny hand in his own. 'Bad things are happenin' to your mom, we wanna make sure you're safe.' Emma didn't look at him, still looked down at Jennifer though there was nothing left to see, just a discarded set of clothes lying there in the street, nameless clothes, belonging to nobody, filthied by the rain.

Then a shout went up and the horses broke through, and the ring that had remained stable around Jennifer's disintegration finally gave way. The stranger held Emma to him, kept her close against his body so she shouldn't be seen, started to pull her away. People were sucked into the now empty space and the pile of soaking clothes was on the verge of being engulfed when Emma broke free from the man and rushed back towards it. Time itself seemed to eddy and curve for her; there's a hydro-dynamics in there somewhere, too. Darting between the forest of legs, she shot out a hand and grabbed her mother's bag – or did it fly up towards her? – then turned and ran back to the stranger. No sooner had she gone than time reasserted itself and the tangle of horses' legs and humans came trampling in and Jennifer's clothes were instantly torn to shreds.

The stranger held her again and manoeuvred her south. Behind them a full-scale battle had broken out between the revellers and the police. Hands sprang up from the mass and tugged at the nearest policemen, trying to unseat them from their steeds. Terrified, the coppers lashed out left and right with their truncheons, telescopic devices that extended to a full three feet, catching people indiscriminately across their shoulders and heads. Off to the left someone dressed in a kilt was yelling, 'They tried to wipe out the bagpipes three hundred years ago, but they're two thousand, three thousand, four thousand years old.' Whoever it was had a set of pipes with him and now he swung them into position, put the mouthpiece to his lips and began to heave out a Scottish battle tune at breakneck speed. A roar went up from the crowd and they pitched into the police with renewed vigour. On top of the tube station, officers stood with a compound-lens camera taking head shots of those in the crowd, ten thousand every ten seconds. The pictures were captured in digital format and fed down a cable to a portable up-link which sat on the rooftop next to the camera. This beamed them up into the sky, up and up, until they reached a satellite high above the earth and were bounced back down to Scotland Yard. There, each face was separated out by computers which then churned through vast databanks searching for matches. As she was led away, Emma reached her hand down inside Jennifer's bag and felt for Joel's nose. When she found it, she held on to it tightly. It was warm.

To the sea

Jennifer ran and ran, laughing as she went. She flowed away from the intersection, beneath and around the frightened feet of the crowd. She disappeared down gutters gratings storm drains, splashed over parapets and down the brick sides of bridges, dripped off overhangs and arches, slid into gardens and filtered her way through the earth. She spread out across the city, eased into sewers and basements, sped along underground railways, made her way down to the Thames. She was lapped up by dogs, sprayed out by cars, sneezed in by rats. She crept her way through pores into bloodstreams. She seeped into cisterns and osmosed into plants. When the storm was over and the sun came out she disappeared into the air and was breathed into lungs, sucked into engines, swollen as clouds and blown this way and that by the buffeting winds. She sat in toilets, played from fountains. Pigeons pecked at her and ducks paddled on her. Birds flew through her, crops drank from her. She was everywhere and nowhere, a sprite of the city, a queen of the land. She did nothing, thought nothing; did everything, thought everything. She matched herself with the great movements of liquid, with the strata of weather and groundwater, pipelines and plumbing, flora and fauna, mist and sea. She aligned herself with the circuits of evaporation and precipitation which power these planes and enable movement between them. She slept in lakes and danced down rivers. Replete with chemicals and minerals, she energised soil and plant, plant and animal, animal and air, linking the cells of the biosphere. Fish spawned in her, dew formed from her. Snow snowed by her. People washed in her, swam in her, lived through her. She was everywhere now and, for her, this was the solution.

AFTERWORD

A dog called Om

Some time later, Emma stepped off a train and on to the light gravel of the station platform at Stratford-upon-Avon. She no longer wore her green coat; it had been replaced with blue dungarees and a black Puffa jacket. Her hair had been cropped short and the new haircut made her look a little less ugly. It was a bright day, crisp, autumnal, a Saturday. She watched the train draw out, then went up the stairs and over the tracks, down again and out into the weak winter sun. The trees were bare, the last remnants of the leaves a dark sludge beneath her trainers.

She left the station and began to walk north, back over the tracks via the road bridge and past all those Bed & Breakfasts that had bordered that roadside for ever. The air was sharp after London, clean and brisk. The houses were detached, screened by low walls and privet. She seemed to know where she was going.

She passed a school and its playing fields where other children were hot–cold with their games. Their yells knocked back and forth between the buildings, counterpointed by the peep of the schoolteachers' whistles. Although it was late morning a mist hung above the grass. Dried pats of mud with neat holes bored through them, imprints of football boots, were strewn across the pavement in front of her.

She walked for about half an hour before she reached what was left of the Last Resort, but she passed it, as most did, without so much as a thought. It took her another hour to walk eastwards along the roads skirting Stratford to the entrance to the civic tip. The gates were open and she walked through them, and beneath the wooden cross-beam that prevented lorries from entering. The track was paved and well-kempt but at either side steep banks reared up behind the pale-grey edging stones. Brambles nettles hawthorn crowded down them, tussling for space.

464

Unripe blackberries hung thin and raw from studded boughs, and sparrows and blackbirds chuckled among the dark tangle.

Emma reached the metal viaduct and passed underneath, ignoring the traffic light, knowing that there was nothing approaching. Round the corner there was bustle and noise: several cars were parked there and their occupants were throwing boxes of junk into massive green skips or feeding empty bottles into colour-coded metal containers. To the north, men unloaded refrigerators into a hole in the ground. Emma ignored them all, walked past them to the edge of the tarmac and followed a trail laid by caterpillar tracks. Some hundred yards further on she came to the landfill, the midden, dead now, the same one Jennifer had used. The junk had been levelled and the meniscus of rubbish lapped up the earthy banks to within a metre or two of her feet. At one end about a third of the pit was already filled in with topsoil and clay, but the diggers stood idle now, their drivers busy downing Saturday pints at the pub.

She stood at the edge of the pit, breathed it in, steadied herself under the assault. This was shattered relationship, densely packed, dynamic upon dynamic laid down like sedimentary rock. Potentials buzzed from item to item, from one discarded object to another, as if each broken thing were a tesla coil of emotion. Rotting sofas with entire families encrusted upon them, infested mattresses with twenty years of marriage in their springs, broken vases, standard lamps, bicycles that knew so many miles. Plates with a thousand meals ingrained on their faces, cane chairs with quivering buttocks lost in their splits, typewriters with love letters hidden in their ribbons, telephones strangled by long strings of sound. Record players silenced by too much vibration, books whose pages held the memories of thumbs, baths ringed with layers of limestone and skin, mirrors filled with rooms in reverse.

Crows wheeled above it all, points on the vortex that spun out of all of this dying technology. Emma watched them for a while, wondering, probing, then turned and inched her way down into the pit. Once safely down, she started out across the surface of rubber wood plastic and steel, going slowly and testing each step before trusting it. She let herself be guided across, the cracked clocks and broken shelves signposting the way for her, until somewhere out in the middle she found what she'd been looking for.

It was the television, Donald's old box and the centrepiece of Jennifer's movie matinée parties. There was not much left of it now. The screen was cracked and the control panel caved in, and the thing looked to the sky, forlorn, as if waiting for one last viewer to come from the heavens and scry it. It had been cursed while alive to form a link in the world, to fold space into colours and flickers. But nothing could do that for long.

465

Emma looked at it: it would do. Picking up a rusty golf club she swung it at the TV and smashed in the screen, hitting the tube again and again, splintering the glass into fragments. Struggling now, she heaved the set up by a corner and rolled it over, emptying out the shards before rolling it back. She wrapped her hand in an old piece of fertiliser bag and picked out the last of them, then set the thing upright, directing it up at the sun. And then she crawled inside.

Folding herself up like one of its pictures, she worked her way in and made a nest of the hulk, fitting herself to its shape. Here she was, an everyday girl in an everyday place. From the dump all around her, the motion of the crows, the events of the sky, she drew strength. She had lost her parents so, like them, she had to grow up, shoulder her responsibilities, take the world into herself. She'd been there an hour when her skin began to blister and breathe, forming thousands of stomate-like openings through which pale filaments began to protrude. Her cloth-ing started to rustle and bulge as these hyphae sought a way out, eventually exiting through her collar and waistband and cuffs, as her mother had done when trapped in her clothes a few weeks before. Once free, they quickly filled the space of the old television, then ate into its housing, stripping molecular compounds from the wood and the metals, and using them to build novel types of lignin and bark.

A core thus established, they plunged down into the tip, infiltrating the products that had been dumped there, drawing on the minerals and the memories and the festering emotions stored up within. In this way a wider root system was formed, an enormous rhizome that broke down the old technology, sucked it dry. At the base of the pit Emma found clay, pierced it with radicles, increasing proportions of smectite and kaolinite as she did so, changing the geological balance beneath; nearer the ground she pene-trated the topsoil and sought partners symbionts parasites and hosts. Every-thing she found was drawn in, made use of: ascomycetes and zygomycetes helped her to integrate with the nature around her, basidiomycetes donated psilocybin that helped her to think, roots of oak and ash linked her with the wind and sky, angiosperms taught her the circling ways of the insects, rubber and concrete lent her resilience and strength, plastics and chemicals helped her adapt and taught her more of the ways of the human.

Within days, she started to put forth new shoots and by the time a week had gone by the tip was verdant, a bower of lianas made strong with metals from motors and fibres from linen, lianas which fluttered like bunting with rich green leaves whose impossible sheen was achieved by the leaching of fluids from discarded cans of furniture polish and industrial cleaner. More crows began to circle around, drawn by the tempting secretions Emma leaked from her limbs. Their droppings enriched the tips with the ammonium and calcium phosphates she hungered for, and before long she would puff spores on to their wings so that they could carry her progeny forth.

She was a lake now, a tiny ocean whose vascular currents were home to microbes and viruses, viroids and pentastomes and other organisms too varied to count, an ecology complete in itself, a replay of the birth of the biosphere. At the centre her old body lay curled, its limbs and the television around them no longer distinguishable from the creak and vegetable spurl, her mind distributed among the autotrophic cells that made up the thicket she'd become. But the TV set still worked as a focus. With her shiny leaves all angled towards it Emma channelled photons into the old wooden box, made it her eye. Through it, silently and in her own time, she watched the skies, scanned the stratosphere, reached out into space for the message she guessed would come soon, a new type of chloroplast that with a biological gamble, a spin of the wheel, a roll of the dice, urged itself on to a strange photosynthetic reaction, the like of which had never before been seen.

For she wasn't alone. High above, skidding round the dip of the planet and sending out signals, a motor-cycle rider on gravity's grim wall of death, is a dark moon of flesh and technology. No one can tell where it starts, where it ends, no one can decipher the orders it gives. It's a point of view, a remote camera, it's something that cares that the planets align in a series of curves. It's a metal egg, a cosmic egg, it's oeuf and oeuvre. Inside its cells things burble and spoil. It's a series of loops and dead-ends and exertions with no sense of itself. It has drives and dynamics, but can't scent or see them. It's not a sphere, more a plane, a wafer of lattice and flux that, like Emma below, creates its own space, its own time. It expands, but not outwards – outwards and inwards mean nothing to it. It envelops and probes, but never equally, never with measure. It heads off in countless directions from multiple centres and goes nowhere. It's frogspawn, bacteria. It's a hopeless god, a lost cause, a blind harbour-master, a crazed midwife, a corrupted disk, a mongrel pup. It is a node, an eddy, a storm, a singularity. It is only something, not one thing. It's a man called machine. It's a dynamic called data. It's a dog they call Om. The only word, perhaps, that is not an instruction.

If such a thing is possible, that is.

ACKNOWLEDGEMENTS

I am indebted to Hillel Schwartz's essay 'Torque: The New Kinaesthetic of the Twentieth Century' (published in *Incorporations*, Zone, 1992) for the identification of the links between Wilbur Wright, Isadora Duncan and comptometer operators, and to Paul Virilio's *The Aesthetics of Disappearance* (trans. Philip Beitchman, Semiotext(e), 1991) for isolating the phenomenon of picnolepsy and uncovering the disappearance fantasies of Howard Hughes.

The description of Nadine's pre-frontal leucotomy owes a great deal to Geoffrey Knight's 'The Orbital Cortex as an Objective in the Surgical Treatment of Mental Illness' (*British Journal of Surgery*, 1964, Vol. 51, no. 2, February). The translation of Himmler's speech at Poznan is taken from Martin Gilbert's *The Holocaust – the Jewish tragedy* (Fontana, 1987). The launch vehicle characteristics of Sputnik I, diagram and text, are copyright Mark Wade and taken from his website (solar.rtd.utk.edu/~mwade/spaceflt.htm) and the Dostoevsky excerpt is taken from Fyodor Dostoevksy, *The Gambler* (trans. Jessie Coulson, Penguin, 1966). I am grateful to the Athlone Press for permission to quote from *Difference and Repetition* by Deleuze, translated by Paul Patton, 1994; to Flammarion for permission to quote from *Angels* by Michel Serres, translated by Francis Cowper, 1995; and to Gollancz for permission to quote from *Invisible Man* by Ralph Ellison, 1953.

Details of Joel's shoe computer are largely taken from *The Newtonian Casino* by Thomas A. Bass (Penguin, 1991) and of SABRE and SAGE (and a few other technological snippets) from *Computer* by Martin Campbell-Kelly and William Asprey (Basic Books, 1996). I am indebted to Sadie Plant for ideas about Ada Lovelace, to Nick Land for setting me straight, and to Mark and Dianna McMenamin's *Hypersea* (Columbia University Press, 1994) for the concept of, well, hypersea.

Finally, immense thanks to Pauline, Hari, Hannah, Jonny, Katie, Josh and the Pig – couldn't have done it without you.

THE BIOGRAPHICAL DICTIONARY OF MANAGEMENT

Volume 1

A–J

GENERAL EDITOR

Morgen Witzel

THOEMMES PRESS

First published in 2001 by

Thoemmes Press
11 Great George Street
Bristol BS1 5RR, England

http://www.thoemmes.com

The Biographical Dictionary of Management
2 Volumes : ISBN 1 85506 871 0

© Thoemmes Press, 2001

British Library Cataloguing-in-Publication Data
A CIP record of this title is available from the British Library

Typeset in Sabon at Thoemmes Press.
Printed and bound in the UK by Antony Rowe Ltd.
This book is printed on acid-free paper, sewn, and
cased in a durable buckram cloth.

CONTENTS

INTRODUCTION

The idea for this project came, as ideas for many good projects do, during a conversation after lunch. Instinctively, we felt the idea seemed right, and it took only about a minute to decide to take the project forward. That was the easy part.

It would have been simple enough merely to make a list of the great and the good in business management and then commission biographies of them. Similar projects have been done in the past: as such, they are valuable historical records and highly useful reference tools (some of these are listed in the General Bibliography). Our goals, however, were slightly different. Specifically, we were interested not just in management as it is today, but also in the historical aspects of the development of management. There is, as many readers of this volume will know, some debate within the management community as to whether the past holds any real value for management today. There is neither time nor space here to go into this argument in detail.[1] Suffice it to say that we believe that management is a dynamic set of ideas and concepts, one which evolves over time. The study of management's past is therefore important in explaining its present.

That given, we wanted to see whether a biographical collection such as this could perhaps tell us more about the nature and historical development of management as both a commercial concept and a social force. To do this, we felt we needed to get away from more traditional models of business history.[2] The current paradigm of study of business history is – correctly – value-neutral in that it tends to regard all the businesses within a field of study – industry sector, national economy, etc. – as equally worthy of study regardless of the quality of their management. The study of the failures is every bit as important as the study of the successes. The focus that we had chosen, however, meant that inevitably we were going to have to be much more selective. We came to the conclusion that our main interest was not in the *managers* as individuals, but in *management* as a set of ideas and practices. We wanted to see if we could use the study of the people to tell us more about their ideas.

We were not the first to take this view. A number of other attempts have been made in the past to use both business history and management history to explain how and why

---

[1] Those interested in some rebuttals of the 'history is bunk' argument may be interested to read Karl Moore and David Lewis's *Foundations of Corporate Empire* (2000) or Chapter 2 of Morgen Witzel's *Builders and Dreamers* (2001).

[2] We are making a distinction here between business history, the study of economic institutions, and management history, the study of the ideas, practices and people by which those institutions are governed. Clearly there is considerable overlap between the two concepts; we do not favour the view found in some academic circles that 'business' and 'management' are concepts best discussed separately. Here, our aim is to look at the evolution and development of management: the importance and relevance of this to business is, we hope, obvious.

management has developed, and several different models have been employed. An early influence was John P. Davis, the American lawyer and historian whose posthumously published book *Corporations* (1905) explores how the modern business corporation developed. Davis takes an evolutionary approach: he sees corporations as social forms which evolve according to the needs of society at a particular time and place. He also takes the view of the *longue durée*; he sees the corporation as an ancient form that has gone through many guises. Crucially from our point of view, he sees corporations as combining social form with social function: how corporations meet their goals and the goals of society depends on how they are managed. Davis's views lent weight to our own conviction that management was not – as some modern writers imagine – something that sprang up fully formed, like Athena from the head of Zeus, in the late nineteenth or early twentieth centuries. Rather, it is an ancient concept, one that has come down through the centuries in many shapes and forms but remains surprisingly unchanged in at least some of its essential features.

The second model that interested us was that adopted by Herbert N. Casson, who during his career as a journalist (he had previously been a Methodist preacher and a socialist agitator, and would later go on to be a leading exponent of scientific management), wrote several important biographical works, most notably *Romance of Steel* (1907), which described the meteoric rise of the American steel industry in the late nineteenth century. Casson, like Davis, is rarely studied these days; the fact that he wrote with considerable flair and energy and in a style which suggests a strong affinity for his subjects may have harmed his reputation – it is, of course, possible for an academic writer to write too well, as someone once said of Francis Parkman – and his many imitators have focused more on the 'romance' and less on the 'business'.[3] But Casson's own work is serious in its intent. His aim is to discover how and why the steel barons succeeded, and his chosen method is to examine their lives and working practices. Reading *The Romance of Steel*, one is aware of watching the progress of two journeys: one is that of Schwab, Carnegie, Frick, Elbert Gary and their fellows towards the positions of power and wealth they came to occupy; the other is that of Casson himself, exploring the nature and roots of management, and steadily formulating the ideas that, a few years later, he would use to advantage when becoming one of the world's leading management consultants.

Biography, too, was one of the tools used by Lyndall Urwick and Edward Brech some years later. Two of the most important figures in the small pantheon of management history, Urwick and Brech, in partnership or singly, have given us some of the field's most valuable work. Their three-volume collaboration, *The Making of Scientific Management* (1947–9), is a very detailed account of the great movement which, between about 1890 and 1930, did so much to shape modern management, and includes a volume of biographies of leading figures from both the United States and Europe. Some years later, Urwick edited *The Golden Book of Management* (1956), a collection of short biographies of some seventy pioneer thinkers and practitioners (again, mostly involved with the scientific management movement). Edward Brech has gone on to compile a five-volume history of management in Britain, which, though not strictly speaking biographical, nonetheless contains much information on the pioneers of management thinking and practice in this country.[4] The work of Urwick and Brech thus combines analytical and

---

[3] William Henry Beable's *The Romance of Great Businesses*, published in 1926, is a good – or perhaps bad – example of this genre.

[4] Edward Brech has done much to keep the torch of management history burning in Britain since the 1950s, and scholars not only in this country but around the world owe him a debt; we are honoured to have had his participation and advice on this project. His five-volume work *The Evolution of Modern Management* will be published by Thoemmes Press in 2002.

descriptive approaches to organizational and managerial thinking with biography. As they comment in the introduction to the opening volume of *The Making of Scientific Management*:

> No student of Scientific Management can comprehend his subject unless he sees behind the text book technique, the reflection of the individual human beings who have lived and laboured to add to our store of exact knowledge.
>
> (Urwick and Brech 1947–9: 19)

Where Casson is more didactic, urging that students of management should learn directly from the careers of great managers, Urwick and Brech see biography as one of a package of tools, essential to understanding the context of developments in management. Like Casson, they emphasize the essentially human nature of management, even scientific management.

The doyen of business historians, Alfred Chandler, does not use biography explicitly as a tool, but his approach, particularly in his early work *Strategy and Structure* (1962), has biographical overtones. A historian rather than a businessman, Chandler's method is more heavily grounded in theory than that of the writers mentioned above. In *Strategy and Structure*, he sets out to describe a particular evolutionary change in the way that businesses were organized and managed in the United States. His vehicle for doing so is four highly detailed case studies of firms that pioneered this transition. As noted, he does not use biography as such, but accounts of the careers of the managers who made the innovations – Pierre du Pont, Alfred Sloan, Robert Wood, Walter Teagle and their associates – run strongly through the narrative. Chandler's approach shows us how the study of mana*gers* can illuminate the study of manage*ment*.

Looking at these four approaches, it seemed that all had commendable features. The *longue durée* approach of Davis, the explicit focus on biography of Casson, the belief that a knowledge of the people involved is a key part of the study of management as postulated by Urwick and Brech, and finally the use of the study of managers to further the study of management that appears in Chandler's work, all confirmed our view that a set of biographical studies aimed at exploring the nature and development of management would have real value. This core proposition in mind, we turned our attention to selecting the subjects for study.

How the Entries were Selected
This was always going to be one of the most difficult stages of the process. We decided, in the end, to restrict the total number of entries to around 600, the number best suited to the span of control of a relatively small editorial board and production team, and which could be produced in relatively short order. Speed was felt to be important: because management is such a dynamic subject, and because we knew from the outset we would be including many subjects who are still highly active in their fields, we needed to produce the body of work relatively quickly if the material was to remain in date. Six hundred entries would not give us complete coverage of the subject – nor indeed would 6,000 – but it would, we felt, be sufficient to cover all the major fields of activity.

When selecting the 600 who would go forward and have entries commissioned on them, we were guided first by our desire to use the project to learn more about the nature and evolution of management. It followed, then, that anyone selected would have to have made some contribution, in terms of either thought or practice. From the beginning, we were

determined that both management professionals and academics would be represented. Management, if we may grossly paraphrase Thomas Edison, is 10 per cent observation and 90 per cent perspiration; but that 10 per cent has had an important impact, especially in the last century. The relationship between academia and professional managers is often an uneasy one, but few can doubt the necessity or importance of both.[5]

Some of the important trends and developments we wanted to cover, however, were not the work of a single innovator or innovative group. In some other cases, particularly in earlier times, the historical picture is more indistinct and those who had the great ideas and made the advances are not known to us; all we can see are the consequences of their ideas in the changing nature of management over time. As well as picking those who made direct contributions to the development of management, then, we determined that in special cases we would pick outstanding figures who could serve as exemplars. We do not yet know in detail how the Ningbo Guild came to dominate the domestic financial markets of eastern China in the early twentieth century, but we do know that Yu Yajing was a leading member of the guild, and we have enough information about him to construct a brief biography which shows how both he and the institutions he was part of operated. Eddie Rickenbacker and Grant McConachie made no startling contributions to management as a discipline, but they are both in their separate ways outstanding examples of how managers operated in new and emerging industries (in this case, airlines). Judicious use of these examples, then, could help give us a more complete and rounded picture of the development of management.

How then to select our 600 from the multitudes clamouring for attention? We needed to ensure that our final selection did the following. First, it had to cover the whole evolution of management, from the time of the first managed institutions to the present. It would be pointless to pretend that management in Mesopotamia 4,000 years ago was just the same as management today, or that *Duties of the Vizier* is of the same value to the modern manager as *Management: Tasks, Responsibilities, Practices* by Peter Drucker, and modern entries (that is, covering people active from about 1850 onwards) were always going to dominate. The aim when picking the entries covering earlier figures was to show only those whose ideas and practices could shed light on the slow evolution of management over that time. Around 10 per cent of subjects in the dictionary lived and worked before 1800, and we think this is about the right balance.[6]

Second, the selection had to be global. A common failing of business and management histories published in the West is that they do not look outside the relatively narrow cultural confines of the Anglo-Saxon business world: even Japan gets only minority coverage in most cases. But China, Korea, France, Germany, Italy, Poland, Czechoslovakia, India and Brazil all have, or at some point have had, thriving management cultures of their own. Often these cultures show up as fascinating hybrids, mixes of ideas and practices borrowed from the English-speaking nations (we include Canada and Australia in this

---

[5] Malcolm Warner, in his introduction to the *IEBM Handbook of Management Thinking*, makes the excellent point that the sources of management thought have also changed in nature. A hundred years ago, the prime generators of new thinking were practitioner-theorists like Taylor, Ford, Dennison, Gulick and Urwick; today's management gurus are nearly all academics. That tendency will be noted in this volume; very many of the subjects born after 1900 worked or work in academia, while very few of those born before 1900 did so.

[6] Daniel Wren, in his *The Evolution of Management Thought*, provides an excellent account of how management ideas emerged long before business became 'big business'; the reader is strongly recommended to this work.

category along with the United States and Britain) with home-grown cultural attributes and concepts. Karel Adamiecki, Tomas Bat'a, Henri Fayol, Gabriel Campion, Roberto Simonsen, Jehangir R.D. Tata and Li Ka-shing have all in their various ways exercised an influence over management practices in different parts of the world; and if those practices have largely remained out of the view of those of us in Britain and America then perhaps it is high time they were brought into our line of vision and studied along with our own systems. With over a hundred entries on Asian managers and thinkers and at least some coverage of the other cases mentioned above, we think we have done these varied cultures at least partial justice.

Third, as becomes clear to anyone studying the subject in depth, management is something of a palimpsest. This may not be immediately clear when looking at the discipline as a whole. But dissect it into its component parts, and you will find ideas borrowed from economics, from sociology, from psychology, from political science, from philosophy, from the physical sciences – and yes, even from history. To understand as much as possible about the origins of management, therefore, it was clear that we were going to have to go outside management and study some of those figures from whom management practitioners and academics have drawn inspiration.

This attitude will, we realize, not find universal agreement. There are those who believe that management is management, and that's that. They will be outraged to find economists and sociologists, historians and futurists, writers on military affairs and on civil administration jumbled up with marketing gurus and leaders of industrial conglomerates. Why, they will cry, are all these non-managers included, taking up space which could have been allocated to *real* managers? What on earth are a king, four saints and a field marshal doing in a biographical dictionary of management?

The answer to the last will, we hope, be clear to anyone who reads the entries.[7] But the case illustrates our point. As John Davis and later writers, most notably the writer on organization James Mooney (regarded by some as Alfred Sloan's *eminence grise* at General Motors), have made clear, two of the most important models followed by the early thinkers on organization were the medieval church and the army. The church provided not only a model of organization but also a powerful influence on the foundational thinking on business economics and ethics, influence which is still apparent to this day even though its source has been forgotten. Frederick II and other writers on strategy and military organization like Clausewitz and Jomini were read and digested by the late nineteenth and early twentieth-century writers on management, just as Sunzi (Sun Tzu) and Miyamoto Musashi continue to be popular in many quarters today. More specifically, Helmuth von Moltke's crushing victory over the French army made a deep impression on the watching world, not least on the young future management guru Harrington Emerson, who went on to turn Moltke's 'line and staff' organization into a universally recognized management concept. Moltke may be an unlikely hero of the management revolution, but he should be counted as one nonetheless.

We had, then, a set of criteria for selection. The selection process itself was done by means of a list of potential names which circulated among the editors for several months, with names being progressively added and crossed off. Many names, of course, selected themselves, their importance being obvious. Others had their champions and detractors. At one point the list had reached over 800 names. Some names we had hoped to include then

---

[7] Frederick II of Prussia, Aquinas, Bernardino of Siena, Benedict of Cluny, Bernard of Clairvaux and Moltke.

de-selected themselves when it became clear that no biographical information whatsoever was available; others, on closer inspection, turned out to be not so significant as originally considered. The most common reason for falling off the list was that in the end no one could think of any notable achievements the subjects had made (apart from making a lot of money, or perhaps losing it), and the trends they represented were well covered elsewhere. Eventually we got the total down to just over 600.

The End Result

Did we get the balance right in the end? The reader will have to be the judge of that. There is still a preponderance of entries on US subjects, which may irritate those who take a global view; but it would be wrong and foolish to deny the gigantic achievements of American business and scholarship in this field. American readers, on the other hand, may be annoyed that figures from American history whom they considered to be important have been left out to make way for more 'peripheral' Europeans or Asians; to them we can only repeat the need for a global view outlined above, and express our hope that all the major schools and trends are at least represented. Some industries have been covered in depth: there are many US railwaymen from the nineteenth century, and many subjects who were and are involved in high-technology industries in the late twentieth century. The focus on these industries is, we believe, necessary given that developments in management in these sectors have had a considerable impact on the concepts of management more generally. The management systems of the railways, as Chandler has shown, had become almost universal in the United States by the end of the nineteenth century; concepts in information management, technology management and virtual working pioneered in the technology industries had likewise become widely diffused by the end of the twentieth century. 'New' sectors have always been the most fertile in terms of innovations in management and practice and were always going to get special attention. The result, however, is that some other sectors may have been under-represented.

Have we succeeded in what we set out to do, to learn more about 'the nature and historical development of management as both a commercial concept and a social force'? Again, the reader will need to judge. Our own view is that, taken as a whole, the project is greater than the sum of its parts. Studying the 600 people in these volumes *will* help to clarify views of what management is and was, and maybe also of what it will be.[8] Each of the 600 is like a tile in a mosaic, each offering the reader a little piece of a much larger picture of management.

There is just space remaining to offer a few comments on that picture. The most immediate and obvious feature of the 600 is their diversity. By this we do not mean their different cultural backgrounds or the different industries in which they worked; these, considering our selection criteria, are a given. The real and astonishing diversity is in their backgrounds, their attitudes and their beliefs. Some came from backgrounds of dire poverty or were refugees, others were born with silver spoons in their mouths. Some struggled long and hard for success, others found it quickly. Some were kind and caring to their employees, others were ruthless.

Any reader hoping, for example, that this collection will provide unqualified support for an ethical view of business is likely to be disappointed. A surprisingly large number of those

---

[8] Such study cannot be gained from this dictionary alone, of course, and our bibliographies have been designed to help readers explore each of the individuals discussed in more detail.

studied here did indeed have strong ethical views, but there were plenty of exceptions. The working practices and ethical views of Jan Coen, Richard Arkwright, William Ellison and Cornelius Vanderbilt may seem repugnant today, but this makes no difference to their success as managers and business leaders in their time. Isaac Singer, Billy Butlin and William Whiteley lived their private lives outside the ethical norms of their times; their businesses seem to have fared none the worse for this.[9]

Generalizations are hard to come by. Reading through this collection, the reader is more likely to be struck by the realization that each of the figures presented here is unique, sometimes startlingly so. Their personalities often cannot be denied: behind the ideas and the achievements we see clearly the flesh and blood and minds. Sometimes the pathos is real: here is George Eastman, committing suicide when his life lost all meaning; there is Joseph Pulitzer, blind and racked with pain; somewhere is Oscar Deutsch staying at his desk while eaten up with cancer; while somewhere else are Edwin Gay and Montagu Norman dying with the belief that they had been failures, almost oblivious to their titanic achievements. And if these pictures provoke in our minds and hearts a reaction of sympathy or pity that has nothing to do with management, then we can remember that, as Urwick and Brech pointed out, if we know the people behind the ideas, we are somewhat closer to knowing the ideas themselves.

This is not, then, a work which concentrates on providing neat, generalized, universal principles for management. Yet those principles do exist, and are evident. Over and over again we see mentioned the qualities that have led to success: hard work, attention to detail, focus, intelligence, analytical ability, the ability to communicate, an understanding of the needs of customers, the ability to create and manage relationships, creativity, leadership, the ability to inspire loyalty, foresight. None of the 600 has all these qualities; anyone who did so would be superhuman. All have at least some of these qualities, however, and most of our subjects probably had or have the majority of these attributes. We come back here to the notion of the mosaic: each individual figure studied gives us part of the picture. Taking them all together, we get a view of what the whole might be like.

One generalization might well stand. In each of the entries there is an Idea. Usually, this Idea was created and/or developed and improved by the subject himself or herself. Sometimes, with the exemplar figures mentioned above, the Idea is a larger trend or force which the subject is following. Each figure, whether a manager or business leader, an academic who has studied the world of business, or someone working and thinking in a related field, has had a vision of something that they personally can achieve and do. Sometimes the Idea has been highly personal, relating to the person's own success; sometimes it has encompassed the destiny of great organizations and nations. We might speak of these things as creativity or innovation, but already these are becoming loaded concepts in management-speak. A better phrasing perhaps comes from Iris Origo, who remarked in her study of Francesco Datini, the small businessman who in part through his superb information-management skills and in part through determination and focus on his goals, elbowed his way into the risky world of international trade just before 1400:

---

[9] If the reader wishes to see an example of this contrast, consider reading the first and last entries in this dictionary: Ernst Abbé, the inspirational leader of Carl Zeiss Jena whose policies on social welfare were later adopted by many governments; and Basil Zaharoff, the 'Merchant of Death', whose unscrupulous marketing methods helped to start the First World War!

the fundamental distinction between the international merchant and the 'little man' did not consist in whether his trade was wholesale or retail, or even in the quantities of his merchandise, but rather in the outlook of the two different kinds of men. (Origo 1957: 89)

Truly to understand management, to get right to its roots and understand it, we have to think of it not as a set of practices or a cluster of academic studies, but as a set of ideas. It is to the greater understanding of those ideas that we hope this dictionary has made some contribution.

Morgen Witzel
Northlew, Devon
2001

References

Casson, H.N. (1907) *The Romance of Steel: The Story of a Thousand Millionaires*, New York: A.S. Barnes.

Chandler, A.D. (1962) *Strategy and Structure: Chapters in the History of American Industrial Enterprise*, Cambridge, MA: MIT Press.

Davis, J.P. (1905) *Corporations*, 2 vols, New York: G.P. Putnam's Sons.

Moore, K. and Lewis, D. (2000) *Foundations of Corporate Empire: Is History Repeating Itself?*, London: FT Prentice Hall.

Origo, I. (1957) *The Merchant of Prato*, London: Jonathan Cape.

Urwick, L.F. (1956) *The Golden Book of Management*, London: Newman Neame.

Urwick, L.F. and Brech, E.F.L. (1947–9) *The Making of Scientific Management*, 3 vols, London: Management Publications Trust; vols. 1–2, repr. Bristol: Thoemmes Press, 1994.

Warner, M. (1998) 'Introduction', in M. Warner (ed.), *IEBM Handbook of Management Thinking*, London: International Thomson Business Press, xvi–xxix.

Witzel, M. (2001) *Builders and Dreamers: The Making and Meaning of Management*, London: FT Prentice Hall.

Wren, D. (1994) *The Evolution of Management Thought*, 4th edn, New York: John Wiley.

ACKNOWLEDGEMENTS

To bring a project of this size from concept to printed page in a little over eighteen months is a remarkable thing. I say this not to boast, but to express my gratitude to all those who have supported and backed this project from the beginning. Any thanks must begin with the members of the editorial board, whose enthusiasm for this project has been vital to keeping it going and whose suggestions and participation in the early debate about what we should be doing have helped shape the final work. I am grateful as well to Edward Brech, John Dunning, Richard Trahair, Tom White, Peter McKenzie-Brown, Steve Koerner, Denny Diehl and Gita Piramal for making valuable suggestions later in the process, and to Tim Ambler for giving the headword list a final review. A special note of thanks should go to Bill Gardner for assembling a fine team of writers at the University of Mississippi, and to Louis Cain for agreeing to review the project for us at an early stage.

I am grateful to Keith Moore at the Institute of Mechanical Engineers, Carol Morgan at the Institute of Civil Engineers, Daniel Wood at Arthur D. Little and Barbara Jones at Lloyds Register of Shipping for tracking down information on some of the more obscure figures. My thanks too to the public relations office at the Harvard Graduate School of Business Administration for their kindness and help, and thanks also to Max Boisot for kindly sending us his CV. Marilyn Livingstone has provided research support and has generally been of invaluable aid in the last few months of the project, not least in helping to deal with the recalcitrant technology that threatened to disrupt everything at the eleventh hour. Finally, the staff at the London Library have been, as ever, full of assistance, support and understanding.

At Thoemmes Press, thanks go to Rudi Thoemmes, Nicola Everitt, Marie Spicer, Andrea Mallett, Alan Rutherford and Chris Albury for all their ideas and help. Katia Hamza has done an outstanding job of copy-editing under pressure, and it has been a real pleasure to work with her. Last of all – the position of honour – may I thank Jane Williamson, whose patience and support have helped make this project real.

MW

HOW TO USE THE *DICTIONARY*

The *Dictionary* contains entries on approximately 600 important thinkers and practitioners in the history of management. The title of each entry gives the subject's name and dates of birth and death, where known. As far as possible, we have used the subjects' given names; thus Lord Beaverbrook appears under AITKEN. In the case of Chinese subjects, we have followed the usual modern convention of using Pinyin romanization for historical figures and for figures from the modern People's Republic of China (thus SUNZI, DENG Xiaopeng), but Wade-Giles romanization for subjects from Hong Kong and other overseas Chinese communities (for example, LIEM Sioe Liong). Further biographical details, again where known, are given in the opening paragraph or paragraphs of each entry. The remainder of each entry discusses the subject's work, writings, ideas and contribution to the history of management.

Bibliographies have been included with the great majority of entries. These should not be taken as full and complete bibliographies, which in some cases would take up many pages. Many of the subjects published very widely, often on many subjects apart from management, and many have also been the subjects of vast bodies of literature. We have tried to restrict bibliographies to the most important and relevant works to the subject at hand. Where possible, we have included the standard biography of each subject, and readers are referred to these for further bibliographical details.

Within the body of the entries there is a cross-referencing system referring to other entries. Names which appear in small capitals (e.g. DRUCKER) are themselves the subjects of entries in the *Dictionary*, and the reader may refer to these entries for more information.

Two indexes are provided. One is an index of names, which includes not only subjects of entries but also other prominent or significant figures whose names appear in the *Dictionary*; this may be useful in helping readers to trace the influences of individuals or groups on modern management thinking. The other is an index of subjects and terms which appear in the *Dictionary*; this will allow the reader to examine different aspects and approaches to ideas and concepts such as scientific management, efficiency, knowledge, and so on. We regret that space has precluded an index of corporations, organizations and institutions mentioned in these volumes; while theoretically valuable, such an index would in practice be very large and unwieldy.

GENERAL BIBLIOGRAPHY

The following were used in the preparation of this dictionary, and will contain further information on many of the subjects included.

Standard Reference Works

American National Biography (1999) ed. J.A. Garraty and M. Carnes, Chicago: Gale Research Incoporated.

Dictionary of National Biography (1885) ed. L. Stephen and S. Lee, first published London: Small, Elder and Co.; supplements cover the period up to 1980.

Who's Who 2000, London: A. & C. Black.

Who's Who in the USA 2000, New Providence, NJ: Marquis.

Who Was Who, London: A. & C. Black.

Who Was Who in the USA, New Providence, NJ: Marquis.

Works Specifically Concerning Management History

Brands, H.W. (1999) *Masters of Enterprise: Giants of American Business from John Jacob Astor and J.P. Morgan to Bill Gates and Oprah Winfrey*, New York: The Free Press.

Collins, J.C. and Porras, J.I. (1997) *Built to Last*, Berkeley, CA: University of California Press.

Crainer, S. (2000) *The Management Century*, San Francisco: Jossey-Bass.

Crainer, S. and Clutterbuck, D. (1990) *Makers of Management*, London: Macmillan.

Davis, W. (1987) *The Innovators: The Essential Guide to Business Thinkers*, London: Ebury Press.

Drury, H.B. (1915) *Scientific Management: A History and Criticism*, New York: Columbia University Press.

Duncan, W.J. (1989) *Great Ideas in Management*, San Francisco: Jossey-Bass.

Gabor, A. (1999) *The Capitalist Philosophers*, New York: Times Business.

George, C.S. (1968) *The History of Management Thought*, Englewood Cliffs, NJ: Prentice-Hall.

Gough, J.W. (1969) *The Rise of the Entrepreneur*, London: B.T. Batsford.

Ingham, John N. and Feldman, Lynne B. (1994) *African-American Business Leaders: A Biographical Dictionary*, Westport, CT: Greenwood Press.

Jeremy, D.J. (ed.) (1984–6) *Dictionary of Business Biography*, 5 vols, London: Butterworths.

Leavitt, J.A. (1985) *American Women Managers and Administrators: A Selective Biographical Dictionary of Twentieth-century Leaders*, Westport, CT: Greenwood Press.

Parkinson, C.N. (1977) *The Rise of Big Business*, London: Weidenfeld and Nicholson.

Piramal, G. (1996) *Business Maharajahs*, New Delhi: Viking.

Pollard, S. (1965) *The Genesis of Modern Management*, London: Edward Arnold.

Tsutsui, W.M. (1998) *Manufacturing Ideology: Scientific Management in Twentieth-century Japan*, Princeton, NJ: Princeton University Press.

Urwick, L.F. (ed.) (1956) *The Golden Book of Management: A Historical Record of the Life and Work of Seventy Pioneers*, London: Newman Neame.

Urwick, L.F. and Brech, E.F.L. (1947–9) *The Making of Scientific Management*, 3 vols, London: Management Publications Trust; vols 1–2, repr. Bristol: Thoemmes Press, 1994.

Warner, M. (ed.) (1998) *IEBM Handbook of Management Thinking*, London: International Thomson Business Press.

Wren, D. (1994) *The Evolution of Management Thought*, 4th edn, New York: John Wiley.

—— (ed.) (1997) *Early Management Thought*, Brookfield, VT: Dartmouth.

Wren, D. and Greenwood, R.G. (1998) *Management Innovators: The People and Ideas That Have Shaped Modern Business*, New York: Oxford University Press.

LIST OF CONTRIBUTORS

Editorial Board

Tim Ambler, Department of Marketing
  Research Fellow, London Business School
Greg Bamber, Graduate School of
  Management, Griffith University
George Bickerstaffe, London
John Dunning, Professor Emeritus,
  University of Reading
Kris Inwood, Department of Economics,
  University of Guelph, Ontario
Anne Jenkins, University of Leeds
David Charles Lewis, Los Angeles,
  California
Liu Zenan, MTM Partnership, London and
  Beijing
Karl Moore, Faculty of Management,
  McGill University, Montreal and
  Templeton College, Oxford
Sasaki Tsuneo, College of Economics,
  Nihon University
Sawai Minoru, Graduate School of
  Economics, Osaka University
Daniel Wren, Professor Emeritus,
  University of Oklahoma
Malcolm Warner, Judge Institute of
  Management Studies, University of
  Cambridge

Contributors

AT   Abe Takeshi
      Professor of Business History
      Graduate School of Economics
      University of Osaka

MA   Mie Augier
      Stanford University, California

RB   Roger Backhouse
      Professor, Department of
      Economics
      University of Birmingham

GB   Greg Bamber
      Professor, Graduate School of
      Management
      Griffith University, Australia

CB   Clayton Barrows
      Associate Professor, School of Hotel
      and Food Administration
      University of Guelph, Ontario

BPB   Bob Batchelor
      San Rafael, California

MB   Markus Becker
      Assistant Professor, Department of
      Marketing
      University of Southern Denmark

PB   Philippe Bernoux
      University of Lyons

REB   Richard E. Boyatzis
      Professor, Department of
      Organization Behaviour
      Case Western Reserve University,
      Cleveland, Ohio

BB   Brian Brennan
      Calgary, Alberta

KDB   Keith D. Brouthers
      University of East London Business
      School

JAEB Jo Ann E. Brown
      The School of Business
      Administration
      University of Mississippi

CC   Charles M. Carson
      The School of Business
      Administration
      University of Mississippi

FC-B Flora Cheung-Birtch
      Judge Institute of Management
      Studies
      University of Cambridge

SC   Simon Coppock
      London

HC-H Hunter Crowther-Heyck
      Assistant Professor, Department of
      the History of Science
      University of Oklahoma

DD   Dennis Diehl
      Newcomen Society USA

WJD   W. Jack Duncan
      Professor, Graduate School of
      Management
      University of Alabama

DF   David S. Ferguson CSP
      Santa Rosa, California

TG   Timothy J. Gilfoyle
      Professor, Department of History
      Loyola University, Chicago

LG   Laurel D. Graham
      Associate Professor, Department of

      Sociology
      University of South Florida

RG   Regina Greenwood
      Department of Industrial and
      Manufacturing Engineering and
      Business
      Kettering University, Chicago

WJH   William J. Hausman
      Professor, Department of Economics
      College of William and Mary,
      Virginia

JCH   Jimmy C. Hinton
      The School of Business
      Administration
      University of Mississippi

JH   Jill Hough
      Assistant Professor of Management
      University of Tulsa, Oklahoma

IK   Ishikawa Kenjiro
      Professor, Faculty of Commerce
      Doshisha University

AJ   Anne Jenkins
      University of Leeds

MJ   Matthew Jones
      Judge Institute of Management
      Studies, University of Cambridge

PJ   Patrick Joynt
      Professor
      Henley Management College and
      Bodo Management School, Norway

KM   Kasuya Makoto
      Professor, Faculty of Economics
      University of Tokyo

EK   Eileen P. Kelly
      Professor
      Ithaca College School of Business,
      New York

KAK   K. Austin Kerr
Professor, Department of History
Ohio State University

TK   Thomas Kochan
Professor of Work and Employment
Research
Sloan School of Management,
Massachusetts Institute of
Technology

SK   Stephen Koerner
Victoria, British Columbia

KT   Kuwahara Tetsuya
Professor of International Business
History
Graduate School of Business
Administration, Kobe University

FSL   Frederic S. Lee
Professor, Department of
Economics
University of Missouri–Kansas City

BL   Barbara Lesko
Department of Egyptology
Brown University, Rhode Island

LL   Leonard Lesko
Professor of Egyptology
Brown University, Rhode Island

DCL   David Charles Lewis
Los Angeles, USA

ML   Marilyn Livingstone
Department of Modern History
Queen's University of Belfast

DM   David Mason
Professor, Department of History
Young Harris College, Georgia

MS   Matsumura Satoshi
Professor, Faculty of Economics
Kanagawa University

PM-B   Peter McKenzie-Brown
Calgary, Alberta

KJM   Karl J. Moore
Professor, Faculty of Management
McGill University, Montreal

OT   Okazaki Tetsuji
Professor, Faculty of Economics
University of Tokyo

PP   Peter B. Petersen
Johns Hopkins University,
Maryland

GP   Gita Piramal
Bombay, India

AP   Anastasia Pseiridis
Judge Institute of Management
Studies, University of Cambridge

QY   Qu Yuxiu
School of Business Administration
University of Wisconsin at
Milwaukee

DR   Domagoj Racic
Trinity College, Cambridge

BR   Bradley R. Rice
Professor, Department of History
Clayton College and State
University

MR   Martin Ricketts
Professor
University of Buckingham

KR   Khalil Rohani
Department of Consumer Studies
University of Guelph, Canada

CR   Chris Rowley
Department of Human Resource
Management and Organization
Behaviour

City University Business School,
London

STR   Stephen Todd Rudman
Judge Institute of Management
Studies, University of Cambridge

SJ   Sasaki Jun
Associate Professor of Economic
History, Faculty of Economics
Ryukoku University

ST   Sasaki Tsuneo
Professor, College of Economics
Nihon University, Tokyo

SM   Sawai Minoru
Professor, Graduate School of
Economics
Osaka University

ShM   Shinomiya Masachika
Professor
Kanto Gakuin University

DBS   David B. Sicilia
Professor, Department of History
University of Maryland, College
Park

HPS   Peter Starbuck
Oswestry, Shropshire

TS   Timothy Sullivan
Professor, Department of
Economics
Towson University, Maryland

DS   David G. Surdam
Adjunct Associate Professor of
Economics, Graduate School of
Business, University of Chicago

RT   Richard Trahair
School of Social Sciences
LaTrobe University, Australia

UM   Udagawa Masaru
Professor of Business History
Hosei University

RV   Robert Vanderlan
Department of History
University of Rochester, New York

PW   Peter Walton
Professor, Department of
Accounting and Control
ESSEC Business School, Paris

WTW   W. Thomas White
Curator
James J. Hill Library
St Paul, Minnesota

MLW   Morgen Witzel
Northlew, Devon

MZ   Milan Zeleny
Professor, Graduate School of
Business
Fordham University, New York
and The Tomás Bat'a University
Zlin, Czech Republic

CHRONOLOGICAL LIST

*fl. c.*2000 BC–1800 BC	Ana-é	Businesswoman
*c.*1900 BC–1875 BC	Pusu-ken	International business manager
*c.*1520 BC	Anonymous	Author of *Duties of the Vizier*
(1325? BC–1241 BC)	Ramose	Scribe
(13th century BC)	Neferhotep the Elder	Tomb builder and foreman
*c.*1300 BC	Sinaranu	International business owner-manager
fl. 891 BC–859 BC	Itobaal	Priest-king of Tyre
7th century BC	Guanzi	Writer on economics and philosophy
640 BC–561 BC?	Solon of Athens	Entrepreneur and political leader
6th century BC	Laozi	Philosopher and sage
551 BC–479 BC	Confucius	Philosopher and sage
*fl. c.*4th century BC	Sunzi	Writer on military strategy
400 BC?–350 BC?	Pasion of Athens	Banker
384 BC–322 BC	Demosthenes of Athens	Orator and politician
*fl. c.*321 BC–*c.*296 BC	Kautilya	Philosopher
*c.*280 BC–233 BC	Han Feizi	Philosopher
fl. 1st century BC	L. Aelius Lamia	International business owner-manager
fl. 1st century BC	Caraeus Plancius	Business manager
fl. 1st century BC	Caius Rabirius Postumus	Business manager
fl. 1st century BC	Publius Sestius	Business manager
116 BC–28 BC	Marcus Terentius Varro	Writer
2nd century AD	A. Decius Alpinus	Manufacturer of tiles and pipe
fl. late 4th century AD	Vegetius	Writer on military management
*c.*480–*c.*535	Benedict of Nursia	Monastic leader
1081–1151	Suger	Abbot
1090–1153	Bernard of Clairvaux	Theologian and monastic leader
*c.*1115/20–1180	John of Salisbury	Teacher and philosopher
*c.*1130–1198	Richard Fitz Neal	Clergyman and civil servant
*c.*1140–1205	Hubert Walter	Clergyman and civil servant
fl. 1190–1236	Thomas of Chobham	Theologian
d. 1268	Henry de Bracton	Lawyer
1224/6–1274	Thomas Aquinas	Theologian and philosopher
1248–1307	Benedetto Zaccaria	Merchant and naval commander
fl. 1260–1290	Walter of Henley	Writer on estate management
*c.*1290–1369	William de la Pole	Merchant and banker
fl. 1310–1347	Francesco Pegolotti	Manager and writer
*c.*1335–1410	Francesco Datini	Merchant
1380–1444	Bernardino of Siena	Theologian and proto-economist
1389–1464	Cosimo dei Medici	Businessman
1394–1455	Giovanni Benci	Banker and manager
*c.*1412–1454	Giovanni Ingherami	Banker

1795–1872	James Gordon Bennett	Newspaper owner and editor
1797–1879	Daniel Drew	Financier and railway owner
1800–1891	Helmuth von Moltke	Field marshal
1803–1876	Titus Salt	Textiles manufacturer
1803–1887	Joseph Whitworth	Engineer
1806–1859	Isambard Kingdom Brunel	Civil engineer
1806–1873	John Stuart Mill	Economist and philosopher
1808–1874	J. Edgar Thomson	Railway owner
1808–1892	Thomas Cook	Travel agent
1809–1884	Cyrus McCormick	Inventor and manufacturer
1810–1877	Aristide Boucicaut	Department store owner
1810–1890	Oliver Winchester	Firearms manufacturer
1810–1891	Phineas T. Barnum	Showman and circus owner
1811–1875	Isaac Singer	Sewing machine manufacturer
1811–1882	Edward Clark	Lawyer and sewing machine manufacturer
1812–1887	Alfred Krupp	Arms manufacturer
1812–1905	Henry Varnum Poor	Journalist and businessman
1813–1889	Irineu de Sousa	Industrialist and banker
1813–1892	Jean-Gustave Courcelle-Seneuil	Economist
1813–1897	Isaac Pitman	Inventor of phonography
1814–1862	Samuel Colt	Firearms manufacturer
1816–1892	Werner von Siemens	Engineer
1816–1899	Paul Julius Reuter	News agency proprietor
1818–1883	Karl Marx	Economist
1818–1898	William Deloitte	Accountant
1820–1895	Friedrich Engels	Economist and industrialist
1820–1910	Florence Nightingale	Reformer of hospital nursing
1820–1914	Donald Smith	Fur trader and railway builder
1821–1877	Minomura Rizaemon	Business manager
1821–1885	William H. Vanderbilt	Railway magnate
1823–1901	Li Hongzhang	Government official
1825–1898	John Swire	Shipowner and merchant
1828–1914	Hirose Saihei	Industrialist
1829–1906	Levi Strauss	Clothing manufacturer
1830–1913	Henry Flagler	Oil company executive and hotel owner
1831–1888	John Pemberton	Soft drinks manufacturer
1831–1895	Edward Harland	Shipbuilder
1831–1897	George Pullman	Railway sleeping car builder
1831–1907	William Whiteley	Department store owner
1834–1896	William Morris	Textiles and furnishings manufacturer and designer
1833–1896	Alfred Nobel	Explosives manufacturer
1834–1885	Iwasaki Yataro	Businessman
1835–1885	Godai Tomoatsu	Financier and industrialist
1835–1901	Fukuzawa Yukichi	Writer on economics and management
1835–1919	Andrew Carnegie	Industrialist and steel maker
1836–1892	Jay Gould	Railway owner and financier
1836–1925	Joseph Rowntree	Chocolate manufacturer
1837–1899	Thomas Ismay	Shipowner
1837–1913	J.P. Morgan	Banker and financier
1838–1916	James J. Hill	Railway owner
1838–1921	Yasuda Zenjiro	Businessman
1838–1922	John Wanamaker	Department store owner
1839–1884	John Player	Tobacco manufacturer

1839–1922	George Cadbury	Chocolate maker and social reformer
1839–1937	John D. Rockefeller	Oil company owner
1840–1905	Ernst Abbé	Scientist and optical equipment maker
1840–1931	Shibusawa Eiichi	Banker and industrialist
1841–1888	B.F. Goodrich	Tyre maker
1841–1915	Thomas Jackson	Banker
1841–1917	Edwin Waterhouse	Accountant
1841–1925	Henri Fayol	Mining engineer and writer on administration
1842–1913	Arthur Chamberlain	Industrialist
1842–1919	John Brunner	Chemicals manufacturer
1842–1924	Alfred Marshall	Economist
1843–1915	William Cornelius Van Horne	Railway builder
1843–1917	Arthur Liberty	Department store owner
1844–1913	Aaron Montgomery Ward	Mail order retailer
1844–1919	Henry J. Heinz	Food producer
1844–1922	John Patterson	Office equipment manufacturer
1844–1924	Henry R. Towne	Engineer
1845–1905	Georges Nagelmackers	Railway entrepreneur
1845–1920	Theodore Vail	Post office and telephone company executive
1846–1911	Jack Daniels	Distiller
1846–1914	George Westinghouse	Inventor and engineer
1847–1911	Joseph Pulitzer	Publisher
1847–1922	Alexander Graham Bell	Inventor of the telephone
1847–1924	William Pirrie	Shipbuilder
1847–1931	Thomas Edison	Inventor
1848–1898	Sakuma Teiichi	Printer and publisher
1848–1916	Joseph Beecham	Pharmaceuticals maker
1848–1919	Edward Holden	Banker
1848–1938	Masuda Takashi	Manager
1849–1917	William Knox D'Arcy	Mining and oil company executive
1849–1936	Basil Zaharoff	Arms dealer
1850–1915	A.G. Spalding	Baseball team owner and sporting goods maker
1850–1917	Katekura Kanetaro	Textile maker and industrialist
1850–1918	R.J. Reynolds	Tobacco manufacturer
1850–1927	Henry Huntington	Railway magnate
1850–1931	Jesse Boot	Retail chemist
1850–1936	Henri Le Chatelier	Chemist, writer on scientific management
1851–1920	Yamanobe Takeo	Textiles manufacturer
1851–1925	William Lever	Soap manufacturer
1851–1927	Charles Mellen	Railway and shipping magnate
1851–1928	Horace Darwin	Scientific instrument maker
1852–1901	Joseph Slater Lewis	Engineer and writer on management
1852–1912	Christopher Furness	Shipowner and shipbuilder
1852–1919	Frank Woolworth	Chain store retailer
1852–1943	Hans Renold	Engineer
1853–1927	Marcus Samuel	Oil company executive
1853–1931	Harrington Emerson	Engineer and efficiency expert
1853–1936	Henry Wellcome	Pharmaceuticals maker
1854–1901	Nakamigawa Hikojiro	Executive, Mitsui
1854–1931	Charles Parsons	Engineer
1854–1932	George Eastman	Film and camera manufacturer
1854–1939	David Gestetner	Office equipment manufacturer
1856–1915	Frederick Winslow Taylor	Engineer and management consultant

1856–1915	Booker T. Washington	Civil rights leader and educator
1856–1930	Daniel Guggenheim	Industrialist and mine-owner
1856–1935	Frederick Halsey	Engineer
1856–1936	Charles de Fréminville	Engineer, writer on scientific management
1856–1945	Kawakami Kin'ichi	Banker and industrialist
1857–1929	Thorstein Veblen	Economist
1857–1944	Ida Tarbell	Journalist
1858–1932	Dan Takuma	Engineer, head of Mitsui
1858–1947	Gordon Selfridge	Department store owner
1859–1947	Sidney Webb	Socialist and writer on labour
1860–1929	Hermann Hollerith	Computer developer
1860–1931	Hibi Osuke	Department store owner
1860–1937	Edward Filene	Retailer
1860–1939	Carl Barth	Engineer
1860–1951	William Kellogg	Food manufacturer
1861–1919	Henry Laurence Gantt	Engineer and consultant
1861–1932	William Wrigley	Chewing gum manufacturer
1861–1937	L.F. Swift	Meat packer
1861–1942	Robert Bosch	Engineer and industrialist
1861–1947	William C. Durant	Motor car manufacturer
1862–1903	John P. Davis	Lawyer and historian
1862–1934	William Procter	Consumer goods manufacturer
1862–1939	Charles M. Schwab	Industrialist and steel maker
1862–1945	John R. Commons	Economist
1863–1914	Richard Sears	Mail order retailer
1863–1935	Arthur D. Little	Chemist and management consultant
1863–1947	Henry Ford	Motor car manufacturer
1863–1951	William Randolph Hearst	Newspaper owner and publisher
1864–1920	Max Weber	Sociologist
1864–1932	Lawrence R. Dicksee	Accountant and academic
1864–1950	Ransom E. Olds	Motor car manufacturer
1865–1940?	Yu Yajing	Banker
1865–1952	Dexter Kimball	Academic and writer on organizations
1866–1915	Hans Schönitz	Writer on business administration
1866–1933	Karel Adamiecki	Engineer
1866–1939	Henri Deterding	Oil company executive
1866–1941	Herbert Austin	Motor car manufacturer
1866–1944	Otaguro Juguro	Manager
1866–1944	Kaneko Naokichi	Manager
1867–1922	Walther Rathenau	Industrialist and politician
1867–1928	John Lee	Writer on management
1867–1930	Toyoda Sakichi	Textiles manufacturer
1867–1934	Muto Sanji	Textiles manufacturer
1867–1946	Edwin Gay	Economic historian and dean of Harvard Business School
1867–1949	Sanford Thompson	Engineer and builder
1868–1916	Robert Hoxie	Academic and writer on scientific management
1868–1924	Frank Gilbreth	Consultant and writer on scientific management
1868–1930	Alfred Mond	Manufacturer of chemicals
1868–1933	Mary Parker Follett	Political and scientist
1868–1938	Harvey Firestone	Tyre manufacturer
1869–1948	Mohandas Gandhi	Political leader and philosopher
1869–1951	Herbert N. Casson	Writer and consultant

Chronological list

1869–1955	Walter Dill Scott	Psychologist and writer on advertising
1869–1957	Annie Turnbo-Malone	Maker of cosmetics and hair care products
c.1879–after 1925	Ma Ying-piao	Department store owner
1870–1945	Nishida Kitaro	Philosopher
1870–1949	A.P. Giannini	Banker
1870–1954	Pierre du Pont	Gunpowder and motor car manufacturer
1870–1959	Pierrepont Noyes	Manufacturer of tableware
1871–1950	Montagu Norman	Banker
1871–1954	Benjamin Seebohm Rowntree	Chocolate maker
1872–1936	James Couzens	Motor car manufacturer and politician
1873–1928	Edward Cadbury	Chocolate maker
1873–1935	John North Willys	Motor car manufacturer
1873–1944	Philip Hill	Financier
1873–1944	Noguchi Shitagau	Founder of Nichitsu *zaibatsu*
1873–1947	William McLintock	Accountant
1873–1955	Eugen Schmalenbach	Economist and accountant
1873–1956	Takeo Toshisuke	Engineer and steel maker
1873–1957	Kobayashi Ichizo	Railway and department store owner
1874–1948	Wesley Clair Mitchell	Economist
1874–1951	Odaira Namihei	Founder of Hitachi
1874–1956	Thomas J. Watson	Computer manufacturer
1874–1961	Harry McGowan	Chemicals manufacturer
1874–1962	Owen D. Young	Lawyer and executive
1875–1935	Edward T. Elbourne	Engineer and consultant
1875–1937	Eric Geddes	Civil servant and executive
1875–1940	Walter Chrysler	Motor car manufacturer
1875–1966	Alfred P. Sloan, Jr	Motor car manufacturer
1875–1971	James C. Penney	Chain store owner
1875–1971	Matsunaga Yasuzaemon	Public utilities manager
1876–1932	Tomás Bat'a	Shoe manufacturer
1876–1935	Moritz Weyerman	Academic, writer on business administration
1876–1936	Roberto Michels	Economist and political scientist
1876–1943	Paul T. Cherington	Academic, writer on marketing
1876–1946	Heinrich Nicklisch	Writer on management
1876–1947	Samuel Courtauld	Textiles manunfacturer
1876–1962	Arch W. Shaw	Writer, editor and publisher
1877–1934	Ivy Lee	Public relations consultant
1877–1944	Louis Renault	Motor car maker
1877–1952	Henry Dennison	Businessman and writer on organization
1877–1963	William R. Morris	Motor car maker
1878–1936	André Citröen	Motor car maker
1878–1944	Horace Hathaway	Engineer
1878–1952	Ohkohchi Masatoshi	Engineer and executive
1878–1962	Walter Teagle	Oil company executive
1878–1966	Elizabeth Arden	Salon owner and maker of cosmetics
1877–1956	Godo Takuo	Engineer
1878–1972	Lillian Gilbreth	Consultant and writer on scientific management
1879–1940	Ueda Teijiro	Academic, writer on business administration
1879–1945	Iwasaki Koyata	Manager
1879–1948	William Knudsen	Motor car manufacturer
1879–1961	Torii Shinjiro	Distiller
1879–1964	William Maxwell Aitken	Newspaper magnate
1879–1969	Robert E. Wood	Army officer and retailer

1880–1943	Ohara Magosaburo	Textiles manufacturer
1880–1949	Elton Mayo	Pyschologist, writer on human relations
1880–1967	Aikawa Yoshisuke	Founder of Nissan
1881–1936	Charles Knoeppel	Writer on organization
1881–1956	William Boeing	Aircraft manufacturer
1881–1958	Arthur Cutforth	Accountant
1881–1960	Yamashita Okiie	Industrial engineer
1881–1968	Charles Sorenson	Motor car manufacturer
1882–1967	Henry Kaiser	Contractor and shipbuilder
1882–1974	Samuel Goldwyn	Motion picture producer
b. 1882	Lewis Haney	Economist and writer on organization and marketing
b. 1882	L.D.H. Weld	Economist and writer on marketing
1883–1932	Gilbert Garnsey	Accountant
1883–1946	John Maynard Keynes	Economist
1883–1950	Joseph Schumpeter	Economist
1883–1957	Ueno Yoichi	Psychologist and management consultant
1883–1971	Coco Chanel	Fashion designer
1884–1957	James D. Mooney	Motor car manufacturer
1884–1975	Melvin T. Copeland	Writer on marketing
1885–1952	Montague Burton	Clothing retailer and manufacturer
1885–1957	Louis B. Mayer	Motion picture executive
1885–1981	Idemitsu Sazoh	Oil company executive
b. 1885	Cornelia Stratton Parker	Novelist and writer on labour
1886–1944	Charles Bedaux	Management consultant
1886–1961	Chester Barnard	Executive and writer on organization
1886–1963	Harold Bellman	Building society chairman
1885–1963	John Spedan Lewis	Department store chairman
1886–1964	Karl Polanyi	Economist
1887–1951	Edwin Booz	Management consultant
1887–1978	William McKnight	Manufacturer of industrial and adhesive products
1887–1979	Conrad Hilton	Hotelier
1888–1976	Walter Carpenter	Chemicals manufacturer
1888–1972	J. Arthur Rank	Food manufacturer and film-maker
1888–1989	T.O.M. Sopwith	Aircraft manufacturer
1889–1937	James McKinsey	Management consultant
1889–1948	Roberto Simonsen	Industrialist and engineer
1889–1971	Samuel Bronfman	Distiller and seller of wines and spirits
1889–1971	John Reith	Broadcaster
1889–1976	Ishibashi Shojiro	Tyre manufacturer
1890–1947	Kurt Lewin	Psychologist
1890–1948	Fred Clark	Academic, writer on marketing
1890–1973	Edward Rickenbacker	Fighter pilot and airline executive
1890–1980	Harlan Sanders	Restaurateur
1890–1982	Philip Sargant Florence	Industrial economist
1891–1969	Sidney Weinberg	Banker
1891–1969	Thomas North Whitehead	Academic, writer on organization and labour
1891–1971	David Sarnoff	Media executive
1891–1973	Ludwig von Mises	Economist
1891–1973	Ordway Tead	Publisher, writer on personnel management
1891–1983	Lyndall Fownes Urwick	Management consultant and writer
1891–1984	Konrad Mellerowicz	Writer on management theory
1892–1938?	Nikolai Kondratieff	Systems theorist and economist

1892–1962	A.T. Kearney	Management consultant
1892–1976	J. Paul Getty	Oil company owner
1892–1986	Marcel Dassault	Aircraft manufacturer
1892–1993	Luther Halsey Gulick	Writer and consultant on public administration
1893–1941	Oscar Deutsch	Cinema owner
1893–1943	Edsel Ford	Motor car manufacturer
1893–1966	Nishiyama Yataro	Steel maker
1893–1967	Victor Gollancz	Publisher
1893–1976	Mao Zedong	Revolutionary and political leader
1894–1951	Oliver Sheldon	Writer on the philosophy of management
1894–1952	Toyoda Kiichiro	Motor car manufacturer
1894–1957	George Merck	Pharmaceuticals manufacturer
1894–1964	Norbert Wiener	Mathematician and writer on cybernetics
1894–1976	Roy Thomson	Media magnate
1894–1982	Geoffrey Vickers	Lawyer, writer on leadership
1894–1983	Ghanshyam Das Birla	Industrialist
1894–1989	Matsushita Konosuke	Maker of electronics equipment
1895–1971	Adolph Berle	Lawyer and economist
1895–1977	Araki Toichiro	Business consultant
1895–1990	Lewis Mumford	Historian and cultural critic
fl. c. 1896–1902	F.G. Burton	Engineer and writer on management
1896–1945	Masuchi Yojiro	Writer on management theory
1896–1950	Otsuka Banjo	Steel maker and industrialist
1896–1959	Gabriel Campion	Writer on business administration
1896–1970	Hirai Yasutaro	Professor of business administration
1896–1972	Howard Johnson	Hotelier and restaurateur
1896–1975	Nakanishi Torao	Academic, writer on business administration
1896–1988	Gardiner Means	Businessman and writer
1897–1961	Baba Keiji	Academic and writer on organization
1897–1984	Erich Gutenberg	Economist and writer on management
1898–1967	Henry Luce	Publisher
1898–1974	Fritz Roethlisberger	Academic, writer on human resource management
1898–1979	André Meyer	Banker and financier
1898–1980	Kamiya Shotaro	Motor car manufacturer
1898–1990	Armand Hammer	Oil company owner
1899–1977	Kikawada Kazutaka	Public utilities executive
1899–1980	William Butlin	Holiday camp owner
1899–1981	Juan Trippe	Airline executive
1899–1983	Walter Puckey	Engineer and management consultant
1899–1990	Erich Kosiol	Mathematician and economist
1899–1992	Friedrich von Hayek	Economist
1899–1999	Abol Hassan Ebtehaj	Banker and economist
1900–1936	Fritz Schönpflug	Economist and writer on management
1900–1980	Edward Lewis	Electronic equipment manufacturer
1900–1985	John Marriott	Hotelier and restaurant owner
1900–1993	W. Edwards Deming	Quality guru
1901–1966	Walt Disney	Motion picture maker
1901–1972	Ludwig von Bertalanffy	Biologist and pioneer of systems theory
1902–1982	Siegmund Warburg	Banker
1902–1984	Ray Kroc	Restaurant owner
1903–1971	William Hill	Bookmaker
1903–1981	Rensis Likert	Psychologist and writer on organization
1903–1987	Bertrand de Jouvenel	Futurist

1904–1993	J.R.D. Tata	Airline owner and industrialist
1904–1994	Yamamoto Yasujiro	Academic, writer on business administration
1904–1997	Deng Xiaopeng	Political leader and economic reformer
1904–	Joseph Juran	Writer on management and quality control
1905–1982	Ayn Rand	Novelist and philosopher
1905–1983	William Pilkington	Glass manufacturer
1905–1987	James Burnham	Philosopher
1905–1991	Baba Katsuzo	Economist
1906–1962	Enrico Mattei	Oil company executive
1906–1964	Douglas McGregor	Writer on organization
1906–1977	Aleksei Stakhanov	Coal miner
1906–	Honda Soichiro	Motor car manufacturer
1908–1970	Abraham Maslow	Psychologist
1908–1996	Takamiya Susumu	Writer on business administration
1908–1997	Ibuka Masaru	Electronics manufacturer
1908–	John Kenneth Galbraith	Economist
1908–1984	Harold Koontz	Writer on management
1909–1965	Grant McConachie	Airline executive
1909–1991	Edwin Land	Designer and maker of photographic equipment
1909–1993	C. Northcote Parkinson	Historian
1909–1993	Eric Trist	Psychologist and writer on organization
1909–1995	Henry Benson	Accountant and auditor
1909–	Peter Drucker	Management writer and guru
1909–	Shingo Shigeo	Industrial engineer and consultant
1910–1973	Allan Flanders	Writer on industrial relations
1910–1988	Fujisawa Takeo	Motor car manufacturer
1910–1994	Jack Barbash	Economist and writer on industrial relations
1910–1997	Harold Geneen	Industrialist
1910–	Edward Brech	Consultant and historian of management
1910–	Ronald Coase	Economist
1911–1977	Ernst Schumacher	Economist
1911–1980	Marshall McLuhan	Writer on media and communications
1912–1985	Axel Springer	Publisher
1912–1990	Ohno Taiichi	Engineer and quality control guru
1912–1996	David Packard	Computer maker
1912–	Milton Friedman	Economist
1913–1994	Robert Jungk	Futurist
1913–2001	William Hewlett	Computer manufacturer
1913–	Tom Burns	Academic, writer on organization
1913–	C. West Churchman	Writer on systems thinking and operations research
1914–1993	Thomas J. Watson, Jr	Computer manufacturer
1914–1996	Edith Penrose	Economist
1914–	John Dunlop	Writer on industrial relations
1915–1976	Jose Maria Arizmendiarrieta	Priest and co–operative founder
1915–1989	Ishikawa Kaoru	Quality control guru
1915–	Chung Ju Yung	Industrialist
1915–	Paul Samuelson	Economist
1916–1971	Joan Woodward	Academic, writer on organization
1916–2001	Herbert Simon	Philosopher and writer on organization
1916–	Robert McNamara	Motor industry executive, politician and banker
1917–1987	Henry Ford II	Motor car manufacturer

1927–	Yamanouchi Hiroshi	Computer games manufacturer
1927–	John Dunning	Academic, writer on international business
1928–	Geert Hofstede	Academic, writer on organization and culture
1928–	Li Ka-shing	Property developer and tycoon
1928–	James G. March	Academic, writer on organization
1928–	Eleanora Masini	Futurist
1928–	Edgar Schein	Psychologist
1928–	Alvin Toffler	Futurist
1929–	Amitai Etzioni	Sociologist
1929–	Berry Gordy	Music industry executive
1930–1985	Laura Ashley	Clothing manufacturer and retailer
1930–1997	Donald Schön	Sociologist
1930–	Peter Checkland	Writer on systems
1930–	Arie de Geus	Consultant, writer on knowledge management
1930–	Mark McCormack	Sports agent
1930–	Richard Nelson	Economist
1930–	Immanuel Wallerstein	Sociologist and political economist
1931–	Roberto Goizueta	Soft drinks manufacturer
1931–	Herb Kelleher	Airline executive
1931–	Philip Kotler	Academic, writer on marketing
1931–	Rupert Murdoch	Media magnate
1932–	Dhirajlal Ambani	Industrialist
1932–	Charles Handy	Management writer and philosopher
1932–	Inamori Kazuo	Ceramics manufacturer
1932–	Jay Lorsch	Academic, writer on organization
1932–	Raymond Miles	Academic, writer on organization and strategy
1932–	Oliver Williamson	Economist
1933–	Edward de Bono	Writer on thinking and creativity
1933–	Amartya Sen	Economist
1934–	Mihalyi Csikszentmihalyi	Academic, writer on creativity
1934–	Ralph Nader	Consumer rights advocate
1934–	Mary Quant	Fashion designer
1934–	William Starbuck	Academic, writer on organization
1935–	Hanawa Yoshikazu	President of Nissan
1935–	Nonaka Ikujiro	Academic, writer on organizational knowledge
1935–	Jack Welch	Executive, General Electric
1935–	Sidney Winter	Economist
1936–	Andrew Grove	Semiconductor maker
1937–	Peter Ueberroth	Baseball commissioner
1938–	Rahul Bajaj	Motor vehicle manufacturer
1938–	Lester Thurow	Economist
1938–	Phillip Knight	Sporting goods manufacturer
1938–	Ted Turner	Media magnate
1939–	Thomas J. Burrell	Advertising executive
1939–	Fritjof Capra	Systems thinker and ecologist
1939–	Dhanin Chearavanont	Industrialist
1939–	Henry Mintzberg	Academic, writer on strategy
1939–	John Stopford	Academic, writer on international business and strategy
1941–2001	Donella Meadows	Futurist
1941–	Percy Barnevik	Executive
1941–	C.K. Prahalad	Academic, writer on strategy
1942–	Tony Buzan	Writer on creativity
1942–	Michael Eisner	Media executive

1942–	Robert D. Haas	Clothing manufacturer
1942–	Lee Kun-hee	Industrialist
1942–	Tom Peters	Management consultant
1942–	Anita Roddick	Cosmetics retailer
1943–	Max Boisot	Academic, writer on organizations and anthropology
1943–	Rosabeth Moss Kanter	Sociologist and writer on management
1943–	Gareth Morgan	Academic, writer on organizations
1943–	Ohmae Kenichi	Management consultant
1943–	Rodolfo Terragno	Lawyer and journalist
1944–	Jim Clark	Software designer and maker
1944–	Larry Ellison	Sofware designer and maker
1944–	Anthony Hopwood	Accountant
1944–	Jürgen Schrempp	Motor vehicle manufacturer
1944–	Henry Kravis	Financier
1945–	Charles Snow	Academic, writer on organization and strategy
1946–	W. Brian Arthur	Academic, writer on systems
1946–	James Beniger	Sociologist
1946–	N.R. Narayana Murthy	Information technology manufacturer
1946–	Robert Reich	Political economist and writer on labour
1946–	Peter Schwartz	Futurist
1947–	Thomas Kochan	Academic, writer on industrial relations
1947–	John Kotter	Writer on leadership
1947–	Michael Porter	Academic, writer on strategy
1947–	Peter Senge	Writer on knowledge and organizations
1948–	Nancy Adler	Academic, writer on cross-cultural management
1948–	Sumantra Ghoshal	Academic, writer on international management
1948–	Michael Hammer	Academic, exponent of re-engineering
1950–	Mitch Kapor	Software designer
1950–	David J. Teece	Writer on strategy
1954–	Gary Hamel	Writer on strategy
1955–	Tim Berners-Lee	Developer of the World Wide Web
1955–	Bill Gates	Software designer and maker
1955–	Steve Jobs	Computer designer and maker
1958–	Son Masayoshi	Software designer and internet entrepreneur
1959–	Ricardo Semler	Manufacturer of food processing machinery
1963–	Mikitani Hiroshi	E–commerce entrepreneur
1965–	Michael Dell	Computer manufacturer

A

ABBÉ, Ernst Carl (1840–1905)

Ernst Carl Abbé was born in Eisenach, Saxe-Weimar (now Germany) on 23 January 1840 and died in Jena, Germany on 14 January 1905. The son of a textile worker, he won scholarships which enabled him to attend university. He studied at the universities of Jena and Göttingen, taking a degree in physics and then a doctorate in thermodynamics in 1861. After a teaching in Frankfurt am Main, Abbé returned to Jena to teach mathematics and physics. In 1870 he was appointed professor of physics, and in 1878 was named director of the university's astronomical observatory. In 1871 he married Elise Snell, daughter of a fellow professor; they had two daughters.

In 1846 a craftsman named Carl Zeiss had opened a small workshop in Jena for the manufacture of optical instruments. Like Horace DARWIN at Cambridge later in the century, Zeiss was able to grow a successful business based on his contacts with the university's scientific community. Zeiss encountered limits to the resolution that could be achieved in microscopes and other optical instruments given current manufacturing methods, and in 1866 he turned to Abbé for assistance. Abbé, studying the problem, developed the diffraction theory of image formation, which not only led to the technical solution of many of Zeiss's problems but continues to be a major underpinning of optical theory to this day. The development of diffraction theory not only made his name as a scientist, it also made him

wealthy. Abbé and Zeiss worked well together and shared many common views, and in 1876 Abbé became a partner in the instrument-making business.

Abbé proved to be a natural businessman. Carl Zeiss gradually handed over more control to the younger man, and Abbé was given a free hand to develop the firm. He saw applications for optics in many fields, and, as well as microscopes and telescopes, began making optical projection equipment, photographic equipment, telescopic sights and measuring instruments. Innovation was a key feature of the Carl Zeiss business; Auerbach (1903) says that at least one new product was launched each year. In the late 1870s a purpose-built factory was erected on the outskirts of Jena, and this was constantly added to as the works expanded.

After Carl Zeiss's death in 1888, Abbé formed a brief partnership with the latter's son, but by 1890 had become sole proprietor. In 1896 he made over ownership of the business to the Carl Zeiss Foundation, remaining on the board as a director and *de facto* general manager until his retirement on health grounds in 1903. All profits from the business went to the Foundation, which gave the majority to the University of Jena and divided the residue among the workers according to a profit-sharing scheme.

Abbé was a strong believer in industrial democracy. He believed that workers had the right to be heard and represented on major issues that affected the business. He paid high

wages: profit sharing was considered an additional perquisite, not the main form of remuneration. He believed in guidance rather than control, and like other high-technology entrepreneurs (notably Robert NOYCE), tended to set targets and ask his workers to meet them while giving them considerable freedom in the execution of their tasks. This was considerably at variance with standard practice in Germany at that time.

Abbé also attracted much attention for his workplace and social reforms. A sick fund had already been set up in 1875, and this was progressively extended to cover illnesses of up to one year's duration. A company pension scheme was established in 1888; paid holidays and compensation in the event of layoffs were introduced, and in 1900 the working day was cut back to eight hours. The reforms at Zeiss attracted attention throughout Germany, and served as models for social legislation in several German states.

BIBLIOGRAPHY

Auerbach, F. (1903) *The Zeiss Works and the Carl-Zeiss Stiftung in Jena*, trans. S.F. Paul and F.J. Cheshire, London: Marshall, Brookes and Chalkley, 1904.

Sponsel, H. (1957) *Made in Germany: Die dramatische Geschicte des Hauses Zeiss*, Gutersloh: C. Bertelsmann Verlag.

MLW

ACKOFF, Russell L. (1919–)

Russell Ackoff was born in Philadelphia on 12 February 1919. He graduated from the University of Pennsylvania in 1941 with a degree in architecture, but was inspired by the course in modern philosophy given by C. West CHURCHMAN, which sparked off a lifetime friendship and a productive collaboration between himself and Churchman. As an academic, Ackoff made a significant contribution to a number of fields in business and management, most notably operations research and interactive planning.

Ackoff began his academic career in 1941 when he joined the University of Pennsylvania as an assistant instructor in philosophy. During the Second World War he served in the US Army, but continued his correspondence with Churchman and completed his Ph.D. in 1947. He subsequently worked as assistant professor in philosophy and mathematics at Wayne University in Detroit, before moving to the Case Institute of Technology in 1951, where he became professor of operations research and director of the Operations Research Group, meanwhile taking up visiting professorships in the UK and Mexico. He returned to the University of Pennsylvania in 1964 and took a series of professorships and chairmanships in the departments of systems sciences and management science. Throughout his academic career he won significant acclaim and was awarded honorary doctorates (from the University of Lancaster, Washington University and the University of New Haven) and many prizes for his contribution to planning, and training and development.

Together with Churchman, he is acknowledged as the co-founder of the field of operations research. Their book *Introduction to Operations Research* (Churchman *et al.* 1957) was the first international textbook in the field. After the Second World War, when the growth in demand rose, operations research set out to address the problems of industry posed by this growth by applying a scientific method to improving production efficiency. The field of operations research grew in importance during that decade. It is characterized by a systems orientation and an interdisciplinary approach.

A practical person and practitioner-oriented academic, Ackoff has been driven by a commitment to participation. This

comes out most clearly in his work on interactive planning and the circular organization, which is a form of democratic hierarchy.

As the problems of production capacity receded in the 1960s, Ackoff moved towards addressing new corporate problems of strategic planning. His approach concerned what he called the 'purposeful systems' of corporations, and the systems of interacting problems that they faced. He formulated his ideas as a participatory approach known as 'interactive planning'. This aims to encourage people to conceive unconstrained idealized designs for the future, and to invent ways of realizing them. Ackoff believes that many obstructions to change reside in the minds of participants rather than in the problem context itself, and that many of these are unwitting assumptions. Interactive planning aims to free participants from these constraints by asking them to focus on an ideal future in which all constraints have been removed. When finding ways to achieve their desired future, participants are no longer plagued by obstructions. The ideas of interactive planning are set out in Ackoff's book *Creating the Corporate Future* (1981).

In interactive planning, Ackoff first advocates 'formulating the mess (or system of interacting problems)' by systems analysis, by clarifying obstructions and by making projections of plausible future performance should the current situation continue. This produces a reference scenario. Next comes a phase of 'ends planning' to design an ideal future, which must be both technologically feasible and lead to a learning organization. The 'means planning' phase closes the gap between the current reference scenario and the ideal future, and requires much creativity. The participation in the planning generates both motivation and commitment, and facilitates implementation of the plans. Interactive planning offers many benefits, although it has been criticized for its naive assumption that all participants are willing and able to engage in open debate, free of all power plays.

Ackoff later developed the concept of the circular organization, again to promote the cause of participation in the running of an organization. In *The Democratic Organization* he sets out the three main principles of participation through structure: (1) the absence of an ultimate authority; (2) the ability of each member to participate directly or through representation in all decisions that affect him or her directly; and (3) the ability of members to make and implement decisions that affect no one other than the decision maker(s). The circular organization enhances people's chances of participating and making rapid and meaningful contributions, and it increases flexibility in response to changing circumstances, although much depends on the rules governing the organization. Although it fails perhaps to take into account more fuzzy-edged boundaries between and within organizations, it offers a creative alternative to the dominant vertical hierarchy of many organizations, and it does so in a way that is complementary to their existing structure. As an adaptation rather than a revolution, it may be easier for firms to adopt.

Ackoff has constantly reiterated the need for involvement with his motto 'plan or be planned for'. He has shown himself to be future-oriented throughout his career, and committed to improving the future by establishing what can be done now to create the future rather than trying to ascertain what the future will be independently of our actions now.

Ackoff has devoted much time to applying his concepts to solving the problems and conflicts of numerous large public and private sector organizations. He has used his deep insights and experience, together with his irrepressible wit, to publish many astute fables on business and management. He will no doubt be remembered in management circles for this astuteness and charm, as well as his commitment to participation and creative problem solving in bringing about a better future.

BIBLIOGRAPHY
Ackoff, R.L. (1981) *Creating the Corporate Future*, New York: John Wiley.
────── (1991) *Ackoff's Fables*, New York: John Wiley.
────── (1994) *The Democratic Organization*, New York: Oxford University Press.
Ackoff, R.L. and Emery, F.E. (1972) *On Purposeful Systems*, London: Tavistock Institute.
Ackoff, R.L. and Sasieni, M. (1968) *Fundamentals of Operations Research*, New York: John Wiley.
Churchman, C.W. and Ackoff, R.L. (1950) *Methods of Inquiry*, St Louis, MO: Educational Publishers.
Churchman, C.W., Ackoff, R.L. and Arnoff, E.L. (1957) *Introduction to Operations Research*, New York: John Wiley.
Flood, R.L. (1998) 'Ackoff, Russell L.', in M. Warner (ed.), *Handbook of Management Thinking*, London: International Thomson Business Press, 1–7.

AJ

ADAMIECKI, Karel (1866–1933)

Karel Adamiecki was born in Dabrowa Gornicza, Poland on 18 March 1866 and died in Warsaw on 16 May 1933. The son of a mining engineer, he was educated at the Higher Technical School in Lodz and then at the University of St Petersburg, Russia, where he took an engineering degree in 1891. From 1891 to 1906 he worked as an engineer in steelworks in Poland and Russia. From 1906 to 1918 he was a consulting engineer, serving also as managing director of a ceramic works in Korwinow, Poland. From 1919 onwards he taught at Warsaw Polytechnic, becoming that institution's first professor of organization and management. He was also co-founder of the Polish Institute of Scientific Management in Warsaw in 1925.

Adamiecki is notable for his independent formulation of a series of scientific principles of organization and management in the 1890s. He developed what he called a 'theory of harmonization', which showed how production should be planned and controlled using an organized series of teams. His 'harmonograms' were graphic devices – in effect, process maps or flow charts – showing how the various stages of production should be managed by different teams working under the same direction. In 1903, the same year that Frederick W. TAYLOR published his famous paper on shop management, Adamiecki presented the results of his experiments with harmonograms to the Society of Russian Engineers in Ekaterinoslav; the two men were not aware of each other's work, but their theories bore striking similarities. The harmonization system was widely adopted in Russia and Poland, with significant results, production increasing by as much as 400 per cent in some cases.

Following the First World War, Adamiecki became involved in teaching and also in establishing links with scientific management movements in other countries. He was named vice-president of the International Committee for Scientific Management in 1896, and joined the board of the International Management Institute in Geneva on its foundation in 1927. Perhaps fortunately, he did not live to see the end of the thriving Polish scientific management community following the invasion and occupation of Poland by Nazi Germany and Soviet Russia in 1939.

BIBLIOGRAPHY
Adamiecki, K. (1948) *Harmonizacja Pracy* (Harmonization of Labour), Warsaw: Instytut Naukowy Organizacji i Kierownictwa.
Urwick, L.F. (ed.) (1956) *The Golden Book of Management*, London: Newman Neame.

ADLER, Nancy J. (1948–)

Nancy Adler was born in 1948 and educated at the University of California at Los Angeles (UCLA), where she received an AB in economics, and an MBA and Ph.D. in management. Since 1980 she has been a member of the faculty of management of McGill University in Montreal, where she is currently professor of organizational behaviour and cross-cultural management. She has been a visiting professor at leading universities, and a consultant to organizations and governments throughout the world. She is a fellow of both the Academy of Management and the Academy of International Business. In 1991 she was named the leading university professor in Canada in all disciplines. She is noted for her work on cross-cultural management, and also for her studies of the role of women in international management.

Adler's studies of cross-cultural management have produced a large quantity of research that is both academically rigorous and relevant to global managers. She defines cross-cultural management as 'the study of the behavior of people in organizations located in cultures and nations around the world' (1983: 231). Surveying articles on organizational behaviour published in leading American management journals in the period 1971–80, she found that less than 5 per cent of these articles focused on cross-cultural issues, and the majority of these were single-culture studies. She concluded that 'growing internationalism demands that a narrow domestic paradigm be replaced with one that can encompass the diversity of a global perspective' (1983: 231).

Adler's research addresses questions that are of importance to international managers, yet have received comparatively little previous academic attention. An example is the question of whether North American firms can successfully assign women managers to work in Asian countries, nations where women traditionally have not held management positions. Her study of North American women managers working in Asian countries (Adler 1987) found that, contrary to what prevailing opinion would have predicted, the women surveyed were overwhelmingly successful. Adler's interviews with women managers working in Asia revealed the presence of what she identifies as the '*gaijin* syndrome' (*gaijin* being Japanese for 'foreigner'). North American women managers are, like their male colleagues, seen as and treated as foreigners, and are not expected to act like local women. Therefore, local cultural rules limiting access of local women to managerial positions do not apply to foreign women (Adler 1987: 186–7).

Adler has created a model for viewing the role of female managers within the changing business dynamics of transnational corporations engaged in global competition (Adler 1993). The impact of transnational corporations on women managers has been primarily positive, with transnational firms including and involving women managers in ways that domestic, multi-domestic or multinational firms do not (Adler 1993: 4). One of these positive impacts has been that transnational corporations have begun to send women abroad as expatriate managers. The '*gaijin* syndrome' is not confined to Asia, and in most countries foreign women managers are viewed first and foremost as foreign managers and only secondarily as women. Thus local clients and colleagues accord them the respect necessary for success (Adler 1993: 6).

Adler's strength as a scholar is exemplified by her willingness to recognize situations in which cross-cultural management researchers learn that, in her words 'we know that we don't know' (Adler *et al.* 1989: 73). The quotation is from a study by Adler and colleagues conducted in the People's Republic of China. This study attempted to investigate Chinese managerial behaviour using a survey instrument previously used in Europe and North America to assess managers' conceptions of management. The attempt failed, but investi-

gating why it failed yielded important methodological insights regarding use of Western-based methodology in non-Western research sites (Adler *et al.* 1989: 61–2).

After recognizing that the methodology chosen was inappropriate, the article observed that the question now to be addressed is 'to discover a better way to learn' (Adler *et al.* 1989: 72). Nancy Adler's work in cross-cultural management has significantly contributed to that discovery process. Through her research, teaching and advocacy within academia, she has pioneered development of a globally relevant organizational science.

BIBLIOGRAPHY
Adler, N.J. (1983) 'Cross Cultural Management Research: The Ostrich and the Trend', *Academy of Management Review* 8(2): 226–32.
—— (1984) 'Understanding the Ways of Understanding: Cross-cultural Management Methodology Reviewed', in *Advances in International Comparative Management*, Greenwich, CT: JAI Press, 31–67.
—— (1987) 'Pacific Basin Managers: A *Gaijin*, Not a Woman', *Human Resources Management* 26(2): 169–91.
—— (1988) 'Women in Management Worldwide', *Interntional Studies of Management and Organization* 16(3–4): 3–32.
—— (1993) 'Competitive Frontiers: Women Managers in the Triad', *International Studies of Management and Organization* 23(2): 3–22.
—— (2000) *International Dimensions of Organizational Behavior*, 4th edn, Cincinnati, OH: South-Western College Publishing.
Adler, N.J. and Izraeli, N.D. (1994) *Competitive Frontiers: Women Managers in a Global Economy*, Cambridge: Blackwell.
Adler, N.J., Campbell, N. and Laurent, A. (1989) 'In Search of an Appropriate Methodology: From Outside the People's Republic Looking In', *Journal of International Business Studies* 20: 61–74.

SR

AGNELLI, Giovanni (1921–)

Giovanni Agnelli, usually known as Gianni to distinguish him from his grandfather, was born in Turin, Italy on 12 March 1921, the son of Edoardo Agnelli and Virginia Bourbon del Monte, Princess of San Faustino. He inherited the family business interests, including the auto manufacturer Fiat, on the death of his grandfather in 1945. The first Giovanni Agnelli, a Piedmontese landowner and former cavalry officer, was a founding partner of Fiat (more properly FIAT, or Fabbrica Italiana di Automobili Torino) in 1899. A combination of high-quality engineering and design and a marketing strategy that focused on small, affordable cars helped the company to grow rapidly, and by 1906 it had entered the export market. In 1908 a share-dealing scandal forced Agnelli and his directors to resign, and Agnelli himself faced criminal charges; however, the ensuing trial saw his acquittal, and in 1909 he took control of the company once more. To avoid further such problems, Agnelli began cultivating relationships with key political figures, including liberal leader Giovanni Giolitti and the young Benito Mussolini. Fiat did well out of the First World War, and by 1918 it was the third largest company in Italy. During the 1920s and 1930s Agnelli and Fiat were closely associated with Mussolini; Agnelli himself was made a senator for life in 1923, and the company continued to grow.

Gianni Agnelli was raised in luxury. His father was killed in an air crash in 1935, and Gianni became heir to the Fiat empire. He

served in the Italian army in the Second World War, in Russia and North Africa. After the fall of Mussolini in 1943, he returned to Italy and fought on the side of the Allied forces, becoming a liaison officer with the US Army and cultivating good relations with many senior officers. His new wife, the Neapolitan princess Marella Caracciolo di Castigneta, was also half-American.

Following the death of his grandfather in December 1945, Agnelli became the head of Fiat, and one of the wealthiest men in Europe. According to Friedman (1988), for the next twenty years Agnelli devoted himself to a hedonistic, jet-set lifestyle, taking little interest in Fiat and leaving its management in the hands of professionals like Vittorio Valletta, the long-serving chairman. Yet it is likely that Agnelli's political connections, particularly with the United States, were important in securing the Marshall Plan aid money for the firm that allowed it to rebuild and grow very quickly after the war. Clearly, too, the obvious managerial and leadership abilities shown by Agnelli on taking up the chairmanship in 1966 did not come from nowhere. Agnelli himself has referred to Valletta, a former professor of banking and a highly able general manager, as his mentor.

Agnelli took over the reins of Fiat at a bad time: the company had run up huge debts, and industrial disputes and Red Brigade terrorism were threatening to bring it to its knees. Agnelli estimated that by 1969, one person-day in five was being lost through absenteeism and industrial action. His response was to appoint a tough new managing director, Cesare Romiti, former head of Alitalia. Romiti's brief was twofold: first, Fiat needed to expand and diversify, and second, it needed to break the strength of the unions. In both tasks, Agnelli and Romiti were successful. By 1980 industrial peace had largely been restored, paving the way for rapid technological upgrading of Fiat's factories, including large-scale automation. Meanwhile, numerous acquisitions and investments assisted Fiat's rapid growth, to the point

where by 1990 the group was estimated to account for about 5 per cent of Italy's gross domestic product. Many of the acquisitions were in rapidly growing high-technology sectors, but Fiat also acquired a number of rival car-makers including Alfa Romeo, Lancia, Ferrari and Maserati.

Agnelli stood down as chairman in 1996. By this point, Fiat was running into difficulties once more. Its share of the domestic car market was declining, and aggressive rivals were challenging its dominance in many high-technology sectors. Several senior Fiat managers were implicated in the *Mani Pulite* (Clean Hands) investigations into corruption, and former managing director Cesare Romiti was indicted on two charges in 1998. Agnelli's designated heir, his nephew Giovanni Agnelli, died of cancer in 1996; this was a particular blow, as the younger Agnelli had already proved his talents as chairman of the motor scooter-maker Piaggio, and was widely seen as a member of a younger, incorruptible and more free market oriented generation. Analysts began speculating that Fiat's decline might be terminal. In early 2000, Fiat announced a strategic alliance with General Motors (GM) that gave the latter a 20 per cent stake in Fiat, and it was widely assumed that Fiat was destined to be swallowed up by the US giant, and that the Agnelli connection with the firm would soon end.

This assumption may have been premature. In November 2000, Agnelli told the *Financial Times* that he had no intention of relinquishing control of Fiat; rather, the GM alliance was seen as offering Fiat better access to the US market, especially for its Ferrari and Maserati sports cars (Barber and Betts 2000). At the same time, using the cash generated by the GM deal, Agnelli holding companies went on a spree of acquisitions during the spring and summer of 2000, further strengthening and diversifying the company portfolio. Though the future of the car-making division may remain unclear, Fiat is the largest employer in Italy after the state; there is clearly much more

to Fiat than cars, and much more to the Agnellis than Fiat. Family control too is being provided for, with Agnelli's twenty-two-year-old grandson John Elkann being elected to the board in 1997.

Agnelli has maintained that he is not a manager: 'he sees himself as a leader, a man who sets the course for others to follow' (Davis 1987: 260). In this, he resembles earlier figures such as John D. ROCKEFELLER, who regarded his role as the mapping out of strategy, with implementation left to subordinates. This is also not an uncommon model in modern European, especially Italian, family capitalism, where the leader's primary role is to chart the company's future. A man of active imagination and immense energy, he is also described as restless and impatient; according to Davis (1987), he has never been known to sit still during a Fiat board meeting. He is also an outstanding networker, not only within Italy, where networking with other business leaders and politicians is essential (Friedman 1988), but also abroad. Many of his networks depend on personal friendships, or at least feelings of trust. In the 1960s, his close personal relationship with Henry FORD II nearly brought about a merger with Ford; in the late 1990s, Agnelli called off a proposed alliance with DaimlerChrysler on the grounds that he did not feel he could he trust the latter's leaders, and the successful conclusion of the alliance with GM depended on such trust being built. In this light, Agnelli's patronage of Formula One motor racing and the Juventus football club, often viewed as relics of his playboy days and evidence that he does not take business seriously, might instead be viewed as an essential part of his networking activities.

Contemporaries regard him as an original thinker; John Kenneth Galbraith commented that Agnelli was one of the few industrialists who thought for himself, rather than simply repeating fashionable clichés (Davis 1987). Few of Agnelli's ideas on management have been committed to writing, and fewer still have been translated into English, but a paper he produced in 1969, three years after taking control of Fiat, might be regarded as his manifesto. In this paper, Agnelli looked at the concept of the 'management gap', usually defined as the gap between needs for management and actual management resources within firms. The real gap, says Agnelli, is between what managers are *capable* of doing and what it is *possible* for them to do. Science and technology constantly open up new management opportunities, yet few managers are capable of taking full advantage of these. To do so requires, on the part of the manager, a blend of science and art, intuition and culture. This is all the more important, he says, because (1) corporations are primary sources of innovation and advancement within society, and (2) corporations interact with society and are a powerful influence on it. The management gap, therefore, is a social issue, not just a business problem. He goes on to give his own definition of management:

> The professional function of the manager should be the integration of men on the job, so as to obtain from each and all of them the maximum of creativity and responsibility. For this reason the manager must be credible when he indicates the goals to be achieved and when he evaluates his staff ... To fulfil these roles, the manager must have understanding, flexibility, and imagination. These are personal characteristics, and they are of basic importance.
> (Agnelli 1969: 266–7)

Managers must be open to innovation and able to anticipate future developments. Most of all, they must be aware of the social relations between the firm and the community, and must

cooperate with political leaders and public officials to harmonize goals, means, and timing of development programs; the manager, in this connection, should help to

develop a through and efficient utilization of all resources. His standing in the community should reflect his personal qualities rather than his role as head of the firm.
(Agnelli 1969: 267)

Agnelli himself conformed closely to this description, which sums up not only his own attitude but also the attitudes of many modern European family capitalists. An outstanding leader in his own right, Gianni Agnelli is also an excellent case study of how the family capitalism model of management can adapt and thrive in changing business environments.

BIBLIOGRAPHY

Agnelli, G. (1969) 'Closing the Management Gap', *Conference Board Record*; repr. in P. Krass (ed.), *The Book of Management Wisdom*, Chichester: John Wiley, 2000, 261–7.
Barber, L. and Betts, P. (2000) 'Agnelli Rubbishes Rumours that Fiat is For Sale', *Financial Times* 23 November: 15.
Davis, W. (1987) *The Innovators: The Essential Guide to Business Thinkers*, London: Ebury Press.
Friedman, A. (1988) *Agnelli and the Network of Italian Power*, London: Harrap.

MLW

AIKAWA Yoshisuke (1880–1967)

Aikawa Yoshisuke (also known as Ayukawa Gisuke), founder of the Nissan *zaibatsu*, was born in Yamaguchi City, Yamaguchi prefecture on 6 November 1880 and died in Tokyo in 1967. After graduating from the University of Tokyo's Mechanical Engineering School, Aikawa worked for a short time for Toshiba as a factory worker. Soon after, he went to the United States for two years, where he studied malleable cast iron technology at foundries in New York State. Back in Japan in 1910, with the help of relatives and with the expertise he had gained from studying abroad, he established the Tobata Foundry. This firm grew into the Nissan Motor Company, Ltd, which went on to manufacture Datsun automobiles in northern Kyushu. During the First World War, the Tobata Foundry expanded the market for malleable cast iron.

During the depression that followed the First World War in Japan, Aikawa diversified his business by acquiring the Teikoku Foundry in 1921, Kizugawa Engineering in 1922, Toa Electric in 1922 and Yasugi Steel in 1925, among others. During the course of company expansion and diversification, he established the Kyoritsu Enterprise holding company in 1923, combining the Tobata Foundry and the other companies he had acquired. In this new organization, Aikawa instituted a combine-style management system, but this did not work well; Kyoritsu also encountered difficulties in financing the companies it held. Unfortunately, Kyoritsu's initial funds were embezzled during the acquisition process. In 1926 the combine was dissolved when Kizugawa Engineering and the Teikoku Foundry merged with the Tobata Foundry.

In 1928 Aikawa took over Kuhara Mining, which was then on the verge of bankruptcy under the management of Fusanosuke Kuhara, Aikawa's brother-in-law. Aikawa reorganized Kuhara Mining into a holding company called Nihon Sangyo (Nissan), combining Kuhara-related companies and the Tobata Foundry. Aikawa realized his plan to make Nissan a combine by capitalizing on the stock market boom that took place after the Manchurian Incident of 1931. During this boom, he gained a huge amount of premium money through setting up initial public offerings of his many companies. By taking this new capital and establishing new companies and acquiring existing ones, Aikawa turned Nissan into a powerful *zaibatsu*. With eighteen directly

related companies, such as Nihon Mining, Hitachi, Nissan Motors and Nippon Suisan (Nihon Fishery, Nissui), and with fifty-nine affiliates under its umbrella, Nissan became Japan's third largest combine after the giants Mitsui and Mitsubishi.

Nissan's launch into the automobile industry was unique among Japanese companies. Aikawa did not think the Tobata Foundry could develop if it stayed within the malleable iron industry, and planned instead to expand into the automobile industry. In the late 1920s Aikawa began preparations for the production of malleable iron automobile parts at the Tobata Foundry, including special steel parts from Yasugi Engineering and electrical parts from Toa Electric. Indeed, many of his companies contributed parts and expertise to this effort. But after the great Kanto earthquake in 1923, Ford and General Motors had started to assemble cars in a shattered Japan, and the American manufacturers dominated a Japanese market in which only three Japanese manufacturers – Tokyo Ishikawajima Shipbuilding, Tokyo Gas and Electric and DAT Motor Manufacturing – had survived. In 1931 Aikawa bought most of DAT Motor's shares, and in 1933 he began full-scale automotive manufacturing by establishing Nissan Motors. Although he failed to merge GM Japan and Nissan Motors in 1936, Nissan managed to establish its truck production line a year later.

In 1937 Aikawa moved Nissan to Manchuria, reorganized it into the Manchuria Heavy Industry Company (Mangyo) – a quasi-government corporation – and became its first president. Although there had been a request from the Japanese army, the main factor behind Aikawa's decision to move his operations to Manchuria was Japan's wartime economy, in which financial management was becoming very difficult. This led to Aikawa's decision to seek new ground and establish a huge heavy industry combine in Manchuria. But Nissan's withdrawal from Japan and Aikawa's Manchuria development plan never

succeeded, and this led to serious financial problems for Mangyo. Failing to receive foreign capital was the most serious of the company's problems. In 1942 Aikawa resigned as president of Mangyo, and the end of the Second World War saw the dissolution of the company.

After the war Aikawa was imprisoned as a war criminal and banned from public service. Upon rehabilitation, he found his way into the political world and was twice elected to Japan's House of Councillors. In 1956 he established the Japan Small and Medium Enterprises Political League and became its president.

UM

AITKEN, William Maxwell, 1st Baron Beaverbrook (1879–1964)

William Maxwell (Max) Aitken was born in Maple, Ontario, Canada on 25 May 1879, to William and Jean Aitken, and died in London on 9 June 1964. His father was a Presbyterian minister. Aitken grew up in New Brunswick and after attending school, chose a business career, having no enthusiasm for academia. He sold sewing machines and then bonds, and became an insurance agent. He moved to Halifax in 1900 where, with the rise of capital markets in Toronto and Montreal, he carved out a niche for himself as a bond and securities salesman.

Aitken developed his own unorthodox business methods. When people came into his office, they would find no chairs, only Aitken standing all day before a lectern. This discouraged them from staying, getting comfortable and socializing. He read his mail first thing in the morning and drove his staff hard, but was polite to them, 'suggesting' rather than demanding. While he did not pay them well, he

promoted staff from within, instead of hiring outsiders.

In 1906 Aitken married Gladys Drury and moved to Montreal. Here he bought and sold a number of companies, including the Montreal Trust, and, through his mergers, created much of the early twentieth-century Canadian business establishment, including the Steel Company of Canada and the Calgary Power Company. Aitken also merged thirteen cement companies into Canada Cement Company, but scandal surrounding the latter persuaded Aitken to liquidate his $5 million holdings and emigrate to Britain in 1907.

Aitken soon found a new career in Conservative politics. He formed a friendship with Conservative leader Andrew Bonar Law, and became his private secretary. In 1910 Aitken stood for the House of Commons in the riding of Ashton-under-Lyne, was elected, and served six years as a Conservative MP. He was as shrewd a broker in politics as he had been in business. He played an important role in ousting the Liberal government of Herbert Asquith and replacing it with a coalition led by David Lloyd George. Aitken was rewarded with a peerage and called himself Lord Beaverbrook, after a stream in New Brunswick.

By this time Beaverbrook had also broken into journalism. He was an astute manager with a flair for marketing. In 1916 he bought the ailing *Daily Express* to support the Tory cause. The paper lost around £250,000 in 1916, but by 1917 Beaverbrook had cut its losses to £70,000. By 1919 the paper was making a profit, becoming a mass circulation daily with 4 million readers. Beaverbrook also acquired the *Sunday Express* in 1918 and the *Evening Standard* in 1923. Beaverbrook's success as a newspaper baron was due to his clever marketing. His papers were strongly nationalist, advocating free trade and closer unity within the British Empire/Commonwealth and isolation from Europe.

Beaverbrook's greatest achievement came during the Battle of Britain in 1940. Prime Minister Winston Churchill made him minister of aircraft production in May 1940. Beaverbrook ran the ministry as an entrepreneur, not a bureaucrat, finding unorthodox solutions to crucial production problems. He shunned routine, calling his staff with orders at two in the morning and juggling two or three meetings simultaneously. Crucial decisions were often taken over a meal of cold chicken. He drove his subordinates mercilessly, but achieved phenomenal results: aircraft production rose from 719 planes in February 1940 to 1,601 in August. When the aircraft factory at Bromwich castle failed to meet targets, Beaverbrook brought in female volunteers from all over Britain. Working two shifts, they would make 11,500 Spitfires by the end of the war. Beaverbrook waged unremitting warfare against standard operating procedure. He often invoked Churchill's authority when raiding supplies from other departments. He quickly became a legend, in the eyes of many a hero second only to Churchill himself.

Beaverbrook entered the War Cabinet in October 1940, became minister of supply in 1941, lend-lease administrator in the United States in 1942 and Lord Privy Seal in 1943. His bold and lean style of enterprise promoted popular journalism in England and revolutionized war production. He resigned from the Conservative Party in 1949 but continued to influence public opinion through his papers, being a strong opponent of British entry into the European Common Market up until his death.

BIBLIOGRAPHY

'Beaverbrook, William Maxwell Aitken, 1st Baron' (1940) *Current Biography, Who's Who and Why, 1940*, ed. M. Block; repr. ed. C. Moritz, New York: H.W. Wilson, 1971.

Chisholm, A. and Davie, M. (1993) *Lord Beaverbrook: A Life*, New York: Alfred A. Knopf.

DCL

ALPINUS, A. Decius (2nd century AD)

Descended from a long line of Roman knights, A. Decius Alpinus was a Roman manager in the brick, tile and pipe industry who operated in Vienna and southern Gaul in the reign of Pius Antoninus (138–61). His ancestor was likely Quintus Decius Alpinus, who served in the region of Geneva in the reign of Augustus (27 BC–AD 14).

The career of A. Decius Alpinus, known only from a few Roman inscriptions, shows a manufacturing firm that possessed some of the features of a multinational company. Alpinus engaged in cross-border trade, managed subsidiaries and employed agents. According to Aubert (1994), manufacturing in Roman Italy in the early centuries of the republic operated on a small scale, with little independent workshops serving local needs for tools and clothing. As Rome grew in size and became an empire, markets developed for primitive mass production industries in brick, tiles, jugs, tableware, lamps, glass, metal and stoneware. Due to the volume of goods they had to create and market, they could not organize themselves in the same way as the older independent entrepreneurs, but instead used managers and agents:

> In its most extreme form, the whole economic process would splinter either vertically (with marketing gaining independence from manufacturing) or horizontally (with the opening of branch factories and outlets), or both ways. When this phenomenon occurred, entrepreneurs had to rely on agents and middlemen.
>
> (Aubert 1994: 202)

Businesses such as those of Decius, engaged in making bricks, lamps and other finished goods, began to concentrate in a few centres, although independent workshops continued to exist. The larger firms sought distant markets and often employed slaves or freedmen as their marketing and distribution agents, some of whom managed subsidiary workshops near their new markets which lowered shipping costs: 'In addition, the producers were able to respond faster to market fluctuations by adjusting the quantity and/or the quality of their production' (Aubert 1994: 216–17).

Roman brickmakers usually concentrated in villas and stamped their products. These stamps showed the name of the *dominus* (lord), as well as the *officinatores* (managers), who transferred from one location to another. The system also allowed consumers to locate – and even sue – the manufacturer.

The large number of items found in southern France stamped with 'CLARIANVS/A DECI ALPINI' hints very strongly that Alpinus operated in Vindobona (Vienna) and awarded his slave Clarianus a subsidiary mandate to make and sell bricks, pipes and tiles in the French Alps and the Rhone basin. By both producing and selling across boundaries in this way, Alpinus's firm took on some of the attributes of a multinational firm.

BIBLIOGRAPHY
Aubert, J.-J. (1994) *Columbia Studies in the Classical Tradition*, ed. W.V. Harris, vol. 21, *Business Managers in Ancient Rome: A Social and Economic Study of Institores, 200 B.C.–A.D. 250*, Leiden: Brill.

Moore, K. and Lewis, D. (1999) *Birth of the Multinational: 2000 Years of Ancient Business History from Ashur to Augustus*, Copenhagen: Copenhagen Business School Press.

DCL

AMBANI, Dhirajlal Hirachand (1932–)

Dhirajlal Hirachand (better known as 'Dhirubhai') Ambani was born on 28

December 1932, the third of five children of Jamna and Hirachand Ambani, in the village of Chorwad, Junagadh district, Gujarat, India, not far from Porbander, the birthplace of Mahatma GANDHI. His father was the local schoolteacher.

In India, then as now, schoolteachers are not well paid; only the youngest son of the Ambani family would receive a college education. As soon as Dhirubhai had matriculated, it was time to shut his books and find work. His elder brother was in Aden, a port city now part of Yemen but then a British crown colony, and he sent back a message that jobs were available. At the age of seventeen, Dhirubhai reached Aden. Shell, which had set up a refinery in Aden in 1953, paid his first paycheque of Rs300 a month as a petrol-pump attendant. From filling gas, Ambani rose to become a sales manager, then graduated to clerking in a general merchandising firm, A. Beese and Company (an affiliate of Burmah Shell). Here he worked for the next five years, all the while improving his Arabic. By the time he left Aden, his salary had risen to Rs1,100.

As a tiny cog in an insignificant subsidiary of Burmah Shell, Ambani watched the global giant's workings with growing fascination:

Our backgrounds were so different. At that time we were worried about spending even ten rupees and here this company would not hesitate to send a telegram worth five thousand rupees. They didn't care. Whatever information must come, must come. In those days there were no telexes. So they used to send telegrams of five thousand words, even twenty thousand words. It wasn't an extravagance. It was the need for doing the right thing at the right time. (Piramal 1996: 20)

The lessons broadened Dhirubhai's fertile mind: 'I had dreams of starting a company like Burmah Shell.' Unlike most teenagers, Ambani had the ability and the doggedness to turn fantasy into reality. He founded a brash company which challenged the established groups and their way of conducting business. He fought for and seized paper licences, converting them into large textile mills and huge petrochemical complexes.

In the process of building Reliance Industries into one of India's top ten companies, Ambani rewrote management theories, fought with India's most fearsome newspaper, made friends with prime ministers and became the only businessman to be lampooned as often as a politician. He first nailed his nameplate onto an office door in 1966. From next to nothing, within two decades sales had ballooned to Rs9 billion by 1986, a growth rate of 1,100 per cent. But Ambani was not satisfied. Sitting at his desk one day in 1984, he drew up a flow chart. If he built such and such a factory, added a division here and a unit there, Reliance could become a Rs80 billion company ten years down the road. Sceptics laughed when he announced his plans but he proved them wrong. In 1995 sales reached Rs78 billion; at the time of writing, sales are Rs87 billion.

But it is not his classic rags-to-riches story that makes Ambani famous and fascinating so much as his status as a messiah in the stock market. He became a cult figure not for what he did, but for what he stood for: the ordinary shareholder. His appreciation of the small investor stemmed from his own background. He knew what it was like to be poor. Banks had in the past often turned him down when he needed money to build his factories, so he had turned for support to the only other source: the public. Mobilizing money directly from small investors was a major departure from standard business practice in India. But by offering a steady appreciation of Reliance shares, Ambani's 'family' of investors multiplied rapidly. Ambani's modern way of thinking can also be seen in his second achievement: the idea that Indian manufacturing should be world class both in terms of size and quality. 'My commitment is to produce at the cheapest price and best quality,' he insisted. 'Think big, think fast, think ahead' (personal correspondence, 1996).

Inevitably his rise as been accompanied by controversy. The corporate world in India is split down the middle between those who consider him a visionary and those who label him a manipulator. A legion of critics accuse Ambani of obtaining special favours from the government so that he can achieve his motto 'where growth is a way of life'. To them, Ambani has just one response: 'Ideas are no man's monopoly. Those who criticize me and Reliance's growth are slaves to tradition'. He adds: 'controversy is the price to be paid for success. Not so long ago I was just a riffraff boy. And when an elephant walks, dogs bark' (Ambani 1993: 56). Asked once what as the secret of his success, he answered: 'One must have ambition and one must understand the minds of men' (Piramal *et al.* 1999: 11).

BIBLIOGRAPHY
Ambani, D. (1985a) 'I Will Salaam Anyone in the Government', *India Today*, 30 June: 89.
—— (1985b) 'Nothing Less than the Best', *Business India*, 17 June: 89.
—— (1989) 'Success is My Worst Enemy', *India Today*, 31 October: 118.
—— (1990) 'I Do Not Consider Myself Cleverer Than My Colleagues', *Business India*, 28 April: 48.
—— (1993) 'Business is My Hobby', *Business India*, 20 December: 56–8.
Ghoshal, S. and Ramchandran, J. (1996) *Reliance Industries Ltd: A Case Study*. London: London Business School.
Piramal, G. (1996) *Business Maharajahs*, New Delhi: Viking.
Piramal, G., Piramal, A., Piramal, R. and Beriwala, M. (1999) *Business Mantras*, New Delhi: Viking.

GP

ANA-É (*fl. c.*2000 BC–1800 BC)

Ana-é was a subject of the Old Assyrian Kingdom, which is traditionally dated to around 2000 BC–1800 BC. She and contemporaries such as Lamassi, Walawala and Kulziya are among history's first recorded female business executives and property owners.

Ancient Assyrian merchants such as PUSU-KEN, the husband of Lamassi, founded the earliest cross-border enterprises (Larsen 1976, 1977; Orlin 1970). The businesses were managed from Ashur, the Assyrian capital, by a family patriarch who employed members of his family as permanent agents in the distant trading colonies of Anatolia. When their husbands journeyed by donkey to Asia Minor, women such as Ana-é and Lamassi managed the business at home. They supervised the weaving of textiles in Ashur, which were then shipped to Kanesh for sale.

Initially travelling alone or with their sons, the Assyrian traders of Anatolia later brought their wives with them, or married wives from among the native population. Here again, the wives as well as their husbands took part in business transactions. The Kanesh tablets KA 1008 and KA 1030, now in the Istanbul Archaeological Museum, tell of a transaction in which the husband of Walawala sells her a slave girl called Suppi-Anika. The slave is paid for in silver and the deal is notarized before Tahlama and Histahsu and their fathers.

Another tablet, KA 165, a marriage contract between Zabarasna and his bride Kulziya, indicates that Assyrian women enjoyed full property rights. Both Zabarasna and Kulziya agreed that their Anatolian house would be their common property, but that in the event of divorce it would be divided between them. Both may well have been elderly, for two heirs are named as well.

These tablets suggest that commerce and business management was not restricted by gender, even in earliest antiquity.

BIBLIOGRAPHY
Aubet, M.E. (1996) *The Phoenicians and the West: Politics, Colonies and Trade*, trans. M. Turton, Cambridge: Cambridge University Press.
Istanbul Archaeological Museum (n.d.) 'Contract concerning the Sale of a Slave Woman', Ataman Hotel, Göreme/Nevehir, Turkey, http://www.atamanhotel.com/cappkultepe-115.html, 30 November 2000.
—— (n.d.) 'Marriage Contract', Ataman Hotel, Göreme/Nevehir, Turkey, http://www.atamanhotel.com/cappkultepe-116.html, 30 November 2000.
Larsen, M.T. (1976) *The Old Assyrian City-state and its Colonies*, Copenhagen: Akademisk Forlag.
—— (1977) 'Partnerships in the Old Assyrian Trade', *Iraq* 39(1): 119–43.
Moore, K. and Lewis, D.C. (1998) 'The First MNEs: Assyria Circa 2000 BC', *Management International Review* 2: 95–107.
Orlin, L. (1970) *Assyrian Colonies in Cappadocia*, The Hague: Mouton.

DCL

ANONYMOUS, *see* Duties of the Vizier

ANSOFF, H. Igor (1918–)

H. Igor Ansoff was born in Vladivostock, Russia on 12 December 1918 and immigrated to the United States with his parents in 1935. He pursued courses in higher education at the Stevens Institute of Technology (ME, MSc) and Brown University (Ph.D.). Initially, Ansoff worked for the RAND corporation (1948–56) in the project management office. Later he joined Lockheed Aircraft Corporation (1956–63), where he became a member of the Diversification Task Force. During this period Ansoff helped develop concepts of firm strategy and product/market diversification (Antoniou 1997).

Ansoff's academic career started in 1963 when he joined the faculty of Carnegie Mellon University. In 1968 he moved to Vanderbilt University as dean of a new graduate management School. Ansoff spent seven years (1976–83) in Europe with a joint appointment as professor at the European Institute for Advanced Studies and the Stockholm School of Economics. He returned to the United States in 1983 to head the strategic management area at the United States International University in San Diego, California (Antoniou 1997).

Ansoff, one of the pioneers of strategic management, has often been referred to as the father of strategic management. His industrial experience appears to have been the catalyst to many of the strategic management concepts he was to write about in his later career. The product–market matrix, strategic contingency theory and strategic decision making all were initially developed based on his experiences working in industry. During his academic career, Ansoff concentrated on developing prescriptive strategic management solutions for managers, with little emphasis on empirical testing.

Unlike many fellow scholars, Ansoff's contributions to strategic management have been very broad and are difficult to summarize. Two early contributions have become foundations for strategy. First to be developed was Ansoff's product–market matrix (Ansoff 1957). Ansoff proposed that firms wishing to diversify had to make choices between product and market diversification (or a combination). His product–market matrix provided managers with four strategic diversification options. First, managers could choose to diversify their product line extension while maintaining their

current market focus (i.e., sell new products/services to existing customers). Second, managers could maintain their current product line but expand their markets (i.e., sell current products to new customers, by expanding either geographically or a different customer set). Third, managers could choose to maintain both their current product and market mix. The final choice was to expand both the product line and markets. So popular has Ansoff's strategic product–market matrix become that today it is included in most textbooks on strategic management, international business and marketing.

Ansoff's second major contribution was to extend the work of Alfred CHANDLER (1962) and develop the contingency view of strategic management (Ansoff 1965, 1972, 1988). The contingency view, also called strategic alignment or strategic fit, suggests that firms can maximize their performance by aligning their strategy and organizational capabilities (including structure) with the turbulence (dynamism and volatility) of the environment. Ansoff continued to develop his contingency view, and in the 1990s, with the assistance of a group of Ph.D. students, provided empirical support for his model (Ansoff and Sullivan 1993).

Ansoff's (1988) view of strategic contingency theory differs from other scholars' in several important ways. First, Ansoff maintained that the environment is composed of four distinct, yet related factors: complexity, familiarity, rapidity of change and visibility of change. Complexity and familiarity are similar to more recent concepts of environmental dynamism. These two factors are concerned with the degree of change occurring in the environment and the ability of firm management to understand these changes. Rapidity and visibility of change are similar to recent concepts of environmental volatility. These factors are concerned with the frequency of change and the ability of firm managers to identify the changes before they impact the organization. Hence, Ansoff helps provide a better understanding of the dynamics of the business environment.

Second, Ansoff's (1988) contingency model is concerned with the aggressiveness of the strategies firms pursue. Unlike other strategy scholars, Ansoff does not offer a set of 'generic strategies' but suggests that strategies selected need to match the turbulence of the environment faced by the firm. Ansoff maintains that when firms are in low turbulent environments they need to use stable strategies (which he defines as procedure-oriented). As the level of environmental turbulence increases, he suggests the aggressiveness of the strategy also needs to increase. Hence, in highly turbulent environments firms should pursue aggressive innovative strategies.

The third part of Ansoff's (1988) contingency model is concerned not just with the structure of the organization but with firm-level capabilities. While Chandler (1962) found strong evidence that organizational structures need to change with changes in strategy, Ansoff took this thinking further and suggested that not only structures need to change but that other firm capabilities may also need to change as strategies change (Tavernier 1976). Further, he suggested that these capability changes were not driven by changes in strategy (as Chandler's work suggested) but that it was changes in the environment that triggered both the change in strategy and the change in capabilities. Ansoff's conceptualization of capabilities tends to be similar to what we now call resources (Barney 1991) or core competencies (Prahalad and Hamel 1990) (see HAMEL; PRAHALAD). Ansoff (1988, 1979, 1972; Ansoff et al. 1976) suggested that organizational capabilities include five different factors: organizational values, managerial competencies, organizational structure, processes and technology. Organizational values are concerned with the culture of the organization. These cultural beliefs influence the objectives and goals of the organization, and its norms and values, as well as the reward and penalty systems within the organization. Managerial competencies include the skill, aptitudes, knowledge, risk propensity and depth of experience of the management team. Organizational structure is concerned with the

responsiveness of the structure to change, job definitions, informal power, information channels and capability for self-renewal. Processes include problem recognition and analysis, decision making, communication, motivation and follow-up processes. Finally, the technology component of organizational capabilities includes systems and procedures, environmental surveillance, planning, delegation, participation, control and computer systems. Ansoff suggests that these five sets of factors, as well as the strategic aggressiveness of the firm, must align with the turbulence level of the environment to achieve superior performance.

Ansoff has also made major contributions in the area of strategic decision making. In his article in *Strategic Management Journal* (1987), he summarizes ideas initially explored in his 1979 book. In these works he provides a detailed discussion of the factors that impact strategic decisions. Among these factors are power, culture and leadership.

Ansoff suggested that strategic decisions might be impacted by the power structure of an organization. Power structures are conceptualized as autocratic, decentralized and distributed. These three structures attempt to describe the number and sources of power in an organization. Autocratic power structures usually are highly centralized with little influence by middle managers or external parties, while distributed power structures have numerous power-sharing groups both inside and outside the organization. Further, Ansoff describes three representative methods for exercising power: coercive, consensual and bargaining. He suggests that different groups attempt to influence organizational decision making by exercising their power in different ways.

Ansoff (1979) devotes one full chapter to discussing organizational culture and how culture may impact strategic decisions. He relates the type of culture required in differing environments, and details eight attributes of culture that may be important. Three types of leadership are discussed, and their impact on strategic

decisions and internal politics is described. Ansoff also highlights the importance of different leadership types based on different strategic opportunities. Finally, he presents a detailed model of firm decision making which includes influences from internal and external stakeholders, political aspirations, power structures, perceptions of the environment, managerial aspirations, past performance, culture and capabilities. Although first developed in 1979, Ansoff's decision model is as advanced as any model put forth today.

Ansoff closes the book with a few chapters on strategic change, how firms recognize change, and how and why they respond as they do to change. Ansoff relates change management to decision making because the ability of a firm to recognize and respond to change appears to be influenced by the same factors that influenced other strategic decisions.

As MINTZBERG (1994) describes it, strategic planning was the initial direction to strategy, yet based on unsatisfactory results, and more was needed. By the mid-1970s Ansoff (Ansoff *et al.* 1976; Ansoff 1972; Tavernier 1976) had recognized the shortcomings of traditional strategic planning and had begun providing a solution through his work on strategic management and strategic adaptation. Although Ansoff's early work focused on strategic planning (1965), he quickly adjusted his theories, based on real-world observations, to focus on a more complete model of strategic management that included implementation of strategies as well as strategic planning (Ansoff *et al.* 1976; Tavernier 1976; Ansoff 1988). In his revised book *The New Corporate Strategy* (1988), he devotes the first half to strategic planning and devotes the second half to problems/solutions of implementation and adaptation. He was an enthusiastic proponent of expanding traditional strategic planning into a more comprehensive strategic management concept.

Ansoff (Ansoff 1971; Ansoff *et al.* 1976; Tavernier 1976) also detailed some of the problems of strategic planning including resistance to change and the need for strategic lead-

ership. He spoke about the need to change organizational capabilities to take advantage of new opportunities provided by a rapidly changing environment. He discussed problems of organizational culture and how implementing new strategies often meant changing long-held cultural beliefs. As in his other work, Ansoff continued to stress the driving force played by the environment and the need to maintain alignment between the environment, firm capabilities and firm strategy.

His work on change management (Ansoff 1979) was an attempt to provide a prescriptive dynamic technique for managers to expand strategic planning into the domain of strategic management. In this work he not only describes the sources of resistance to changes in organizational strategy and capabilities, but also describes four methods for overcoming resistance to change.

Because he recognized that strategic planning was static and that a more dynamic strategic management approach was needed, Ansoff (Ansoff *et al.* 1976) introduced the concept of planned learning as an alternative to either adaptive learning or planned change. He suggested that adaptive learning is most common and normally triggered by changes in the environment that the firm can no longer ignore. Adaptive response is normally to cut costs or increase marketing; however, the persistence of the environmental signals (poor results) continues. At this point adaptive learners attempt to find better strategies (product/markets) and make adjustments to structures (organizational capabilities). Ansoff contends that there are several problems with adaptive learning, including (1) the slow speed of recognizing the need to change which endangers the firm and results in poor performance, and (2) the additional losses accumulated during the strategy/structure search and implementation periods.

Planned change, Ansoff maintains, means that managers extrapolate the present environment into the future and then plan future changes in strategy and structure before they are needed. Hence, planned change suggests that

firms will minimize any losses due to development of new strategies and structures when the time to change arrives. Yet again Ansoff finds fault with this theory suggesting that (1) changes in the environment may not be linear and, therefore, managers may not be in a position to extrapolate them, and (2) managers may be unwilling/unable to conceptualize strategies/structure which differ significantly from historically/culturally held belief systems. Hence, managerial cognitive limitation may make planned change ineffective.

The alternative to these two strategic management methods is what Ansoff (Ansoff *et al.* 1976) calls planned learning. He states that 'excessive overplanning can be as unproductive as impulsive recourse to trial and error' (Ansoff *et al.* 1976: 72). He therefore suggests a technique that combines the benefits of both adaptive learning and planned change. Planned learning involves using organizational flexibility, testing of potential strategies/capabilities prior to implementation, and a pacing element which prioritizes potential changes.

The above discussion was intended as an introduction to Ansoff's major contributions to the field of strategic management. However, Ansoff was a prolific thinker and made numerous other valuable contributions, two of which are summarized below.

Ansoff was well aware that changes in the environment would drive changes in the products/services firms provided and the markets they served (Ansoff 1971). This, he knew, meant that managers would have to deal with change. Change would sometimes be rapid, other times slow. What was needed was a systematic method of determining how to respond to change. In an attempt to provide managers with prescriptive tools for identifying, planning for and managing changes in the environment, Ansoff developed both an issues management (Ansoff 1980) and a surprise management (Ansoff 1976) system. These systems, he suggested, can help managers systematically address changes in the environment by managing environmental scanning, strategy

capabilities development, and implementation. These tools provide managers with a systematic set of decision rules, which provides a framework for evaluating the type, degree and intensity of strategic management adaptive behaviour required in a firm. The issues management system is concerned with managing both strong and weak environmental signals, while the surprise management system address the importance of planning for major, potentially damaging, discontinuous shifts in the business environment.

Ansoff was also an early exponent of the use of technology in strategic management. In fact, one of the major internal capabilities in Ansoff's contingency model was technology, especially computer technology. Further, Ansoff (1986) has written about the role played by computers in aiding management during the strategic management process.

Much of Ansoff's writing is very technical, and therefore readers without background knowledge may find it difficult to understand. However, Ansoff and McDonnell (1990) provide a highly readable general overview of Ansoff's many ideas, concepts and models.

Ansoff's contributions to the field of strategic management were far ahead of his time and, perhaps because he was more interested in developing theory than in testing it, much of his work remains unexplored. Many of today's 'original' insights have their roots in Ansoff's work during thirty-five years as a strategic management scholar. Despite advances in the field, those interested in strategic management will still find it beneficial to look closely at Ansoff's work.

BIBLIOGRAPHY

Ansoff, H.I. (1957) 'Strategies for Diversification', *Harvard Business Review* (September–October): 113–24.
—— (1965) *Corporate Strategy*. New York: John Wiley and Sons.
—— (1971) 'Strategy as a Tool for Coping with Change', *Journal of Business Policy* 1(Summer): 3–7.
—— (1972) 'The Concept of Strategic Management', *Journal of Business Policy* 2(4): 2–7.
—— (1976) 'Managing Strategic Surprise by Response to Weak Signals', *California Management Review* (Winter): 21–33.
—— (1979) *Strategic Management*, New York: John Wiley and Sons.
—— (1980) 'Strategic Issues Management', *Strategic Management Journal* 1(2): 131–48.
—— (1986) 'Competitive Strategy Analysis on the Personal Computer', *Journal of Business Strategy* 6(3): 28–36.
—— (1987) 'The Emerging Paradigm of Strategic Behavior', *Strategic Management Journal* 8: 501–15.
—— (1988) *The New Corporate Strategy*, New York: John Wiley and Sons.
Ansoff, H.I. and McDonnell, E. (1990) *Implanting Strategic Management*, 2nd edn, New York: Prentice Hall.
Ansoff, H.I. and Sullivan, P.A. (1993) 'Empirical Proof of the Paradigmic Theory of Strategic Success Behaviors of Environmental Serving Organizations', in D.E. Hussey (ed.), *International Review of Strategic Management*, New York: John Wiley and Sons, vol. 4, 173–203.
Ansoff, H.I., Declerck, R.P. and Hayes, R.L. (1976) *From Strategic Planning to Strategic Management*, New York: John Wiley and Sons.
Antoniou, P. (1997) 'Ansoff, H. Igor', in M. Warner (ed.), *International Encyclopedia of Business and Management*, London: Routledge, vol. 1, 224–8.
Barney, J. (1991) 'Firm Resources and Sustained Competitive Advantage', *Journal of Management* 17(1): 99–120.
Chandler, A.D. (1962) *Strategy and Structure: Chapters in the History of the American Industrial Enterprise*, Cambridge, MA: MIT Press.
Mintzberg, H. (1994) *The Rise and Fall of Strategic Planning*, New York: Prentice Hall.

Prahalad, C.K. and Hamel, G. (1990) 'The Core Competence of the Corporation', *Harvard Business Review* (May–June): 79–91.

Tavernier, G. (1976) 'Shortcomings of Strategic Planning: An Interview with H.I. Ansoff', *International Management* (September): 45–7.

KB

AQUINAS, Thomas (1224/6–1274)

Thomas Aquinas was born at some time in the years 1224–6 at Roccasecca, near Naples, Italy. The younger son of an Italian noble family, he was educated at Monte Cassino and the University of Naples before joining the Dominican order in 1244. He continued his education at Paris and Köln, in part under the tutelage of Albertus Magnus. A true internationalist, Aquinas travelled widely during his teaching and administrative career with the Dominicans, working in Naples, Rome and Orvieto, and twice serving as professor of theology at Paris. He died at Fossanova, Italy on 12 March 1274, while travelling to attend a church council in Lyons. He was canonized in 1323.

Aquinas towered over his contemporaries, both intellectually and physically (he was well over six feet tall). His philosophical project was the harmonization of Christian theology with classical philosophy, especially that of Aristotle. His major works, particularly *Summa theologiae* and *Summa contra gentiles*, became the focal point of scholastic thought; their influence persisted through the Renaissance, and in the twentieth century 'Thomism' was revived by philosophers such as Jacques Maritain. He remains a pivotal thinker in the Western, especially Catholic, intellectual world.

Aquinas understood the importance of economics, and makes a number of references to the conduct of business. His most important and enduring influence has been in the area of ethics. He is in large part responsible for the view that being 'ethical' consists in working towards some previously determined end which can be described as good; deviation from the path towards that goal is 'unethical' (Kretzmann and Stump 1998). His view of ethics is therefore a practical one, and its influence can be seen very strongly in modern codes of business ethics which prescribe standard forms of ethical behaviour; deviation from the code is to risk being unethical.

Much attention has focused on Aquinas's concept of the 'just price'. Earlier writers such as O'Brien (1920) and HANEY believed that the scholastics saw price as reflecting an object's inherent value. Later scholars, notably Dempsey (1935) and De Roover (1955, 1958) disputed this. In their view, Aquinas did not regard value as inherent in an object; were this so, says Aquinas at one point, then a mouse, which is sentient, would be valued more highly than a pearl, which is inanimate (Dempsey 1935: 481). Instead, Aquinas believed that the 'just price' was the price set by the market through the relationship between buyer and seller, the natural price being created by the interplay of supply and demand. This price reflected natural justice for both parties. He further notes that sellers can create what we would now call 'value-added' by influencing the availability, nature or quality of goods, and by assuming greater risks in times of scarcity.

Aquinas's views in this respect are of considerable importance, and are reflected in many early works on marketing, particularly those concerned with pricing theory. His arguments are not materially different from those of, for example, Moriarty (1923) on the nature of marketing. Though largely unknown by business people today, Aquinas's ideas have had a significant impact on the development of both business ethics and marketing.

BIBLIOGRAPHY

De Roover, R. (1955) 'Scholastic Economics: Survival and Lasting Influence from the Sixteenth Century to Adam Smith', *Quarterly Journal of Economics* 69(2): 161–90; repr. in M. Blaug (ed.), *St Thomas Aquinas*, Aldershot: Edward Elgar, 1991, 67–96.

—— (1958) 'The Concept of Just Price Theory and Economic Policy', *Journal of Economic History* 18: 418–34; repr. in M. Blaug (ed.), *St Thomas Aquinas*, Aldershot: Edward Elgar, 1991, 97–113.

Dempsey, B.W. (1935) 'Just Price in a Functional Economy', *American Economic Review* 25: 471–86; repr. in M. Blaug (ed.), *St Thomas Aquinas*, Aldershot: Edward Elgar, 1991, 1–16.

Kretzmann, N. and Stump, E. (1998) 'Aquinas, Thomas', in E. Craig (ed.), *Routledge Encyclopedia of Philosophy*, London: Routledge, vol. 1, 326–50.

Moriarty, W.D. (1923) *The Economics of Marketing and Advertising*, New York: Harper and Bros; repr. Bristol: Thoemmes Press, 2000.

O'Brien, G. (1920) *An Essay on Medieval Economic Teaching*, London: Longmans Green.

MLW

ARAKI Toichiro (1895–1977)

Araki Toichiro was born in Tokyo on 25 December 1895, and died there on 15 May 1977. After graduation from the applied chemistry course of Tokyo Technical College in 1916, Araki worked for two years with Fujikura Electric Wire Company, Ltd. In 1918 he passed the examination given by the Ministry of Agriculture and Commerce for study abroad, and went to Akron University in Ohio to study chemistry. After receiving his master's degree, however, he changed his concentration from chemical engineering to industrial engineering and scientific management. He met and studied with two of the most influential industrial engineers in the United States, Lillian GILBRETH and Harrington EMERSON.

After his return to Japan in 1922 Araki joined UENO Yoichi, one of the most famous promoters of scientific management in Japan, in the creation of the Industrial Efficiency Research Institute of Kyochokai, a research institute for the study and solution of social problems. The next year he founded his own Araki Efficiency Centre, and launched a growing consulting business. The list of his clients included not only small firms but also large companies such as Nippon Kokan (NKK), Asano Cement, Yokohama Dock, Union Beer, South Manchurian Railway and Nippon Gakki. At NKK he changed the layout of machinery to speed up the production flow, and promoted the transition from twelve-hour shifts to eight-hour shifts in order to eliminate less efficient work. In 1930 the Ministry of Commerce and Industry established a Production Management Committee under its Industrial Rationalization Bureau, and Araki was appointed as a member of this body along with other prominent industrial engineers.

From 1937–40 Araki was consulted by Konishiroku Photo Industry (now Konica) on how to increase production under the wartime planned economy. In order to boost labour incentives, he advised the introduction of a premium system in the context of a reformed wage system. His advice, however, could not be implemented due to the strong opposition of a superintendent dispatched from the army, who said, 'Shame on you for trying to make human beings work by wage incentives. You should have them work by means of spiritual guidance, not treat them as mere material resources' (Araki 1971: 51).

From 1949 Araki resumed his consulting business, taking on the case of the Yamaichi Securities Company. There he achieved bril-

liant success through the integration of the branches in an effective system of communications system, as well as budget control, rationalization of the wage system and mechanization of office work. The Araki Efficiency Centre was reorganized into the Nihon Management Efficiency Institute, expanding its staff in 1950. In 1951 the Japan Management Consultant Association was established as an official body of management consultants. Araki was appointed vice-president of the association, and became its president in 1957. He also assumed various other posts including president of the Japan Efficiency Federation, vice-president of the Consulting Association for Small Business, and adviser to the Japan Productivity Centre.

BIBLIOGRAPHY

Araki T. (1971) *Noritsu Ichi Dai Ki* (Biography of Efficiency), Tokyo: Nihon Noritsu Kyokai.

Gordon, A. (1989) 'Araki Toichiro and the Shaping of Labor Management', in T. Yui and K. Nakagawa (eds), *Japanese Management in Historical Perspective*, Tokyo: University of Tokyo Press.

Ikai S. (1991) *Gori no Nekkikyu* (A Hot-air Balloon of Rationality), Tokyo: Shikai Shobo.

SM

ARDEN, Elizabeth (1878–1966)

Elizabeth Arden was born Florence Nightingale Graham in Woodbridge, Ontario on 31 December 1878, the daughter of William and Susan Graham. She died in New York City on 18 October 1966. She married Thomas Jenkins Lewis in 1915; after divorcing him in 1934 she married Prince Michael Evlanoff in 1944, but divorced him in 1946.

After leaving school she trained as a nurse, moving to New York in 1907. In 1908 she took a clerical job in a beauty salon, learned about facial massage and cosmetics, and in 1909 opened a salon with a partner, Elizabeth Hubbard. In 1910 the partnership broke up and Graham opened her own salon, changing her name to Elizabeth Arden, a name she felt more appropriate for her profession (the surname came from the title of a Tennyson poem). By 1914 she was producing her own cosmetics, and opened a branch in Washington, DC; more branches followed, including one in Paris in 1922. By the 1930s she was selling a range of over 300 cosmetics, and had established salons across the United States and Europe.

As well as developing the mass production of cosmetics and adapting the chain store concept to beauty salons, Arden also pioneered the 'beauty farm' or 'health farm' in 1934, when she started up Main Chance Farm, a residential establishment which provided health and beauty care, including exercise routines, and advice on diet and nutrition. A second farm was established in Arizona in 1947, and the model for 'health tourism' has been widely copied.

Arden was exacting in her search for quality, and also understood the needs of her market, mainly wealthy women; her managerial ability lay in seeing the potential for adapting the beauty business to models worked out in other sectors. Much of her early success was due to her first husband, who acted as her general manager and organized the business on a sound footing. Arden herself was a harsh employer who reportedly gave more care to her racehorses than to her staff; in 1945 she was the leading racehorse owner in the United States in terms of prize money won, and her horses featured on the cover of *Time* magazine. Her later career featured a bitter personal feud with her competitor, Helena Rubenstein, a rivalry which both women exploited to considerable public relations advantage.

ARGYRIS, Chris (1923–)

Chris Argyris was born in Newark, New Jersey on 16 July 1923, the son of Stephan and Sophia Argyris. He grew up in Greece and New Jersey. According to Lundberg (1998), Argyris had in some respects a difficult childhood, particularly at school where he was a member of a minority group and had – initially – a limited command of English. This experience 'instilled in him two enduring characteristics: a propensity to examine himself carefully to discover his deficiencies, and a desire to work hard to change himself' (Lundberg 1998: 19). He served as an officer in the US Army Corps of Signals during the Second World War, and afterwards went to Clark University, from which he graduated with an AB in 1947. He completed his MA at Kansas University in 1949, and his Ph.D. at the School of Industrial and Labor Relations at Cornell University in 1951. He married Renee Brocoum in 1950; they have two children.

On completing his Ph.D., Argyris joined the faculty of Yale University. He served as director of research in labour from 1951 to 1954, associate professor from 1954 to 1959, and professor of business administration from 1960 to 1965; he was Beach Professor of Academic Services from 1965 to 1971. He then moved to Harvard University, where he has been James Bryant Conant Professor of Education and Organizational Behavior since 1971. He has held a number of other posts, including membership of the board of directors of National Training Laboratories and special consultant on human relations to the secretary of health, education and welfare, and has been associated with institutions as varied as the Ford Foundation, the National Institute of Mental Health, and the Air Force Personnel and Training Center.

The capacity for self-analysis which Argyris developed at an early age was soon extended to the study of others, both as individuals and groups. In his early work (Argyris 1957, 1960, 1962), he noticed what he termed a basic incongruence between the needs of individuals and the demands of organizations. Organizations, as they are usually structured, are hierarchical and control-centred. Communication is largely top-down. Managers, in guiding the efforts of those below them, impose strict limits on those efforts and on those people. Individuals, on the other hand, are independent, active, self-aware entities. In fact, as people grow more mature and wiser, these attributes tend to be enhanced. Experienced and knowledgeable people – who arguably make the best employees – are those most likely to be independent in thought and to find the internal climate of organizations restrictive. In other words, it is those employees with the greatest potential who are being most heavily restricted by the organization and its structure.

The result, in terms of organization culture, tends to be disbelief, distrust and inhibition. The trust and loyalty which the organization should be encouraging are not there. Instead, in frustration, people may even take negative steps towards the organization, reducing their work output, 'gold-bricking' or even leaving the organization altogether; high staff turnover can be read as one sign of an organization in which individual needs are being suppressed by organizational constraints.

One of the consequences of this incongruence can be the erection of barriers to organizational change. Argyris (1970, 1971, 1980, 1982) describes how what he calls 'defensive routines' inhibit change, retarding its progress or even blocking it altogether. These defensive routines are actions taken by employees or groups of employees for the specific purpose of warding off changes which they perceive to be dangerous or threatening. While some of these routines are obvious, others are much less so. The most problematic routines to deal with, says Argyris, are those undertaken for what are perceived as positive reasons. Defensive routines are not necessarily undertaken for selfish reasons: people may use them to 'support' the organization against changes

which they believe would damage it, or to 'protect' other employees whom they believe to be vulnerable to unwanted change, or because they wish to be 'realistic' about the prospects for change. Many of these routines become so embedded in the organization that even the change strategies designed to overcome them begin to take on a defensive nature themselves.

How, then, to overcome these barriers and manage change? In the next phase of his work, Argyris turned to both his own background in psychology and to colleagues in sociology, most notably Donald SCHÖN, with whom Argyris had an extremely fruitful collaboration in the 1970s. Together, they developed the theory of 'action science'. Argyris and Schön decided to switch their attention from observed behaviour to the actual processes of reasoning, to get at the causes and sources of behaviour, specifically the knowledge and routines employed when planning and undertaking actions. The term 'action science' was developed as an alternative to the concept of 'normal science' as elaborated by T.S. KUHN. For Argyris, the static studies employed by conventional rigorous research are divorced from reality; science needs to be part of action, and vice versa. As he says: 'Action is how we give meaning to life ... Actionable knowledge is not only relevant to the world of practice, it is the knowledge that people use to create that world' (Argyris 1993: 1).

At the core of action science is learning and the circulation of knowledge. It is the circulation and use of knowledge, says Argyris, that leads to effective change; therefore the emphasis should be on the knowledge, not the change processes. He distinguishes between single-loop learning, in which feedback is used to alter actions, and double-loop learning, in which feedback is used to question the underlying assumptions on which action is based. Truly effective change, he says, must be based on double-loop learning. Here the problem of defensive routines becomes important once more: many people within the organization, through motives as various as pride in the status quo and fear of uncertainty, may resist double-loop learning as it threatens their own previously held beliefs and convictions. Time and effort must be spent breaking down these routines before double-loop learning can be put into place.

Action science is not a panacea, and the pitfalls for the researcher and change agent are many. But the concept has two important advantages: first, the research aspect of action science generates considerable quantities of new knowledge about the organization; second, the action this research calls for ensures a wide circulation of this knowledge. The breaking down of defensive routines calls for patience and persistence, but the new knowledge generated can itself be a powerful resource for doing this. Above all, perhaps, action science provides a clarity which other forms of research do not; as Lundberg comments, 'perhaps the most distinctive feature of action science is that is has the potential to uncover its own contradictions and alter its own learning processes accordingly' (Lundberg 1998: 22). This dynamism and flexibility means action science can be configured to a variety of organizational needs.

In the 1970s and again in more recent work (for example, Argyris 2000), Argyris has also paid attention to the role of the change agent. He is particularly critical of the forms of research which change agents use to gather information. He notes that research into the functioning of organizations tends to have some of the faults found in those organizations themselves. That is, it tends to be top-down and directive, with the researchers controlling the research programme and defining the tasks that subjects would undertake. This tends to distort the results. Argyris discovered that the results of studies of organizational behaviour seldom matched actual behaviour; there was a further incongruence, between what people actually *did* and what they *said* they did. This problem further fuels his belief in the need for action science, which, by shifting away from behaviour to knowledge

and beliefs, has a capacity to get closer to the heart of the problem. The importance of a neutral, value-free change agent cannot be overstressed, but even these agents – such as consultants – can unwittingly reinforce or even create defensive routines. Ultimately, it is not so much the character of the agent that matters as the quality of the change created.

Argyris's work has not been universally accepted. His writing can be dense and impenetrable to the layman, and he has been accused of focusing too much on conceptual thinking and not enough on the practicalities of actually implementing action science. However, his conceptualizations of learning flows, knowledge in action and defensive routines are becoming increasingly relevant in modern knowledge-based businesses as we learn more about how knowledge functions and is controlled and distributed within organizations.

BIBLIOGRAPHY

Argyris, C. (1957) *Personality and Organization*, New York: Harper.
—— (1960) *Understanding Organizational Behaviour*, Chicago: Dorsey.
—— (1962) *Interpersonal Competence and Organizational Effectiveness*, Chicago: Dorsey.
—— (1964) *Integrating the Individual and the Organization*, New York: Wiley.
—— (1965) *Organization and Innovation*, Chicago: Irwin.
—— (1970) *Intervention Theory and Method*, Reading, MA: Addison-Wesley.
—— (1971) *Management and Organizational Development*, New York: McGraw-Hill.
—— (1972) *The Applicability of Organizational Sociology*, Cambridge: Cambridge University Press.
—— (1976) *Increasing Leadership Effectiveness*, New York: Wiley.
—— (1980) *Inner Contradictions of Rigorous Research*, New York: Academic Press.
—— (1982) *Reasoning, Learning and Action*, San Francisco: Jossey-Bass.
—— (1993a) *On Organizational Learning*, Oxford: Blackwell; 2nd edn 1999.
—— (1993b) *Knowledge for Action: A Guide to Overcoming Barriers to Organizational Change*, San Francisco: Jossey-Bass.
—— (2000) *Flawed Advice and the Management Trap: How Managers Can Know When They're Getting Good Advice and When They're Not*, Oxford: Oxford University Press.
Argyris, C. and Schön, D. (1974) *Theory in Practice*, San Francisco: Jossey-Bass.
—— (1978) *Organizational Learning*, Reading, MA: Addison-Wesley.
Argyris, C., Putnam, R. and Smith, D. (1985) *Action Science*, San Francisco: Jossey-Bass.
Lundberg, C. (1998) 'Argyris, Chris', in M. Warner (ed.), *IEBM Handbook of Management Thinking*, London: International Thomson Business Press, 18–23.

MLW

ARIZMENDIARRIETA, José Maria (1915–76)

José Maria Arizmendiarrieta was born in the village of Marquina (Markina) in Spain's Vizcaya province on 22 April 1915. He died in Mondragón in Gipuzcoa province. At the age of three he lost the sight of one eye in an accident. He became aware of his calling as a priest at an early age, and at twelve entered a theological preparatory school. During the Spanish Civil War Arizmendiarrieta, like many of his fellow Basques, supported the Republican cause against General Franco. In

1937, when the Basque region was taken by forces loyal to Franco, Arizmendiarrieta and many of his fellow priests were arrested, and sixteen were shot; Arizmendiarrieta was spared apparently through an oversight. Released, he resumed his training as a priest, and in 1941 was sent to the town of Mondragón (whose previous priest had been one of those executed in 1937), where he remained until his death.

The Basque region suffered both economic deprivation and political persecution under Franco. Arizmendiarrieta's first attempts to help his new community were fairly traditional, organizing social activities and a sports club. He was strongly aware, however, that the greatest need was for economic prosperity to combat the region's crippling poverty. In 1943 he established a small technical college in the town, supported by donations from local people. The college, which survives today as the Mondragón Eskola Politeknikoa, provided technical and engineering education and helped graduates find jobs in factories.

In 1956 five graduates from the college, unable to raise capital to start their own business, decided instead to set up a cooperative to manufacture oil stoves and lamps. This business, called Ulgor (now Fagor), could not have been established without the support of Arizmendiarrieta, who helped the cooperators find members and premises. Ulgor flourished, and was soon joined by other cooperative businesses such Arrasate and Eroski. In 1959 Arizmendiarrieta founded the Caja Laboral Popular, a cooperative savings bank which helped fund further cooperative ventures; in 1967 he led the founding of a cooperative social security department, and in 1967 he was the moving force behind the establishment of a research department, which in 1974 became a cooperative in its own right – Ikerlan.

Although Arizmendiarrieta did not take a direct hand in managing the cooperatives, his was the guiding spirit which moved them all. As the Mondragón Cooperatives Corporation (the umbrella organization which coordinates the activities of the cooperatives) says in its history,

Arizmendiarrieta 'became a model and point of reference for all cooperators' (MCC 2000).

Arizmendiarrieta's philosophy was based on notions of democracy and empowerment, combined with a sound knowledge of sociology, economics and the factors of production; among his influences were Herbert Marcuse, Jacques Maritain, John Kenneth GALBRAITH and Karl MARX. He believed that cooperation could become an effective alternative to capitalism. He was not an unthinking anti-capitalist, but rather a pluralist who believed that there were many approaches to the market; what he disliked and feared was the total dominance of capitalism to the exclusion of other forms:

In the mind of the co-operators is the idea that future society probably must be pluralist in its organisations, including the economic. There will be action and interaction of publicly owned firms and private firms, the market and planning, entities of paternalistic style, capitalistic or social. Every juncture, the nature of every activity, the level of education and the development of every community will require a special treatment ... not limited to one form of organization, if we believe in and love man, his liberty, and justice, and democracy.

(Whyte and Whyte 1989: 253)

His pluralistic approach plus his belief in individual empowerment helped to enable the men and women of this remote mountain town to become successful managers and entrepreneurs. Today, the Mondragón Cooperatives Corporation contains around 120 cooperatives with operations in twenty-three countries and a combined annual turnover approaching $6 billion; it is the eighth largest business entity in Spain. So effective has management been within the group that only one of the cooperatives has ever gone bankrupt. Arizmendiarrieta's greatest legacy is that he has shown that pluralistic forms of management can be and are successful.

BIBLIOGRAPHY

Bradley, K. and Gelb, A. (1983) *Co-operation at Work: The Mondragón Experience*, London: Heinemann.

MCC (2000) 'The Mondragón Experience', http://www.mondragon.mcc.es/ingles/experiencia.htm, 22 February 2001.

Ormachea, J.M. (1993) *The Mondragón Cooperative Experience*, Mondragón: Mondragón Cooperative Corporation.

Whyte, W.F. and Whyte, K.K. (1989) *Making Mondragón: The Growth and Dynamics of the Worker Cooperative*, Ithaca, NY: ILR Press.

MLW

ARKWRIGHT, Richard (1732–92)

Richard Arkwright was born in Preston, Lancashire on 23 December 1732. He died in Cromford, Derbyshire on 3 August 1792, probably from a heart ailment. Arkwright's family had lived in and around Preston for generations (in later life he would joke that the progenitor of his family was Noah, 'the first arkwright'). His father, Thomas Arkwright, was a tailor; he himself was the youngest of thirteen children. He received a rudimentary education at home, and was then apprenticed to a barber. In 1750 he moved to Bolton, where he was able to set up his own barber-shop and eventually branch out into wig-making; by 1762 he had added a tavern to his business interests. In 1755 he married Patience Holt, who bore a son (also called Richard) before dying just over a year later. In 1761 he married Margaret Biggens, and the couple had one daughter, Susanna, before separating around 1779.

Quite when Arkwright's interest in cotton-spinning machinery began is difficult to date, but his interest was by no means unique; the Enlightenment in Britain was a time of great scientific and technical advances, particularly in mechanics, and interest was widespread. From the 1740s onward there had been a number of experiments with cotton-spinning machines. In 1767 Arkwright teamed up with John Kay, a clockmaker from Bury who already had some patents to his name. According to most accounts, Arkwright had the idea for a spinning frame, a powered machine which would spin cotton using a system of rollers. Lacking the technical expertise to put the idea into execution, he called on Kay's skills to build the first working models. However, Kay had also worked with the inventor Thomas Highs, who later claimed that Kay and Arkwright had stolen his own ideas. Accusations of theft of intellectual property dogged Arkwright for the rest of his life.

Regardless of whether the original idea was Arkwright's, there can be no doubt that he exploited it with great ability. In 1768 he moved from Preston to Nottingham, then a centre of cotton manufacturing, and with two partners, David Thornley and John Smalley, set up a horse-powered mill for spinning cotton yarn. The experiment worked, but more capital and a better source of power were needed for full commercial exploitation. With two new partners, Samuel Need and Jedediah Strutt, Arkwright built a second mill at Cromford in Derbyshire, using water power (his spinning frame is thus more usually known as the 'water frame').

The new mill was a success, and Need and Strutt began buying the yarn it produced for their own hosiery manufacturing concerns. The next obstacle to full commercial exploitation was regulatory. Arkwright's raw material, Indian cotton, was subject to a high import tariff, a protectionist measure which had been enacted for the benefit of the Lancashire woollen industry. Intense lobbying by Arkwright and his partners succeeded, in 1774, in gaining an exemption for raw cotton to be used for manufacturing in England. The com-

bination of free trade and new technology set the scene for a boom in the cotton industry throughout the north of England; cotton imports, which amounted to 4.7 million pounds weight in 1771, had reached 56 million pounds by 1800.

Arkwright, meanwhile, was about to demonstrate both his organizational skills and his understanding of intellectual property to the fullest. From 1771–5 he was involved in continuous improvement and expansion of his Cromford mill. His aim was to produce a single machine which would handle not only spinning cotton yarn but also all the preparatory processes including carding, drawing and roving. No contemporary accounts survive which tell exactly how Arkwright developed these processes, but it seems clear that, although he used individual devices invented by others along with ones he invented himself, the concept of the continuous process was his alone. The actual work of building and testing the new machines was difficult; capital was not in short supply, but skilled workmen were. Only clockmakers had the necessary skills and tools to create the fine-precision machinery Arkwright needed, and these were recruited wherever they could be found (some years later, during the great boom in factory construction, Londoners found that there were almost no clockmakers left in the capital; all had gone north to build factories). Direct supervision of the designs and building process was undertaken by Arkwright himself, who seems to have carried most of the designs in his head.

By 1775 he had succeeded, and promptly patented his new process. This was the true heart of the factory system: a single machine process, capable of continuous production through multiple stages, driven by a permanent supply of power and capable of being worked in shifts. Its commercial potential was enormous, far beyond the capabilities of one man or even a small group to exploit. Arkwright knew this well; apart from building new mills of his own, he sold licences to other

groups of capitalists who wished to build mills using his designs. Often he also invested sums of his own in these licensed mills. By 1780, as many as fifteen Arkwright-patent mills were operating, either directly owned or under licence. Arkwright himself reckoned they employed as many as five thousand people.

In fact, the Arkwright patent on the spinning process was indefensible in both theory and practice. Although the design for the overall process was Arkwright's own, many of its components were not; he had borrowed freely from other engineers and inventors during the design process. Further, although some entrepreneurs bought licences from him, others simply pirated the design and set up mills without licences. In 1781 Arkwright took nine of these pirate mill owners to court, but lost the case on the grounds of lack of specificity in the patent, which was then declared null and void.

Arkwright seems to have been unperturbed by this setback. Nor did the Chorley riots of 1779, when rioting workers sacked and burned a newly built mill in Lancashire, cause him more than a momentary setback. He was already a very rich man, with plenty of capital to exploit in expanding still further, and well able to absorb the loss of Chorley; and he was ahead of his rivals in terms of both technological abilities and skilled workers. The six years from 1775–81 had allowed him to build up a priceless competitive advantage.

Now, rather than selling licences, he sold water frames and other machinery to those who did not wish to build their own. By 1794 his sales of original equipment alone had amounted to £60,000 (Fitton 1989: 91). Of his original partners, Samuel Need died in 1781 and the partnership with Strutt came to an end, but Arkwright created many further partnerships. His son had by now joined the business and was involved in many new ventures. Sometimes Arkwright simply invested in ventures without requiring control, as when he financed Samuel OLDKNOW's first mill, or advised David Dale on the establishment of the mills at New Lanark (later con-

trolled by Robert OWEN). More often, however, he took a large share of equity and control. His partnerships in these instances were carefully chosen. For instance, for a new mill in Manchester in 1786 he took into partnership two local cotton merchants, William Brocklehurst and John Whittenbury. These men were also involved in a variety of further partnerships with other merchants and businessmen. By bringing them into the business, Arkwright not only secured their capital but tapped into their business networks.

As well as partnerships with other merchants, Arkwright developed a core of highly skilled senior managerial and technical staff. These were often moved around from one Arkwright concern to another, especially when new mills were planned. They were also in great demand elsewhere. The most famous example of an ex-Arkwright man going onto greater things is Thomas Marshall, a former mill superintendent who introduced Arkwright's methods to New England in 1791 and founded the US cotton industry.

Technological experimentation and advancement were a constant preoccupation with Arkwright. In particular, he was interested in power generation. Water power had the drawback of limiting location: plants had to be sited where streams generated sufficient force to turn the water wheels, and also in areas where there was no risk of the water freezing in winter. In the 1780s Arkwright began experimenting with steam engines, using NEWCOMEN's original designs, but found them unsatisfactory. His interest in steam, however, brought him to the notice of Matthew BOULTON and James WATT, then in the process of improving Newcomen's designs. Much correspondence ensued, and steam was experimented with on several occasions; however, widespread adoption of steam power did not begin until after Arkwright's death.

Arkwright, as the founder of the factory system, is often criticized for many of its abuses, particularly in terms of the health and safety of employees and child labour. Like most mill owners of his day, he used workers as young as eight in many of his mills, though his son later put a stop to this practice. In terms of health and safety, his mills seem to have been better than some but worse than others. He was by no means as enlightened as Robert Owen, but visitors to his factories reported them to be clean, sanitary and well ventilated (by no means the usual case among his competitors). Workers put in long hours – Arkwright factories were on continuous production, and twelve-hour shifts were the norm – but were paid better than in other concerns, and Arkwright not only paid bonuses but spent considerable sums on housing and occasional entertainments for his workers. Paternalistic this certainly was, but it ensured that Arkwright employees had a better standard of living – and life expectancy – than those who worked in some other mills.

Many commentators (Fitton 1989; Chapman 1992; Langlois 1999) credit Arkwright with the founding of the factory system, and it seems correct to assume that his combination of organizational genius and ability to use and exploit new technologies not only enriched him personally but contributed to the broader revolution in business and the economy. The impacts of that system were, of course, enormous, but exactly what those impacts were continues to be the subject of debate. Karl MARX and his followers believed that the main impact of the factory system was that it concentrated capital and allowed for greater exploitation of labour, and by and large this remains the orthodox view today. More recently, however, transactions costs theorists such as North and WILLIAMSON have argued that the factory system allowed for greater efficiency, as it reduced transactions costs and lowered the costs of coordination and monitoring quality. Langlois (1999) believes that the real revolution lay not in the concentration of capital or of labour, but in the switch of emphasis from *product* to *process*. In contracting or putting-out systems, the main methods of producing goods prior to the

factory system, the business owner could only monitor the end product; he or she had no control over the process. By bringing the process under direct managerial control, Arkwright could concentrate on engineering that process to produce high-quality output at lower cost. In Langlois's view: 'The factory system arose because growth in the extent of the market ... opened up entrepreneurial possibilities for high-volume throughput. This meant not only an extended division of labour but also investment in new capabilities ... that, by making production more routine, permitted lower unit costs' (1999: 47).

From a tailor's son, Arkwright had risen to be a power in the land. He was knighted in 1786, ostensibly for making a speech congratulating King George III on his escape from an assassination attempt; in 1787 he was made high sheriff of Derbyshire. He began building a grand new manor house at Cromford. A compulsive worker who was poor at delegation, he continued to be at his desk from 5 a.m. to 9 p.m. every day, and unsurprisingly began to develop heart problems, but worked on until his final illness. When he died, 2,000 mourners attended his funeral in Cromford.

Arkwright was one of the central figures of the Industrial Revolution in England and Scotland, a prime mover in the technological advances of the period and one of the founding fathers of the factory system. Although controversy surrounds his claims to inventions such as the spinning frame, even his bitterest critics have not denied his entrepreneurial skills. Fitton, author of the only scholarly biography of Arkwright, describes him as 'a business genius of the first order. The founder of the modern factory system, he was the creator of a new industrial society that transformed England ... into the workshop of the world' (Fitton 1989: 1).

BIBLIOGRAPHY

'Arkwright, Sir Richard' (1885) in L. Stephen and S. Lee (eds), *Dictionary of National Biography*, London: Small, Elder and Co., vol. 2, 81–6.

Berg, M. (1985) *The Age of Manufactures: Industry, Innovation and Work in Britain, 1700–1820*, Oxford: Blackwell.

Chapman, S. (1992) *Merchant Enterprise in Britain*, Cambridge: Cambridge University Press.

Fitton, R.S. (1989) *The Arkwrights: Spinners of Fortune*, Manchester: Manchester University Press.

Fitton, R.S. and Wadsworth, A.K. (1958) *The Strutts and the Arkwrights 1758–1830: A Study of the Early Factory System*, Manchester: Manchester University Press.

Guest, R. (1823) *A Compendious History of the Cotton Manufacture; With a Disproval of the Claim of Sir Richard Arkwright to the Invention of its Ingenious Machinery*, Manchester: Joseph Pratt.

Langlois, R.N. (1999) 'The Coevolution of Technology and Organisation in the Transition to the Factory System', in P.L. Robertson (ed.), *Authority and Control in Modern Industry*, London: Routledge, 36–55.

Pollard, S. (1965) *The Genesis of Modern Management*, London: Edward Arnold.

MLW

ARROW, Kenneth Joseph (1921–)

Kenneth Joseph Arrow was born in New York City on 23 August 1921. He was educated at the City College of New York, graduating with a degree in social science and mathematics, and then at Columbia University, where he gained an MA in mathematics in 1941. He served in the US Army from 1942 to 1946, reaching the rank of captain, and then returned to Columbia to study for his Ph.D., which he

completed in 1951; at the same time he was research associate and assistant professor at the Cowles Commission for Research in Economics at the University of Chicago. He served as a consultant to the RAND Corporation for many years from 1948, and as an economic adviser on the US Council of Economic Advisors. In 1949 Arrow became acting assistant professor at Stanford University, where he rose rapidly through the academic ranks, becoming a professor in 1953. He moved to Harvard in 1968, and finally returned to Stanford in 1979 as professor of economics and operations research. He married Selma Schweitzer in 1947, and has two sons.

One of Arrow's first well-known works was his development of a general impossibility theorem (published in 1951 as *Social Choice and Individual Values*). Based on his doctoral thesis, this work set out to ascertain what conditions (if any) allowed group decisions to be rationally and democratically derived from individual preferences. Arrow set out four conditions that had to be satisfied by any method of relating individual preferences to social choices. He proved that the four conditions are contradictory, and thus that it is impossible for any social welfare function to satisfy them all simultaneously. Arrow confirmed that democratic decision making as traditionally understood was, in principle, impossible. The impossibility theorem shows that there is not, and in principle cannot be, any perfect form of government. This led to the development of public choice economics. He later developed theories of social choice that allow decisions to be made in situations of multiple criteria, particularly in cases with conflicting and incommensurable criteria.

His work in developing the general equilibrium theory of economies and welfare economics was also of considerable importance. He used new mathematical techniques to provide better and more general proofs of the existence and uniqueness of general competitive equilibrium, proved that all competitive equilibria are optimal, and that all optimal states can be achieved through the competitive market process.

The economics of information, uncertainty, risk-bearing and insurance was the third of Arrow's three main fields of work (social choice theory and his work on general equilibrium theory being the other two). He was a pioneer in developing and applying the concepts of uncertainty and risk to economic analysis. He found that the efficient (Pareto's definition) use of resources in uncertainty depends partly on relationships or controls extraneous to the price mechanism, such as family ties, moral principles and so on. He argued that 'the uncertainties about economics are rooted in our need for a better understanding of the economics of uncertainty; our lack of economic knowledge is in good part our difficulty in modelling the ignorance of the economic agent' (Arrow and Raynaud 1986). A substantial amount of his work was directed towards this difficulty.

In addition to the considerable importance of each of Arrow's individual contributions, his contribution to economic thinking is significant for its breadth as well as for articulating new problems and promoting new paths for research. He was continually motivated to demonstrate that economic reasoning could be of real practical use to the problems of industrial decision makers of the time. Consequently, he worked on a diverse range of applied problems including the economics of medical care and health insurance (which broke new ground in the field, focusing particularly on the role of differential information), building theory and models of discrimination, impacts on urban economic development, social responsibility and economic efficiency, environmental preservation and irreversibility. Other significant papers by Arrow contributed to the stability analysis of market models, optimal inventory theory, mathematical programming and statistical decision theory.

Although highly technical, Arrow's work was concerned with basic economic issues and

pressing social problems. He concerned himself with the most fundamental questions in economics, such as can the economic system achieve an equilibrium, and if so, how should it be evaluated in terms of social welfare? Can non-market choice rules be used instead of, or as an addition to, the market, and if so, how do these collective choice rules perform? Can the economic system function smoothly with uncertainty and imperfect information, and how might economic institutions be changed in the face of that uncertainty?

Arrow's career was long and outstandingly productive, and his many contributions to economic theory were well recognized by his colleagues, who acknowledged his unfailing genius and good humour. More publicly, he was recognized with the award of the Nobel Prize for Economics in 1972, in addition to many other awards and thirteen honorary doctorates. The Nobel Memorial prize was awarded (jointly with John Hicks) for his pioneering work to general economic equilibrium theory and welfare theory. Arrow was also cited by the Swedish Academy of Science for his contributions to growth theory and decision theory.

BIBLIOGRAPHY

Arrow, K.J. (1951) *Social Choice and Individual Values*, New York: Wiley.
—— (1971) *Essays in the Theory of Risk Bearing*, Amsterdam: North Holland.
—— (1974) *The Limits of Organization*, New York: W.W. Norton.
—— (1983–5) *The Collected Papers of Kenneth J. Arrow*, 6 vols, Cambridge, MA: Harvard University Press.
—— (1985) *Applied Economics*, Cambridge, MA: Belknap Press of Harvard University Press.
Arrow, K.J. and Raynaud, H. (1986) *Social Choice and Multicriterion Decision-making*, Cambridge, MA: MIT Press
Fisher, R.C. (1987) 'Kenneth J. Arrow', in R. Turner (ed.), *Thinkers of the Twentieth Century*, London: St James Press.
Oppenheimer, P.M. (1983) 'Arrow, Kenneth Joseph', in A. Bullock and R.B. Woodings (eds), *Fontana Biographical Companion to Modern Thought*, London: Collins.
Wasson, T. (ed.) (1987) 'Arrow, Kenneth J.', in *Nobel Prize Winners*, New York: H.W. Wilson Co.

AJ

ARTHUR, William Brian (1946–)

William Brian Arthur was born in Belfast on 21 July 1946, into a Catholic family living in a Protestant neighbourhood. He studied electrical engineering at Queen's University, Belfast, where he graduated with a first-class degree in 1966. He spent the following year studying for an MA in operations research at Lancaster University, and then moved to the University of Michigan to study mathematics, where he received his master's degree in 1969. He subsequently studied at the University of California at Berkeley, where he received an MA in economics and a Ph.D. in operations research in 1973. He then worked at the Population Council in New York, researching population and economic development in South Asia and the Middle East. In 1977 he was appointed a research scholar at the prestigious International Institute for Applied Systems Analysis in Austria, and conducted research on population economics and optimization theory.

From 1983 to 1996 Arthur was Morrison Professor of Population Studies and Economics, the youngest endowed-chair professor at Stanford University. He co-founded and chaired the Morrison Institute of Population Studies. In 1988 Arthur joined the Santa Fe Institute (SFI), an independent

research institute in New Mexico, specializing in the development of the complexity sciences. He became the first director of the economics research programme at SFI, exploring the economy as an evolving complex system, and later joined the steering committee and board of trustees. At the time of writing he is Citibank Professor there, and is also a Coopers and Lybrand Fellow.

In his many papers Arthur pioneered the study of positive feedbacks or increasing returns in the economy, and in particular their role in magnifying small, random events. His interest in the history of technology and his study of the rise of Silicon Valley led Arthur to describe economics of the knowledge age as characterized by increasing returns, rather than the diminishing returns of traditional industrial economics, which are governed by the finite limits of physical resources, and hence lead to rising costs and decreasing returns. In contrast, in the world of information and the software industry, once the initial investment has been made, returns increase as each copy is sold.

Arthur developed a theoretical framework for economic allocation under increasing returns during the 1980s, which he published in his book *Increasing Returns and Path Dependence in the Economy* (1994). He asserts that high-technology industries operate under conditions of increasing returns, and that as modern economies have shifted towards high technology, the nature of competition, business culture and appropriate government policy are altered. Arthur's work highlights the importance of building up market share and the user base in developing corporate strategy in these markets. The once controversial concept of increasing returns is now widely accepted by economists as well as those working in technology industries.

Arthur identified three separate characteristics that contribute to increasing returns in high technology. The first is the high up-front costs of developing a product; the second are the so-called 'learning effects', which keep customers with the product they have learned to use. The third are 'network effects'. 'Network effects' occur as more and more people adopt a product, increasing the likelihood of others adopting it. This is due to the drive to minimize learning and maximize compatibility.

The combination of network effects and increasing returns means that companies or technologies that gain a dominant position early on tend to increase their domination. This he describes as resulting in 'lock-in' to a particular product or technology. Which product becomes locked in is dependent on the historical path of small events encountered along the way. These small events may be anything from chance meetings, sudden changes in regulations or clever strategizing, and are magnified by the force of increasing returns.

His 1990 article 'Positive Feedbacks in the Economy', published in *Scientific American*, brought his work to the attention of the lawyers in the anti-trust case brought against the software giant Microsoft. Arthur's theories helped legislators and lawyers make sense of economic activity in the new high-technology markets, and influenced the development of new precedents in anti-trust legislation.

Arthur himself notes that the concept of monopoly in high-technology industries is no bad thing, as it acts as a motivator for innovation. The many sources of increasing returns in this sector make monopolies almost inevitable; however, he notes that they are short-lived, temporary monopolies that exist only until the next wave of technology emerges. Problems arise when an extant monopoly suppresses innovation in the industry, and when the monopoly is unfairly used to gain advantage in a separate market.

Arthur continually challenged traditional economic thinking in his work, and is an outspoken critic of academic economists that focus too much on the formal neoclassical economic models developed in the first half of the twentieth century, and too little on how the world works. He emphasizes, however, that

the theories of increasing returns are not in opposition to classical economic theories based on the assumption of diminishing returns, but complementary to them.

He met considerable opposition to his ideas on increasing returns at the outset. Many of these criticisms relate to ideologies of the 'rightness' of the market mechanism, which is challenged by Arthur's work on lock-in. However, Arthur is clear that he is an admirer of the free market mechanism. What he suggests, however, is that under the conditions of increasing returns, markets become unstable and can lock in to the dominance of one product, and occasionally lock in to less than optimal products, as illustrated by the widespread take up of the DOS operating system and the VHS video format. He emphasizes that the key point is not whether the product locked in is better or worse than others, but that these markets are unstable and tend to become temporarily dominated.

Arthur was awarded the Schumpeter Prize in Economics in 1990 and a Guggenheim fellowship in 1987, both for his work on increasing returns. Amongst his other research work, he has focused upon the role of cognition in the digital economy, in particular formulating economic theory to describe how human agents formulate problems in indeterminate situations. His pioneering contribution to economic theory has won much acclaim for explaining the dynamics of the emerging technology-dominated economy, and for shedding new light on strategy in such an economy.

BIBLIOGRAPHY
Arthur, W.B. (1990) 'Positive Feedbacks in the Economy', *Scientific American* (February): 92–9.
—— (1994) *Increasing Returns and Path Dependence in the Economy*, Ann Arbor, MI: University of Michigan Press.
—— (1994) 'Vita', http://www.santafe.edu/arthur.htm, 15 March 2001.
Arthur, W.B., Lane, D. and Durlauf, S. (eds) (1997) *The Economy as an Evolving Complex System II*, Reading, MA: Addison-Wesley.
Gates, D, (1998) 'The PreText Interview', *PreText Magazine* May/June(6), http://www.pretext.com, 15 March 2001.
Kurtzman, J (1998) 'An Interview with W. Brian Arthur', *Strategy & Business*, Quarter 2, http://www.strategy-business.com/thoughtleaders/98209, 15 March 2001.

AJ

ASHLEY, Laura (1925–85)

Laura Ashley was born Laura Mountney in Dowlais, near Merthyr Tydfil, South Wales on 7 September 1925. She died on 17 September 1985 in Coventry of injuries received falling down stairs at her daughter's home in the Cotswolds three days earlier. She married Bernard Ashley in 1949. After a period in the Women's Royal Naval Service (Wrens) and working for the National Federation of Women's Institutes, Ashley and her husband launched a small business, based out of their own home, making items such as tea towels and table mats featuring authentic nineteenth-century designs. They later moved into clothing design, selling scarves and then a full range of clothing through high-street retailers and departments stores. Initially Ashley printed her own fabrics and tailored her own clothes in her home, selling personally to small shops and boutiques in London. Her designs caught on; the family, which now included two children, moved to a farmhouse in Surrey where there was more space to develop production facilities. Later, factories were established in Wales and Kent. The company opened its first shop in London in 1968 and continued to expand, reinvesting profits in new shops and production facilities. By the

1970s Laura Ashley was an international brand name, selling clothing through over 200 of its own outlets around the world. Ashley received the Queen's Award for Export Achievement in 1977, and was offered an OBE, but turned it down because no similar offer was made to her business partner and husband (he was later knighted, in 1987). The company was floated on the stock market in 1985, shortly before her death.

Ashley, like all successful clothing designers and retailers, found an unsatisfied want among potential customers and set about designing products to fulfil it. In her case, she tapped into a postwar nostalgia for the values and, especially, the arts and design of nineteenth-century Britain. Like William MORRIS, she saw the social and cultural values of design, and realized that 'heritage', as it later came to be known, was an increasingly important value in modern Britain. Part of her success was that she ran counter to contemporary cultural trends; while other designers such as Mary QUANT strove to stay ahead of 1960s culture, Ashley's designs reached out to women who felt alienated by that culture and wished to remain with the familiar. The 'heritage' brand image was backed up by clothing designs that were simple, functional, and yet attractive and feminine. The image had international appeal, and Laura Ashley clothes sold well in the United States and were wildly successful in Japan, generating the not unusual marketing phenomenon of nostalgia for another culture's past. The Laura Ashley organization was also strongly integrated vertically; Bernard Ashley, who controlled the organizational and financial side of the business, maintained that Laura Ashley was the only international clothing company in the world to control all its own production, distribution, marketing and retailing. Since Laura Ashley's death the company has lost direction and has failed to replace her creative and design genius.

ASTOR, John Jacob (1763–1848)

John Jacob Astor was born in Waldorf, near Heidelberg, in the German state of Baden on 17 July 1763 and died in New York on 29 March 1848. His father, Jacob, a struggling butcher, raised John on his own after his wife Maria died in 1766. Apprenticing in the family shop, he later learned English while working for his brother in England between 1779 and 1783, and then sailed for America.

Astor settled in New York City, the ideal base for an aspiring fur trader. He married Sarah Todd in 1785. Brands (1999) relates how he journeyed up the Hudson, Mohawk and other inland waterways, buying otter and beaver pelts from the British colonies in Canada and the natives in western New York, and selling them to New Yorkers and Europeans. He then peddled imported goods to his native and Canadian suppliers. By 1800 Astor was America's leading fur trader, following the westward course of settlement to buy furs from the British in the territories of Ohio and Michigan. His operation also included Upper and Lower Canada.

Astor was the first American entrepreneur to think not only continentally but globally. Shortly after Lewis and Clark's overland journey to the Pacific (1808), he first tried to set up a trading post on the Columbia River, but this fell into the hands of his British competitors. But by 1809 Astor was selling American furs in China, Chinese goods in Europe, and European goods in America, all of which were carried in his own fleet. The war of 1812 helped the American Fur Company monopolize the American fur trade by securing preferential legislation from Congress. Between 1825 and 1830 it controlled the fur trade in the emerging American Midwest, then filling up with settlers.

Following the war, Astor's fleet of eight ships, led by the *Severn*, the *Magdalen* and the *Beaver*, resumed their global voyages. Leaving New York, they sailed to Latin America, the Pacific Coast, Hawaii, China, around to

Europe and back to New York. He was America's first global trader, carefully watching the world market for every advantage. This global trade eventually yielded diminishing returns, and by 1827 Astor had sold his fleet, concentrating instead on fur trading in the Midwest.

Astor also served as a director of the New York branch of the Bank of the United States from 1816 to 1819, where he attempted to pursue fiscally conservative policies but was outvoted. He then settled in Europe, while attempting to manage the American Fur Company from abroad. By 1834, Astor realized that the age of the fur trader was passing. He had found in the meantime a new outlet for investment: real estate. Astor knew that the price of land in New York could only rise as the city's population swelled. As early as 1803 he had $180,000 invested in New York properties; by 1820, he had over $500,000, and by 1826 Astor owned 174 properties which provided him with $27,000 a year (Brands 1999). Following his retirement from the fur business, he invested a further $830,000 in real estate, becoming the largest property owner in the New York City. The quintessential manager of his day, John Jacob Astor died worth $10 million, the wealthiest tycoon in early nineteenth-century America.

BIBLIOGRAPHY

'John Jacob Astor' (1999) *McGraw-Hill Encyclopedia of World Biography*, Detroit, MI: Gale Research Inc., vol. 1, 351–2.
Williams, K.H. (1999) 'Astor, John Jacob', in J.A. Garraty and M. Carnes (eds), *American National Biography*, New York: Oxford University Press, vol. 1, 696–9.

DCL

AUSTIN, Herbert (1866–1941)

Herbert Austin was born at Little Missenden, Buckinghamshire on 8 November 1866, the son of a struggling farmer. He died at Longbridge, near Birmingham on 23 May 1941. He was educated at a local school, Rotherham Grammar School and finally Brampton Commercial College. Having displayed a talent for drawing, he ventured briefly into an architecture apprenticeship, but it held little appeal for him. Soon after he was persuaded by his uncle (also an engineer) to make his way in Australia's land of promise. At the age of seventeen he sailed to Melbourne where he took up a two-year mechanics apprenticeship under a Scottish engineer. He worked as an engineer in a number of firms in Melbourne, and attended Hotham Art School in his spare time. It was in Melbourne too that Austin met and married Helen Dron on 26 December 1887. He took up a position managing an engineering workshop developing a new sheep-shearing machine, and shortly after joined Wolseley Sheep Shearing Machine company as an engineer, and later as manager of the newly formed British subsidiary company, before returning to England in 1893. The time spent in the Australian outback impressed upon him the importance of eliminating the vast distances between settlements so as to reduce social isolation. He later declared that it was not long after this experience that he recognized his life's purpose was to motorize the world by supplying the most basic form of motorized transport.

As head of Wolseley in England, Austin ventured into the manufacture of automobiles. During a slack period at the factory in 1895, he turned his hand to building an experimental motor car, some two or three years after examining early, crude internal combustion engines in Paris. Austin had to build his cars largely at the weekend, as an adjunct to his existing business. By the end of 1896 he had a second car ready for the National Cycle Exhibition at Crystal Palace. In 1899 a

thousand-mile endurance race from London to Edinburgh and back was staged, and Austin, driving his own car, won the Class B category. The success of his first four-wheel car led Vickers to finance a separate Wolseley Tool and Motor Car Company with Austin as general manager, putting one of Austin's car designs into production. Progress was slow, but profits were made in 1902 and 1903. Austin left in 1905 to set up the Austin Motor Company at Longbridge. Much later in his career, he tried unsuccessfully to outbid William R. MORRIS and buy the Wolseley Motor Company.

Austin Motor Company grew slowly; in his first year Austin made twenty-three cars. Progress was steady rather than spectacular, and was impeded by the proliferation of models which the company did not rationalize until 1913. By this time he employed 1,900 people and was making 900 cars a year. There was no production line but Austin, who prided himself on the high quality of his product, modified the design of some of his machine tools to make production more efficient. Most of the components were made in-house, as Austin preferred to use an integrated production system, unlike his rival Morris who preferred to obtain as many parts as possible from outside suppliers.

During the First World War demand fell and Austin was compelled to lay men off. Struggling to keep going, the firm survived by taking on subcontracting and producing machine tools, and, ironically, making wooden wagons and horsedrawn ambulances for the government. Soon after, the firm won a life-saving £500,000 contract to supply vehicles to the Imperial Russian Army. By the end of 1914 Longbridge had started to manufacture shells, and the plant was extended vastly with government subsidies to make ammunition as its main product. Austin developed machine tools to speed up the traditional manual construction of shells. By the end of the war the factory had expanded to employ 20,000 workers, ten times the number working there before the war. The company had made substantial profits, and Austin was made a Knight of the British Empire in 1917 in recognition of his war effort; he also received the Order of Leopold, awarded by the Belgian monarch.

After the war, Austin devoted himself to a thorough and expensive conversion of the government munition works. He laid out his new buildings from scratch according to workflow principles. He aimed for complete standardization and kept parts to a minimum for each model, establishing a production practice that is still followed by manufacturers today. But by 1920 the firm had a million-pound overdraft and substantial other debts. When sales slowed, Austin was in deep trouble. He had concentrated on the higher horsepower and higher price end of the market, and this meant disaster when the 1920–21 recession took hold. In 1920 General Motors entered into talks to buy Austin Motor Company, but these failed. In May 1921 the receivers were called, in but Austin managed to persuade them to grant the company a reprieve. While the figures were worsening over the next year, Austin was producing the new Austin Twelve. Its first models were financed by selling off stocks and plant. The car sold well, and the company started to pay off its debt.

Austin acknowledged in 1921 that his firm should move into the cheaper end of the burgeoning market for cars of medium power, size and price. He developed his new small car in isolation from Longbridge, where he and his colleagues regarded each other with mild mutual suspicion. He constructed an office in his home at Lickey Grange and worked there around the clock with a young, enthusiastic designer, Stanley Edge. The resulting innovative Austin Seven was widely acknowledged as a masterpiece. It was priced at only £25 more than the most expensive motorcycle sidecars, making inroads into that market. It also fell on the right side of the horsepower tax. It had a high power-to-weight ratio and was simple to operate, making it a great success with the public. Austin further secured its success by

demonstrating its competitive performance, at Brooklands and Monza in 1923. The Seven sold remarkably well from the outset, and by 1928 over 22,000 a year were being produced, accounting for half the firm's output. Much of Austin's growth was due to the longevity of this popular model.

General Motors tried again to buy Austin in 1924 but failed, while Austin the same year proposed a merger with Austin, Morris and Wolseley; but Morris declined and proceeded to buy Wolseley himself in 1927. Market concentration continued and in 1929 Morris, Austin and Singer controlled 75 per cent of the British market.

Austin, who had a passion for designing production processes, modernized his plant again when finances returned to a healthy position. He introduced improved machining and assembly, cellulose paint and moving conveyor assembly lines, and by 1926 had complete pressed steel bodies manufactured to his design, all of which were important innovations in car production. Improved production efficiency allowed Austin to slash the price of the Seven by almost 50 per cent in seven years. Austin emphasized high quality in all his models, and would invariably insist that only the best materials and the highest workmanship were good enough for his new products. This policy resulted in unsurpassed reliability and an excellent reputation.

Innovation at Austin was seen not as a continuing industrial imperative but as an imaginative process to be stimulated when the need arose, to combat critical adversity in 1921 or to withstand aggressive competition in the 1930s. This conservative strategy allowed him to minimize the uncertainty during the company's postwar history.

Having formerly defended their own industry's protected position, Morris and Austin were nonetheless quick to condemn a collusive agreement between British steel-makers and the international steel cartel. In 1934 Austin approached the steel-makers asking for a reduction in price. He suggested that the British manufacturers should jointly install an up-to-date strip mill like those of the Americans. They refused, and Austin attempted to enter the sheet steel trade by setting up Tunstall Steels. Morris also attempted a venture into steel production; however, both failed.

Austin's influence was widespread, and his professional career included the presidency of the Institute of British Carriage and Automobile Manufacters, the Institute of Automobile Engineers, the Institute of Production Engineers, the British Cast Iron Research Association, and the Society of Motor Manufacturers and Traders. In recognition of his contribution, Austin was honoured with a peerage, bestowed in 1936, with the title of Baron Austin of Longbridge.

Before 1914 Austin could be described as an archetypal inventor-entrepreneur bent on making a success of his own enterprise, although Austin's motivation appears to have had little to do with a stereotype maximization of profit or revenue. However, after the death of his son in 1915, owner-entrepreneurship held few attractions for him. Creative application through invention, engineering and design became more important to him than the permanence of his company. Austin frequently made bold decisions, as evidenced by his determination to build a large factory in Nizhni Novgorod in the Soviet Union (operated by the Austin Company of Cleveland) which opened at the beginning of 1932. It reached a production level of 117,000 cars in 1938.

Austin's ambitions were to motorize the common man and to preserve his firm's reputation as a maker of vehicles of high quality and low cost. 'Life has taught me', he wrote in 1929, 'that nothing worthwhile is accomplished without untiring exertion and interminable application, fortified and inspired by very definite purpose.' Survival and success in business, he maintained, was due to something more than the mere exigencies of commercialism – to some guiding force whose energy is drawn from the distant objective, to a purpose transcending the accumulation of wealth.

Management discussions at Austin concentrated on costs, profit margins and break-evens; finance was the determining factor limiting the levels of sales, despite higher demand for the cars. Austin Motor Company had a high concentration of ownership, yet Austin himself had less personal dominance over the firm than did Morris, for example. Like other motor manufacturers, Austin had a small board of directors, but little interlocking with other large producers and little separation of ownership from control. The unions grew in strength substantially from 1913 to 1939, when large numbers of semi-skilled workers joined the unions. Workers at Austin became largely unionized quite quickly, and won better wages and working conditions, though Austin himself was frustrated by the shift in attitudes towards collectivism embodied by the unions, which in his opinion hindered society's adaptation to modern industrial development.

Austin was described as a remote figure, a dour man, brusque, but very well respected and hard-working. Widely referred to as 'Pa' Austin, he dressed and spoke plainly; he neither drank nor smoked and he carefully examined potential employees for evidence of such habits. Like Morris, Austin was not opposed to comfort but loathed excessive luxury without purpose. He was forthright and serious-minded but unsophisticated; he was elected MP for Kings Norton and served from 1919 to 1925, but his political naivety turned to disillusionment with the House of Commons. Like Morris, he had conservative political views.

Although work dominated his life, Austin was very fond of music, particularly opera, and had played the violin as a young man. He declared that there was a powerful link between good music and good engineering. Morris described him as one of the best motor engineers in the world, whose contribution to the development of the motor industry in the early days far exceeded his own. Austin was a prolific inventor, and apart from motor cars his interest ranged from improvements to sheep-shearing machines and cream separators, to machine tools and similar appliances.

He died from pneumonia, at his desk in Lickey Grange close by the Longbridge works, in May 1941. His death was mourned by a great number, and 15,000 workers stood along half a mile of the road outside the factory, in silent tribute as the funeral cortege drove past. He is buried at Lickey Church, alongside his wife Helen.

BIBLIOGRAPHY

Bardou, J. P., Chanaron J.-J., Fridenson, P. and Laux, J. M. (1982) *The Automobile Revolution: The Impact of an Industry*, Chapel Hill, NC: University of North Carolina Press.

Church, R. (1979) *Herbert Austin, The British Motor Car Industry to 1941*, London: Europa Publication.

Lambert, Z. E. and Wyatt R. J. (1968) *Lord Austin the Man*, London: Sidgwick and Jackson.

AJ

B

BABA Katsuzo (1905–91)

Baba Katsuzo was born in Hikone City, Shiga prefecture on 14 March 1905 and died in Fukuoka on 29 October 1991. He graduated from Osaka Commercial School and went on to attend Hikone Higher Commercial School, graduating from this institution in 1926. He worked briefly for the Bank of Japan before enrolling in the economics department of the Imperial University of Kyushu in April 1927. Here he studied Marxist economics under Professor Sakisaka Itsuro, a great authority on this brand of economics. Baba graduated from the university in March 1936. He was adopted as a deputy assistant, and then invited to be a lecturer in the department of economics, taking up the post of assistant professor in April 1936. In October 1945 he became a full professor, and in August 1952 received his doctorate in economics. In March 1968 he withdrew from Kyushu University owing to mandatory retirement; after that he was successively a professor at Seinan Gakuin University and Hiroshima Missionary University.

The Marxist theory of business administration, or individual capital theory, was created in Japan by NAKANISHI Torao. Although Nakanishi himself later changed his views, the concept of individual capital theory was adopted and greatly expanded by Baba. In academic circles in business administration in Japan from the late 1950s, there was bitter controversy within the Marxist school. One of the points of controversy was a methodologi-

cal problem in the study of business administration concerning the five-step theory proposed by Baba. This theory was first published in 1938, in an article entitled 'Scrutiny of Individual Capital Movement Theory in the Science of Business Administration', which appeared in the journal *Accounting*; interest in it was aroused when MITO Tadashi took up the paper at an annual meeting of the Japan Society of Business Administration in 1955.

Starting from the idea of individual capital theory dependant on MARX's *Das Kapital*, Baba reconstructed the theory and described it as also having the characteristics of a theory of management techniques. He was critical of the understanding of individual capital as dealt with by Nakanishi, believing that as an objective of study it was too abstract. He insisted that individual capital should be understood by dividing it into five steps, starting with an abstract and general step, and ending with a more concrete and individual step. These steps in the understanding of individual capital were as follows: (1) a step where social and total capital are not separate; (2) a step where individual capital is a constitutional element of social and total capital; (3) a step where individual capital creates competition between the different categories; (4) a step where individual capital creates competition within the same category; and (5) a step where individual capital is divided into owned capital and borrowed capital, a reality in the conscious control of the capitalist who plans, guides and controls it. Baba also insisted that the science

of business administration should take up the
notion of individual capital as it exists in
concrete fashion in the final step, above, and
make this the objective of study.

Baba's theory of the five-step understanding
of individual capital aimed at integrating the
economics of *Das Kapital* with management
techniques of planning and control. He was
well-versed in the techniques of bookkeeping
and accounting, and used this understanding
to analyse business finance and labour
problems from a fundamental basis of
Marxist economics.

BIBLIOGRAPHY

Baba, K. (1938) 'Keieigaku ni okeru
Kobetsu Shihonsetsu no Ginmi' (Scrutiny
of Individual Capital Movement Theory
in the Science of Business
Administration), *Accounting* 43(6):
835–54.
——— (1947) *Kogyo Keiei to Rodo
Mondai* (Business Administration and
Labour Problems), Fukuoka: Kyushu
Sangyo Rodo Kagaku Kenkyusho.
——— (1951) *Genka Shokyaku Ron* (A
Depreciation Theory), Tokyo: Chikura
Shobo.
——— (1957) *Kobetsu Shihon to Keiei
Gijyutsu: Keieigaku no Houhou oyobi
Romu no Konpon Mondai* (Individual
Capital and Management Technology:
Methodology of the Science of Business
Administration and Fundamental
Problems of Labour), Tokyo: Yuuhikaku.
——— (1965) *Kabushiki Kaisha Kinyu
Ron* (Corporate Finance Theory for Joint
Stock Companies), Tokyo: Moriyama
Shoten.
——— (ed.) (1968) *Keieigaku Houhou
Ron: Kobetsu Shihonsetsu no Tenkai*
(Methodology of the Science of Business
Administration: Development of
Individual Capital Theory), Kyoto:
Minerva Shobo.

ST

BABA Keiji (1897–1961)

Baba Keiji was born in Kawachi-gun, Osaka
prefecture on 22 May 1897. He died in Tokyo
on 10 August 1961. From the time of his graduation from the First High School in Osaka, he
developed an ambition to amalgamate the
study of engineering, economics and business
administration. After graduating from the
department of electrical engineering in the
faculty of engineering at the Imperial
University of Tokyo in 1920, he returned to
the same university and entered the faculty of
economics. In 1923 he graduated again, this
time with a degree in economics, and enrolled
in postgraduate studies. In 1925 he was
appointed as an assistant at the faculty of economics, and studied abroad in Germany,
France, Britain and the United States from
1927 to 1930. In 1931, after returning to
Japan, Baba was appointed professor at the
University of Tokyo, lecturing on commerce
and the science of business administration until
he reached the age of mandatory retirement in
1957. He was a scholar of strict morals and
uprightness, and a lover of solitude. He wrote
many books.

When Baba started his study of business
administration, the German economics of
business administration was very influential
in Japan. But Baba was not in favour of
handling this science by the German method
alone. He intended to reconstruct the science
of administration in his own way, by treating
administration as a science with its own conceptual objective and by taking in both
German economics of business administration
and American management theory.
Accordingly, he first studied scientific methodology. He studied the position of the neo-
Kantian School, including figures such as
Heinrich Rickert, Max WEBER, Alfred Amonn
and others, and especially the phenomenology
of Edmund Husserl. Baba concluded that
business enterprises, as a conceptual objective
of the science of business administration, were
organizations linked by a series of relation-

ships between specialized departments and at the same time maintaining a unified government of the economic unit as a whole. Economics analyses the economy by paying attention to the social exchange relation and the social division of labour, whereas the science of business administration considers governmental relations and specialization relations within the management and organization of an individual enterprise. The former is a problem of management, whereas the latter is a problem of business finance and production. Baba insisted that the fundamental problem of the study of business administration was to grasp both the stream of value and the relations between people within the organization in a unified way.

Baba was distinctly aware that the twentieth century was a period of technology and organization, and conducted research on the relationships between technology, management, economy and society. On the other hand, he took it for granted that an organization was comprehended as a conceptually unified human mass, and that the organizational members' actions were oriented in a single direction by the adjusting forces that brought about this unification. But organizational behaviour does not necessarily coincide with the direction of an organization. This is because the organization, as a concept, is not necessarily distinctly formulated by its organizational members; instead, it is often comprehended only at an emotional level. Furthermore, the nature of causal relations in the development of organizations is very often misunderstood. In addition, owing to the diversity of the individual elements of the organization and the ensuing conflicts between these elements, the unity of the organization is always damaged. The various forces acting on the organization constantly create new linkages and relationships, and the result is an 'indefinite-form process' in which new relationships are brought about without cessation and are often in an uncontrollable state. Awareness of this dynamic process is fundamental to under-standing organizations, according to Baba. He was critical of static theories of organization and management, and advocated a dynamic organization process theory similar to the organization theory of Chester BARNARD.

After the Second World War, Baba frequently visited the US Culture Center in Tokyo, where he studied the literature on US organization and management theory. From 1948 he began introducing human relations theory and the ideas of Barnard and Herbert A. SIMON into Japan. In 1959 he established the Academic Association for Organizational Science, and made great contributions to the development of the science of organization and diffusion of the interdisciplinary approach in Japan.

BIBLIOGRAPHY
Baba K. (1926) *Sangyo Keiei no Shokuno to Sono Bunka* (The Functions of the Industrial Administration and Its Dividing), Tokyo: Daito Kaku.
——— (1931) *Keieigaku Houhou Ron* (The Methodology of the Science of Business Administration), Tokyo: Nihon Hyoron Sha.
——— (1933) *Gijyutsu to Keizai* (Technology and Economy), Tokyo: Nihon Hyoron Sha.
——— (1934) *Keieigaku no Kisoteki Shomondai* (The Fundamental Problems of the Science of Business Administration), Tokyo: Nihon Hyoron Sha.
——— (1936) *Gijyutsu to Shakai* (Technology and Society), Tokyo: Nihon Hyoron Sha.
——— (1941a) *Soshiki to Gijyutsu no Mondai* (Problems of the Organization and Technology), Tokyo: Nihon Hyoron Sha.
——— (1941b) *Soshiki no Kihonteki Seikaku* (The Fundamental Character of Organization), Tokyo: Nihon Hyoron Sha.
——— (1947) *Soshiki no Choseiryoku to*

Sono Sho Rinenkei (The Adjustment Force of the Organization and Its Ideal Types), Tokyo: Nihon Hyoron Sha.
——— (1954) *Keieigaku to Ningensoshiki no Mondai* (A Problem of the Science of Business Administration and Human Organization), Tokyo: Yuuhikaku.

ST

BABBAGE, Charles (1792–1871)

Charles Babbage was born on 26 December 1792, possibly at Teignmouth in Devon (though Moseley, 1964, mentions Totnes and Kyman, 1985, gives the place of birth as Walworth, Surrey), the son of a prominent banker. He died in London on 18 October 1871. Babbage was educated at schools in Devon and Middlesex, although the *Dictionary of National Biography* states that in his main field of interest, algebra, he was self-taught. He entered Trinity College, Cambridge but later moved to Peterhouse, from whence he graduated in 1814. Among his closest friends at Cambridge were John (later Sir John) Herschel and George Peacock, with whom he later co-founded the Astronomical Society (1820); other acquaintances included the physicist Humphrey Davy and the engineer Isambard Kingdom BRUNEL.

After graduation Babbage settled briefly in Devon, where he married, but by 1815 he was living in London, already a rising star in scientific circles. In 1816 he was elected a Fellow of the Royal Society. He was also a founder of the London Statistical Society, one of the most important associations of scientists and political economists in the early nineteenth century. In 1828 he became Lucasian Professor of Mathematics at Cambridge, a post which he held for eleven years, although he seems never to have given any lectures.

Around 1820 Babbage began his first serious effort to develop a calculating engine, the so-called 'difference engine'. Mechanical calculators had been developed as early as the sixteenth century; the philosopher Blaise Pascal had designed one example, and other inventors since had designed, and even sold commercially, various types of calculating engine. Babbage, who had studied these earlier models while at Cambridge, became convinced of their wider potential. His first view was that calculating engines, faster and more accurate than human calculations, could correct errors in astronomical tables and thus make marine navigation more accurate and safer, but he quickly realized that such engines could have much broader applications in commerce, industry and government.

Babbage's difference engine was in effect an advance, although an important one, on earlier types (the name 'difference engine' stems from the fundamental principle of calculation involved, the method of finite differences). A first example, constructed by Babbage between 1820 and 1822, was a success, and he then received government and private backing for a far larger and more complex model. Unfortunately, at this point Babbage's own intransigent personality came into play and he began to quarrel, first with his government backers and then more disastrously with his partner Joseph Clement, the engineer responsible for building the engine. When in 1828 relations between them broke down, Clement seized all of the notes and blueprints for the engine and refused to return them.

By this time Babbage's mind was already turning to a far more radical innovation, the analytical engine. Unlike the difference engine, which was intended only for making tables, the analytical engine was a programmable automatic calculator capable of a number of different functions. It used a punch-card system, previously developed for Jacquard power looms, to input instructions, and returned data in the form of a printout. Most important of all, the machine was designed to be able to store data in memory.

When the idea of the analytical engine was announced, it was widely derided as impractical. Babbage continued to have notable supporters, including the Duke of Wellington who invested £5,000 in the project. He was also assisted for a time by Ada, Countess of Lovelace, daughter of Lord Byron and a mathematician whose genius exceeded Babbage's own. But, crucially, the government of the day withheld its support. A part of the analytical engine was constructed, but by the 1840s Babbage had exhausted his own private capital and that of his investors. He and the Countess of Lovelace developed a mathematical scheme for winning large amounts of money betting on horse races, but the inevitable failure of this involved the loss of further capital. His personal disappointments grew; he stood twice for parliament in the Finsbury constituency, and was rejected both times. His wife had died young, and the premature death of the Countess of Lovelace was a further blow. He became increasingly irascible in later years, and devoted much time to a campaign against street musicians, whose noise, he claimed, was ruining his nerves and his health. By the time of his own death in 1871 he was virtually alone, and only a handful of people attended his funeral.

After his death, Babbage's work lay neglected until the 1940s, when the British scientist Alan Turing and his colleagues, then in the process of developing computers for code-breaking during the Second World War, realized that Babbage had in effect already invented the programmable computer. The second half of the twentieth century saw a great upsurge in interest in Babbage's scientific work, and he is now generally recognized as the 'father of the computer'.

The invention of the computer alone would have ensured Babbage a place in the history of management, but, as noted, Babbage always sought practical application for his inventions. His most important book, *The Economy of Machinery and Manufactures* (1835), sets out his vision of the role of technology in industry.

As Kyman (1985) points out, Babbage was thus the first political economist to stress the central role of manufacturing in terms of national prosperity. Kyman notes too that Babbage's detailed descriptions of the roles – and potential future roles – of technology in many different industries were largely the result of his own personal investigations and researches in hundreds of factories in Britain and continental Europe.

Technology, Babbage believed, was on the point of revolutionizing production. This would have many benefits, not only in improving firms' profits but also in improving conditions for workers in industrial concerns. In this he anticipated the view of thinkers on scientific management, such as F.W. TAYLOR and Harrington EMERSON (Urwick and Brech 1947), who also stressed the need to improve working conditions. However, he also warned that increasing mechanization would bring its problems, particularly with regard to labour relations. To head off these problems, he called for a new approach to the organization of labour in manufacturing industries:

> It would be of great importance if, in every large establishment the mode of payment could be so arranged, that every person employed should derive advantage from the success of the whole; and that the profits of each individual, as the factory itself produced profit, without the necessity of making any change in wages.
>
> (Babbage 1835: 251)

The results of such a profit-sharing system, Babbage believed, would be fourfold:

1. That every person engaged [in the factory] would have a direct interest in its prosperity ...

2. Every person concerned in the factory would have an immediate interest in preventing any waste or mismanagement in all departments.

3. The talents of all connected with it would be strongly connected to its improvement in every department.

4. None but workmen of high character and qualifications could obtain admission into such establishments.

(Babbage 1835: 257)

In all four points, Babbage directly anticipates the bonus schemes and profit-sharing schemes developed in the 1890s and after.

Unusually for writers of his time, Babbage goes beyond issues relating to simple production and consumption and also examines the selling and marketing process. The introduction of technology was also necessary, Babbage believed, to improve the quality of goods. In two chapters, 'On the Influence of Verification on Price' and 'On the Influence of Durability on Price' (1835: 134–51), Babbage notes the effect of product quality on the price which goods can command in the market. Not only actual product quality is concerned, but also *perceived* product quality. Babbage argued that customers, when assessing the quality of goods before purchase, incur *costs*, in terms of time and sometimes also of money. The level of cost varies according to the good. The quality of loaf sugar, for example, can be verified quickly, usually on sight. The quality of tea takes longer to ascertain, and verification usually requires consumption of some portion of the product. Manufacturers can partially overcome this problem by sending quality signals to the customer, the most common of which is the maker's mark or trade mark (ancestor of the modern brand mark). So long as this mark is backed up by consistent product quality, manufacturers will be able to charge a premium price and thus make greater profits – or, at least, maintain profitability in the face of increasing competition. Babbage was thus the first writer on management to make explicit the connections between product quality, price and profit, and he had also begun to explore issues relating to branding and customer loyalty.

The dominant theme of Babbage's work, however, is the need for business management – and indeed all human activities – to be carried out according to scientific principles. His calculating engines were intended to assist in the implementation of those principles; technology was not an end in itself, but a means to a higher end of greater prosperity, better incomes and living conditions for workers, and a more ordered and rational society. Like most men of his time, Babbage saw no distinction between business and society; the two were interdependent parts of a whole.

Babbage's influence has been profound. His shift in focus to manufacturing as the centre of the national economy was adopted by all later writers on political economy; MARX refers explicitly to Babbage on several occasions, and as Kyman (1985) points out, John Stuart MILL's *Principles of Political Economy* assumes the reader has read and is familiar with Babbage. Less explicitly, Alfred MARSHALL's theories of the firm and Max WEBER's ideas on rationalism show influences of Babbage. In terms of straightforward management theory, we have seen how Babbage prefigured scientific management on a number of levels, and also occupies a place in that current of thought which links business ethics with managerial efficiency. His technical, economic and managerial ideas played a significant role in the development of the modern management paradigm.

BIBLIOGRAPHY

Babbage, C. (1830) *Reflections on the Decline of Science in England and Some of its Causes*, London: B. Fellowes.

—— (1835) *The Economy of Machinery and Manufactures*, London: Charles Knight.

—— (1851) *The Exposition of 1851*, London: John Murray.

'Babbage, Charles' (1885) in L. Stephen and S. Lee (eds), *Dictionary of National Biography*, London: Small, Elder and Co., vol. 2, 304–6.

Blaug, M. (ed.) (1991) *William Whewell (1794–1866), Dionysius Lardner (1793–1859), Charles Babbage (1792–1871)*, Pioneers of Economics vol. 19, Aldershot: Edward Elgar.

Kyman, A. (1985) *Charles Babbage: Pioneer of the Computer*, Oxford: Oxford University Press.

Morrison, P. and Morrison, A. (eds) (1961) *Charles Babbage and His Calculating Engines*, New York: Dover.

Moseley, M. (1964) *Irascible Genius: A Life of Charles Babbage, Inventor*, London: Hutchinson.

Urwick, L.F. and Brech, E.F.L. (1947) *The Making of Scientific Management*, vol. 1, *Thirteen Pioneers*, London: Management Publications Trust; repr. Bristol: Thoemmes Press, 1994.

MLW

BAJAJ, Rahul Kumar (1938–)

Rahul Kumar Bajaj was born on 10 June 1938 in Calcutta, to Savitri and Kamalnayan (1915–72) Bajaj, but lives in Pune where he has worked for most of his life. The Bajaj family has been in the limelight for at least three generations, making for a unique childhood. Rahul's grandfather, Jamnalal Bajaj (1889–1942), was a close friend of Mahatma GANDHI and Jawaharlal Nehru, an active participant in the nationalist movement against the British Raj and treasurer of the Congress Party. Between 1939 and 1947, most adult members of the Bajaj family found themselves behind prison bars in the cause of Indian freedom. The political tradition continued into the next generation. Kamalnayan was a member of parliament who broke away from Indira Gandhi when the Congress Party split in 1969.

While Rahul Bajaj has remained away from active politics, on several occasions he has taken up the cudgels for the 'national' interest. 'Today, when the buzzword is globalization, it is presumed that consumer interests will equally serve national interest but this is not necessarily so', he feels (interview, 23 October 2000). His vociferous demand for a 'level playing field' for Indian corporates made him a minority of one. At the same time, Bajaj led the demand for better corporate governance by Indian firms and has influenced recent legislation in this area.

Bajaj grew up in a Spartan atmosphere, exceptional for a business family. The family's elegant flat in Bombay was a far cry from Gandhi's ascetic ashram at Wardha, but Bajaj's upbringing and values were more middle class than aristocratic. Given this background, it was no surprise that Bajaj chose to live inside the scooter factory complex when he joined the firm in 1965. 'Actions speak louder than words. I did not and do not believe in absentee landlordism,' he declared (Piramal 1996: 94).

He became CEO of Bajaj Auto in April 1968 and under his leadership the company manufactured a product so popular with the Indian middle classes that it had a ten-year waiting list, a product which could be sold within hours of purchase for triple and quadruple the original price. Yet the Congress government refused to permit the company to expand its manufacturing facilities. 'My blood used to boil. The country needed two-wheelers and I was not allowed to expand. What kind of socialism is that?', argued Bajaj. 'But thank goodness I was never actually penalized, though I was ready to go to jail for excess production just as both my parents had for the freedom struggle' (Piramal 1996: 104).

In this situation, Bajaj adopted a value-for-money business model, following the dictum 'if your customer wants stainless steel, don't give him platinum' (Piramal *et al.* 1999: 41). He refused to find ways to exploit the monopoly regime by raising prices, preferring instead to develop highly reliable, totally standardized scooter models at the lowest possible price by

continuous innovation in cost reduction, a model that made great strategic sense and great social sense.

Restrictions were lifted when the industry was liberalized in 1984, paving the way for global two-wheeler companies such as Honda to establish their own facilities in India. Bajaj promptly seized the opportunity, and in the 1980s Bajaj Auto was the fastest-growing company in India and the fourth largest two-wheeler manufacturer in the world. Sales grew from Rs 519 million to Rs 18.5 billion, a growth rate of 1,852 per cent. An autocratic manager ('I don't take a vote. I make the decision. I ask for other people's opinions in key matters and I give them a fair hearing. But I don't believe in consensus decision making', Piramal 1996: 133), Bajaj's tight control on costs and emphasis on economies of scale resulted in an extremely profitable operation, where Bajaj scooters were 20 per cent cheaper than those of the nearest competitor and yet enjoyed a 20 per cent profit margin. As he says, 'competition is the only guru in today's world' (Piramal *et al.* 1999: 34).

BIBLIOGRAPHY

Bajaj, R. (1991) 'The Raj and Me', *India Today*, 15 August: 28.

Bajaj, S. (1991) *God's Plan Works: An Autobiography*, Bombay.

Belle, N. (1988) 'Rahul Bajaj: A Passion for Excellence', *Gentleman* (March): 33–42.

Budhiraja, S., Piramal, G. and Ghoshal, S. (1999) *The Transformation of Bajaj Auto Ltd: A Case Study*, London: London Business School.

Business India (1979) 'The House of Bajaj and Ethics in Business', 22 January: 22–38.

Ghoshal, S., Piramal, G. and Bartlett, C. (2000) *Managing Radical Change: What Indian Companies Must Do To Become World Class*, New Delhi.

Kulkarni, V. (1951) *A Family of Patriots*, Bombay.

Lomax, D. (1986) *The Money Makers: Six Portraits of Boardroom Power in Industry*, London: BBC.

Piramal, G. (1996) *Business Maharajas*, New Delhi: Viking.

Piramal, G., Piramal, A., Piramal, R. and Beriwala, M. (1999) *Business Mantras*, New Delhi: Viking.

GP

BARBASH, Jack (1910–94)

Jack Barbash was born in New York City on 1 August 1910 and died on 21 May 1994 in Madison, Wisconsin. Barbash received his bachelor's and master's degrees in economics from New York University. His first professional job was with the New York State Department of Labor. In the late 1930s he and Kitty, his wife and research partner, moved to Washington DC, where they lived with international labour expert Morris Weisz and his family. Over the next two decades Barbash worked for, among other organizations, the National Labor Relations Board, the War Production Board, the Senate Labor Committee, the Department of Education, various individual trade unions and the Congress of Industrial Organizations (CIO). In 1955 he participated in the merger negotiations between the CIO and its rival union federation, the American Federation of Labor (AFL), which created the AFL-CIO. In 1957 he joined the faculty of the School for Workers at the University of Wisconsin, and subsequently was appointed the John E. Bascom Professor of Economics and Industrial Relations, a position he held until his retirement. He was elected president of the Industrial Relations Research Association in 1980 and of the Association of Evolutionary Economics in 1981.

47

Barbash was one of the great trade union intellectuals of the twentieth century. He was influenced by the ideological fervour and skills displayed by socialist and communist union organizers in the 1930s, and by the pragmatic trade union leaders who built the American labour movement during its years of rapid growth from the 1930s through the 1950s. His early books such as *Labor Unions in Action* (1948), *The Practice of Unionism* (1956), *Unions and Union Leadership* (1959) and *Labor's Grass Roots* (1961) drew on his first-hand acquaintance with the leading trade union figures of day such as John L. Lewis, Walter Reuther, David Dubinsky, George Meany and Arthur Goldberg. His writings displayed a keen understanding of how personal leadership and institutional and historical contexts interact to shape events.

Barbash is best known for providing a normative and intellectual framework for the field of industrial relations. His first sketch of this framework was published in a 1964 article, 'The Elements of Industrial Relations', and later expanded into a book of the same title (1985). To him, the field of industrial relations resolves around the search for institutional arrangements that can produce both equity and efficiency. His view was that employment relationships are characterized by a fundamental and enduring conflict between employers' efficiency interests and workers' security interests. Unlike MARX, however, he viewed these interests as a natural and enduring aspect of the structure of employment relationships. Conflicting interests would be present under any economic or political regime, not just under capitalism. But workers and employers also have some shared, common interests, and therefore the task of industrial relations institutions in general, and collective bargaining in particular, is to resolve these legitimate differences and search for solutions to shared problems. In this regard, Barbash was the leading third-generation spokesman for the Wisconsin School of Industrial Relations, founded on the ideas of Professor John R. COMMONS in the decades prior to the New Deal and carried on thereafter to the 1950s by Professor Selig Perlman.

Underlying all his work was an intellectual interest in what he often called 'the labor problem'. One of his favourite questions to students was: 'Do unions cause labour problems or do labour problems cause unions?' His answer was that both were true statements. Unions arose because employees needed collective strength to represent their interests at work, but, once created, the institutional needs of unions and the politics inside both union and employer bargaining organizations added additional issues and conflicts to the employment relationship.

While most of his writing focused on explaining or interpreting how labour and management structures and processes evolved, Barbash was most influential in laying out the normative premises for what industrial relations as an intellectual field of study and as a profession should strive to achieve. He chose, for example, to address the issue of 'values' in industrial relations in his 1980 presidential address to the Industrial Relations Research Association:

In a liberal society, the business of industrial relations is more than technique and know-how. It is also the values to which technique and know-how are directed. Equity, due process, fairness, rights, reasonableness, participation, incentive, alienation, privacy, democracy, self-determination, good faith, mutual survival, incrementalism, pragmatism, job satisfaction, order – these are some of the values that our field has embedded into the practice of collective bargaining.

(Barbash 1980: 7)

His election to the presidency of the Association of Evolutionary Economics served to recognize Barbash's standing as one of the leading 'institutional' economists of his generation. Institutional economists seek to analyse

the interplay of market forces with structural, political and legal factors, and use a blend of historical and empirical techniques to analyse economic events. Barbash was at his best when analysing and writing about how labour institutions fit with and evolved in democratic societies and capitalist economies.

Barbash was as well known for his considerable teaching and oratorical skills as for his writing. His courses on capitalism and socialism, trade unionism and industrial relations theory were sought out by generations of students at the University of Wisconsin, and have been replicated by faculty at other leading universities throughout the country. His educational impact, reaching far beyond Wisconsin, is perhaps his greatest and most lasting legacy.

BIBLIOGRAPHY

Barbash, Jack (1948) *Labor Unions in Action*, New York: Harper and Brothers.
—— (1956) *The Practice of Unionism*, New York: Harper and Row.
—— (ed.) (1959) *Unions and Union Leadership: Their Human Meaning*, New York: Harper and Row.
—— (1961) *Labor's Grass Roots*, New York: Harper and Row.
—— (1964) 'The Elements of Industrial Relations', *The British Journal of Industrial Relations* 2 (March): 66–78.
—— (1980) 'Values in Industrial Relations: The Case of the Adversary Principle', in B. Dennis (ed.), *Proceedings of the Thirty-second Annual Meeting of the Industrial Relations Research Association*, Madison, WI: Industrial Relations Research Association, 1–9.
—— (1985) *The Elements of Industrial Relations*, Madison, WI: University of Wisconsin Press.

TK

BARNARD, Chester Irving (1886–1961)

Chester Irving Barnard was born in Malden, a provincial town in the vicinity of Boston, Massachusetts on 7 November 1886, the son of a mechanic. He died in New York on 7 June 1961. When he was five years old his mother, Mary Putnam Barnard, passed away, and Barnard was taken in by his maternal grandfather, a goldsmith. The family was poor but cultured and there was always a warm atmosphere full of music and philosophy. This environment exercised great influence over Barnard. His father remarried, and later a half-sister was born.

Since his father was unable to afford to send his son to higher education, Barnard worked for a piano factory in the neighbouring town of Lynn after he graduated from grammar school. While working in the factory, he mastered the skills of piano tuning. As well as working in the factory, he studied hard and was later admitted to Mount Hermon School on a scholarship thanks to his good marks. In 1906 Barnard went to Harvard University to study economics. While at university he also took on various part-time jobs including managing a dance band, piano tuning and translation. Although he had obtained almost all of the credits required for graduation before he became a senior, Barnard left Harvard University in 1909 without finishing his degree. He asked his uncle to introduce him to a family acquaintance, W.S. Gifford, then chief of statistics of AT&T. Through Gifford he got a job with the company's statistics department with a weekly salary of $11.50.

Barnard's first work was the translation of foreign documents concerning telephone charges. He soon became a commercial engineer, and came to be regarded as the most proficient expert in the Bell System owing to his study of telephone charges. He was then transferred to a managerial job. In 1922 he was appointed assistant to the vice-president and general manager of Pennsylvania Bell Telephone Company. In 1926 he was

promoted to the post of vice-president in charge of sales. In 1927 he assumed the post of the first president of New Jersey Bell Telephone Company, and remained in this post for twenty-one years until retiring in 1948.

Barnard, who was highly public spirited, also engaged in many unpaid public activities. In the 1930s he was appointed head of the local public utility company in New Jersey. In October 1931, during the Great Depression, he organized New Jersey's Emergency Relief Administration at the request of the state's governor. During the Second World War, in 1941 he assumed the post of special adviser of the Secretary of Finance, and from 1942 to 1945 was chairman of the United Service Organization, which was organized by volunteers for the purpose of providing various services to the soldiers fighting at the front. In 1946 he was appointed adviser to the American delegation to the United Nations Atomic Power Committee, and he served as a member of the president's ad hoc committee concerning the unification of the governmental medical service. In 1948, after resigning from the presidency of New Jersey Bell Telephone, Barnard assumed the post of director-general of the Rockefeller Foundation.

While president of New Jersey Bell Telephone, Barnard was on friendly terms with many academic researchers. Taking up the sociology of Vilfredo Pareto as a common interest, he came to be friendly with the biochemist L.J. Henderson. It was Henderson's influence that led Barnard to write his major book. The Lowell Institute at Harvard University held open classes every year, and Henderson recommended Barnard as a lecturer to the president, A. Lawrence Lowell, who was looking for a speaker for the year 1937. Barnard was invited to give a series of eight lectures in November–December 1937. The manuscripts for these lectures were arranged and published under the title *The Functions of the Executive* (1938).

Barnard felt that the research on organization and management which had been conducted up until that time was not in accord with his own business experiences. He made up his mind to construct a new theory as an action analysis of organizations based on a realistic human model. He denied the validity of conventional management theory, which held that humans are driven by economic motives to take actions rationally in order to achieve the maximum realization of benefit to themselves. Replacing this unrealistic understanding of humans, called the 'economic man model', Barnard placed instead at the basis of his theory a human figure who has his or her own intentions and psychological factors (i.e. a variety of motives), and makes decision and takes actions on his or her own responsibility even though he or she is subjected to many restraints.

To realize their goals, people often develop cooperative relationships with each other. An individual person requires that his or her own abilities be enhanced in order to realize his or her purpose and as a strategic decision, chooses cooperation with other people as a method of achieving that purpose. This is often seen throughout society. However, such cooperation can take different forms. Barnard defines cooperation generated in this manner as a system of physical, biological, personal and social components, which are in a specific systematic relationship by reason of the cooperation of two or more persons for at least one definite end.

The only factor common to the various kinds of concrete cooperative system we experience, says Barnard, is organization. That is to say, when all the concrete and specific elements possessed by a cooperative system are removed, the element which remains is a system of various kinds of force in concert with each other. In this sense, organization is a system of consciously coordinated activities or forces of two or more persons. It is a construct analogous to the field of gravity or electromagnetic field. This system is invisible, but it certainly exists.

An organization comes into existence when (1) there are persons able to communicate

with each other; (2) those persons are willing to contribute action; and (3) they wish to accomplish a common purpose. These are necessary and sufficient conditions for the formation of the organization.

The problem as to whether the formed organization can remain continuously in existence depends on whether the double equilibrium of the organization as a system can be maintained. The organization, which is a system constituted by various kinds of forces, will come to a rupture unless, first, an equilibrium can be brought about *between* the system and its external environment, and, second, internal equilibrium can be maintained concurrently *within* the system. This internal equilibrium is the balance of the elements of organization; the communications which link the common purpose of the cooperative activity with the organization's members' willingness to make their personal contributions are particularly important. The external equilibrium of the organization, on the other hand, is the result of the effectiveness and efficiency of the organization. The *effectiveness* of the organization resides in the adequacy of organizational purpose, and therefore can be defined as the organization's ability to accomplish that purpose. Accordingly, effectiveness is founded in a technological sense on the rationality of the measures chosen for achieving that purpose. The *efficiency* of the organization, on the other hand, depends on the degree of satisfaction derived by the members of the organization from making their personal contribution and the incentives which they have to work. Even if organizational effectiveness is strong, organizational members' willingness to contribute cannot be maintained if the realization of the common purpose does not result simultaneously in the satisfaction of their own needs and the meeting of their own personal goals. If this does not happen, the organization as a cooperative system is unable to obtain the required level of contributive activity from its members, and thus begins to

decline, finally becoming extinct. Therefore, if the organization is to continue in existence, it is necessary to maintain these two equilibria simultaneously.

The alignment of the various forces involved in cooperative activity so as to maintain dual equilibrium, and thus the organizational system as a whole, is the function of the executive. The work of the executive relates to the elements of the organization in its content, and is comprised of the following: (1) establishment and maintenance of a communication system; (2) promotion of incentives to all organizational members so that they work to achieve cooperation; and (3) the development and articulation of the organziation's common purpose. Within the organization, a variety of desires, ideals, values and so on are held by its members. Unless these differing views can be aligned with a unified and settled set of overall organizational values, no effective organizational activity can be carried out; neither the effectiveness nor the efficiency of the organization can be realized. Leaders within the executive function must make decisions concerning the selection standards to which the organization's members must conform when they make organizational choices. Barnard insists that this is a moral aspect of leadership, and that the responsibility imposed on the executive is not to subject employees to reprimand, but gradually to establish an adequate criterion of value judgement for organizational behaviour.

Barnard's theory emphasizes the scientific analysis of organizational behaviour by placing importance on the choices that are involved in organizational activity and decision making. This new approach to the organization as a system made possible many new developments within the science of business administration. In this sense, Barnard can truly be said to be a giant who opened up the frontiers of the study of modern business organizations.

BIBLIOGRAPHY

Barnard, C.I. (1938) *The Functions of the Executive*, Cambridge, MA: Harvard University Press.

—— (1948) *Organization and Management: Selected Papers by Chester I. Barnard*, Cambridge, MA: Harvard University Press.

Iino H. (1978) *Barnard Kenkyu: Sono Soshiki to Kanri no Riron* (Study on Barnard: His Theory of Organization and Management), Tokyo: Bunshindo.

Katoh, K. (1996) *Barnard to Henderson: The Functions of the Executive no Keisei Katei* (Barnard and Henderson: The Formation Process of *The Functions of the Executive*), Tokyo: Bunshindo.

Wolf, W.B. (1972) *Conversation with Chester I. Barnard*, Ithaca, NY: Cornell University Press.

—— (1974) *The Basic Barnard: An Introduction to Chester I. Barnard and His Theories of Organization and Management*, Ithaca, NY: NYSSILR.

Wolf, W.B. and Iino H. (eds) (1986) *Philosophy for Managers: Selected Papers of C. I. Barnard*, Tokyo: Bunshindo.

ST

BARNEVIK, Percy (1941–)

Percy Barnevik was born in Simrishams, Sweden on 13 February 1941. His family ran a small print shop which employed around fifteen people. Working in the family shop, according to biographer Manfred Kets de Vries (1999), helped to shape his future philosophy of management. Here he learned thrift, efficiency, meeting deadlines and personal responsibility. Barnevik's experience taught him, says De Vries, that when company units and teams were small and personal, employees worked better and were more committed to quality performance. Where several thousand people were together in a workshop, however, the whole process became anonymous.

In 1960 Barnevik entered the Gothenburg School of Economics, where he obtained his MBA in 1964. While working as an intern at the Swedish pulp and paper company Mölnycke, he was offered a scholarship at the Stanford Business School, which he entered in 1965–6. At Stanford, he studied systems analysis. He married Aina Orvarsson in 1963.

Following his education at Stanford, Barnevik went to work for the consulting firm of Datema, where he was able to network and rise within the ranks. Soon he was managing systems for the Swedish Axel Johnson Group. By 1969 he was working for the Swedish tool firm Sandvik, where he solved their information systems problems. Barnevik put together his own team and eventually restructured the company. To learning the lesson of working with small units, Barnevik added the importance of management and control of accounting.

Between 1975 and 1979 Barnevik took on Sandvik's faltering US subsidiary. Within four years, he had tripled sales to $250 million and captured part of the market from General Electric and United States Steel. Sandvik in the USA became a laboratory for Barnevik's ideas on decentralization. No workshop was larger than 250 people. Here he also had his first experience of working in a large, continental market.

Returning to Sweden in 1979, Barnevik was approached by Marcus Wallenberg, who offered him the opportunity of managing Sweden's famous electrical equipment maker, Allmanna Svenska Elektriska Aktiebolaget (Swedish General Electric Company), commonly known as ASEA. ASEA in 1980 was a firm of 40,000 faced with declining demand for its products. Barnevik found a state-of-the-art technical company in which administration was highly centralized and communication between the Swedish and

foreign operations was deficient. The firm valued technical expertise and selected electricians rather than businessmen as managers. Employees enjoyed lifetime security.

Barnevik sought to create a company that could compete in an emerging global economy. His first step (De Vries 1999; Barham and Heimer 1999) was to redirect the priority to the customer. The engineering sector was divided into product divisions where production, contracting and marketing were combined under a single division manager for each product. The company was decentralized into forty profit centres, each of which had sweeping jurisdiction and responsibility. Production and marketing were coordinated at the local level. Unprofitable plants were closed, and head office staff were trimmed from 2,000 to 200. These were hard decisions for Barnevik, as whole towns often depended upon an ASEA plant. Barnevik, however, did not believe in management through toughness alone; he felt one needed to have empathy for those being downsized. Barnevik ended unprofitable contracts designed simply to maintain employment. He cut inventories and put pressure on debtors, seeking to uncover all unused capital assets in the firm.

Between 1980 and 1983 ASEA quintupled its earnings, but Barnevik also had long-term goals for the company. Research and development were essential to the future, and profits were essential to research and development. In order to secure them, ASEA would have to change from an export-oriented company to a multinational with direct investment and marketing operations abroad. ASEA would have to develop local sales forces in foreign countries and transfer Swedish expertise and technology to them. ASEA would set up production in host countries. Where possible, ASEA bought local firms so as not to appear as an 'invading' Swedish company out to saturate the market. Barnevik also concentrated on leading-edge technologies and picked his markets carefully, including robots, transportation equipment and services.

In 1981 Barnevik reorganized the international management structure. Each ASEA subsidiary product office had previously reported only to its product division office in Sweden. Now, it would also report to a manager in the host country. This would allow ASEA to appear as, for example, a Canadian or US firm rather than a 'Swedish' one. Division managers had to become more profit-minded, and country managers had to work with them. All this increased mutual accountability.

Barnevik's initial goal was to make ASEA a 'Nordic' company with a strong market presence in Norway, Denmark, Finland and Iceland. The next phase of expansion in the 1980s targeted the European Community, Japan and Asia, and, especially, the USA. In 1987 Barnevik presided over the landmark merger of ASEA with BBC Brown Boveri Ltd of Baden Switzerland. The new company, known as Asea Brown Boveri Ltd (ABB), was headquartered in Zurich. ABB, however, was to be neither a Swiss nor a Swedish company, but rather a global firm. Each of the two founding firms owned 50 per cent of ABB. The new business grew rapidly in the first three years of its existence, expanding through acquisitions and joint ventures, acquiring over fifty companies and expanding into Eastern Europe as well as Asia.

Barnevik, who was the new firm's CEO, applied all of the strategies he earlier perfected in the older, more Swedish ASEA. In a 1991 interview with William Taylor *of Harvard Business Review*, he described ABB not as a multinational but as a *transnational* company, one that had no national identity, and that could be both a global firm worldwide and a local firm in each of the countries in which it operated.

The key to 'thinking global' while 'acting local' was the matrix organization Barnevik developed at ASEA and perfected at ABB. First, there were the functional or segment managers in electricity, turbines and other activities, who operated globally. Second, each group of ABB units in a given country also

had a country manager, and each unit was capable of operating on its own. ABB companies in the USA operated as US companies, those in the UK as UK companies. It was a scheme combining radical decentralization with the ability to shift resources and strategies around the globe.

In the 1990s Barnevik confronted the challenge of globalization with a strategy of downsizing ABB operations in North America and Western Europe while increasing his investment in the areas where markets and capitalism were still growing. By the middle of the decade there were thirty ABB firms in Central Europe and the former Soviet Union, and over a hundred plants and centres in Asia. According to Taylor (1991) and Branegan (1997), ABB in 1997 had over 200,000 employees in 140 countries, 50,000 of which worked in Asia or the former Soviet bloc. It comprised over 1,000 firms and was worth almost $40 billion. Its penetration of the Indian market was highly successful. Between 1995 and 1997 ABB was described by the *Financial Times* as Europe's most admired company. Barnevik and ABB were regarded as the prototypical model for cross-border firms of the twenty-first century, combining innovative management and strong global direction with small, manageable units and consciousness of national and local sensitivities.

In early 1997, Barnevik accepted the offer of the Wallenberg family to manage Investor AB, the giant Swedish holding company with holdings in Saab, Ericsson, Scania and a number of other major Swedish firms. Barnevik is still active with ABB, though he has turned management over to his successor Göran Lindahl. He remains chairman of the board of Sandvik, and sits on the board of General Motors; he is also chairman of the multinational drug company AstraZeneca PLC.

In his youth Percy Barnevik acquired the habits of punctuality and efficiency, together with the perfectionism, that have made him an excellent manager. He has, however, been anything but hidebound, welcoming the input of those under him. According to one subordinate, Arne Olsson, Barnevik's position was like that of the centre of a wheel:

When Percy starts something, he asks people to give him some ideas or write a paper. He works like hub in a wheel. He has a number of spokes and works with and by those spokes. He sends signals through the spokes and gets information back and uses different spokes as appropriate. Being in the middle of the wheel, he gets a fantastic view. With his computer-like skills, he then processes all this information and out comes something very good.

(Barham and Heimer 1999: 12)

BIBLIOGRAPHY
Barham, K. and Heimer, C. (1999) *ABB, The Dancing Giant: Creating the Globally Connected Corporation*, London: Pitman.
Branegan, J. (1997) 'Global Business Report/Movers and Shakers: Percy Barnevik', *Time* 149(9): 3 March; http://www.time.com/time/magazine/1997/dom/970303/global_busine.percy.html, 6 October 2000.
De Vries, M. Kets (1999) *The New Global Leaders, Richard Branson, Percy Barnevik, David Simon and the Remaking of International Business*, San Francisco, CA: Jossey-Bass.
Taylor, W. (1991) 'The Logic of Global Business: An Interview with ABB's Percy Barnevik', Web presentation based upon article for *Harvard Business Review* (March–April 1991); repr. no. 91201, http://barney.sbe.csuhayward.edu/~skamath/powerpoint/mgmt6710_s81/sld001.htm, 8 October 2000.

DCL

BARNUM, Phineas Taylor (1810–91)

Barnum was born in Bethel, Connecticut on 5 July 1810. He died on 7 April 1891 at his home in Bridgeport, Connecticut, following a stroke. After the death of his father, a local tavern-keeper, in 1825 Barnum worked as a store clerk to support his family and then went into business for himself, running a store, selling lottery tickets and editing a newspaper. He married Charity Hallett in 1829 and the couple settled permanently in New York, where they kept a boarding house.

In the 1830s Barnum made several attempts to break into show business, managing travelling shows and circuses. All the ventures failed, usually because they were poorly capitalized. His breakthrough came at the end of 1841 when he bought Scudder's American Museum, a fixed-site attraction on Broadway in New York. Barnum saw his opportunity: New York was growing rapidly, and its citizens lacked opportunities for entertainment. The Museum, a collection of stuffed animals and curios, was renamed Barnum's American Museum, and greatly expanded to include such attractions as ventriloquists, living statuary, educated dogs, music and dancing, jugglers, giants, dwarves, panoramas and dioramas of famous scenes such as Niagara Falls, and 'the first English Punch and Judy in this country' (Barnum 1889: 57).

Thanks to Barnum's flair for advertising, the attraction was immediately successful. He then moved into theatrical management, managing the Swedish singing star Jenny Lind and the midget entertainer General Tom Thumb. In 1865 he launched a new travelling circus, much larger and more successful than previous attempts. When his circus's success was challenged by a competitor, owned by James Bailey, Barnum's response was to suggest a merger; the result, Barnum and Bailey's Circus, married Barnum's marketing flair with Bailey's organizing abilities, and dominated the market into the twentieth century. Barnum continued to tour with the circus until well into his seventies; by this time his fame was such that he himself was one of the star attractions of the show.

As a marketer, Barnum did not conduct research into customer needs and then set out to meet them; instead, he designed products and then worked tirelessly to stimulate demand, using every available form of promotion. As he says, 'I often seized upon an opportunity by instinct, even before I had a very definite conception as to how it should be used, and it seemed, somehow, to mature itself and serve my purpose' (Barnum 1889: 57). His instincts told him that publicity was often cheaper and more effective than advertising, and he cultivated newspaper editors such as Horace Greeley in hopes of placing favourable stories; but he could turn even bad publicity to his benefit. His primary aim was volume business, and he frequently undercut competitors in order to gain a larger share of the market.

Barnum's showmanship, which often verged on self-parody, became in the end an attraction in itself, rather as some modern advertisements become as famous as the products they promote.

Barnum pioneered many of the techniques used in modern marketing, especially publicity and below-the-line promotions. He is often accused of cynicism – the phrase 'there's a sucker born every minute' is attributed to him – but he himself believed that he was neither more nor less dishonest than any business person: he once asked, 'In what business is there not humbug?' (Werner 1923: 274).

BIBLIOGRAPHY
Barnum, P.T. (1889) *Struggles and Triumphs, or, Sixty Years' Recollections of P.T. Barnum, Including His Golden Rules for Money-Making*, Buffalo, NY: The Courier Company.
Werner, M.R. (1923) *Barnum*, New York: Harcourt, Brace and Co.

MLW

BARTH, Carl George Lange (1860–1939)

Carl George Lange Barth was born in Christiana, Norway on 28 February 1860 and died in Philadelphia on 28 October 1939. After technical training at the Horten Technical School, an apprenticeship at the Navy Yard at Oslo and a period of teaching mathematics, he emigrated to the United States in 1881. From 1881 to 1895 he worked for the machine tool maker William Sellers and Company in Philadelphia, rising from draughtsman to chief designer. From 1895 to 1897 he worked as a draughtsman and designer in St Louis, and from 1897 to 1899 as an instructor in mathematics with the International Correspondence Schools and then the Ethical Culture School in New York. In 1899 he was invited by Frederick W. TAYLOR to join the latter's team at Bethlehem Steel Company, where his strong mathematical abilities helped Taylor solve a number of problems which had confronted his production system. His technical accomplishments there included the design of the Barth slide-rule and the formula of twelve variables which was incorporated into Taylor's *Shop Management* (1903).

Leaving Bethlehem in 1901, when Taylor and his followers were dismissed shortly before the takeover of the firm by Charles M. SCHWAB, Barth became a consulting engineer, working with Taylor and his team at several other factories, notably the Link-Belt Company in Philadelphia, and, with Horace HATHAWAY, at the Tabor Manufacturing Co. Within the team, Barth became known as the 'systems man' who would implement the systems Taylor designed, working out the technical bugs as he did so. He was noted for his attention to detail and strong technical abilities, and frequently designed the machinery to support Taylor's production systems.

Barth was an early supporter of Harvard Business School and its first dean, Edwin GAY; he was the first of the Taylor team to lecture there, and held a formal post as lecturer on scientific management from 1911 to 1916 and

from 1919 to 1922. From 1914 to 1916 he also lectured on scientific management at the University of Chicago. He retired in 1923. Without Barth's technical genius, Taylor's system would have had much less impact and been less effective.

BIBLIOGRAPHY
Drury, H.B. (1915) *Scientific Management*, New York: Columbia University Press.
Urwick, L.F. (ed.) (1956) *The Golden Book of Management*, London: Newman Neame.

BAT'A, Tomás (1876–1932)

Tomás Bat'a was born in the small Moravian town of Zlín on 3 March 1876. He died on 12 July 1932 in a plane crash near Zlín. The Bat'a family had been cobblers for nine generations, starting in 1580; Tomás himself made his first pair of shoes at the age of six. In 1891 he left for Vienna and started his first enterprise, which was unsuccessful. He learned the hard way that the market is more important than production (Bat'a 1992). In 1894, with his sister Anna and brother Antonin, he founded a shoemaking company in Zlín, the Antonin Bat'a Company. Their invested capital was 800 Austrian guldens (about £210).

This enterprise too did not go well. Antonin Bat'a quickly ran up a debt of 8,000 guldens and signed a 20,000 guldens promissory note. The imminent threat of bankruptcy was a life-shaping influence on Tomás Bat'a. To avoid bankruptcy was a matter of honour and morality to him, and he worked harder than ever. In 1895 he introduced a successful innovation: linen shoes with leather soles. In 1900 he built his first factory, hired fifty employees and formed a public company, T. and A. Bat'a. In 1904 he went to the United States, where he was impressed by the seemingly

classless, democratic society of equals. In 1911 he returned to the United States to study machine-based production, and to purchase suitable tools and machines.

The First World War brought him a sizeable order for 50,000 pairs of shoes from the army, which he spread among all the shoemakers in Zlín. His only son, Tomás (or 'Tomík') was born in the same year. At the time of writing, 'Tomík' still lives in Toronto, now known as Thomas Bata, Jr, and the conglomerate Bata International is managed by his sons.

By 1917 the production of T. and A. Bat'a had reached 10,000 pairs a day and 5,000 people were employed in the factory. In 1919 Bat'a went to the United States for the third time. He visited Henry FORD and studied his mass-production lines. He visited Chicago and its Czech community, met the successful Czech industrialist Vlcek in Cleveland, and was more than impressed by Endicott Johnson, the largest shoemaking factory (making 100,000 pairs a day) in Binghamton, New York.

In 1922, when the Czech currency was radically revalued, Bat'a responded by cutting his prices by 50 per cent and thus securing his markets and exports. In order to achieve this, he lowered the wages of his employees (or 'associates', as they were called), but in return he provided discounted groceries and consumer goods, services and subsidized housing to his workers. In 1923 Bat'a was elected Mayor of Zlín. The combination of global business and local political power allowed him to improve Zlín and its environs considerably and turn a small town into an innovative European city.

During the period 1924–6 Bat'a introduced a number of major innovations, and what became known as the Bat'a system of management started to take shape. First, the participation of workers in both corporate profits and losses was introduced. Second, individual workshop autonomy was brought in, allowing the workers to take responsibility for their own workshop team's decision making.

Finally, in 1926, he introduced electric machines ('electrical robots', as he called them), which allowed for individual and independent relocation of machinery, quick decoupling of production lines and on-line preventive maintenance, all forming the foundations of flexible manufacturing.

Workshop autonomy and employee profit sharing were unprecedented moves which put Bat'a far ahead of his competitors and even of many world-class companies of today. The earnings of his workers shot up to six to eight times the industrial average of the day. 'Every worker a capitalist' was Bat'a's slogan, earning him the wrath, hate and envy of socialist politicians, international communists and labour unions worldwide. Bat'a had stepped dangerously out of the crowd. His new assembly lines, far surpassing Ford's productivity, increased production by 75 per cent in 1927 alone. The number of employees rose by 35 per cent and productivity soared. In 1928 Czechoslovakia became the largest shoe exporter in the world.

In 1929 the US stock market crash and the onset of worldwide economic depression brought increased tariffs on shoe imports. Bat'a responded by incorporating company affiliates abroad, and soon was expanding around the world. His ventures to Switzerland, Germany, Egypt, India, China and the United States were extremely successful. In 1930 Bat'a was making 100,000 pairs a day, while introducing a five-day working week of forty-five hours. In order to get closer to his customers, Bat'a started opening his own retail centres: there were 666 new retail stores in thirty-seven countries by 1932. Trade unions, industrialist lobbies, socialists and communists alike agitated against the 'Bat'a antisocial system'. The private Bat'a Corporation was founded in 1931 and the original public company T. and A. Bat'a was dissolved.

During the Depression, in 1931 alone Bat'a built nine new factory buildings in Zlín. He also built the first skyscraper in Europe, with the famous 'office in the elevator', two ware-

houses, a gas works, a department store, six dormitories for young male and female apprentices, the private Bat'a School of Work, 500 new family houses for employees and a new airport at nearby Otrokovice.

Only fate or an act of God could stop Tomás Bat'a. In 1932, at the age of fifty-seven, he was killed in a plane crash while taking off from Otrokovice airport for an urgent business meeting in Switzerland. However, the Bat'a system of management and the Bat'a corporation survived. Tomás's halfbrother, Jan A. Bat'a, took over the company. Jan was an entrepreneurial genius in his own right and during 1932–8 the company went through unprecedented growth and worldwide expansion. In June 1934, a forty-hour working week was introduced. By 1936, 58 million pairs of shoes were manufactured and sold yearly by the Bat'a enterprises. Jan Bat'a too became a legend, travelling around the world, visiting prewar Japan (and predicting its later industrial miracle), introducing innovative technologies and displacing a mountain from one side of the river to another as part of an anti-flood regulatory project. The number of Bat'a companies abroad grew to sixty-three in 1937. In Czechoslovakia alone, Bat'a produced 47.8 million pairs of shoes in that record year. The company employed over sixty-five thousand people worldwide.

In 1939, after the Munich sellout and the betrayal of Czechoslovakia by France and Britain, Hitler's armies marched into the country. Tomík Bat'a went to Canada, where he established the Bata Shoe Corporation of Canada in Frankford, Ontario; he renamed the place Batawa. Jan A. Bat'a left Czechoslovakia for the United States in early 1939, after trying unsuccessfully to save the company from Nazi control and military takeover. For his efforts with the German authorities in 1939, Jan was blacklisted by the Allies and in 1941 was forced to leave for Brazil, where he pursued a remarkable career well into the 1950s.

On 20 November 1941, the US Army air forces bombed Bat'a factories in Zlín, dropping some 260 bombs, destroying or damaging ten factory buildings and sixty-two residential houses. After that, the Bat'a enterprises in Czechoslovakia entered a rapid and irreversible decline. On 27 October 1945, the Bat'a company was nationalized and in 1946 renamed Bat'a, n.p. Zlín. As a national company under communist rule, the enterprise never recovered. All the best managers and employees left, the Bat'a system was abandoned, and knowledge accumulated over some fifty years was quickly dissipated. In 1947 Jan Bat'a was tried in absentia for crimes against the state. The communist court sentenced him to fifteen years in prison and confiscation of his entire property. In 1949 the communists renamed the company to Svit n. p. Gottwaldov, also renaming Zlín to Gottwaldov after the first communist president, Klement Gottwald. The end of Bat'a and his legacy in Czechoslovakia seemed complete.

From 1931 when it went private, the Bat'a firm became independent of financial capital and banks. From that year onwards, the company financed itself exclusively from its own resources, apart from the savings of employees in their personal accounts. This enabled the emergence of an original and autonomous system of management known as the Bat'a system. Its main purpose was to ensure that every one of the 67,000 employees worked efficiently and effectively. The principle of maximum output from each individual was not negotiable.

The company did not have any written organizational regulations or rules, mission statement or any other symbolic trappings. The company was rooted in knowledge, that is in the coordination of action, not in the fashionable symbolic description of action. The system of company management has never been published; the first ever conference on the Bat'a system was held in May 2001 in Zlín. No organizational regulations

were issued until 1956, by the communist managers of the then state-owned company.

The main feature of the Bat'a system and organization was the division of the entire company into small and economically independent accounting units, like workshops, cells, teams or modern amoebae. The flat organization consisted of cobbler workshops, purchasing departments, sales departments and an analysis department. Every shop and its various supporting departments became independent accounting and entrepreneurial units.

When contracting with one another, these business units behaved as if they were external, market-driven companies. Every unit bought raw materials or prefabricated products from a preceding unit and, after having carried out its part of the work, it either sold the product to the following department or as a final product to the sales department. The internal market of Bat'a was a clear precursor to independent profit centres or the famous 'amoeba system' at the Japanese Kyocera Corporation.

If the quality of the product was lower than required, the accepting unit was offered a discount price. The calculation centre and the management checked the business contracts and the unit prices. Each of the units was headed by a manager fully responsible for its operations and profits. Such organization did not allow any concealment of losses or damages that would have to be assumed by other departments. Every six months, the accounting office issued a survey of business units, with their names and numbers. A privileged position, but also material responsibility, was reserved for the calculation, purchasing, sales and personnel departments, as well as the accounting office.

The company determined fixed, market-based transfer prices for six months and the internal units cleared their accounts at these prices. The analysis department followed price developments outside the company very closely and watched the prices paid by the purchasing department. These prices encouraged the 'buyers' (internal customers) to settle their disputes as quickly as possible so that no losses could arise.

According to Bat'a planning principles, supplies had to be ensured for the whole six months by the supply norms consistent with keeping the price and quality according to the reference products. Discounts for early invoice payments were applied, as well as other measures aiming at increasing the profit of the 'buying' department. Other units were motivated in similar ways.

The Bat'a system of retailing was based on strong disintermediation. The company built its own retail stores with the intention of lowering sales costs (to lower shoe prices and to increase profits) and of operating production more efficiently by keeping better control of the amount of goods in stock. The standard design stores were divided into several types, and for each type the number of shoe samples and number of shoes in stock was established. Shoe and stocking repair shops were installed in every store. In the larger stores there was also a pedicure service. The store managers paid a security deposit upon their appointment to head position. They were interested in sales, because they paid all overhead costs, the salaries of their employees, for advertising and so on. They tried to sell as much and as quickly as they could because there was a danger that they would have to pay the price difference at the price discount declared by the company (for example, for seasonal shoes) from their share of the profit. The level of expertise of store staff was closely monitored from Zlín. There were more than 2,000 stores with 8,000 staff workers in 1937.

Perhaps the most important unit in the company headquarters was the analysis department. Its workers were highly trained and reported directly to the chief executive. They carried out preliminary calculations and continually processed the data. They determined the internal clearing prices. In this way, the analysis department was the primary tool used by the company's top management to lower production costs and increase profits.

Many observers admired the efficiency of Bata's intra-company accounting, which computed weekly balances and wages without using complex computing technology. The weekly balance, including that of the extra-mural departments, had to be completed by Friday evening so that the data were ready for the conference of managers held every Saturday. The reconciliation was carried out manually, and adverse data were marked in red. No written analyses were prepared for the conference. Monday and Tuesday were intentionally selected as paydays so that the employees could not spend their money on Saturday and Sunday without having time to think about it.

One of the prerequisites of manufacturing cheap quality shoes was production volume, even at the cost of a rather limited range. Mass production required standardization of process, which was carried out very consistently, not only in shoe production but also in technology. Everything functional was gradually standardized: factory halls, machines and their interchangeable parts, shop equipment (shelves, chairs, counters). The decimal system was consistently introduced everywhere, in the numbering of buildings, doors, production data and so on.

Tomás Bat'a required that everything necessary for production had to be of top quality: 'The best in the world is good enough for us,' he insisted. In 1929 the daily production per worker reached 12.5 pairs of shoes, which was three times higher than in other factories in Czechoslovakia. In the United States at the time, peak daily productivity was five pairs of shoes per worker. Substantially more efficient methods and forms of management, as well as better organization, are the explanation for these radical differences.

Although profit sharing was not an entirely new idea, other companies distributed extra money after the annual balance report was prepared behind closed doors. This was unacceptable to the open-book thinking and policy of Bat'a. He operated under the following principles:

1. Profit accounting must be carried out as soon as possible, i.e. weekly.

2. Each participant must calculate his or her share himself.

3. Profit participation must relate to small departments so that every employee is able to influence the running of his workplace.

The size of individual employee share depended on the importance of the work. Foremen, masters and workers shared in profits only. Managers and members of the board of directors participated in losses as well. The workers' profit share amounted to about 20–30 per cent of their wages. The profit shares of the higher ranked often exceeded their basic income many times over.

The concept of autonomy was also introduced into purchasing, social institutions, restaurants, cinemas, the hospital and other ancillary functions. The profit share was paid weekly, half in cash, the rest to the worker's personal account at an interest rate of 10 per cent per year. At any time, an employee could withdraw a quarter of his savings for necessary purchases, apartment furnishings and so on. On leaving the company the employee was paid out all his savings after the guaranty, which the employee signed when joining the company, expired. Bat'a regarded these deposits as a part of the moral bond between company and workers.

The profits were computed locally (at a work centre) and divided into two equal parts: one for the company, the other for the workers. The share of profits was paid out without regard to losses in other workshops and without regard to the results of the whole company. Every week the balances were displayed for public scrutiny. Open-book management was one of the pillars of the system.

Each worker was reimbursed according to a rate calculated for each operation according to the efficiency and importance of the work. Salaries were not allowed to drop below a weekly minimum. Profit participation was

divided into three categories. A participant was entitled to a plain profit share, a foreman to a double share, and a master to 10 per cent of half of the profit allocated to his workers. Despite the fact that workshop autonomy and profit sharing required constant calculation and accounting, the amount of paperwork and bureaucracy did not increase. Unskilled workers in Czechoslovakia earned 150 Kr., but at Bat'a they earned 280 Kr. Such wages were not surpassed even in the most developed countries in Europe.

To summarize the basic principles of the Bat'a system of management:

1. Bat'a's management ensured that every employee felt satisfied with his or her income. The workers had to calculate their wages themselves after they had completed their work.

2. The company was fully decentralized into autonomous accounting units, and relied on an independent analysis department to make intra-company markets work.

3. Financial statements were prepared weekly. Simplicity and speed were among the basic administrative principles.

4. Heads and managers had to compensate the firm from their personal accounts where their workers caused damage, even if they themselves were not directly to blame.

5. When accepting delivery of goods, stock workers were forbidden to look at the invoice or the bill of delivery, but had to issue a receipt. The control of received material was thus assured.

In terms of machinery and technology management, Bat'a surpassed many of today's practices. He never hesitated to replace a good machine with a better one, even if the original was not yet worn out. He did not wait for someone else to start machine production, but began constructing and manufacturing the nec-essary machines himself, always aiming at greater efficiency. In an effort to repair machines as quickly as possible, Bat'a intro-duced standardization of the parts and forbade maintenance workers to use files or hammers (which might damage machines) in repair work.

In order to be able to move machines from place to place, he scrapped belt transmissions, hitherto standard in mass production. Every machine was furnished instead with an inde-pendent platform with its own electric motor. It was therefore easy to reconfigure or introduce assembly lines. By introducing a two-storey conveyor belt (one storey being heated), he accelerated the drying of the shoes. He did not bother to have his remarkable inventions patented: he knew that competitors could never catch up with him. Only in the 1950s did similar technologies appear in the United States.

Small productivity improvements were abundant, far surpassing even current prac-tices. Identical forms, printed in many lan-guages, received from subsidiary companies abroad, were processed in Zlín, and because the forms were standardized employees could process them without needing to speak a par-ticular language. Every head employee had his own signal in Morse code. On hearing it from his pager – no matter where he was – he called in from the nearest telephone. The simplest signal was reserved for the Chief: a dot. All this took place many decades before the pager became widely used in the West.

Smoking and alcohol were forbidden throughout the entire premises of the Bat'a works. The administrative employees worked in spacious offices; sometimes the whole floor of the administration building was a single office. Separate rooms were available for meetings with clients. Large administrative losses due to useless telephone calls, chats at water coolers, drinking coffee and other inef-fective activities were eliminated.

Bat'a was strongly opposed to asking for governmental support, help or bailouts, as opposed to the current Czech business culture

which is increasingly focused on fighting for meagre governmental handouts. Bat'a analysed the 1922 currency revaluation as follows:

> Our storehouses are overfilled with goods, sales are stagnating, exports have collapsed, production is at its lowest level, people need shoes but they have no money. It is useless to demand any sort of relief from the government (tax, customs, and postage). It is not possible to keep firing workers, who would then make further demand on unemployment welfare from the State. If factories are closed down, the State will lose its tax income and an unemployed worker will not buy shoes even at a half price. That is why the production has to be kept going at any cost.
> (Bat'a 1992)

Instead, Bat'a chose to rely on his own people. At a rally of employees on 11 March 1924, he told them:

> We are granting you a share in the profits not because we feel a need to give money to people out of the goodness of our hearts. No, in taking this step we have other goals. By doing this, we want to achieve a further decrease of production costs. We want to reach the situation in which shoes are cheaper and workers earn even more. We think that our products are still too expensive and workers' salaries too low.
> (Bat'a 1992)

To be a strong example, in work, decision making and determination, always and everywhere, was the key: 'Because no textbook exists ... I decided to produce my own system, which – I hope – would help Mankind' (Bat'a 1992). Strong ethics, moral convictions and service to the public were great innovations in that less than admirable era in business: 'Our company started to grow at an incredible rate after our employees became convinced that our attitude – both towards them and towards our customers – was strictly moral' (Bat'a 1992).

Bat'a's view of Europe and its ills was also decades ahead of slowly emerging thinking on integration:

> The European trade and industry ... presents a very sad scene. Nations saddled with import duties are crushing their neighboring nations ... It cannot be denied that the strength of the American industry and great wealth of the Americans owes to the fact that the USA has created a single market. The duty of European nations – the cradle of trade and industry – should be to produce and sell, not to dig deep trenches between individual states in the form of high duties and tariffs.
> (Bat'a 1992)

The life of Tomás Bat'a is a great story of great personal and corporate achievements, incredible tragedies and continuous production of the only lasting knowledge: knowledge in action. He was one of the most complete systems-oriented and knowledge-producing entrepreneurs of the twentieth century. He left us the legacy of the Bat'a system of management, one of the most fully integrated organizational and management systems yet developed. The Bat'a system is the precursor to many of the best management practices of today. Its main building blocks amount to modern components of the new economy: high technology, knowledge management, innovation strategy, global competitiveness, team autonomy, employee wealth sharing, global networks, industrial ecology, supplier/customer networks, business ethics and service to the public. The Bat'a system integrates all these and more dimensions into a seamless and effective package of true managerial excellence.

BIBLIOGRAPHY

Bat'a, T. (1992) *Knowledge in Action: The Bata System of Management*, Amsterdam: IOS Press.
Cekota, A. (1944) *The Battle of Home*, Toronto: Macmillan.

Cekota, A. (1968) *Entrepreneur Extraordinary: The Biography of Tomas Bata*, Rome: Edizioni Internazionali Soziali.

Hindus, M. (1947) *The Bright Passage*, New York: Doubleday.

Vlcek, J. (1971) 'Das Bata-Führungssystem', *Industrielle Organisation* 40(11): 615–19.

Zeleny, M. (1986) 'The Roots of Modern Management: Bat'a System', *Human Systems Management* 6(1): 4–7.

—— (1988) 'Bat'a System of Management: Managerial Excellence Found', *Human Systems Management* 7(3): 213–19.

—— (1996) 'Bata System of Management', in M. Warner (ed.), *International Encyclopedia of Business and Management*, London: Routledge, 351–4.

—— (1997) 'Bata, Tomas', in M. Warner (ed.), *IEBM Handbook of Management Thinking*, London: International Thomson Business Press, 49–52.

—— (1998) 'Bata System of Management', in M. Warner (ed.), *IEBM Handbook on Human Resources Management*, London: International Thomson Business Press, 359–62.

MZ

BEAVERBROOK, LORD, *see* Aitken

BEDAUX, Charles Eugéne (1886–1944)

Charles Eugéne Bedaux was born in Paris on 11 April 1886 into a lower middle-class family. He committed suicide in a US military prison on 18 February 1944 while awaiting trial on charges of treason. Details of his early career are patchy, and little is known about his education or early work; Ungar (1997) suggests he may have been involved in running a brothel in his late teens. At the age of twenty he emigrated to the United States, where his first job was as a construction worker digging tunnels for the New York City subway. He subsequently became a salesman, selling everything from life insurance to toothpaste.

In his late twenties, Bedaux moved to Grand Rapids, Michigan, where he took a job with a furniture manufacturer. Studying the movements of the workers, he hit upon a way of improving the accuracy of productivity and performance measurement in the workplace. His system was in essence an improvement on earlier systems of performance measurement developed by Frederick W. TAYLOR and Sanford THOMPSON. The latter's time study method involved breaking each job into its smallest components and then measuring the standard times required to achieve each component to create a total time required for the job. However, this system had been heavily criticized, not least for failing to take into account the effect of worker fatigue on performance (Kessler 1998).

Bedaux, like other observers, noticed that as workers became tired, their performance declined and standard tasks took longer. Giving workers rest breaks also tended to distort the picture, as it was not clear how much rest was needed to achieve optimal performance. Bedaux's solution was to factor the required time for rest into the task time. He developed what he called a 'relaxation curve', a tool for measuring the amount of rest employees required to achieve optimum task performance. With the rest period factored into the work, tasks could now be broken down into universal units or 'B units' (also sometimes known as 'work units' or 'allowed minutes') by which productivity could be measured and standards set. Bedaux also used the B-unit method to form a rating system for bonuses; workers who performed tasks faster

than the minimum B-unit requirement had their speed of work measured and were then paid bonuses proportional to how far they exceeded this floor level.

Kessler (1998) notes that the Bedaux system had considerable advantages over earlier systems. One of the most important of these was that it could be applied across and between departments. By paying bonuses based on workers' ability to perform tasks rather than on the actual task (as in piecework systems), firms could apply the same system universally rather than having to develop new systems for each workshop or department. However, the system was highly complex and this, says Kessler, led to two disadvantages: first, the system was difficult to implement correctly, and second, workers found it difficult to understand the rationale behind the system and to know whether they were being treated fairly. Both these problems led to worker unrest in many plants where the Bedaux system was introduced.

Nonetheless, the promise of a standardized system which could be implemented across the board held great appeal for many companies, and Bedaux's persuasive salesmanship may have helped. He established his first consultancy firm in Cleveland, Ohio, advising firms on how to implement his system, and rapidly built up a network of consultancies across the United States and then in Europe. During the 1930s as many as 1,000 firms were using the Bedaux system around the world. Curiously, given earlier resistance to the scientific management movement, the system was particularly popular in Britain, where it was adopted by firms such as ICI and Lucas, which were already dominated by strong centralizing managements. Many of these firms suffered from severe labour disruption as a result, but it is difficult to assign blame for this entirely to Bedaux; his original idea seems to have been genuinely motivated by a desire to be fair to both workers and employers. He cannot be held solely to blame for the failures in execution of the system,

although his consultants were usually involved in the initial application.

Although he had become an American citizen and had married an American, Bedaux returned to France in 1927, a wealthy man. He bought a sixteenth-century chateau, and became the darling of Parisian society. Among his friends was the Prince of Wales, who briefly became King Edward VIII and then abdicated to become Duke of Windsor; the Duke married Mrs Wallis Simpson at Bedaux's chateau. Among the more bizarre events of his life was the Charles E. Bedaux Sub-Arctic Expedition of 1934, when Bedaux attempted to pioneer an overland route through the wilderness from Edmonton, Alberta to Telegraph Creek, British Columbia and ultimately to Alaska. Expedition members included Bedaux himself, his wife, his mistress, several surveyors and a Hollywood cinematographer; supplies included large quantities of champagne, caviar and ball gowns for the ladies. Plagued by equipment failures, the 'Champagne Expedition' had to be abandoned before it reached its destination.

Bedaux's ideas on workplace efficiency had broadened into a more general technocratic philosophy, and he became an advocate of the application of scientific methods to social and political control. This led him into increasing involvement with right-wing politics. According to Kessler, 'he had a strong sense of mission, believing that poverty could be eradicated if production was organized on his methods and that an efficient society could be created if led by engineers and technocrats' (1998: 53). After the fall of France in 1940 he served as a technical adviser to the Vichy government and also to the occupying Nazi regime in northern France. In 1942 he went to North Africa where he began work on a project to lay a pipeline across the Sahara desert, and was captured by Allied forces at the end of the year. Still a US citizen, he was charged with treason and flown back to the United States, but took an overdose of bar-

biturates before he could be brought to trial. Conspiracy theorists continue to believe that he was murdered by the FBI, for motives unknown.

BIBLIOGRAPHY

Kessler, I. (1998) 'Bedaux, Charles E.', in M. Warner (ed.) *IEBM Handbook of Management Thinking*, London: International Thomson Business Press, 53–6.

Ungar, G. (1997) *The Champagne Expedition*, Ottawa: National Film Board.

MLW

BEECHAM, Joseph (1848–1916)

Joseph Beecham was born in Wigan, Lancashire on 8 June 1848 and died in London on 23 October 1916. Beecham was educated at a free school and then (when his family moved to St Helens) at the Church of England Moorflat School, showing great facility for mental arithmetic and an interest in music, cricket and cycling. Already working part-time for his father, Thomas Beecham, Joseph left school in the early 1860s to work full-time, working (by his own account) more than eighteen hours a day. His father had a turbulent personal life and a domineering personality: a scandalous separation from Joseph's mother was only brought to an end by her death in 1872 (his father was to marry twice more) and, although Thomas Beecham officially ceded control of the firm to his son in 1881, Joseph remained a salaried employee for most of the next decade. Joseph married Josephine Burnett, with whom he had eight children before they too separated in 1901. Beecham was a councillor (1889) and mayor (1899, 1910–11) in St Helens, and became a passionate benefactor of the arts with an impressive collection of British landscape paintings (including Constables and Turners). He was also a keen supporter of his son Thomas Beecham's (later Sir Thomas Beecham) successful efforts to became a world-famous conductor, after realizing that his son was not suited for work in Beecham's publicity department. Joseph Beecham was knighted (1912) and then made a baronet (1914). In 1914 he bought the Covent Garden estate (including the market, Drury Lane Theatre and the Covent Garden Opera House) for an unprecedented £2 million; complications from this sale were unresolved at his death.

Beecham's two key contributions to the firm were in advertising and overseas expansion. He increased advertising expenditure six-fold to £120,000 (1884–91), and brought to this area of the business a surprising (given his introverted nature) creative flair. Whereas his father's advertisements had been prosaic and pedagogic, Joseph Beecham's tried to entertain. For publicity purposes, he published albums of music with titles such as 'Beecham's Music Portfolio: A Wonderful Medicine', gave away kazoos and issued cheap illustrated handbooks in their millions. He also set up ingenious publicity stunts: the arrival in 1891 of the Prince of Wales's ship in Bombay Harbour was celebrated by a flotilla of small yachts with adverts for Beecham's Pills on their sails; a jocular open letter claimed that Beecham's Pills would have prevented the eponymous wife's suicide in the sensational play, *The Second Mrs Tanqueray*; a caricature of Gladstone recommended Beecham's Pills for problems with 'The Grand Old Magician's Irish Policy', and a topical picture of a suffragette in men's clothes carried the slogan 'Since taking Beecham's Pills I have been a New Woman'. Significantly, in 1909 Beecham was appointed a director of Pears Soap, another of the principal players in the expansion of Victorian advertising.

Overseas, Beecham opened up markets neglected by his father. He appointed export

agents throughout the vast British Empire and beyond, supported by huge marketing campaigns. Beecham also personally supervised a manufacturing subsidiary in New York, crossing the Atlantic some sixty times. His cosmopolitanism is summed up in his claim to have 'bought his tie in Cairo, his coat in Australia and his boots in San Francisco' (Corley 1984: 244). He was also knighted by the Tsar of Russia for his sponsorship of a season of Russian ballet in London.

BIBLIOGRAPHY

Beecham, T. (1944) *A Mingled Chime*, London: Hutchinson.

Corley, T.A.B. (1984) 'Sir Joseph Beecham', in D.J. Jeremy (ed.), *Dictionary of Business Biography*, London: Butterworths, vol. 1, 243–6.

Hindley, D. and Hindley, G. (1972) *Advertising in Victorian England, 1837–1901*, London: Wayland.

Lazell, H.G. (1975) *From Pills to Penicillin: The Beecham Story*, London: Heinemann.

SC

BELL, Alexander Graham (1847–1922)

Alexander Graham Bell was born in Edinburgh on 3 March 1847, the son of Melville and Eliza Bell. He died in Baddek, Nova Scotia on 2 August 1922. He married Mabel Hubbard in 1877. Bell studied anatomy and physiology at the University of London, and became very much involved in the study if deafness; both his mother and wife were deaf (he met his wife while teaching at the Boston School for Deaf Mutes, where she was a pupil), and he was a friend of Helen Keller. His family moved to Boston in 1870 after the death of a brother and a sister from tuberculosis, and

Bell became a professor of physiology at Boston University. He also began conducting experiments with sound apparatus, initially in hopes of developing a hearing aid. In this he was not successful, but he did discover a method of transmitting sound via electric signal over wires, and on 7 March 1876 was granted a patent for a telephone transmitter; the first successful transmission was made only a few days later, in Boston.

Bell continued to develop his telephones with experiments in Boston and Brantford, Ontario, where his parents had settled. The Bell Telephone Company was founded in 1877, although Bell himself took little part in running it; much of the work in bringing the telephone to a broader commercial market was done by Theodore VAIL and also by Bell's rival Thomas EDISON, who had also been working on a telephone and who now made a number of improvements to Bell's design. Bell himself went on to patent a number of other devices, including the photophone, a device for transmitting sound on a beam of light, and techniques for teaching speech to the deaf. In 1885 he settled on Cape Breton Island, Nova Scotia, and there took up an interest in designing aircraft; the *Silver Dart*, designed by Bell and Glenn H. Curtiss, and piloted by J.A.D. McCurdy, became the second successful powered aircraft design after the *Flyer* of Orville and Wilbur Wright, and marked the beginning of Canadian aviation.

Bell was not a manager *per se*, although he appreciated the enormous commercial significance of telephones. His approach to the telephone, as to the aeroplane and his work with the deaf, centred around his belief in the value and importance of communication. The ability to communicate was essential in any sphere, personal, social or commercial, and his life's work was devoted to improving communication by whatever means.

BELL, Daniel (1919–)

Daniel Bell was born Daniel Bolotsky in Brooklyn, New York on 10 May 1919, of Eastern European Jewish parentage. His early years were harsh and painful: his father died when he was six months old, and his mother had to work in a factory and placed him in a day orphanage.

Like many in his community, during the 1930s Bell was attracted to socialism, having joined the Young People's Socialist League in 1932, at the precocious age of thirteen. Several years later he entered the City College of New York, graduating with a BSc degree in 1938. By this time he was a very articulate young spokesman for socialism in a country where the ideology had little appeal, particularly with the coming of Franklin Roosevelt's New Deal after the latter's election in 1933.

Bell continued writing for the socialist *New Leader*, serving as its editor between 1941 and 1945, and then writing for *Fortune* magazine between 1948 and 1956. Here he applied his knowledge of sociology to labour and business issues. After a brief sojourn in Paris with the Congress for Cultural Freedom, Bell entered the graduate programme in sociology at Columbia University in the autumn of 1957. Earning his doctorate in 1960, he then taught sociology at Columbia until 1969, when he moved to Harvard.

By the 1950s Bell had moved a long way from his youthful socialism. In 1960, he published his first noteworthy book, *The End of Ideology*. At a time when John F. Kennedy and Richard Nixon were running for the presidency of the United States on virtually identical platforms, Bell saw a Western world in which class war and class ideologies were things of the past and welfare capitalism worked in harmony with the public sector. Marxism, discredited by de-Stalinization and the Hungarian Revolution of 1956, was now irrelevant in the United States, where workers had company pensions, mowed their lawns in Levittown, and drove Chevrolets and Fords.

However, Bell's 'end of ideology' argument was premature, for an anarchist and ecological left and a libertarian, populist right plunged the 1960s into turmoil. The 1972 US presidential campaign between Nixon and South Dakota Senator George McGovern was sharply polarized.

Bell was a noted futurist, and served on the Presidential Commission on the Year 2000, where he published his next major work. *The Coming of Post-industrial Society: A Venture in Social Forecasting* (1973) was a landmark. Bell defined a postindustrial society as one in which most of its work force operated in the tertiary or service sector. The concept began to germinate in Bell's mind as early as the 1950s, when his articles in *Fortune* dealt with the rise of service industries. Bell drew on the work of sociologist Colin Clark's *The Conditions of Economic Progress* (1940), which divided economies into primary (agricultural), secondary (industrial), and tertiary (service) sectors. Bell first used the term 'post-industrial' in a lecture in the summer of 1959 in Salzburg, and in 1962 he published a paper for the Boston Forum on 'The Post-industrial Society: A Speculative View of the United States in 1985 and Beyond'.

The Coming of Post-industrial Society opened with a discussion of some predictions of Bell's original mentor, Karl MARX. The Marx that Bell discussed, however, was not that of volume 1 of *Das Kapital* but that of the posthumous volume 3. Here Marx's writings, edited by Friedrich ENGELS, predicted the separation of ownership from control in the management of enterprises and the rise of a white-collar administrative class larger than the working class. Bell saw the prophecies of the late Marx as much more applicable than the earlier ones, given that the class war predicted in the *Communist Manifesto* of 1848 had not taken place. In the early 1970s, Africa and Asia still employed 70 per cent of their labour force in the primary sector, while Western Europe, the Soviet Union and Japan employed a majority in the secondary sector. Only in

the United States had the postindustrial society arrived, with a majority (60 per cent) of the work force in the tertiary sector.

Postindustrial society was also characterized by the primacy of professionals, technocrats and theoretical knowledge. 'Industrial society', wrote Bell, 'is the coordination of machines and men for the production of goods. Post-industrial society is organized around knowledge ...' (Bell 1973: 20). He argued that economies in the twentieth century operated by trying to predict and plan the future. The First World War had inaugurated an era in which applied science and technology began to assume a major economic and social role. John Maynard KEYNES provided a theory as to how government could fine tune the business cycle, and computers and statistics provided the tools and models as to how this could be done. Technological change in the nineteenth century was often unplanned, but that of the twenty-first century would be anticipated and even planned. Business productivity and profits became more dependent upon conscious theoretical knowledge. If United States Steel represented the ideal corporation of the 1920s, General Motors represented that of the 1950s, and International Business Machines (IBM) that of the 1970s.

In the remainder of the book, Bell elaborates upon the uniqueness of postindustrial society and the changes in occupations that characterize it. Focusing upon the importance of knowledge and technology, Bell predicted that the corporation would remain the dominant form of business organization through to the year 2000. In place of the old divisions between capitalism and socialism, he saw a tension between 'economizing' and 'sociologizing' modes in both systems. The former stressed short-term profits and efficiency while the latter looked at broader criteria. The main conflict in this new kind of society would be that between the new technocratic elite and the more populist masses: 'Now wealth, power, and status are not dimensions of class, but values sought or gained by classes' (Bell 1973: 43). The new leaders of society would be scientists, professors, programmers and engineers rather than steel-makers or manufacturers.

Bell looked at some of the cultural implications of the new economic order in his next major work, *The Cultural Contradictions of Capitalism* (1976). Here Bell reversed the Marxist idea that economics determines culture. Instead, Bell argued, there was now a radical tension between society and art. Society was ruled by economic efficiency and logic, while in the arts the self and what appealed to it were taken as the basis for value. *The Cultural Contradictions of Capitalism* drew its name from the paradox of a society grown wealthy from the virtues of hard work and self-denial, which then repudiated these virtues. The revolt against the Puritan work ethic, however, was not a recent development; it went back to the eve of the First World War. Nineteenth-century USA was a place of hard-working farmers and town merchants ruled by self-discipline and strong moral codes. By 1913, a new cultural elite, in a country grown prosperous from these very virtues, began to attack them. Walter Lippmann (1889–1974), John Reed (1887–1920) and Van Wyck Brooks (1886–1963) spearheaded this attack upon Victorianism. Affluent young bohemians settled in Greenwich Village and San Francisco, reading Marx, Friedrich Wilhelm Nietzsche and Sigmund Freud, promoting birth control, free love, homosexuality and the rights of African-Americans and immigrants. Self-expression replaced self-discipline.

The unprecedented affluence of the 1920s, with its New Era capitalism based upon the automobile, encouraged the spread of this new ethic of hedonism, which was a consumption rather than a production ethic. According to Bell 'A consumption society was emerging, with its emphasis on spending and material possessions, and it was undermining the traditional value system, with its emphasis on thrift, frugality, self-control, and impulse renunciation' (Bell 1976: 64–5). The cinema provided new role models for youth, with new,

more libertine and materialistic values; the automobile offered a private sanctum for sexual experimentation away from parents and local moralists.

The Great Depression and the Second World War slowed the trend to the consumption ethic, but it returned with a vengeance to dominate US culture in the affluent 1950s and 1960s. Nowhere was this more evident than in the individualistic lifestyle of southern California. A 'fun' morality, largely sexually oriented and an obsession with self-esteem, said Bell, had replaced virtue, but this had left capitalism with no restraining ethic. The US business ethic was no longer work and produce, but consume and enjoy. This was demonstrated by the growth of businesses in photography, travel, fashion and especially entertainment. Bell even saw the theory of Marshall McLUHAN that 'the medium is the message', that form is more important than content, as another indicator of the temper of the age. For Bell, the 1960s counter-culture was far from a rebellion but merely an extension of the hedonism of the 1950s, an attack upon values that had faded decades before. Religion and morality were replaced by psychology.

All of this, Bell insisted, stemmed from the very contradictions of a capitalism that seemed to be digging its own grave not by any economic contradictions, as Marx had envisioned, but by the fact that it produced the very affluence that undermined its own work ethic:

On the one hand, the business corporation wants an individual to work hard, pursue a career, accept delayed gratification – to be, in the crude sense, an organization man. And yet, in its products and its advertisements, the corporation promotes pleasure, instant joy, relaxing, and letting go.
(Bell 1976: 71–2)

In 1999, Bell, now a Harvard professor emeritus, published a third edition of *The Coming of Post-industrial Society*, with a new foreword of over seventy pages. In it, he updated his tentative vision of a dawning postindustrial age. Bell observed that his term was now a part of the common language; political leaders now used it frequently. In 1973 the United States had been the only postindustrial country, but now Britain, Japan and most of Western Europe had joined the United States. Bell now saw the economy divided into *five* sectors: (1) primary: agriculture, (2) secondary: industry, (3) tertiary: transport and utilities, (4) quaternary: trade and finance, and (5) quinary: health and education. Postindustrial technology was being organized around microprocessors instead of motors. Economic geography had in the past determined where businesses located. With communication and knowledge becoming all-important, businesses would now cluster around universities and suburbs, not mines, rivers and cities. Considerations of time now overshadowed those of space. Markets 'are no longer places but networks', being everywhere at the same time when millions of pounds and dollars can move across borders with the click of a mouse (Bell 1999: xlvii). Bell found that in the postindustrial world, developing nations, such as those of Africa, which were living by exports of food and raw materials would be in serious trouble, for new technologies would eliminate demand in their markets. In the new global economy, each country was losing control over its currency and maybe even its culture as private global television networks such as the Cable News Network (CNN) rivalled state and national ones. Tastes and entertainment were becoming international. Postindustrial society, argued Bell, had also spawned a new knowledge class which was not conservative so much as libertarian, and a labour force in which women composed fully half of the managerial class.

Unlike Marx, Bell has abhorred violent revolution and radical socialist solutions. He has nevertheless sought to do for the late twentieth century what Karl Marx did for the nine-

teenth. He wished to present a comprehensive theory relating economic and social change. In this he succeeded, becoming the leading interpreter of the postindustrial age.

BIBLIOGRAPHY

Bell, D. (1973) *The Coming of Post-industrial Society, A Venture in Social Forecasting*, New York: Basic Books.

——— (1976) *The Cultural Contradictions of Capitalism*, New York: Basic Books.

——— (1999) 'The Axial Age of Technology, Foreword: 1999', in *The Coming of Post-industrial Society, A Venture in Social Forecasting*, 3rd edn, New York: Basic Books, ix–lxxxv.

'Bell, Daniel' (1999) *McGraw-Hill Encyclopedia of World Biography*, Detroit, MI: Gale Research Inc., vol. 2, 132–3.

Clark, C. (1940) *The Conditions of Economic Progress*, London: Macmillan.

DCL

BELLMAN, Charles Harold (1886–1963)

Harold Bellman was born in London on 19 February 1886 and died there on 1 June 1963. Although he was born in Paddington in London, Bellman considered himself a Cornishman (both his parents were from Penzance). He was a lifelong Methodist and popular lay preacher, and his wife, Kate Peacock, was a Sunday School teacher when they met (they married in 1911). Within a year of leaving school at the age of fourteen, Bellman had passed the clerks' examinations for the Railway Clearing House and gained promotion (despite finding the job extremely boring). Barred from active service in the First World War on medical grounds, Bellman joined the Ministry for Munitions, where his wartime services won him an MBE. In 1918 he became a part-time board member of the Abbey Road and St John's Wood Building Society, and by June 1920 was working there full time. Within ten years, he had been promoted from secretary to managing director, and in 1937 was appointed chairman. Knighted in 1932, Bellman was also granted the Légion d'Honneur and Australian Order of Merit.

A believer in 'alert general intelligence' rather than 'highly gifted specialists' (Bellman 1947: 258), Bellman made certain he learned everything about the operations of the Abbey Road Society. He and his father both had been members of the Society (Bellman was born in a house that was purchased with an Abbey Road mortgage), and Bellman now worked there as cashier, counter clerk and surveyor's assistant. He redesigned publicity materials, persuaded the directors to pay for modest advertisements (their success enabled him to employ a professional agency) and generated publicity through exhibits at the Ideal Home Exhibition and popular books promoting the building society movement.

Bellman emphasized the building society as a society through friendly advertisements, the quarterly publication of the *Abbey Road Journal* for society members, and the introduction to the annual general meeting of concerts and guest speakers (demand for tickets outstripped supply). He also established a branch network: by 1934 the four London offices had been expanded to eight, along with nearly 100 branches and agencies in the rest of country. While these intermediaries had to be paid commission – unusual at the time – they enabled Abbey Road to offer improved and more personal service. Finally, Bellman increased the proportion of the price of a property that could be loaned to a house purchaser from 80 to 90 per cent on condition that the borrower take insurance against default, persuaded builders to put up security on behalf of purchasers, reduced fees and fines, and had the interest on deposits calculated on a daily

basis. All these combined to make the society highly approachable and attractive to prospective customers.

As chairman of the Abbey Road Building Society, Bellman oversaw a unique period of growth in the building society movement. He believed in growing the market rather than winning market share from competitors, and sought wherever possible to publicize the building society movement as a whole. From 1933 he sought to establish a code of practice to protect building societies against rash loans, and in January 1944 he presided over the merger of Abbey Road with the National Building Society, becoming joint managing director and chairman of the new Abbey National. Before the First World War, Abbey Road had been the fifteenth largest building society in Britain with assets of around £1 million, and it was still operating from a single office until the early 1930s; but by the Second World War it had become the second largest building society. After the 1944 merger, the Abbey National's combined assets were £82 million, 10.3 per cent of the total assets of all British building societies.

BIBLIOGRAPHY

Bellman, C.H. (1927) *The Building Society Movement*, London: Methuen.
—— (1935) *The Thrifty Three Millions*, London: Abbey Road Building Society.
—— (1947) *Cornish Cockney: Reminiscences and Reflections*, London: Hutchinson.
Cleary, E.J. (1965) *The Building Society Movement*, London: Elek Books.
—— (1984) 'Sir Charles Harold Bellman', in D.J. Jeremy (ed.), *Dictionary of Business Biography*, London: Butterworths, vol. 1, 273–8.
Jeremy, D.J. (1998) *A Business History of Britain, 1900–1990s*, Oxford and New York: Oxford University Press.

SC

BENCI, Giovanni d'Amerigo (1394–1455)

Giovanni d'Amerigo Benci was born in Florence, into a middle-class family, and died there in mid-July 1455. He married Ginevra di Peruzzi in 1431, and they had eight children before her death in 1444; he also had at least one illegitimate child by a slave girl. In 1409 he joined the Rome office of the Medici Bank, then a relatively small business, where he served as an office boy. Adept at double entry bookkeeping, by 1420 he had risen to be the branch's chief accountant. In 1424 the Medici made their first attempt at expansion north of the Alps, and Benci was sent to Geneva to help set up a new branch there. At this point he was still a salaried manager, albeit on the very high salary of 115 florins a year, but with the formal establishment of the Geneva branch he was given a junior partnership. In 1433 he set up a temporary office in Basel and successfully managed a complex banking business during the term of the Council of Basel. By 1435 he had come to the attention of the senior management of the Medici Bank, and Cosimo dei MEDICI called Benci back to Rome and made him general manager of the entire business, jointly with Antonio Salutati. Benci was also put in charge of the Tavola, the Medici's banking and foreign exchange operation, which had been suffering losses; thanks to his accounting skills and energy, the Tavola was soon restored to profit.

Salutati died in 1443, and Benci then served as sole general manager until his own death. He had won the trust and respect of Cosimo dei Medici; the surviving records show him to have been 'a very efficient business man with an orderly and systematic mind' (de Roover 1963: 57). It was during his period as general manager that the Medici reached the height of their expansion and power, developing branch offices across Western Europe and building up agency relationships in Asia, and diversifying spectacularly into cloth manufacturing, financial services and international

trade. The Medici relied on him utterly, and in return rewarded him fully: he became one of the *maggiori*, the senior partners of the business, and at his death left his heirs an estate valued at over 46,000 florins.

Benci was one of the great managers of his age, and his efforts helped make the Medici Bank the greatest international business of the fifteenth century. He was a skilled financial manager and organizer, demonstrating to the full his abilities in these areas both in Geneva and later in Florence. Sadly, his successors were not of the same quality, and the business declined progressively in later years, finally failing in 1494.

BIBLIOGRAPHY

de Roover, R. (1963) *The Rise and Decline of the Medici Bank*, Cambridge, MA: Harvard University Press.

MLW

BENEDICT OF NURSIA (c.480–c.547)

Saint Benedict was born in the central Italian town of Nursia and died at his abbey of Monte Cassino. Educated in Nursia and Rome, he opted for a religious life. After three years as a hermit, he was invited by a group of monks to be their abbot (the leader of their community). But when Benedict attempted to instil discipline and rule into the community, the monks objected, even attempting to poison him. The experience left Benedict convinced that monastic communities could only function if they were subject to strong leadership and rules.

By around 525, Benedict had founded a new monastery at Monte Cassino in central Italy, and had promulgated the first version of his rule for monastic communities. The Rule of St Benedict is divided into seventy-three precepts, which lay out the duties of members of monastic communities. The rule begins with a statement of goals: monks are to dedicate their work to the glory of God. The remainder of the rule specifies how those goals should be carried out, setting not only times of work, meals, prayer and rest, but also the hierarchy and chain of command within each monastery. Supreme over all was the abbot, who directed the affairs of each monastery; below him were subordinate officers such as the treasurer, and then came the general chapter of monks. The monks were to obey the orders of the abbot, but those orders had to be explained in regular meetings of the chapter, where monks could voice their own views of the abbot's decisions.

Earlier sets of monastic rules had been written, but none had been widely accepted. Benedict's rule, which was simple and easy to follow, was immediately successful and was promptly adopted by other monastic communities. By the time of Benedict's death there were more than thirty monasteries following his rule; by 600 there were hundreds across Europe, and the Benedictines had been organized formally into a monastic order with all monks reporting to an abbot and chapter. The system ultimately fell into decay, as there was a lack of central control over the monasteries and no way of checking abuses or deviations from the rule. The Cluniac reforms of the eleventh century remedied this defect, and in the twelfth century the rival Cistercian order led by Saint BERNARD OF CLAIRVAUX took the concept of the monastic corporation still further.

Benedict and his immediate followers had taken the first step in establishing a centralized corporate organization within the church, and thence more broadly in society. Monastic organization was one of the contributing influences on European business organization in its formative period. The economist John Davis commented that 'Christianity has contributed to the progress of civilization in two ways: directly through its qualities as a form of religion, and indirectly through the system of

social organization incidentally involved in its exercise' (1905: 35). MOONEY and Reilley (1939) saw the monastic structure, with the abbot both governing the chapter and responsible to it, as a precursor to the 'line and staff' principle of organization.

BIBLIOGRAPHY
Cary-Elwes, C. (1988) *St Benedict and His Rule*, London: Catholic Truth Society.

Davis, J.P. (1905) *Corporations: A Study of the Origin and Development of Great Business Combinations and their Relation to the Authority of the State*, New York: G.P. Putnam's Sons.

Kennedy, M.H. (1999) 'Fayol's Principles and the Rule of St Benedict: Is There Anything New Under the Sun?', *Journal of Management History* 5(5): 269–76.

McCann, J. (1937) *Saint Benedict*, London: Sheed and Ward.

Mooney, J.D. and Reilley, A.D. (1939) *The Principles of Organization*, New York: Harper and Bros.

MLW

BENIGER, James R. (1946–)

James Beniger was born in Sheboygan, Wiconsin on 16 December 1946. He graduated with a BA *magna cum laude* from Harvard University in 1969, then took his master's degree from the University of California at Berkeley in 1973 and his Ph.D. from the same institution in 1978. After completing his BA he worked as a journalist for several years, as a staff writer for the *Wall Street Journal* and later, briefly, with the *Minneapolis Star*. He has taught sociology at Princeton and Yale Universities, and is currently associate professor of communications and sociology at the University of Southern California. In 1989 he advised the then Soviet Academy of Sciences on the 'informatization' of the Russian economy. He married Kay Ferdinandsen in 1984; they have two children.

A sociologist who writes on issues such as communication and globalization, Beniger has also had an influence on modern management thinking, particularly relating to issues such as information and control. In his major work, *The Control Revolution* (1986), Beniger advances the view that modern society is dominated by institutions which aim to achieve control. These institutions include among them business corporations and other commercial organizations. One way in which control is exercised is through the control of the flow of information. By altering or stopping up information flows, one of the key components of modern society, institutions can achieve greater control over constituent groups such as customers, employees and society at large. As these large institutions are the only organizations with the power to affect information flows in this way, it is logical that they will achieve more control as time passes.

Beniger's work has echoes of earlier control theories, notably that advanced by James BURNHAM, although Beniger is more concerned with the means of control than the motives for it. It is notable, however, that in an age when many theorists argue that more information means more freedom and competitiveness in markets, Beniger is suggesting that it might actually mean less.

BIBLIOGRAPHY
Beniger, J.R. (1983) *Trafficking in Drug Users: Professional Exchange Networks in the Control of Deviance*, Cambridge: Cambridge University Press.

—— (1986) *The Control Revolution: Technological and Economic Origins of the Information Society*, Cambridge, MA: Harvard University Press.

BENNETT, James Gordon (1795–1872)

James Gordon Bennett was born in Keith, Scotland 1 September 1795. He died in New York City, following a stroke on 1 June 1872. After emigrating to New England, he spent some twenty years working as a journalist in Boston, Charleston and New York. In 1832 he started his own newspaper, the New York *Globe*, but this soon failed. In 1835 he tried again, with capital of $500 and an office in a basement on Wall Street, from where he launched the New York *Herald*. This paper survived and flourished, and ultimately made Bennett, its owner and editor for nearly four decades, a very wealthy man.

In New York in the 1830s there were many newspapers, mostly with small circulations and usually owned by competing business and/or political interests; their primary purpose was to serve as propaganda organs for their owners. Bennett's innovation was to see the news, and more particularly newspapers, as a commodity that could be sold like any other. The *Herald* formula had two ingredients. First, Bennett aimed to print news of events, rather than opinions of political elites, and his paper was therefore independent of the establishment of the day. Second, he printed the news that he thought ordinary people wanted to read: 'sin, science, and sensation' (Huntzicker 1999: 15). In 1836, the paper closely followed the police investigation into the murder of a prostitute, reporting the entire affair in graphic detail. Among the journalistic innovations were reports of interviews with police and detectives and eye-witness accounts of the murder scene. Circulation soared.

Bennett's press was dubbed 'yellow journalism', and in 1840 the other New York papers launched the so-called 'Moral War', attempting to drive Bennett out of business through pressure of public opinion. He defended himself so vigorously in print that circulation of his paper actually went up. Bennett had realized that the fierce struggle between the papers was actually expanding the market, as the furore over the Moral War led more and more people to buy papers.

More than any other editor of his generation, Bennett understood the power of the press. He once wrote: 'A newspaper can send more souls to Heaven, and save more from Hell, than all the churches or chapels in New York – and make money at the same time' (Mott 1941: 232). A curious mix of moral crusader, populist journalist and hard-headed businessman, Bennett knew that his paper's survival depended on its continually being able to report more and better news than its rivals. In 1862, during the American Civil War, the paper published a complete order of battle of the Confederate Army. This caused a sensation in New York, and Bennett was investigated as a possible Confederate spy; in fact, his reporters had pieced together the information from Southern newspapers smuggled into New York. Bennett was also the first to employ 'celebrity' writers such as Mark Twain, and was a great spotter of journalistic talent; it was Bennett who gave Henry Stanley his first break in journalism. By 1870 he had made the *Herald* the most successful newspaper in North America, through a combination of shrewd knowledge of his market, careful attention to detail in his product, and the ability to extract the best from those who worked for him. By doing so, he revolutionized journalism, and became the prototype of media barons such as William Randolph HEARST and Joseph PULITZER.

Bennett's son, also James Gordon Bennett (1841–1918), took over the management of the *Herald* in his father's later years. It was the younger Bennett who gave Stanley the cryptic order 'Go and find Livingstone!', which made Stanley's career and arguably changed the course of African history. He was an autocratic and domineering man who, unlike his father, would not delegate management; he once asked for a list of staff who were believed to be indispensable and, on receiving the list, summarily dismissed the lot, commenting that: 'On my newspaper, no one is indispensable.'

He nevertheless ran the *Herald* competently until the early years of the twentieth century, when his own powers began to fail and he lost control of the paper, which soon after merged with the *Tribune*.

BIBLIOGRAPHY

Carlson, O. (1942) *The Man Who Made News*, New York: Duell, Sloan and Pearce.
Huntzicker, W. (1999) *The Popular Press, 1833–1865*, Westport, CT: Greenwood Press.
Mott, F.L. (1941) *American Journalism: A History of Newspapers in the United States through 250 Years*, New York: Macmillan.
Seitz, D.C. (1928) *The James Gordon Bennetts*, Indianapolis, IN: Bobbs-Merrill.

MLW

BENNIS, Warren (1925–)

Warren Bennis was born in New York City on 8 March 1925. After graduating from high school, Bennis served in the US Army from 1943–7. At the age of nineteen, he was one of the youngest infantry commanders to serve in the European theater during the Second World War, and was decorated with the Purple Heart and the Bronze Star. The lessons he learned in the army served him well, as it was the first organization that he was able to observe up close and in depth. Among these lessons were the effects of good and bad leadership upon morale, as well as the influence of command-and-control leadership and institutional bureaucracy.

After leaving the army, Bennis attended Antioch College from 1947 to 1951. Inspired by Antioch's progressive campus culture, Bennis wrote a series of satirical articles in the college literary magazine which were intended as challenges to the positions of more orthodox university figures. Douglas MCGREGOR, the president of Antioch College (1948–54), had a great influence on Bennis. McGregor came from Massachusetts Institute of Technology (MIT), where he had founded the industrial psychology department; in 1954 he returned to MIT, where he pioneered the study of human relations and organizational behavior.

In 1951 Bennis was admitted to MIT on the basis of his perfect academic record at Antioch and McGregor's letter of recommendation. After obtaining his Ph.D. in economics and social science, Bennis taught social psychology for a year (1955–6) as an assistant professor at MIT. Also in 1955, he was invited to Bethel, Maine, the summer headquarters of the National Training Laboratories (NTL). Founded by the psychologist Kurt LEWIN in 1947, NTL paved the way for intriguing research into a new social invention called T-groups (the T stood for training). Bennis learned much from leading empirical studies of the processes and outcomes emerging from T-groups. Later that year, he and Herbert Shepard published two articles on 'natural groups' in *Human Relations*, in which they described the stages of group development (Bennis and Shepard 1956; Shepard and Bennis 1956).

Bennis left MIT in 1956 to take a position at Boston University for three years. He also conducted research and taught courses at Harvard University. He returned to MIT at Douglas McGregor's invitation in 1959. He served on the faculty of MIT's Sloan School of Management, and later succeeded McGregor as chairman of the Organizational Studies Department. With Ken Benne and Bob Chin, he produced his first book, a selection of readings entitled *The Planning of Change* (1961). He also published another book, *Interpersonal Dynamics: Essays and Readings on Human Interaction,* in collaboration with Edgar SCHEIN, Dave Berlew and Fritz Steele.

From 1956 to 1967 his output was prodigious, including seventeen books and over 250 articles. He also consulted extensively as a leading organizational theorist and a pioneer in organization development.

In 1967 Bennis came to the State University of New York (SUNY) at Buffalo at the invitation and persuasive appeal of the incoming president, Martin Meyerson. He initially served as provost before assuming the roles of Vice President of Academic Development and Acting Executive Vice President of SUNY. During his tenure in these positions, Bennis learned a great deal, especially in regard to his thoughts about change. He learned that, to achieve and sustain change in an organization, the thoughts and beliefs of current members must be taken into account. He also realized that if a vision is not sustained by action, it is meaningless. In 1973, Bennis reflected on his experiences at SUNY-Buffalo in *The Leaning Ivory Tower*.

Bennis left Buffalo in 1971 to become president of the University of Cincinnati (1971–8). At the beginning of his tenure, he was disturbed by the tendency of routine work to divert his time and attention away from the more important non-routine work, such as creative planning and fundamental organizational change. He found that leaders of other institutions were bothered by the same problem. He resolved to be a president 'who led, not managed' (Bennis 1993: 31). In fact, Bennis was actively learning how to lead. From his experiences, he learned a number of important things about leaders and leadership, many of which were later captured in his book, *On Becoming a Leader* (1989). Thus, Bennis's experience as a real leader at both SUNY and Cincinnati helped him shape his thoughts about leadership. Witnessing at first hand the troubles that modern leaders encounter enabled him effectively to bridge the gap between leadership theory and practice in his subsequent writings.

Since 1979, Bennis has been a university professor and Distinguished Professor of Business Administration at the University of Southern California's (USC) Marshall School of Business. At USC, he has been able to consolidate what he learned 'about self-invention, about the importance of organization, about the nature of change, about the nature of leadership – and to find ways to communicate those lessons' (Bennis 1993: 35). In 1991 he became founding chairman of the Leadership Institute at USC. The institute has transformed the Marshall School into an intellectual centre for studying executive leadership. While the institute was the first of its kind in the United States, it has served as the prototype for some fifteen subsequent centres, including one at Harvard.

Bennis's influence has been profound. His contributions stem not from an analysis of what has already happened, but from his foresight into what may happen. In a landmark 1964 *Harvard Business Review* article, he and co-writer Philip Slater claimed that 'Democracy is Inevitable.' While this idea sounded outrageous at the time, it was supported in 1990 by the dramatic revolution of Eastern Europe and the demise of the Soviet Union. In 1966, Bennis published an article titled, 'The Coming Death of Bureaucracy', in which he argued that the old command-and-control, pyramidal organizational structures would be replaced by adaptive, rapidly changing temporary systems. His subsequent work – particularly *The Temporary Society* (1968), also co-authored with Phil Slater – explored new organizational forms. Bennis envisaged organizations as adhocracies – roughly the direct opposite of bureaucracies – freed from the shackles of hierarchy and meaningless paperwork.

In the 1980s, Bennis and others moved the study of leadership to a new stage. His book, *Leaders* (1985), co-authored with Burt Nanus, was a huge success. The authors argued that leadership is not a rare skill; leaders are made rather than born. Leaders are usually ordinary or apparently ordinary persons rather than charismatic individuals. Leadership is not

solely the preserve of those at the top of the organization; it is relevant at all levels. Finally, leadership is not about control, direction and manipulation. *Leaders* and another best-seller, *On Becoming a Leader* (1989), were translated into twenty-one languages. His latest books, *Organizing Genius: The Secrets of Creative Collaboration* (1997) and *Co-Leaders: The Power of Great Partnerships* (1999), bring together the major themes of life's work: leadership, change, great groups and powerful partnerships.

Since he began his career over forty-five years ago, Bennis has authored or edited over twenty-six books, a number that continues to expand. He has also written over 1,500 articles in publications such as *Harvard Business Review*, *Wall Street Journal*, the *New York Times*, *Psychology Today*, *Esquire*, *Atlantic Monthly*, and many management publications. He was the founding editor of Addison-Wesley's Organization Development series. In 1998, Jossey-Bass Publishers introduced a new imprint for innovative books on change leadership – Warren Bennis Books.

Bennis has been an adviser to four US presidents, and currently serves on the boards of Antioch College, the Claremont University Center and Graduate School, Harvard's Center for Educational Leadership, the Salk Institute, and the Center for Professional and Executive Development at Hughes Aircraft. He is a founding director of the American Leadership Forum, and has served as director of Gemini Consulting, the Foothill Group and First Executive, and on the national boards of the US Chamber of Commerce and the American Management Association. In the international arena, he was the US Professor of Corporations and Society at the Centre d'Études Industrielles in Geneva, the Raoul de Vitry d'Avenecourt Professor at INSEAD in Fontainbleau, a professor at IMEDE in Lausanne, and a founding director of the Indian Institute of Management in Calcutta. Finally, Bennis has been a consultant for a wide variety of Fortune 500 firms, including Chase Manhattan Bank, Polaroid, Ford Motor Company, TRW, McKesson Equitable Life, Starbucks, Anderson Consulting, Linkage Inc. and Booz Allen.

Over the years, Warren Bennis has received numerous honours in recognition of his outstanding achievements and contributions. In addition to being the recipient of eleven honorary degrees, Bennis received the 1987 Dow Jones Award for 'outstanding contributions to the field of collegiate education for business'. He twice received the prestigious McKinsey Foundation Award for the best book on management: in 1967 for *The Temporary Society,* and in 1968 for *The Professional Manager.* In 1986, he received the First Annual Award from University Associates, and was presented with the Pericles Award from the Employment Management Association. Other honours include being admitted to *Training Magazine*'s Hall of Fame, the Distinguished Service Award from the American Board of Professional Psychology (its highest honour) and the Perry L. Roher Consulting Practice Award from the American Psychological Association.

Throughout his career, Bennis's ideas and research on leadership have always been cutting edge. He argues that the study of leadership, because of its practice-oriented nature, must link theory to the real world. From his experience as a leader, Bennis can serve as a model for connecting theory to practice. Although he has not held a formal leadership position since 1979, his studies remain firmly anchored in the real world. For example, he wrote *Leaders* after interviewing ninety US leaders. Such efforts have enabled him to have a far-reaching and sustained influence on the study and practice of leadership, an influence that continues in the twenty-first century.

BIBLIOGRAPHY
Bennis, W.G. (1966) 'The Coming Death of Bureaucracy', *THINK* 32(November–December): 32–3.
—— (1973) *The Leaning Ivory Tower,*

San Francisco: Jossey-Bass.

—— (1989) *On Becoming a Leader*, Reading, MA: Addison-Wesley.

—— (1993) *An Invented Life: Reflections on Leadership and Change*, Reading, MA: Addison-Wesley.

—— (1997) *Managing People is Like Herding Cats*, Provo, UT: Executive Excellence Publishing.

Bennis, W.G. and Biederman, P.W. (1997) *Organizing Genius: The Secrets of Creative Collaboration*, Reading, MA: Addison-Wesley.

Bennis, W.G. and Nanus, B. (1985) *Leaders*, Reading, MA: Addison-Wesley.

Bennis, W.G. and Shepard, H.A. (1956) 'A Theory of Group Development', *Human Relations* 9: 415–37.

Bennis, W.G., and Slater, P.E. (1964) 'Democracy is Inevitable', *Harvard Business Review* (March–April): 51–9.

—— (1968) *The Temporary Society*, New York: Harper and Row.

Bennis, W.G., Benne K.D. and Chin R. (1961) *The Planning of Change: Readings in the Applied Behavioral Sciences*, New York: Holt, Rinehart and Winston.

Heenan, D.A. and Bennis, W.G. (1999) *Co-leaders: The Power of Great Partnerships*, New York: John Wiley.

Shepard, H.A. and Bennis, W.G. (1956) 'A Theory of Training by Group Methods', *Human Relations* 9: 403–14.

Who's Who In The World (1991–2), 10th edn, Chicago: Marquis Who's Who, Inc.

QY

BENSON, Henry Alexander (1909–95)

Henry Alexander Benson was born in Johannesburg, South Africa on 2 August 1909 and died in London on 5 March 1995. The grandson of one of the four Cooper brothers who had founded the firm of Cooper Brothers in London in the nineteenth century, he was educated in South Africa and then entered the family firm at the age of sixteen in 1926. He stayed with the firm, apart from service in the Second World War, until retirement in 1975, at which point he became a special adviser to the governor of the Bank of England.

The scion of a British accounting dynasty, Benson (who was to become Sir Henry, and later, Lord Benson) was a major player in international auditing and accounting, and dominated the London accounting stage for several decades. He was the founding chairman of the International Accounting Standards Committee (IASC), now the world's lead rule-maker in accounting, as well as being a major force in the creation of Coopers and Lybrand, now part of PricewaterhouseCoopers, the largest international audit firm. He was also an adviser to several British governments.

Benson's most visible achievement was the creation of the IASC. The idea for this was first put forward by Benson in the corridors of a world accounting congress in Sydney in November 1972, and by June 1973 he had written the constitution, had it signed by the nine founding countries (the UK, the United States, Canada, Australia, Japan, Mexico, France, Germany and the Netherlands) and was chairing the first meeting of its board. The IASC sets accounting standards which are the benchmark for the financial reports of non-American multinationals, and which are also used by many countries as national accounting rules. Its standards were endorsed in 2000 by the International Organization of Securities Commissions for use on all major stock exchanges for foreign listings. The European Commission has also adopted IASC standards as the road to harmonization of reporting by all listed European companies. By the year 2005 all listed European companies will be obliged to follow IASC rules rather than national rules. The IASC has become the world's leading standard setter, by which

national regulators increasingly must be advised.

There is some dispute about the road which led to the IASC. Benson's story, followed consistently throughout his life and set out, for example, in his autobiography (Benson 1989), is that the IASC was a logical progression of ideas arising from internationalization of business. He was very active in international business and had the foresight to see that this was the path of future evolution. As an auditor, he was increasingly aware that different financial reporting rules pertained in different countries, making cross-border activity more difficult. As formal rule-making structures began to evolve in individual countries, he felt there was a need to provide some instrument which would help countries bring their rules closer together rather than moving them further apart. This led him, when president of the Institute of Chartered Accountants in England and Wales (ICAEW), the premier British auditing body, to form in 1966 a joint study group with the US and Canadian professional bodies. This body was supposed to study accounting issues and suggest solutions acceptable to the three countries.

Benson maintains that he was approached at the world congress in 1972 by a number of other countries which wanted to join the study group, and the IASC evolved from that. It was formed by professional audit and accounting bodies, and financed by them. Benson succeeded in having the organization based in London, rather than New York, by the expedient of persuading the ICAEW to pay for office accommodation in the early years.

Other accountants do not entirely endorse this account. The United States was represented during negotiations by Wallace Olson of the American Institute of Certified Public Accountants, and he claims (Olson 1982) that both Japan and Mexico were included in the original nine members purely on American insistence that they be approached.

Sir Douglas Morpeth, president of the ICAEW in 1972–3 and co-author of the IASC constitution, shares the view (Bocqueraz and Walton forthcoming) that the UK was heavily involved in entry to the European Union at that time (the UK joined the Common Market in 1973) and that the UK profession was worried about pressures to harmonize European accounting on the German model. The IASC was seen as a vehicle which would champion Anglo-American accounting and act as a counter-influence to the commission. In practice, this is exactly what has happened as the commission has since 1995 moved progressively towards use of IASC standards for the annual accounts of large groups.

Whatever the motivations, it was Benson who took the initiative to found the international accounting standard setter, and it was his commanding personality and considerable influence which established the IASC and gave it credibility. When he stood down as chairman, he continued to support the organization publicly and privately, for example (Benson 1978) attacking the United Nations for straying into IASC territory by wanting to write accounting standards. He made his last public appearance at the IASC's twentieth anniversary conference in June 1993.

While the IASC is Benson's most public monument, he had an extremely active professional life (the IASC rates only twelve pages in his autobiography). Cooper Brothers was a respectable and sizeable audit firm by the standards of the time when Benson joined, but had only three or four offices and about 150 staff. When Benson retired in 1975 it had nearly 20,000 employees worldwide in 332 offices. Benson was made a partner in 1934 but went off to join the Grenadier Guards in the Second World War. He was eventually demobilized with the rank of brigadier after a very varied army career. Amongst other things, he was called on to reorganize the control systems of the Royal Ordnance factories to make them more effi-

cient. From this he drew not only a belief in the value of harmonized systems, but also good connections with the government and civil service which were to stand him in good stead later.

After the war the returning generation took over the reins of the firm, and while senior partner John Pears ran the firm, Benson put his energies into development, seeing international business as the way ahead. The firm set out on an aggressive expansion drive, opening offices in several countries. In 1955 they had about 1,000 employees and a network of thirty-five offices. The next stage was reached in 1957 when the firm merged with a US audit firm, Lybrand, Ross Brothers and Montgomery, later trading worldwide as Coopers and Lybrand. The firm eventually merged with Price Waterhouse in 1998 to become PricewaterhouseCoopers, by far the largest of the Big Five international audit firms.

Benson was known and trusted by a series of prime ministers from Harold Wilson to Margaret Thatcher. He participated in many committees and his firm received a number of government appointments from 1945 onwards. Amongst other tasks, Benson advised the Heath government during the collapse of the Rolls-Royce aircraft engine company in the early 1970s. He was a special adviser to the governor of the Bank of England for seven years, and also chaired the royal commission on legal services (1976–9), for which he received a life peerage in 1981.

Henry Benson was a considerable force in international accounting. The way in which multinationals report their results, as well as the way in which international audit firms operate, has been directly influenced by his work. The IASC, the institution which he created, is the world's accounting standard setter of reference.

BIBLIOGRAPHY
Benson, H. (1978) 'Danger! A Corporate Report from the UN', *Accountancy*

(May): 3–14.
—— (1989) *Accounting for Life*, London: Kogan Page/ICAEW.
Bocqueraz, C. and Walton, P. (forthcoming) 'Creating a Supranational Regulator: The Role of the Individual and the Mood of the Times. A Case Study of Change in Accounting'.
Olson, W.E. (1982) *The Accounting Profession, Years of Trial: 1969–1980*, New York: AICPA.

PW

BERLE, Adolf Augustus, Jr (1895–1971)

Adolf Augustus Berle was born in Boston Massachusetts on 29 January 1895 and died in New York City on 17 February 1971. He received his BA (1913) and MA (1914) from Harvard and his LLB in 1916 from Harvard Law School, and entered law practice in New York City. After service in the First World War, he returned to New York to practice corporate law. He went on to a career as a successful corporate lawyer, diplomat and close adviser to President Franklin D. Roosevelt.

The United States in the 1920s was undergoing the economic boom exemplified by the phrase 'the Roaring Twenties', and Berle's specialization in the emerging law of corporation finance gave him an excellent view of the operation of securities markets unencumbered by government regulation. Berle also earned a reputation as a legal scholar, writing many articles on his specialization. He taught at Harvard Business School, and joined the faculty of Columbia University Law School in New York. At Harvard he met Professor William Ripley, whom he later acknowledged as a major influence (see preface to Berle and Means 1932). Ripley's 1927 book *Main Street and Wall Street* was a description of the tumul-

tuous world of contemporary corporation finance and securities trading, written for general audiences. The book, which cited or mentioned Berle's writings several times, argued that individual shareholders of large corporations were powerless against management.

Through Ripley, Berle obtained a foundation grant in 1927 for an interdisciplinary study of American corporations, and hired Gardiner MEANS, a graduate student in economics at Columbia, as research economist (Schwarz 1987: 51). The product of their research was *The Modern Corporation*, published in 1932. *The Modern Corporation*'s then revolutionary thesis, supported by Means's statistics, was that modern corporations represented unprecedented aggregations of economic power, subject not to the control of their shareholder-owners, but to that of professional managers. The 200 largest non-banking corporations in the United States possessed close to one-half of the non-banking wealth of the country, or almost one-quarter of the total national wealth (Berle and Means 1932: 19). Within these large corporations, control was separated from ownership. With so many shareholders, individual shareholders did not hold enough shares to be able to exercise control over management. Direction of the corporation passed from shareholders to professional, employed managers, who owned relatively few shares in the corporations employing them, and whose interests were in conflict with those of shareholders (1932, Book 2, chaps 5–6).

Because private owners no longer controlled corporations, and corporations possessed enormous and growing economic power, some arrangement had to be found to prevent possible abuse of that power. The historical significance of *The Modern Corporation* lies in Berle and Means's suggested solution. This was founded on the idea that 'neither the claims of ownership or those of control can stand against the paramount interests of the community' (1932: 312). *The Modern Corporation* did not offer a programme to protect the interests of the community versus large corporations. Yet the book's successful intellectual challenge to *laissez-faire* property rights concepts was, in Berle's words, 'causative both in the development of legal and economic theory and in policies and measures of the United States government' (1932, preface to the revised edn: vii). *Time* Magazine may not have exaggerated when it called *The Modern Corporation* 'the economic Bible of the Roosevelt administration' (Hessen 1983: 279).

The Modern Corporation's continued importance rests not in economic history but in its recognition of the relationship between improved corporate governance through enhanced shareholder protection, increased shareholder value and efficient capital markets (Bratton 2001). In *The Modern Corporation*, Berle offered specific recommendations for protection of shareholders (Book 2, chaps 7–8; Book III, chaps 3–4). The recommendation that rules be imposed 'requiring general disclosure by the corporation of all material facts tending to change open [public securities] market appraisals' (Berle and Means 1932: 289) formed the basis of the US Securities Exchange Act of 1934. As Professor Bratton points out in his incisive article, improved corporate governance through enhanced fiduciary standards, and open public securities markets are issues that have a 'global venue'. In the future it is likely that *The Modern Corporation* will be 'causative in policies and measures' of governments throughout the world (Bratton 2001).

The Modern Corporation continues to justify the encomium: 'one of the most influential books of the twentieth century' (Moore 1982: 236). It provided intellectual support for the government intervention in the economy that was the centrepiece of Roosevelt's 'New Deal'. Yet its significance goes beyond economic history. Managers, investors, scholars and government officials are still wrestling with the problems stemming

from the separation of ownership and control in large corporations described in the book. Later authors influenced by the book included figures as various as James BURNHAM, whose study of *The Modern Corporation* led him to conclude that ownership would follow control and ultimately pass to the managers, and Alfred CHANDLER, who not only accepted the thesis of the separation of ownership and control but saw it as the basis of an American style of 'managerial capitalism' which was in many ways superior to other forms.

BIBLIOGRAPHY

Berle, A.A., Jr and Means, G.C. (1932) *The Modern Corporation and Private Property*, New York: Harcourt, Brace and World, 1967.

Bratton, W.W. (2001) 'Berle and Means Reconsidered at the Century's Turn', *Journal of Corporation Law* 26.

Herman, E. (1981) *Corporate Control, Corporate Power*, Cambridge: Cambridge University Press.

Hessen, R. (1983) 'The Modern Corporation and Private Property: A Reappraisal', *Journal of Law and Economics* 26(2): 273–90.

Moore, T.G. (1982) 'Introduction to "CORPORATIONS AND PRIVATE PROPERTY", A Conference Sponsored by the Hoover Institution', *Journal of Law and Economics* 26(2): 235–6.

Ripley, W.Z. (1927) *Main Street and Wall Street*, Boston: Little, Brown.

Schwarz, J. (1987) *Liberal: Adolf A. Berle and the Vision of an American Era*, New York: Free Press.

SR

BERNARD OF CLAIRVAUX (1090–1153)

St Bernard was born near Dijon, Burgundy, the son of a noble family. He died at his monastery of Clairvaux in 1153, and was canonized in 1174. In his early twenties, Bernard joined the newly founded Cistercian order of monks, who were more ascetic and more disciplined than the older established Benedictine order. Bernard's organizational and intellectual powers were such that he quickly rose to high positions, and in 1125 he was chosen to lead a new monastic foundation at Clairvaux. Clairvaux became the centre of an astonishing expansion: over the next half-century, hundreds of Cistercian monasteries were established across Western Europe. Bernard himself became the most famous orator and theologian of his day, disputing with Peter Abelard and preaching the Second Crusade in 1147.

Pious and ascetic, Bernard was one of a minority of late medieval theologians who believed that trade and commerce were inherently sinful. (He would have been horrified to have been included in a collection such as this.) Ironically, the organization which he led not only had a lasting influence on the shape of business organization, but was also a highly successful multinational commercial enterprise.

Like St BENEDICT before him, Bernard designed a rule for monks that not only specified the duties of individuals but also organized and structured monastic activity. As to the organization of individual monasteries, Bernard did not greatly depart from the original Benedictine rule; the major change was in the overall structure of the order. As the Cistercian order expanded, each monastery sent out parties of monks to colonize new sites and establish new monasteries. The first house in the process was known as the 'founder house', and the new monasteries were known as 'daughter houses'. As the daughter houses grew, they in turn became founder houses, establishing colonies of their own. This system

was also used for organizational control: founder houses were responsible for order and discipline in their own daughter houses. As most monasteries were both founder houses and daughter houses simultaneously, this made for a pyramidal yet highly fluid form of control, with abbots at once inspecting other houses and reporting on the affairs of their own house to a higher authority. General chapters of the order, usually held once every three years, brought all abbots together in conference, usually at one of the original founder houses such as Clairvaux.

The resulting organization was both flexible and easy to control, and an ideal vehicle for entrepreneurship. In order to make the order independent, Bernard's strategy was to colonize waste lands such as forests, moors and swamps and make them productive. This strategy was highly successful. For example, one monastery in The Netherlands cleared and drained 25,000 acres of swamp in a few years, turning it into one of the richest farms in the region. The larger monasteries divided their lands into production units known as granges, and often these granges specialized in particular products, such as wine-making, fruit-growing, iron-mining, coal-mining or even banking. There was considerable internal trade between monasteries with specialist granges.

The medieval corporation *par excellence*, the Cistercians used their organizational assets both for religious purposes and to develop what was in effect a diversified multinational corporation. So widely recognized was the administrative skill of the Cistercians that their abbots were often called in as advisers or consultants to governments on special works projects or new taxes.

BIBLIOGRAPHY

Evans, G.R. (2000) *Bernard of Clairvaux*, Oxford: Oxford University Press.

Murphy, S. (1998) 'Bernard of Clairvaux', in E. Craig (ed.), *Routledge Encyclopedia of Philosophy*, London: Routledge, vol. 1, 753–4.

Witzel, M. (1998) 'God's Entrepreneurs', *Financial Times Mastering Management Review* 18: 16–19.

MLW

BERNARDINO OF SIENA (1380–1444)

San Bernardino of Siena was born Bernardino degli Albizzeschi on 8 September 1380 in Massa Maritima, Italy, the son of the Sienese governor of the town. He died at Aquila on 20 May 1444, probably of exhaustion brought on by overwork. Orphaned at an early age, he was attracted to the religious life and joined the order of the Observant Friars in 1403. From 1417 on he attracted increasing fame as a preacher, travelling throughout Northern Italy and drawing large crowds. In 1433 he was appointed Vicar-General of the Observant Friars, but continued his preaching tours whenever his official duties allowed. It was while on one such tour that he died. Bernardino was canonized just six years after his death. A preacher and theologian of only moderate importance, Bernardino attracted much attention in the twentieth century for his views on economics.

Bernardino's economic thought is to be found in a series of fourteen sermons, *De contractibus et usuris* (On Contracts and Usury), themselves part of a larger series of sermons, *De evangelio aeterno* (Concerning the Eternal Gospel). Bernardino did not publish the sermons himself; rather, the texts were taken down verbatim by a devoted follower in his audience (the faithfulness with which the texts reproduce Bernardino's words can be judged from the frequent inclusion of asides such as injunctions to children to stop making noise, or requests to chase away stray dogs).

In economics, Bernardino was a follower of AQUINAS, and he developed more fully many of the latter's ideas such as that of the just price and the relationship between price and value; he also argued for the superiority of private property over that which is communally held. In his preachings on business ethics, while condemning fraud and deceitful practices, he upholds a view that trade and business are not inherently sinful, and indeed have many valuable social functions; business is a legitimate activity, especially if it benefits society as a whole. In this context he argues for what we would now call greater transparency, urging business people to keep accounts and records so that they could prove their own integrity if required.

In sermon 33, Bernardino looks at the qualities which make a good manager. Recognizing, as De Roover (1967) notes, that managers of exceptional ability are rare, he tries to define the factors that make up that ability. A good manager, Bernardino says, should have four qualities: he should be efficient, he should accept the responsibilities of his position, he should be a hard worker, and he should be willing to accept and assume risks. In terms of efficiency (*industria*), Bernardino notes that managers should be well informed about market conditions and opportunities, and attentive to detail, 'which in the conduct of business is most necessary' (quoted in De Roover 1967: 13). Bernardino's sermon 33 thus may be regarded as one of the first attempts to define managerial competence.

BIBLIOGRAPHY

De Roover, R. (1967) *San Bernardino of Siena and Sant'Antonio of Florence: The Two Great Economic Thinkers of the Middle Ages*, Boston: Baker Library, Harvard Graduate School of Business Administration.

Origo, I. (1962) *The World of San Bernardino*, London: Jonathan Cape.

Trugenburger, A.E. (1951) *San Bernardino da Siena*, Rome: Officina poligrafica laziale.

MLW

BERNERS-LEE, Tim (1955–)

Tim Berners-Lee was born in London on 8 June 1955. Raised in London in the 1960s, Berners-Lee was encouraged to think unconventionally by his parents, who met while working on the first commercially sold computer (the Ferranti Mark 1). He developed a love for electronics. He attended Emmanuel School in London from 1969 to 1973 and then Queen's College Oxford, graduating in 1976 with a BA in physics with first-class honours. He has since received a variety of honorary degrees, is an Honorary Fellow of the Institution of Electrical Engineers, and a Distinguished Fellow of the British Computer Society.

Upon graduation from Oxford, Berners-Lee was employed by Plessey Telecommunications, a major UK telecommunications equipment manufacturer, in Poole, Dorset. While employed there he worked on distributed transactions systems, message relay and bar code technologies. He joined D.G. Nash Ltd in Ferndown, Dorset in 1978, where he wrote software for intelligent printers and a multitask operating system until 1980. Following this, Berners-Lee spent a year and a half as an independent consultant. During a six-month stint at the European Particle Physics Laboratory (CERN) in Geneva, he developed a program for storing information (named Enquire, and never published) that formed the conceptual basis for the World Wide Web (WWW).

From 1981 to 1984 Berners-Lee worked on the technical design of graphics and communications software, and a generic macro language. In 1984 he took up a fellowship at

CERN and worked on real-time systems for scientific data acquisition and system control. In 1989 he proposed a global hypertext project based on his earlier Enquire program, and work began in October 1990. This resulted in the development of three standards for weaving documents into the WWW: uniform resource locators (URLs), hypertext markup language (HTML) and hypertext transfer protocol (HTTP). This technology became available on the Internet in the summer of 1991. Berners-Lee continued to refine the design of the WWW through 1991–3 at CERN.

In 1994 he joined the Laboratory for Computer Science at the Massachusetts Institute of Technology (MIT) to direct the World Wide Web Consortium (W3C), which was designed to coordinate WWW development worldwide. He is presently director of W3C, and became the first holder of the 3Com Founders chair at MIT in 1999. His book, *Weaving the Web*, written with Mark Fischetti and published in the autumn of 1999, tells his story of the creation of the WWW and outlines his philosophy of an open-access, self-policing Web. It also deals with issues such as privacy, censorship, influence of software companies and his vision of where the Web is headed.

Unlike many of his contemporaries, Berners-Lee has not become wealthy from the new technology. He believes that proprietary control of the Web would have prevented its success. 'People only committed their time to it because they knew it was open, shared: that they could decide what happened to it next ... and I wouldn't be raking off 10 per cent!', he said in a *Time* interview (1999) He has received numerous awards for his work from the scientific, communication, computer and technology communities, along with an OBE (2000).

Eric Schmidt, CEO of Novell, has called Berners-Lee 'the unsung hero of the Internet'. He continued, referring to computer networking, 'If this were a traditional science, Berners-Lee would win a Nobel Prize. What he's done is that significant' (quoted in Lohr 1995). In 1999 *Time* listed him as one of the 100 most influential minds of the twentieth century. Berners-Lee's achievement ranks as one of the great technological advances which have profoundly affected management, along with earlier achievements such as the computer, the telegraph, electricity, the factory system and printing. Although he is not himself a business manager as such, his influence on the modern shape of management – through both his technology and his philosophy of its use – has been profound.

BIBLIOGRAPHY

Anon. (2000) 'Longer Biography', http://www.w3.org/People/Berners-Lee/Longer.html, 5 March 2001.

Berners-Lee, T. and Fischetti, M. (1999) *Weaving the Web*, San Francisco: Harper San Francisco.

Lohr, S. (1995) 'His Goal: Keeping the Web Worldwide', *New York Times Business Day*, 18 December, http://www.w3.org/People/Berners-Lee/951217-NYT/951217-NYT-1.gif, 5 March 2001.

Time (1999) 'Interview with Tim-Berners Lee', 29 September, *Time Magazine Transcripts*, http://www.time.com/time/community/transcripts/1999/092999berners-lee.html, 5 March 2001.

JW

BIRLA, Ghanshyam Das (1894–1983)

Ghanshyam Das Birla was born in Pilani, Rajasthan, India on 10 April 1894 and died in London on 11 June 1983. Starting his business career as a jute broker at the age of sixteen, Birla migrated from the deserts of Rajasthan to a rented room in Calcutta with one of his three brothers. Sleeping, cooking and washing were all done in that one room. This was in 1910; by

1939 Birla Brothers were India's thirteenth largest business group. The Tatas, headed by J.R.D. TATA, were the largest; the firms in between were mostly British.

Birla's s energy and long business career made a mark on the era he lived in, and his personal interests led to four areas of achievement. A close friend of M.K. GANDHI, Birla played both a financial and a political role in the Freedom Movement, which won independence for India from the British Raj in 1947. Birla also created from scratch India's second largest business conglomerate (after the Tatas). An economic nationalist who believed in the power of corporate unity, he established several trade and industry lobby groups, most notably the Federation of Indian Chambers of Commerce and Industry (FICCI). Finally, he was a philanthropist on a vast scale: the Birlas built temples, hospitals, schools and colleges all over the country.

Birla's story is interesting, not just because of the money he made, but also because of *how* he made it. He preferred to buy technology than enter into partnerships. His companies were generally greenfield projects, and he often pioneered particular business sectors in India. To build a jute mill, he had to break the stranglehold that British – mainly Scottish – businessmen had on this industry. To build Hindalco, one of India's largest aluminium companies, he had to hack his way through jungles, real and bureaucratic. His empire-building spree preceded licensing. Prime Minister Indira Gandhi's administration introduced the Monopolies and Restrictive Trade Practices Commission in 1964, but the draconian 'License-Permit Raj' flourished mainly in the 1970s and 1980s. Thus during the most aggressive period of Birla's growth, he had no power to block others, no licence to print money as has been imputed to him. During the British Raj he competed with multinationals in a colonial environment where his biggest competitors were on clubbing terms with the ruling elite; after independence, not only was he strait-jacketed by licensing like everyone else,

but he also had to contend with the active hostility of the Nehru–Gandhi dynasty which launched several tax investigations into the source of Birla wealth.

A letter to the prime minister's office, dated 20 April 1953, reveals the frustrations Birla faced:

> We have received proposals from Britain for manufacturing explosive substances and from Germany for starting a steel factory in collaboration. I am now sixty and am least interested in starting some new business merely for more money. My only interest is greater production in the country. I just want to know whether I can proceed in the matter. I want no commitment from the Government but only want to know the policy of the Government in such matters. (Quoted in Piramal 1998: 124)

There was no reply from prime minister Jawaharlal Nehru, Indira Gandhi's father.

Birla was as much associated with industry as with the freedom movement and philanthropy. Mahatma Gandhi considered him both a friend and a counsellor. Birla preferred to describe himself as an 'unofficial emissary and honest interpreter' between Gandhi and the British. It was from Birla's Bombay house that Gandhi launched the 'Quit India' Movement; and it was in the garden of Birla's Delhi house that Gandhi was assassinated.

His formal education had ended when he was about ten, although a tutor was later hired to teach him the rudimentary elements of bookkeeping and enough English to read and write telegrams. Later in life, Birla persuaded the Massachusetts Institute of Technology to help him build the Birla Institute of Technology and Science (BITS) at Pilani, now one of India's finest education complexes. In one year Birla opened 400 schools, generally offering free or heavily subsidized primary education. He taught himself to read, think and write on religion, medicine, history and current affairs, English and Indian literature, as

well as most aspects of India's economic problems.

But what kind of management thinker was Birla? Three characteristics made him possibly India's most outstanding business leader. He was a rebel; he had a modern mind; and he could happily accept opposites at the same time. To be a rebel requires an enormous commitment to untested values. To have a modern mind requires tremendous moral courage. And the ability to marry opposites requires humanity and tolerance for the weaknesses of others.

Birla was a man of strange contrasts. One of his favourite sayings was 'money is easy to make but difficult to spend properly'. The motto, not very tactfully, decorates many Birla factories and offices. The founder of BITS Pilani did not believe in formal degrees: none of his sons were graduates, and he favoured pedigree over merit certificates while recruiting. In business, Birla disliked speculation, although the family fortune had been built on it. The Birlas were devoid of a political tradition, but Birla plunged into the national movement with complete abandon. The unresolved conflict between his pragmatism and morality was but one the many contradictions in his character. Birla did not think twice before saying: 'My grandsons disagree with me but I think caste is what holds this country together. Abolish caste and India is in trouble' (Jack 1983: 14). Could this be the same man who so staunchly supported Gandhi's Harijan (Untouchables) campaign and was even president of the Harijan Sevak Sangh (Society to Help Untouchables)?

Birla's business approach was equally eclectic. A distinctly autocratic manager, he relied on his 'monkey brigade' (this was the name he gave his sons, grandsons, nephews and assorted family members in the firm) who not only followed what he started but showed considerable initiative of their own. Above them was Birla's small but tough core team of intensely loyal executives who shared his values, values which favoured profit over the customer. Loyalty was not one-sided. In 1930 Birla silently bore a Rs7.5 million loss caused by a manager in a hessian deal. 'This brought Birla Brothers to the brink of disaster but GD's support to him remained unaffected,' recalled a peer (Piramal 1998: 141).

Another trait was his vigorous optimism. For example, after the war with Pakistan which followed close on the heels of the humiliation by China (1962), many Indians were feeling gloomy. Birla, on the contrary, told the *New York Times* that: 'India had emerged as a nation with self-confidence, solidarity, conscious of a new destiny and also the will to chart a new course on broader horizons' (Birla Group 1984: 140).

In his youth, a rebellious Birla overthrew many caste conventions. He refused to do *priaischit* (penance) on returning from an overseas trip. He split the Marwari clan over marriage traditions. However, his attitude to women remained conservative to the end. He provoked men's emancipation in Marwari society but not women's. Something of a dandy, he loved good clothes and fine furniture, but his personal needs were austere and spartan and became more so with age. Some say he did not know how to enjoy the pleasure of life. He himself felt that Hinduism provided him with all he needed. The opening sentence of his autobiography, *In the Shadow of the Mahatma*, is illuminating: 'This is a book about the importance of knowing people, about the value of personal contact.' Birla had few illusions about people: 'Contact reveals truth and sometimes even unpleasant truths, but in the main the good we discover in others by knowing them better far outweighs the evil as my story shows' (Birla 1953: 1).

Wealth can attract envy, not necessarily admiration, and India is not a society that admires success, especially business success. Hinduism exhorts one not to work for the fruit of one's labour. Islam disapproves of the giving and receiving of interest. But a passion for work made Birla a rich and powerful man. Consequently, he evoked admiration, but in a

somewhat reluctant, slightly resentful way. As one of Birla's many biographers has said: 'Capitalists on so grand and unrepentant a scale tend to be regarded with suspicion in an ostensibly socialist society' (Ross 1986: 14).

BIBLIOGRAPHY

Birla, B.K. (1994) *A Rare Legacy*, Bombay (originally published in Hindi as *Swantah Sukhaya*).

Birla, G.D. (1953) *In the Shadow of the Mahatma*, London: Longmans.

—— (1956) *Atulanada Chatterjee*, Calcutta.

—— (1977) *Bapu – A Unique Association*, 4 vols, Bombay.

—— (1981) *India's March Towards Freedom 1935–1947*, New Delhi.

Birla, K.K. (1987) *Indira Gandhi: Reminiscences*, New Delhi.

Birla Group (1983a) *The Path to Prosperity: A Collection of Speeches and Writings of GD Birla*, Bombay.

—— (1983b) *Words to Remember*, Bombay.

—— (1984) *The Glorious 90 Years*, Bombay.

Burman, D. (1957a) *The Mystery of Birla House*, Calcutta.

—— (1957b) *TTK and Birla House*, Calcutta.

Jack, I. (1983) 'The King is Dead', *Sunday*, 26 June: 14–27.

Jaju, R.N. (1985) *G.D. Birla: A Biography*, New Delhi.

Piramal, G. (1998) *Business Legends*, New Delhi: Viking.

Ross, A. (1986) *The Emissary: GD Birla, Gandhi and Independence*, London: Collins Harvill.

Timberg, T.A. (1978) *The Marwaris: From Traders to Industrialists*, New Delhi: Vikas.

GP

BOEING, William Edward (1881–1956)

William Edward Boeing was born in Detroit, Michigan on 1 October 1881 and died in Puget Sound on his yacht on 28 September 1956. His German immigrant father died in 1890, and Boeing was raised by his Austrian-born mother. After attending private schools in both the United States and Switzerland, he studied engineering at Yale University, from whence he graduated in 1904. Aviation was the furthest thing from Boeing's mind in 1903 and 1904 when Wilbur and Orville Wright were creating the first aeroplane. He wanted to be a lumber manager, and, relocating to the state of Washington in 1904, built up one of the most successful lumber businesses in the state.

Boeing's life and that of Seattle and the United States changed forever when, on 4 July 1914, he flew for the first time as a passenger in a Curtiss seaplane. He instantly fell in love with aircraft. By 1915 the thirty-four year old Boeing was not only taking flying lessons but had set up a partnership with fellow engineer, Conrad Westervelt, to build his own seaplane. He set up a small hangar in Seattle, and in 1916 the B&W flying boat made its maiden voyage. Westervelt soon dissolved the partnership, but not before telling Boeing that the US Navy might be interested in his plane.

In November 1916 Boeing set up the Boeing Airplane Company, which during 1917 and 1918 laboured to fill an order for twenty-five Curtiss seaplanes. Military contracts would be the lifeblood of Boeing for many years, even though Boeing's real love was commercial aviation. In 1926 he lamented, 'Can't we build anything but warplanes?' (Ingells 1970: 28). The firm almost went bankrupt in 1919 but was saved by some new government contracts. One of the planes Boeing created was a large multi-engined triplane called the Ground Attack Experimental. Commercial aviation in the meantime was coming into its own, and Boeing was determined to help shape it. When the Post Office began airmail deliveries between Seattle and Vancouver, British

Columbia on 27 December 1919, Boeing's B-1 seaplane, his first commercial aeroplane, made the deliveries.

In the early 1920s the United States led in neither military nor commercial aviation. American pilots in the First World War had flown French Spads. American aviation finally found an ally in President Calvin Coolidge (1923–9). Under Coolidge's administration the Army Air Corps was created, and the Air Mail and Air Commerce Acts were passed in 1925 and 1926. The Federal government's desire to stimulate commercial and military aviation created a windfall market for Boeing aircraft.

Boeing employed some 500 workers in 1926. Even then he had a vision of an airline and airmail industry that would rival both the railroads and the rising power of the automobile. The government in 1926 was beginning to privatize airmail services, and Boeing won the contract for the Illinois to California route. The Boeing 40 and the Boeing 40A were light and powerful enough to carry half a ton of mail and two passengers between Chicago and San Francisco for a cost lower than that of any competitor.

However, even before Charles A. Lindbergh's flight from New York to Paris in May 1927 created an aviation mania, Boeing was already facing stiff competition from Henry FORD (Ingells 1970). Ford Trimotors were already flying between Detroit, Chicago and Cleveland, and Ford had even built his own terminals. Boeing, in response, also began to internalize his operation. He formed, with his engine supplier Pratt and Whitney and Hamilton Propellor, the United Aircraft and Transportation Corporation. United bought the planes Boeing made. The new combined firm lasted for five years, and acquired routes from Seattle to Chicago and down the west coast to San Diego, as well as from Chicago to Fort Worth and to New York. Competition with Ford's airline, the ancestor of Trans World Airlines (TWA), which flew from New York to Los Angeles,

spurred Boeing to develop even more advanced planes such as the Boeing 80A, which carried eighteen passengers.

Boeing's efforts to remain on the leading edge of aviation technology and to control commercial aviation allowed his company to weather the Great Depression. Boeing had a brand name, long experience and financial stability. There were few Boeing layoffs during the 1930s. In the meantime, competition from Ford and Martin drove Boeing into revolutionary designs that eventually helped make the United States second to none in both civilian and military aviation. The wooden biplanes of the 1920s were now replaced by steel monoplanes. Boeing's major coup in aviation was the Boeing 247. First flying in 1933, the sleek, twin-engine 247 was the forerunner of all modern bombers and airliners. It was all metal, had retractable landing gear and trim tab elevators, and obliterated all competition until Douglas Aircraft countered with the famous DC-3 (Ingells 1970).

Boeing's 247 was the prototype for even bigger planes such as the 299, which eventually became the famous B-17 Flying Fortress four-engine bomber. The Seattle firm began to expand once again in 1936 as Hitler's new Luftwaffe presented a formidable challenge. Boeing had almost 3,000 employees in 1938, and almost 29,000 on the eve of Pearl Harbor in 1941. The B-17 became Boeing's first principal contribution to victory. The aeroplane was mass produced by the thousands by Ford and other plants as well as by Boeing, and was deeply loved by the bomber pilots who flew it. It was sturdy and dependable: B-17s would return home from daylight bombing raids over Germany sometimes with a rudder or elevator missing, or three engines crippled, but still flying. The Flying Fortress was too short-range for the Pacific war, but by 1944 the faster and longer-range Boeing B-29 Superfortress was bombing the Japanese home islands from the Marianas, ultimately dropping the two atomic bombs.

After the war, Boeing had a much more difficult time than, for example, General Motors, in reconverting to a peace-time economy. It tried to diversify into consumer goods, but with little success. The intensification of the Cold War, however, sustained the firm. The B-47 Stratojet, produced in the hundreds, became the backbone of the American nuclear deterrent in the early 1950s. By 1956 the giant B-52 Stratofortress, still in service after forty years, had begun to replace the Stratojet.

Boeing had retired from active participation in his firm in 1933. He did not live to see the success of his greatest product, his airliners. The Boeing 707 went into service at the end of the decade, and the company sold hundreds not only to American carriers but to most international airlines as well. The same success was repeated later in 1970 with the giant 'jumbo' 747, which had a B-52's intercontinental range and could carry around 500 passengers. The 727, which could fly from smaller airports, opened even small cities to the global economy of jet travel. Since the 1970s Boeing's jets have dominated the market for global air travel, although by the 1990s European Airbus Industries, subsidized in part by European governments, was cutting into the Boeing market.

Boeing created an innovative, internalized enterprise that went on to dominate much of world aviation. He was the most successful aircraft-maker in history: his bombers helped to win the Second World War and wage the Cold War, and his company's airliners have helped create the global economy.

BIBLIOGRAPHY

Ingells, D.J. (1970) 747: Story of the Boeing Super Jet, Fallbrook, CA: Aero Publishing.

DCL

BOISOT, Max Henri (1943–)

Max Henri Boisot was born on 11 November 1943. He trained as an architect, first at Cambridge, where he took a BA (1966) and diploma (1968) in architecture, and then at the Massachusetts Institute of Technology where he took a master's degree in city planning and also a master's in management in 1971. Later qualifications include a Ph.D. from the Imperial College of Science and Technology in London. After working as a manager with a subsidiary of the Trafalgar House corporation in London, he co-founded the architectural and planning partnership Boisot Waters Cohen in London in 1972. From 1975 to 1978 he was a consultant on building and architectural projects in France and the Middle East. His move into management studies came in 1979, when he joined the Euro-Asia Centre at INSEAD, where he remained for two years. From 1981 to 1986 he was associate professor at the École Supériéure de Commerce de Paris, teaching international business, business policy and organizational theory.

Boisot's time with the Euro-Asia Centre helped reinforce his interest in managing across cultures. He was one of the prime movers behind the China–EC Management Programme, the first MBA programme to be run in the People's Republic of China, and from 1984 to 1989 was dean and director of the programme in Beijing. The programme has today evolved into the China–Europe International Business School (CEIBS) in Shanghai, where Boisot remains a visiting professor. In 1994 he also set up the Euro–Arab Management School in Granada, Spain, for the European Commission. He is currently professor of strategic management at ESADE at Barcelona, and has links with many other universities around the world. He is widely known as a consultant to businesses and organizations such as the World Bank and the European Commission. In 2000 Boisot was the winner of the Igor Ansoff Strategic Management Award.

As well as his pivotal role in introducing Western-style management education into China following the economic reforms begun by DENG Xiaopeng, Boisot has also written extensively on organizations and culture, especially on the circulation of information and knowledge inside organizations. His first major work, *Information and Organizations* (1987), introduced a number of innovative ideas. In the opening chapters of the book, Boisot argues for a cultural approach to the study and science of organization, on the grounds that organizations are made up of people who are in effect cultural beings and who do not react as deterministic theories of management say they should:

> Industrial management, until a decade or so ago, fancied itself to be a pretty scientific business, proceeding with a ruthless determination down the probabilistic branches of decision trees only to find monkeys masquerading as workers, sitting on the extremities and thumbing their noses at them. The 'expected values' that were lying at the ends of the branches were not those of management science; they were those of disgruntled, refractory blue collar workers waiting in ambush.
>
> (Boisot 1987: 14)

Culture, says Boisot, is not a superficial set of similar and/or different features – it goes to the heart of how organizations function. Nowhere is this more evident than in the ways in which different cultures structure and share information. Using the techniques of anthropology – themselves a novelty in management studies at the time – and his own widespread experience of working in different cultures, Boisot developed the theory of 'culture space' or C-space, within which knowledge management takes place. Knowledge itself can be classified along two dimensions: codification and diffusion. On the codification dimension, *codified* knowledge is that which can be easily set out and transmitted, while *uncodified* knowledge

is more implicit and difficult to transmit. *Diffused* knowledge is knowledge that is readily shared, and *undiffused* knowledge is knowledge that is not readily shared. Using these two dimensions, then, Boisot develops a fourfold typology of knowledge:

1. Proprietary knowledge (codified but undiffused).

2. Personal knowledge (uncodified and undiffused).

3. Public knowledge (codified and diffused).

4. Common sense (uncodified and diffused).

Boisot also develops a set of four types of organizational culture, each of which relates to one of the types of knowledge above. Cultures in which public knowledge predominates he describes as *markets* where knowledge has some attributes of a commodity, and is easily exchanged and shared. Cultures in which proprietary knowledge predominates he describes as *bureaucracies*; here knowledge is codified and formalized but is not readily shared. Cultures in which personal knowledge predominates are called *fiefs*; here knowledge tends to be both implicit and not readily shared, with knowledge transmission governed closely by those who possess it. In the fourth type, *clans*, knowledge is uncodified but tends to be more readily shared through common values and attributes.

This relatively simple model is capable of great elaboration, and Boisot goes on to show that it can be used to understand not only the transmission and use of knowledge within and between organizations, but also how guardians of knowledge use their control to maintain their own power. He has continued to develop these concepts and themes in his later work, notably *Information Space* (1995) and *Knowledge Assets* (1998). Boisot's application of anthropological and cultural principles to the understanding of

knowledge was far ahead of its time in the 1980s; although it aroused only moderate interest when it first appeared, *Information and Organizations* can now be regarded as one of the most important management books of the 1980s. Boisot's work later came to the attention of writers on information and knowledge management, and he is now regularly cited as one of the pioneers of the field.

BIBLIOGRAPHY

Boisot, M. (1987) *Information and Organizations: The Manager as Anthropologist*, London: Fontana.

—— (ed.) (1994) *East-West Business Collaboration: The Challenge of Governance in Post-socialist Enterprises*, London: Routledge.

—— (1995) *Information Space: A Framework for Learning in Organizations, Institutions and Culture*, London: Routledge.

—— (1998) *Knowledge Assets: Securing Competitive Advantage in the Information Economy*, Oxford: Oxford University Press.

MLW

BOOT, Jesse (1850–1931)

Jesse Boot was born in Nottingham on 2 June 1850 and died in Jersey on 13 June 1931. He was the only son of a Wesleyan preacher and herbalist, John Boot. After his father died, the ten-year-old Jesse worked to support his mother and sister. Too poor to produce his own lines, from 1874 Boot began to sell cut-price patent medicines, establishing a formula of bulk purchasing to reduce resale prices which he used throughout his career with great success. He built up a chain of retail chemists, gradually expanding beyond Nottingham. He spent more than two decades working punishingly long hours: 'My health suffered so much ... that at thirty-six anybody could have had my business very cheap' (Weir 1994: 31). In 1886 he suffered a breakdown which forced him to take a holiday; while on Jersey, he met his future wife, Florence Anne Rowe, in a small bookshop.

By the early 1890s Boot was fighting exhausting battles with rival retail chains based in Bristol, Leeds, London and Plymouth. He formed a partnership with James Duckworth, who ran a chain of grocery shops in Lancashire and acquired Day's chain in the south-east of England in 1901. Thereafter expansion was rapid. From thirty-three shops in 1893, Boot's and Company had expanded to more than 560 shops by 1914 and was the largest retail chain in the world.

Lacking confidence in his son, Boot continued working despite crippling arthritis (he had to be carried everywhere), before finally selling the firm for more than £2 million to Louis K. Liggett's Rexall group in the United States. He then retired to Jersey and the South of France. Fearing the effects of his wife's expensive tastes on his hard-earned fortune, Boot became a generous benefactor, providing municipal parks and hospitals, and funding the rebuilding of University College, Nottingham (from abroad, he supervised details down to the location of the flowerbeds). His generosity to the Liberal Party had already secured Boot a knighthood (1909) and baronetcy (1916), and in 1928 he was rewarded with the title First Lord Trent of Nottingham.

In 1877 Boot had gained the financial support of local businessmen for a series of advertisements in the *Nottingham Daily Express*: as a result, his profits grew from £20 to £100 a week. As his business grew, Boot set up departments dedicated to shop displays and packaging, and conducted national advertising campaigns that claimed: 'Largest, Best & Cheapest – Branches Everywhere' (Weir 1994: 35). His commitment to inventive branding and

marketing was typified by the flagship department store built in the fashionable Gothic style in Nottingham in 1903; his wife Florence was responsible for its interior decoration. Florence also took a personal interest in the welfare of 'her girls' working in Boot's shops and warehouses, and established Boots 'No. 2 Department' for stationery, books and other 'fancy goods'. Boot pursued creative diversification while continually strengthening his proprietary lines (he began large-scale chemical manufacturing during the First World War).

Boot made two significant contributions to pharmaceutical retailing. First, his legal skirmishes resulted in a House of Lords decision to allow qualified pharmacists to work for limited companies. Thus Boot was able to sell prescription drugs from his stores and, more importantly, employ well-qualified managers to run his branches. Second, the need to finance his company's extraordinary expansion meant Boot had to introduce innovative means of share distribution. Rather than quote shares on the stock exchange, they were sold in Boot's high-street shops, with his managers earning commission on the sales. This measure was a great success: initially financed by Nottingham professionals and businessmen, Boot's and Company was soon mostly financed by customer shareholders.

BIBLIOGRAPHY

Boots Web site (2000) http://www. boots.co.uk, 15 May 2001.

Chapman, S.D. (1974) *Jesse Boot of Boots the Chemists*, London: Hodder and Stoughton.

────── (1984) 'Jesse Boot', in D.J. Jeremy (ed.), *Dictionary of Business Biography*, London: Butterworths, vol. 1, 374–7.

Jeremy, D.J. (1998) *A Business History of Britain, 1900–1990s*, Oxford and New York: Oxford University Press.

Weir, C. (1994) *Jesse Boot of Nottingham*, Nottingham: The Boots Company.

SC

BOOZ, Edwin George (1887–1951)

Edwin George Booz was born in Reading, Pennsylvania on 2 September 1887, the son of Thomas and Sarah Booz. He died in Chicago on 14 October 1951. He married Helen Hootman in 1918, and they had two children. He attended Northwestern University, taking an AB in 1912 and an AM in 1914. In the latter year he also set up his own consultancy business, Edwin G. Booz Engineering Surveys. Like most of the early consultants, Booz called himself an 'efficiency expert' (the term 'management consultant' is of later origin), but the services he offered were wide-ranging. Like Arthur D. LITTLE, who had established his consultancy business in 1905, Booz was usually called in to solve specific technical problems, but often found that the demand for his services quickly widened as the solution to each problem uncovered other problems further along the line. Booz's firm offered advice on everything from plant location to marketing strategy. Not a functional expert himself (indeed, Booz, only twenty-seven when he went into the business, had little practical business experience), he based his advice on common sense and good judgement, qualities which he found lacking in many business leaders: famously, he once told one company president that the only thing wrong with his company was the man in charge.

Booz was a considerable success as a consultant, and his reputation grew. He served in the US Army 1917–18, finishing as a major on the staff of the Inspector General, with special responsibility for business organization. After the war his business grew rapidly. Booz hired technical experts in a variety of fields, many of them trained at Northwestern or the University of Chicago, which he used as his talent pool in much the same way that Little recruited from the Massachusetts Institute of Technology. The firm expanded to include offices in New York, Minneapolis and Los Angeles. Clients included Montgomery Ward, Western Union, RCA, Columbia Pictures and Sperry Corp.

The Second World War also brought a great boost to the business, as companies involved in war work sought to increase production capacity rapidly; Booz and his team did much to ensure that such teams grew without sacrificing efficiency. The business survives today as Booz, Allen and Hamilton, one of the largest and most prestigious management consultancies in the world.

BOSCH, Robert (1861–1942)

Robert Bosch was born in the village of Albeck in Swabia, Germany on 23 September 1861, the son of Servatius Bosch, a farmer, and his wife Maria. He died in Stuttgart, Germany on 12 March 1942. Educated in Ulm, Bosch apprenticed as a mechanical engineer and then took a number of different jobs in the towns and cities of south Germany, all the while enhancing his knowledge of his profession. He also learned some accounting skills, and briefly attended Stuttgart Technical University. In 1884 he went to the United States, where he learned electrical engineering in the workshops of Thomas EDISON. Returning to Germany, he used his savings and an inheritance from his father to set up a workshop in Stuttgart, where he repaired machines and also designed and patented a magneto ignition system for use with internal combustion engines. The device was first used with stationary engines, but was demonstrated for use in a motor vehicle for the first time in 1897 and was adopted by the carmaker Daimler in 1902. By 1910 Bosch was exporting magnetos to Britain and the United States, and his system was used by almost every car-maker in the world. The export market was closed during the First World War, but in the 1920s Bosch reemerged on the international scene as a designer and major competitor in automobile components ranging from fuel pumps to windshield wipers. The

company also diversified into areas such as refrigerators.

Bosch was a progressive employer, so much so that other industrialists nicknamed him 'Red Bosch'. He introduced an eight-hour working day in 1906, paid high wages and introduced a holiday pay scheme. His policy was one of enlightened self-interest: he believed that high wages led to high profits, not the other way around. He encouraged research and development both within the firm and in society generally, and as a philanthropist he funded research in many fields of science and medicine as well as in educational institutions. He believed strongly in international peace and cooperation, and the rise of the Nazis and the outbreak of the Second World War were a bitter disappointment to him. The culture of innovation and philanthropy that he instilled in his firm, Robert Bosch Gmbh, survives in large measure intact to this day.

BIBLIOGRAPHY
Heuss, T. (1987) *Robert Bosch*, Stuttgart: Deutsche Verlanganstalt.

BOUCICAUT, Aristide (1810–77)

Aristide Boucicaut was born in Bellême, Normandy and died in Paris. Little is known of his early life, but after joining his father's hat-making business and eking out a somewhat precarious business selling hats in the market towns and fairs of Normandy, at the age of twenty-five Boucicaut decided to seek his fortune in Paris. Here he found a job as a clerk in a clothing and drapery business, and soon rose to a management position. Around this time Boucicaut met and married Marguerite Guerin, who later became his business partner.

In 1848, with capital provided by a friendly backer, the Boucicauts opened their own

drapery shop; by 1852 the shop was profitable enough that they were able to buy out their backer. The shop, Au Bon Marché, became one of the most fashionable in Paris, and the Boucicauts began to introduce the marketing innovations that would make them famous: a welcoming atmosphere where customers were encouraged to browse and try goods they liked, fixed prices and a fair pricing policy with low margins, and a diverse range of goods. Au Bon Marché also introduced quality guarantees with money back for defective goods, home delivery and mail order. By the late 1850s the premises had expanded, and the shop had gone from being a high-class drapers to the world's first true department store. In 1872 Au Bon Marché closed its original shop and reopened in new, still larger premises. Even this building proved insufficient, and a further expansion was added in 1876; one of the architects of the new wing was Gustave Eiffel, who built in a highly modern style using steel and glass. The store became the wonder of Paris and attracted tourists from all around the continent; it also inspired imitators, both in Paris and in other major cities in Europe and the United States.

After Aristide Boucicaut's death in 1877, Marguerite Boucicaut ran the business for a further ten years and oversaw more expansion and further development of the company's offering. Au Bon Marché was widely used as a model for other ventures, and Marguerite Boucicaut's acumen was spoken of with respect by other department store magnates such as John WANAMAKER.

BOULDING, Elise (1920–)

Elise Boulding was born Elise Bjorn-Hansen in Oslo on 6 July 1920, daughter of Joseph Bjorn-Hansen, an engineer, and his wife Birgit. She received her BA in English from Douglass College in 1940 and married Kenneth Boulding, the noted economist, in the following year. She took an MS in sociology from Iowa State University in 1949, and a Ph.D. from the University of Michigan in 1969. She began her academic career in 1967, when she joined the sociology faculty of the University of Colorado at Boulder, where she became professor of sociology in 1971. She moved to become professor and chair at Dartmouth College, New Hampshire in 1978. Since 1985 she has been professor emerita of sociology at Dartmouth College.

Along with her husband Kenneth Boulding, she was among the founders of the field of peace and conflict research, and was a prolific author and activist on the subject. She further contributed to the development of the field through the many positions she held in influential organizations. Notable among these were the International Peace Research Association, where she served as secretary-general and foundation president; the Women's International League for Peace and Freedom, which she chaired from 1967 to 1970; and many others, including the Project on Conditions for a Just World Peace and the National Academy of Peace and Conflict Resolution. Boulding received many awards for her work towards a just peace, and continued to write well into her seventies. In 1990 she was nominated for the Nobel Peace Prize.

The breadth of Boulding's work is significant, and ranges from transnational and comparative cross-national studies on conflict and peace to social development, world order, women in society and futures studies. She did much pioneering work with the United Nations University on its Human and Social Development program and the Household, Gender and Age project (see MASINI). The major themes of her work were the idea of the world as a dynamic, evolutionary, complex and diverse system, and the idea of how powerfully human visioning of the 'totally other' (radically different) can transform that system.

Boulding's work in futures studies began in

1961 when she translated Fred Polak's classic text *The Image of the Future* (1953) from the Dutch. She developed Polak's concept of images of the future and brought it into the mainstream of futures thinking, demonstrating how it could become the centrepiece of practical future-oriented action. She wrote a number of futures works including *The Social System of the Planet Earth* (1980), *The Future: Images and Processes* (1995), both with Kenneth Boulding, and *Building a Global Civic Culture* (1988). This last explores a number of important conceptual, organizational and human innovations for a more just and sustainable future. As Slaughter (1996) describes, the book also considers problems of knowledge in high-technology cultures, and how to recover a broader range of ways of knowing.

The mother of five children and with grandchildren, Boulding believed strongly in the value and role of the family in society, and she chaired the Parenting Center in Boulder, Colorado in the late 1980s. Her Quaker beliefs are evident throughout her writings, most obviously in *One Small Plot of Heaven: Reflections of a Quaker Sociologist on Family Life* (1989). These beliefs not only provided her with a strong foundational philosophy for her work in peace and conflict research, but were the basis for her pioneering contribution to the ethics of futures studies. She wrote a number of works addressing what she saw as neglected sectors of society, namely women and children. Amongst the most important of these are the *Handbook on International Data on Women* (1979b), *The Underside of History: A View of Women through Time* (1976) and *Women in the Twentieth Century World* (1977). She worked to bring women's issues to the fore in the work of various United Nations University programmes. She was engaged in work to establish the rights of children and the elderly, culminating in her book *Children's Rights and the Wheel of Life* (1979a), which reviews the lack of rights given to children until the age of twenty-one. In

reviewing the age classifications and associated legal frameworks imposed in our society, she has been the forerunner of current societal debates about the age of responsibility and maturity with regard to serious crime, sexual consent and consent for medical treatment amongst children.

Boulding was concerned with increasing women's participation in policy and decision making. She notes that 'most female experience with participation in mixed settings is negative when it comes to agenda-setting, policy planning and decision making', and concluded that 'the distinctive contributions of women's culture cannot be made under such circumstances' and that there should be coexisting all-women's groups in which that culture can be nurtured, buttressed by strong separatist strategies of social innovation. She claims that the significance of these separatist strategies is that they provide working models of how things could be in the future. She sums up her view of the path forward for women's involvement thus:

The trip to the 'over-side' for women has to be a shuttling back and forth between women's and mixed spaces until women are socially strong enough and organisational structures have become open enough to sustain the feminist input into public life in its economic political and cultural dimensions.

She asserts that the sectors of society best equipped to replace hierarchy with decentralist structures, based on non-hierarchical communication are the women's movements.

Boulding has spent a productive lifetime working for peace, justice and the future. She continuously challenged the status quo in society, and tackled the development of a new social order from global, ethical and gender perspectives, with practical and valuable contributions. She is also recognized for her pioneering work in the ethics of futures studies and decision making.

BIBLIOGRAPHY

Boulding, E. (1977) *Women in the*

Twentieth Century World, New York: John Wiley.

—— (1979a) *Children's Rights and the Wheel of Life*, New Brunswick, NJ: Transaction Publishing.

—— (1979b) *Handbook on International Data on Women*, London: Sage.

—— (1988) *Building a Global Civic Culture*, New York: Teachers College Press.

—— (1989) *One Small Plot of Heaven: Reflections of a Quaker Sociologist on Family Life*, Wallingford, PA: Pendle Hill Publications.

—— (1992) *The Underside of History: A View of Women through Time*, London: Sage.

Boulding, E. and Boulding, K.E. (1995) *The Future: Images and Processes*, London: Sage.

Boulding, K.E., Boulding, E. and Burgess, G.M. (1980) *The Social System of the Planet Earth*, Reading, MA: Addison-Wesley.

Slaughter, R.A. (1996) *The Foresight Principle*, Twickenham: Adamantine.

AJ

BOULTON, Matthew (1728–1809)

Matthew Boulton was born in Birmingham on 14 September 1728 and died on 17 August 1809. He studied drawing and mathematics, becoming a hardware manufacturer by developing a new method of inlaying steel. His success in selling watch-chains, buckles and other personal items allowed him to expand his business in 1762, with a highly significant investment in an expansive facility outside Birmingham called the 'Soho establishment'.

Five years later, Boulton solved a challenge to improve watermill flow by building an improved version of the existing steam engines designed by Thomas Savery and Thomas NEWCOMEN. In 1769 he formed a partnership with James WATT to leverage the importance of these new steam machines. In particular, the new technology was applied to the manufacture of coinage, and Boulton and Watt developed a considerable business in the manufacture of silver and copper coins. Their coins were exported for the Sierra Leone Company, the East India Company and to St Petersburg for the Russian government. In return for the latter sales, Boulton received valuable sums of medals and minerals from Siberia and monies from Russia.

The Soho plant also developed and patented a very high-quality process of copying oil paintings. The process involved one of the earliest uses of the Bernoulli principle, that if water flows through a pipe and arrives at a part in which the pipe is suddenly contracted, this will greatly increase the velocity of the fluid. The ingenious application of this principle did not reappear until 1792.

Boulton also showed off his skills with an early display of micro-engineering. Promising to impress a distinguished mechanical fair in France, he displayed a well-shaped needle of his own making. The common-looking needle at first impressed none of the examiners, until Boulton disassembled the needle, revealing it to be six needles in one, all beautifully made.

Boulton died at the age of eighty-one, having advanced the useful arts and promoted commerce in his country. He was buried at Handsworth, near the Soho factory, with six hundred workmen each receiving a silver medal struck to honour his life. He was credited with an amiable disposition and character, as well as the breadth of mind that allowed him to work with others and broaden the success of his work through partnerships.

BIBLIOGRAPHY
Dickinson, H.W. (1937) *Matthew Boulton*, Cambridge: Cambridge University Press.

Howe, H. (1858) *Lives of Distinguished*

European Mechanics, New York: Harper and Brothers, 327–30.

Urwick, L.F. and Brech, E.F.L. (1949) *The Making of Scientific Management*, vol. 2, *Management in British Industry*, London: Management Publications Trust; repr. Bristol: Thoemmes Press, 1994.

DD

BRACTON, Henry de (or Bratton: d. 1268)

Virtually nothing is known of Henry de Bracton's (sometimes known as Bratton) origins or education, and there is no certain date of birth available; indeed, there is some controversy regarding his place of origin and his educational background. His first appearance in the records occurs in 1245, when he was acting as an itinerant justice, and throughout the 1250s and 1260s he appears as a justice involved in a range of legal activities, from general assizes to specific inquiries into the inheritance of land. Bracton's judicial activities were frequently concerned with disputes over the ownership and inheritance of private property, a central concern of medieval justice. Just as Richard FITZ NEAL's career was primarily involved with the affairs of the exchequer, so Bracton's was almost entirely concerned with the law. In the early part of his career, many of his cases were concerned with issues in counties in the West Country (Cornwall, Devon, Dorset and Somerset), and this fits well with his biographer's opinion that he was born in Devon, as does his appointment as protector of Witham Abbey in Somerset. In the latter part of his career, Bracton was involved in cases concerning other parts of the country, most notably in 1259 in a special assize for Gloucestershire and Herefordshire. It is clear that between assizes in local areas, Bracton was resident either at Westminster or in attendance on the king's court when it was itinerant. He often appears as one of those who authorized the issue of close letters of appointment and commission. The favour of the king is shown in the grant of a property in London, as well as certain rights in Selwood forest and in the forest of Mendip.

Bracton's legal career was no more spectacular than that of many of his contemporary justices, and his reputation for later generations lies almost entirely in his authorship and compilation of a key treatise on the state of English law in the mid-thirteenth century, *De legibus et consuetudinibus Angliae*. His was not the first treatise of its type – a shorter and less comprehensive volume had been produced some eighty years before in the reign of Henry II. Bracton's treatise, however, is more complete in its treatment of all aspects of available law, and moreover was written at a time when justices and other participants in the legal world were reaching new heights of professionalism and specialization.

The treatise was partly an analysis of the precedents which underpinned English common law in the mid-thirteenth century (the treatise dates from *c*.1240), but it also importantly contains an examination of the principles which lay behind these precedents. Bracton also provides a succinct definition of the king's place in the legal structure of the country, when he states that whilst all law emanates from the crown, a king must also stand beneath God and the law. Much of the work is concerned with the conveyancing of property, by sale, inheritance and grant to the church. Bracton's description of the circumstances of property conveyance provides very early evidence of both the development of written records and of the English language when he records that in order for a conveyance to be legal an agent of a donor of land must have 'bothe writ and chartre'.

The importance and influence of Bracton's treatise can be gauged by the number and frequency of editions which were produced in

the 300 years after its creation. Copies of it were clearly used by authors of fourteenth-century legal works, and parts of it were printed in 1557, with a full printed copy being published in 1569. It was also cited in the judgement of Charles I and by Milton in his *Defence of the People of England*. Bracton himself remained a rather obscure person to the end of his life, and his date of death can only by inferred by the reallocation of his properties, which occurred in 1268. His legacy was a contribution to the professionalization of justice and of administration more widely.

BIBLIOGRAPHY

Bracton, H. de (1968) *De legibus Angliae*, ed. Samuel E. Thorne, Cambridge, MA: Selden Society and the Belknap Press of Harvard University Press.

'Bracton, Henry' (1885) in L. Stephen and S. Lee (eds), *Dictionary of National Biography*, London: Small, Elder and Co., vol. 10, 1052–5.

Clanchy, M.T. (1993) *From Memory to Written Record, England 1066–1307*, Oxford: Blackwell, 2nd edn.

ML

BRAVERMAN, Harry (1922–76)

Harry Braverman was born in Brooklyn, New York on 9 December 1922 to Polish-Jewish parents, and died there of lymphoma on 2 August 1976, at the age of just fifty-three. He attended City College, New York in 1937, but left after only one year in order to seek work. Braverman did eventually graduate some twenty-five years later, from the New School of Social Research in New York in 1963. His working life was bifurcated between several skilled manual jobs (1938–51) and white-collar employment (1951–76). He began his working life with a four-year apprenticeship (1938–42) as a coppersmith in Brooklyn naval shipyard, and he worked at this for a further three years, supervising up to twenty workers. He was then drafted into military service in 1945, when he repaired locomotives for the Union Pacific railway in Cheyenne, Wyoming. After demobilization Braverman moved to Youngstown, Ohio, where he spent seven years in steel fabrication at various trades, including pipe fitting, sheet metal work and layout, and also in two plants which fabricated heavy steel plate and structural steel into equipment for the basic steel industry, such as blast furnaces. Later he was a journalist and editor (1954–60) and entered publishing, becoming in turn editor, general manager and vice-president of Grove Press (1960–67) and director of Monthly Review Press (1967–76).

It was this working background, especially his observations on the rationalization and erosion of craft work, that created and polished the lens through which Braverman examined life and work, and forged the template for his analysis and writing. While he wrote an early book on the future of Russia and the Soviet Union and also pieces as a journalist and book reviewer, he remains best known throughout much of the world for *Labor and Monopoly Capital* (1974). This was a broad-ranging and seminal book on the labour process, which proved to be the anvil on which his reputation was forged, shaped and tempered.

A long-time Marxist and activist, Braverman joined the Socialist Workers' Party in the 1930s. He left with a group of others in 1954 and helped set up the magazine *The American Socialist*, which he also edited (1954–60). During the 1950s, in addition to his journalism, he wrote numerous book reviews and summaries for the Book Find Club. These high-quality pieces attracted the attention of the New York publisher, Grove Press, which recruited Braverman to work for it, where he displayed considerable business and management acumen. He subsequently moved to Monthly Review Press as a return to socialist

publishing, and it was here that he wrote his major work.

Braverman was never an academic as such. Indeed, he disliked what he saw as 'ivory tower' academics and those whom he labelled as not grounded in the world of work, although ironically, many academic careers were subsequently made on the bandwagon his book set in motion and the publications it engendered. Crucially, the views and themes in his famous book were driven by his particular approach, which was underpinned by his own experiences, observation and political outlook. Therefore, he theorized from his own work experience 'upwards', as he viewed the best methodology as being reflection on lived experience by the politically engaged. For Braverman, this was a far superior approach compared to what he saw as the inaccuracies of the academic and official descriptions of work. He believed that the literature on technical and management trends was based on little genuine information, and was too vague and general and full of 'egregious errors'.

Labor and Monopoly Capital was both highly influential and heavily criticized. In the wake of his book and thesis, Marxist analysis and work was revitalized and popularized (see Thompson 1989). Debate on the labour process developed, spread and lapped along many academic shores (Knights and Willmott 1990). These include the areas of history and labour economics (for example, Zimbalist 1979; Edwards 1979); industrial sociology (Littler 1982); industrial relations (Kelly 1982; Wood 1982, 1989; Edwards 1986); economics (Friedman 1977); organizational studies; economic history; and industrial geography, amongst others.

Braverman's book went on to gain an almost iconic status. It remains a classic, and for most people it is the main plank underpinning Braverman's reputation. He began the book in the late 1960s, working on it during the evenings while continuing with his 'day job'. The book's 450 pages are organized into an introduction and twenty chapters in five

parts. The first part is 'Labor and Management', with chapters on labour and labour power, the origins of management, the division of labour, scientific management, the primary effects of scientific management, and the habituation of the worker to the capitalist mode of production. Second is 'Science and Mechanization', with chapters on the scientific-technical revolution, the scientific-technical revolution and the worker, machinery, and further effects of management and technology on the distribution of labour. Third is 'Monopoly Capital', with chapters on surplus value and surplus labour, the modern corporation, the universal market and the role of the state. Fourth is 'The Growing Working-class Occupations', with chapters on clerical workers, and on service occupations and retail trade. Fifth is 'The Working Class', with chapters on the structure of the working class and its reserve armies, the 'middle layers' of employment, productive and unproductive labour, and a final note on skill.

Braverman built on MARX's writings concerning the so-called labour process. This can be seen as involving the means by which 'raw materials' and 'objects' (in manufacturing and services) were transformed by human labour into 'products' for use, and 'commodities' to be exchanged. Therefore, the core of the labour process approach rests on the belief that the capacity to work was utilized as a means of producing value (Thompson 1989). The following points are important to this. First, the capital–labour relationship was essentially exploitative as the surplus value from work activities accrued to capital. Second, the 'logic of accumulation' required capital continually to develop the production process and cheapen the costs of production. Third, continued development of the production process required the establishment and maintenance of both general and specific 'structures of control'. Fourth, the resultant 'structured antagonism' relationship included systematic attempts by capital to obtain cooperation and consent, with a continuum of worker

responses, from resistance to accommodation and compliance and consent. Thus, the problem of 'work' was about control and how managers ensured the maximum degree of effort for the minimum amount of reward. The solution was to extend the division of labour, separating the conception of work from its execution, and deskilling the work force. This would not only increase productivity and reduce labour costs, but also generate more compliant workers.

Braverman's thesis can be seen succinctly in the book's subtitle: *The Degradation of Work in the Twentieth Century*. In particular, Braverman analysed the effects of technology and scientific management on the nature of work. As we have noted, he disbelieved 'official' views in several areas, including the assertions that skills had been upgraded, that greater education time naturally meant more skilled or knowledgeable work, or that formal designations corresponded with actual skills. Rather, for Braverman, the drive for efficient production required managerial control of workers, excluding workers from control and ownership of knowledge and skills acquisition. This led to poorer quality and experience of labour. These processes applied to jobs across the employment spectrum, from manufacturing to services, and from design to clerical work. This degradation or 'deskilling' thesis suggested an underlying drive within capitalism to substitute less skilled or unskilled for skilled work.

Thus, the fundamental industrial relationship during the twentieth century was one of management exploitation and 'degradation' of labour by deskilling work, and this was through the use of Taylorism (see TAYLOR), scientific management techniques and work study to support the achievement of capital's objectives. Therefore there was the technical division of labour, involving the breaking down of tasks within former crafts at the initiative of employers in order to increase efficiency. The application of work study techniques facilitated this disintegration of work into compo-

nent tasks which could then be allocated to individuals (specialization). Management thereby cheapened the individual's input value to the production process (with tasks requiring less training, skill and responsibility), tied the individual more directly to the technical system (especially assembly lines) and made individuals or groups capable of being subjected to production output controls (such as bonus payments, quotas and so on). This thesis of Braverman's also presented management as a 'control' function. Management's basic task was to design, control and monitor work tasks and activities so as to ensure the effective extraction of surplus value from the labour activity of employees.

Further elements within the thesis concerned 'class'. There was a belief that there would develop a homogenization of socioeconomic classes; all workers would come increasingly to regard themselves as part of the 'working class' as they were subject to the same type of work controls and conditions as were manual workers. Braverman explored in depth the US class structure and its changes, which he saw as evolving from the self-employed to waged employees and a division into manufacturing and services and occupations engaged in jobs officially designated as skilled, but actually not so.

Braverman and his thesis can be attacked on several grounds (some of these are summarized in Noon and Blyton 1997). On the one hand, there is the antithesis and total opposition of the 'upskilling' camp. For the prophets of this group, technology actually increased skills, job satisfaction and so on. One strand of this concerns the ideas behind 'flexible specialization'. A wide range of more 'friendly fire' also rained down on Braverman. First, he was criticized for his broad brush universalism and limitations stemming from his US-centric bias. His ideas fitted less well in some societies, such as Japan and Germany. Capitalisms varied and were embedded in sociocultural and institutional contexts which imposed and impinged variously on trends and develop-

ments in work and the employment relationship.

Second, how skill was viewed and defined by Braverman was problematic. The implication was that skill was composed of technical components which could be objectively evaluated and observed. Yet his focus on 'objective' features of skill ignored 'tacit' skills and their importance, and the need for them in even formally 'unskilled' work, and those connected to gender or personality, such as services and emotions. Skill was also socially constructed, and a 'label' often negotiated and fought over irrespective of defined skill levels. He also exaggerated and romanticized the typicality and prior situation of skilled craft workers, and overlooked skill transfer possibilities. Indeed, management may well see it as advantageous in certain circumstances to upgrade rather than deskill employees.

Third, a major problem concerns Braverman's failure to explore and integrate ideas of 'social action' (although he may well have come to address this given time, of course). He oversimplified and homogenized both management and workers, ignoring alternative tactics, and strategies and control mechanisms. Organizations are viewed over-rationally, as carefully, consciously and ruthlessly adopting policies. Yet, often decisions are made for a variety of reasons, with influences ranging from sectional interests to 'muddling through' and mistakes. Workers are heterogeneous, for example, by skill, gender and so on. Neither are they totally compliant, as they have resisted, challenged or modified deskilling to varying degrees, with some influence or control of their work situation via individual and collective action and organized labour. This is evidenced by the operation and power of so-called 'restrictive practices' at specific times and places. Indeed, managerial moves from 'simple' to 'technical' (mechanical assembly lines) and 'bureaucratic' (rules, procedures, regulations, internal labour markets) control (Edwards 1979) can be seen as responses to this. Likewise, in the concept of

segmented labour markets (and now in the fashionable guise of the 'flexible firm') organizations can divide workers. 'Core' and 'central' employees (whose role, skill and expertise are required for the viability of the organization) are distinguished from 'peripheral' or 'marginal' workers (with fewer links to an organization's success). This can lead to a fragmentation of interests and less effective resistance to control. Similarly, while 'direct control' was exercised through the application of scientific management, 'responsible autonomy' (Friedman 1977) can also be applied. This involves expanding or enhancing the employee's job situation so that it appears to allow some degree of self-control, but this is constrained and allowed only in areas and in a direction which supports management and organizational objectives. Thus, management has a variety of control methods. Furthermore, Braverman understates the degree of consent and accommodation by employees. This includes the view that work forces can consent to their own subordination (Burawoy 1979).

Fourth, there remains another major problem at the very heart of the Bravermanite thesis. It exaggerates and overstates management's unity, the coherence and consistency of strategy formulation, and the dominance and centrality of control, labour and work design in managerial thought and decisions. It underestimates the diversity, complexity (and competing nature) of management and broader business objectives. Control is not an end in itself, but rather is of interest only to the extent that it impacts on profits, dividends, share price and so on. All too often labour is a peripheral issue, or one that is dealt with in an ad hoc and 'fire-fighting' manner, not as a central issue, strategically or coherently.

Nevertheless, despite this plethora of criticisms and problems, the importance and continuing resonance of Braverman's views and thesis are apparent. This is indicated by such factors as the following. If, as argued by some (Armstrong 1988; Thompson 1989), a more subtle reading of Braverman is used, this

weakens many of the criticisms. For example, work deskilling and degradation can be seen not as a universal 'iron law' operating in all cases, but as more of a 'tendency'. In addition, Braverman still provides a wealth of interesting description, cases and analysis of the evolution, development and roles of labour, management, capital and state. He usefully combines and links employee behaviour, industrial relations and questions of work design and organization, as well as management control to the political economy and wider, more macro issues and themes. Indeed, since its appearance, *Labor and Monopoly Capital* has not been out of print; it has sold over 120,000 copies in English, and still has an average of 2,000 annual sales; it has been translated into French, Italian, German, Dutch, German, Swedish, Norwegian, Spanish, Portuguese, Greek and Japanese, and remains the publisher's best-seller (Smith 1998). Braverman was also the catalyst for a huge volume of work by others, and his thesis remains an important perspective on a range of academic areas. Many courses in these fields contain coverage of his work as well as its followers and protagonists, while words related to his work have entered the lexicon of many academic fields.

Interestingly, Braverman's scepticism of official views on skills, the expansion of education equating to more skilled work and formal designations of skill also retain their importance, value and salience. His work serves as a counter and foil to much of the more banal posturing and platitudes propounded in this area, with talk of 'revolutionary' changes, such as the e-business phenomenon, and by those naively propounding technology's universalism and automatic utopia, with 'benefits' such as upskilling, job enrichment and so on. That technology may have a darker side can be seen in the grim panopticon-like employment conditions it has allowed in the increasingly numerous telephone 'call centres', with their close surveillance and control. As such, Braverman remains worth reading for those who have not done so and would repay rereading for those who need to refresh themselves.

Braverman became the main reference for many debates in diverse areas of management and business studies. He did much to put Marxist analysis back on the map, (re)launch and sustain many academic careers and fill the bookshelves of libraries and generations of academics and students. His ideas and views, while correctly criticized in some aspects, nevertheless still contain useful insights and analysis. As such, Braverman continues to resonate on into the twenty-first century.

BIBLIOGRAPHY

Armstrong, P. (1988) 'Labor and Monopoly Capital', in R. Hyman and W. Streeck (eds), *New Technology and Industrial Relations*, Oxford: Blackwell, 143–59.

Braverman, H. (1963) *The Future of Russia*, London: Collier Macmillan.

—— (1974) *Labor and Monopoly Capital: The Degradation of Work in the Twentieth Century*, New York: Monthly Review Press.

—— (1976) 'Two Comments', *Monthly Review* (June): 18–31.

Burawoy, M. (1979) *Manufacturing Consent: Changes in the Labor Process Under Monopoly Capitalism*, Chicago: University of Chicago Press.

Edwards, P. (1986) *Conflict at Work*, Oxford: Blackwell.

Edwards, R. (1979) *Contested Terrain: The Transformation of Work in the Twentieth Century*, London: Heinemann.

Friedman, A. (1977) *Industry and Labour: Class Struggle at Work and Monopoly Capitalism*, London: Macmillan.

Kelly, J. (1982) *Scientific Management, Job Design and Work Performance*, London: Academic Press.

Knights, D. and Willmott, H. (eds) (1990) *Labour Process Theory*, London: Macmillan.

Littler, C. (1982) *The Development of the*

Labour Process in Capitalist Countries,
London: Hutchinson.

Noon, M. and Blyton, P. (1997) *The Realties of Work*, London: Macmillan.
Smith, C. (1998) 'Braverman, Harry', in M. Warner (ed.), *IEBM Handbook of Management Thinking*, London: International Thomson Business Press, 86–93.
Thompson, P. (1989) *The Nature of Work: An Introduction to Debates on the Labour Process*, London: Macmillan.
Wood, S. (ed.) (1982) *The Degradation of Work? Skill, Deskilling and the Labour Process*, London: Hutchinson.
—— (ed.) (1989) *The Transformation of Work? Skill, Flexibility and the Labour Process*, London: Unwin Hyman.
Zimbalist, A. (ed.) (1979) *Case Studies in the Labour Process*, New York: Monthly Review Press.

CR

BRECH, Edward Francis Leopold (1910–)

Edward Brech was born in London. After taking a BA and BSc in economics from the University of London, he went into business in the City of London. Much of his professional career with the consulting firm Urwick Orr and Partners, where he worked closely with the company's founder, Lyndall Fownes URWICK and became one of Britain's leading management consultants in his own right, particularly in the construction industry. He also played a significant role in the establishment of training courses for managers, especially at the London Polytechnic, and lectured and taught there and at a number of other training institutions. After leaving Urwick Orr he served from 1965 to 1970 as chief executive of the Construction Industry Training Board, and from 1971 to 1975 was chairman of the engineering firm Certex. From 1974 to 1985 he chaired the contract leasing firm Intext. After retiring from business in 1985 Brech devoted himself to his long-standing interest in researching the history of British management, and to that end in 1992 became the world's oldest Ph.D. student, enrolling at the Open University School of Management; he completed his Ph.D. in 1995. Among his professional awards are the James Bowie Medal for contributions to the advancement of management practice in Great Britain (1955), a fellowship of the International Academy of Management (1961) and a life membership of the British Institute of Management (BIM) in 1990 in recognition of fifty years of service to the BIM and its predecessors.

Brech is today best known for his writings, which fall into two categories: writings on the practice of management, and writings on the history of management in the UK. The former include most notably *Management: Its Nature and Significance* (1946), which continued in print into the 1960s and was very popular in both Europe and Japan; *The Principles and Practice of Management* (1953); and *Organization: The Framework of Management* (1957), the latter serving for some time as one of the major texts on organization in US business schools. Brech has been a consistent supporter of the view that management needs to be conducted according to fundamental principles: he defines management as being 'concerned that the job gets done, and done efficiently. Its tasks all centre on decisions for planning and guiding the operations that are going on in the enterprise' (Brech 1953: 9). His concept of management thus owes more to the broad, holistic approach to management espoused by EMERSON and CASSON than to the narrowly functional approach of TAYLOR and some of his followers, although in his writing Brech frequently praises Taylor and makes explicit note of his contribution to modern management thought and practice. During the 1950s and 1960s

Brech and his contemporary Walter PUCKEY helped keep British management writing and education alive in the face of the onslaught of post Second World War Americanization, and ensured that contemporary British writers would have a basis on which to build.

Brech's historical writings are of great significance for the history of management. In 1948–9 he and Urwick together produced the seminal three-volume *The Making of Scientific Management*, which remains to this day a central reference point for any student of the movement, and virtually the only reliable work on the early history of the British branch of the movement. Their reprise of the contributions of figures such as F.G. BURTON, Joseph Slater LEWIS and Edward ELBOURNE has ensured that the work of these British pioneers of management thought lives on; they also give due weight to the activities of French writers and thinkers such as LE CHATELIER and FRÉMINVILLE. Volume 3 of the set, covering the research in human relations carried out at the Hawthorne plant by Elton MAYO and Fritz ROETHLISBERGER, is widely regarded as the definitive summary of that work and its results. Since retiring from full-time work, Brech has devoted his energies to the history of management in Britain; the result, his five-volume *The Evolution of Modern Management*, will be published in 2002. For both the breadth of his interests and for his work in rescuing the history of British management, Brech is one of the most important British management writers of all time.

BIBLIOGRAPHY
Brech, E.F.L. (1946) *Management: Its Nature and Significance*, London: Pitman.
—— (ed.) (1953) *The Principles and Practice of Management*, London: Longmans Green.
—— (1957) *Organization: The Framework of Management*, London: Longmans Green.
—— (2002) *The Evolution of Modern Management*, 5 vols, Bristol: Thoemmes Press.
Urwick, L.F. and Brech, E.F.L. (1948–9) *The Making of Scientific Management*, London: Management Publications Trust, 3 vols; vols 1–2 repr. Bristol: Thoemmes Press, 1994.

MLW

BRONFMAN, Samuel (1889–1971)

Samuel Bronfman was born on 27 February 1889 either at Soroki, Bessarabia or en route to Canada from Russia (Newman, 1978, gives sources for both versions). He died of prostate cancer at Montreal, Quebec on 10 July 1971. The third son of a Jewish tobacco farmer who fled the pogroms in tsarist Russia, Bronfman spent his early life in Brandon, Manitoba. He left school at fifteen to join his father Ekiel and his brothers Abe and Harry, selling firewood in the summer and frozen whitefish in winter, and also selling half-broken wild horses to Manitoba farmers. The family enterprise flourished. In 1903, the Bronfmans were able to make a $5,000 Cdn down payment on the Anglo-American Hotel in Emerson, Manitoba. The hotel business boomed with construction of the Canadian Northern and Canadian Pacific railways, and within a few years the Bronfman family were running hotels in Winnipeg, Saskatchewan and Ontario. In his early twenties, Samuel Bronfman took charge of the family's largest investment, the $190,000 Cdn Bell Hotel in Winnipeg. Under his astute management, the hotel earned $30,000 Cdn profit a year. Bronfman made other investments, including a venture in muskrat furs that netted him $50,000 Cdn.

When prohibition came to Manitoba in 1916, the Bronfmans decided to quit the hotel business and turn their energies toward what

became known in Canada as the inter-provincial package liquor trade – selling spirits through the mail. Samuel purchased the Bonaventure Liquor Store Company in Montreal, and stocked his warehouse with spirits produced by Canadian distilleries as he sought to satisfy a growing list of mail-order customers. He augmented his stock with imports of quality British brands. During the early 1920s the Bronfmans supplied much of the liquor exported from Canada, where it was largely legal, to the United States, where it was not. Prohibition drove US bootleggers and speakeasy operators towards Canada in search of liquor, and the Bronfmans served them from the French-owned islands of St Pierre and Miquelon, 24 kilometres (15 miles) off the Newfoundland coast.

In 1925 Samuel and his brothers Allan and Harry bought a distillery in Montreal and established a partnership with the Distillers Company of Edinburgh and London, manufacturer of such well-known Scotch brands as Haig, Black and White, Dewar's and Johnnie Walker. Three years later, Bronfman bought the Joseph E. Seagram and Sons distillery in Waterloo, Ontario. Deciding that prohibition could not last forever, he began to stockpile supplies. When US prohibition ended in 1933, Seagram was poised to serve the US hotel and liquor store market from one of the world's largest reserves of rye and bourbon whiskey.

Success in the United States made Seagram very profitable and led to the company's expansion throughout the world. Seven Crown and Seagram's VO became the world's largest-selling brands of whiskey. Under Bronfman's leadership, the company invested in wineries and distilleries, acquiring control of such brands as Chivas Regal scotch, Captain Morgan's rum, Mumm's champagne and Barton and Guestier wines.

In 1957, Bronfman, known to his family as 'Mr Sam', handed control to his son Edgar Miles Bronfman, who continued to increase Seagram's holdings in wine and spirits and also diversified into other industries including motion pictures and Broadway musicals. By 1965, Seagram's annual sales in 119 countries were estimated at more than one billion Canadian dollars. The company continued to grow and diversify after Bronfman's death; in 1995, Seagram became a major company in the entertainment field with its purchase of 80 per cent of the US entertainment conglomerate MCA. As of January 1995, Seagram had annual sales of $7.6 billion Cdn, assets of $18.2 billion Cdn and 15, 800 employees.

BIBLIOGRAPHY

Marrus, M.R. (1991) *Mr. Sam*, Toronto: Viking.
Newman, P.C. (1978) *Bronfman Dynasty: The Rothschilds of the New World*, Toronto: McClelland and Stewart.

BB

BRUNEL, Isambard Kingdom (1806–59)

Isambard Kingdom Brunel was born in Portsea, Hampshire on 9 April 1806, and died in London on 15 September 1859 after suffering a stroke. His father, Sir Marc Isambard Brunel, was a French naval officer who immigrated to the United States before settling in Britain; his great achievement in that country was the design and construction of the Thames Tunnel in London. Isambard Kingdom Brunel, after education in Hove, Caen and Paris, joined his father's engineering business and was his deputy on the construction of the Thames Tunnel, where he won respect for both his engineering skill and his personal courage. On several occasions he risked his own life to rescue workmen when the tunnel works flooded, and was once badly injured.

Brunel's main attention was focused on the new revolution in transport, based on the great advances in steam power made by the likes of

BOULTON and WATT. George STEPHENSON had already demonstrated the possibilities inherent in the railways. Brunel's own greatest achievements as an engineer were in railways and shipbuilding. In 1833 he surveyed the Great Western Railway from London to Bristol, and oversaw its construction from 1833 to 1841; he later designed most of the railways in the west of England and also worked in Ireland and Italy. By 1835 he was working on designs for steam-powered ships, and built three of the most famous steam vessels of all time: the wooden-hulled *Great Western*, launched in 1838; the *Great Britain*, the first iron-hulled steam vessel ever built; and finally in 1858 the *Great Eastern*, another iron-hulled ship which, with a displacement of 32,000 tons, was also by far the largest ship ever built. The expense and strain of building the *Great Eastern* caused a deterioration in Brunel's health, and he died only a year later.

A short man, standing just over five feet tall (he often wore top hats to make himself appear taller), Brunel was also a workaholic who would spend sixteen to eighteen hours a day in his office, frequently eating and sleeping there. He was noted for his attention to detail: he designed not only the railway lines but also the stations and rolling stock, with attention to small details such as the shapes of lamps and the quality of coffee in railway waiting rooms. Though not a seaman, he wrote personally detailed memoranda describing the duties of the captain and chief engineer of the *Great Eastern*.

An engineering genius, Brunel was also an entrepreneurial spirit who fully understood the commercial possibilities of his designs, and positioned himself so as to capitalize on them. He had his technical knowledge at his fingertips, and seemed always to be able to solve any new problem as it arose. His knowledge and his energy meant that he naturally assumed command of any new venture. The directors of his projects deferred to him even when he did not have any financial interest in the project; he was the *de facto* general manager of Great

Western Railway. Once he had a project in mind, he would put together a consortium of financiers and backers, who would in turn hand him near total control. He was a first-class networker, in both business and intellectual terms, and corresponded constantly with scientists and engineers such as Stephenson and Michael Faraday.

In personal terms he was an autocrat who ruled his personal staff with a rod of iron but rewarded those who were loyal to him and had talent. He had strong views on business ethics and deplored unscrupulous business methods, but argued for self-regulation among the railways, not government interference. His abilities as an organizer and networker marked him out from the ordinary engineer or inventor, and his career provides a useful model for technological entrepreneurs wishing to control and manage their own projects.

BIBLIOGRAPHY
Brunel, I. (1870) *The Life of Isambard Kingdom Brunel, Civil Engineer*, London: Longmans; repr. Newton Abbott: David and Charles, 1971.
Hay, P. (1973) *Brunel: His Achievements in the Transport Revolution*, London: Osprey.

MLW

BRUNNER, John Tomlinson (1842–1919)

John Tomlinson Brunner was born in Liverpool on 8 February 1842, the son of John Brunner, a Swiss immigrant, and his wife Margaret. He died in Liverpool on 1 July 1919. He married twice, to Salome Davis in 1864, and, after her death, to Jane Wyman; he had seven children in all. After education at St George's House, in 1857 he became a clerk with a shipping firm. In 1861 he joined the

chemical manufacturing firm Hutchinson and Sons in Widnes, and over the course of the next twelve years rose from office clerk to general manager. While with Hutchinson he met the chemist Ludwig Mond, also an employee of the firm, and the two decided to go into business together. Mond negotiated a licence to produce ammonium soda from the patent holders, the Belgian firm of Ernest and Alfred Solvay, and in 1873 the firm of Brunner, Mond was established, with a factory at Withington, Cheshire producing soda ash.

While Mond provided the technical expertise for the new venture, Brunner provided the organizational and management skills. Some of these skills had been acquired through on-the-job experience at Hutchinson and Sons, where he was responsible for accounting and personnel management; he also turned out to have a natural ability at business-to-business marketing. So sound was the commercial organization he established that the new company was trading at a profit by the end of its second year, and from the late 1870s onward it expanded steadily. Brunner, Mond went public in 1883; by 1890 they were producing 10,000 tons of soda ash annually. Markets were developed first in Britain and North America, but later also in the Far East and Australia, and in the 1890s Brunner, Mond was one of the first Western chemical companies to trade in volume with China and Japan. Brunner became chairman of the firm in 1900, and in the period before the First World War saw off a number of competitors, either through acquisition or by driving them out of the market.

Brunner was also active in politics, serving as a Liberal MP from 1885 to 1910. He was made baronet in 1895, and a privy councillor in 1906. He retired in 1918, being succeeded in the chair by his son Roscoe, and he died just a year later. The company later came under the control of Ludwig Mond's son Alfred MOND and evolved into Imperial Chemical Industries (ICI).

One of the more interesting aspects of the operations of Brunner, Mond concerns their personnel management and education policies. As Kidner (1986) points out, most firms at the time preferred to hire young men or boys and train them from the ground up, promoting them internally to positions of seniority; indeed, Brunner himself began his career this way. But with manufacturing becoming increasingly technologically complex, in terms of both products and processes, some manufacturers began considering the possibility of bringing in educated older men and training them for senior management. Brunner, Mond was one of the first firms in Britain to experiment in this respect, hiring in the 1880s several university graduates with chemistry degrees as, in effect, management trainees. The company also began providing technical training for junior employees, helping them to learn more about the product and process technologies with which they were working. This emphasis on education almost certainly accounts for much of the efficiency and profitability of Brunner, Mond during its years of rapid growth.

BIBLIOGRAPHY
Kidner, A. (1984) 'Brunner, Sir John Tomlinson', in D.J. Jeremy (ed.), *Dictionary of Business Biography*, London: Butterworths, vol. 1, 484–6.
Reader, W.J. (1970) *Imperial Chemical Industries: A History*, Oxford: Oxford University Press, 2 vols.

BÜLOW, Dietrich Adam Heinrich von (1757–1807)

Heinrich von Bülow was born in Prussia in 1757, and died in prison at Riga (modern Latvia) in 1807 (exact dates are not known). He came from a distinguished Prussian military family; his elder brother General Friedrich Wilhelm von Bülow rose to high rank in the

Prussian army, and commanded the army corps that came to the aid of the Duke of Wellington at Waterloo. Bülow himself served in the Prussian army from 1773–89, and on retirement devoted himself to writing on military issues. He published his major work, *Geist des neuen Kriegssystems* (The Spirit of the Modern System of War), in 1799, and went on to write a further fifteen works, culminating in *Der Feldzug von 1805: militärisch-politisch betrachet* (The Campaign of 1805: From a Military-political Point of View) in 1806. This last work was a scathing criticism of the Prussian army and state in the wake of the defeats by Napoleon Bonaparte in 1805–6. Bülow was arrested on charges of insanity in early 1807 and was imprisoned first at Kolberg and then at Riga, where he died, apparently as a result of his maltreatment in prison.

Geist des neuen Kriegssystems attempted to set out a new 'system' for the making and waging of warfare, though as Palmer (1986) points out, there was little that was new about this work. However, Bülow did, for the first time, define and establish 'strategy' and 'operations' as terms in their own right, words which have since entered the lexicon of both military science and business management. These basic concepts were developed more fully in the work of JOMINI and CLAUSEWITZ.

Following the defeat of Prussia at the battle of Jena-Auerstadt in 1805, Bülow began developing a new approach to strategy. Writers and thinkers since the time of DEMOSTHENES had compared business to war, but in *Der Feldzug von 1805* Bülow stood the metaphor on its head. He argued that war needed to be treated like business; the military force available to a nation was its 'capital', which needed to be kept in circulation. Concentration of capital and assets at the appropriate points would yield a return on investment, and capital had to be flexible so that it could be concentrated quickly where needed. This new approach emphasized strategic goals over processes and methods. Unfortunately for himself, in the same work Bülow overplayed his hand in criticizing the

Prussian authorities. His arrest and death followed not long after the publication of *Der Feldzug von 1805*.

Bülow has been described as 'irresponsible, vain and vague' (Palmer 1986: 119), and as a military thinker he has only limited merit. His most valuable legacy in management terms is his development of the concept and importance of strategy in truly modern terms. He is a shadowy but nonetheless important figure in the continuum of thinkers on military science from Frederick the Great (see FREDERICK II) to MOLTKE, who were in turn an important influence on the management writers of the late nineteenth and early twentieth century, most notably James MOONEY.

BIBLIOGRAPHY

Bülow, H. von (1799) *Geist des neuen Kriegssytems*, trans. as *The Spirit of the Modern System of War*, London, 1806.

—— (1806) *Der Feldzug von 1805: militärisch-politisch betrachet* (The Campaign of 1805: From a Military-political Point of View), Leipzig.

Palmer, R.R. (1986) 'Frederick the Great, Guibert, Bülow: From Dynastic to National War', in P. Paret (ed.), *Makers of Modern Strategy*, Princeton, NJ: Princeton University Press, 91–119.

MLW

BURNHAM, James (1905–87)

James Burnham was born in Chicago on 22 November 1905, the son of Claude and Mary Burnham, and died at home in Kent, Connecticut on 28 July 1987. His family background was one of relative affluence, his father being a vice-president of the Burlington Railroad. Burnham was well educated, taking his BA in philosophy from Princeton University

in 1927 and an MA in the same subject from Balliol College, Oxford in 1929. In 1930 he was appointed to teach philosophy at New York University, where he remained until 1953. He married Marcia Lightner in 1934; they had three children.

In the early 1930s, like many others of his background, Burnham was strongly drawn to communism, especially the brand espoused by Leon Trotsky. In 1935 he joined Trotsky's Fourth International Party, and wrote frequently for journals such as *New International* and *Partisan Review*. It is not known if he ever met Trotsky, who was then in exile in Mexico, but the two were frequent correspondents. Again like many others, Burnham became disillusioned with the Soviet state of Josef Stalin, and particularly by the alliance between the USSR and Nazi Germany on the eve of the Second World War. He quarrelled violently with Trotsky over the question of whether the USSR was in fact a socialist state (with Burnham maintaining that it was not). In March 1940 Burnham resigned from the party, continuing his polemic with Trotsky up until the latter's murder by Stalin's agents a few months later.

Although Burnham had rejected communism as a political ideology, he remained strongly influenced by Marxist thought, in particular the concept of the dialectic as a historical force. The next phase of his thought was characterized by a strong rejection of authoritarianism, in which category Burnham included not only fascism and Stalinism but also milder forms of state intervention such as Roosevelt's New Deal in the United States. His best and most influential books, *The Managerial Revolution* (1941) and *The Machiavellians* (1943), come from this period. In both works, his primary theme is power. Following the Marxist dialectic, he maintained that in any society there are two elite classes of people, those who have power and those who are attempting to take it. Both these groups are minorities, not representative of or working in the best interests of the masses.

From this position, Burnham moved almost inexorably towards libertarianism. In 1955, after leaving academia, Burnham took a post as a senior editor of the right-wing American journal the *National Review*, working closely with founder and owner William F. Buckley, Jr. Buckley and Burnham became close friends, and to Burnham is ascribed a role in toning down some of the journal's more radical right-wing views. He remained a bitter opponent of not only the USSR and its policies but of all those who advocated dealings with it; in *Suicide of the West* (1964), he accused Western liberals of opening up the Third World to Soviet domination through the withdrawal from empire. As well as Buckley, his admirers included Ronald Reagan, who, after becoming president of the United States, awarded Burnham the Presidential Medal of Freedom (1983). He had by then retired from the *National Review* after suffering a stroke in 1978.

In *The Managerial Revolution*, Burnham sets out an alternate view of social transformation from that espoused by MARX and his followers. In most types of society, says Burnham, the control of the means of production is in the hands of a small group. This group uses this power to give its members 'preferential treatment in the distribution of the products of those instruments' (1941: 56). Control alone, says Burnham, is never the ultimate end; elites use their control to determine both what is produced, and who receives the goods and services produced and in what quantity. Control of access and preferential treatment in distribution are thus closely related.

Marx hard argued that, just as the bourgeoisie had taken control of the means of production from the land-owning aristocracy, so in time the workers would take control from the bourgeoisie. Burnham, by 1941, believed Marx had been living in a fool's paradise. Rapid technological advance combined with the progressive de-skilling of workers through the division of labour meant that workers no

longer had the capacity to take control; they lacked the skills to operate the means of production, even if they could manage to take *de facto* control.

Instead, said Burnham, a new class was rising to challenge the bourgeoisie, whom Burnham usually prefers to call the 'capitalists'. This was the 'new middle class': 'the salaried executives and engineers and managers and accountants and bureaucrats and the rest, who do not fit without distortion into either the "capitalist" or "worker" category' (1941: 48). Increasingly, these professional managers were removing control of instruments of production from the hands of the capitalists. He describes how this process happens, as the capitalists, who own those instruments, increasingly delegate their authority to others:

The big capitalists, legally the chief owners of the instruments of production, have in actual life been getting further and further away from those instruments, which are the final source and base of social dominance. This began some time ago, when most of the big capitalists withdrew from industrial production to finance ... the control necessarily became more indirect, exercised at second or third or fourth hand through financial devices. Direct supervision of the productive process was delegated to others, who, particularly with the parallel development of modern mass-production methods, had to assume more and more of the prerogatives of control – for example, the all-important prerogative of hiring and firing (the very heart of 'control over access to the instruments of production') as well as organization of the technical process of production.

(Burnham 1941: 95)

So far, this looks like nothing more than the separation of ownership and control thesis advanced by Berle and Means in the previous decade. Burnham, however, believed that Berle and Means had not followed the concept through to its logical conclusion: that the managers, once they have achieved control, will then proceed to take ownership. In fact, says Burnham, the separation of ownership and control is largely an appearance: 'Ownership *means* control; if there is no control, then there is no ownership... If ownership and control are in reality separated, then ownership has changed hands, to the "control", and the separated ownership is a meaningless fiction' (1941: 87–8). And, by allowing managers control over the means of production, the capitalists had sown the seeds of their own doom:

Control over access is decisive and ...will carry control over preferential treatment in distribution with it: that is, will shift ownership unambiguously to the new controlling, a new dominant, class. Here we see, from a new viewpoint, the mechanism of the managerial revolution.

(Burnham 1941: 90)

The managerial revolution, says Burnham, is a struggle for power, in which the world is making the transition from a capitalist or bourgeois society into a managerial society. Moreover, the managers will be successful; the capitalists have neither the will nor the means to withstand them. From the perspective of the managers, they *must* take control in order to consolidate their own position. As long as they lack control, they can be hired and fired by the capitalist owners like any other employee, and their own privileged position – their own preferential access to distribution – will be lost. And in order to consolidate their control, they will take ownership as well.

Managerial control would not be exercised directly, however; on their own, managers were incapable of defeating the forces of capital. Burnham notes that there is little sense of a collective cause among managers, and it seems unlikely that they will unite to challenge the capitalists directly. Instead, he

believes, they will take steps to exercise control over the state. It is the state which will be the managers' primary tool; state intervention and control will be the means by which they take over the means of production. 'Fusion with the economy of the state', he believed, offered managers their best chance of becoming the ruling class (Burnham 1941: 120).

That this revolution would be global in nature, Burnham did not doubt; forty years before globalization became a popular concept, he had already noted how 'the modern world is interlocked by myriad technological, economic, and cultural chains' (1941: 4). He predicted too the rise of economic superpowers dominating lesser states and, several decades before OHMAE's elucidation of the 'triad' theory, wrote that the United States, Japan and Europe would dominate the world between them (Burnham 1941: 167–8). George Orwell, who had read and critiqued *The Managerial Revolution* (Orwell 1946), borrowed elements of Burnham's theory for his novel *1984*.

What is particularly startling is Burnham's assumption that the managerial revolution would lead to totalitarianism. He saw German National Socialism and Soviet Marxist-Leninism as both being 'managerial ideologies'; in both states, wealth was concentrated in the hands of the upper classes, even more so than in the United States (this had been one of the causes of his argument with Trotsky). Although he does not say so explicitly, his argument implies that managers will develop a form of class consciousness, sufficient to allow them to recognize common interests and take concerted action using the state as a tool. At the time he was writing, this view would not have seemed far-fetched. Following the Wall Street crash of 1929, corporatism was in the air as corporations sought to defend their shrinking markets through alliances and combinations with government, trades unions and each other. Competition was seen by many as wasteful and ruinous; the free market was

regarded by many even in high positions in industry with suspicion. As for managers themselves, they were being urged by writers such as Herbert CASSON to become more professional in their approach and to develop a stronger self-identity as managers.

In his subsequent work, *The Machiavellians*, Burnham looks once again at the question of power – who has it, and how they acquire it – in societies and organizations. His hero here is Niccolò MACHIAVELLI, whom Burnham sees as a hero; Machiavelli, to him, is not a preacher of amoral political doctrines but a man who dares to tell the truth about how power is acquired and used. After him, Burnham lists a number of 'Machiavellians', scientists and writers who have explored the social foundations of power, including Gaetano Mosca, Georges Sorel, Roberto MICHELS and Vilifredo Pareto. Building on their work, Burnham sees all societies as characterized by a near-constant struggle between elites and non-elites; the rule of the former is based on a combination of force and fraud, constraining those groups who wish to overthrow the elites to use the same methods. The managers will triumph over the capitalists, he believes, because they have a greater will to win and because they believe their own survival as a class to be at stake.

The relationship between business and political control described here is an interesting one. Business stability requires political and economic stability; in the fifteenth century, Cosimo dei MEDICI had seized political power precisely to ensure such stability. In Aldous Huxley's novel *Brave New World*, of which Burnham certainly knew, a similar situation obtained. Burnham believed that if political control was threatened, the elites would move to secure their own position; thus the managers would take control of the state, pushing the capitalists out of the dominant position.

Ultimately, however, this did not happen. Managers – like workers – remained more attached to their national, organizational and local identities and stayed largely loyal to the

capital-owning classes. Burnham failed to foresee this, and he failed also to predict that managers would develop the ability to acquire ownership through the mechanisms of the market rather than turning to the state. By the 1990s, thanks to devices like executive share-ownership plans, mangers were well on their way to entering the owning classes, and the separation of owner and manager, like that of ownership and control, was beginning to blur. But if the managerial revolution did not turn out as Burnham predicted, his underlying thesis, that the growth of professional management was both part of and had a strong influence on the greater social changes of the twentieth century, remains a powerful one.

BIBLIOGRAPHY

Burnham, J. (1941) *The Managerial Revolution: Or, What is Happening in the World Now*, London: Putnam.
—— (1943) *The Machiavellians: Defenders of Freedom*, London: Putnam.
—— (1947) *The Struggle for the World*, London: Jonathan Cape.
—— (1964) *Suicide of the West: An Essay on the Meaning and Destiny of Liberalism*, London: Jonathan Cape.
Francis, S.T. (1984) *Power and History: The Political Thought of James Burnham*, New York: University Press of America.
Geiger, R. (1959) *Die Entwickzungstedenzen des Kapitalismus bei Keynes, Schumpeter and Burnham*, Winterthur.
Orwell, G. (1946) *James Burnham and the Managerial Revolution*, London: Socialist Book Centre.

MLW

BURNS, Tom (1913–)

Tom Burns was born in London on 16 January 1913, the son of John Burns, a labourer, and his wife Hannah. He took a BA from the University of Bristol, and then worked as a schoolteacher from 1934 to 1939. During the Second World War he served with the Friends' Ambulance Unit, in Scandinavia and the Far East, and was for three years a prisoner of war. Following the war he worked with the West Midland Group on Postwar Reconstruction and Planning from 1945 to 1949, and then became a lecturer at the Social Sciences Research Centre at the University of Edinburgh, where he spent the remainder of his professional career; he was made senior lecturer in 1952, reader in 1961 and professor of sociology in 1965. He was made a fellow of the British Academy in 1972, and was a visiting professor at Harvard University from 1973 to 1974. He married Mary Clark in 1944; they have five children. Burns retired from the University of Edinburgh in 1981. As well as his work on organizations he has also written and translated a number of books on sociology and on literature.

A sociologist by training and inclination, Burns became interested in the application of sociological principles to business organizations after he joined the University of Edinburgh. His outlook was further broadened through his collaboration in the late 1950s and early 1960s with the psychologist George Stalker, with whom Burns produced his best-known and most influential work, *The Management of Innovation* (1961). Somewhat unusually for a scholar of his time and in his discipline, Burns also takes a historical view. He starts from the position that business organizations, and the models of management that govern them, have evolved according to social and economic needs.

In the eighteenth century, according to Burns (1963), a combination of new technology and new philosophical approaches to the physical sciences enabled men such as Richard

ARKWRIGHT to develop the factory system. The factory system was well suited to the environmental and social conditions in which it developed, with factories being focused on one type of production (usually textiles) and using a combination of powered technology and labour. The last point is important; citing Andrew URE, Burns says it is not only the *division* of labour that is important in achieving efficiency, but also the *recombination* of labour under the aegis of the entrepreneur, ensuring that the various divided efforts of the labourers are directed towards the end of the enterprise.

In the late nineteenth century, further technological improvements, especially in transportation and communications, as well as the development of new markets and growth in demand from old ones, spurred organizations to grow and diversify, developing much greater ranges of product. These large-scale diversified organizations required more technical staff and more administrators if they were to remain efficient; Burns notes how the proportion of administrative staff in British factories grew from 8.6 per cent in 1907 to 20 per cent in 1948 (Burns 1963). In these new organizations, administrative control became a priority, and loyalty to the organization was one of the key demands made on workers and managers alike. This tendency to bureaucracy became greater, says Burns, as the rate of technology advance slowed and markets matured. He makes a telling observation at this point:

An industry based on major technological advances shows a high death-rate in its early years; growth occurs when the rate of technical advance slows down. What happens is that consumer demand tends to be standardized through publicity and price reductions, and technical production is consequently restrained. This enables companies to maintain relatively stable conditions, in which large-scale production is built up by converting manufacturing processes into routine cycles of activity for machines or semi-skilled assembly hands.
(Burns 1963: 18).

The phenomenon which Burns here describes can be seen in many industries in the early years of the twentieth century, especially in the United States. Early theorists in areas such as economics and especially marketing sought to create greater standardization, to rein in the flow of new products and to educate consumers into an acceptance of the status quo; some, such as Paul CHERINGTON and even more so Fred CLARK, were positively critical of consumer demand as a force capable of working against the firm's best interests if it is not properly managed through advertising and sales efforts. The phenomenon of high death rate in industries with rapidly advancing technology was also observed later in the century in Silicon Valley and elsewhere in the computer industry, and this may offer pointers to the future of this industry.

But, says Burns, there is a way in which firms can make themselves better equipped to survive in such conditions, and that is by adopting an organizational form which is more adapted to the management of change and innovation. He conceptualizes the early twentieth-century model of organization as a *mechanistic* model, and compares it to the formal-rational bureaucracy described by Max WEBER. To survive in changing conditions, says Burns, firms need to look at moving to an *organic* or *organistic* model. Whereas mechanistic organizations are hierarchical and bureaucratic with clearly defined roles and tasks, focused on top-down control with vertical communications systems, organistic organizations are more fuzzy; tasks and boundaries are perceived to change and evolve according to needs and pressures, control is less rigid and horizontal communications also come into play.

In Burns and Stalker (1961) these two models are placed at extreme points on a continuum; it is recognized that no organization is

ever wholly one or the other. It is clear, however, that Burns and Stalker believe that the organistic form is far better suited to the needs of managing innovation and change. The mechanistic model may be more effective in mature or static industries (although there is doubt about even this), but it cannot survive in industries in which rapid change is the order of the day. However, making a transition to an organistic form is rarely easy. If it were simply a case of altering the organization's structure and reporting and control systems, what Burns and Stalker call the organization's 'formal authority system', then the difficulties might be lessened. However, many firms attempt to change their formal authority systems without recognizing that two other aspects of the organization need to be considered as well. First, there is the personal self-interest of the managers and workers within the firm, who fulfil certain social and economic needs by being part of the organization. Burns and Stalker refer to this as the 'career structure' and refer explicitly to the effect that organizational change can have on personal promotion prospects, but it is clear that a wide variety of personal needs and emotions come into play here. Second, there is what they refer to as the organization's 'political system', a reference to the internal power structures that pervade every organization, sometimes parallel to and sometimes running against the grain of the formal authority system.

The analysis of these three systems individually is not particularly new: descriptions of the career system can be found in human resource management literature from the 1920s onward, and the concept of the political system goes back to MACHIAVELLI. The great contribution by Burns and Stalker was to show how all three systems coexist and interrelate within organizations. Any change management programme needs to consider not only the three systems separately but the interaction between them.

The problem with change programmes is that they tend to affect all individuals at all three levels; a change in the formal authority system may be perceived as blocking personal advancement and/or reducing or inhibiting political control. Individuals respond by attempting to block or amend change routines. These attempts Burns and Stalker describe as 'pathological systems', responses to change which resemble the 'defensive routines' described by Chris ARGYRIS. Pugh (1998) shows how Burns and Stalker categorize these pathological systems into three classes. First, there is the *ambiguous figure system*: responsibility for decisions which should rest with senior managers is delegated to people outside the chain of control, bypassing the formal organization and creating uncertainty and confusion. Second, there is the *mechanistic jungle*, whereby organizations respond to pressures for change not by becoming more organistic but by proliferating their existing bureaucracy. The third response is the *superpersonal system*, where responsibility that should rest with individuals is instead delegated to committees. In the short term this may have its advantages, but Burns and Stalker believe that a permanent system of committees leads to inefficiency and a division of political leaders.

As Pugh points out, the title of *The Management of Innovation* can be somewhat misleading. Instead of discussing innovation *per se*, Burns and Stalker are more concerned with the organizational conditions which allow innovation to flourish. They are not alone in this emphasis. Successful innovators such as William HEWLETT, for example, hold that a supportive organizational culture is essential for successful innovation, and examples from practice bear out the view that innovative businesses are more likely to have organistic than mechanistic models of organization. Burns himself conducted an important later survey of the British Broadcasting Corporation (BBC) which showed how entrenched political systems can hamper attempts to implement organizational change (Burns 1977).

BIBLIOGRAPHY
Burns, T. (1954) *Local Government and Central Control*, London: Routledge.
—— (1963) 'Industry in a New Age', *New Society* (31 January): 17–20; repr. in D. Pugh (ed.), *Organizational Theory: Selected Readings*, London: Penguin, 1977, 99–110.
—— (ed.) (1967) *Social Theory and Economic Change*, London: Tavistock Publications.
—— (ed.) (1969) *Industrial Man: Selected Readings*, London: Penguin.
—— (1977) *The BBC: Public Institution and Private World*, London: Macmillan.
Burns, T. and Stalker, G.M. (1961) *The Management of Innovation*, London: Tavistock Publications.
Pugh, D. (1998) 'Burns, Tom', in M. Warner (ed.), *IEBM Handbook of Management Thinking*, London: International Thomson Business Press, 94–8.

MLW

BURRELL, Thomas J. (1939–)

Thomas J. Burrell was born in the Chicago suburb of Englewood on 18 March 1939, the son of a tavern-keeper and a beautician. Englewood was a black urban ghetto characterized by gang violence and race riots, in which Burrell grew up as something of an outsider. He did not do well at school, and was a failure in his first attempt to go to university; after dropping out he worked for a short time on an assembly line. Resolved to make a success of his career, and remembering a high-school aptitude test which showed he might make a good advertising copy-writer, he returned to Roosevelt University in 1957 and took a degree in English and advertising. In 1960 he took a job in the mailroom of Wade Advertising Agency in Chicago and began learning the business from the ground up, and on graduation the following year, Wade promoted him to copywriter; probably the only black advertising copywriter in Chicago, and one of the few in the country.

Through the 1960s Burrell worked with a succession of agencies, including Leo Burnett in Chicago and Foote, Cone and Belding in London. He proved to be a talented copywriter for television advertisements in particular, and was involved in a number of high-profile campaigns. Like other black members of creative teams in the industry, however, he was continually frustrated by the inability and/or lack of inclination of advertisers to appeal to the black market. Despite the rise of the civil liberties movement in the United States and consequent pressures on advertisers to recognize blacks in their advertising, the number of black subjects appearing in television advertisements was small and the ads themselves remained largely focused on the white market.

Believing he could break through in this sector of the market, Burrell and two colleagues established the Burrell McBain agency in Chicago in 1971 in a single-room office. Burrell believed that the best way to reach black viewers was not through promoting product features, but through 'lifestyle' advertising: 'to create and celebrate an image of black people that is positive and uplifting, which at the same time reflected positively upon the product' (Ingham and Feldman 1994: 124). He persuaded advertisers that this strategy would work, and quickly picked up high-profile clients such as Crest, Coca-Cola and McDonald's. In each case, he convinced the advertisers that their product-centred advertisements for the white market would not succeed with black consumers, and developed successful campaigns which centred on the core values of the black community. By 1980 Burrell's agency was by far and away the largest black-owned advertising agency in the country.

In the 1980s Burrell began moving out of advertising to purely black consumers and towards the general market. While product-oriented advertisements aimed at the white market would have limited appeal to black consumers, Burrell believed the reverse was not true: 'lifestyle' advertising would appeal to white consumers. His lifestyle advertisements for the general consumer market were widely imitated and won his agency several awards. His work has not only brought greater aware-ness of the needs and values of black con-sumers in the United States, it has also con-tributed greatly to general knowledge of consumer motivation and responsiveness to advertising. It has brought great success to his company, Burrell Communications, which had billings of $178 million in 1998 and was ranked the seventy-eighth largest advertising agency in the United States.

BIBLIOGRAPHY
Ingham, J.N. and Feldman, L.B. (1994) *African-American Business Leaders: A Biographical Dictionary*, Westport, CT: Greenwood Press.

MLW

BURTON, Francis George (*fl. c.*1896–1902)

Almost nothing is known of the personal life of Francis George Burton, save that he served as secretary and general manager of the Milford Haven Shipbuilding and Engineering Company, Ltd in Pembrokeshire, Wales. He does not appear to have been a member of any of the professional guilds or societies asso-ciated with his sector of industry, nor does he appear to have been associated with any training institutions. What little we know of his personal interests is what can be gleaned from his books, which are among the earliest of the modern era in Britain – or anywhere – to deal specifically with the problems and tasks of management.

Burton, as he comes across in his writing, was typical of many late Victorian managers in that he saw his country's commercial interests and economic interests in much the same light, and even to some extent intertwined. Britain was threatened by competition from foreign powers, especially the rising industrial strength of old opponents such as Germany, France and Russia, but also the United States. To compete and win, Britain needed a strong navy and a well-founded and well-organized man-ufacturing base. In both the military and com-mercial spheres, the key to success was orga-nization, the application of the principles of the scientific revolution to business and, especially, technical training. Perhaps his most revealing – certainly one of the more unusual works of management literature – is *The Naval Engineer and Command of the Sea* (1896a), a fictional account of the British Navy fighting two imag-inary wars, one with the French and then another with the Americans. In both cases the Royal Navy is victorious, thanks to the supe-riority of its technology and the high rates of technical training of its engineers. Training, technology and systems were Burton's man-agerial watchwords.

For all his emphasis on systems, however, Burton was not a rigid thinker. His two books on accounting – *Engineering Estimates and Cost Accounts* (1896b), based on an earlier series of articles in the magazine *Engineering*, and *Engineers and Shipbuilders Accounts* (1902), drawing on the work of Lawrence DICKSEE – show that while Burton believed strongly in the need for organizational flexi-bility, the need, he said, was for uniformity of principle, not uniformity of detail (1896b: 4). In the earlier work, he also dwelt on the impor-tance of sharing knowledge within the orga-nization so as to achieve both greater efficiency and greater accuracy; a manager not in pos-session of all the facts inevitably runs a greater

risk of error. Burton is one of the first writers to argue for a systematic approach to knowledge transmission and dissemination, one of the key elements of knowledge management.

Burton's most popular work was *The Commercial Management of Engineering Works* (1899). This book is primarily noteworthy as an early – not altogether successful – attempt to show the broad nature of management. His definition of management is worth reproducing at length:

> The term 'Commercial Management' is a very comprehensive one, and includes a great deal more than making office arrangements, compiling catalogues, purchasing stores and selling products ... It has its *content* in a profitable workshop, and therefore includes everything which affects the profit and loss account, whether it be initially of a technical or commercial character. It is supreme over technic, in so far as the employment thereof is concerned; it is subordinate to technic, because no commercial management can in these days be successful which is purely empiric in character and neglectful of scientific deduction and knowledge. The problem presented is a very wide one, and requires in its solver broad and extensive observation of men as well as books, as well as the possession of personal qualifications which may be indicated but which cannot be imparted.
>
> (Burton 1899: 1–2)

Management, then, has as its province any activity which affects the profitability of the firm. Like Herbert CASSON, Burton distrusts personal experience, seeing it as less valuable than adherence to systems. Again, however, he stresses that systems must reflect the real situation that the company finds itself in, and must be capable of adaptation and change (1899: 2).

Unfortunately, as Urwick and Brech (1957: 148–9) point out, Burton does not go on from this promising beginning. An accountant by training and by nature, he uses most of the book to describe production and control systems in detail. The work is thus very practial, and Urwick and Brech comment that its audience undoubtedly found it highly useful, but it does not follow up the philosophical and theoretical issues raised in the introduction. Only in one short chapter, that on the role of the general manager (chap. 3) does Burton expand on this all-embracing nature of management. He defines the general manager as 'the officer on whom, above all others, the profits of the company depend' (Burton 1899: 20), the person responsible for both the system of supervision, and the firm's *esprit de corps* and morale of employees, both of which are necessary for success. The general manager is responsible not only for discipline but also for seeing that justice is done to employees and within the firm. A primary duty is the selection of staff, ensuring that the right person is in the right place doing the right job. Burton also stresses the importance of technical qualifications, but suggests the general manager should be an all-rounder rather than a highly trained specialist:

> It is almost superfluous to say that the manager should be a highly-qualified engineer; not necessarily an eminent specialist, but a good all-round man, who has sufficient grasp of all the departments to appreciate at their proper worth the reports and suggestions made by those immediately in charge of them ... by his general technical knowledge and common sense he must be able to reconcile their conflicting claims and direct them all to the making of a profitable revenue account ... it must be ability which duly estimates the correlation of all forces, not the monastic scholarship which severs its own individual researches from all others.
>
> (Burton 1899: 24)

A later chapter (chap. 14) dwells on the importance of good staff relations and on

systems for ensuring both high rates of productivity and good staff morale, which Burton sees as interrelated. He remarks again on the importance of justice: workers must feel they are being treated fairly and honourably, or else no system of discipline can be expected to work smoothly. In terms of recruitment, emphasis is placed on the 'character' of employees. The second half of the chapter, which is more interesting, compares the various systems of incentives which had been developed in the last decade of the nineteenth century: profit sharing, the most commonly used system in Britain; employee participation, in particular the system developed at the National Cash Register Company in the United States; and piecework systems, then coming into vogue in the United States, particularly analytical and differential piecework systems (the latter having been recently developed by F.W. TAYLOR). Burton particularly favoured the Taylor system; he was dubious about profit sharing, but conceded that it had been introduced successfully in several firms.

The second edition of 1905 contains an interesting chapter on the German system of management. This system, used in German factories before the First World War, was founded on Taylor's principles of scientific production, marrying them to a system of inspection and control derived from the Prussian Army. These quasi-military plants were, says Burton, highly efficient.

Urwick and Brech (1957) were somewhat critical of *The Commercial Management of Engineering Works*, believing it to be too technically oriented and too much focused on production, contrasting it unfavourably with the earlier *The Commercial Organisation of Factories* by Joseph Slater LEWIS. The criticism is valid, given that Burton clearly recognized that the manager's real role was much broader. However, allowance needs to be made for personal method. Not unlike Harold GENEEN half a century later, Burton focused on accounting

and production as the bottom line for both efficiency and profits. Not a generalist himself, he recognized the need for a more general approach. Credit needs to be given for this recognition, and Burton can claim a place in the early twentieth-century British tradition of management as a holistic discipline, at once both art and science – a tradition which was sadly eroded as the century went on.

BIBLIOGRAPHY

Burton, F.G. (1896a) *The Naval Engineer and Command of the Sea: A Story of Naval Administration*, Manchester: The Technical Publishing Co., Ltd.
—— (1896b) *Engineering Estimates and Cost Accounts*, Manchester: The Technical Publishing Co., Ltd.
—— (1899) *The Commercial Management of Engineering Works*, Manchester: The Scientific Publishing Co., Ltd; 2nd edn, 1905.
—— (1902) *Engineers and Shipbuilders Accounts*, London: Gee and Co.; 2nd edn, 1911.
Urwick, L.F. and Brech, E.F.L. (1947) *The Making of Scientific Management*, vol. 2, *Management in British Industry*, London: Management Publications Trust; repr. Bristol: Thoemmes Press, 1994.

MLW

BURTON, Montague Maurice
(1885–1952)

Montague Maurice Burton was born in Kurkel, Lithuania on 15 August 1885, the son of Hyman and Rachel Ossinsky (he adopted the name Montague Burton in 1904). He died in Leeds, Yorkshire on 21 September 1952. He married Sophia Marks in 1909. After education in an Orthodox Jewish parochial school,

Burton came to Britain in 1900 to escape anti-Semitic pogroms in his homeland. Settling in Chesterfield, Derbyshire, he learned English and began to work as a shop assistant. Ambitious and eager to make his fortune, in 1904, using a little borrowed capital, he set up a clothing shop in Chesterfield. In 1909 he moved to Sheffield and opened a second branch there; in the following year, shops were opened in Manchester, Leeds and Mansfield. Burton's younger brother Bernard came into partnership with him in 1913 and a third partner, the tailor Ellis Hurwitz, joined later that year.

The expanding of the partnership accompanied one of the distinctive features of the Burton enterprise: the vertical integration of his business up from retailing to manufacture of clothes and, ultimately, to manufacturing textiles. The first clothing factory was established in Leeds in 1914 under the management of Hurwitz; by 1925 this had grown to be a vast enterprise employing 5,000 people (Sigsworth 1986). In the 1930s more factories were established in Lancashire, allowing Burton to have full control over product design and quality, from the weaving of the wool to the tailoring of the suits and the design of the shops. This kind of vertical integration is seldom seen in the garment industry – Laura ASHLEY in the twentieth century is one of the few other examples – and the management of so complex and diverse a business is to say the least difficult. Burton, however, was more than equal to the task.

It is for retailing, however, that Burton is best known. From 1910 onwards he expanded his retail business very rapidly. By 1918 he had fifty-one shops; by 1928 there were 364 and by 1939 there were 600, making Burton's easily the largest retail chain in the world (Sigsworth 1986). Most were concentrated in Britain, although there were some outlets in Ireland and on continental Europe; in general, however, Burton tended to stick to the market he knew best. His main product offering was high-quality affordable men's suits and accessories (moves into making and selling women's clothing did not come until after the Second World War). He had a genius for picking prime retail locations for his shops, and was adamant about shop design and layout; he insisted that, as far as possible, all shops had to be laid out in the same way and have a uniform appearance so as to project a consistent brand image to customers. A teetotaller, he banned alcohol in any part of his business and, in an effort to woo patrons away from public houses, built billiards on the floor above many of his shops in an effort to provide alternative recreation to drinking, and, incidentally, bring more potential customers past his shop windows and through his front doors. Altruism and sound business practice were here well combined.

Patriarchal in his management style, Burton took a strong interest in the welfare of his workers, and his new factories in the 1920s and 1930s were built equipped with a wide variety of health, recreational and social facilities for workers. He understood the value of good relationships with employees and believed he had a paternal duty to look after their physical and moral well-being. A philanthropist and patron of the arts, he was also an ardent Zionist and supporter of both the League of Nations and the United Nations. Burton was knighted in 1939.

BIBLIOGRAPHY
Redmayne, R. (ed.) (1951) *Ideals in Industry*, Leeds: Montague Burton.
Sigsworth, E.M. (1984) 'Burton, Sir Montague Maurice', in D.J. Jeremy (ed.) *Dictionary of Business Biography*, London: Butterworths, vol. 1, 526–31.

MLW

BUTLIN, William Heygate Edmund Colborne (1899–1980)

Billy Butlin was born in Cape Town, South Africa on 29 September 1899, and died at his home on Jersey on 12 June 1980. His parents' marriage dissolved when he was young, and Butlin's mother remarried and took her son to Canada. Butlin left school at twelve; in 1915 he joined the army, serving with the Canadian Mounted Rifles during the First World War. After the war he returned briefly to Canada, then took passage to Britain and went to work for his uncle, a showman in the West Country.

Butlin quickly became a highly successful showman himself, running hoopla stalls and fairground attractions. In the mid-1920s he set up a seaside amusement park at Skegness, and followed this with nine more parks. He developed many new attractions, such as the Dodgem, which he imported from the United States. By 1930 he was a wealthy man.

Butlin then turned to designing and building holiday camps. According to his own account (Butlin and Dacre 1982), the inspiration for these came from the realization, while on holiday in the mid-1920s, that there was nowhere for working-class families to holiday comfortably. In the 1930s, there were more wage earners in Britain than ever before, and Butlin had identified a major market opportunity.

The first Butlin's camp, which opened in 1936 next to the amusement park at Skegness, was the first purpose-designed all-in holiday resort ever built. It included accommodation for 2,000 people (later expanded to 5,000), dining and recreation halls, games rooms, tennis courts, bowling greens, a boating lake and a swimming pool, and also a chapel with full Sunday services. The emphasis was on 'wholesome family entertainment' (campers also had free admission to the nearby amusement park). The public response showed that Butlin had got his market right: the camp was almost immediately full and was turning a profit within a few months.

During the Second World War Butlin organized hostels for munitions and factory workers, for which he received the MBE, and organized leave centres for British troops in Europe. Resuming his business in 1945 he continued his expansion, with seven camps around Britain by 1962. The advent of cheap air travel in the 1960s began cutting into Butlin's business; he retired in 1968, and the company was sold for £43 million in 1972.

Butlin was knighted in 1964. He married three times, and there were six children from the various marriages, two of whom predeceased him. The first two marriages are said to have been unhappy, and before divorcing his first wife Butlin lived with her sister for a number of years. His private life is thus in contrast to the atmosphere of his camps, where good cheer and strong morals were provided (or enforced) in equal measure.

A natural-born entrepreneur, with almost no formal education, Butlin had a fine grasp of the essentials of management. He proved himself an excellent organizer and motivator, and understood the psychology of both staff and customers, commanding loyalty from both in almost equal measure. Most of all, he showed how an understanding of consumer behaviour and motivation combined with sound management could open up new business sectors almost overnight, thus pioneering the mass leisure industry. Butlin's model has been considerably developed and refined, but the basic principles continued to be used, most notably by Gilbert TRIGANO in his up-market Club Med resorts.

BIBLIOGRAPHY
Butlin, W.E. and Dacre, P. (1982) *The Billy Butlin Story: 'A Showman to the End'*, London: Robson Books.
Jeremy, D.J. (1984) 'Sir William Heygate Colbourne Butlin', in D.J. Jeremy (ed.), *Dictionary of Business Biography*, London: Butterworths, vol. 1, 535–41.

MLW

BUZAN, Tony (1942–)

Tony Buzan was born in London in 1942. He graduated from the University of British Columbia with a degree in psychology in 1964, and subsequently lectured on psychology at the university. He later studied neurophysiology, neurolinguistics, semantics and perception in his quest to understand how people learn. He returned to London to take up the post of editor of the international journal of Mensa (the high-IQ society) from 1968, where he remained until 1971. At that time he was also involved in teaching people with learning difficulties, using his newly developed methods. He was invited to host an educational series called *Use Your Head*, which developed into a twenty-five year collaboration with the British Broadcasting Corporation (BBC) and resulted in his popular book of the same title, which was first published in 1974. A former successful athlete himself, Buzan has been a coach to the British Olympic rowing and chess squads, as well as a prize-winning poet.

Buzan's career as a writer on the functioning of the brain and mental powers has been concerned with the development of studying and learning skills. These include reading skills, memory, creativity, analytical thinking, logic, vision, communication, comprehension and concentration. Although he is best known for inventing and popularizing mind-mapping techniques, he has worked constantly at the development and inclusion of a wide range of techniques in all forms of educational activity. The motivation for his work was the premise that humans are believed to use only a tiny proportion of the potential of their brains.

Buzan developed the concept of 'mental literacy' and invented the 'mind-map' technique in the late 1960s. The mind map is a graphic technique that facilitates the unlocking of the brain's potential. It does this by harnessing the full range of cortical skills including word, image, colour, number, logic, rhythm and spatial awareness. As Buzan describes, drawing on the Nobel-prize-winning work of Roger Sperry, the more the different activities of the brain are integrated, the more synergetic the brain's performance becomes. Each separate intellectual skill enhances the performance of other intellectual skills.

Mind maps, often used for assembling an overview, structuring complex information and for brainstorming, are also a useful memory tool, according to Buzan. In fact, Buzan came to the development of mind maps in an attempt to develop tools that aided memory for studying and revising. The technique makes use of imagination, association and location, the basic principles identified by the Greeks as central to memory power. In developing the technique, Buzan was influenced by the writing of science fiction author A.E. van Vogt for his ideas on general semantics theory, which emphasizes that all knowledge is a giant map of associative networks. The work of Evelyn Wood on note-taking also influenced Buzan; Wood recommended breaking away from linear note-taking, and instead using words or phrases on lines emanating from a central geometric shape. Buzan began to use mind mapping in order to structure his thoughts on the mind-mapping technique itself and, in collaboration with his brother, Professor Barry Buzan, produced his first book on the subject, *The Mind Map Book* (1971).

One of Buzan's most popular books, *Use Your Head* (1974), regarded as his classic text, was voted one of the thousand greatest books of the last millennium, and one that should be read for this millennium. It has sold over a million copies and has recently been updated and reprinted. The considerable success of the mind map is due to its ability to gather and structure large amounts of data, and its facilitation of creative thinking by allowing new associations and linkages to emerge. Buzan continues to strive to reach the popular audience so that his techniques will be open to as many people as possible. He lectures widely, and has produced television and radio programmes, and software tools in order to facilitate this objective.

Amongst his other innovations are the founding of the World Memory Championships ('Memoriad') and the successful Mind Sports Olympiad (he himself held the world's highest 'creativity IQ' in 2000). He is chairman of the Brain Foundation and has also founded the Brain Trust Charity, which conducts research into thought processes and mechanisms of thinking. Its aim is to maximize the ability of individuals to unlock the potential of their brains. The drive for Buzan's work has been the belief that improved learning and clearer thinking will enhance human performance. Throughout his career Buzan has also worked closely with those labelled as dyslexic and 'learning disabled'.

Buzan's work raised the profile of creativity in management in practitioner and development circles alike, as well as self-help and personal development audiences. The considerable popularity of his books, which have together sold over three million copies, illustrates the widespread use of mind mapping as a problem-solving and learning technique.

BIBLIOGRAPHY
Buzan, T. (1977) *Make the Most of your Mind*, London: Pan.
—— (1974) *Use Your Head*, London: BBC Publishing.
—— (2000) 'Tony Buzan CV', http://www.mind-map.com/MM/training/tonycv.htm, 15 March 2001.
Buzan, T. and Buzan, B. (1971) *The Mind Map Book*, London: BBC Books.
Buzan, T. and Keene, R. (1994) *Buzan's Book of Genius and How to Unleash Your Own*, London: Stanley Paul.

AJ

C

CADBURY, Edward (1873–1948)

Edward Cadbury was born in Birmingham on 20 March 1873 and died there on 21 November 1948. He married Dorothy Hewitt in 1896; the couple had no children. He joined the family firm of Cadbury brothers, working with his father Richard and more notably his uncle, George CADBURY. Although he is best known today for his book *Experiments in Industrial Organization* (1912), which largely describes the work of his father and uncle, he was himself an energetic and talented manager who not only carried on their pioneering work in labour relations and social welfare, but also oversaw a great period of growth for the firm. While still in his twenties, Edward Cadbury took charge of exports and oversaw Cadbury's great export drive before the First World War. After the war, as high postwar tariffs began cutting into export sales, Cadbury changed strategies and began instead to expand production overseas, developing factories in Canada, Australia and other countries, turning Cadbury into a true multinational. He also emphasized operational planning and output management, and established the company planning office in 1913, one of the first such in a British firm. He was finally in charge of the women's works department, and took a great interest in advancing the welfare and role of women in the workplace.

Experiments in Industrial Organization is a meticulous documentation of the Cadbury system, organizationally and in welfare terms.

Particularly noteworthy is the emphasis on education, which played a key role in the Cadbury ethos; it was thought that knowledgeable employees were good employees. A full educational programme including art, science, history, geography and French along with mechanical and technical subjects was provided by the works school. Cadbury also had a comprehensive health care system, with staff doctors and nurses in attendance not only at the workplace but also at employees' homes. The emphasis was on keeping employees both mentally and physically fit.

In wages policy, a mixed system was adopted, with a basic wage supplemented by piecework. There was also a merit scheme, in which workers could earn bonuses for quality work. The overall philosophy was that the wage of each worker should be determined by his or her value to the firm; there was no blanket wage policy.

Employee involvement took several forms. Directly, employees could make contributions through a suggestion scheme. Suggestions could be put forward for new products, new production methods, new administrative or management procedures, or 'any suggestion on any other subject, so long as it relates to the works at Bournville in some way' (Cadbury 1912: 212). Prizes were given for the best suggestions. Edward Cadbury tracked the number of suggestions carried forward, and found that over time around 20 per cent on average were accepted, and 5–10 per cent were carried forward and put into practice.

Indirectly, employees had a voice through two powerful committees: the Men's Works Committee and the Women's Works Committee. Made up of a mixture of board nominees, foremen and workers and chaired by a director (Cadbury himself chaired the women's committee), the committees had power of scrutiny over plans for new machinery, buildings and other facilities, health and safety, employee complaints, cases of employee distress and many other issues. It is notable that the women's committee had virtually the same powers as that of the men.

Although in many ways highly paternalistic, Cadbury broke new ground in terms of employee involvement and participation. Cadbury himself was in no doubt that the results could be seen in terms of higher levels of productivity and innovation, and during his time Cadbury was one of the most admired firms in Britain.

BIBLIOGRAPHY
Cadbury, E. (1912) *Experiments in Industrial Organization*, London: Longmans, Green and Co.
Cadbury, E. and Shann, G. (1906) *Women's Work and Wages*, London: T. Fisher Unwin.
—— (1908) *Sweating*, London: Headley Brothers.
Wagner, G. (1987) *The Chocolate Conscience*, London: Chatto and Windus.
Williams, I.A. (1931) *The Firm of Cadbury 1831–1931*, London: Constable.

MLW

CADBURY, George (1839–1922)

George Cadbury was born in Edgbaston, Birmingham on 19 September 1839, and died at home in Northfield, Birmingham on 24 October 1922. His father, John Cadbury, was a Quaker and chocolate-maker; his mother was a temperance worker. George Cadbury was educated at a Quaker school in Edgbaston, but left school early after the death of his mother. After a period working for Joseph ROWNTREE, Cadbury joined the family firm, Cadbury Brothers. In 1861, aged twenty-one, he and his older brother Richard took control of the firm following their father's death. The business had gone into decline, and the brothers worked twelve hours a day, six days a week, to turn it around. A devout Quaker, George Cadbury taught Sunday school every week and abstained from alcohol, tobacco, coffee and tea.

The Cadbury business grew rapidly. By 1900 it had a turnover of £1 million; by 1912 this had reached £2 million, and by 1920 £8 million, outstripping all its rivals. Upon the death of Richard Cadbury in 1899, Cadbury Brothers became a limited company. Though some preferred shares were later issued, control remained strongly in family hands; Cadbury was a strong believer in family control. He had six children from his two marriages (to Mary Tylor in 1873 and, after her death in 1887, to Elizabeth Taylor); two of his sons, George and Edward CADBURY, followed him into the firm, as did two of Richard's sons.

George Cadbury is most famous for planning and building the model town of Bournville. When, in 1879, it became clear that the company's factory in central Birmingham was not large enough to support continued expansion, the Cadburys built a much larger factory on a greenfield site on the outskirts of the city. Along with the factory they built large-scale housing and public amenities for their workers, borrowing ideas from earlier schemes such as Robert OWEN's New Lanark. Bournville became the most famous of the late Victorian 'social experiments' that combined industrial management with social reform.

As Gardiner (1923) points out, Cadbury's social experiment was never *solely* about social reform. What was good for the community was good for the company, and vice versa; the innovations that pleased Cadbury most were those which benefited employees and the firm in equal measure. For example, swimming baths were built near the factory, and employees were encouraged to use these; this both improved employee health and fitness, and improved cleanliness in the factory.

Cadbury reduced working hours, on the grounds that shorter hours led to greater efficiency. He paid well; in hard times he preferred to lay off workers rather than cut pay, on the grounds that it was immoral to ask employees to work for low wages. He also promoted industrial democracy, and was one of the first employers to introduce works councils. His employment practices were not wholly progressive, however; female employees who married were dismissed, on the grounds that having a wife as a wage earner was bad for a man's morals.

Cadbury, like LEVER, John LEWIS and other British industrialists of the late nineteenth and early twentieth centuries, showed that it was possible to combine business growth with ethical behaviour. The Bournville experiment was an outstanding success, and greatly influenced British management thinking for the next half-century.

BIBLIOGRAPHY

Cadbury Brothers Ltd (1922) *George Cadbury 1839-1922: Memorial Number of the Bournville Works Magazine*, Birmingham: Cadbury Brothers Ltd.

Gardiner, A.G. (1923) *Life of George Cadbury*, London: Cassell.

Murray, B.G. (1984) 'George Cadbury', in D.J. Jeremy (ed.), *Dictionary of Business Biography*, London: Butterworths, vol. 1, 547–54.

MLW

CADBURY, George Adrian Hayhurst (1929–)

Adrian Cadbury was born on 15 April 1929 in Birmingham, the son of Lawrence Cadbury. His father and his uncle Edward CADBURY were the sons of George CADBURY, who had managed the spectacular growth of the Cadbury chocolate-making firm in the late nineteenth century. Educated at Eton, Adrian Cadbury served in the Coldstream Guards in 1948–9 before going on to King's College, Cambridge. A rower, he competed in the 1952 Olympic Games, where his team placed fourth in their event. He served as deputy chairman of Cadbury Schweppes from 1969 to 1974, and chairman from 1975 to 1989. He is described as one of the driving forces behind the merger of Cadbury and Schweppes in 1969 (Krass 1996). Following retirement from Cadbury-Schweppes, he was a member of the Panel on Takeovers and Mergers from 1990 to 1994, and served on the Economic and Financial Policy Committee of the Confederation of British Industry (CBI). He has held a number of other public and civic appointments, including president of the Birmingham Chamber of Commerce and Industry and chancellor of Aston University. He married twice, to Gillian Skepper in 1956 and, following her death in 1992, to Susan Sinclair in 1994. Adrian Cadbury was knighted in 1977.

In 1991 Cadbury was appointed chairman of the Cadbury Committee on the Financial Aspects of Corporate Performance, established by the London Stock Exchange, which investigated financial management and corporate governance generally. The recommendations of the committee and its code of best practice, published in 1992, have been adopted as policy guidelines in Britain – companies listed on the London Stock Exchange are required to comply with them – and have been influential in regulation and self-regulation elsewhere.

In the tradition of his father, uncle and grandfather, Adrian Cadbury is noted for his strong ethical approach to business and man-

agement. According to Krass (1996: 244), Cadbury emphasizes the individualistic nature of employees, and believes that their expectations and desires in life should receive explicit recognition in the workplace. The answer to the problems of control which this could create is to ensure that employees are strongly motivated towards achievement and success; this lessons the need for supervision, and ensures that top management can spend more time planning and leading, secure in the knowledge that all the individual members of the firm, rather like the members of a rowing team, are pulling together. He emphasizes that ethical behaviour must come from the top, and that leaders are responsible for ethics along with other matters of policy.

Cadbury's most important work is *The Company Chairman* (1995), a highly successful work both in Britain and abroad, and one of the few modern works to investigate in detail the increasingly demanding role of chairman of the board in a large modern corporation. Defining the role of the chairman, Cadbury says the first and foremost responsibility is to ensure that the board of directors itself runs smoothly and exercises its supervisory duties in an appropriate manner, particularly in areas such as setting corporate strategy. However, there are other duties as well. Increasingly, the chairman is becoming responsible for the company's external relations, while the managing director or chief executive officer retains responsibility for internal relations. Externally, the chairman has two important tasks. The first of these is to maintain good relations with shareholders; the second is to manage the company's responsibility to society.

Corporate social responsibility is, in Cadbury's view, a contract with society. He argues that 'companies are licensed by society to provide the goods and services which society needs. The freedom of operation of companies is, therefore, dependent on their delivering whatever balance of economic and social benefits society currently expects of them'

(Cadbury 1995: 147). Part of that contract 'is that companies shall not pursue their immediate profit objectives at the expense of longer-term interests of the community' (1995: 147).

In the future, Cadbury believes, corporate governance will increasingly come to be affected by these two factors: the power and demands of shareholders, and the demands of broader society that companies fulfil their social contracts. Frequently, these two interests will collide. A major element of the company chairman's role is to find the best means of ensuring that both interests are satisfied. This is clearly only a very sketchy summary of this thoughtful book, which should be seen as one of the best and most balanced studies of the practical aspects of corporate leadership yet produced.

BIBLIOGRAPHY
Cadbury, A. (1995) *The Company Chairman*, 2nd edn, Hemel Hempstead: Director Books.
Krass, P. (1996) *The Book of Leadership Wisdom*, Chichester: John Wiley.

MLW

CAMPION, Gabriel L. (1896–1959)

Gabriel Campion was born in Charleville, France on 17 January 1896. He died while on a round the world trip on 26 October 1959, near Ceylon. Campion studied jurisprudence and economics at the faculty of law at the University of Paris. After graduation, he entered the world of business and finance. From April 1921 to January 1954 he worked for the ministry of finance as financial audit officer. In 1937 he was engaged in the negotiation of a loan to Yugoslavia as plenipotentiary ambassador. In 1941 he was appointed the governmental member of the Morocco

National Bank. He also took up the post of president of the Paris Bank Association.

After the Second World War, many French universities established associated research institutes, and set out to develop independent programmes in management education, which had been a monopoly of the Grandes Écoles. In 1956 Paris University established a management research institute, which is now the Institute d'Administration des Entreprises de Paris (IAE). Faculty members were invited both from academic circles and the business world. Campion, a proficient businessman in the financial world and also concurrently president of the Bank Association in Paris, took up a post at the research institute. His lectures developed for the institute were published as the two-volume *Traité des entreprises privée*, the volumes appearing in 1945 and 1948. These books are the first academic work in France devoted to the major problems in all areas of business administration. Volume 1 was awarded the French Academy Prize.

France is an advanced nation in both the study of business administration and in management education. Regrettably, however, this fact is not well known, and many French people themselves are unaware of it. Yet in terms of management education, the École Superieur de Commerce de Paris (ESCP) was established as an agency of high commercial education in 1819. In addition, in 1881 the second commercial higher education agency, the Hautes Études Commerciales (HEC) was established in Paris. Commercial higher education agencies were established all over France. In comparison, in the United States the Wharton School was not established at the University of Pennsylvania until 1881. The first German commercial university was established in Leipzig in 1889; in Japan, Tokyo Commercial University (now Hitotsubashi University) was established in 1920. In terms of academic research associations, the first German association was established in 1924, with the first French organization following closely after in 1925; the first Japanese associ-ation was established in 1926, and the first US association not until 1936. When Campion arrived on the scene, he was thus part of an already growing tradition of French management thought and education.

Campion's main contribution was his theory of business administration. This theory was constituted on the premise that by absorbing the general equilibrium theory of M.E.L. Walras in a critical manner, a unified administration theory could be constructed that would combine the economics of business enterprises with the administration theory originally formulated by FAYOL. By examining services and products together with the concept of general equilibrium in the markets for capital and its performance as laws, Walras had expanded macroscopically the theory of entrepreneur's functions as being a combination of the production elements. Campion set out to expand Walras's theory microscopically. He defined the enterprise as a combination of those production elements which had technological aspects and those which had commercial aspects, on the assumption that this combination would bring about something new, a whole greater than the sum of its parts. A doubt arises as to the conditions under which the business enterprise would be able to remain in continuous existence. Campion determined that the conditions for existence reside in the principles of autonomy, cooperative labour and competition: these were the factors that would allow the business to survive. According to Campion, the essence of the business enterprise does not reside with profit-making, but instead in its capacity for autonomy and risk-taking. Thus his theory of the business enterprise not only covers enterprise for profit, but also deals with all business enterprises assuming technological and commercial risks through their autonomy. He takes it for granted that the essence of the functions of the executive, as seen above, is the combination and adjustment of production elements to achieve the enterprise's goals.

BIBLIOGRAPHY

Campion, G.L. (1943) *Economie privée: organization, financement et exploitation des enterprises* (Private Economy: Organization, Finance, and Administration of Enterprises), Paris: Centre d'Information Interprofessionnel.

—— (1945–8) *Traité des enterprises privées* (Introduction to Private Enterprises), 2 vols, Paris: Presses Universitaires de France.

ST

CAPRA, Fritjof (1939–)

Fritjof Capra was born in Vienna, Austria on 1 February 1939. He received his Ph.D. in theoretical physics from the University of Vienna in 1966, and subsequently engaged in research in particle physics at the University of Paris (1966–8), the University of California at Santa Cruz (1968–70), the Stanford Linear Accelerator Center (1970), Imperial College London (1971–4) and the Lawrence Berkeley Laboratory at the University of California (1975–88). He also taught at the University of California (at Santa Cruz and Berkeley) and San Francisco State University. However, it was his innovative exploration of the parallels between the modern physics and Eastern mysticism, in *The Tao of Physics* (1975), that brought him recognition. It also paved the path to his future work as a systems theorist and activist primarily concerned with the promotion of an ecological or holistic worldview. In his next book, *The Turning Point* (1982), he argued that Western science, as well as the economic and social systems, which are based on mechanistic thinking in the spirit of René Descartes and Isaac Newton, have reached their limits. Consequently, he called for drastic changes based on the adoption of a holistic paradigm of thought and social action, a view that would recognize the interconnectedness of all aspects of life. Capra's radical criticism of current science and social organization also stimulated his popularity among the adherents of New Age ideas. At the same time, he became one of the most poignant voices of the ecological movement.

In 1984 Capra co-authored a book on the rise of the ecological politics (*Green Politics*, with Charlene Spretnak) and co-founded the Elmwood Institute in Berkeley, California, a network of thinkers and activists dedicated to promotion of the ecological paradigm. A group of authors gathered by this think tank, including Capra himself, wrote *EcoManagement* (1993), the first guide for the 'ecological auditing' of business and the reduction of its impact on the environment. The book provided practical guidelines for examinations of business organizations and their operations, including product design, manufacturing, management techniques, corporate culture and goals, in relation to their long-term ecological sustainability. In 1995 Capra and Günter Pauli co-edited the book *Steering Business Towards Sustainability*, a review of ways to motivate corporations to integrate sustainable development into their core strategic considerations. In *The Web of Life* (1996) Capra presented a synthesis of systems thinking applied to living systems and promoted the concept of 'ecological literacy', defined as 'understanding the principles of organization of ecological communities (i.e. ecosystems) and using those principles for creating sustainable human communities' (Capra 1996: 289). He suggested that the principles of ecology should become manifest in areas such as management, politics and education. This view is reflected in Capra's current role as the founding director of the Center for Ecoliteracy, an educational organization dedicated to introducing environmental education and systems thinking into schools. Capra is also on the faculty of Schumacher College, an institution for eco-

logical studies in Britain. He has lectured widely to lay and professional audiences across Europe, Asia, and North and South America.

BIBLIOGRAPHY

Callenbach, E. *et al.* (1993) *EcoManagement: The Elmwood Guide to Ecological Auditing and Sustainable Business*, San Francisco: Berret-Koehler.

Capra, F. (1975) *The Tao of Physics*, London: Wildwood House.

—— (1982) *The Turning Point: Science, Society and the Rising Culture*, London: Wildwood House.

—— (1996) *The Web of Life: A New Synthesis of Mind and Matter*, London: HarperCollins.

Capra, F. and Pauli, G. (eds) (1995) *Steering Business Towards Sustainability*, Tokyo: United Nations University Press.

Capra, F. and Spretnak, C. (1984) *Green Politics*, New York: E.P. Dutton.

DR

CARNEGIE, Andrew (1835–1919)

Andrew Carnegie was born in Dunfermline, Scotland on 25 November 1835 and died in Lennox, Massachusetts on 11 August 1919. His father, Will Carnegie, and his mother Margaret were unemployed weavers, thrown out of work by the new industrial technology of the factory system. Impoverished by Britain's Industrial Revolution, the Carnegies took advantage of family ties to leave their home in Dunfermline and settle in Pittsburgh, Pennsylvania in 1848.

By 1853, Pittsburgh was a growing centre of about 50,000 people earning a living in coal and lumber. The city seemed sure to profit from the USA's dawning industrial age. The region where the tributaries of the Ohio river joined was rich in iron ore, bituminous coal and limestone. Already Pittsburgh boasted sixteen iron mills, and the nearby city of Connellsville was becoming the coke capital of the United States. When Carnegie arrived, a number of small plants and iron industries competed to service the local market.

Carnegie, then aged thirteen, had to enter the work force immediately. Like many immigrants, he was able to succeed not only by his dedication to hard work and learning on the job, but through the networking and support of his fellow Scottish immigrants. He began working as a bobbin boy in a textile factory owned by a fellow Scot, and from there graduated to another Scottish-owned factory where he managed the boiler room. The fact that his new boss could not write well enabled Carnegie to begin to help him with his books.

Carnegie was never one to neglect new ideas or methods of doing things, and this would be a paramount factor in his rise. He helped his boss during the day while studying accounting at night. His diligence soon led his boss to refer him to the Pittsburgh Telegraph Company. This new opportunity was the key to Andrew's future. Hired as a messenger, he was suddenly placed in contact with prominent Pennsylvania businessmen, whom he quickly impressed with his initiative. Seeing a future in new skills and technologies, he mastered Morse code.

By 1853, Andrew Carnegie was working as a telegraph operator, placed in one of the most strategic locations an entrepreneur could be. Western Pennsylvania boasted rich deposits of coal and oil, and had a lead in the railway and telegraph industries that, in the 1850s, were beginning to transform the United States. Carnegie was acquiring both networks and skills in a new economy that was poised on the verge of a take-off that would be accelerated by the Civil War. All his business dealings gave him expert market knowledge.

Carnegie took another major step at seventeen when he was hired to be the personal

telegrapher of Thomas Scott, a prominent executive in the powerful Pennsylvania Railroad (the Penn). He worked for the Penn from 1853 to 1865, learning the skills of management, cost accounting, coordination of markets and personnel in an operation that extended from Philadelphia to Chicago. In his career at the Penn, Carnegie showed a remarkable initiative. When a derailment took place, he intervened, forging Scott's signature on an order to get the trains moving. In doing this he risked his entire career, but the risk paid off handsomely when he succeeded and Scott was impressed. By 1859, aged twenty-four, Carnegie was superintendent of the whole Penn Western Division.

In the meantime, he had become a successful investor due to dividends from some stocks he had acquired cheaply with Scott's help. When Scott entered into the partnership of the new Woodruff Sleeping Car Company, Carnegie was given 13 per cent of the shares, adding $5,000 a year to his income. Carnegie then proceeded to sink this new capital into the emerging oil industry. Less cautious than Ohio's John D. ROCKEFELLER, who would invest in refining, Carnegie, with capital to risk and spare, invested in the oil boom which swept Western Pennsylvania on the eve of the Civil War. He formed an oil partnership called Columbia Oil, and in the first year made a near 50 per cent profit on his investment.

The Civil War launched the fortunes of many of the USA's greatest tycoons, especially the giants Carnegie, Rockefeller and J.P. MORGAN. Columbia did so well that the one-time bobbin boy, making fifty dollars a year in 1848, earned almost $50,000 a year by 1863. He now managed a series of industries, including the Keystone Bridge Company, Union Iron Mills, the Superior Rail Mill and the Pittsburgh Locomotive Works. By 1868 he also had a share in Union Pacific, Western Union and the Pullman Palace Car Company. Carnegie, however, saw that his future and that of the United States lay in steel. Railroads, oil and steel formed a synergy in which growth in one

stimulated growth in the others. As Americans fought to preserve the Union and poured westward into California, the Plains and the Rockies, forging a continental market linked by railways, Carnegie recognized that railroads needed locomotives, rolling stock, rails and bridges.

Iron-making in the United States in the 1850s and even 1860s was still a slow business. Britain dominated the techniques and the market. British and early US foundries converted iron ore into pig iron by expelling the impurities. The more impurities one expelled from iron, such as oxygen, carbon or phosphorous, the stronger the iron would be. US iron-makers used charcoal and, at first, hard anthracite coal in their smelting process. As the railroads crossed the Alleghenies and joined the Northeast to the growing states of the Midwest, the demand for iron rails became insatiable. The coke ovens of Connellsville quickly became a major source of cheaper US pig iron, now smelted with the soft bituminous coal of Western Pennsylvania.

Carnegie set up the Cyclops Iron Works in 1864 and the following year he resigned from the Penn, never to work for a salary again. As the network of rail lines in the Northeast and Midwest turned into a thick web that thrust its strands into places such as Nebraska, Colorado, Texas and California, more trains ran on them and the trains were heavier. Iron rails wore out very quickly. Carnegie proposed to market sturdier and better rails. Telegraphy and railroads revolutionized the economy in the 1840s and 1850s, and Carnegie saw the potential of both. The same was true of steel, which was far sturdier than iron, but steel was too expensive to be profitably used at that time.

Carnegie, however, was aware that Henry Bessemer in 1856 had developed a cheap means of making steel by blowing compressed air through molten iron. The process, developed at the same time by William Kelly in the United States, was patented in 1866, opening the door for the commercial production of a

metal that was far sturdier than even the purest wrought iron. Carnegie quickly decided that instead of diversifying in railroads, oil and iron, he would throw all his resources into the essential new technology of steel, and excel at it. Setting up Carnegie, McCandless, and Company, he proceeded to hire the world's leading expert on Bessemer steel to design the state-of-the-art Edgar Thomson Steel Works, on the field where George Washington and General Braddock had been defeated by the French in 1754. The works, built by Carnegie engineer Alexander Holley (1832–82) between 1873 and 1875 were named after Pennsylvania Railroad President John Edgar THOMSON. Investing in a new plant in the depths of the 1873 depression seemed foolish to many, but Carnegie had the resources to do it, thanks to the careful and cautious management of his assets. The severe deflation, moreover, cut his costs and weeded out his potential competitors. Situated at the junction of the Allegheny, Monongehela and Ohio Rivers, and close to the Penn and B&O rail yards, the Thomson Works had easy access to coal, iron, oil and customers.

Rivers and rail lines gave the Thomson Works access to the newly discovered deposits of soft, easily-mined low-phosphorous iron ore found in Upper Michigan, and the soon to be uncovered beds of eastern Minnesota. By 1900 the Mesabi Range would provide one-third of all US iron and one-sixth of all the iron in the world. If Minnesota would provide the raw materials of US power, Carnegie would provide the means to turn it into the finished steel that guaranteed that power.

The new steel-maker's management skills allowed him, like Rockefeller, to outproduce and undercut any rivals. Carnegie possessed superior market intelligence and technology, and used both to his advantage. He applied his management experience learned on the railroad to control his costs systematically. For Carnegie, controlling costs was the key to profit, for costs were far more predictable than earnings. Unlike others, Carnegie knew well in advance whether a given year would show a profit or a loss. He could set his prices wherever he needed to keep his plants running at full capacity. He could threaten to undercut his competitors for, unlike them, he knew his steel cost fifty dollars a ton.

The millions Carnegie saved were ploughed into investments in new steel-making techniques. Quickly, the USA began to overtake Britain in steel production. In 1870, Britain produced 292,000 tons of steel to the USA's 69,000; by 1880 the USA, led by Carnegie, was catching up with 1,247,000 to Britain's 1,375,000. By 1890 Carnegie, and what was left of his competition, forged ahead: 4,217,000 to 3,679,000. By 1900 the giant Carnegie combine dominated a steel industry that produced twice as much steel as did Britain: 10,188,000 tons versus 5,050,000 tons in a world steel market of 28,273,000 tons.

Carnegie knew well that innovation cut costs and created profits, market shares and jobs. He was eventually able to make ever-larger steel production runs at no higher cost. He invested heavily in research to allow his firm to cut out any redundant steps in the process. Molten iron was poured directly into the steel converters, and steel ingots were loaded onto moving flatcars. Carnegie soon applied the new open-hearth process pioneered by Englishmen Sidney Thomas and Percy Gilchrist, which meant cheaper, faster and better steel production. By the 1890s this new steel was replacing Bessemer steel. Carnegie recognized what his British (and US) competitors did not: that investment in new plants and techniques might seem more risky and expensive at first, but that the productivity and market-share advantages would eventually even the score. Carnegie's cheaper, higher-quality steel captured the market from that produced by firms which still clung to the techniques of the 1860s in the 1880s and 1890s. From $200 per ton in 1810, the price of steel was reduced to $20 per ton by 1900. In 1860 iron-makers were shipping 100,000 tons of ore from Michigan; by 1900 Carnegie con-

trolled the lion's share of over 10 million tons coming largely from the Mesabi.

Carnegie was a pioneer in mass production before Henry FORD. Machinery loaded his blast furnaces and dumped pig iron onto freight cars. Carnegie was now able to build blast furnaces that were 30 metres high, cutting his labour costs in half. Because of this and other innovations, Carnegie Steel prospered during the 1890s depression, expanding by 75 per cent while other firms were going under. Carnegie's strategy was to develop economies of scale, know the contours of the entire market, and gain as much market knowledge as possible to anticipate shifts ahead of time. According to his partner Charles SCHWAB, Carnegie's success was due to his ability to anticipate competitors in manufacturing better and cheaper than they did.

By the late 1880s Carnegie was riding a railway boom that saw the construction of many lines in the West and the South. He sensed that the market for steel rails would soon be saturated, while vast new markets for steel structures were opening up everywhere. The United States was fast becoming an urban nation as ranks of immigrants and displaced farmers flocked to the cities. A boom in construction of skyscrapers, steel-braced offices, elevated trains, trolleys, utility lines and bridges meant one thing for Carnegie: an enormous new market for all kinds of steel products.

Carnegie rose to the new challenge in the boldest manner possible, through vertical integration. He placed Henry Clay Frick in charge of rationalizing all Carnegie operations. The vast new mines of Minnesota were leased from the Rockefellers. Carnegie used Rockefeller's rolling stock and shipping, but soon bought his own ore ships and set up his own mining subsidiary, the $20 million Oliver Iron Mining Company. To further internalize his operations, Carnegie built his own rail line from Conneaut, Ohio, on the shores of Lake Erie, to Pittsburgh. Iron could now be mined, shipped and turned into steel without ever leaving Carnegie's control. The depression of the 1890s, the worst in US history at that time, only dented Carnegie's growth, with his annual profits still averaging $4 million a year between 1893 and 1896.

In spite of his enormous wealth, Andrew Carnegie remained socially progressive. He read widely, including the Bible, the classics, Shakespeare, Macaulay, Darwin and the works of the social Darwinist philosopher Herbert Spencer. Believing that all was well since all grew better, he, like J.P. Morgan and John D. Rockefeller, modified the freewheeling ideology of unrestrained market competition. Carnegie's own idea was that big firms like his own were actually good for competition because they would attract new enterprises and new money. Meanwhile, mass production and the application of technology and rational management would raise everyone's living standards.

Andrew Carnegie's philosophy, set forth in his 1889 *Gospel of Wealth* and his *Autobiography*, was a remarkable synthesis of social Darwinism and philanthropy in which the law of competition applied to firms more than individuals. *The Gospel of Wealth* contained in a single volume a defence of inequality linked to one of the strongest statements of *noblesse oblige* ever penned by a business leader. The revolution in productivity Carnegie had done so much to perfect now enabled the poor to 'enjoy what the rich could not before afford'. The only thing that made this possible was 'the concentration of business industrial and commercial, in the hands of a few; and the law of competition between these' as being beneficial and essential for the survival of the human race. Managers in this world must of necessity make as much profit as they could (Hacker 1968: 359).

Carnegie's defence of business concentration provoked a highly critical response, particularly in Britain, which linked the rise of firms such as Carnegie's to the growing disparity of rich and poor. In the British journal *Nineteenth Century*, Carnegie replied in 1891 by showing that the prosperity of the million-

aire was inseparable from that of his fellow citizens: 'In a country where the millionaire exists there is little excuse for pauperism; the condition of the masses is satisfactory just in proportion as a country is blessed with millionaires' (Hacker 1968: 360). Large companies created wealth, not destroyed it. There were hardly any millionaires in all of Asia, more in Britain than in all of Europe, and even more in the United States, where a worker could make twice as much as in Britain and four times as much as in Europe. Millionaires created wealth for everyone, and would make no money by exploiting their workers. The higher the wages an employer paid, the higher would be his profits.

Andrew Carnegie was one of the most progressive employers of the Gilded Age. He paid his workers well, and acknowledged their right to form trade unions. He disdained the use of strike breakers. His reputation as a benevolent merchant prince was, however, to be forever tarnished by the bitter Homestead strike of 1892, for which he was not directly responsible. Carnegie had left the Homestead operation in the hands of Frick, whose philosophy of management was far more rigid than his own. When the steelworkers' contract came up for renewal, Frick rolled back their wages in a deepening recession. The workers, who mistrusted Frick, perceived an attempt on the part of management to destroy the union. Acting high-handedly, Frick sent a private army of Pinkertons (private detectives and security guards) to occupy the steel mills. One of the most ferocious industrial battles in US history then took place, with workers attacking the Pinkertons with a cannon and pouring oil into the Monongehela, which was then set on fire. Seven died and the Pennsylvania militia had to restore order. Frick himself was wounded by an anarchist agitator. The mills reopened, with non-union labour. Carnegie, in Scotland at the time, did nothing on behalf of the workers, but supported Frick. As a result, his progressive reputation received a blow from which it never fully recovered. According to the *St. Louis*

Post-Dispatch: 'Three months ago Andrew Carnegie was a man to be envied. Today he is an object of mingled pity and contempt' (Smith 1984: 477). Homestead produced a great deal of soul-searching in Carnegie, which served to reinforce his philanthropic instincts.

Although he lived in a time in which the trust and the limited liability corporation were fast taking over US management, Carnegie still expressed a preference for the partnership form. In a corporation, bankers and promoters were too close to the seat of power to permit the best management decisions to be made. Carnegie felt that in his partnership of thirty-two executives, which resembled a giant replica of the ancient Roman publican partnership, the input and expertise of men like Frick and Schwab were indispensable to his success. In his huge operation, Carnegie saw himself merely as the first among equals and gave his partners due credit for their mutual success.

Nevertheless, Carnegie in 1900 defended the trust and corporate forms as essential in concentrating capital, accessing a national market and cheapening the cost of goods. In a piece entitled 'Popular Illusions about Trusts', he linked low prices to the scale of production: to 'make ten tons of steel a day would cost many times as much per ton as to make one-hundred tons ... the larger the scale of operation, the cheaper the product' (Hacker 1968: 361).

In spite of all his success, Carnegie by 1900 faced a challenge from one of the few powerful enough to challenge him. The banker J.P. Morgan was now branching into the steel industry and cutting into Carnegie's vast market. The new Morgan steel firms were no match for Carnegie, but it would take a decade to put them out of business, and Andrew Carnegie, at sixty-five, was not up to the struggle. Morgan had two assets: his money, and Charles Schwab. Schwab insisted that the steel industry now needed more, not less, specialization, as both Carnegie and his rivals sought to make the same kinds of steel.

Schwab argued that plants should concentrate on rails, girders or pipes and relocate to the most cost-efficient locations, and envisioned an amalgamation of most (but not all) steel companies into one large firm. Morgan, dreading the prospect of a steel war with the Carnegie colossus, liked what he heard and offered $400 million for the Carnegie Company. Carnegie finally accepted $492 million in 1901.

Carnegie retired from the business world, leaving as his legacy the $1.4 billion United States Steel Corporation, a gargantuan trust made up of the Carnegie, National Steel, National Tube, American Steel and Wire, American Steel Hoop, American Tin Plate, American Sheet Steel, American Bridge, Shelby Steel Tube Companies and the Lake Superior Consolidated Iron Mines with all of its fleet, mines, and rail lines. Having never totally buried his egalitarian origins, he now devoted his life to donating some $350 million to libraries, parks, universities, trust funds and the cause of world peace, until his death in 1919.

After the American Civil War, steel became the key index of world power. The fact that the United States became the foremost steel-producing power in the world was due in part to its immense resources and huge domestic market, but the role of Andrew Carnegie and his prudent, innovative management was central. Carnegie's contributions to the advancement of US management were enormous in terms of both ideas and accomplishments. He created almost single-handedly the industry that made the United States the most powerful country in the world. Without him, Ford, General Motors, Boeing and Allied victory in both world wars would have been impossible. He pioneered the understanding that specialization and determined investment in new technologies was the key to both a firm's and a nation's competitiveness. Carnegie also led the way in systematic cost accounting which, coupled with a knowledge of past and present market conditions, gave him a great advantage over his rivals. Finally, his advanced views on labour relations and corporate phil-anthropy, despite Homestead, foreshadowed the welfare capitalism of the 1950s.

BIBLIOGRAPHY
Hacker, L.M. (1968) *The World of Andrew Carnegie: 1865–1901*, New York: Lippincott and Co.
Smith, P. (1984) *The Rise of Industrial America: A People's History of the Post-Reconstruction Era*, vol. 6, New York: McGraw-Hill Book Company.
Wall, J.F. (1970) *Andrew Carnegie*, New York: Oxford University Press.

DCL

CARNOT, Lazare Nicolas Marguerite
(1753–1823)

Lazare Carnot, the 'Organizer of Victory', was born in Nolay, Burgundy on 13 May 1753, the son of a local lawyer and judge. He died on 2 August 1823 in Magdeburg, Germany, possibly of cholera. Educated at Autun and the Engineering School in Paris, he joined the artillery service in 1773 and was promoted to captain in 1783. He became known as a writer on scientific and military affairs, especially fortifications; he also became involved in left-wing politics, and was friendly with Maximilian Robespierre.

Following the French Revolution of 1789, Carnot was elected a member of the Legislative Assembly in 1791. He was an influential member of the Jacobins, the left-wing party that seized control in 1793, and that year became a member of the ten-man Committee of Public Safety, headed by Robespierre, which ruled France and used the guillotine to purge political opposition ruthlessly. At the same time, a coalition of foreign powers had defeated French armies in the field and was poised to invade. Carnot, who possessed both

great energy and great organizational abilities, reformed the French army and, in the words of Dupré (1940: 100), 'in eighteen months, staffed and directed to victory the fourteen raw armies raised by the revolution'. The new French armies repulsed the invaders on every front.

Carnot survived the counter-revolution of Thermidor 1794, when Robespierre and his colleagues fell, and kept a seat on the five-man Directory which took over government, continuing to organize and manage the French military machine. Ousted in the coup of 19 Fructidor 1797, he spent two years in exile in Bavaria, but was invited to return by Napoleon, who had risen to power through his command of the armies Carnot had organized. In 1807 he retired from all public offices in order to devote himself to writing, but in 1814 served briefly on Napoleon's staff; in 1815, on Napoleon's return from Elba, Carnot again offered his services and was made Minister of the Interior. Napoleon ennobled him as a count on the day of the Battle of Waterloo. Following the Bourbon restoration, Carnot went into exile once more, and remained in Germany until his death.

Carnot was one of the greatest organizers of all time. He worked almost continuously, and oversaw every aspect of the military machine, including recruitment, training, equipment and promotions, even on occasion taking to the field to oversee his generals directly. He was a great cutter of red tape, and often issued orders in his own handwriting on memorandum paper, with little or no formality and bypassing established chains of command. His memory was prodigious, and he was a master of detail. Most of all, he managed to centralize the control of military affairs, and ensured that the French army was directed by a single controlling will. His organizational genius was greatly admired by MOLTKE, and influenced the organizational thinking of the early proponents of scientific management.

BIBLIOGRAPHY

Amson, D. (1992) *Carnot*, Paris: Perrin.
Carnot, H. (1907) *Mémoires sur Lazare Carnot 1753–1823*, 2 vols, Paris: Hachette.
Dupré, H. (1940) *Lazare Carnot: Republican Patriot*, Oxford, OH: Mississippi Valley Press.
Reinhard, M. (1994) *Le Grand Carnot: Lazare Carnot 1753–1823*, Paris: Hachette.

MLW

CARPENTER, Walter Samuel, Jr (1888–1976)

Walter Samuel Carpenter was born in Wilkes-Barre, Pennsylvania on 8 January 1888 and died in Wilmington, Delaware on 2 February 1976. The son of an engineering contractor, also named Walter Samuel Carpenter, and his wife, Belle Carpenter née Morgan, Carpenter attended public schools in his hometown and graduated in 1906 from Wyoming Seminary, a prep school in nearby Kingston, Pennsylvania. He then entered Cornell University, where he planned to earn a degree in civil engineering. He never finished his degree. He worked at Du Pont every summer during his first three years at Cornell, and left university during his senior year to take a full-time job with the company in Chile's barren north coastal region. There he assumed responsibility for purchasing the vast tonnage of sodium nitrate needed for Du Pont's explosives operations.

The Chilean nitrate market was very competitive but Carpenter did well, obtaining the immense quantities Du Pont needed. After two years in Chile, in 1911 he was assigned to work in the development department at Du Pont's corporate headquarters in Wilmington,

Delaware. In 1917, as the United States entered the First World War and the market for Du Pont explosives expanded, Carpenter was appointed director of the firm's development division. By 1919 he was a vice-president and, at the age of thirty-one, the firm's youngest director and executive committee member. The firm's three principals, the cousins Irénée, Lammot and Pierre DU PONT, were reshaping the family company at this time, and Carpenter was one of the key people they relied on as they moved forward.

Carpenter was involved in the early negotiations that were to carry Du Pont into such products as ammonia derivatives, rayon, celluloid and lacquers. Each became significant in the development of the new chemical and product divisions that fuelled the company's growth: Ammonia led to the manufacture of polychemicals. Rayon was a staple for developing the textile fibres division. Celluloid led to plastics, and lacquers became the foundation for Du Pont's paint manufacturing business.

In 1922 Carpenter was named treasurer of Du Pont, and successively served as a member of the finance committee, vice-chairman of the executive committee and chairman of the finance committee. In the latter role, he maintained Du Pont's investment in research and promoted the construction of new plants for new products. In 1927 he was one of a group of Du Pont executives elected to the board of General Motors after Du Pont made a major investment in the latter firm. He served on the General Motors board until 1959.

In May 1940 Carpenter succeeded Lammot du Pont to become the first president of Du Pont who was not a member of the du Pont family. With the United States poised to enter the Second World War, Carpenter spearheaded Du Pont's participation in a vast government production programme in which the firm designed, built and operated fifty defence plants, ranging from relatively small units to an engineering works in Hanford, Washington, where plutonium for the first atomic bomb was made.

After the war, Carpenter changed the business focus of the company to achieve production levels more suited to a peacetime economy, then stepped down as president in favour of Crawford Greenwalt. Carpenter became chairman of the board and served for fourteen years. In 1962 he accepted the rarely bestowed title of honorary chairman, which he held until 1975 when, at the age of eighty-seven, he chose not to stand for re-election. He thus ended a sixty-five-year career with Du Pont. At that point, the firm was manufacturing more than 1,600 chemical products, and had plants or offices in thirty-four states and several countries.

Carpenter died at his home in Wilmington at the age of eighty-eight. His peers remembered him as a thoughtful man who was able to grasp key points quickly, and who could see future needs and opportunities clearly. They also remembered him as a strong proponent of owner-management of large industrial firms, and how he saw this as one of the competitive advantages Du Pont wielded over the course of its long history. Carpenter was a firm believer in the philosophy that managers should have a stake in the company beyond their salaries by becoming major stockholders.

BIBLIOGRAPHY
Cheape, C.W. (1995) *Strictly Business: Walter Carpenter at Du Pont and General Motors*, Baltimore, MD: Johns Hopkins University Press.

BB

CASSON, Herbert Newton (1869–1951)

Herbert Newton Casson was born in Odessa, Ontario on 23 September 1869. He died at home in Norwood, Surrey on 4 September

1951. His father, the Reverend Wesley Casson, was a Methodist missionary from County Durham in northern England; his mother, Elizabeth Jackson, came from an immigrant family in Brantford, Ontario and had in her youth been known as 'the Belle of Brantford'. During Casson's youth the family moved around the remote bush towns of northern Ontario, as his father was posted to a new church every three years. The years 1877–80 were spent in the frontier province of Manitoba, whose population was still mostly nomadic Plains Indians and Métis (mixed race) peoples; years later, Casson recalled vividly the sight of armed Métis horsemen riding into the trading post where his father's church was located (Casson 1931). The family returned to Ontario in early 1880, shortly before the outbreak of the Métis rebellion led by Louis Riel.

Although he says he had no formal education until the age of seventeen, the years on the frontier taught Casson a great deal, including self-confidence and self-reliance. In his youth, he recalled, people turned their hands to everything necessary to make a living; if you did not know how to do something, then you learned. By the time Casson went to Victoria College (now part of the University of Toronto) in 1890 on a theology scholarship, he had acquired a hunger for knowledge, both theoretical and practical. The almost compulsive desire for learning is one of the constant features of his life:

I have found that knowledge is infinite. The longer I live, the more I realize that what I know is only a very small thing. On every road I have travelled, I have found there is no end to it. Every man who wishes to live a worth-while life must keep on learning as long as he has breath. I dare say that when my doctor tells me I have only three more days to live, I shall begin to study coffins.

(Casson 1931: 231–2)

Although Casson wished to study philosophy, the scholarship granted by the Methodist church would only allow him to study theology. Undeterred, he obtained permission to double up his courses and graduated with a joint degree from Victoria College in 1892. He was immediately offered a position by the church. He had not yet been ordained, but there was a shortage of ministers and Casson was given the church at Owen Sound, Ontario late in 1892, along with a small salary. Just twenty-three, he threw himself into his job, starting a temperance movement soon after his arrival. Quite what happened next, Casson does not relate, stating only that men flocked to his church, but women left it in large numbers. In the following year he was tried by the Methodist church council for heresy and found guilty. He resigned his position and went south to Boston, where he found work with a publishing company.

His brief career as a Methodist clergyman had given Casson a sense of social responsibility, and also seems to have encouraged a desire to rebel. In Boston in 1893 he visited the immigrant slums on the south side of the city and was shocked by the terrible poverty he found there. He became, almost overnight, a socialist; within a few months he was one of the USA's leading 'Red' agitators, leading mass demonstrations in Boston, drawing audiences of thousands to his lectures and rallies, and establishing links with socialist leaders elsewhere. Among the friends he made in this period – names he still mentions with affection forty years on – were the British socialist leader Keir Hardie, the American trade union boss Samuel Gompers, and Walter Vrooman, later co-founder of Ruskin College, Oxford. It was Hardie, Casson recalled in his memoirs, who first put into his head the idea of going to Britain (Casson 1931).

In 1898, following the destruction of the US battleship *Maine* in the port of Havana, Cuba, war fever swept the United States, fomented by newspaper owners like William Randolph HEARST and Joseph PULITZER. Casson, opposed

to the war for both personal and ideological reasons, tried to organize a pacifist movement. Almost unanimously, his followers deserted him, clamouring in support of the war movement. Many years later, writing his autobiography, Casson's tone still betrays his bitterness: 'Everything that I had built up in six years was destroyed in a week' (Casson 1931: 57).

Seeking refuge from the crushing of his hopes, Casson joined what he thought would be a group of like-minded people, the Ruskin Colony, a socialist commune founded in Tennessee the previous year. He was bitterly disappointed. He found at Ruskin not the camaraderie of true socialists working together for a goal, but a group of quarrelling, factionalized, suspicious people living together in filth and abject misery on a diet of rice and beans. He stayed for six months, by the end of which the scales had fallen from his eyes. He wrote later:

> this strange adventure cured me of all sympathy with Socialism or Communism. It swept my mind clear of all the plausible theories of social democracy. It opened my eyes to the fact that there is no tyrant like the mob – that the most efficient thing in every nation is the leadership of the 'Efficient Few' ... As soon as I left Ruskin Colony, I became a defender of civilization.
>
> (Casson 1931: 60–61)

After some heart searching, he resolved on a complete change of course. As he puts it simply: 'I had seen the best the Communism could do. And now I wanted to see the best that could be done by private Capitalism' (Casson 1931: 65). He had heard something of the reputation of John PATTERSON at National Cash Register, and travelled north to visit the latter's factory in Dayton. The meeting with Patterson and his tour of the Dayton plant, clean and well-ventilated with comfortable dining and health facilities for the workers,

made a deep impression; he described the passage from Ruskin to Dayton as one from squalor to opulence. Around this time too, Casson met and married Lydia Kingsmill Commander.

Casson had always had an ability to write, and he now went to New York, where he quickly found a job with Arthur Brisbane at the *New York Evening Journal*; here he spent six months learning the newspaper trade. He was then offered a job by Joseph Pulitzer on the *New York World*, and accepted (apparently ready to forgive Pulitzer's role in the war fever of 1898). The *World* at this point was abandoning its downmarket competition with the Hearst papers and was beginning to set new standards for quality journalism. Casson, after an interval, was made editor of the *World*'s Forum Page, where he made a speciality of interviewing people in positions of power. An early break came when he persuaded the notoriously taciturn President Grover Cleveland to grant him an interview. The two men became friendly, and Casson remained a confidante of Cleveland for many years. From politicians and leading academics Casson went on to interview inventors and scientists, including Marconi, Tesla, EDISON and BELL, and then businessmen such as Edward FILENE and John WANAMAKER. He became a leading member of the New York literary scene, friendly with Mark Twain and other leading writers. Among his coups was the first published interview with the brothers Orville and Wilbur Wright, shortly after their first powered flight at Kitty Hawk, North Carolina.

In 1905 the editor Frank Munsey offered Casson a job on *Munsey's Magazine*, with a brief to write a series of profiles of the steel barons. This later became Casson's first book, *The Romance of Steel: The Story of a Thousand Millionaires*, published in 1907. From this success he went on to write on the combine harvester industry and the development of the telephone; he also produced a biography of Cyrus Hall McCORMACK at the

request of the latter's widow. His pen portraits of American business leaders at the beginning of the century are still highly evocative: Andrew CARNEGIE he describes as 'one of the most original and sagacious men I have ever known'; Henry Clay Frick was 'a man of steel – keen, hard, competent'; Charles M. SCHWAB was 'always uncomfortable in the midst of his grandeur'; of J.P. MORGAN in a rage, 'the very look of him made my knees shake (Casson 1931: 107–15). Most moving of all, perhaps, is his decription of Joseph Pulitzer, blind, ill, gnawed by doubt, 'tearing his life into shreds and tatters' as he sat at the heart of his publishing empire (Casson 1931: 76).

Casson's research on the telephone industry had made him friends among the senior executives of Bell, and as a favour he did some publicity work and copy-writing for them. He later did the same for the cities of Buffalo and Denver. When Standard Oil found itself under public pressure following the publication of Ida M. TARBELL's *History of the Standard Oil Company* in 1904, the younger John D. Rockefeller, who knew Casson, recommended him to the company's executives; Casson helped manage Standard's public during the fight against the anti-trust suit filed by the US government, and became friendly with H.K. McCann, the company's advertising manager.

Casson was now working in the heart of American business, and his knowledge of varied business methods and far-flung network of contacts brought him to the attention of Harrington EMERSON, the efficiency expert and one of the country's leading business consultants. Emerson wrote to Casson in the spring of 1908:

He said: 'Perhaps you are not aware of it, but you have become an Efficiency Expert. Why not come and join my organization?' I went and became his partner. I may say that I was fascinated with him. I found that he knew clearly what I had discovered for myself vaguely.

(Casson 1931: 152)

Casson worked with Emerson for about a year, helping to publicize Emerson's work and becoming immersed in the details of this new movement. He perceived that the principles behind the efficiency movement, hitherto applied primarily to production techniques, could also be applied to marketing, especially to advertising and sales. He tried to persuade Emerson to develop business in this direction, but Emerson had doubts as to whether efficiency methods would work in marketing. Undaunted, Casson left Emerson and spent the following year researching and writing a book, *Advertisements and Sales* (1911). Shortly thereafter, Standard Oil was broken up at the successful conclusion of the government's anti-trust suit, and Casson's friend H.K. McCann found himself out of a job. Pooling their capital, Casson and McCann founded the H.K. McCann Advertising Company in 1911, based on the principles Casson had described in his book. Casson sold out his share of the partnership in early 1914, doubling his money. He later commented wryly that if he had kept his shares he would have become rich many times over; the H.K. McCann Company went on to become McCann-Erickson, one of the world's largest and richest advertising companies.

In 1914, however, Casson had decided that he wanted to retire, and revived his old dream of settling in England. In April 1914 he bought a house in Norwood, suburb of London, and settled his family there. A few months later the First World War broke out, and British industry went onto a war footing. Casson resolved to help his adopted country in any way that he could. Discovering – to his horror – that the efficiency movement was almost unknown in Britain, he set about publicizing it. He began programmes of lectures on efficiency and its merits for the managers of factories, most notable being the course of six lectures at the Manchester firm of Mather & Platt which the company itself later published (Casson 1917). He set up a publishing company and began writing a stream of books on efficiency

and on management more generally; he also founded a journal, *Efficiency*, patterned partly on Arch SHAW's American journal *System*, which he published and also wrote in large part. Thus Casson embarked on his fifth and final career, as one of Britain's leading management consultants. He continued to write and publish through the 1920s and 1930s, and was in demand in Britain and around the world as a public speaker. In 1950 he embarked on a ten-month lecture tour of Australia, New Zealand and Fiji. He died shortly after his return.

Casson remains best known today as one of the first writers to introduce the work of Emerson and of Frederick W. TAYLOR to Britain, and as one of the most prominent early apostles of scientific management in that country. But there was much more to his work than that. His publications amount to some 170 books, and even if some of the later texts are repackaged versions of earlier works, the breadth of his interests was still great. He continued his emphasis on applying the principles of efficiency to marketing and sales; he also wrote a number of what would now be described as 'self-help books' for managers, encouraging them to improve their learning and reasoning abilities. Often these had catchy titles such as *Fifty-two Ways to Be Rich* or *Fourteen Ways to Increase Profits* and were little more than collections of aphorisms. But there is still a considerable body of work which focuses on the nature of management itself. Through much of his later writing, Casson is consciously trying to explain what management *is*, often to managers who had never considered the subject before.

One of the greatest failings in management, he found, was a reliance on tradition rather than reason and study:

Managers had never studied management. Employers had never studied employership. Sales managers had never studied the art of influencing public opinion. There were even financiers who had never studied finance. On all hands I found guess-work and muddling ... A mass of incorrect operations was standardized into a routine. Stokers did not know how to stoke. Factory workers did not know how to operate their machines. Foremen did not know how to handle their men. Managing directors did not know ... the principles of organization... . Very few had LEARNED how to do what they were doing.
(Casson 1931: 222–3)

The result is confusion, error and myth: 'There are nearly as many myths and delusions in business as there were in ancient philosophies and religious. I have seen many an industrial process that was as absurd as a ceremonial in a temple in Thibet' (Casson 1931: 227).

To learn, Casson, concluded, it was necessary for a manager to swallow his pride and turn to the outside for help. One common objection to his work that he encountered throughout his consultancy career was from managers who believed that only they knew how their business worked. Casson believed this was impossible: no individual could know how the whole of a business worked, especially not a large business. As a result, managers mistook their own partial knowledge for knowledge of the whole. Following his lifelong credo, Casson says there is always room to learn, and expresses this in his usual robust fashion:

If a man says: 'I know all about my own business' he is ready to die; he is finished; he cannot go on amongst ordinary men any more; he knows to much. The only finished man is a dead man.
(Casson 1917: 3)

Bringing in outsiders cannot only provide new or missing knowledge, it can also shake up and alter ways of thinking. In his lectures at Mather & Platt, Casson noted how many managers take their work for granted. They

ask 'how' a thing is done, but they rarely ask the much more important question of 'why' it is done in a particular way. Outside consultants, by asking these kinds of questions, force managers to question and challenge their own beliefs and arrive at new ways of looking a things (Casson 1917). Although he also provided technical support, it was this challenging and analytical approach that lay at the core of Casson's business and consulting philosophy:

> When a man has studied many books and businesses, the secret of his success as an Efficiency Expert is not at all his cleverness. He may not be clever at all. He succeeds because of the magic of the SCIENTIFIC METHOD – because he notices, studies, leans and creates. He searches for facts. He doubts what he is told. He cares nothing for opinions. He looks at a business with sharp eyes, as a small boy looks at a circus. He follows up clues. He takes nothing for granted. He studies the business as a whole, and his purpose is to increase the percentage of the result.
>
> (Casson 1931: 226)

Casson, like Peter DRUCKER two decades later, believed that management is purposive action; in his philosophy, management is about getting things done. His approach is first to define action as 'the creation of causes that are likely to produce a certain desired effect'; the manager must 'first study the nature of the desired effect, then create the causes that are most likely to produce it' (Casson 1935: 13). He classes actions in two types: *routine*, doing what was done before, and *creative*, doing something new. Routine action is important and necessary, but creative action is what takes companies forward. Creative action includes staff training, finding customers, planning, employee relations, advertising and so on. He calls for an 'action habit of mind' to be developed in managers, and comments that there is too much fear in the business world, especially

fear of authority and fear of failure, and fear in turn inhibits action. He also argues for the importance of creativity (Casson 1928: 149), and is particularly admiring of the firm of Cadbury, which he regarded as being the best example in the world of a firm that had stimulated and harnessed the creativity of its employees (Casson 1928: 165). He argued that every firm should conduct research to generate new knowledge: there should be a nucleus of creative thinkers, which should be as large as possible (Casson 1928: 163).

Casson had a strong authoritarian streak, and he sometimes talked of progress being the result of the 'efficient few' pushing against the opposition of the many. He believed that leadership is essential to overcoming the barrier of inertia that he sees everywhere, in work as well as in society. Yet his model of organization was not simply command and control. Like Emerson, he pushed for the adoption of the line and staff model of organization, and believed discipline to be important. But authority alone cannot manage a successful company (Casson 1935: 20). Managers must also learn to motivate their employees, to make them feel respected and part of the organziation for which they work. Real authority, says Casson, derives from the respect rather than ranks or titles. He also takes a dynamic view of how businesses function, and advocates planning and process engineering: 'Work travels. Every job has a Cook's Tour through the factory; and it should not start until its journey has been planned and everything made ready for it' (Casson 1935: 25).

Casson developed an organic model of organization which used the human body as a metaphor; this was widely influential, being cited by early writers on organization such as Charles KNOEPPEL. He also became increasingly interested in psychology and the motivations for human action, in terms of both marketing and organizational study. *Human Nature* (1918) is an attempt to explain some of the basics of motivational theory to managers, and makes a useful distinction between those

motivating factors which relate to our individual needs and those which relate to our social needs; he classes these as *centrifugal* and *centripetal* needs, respectively:

> Each set of qualities needs to be offset by the other. If a man has centripetal qualities only, he is mere raw material. He is undeveloped. He has no personality. If he has centrifugal needs only, he is a crank, an outlaw, a genius or a lunatic.
>
> (Casson 1918: 191)

The need for balance, in organizations and in people, is constantly stressed. The same principles are considered in relation to marketing, notably in his earlier *The Axioms of Business* (1915), in which he argues that an understanding of consumer motivations and needs is the key to successful sales. Price, he says, is overrated as a factor; it does not matter so much as the nature of the proposition (Casson 1915: 64), and it is actually quite difficult to set prices too high:

> I once saw a millionaire Pittsburgher buy a painting of a cow for £11,000. He could have bought the cow herself for £15. But the painting had become famous. It was the only one of its kind. Everybody wanted it. And the Pittsburgher wanted it more than he wanted £11,000.
>
> (Casson 1915: 65)

How strong was Casson's influence? The question is difficult to answer. As noted, he was constantly in demand as a lecturer and speaker for the last forty years of his life, and his books between them sold at least half a million copies, possibly many more. Yet, as every management writer knows, it is one thing for an audience to receive a message, and quite another for them to act upon it. There is no indication that British industry as a whole responded on a wide scale to Casson's message; although as much of his consultancy work was with small and medium-sized firms,

it may be that records simply do not survive.

Yet he was, and to some extent still is, a powerful influence. He brought the techniques of American scientific management and efficiency to Britain during the First World War, at a time when few others in the country were more than dimly aware of them. He paved the ground for the acceptance of these techniques in many quarters by arguing strenuously that they were not 'American methods' but universal principles: scientific management had been invented in the USA but was no more 'American' than electricity or the principles of astronomy.

His style of writing is terse and full of aphorisms, some of which can be quite abrasive, such as: 'Almost every works needs a bigger scrapheap. There are many obsolete machines inside that should be outside' (Melluish 1948: 133), and 'It would be far safer, sensible and more profitable to dismiss a do-nothing director and to put a bag of sand in his chair' (Melluish 1948: 134). His writing was determinedly populist, and would pass few tests of academic rigour: he repeats himself frequently, and some of his bases for argument, notably those resting on the physical sciences, are decidedly shaky. Yet against this, he had a powerful vision of what management could and should be, a strong philosophy based on some surprisingly modern concepts such as dynamic organization and, above all, the need for continuous learning. He deserves to be remembered as one of the twentieth century's great management writers.

BIBLIOGRAPHY

Casson, E.F. (1952) *The Life and Thoughts of Herbert N. Casson*, London: Efficiency Magazine.

Casson, H.N. (1907) *The Romance of Steel: The Story of a Thousand Millionaires*, New York: A.S. Barnes.

—— (1909) *Cyrus Hall McCormack: His Life and Work*, Chicago: A.C. McLurg and Co.

—— (1911) *Advertisements and Sales: A*

Study of Advertising and Selling from the Standpoint of the New Principles of Scientific Management, London: Pitman.

—— (1913) *Advertisements and Sales*, London: Pitman.

—— (1915) *The Axioms of Business*, London: Efficiency Exchange.

—— (1917) *Lectures on Efficiency*, Manchester: Mather and Platt.

—— (1918) *Human Nature*, London: Efficiency Magazine.

—— (1927) *Men at the Top: Twelve Tips on Leadership*, London: Efficiency Magazine.

—— (1928) *Creative Thinkers: The Efficient Few Who Cause Progress and Prosperity*, London: Efficiency Magazine.

—— (1929) *The Twelve Worst Mistakes in Business*, London: Efficiency Magazine.

—— (1931) *The Story of My Life*, London: Efficiency Magazine.

—— (1935) *How to Get Things Done*, London: Efficiency Magazine.

—— (1937) *What Makes Value?*, London: Efficiency Magazine.

—— (1939) *Making People Want to Buy*, London: Efficiency Magazine.

—— (1941) *Efficient Management*, London: Efficiency Magazine.

—— (1949) *The Business Omnibus*, London: Efficiency Magazine.

Kauffmann, K. and Kruse, U.J. (1928) *The Brain-workers' Handbook*, trans. F.H. Burgess and H.N. Casson, London: Efficiency Magazine.

Melluish, W. (ed.) (1948) *Effiency for All*, Kingswood: The World's Work Ltd.

Wirz, A. (1986) *Efficiency: Herbert Cassons Philosophie des Erfolgs*, Zurich: O. Füssli.

MLW

CHAMBERLAIN, Arthur (1842–1913)

Arthur Chamberlain was born in Camberwell, Surrey on 11 April 1842, the son of Joseph and Caroline Chamberlain. He died at Ottery St Mary, Devon on 19 October 1913 after a long illness. He married Louisa Kenrick (whose twin sister married his brother Joseph, the prominent Liberal Unionist politician and himself a successful businessman); they had nine children. After education at University College School in London, he joined the family manufacturing firm, Nettlefold and Chamberlain. Later he joined another firm, the brassfounders Smith and Chamberlain; selling his shares, he then established a partnership with George Hookham which manufactured and sold electrical equipment. This business was sold in 1898, and Chamberlain used his profits to invest in a number of other businesses in the Midlands.

Chamberlain's reputation was that of a 'company doctor', and he came to specialize in the rescue and turnaround of ailing firms. On several occasions shareholders called on him to take over failing firms, and each time he was able to salvage something from the wreckage; sometimes the firms in question went on to be highly successful. His greatest success was with the ammunitions manufacturer Kynoch. The board of Kynoch called on Chamberlain to investigate the affairs of the firm in 1888, after it had run up substantial losses and managing director and founder George Kynoch had been forced to resign. Chamberlain took over as chairman in 1889. He found the firm in confusion, with several loss-making divisions, no organizational structure and an appalling safety record (Smith, 1986, relates that explosions were frequent, as the workers used to cook their breakfasts over candles alongside the lines where cartridges were being filled with black powder). He proceeded to turn the 'desperately sick' firm around:

> He made a clean sweep, paying attention to the operation of the works, costs, stock

144

and purchasing, making many workers redundant. Quality control was introduced to eliminate cartridge rejection and to regain the reputation of the company. A metallurgist was appointed. Advertising was used. Annie Oakley, for instance, was seen using Kynoch's Eley cartridges.

(Smith 1986: 635)

So effective were Chamberlain's management methods that Kynoch not only returned to profit but began rapidly to expand. New plants were built, employment increased and new machinery was installed to increase production. In 1892 Chamberlain began exploring the idea of replacing black powder with cordite, and by 1895 Kynoch had begun making cordite cartridges for the army's Lee-Enfield rifle. By the turn of the century it was the largest ammunition-maker in the country.

Chamberlain's management philosophy was summed up in a privately printed work, *The Book of Business*, which he produced for his children. He was, for his time, an enlightened employer, one of the first in the country to introduce the forty-eight hour working week, and he greatly improved health and safety conditions in all his businesses. Chamberlain supported better education and training for people making a career in business. His most interesting view concerned the importance of the human element in business:

the human element, in your workmen, your customers, your opponents, your colleagues or yourself, is the main factor: and of the human element, which enters then so largely into business, it is impossible for me to predict anything with certainty, except, that you can control it, *if you know how*.

(Quoted in Smith 1986: 637)

Chamberlain's managerial significance lies in his gift for extracting the essentials from a failing business and concentrating on those until the business returns to profit once more.

His abilities as a turnaround specialist would be sorely missed by British industry in the decades to come.

BIBLIOGRAPHY

Elletson, D.H. (1966) *The Chamberlains*, London: John Murray.
Smith, B.M.D. (1984) 'Chamberlain, Arthur', in D.J. Jeremy (ed.), *Dictionary of Business Biography*, London: Butterworths, vol. 1, 633–43.

MLW

CHAND, Fateh (*c*.1680–1744)

Fateh Chand, more usually known as Jagat Seth, was probably born, and probably died, in Murshidabad, Bengal. His family were Jains, who had been involved in banking for some generations; they came originally from Jodhpur, but had settled in Bengal some years before. Their rise to prominence began in the late seventeenth century with Manik Chand, who was personal banker to the Mogul Emperor Aurangzeb. Being childless, Manik Chand adopted his nephew Fateh Chand as his heir.

Assuming control of the bank in 1714, Fateh Chand became the most powerful financier in India. Following his uncle's example, he cultivated good relations with the Mogul emperors. He supported the Emperor Farrukhsiyar against a rival claimant, and was rewarded with an emerald seal and the hereditary title Jagat Seth (Banker to the World). (Sources say the title was awarded in 1723, but if so, it must have been awarded by a different emperor, as Farrukhsiyar was deposed and murdered in 1719.) He also extended his banking network. Manik Chand had established branches in Patna and Dacca, the sites of royal mints; Fateh Chand extended the

network of branches (*kothis*) all across North India to Delhi, the imperial capital. He cultivated relationships with banking houses in other parts of India, such as the Chellabys of Surat and the Chettys of Coromandel, helping to establish a financial structure which covered all of India. In Bengal, meanwhile, he cemented his hold over the finances of the province. He established a mint at Murshidabad, and took control of all revenue collection and taxation (*diwani*), and all currency exchange in the province. The emperors regarded him as equivalent in power to the Nawab, or governor, of Bengal. Foreigners, too, admired him: Edmund Burke later compared the family of Jagat Seth to the Bank of England, while the East India Company's Robert Clive said they were richer than any business in London. Modern observers have variously compared them to MEDICI and ROTHSCHILD.

One of the great banking innovations of the period, in which Fateh Chand seems to have played a major role, was the development of the bill of exchange (*hundi*). This was made possible by the development of the banking networks referred to above. In the seventeenth century, the revenues of Bengal were sent to Delhi in the form of cartloads of specie; Jagat Seth reformed the system so that a single bill of exchange could be sent from Murshidabad to Delhi and drawn on his agents in the capital. He also seems to have encouraged the rapid development of trade in bills of exchange.

From the 1720s onward, aware of his power, the East India Company took pains to cultivate Fateh Chand. He in turn seems to have regarded them as useful commercial partners, but nothing more. After his death, however, his successors grew closer to the British. The Mogul Empire was breaking up under the pressures of civil war and foreign invasion, and Bengal was one of many provinces that shook off imperial control; in these circumstances, the East India Company may have looked like a stabilizing force. In 1757 the second Jagat Seth, Fateh Chand's grandson Mahatab Chand, sided with the Company against Siraj-ad-daula, Nawab of Bengal, and helped secure his overthrow. In 1763, the anti-British Kasim Ali seized Bengal and declared himself Nawab, and Mahatab Chand and his cousin Swarup Chand were both murdered by Kasim's troops. Khoshal Chand, the third Jagat Seth, tried to rebuild the business, but by now he was facing increasing competition from both British interests and new rising local houses such as that of Bolakida. Long (1869) records that by the mid-nineteenth century Fateh Chand's descendants were pensioners of the British in Calcutta. The last Jagat Seth died in 1912.

BIBLIOGRAPHY

Bhattacharya, S. (1969) *The East India Company and the Economy of Bengal from 1704 to 1740*, Calcutta: K.L. Mukhopadhyay.

Jain, L.C. (1929) *Indigenous Banking in India*, London: Macmillan.

Long, J. (1869) *Selections from the Unpublished Records of Government for the Years 1748 to 1767 Inclusive*, Calcutta: Office of the Superintendent of Government Printing, vol. 1.

MLW

CHANDLER, Alfred Dupont, Jr (1918–)

Alfred Dupont Chandler was born in Guyencourt, Delaware on 15 September 1918, one of five children of Alfred Dupont Chandler and his wife, Caroline Johnston Ramsay. His great-grandfather was the business journalist Henry Varnum POOR, one of the founders of Standard and Poors, and there were also family connections with the du Ponts. After schooling he attended Harvard University, graduating in history in 1940. Among his classmates at Harvard was future US president John F.

Kennedy; both men were members of the Harvard sailing team, and both joined the US Navy in the Second World War. Chandler finished the war with the rank of lieutenant-commander in the US Navy Reserves. Demobilized in 1945, he began graduate studies at the University of North Carolina, but in 1946 returned to Harvard to take his Ph.D. writing his thesis on Henry Poor (later published in 1956). In 1950 he was appointed to a teaching post at the Massachusetts Institute of Technology, where he taught history until 1963; from 1963–71 he was professor of history at Johns Hopkins University, where he was also editor of the presidential papers of Dwight D. Eisenhower. In 1971 he became professor of business history at Harvard; he is currently professor emeritus.

Unusually for a modern business school, Harvard has a long tradition of the teaching and researching of business history, which can be traced back to its founding dean, Edwin GAY, and which continued through later scholars such as N.S.B. Gras and Henrietta Larson. Chandler's achievement has been to make business history a part of the core curriculum at Harvard, and to instil in students a respect for and understanding of historical processes in business. Although his own historical work is open to criticism, he has set a benchmark for business historians in terms of both breadth of thinking and relevance to the practical problems of business.

It is Chandler's writing, however, rather than this teaching which has had the greatest impact. He has produced three seminal books – Strategy and Structure (1962), The Visible Hand (1977) and Scale and Scope (1990) – all of which have had great impact and all of which have been bestsellers. The Visible Hand, indeed, became the first business book to win a Pulitzer prize. A historian rather than a business academic, Chandler's writing has demonstrated how historical thinking can be applied to the problems of business. He achieved this first in his work on Henry Poor, which focused on Poor himself and his influ-

ence and impact on the growth of the American railways; and second, and perhaps most successfully, in Strategy and Structure, when he looked at corporate responses to the problems of diversification in the first half of the twentieth century. In these first two works, the scope of his enquiry was limited to a few organizations or businesses. In the later works, The Visible Hand and Scale and Scope, Chandler broadens his focus and becomes more general, looking for common patterns across and between national business cultures.

In Strategy and Structure, Chandler observes the growth of the large diversified corporation in the United States. He particularly notes the appearance of the multidivisional form (M-form), in which diversification proceeds by the establishment of a number of semi-independent operating divisions, focused either geographically or on a particular group of products, the whole being subject to the managerial oversight of corporate headquarters. The net effect is the partial devolution of power and control from headquarters to the heads of the divisions. Chandler notes that many of the successful firms in the United States between 1920 and 1960 had adopted the M-form. The core of the book is taken up with four case studies of such successful firms: Du Pont, General Motors, Standard Oil (New Jersey) and Sears Roebuck. Each of the four approached diversification and adaptation to the M-form in a different way and for different reasons; indeed, some were more successful than others in their implementation of it. Interestingly, much of the book then focuses on the organizational dynamics of each case, as Chandler follows the decision to adapt and the processes of adaptation through to their conclusion. In each case, the reorgnization had a champion: Pierre DU PONT at Du Pont and later at General Motors, Alfred SLOAN at General Motors, Walter TEAGLE at Standard Oil and General Robert WOOD at Sears Roebuck. It was the relationships between these men and their executives and employees that to a large extent determined the shape

and success of the reorganization in each case, and one often overlooked aspect of this work is the way in which it highlights the close links between leadership and corporate reorganization or rejuvenation.

What do these case studies tell us? For Chandler, of primary importance is the link between corporate strategy and corporate structure. He defines strategy as 'the determination of the basic long-term goals and objectives of an enterprise, and the adoption of courses of action and the allocation of resources necessary for carrying out these goals' (Chandler 1962: 13). Structure, in turn, is

the design of organization through which the enterprise is administered ... It includes, first, the lines of authority and communication between the different administrative offices and officers, and, second, the information and data that flow through these lines of communication and authority.

(Chandler 1962: 14)

In Chandler's view, the choice of structure is an organizational decision which is dependent on the choice of strategy: 'The thesis ... is then that structure follows strategy and that the most complex type of structure is the result of the concatenation of several basic strategies' (Chandler 1962: 14).

'Structure follows strategy' is both the theme of this work and its fundamental lesson. In the four case studies given, the companies in question were faced with the need to make a fundamental shift in strategy, resulting from changes in population, income, technology, etc. in their core markets. The strategy chosen by the executive was one of diversification; the M-form structure was the organizational response to this strategy. It must be emphasized that this is a historical account. In *Strategy and Structure*, Chandler is describing how and why the M-form, which appears to be the most powerful – though by no means the only – organizational model adopted by

large American firms, came to be. He is *not* saying, at least not overtly, that this is the one best model of organization. While he remains firm in his conviction that structure follows strategy, he concedes that different strategies require different structures. However, as Whittington (1998) notes, this did not stop McKinsey and Company consultants from selling the M-form as the ideal organizational structure around the world in the 1960s.

In *The Visible Hand: The Managerial Revolution in American Business*, Chandler both expands on the themes of *Strategy and Structure* and develops new ones. It was clear in the earlier work that one of the key elements in the successful reorganization and transition to the new form was the quality of a firm's management. In *The Visible Hand*, then, Chandler looks at a parallel phenomenon to the rise of the M-form and one that may be connected to it: the rise of professional management. His basic thesis is that the rise of large-scale business was accompanied by the growth of a professional managerial class, and that there was a basic separation of ownership and control. (Interestingly, Chandler makes only passing reference to the earlier thesis on this subject by BERLE and MEANS; likewise, despite the subtitle of his own work, BURNHAM's *The Managerial Revolution* is referred to only in a footnote.)

In *The Visible Hand*, Chandler sets out to chart this process. Prior to the American Civil War, businesses in the United States were usually small, localized, and family owned and controlled. Larger, multi-unit enterprises began to emerge 'when administrative coordination permitted greater productivity, lower costs, and higher profits than coordinated by market mechanisms' (Chandler 1977: 6). Business activities which had been carried out between firms could not be internalized within a firm, with corresponding advantages in terms of control and economy of scale. The 'visible hand' of the title is a direct reference to Adam SMITH, who postulated an 'invisible hand' of market forces which guided and regulated

activity; the 'visible hand' is that of professional management, which can also provide guidance and control of business activity.

The advantages of internalization, says Chandler, could not be achieved until a managerial hierarchy had been put in place. Growth is thus a self-perpetuating process; firms need to grow in order to be able to put in place the management structure that allows them to achieve internalization of activity, which in turn permits further growth. Eventually, says Chandler, once a hierarchy has been established it becomes 'a source of permanence, power, and continued growth' (Chandler 1977: 13). As the business grows, the salaried managers within its upper ranks become more highly skilled and their work becomes more technical and complex. As this process of growth in size and complexity continues, the owners of the business find that they can no longer directly control the business, and increasingly delegate that control to the managers, leading to the aforementioned separation of ownership and control. This in turn leads to a changing strategic emphasis; professional managers, says Chandler, are more likely to emphasize long-term growth and stability than short-term profits. Finally, the size, economic power and strategic direction of these large business units changes and alters the economy itself, especially the industry sectors in which these firms operate. The final picture is a transition to what Chandler calls 'managerial capitalism', in which the chief decisions that determine the present and future trajectory of the business enterprise are made by its professional managers.

Tracing the historical origins of this shift in power, Chandler goes back to the mid-nineteenth century. Describing a picture which has become widely accepted by business historians, he says:

The first modern enterprises were those created to administer the operation of the new railroad and telegraph companies. Administrative coordination of the movement of trains and the flow of traffic was essential for the safety of passengers and the efficient movement of a wide variety of freight across the nation's rails. Such coordination was also necessary to transmit thousands of messages across its telegraph wires. In other forms of transportation and communication, where the volume of traffic was varied or moved at slower speeds, coordination was less necessary.

(Chandler 1977: 485)

He goes on to point out that when other industries began to grow, companies within them often borrowed the techniques already developed in the railway and telegraph industries; and indeed, it can be observed that many of the most prominent business managers of the late nineteenth century had at least some background in either industry. So, the railways and the telegraph had a dual function: they developed techniques for coordinated management of large organizations over large geographical space, and they provided marketing and distribution opportunities which made physical growth possible. He uses the example of the meat-packing industry, firms such as Armour and Swift, which was enabled by the railways to develop large vertically integrated organizations based on the large-scale rearing of livestock in the West and Midwest and selling meat in the urban centres of the East. Other industries, such as steel, coal and oil, were also enabled to grow in this fashion. And, as firms and sectors grew, they developed management hierarchies and underwent their strategic transformations each in turn, thus creating the managerial revolution.

The growth described above gave US companies enormous advantages in terms of both economies of scale and economies of scope. Further, the internalization of management activity created advantages in terms of transaction costs. The costs of transactions conducted through a market were usually higher than those conducted within the firm through

an efficient management hierarchy; thus vertical integration, for example, could make firms more effective competitors. For Chandler, this was the secret of US global success in the period 1930–70. To demonstrate his thesis, in his third major work, *Scale and Scope*, he compared and contrasted US 'competitive managerial capitalism' with the models he saw as dominating the economies of two of the USA's chief rivals, Britain and Germany. Germany, said Chandler, was dominated by what he calls 'cooperative managerial capitalism'. That is, German firms adopted a model of business much like that of the United States, characterized by hierarchies of professional managers, but for a variety of social and cultural reasons they preferred to conduct networks of inter-firm alliances rather than engage in full-scale competition. This professionalism, in his view, did much to explain Germany's economic resurgence after the Second World War. The British economy, on the other hand, comes in for severe criticism. Britain clung for far too long (in Chandler's view) to a model which he describes as 'personal capitalism', whereby the owners of businesses continued to exercise control and failed to hand over to professional managers. This lack of evolution stifled the growth and competitiveness of British industry and was a major factor in its postwar decline.

Scale and Scope has been roundly criticized, especially outside the United States. Of Chandler's major works, it is probably the least successful, in that it does not fully demonstrate its thesis: that the transition to 'competitive managerial capitalism' enabled the United States to achieve economic power over and above that of its main rivals. Arguments can be advanced against this thesis on many levels. It is not at all clear that US economic dominance is due *solely* to any particular managerial form or structure. Chandler may also have been guilty of selecting his data to fit his thesis; neither the Far East nor southern Europe, especially Italy, where there have been and continue to be many examples of successful

firms based on personal/family models of capitalism, figure in his analysis. His analysis of the British case also has flaws: professional management had advanced rather more rapidly in Britain than he allows, and there is a tendency to discount successful British firms that were managed personally by their owners, such as Imperial Chemical Industries in the 1920s (see MOND). Even in the United States, the dominance of managerial capitalism seems questionable, and in some cases participation by the owner's descendants and family in day-to-day management continues to this day. Chandler, it seems, does not seem to recognize that the owner of a business can also be at one and the same time a highly professional and efficient manager.

Other criticisms have been levelled at his work more generally. Whittington (1998: 99) suggests that Chandler has a 'rosy view of the historical origins of modern US capitalism' occasioned by his own family and personal connections to some of its leaders. David TEECE has suggested that Chandler's emphasis on the M-form is itself becoming out of date, as the new business era now beginning will emphasize flexibility and speed of response over economies of scope and scale (Teece 1993); if Teece is correct, the business of the future will be prepared to put up with higher transaction costs in order to concentrate on core capabilities and innovation.

Despite these criticisms, Chandler's work has undeniable strengths. Although there are occasional flaws, his description of the evolution of large-scale US businesses and the simultaneous development of new techniques of professional management is clear and logically sound. He notes how changes in one sector, such as transportation, can have knock-on effects for many other sectors; a revolution in one business can lead to much more widespread change. His work on the relationship between strategy and structure remains pivotal to modern strategic thinking. Above all, perhaps, he has created an awareness that management is a historical concept, one that

has developed over time and will continue to do so. His style of historical analysis, if not necessarily his conclusions, provides a sound platform for the consideration of future trends, and brings the role of historical understanding squarely to the centre of management thinking.

BIBLIOGRAPHY

Chandler, A.D. (1956) *Henry Varnum Poor: Business Editor, Analyst, and Reformer*, Cambridge, MA: Harvard University Press.

—— (1962) *Strategy and Structure: Chapters in the History of the American Industrial Enterprise*, Cambridge, MA: MIT Press.

—— (1977) *The Visible Hand: The Managerial Revolution in American Business*, Cambridge, MA: Harvard University Press.

—— (1990) *Scale and Scope: The Dynamics of Industrial Capitalism*, Cambridge, MA: Harvard University Press.

Chandler, A.D. *et al.* (eds) (1997) *Big Business and the Wealth of Nations*, Cambridge: Cambridge University Press.

McGraw, T.K. (1988) *The Essential Alfred Chandler: Essays Towards a Historical Theory of Big Business*, Boston, MA: Harvard Business School Press.

Teece, D.J. (1993) 'The Dynamics of Industrial Capitalism: Perspectives on Alfred Chandler's *Scale and Scope*', *Journal of Economic Literature* 31: 199–225.

Whittington, R. (1998) 'Chandler, Alfred Dupont, Jr', in M. Warner (ed.) *IEBM Handbook of Management Thinking*, London: International Thomson Business Press, 99–104.

MLW

CHANEL, Gabrielle Bonheur (1883–1971)

Coco Chanel was born in Saumur in the French province of Auverne on 19 August 1883. She died in Paris on 10 January 1971. Orphaned at the age of six, she was educated at a convent school in Aubazine. From 1900 to 1905 she worked as a clerk in a hosiery shop in the town of Moulins, and from 1905 to 1908 she was a night-club singer in Moulins and Vichy, where she adopted the nickname 'Coco'. She then moved to Paris, where friends helped her raise money to set up her first business, a hat boutique. Other ventures followed, and Chanel began designing and making her own clothes. Her designs, particularly those influenced by masculine tailoring, quickly caught on, and in the 1920s and 1930s she dominated the Paris fashion scene. She was also the centre of a glamorous social set and was personally linked to a number of artists and members of high society, including the composer Igor Stravinsky and the Duke of Westminster.

During the Second World War Chanel remained in German-occupied Paris continuing to do business, and also had a liaison with a German army officer. Following the liberation of Paris she was briefly arrested by the French police on suspicion of collaboration, and lived in semi-exile in Switzerland for some years. In 1954 she launched her 'comeback' collection, including one of the most famous items of twentieth-century women's wear, the 'little black dress'. She continued to direct her fashion empire, which included perfume and cosmetics, into the 1960s.

Chanel's most famous dictum was: 'Fashion changes; style remains.' Her view was that genuine quality would have continuous appeal beyond the short-term and whimsical demand generated by ever-changing fashions. Her clothes and perfumes, especially the famous Chanel No. 5, had universal appeal; she provided haute couture to the jet-set and dressed the stars of Hollywood's Universal Studios, but she also knew how to appeal to

ordinary women. Her greatest talents as a manager were her understanding of the universality of good design, and her ability to develop a marketing strategy that would allow her philosophy of design to appeal to different market segments in different ways. She remains an excellent case example of successful product design and marketing, and also of female entrepreneurship in a hitherto male-dominated industry.

CHEARAVANONT, Dhanin (1939–)

Dhanin Chearavanont was born in Bangkok, Thailand on 19 April 1939, the youngest son of Chin Ek-chor, an immigrant from Shantou province. Chin and his brother had arrived in Bangkok in the 1920s and set up an agricultural business, Chia Tai, importing vegetable seeds from China, and sending back agricultural produce and livestock. This firm grew to a position of dominance in the market, but the coming of the Second World War meant the end of the China connection and the firm consolidated in Thailand. Chearavanont was educated at schools in Thailand and Hong Kong, graduating from the Hong Kong Commercial College in 1956 and then joining his brothers in the family firm. Like most Chinese emigrants to Thailand, they took Thai equivalents to their Chinese names.

In 1963, despite being the junior sibling, Chearavanont was made managing director of the company, which had by now expanded into operating feed mills and was known as Charoen Pokphand. His energy and ability to manage a network of contacts at once made their mark. Among his most important contacts was Chin Sophanpanich, the Thai-born Chinese banker whose Bangkok Bank was for a time the largest bank in Asia, and who also provided substantial capital to other overseas Chinese entrepreneurs including LIEM

Sioe Liong and Robert KWOK. The contact with Chearavanont was particularly close, however, and Charoen Pokphand seems to have had access to almost limitless amounts of capital. In the 1970s the company moved into contract farming and agricultural wholesaling on a very large scale, quickly rising to a position of dominance in Thai agribusiness. In the late 1970s Charoen Pokphand also moved into large-scale fish farming, particularly of shrimps.

The emphasis on food production led to a natural movement downstream into restaurants and food retailing. In the 1980s Charoen Pokphand (now CP Group) acquired a number of high-profile franchises, most notably that for the 7–11 chain stores; by the end of the decade, CP was also the largest food retailer in the country. Guided by Chearavanont, who became president of the company in 1979 and chairman in 1989, CP rode on the back of Thailand's phenomenal economic growth in the 1990s and diversified into many fields including telecommunications, the manufacture of motorcycles, and oil and gas extraction. The company also invested heavily in China, becoming one of the largest foreign investors there; in 1990 Chearavanont was appointed one of the Chinese government's advisers on Hong Kong. By 1997 the group owned 250 companies in Thailand, Hong Kong and China, and Chearavanont's own net worth was estimated at $5.5 billion. The Asia crisis of 1998, which began in Thailand and hit that country hardest, forced CP Group to retrench, but by 2000 the group had weathered the storm and was expanding once more.

CP Group exhibits many of the managerial characteristics of overseas Chinese businesses. All three of Chearavanont's brothers and all three of his children are involved in the business along with him, and there is a strong Confucian family ethic pervading the business, at least at the highest levels. At the same time, as Hiscock (1997) notes, the company has some distinctive characteristics.

Although it has diversified widely, it has also stuck firmly by its core agribusinesses, and it was probably these that pulled the group through the Asia crisis. These businesses are particularly well managed, and Chearavanont has shown himself to be a considerable innovator in agriculture management and practice, spending large sums on research and development and deploying new technology where possible. He has shown an ability to manage business on a high-technology basis even in a largely agrarian economy by sticking to a mix of traditional methods and new innovations.

BIBLIOGRAPHY
Hiscock, G. (1997) *Asia's Wealth Club*, London: Nicholas Brealey.

MLW

CHECKLAND, Peter Bernard (1930–)

Peter Bernard Checkland was born in Birmingham on 18 December 1930, the son of a grocery store manager. He was educated at George Dixon's Grammar School in Birmingham and joined the RAF directly from school, serving for two years as a sergeant instructor from 1948 to 1950. He won a Casberd Scholarship of St John's College, Oxford to study chemistry, where he obtained a first-class degree in 1954. Leaving Oxford, he took a job at ICI Fibres where he moved up through the ranks over the next fifteen years, finishing as group manager. As he moved into management roles, Checkland was disappointed to find that the books on management science held little relevance to his job. He was looking for work on management practice that gave an emphasis to maintaining relationships, rather than what he described as the 'goal-seeking' approaches of traditional management science.

Checkland's interest in management and the concept of systems grew as he explored these issues, and he moved from ICI to take up a position at Lancaster University, where he quickly became professor of systems. He led an action research project to explore the usefulness of systems engineering techniques in tackling real management problems. The researchers discovered that the methodology had to be changed radically in order to cope with the complexity and ambiguity in real managerial situations. This was the beginning of Checkland's soft systems methodology (SSM), for which he is best known.

Checkland wanted to develop a side of systems thinking that was distinct from the 'hard' systems thinking, usually called systems engineering, and the systems analysis used for decision making. These approaches he described as 'embodying a poverty-stricken goal-seeking model that focused on "how to do it" rather than "what should be done"' (Jackson 1998: 106). Checkland was striving to develop systems methodologies that were relevant to those working in 'soft' problem situations where goals, objectives and the systems themselves were problematical, as well as the means of resolving the situation.

Jackson (1998) describes the three major intellectual developments of SSM as the notion of 'human activity systems' as distinct from physical systems or social systems. This is described as a systems model of the activities people need to undertake in order to pursue a particular purpose. The models used in SSM could not be representations of the real world; as there is often disagreement about the nature of the situation, the models would be epistemological devices used to find out about the world. Also, the models used are contributions to a debate about possible change, and as such part of a learning process.

The initial formulation of SSM outlined seven steps (Checkland 1981) that explore the nature of the problem situation and compare conceptual models of relevant systems with the real world, in the exploration of possible

153

actions to improve the situation. Checkland emphasizes that there is never a 'solution', merely the emergence of another different problem situation. Thus participants are continually learning and having their attitudes and perceptions challenged. SSM, then, is a cyclic learning process, developed upon VICKERS' account of the way in which appreciative systems originate, develop and change.

Checkland soon wanted to develop the original formulation of SSM to emphasize the interrelationships between situational logic and situational change. In his second development of SSM, he gave equal attention to the cultural stream of analysis and the logic-based stream of analysis. The cultural analysis centres on the intervention itself, the problem owners and problem solvers, as well as the social roles and norms, and finally the power and politics of the situation. This model is referred to as the two-strands model of SSM. Checkland further developed the use of SSM by distinguishing its use into Mode 1, where the methodology is external and dominates the proceedings, and Mode 2, where interactions are situation-driven and which allows managers who have internalized the procedures of SSM to make sense of the situation. The continual development of the methodology based on research and practical experience of its use has contributed to its continued success and applicability to the world of business. Checkland's approach has also been widely applied in the field of information systems.

Checkland's contribution has been acknowledged by the academic community with honorary doctorates from City University and the Open University. He was the first recipient of the Most Distinguished and Outstanding Contributor Award of the methodologies group of the British Computer Society (1995), and the first recipient (jointly with Sir Geoffrey Vickers) of the Medal for Outstanding Contribution to Systems thinking from the UK Systems Society (1997).

Checkland's intention to develop systems thinking in management beyond the harder application that became mainstream in operations research had echoed the concerns of ACKOFF and CHURCHMAN's concerns with that field. More recently, Peter SENGE has similarly been concerned with softening systems dynamics thinking. From the beginning, Checkland was determined to take systems thinking beyond the abstractions of general systems theory, and to move beyond 'goal-seeking' scientific method in management. His aim was to develop a means of making systems thinking practicable and useful in the real life of managers where maintaining relationships was equally, if not more important. This he has largely done with the development of SSM. It represents a significant step forward in the application of systems thinking to management, particularly in acknowledging the cultural side of problem solving.

BIBLIOGRAPHY

Checkland, P.B. (1981) *Systems Thinking, Systems Practice*, Chichester: Wiley.
Checkland, P.B. and Scholes, J. (1990) *Soft Systems Methodology in Action*, Chichester: Wiley.
Jackson, M.C. (1998) 'Checkland, Peter Bernard', in M. Warner (ed.), *IEBM Handbook of Management Thinking*, London: International Thomson Business Press.

AJ

CHERINGTON, Paul Terry (1876–1943)

Paul Terry Cherington was born in Ottawa, Kansas on 31 October 1876, the son of Fletcher and Caroline Cherington, and died in New York on 9 April 1943. Cherington received his bachelor's degree from Ohio Wesleyan University, then took a masters degree at the University of Pennsylvania in

1902. From 1897 to 1902 he was assistant editor of *The Manufacturer*, a journal published by the Philadelphia Commercial Museum; he went on to become the museum's director of publications from 1902 to 1908. In 1908 he was recruited to the faculty of Harvard University, and was one of the founder members of the new Harvard Business School, established that same year. Cherington worked closely with Dean Edwin GAY, and was responsible for the development of courses on marketing and advertising; he was regarded as a very gifted teacher, and his courses, always oversubscribed by students, helped shape future generations of teaching and research. He was also co-founder of Harvard's Bureau of Business Research, which he directed until 1919. He conducted the bureau's first major investigation, into the state of the shoe industry; the impression this survey made on him can be judged by the frequent references to shoemaking and shoe marketing in his later books. Melvin COPELAND, long-serving professor of marketing at Harvard and himself a major figure in marketing's development, regarded Cherington as something of a mentor. Also while at Harvard, in 1911 Cherington married Marie Richards; the couple had two sons.

Cherington was appointed assistant professor at Harvard in 1913, and professor of marketing in 1918. He left Harvard in the following year, taking up a post as secretary of the National Association of Wool Manufacturers from 1919 to 1922, and then was director of research for J. Walter Thompson from 1922 to 1931. He continued to hold academic posts: he was professor of marketing at Stanford University from 1928 to 1929, and taught at New York University from 1932 to 1935. From 1933 to 1938 he was a partner in the market research firm Cherington, Roper and Wood, working with one of the pioneers of opinion polling in the United States, Elmo Roper. Roper and Cherington predicted the results of the 1936 presidential election with great accuracy, and this helped to raise the

profile of opinion polling very significantly, so that it became an important tool in both business and political management. In 1939 Cherington became a partner in McKinsey and Company. He also held a number of posts on government and university committees. He retired in the late 1930s.

He was a gifted teacher and highly original thinker and writer; among marketing academics, Cherington stands second only to Philip KOTLER in terms of importance and influence. Although Cherington's major influence was through his teaching and work, his writings were and remain important. He was one of the pioneers of the academic discipline of marketing, and his works not only show the problems which the early marketers were anxious to solve, but betray the influences and ideas they used to solve them. His two major works are *The Elements of Marketing* (1920), which was highly influential and had many imitators, and *The Consumer Looks at Advertising* (1928), which reflects back on almost two decades of observation and practice. *Advertising as a Business Force* (1913) is an early casebook, written as an instruction aid while Cherington was still at Harvard. Of his remaining works, the most important is *People's Wants and How to Satisfy Them* (1935) which draws heavily on sociology and political science.

Cherington begins by considering why marketing suddenly became important in the first two decades of the twentieth century. The perceived wisdom at the time – as indeed it is today amongst some business historians – is that marketing emerged as a result of overproduction; large-scale production meant that, for the first time in history, manufacturers could make goods faster than they could sell them. It was therefore necessary to adopt marketing techniques to stimulate demand. Cherington does not fully accept this. Overproduction was indeed a factor, and he remarks that the ready availability of capital and labour in the United States meant there was more stimulus to overproduction

than before (Cherington 1920: 5). However, the real consequence of large-scale production, he feels, is the breaking of the direct link between producer and consumer (1920: 1–2, 11).

Small, jobbing producers (such as shoe-makers) can and often do sell directly to their end consumers, even making goods to order. They know their customers well, often personally, and can measure accurately their needs, wants and demands. The assemblage of capital, labour and raw materials required for large-scale production, however, means that this is no longer possible: goods are produced not for sale or consumption now, but at some point in the future. This leaves producers with the tasks of trying to anticipate demand of an unknown nature at an unknown future point, and of then trying to ensure that their goods are actually sold at a price which recoups the cost of production, transport and distribution (Cherington 1928: 14–15).

Nor is it just the production factor that has changed: 'the conditions surrounding consumption have had quite as distinct an influence upon these problems and the mechanism which has been developed for their solution' (Cherington 1920: 3). Better education, greater mobility and increasing urbanization are just some of the factors that are causing consumer demand to change and evolve. Both changes in production and in consumption have resulted in 'maladjustments' between producer and consumer (1920: 3). It is the task of marketing to correct these.

The Elements of Marketing is, unsurprisingly, focused to a great extent on distribution. This was, after all, the key marketing problem that manufacturers had to solve at the time; product and price were important but less pressing than the fundamental issue of getting the product from the factory gate to the customer in an era when large-scale, long-distance transportation and communication were still in the throes of development.

Cherington even debates whether 'marketing' is the correct term to use; he feels 'merchandise distribution' would be more accurate than 'marketing', which has connotations of 'provisioning a household', but concedes that the former term is awkward to use (1920: 1).

Setting this problem aside, he goes on to define the fundamental task of marketing: 'to effect a transfer of ownership of goods in exchange for what is considered to be an equivalent' (1920: 6). This is the *task*; the fundamental *activity* is 'to bring a buyer and a seller together in a trading mood' (1920: 9). This 'trading mood' assumes a predisposition by both parties to make the transaction; that predisposition can be assumed on the part of the seller, and later in the book Cherington describes how it may be stimulated in the buyer through branding and advertising.

In this definition, Cherington says, the essence of marketing has not really changed; the basic task of effecting a change of ownership in goods is faced by all businesses, no matter what their size.

> The increased complexity of modern marketing is not due to any change in the inherent nature of the elemental task of marketing, namely, effecting a change in the ownership of merchandise. It apparently arises partly from the addition of other supplementary tasks not necessary until recently; and partly from the development of more indirect forms for this task itself.
>
> (Cherington 1920: 5)

He classifies these tasks in three groups: (1) merchandise functions, (2) auxiliary functions and (3) sales functions.

The greatest amount of space is given to the first group. Merchandise functions are intended specifically to correct the 'maladjustments' in the market process between producer and consumer. These, says Cherington, come in four different types:

(1) those between the quantity of merchandise produced and that sought for consumption; (2) those between the quality of merchandise produced and the various grades sought for consumption; (3) those between the time of production and the time of consumption; and (4) those between the place of production and the place of production.

(Cherington 1920: 14)

Each of these can be dealt with by the corresponding merchandise function, namely (1) assembling, (2) grading and classing, (3) storage and (4) transporting. *Assembling* in this context means delivering the appropriate quantity of the appropriate goods to the customer; *grading and classing* involves ensuring that the goods are of the appropriate quality; *storage* involves the holding of goods already produced until the consumer is ready to purchase them; and *transporting* ensures that the goods are delivered to a geographical point where the consumer is willing to make a purchase.

Auxiliary functions are twofold: (1) financing and (2) the assumption of risk. Cherington and his contemporaries considered both of these to be of great importance. Firms at the time tended to think of distribution as a cost-free activity, a belief which Cherington strongly corrects: large-scale distribution is very costly and requires capital, from either inside or outside the producing firm. The assumption of risk usually requires two strategies: insurance to protect the actual goods from damage during distribution, and hedging activities in case market forecasts turn out to be wrong and goods remain unsold.

Sales functions relate to the actual exchange, and also to the stimulation of demand on the part of the consumer. Cherington was an early believer in the power and efficacy of advertising, in an era when large-scale advertising was widely criticized for being inefficient and wasteful. Acknowledging that advertising and distribution costs could make up more than half the sale price of some goods, Cherington believes these costs are justified if consumers are ready to pay them. Advertising and selling he sees as a service to the consumer. The role of advertising in particular is to provide information to the consumer. Advertising does not make the buying decision; it allows the consumer to make that decision in better informed manner (Cherington 1928: 74).

Cherington argues that consumers must become better informed and more educated, for their own good and that of the economy. When consumers have better information on which to base their choices, he says, inefficient and unfit producers will be eliminated, making the whole economy stronger (1928: xi). In *The Consumer Looks at Advertising*, Cherington moves the emphasis away from distribution and more towards understanding the consumer. The key principle here is the consumer's 'will to buy' (1928: 38). This demand factor, he says, 'is not a spineless effect, but a restless and irresistible cause' (1928: 38) and is the starting point for the consideration of all business problems. He spends some time breaking down the will to buy into separate motives, making distinctions between needs (the demand for necessities) and wants (the demand for non-necessities).

In *People's Wants and How to Satisfy Them* (1935) Cherington moves away from a consideration of purely marketing problems and looks at some of the social issues surrounding demand. Most people, he says, will aim to have a 'good life' in both spiritual and material terms. There are two ways of attempting to provide such a good life: the planned economy, which attempts to design the good life, and the free market, which allows the good life to evolve through the mechanisms of individual choice. The first society is rigid, the second is mobile and flexible. In this context, Cherington argues against measures undertaken to ensure business stability. The last thing businesses need is stability, as this usually means stag-

nation; instead, they should be constantly challenged by changing market conditions and consumer wants (1935: 161).

BIBLIOGRAPHY

Cattell, J.M., Cattell, J. and Ross, E.E. (1941) *Leaders in Education*, 2nd edn, Lancaster, PA: The Science Press.

Cherington, P.T. (1913) *Advertising as a Business Force*, New York and London: Pitman.

—— (1920) *The Elements of Marketing*, New York: Macmillan.

—— (1928) *The Consumer Looks at Advertising*, New York: Harper and Brothers.

—— (1935) *People's Wants and How to Satisfy Them*, New York: Harper and Brothers.

Cruikshank, J.L. (1987) *A Delicate Experiment: The Harvard Business School 1908–45*, Boston: Harvard Business School Press.

MLW

CHRYSLER, Walter Percy (1875–1940)

Walter Percy Chrysler was born in Wamego, Kansas on 2 April 1875 and died at his estate on Long Island, New York on 18 August 1940. The third of four children of a train engineer, Henry Chrysler, and his wife, Anna Breyman, Chrysler grew up in a neighbourhood which he described as tough ('if you were soft, all the other kids would beat the daylights of out of you', Chrysler 1973), and in response he developed an aggressive, quick-tempered personality. Chrysler played the drum, clarinet and tuba in the Ellis Band, having learned to read music at piano lessons. He left Ellis High School in 1892 and refused to go to college, wanting to work with machines instead. When his father refused to sponsor him as an apprentice, he took a job as a sweeper in the local Union Pacific railroad shop. His father relented and he took up his apprenticeship a few months later.

Chrysler was driven by a passion to learn about machines and engineering, and stayed up all night learning practical mechanics as he repaired locomotives. He described this as an exciting time: 'Not books, but the things themselves were teaching me what I wished to know' (Chrysler 1973). He also took correspondence courses on engineering from Salt Lake City Business School. In 1897 he finished his apprenticeship, a competent and spirited young mechanic. Years later he said, 'even now I can lie in bed at night and tell, from the sound of a distant locomotive as it labours with a heavy train whether its valves are rightly set' (Chrysler 1973).

His impatience with incompetence and his authoritarian manner meant that he moved frequently as a journeyman, six times in the three years to 1900. He then moved to the Denver and Rio Grande Western Railroad in Salt Lake City, and in the following year he married his childhood sweetheart Della Forker, the daughter of an Ellis shopkeeper. He was quickly promoted through the management ranks, and constantly sought new challenging positions, rising to be superintendent in charge of design of locomotives and the production process. His reputation grew when he turned an unprofitable plant into a money-maker.

In 1912 he was invited to manage the world's second largest car plant, the Buick Motor Company in Michigan, owned by General Motors. He had been fascinated by cars ever since he had bought a Locomobile in 1908, which he had completely disassembled and reassembled before putting it on the road. He was given the freedom to reorganize Buick's production, and more than doubled Buick's output while reducing the plant's payroll by a quarter. His innovations included comprehensive piecework schedules, cost-accounting methods and redesigned produc-

tion processes. He conducted daily inspection tours in the vast plant, looking for ways to improve efficiency. He directed innovation, including the invention of special-purpose machines and assembly-line methods that amounted to true mass production. By 1915 he demanded and got a substantial pay rise that allowed him to buy General Motors stock; in the following year he was offered $500,000 a year to remain as president of Buick and vice-president of General Motors. He drew most of his salary as stock and quickly amassed a significant fortune. Three years later he resigned from the firm and the industry, having opposed General Motors' strategy of acquisitions, led by William C. DURANT.

Chrysler was persuaded to step in to rescue Willys Overland in 1920, the car-maker founded by John North WILLYS, with a salary of $1 million a year. However, the huge debt burden dragged the company down and it went into receivership. But Chrysler had recruited a team of the Willys engineers to design a radically new high-performance, moderately priced car. He had become chairman of the reorganizing committee of Maxwell Motors, and was duly made president of the restructured firm. The design team developed the new car, the Chrysler Six, and unveiled it in January 1924. It was low slung, had a short wheel base (which facilitated manoeuvrability), a high-compression engine and four-wheel hydraulic brakes. The car was an immediate sensation, and Chrysler was able to capitalize on its publicity to obtain the capital he needed to mass produce the Chrysler Six. It sold well and the company made a $4 million profit in 1925. The company was renamed Chrysler Corporation that year.

Three years later, in 1928, Chrysler had earned $46 million in profit and was the country's third largest car manufacturer. To break into the low-priced market dominated by Ford and General Motors, Chrysler acquired Dodge Motor Company. This allowed Chrysler to sell the popular Dodge car and simultaneously double the number of dealers for its own models. The acquisition also lowered the cost of basic components, preparing the way for the Plymouth, the 1928 entry into the low-priced market.

Although a great technological innovator, Chrysler was markedly less innovative when it came to the management of the work force. During the early years of growth Chrysler's workers faced virtually unlimited management control; Chrysler combined paternalism with support for strict plant discipline by the foremen. Conditions were poor, although conditions improved slightly following the acquisition of Dodge; improvements included group life insurance, free dances for employees and a welfare department. However, as the Great Depression of 1929–33 took hold, no jobs were safe and even skilled workers were laid off.

During the Depression, Chrysler directed the company's retrenchment, running his factories at less than 40 per cent capacity in 1932–3, but all the while continuing to fund fully his research and development capability. As the economy began to recover in 1933, the company introduced new body styling and improved suspension to enhance passenger comfort. Its strong sales enabled the company to surge ahead of Ford to become America's second largest car maker after General Motors.

Chrysler's last great project was the construction of the seventy-seven storey Chrysler building in new York City. Inspired by the Eiffel Tower, and fuelled by a desire by Chrysler to invest his fortune in something solid, it was for a short time in 1930 the tallest structure in the city. His wife died in 1938, and her death contributed to Chrysler's decline and death in 1940.

Chrysler was a major player in the US automotive industrial revolution. He is credited with personally bringing technological and managerial knowledge from the railroad industry into the automotive industry. Building on that knowledge, he developed modern mass-production methods at Buick, which paralleled the more famous developments by FORD.

CHRYSLER

BIBLIOGRAPHY
Chrysler, W.P. (1937) *Life of an American Workman*, New York: Dodd, Mead and Co.

AJ

CHUNG Ju-yung (1915–)

Chung Ju-yung was born in the village of Asan in Kangwon province of what is now North Korea on 25 November 1915, the eldest of the eight children of Chung Bong-shik and Han Sung-shil. After completing high school in Songjun in 1930, he left home and became a railway construction worker near Wonsan. He returned home and then left again several times, taking various jobs and also studying bookkeeping. In 1933 he went south, taking a job on the docks at Inchon, and then working as delivery boy for a rice store. He stayed at this job for four years, learning the business. In 1938, with a little accumulated capital, he started his own rice store in Seoul. However, this store was forced to close in the following year when the Japanese military government prohibited Koreans from owning rice stores. Around this time Chung married Byun Jung-suk, the daughter of a family from his home town.

In 1940 Chung and a partner set up a vehicle repair workshop in Seoul, but in 1943 this too was closed by the government. Chung then purchased a small fleet of trucks and won a contract to haul ore from a gold mine in Hwanghae province, which kept him going through the war. In 1946 he returned to Seoul and set up another repair business, Hyundai Auto Service. Seeing opportunities in construction, however, in the following year he set up the Hyundai Civil Works Company. During the 1950s the construction industry in Korea boomed and Chung won major con-

tracts for building work and infrastructure, including in 1959 the contract to rebuild the port of Inchon. By 1960, Hyundai was the largest construction company in Korea. By 1965 the company was working overseas in Thailand and Vietnam, and bidding for contracts in Alaska and Australia.

In 1968 a joint venture with Ford took the car business from repair to assembly with the launch of the Kortina, the first car to be built in Korea; by 1976, with the launch of the Pony, Hyundai was building its own designs. The company had also moved into shipbuilding, and won contracts to build supertankers, which catapulted it into the top league of world shipbuilders. The construction industry also continued to advance, particularly in Saudi Arabia and the Persian Gulf, where it specialized in the building of pipelines and oil terminals. By now Hyundai was the largest company in Korea, and Chung was a figure of world prominence; he was named chairman of the organizing committee for the 1988 Seoul Olympics, and was the first Korean businessman to visit the USSR and North Korea. In 1992 he ran for election as president of South Korea, but this was to be his downfall. Kim Young-sam, who won the election, launched a series of legal and tax investigations into Hundai and found that Chung had illegally used Hyundai money to finance his election campaign. Tried and convicted, he was given a three-year suspended sentence, and in 1995 stepped down in favour of his son, Chung Mong-koo.

Chung, along with his rival Lee Byung-chul at Samsung, was responsible for creating a new business form, the *chaebol*. Like overseas Chinese businesses and also like Japanese *keiretsu*, *chaebols* such as Hyundai are diversified conglomerates with a strong vertical hierarchy, and much authority resting with the office of the chairman. *Chaebols* also have a strong Confucian ethic, with an emphasis on family-style relationships within the firm; external networking is also important, and throughout his career Chung placed much

emphasis on cultivating good relationships, with government in particular. However, the level of diversification tends to be lower than in Chinese and Japanese organizations, and there is also a strong emphasis on functional specialization. Chung himself did not maintain a large headquarters or professional staff, working directly with the heads of divisions and subordinate companies to coordinate policy. Although Hyundai had a central planning department, its main function was to allocate resources once policy had been decided upon. This comparatively simple organizational form, autocratic though it was, allowed Chung to build Korea's largest business and a personal fortune estimated in 1995 at $6.2 billion. His son, Chung Mongkoo, has maintained the company's position, although its dominance is now being challenged by the more aggressive Samsung led by Lee Kun-hee.

BIBLIOGRAPHY
Hiscock, G. (1997) *Asia's Wealth Club*, London: Nicholas Brealey.

MLW

CHURCHMAN, C. West (1913–)

C. West Churchman was born in Mount Airy, Pennsylvania in 1913. He was brought up in a Quaker background which undoubtedly contributed to his enduring moral and ethical stance. He studied philosophy and logic at university, and obtained his Ph.D. from the University of Pennsylvania in 1936. Shortly after, he joined the faculty there as an assistant professor. One of the first courses Churchman offered was 'Modern Philosophy' in 1939, which was attended by Russell Ackoff. The two quickly established what became a lifelong friendship. They worked closely together for twenty years, and established the field of operations research (OR).

During the Second World War Churchman became head of the statistical section of the Frankford Arsenal. He was made a professor at the University of Pennsylvania when he returned in 1946. In 1947 he moved to Wayne University in Detroit, where he and Ackoff published *Methods of Inquiry* (1950). Churchman was concerned to apply his philosophy to industrial and government problems and moved, with Ackoff, to the Case Institute of Technology in 1951, where they set up the Operations Research Group with this aim. Churchman and Ackoff also produced, in collaboration with E.L. Arnoff, the first international textbook on OR, *Introduction to Operations Research* (1957). The book set out the philosophical aspects of an interdisciplinary approach to real-world problems, as well as setting out the techniques of OR such as linear programming, inventory control and production scheduling. This and their subsequent work was well received. Churchman was editor-in-chief of *Philosophy of Science* from 1949 to 1959 and of *Management Science* from 1956–61, and was made president of the Institute of Management Sciences in 1962.

However, Churchman became frustrated with the developments in OR during the 1960s as the techniques were increasingly used without reference to whole systems. He moved away from the field of OR to concentrate upon systems thinking. He similarly resigned as editor of *Management Science* because he felt that the journal's increasingly mathematical contributions were science for its own sake and were of little practical benefit to humankind. Churchman called relentlessly for a critically reflective and moral practice of science. This position included the awareness of and concern for future generations, again showing his naturally ethical and systemic tendencies, and the basis of many futurists' beliefs.

Churchman moved to the business school at University of California at Berkeley in 1958 to direct a Centre for Research in Management Sciences. The work he did there explored management as a philosophical challenge, testing people's capacity to appreciate the ethics of whole systems. He developed his systems thinking in the production of his next four books, *The Systems Approach* (1968), *Challenge to Reason* (1968), *The Design of Inquiring Systems* (1971) and *The Systems Approach and Its Enemies* (1979). The questions he raised in these books are still being addressed today. He remained at Berkeley, finally becoming professor emeritus of the business school there in 1981.

The two main strands of Churchman's thinking that endured throughout his long career were his systems perspective, and his concern and strong commitment for ethical alertness. He also believed that the two were entwined, that ethical alertness came from thinking systemically. His work was concerned always with humanity in scientific research. Churchman believed that an ethical and moral stance should be integrated into management practice and thinking, rather than being addressed as an afterthought.

Churchman can be described as a founder of the modern systems approach. Systems, to Churchman, are not existing identifiable entities, but 'whole systems judgements', that is judgements made in the knowledge of the totality of relevant conditions. His contributions to systems thinking were to define a systems teleology setting out the conditions under which a system could demonstrate purposefulness; and establishing ways of bounding problem contexts using concepts such as 'sweep in' (developing knowledge of the totality of relevant conditions), 'unfolding' (giving structure to problem contexts) to make explicitly 'boundary setting'. He gave emphasis to the notion that boundary setting is a matter of choice and can only ever result in partial boundaries. His systems

approach was the forerunner to work on soft systems thinking, developed by Peter CHECKLAND, and critical systems thinking, developed at the University of Hull in the 1980s.

Churchman is a philosopher who strove to apply philosophy, and science generally, to the betterment of humankind, in the field of management. He is renowned for his contribution to systems thinking, the establishment of OR and his contribution to the debate on the ethics of science. He also made contributions to research methodology, logic, modelling complex problems, and the world *problematique* of futures studies. He was an all-round thinker and an excellent writer with a knack for bringing his thinking into clear relief with the use of poetry, stories and example problems. His work continuously called for the recognition of the importance of wisdom and hope in management science. The importance of Churchman's contribution was recognized with his nomination for the Nobel Prize for Social Sciences in 1984.

BIBLIOGRAPHY

Churchman, C.W. (1948) *Theory of Experimental Inference*, New York: Macmillan.

——— (1968) *Challenge to Reason*, New York: McGraw-Hill.

——— (1968) *The Systems Approach*, New York: Delta.

——— (1971) *The Design of Inquiring Systems*, New York: Basic Books.

——— (1979) *The Systems Approach and Its Enemies*, New York: Basic Books.

Churchman, C.W. and Mason, R.O. (1976) *World Modelling: A Dialogue*, Amsterdam: North Holland.

Churchman, C.W., Ackoff, R.L. and Arnoff, E.L. (1957) *Introduction to Operations Research*, New York: Wiley.

Churchman, C.W., Auerbach, L. and Sadan, S. (1975) *Thinking for Decisions: Deductive Quantitative Methods*, Chicago: Science Research Associates.

Flood, R.L. (1998) 'Churchman, C. West', in M. Warner (ed.), *Handbook of Management Thinking*, London: International Thomson Business Press, 122–7.

AJ

CITRÖEN, André (1878–1936)

André Citröen was born in Paris on 2 May 1878, the youngest of three brothers. He died probably in Paris on 3 July 1936. His father was a Jewish diamond merchant, who settled in Paris in about 1872; he killed himself to escape anti-Semitic persecution when André was six years old. Citröen went to the Lycée Condorcet, and on to the École Polytechnique at the early age of sixteen. After graduation in 1898, he started his first business at the age of twenty-two, when he came up with an idea for a new type of gear and established a gear-cutting shop. The company became very profitable and grew until in 1913 it became the Société Anonyme des Engrenages Citröen, with a capital of three million francs.

In 1905 he took an order to make 500 automobile engines. Although he lost money on the contract, it was his first entry into the automotive industry, which he believed had great potential. His reputation as a successful businessman and engineer spread, partly thanks to his gregarious nature. His second venture began when he was brought in to advise the board of Mors, a failing automotive company in Paris, and took over the firm in order to save it. After two years he returned the company's finances to the black, although its fortunes remained turbulent for some time. The company became the foundation of Citröen SA.

Although production and sales reached new heights, Citröen had not been able to reduce production costs or reduce short-term debt,

and the company again made a small loss in 1913. His response was a complete reorganization of the factory to improve workflow. This was done to such good effect that his factory became a showcase for visiting engineers, who reported that 'What might be called American methods are seen in their best form' (Laux 1976). The careful inspection of incoming materials and parts was also an important part of his production changes. Again, Citröen succeeded in turning the company round and it began to grow. The start of the First World War bolstered the growth of the firm as demand for military hardware and munitions rose.

Citröen took this opportunity to build a new concern in Paris to make shells using an American-style automobile mass-production system he had seen in the United States in 1912. He became a renowned munitions manufacturer during the First World War, producing high-quality shells very quickly. At the end of the war Citröen converted his munitions plant to automobile manufacturing. Possession of efficient production technology gave the firm a tremendous advantage in that it could produce high-quality cars more cheaply than the competition. By 1929 Citröen had more than 30 per cent of car sales in France. The company aimed at the mass market, producing a modern product but a limited range of cars. This product strategy was in direct contrast to that of Citröen's rival RENAULT, who lost ground by focusing stubbornly on a wide range of cars. Citröen kept improving his production facilities, again outdoing Renault by being the first to install full-moving assembly lines in 1919.

To expand sales Citröen, like his competitors, recruited more dealers and established more sales outlets at home, in the colonies and abroad. Unusually for the time, his advertising campaigns often targeted women. He also displayed an international perspective and quickly established a factory in Britain in 1926, following this with plants in Italy, Germany and Belgium. In the interwar

decades Citröen vied with Renault as the largest French automobile producer. Financially, Citröen continued playing his creditors off against one another, and the firm was plagued with financial instability. When the depression struck in the 1930s, the firm fell into the hands of his financiers. He died shortly after, in 1936.

Unlike Renault, Citröen was happy to work with a team and he had a good eye for choosing subordinates, both in engineering and in management. His taste for innovation in the engineering field kept the firm at the forefront of developing automobile technology, introducing the pneumatic suspension which Citröen cars still use today, and headlights that could be steered to see round bends (in fact these had the unfortunate habit of sticking, leaving drivers suddenly blind to the road ahead.).

Citröen was a risk-taker, and by all accounts was an inveterate gambler. His finances were constantly shaky, and he was frequently under pressure from his banks. One of his many saving graces was his well-known skill as a speaker, which he put to good use stalling creditors as well as in advertising his cars. His panache gave the firm a distinctive marketing flair, which, coupled with his bold technological innovations in the cars and his constant striving to increase production efficiency, made the firm one of the leading pioneers of the automobile industry. His inability to shore up the precarious financial situation was partly due to his own nature and partly due to the structure of financial control that had emerged from the takeover of Mors.

BIBLIOGRAPHY

Bardou, J.P., Chanaron, J.-J., Fridenson, P. and Laux, J.M. (1982) *The Automobile Revolution: The Impact of an Industry*, Durham, NC: University of North Carolina Press.
Laux, J.M. (1976) *In First Gear: The French Automobile Industry to 1914*, Liverpool: Liverpool University Press.
Reynolds, J. (1997) *Andre Citröen: The Man and the Motor Cars*, New York: St Martin's Press.

AJ

CLARK, Edward (1811–82)

Edward Clark was born in Athens, New York on 19 December 1811, the son of Nathan and Julia Clark. He died of typhoid at his home near Cooperstown, New York on 14 October 1882. He was educated at the Lenox Academy and at Williams College in New York, and was admitted to the bar in New York in 1834. He married Caroline Jordan in 1836. In 1838 he and his father-in-law, Ambrose Jordan, established a law practice in New York City. In 1848 Clark represented an impoverished inventor, Isaac SINGER, in a patent suit; unable to pay his legal bills, Singer instead gave Clark a one-third share in his patents. This apparent piece of charity work paid off when in 1850 Singer developed and marketed the first sewing machine. Clark bought out another partner and became an equal partner in the firm with Singer. During the period 1853–6 Clark represented the firm through a series of patent suits initiated by Singer's rival Elias Howe, and negotiated the patent pool arrangement that ultimately settled the issue.

This issue resolved, Clark took over the management of the firm's sales efforts. He tried selling territorial rights, in effect a franchise to sell Singer machines within a given region, and using commission sales agents, both with little success. Clark then decided to recruit his own sales force, beginning by recruiting workers from the Singer factory who showed some aptitude for sales; these men, who knew the machines well, were better able to describe the product features to customers. The sales force were trained to give demon-

strations of the machine and instruct house-wives in how to use it (for its time, the sewing machine was a very high-technology piece of equipment) and also to provide repairs. Clark extended credit to purchasers through a form of hire-purchase agreement. By the mid-1860s the firm had expanded its sales operation to include agencies in Britain and Germany; in 1882 the first European factory was opened in Glasgow. In the 1870s Clark devoted himself to rationalizing the company's marketing operations, among other things installing a formal reporting structure which allowed data and information from salesmen in the field to be passed quickly back to headquarters and analysed. Clark also undertook reforms in the firm's operations and management structure. Although Singer's was the mechanical and design genius that enabled the firm to produce a high-quality product, Clark's was the management expertise which allowed it to grow and become the world leader in its field.

BIBLIOGRAPHY

Davies, R.B. (1976) *Peacefully Working to Conquer the World: Singer Sewing Machines in Foreign Markets, 1854–1920*, New York: Arno.

CLARK, Fred Emerson (1890–1948)

Fred Emerson Clark was born in Parma, Michigan on 26 August 1890 and died at Evanston, Illinois on 26 November 1948. The son of Guy and Ida Clark, he was educated at Albion College and the University of Illinois, where he took his Ph.D. in 1916. He married Carrie Patton in 1915, and they had one son. Clark held a variety of short-term posts including instructor in commerce and industry at the University of Michigan (1916–17), professor of business administration at the University of Delaware (1917–18), and assis-tant professor of economics at Michigan (1918–19). In 1919 he moved to Northwestern University, where he remained for the rest of his career, first as assistant professor of economics and marketing and then, from 1923, as professor of marketing. He also served as director of the Graduate School of Commerce at Northwestern from 1937 to 1947.

Clark was one of the group of academics, also including Homer Vanderblue and Walter Dill SCOTT, who established Northwestern University as a leading centre for marketing study and research, a tradition which has continued at Northwestern down to the present day under Philip KOTLER. He was by all accounts a highly effective teacher. The early marketing courses at Northwestern were modelled on those developed at Harvard Business School by CHERINGTON and COPELAND, but Clark and his colleagues made alterations and improvements. They put a stronger emphasis on consumer psychology, gradually shifting the emphasis away from distribution and price issues and towards greater consideration of product and promotion. They also expressed concern that the Harvard system was too 'functional', and both Clark and Vanderblue called for a more integrated approach to marketing.

Clark's basic conceptualization of marketing is outlined in his *Principles of Marketing* (1924). He defines marketing as 'those efforts which effect transfers in the ownership of goods, and care for their physical distribution' (1924: 1). The need for marketing, he says, stems from the division of labour, 'particularly as manifested in large scale production and in the localization of industry' (1924: 1).

This division of labor, in turn, is due to the diversity of human wants – a diversity which arises not merely from the demand for the prime necessities of life, but from that far greater number of acquired wants which result from the seemingly limitless

165

possibilities for human beings to expand and develop their desires.

(Clark 1924: 1).

At the heart of marketing are two processes, concentration and dispersion. Goods are first collected by a marketing organization from producers and gathered at a central point. They are then dispersed to individual customers. The marketing organization rests on this focal point, where concentration ends and dispersion begins. Clark was much preoccupied with problems of marketing efficiency, and argued that both processes needed to become simpler and cheaper, or else the cost of the marketing system would outweigh its value. The vagaries of consumer demand, coupled with slowness of response by marketing organizations, meant that technical inefficiencies were a constant problem. Consumers demanded both a greater range of products and higher levels of service, and these could not be provided without an increase in cost to the system. These inefficiencies are, he says, an inevitable consequence of the free market, and cannot be escaped unless the entire competitive system is scrapped.

Recognizing this to be impossible, Clark calls instead for greater integration within the marketing system. In particular, he believes that there needs to be greater cooperation between consumers and producers, allowing for the pooling of information that would help producers predict demand more accurately, improve their physical distribution systems and eliminate unnecessary middlemen. Clark's ideas on the need to link consumers and producers more directly within the context of a free market were in advance of their time.

BIBLIOGRAPHY
Cattell, J.M., Cattell, J. and Ross, E.E. (1941) *Leaders in Education*, 2nd edn, Lancaster, PA: The Science Press.
Clark, F.E. (1921) 'Criteria of Marketing Efficiency', *American Economic Review* 11: 214–20.
—— (1924) *Princples of Marketing*, New York: Macmillan.
—— (ed.) (1924) *Readings in Marketing*, New York: Macmillan.
Clark, F.E. and Weld, L.D.H. (1932) *Marketing Agricultural Products in the United States*, New York: Macmillan.

MLW

CLARK, Jim (1944–)

Jim Clark grew up, impoverished, in the Texas panhandle town of Plainview. The product of a broken home, Clark was suspended from high school at the age of sixteen and never returned. Eager to escape the confines of Plainview, at the age of seventeen he joined the navy and, after nine months at sea, surprised his instructors by getting the highest score of his class in a maths test. This resulted in his going to night school to earn his high school equivalency. In 1970 he graduated from the University of New Orleans with a BS in physics, and received his MA in physics from the same institution in 1971. He went from there to the University of Utah and graduated with a Ph.D. in computer science in 1974.

After university, Clark landed a job with the University of Santa Cruz as an assistant professor, and was already thinking of bringing 3-D computing to engineers. From 1979 to 1982, while working as an associate professor at Stanford University, he further developed his 3-D graphics work, and designed a computer chip which would later allow engineers to model designs on relatively inexpensive computers, saving them months of work and thousands of dollars. He dubbed his invention the 'Geometry Engine', and with the help of a $25,000 start-up loan from a friend and a handful of his students, whom he hired in 1982, Silicon Graphics Inc. (SGI) was born.

Silicon Graphics is probably most famous for the workstations it produced to create special effects for films such as *Jurassic Park* and *Forrest Gump*. Clark served as chief technical officer and chairman of the board until his departure from the firm in 1994. In order to finance the operation, Clark was forced to sell off much of his stock holdings to venture capitalists, and his frustration grew as his influence waned. A falling out with CEO Ed McCracken convinced Clark to move on. He later observed, 'I felt that someone had taken away one of the passions of my life' (*Business Week* 1998). Although the company had become a billion-dollar operation, the selling off of Clark's stocks whittled his share to $16 million.

In 1994 Clark, along with Marc Andreesen, a 22-year-old genius who had helped to create the Mosaic Web browser at the University of Illinois, founded Netscape Communications. Clark recruited James Barksdale to be CEO, and Andreesen rounded up the rest of Mosaic's core engineering team to develop and launch the Internet browser. The company thrived and in August of 1995 Netscape made headlines as the most successful initial placement offering (IPO) in the history of the United States. A $5-million investment by Clark in 1994 brought him 19 per cent of the company, and would ultimately make him the first Internet paper billionaire.

In 1995 Clark, who had been frustrated in his dealings with the health care system following a motorcycle accident in the early 1990s, founded Healtheon. His aim through Healtheon (later named Healtheon/Web MD Corp. in November 1999, and shortened in September 2000 to Web/MD Corp.) was to create a system that would slash red tape and create centralized information services to connect doctors, insurers, pharmacies and patients. The company had a rocky start in the first year, but the hiring of Mike Long as CEO and the willingness of investors to back Internet companies propelled the company into a billion-dollar operation. Clark is a major

shareholder, and was chairman until his resignation in October 2000. Clark has also invested and served on the boards of My CFO, a personal finance site for the ultra-rich, and Shutterfly.com, an online photo-processing and delivery service. He is also very involved with a project to computerize totally the operation of his 150-foot, $30-million sailboat, *Hyperion*.

As the only person to have been involved in three start-up companies which each grew to over a billion dollars in value, Clark presents an interesting case study for both entrepreneurship and the management of innovation. Like other techno-entrepreneurs such as Mitch KAPOR and Robert NOYCE, he seems to derive more satisfaction from the start-up process; although he places less of a premium on personal control, he still sometimes appears to find growth to be an inhibiting rather than an enabling factor.

BIBLIOGRAPHY

Business Week (1998) 'Jim Clark is Off and Running Again', http://www.businessweek.com/1998/41/b3599112.htm, 5 March 2001.

Clark, J. (1999) *Netscape Time*, New York: St Martin's Press.

Lewis, M. (1999) *The New New Thing: A Silicon Valley Story*, New York: W.W. Norton.

JW

CLAUSEWITZ, Karl von (1780–1831)

Karl von Clausewitz, the son of a retired army officer, was born in Burg, Germany on 1 June 1780. He died of cholera at Breslau (modern Wroclaw, Poland) on 16 November 1831. He was commissioned in the Prussian army in 1793. He attended the military school in Berlin from 1801 to 1804, then joined the general

staff in 1804, serving under General Scharnhorst. He assisted Scharnhorst in the reorganization of the Prussian army following the defeat by Napoleon in 1806. In 1812 he served with the Russian army that defeated Napoleon, and in 1815 he was a senior staff officer in the Waterloo campaign. In 1818 he was appointed director of the War College in Berlin, where he began writing his major work, *Vom Kriege* (On War). He died while serving with the Prussian army during the Polish revolution of 1830–31.

Clausewitz is known today as the most important writer on military science in the Western world; worldwide, his fame is exceeded only by that of SUNZI (Sun Tzu). *Vom Kriege* is studied by cadets at nearly every military academy, and has been referred to by every almost every subsequent writer on strategy. Deeply influenced by Kant and other German philosophers of the Enlightenment, Clausewitz applied techniques such as critical reasoning to war, looking for a bridge between theory and practice. While contemporaries such as BÜLOW and JOMINI stressed an abstract, almost mechanistic approach to strategy which sought to eliminate chance and human error, Clausewitz tried to come to terms with the moral and psychological aspects of war.

Central to his view of strategy and warfare in general was the relationship between theories of war and war itself. War is not an independent phenomenon; it is waged for a purpose, one that is determined by the will of the commander. There is a difference between the purpose of war and war itself; the latter is simply 'an act of violence meant to force the enemy to do our will' (1819: 90). It is easy to set a purpose for war, and easy too to make plans for the defeat of the enemy and set these plans in motion. However, it is another matter to carry out these plans as intended, and leaders are constantly beset with the problem of staying true to their own purposes. In taking this view, Clausewitz acknowledges a debt to MACHIAVELLI, whose works on war and politics were familiar to him.

The key factor is 'friction': 'countless minor incidents – the kind you can never really foresee – combine to lower the general level of performance, so that one always falls far short of the intended goal' (1819: 119). Friction, says Clausewitz, is what distinguishes real war from war on paper (1819: 119). Strategic planning is based on statistical facts; but real war can never amount to more than probabilities. Many factors lead to friction, but none is more important than the moral factors, the courage and ability of the leader, the experience and spirit of the troops. Should these fail at any point, previously determined plans will be jeopardized. As a result, he says, 'Everything in strategy is very simple, but that does not mean that everything in strategy is very easy' (1819: 178).

These basic Clausewitzian principles – that strategy is subordinate to purpose, and that the achievement of any given strategic goal is never certain – have informed much strategic thinking and writing since. Clausewitz was a powerful influence on MOLTKE, and through him on the scientific management movement.

BIBLIOGRAPHY
Clausewitz, K. von (1819) *Vom Kriege*, ed. and trans. M. Howard and P. Paret, *On War*, Princeton, NJ: Princeton University Press, 1984.
Parkinson, R. (1971) *Carl von Clausewitz*, London: Wayland.

MLW

CLEGG, Hugh Armstrong (1920–95)

Hugh Armstrong Clegg was born in Truro, Cornwall on 22 May 1920 and died in Kenilworth, Warwickshire on 9 December 1995. The son of a Methodist minister, he joined the Communist Party while head boy of

Kingswood School, Bath. He went to Magdalen College, Oxford, but his studies were interrupted by the Second World War. Following five years in the army as a telephone engineer, Clegg returned to Oxford, taking the best degree of his year. The famous labour scholar G.D.H. Cole introduced him to industrial relations. He joined the newly founded Nuffield College as a student working on a union history. In 1949, at the age of twenty-nine, he was elected a Nuffield College fellow. Here his long-term partnership (and division of labour) with the more theoretically inclined Allan FLANDERS developed and flourished. Clegg later moved to the University of Warwick as professor of industrial relations (1967–79) and director of its Industrial Relations Research Unit (1970–74), helping establish the Unit as an internationally pre-eminent centre for multidisciplinary and rigorous research and teaching.

Clegg's academic career was interspersed with numerous bouts of policy and practice work, as he served on official enquiries and arbitrations. He was a member of many committees, on railway pay (1958–60), on the docks (1964–5) and on local authority pay (1970), served on the Royal Commission on Trade Unions and Employers Associations (1965–8), the National Board for Prices and Incomes (1966–8) and the Council of Advisory, Conciliation and Arbitration Service (1974–9), and was chairman of the Standing Commission on Pay Comparability (1979–80).

A prolific writer, his work includes many monographs on particular events, industries, occupations and previously ignored subjects. He also wrote on union history, industrial democracy, and comparatively and theoretically on unions and collective bargaining. There was also the path-breaking founding text of the influential 'Oxford School of Industrial Relations' (Flanders and Clegg 1954), of which he, along with Flanders and FOX, was a key member. This text catered for teachers and students and was for the use of 'practitioners' (including unionists and civil servants); it ran through five reprints, with two evolutions as eponymous texts (Clegg 1970; Clegg 1979).

Common themes run through much of Clegg's work as a pluralist opposed to radical change, a compass to which he remained true. This includes his famous maxim that 'an ounce of fact is worth a pound of theory', as he was concerned that many theories were based on little evidence. A second overarching concern was his view of what industrial relations 'was', with a focus on formal institutions. A third theme concerns the belief in, and support for, collective bargaining and interest in its structure and optimal level. A fourth area concerns employees' democratic 'rights'. Another theme was noted early, namely his 'keen sympathy with trade unionists and the purposes of trade unionism' (Clegg 1954: xiii).

Clegg can be considered one of the most influential scholars of industrial relations in the twentieth century. While it may be argued that many academics have little impact on 'real lives', as many practitioners do not read their works, Clegg had influences via the 'sharp end' of practice. His empiricism laid solid foundations for the subject, and continues to cast a light over it. Clegg was an impressive personality and inspired considerable personal loyalty, which gave the 'Oxford School' a resilience it might otherwise have lacked. In terms of his work regime, academic credentials, personality and the way he was held in esteem, tribute was paid at the memorial service held for him at Nuffield where Lord McCarthy, his former student, succinctly concluded: 'we will not see his like again'.

Acknowledgements
Thanks to Willy Brown, Rod Martin and Pat McGovern for earlier comments.

BIBLIOGRAPHY
Clegg, H.A. (1950) *Labour Relations in London Transport*, Oxford: Blackwell.
—— (1951) *Industrial Democracy and Nationalization*, Oxford: Blackwell.

—— (1954) *General Union A Study of the National Union of General and Municipal Workers*, Oxford: Blackwell.

—— (1960) *A New Approach to Industrial Democracy*, Oxford: Blackwell.

—— (1964) *A History of British Trade Unions*, vol. 3, Oxford: Oxford University Press.

—— (1970) *The System of Industrial Relations in Great Britain*, Oxford: Blackwell.

—— (1971) *How to Run an Incomes Policy, and Why We Made Such a Mess of the Last One*, London: Heinemann.

—— (1976) *Trade Unionism under Collective Bargaining: A Theory Based on Comparisons of Six Countries*, Oxford: Blackwell.

—— (1979) *The Changing System of Industrial Relations in Great Britain*, Oxford: Blackwell.

—— (1990) 'The Oxford School of Industrial Relations', *Warwick Papers in Industrial Relations*, IRRU, University of Warwick, 31.

Clegg, H.A. and Adams, R. (1957) *The Employers Challenge: A Study of the National Shipbuilding and Engineering Disputes of 1957*, Oxford: Blackwell.

Clegg, H.A. and Chester, T.E. (1957) *Wages Policy and the Health Service*, Oxford: Blackwell.

Clegg, H.A., Fox, A. and Thompson, A.F. (1964) *A History of British Trade Unions*, vol. 1, Oxford: Oxford University Press.

Clegg, H.A., Killick, A.J. and Adams, R. (1961) *Trade Union Officers: A Study of Full Time Officers, Branch Secretaries and Shop Stewards*, Oxford: Blackwell.

Flanders, A. and Clegg, H.A. (1954) *The System of Industrial Relations in Great Britain*, Oxford: Blackwell.

CR

COASE, Ronald (1910–)

Ronald Coase was born in Willesden, near London on 29 December 1910. He attended the London School of Economics, where he took a degree in commerce; among his influences there was Arnold Plant. In 1931 he visited the United States on a scholarship, where he conducted a study of variations in the structure of firms across industries. Returning to Britain, he joined the faculty of the London School of Economics, where he taught until 1951. During the Second World War he was engaged in government work at the offices of the War Cabinet. In 1951 he emigrated to the United States, teaching variously at the State University of New York at Buffalo, Stanford University and the University of Virginia before settling at the University of Chicago Law School, where he remained from 1964 to 1981. He was editor of the highly influential *Journal of Law and Economics*. He received the Nobel Prize for Economics in 1991.

Coase is one of the most influential economic thinkers of the twentieth century. Unlike most other well-known economists of the era, who tended to concern themselves with the great macroeconomic issues of their times – Maynard KEYNES with unemployment, Milton FRIEDMAN with inflation and monetary theory – Coase focused on fundamental microeconomic questions. The result was a set of contributions which lay dormant for years before their implications became widely recognized. In the last quarter of the twentieth century, papers by Coase written in the 1930s and early 1960s became the foundation for whole new subdisciplines in economics.

For management theorists and students of business structure, Coase's work is of central importance. Indeed, as memories of the mass unemployment of the interwar years faded and the inflationary pressures of the 1960s and 1970s began to die away, long neglected issues of economic organization came once more to the fore. The collapse of the planned economies of Eastern Europe; the growth of

multinational enterprise and the rise of globalization; the privatization of industries in the mixed economies of the West; the establishment of new regulatory agencies at both national and international levels; the advance of new technologies especially in the field of electronic communications: all this upsurge of organizational experiment and change reflected the urgency of the basic question at the heart of Coase's work. What determines the best organizational structure for the conduct of business?

In 1937 Coase had asked this question in a paper entitled 'The Nature of the Firm'. Why are some firms large and others small? Why are some vertically integrated while others specialize in a particular stage of production and trade with upstream and downstream firms across markets? Why do some firms control production activities in overseas countries while others simply purchase inputs from independent foreign suppliers? Coase's answer was simple. Firms will often find it profitable to undertake the supply of inputs themselves because 'there is a cost of using the price mechanism'. Transacting with other economic agents across markets is costly. If it were not costly to transact, the very existence of the 'firm' would be impossible to explain. Finding a suitable supplier, bargaining over the price, assessing reliability, explaining what is required, renegotiating at contract renewal, enforcing the contract terms; all these activities are costly. In the firm, some of these costs are reduced. When a supplier joins a 'firm', Coase argued that 'authority' replaces bargaining. Contracts within the firm are durable and non-specific. They permit the 'employer' to give (within limits) instructions to 'employees' or within firm 'suppliers' and to avoid the costs of frequent renegotiation.

On the other hand, there are also costs of organizing transactions within a firm. If decision making becomes too centralized and the firm becomes too 'bureaucratic', its administrative costs will rise. If this were not so, it would be efficient to organize the entire economy as one giant firm – as was indeed disastrously attempted in the planned economies. For Coase, the optimal scope of the firm is determined by the equality of marginal 'transactions cost' in the market and marginal 'organization cost' within the firm. As the firm grows and extends its activities, a point will come where the cost of organizing an additional transaction within the firm will rise to the level at which it can be transacted across the market. This will mark the 'boundary' of the firm.

The study of transactions costs is the core of Coase's contribution to economics. Before Coase, students of economic organization had been well aware of many of the factors to which Coase drew attention. But until Coase's brilliant identification of a class of costs labelled transactions costs, it was difficult for the study of economic organization to progress further than a form of applied common sense. Hitting on the right conceptual framework can be crucial to all forms of scientific advance. For several centuries, the costs of labour and capital had been familiar ideas. The startling organizational innovations of the first Industrial Revolution with the channelling of flows of labour, raw materials and capital resources through the factory system may have so overwhelmed the senses that the very din drew the attention towards technology and physical processes and away from the problem of transacting. Perhaps it is no accident that the communications revolution of the late twentieth century and the relative decline of manufacturing has tugged the attention back towards a more subtle type of cost – transactions cost – though one which is recognized as a powerful reality by every practical business person.

Modern work on business enterprise is heavily indebted to Coase's framework. Some explanations of multinational expansion, for example, rely on the costs of transacting in certain types of knowledge. A well-defined and protected patent right, for example, would permit a firm to license technology worldwide

and thus to avoid multinational expansion. Other types of knowledge, however, may be vulnerable to theft, or may be impossible to codify and thus to trade. The 'core competence' of a firm or its 'competitive advantage' will often be made up of skills or reputational advantages which can be exploited only by means of internal expansion. Modern management thinking along these lines is thus profoundly 'Coasian' in its emphasis.

Public policy has also increasingly had to wrestle with Coase's problem of firm versus market. Privatized utilities, for example, have been broken into vertically disintegrated structures in order to encourage competition at those stages which are not naturally monopolistic. Transactions costs have thereby been incurred. Contracts now link electricity generation, transmission, distribution and retailing where once there was simply internal administration. The costs of contracting are thrown into sharp relief when 'qualitative' aspects of an industry's output such as its safety or reliability are involved. Sometimes competition between suppliers can be expected to improve service standards which are difficult to measure. Where consumers cannot 'observe' these qualitative factors at low cost, however, and where they are unable to switch to alternative suppliers, contracting can give rise to great problems. As Britain found in the early twenty-first century, the supply of 'safety' on the rail system is costly to produce by means of a set of contracts between track provider and train operating companies.

Coase's work forms the basis not only for modern work in the structure of business organization but also for the whole subdiscipline of 'law and economics'. In 'The Problem of Social Cost' (1960), Coase noted that if one person's activities adversely affected others (there were external costs) a solution could be found either through government intervention or through contract and agreement. Once more the choice would depend upon the costs of internal administration versus the costs of transacting. If transactions costs were negligible, all the

law would need to do would be to define property rights clearly. If people have a property right to clean water in a river, for example, a firm wishing to pollute the river would have to purchase the right to do so from the people affected. Presumably the firm would only go ahead if it were more than able to pay compensation to the people who would suffer. Conversely, if the firm had the right to pollute the river, those expecting to lose from the pollution could bribe the firm to reduce its emissions into the watercourse. Either way, bargaining would proceed until all the gains from trade were exhausted and social efficiency was achieved.

By using some celebrated legal cases from English common law, Coase illustrates the reciprocal nature of external harm. He does not pass judgement on who 'ought' to have the property rights – the complainant protesting about grinding noises or the apothecary wishing to pursue his trade – but merely observes that bargaining between the two litigants will, however the rights are assigned, be mutually advantageous. Transactions costs are once more central to the argument, however. In the face of very great bargaining and other transactions costs, it will obviously matter to whom property rights are assigned. This has led to the idea that the courts should 'mimic the market' and assign property rights to the party that values them most highly, and thus to the party that would be expected (in the absence of transactions costs) to purchase them (see Posner 1973). A further conclusion was that reducing transactions costs and encouraging private bargains was an important aspect of policy towards social cost. Establishing property rights in environmental resources and permitting trade in such rights has been an important addition to environmental policy because it supplements what would otherwise be complete reliance on administrative solutions. The imposition and policing of centrally set standards, instructing firms to operate in particular ways using specified technology, or the introduction of taxes on particular activi-

ties all rely on the centralized evaluation of costs and benefits rather than decentralized private agreement.

It is sometimes mistakenly thought that Coase is an advocate of market transacting over other solutions to organizational problems. As can easily be seen from the above, this is a misconception. For Coase, efficient economic organization is about economizing on all costs including the costs of 'market contract' and the costs of 'internal' administration. There is no single 'best' form of organization suitable for all circumstances. His reputation for supporting market processes probably derives from the fact that, in the context of the time at which his ideas were first developed, the claims of central administration were rather widely endorsed by many economic thinkers. In the 1930s and 1940s, for example, the advantages of central planning over the market were urged by theorists who greatly underestimated the information and control problems that would be encountered. Similarly, in the 1960s it was somewhat uncritically assumed, even by relatively free market economists, that the problem of social cost could only be solved by central government action and that this represented one of the 'classic' justifications for the existence of the state.

Given prevailing opinion, therefore, Coase's ideas tended to lend support for experiments with market transacting. Hence his support for creating private property rights in the broadcasting spectrum (Coase 1959) and allocating these by means of a competitive auction rather than by administrative fiat. Hence his interest in historical examples of people overcoming apparently high transactions costs in order to achieve a social goal. Even the lighthouse, that archetypal 'public good' mentioned in every public finance textbook, was introduced in England without recourse to government finance (Coase 1974). Nothing in Coase's view of the world, however, establishes the universal supremacy of contract. Indeed, the very notion of 'transaction cost' is in one sense subversive of markets and was introduced by Coase initially as an explanation of non-market forms of organization.

Coase's initial conception of transactions cost has been greatly refined by other theorists. His distinction between 'market' and 'firm' as involving a simple contrast between voluntary contract and the exercise of 'authority' has been subject to much criticism. Firms can monitor outside 'independent' suppliers just as they may offer incentive contracts and a large measure of independent initiative to those within. Modern 'property rights theorists' have developed new ways of explaining why it is sometimes advantageous to 'own' a supplier and sometimes not (for example, Hart 1995). The 'New Institutional Economists' have analysed 'transactions' with greater sophistication than Coase's original framework provided (for example, WILLIAMSON 1985). However, all these scholars openly acknowledge the debt that they owe to the remarkable contributions of Ronald Coase.

BIBLIOGRAPHY

Coase, R.H. (1937) 'The Nature of the Firm', *Economica*, new series, 4(16): 386–405.

—— (1959) 'The Federal Communications Commission', *Journal of Law and Economics* 2: 1–40.

—— (1960) 'The Problem of Social Cost', *Journal of Law and Economics* 3: 1–44.

—— (1974) 'The Lighthouse in Economics', *Journal of Law and Economics* 17(2): 357–76.

Hart, O. (1995) *Firms, Contracts and Financial Structure*, Oxford: Clarendon Press.

Posner R.A. (1973) *Economic Analysis of Law*, Boston: Little, Brown.

Williamson, O.E. (1985) *The Economic Institutions of Capitalism: Firms, Markets, Relational Contracting*, New York: The Free Press.

MR

COEN, Jan Pieterszoon (1587–1629)

Jan Pieterszoon Coen was born in Hoorn, the Netherlands on 8 January 1587. He died of fever in Batavia on the island of Java (now Djakarta, Indonesia) on 21 September 1629. The son of a merchant, he received a good education; he was fluent in six languages and was also a trained mathematician. In 1607, aged twenty, he joined the newly incorporated Dutch East India Company as an under-merchant and sailed as a passenger on one of the Company's merchant vessels to the East Indies. The Company, founded in 1602 and incorporated in 1606, had been founded primarily to exploit the spice trade between the East Indies and Europe; its merchants were attempting to corner the market in spices in the face of opposition from Portuguese and English traders. The competition between these traders, although primarily commercial in nature, often had violent overtones; in the early seventeenth century the dividing lines between maritime trade, warfare and piracy were blurred, especially outside European waters.

Coen's first voyage to the East Indies was a success, and he was promoted to upper-merchant and sent back to Java in 1612, this time in command of a ship. Thereafter his rise was rapid; in 1613 he became president of the important factories, or trading stations, at Bantam and Jacatra, and in 1614 he became director-general of all the posts on Java. He defended his position vigorously against the encroachments of the British East India Company, using both economic and military means, even though his forces were often weaker than those of the British traders. In 1617 the ineffective governor-general of the East Indies, Laurens Reael, resigned in a dispute with the Seventeen, the governing council of the Company, and Coen was appointed as his successor. During the next five years Coen efficiently consolidated Dutch hold over the spice trade, driving the British from post after post through commercial deals with local rulers which excluded the British

from the trade; and where these could not be reached he used force.

Coen's achievements during this time have been overlooked by British historians, who have been preoccupied with the plight of the defeated British East India Company; even recent writers like Milton (1999) have been more interested in blackening Coen's character than examining his achievements. In fact, these were considerable. With slender resources, never more than a dozen ships and a few hundred men, he maintained a string of trading stations spread across 3,000 kilometres (2,000 miles) of the Indonesian archipelago. Opposed by hostile indigenous powers and foreign trading companies, he not only consolidated his trade but drove his foreign rivals out; by 1622 the British East India Company had abandoned all its factories in the Indies east of Sumatra, and thenceforth concentrated on India.

Coen achieved his goals by a mixture of efficiency and ruthlessness. Modern accounts focus on his military exploits, but he was a highly efficient commercial manager as well. He inspected the accounts from all posts in the East Indies and demanded to know the reasons for any delays or failures. He set targets for increasing the volume of spices traded, and ensured his factors met them. His relationship with the Seventeen was usually stormy, but the meteoric rise in trade and profits under Coen's governor-generalship attested to the success of his methods.

Coen set the blueprint for subsequent overseas trading ventures. He learned early the lesson that in the often chaotic political situation in the Far East, the Company would have to achieve a measure of political control if it were to safeguard its commercial interests. Violence had to be used if trade were to prosper. As he told the Seventeen in 1614, 'trade with India must be conducted and maintained under protection and the favour of your own weapons, and that the weapons must be supplied from the profits enjoyed by the trade, so that trade cannot be maintained without

war or war without trade' (Day 1904: 46). This attitude is of course reprehensible by today's standards, but was a common one at the time. Coen differed from his colleagues and rivals only in that he had the willpower and the ruthlessness to carry his chosen strategy through to the end. A hundred and fifty years later, Robert Clive and Warren HASTINGS chose the same strategic option for the British East India Company, taking a measure of political control and laying the foundations of empire in India.

Coen also argued for freedom of action for merchants in the field; it was impossible, he said, for the Seventeen in Amsterdam to control efficiently the Company's work on the far side of the world. He believed that the Seventeen should set policy and then allow its managers to carry out the policy in ways they saw fit. He went so far as deliberately to mislead the Seventeen on some occasions; in 1619 he wrote to them in his usual direct style: 'I swear to you by the Almighty that the Company has no enemies who do so much to hurt and hinder it, as the ignorance and thoughtlessness (do not take ill of me) which obtain among Your Honours, and silence the voice of the reasonable' (Day 1904: 90). This lesson too was learned by later overseas commercial enterprises, whose governors tended to opt for indirect rather than direct control.

In 1623 Coen was recalled to the Netherlands and given a hero's welcome. He married Eva Ment, the daughter of an Amsterdam merchant, in 1624. In 1627, with the situation in the Indies deteriorating again, the Seventeen asked Coen to return as governor-general. He died two years later, aged forty-two. He was by no means a pleasant or an admirable man, but of his success there can be little doubt. As Colenbrander points out, his efforts ensured that the Dutch East India Company would grow and prosper for another two centuries; for generations, the name 'Coen' was synonymous with the Company's success (Colenbrander 1934: 448).

BIBLIOGRAPHY

Colenbrander, H.T. (1934) *Jan Pieterszoon Coen*, s'Gravenhage: Martinus Nijhoff.

Day, C. (1904) *The Policy and Administration of the Dutch in Java*, New York: Macmillan.

Hyma, A. (1942) *The Dutch in the Far East: A History of the Dutch Commercial and Colonial Empire*, Ann Arbor, MI: George Wahr.

Milton, G. (1999) *Nathaniel's Nutmeg*, London: Sceptre.

MLW

COLT, Samuel (1814–62)

Samuel Colt was born in Hartford, Connecticut on 19 July 1814, the son of Christopher and Sarah Colt. He died in Hartford on 10 January 1862. In 1856 he married Elizabeth Jarvis; the couple had four children. Colt's father was a textile merchant, whose business failed when Colt was still a boy. Working as indentured labourer from the age of ten, Colt developed an interest in firearms and explosives. He attended Amherst Academy, where at the age of sixteen he designed a fireworks display for the Fourth of July celebrations; this misfired literally as well as figuratively, and the school building was burned to the ground. Anticipating expulsion, Colt left the school and took a job as a merchant seaman. According to legend, it was while on a voyage to Calcutta that he first developed the idea of the revolver. In fact, his was not the first such design; patents for revolvers had been issued in the United States as early as 1913, and it is likely that Colt knew of these (Hosley 1996: 47).)

Returning home, Colt took a job in a textile factory, and then at the age of eighteen found work as a travelling salesman, touring New

England selling nitrous oxide (laughing gas). He proved himself an adept salesman; he called himself Dr Colt, and quickly mastered the techniques of promotion. He used his earnings from this job to build prototypes of his revolver, and in 1835–6 took out US, British and French patents. In 1836, having found financial backing, he established his first factory in Paterson, New Jersey. Although Colt's revolvers proved effective, the US Army showed no interest and there was at this point little civilian demand; the company failed in 1842.

The turning point in Colt's fortunes came when Captain Samuel Walker of the Texas Rangers wrote to Colt with an enthusiastic endorsement of his revolvers, explaining how the quick-fire weapons effectively evened the odds when fighting against superior numbers. Realizing that here was a valuable source of publicity, Colt returned to Connecticut. The Connecticut River valley was already a centre of arms-making, on its way to becoming what Hosley (1996) calls America's first centre of machine-based manufacturing. He first contracted with the arms-maker Eli Whitney Jr to make revolvers according to Colt's designs, while Colt himself promoted and sold the weapons.

It was at this point that Colt began deliberately to create the image of his revolvers, an image that was to become their single most important selling point. Rugged and durable though his guns were, they were not as good as some other designs, notably the English-made Adams revolver. What Colt was selling, however, was not so much the gun itself as its image. Hosley notes that the 1850s were the time of the beginning of the opening of the American West, when the pioneer and frontiersman became role models of great stature; this was the gun used by the Texas Rangers, by pioneers in their desperate battles with Indians, and the romance of the frontier began to cling to the product. This was also the beginning of the USA's gun culture, when it became popular and fashionable to own and use firearms. Colt certainly capitalized on the first, and probably

contributed in no small way to the second (Hosley 1996: 72).

Colt developed his own image as well: in the 1850s he began calling himself 'Colonel Colt' (a title to which he had no more claim than the Dr Colt of his days selling laughing gas) and embarked on an assiduous campaign of self-promotion. Like his contemporary P.T. BARNUM, he deliberately cultivated myths about himself, which added to the stature of his products. In the meantime, he was a ruthless salesman who had few scruples about his clients. One of his first major contracts was to the army of Ottoman Turkey; during the Crimean War he sold arms to both Russia and England, and the Irish Fenians and Garibaldi's Redshirts were among his other customers.

But there was more to Colt than shrewd marketing. He knew that, given that his guns were often used in life-and-death situations, quality was essential; even a few stories of guns jamming in action could ruin the product's reputation. Further, like Richard ARKWRIGHT in England eighty years before, he realized that there was sufficient demand to make large-scale machine production possible. Accordingly, two years after teaming up with Whitney he resolved to build his own factory and run it on mass-production lines. Skilled workers were recruited from all over New England and Europe to build and run the factory machinery, and the talented engineer Elihu Root was hired as factory superintendent. High-speed automated production was the centre of Colt's concept of the factory; he later calculated that 80 per cent of his production costs were machine costs, while only 20 per cent were human labour costs, an astounding ratio for the time. Machine production ensured that quality could be engineered in, while maintaining a level of production high enough to meet demand.

Colt has sometimes been compared to Arkwright, not only for his appreciation of the importance of the factory system, but for his role in spreading that system and introducing it broadly into US industry. Colt's success

inspired many emulators. Former Colt employee Christopher Spencer set up his own factory in 1860, making tube-fed magazine rifles of his own design, the famous Spencer rifle which was widely adopted by the Union army in the American Civil War; later, Oliver WINCHESTER adopted many of Colt's methods in making and selling his rifles. As in Arkwright's England, skilled artisans trained in the firearms factories helped spread factory techniques and methods into other industries as well. Colt is seen as an important anticipator of the systems of mass production based on division of labour, analysed in detail by F.W. TAYLOR and put into effective practice by Henry FORD. Hosley sums up Colt's contribution and abilities:

Indeed, Colt's greatest invention was not repeating firearms – he had plenty of competition – but the system he built to manufacture these and the apparatus of sales, image management and marketing that made his guns ... the most popular, prolific and storied handgun in American history. Colt was the Lee Iacocca of his generation, a man whose name and personality became so widely associated with the product that ownership provided access to the celebrity, glamour and dreams of its namesake. What Colt *invented* was a system of myths, symbols, stagecraft and distribution that has been mimicked by generations of industrial mass marketers and has rarely been improved upon.

(Hosley 1996: 73–4)

Colt had been suffering from rheumatism in 1858, and a combination of disease and overwork brought about his death at the age of forty-eight. His wife Elizabeth Colt took over the firm and guided it through its greatest period of prosperity, from 1870 to 1890, when famous designs such as the Colt .45 Peacemaker dominated the market. She sold the firm in 1901.

BIBLIOGRAPHY

Hosley, W. (1996) *Colt: The Making of an American Legend*, Amherst, MA: University of Massachusetts Press.

Rohan, J. (1935) *Yankee Arms Maker*, New York: Harper and Row.

MLW

COMMONS, John Rogers (1862–1945)

John Rogers Commons was born in Hollansburg, Ohio on 13 October 1862 and died in Raleigh, North Carolina on 11 May 1945. His early life provides important guidance to understanding his work. He was born in the midst of the American Civil War, to parents who were both staunch anti-slavery advocates. Ohio was part of the Union, but the area in which Commons was born and raised was known for sympathy with slavery, and Commons probably acquired experience in the upholding of unpopular causes very early in life. Commons's father was an unsuccessful businessman. One of his failed ventures was newspaper publishing, through which John learned the printer's craft. This provided him with a means of support as well as first-hand experience in working at a trade – experience unique to economists of that era.

Commons began his education in Ohio at Oberlin College in 1882, where he supported himself by working as a printer. After an education interrupted by emotional problems, Commons obtained an AB degree in 1888 and entered graduate school at Johns Hopkins University in Baltimore, Maryland. He did not receive his doctorate, either for financial or for academic reasons, and left Johns Hopkins in 1890. In the nine years that followed he taught at Wesleyan University, Oberlin, Indiana University and finally Syracuse University. The rapid succession of academic

posts reflected the views of university admin- istrations that Commons was a 'radical'. This reputation resulted from Commons's interest in several American reform movements of the era, including temperance, socialism and the 'Single Tax' movement of Henry George.

In 1904 Commons obtained an appoint- ment in the department of political economy at the University of Wisconsin through Richard Ely, under whom he had studied at Johns Hopkins. He remained at Wisconsin until retirement in 1932, and it was here that he pio- neered academic research into the history of labour in America. At the same time he became involved with the administration of Wisconsin governor Robert LaFollette, one of the leaders of the American 'Progressive' political movement. In response to America's rapid industrialization the Progressives advocated incremental changes to American laws and political institutions. Their goal was to enable American democracy to cope with dislocations caused by the new industrial society, without abandoning capitalism. Commons played an active role in the Progressive legislative pro- gramme, and was instrumental in drafting Wisconsin's civil service law (1905), the law regulating companies providing public utility services (1907) and the law creating the Wisconsin Industrial Commission (1911).

At the same time, Commons investigated the new industrial economy through detailed studies of the history of American industry and labour, including contemporary field research. He took over from Ely the director- ship of a project to complete 'a history of industrial democracy in the United States'. With the aid of graduate students, he pub- lished the eleven-volume *A Documentary History of Industrial Society* (1910–11) and the first two volumes of the *History of Labor in the United States* (1918). Two more volumes of this work were published in 1935.

The literature concerning Commons is volu- minous, and now includes at least 71,000 cita- tions on the World Wide Web. However, Commons's economic theory is best summa- rized in his own words. The following summary is taken from his article 'Institutional Economics', published in the *American Economic Review* in 1931. Commons defines an 'institution' as 'collective action in control, liberation and expansion of individual action'. Collective action ranges from unorganized custom to what Commons calls 'organized going concerns', which include the family, cor- porations, trade unions and the state. This control of one individual is intended to, and does, lead to gain or loss to another individual. Control leads to duty, that is, conformity to col- lective action. It also leads to credit, that is security created by the expectation of individ- ual conformity. Commons calls this 'incorpo- real property'. Collective control can also take the form of prohibition of certain behaviour. This can create liberty in a person immunized against such behaviour, but a corresponding loss of liberty to a correlative person. As example, Commons cites the goodwill of a business, which he identifies as 'intangible property'.

The state, a cartel, a cooperative association or a trade union lays down and enforces rules determining for individuals this bundle of cor- relative and reciprocal economic relationships. These rules indicate what individuals can, must or may do or not do, enforced by collective sanctions. Analysis of these sanctions forms the correlation of economics, jurisprudence and ethics that is the prerequisite to the theory of institutional economics. Institutional econom- ics goes back to David Hume, who, according to Commons, found the unity of economics, jurisprudence and ethics in the principle of scarcity, and the conflicts of interest that scarcity produced. According to Commons, Adam SMITH isolated economics from the other two social sciences on assumptions of divine providence, earthly abundance and the result- ing harmony of interest. Ethics consists of rules of conduct arising from the conflict of interests in turn arising from scarcity, and enforced by moral sanctions. Economics deals with the same rules of conduct enforced by the collective

sanctions of profit and loss in case of obedience or disobedience; jurisprudence deals with the same rules enforced by the organized sanction of violence.

For Commons, collective action is more than control or liberation of individual action; it is the expansion of the will of the individual 'far beyond what he can do by his own puny acts. The head of a great corporation gives orders, whose obedience, enforced by collective action, executes his will at the ends of the earth' (Commons 1931: 519). To Commons, individual actions are really transactions, instead of either individual behaviour or the exchange of commodities. It is this shift in emphasis away from individual actors and commodities, to transactions and rules governing collective action, that marks the transition from what Commons calls the classical and hedonic schools of economics to institutional economics. Classical and hedonic economists founded their theories on the relation between individual and nature, but, in Commons's view, institutionalism is a relation between individual and individual.

The smallest unit of the classical economists was a commodity produced by labour; the smallest unit for hedonic economists was the same or similar commodity enjoyed by ultimate consumers. In contrast, for institutional economists the smallest unit is a 'unit of activity', a transaction with its participants. Transactions intervene between the labor of the classic economists and the pleasures of the hedonic economists, simply because it is society that controls access to the forces of nature, and transactions are not the 'exchange of commodities' but the alienation and acquisition, between individuals, of the rights of property and liberty created by society.
(Commons 1931: 519–20)

Transactions are the means, under operation of law and custom, of acquiring and alienating legal control of commodities, or legal control of the labour and management that will produce and deliver or exchange the commodities and services, forward to the ultimate consumer (Commons 1931: 525).

Based on studies of economic theory and of judicial decisions, Commons identified three types of transactions: *bargaining, managerial* and *rationing*. Bargaining transactions derive from the market, representing the best two buyers and the best two sellers in that market. Bargaining transactions rest on the assumption of equality of willing buyers and sellers. There are four types of conflict of interest in bargaining transactions: competition, discrimination, economic power and due process. To govern them, the courts have fashioned four types of working rules.

Where both the two buyers and the two sellers are competitors, the courts, guided by custom, have created a long line of rules on fair and unfair competition. One of the buyers will buy from one of the sellers, and one of the sellers will sell to one of the buyers. Out of this type of transaction, custom and judicial decisions have created rules of reasonable and unreasonable discrimination. At the close of the transaction one seller, by operation of law, transfers title to one of the buyers and one of the buyers transfers title to money or a credit instrument to one of the sellers. Out of this purchase and sale arise the issues of equality and inequality of bargaining power, and rules of reasonable and unreasonable value. Finally, in the American system of jurisprudence, custom and judicial rules governing all of these transactions are subject to the ultimate review of the United States Supreme Court, on grounds that the custom or decision involves a taking of property or liberty without due process of law.

Unlike the assumption of equality of the parties in bargaining transactions, the assumption in managerial transactions, by which actual wealth is produced, is inequality. One party is the manager, executive or foreman, and gives orders. The workman or other subordinate must obey. Yet here also, custom and

courts decisions develop rules as to what are reasonable and unreasonable commands, and what obedience is required.

Rationing transactions differ from managerial transactions in that the superior is a collective superior, while the inferiors are individuals. These transactions involve rationing of wealth or purchasing power to subordinates without bargaining, but with negotiation. Commons gives the example of the budget established by a company's board of directors, or the negotiations leading up to enactment of legislation favoured by economically powerful interests.

Commons's economic theory of transactions did not meet a favourable reception during his lifetime, or for some time thereafter. Even economists who respected his contributions to labour economics and social legislation were critical of this aspect of his work. Part of the criticism resulted from what some saw as Commons's 'fixation' and 'infatuation' with the legal basis of economic activity (Chamberlain 1964: 92–3). With time that view has changed, and Commons is rightfully credited as anticipating the work of the Nobel laureate Ronald COASE and developments in transaction costs theory led by WILLIAMSON (Van de Ven 1993: 150–51).

By contrast, Commons's contributions to labour economics and social legislation were immediately acknowledged. In Commons's view the employment relationship, like other transactions, was subject to institutional modification through court decisions and legislation. His emphasis on collective action as a means of expanding the power of the individual, along with his own work experience and field research, made him an important advocate of trades unions and their right to bargain collectively on behalf of members. Commons's influence was apparent in the National Labor Relations Act, which codified trades unions' right to legal recognition and to bargain collectively. This law has served as a model for labour legislation in several countries, including the 1979 legislation in the UK.

The law was drafted by Senator Robert Wagner, a member of the American Association for Labor Legislation, whose executive secretary was a former Commons student. Another former student drafted the Social Security Act (Chasse 1997: 941).

Despite early flirtations with socialism, Commons was not a foe of capitalism. He was a friend of Samuel Gompers, one of the founders of the modern American trades union movement. They held a common view that the American labour movement should concentrate on economic gains, and avoid political involvement in efforts to eliminate capitalism (Oser and Blanchfield 1975: 399).

In 1919 Commons and some of his students conducted field research at thirty American businesses, 'looking for successful experiments in labor management' (Commons 1921: 281). Commons reported that: 'What we find that labor wants, as a class, is wages, hours and security, without financial [managerial] responsibility, but with power enough to command respect' (1921: 282). Capitalism 'is not the blind force that socialists supposed, and not the helpless plaything of demand and supply, but it is Management' (1921: 286). Commons foresaw that workers' focus on security in a well-paying job with fair treatment would confer opportunity and responsibility on management. Modern industrial relations and organizational behaviour are the study of the exercise of that responsibility, and Commons is also rightfully recognized as one of its founders (Van de Ven 1993: 139).

Commons also influenced the work of another Nobel laureate, Herbert SIMON. Commons's concept that transactions within institutions are governed by 'working rules' developed in part through bargaining influenced Simon in his creation of a 'new institutional economics for managers that studied bargaining inside bureaucracies' (Waring 1991: 52–3). Finally, Commons made another enduring contribution to the study of organizations through his emphasis on and skill in doing field research. Commons could never

be confused with economists such the ones that Barbara Bergmann was referring to when she asked 'Why do most economists know so little about the economy?' (Bergmann 1986). In the words of Joseph Dorfman: 'few economists were as aware as he of the need to come to grips with the facts of the economic scene if society was to progress' (Dorfman 1949: 193). This is a fitting legacy.

Commons's life spanned a period of dramatic change in the United States, as an agrarian economy was displaced by industrialization. His detailed empirical studies of American society and the economy played a pivotal role in the enactment of social legislation during the first third of the twentieth century. As important as these activities were, his work retains equal contemporary significance. His theoretical work on institutional economics stressed the importance of the institutions of capitalism, especially the legal system. His emphasis on economic transactions provided the theoretical foundation for the later work of many others. Commons rejected the classical economists' view of labour as a commodity. His analysis of employer–employee relations in transactional terms recognized the conflicts inherent in the employment relationship. He emphasized the roles of bargaining and of institutional change in ameliorating these conflicts. He advocated legislation legitimizing trade unions and regulating working conditions and employment security.

BIBLIOGRAPHY
Bergmann, B. (1986) 'Why Do Most Economists Know So Little about the Economy', in B. Bowles et al. (eds), Unconventional Wisdom: Essays in Economics in Honor of John Kenneth Galbraith, Boston: Houghton Mifflin, 31–7.
Chamberlain, N.W. (1964) 'The Institutional Economics of John R. Commons', in C.E. Ayres, N.W. Chamberlain, J. Dorfman, R.A. Gordon and S. Kuznets, Institutional Economics: Veblen, Commons and Mitchell Reconsidered, Berkeley, CA: University of California Press, 61–94.
Chasse, J.D. (1997) 'John R. Commons and the Special Interest Issue: Not Really Out of Date', Journal of Economic Issues 31(4): 933–49.
Commons, J.R. (1921) 'Industrial Government', International Labour Review 1(1); repr. in International Labour Review 3(4): 281–6, 1996.
—— (1924) Legal Foundations of Capitalism, Madison, WI: University of Wisconsin Press, 1959.
—— (1931) 'Institutional Economics', American Economic Review 26: 648–57; repr. in
Gherity, J.A. (ed.) (1964) Economic Thought: A Historical Anthology, New York, Random House, 515–26.
—— (1934a) Institutional Economics: Its Place in Political Economy, Madison, WI: University of Wisconsin Press, 1959.
—— (1934b) Myself, An Autobiography, Madison, WI: University of Wisconsin Press, 1963.
—— (1950) The Economics of Collective Action, ed. K. Parsons, Madison, WI: University of Wisconsin Press, 1970.
Commons, J.R., Phillips, U.B., Gilmore, E.A., Sumner, H.L. and Andrews, J.B. (eds) (1910) A Documentary History of American Industrial Society, 10 vols, New York: Russell and Russell, 1958.
Commons, J.R. et al. (1935) History of Labor in the United States, vols 3–4, New York: Macmillan.
—— (1966) History of Labor in the United States, New York: A.M. Kelley, reprint of the 1918 edition, vols 1–2.
Dorfman, J. (1949) The Economic Mind in American Civilization, New York: Viking, 277–94.
Oser, J. and Blanchfield, W. (1975) The Evolution of Economic Thought, 3rd edn, New York, Harcourt, Brace, 383–400.
Van de Ven, A. (1993) 'The Institutional

Theory of John R. Commons: A Review and Commentary', *Academy of Management Review* 18(1): 139–51.

Waring, S.P. (1991) *Taylorism Transformed*, Durham, NC: University of North Carolina Press, 52–3.

Wisconsin Lawyer (n.d.) 'Wisconsin's Legal History: John R. Commons', http://www.wisbar.org/wislawmag/archive/history/commons.html, 1 November 2000

SR

CONFUCIUS (551 BC–479 BC)

The philosopher Kong Qiu (K'ung Ch'iu), known to the West as Confucius, was born in 551 BC in the state of Lu in northeastern China. At this time, the Zhou emperor was very weak and the country was dominated by competing warlords. Little is known of Confucius's childhood, and what is known is often embellished with myth. He appears to have been the son of a military officer and an impoverished member of the *shi* (lesser nobility). He married at the age of nineteen, and appears to have worked as a minor bureaucrat in charge of grain, flocks and herds. As tutor to the reigning duke of Lu from about 518 BC to 501 BC, Confucius became involved in the power struggle among the rival clans of the Meng, Ji and Shu. Serving after 501 BC as magistrate and then justice minister of Lu, Confucius tried and failed in his efforts at mutual disarmament of the three feuding clans. Expelled from Lu, Confucius and many of his followers became itinerant teachers throughout eastern China, where many state rulers welcomed them. He died in 479 BC, mourned by his disciples.

Confucius is generally regarded as the foundational philosopher of Oriental civilization. His teachings of moral virtue, reverence for authority and the sanctity of family not only form the basis of over two millennia of Chinese tradition, but have also been a vast influence upon the business culture of much of the Far East, including Japan.

In his youth, Confucius was fascinated by Chinese tradition and ritual, and came to see his calling in imparting that tradition and ritual to present and future generations. He began to educate himself in ancient Chinese lore, and then to teach others. Liu (1955) calls him the founder of private education in China, for all such teaching was traditionally handled by the state. Confucius taught an intensely conservative ethical system which sought to restore the fallen status of moral tradition, family and kingdom in a time of disorder and corruption. As summarized in Book 1, verse 2 of *The Analects* (a collection of his maxims edited at a much later date):

Master Yu said, those who live in private life behave well towards their parents and elder brothers, in public life seldom show a disposition to resist the authority of their superiors. And as for such men starting a revolution, no instance of it has ever occurred. It is upon the trunk that a gentleman works. When that is firmly set up, the Way grows. And surely proper behaviour towards parents and elder brothers is the trunk of Goodness?

(Confucius 1938: 83)

The Confucian ethic was essentially a statist and highly altruistic one which emphasized duties rather than rights. In its original form, it denigrated the acquisitive individualism of the entrepreneur: Confucius grieved when his disciple Zukong became a thriving businessman. In Book 4, verse 2 of *The Analects*, Confucius maintained that a truly Good person was content with Goodness alone; a merely wise person was good because it paid to be so. This thought was developed in verse 5: 'Wealth and Rank are what every man desires; but if they can only be retained to the

detriment of the Way he professes, he must relinquish them' (Confucius 1938: 102). Confucianism became the state philosophy under the Han Dynasty (202 BC–AD 9), when its disciples opposed public investment in salt and iron. In their view, promoting a business rather than a purely agrarian economy, would lead peasants to neglect farming and rulers to become profit-minded, and the entire population would become acquisitive.

During the later Song Dynasty (916–1279) Confucianism came to terms with the market, although its civic and familiar ideals remain a major factor. Most notably, amongst the overseas Chinese community in countries such as Taiwan and Singapore and now increasingly in post-Mao China itself, Confucianism has a direct effect on how businesses are organized and managed. The 'Chinese family business' has been the main vehicle for the spectacular economic successes of the overseas Chinese in the past fifty years, and this business model is largely structured on Confucian lines. Observers such as Francis Fukuyama (1996), Hill Gates (1996) and S. Gordon Redding (1990) have noted the family-based structure of past and present Chinese businesses. Families had rights far more than individuals. A Chinese boss will turn his firm over to his son; a Japanese boss to a professional manager.

Confucian concepts of duty and responsibility are also important in Japan, but they are applied differently. In China, the firm is built around a biological family that, according to Gates (1996), is not inclusive. In Japan, the firm *becomes* a big adoptive family. Japanese business culture, says Fukuyama, is more trust-oriented than Chinese, allowing for big non-family corporations to flourish.

The respect one shows to one's manager, the intense stress upon modesty and conformity in the workplace, the governing of business life by endless unwritten rules known as *kata*, the company exercises and lectures described by Gannon were all rooted in Confucian ideals. Workers and managers identify themselves by their status, not their wealth, and traditionally devote themselves to their company, often more than to their family, something the Chinese would rarely consider. In return, the Japanese company would devote itself not only to its workers, but also to its customers and to the prosperity of Japan as a whole. Long-term honour-bound arrangements were made with banks and suppliers (McMillan 1996). The influence of Confucian concepts of honour and self-sacrifice are evident. An American goes into business to make money; a Japanese does so to serve society as well as to make money.

BIBLIOGRAPHY

Chen, M. (1995) *Asian Management Systems*, London: Routledge.

Confucius (1938) *The Analects of Confucius*, trans. A. Waley, New York: Vintage Books.

—— (1981) 'The Gentleman', from the *Analects*, trans. M. Coyle in P.B. Ebrey (ed.), *Chinese Civilization and Society, A Sourcebook*, New York: The Free Press, 13–14.

'Confucius' (1999) *The McGraw-Hill Encyclopedia of World Biography*, Detroit MI: Gale Research, Inc., vol. 4, 197–200.

Crow, C. (1938) *Master Kung: The Story of Confucius*, New York: Harper and Brothers.

Day, C.B. (1962) *The Philosophers of China: Classical and Contemporary*, New York: Philosophical Library.

Fukuyama, F. (1996) *Trust: The Social Virtues and the Creation of Prosperity*, New York: The Free Press.

Gannon, M.J. (1994) *Understanding Global Cultures: Metaphorical Journeys through 17 Countries*, Thousand Oaks, CA: Sage Publications.

Gates, H. (1996) *China's Motor: A Thousand Years of Petty Capitalism*, Ithaca, NY: Cornell University Press.

Liu W. (1955) *Confucius: His Life and*

Time, New York, The Philosophical Library.

McMillan, C.J. (1996) *The Japanese Industrial System*, 3rd rev. edn, New York: Walter de Gruyter.

Redding, S.G. (1990) *The Spirit of Chinese Capitalism*, New York: Walter de Gruyter.

'The Debate on Salt and Iron' (1981), trans. P.B. Ebrey, in P.B. Ebrey (ed.), *Chinese Civilization and Society: A Sourcebook*, New York: The Free Press, 23–9.

DCL

COOK, Thomas (1808–92)

Thomas Cook was born at Melbourne, Derbyshire on 22 November 1808 and died at Stonegate, Sussex on 18 July 1892. His father died when he was four; apprenticing as a carpenter, he moved to Loughborough in Leicestershire where he later found employment with a publisher. The Cooks had been a strict Baptist family, and Cook now became active in the association of Baptists; in 1828 he was appointed Bible reader and missionary for Rutland, in which capacity he travelled several thousand years on foot. In 1832 he moved to Market Harborough, where he took up his trade as a wood-turner and continued his missionary work. He married Marianne Mason in 1832 and they had one son, John Mason Cook, born in 1844. Around this time too, Cook took the pledge and remained a teetotaller throughout his life. In 1840 he was appointed secretary of the Market Harborough branch of the South Midlands Temperance Association.

In 1841 Cook and members of his branch wished to attend a temperance meeting in Leicester. Cook had the idea of approaching the recently built South Midlands railway, which connected the two places, and of asking to hire a special train to convey the party to and from the meeting. The journey duly took place on 5 July 1841. According to Pudney (1953), this was not (as is often claimed) the first railway excursion in Britain, as several other similar ventures had been organized in previous years. It did, however, set Thomas Cook to thinking about other possibilities. The first true pleasure trip was organized in 1845, a railway day excursion from Nottingham, Derby and Leicester to Liverpool and back. Cook struck a deal with the railway to arrange cheap fares, took a commission on the tickets sold, and organized the passengers at either end. The excursion was highly successful and profitable, as were the many that followed it.

Over the following decade Cook expanded his business very rapidly. As well as local trips such as country-house visits, excursions to Wales and Scotland were also organized, some lasting for a week or more. In what became the organization's standard procedure in later years, Cook always travelled the route of each excursion in advance, inspected hotels and facilities and made prior arrangements, paid for all facilities to be used, and even wrote guidebooks for the use of the excursionists. Cook thus assumed the entire cost risk of the excursion, leaving the travellers to pay a fixed fee which covered all accommodation, travel and food.

In 1851 Cook organized tours to the Great Exhibition in London, which were highly profitable. By this time the railways, alive to the opportunities, had begun taking over the domestic excursion business themselves and were refusing Cook access to their trains. His response was to move overseas. In 1855 he organized excursions to the Paris Exhibition; by the 1860s Switzerland and Italy had been added to the itinerary, and 1869 saw the first tour of Palestine and steamer excursion on the Nile. Round-the-world tours were added in the 1870s. In the 1880s the firm entered the Indian market, organizing tours for wealthy Indians coming to Europe, and even getting

involved in the Mecca pilgrimage trade. By 1890, 1,200 hotels in Europe alone were part of the Cook system, tens of thousands of people annually were taking Cook's tours, and the firm had added banking and currency exchange to the portfolio of services offered to customers.

Cook's system was simple, and relied on two fundamental assumptions about his market, both of which were amply proved. The first was that there were very many middle-class and prosperous working-class families who would enjoy the chance to travel abroad but were deterred from doing so by various risk factors. Foremost among these were lack of familiarity with local customs and cultures, and uncertainty about the costs of travel. Cook laid off the first risk by introducing 'conducted tours' whereby an agent familiar with the local area would accompany the party at all times and solve any travel-related problems as they arose (Cook himself worked as an agent into the 1970s, and his son and grandson both worked as agents, particularly on newly established routes). The second risk was dealt with by developing the all-inclusive holiday package, whereby tourists paid a flat fee which included all travel, accommodation and food. (It did not include alcoholic drinks, which passengers had to purchase themselves; the Cooks were later criticized for being teetotallers yet allowing the sale of wine and spirits on their Nile steamers.)

Cook's second assumption was that railway companies, hotels and restaurants would be willing to reduce their fares provided he could guarantee them a sufficient volume of customers; in other words, they would put the emphasis on turnover rather than unit profit. In this he was correct. Each route covered by Cook's tours had to be worked out in advance, with an often tortuous series of negotiations with many individual railway and steamship companies, hotels, restaurants and even cab drivers and railway porters to ensure that a price was agreed in advance. For a new route in foreign countries, this could take months. At the end of it, however, the Cooks had a new, risk-free service which could be offered to the travelling public at an affordable cost. Quality and price were both guaranteed. The mass tourism industry had been created, and in largely the same form as it exists today.

Cook's success can be measured in two ways: the vast increase in numbers of the travelling public, and the consequent outcry this provoked. In 1890, around the time Cook retired from the firm, more than 3.2 million tickets for Cook's tours were sold. By this time too, the organization was employing more than 1,700 people worldwide, and owned a headquarters building on Ludgate Circus in London and properties elsewhere in the capital. The spread of mass tourism provoked outrage in some quarters. Charles Lever, an English diplomat in Italy, wrote anonymous newspaper articles claiming that the tourists in Cook's parties were convicts whom Australia had refused to accept, and were instead being deported to Italy in the guise of tourists; writing in *Blackwood's* magazine in 1865, he commented that 'these devil's dust tourists have spread over Europe, injuring our credit and damaging our character ... Take my word for it, if these excursionists go on, nothing short of another war ... will ever place us where we once were in the opinion of Europe' (quoted in Pudney 1953: 165). Likewise John Ruskin, appalled at the invasion by mass tourists of the mountains of Switzerland, spluttered to Cook: 'you have made race-courses of the cathedrals of the Earth. Your *one* conception of pleasure is to drive in railroad carriages around their aisles and eat off their altars' (Brendon 1991: 81).

Such rants lost some of their force when, in the 1890s, both Kaiser Wilhelm of Germany and the future King George V of England contacted Cook's to arrange private tours of the Holy Land. A better opinion was offered by the *Times* in its obituary of Thomas Cook: 'They [the Cooks] have organized travel as it was never organized before, and they have their reward in the enormous increase in the

number of travellers ... They have applied the resources of civilization to a very general modern need, and for this they deserve and obtain full recognition' (Pudsey 1953: 19).

Cook, affected by blindness, retired from the business to his country house in Stonegate, where he died. He was succeeded by his son John Mason Cook (1841–99), described by Brendon (1991: 100) as 'a man of outstanding ability and ruthless determination', a great organizer who made his father's broader successes possible. He had begun working full-time for the firm in the 1860s, and was instrumental in organizing the firm and putting it onto a solid commercial footing after the headlong expansion of the first two decades. He did much of the groundwork for routes in the Middle East, Egypt and India, and conducted personally many of the first tours there. Father and son seem to have had the perfect partnership; Thomas Cook's was the marketing genius and entrepreneurial spirit, while John Mason Cook provided the organizational and financial skills. In 1885 when war broke out in the Sudan, John Mason Cook chartered steamers to carry troops and supplies for the Gordon Relief Expedition travelling up the Nile to Khartoum; when most of the steamers were wrecked during the war, Cook built his own ships, starting another travelling tradition that lasts to this day. He died of the after-effects of a fever contracted while conducting Kaiser Wilhelm's tour to Jerusalem in 1898.

BIBLIOGRAPHY

Brendon, P. (1991) *Thomas Cook: 150 Years of Popular Tourism*, London: Secker and Warburg.
Pudney, J. (1953) *The Thomas Cook Story*, London: Michael Joseph.

MLW

COPELAND, Melvin Thomas (1884–1975)

Melvin Thomas Copeland was born in Brewer, Maine on 17 July 1884, the son of Salem and Livonia Copeland. He died in Boston on 27 March 1975. He was educated at Bowdoin College and Harvard University, taking his Ph.D. from Harvard in 1910. He married Else Helbling in 1912; they had two daughters. After teaching at New York University from 1911 to 1912, he returned to Harvard, where he taught for the remainder of his career. He was appointed assistant professor of marketing in 1915 and professor of marketing in 1919, one of the first academics ever to hold those titles. He directed Harvard's Bureau of Business Research from 1916 to 1926.

Copeland played an important role in the early years of Harvard Business School, where he was brought in by the founding dean, Edwin GAY, to introduce new teaching methods such as the case study and classroom discussion. He also wrote a valuable history of the school's first forty years of operation, which is a useful source not only on the school itself but on the history of the development of management education generally. It is as a writer and theorist on marketing, however, that Copeland is best known. His work, notably *Problems in Marketing* (Copeland 1917a), a collection of 175 case studies, by far the richest teaching resource available at the time, and *Principles of Merchandising* (1924), show strongly the influence of earlier work by his Harvard colleague and mentor Paul CHERINGTON, with a continuing strong influence on distribution and management of producer–wholesaler–retailer relations. However, Copeland also shows the influence of emerging psychological theories of consumer demand, as espoused most notably by Walter SCOTT at Northwestern University, the other major centre for marketing study at the time.

Some of Copeland's ideas of marketing were quite advanced for their day. He was one of the first to note that the sales and production func-

tions of an organization do not stand in splendid isolation, but are in fact dependent on each other to a large degree. He also noted that successful marketing can expand the overall demand for a product (Copeland 1924: 8). His work on consumer motivation is very well developed. He warns marketers that whereas the motives of sellers in any given market are usually simple, those of buyers are highly variable and usually complex. He goes on to distinguish between two classes of buyer motive: *emotional* motives and *rational* motives. The former may consists of factors such as emulaton, satisfaction of appetites, pride of personal appearance, securing home comfort, and so on; the latter include such factors as dependability, durability and economy in purchase (Copeland 1924: 162). Copeland's rational motives are based on the features of the product itself, while his emotional motives centre around the use and value of the product to the consumer. He stresses that any given buyer's motives are likely to be a set of multiple motives, including some rational and some emotional motives; he thus conceptualizes what later came to be known as the 'bundle of benefits' which accrue to a consumer when buying a product.

Copeland was also one of the first to make explicit the distinction between marketing to consumers and marketing to businesses, or industrial marketing. Although earlier writers had touched on the differences, Copeland devoted considerable time to the problems of industrial marketing. His *Cases in Industrial Marketing* (1930), providing more valuable case study material, contains a useful introduction which sums up many of the issues involved, including the motivation and buying characteristics of industrial purchasers.

In his later work (Copeland 1951; Copeland and Towl 1947), Copeland turned from the problems of marketing to the nature of management more generally. Managers, he says, are put into positions of authority over others, but that authority is not something that can be assumed as a perquisite of managerial rank:

Real authority is not a power attained by the bestowal of a title or by an entry on an organization chart, by the issuance of a directive or by the laying on of hands. Real authority must be won by the action of the executive himself.

(Copeland 1951: 5)

An appointment to office, he says, is no more than a chance to win authority. He notes the importance of information, and says it is essential for a manager to be well informed if correct decisions are to be reached. For Copeland in the years following the Second World War, the crucial challenge facing managers was the ability to manage change, to keep themselves and their organizations flexible and adaptible, while at the same time maintaining a unity of purpose and a focus on goals. Copeland and Towl (1947) also examine the nature of the relationship between managers in an executive function and the board of directors, and conclude that it is the function of the board to provide leadership and vision, delegating authority as far as possible to the executives beneath them to ensure that vision is met.

In both his writings on marketing and in his views on management in a world of change, Copeland was often ahead of his time; although much of his work is undeniably a product of its own era, many of his ideas sound remarkably modern. His influence on marketing thought and on management pedagogy remains strong to this day.

BIBLIOGRAPHY
Cattell, J.M., Cattell, J. and Ross, E.E. (1941) *Leaders in Education*, 2nd edn, Lancaster, PA: The Science Press.
Copeland, M.T. (1912) *The Cotton Manufacturing Industry of the United States*, Cambridge, MA: Harvard University Press.
—— (1917a) *Problems in Marketing*, Chicago: A.W. Shaw.
—— (1917b) *Business Statistics*, Cambridge, MA: Harvard University Press.

———— (1924) *Principles of Merchandising*, Chicago: A.W. Shaw.
———— (1930) *Cases in Industrial Marketing*, New York: McGraw-Hill.
———— (1951) *The Executive at Work*, Cambridge, MA: Harvard University Press.
———— (1958) *And Mark the Era: The Story of Harvard Business School*, Boston: Little, Brown.
Copeland, M.T. and Towl, A.R. (1947) *The Board of Directors and Business Management*, Boston: Division of Research, Graduate School of Business Administration, Harvard University.

MLW

CORNING, Erastus (1794–1872)

Erastus Corning was born in Norwich, Connecticut on 14 December 1794, to Bliss and Lucinda Corning, and died on 9 April 1872. He played a key role in the coming of railroads, nineteenth-century America's take-off industry. Corning moved to Albany, New York in 1814, where he married Harriet Weld in 1819. He distinguished himself as an entrepreneur in several areas, owning an ironworks by 1826 and becoming president of the Albany City Bank and Mutual Insurance Company in the 1830s. He also became a powerful Democratic politician, and was mayor of Albany from 1833 to 1836.

Corning's greatest achievement was the realization of his vision of a railway along the route of the Hudson, the Mohawk and the Erie Canal, linking New York City with the Great Lakes. In 1827, he chartered the Mohawk and Hudson Railway linking Albany with nearby Schenectady. In the years that followed, seven other entrepreneurs built pieces of line to the west along the Mohawk and Erie Canal. Corning, always the innovator, profited

through the sale of his iron and steel to these lines, and quickly saw the vision of a single line from New York to Buffalo. Settlers and merchants could go west by rail in one-tenth of the time taken by the slow mule-driven barges of the Erie Canal. Before 1851, the New York state legislature had granted the canal a monopoly. When this was revoked, Corning, using his powerful connections in the Democratic party, quickly secured the passage of a bill allowing him to consolidate all the rail lines under his ownership. By 1853 he had accomplished his goal, merging fourteen railway lines to create the New York Central: 'For many years it remained the largest corporate merger in American financial history' (Martin 1992: 247).

Corning was the founder and first president of the New York Central, which was destined, along with the Pennsylvania, to be the most powerful and profitable railroad in pre-Civil War America. 'Corning's entrepreneurial vision had started the avalanche that was railroad expansion ... and he was well paid for his efforts, especially those in behalf of what became the Central in 1853' (Martin 1992: 248). Corning died, secure in the knowledge that he would always be remembered as a builder of the state of New York, and of the federal Union.

BIBLIOGRAPHY
'Erastus Corning' (1999) *McGraw-Hill Encyclopedia of World Biography*, Detroit, MI: Gale Research, Inc., vol. 4, 238–9.
Larkin, F.D. (1999) 'Corning, Erastus', *American National Biography*, ed. J.A. Garraty and M. Carnes, New York: Oxford University Press, vol. 5, 525–7.
Martin, A. (1992) *Railroads Triumphant: The Growth, Rejection, and Rebirth of a Vital American Force*, New York: Oxford University Press.

DCL

COURCELLE-SENEUIL, Jean-Gustave
(1813–92)

Jean-Gustave Courcelle-Seneuil was born into a wealthy farming family in Vauxains, Dordogne prefecture in the Perigord district of France on 22 December 1813. He moved to Paris before 1830, establishing himself as a writer and contributing to several newspapers. He attended law school, where he also studied politics and political economy. Later he returned to Perigord to start a refinery business, but this failed. He returned to Paris shortly before the February Revolution of 1848 to take up an appointment as general manager of state-owned land. His term in office as a public official was fairly short, but did include a visit to Britain.

In 1852, after the disruption of the Second Republic (1848–51), Courcelle-Seneuil emigrated to Chile, where he took up a professorship of political economy at Santiago University, and worked concurrently as a financial adviser to the Chilean government. In 1855 he published a book on the study of business enterprises from an economic point of view, *Traité théorique et pratique des enterprises industrielles, commerciales et agricoles, ou manuel des affaires*, published in Paris. This book is regarded as the first full-fledged study of business administration to come out of France. His first great book on political economy, *Traité théorique et pratique de l'économie politique*, was published in 1858–9. In 1862 Courcelle-Seneuil returned to France, but he continued to receive an annual payment from the Chilean government in return for writing for Chilean newspapers. During the Second Empire (1852–70) he was very active, and published several more books on economics, politics and finance in the years before 1870.

On 4 September 1870, following the defeat of French armies in the Franco-Prussian War and the collapse of the Second Empire, Courcelle-Seneuil was appointed a member of the ad hoc committee which replaced the Conseil d'Etat and took over the emergency government of the country. As well as advising the French government during and after the crisis, he also served on important government committees and was actively engaged in the enactment of laws concerning bankruptcy, the conservation of historic buildings, the protection of abandoned children and many other areas. He continued to be an active writer until the last year of his life. In 1882 he was appointed a member of the Academie des Sciences Morales. To honour his achievements as one of the representative advocates of liberal economic theory, he was also made an officer of the Legion of Honour.

During the Second Empire, the classical school of individualism, liberalism and optimism underwent a revival in French economics. Courcelle-Seneuil attempted to apply the theory of political economy to business enterprises. On the assumption that private profit has something in common with public profit, he took up profit-seeking enterprises as an objective for his research. Thus he sought to examine the features of such enterprises from the standpoint of capital and the use of labour. He regarded business enterprise as a continuous human activity for replenishing human desire, and determined that the fundamental constituent elements of all enterprises are capital and labour. He came to the conclusion that the people in charge of controlling those factors are in fact entrepreneurs.

According to Courcelle-Seneuil, the functions of the entrepreneur reside in combining capital with labour, with the concept of profit maximization as the leading principle. The function of business administration is to predict the future, to procure the necessary materials, direct the workers and convey orders. Slightly in advance of Courcelle-Seneuil, Charles Dupin had pointed out the importance of administrative functions, but it was Courcelle-Seneuil who defined the elements of administration as prediction, procurement, direction and communication. Later, in 1916, Henri FAYOL would follow

much the same model when defining the elements of the management function as prediction, organization, direction, coordination and control. Courcelle-Seneuil, drawing on the French theory of business enterprise originating with Jean-Baptiste SAY, expanded on that theory to develop a full-fledged theory of administration which had an influence for many years to come.

BIBLIOGRAPHY

Courcelle-Seneuil, J.-G. (1855) *Traité théorique et pratique des enterprises industrielles, commerciales et agricoles, ou manuel des affaires* (Introduction to the Theory and Practice of Industrial, Commercial, and Agricultural Enterprises, or Business Handbook), Paris.

—— (1858–9) *Traité théorique et pratique de l'économie politique* (Introduction to the Theory and Practice of Political Economy), 2 vols, Paris.

Richardot, J. (1961) 'Courcelle-Seneuil', in R. d'Amat (ed.), *Dictionnaire de biographie francaise* (Dictionary of French Biography), Paris: Libraire Letouzey et Ane, 954–5.

ST

COURTAULD, Samuel (1876–1947)

Samuel Courtauld was born at Braintree, Essex on 7 May 1876, the second son of Sydney and Sarah Courtauld. He died in London on 1 December 1947, following a serious illness. His grandfather was a founder of Courtaulds silk-weaving firm, for which his father also worked; the firm had become very prosperous in the Victorian period, specializing in the making of black crepe for mourning, and at the end of the nineteenth century patented and specialized in the production of rayon. Courtauld, after an education at Rugby School, spent time in France and Germany learning the silk-weaving business before returning to Britain, where he was appointed general manager of the Courtaulds mill at Halstead in 1901. In the same year he married Elizabeth Kelsey; they had one daughter.

In 1908 Courtauld was appointed general manager of all the company's textile mills. This was not simple nepotism; Courtauld's energy and talent had been recognized by senior management (Coleman 1986). In 1916 he joined the board of Courtaulds Ltd, and in 1921 was made chairman of the board. He guided the company through rapid growth and overseas expansion in the 1920s and then the difficult years of the Great Depression and the Second World War. His managerial style was cautious; Courtauld's policy was to expand the company but to avoid debt and to maintain large financial reserves. The company was able to maintain its position as the market leader in rayon throughout Courtauld's tenure in office.

Today Courtauld is more famous for his patronage of the arts. He was a patron of both the Tate Gallery and the National Gallery in London, and set up the Courtauld Institute of Art at the University of London. He was not, however, an ordinary industrialist with a taste for artwork and the money to indulge it; Courtauld had strong views on the role of art and education in society and the workplace, views which are discussed in detail in his book *Ideals and Industry* (1949). In particular, he believed that an artistic education was important in stimulating creativity. Articles of common use should be beautiful as well as useful, and he saw the relationship of art to craft as being similar to that of the soul to the body; art should infuse craft, and lead to creativity and development in the workplace (1949: 46).

Business organizations, Courtauld felt, have both economic and non-economic functions. One of his favourite sayings was that 'man is

the only non-economic animal'. 'Practically all the activityes of the other animals are directed – directly or indirectly – by the struggle for survival. Only man has developed surplus power which he can turn to immaterial ends, and that power makes him man' (1949: 60–61). This did not mean that economics played no role in human affairs; rather, the economic and the spiritual should go in tandem, and profitability and spirituality are not incompatible.

Like many business leaders and managers of his generation, Courtauld was in favour of closer cooperation between business and labour, but he also believed government should play a major role as well, particularly in education and training; his views at times smack of corporatism. He believed that management should be recognized as a profession, and that managers should have their own professional societies with codes of ethics and conduct.

BIBLIOGRAPHY
Coleman, D.C. (1969–80) *Courtauld's: An Economic and Social History*, Oxford: Clarendon Press, 3 vols.
——— (1984) 'Courtauld IV, Samuel', in in D.J. Jeremy (ed.), *Dictionary of Business Biography*, London: Butterworths, vol. 1, 803–806.
Courtauld, S. (1949) *Ideals and Industry: War-Time Papers*, Cambridge: Cambridge University Press.

MLW

COUTTS, Thomas (1735–1822)

Thomas Coutts was born in Edinburgh, one of four sons of John Coutts, a prominent merchant and banker. He died in London on 24 February 1822. He married twice, to Susannah Starkie in 1763, and after her death in 1814, to the actress Harriet Mellon in 1815. His father had founded one of the first private banks in Scotland, and all four of his sons followed him into the trade. Thomas and Patrick Coutts moved to London in 1750, where they set up an agency for the Edinburgh firm; another brother, James, moved to London in 1755 and went into partnership with a prominent Scottish banker, George Campbell. When Campbell died in 1760, Thomas Coutts joined his brother in the partnership and the name was changed to James and Thomas Coutts. James Coutts was involved in politics (he became an MP in 1762 and left the management of the bank to his brother) and it was probably through his connections that in 1760 King George III named Coutts as his private bankers.

This was a considerable coup, as the royal business gave Coutts access to the highest levels of the court and government. Over the next four decades he built up an impressive list of clients that included not only the king and the Prince of Wales but also prominent politicians such as William Pitt and Charles James Fox, and others including the Duke of Wellington and Lady Hester Stanhope. The bank, guided by Coutts, maintained a reputation for reliability, quality of service and probity. (Absolutely impartial in his business dealings, he lent money not only to the Hanoverian kings but also to Clementina Walkinshaw, former mistress of the pretender Prince Charles Stewart.) Coutts became the bank of the establishment.

Personal banking at this time was becoming much more complex, thanks largely to the growing diversity of government bonds issued to finance the national debt. This in turn gave bankers more scope to invest on behalf of their clients. Coutts, close to the government, was ideally placed in the trade; thanks to his contacts, he could provide information to his clients, and advise them on the investment packages that would suit their needs.

The American Revolution (1775–81) resulted in a financial crisis in London and

nearly a hundred banks failed over a ten-year period, but Coutts was able to weather the storm. Amsterdam, hitherto the centre of European finance, was even more badly damaged, and by 1790 the major Dutch banks had either gone under or relocated to the safer environment of London. The French Revolution further damaged the European centres of finance, and by 1800 London was the acknowledged capital of European banking, with established firms such as Coutts competing with newer bankers such as Baring, Goldsmid and ROTHSCHILD. Coutts, forecasting the trends correctly, began opening up international links in the 1780s, and by 1800 had developed ties with several Swiss banks; through these, he was able to offer private banking services to clients in the Mediterranean and the Levant. With correspondent banks from Lisbon to Bombay, Coutts became the bank of choice for international travellers; British officers serving in Spain were even able to negotiate Coutts drafts with banks in cities within the war zone.

It is difficult to say whether Coutts was an innovator or was simply an adapter to changing conditions. Possibly the distinction in this case is irrelevant; what matters is his achievement. Other banks failed or were dissolved, but his endured. He managed his clients with a skill that allowed him to take on loss-making accounts (such as those of Fox and the Prince of Wales) in the knowledge that they would give him access to contacts that would allow him to turn a profit elsewhere. He understood too the importance of London's emergence as a financial capital, and of the need to build an international network. Above all, he set a standard of service which became part of the Coutts corporate culture and which endures largely to this day.

BIBLIOGRAPHY
Healey, E. (1992) *Coutts & Co: The Portrait of a Private Bank*, London: Hodder and Stoughton.
Witzel, M. (1992) 'Thomas Coutts and the Rise of Modern Banking', *The Strand* (January): 7–9.

MLW

COUZENS, James Joseph, Jr (1872–1936)

James Joseph Couzens was born in Chatham, Ontario on 26 August 1872 and died in Detroit, Michigan on 22 October 1936. One of the original investors in the Ford Motor Company (1903), Couzens rose to the position of vice-president and treasurer of the company before eventually breaking with Henry FORD in 1915. In 1919 he sold his interests to Ford for roughly $30 million and that same year was elected mayor of Detroit. He was appointed to the US Senate in 1922 and was elected to the position two years later, where he served until his death.

Couzens' father migrated from England to Ontario, where he became a soap manufacturer. In an early declaration of independence from his father, the young Couzens insisted that he be known only as James Couzens. In 1890 he moved 80 kilometres (50 miles) across the border to Detroit. He became a car checker for the Michigan Central Railway, then, five years later, left to become a clerk for one of its customers, the Detroit coal dealer Alex Y. Malcomson. This alliance was to prove propitious. Malcomson formed a partnership with the young and struggling Henry Ford in 1902, and assigned his chief clerk to keep track of Ford's expenditures. Couzens, impressed with the operation, within a year scraped together $2,500 to invest in twenty-five shares of stock in the newly formed company, and effectively became its business manager.

Many have argued that Couzens, second only to Henry Ford himself, was responsible for the policies that led to the spectacular early success of the Ford Motor Company.

Although Henry Ford conceived and helped design the Model T, Couzens put in place the structures that helped produce and sell it. He developed the decentralized system of geographically dispersed assembly plants and branch offices, in which branch managers recruited dealers and supervised dealerships that were not owned by Ford but that operated as franchised agencies, thus saving on investment costs. This network of dealers (over 7,000 in 1913) sold the Model T in prodigious numbers.

Couzens also had a strong hand in devising the famous wage offer of five dollars per day, announced in January 1914. The offer, approximately twice the going wage rate at the time, was contrived in part to stave off a growing unionization movement and in part to stop the extraordinarily high labour turnover rate at the Highland Park factory. Thousands – perhaps as many as 10,000 – job applicants converged on the Ford plant as the major financial newspapers of the nation castigated the policy as foolish utopianism or worse. But the immediate result of the policy was not the destruction of the company, or of capitalism, but of continued profits as other costs continued to decline and productivity increased.

Despite his success, Couzens was growing tired of the business, and he and Ford were beginning to have divergent views of where the company was headed. However, the final break with Ford came in 1915 over a political issue: pacifism, which Ford insisted on promoting in pamphlets directed at customers. Couzens objected and offered his resignation on 14 October. Ford accepted on the spot, thus ending Couzens' brilliant managerial career at Ford Motor Company.

Couzens had always had an active interest in Detroit politics, serving as commissioner of street railways (1913–15) even before his resignation from Ford. After his resignation he became commissioner of police (1916–18) and was elected mayor. In a twist of fate, he was appointed in 1922 to the Senate seat that Henry Ford had lost in 1918. Couzens was subsequently elected to the seat. He was considered a Progressive Republican and was a supporter of Franklin D. Roosevelt's New Deal. Couzens was defeated in the Republican primary in 1936, but died before his term expired.

BIBLIOGRAPHY
Barnard, H. (1958) *Independent Man: The Life of Senator James Couzens*, New York: Charles Scribner's Sons.
O'Brien, A.P. (1997) 'The Importance of Adjusting Production to Sales in the Early Automobile Industry', *Explorations in Economic History* 34: 195–219.
Rae, J.B. (1965) *The American Automobile*, Chicago: University of Chicago Press.
Sward, K. (1972) *The Legend of Henry Ford*, New York: Atheneum.

WJH

CROSBY, Philip B. (1926–)

Philip Crosby was born in Wheeling, West Virginia on 18 June 1926. He received a degree in podiatry (his father's profession), but decided not to pursue this career. Leaving the US Navy in 1952, he worked initially on an assembly line. Eventually he became a reliability engineer for the Crosley Corporation in Richmond, Indiana. At the time, Crosby realized 'that the way things worked assumed that nothing would ever be done right, so most of the effort was placed on checking initial results and then correcting them' (Crosby 1996a: xv). This approach to quality was accomplished very formally: papers were written about calculated risk and everyone accepted that there would be mistakes. 'This did not compute with the medical background I had accumulated in the past few years' (Crosby 1996a: xv). Consequently, Crosby

attempted (with little success) to change the corporate outlook that accepted defects. Eventually, he sensed that to advance in his career he needed to move from the Crosley Corporation to a more progressive firm, and found a position as a reliability engineer at the Bendix Corporation in Mishawaka, Indiana, where the company was building the Navy's TALOS missile. Results from Crosby's work at Bendix and the valuable experience he gained there helped him to advance to his next career move.

In May 1957 Crosby and his family moved to Orlando, Florida, where he joined the Martin Company as a senior quality engineer. A few years later he became a department manager at Martin and was in charge of the quality programme for the Pershing missile project. It was here that he developed the concept of 'zero defects' (Crosby 1996a: 80). The idea in this case was not to spot defects in finished products, but to prevent defects from occurring in the first place. Unlike in the Crosley Corporation, defects could not be accepted at any rate in missile construction. Unfortunately, Crosby's approach for zero defects 'was taken by the government and much of the aerospace industry as a motivation program rather than a management performance standard' (Crosby 1996a: 80). However, he took advantage of the opportunities for learning at Martin. During his eight years there, the company grew to approximately 10,000 employees. Crosby considered that the most important thing he learned at Martin was about relationships with people. While some thought that hiring subordinates with a lack of experience was a problem, Crosby considered it an advantage. People with no experience were easier to teach 'the correct way than for them to unlearn their bad habits' (Crosby 1996a: 81).

In 1963, when Crosby became responsible for the quality of the outputs of Martin's suppliers, he attempted to eliminate the need for inspecting and testing incoming materials from suppliers. While this was not completely accomplished, rejections were reduced to a small number and supplier quality improved substantially in just a year: 'This came about when the concept of Zero Defects became an actual working policy for the Purchasing and Quality Management [Department]' (Crosby 1996a: 86).

In 1965 Crosby assessed his future at Martin. He had been on a quick promotion track, 'however, all that was coming to a close. Since I was not an engineer there was no probability that I would go to corporate headquarters' (Crosby 1996a: 86). In May he accepted a position as quality director for ITT, then headed by Harold GENEEN. 'The company [ITT] was not quite $2 billion in revenue when I joined in 1965, but was $20 billion when I left 14 years later' (Crosby 1996a: 86). Reflecting on his prior experience as he started at ITT, Crosby realized that at the Crosley Corporation, acceptable quality levels meant a commitment to doing things wrong. Further, he learned while working at Bendix that he could set a new management standard with zero defects. Then, at Martin, he learned that to be taken seriously the quality outcome of zero defects had to be measured in terms of money. These experiences had helped to formulate his quality philosophy by the time he joined ITT.

As corporate vice-president of ITT for fourteen years from 1965 to 1979, Crosby applied this pragmatic philosophy in real-world settings. The nature of his job meant that he worked with many industrial and service companies around the world. As a result, he found that his approach to the management of quality worked in many types of situations. When, in 1965, top management at ITT decided to focus on quality throughout the corporation, Crosby established four objectives that continue to be part of his overall approach to quality management:

1. Establish a competent quality management program in every operation, both manufacturing and service.

2. Eliminate surprise nonconformance problems.

3. Reduce the cost of quality.

4. Make ITT the standard for quality worldwide

(Crosby 1979: 7)

Another aspect of Crosby's philosophy that also transcends much of his career is his belief that quality is free. In making this point, Crosby uses his 'cost-of-quality concept to demonstrate that quality is free' (Teboul 1991: 112). That is, Crosby believes that 'not achieving quality costs money. He argues that the real cost of quality is the cost of doing things *wrong*' (Thomas 1992: 32). The cost of quality represents expenses that could have been avoided by doing things right the first time. These overall costs, according to Crosby, can be attributed to four specific types of costs.

• Prevention costs: project reviews, design reviews, validation, training, maintenance, improvement projects, design of experiments, operating procedures, guidelines, etc.

• Appraisal costs: tests, inspection, audits, surveys, gathering and processing control data, reports, evaluation of suppliers, certification, etc.

• Internal failure costs: scrap, rework, lost time, reruns, unused capacity, engineering changes, etc.

• External failure costs: returns, recalls, complaints, replacements, compensation, field service, repairs under guarantee, product liabilities, etc.

(Teboul 1991: 112)

Not everyone agrees that quality is free. In considering both short-run and long-run performance goals, Cole considers that 'Philip Crosby is wrong. Except in some trivial cases, "Quality is *not* free." It pays eventually but the investment – particularly of management time and effort – is substantial' (Cole 1995: 209).

Nevertheless, both zero defects and cost of quality are solid parts of Crosby's philosophy. These ideas originated early in his career and continue as major underpinnings of his work today. In 1979, as his work with ITT drew to a close (he went on to set up his own private quality consultancy practice), Crosby stressed that: 'Used as a management tool for the purpose of focusing attention on quality management the COQ [cost of quality] is a positive blessing and serves a unique purpose' (Crosby 1979: 126).

Another articulation of Crosby's philosophy is embraced in his absolutes of quality management. Evans and Lindsay present a good summary of these absolutes.

• The definition of quality is conformance to requirements. Requirements setting is the responsibility of management. Requirements are communication devices and are ironclad.

• The system for causing quality is prevention. The first step toward prevention is to understand the production process. Once this is done, the objective is to discover and eliminate all opportunities for error. Statistical methods are useful in this regard.

• The performance standard is zero defects. Crosby feels that this is widely misunderstood and resisted. He claims that most people accept zero defects as a standard in many aspects of their personal lives and need only be taught and convinced that zero defects is a reasonable and essential standard in their work lives.

• The measurement of quality is the price of nonconformance. Quality cost data are useful to call problems to management's attention, to select opportunities for corrective action, and to track quality improvement over time.

(Evans and Lindsay 1989: 24)

Crosby believes that organizations can learn, and that management should adopt quality management because it is free and beneficial for

the 'bottom line'. He also considers that 'the problem organization will benefit most from his quality management program' (Hunt 1992: 51). In his 1984 book *Quality Without Tears*, Crosby relates the symptoms of such a problem organization: (1) the outgoing product or service normally contains deviations from the published, announced, or agreed-upon requirements; (2) the company has an extensive field service or dealer network skilled in rework and resourceful corrective action to keep the customers satisfied; (3) management does not provide a clear performance standard or definition of quality, so the employees each develop their own; (4) management does not know the price of non-conformance. Product companies spend 20 percent or more of their sales dollars doing things wrong and doing them over. Service companies spend 35 percent or more of their operating costs doing things wrong and doing them over; and (5) management denies that it is the cause of the problem (Crosby 1984: 1–5).

In defining what he means by quality, Crosby emphasizes that 'quality has to be defined as conformance to requirements, not as goodness' (Crosby 1984: 64). That is, quality is conformance to requirements, and non-quality is non-conformance. When Crosby spoke about quality as conformance to requirements, he believed that any product that conformed to its design specifications was high quality. It followed then that 'a Pinto that met Pinto requirements was as much a quality product as a Cadillac that conformed to Cadillac requirements' (Costin 1994: 149). In addition, Crosby emphasizes that quality is not:

• Goodness, or luxury, or shininess.

• Intangible, therefore non measurable.

• Unaffordable.

• Originated by the workers.

• Something that originates in the quality department.

(Hunt 1992: 52)

Crosby considers that an organization's first step in moving toward a major improvement in its quality is to determine its current level of 'management maturity'. In this case, Crosby uses his Quality Management Maturity Grid. Consisting of five stages, the grid evaluates the organization's status in terms of measurement categories such as management understanding and attitude. The five stages of quality management maturity are: (I) Uncertainty; (II) Awakening; (III) Enlightenment; (IV) Wisdom; and (V) Certainty (Crosby 1996a: 32–3). Then, when a firm has determined its present maturity stage on the Quality Management Maturity Grid, it can implement a quality management programme based on Crosby's fourteen steps of quality improvement. These are:

1. Management commitment
2. Quality improvement team
3. Measurement
4. Cost of quality
5. Quality awareness
6. Corrective action
7. Zero Defects planning
8. Employee education
9. Zero Defects day
10. Goal setting
11. Error-cause removal
12. Recognition
13. Quality councils
14. Do it over again

(Crosby 1984: 99)

Each step is designed to move the organization's management style ultimately towards Stage V. At this stage 'conformance to the firms stated quality requirements [is] assured. A Zero-Defects culture is established and the cost of quality is reduced to its lowest possible level' (Hunt 1992: 54).

Crosby is closely associated with the concept of zero defects, which he created at the Martin

Company in 1961. He defines quality as conforming to requirements, and measures quality by the cost of non-conformance. Subsequently, the Crosby approach focuses attention on developing processes and conditions that prevent defects. Consequently, inspection and other non-preventive approaches are not used. Further, he considers that 'statistical levels of compliance program people for failure' (Brocka and Brocka 1997: 61). Although zero defects were used as a motivational tool during the 1960s in the United States, the Japanese, by contrast, 'properly applied zero defects, using it as an engineering tool, with responsibility of proper implementation left to management' (Brocka and Brocka 1997: 62). Unfortunately, zero defects failed in the United States, where responsibility for the implementation was left to the individual worker. Crosby also urged that companies should develop a quality 'vaccine' to prevent non-conformance (defects) (Crosby 1984: 7).

In 1979, when Crosby reviewed his quality management strategy, he considered that concepts instead of techniques were important. That is, popular technique-based programmes were not major concepts. These included, for example, statistical process control and quality circles: 'They were just tools, and properly applied, could be useful' (Crosby 1996a: 136). Instead, Crosby built his Quality College on four absolutes of quality management that had evolved in his own thinking over the years:

1. Quality means conformance to requirements, not goodness.

2. Quality comes from prevention, not detection.

3. Quality performance standard is Zero Defects, not Acceptable Quality Levels.

4. Quality is measured by the Price of Nonconformance, not by indexes.
(Crosby 1996a: 136)

Crosby also found that a major need in terms of improving quality was to change the thinking of top management. If top executives expected defects it would get them, and workers would have similar expectations. However, 'if management established a higher standard of performance and communicated it thoroughly to all levels of the company, Zero Defects was possible' (Costin 1994: 149). Therefore, zero defects must be a management standard instead of a motivational slogan for workers.

In some accounts of quality management the major contributors to the field are identified as W. Edwards DEMING, Joseph JURAN and Crosby. 'In many versions Deming is the protagonist and Juran is a secondary character. In one article, Deming and Juran were portrayed as rivals. A close relative of W. Edwards Deming was quick to point out that this was not the case' (Petersen 1998: 35). While Deming disagreed about the extent of Juran's influence in Japan, he valued Juran as a colleague: 'Members of the Juran Institute are quick to point out that Juran and Deming respected each other, were colleagues, and were not rivals' (Petersen 1998: 35). Crosby, in commenting on Deming and Juran writes, 'If you do what they teach you will do very well. They are dedicated people and worthy of respect' (Bank 1992: 76). However, Crosby does not think that his relationship with Juran is one of mutual respect: 'Dr. Juran seems to think I am a charlatan and hasn't missed many opportunities to say that over the years' (Crosby 1989: 79).

It should also be noted that Crosby gives a good account of himself when compared with the other two gurus, Deming and Juran. Unlike them, Crosby was an excellent speaker and was able to charm corporate executives. If style and manner of presentation are important, Crosby was the best of them all; but others will argue about the depth of Crosby's substance. It is also argued that Crosby's strong projection was overdone. In this regard, Wren and Greenwood claim that 'the most

flamboyant of the leading U.S. quality experts is Philip B. Crosby' (Wren and Greenwood 1998: 217). In contrast, Lee IACOCCA considers Crosby to be the best: 'For my money nobody talks quality better than Phil Crosby. We thought enough of it [Crosby's quality college] that we established our own Chrysler Quality Institute in Michigan, modelled after his operation' (Iacocca 1988: 256–7).

In retrospect, Philip Crosby made a major contribution to the quality movement in the United States during the 1980s and 1990s. Having solid corporate experience, Crosby developed and taught a significant and far-reaching 'quality [management] process that is the basis for many quality improvement programs' (Schmidt and Finnigan 1993: 173). In 1994 he retired from his own consultancy firm, Philip Crosby Associates, in order to write and speak about quality, and also founded Career IV, a consultancy to help grow executives. He reports 'it is wonderful to be able to sit down in the morning and write for several hours without interruption' (Crosby 1994: ix). In his many reflections on his life's work, he adds this parting advice: 'make the customer successful, and that will make the company (and you) shine' (Crosby 1994: 210).

BIBLIOGRAPHY

Bank, J. (1992) *The Essence of Total Quality Management*, New York: Prentice Hall.

Brocka, B. and Brocka, M.S. (1992) *Quality Management: Implementing the Best Ideas of the Masters*, Homewood, IL: Business One Irwin.

Cole, R.E. (ed.) (1995) *The Death and Life of the American Quality Movement*, New York: Oxford University Press.

Costin, H.I. (1994) *Readings in Total Quality Management*, Fort Worth, TX: Harcourt Brace and Co.

Crosby, P.B. (1979) *Quality is Free: The Art of Making Quality Certain*, New York: McGraw-Hill.

—— (1984) *Quality Without Tears: The Art of Hassle-free Management*, New York: McGraw-Hill.

—— (1986) *Running Things: The Art of Making Things Happen*, Mentor Books.

—— (1988) *The Eternally Successful Organization: The Art of Corporate Wellness*, New York: McGraw-Hill.

—— (1989) *Let's Talk Quality: 96 Questions You Always Wanted to Ask Phil Crosby*, New York: McGraw-Hill.

—— (1990a) *Cutting the Cost of Quality*, New York: McGraw-Hill.

—— (1990b) *Leading: The Art of Becoming an Executive*, New York: McGraw-Hill.

—— (1994) *Completeness: Quality for the 21st Century*, New York: Plume.

—— (1995) *Reflections on Quality*, New York: McGraw-Hill.

—— (1996a) *Quality is Still Free: Making Quality Certain in Uncertain Times*, New York: McGraw-Hill.

—— (1996b) *The Absolutes of Leadership*, San Francisco: Jossey-Bass.

—— (1999) *Quality and Me: Lessons From an Evolving Life*, San Francisco: Jossey-Bass.

—— (2000) 'Phil's Page', Philip Crosby Associates, II Inc., http://www.philipcrosby.com, 15 March 2001.

Evans, J.R. and Lindsay, W.M. (1989) *The Management and Control of Quality*, St Paul, MN: West Publishing Company.

Hunt, V.D. (1992) *Quality in America: How to Implement a Competitive Quality Program*, Homewood, IL: Business One Irwin.

Iacocca, L. (1988) *Talking Straight*, London: Sidgwick and Jackson.

Main, J. (1986) 'Under the Spell of the Quality Gurus', *Fortune* 114(4): 30–34.

Petersen, P.B. (1998) 'Reflections about a Most Unforgettable Person: W. Edwards Dening (1900–1993)', in J.W. Cortada and J.A. Woods (eds), *The Quality Yearbook 1998 Edition*, New York: McGraw-Hill, 31–9.

Schmidt, W.H. and Finnigan, J.P. (1992) *The Race Without a Finish Line: America's Quest for Total Quality*, San Francisco: Jossey-Bass.

—— (1993) *TQ Manager: A Practical Guide for Managing in a Total Quality Organization*, San Francisco: Jossey-Bass.

Teboul, J. (1991) *Managing Quality Dynamics*, New York: Prentice-Hall.

Thomas, B. (1992) *Total Quality Training: The Quality Culture and Quality Trainer*, New York: McGraw-Hill.

Wren, D.A. and Greenwood, R.G. (1998) *Management Innovators: The People and Ideas that Have Shaped Modern Business*, New York: Oxford University Press.

PBP

CROZIER, Michel (1922–)

Michel Crozier was born in Sainte-Menehould, France on 6 November 1922, the son of Joanny and Jeanne Crozier. His father was a hardware merchant. He studied in Paris at the Hautes Études Commerciales (HEC), France's leading school for business and administration at the time, and took a BA in 1943; he went on to study literature and law at the Sorbonne and the University of Lille, and also wrote poetry, met Jean-Paul Sartre and dabbled in left-wing politics. In 1947 he went to the United States, where he travelled for a year and studied the American labour movement. He married Cristina Ortega-Salinas in 1952; they have three children.

In 1954 Crozier joined the Centre Nationale de la Recherche Scientifique in Paris, serving as a research associate from 1954 to 1964 and then being appointed professor in 1964. In 1962 he founded and became research director of the Centre de Sociologie des Organisations,

also in Paris. Most of his subsequent career has been with these two organizations, although he has also held other posts: he was professor of sociology at the University of Nanterre (1967–8) and has held visiting professorships at Harvard University and the University of California at Irvine. He has been a consultant to the RAND Corporation, the European Economic Community (now the European Union) and the Trilateral Commission. He holds the National Order of Merit and the Legion of Honour from the government of France.

Crozier takes a sociological approach to the study of organizations, especially bureaucracies. His most famous work, *Le phenomena bureaucratique* (The Bureaucratic Phenomenon) (1963), is largely a study of the French civil service bureaucracy, but later observers such as Thoenig (1998) believe that many of his conclusions are valid in business organizations as well. In *Le phenomena bureaucratique*, Crozier defines a bureaucracy as (1) having a centralized decision-making system; (2) governed by impartial and universally applied rules; (3) very hierarchical, with little contact between the various levels in the hierarchy apart from top-down pressures; and (4) informal power structures which develop parallel to but to some extent outside the formal hierarchy. He sees bureaucracy as a self-perpetuating process, one whose routines tend to go only in one direction; the evolution of a bureaucratic organization serves always to strengthen bureaucratic routines and behaviour, never to weaken them. In practical terms, as Thoenig (1998) comments, this means that bureaucracies are inherently unable to correct themselves or to adapt to errors.

Following lines of thought developed by Herbert SIMON and traceable back to Max WEBER, Crozier sees bureaucracy as in some ways a natural phenomenon. Organizations are certainly a natural response to the human need to organize in order to complete a task. Once an organization has been created, other human needs, particularly those for power

over and dominance of others, also come into play. Those who wish to have such power will work out strategies for achieving it, which they will seek to do by either rising to the top of the administrative hierarchy, taking control of informal power structures, or both. One way of achieving power over others is to create uncertainty in those others, which can be effectively done by denying them access to knowledge which the power-seeker controls. In this way, bureaucratic organizations concentrate power by inhibiting communication; control is achieved through the granting or denying of access to privileged information and persons.

Crozier developed these themes in more detail in his *Le monde des employes de bureau* (The World of the Office Worker) (1965). His later work has focused more on the application of sociological principles to wider society, as in *La societe bloquée* (The Stalled Society) (1970), an analysis of French society and what Crozier perceived as its inbuilt resistance to change, and *Le mal americain* (The Trouble With America) (1980), a discussion of the political and cultural problems faced by the United States. He remains a potent critic of bureaucracy in all its forms, and his work provides useful guidance for those seeking to understand how and why bureaucracies develop in both public and private sectors.

BIBLIOGRAPHY

Crozier, M. (1963) *Le phenomena bureaucratique*, Paris: Editions du Seuil; *The Bureaucratic Phenomenon*, Chicago: University of Chicago Press, 1964.

———— (1965) *Le monde des employes de bureau*, Paris: Editions du Seuil; *The World of the Office Worker*, Chicago: University of Chicago Press, 1971.

———— (1970) *La societe bloquée*, Paris: Editions du Seuil; *The Stalled Society*, New York: Viking.

———— (1976) *Decentraliser les responsibilites* (The Decentralization of Responsibilities), Paris: Documentation Française.

———— (1980) *Le mal americain*, Paris: Fayard; *The Trouble with America*, Los Angeles: University of California Press, 1984.

———— (1987) *État modeste, état modern* (Modern State, Modest State), Paris: Fayard.

Crozier, M. and Friedberg, E. (1977) *L'acteur et le systéme: les contraintes de l'action collective*, Paris: Editions du Seuil; trans. A. Goldhammer, *Actors and Systems: The Politics of Collective Action*, Chicago: University of Chicago Press, 1980.

Crozier, M., Huntington, S.P. and Watanuki, J. (1975) *The Crisis of Democracy: Report on the Governability of Democracies to the Trilateral Commission*, New York: New York University Press.

Thoenig, J.-C. (1998) 'Crozier, Michel', in M. Warner (ed.), *IEBM Handbook of Management Thinking*, London: International Thomson Business Press, 140–44.

MLW

CSIKSZENTMIHALYI, Mihaly (1934–)

Mihaly Csikszentmihalyi was born in Fiume, Italy on 29 September 1934, the son of a diplomat. He emigrated to the United States in 1956 and became a naturalized citizen. He obtained his BA from the University of Chicago in 1959, having trained as a psychologist, and stayed on at the university to move into creativity research as a postgraduate student. He was awarded his Ph.D. in 1965, and returned to the University of Chicago as assistant professor in sociology and anthropology in 1967. He later became professor of behavioural science and then professor of psy-

chology at Chicago. In 1983 he joined the US Social Science Research Council Committee on Development, Giftedness and the Learning Process. He was also appointed to the board of advisers of the Getty Museum and the *Encyclopaedia Britannica*.

Csikszentmihalyi began to study creativity in the mid-1960s, when creativity research, still in its infancy, was part of the emerging social agenda. At that time, creativity research was being recast to provide a way to break out of conservative educational practices which were seen to destroy creative expression (prior to this, creativity research had been pioneered in order to detect creative abilities in areas of national interest during the Cold War). Csikszentmihalyi was fundamentally opposed to these earlier arguments for biological determination of human potential. He explored emotion, cognition and conation as important in the phenomenon of creativity. His early work on personality traits and cognitive processes focused upon artists and art students. He also did substantial work on exploring the nature of the creative process, and the values, roles and personality of artists, making substantial contributions to theory from the 1960s to the mid-1970s.

Csikszentmihalyi emphasized the importance of problem finding, describing intellectual activity as taking place on a continuum between two poles, with presented problems at one end and discovered problems at the other. He describes 'presented problems' as those that are clearly formulated, requiring only the application of accepted method to arrive at expected solution, whereas 'discovered problems' are experienced only as a vague unease and dimly felt emotional or intellectual tension. This work on the nature of problems has been of value in a number of different management fields.

In the 1970s it was demonstrated that IQ is largely unrelated to divergent thinking (classically an important part of the creative process); that there are certain personality traits characteristic of more creative individuals; and that certain kinds of divergent thinking skills can be improved with training and practice. Creativity research developed into asking questions about the nature of creative thinking in various domains and how it develops. Csikszentmihalyi himself turned to a more systemic view of creativity. He enlarged the understanding of the social and cultural context of artistic development, helping to explain why and how certain locales have given rise to a great outpouring of creative work. His work investigating the factors that led to the creative output of Florence in the fifteenth century highlights the importance of the infrastructure that supported artistic endeavour (patrons such as Cosimo dei MEDICI, education, an artistic community). From this work, he came to the conclusion that the study of creativity as a process must take into account the parameters of the cultural symbol system in which the activity takes place, and the social roles and norms that regulate the creative activity.

In contrast to earlier thinking, Csikszentmihalyi concluded that creativity is not an attribute of individuals, but an attribution based on the conditions of the social system, such as judgements of taste, beauty or goodness. Thus, he declared that it is not the creative *person* that should be the focus of attention for creativity research, but the person who is part of the creative *system*. He proposed a systems view of creativity, as the result of the interaction between three subsystems: a domain, a person and a field (the individuals who understand the domain and gatekeep it). Accordingly, personality traits play a role in creative activity by enabling a person to produce variations that, if the other elements of the system are conducive to it, will be selected, preserved and transmitted to future generations as valued contributions.

Csikszentmihalyi emphasized that only by considering the three as a set of continuously interrelated issues would it be possible to move the field of creativity research forward coherently. He notes that the

causal chain between the three is not a simple linear progression from individual variation to social selection to cultural retention and transmission. The system is more intimately connected than that, depending on one's perspective one may be able to see causation in any number of permutations. Moreover new fields and domains emerge, making new kinds of creative behaviour possible.

(Getzels and Csikszentmihalyi 1976)

The systemic view asserts that the specific individual traits associated with creativity will depend on characteristics of the other two subsystems. This framework formed the basis for new creativity research. Csikszentmihalyi noted that psychologists study creativity from an individual perspective, sociologists from an institutional perspective, and anthropologists from a cultural perspective. He called for creativity research to be developed into an interdisciplinary domain to draw together this fragmentation.

A principal contribution of his later work has been the exploration of what he has called 'flow' experiences. He describes 'flow' as an optimal experience while engaged in an all-absorbing activity, and as an autotelic experience, that is one that is rewarding in and of itself. According to Csikszentmihalyi, 'The optimal experience usually occurs when a person's body or mind is stretched to its limits in a voluntary effort to accomplish something difficult and worthwhile' (Csikszentmihalyi and Csikszentmihalyi 1988). This later work followed the theories of intrinsic rewards as a major driver of behaviour, and sought to explore the conditions of people's inner motivation and performance. It has been used to shed light on how the quality of the work experience can be transformed to produce flow experiences. Those activities that are more conducive to flow, as described by Csikszentmihalyi, 'have rules that demand the learning of skills, they set up goals, provide feedback, and they make control possible.

They facilitate concentration and involvement by making the activity as distinct as possible from the paramount reality of everyday existence' (Csikszentmihalyi 1997). Much of his work sets out the framework for the effort to penetrate more deeply into the nature of creativity. He emphasizes that creativity research will fail without recognizing that creativity is not something that takes place inside the head of a person, but is the product of a larger and more mysterious process. His work has been taken up by those advocating a 'whole person' approach to human resource management, and has informed the psychology of entrepreneurship and leadership.

Csikszentmihalyi's work has been driven by his belief that the furthering of creativity (the process of change perhaps most uniquely human, as he describes it) is a worthy human purpose and one most likely to produce knowledge that will provide leverage over the ever more challenging problems humans are likely to confront as our species moves into a new millennium. Csikszentmihalyi's work has contributed greatly to the understanding of human motivation and productivity as well as the implications for the organization of work. All of which has important implications for the organization of work, the effectiveness of organizations and the realization of human potential.

BIBLIOGRAPHY
Csikszentmihalyi, M. (1992) *Flow: The Psychology of Happiness*, London: Rider.
—— (1997) *Living Well: The Psychology of Everyday Life*, London: Weidenfeld and Nicolson.
Csikszentmihalyi, M. and Csikszentmihalyi, I. (1988) *Optimal Experience: Studies of Flow in Consciousness*, Cambridge: Cambridge University Press.
Feldman, D.H., Csikszentmihalyi, M. and Gardner, H. (1994) *Changing the World: A Framework for the Study of Creativity*, Westport, CT: Praeger.
Getzels, J.W. and Csikszentmihalyi, M.

(1976) *The Creative Vision*, New York: John Wiley and Sons.

AJ

CUTFORTH, Arthur Edwin (1881–1958)

Arthur Edwin Cutforth was born in Woodford, Essex on 25 August 1881, the son of Samuel Cutforth, a draper, and his wife Annie. He died in York on 7 April 1958. He married Alizon Farrer Ecroyd in 1920; they had four children. Cutforth was educated at Bancroft's School, Woodford, and Trent College, Derbyshire. Choosing accountancy as a career, he articled in 1900 and took his final examinations in 1905. He joined the firm of Deloitte, Plender, Griffiths and Company in London, and the following year (1906) published his book *Audits*; the book ultimately ran to nine editions. Cutforth went on to become one of the most prominent and respected people in his profession, publishing several books, taking a keen interest in training for accountants and the improving of professional standards, and serving two terms as president of the Institute of Chartered Accounts of England and Wales (ICAEW). He was made CBE in 1926, served as High Sheriff of Hertfordshire in 1937–8 and was knighted in 1938. Ill health forced his retirement in the same year, and he and his wife lived in the Lake District until shortly before his death.

Audits became a standard textbook, and Cutforth and Lawrence DICKSEE were the authorities most often cited in accountancy training schools. Although he did not become involved in teaching to the extent that Dicksee did, Cutforth was strongly involved in the educational movement of the day, focusing his attention on examinations. He stated repeatedly that accountancy as a profession needed the highest possible standards so as to instil confidence in both companies and the public at large. He felt that the purpose of examinations was to ensure that only the very best and most able people entered the profession.

After the First World War, Cutforth became Britain's leading authority on corporate amalgamations. The amalgamation movement, perhaps best exemplified by Alfred MOND, was very active during the 1920s. In Cutforth (1926) he spelled out the three strategic approaches to amalgamation: (1) complete amalgamation, in which the companies concerned are dissolved and a completely new company is formed; (2) merger under a holding company, in which the holding firm is established and a controlling interest in the merging companies' stock is vested in it; and (3) pooling arrangements. Cutforth then discussed the accounting pros and cons of each option. The book also includes a very useful chapter on valuation, focusing on the problems involved in computing net profit and total capitalization. He notes too that in the end, whatever value an accountant might put on a company, its value in the market is worth what a buyer will pay for it, no more and no less; and for many reasons, this figure might be either higher or lower than the valuation. Among other measures, Cutforth argued for greater transparency and openness in financial reporting to assist in valuation.

BIBLIOGRAPHY
Cutforth, A. (1926) *Methods of Amalgamation and the Valuation of the Business for Amalgamation and Other Purposes*, London: G. Bell.
Kitchen, J. and Parker, R.H. (1980) *Accounting Thought and Education: Six English Pioneers*, London: Institute of Chartered Accountants.

MLW

CYERT, Richard Michael (1921–98)

Richard Cyert was born in Winona, Michigan on 22 July 1921 and died in Pittsburgh, Pennsylvania on 7 October 1998. He was educated at the University of Minnesota and graduated in economics in 1943. After serving as officer in the US navy for three years during the Second World War, Cyert entered graduate school at Columbia University, New York in 1946. He completed his degree in 1951. He received many rewards and honorary memberships for his work, and was until his death President Emeritus, and R.M. and M.S. Cyert Professor of Economics and Management at Carnegie Mellon University. He is well known for his contribution to behavioural economics (in particular the behavioural theory of the firm), business administration and Bayesian economics, and for his leadership of Carnegie Mellon University.

Cyert has worked extensively within the fields of behavioural economics, economics in general, decision theory and management. Some of his most important books are *A Behavioral Theory of the Firm*, written with James G. MARCH (Cyert and March 1963) and *Bayesian Analysis and Uncertainty in Economic Theory* with Morris DeGroot (Cyert and Degroot 1987). Professor Cyert came to Carnegie Mellon University (then Carnegie Institute of Technology) in 1948 as instructor of economics, and was successively assistant professor of economics and industrial administration, associate professor and head of the department of industrial management, and finally professor; he was dean of the Graduate School of Industrial Administration (GSIA) (1962–72) and president of the university (1972–90). Even when taking on leadership duties as dean and president, he remained very active in publishing and research. Throughout his career he initiated, contributed to and maintained a keen interest in behavioural economics.

Cyert belonged to that small but select group of economists/political scientists/organization theorists who helped launch and develop the behavioural economic programme in the United States in the 1950s and 1960s, and he was one of the three 'founding fathers' (along with James G. March and Herbert A. SIMON) of behavioural economics, established at Carnegie Mellon during this period. His own interest in behavioural economics started with his doctoral thesis on price-setting in oligopolistic markets. Cyert found that neoclassical theory gave him very little support as a prescription for description of managerial and firm behaviour. As a result, Cyert and his colleagues at Carnegie Mellon University laid the research foundations for a series of contributions to organizational and behavioural approaches to economics and management (Augier and March 2001).

It was during his years as a doctoral student that Cyert realized that for economics to go anywhere it had to begin collaborating with other disciplines, such as organization theory, sociology, management and psychology. This interdisciplinary view was stimulated, encouraged and developed at Carnegie Mellon during his interaction and collaboration with Herbert Simon and James March. This is demonstrated in his attempts to go inside the 'black box' of neoclassical theory of the firm and understand the internal decision-making processes of the firm, especially in his work with James G. March. Their first co-authored paper, 'Organizational Behavior and Pricing Behavior in an Oligopolistic Market', was published in *American Economic Review* in 1955. Eight years later, they published *A Behavioral Theory of the Firm*. In this book, Cyert and March outlined a theory that was built around a political conception of organizational goals, a bounded rationality conception of expectations, and adaptive conception of rules and aspirations, and a set of ideas about how the interactions among these factors affect decision making in firms (Augier and March 2001). They emphasized the idea of problemistic search; the idea that search within a firm is stimulated mostly by problems and directed to

solving those problems, and the idea of organizational learning. In *A Behavioral Theory of the Firm*, organizations learn from their own experiences and the experiences of others.

When *A Behavioral Theory of the Firm* was published, Cyert became the dean of GSIA, but he continued (as did March and Simon) working within behavioural economics, sometimes with other collaborators. With Robert Trueblood, he worked on statistical sampling methods and statistical decision theory (Trueblood and Cyert 1957). In the late 1960s, Cyert began working with Morris DeGroot, who was trained in Bayesian statistics. They published their first paper in 1970, and their book was published in 1987 (Cyert and DeGroot 1987). Most people would probably not be inclined to equate 'Bayesian' economics with 'behavioural' or 'managerial' economics, but, importantly, Cyert's approach to Bayesian economics was both a natural outgrowth of his work with March on behavioural economics and a contribution to behavioural economics itself (Day and Sunder 1996; Augier and March 2001). The argument that Cyert's work on Bayesian economics can be seen as a contribution to behavioural economics is twofold. First, in doing this kind of work, Cyert was interested in building a theory of *real economic behaviour* by taking uncertainty into account (Cyert 1970). This is consonant with modern behavioural emphasis on uncertainty and behavioural aspects of economics. Second, he built on his work with March and the idea of *organizational learning*. An important example of how learning can contribute to the development of Bayesian economics is found in Cyert's work on adaptive utility. Noticing the observable difference between the assumed fixed utility of decision making and the observed choices, Cyert wanted to apply the concept of learning to the concept of utility in such a way that changes in utility functions over time (as a result of learning) could be accounted for. This intertemporal aspect of learning is clearly a behavioural idea.

During his ten years as the dean of the GSIA and eighteen years as the president of Carnegie Mellon University, Cyert applied economics, particularly economics and strategy, to the management of organizations of higher education. Under Cyert's direction, the GSIA became a model institution for other schools in the United States and in Europe. Cyert believed in a close relationship between university and industry, and among his goals as a university president was to improve the quality of the university, and to develop a strategy for doing so within a balanced budget. This was not an easy task, but due to his knowledge of organization theory of management practice, he managed to achieve his goals and to bring Carnegie Mellon University onto the research map as a cutting-edge research institution.

In 1990 Cyert edited a book on university management, *The Management of Nonprofit Organizations*. The book includes several essays by Cyert in which he summarizes his approach to managing universities, drawing from both his training as an economist and his experience as a dean and a university president. A central basis for his writings on management is the distinction between the role of economics as an instrument for improving economic behaviour and its role as a description of that behaviour (Augier and March 2001). Cyert tried to keep the two aspects of economics separate. To him, economic theory represents the ideal-typical behaviour, but it is a poor description of real behaviour. Cyert maintained that economics needs to be behavioural in order to describe behaviour, but as a contributor to management thought, Cyert was a relatively traditional economist. He described his goals as an academic administrator as being to improve the quality of the university and to develop a strategy for doing so with a balanced budget. He advocated the application of economic analysis and decision theory to problems of firms and universities; and he recommended the application of conventional economic notions of marginal analysis, comparative advantage and the mon-

itoring of behaviour and performance measures.

Although Cyert was an economist and thus, as a manager, departed somewhat from the principles he discussed in his work on the behavioural theory of the firm, he did not deviate from these in his understanding of how organizations work. Cyert believed that people make mistakes, and that these are important parts of the description of actual human behaviour. He saw universities and other organizations as deviating from the economic idea of efficient organizations, and portrayed them as being filled with conflict of interest and uncertainty about goals. As a manager, however, he saw these features of organizations as defects to be overcome or minimized.

BIBLIOGRAPHY

Augier, M. and March, J.G. (2001) 'Richard M. Cyert: The Work and the Legacy', in M. Augier and J.G. March (eds), *The Economics of Choice, Change and Organization: Essays in Memory of Richard M. Cyert*, Cheltenham: Edward Elgar.

Cyert, R.M. (1970) 'Implications for Economic Theory of a Behavioral Approach to the Firm', in W. Goldberg (ed.), *Behavioral Approaches to Modern Management*, Goteborg: Foretagsekonomiske institutionen vid Handelshogshkolan I Goteborg.

—— (ed.) (1990) *The Management of Nonprofit Organizations*, Lexington, MA: D.C. Heath and Co.

Cyert, R.M. and DeGroot, M.H. (1970) 'Bayesian Analysis and Duopoly Theory', *Journal of Political Economy* 78: 1168–84.

—— (1987) *Bayesian Analysis and Uncertainty in Economic Theory*, Totowa, NJ: Rowman and Littlefield.

Cyert, R.M. and March, J.G. (1955) 'Organizational Structure and Pricing Behavior in an Oligopolistic Market', *American Economic Review* 45: 125–39.

Cyert, R.M, Dill, W.R. and March, J.G. (1958) 'The Role of Expectations in Business Decision Making', *Administrative Science Quarterly* 3: 309–40.

Day, R. and Sunder, S. (1996) 'Ideas and Work of Richard M. Cyert', *Journal of Economic Behavior and Organization* 31: 139–48.

Cyert, R.M. and March, J.G. and (1963) *A Behavioral Theory of the Firm*, Englewood Cliffs, NJ: Prentice Hall.

Trueblood, R.M. and Cyert, R.M. (1957) *Sampling Techniques in Accounting*, Englewood Cliffs, NJ: Prentice Hall.

MA

D

DAN Takuma (1858–1932)

Dan Takuma was born on 7 September 1858 and assassinated on 5 March 1932. The fourth son of a warrior family in the fief of Fukuoka, at the age of ten he was adopted by the family of Dan, who was chief accountant of the Fukuoka clan.

In 1871, after the Meiji Restoration, Dan joined the European/American inspection delegation headed by Iwakura Tomomi (1825–83), on the orders of the Fukuoka, and went to the United States. He studied colliery engineering at the Massachusetts Institute of Technology (MIT), where he was granted a doctorate in engineering, and returned to Japan in 1878. However, circumstances prevented him from working in coal mining after he returned to Japan, and he instead took up a post as assistant professor at the Imperial University of Tokyo. In 1884 he joined the Kohbu-sho (Engineering Ministry), where he worked in the Miike Colliery Bureau. With the transfer of Miike Colliery to Mitsui in 1889, Dan joined Mitsui, and was made executive director of the Mitsui Colliery General Partnership in 1894. By introducing state-of-the-art facilities to Miike Colliery, Dan renovated its coal-mining technology. He then established a port facility in Ohmuta for coal shipments, and this was followed by the construction of coal chemical factories. Thus Dan's competence as a colliery engineer and his capability as a business administrator were fully demonstrated.

With the establishment of the Mitsui General Partnership in 1909, Dan assumed a post as advisory director. In 1914 he was appointed director-general, assuming the post occupied by his predecessor MASUDA Takashi, and became the head of the business concern known as Mitsui Financial Combine. He adopted an aggressive entrepreneurial policy, founding many and various businesses which went on to form the gigantic Mitsui *zaibatsu*.

In 1916 Dan Takuma joined the Nihon Kogyo Club, an assembly of businessmen from very large enterprises in Japan, and was appointed head director of the club. In 1921 he inaugurated Nihon Keizai Renmei (Japan Economists' League), the first business administrators' body in Japan, and again assumed the post of executive director. Later in 1928, he was appointed the first president of the League. In 1929 he was fiercely opposed to the labour union plan set out by the Hamaguchi Cabinet. Taking leadership in the financial circle, he became involved in a variety of financial and political activities until his assassination by the Ketsumei-Dan, a right-wing group in 1932.

BIBLIOGRAPHY
Late Baron's Biography Editing Committee (ed.) (1938) *Danshaku Dan Takuma Den* (Baron Dan Takuma's Biography), 2 vols, Tokyo: Late Baron's Biography Editing Committee.

ST

DANIELS, Jasper Newton (1846–1911)

Jasper Newton 'Jack' Daniels was born near Lynchburg, Tennessee on 5 September 1846 and died there on 10 October 1911. Jack Daniels was born the tenth and youngest child of a Tennessee family in a region already noted for whisky production. After a dispute with his stepmother, he left home at the age of seven and went to work at a whisky distillery at nearby Louse Creek. The owner, Dan Call, was also a Lutheran preacher. Daniels was well suited to the work and quickly learnt the skills of distilling. By the age of fifteen he was Call's business partner, and two years later he bought Call out and became sole proprietor. Call had been forced to give up his distillery business due to pressure exerted by his largely teetotal congregation ('Rare Jack Daniels' 1951: 103).

Daniels purchased a new site closer to Lynchburg, still the present-day location of his distillery. It is placed near to an iron-free spring, essential for the successful distilling of whisky, in a valley known locally as 'The Hollow'. The distillery produces a so-called 'Tennessee' whisky, which is essentially a variation of bourbon. It comes from a 'sour mash' composed primarily of corn, with some rye and malt added. What distinguishes Jack Daniels and other Tennessee whiskies from 'Kentucky' bourbon whisky is the fact that they are also filtered through charcoal (made from hard sugar maple) and then placed in new charred oak barrels for ageing.

In 1866 Daniels registered his distillery with the United States government, the basis of the company's ongoing boast that it is the oldest registered distillery in the country. For many years thereafter, Jack Daniels whisky was a regional beverage, rarely seen outside of Tennessee and neighbouring states. However, at the turn of the century, this began to change. In 1904 a case of Jack Daniels whisky was sent to the St Louis Exposition and won a Gold Medal. This success was followed by international recognition at the Anglo-American Exposition held in London during 1914. These awards did much to publicize Daniels' whisky, and sales increased accordingly in new markets. Jack Daniels is one of the very few brands of American whisky which sells in any quantity abroad.

Unfortunately, the new markets did little to protect either Jack Daniels or other American distillers and brewers from the growing prohibitionist movement. In 1909, Moore County, which includes Lynchburg, went 'dry,' although the distillery was allowed to sell its products elsewhere. In 1911 this too was prohibited, and the distillery faced a crisis. Daniels himself was by this time out of the picture; in 1905, during a characteristic display of temper, he had kicked his office safe when it failed to open. The incident created a blood clot which led in turn to gangrene and finally to amputation of his leg. He suffered from declining health thereafter, and in 1907 he handed over the distillery to his nephew, Lem Motlow. In 1911, the year Daniels died, the distillery was mothballed and Motlow took up farming. The distillery reopened in 1937, several years after the repeal of nationwide prohibition, although Moore Country remains 'dry' to this day. One of the best-known brand names in the country, the Jack Daniels distillery premises have been added to the National Register of Historic Places.

Despite, or perhaps because of his humble origins, Daniels became something of a dandy and cultivated the image of an American country squire. He always wore a knee-length frock coat, a fawn coloured vest and a planter's hat, and grew an elaborate moustache and goatee, the image that continues to adorn the brand's label. A statue of Jack Daniels dressed in full regalia, erected by the man himself before he died, stands outside on the distillery grounds. Although a 'ladies' man', he never married.

BIBLIOGRAPHY
Green, B.A. (1967) *Jack Daniels's Legacy*, Nashville, TN: Rich Printing Company.

'Rare Jack Daniels' (1951) *Fortune* (July): 103–6.

SK

D'ARCY, William Knox (1849–1917)

William Knox D'Arcy was born in 1849 in Newton Abbot, Devon, the son of William Francis D'Arcy, a solicitor, and his wife Elizabeth. He died in London on 1 May 1917. He was married first to Elena Birkbeck and, after her death in 1897, to Ernestine Nutting; there were five children from the first marriage. D'Arcy was educated at Westminster School. When he was seventeen the family emigrated to Australia, settling at Rockhampton, Queensland, and D'Arcy studied law in his father's office and later became a successful solicitor in his own right. He also developed an interest in mining; Australia in the 1870s and 1880s was still in the grip of gold fever, and traces of gold-bearing quartz had been found in Queensland. A chance encounter with a farmer named Sandy Morgan in 1886 led D'Arcy to the discovery of the Mount Morgan gold reef, which he and his associates developed into one of the richest gold mines in the world. Now very wealthy, at the age of forty D'Arcy retired back to Britain in 1889 and devoted himself to social pursuits for the next decade.

Possibly growing restless, however, he began looking around for other fields of activity. With the growing importance of petroleum and its products, and with his own geological experience, D'Arcy began considering oil exploration. Another chance encounter, with Antoine Kitabji, a former Persian customs officer, led him to consider the possibility of oil in Persia. Making the acquaintance of Sir Henry Drummond Wolff, a former British ambassador to Persia, D'Arcy negotiated a concession with the Shah of Persia granting him permission to prospect for oil throughout most of the country. Although traces of oil were found in many places, and could even be skimmed from surface pools, it remained to be seen whether oil could be extracted in sufficient quantities to justify costs. D'Arcy, spending his gold fortune freely, employed two leading surveyors and drilled first in the west of the country, near Bushehr; coming up empty, they moved north to another location, the Maidan-i-Naftun (Valley of Oil) near the town of Masjid-i-Suliman and adjacent to an ancient Zoroastrian fire temple. Looking as much at the folklore and history of the place as the geological signs, D'Arcy deduced there must be oil in the area and drilled.

He found traces of oil, but by now needed more financial backing. Help came from Donald SMITH, Lord Strathcona and one of the builders of the Canadian Pacific Railway, who put together the Oil Concession Syndicate in 1905 with backing from major producers such as Burmah Oil. D'Arcy and Smith were aware that the Royal Navy was planning to convert from coal-fired to oil-fired engines, and for both patriotic and commercial motives they were anxious to secure a supply of oil for the navy. The next three years were characterized by repeated failures and dogged persistence on the part of D'Arcy. In 1908, however, a large oil field was discovered, and in 1909 the partners in the Concession Syndicate founded the Anglo-Persian Oil Company, with D'Arcy as a director. He continued to be actively involved in the management of the company until his death.

The founder of the Middle Eastern oil industry, D'Arcy had a simple management style: his subordinate staff never numbered more than two, and he preferred to manage actively rather than delegate. His persistence and focus on his goal are remarkable. Most of all, however, at both Mount Morgan and the Maidan-i-Naftun, D'Arcy had a knack of being in the right place at the right time, illustrating well the close nature of the link between luck and good management.

BIBLIOGRAPHY
Beable, W.H. (1926) *The Romance of Great Business*, London.
Ferrier, R.W. (1982) *The History of the British Petroleum Company: The Developing Years 1901–1932*, Cambridge: Cambridge University Press.

MLW

DARWIN, Horace (1851–1928)

Horace Darwin was born at Downe in Kent on 12 or 13 May 1851 (dates vary). He died at Cambridge on 22 September 1928. He married Emma Farrer in 1887, and they had a son, Erasmus, who was killed in the First World War, and two daughters. The fifth and youngest son of the scientist Charles Darwin, Horace Darwin was educated privately before taking his degree at Trinity College, Cambridge. He served an apprenticeship as an engineer with an iron foundry in Kent, returning to Cambridge in 1878. In 1880 he joined a partnership with A.G. Dew-Smith to make scientific instruments for the new scientific laboratories being established at the university, and the Cambridge Scientific Instrument Company was founded in 1881. By 1885 he had acquired a majority of the company's shares and was appointed its chairman. He served as Mayor of Cambridge from 1896 to 1897. During the First World War Darwin served on several government committees and his firm carried out experimental military research; for these services, he was knighted in 1918. In 1921 Cambridge Instrument merged with its sometime collaborator in the instrument-making business, R.W. Paul and Company.

Darwin was the firm's principal designer, and Gee (1986) says that the key to the firm's success was the excellence of its design, word of which quickly spread; by the middle 1980s the firm was building instruments for laboratories and organizations all over the UK and beginning to take orders from abroad. '"Go and talk to Horace Darwin" was the advice given to anyone who needed some delicate new scientific instrument' (Chancellor 1973: 209). But Darwin also employed a highly sophisticated form of relational marketing, using his own and his family's scientific contacts to attract the attention of likely buyers. This was a time and a place when direct advertising was not possible; instead, Darwin made sure his firm's name was known in the market through personal contact and word of mouth. The combination of awareness and reputation for quality meant that potential purchasers of scientific instruments automatically thought first of Darwin and Cambridge Instrument.

Darwin was also the founder of the Cambridge 'cluster' of science-related industries. He believed in collaboration rather than competition, and saw the growth of rival firms as being important in both growing the market and generating new knowledge. Many of his foremen and assistants such as W.T. Pye, Robert Whipple and Henry Tinsley went to other established firms or to establish their own businesses. The development and growth of the Cambridge cluster is by no means the least of Darwin's achievements.

BIBLIOGRAPHY
Chancellor, J. (1973) *Charles Darwin*, London: Weidenfeld and Nicolson.
Gee, D. (1984) 'Darwin, Sir Horace', in D.J. Jeremy (ed.), *Dictionary of Business Biography*, London: Butterworths, vol. 2, 14–17.

MLW

DASSAULT, Marcel (1892–1986)

Marcel Dassault was born Marcel Bloch on 22 January 1892 in Paris and died there on 18 April 1986. The son of a Jewish physician, he seems to have been well educated, but his autobiography gives little detail of his early career. During the First World War, Bloch and his business partner Henri Potez built propellers for French military aircraft. At the war's end Potez carried on building aircraft, while Bloch invested in property and quickly became wealthy. In 1930 he returned to the aircraft industry, set up his own aircraft firm, competing with Potez, and built airliners and bombers for the French Air Force.

During the Second World War Bloch and his brother joined the French Resistance movement. His brother became a general in the *Francs-Tireurs et Partisans*, one of the largest resistance organizations, under the codename *Dassault*; he was captured by the Gestapo and executed. Bloch was also captured in 1944 and sent to Buchenwald concentration camp, where he survived an attack of diphtheria and Allied bombing raids. After the war, in honour of his late brother, Bloch changed his surname to Dassault. He also reportedly converted to Catholicism.

Re-establishing himself in the aircraft industry, Dassault founded the firm Avions Marcel Dassault, which quickly became France's leading military aircraft-maker. His first major success was with the Mystère, a sophisticated ground-attack aircraft (the name, he later revealed, was taken from the title of the novel *Le Docteur Mystère* by Jules Verne, his favourite author). Other now legendary military aircraft designs included the Ouragon, the Etendard and the Mirage, the latter two of which are still in service with many air forces around the world. At a time when many European aircraft-makers were going bankrupt or merging, Dassault went from strength to strength, dominating the market and remaining highly profitable. In 1967 Avions Marcel Dassault finally merged with its only major rival Breguet; Dassault himself retired in 1971. He was also involved in politics, and served as a deputy in the National Assembly from 1951–5 and then from 1958 until his death.

Dassault's postwar success was founded on two key factors: simple, effective designs and good marketing. His aircraft were not over-engineered, and did not require the sophisticated aircrew training needed to fly some contemporary American designs, for example. They also performed extremely well when it most mattered – in combat. Pilots in the Israeli Air Force favoured the Mirage over many other fighter aircraft, and many mourned the replacement of their trusty Mirages with more advanced F-4 Phantoms in the 1970s. Because the designs were simple, they were also cheap and (supported by an extremely liberal French government policy concerning arms exports) Dassault was able to sell his aircraft in many parts of the world. The arms industry is a notoriously difficult one, fraught with high entry costs and barriers, extreme regulatory and political pressures, and strong competition (not to mention ethical and moral issues). Dassault's success in this market was due in no large part to his own ability to discern and meet market needs, allied to networking skills which enabled him to keep on the right side of the relevant governments.

BIBLIOGRAPHY
Carlier, C. (1992) *Marcel Dassault: Le Légende d'un siècle*, Paris: Perrin.
Dassault, M. (1971) *Le Talisman*, Paris: Editions J'ai lui.

MLW

DATINI, Francesco (c.1335–1410)

Datini was born in Prato, Italy probably in 1335, and died there in 1410. His father, a tavern-keeper, and his mother both died of the Black Death in 1348, and Datini and his brother were raised by a foster mother. At age fourteen he went to work as an apprentice for a trader in nearby Florence, and at fifteen, using a small legacy left by his father, he travelled to Avignon, France, then the seat of the papal court and host to a thriving Italian financial and business community. Datini found work in this community, and by 1361 had accumulated enough capital to go into business on his own account. Trading first in arms and armour, by the middle 1360s he had branched out into areas as diverse as cloth, salt, furnishings and works of art. Like many small businessmen of the time, he dealt in both wholesale and retail. By 1378 he had also branched out into banking. He married Margherita Bandini, the daughter of a fellow merchant, in Avignon in 1380; the couple had no children, but they later adopted Datini's illegitimate daughter by a slave girl.

In 1382 the papacy was restored to Rome and Avignon lost some of its commercial importance. Datini returned to Prato, by now a wealthy man, and in 1382 began a further diversification, this time into manufacturing. Investing in a small woollen-cloth business, he poured in capital and greatly expanded the business. According to the terms of the partnership, Datini was to provide the capital while Niccolò di Giunta, the previous owner, provided specialist knowledge of cloth-making and its management. This sort of partnership, with one partner providing capital and the other providing knowledge and expertise, was common at the time.

In 1386 Datini began his bid to enter the lucrative but highly risky world of international trade. His first move was to Florence, where he established a series of partnerships including a retail shop and wholesale/distribution ventures in bulk commodities and luxury goods. Other ventures quickly followed: as well as Avignon, Datini established ventures in Pisa in 1382, Genoa in 1388 and Barcelona in 1392 (with branch offices in Valencia and Majorca). At the peak, Datini was the controlling partner or *capo* in eight businesses in Italy, Spain and France. Typically for the time, each venture was established as a separate partnership (although in many cases the same partner was involved with Datini in more than one venture). Partnerships were of short duration, usually only two years, at which point they were renewed, renegotiated or dissolved at the wish of the partners. Datini always remained diversified, manufacturing and trading in many different goods, a deliberate risk-reduction strategy adopted by many of his peers in a time when the risks associated with physically transporting and distributing goods were very high.

Datini's success is remarkable because, compared with the major international trading houses of his day, he had little capital and no important backers. He did, however, have a talent for gathering information. In addition to his own businesses, he had agents and correspondents in many parts of Western Europe and around the Mediterranean, and he corresponded with these frequently; he seems to have been able to read and write at least eight languages. As his business interests expanded, Datini left the day-to-day management of the branches to partners or to appointed general managers called *fattori*. His own focus was on head-office functions. He organized his own correspondence; as he once wrote to a friend, 'I would look over each of my papers and set them in order and mark them, so that I may be clear about each man with whom I have to do' (Origo 1957: 105). He also kept centralized accounts for each partnership. In the wool manufacturing business, his accounts showed both the cost of each stage of production and the consolidated final production cost, giving him exact information about the financial status of the business. His management of information was an important factor in his

success, but so too was his own ambition and vision. As Origo comments,

the fundamental distinction between the international merchant and the 'little man' did not consist in whether his trade was wholesale or retail, or even in the quantity of his merchandise, but rather in the outlook of the two different kinds of men. (Origo 1957: 89).

Datini's businesses ran into problems when a renewed outbreak of plague in 1399–1400 killed many of his trusted partners in Florence, Prato and Genoa. He closed several businesses and scaled back his activities, going into semi-retirement before his death. Remarkably, his business papers and correspondence have survived almost intact in Prato: the collection, which includes 150,000 letters, 500 account books, 300 deeds of partnership, 400 insurance policies and several thousand other documents including bills of lading, bills of exchange and cheques (Origo 1957: 11), is both testament to Datini's activity and a valuable resource for understanding fourteenth-century business and management practices.

BIBLIOGRAPHY

Istituto Internazionale di Storia economica 'F. Datini' (2000) 'The Datini Company System', http://www.istitutodatini.it/schedule/datini/eng/sistema2.htm, 14 February 2001.
Origo, I. (1957) *The Merchant of Prato*, London: Jonathan Cape.

MLW

DAVANZATI, Bernardo (1529–1606)

Bernardo Davanzati was born in Florence on 30 July 1529 and died there on 29 March 1606. A successful businessman with interests in Italy and France, he was also an important scholar who translated the works of the Roman writer Tacitus and wrote a history of the English Reformation. He wrote two works on economics, of which one, *Notizia dei cambi* (Discourse Upon Coins), was widely read; it was translated into English by John Toland in 1696. His economic thought had some influence on later writers such as William PETTY and John Locke.

In the *Notizia dei cambi*, Davanzati describes how money has evolved and the role it plays in our economy, and discusses why it is necessary for states to ensure that there is an adequate supply of money in circulation. Unusually for economic treatises of the time, however, he also discusses the role of personal preference in variations in demand. People use money, he says, 'to buy all things for the satisfaction of their wants and desires, and so to become happy' (Davanzati 1588: 13). He ascribes two motives to buyers, will and want: that is, the need to purchase, and the power to make purchases to satisfy those needs. Individual circumstances vary greatly: a thing which has little value at one time or place may have great value at another, depending on what purchasers are willing to pay.

As well as dealing with purchasers' needs and motivations, Davanzati also discusses the value of knowledge in market terms. People find it difficult, he says, to obtain knowledge of where the things they need can be purchased, and part of the function of the markets is to supply that knowledge. The most knowledgeable of all players in the market are the merchants, who know where things can be bought and sold – this is the source of their profit:

we can scarce discover those few things that are round about us, and we prize them according as we see them more or less desired at any time, or in any place: whereof the merchants do carefully inform

themselves, and for that reason they know the prices of things better than all others.
(Davanzati 1588: 14).

BIBLIOGRAPHY

Davanzati, B. (1588) *Notizia dei cambi* (Discourse Upon Coins), trans. J. Toland, 1696; http://www.socsci.mcmaster.ca/~econ/vgcm/3ll3/davanzati/coins, 17 February 2001.

Hutchison, T.W. (1988) *Before Adam Smith: The Emergence of Political Economy, 1662–1776*, Oxford: Basil Blackwell.

DAVIS, John Patterson (1862–1903)

John Patterson Davis was born in Niles, Michigan on 27 May 1862. He died in Asheville, North Carolina in early December 1903. He graduated from the University of Michigan with an AM degree in 1885 and trained as a lawyer, being called to the bar in Michigan in 1887 and then practising in Omaha, Nebraska from 1888 to 1892. Returning to the University of Michigan, he took a Ph.D. in 1894, and then taught history and economics at Michigan from 1894 to 1895. By this time his health had begun to deteriorate; he retired to Idaho in search of a better climate, devoting himself to writing and to the practice of law on a part-time basis until his final illness began.

Davis's major work, published posthumously, was *Corporations* (1905), a 600-page study of the evolution of the modern model of the corporation. His starting point was that the corporation was, at the most basic level, a social form. As such, corporations had a tendency to evolve and adapt over time: 'Like all other social forms, corporations are subject to modification: (1) internally, by the influ-ence of their content, the social activity exercised by them, and (2) externally, by the influence of other social forms and social activity' (Davis 1905: 10–11). Social forms have a close relationship with their environment and, like species in the biological world, can undergo changes through contact with other forms.

Davis also makes explicit the link between form and function, the shape an organization takes and its purpose:

Social forms and social functions are intimately interdependent. Lack of adaptation of either to the other must result in modifications in one or the other or both ... If the form, whether originally or as the result of a subsequent more or less arbitrary modification, is unsuitable for a particular function, it must be altered to conform to the character of the function, or perish – unless it be adapted or adaptable to some other social function to which it may be readily transferred.
(Davis 1905: 11)

This adaptation, Davis says, is a historical process:

Corporate forms and functions and the environment by which they are influenced are all products of time. They are all meaningless except as they register past experience or predict future social growth, stagnation or decay. They must therefore be subjected to historical treatment.
(Davis 1905: 11).

He holds that the only way to understand both *how* and *why* corporations have evolved into their present form is to deal with them historically.

This, then, is the lens through which Davis looks at corporations. He believes that each historical era develops the corporations which suit its particular needs for social forms; remarkably for a modern economic writer, he makes no judgements about the past, believing

that an evolutionary process ensures that each era has the most suitable form given its social and cultural characteristics. He traces the development of the corporation through ecclesiastical corporations (church and monasteries), the feudal system, which he sees as a corporation of sorts, municipalities, gilds, and education corporations such as the first universities. In volume 2 he goes on to more purely commercial enterprises such as regulated companies, joint-stock companies and colonial companies, coming finally to the many varieties of modern corporation which he sees as including both profit-making enterprises and non-profit bodies such as universities, charities, fraternities and lodges.

This is an important book: its second chapter remains one of the best and most succinct examinations of the corporation from a social point of view yet written, showing why we associate and how. Only now, a century later, are writers like Moore and Lewis (2001) returning to this theme and exploring the many forms that corporate organization has taken and can take.

BIBLIOGRAPHY

Davis, J.P. (1894) *The Union Pacific Railway: A Study of Political and Economic History*, Chicago: S. Griggs and Co.
—— (1897) 'The Nature of Corporations', *Political Science Quarterly* 12: 273–94.
—— (1905) *Corporations*, 2 vols, New York: G.P. Putnam's Sons.
Moore, K. and Lewis, D. (2001) *Foundations of Corporate Empire*, London: FT Prentice-Hall.

MLW

DE BONO, Edward (1933–)

Edward de Bono was born in Floriana, Malta on 19 May 1933, the son of Professor Joseph de Bono CBE and his wife Josephine. His father was a senior member of Malta's medical faculty. De Bono was educated at St Edward's College, Malta during the Second World War, and later at the Royal University of Malta, where he took his degree in medicine. He studied for an honours degree in psychology and physiology as a Rhodes Scholar at Christ Church, Oxford, and remained there to take a D.Phil. in medicine. He also has a Ph.D. from Cambridge. De Bono worked in the department of medicine at Cambridge University from 1963, first as a research assistant and then as lecturer in medicine, eventually becoming professor of investigative medicine. He is director of the Centre for the Study of Thinking, and the founder and director (1969) of the Cognitive Research Trust in Cambridge, which developed the widely popular CoRT training programme for teaching thinking as a curriculum subject in schools. He is a recent president of the UK Association of Business Executives, which aims to promote management learning. He married Josephine Hall-White in 1971; they have two sons.

De Bono is widely regarded as a major contributor to developing creativity theory and techniques. He began his work by asking whether it might be possible for people to generate new ideas on demand, rather than waiting for inspiration. He theorized that the brain makes sense of the world around it by building up patterns according to experience. This behaviour, although necessary for everyday actions and learning, has the inevitable drawback of confining people to thinking along lines long established by their own experience. De Bono's answer was to develop 'lateral thinking', a term he coined in his book *The Use of Lateral Thinking* (1967), and a concept now widely accepted and used. Lateral thinking (to distinguish from logical, or vertical thinking) concerns the way in which

people perceive the situations around them; its purpose is to generate new ideas and escape from old ones. The major principles of lateral thinking are summarized as:

1. Recognition of dominant or polarizing ideas.

2. The search for different ways of looking at things.

3. A relaxation of the rigid control of vertical thinking.

4. The use of chance and provocative methods in order to introduce discontinuity.

5. Understanding and use of the word 'Po' as an alternative to 'no' (de Bono 1971: 51).

He also distinguished the importance of the role humour plays in lateral thinking. He suggests that what will distinguish similarly energetic and educated people in future will be a superior imagination.

De Bono later applied his lateral thinking techniques to management practice in his book *Lateral Thinking for Management* (1971a), in which he shows the application of his ideas to the development of new products, and new approaches to problem solving and planning. The book emphasizes that creativity is so essential a part of management equipment that it cannot be left to chance or to the gifted amateur.

In his second major contribution, de Bono advocated the use of 'parallel thinking' as opposed to the more traditional argument or adversarial thinking promulgated by Socrates, Plato and Aristotle. This thinking, he explained, is intended only to discover the 'truth' by proving the other side wrong, and lacks a constructive or creative element. Parallel thinking, by contrast, allows all parties to think about an issue with contradictory statements accepted in parallel; these are then reviewed and the way forward is designed from the thoughts contributed. These ideas were published as *Parallel Thinking* (1971b). Much of his work was devoted to the devel-

opment of techniques using visual thinking and games to facilitate lateral thinking and parallel thinking, the most famous of which is his 'Six Hats' technique.

De Bono is also a proponent of the power of positive thinking, and has shown himself to be an implicit futurist and humanist in his writing. Although de Bono believes that the future cannot be designed as there is so much uncertainty, he notes that 'we can design our attitudes so that they are positive and flexible and will allow us to make a fuller use of the benefits which technology has provided'. He also calls for a deeper reflection on our thinking habits:

we need to consider whether we are locked into structures and concepts that prevent positive development. We have to make a deliberate and positive effort to secure a positive future. The call is to arms, not the gun and bomb, but those of the focused power of human thinking unleashed from its pettiness.

(De Bono 1979: 15).

One of de Bono's later projects, the Supranational Independent Thinking Organization (SITO), based in Malta, focuses on finding new ways to resolve conflicts. He argues that previously we have relied on the argument mode in conflict resolution, which is not effective. Instead he proposes focusing on an exploratory mapping and creative design approach.

De Bono has been an active proponent of direct teaching of thinking as a skill, and his thinking lessons are widely used throughout the world by children and adults alike. A prolific author, he has written sixty-two books, translated into thirty-seven languages. His application of creative thinking to management has undoubtedly improved both the techniques and outcomes of problem solving and innovation. Equally importantly, it also allows for the participation of the 'whole person' in the once too formal, 'scientized' discipline of management.

BIBLIOGRAPHY

Berry, N. (1992) 'The Revolutionary Implications of Edward de Bono's Lateral Thinking', *Sunday Times*, 4 October, http://www.edwdebono.com/debono/berry.htm, 15 March 2001.

de Bono, E. (1967) *The Use of Lateral Thinking*, London: Jonathan Cape.

—— (1971a) *Lateral Thinking for Management,* London: Pelican.

—— (1971b) *Parallel Thinking*, London: Viking.

—— (1979) *Future Positive*, London: Temple Smith.

—— (1983) *The Atlas of Management Thinking*, London: Penguin.

AJ

DE GEUS, Arie (1930–)

Arie de Geus was born in Rotterdam on 11 August 1930. He graduated from Erasmus University in Rotterdam with a Master's Degree in Economics. He joined the Royal Dutch/Shell Group in 1951, and spent the whole of his career there until retirement in 1989. During this period he worked in Turkey, Belgium and Brazil, and, for his last ten years with Shell, in the UK, where he was first in charge of Shell's businesses in Africa and South Asia. In 1981 he became coordinator for group planning.

From 1981 to 1988, De Geus was chairman of the Netherlands–British Chamber of Commerce. He was appointed an officer in the Order of Oranje-Nassau by the Queen of the Netherlands in 1988. In 1997 he was awarded an Honorary Doctor of Letters degree by Westminster University. Since his retirement he has advised government and private institutions and has lectured throughout the world. He is a visiting fellow at the London Business School and a board member of the Nijenrode Learning Centre in the Netherlands. Cooperating with Peter SENGE, De Geus has also been involved in the activities of the Center for Organizational Learning at the Massachusetts Institute of Technology.

A practising manager who at later stages of his career turned into a popular management theorist, De Geus achieved prominence through a handful of articles, the most important of which being 'The Living Company' (1997a). This article appeared in *Harvard Business Review*, and subsequently won the McKinsey Award. However, it was the critical acclaim and the best-selling status of his first book, *The Living Company: Habits for Survival in a Turbulent Business Environment* (1997b) that brought him a global audience and recognition as well as a number of awards.

De Geus's main contribution to organization theory is the idea of the 'learning organization' (he shares the credit for its origination and popularization with Peter Senge). The concept itself integrates an old (but increasingly popular) metaphor of the business enterprise as a living being into the modern concern for learning as the key to organizational effectiveness. Since the company is viewed as an organism with a capacity to learn, De Geus explores the analogy further by trying to determine the factors and practices that enable companies to survive and prosper over long periods of time. He argues that most corporations fail because managers are too narrowly focused on the economic activity of producing goods and services, forgetting that their organization's true nature is that of a community of humans with shared values. Moreover, as living systems interacting with their environment, companies should cultivate mutually beneficial relationships with their stakeholders and achieve a harmony of values with them. De Geus's insights correspond to the issues usually debated within the fields of organizational learning and business ethics. His prominence as an interpreter and popularizer of these ideas should not be neglected, but it remains to be

seen whether his thought will have a lasting impact on management theory and practice.

BIBLIOGRAPHY

De Geus, A. (1988) 'Planning as Learning', *Harvard Business Review* 66(2): 70–74.
—— (1997a) 'The Living Company', *Harvard Business Review* (March–April): 51–9.
—— (1997b) *The Living Company: Habits for Survival in a Turbulent Business Environment*, London: Nicholas Brealey.

DR

DE LA POLE, William (*c*.1290–1369)

The date and place of William de la Pole's birth is uncertain, although he was probably the son of a merchant from either Hull or Ravensrode in Yorkshire. He died in Hull on 21 June 1366. His principal biographer (Fryde 1988) points out that due to the family's later prominence (as dukes of Suffolk), much energy has been expended on trying to establish illustrious forbears, to no avail. His probable birth date is *c*.1290–95. Whatever his date of birth, his first appearance in official records was in 1317, when, with his brother (and business partner) Richard, he was responsible for buying the king's wine in Hull. Both brothers appear again as chamberlains of Hull. William was slightly the younger of the two de la Poles. The brothers' involvement with the royal household and the exchequer date from 1322, when they were involved in the purchase of the goods of a rebel against Edward II, and at the same time with the sale of wine to the king's household whilst he was in the north. William's partnership with his brother lasted until 1331, and they were heavily involved in the overseas wool trade out of Hull. During this time William, apparently independently, was lending money to the crown for Edward II's French campaigns in Gascony. These advances of coin amounted to some £1,800 in March 1325 and a further £31,000 in May of that year. Along with the large Italian finance houses such as the Bardi, de la Pole was acting as a major creditor to the crown. Attacks on the Bardi in 1328 benefited de la Pole; he was granted their vacant London house.

Despite their financial support for Edward II in the years before his downfall in 1327, neither of the de la Pole brothers seem to have suffered any ill effects from the political upheavals surrounding the deposition of the king and his replacement by his son, Edward III. Fryde (1988) suggests that this was because of their strong position in Hull and the importance of that town in the defence of the north against the Scots, a defence which became necessary shortly after Edward III came to the throne. Doubtless their immunity also had much to do with loans given to Edward's regents, Queen Isabella and Roger Mortimer, in the months following his accession, at a time when the Italian banks were having difficulties not only in England but also in Florence. The de la Pole family loaned nearly £5,000 to the crown in the first year of Edward III's reign. Further loans amounting to just under £1,000 were given in 1329 and 1330. The overthrow of the two regents and Edward's assertion of personal role made no difference to their relationship with the crown; indeed, Richard de la Pole was one of the only men who retained his position at court throughout the period.

The brothers' partnership was terminated in 1331; the termination itself is one of the very few of their business records to survive. The agreement mentions past quarrels but does not state the reason for the termination at this point. Certainly William had been operating on his own as a financier for much of the period of their partnership, and it may be that he wished to pursue this course whilst his brother did not. By 1331 Richard de la Pole

was firmly established in London, whilst despite his frequent and complex dealings with the exchequer and the crown, William retained his main residence in Hull. The agreement confirms that most of his business was concerned with money lending.

De la Pole's career after 1331 is intertwined with Edward III's finances and military campaigns. He was without doubt the outstanding businessman of his day in terms of the amounts of money which flowed through his hands. His nearest rival, Sir John Pulteney, was worth only a fraction of de la Pole's wealth. Fryde attributes his success to his efficiency and intelligence, but also to 'his unscrupulous, ruthlessness and remarkable capacity to bend the wills of other men to his own' (Fryde 1988: 25). The first part of this opinion is based on a study of de la Pole's accounting procedures, which were very detailed and broke down goods into precisely measured costs per unit of salt, wheat or wool. His accounts were notably better organized than those of his partner in a mid-1330s wool company, and of the royal accounts for wool exports. Clearly de la Pole was a aware of the benefits of maintaining good accounts in order to track the profitability of different commodities and different areas of business.

De la Pole also managed to buy better-quality product (notably wool) for lower prices than his contemporaries, despite or perhaps because he paid his buying agents nearly twice as much commission as others. Furthermore, he employed a larger number of agents than did other merchants. His position in Hull, within easy reach of large quantities of wool, was enviable; he seldom went further than north Lincolnshire or North Yorkshire for his wool supplies, thereby reducing transport costs. His shipments of wool seem also to have suffered less damage in transit than did those of others, perhaps because of his influence over the placement of his goods on board the ships. He preferred to store wool in the Low Countries, where the buyers were located and where warehousing costs were lower than in Hull. De la

Pole did not even own any warehousing in Hull, nor did he own more than a very few ships, preferring to use his influence to negotiate low prices with captains and landlords, and to leave his working capital liquid. Economies of scale and superior organizational ability were clearly key factors in his success.

In addition to his mercantile activities, there is good evidence that de la Pole was making considerable sums by speculating on the gold market at a time (in the late 1330s) when the value of gold was rising rapidly. England did not itself have a gold coinage, only a silver one, so de la Pole must have been heavily involved in European money markets.

For all his success as a merchant and currency speculator, however, it is for his activities as a royal banker that de la Pole is best known. Apart from the Italian banking houses, de la Pole was the largest of Edward III's creditors throughout the 1330s and for much of the 1340s. The large sums lent were not his alone, but rather sourced from many private individuals who used him as a secure outlet for investment. Merchants from the north certainly trusted him to lend money on the expectation of profit, as did some London merchants such as Pultneey. De la Pole's primary value to the crown during a period of very heavy expenditure in the opening years (1338–45) of the Hundred Years' War may have been his ability to conjure up sums of money from a wide variety of sources at short notice and thereby provide the quick injections of cash so necessary to Edward III's government and army. There is reason to believe that he was also a repository for the money of many lay magnates and ecclesiastics, as well as from foreign businessmen. The reasons for his pre-eminence as royal banker are not clear, but certainly personal ability and reputation were contributing factors. The scale of his money-lending activities can be judged by the sums dispersed to the crown in the period June 1338–October 1339, which can be conservatively estimated at £199,000 (the annual tax revenues of the kingdom of England were about one-third of that value).

The result of such complex and crucial financial arrangements with the crown lead to an uneasy relationship between de la Pole and his royal debtor. In 1339, at the height of de la Pole's influence, he was knighted and made one the barons of the exchequer, but just a year or so later, during a political and administrative crisis, he (and several other similar merchants) were arrested and jailed. Although de la Pole emerged from this affair relatively unscathed, and resumed both his mercantile and banking activities, he was again charged and tried on a number of counts in the early 1350s.

The crown's reliance on de la Pole's money caused eventual resentment and a lingering suspicion that the Hull merchant was gaining excessive profits at the crown's expense. After much negotiation de la Pole emerged from the 1353–4 court case with a pardon for his activities, but with his reputation damaged and some of his debts unpaid. He was no doubt associated in the king's mind with a period when his financial embarrassments and the level of his debts precipitated a major political crisis. It is hardly surprising that his major creditor of those years should fall from grace. There is little doubt that de la Pole emerged from all his royal banking a richer, rather than a poorer, man.

The last 12 to 14 years of de la Pole's life were spent largely removed from the financial centre of activity. He continued to trade in wool (often illegally) until the 1360s, and in the last five years of his life expended some time and energy in trying to establish a convent of Poor Clare nuns in Hull. This plan did not come to fruition and, many years after his death, he was finally buried before the altar of the church of St Michael in a Carthusian convent founded by his son, Michael. All of de la Pole's personal wealth was passed on to his son (apart from his wife's dower). Over the decades he had built up a portfolio of land outside Hull and this property laid the foundations of the family estate, and his money and property would later propel the family into the nobility of England.

BIBLIOGAPHY

'De la Pole, William' (1885) in L. Stephen and S. Lee (eds), *Dictionary of National Biography*, London: Small, Elder and Co., vol. 46, 48–50.

Fryde, E.B. (1988) *William de la Pole, Merchant and King's Banker (d. 1366)*, London: The Hambledon Press.

ML

DELL, Michael (1965–)

Michael Dell was born in Houston, Texas on 23 February 1965. He was raised in an upper middle-class neighbourhood in West Houston; his father worked as an orthodontist, while his mother was a stockbroker. As he grew up he listened intently as his parents discussed interest rates and stocks around the family dinner table, which gave him insights into issues involving money. At the age of eight, he applied for a high school equivalency diploma from the back of a magazine, hoping to shortcut the system by eliminating the middleman – the school. By the age of twelve, he had earned $2,000 running a mail-order stamp-trading business.

The success with stamps and other money-making ventures gave Dell a strong sense of entrepreneurship. By the age of sixteen he had figured out a way to turn his summer job selling subscriptions to the *Houston Post* into a highly profitable venture, which netted him $18,000. He realized that targeting newlyweds and new homeowners with personalized letters led to a greater percentage of successful subscriptions. When one of Dell's high school teachers assigned the class the task of filling out a tax return, she was chagrined to find out her student made more money than she did that year.

Although Dell demonstrated a keen understanding of money, his worldview really changed when his parents let him buy his first computer, an Apple II, when he was fifteen years old. The computer was a natural progression for Dell. He had been fascinated with computing and maths since the age of seven, when he bought his first calculator. The first thing he did when he got his computer home was to take it apart to figure out exactly how it worked. As with stamps, Dell realized that his hobby could also be a business opportunity.

Quickly learning about both computers and the nascent computer industry, Dell believed that he could provide better customer service at a competitive price in relation to the computer stores popping up around Houston. Actually, from his perspective, the people working in the computer stores knew relatively little about computers, which they considered simply another big ticket item with a large sales mark-up. Dell began buying upgrade parts, such as memory chips, disk drives and faster modems, and installing them himself in IBM computers. He then sold the computers to people he knew for a tidy profit – all this while still a high school student.

Dell continued to rebuild computers while attending the University of Texas at Austin. While his parents hoped he would follow in his older brother's footsteps and study medicine, he remained focused on the idea of upgrading and selling computers. He recalled the day he left for school: 'I drove off in the white BMW that I had bought with my earnings from selling newspaper subscriptions, with three computers in the backseat of the car. My mother should have been very suspicious' (Dell 1999: 9).

Dell set up shop at the University of Texas and word spread quickly about his computer services. Businesspeople from Austin would trek up to his dorm room on the twenty-seventh floor and drop off or pick up computers. Dell even applied for a vendor's licence to take advantage of the open government bidding process in the state of Texas. Since

Dell had no overheads, he won many bids and dramatically increased revenues. Soon the computer business took up more of Dell's time than his classes. After getting word that his grades were dropping, Dell's parents showed up in Austin for a surprise visit. They called him from the airport to let him know they were in town, which barely gave Dell enough time to hide all the excess computer parts behind the shower curtain in his room-mate's bathroom.

In January 1984 Dell returned to Austin and formally set up a company called PCs Limited. Through word of mouth and an advertisement in the classified section of the local newspaper, Dell sold between $50,000 and $80,000 a month of upgraded computers, kits and components to customers in the Austin area. He left the dorm room and rented a two-bedroom apartment that could accommodate the thriving business. Several months later, Dell incorporated the company as 'Dell Computer Corporation', doing business as PC Limited. The fee to capitalize a company in Texas was $1,000; this was the total amount invested in the fledgling company, and a figure now part of Dell corporate lore.

Soon the business outgrew both the apartment and his parent's wishes for Dell to become a doctor. He dropped out of school after his freshman year and moved his company to a 1,000-square-foot office space in North Austin. Spurred on by the success of Apple and IBM, the personal computer industry exploded in the mid-1980s. Demand far outstripped the available supply. Dell refurbished IBM models, but realized that truly to revolutionize the industry his company would have to produce its own computers. He paid a local engineer $2,000 to build Dell's first 286 model. The company continued to grow at a startling rate, and in 1985 moved into a 30,000-square-foot building, but stayed there only two years before outgrowing that facility as well.

From his earliest days in business, Dell followed the 'direct model', which meant that

the company built the types of computer people wanted and sold them directly to the public, also referred to as 'built to order'. The beauty of the direct model was that it eliminated resellers who marked up the cost of systems and added no value to the selling process beyond serving as a middleman in the system. This model of business allowed Dell to set the prices it charged for computers, and also made the entire production process more efficient. The cost of selling products in the computer industry averaged approximately 12 per cent of revenue, but Dell cut this figure down to 4–6 per cent. Internally, Dell also carried little extra inventory, usually eleven days of product, which eliminated the high costs associated with carrying excessive overheads; a marked difference from other manufacturers, who were forced to add additional cost to the overall price to pay for the overhead. 'While other companies had to guess which products their customers wanted, because they built them in advance of taking an order', Dell explained, 'we knew because our customers told us before we built the product' (Dell 1999: 22). Added together, the combination of high profit margins and low costs fuelled Dell's early success and solidified the advantage of the direct model.

In Dell's first eight years the company grew at an astonishing 80 per cent annually, then slowed slightly to 55 per cent. By the end of 1986, Dell's sales had hit $60 million. In comparison, by 2000 revenues had reached $32 billion. Initially Dell was viewed as a quirky upstart in the computer manufacturing industry, but the giants started to take notice of the band of rogues down in Austin. Companies such as Compaq, Hewlett-Packard and Gateway all tried to mimic Dell's built-to-order philosophy, but faced the problem of eliminating middleman who were firmly in place. This was never a problem which Dell had to worry about. His company delivered on the promises it made to customers, which fuelled greater customer loyalty, brand strength and a lower customer acquisition cost.

Dell's success is built on relationships with both customers and suppliers. Taking the lead in adopting new technological innovations, Dell set itself apart by moving to the Web and doing so profitably.

While it has become apparent that many companies have not been able to figure out how to use the Internet to their advantage, especially after the Nasdaq meltdown in 2000, Dell has been an e-commerce success story. In 1994 Dell launched its Web site with functionality that allowed users to calculate the cost of various configurations. Dell said:

As I saw it, the Internet offered a logical extension of the direct model, creating even stronger relationships with our customers. The Internet would augment conventional telephone, fax, and face-to-face encounters, and give our customers the information they wanted faster, cheaper, and more efficiently.

(Dell 1999: 91).

Internally, Dell utilized the Web to create efficient logistics and distribution systems. The company used the Internet and information technology to reduce obstacles to the flow of information, and to simplify various critical business processes. They allowed customers and suppliers inside the company through Internet browsers to share information and build a virtually integrated organization, linked by information. Since customers could order computers to their exact specifications via the site, it made the entire process more cost-effective. 'The Internet for us is a dream come true,' Dell explained. 'It's like zero-variable-cost transaction. The only thing better would be mental telepathy' (Dearlove and Coomber 2001: 54–5). By December 1996, the first year the company sold via the Internet, Dell's online sales had reached $1 million a day. Two years later, the company boasted Web sales of more than $12 million a day.

Dell himself began an internal Internet evangelism programme, going so far as to dress up

like the famous Second World War Uncle Sam recruitment poster with the caption, 'Michael wants YOU to know the Net' (Dell 1999: 95). He took the lead on the internal campaign so that every Dell employee would understand how the Internet could transform business, especially as it related to the Dell direct model. Today, roughly 50 per cent of Dell's sales are Web-enabled.

One of Michael Dell's strengths is the ability to interpret new trends and find ways to turn them into business advantages. Understanding the pervasive nature of the Internet led Dell to branch out beyond PCs and begin building Web-related products such as servers and storage devices. Dell has also nearly perfected the just-in-time process, so that 84 per cent of orders are built, customized and shipped within eight hours.

Over the last couple of years, Dell's stock has been hit by a worldwide slowdown in PC sales, and uncertainty regarding the American economy, especially after the Nasdaq downturn in early 2000. Dell set the bar so high in terms of growth that otherwise phenomenal growth rates look paltry compared to earlier statistics. In fiscal 2001 Dell grew at 25 per cent, a remarkable figure for most companies, but not for one that grew 59 per cent only three years earlier. Suddenly analysts wondered if the Dell rose had lost its bloom. However, Dell is still the market leader in desktop sales, laptops and workstations.

Critics claim that Dell cannot keep up the pace the company set in the 1990s. But Dell himself fights back. According to business writer Betsy Morris, 'Michael Dell portrays his company as the good guy, the Robin Hood going into battle on behalf of its customers against the bad guys: price gougers with fancy offices and corporate perks and silly old ways of doing things' (Morris 2000: 95). There have been missteps in the history of Dell, such as miscalculating the importance of laptops, but each challenge has brought out new skills in Dell and proven his leadership all over again.

Perhaps Dell's strongest management trait is developing a corporate culture that places the company in continuous growth mode, like a living organism. Under Dell, the company constantly adapts and changes to meet customer needs. Flexibility, speed and information are ingrained components of the Dell corporate DNA. In addition, given all the success Dell has had in the last two decades of the twentieth century, including becoming the youngest CEO of a Fortune 500 company ever, it is easy to overlook the fact that he is still under forty years old and one of the richest men in the world (net worth estimated at $16 billion).

BIBLIOGRAPHY

Dearlove, D. and Coomber, S. (2001) *Architects of the Business Revolution*, Milford, CT: Capstone.
Dell, M. (1999) *Direct from Dell: Strategies that Revolutionized an Industry*, New York: HarperBusiness.
Morris, B. (2000) Can Michael Dell Escape the Box?, *Fortune* (October): 93–110.
Serwer, A. (1998) Michael Dell Rocks, *Fortune* (May): 58.

BPB

DELOITTE, William Welch (1818–98)

William Welch Deloitte was born in London in 1818 and died there on 23 August 1898. Little is known of his background or early life, but he appears to have established his own accountancy practice on Basinghall Street, London by 1845, specializing in insolvencies (his offices were located conveniently close to the bankruptcy courts). To Deloitte goes credit for the practice, now enshrined in law in most countries, of having company accounts examined by external auditors. In 1849 Deloitte, who had gained a reputation for probity and ability,

was approached by the shareholder-auditors of Great Western Railway to assist them in preparing the company's accounts, at a time when the company was undergoing some financial difficulties. Deloitte performed his task so well that both the shareholders and directors were impressed enough not only to appoint him their permanent auditor, but to recommend that the practice of having external auditors be adopted in law.

Over the second half of the nineteenth century, Deloitte continued to be in demand as external auditor for large companies, especially in transportation and engineering. His own business grew and he took on a large number of staff, although unusually for an accountant of his time he rarely took in partners. He continued to be an innovator in accounting practice, developing the double-account system for auditing railway companies (this again was adopted in law as standard practice) and also devising a standard system of hotel accounts. He was called in to investigate several major frauds, again mostly in railway and steamship companies. By the time of his retirement in 1897 he was the most high-profile accountant in Europe. He left behind a number of accounting and auditing methods which have had lasting impact on management reporting and control. The firm he founded is today part of the global accounting and consulting business, Deloitte Touche Ross.

DEMING, William Edwards (1900–93)

W. Edwards Deming was born in Sioux City Iowa on 14 October 1900 and died at his home in Washington, DC on 20 December 1993. His early life was hard. The family farm in Wyoming was unsuccessful, and Deming began working at odd jobs while still a young child to help his family. He received an engineering degree in 1921 from the University of Wyoming and continued his education at the University of Colorado, where he obtained a master's degree in mathematics and physics in 1924. Deming went on to receive a Ph.D. in mathematical physics from Yale University in 1928. However, it was two summers of employment between Yale academic terms that provided what his leading biographer described as one of the most formative experiences of Deming's early career (Gabor 1990: 41). Deming worked as a student intern at the Hawthorne factory of Western Electric Company, a subsidiary of American Telephone and Telegraph (later AT&T) in Chicago. The plant employed 46,000 people, who assembled telephones.

Deming's stay at Hawthorne coincided with the beginning of research there on worker motivation by Elton MAYO and Fritz ROTHLISBERGER that became known as the Hawthorne Investigations (although Deming later insisted that he was unaware of the research while there: Gabor 1990: 42). Deming's experiences at Hawthorne were generally unpleasant. The reality of factory work was evidently a shock. According to Gabor, because of his frontier upbringing, 'Deming had no frame of reference for the demeaning drudgery the workers at the Hawthorne plant had to endure' (Gabor 1990: 42). Hawthorne probably helped shape Deming's dislike of American management and sympathy for American workers. But Hawthorne was also important to Deming in a positive way: it marked his exposure to the work of Walter Shewhart, of American Telephone and Telegraph Laboratories in statistical quality control (SQC).

SQC originated from agricultural research done by Britain's Sir Ronald Fisher. Research into better crop-growing methods was hampered because of the limited number of observations that could be done, due to the length of the growing season. Fisher developed statistical sampling techniques that enabled identification of interactions between multiple variables in crop growing, using a

small number of observations. Fisher's work captured the attention of Shewhart, who was working on industrial quality control problems for Western Electric. Shewhart developed statistical sampling methods that identified variations in the quality of manufactured products. Prior to Shewhart, quality control depended upon inspection after manufacture, based on the TAYLOR's theories (Main 1994: 58–9).

The actual tools of SQC are fairly simple. They begin with the statistical control chart, developed by Shewhart, which measures variations in a process through sampling. Shewhart, and later JURAN, distinguished between 'random' and 'assignable' causes for variation; Deming used the phrases 'common' and 'special' causes for the same concepts (Deming 1986: chap. 11). For Deming, faults (variations) inherent in the system, are 'common'; faults (variations) from transient events are 'special' (Deming 1986: 314). Common or random causes are part of the production process, while transient or assignable causes are identifiable. It is important to be able to distinguish between the two because special causes can be removed through SQC while common causes can only be removed through improving the process itself. This insight was the foundation of Deming's theory of management. The central problem of management was to understand variation. Deming believed that 94 per cent of variation was common (systemic), and thus the responsibility of management, and 6 per cent was special. Thus, management bore the greatest responsibility, and 'the production worker [should be held] responsible only for what he can govern' (Deming 1986: 315).

After receiving his Ph.D. Deming went to work first for the US Agriculture Department, and then the Census Bureau in Washington, DC. Shewhart became both a friend and a mentor, and while in government service, Deming also spent a year in London studying statistical theory under Sir Ronald Fisher. During the 1930s Deming established himself as an authority in statistical sampling theory.

Deming first came to national attention in the United States during the Second World War. He played an important role in teaching SQC to some 2,000 engineers and industrialists involved in military production. In turn, this group went on to teach more than 30,000 others (Boardman 1994: 184). Despite the impact of SQC on American military production, Deming was dissatisfied with what he felt was a serious misapplication of what he and others were teaching. As he put it, 'brilliant applications attracted much attention, but the flare of statistical methods by themselves, in an atmosphere in which management did not know their responsibilities, burned, sputtered, fizzled and died out' (Deming 1986: 487). Following the war Deming joined the faculty of the school of business at New York University. Although angered by what he perceived as disinterest on the part of American management in SQC, he maintained an active consulting practice in statistics with a steady stream of US clients. In 1946 he became a founding member of the American Society for Quality Control. He also consulted for foreign governments regarding applications of statistical sampling to census taking. It was one such assignment that first brought him to Japan.

According to Professor William Tsutsui's incisive study of Deming and the quality movement in Japan (Tsutsui 1996), which draws extensively upon Japanese language sources, Japanese concern for industrial quality predated Deming's arrival. SQC became known in Japan in the 1930s, although it was not systematically applied by Japanese industry prior to 1945, when it was brought to Japan by the American military occupation authorities, the Supreme Commander, Allied Powers (SCAP). American telecommunications engineers assigned to SCAP were detailed to train Japanese engineers so that radios and telecommunications equipment could be mass produced in Japan, to assist in rebuilding the national communications infrastructure. During 1949–50 the engineers conducted

training courses and wrote a textbook on production management. Some of the students in these courses later became leaders of companies such as Matsushita, Fujitsu and Sony (Wren and Greenwood 1998: 207–8). At the same time, the Union of Japanese Scientists and Engineers (JUSE), through its Quality Control Research Group, began offering training seminars in quality techniques (Tsutsui 1996: 305–307).

Deming himself first visited Japan in 1947, at SCAP's invitation, as part of a team of statisticians involved in preparing for the 1951 Japanese census. He travelled throughout Japan and developed an admiration for the country and its people. Through the work of the SCAP production management experts, Japanese engineers and industrialists had become familiar with Shewhart's work, including a book of lectures by Shewhart that Deming had edited. When the SCAP experts returned to the United States, Deming was invited to return to Japan by JUSE to lecture on quality control.

Contrary to legend, Deming's 1950 lectures to Japanese executives and engineers did not involve exposition of what Deming called the 'fourteen points' that formed the basis of his management philosophy (Tsutsui 1996: 309–10; Noguchi 1995: 42). Rather, the lectures to engineers, given as eight-day courses, explained basic SQC principles, including sampling, statistical control charts and Shewhart's 'Plan, Do, Check, Act' cycle, later known in Japan as the 'Deming cycle'. Deming's lectures to top management emphasized the importance of product quality as the key to developing export markets for Japanese products. Deming also stressed to management that quality is meaningless except in reference to whether a product meets customers' needs, and the importance of listening to the customer to ascertain those needs.

Deming's lectures were well attended and well received by both engineers and leading executives. JUSE published a Japanese translation and an English edition of the lectures.

Deming generously donated the royalties to JUSE, which established the Deming prize in his honour in 1951. Within a decade this prize had become, in Tsutsui's words, 'the premier corporate accolade in Japan' (Tsutsui 1996: 309), and a valuable source of publicity for JUSE and the quality movement. Deming returned to Japan in 1951 and 1952 to conduct courses in SQC and market research. Although he travelled to Japan many times thereafter, particularly in connection with Deming prize events, the 1952 courses were the last that he taught there. The Emperor of Japan decorated Deming in 1960.

Although the legend propagated by the American media tells a different story, Deming was neither the only nor the most important American influence on Japan's postwar industrial resurgence. Noguchi Junji, who was a senior member of JUSE and an admirer of Deming, wrote that 'Deming's great legacy was that he opened the way for quality control by statistical methods in Japan' (Noguchi 1995: 36). However, Noguchi and other observers credited Joseph Juran with having a greater influence on Japanese quality management (Tsutsui 1996: 317–9; Green 1992: 17). At the same time, Tsutsui is correct in crediting Deming with an important role as symbolizing, for Japan's fledgling quality movement, the ideal of quality and the imperative for management reform (Tsutsui 1996: 324–5).

The 24 June 1980 NBC television documentary, *If Japan Can, Why Can't We?* presented a different version of events, however. America had faced many shocks during the 1970s, but perhaps none more serious to US business confidence than the capture of American markets by Japanese imported products, especially automobiles and home electronics. The television programme was the first attempt to explain Japanese industrial success to the American public. However, many American multinational companies were already very familiar with their Japanese counterparts through US–Japanese joint ventures

operating in Japan, such as Xerox/Fuji Xerox and Hewlett-Packard/Yokogawa, as well as through the more painful experience of having to compete in the US against Japanese products that American consumers regarded as being superior in quality. Delegations from Ford and General Motors, among other companies, had visited Japan in the 1970s in search of answers. *If Japan Can, Why Can't We?* offered a simple explanation, one which met a favourable reception in America.

Deming had returned to teaching at NYU, and maintained a consulting practice that, at the time of the NBC programme had one US business client, Nashua Corporation. The producers of the documentary somehow learned of Deming, and first interviewed him at his Washington, DC home. Deming was then featured during the final portion of the actual broadcast. While Gabor's 1990 biography simply states that the program 'touted Deming's role in the revival of Japanese industry' (Gabor 1990: 223), Deming's rival Juran (who, according to his biographer, was also invited to appear on the programme, but declined; Butman 1997: 164) was more specific. In Juran's words:

In 1980 there emerged a widely viewed videocast, 'If Japan Can, Why Can't We?' It concluded that Japanese quality was due to their use of statistical methods taught to them by Deming. This conclusion had little relation to reality; however the program was cleverly presented and was persuasive to many viewers.

(Juran quoted in Tsutsui 1996: 323)

Tsutsui concludes that there is ample historical justification for Juran's contention, even though business rivalry may have been involved, since Deming and Juran were consulting competitors. Regardless, the television programme offered an appealing explanation to Americans troubled by Japan's business prowess: the Japanese were so effective because Deming, an American, had taught them to be.

By extension, American companies could do what the Japanese had done by listening to Deming.

Deming's message of commitment to quality was delivered to an American corporate audience that was prepared to be receptive. The basic precept of total quality management (TQM), that quality is the responsibility of everyone in an organization, had been articulated by Dr Armand Feigenbaum of US General Electric in his 1950 book, *Total Quality Control*. Philip CROSBY's book *Quality is Free* (1979), published a year prior to the NBC programme, had been a bestseller. Following the broadcast, demand for Deming's consulting services exploded. Major US corporations, first Ford, then General Motors, Dow Chemical, Florida Power and Light (later, the first American company to win the Deming prize) and others became clients. Deming also began offering four-day seminars, sponsored by a variety of organizations, at which he expounded his philosophy of management. He would continue offering these seminars until a few days before his death.

Deming's philosophy of management is encapsulated in his 'fourteen points for management', set forth in Deming (1986: 23–4). They are:

1. Create constancy of purpose toward improvement of product and service, with the aim to be competitive and to stay in business and to provide jobs.

2. Adopt the new philosophy. We are in a new economic age. Western management must awaken to the challenge, must learn their responsibilities, and take on leadership for change.

3. Cease dependence on inspection to achieve quality. Eliminate the need for inspection on a mass basis by building quality into the product in the first place.

4. End the practice of awarding business on the basis of price tag. Instead, minimize total cost. Move toward a single supplier

for any one item, on a long-term relationship of loyalty and trust.

5. Improve constantly and forever the system of production and service, to improve quality and productivity, and thus constantly decrease cost.

6. Institute training on the job.

7. Institute leadership. The aim of supervision should be to help people and machines and gadgets to do a better job. Supervision of management is in need of overhaul, as well as supervision of production workers.

8. Drive out fear, so that everyone may work effectively for the company.

9. Break down barriers between departments. People in research, design, sales and production must work as a team, to foresee problems of production and in use that may be encountered with the product or service.

10. Eliminate slogans, exhortations and targets for the work force, asking for zero defects and new levels of productivity. Such exhortations only create adversarial relationships, as the bulk of the causes of low quality and low productivity belong to the system and thus lie beyond the power of the work force.

11. a. eliminate work standards (quotas) on the factory floor. Substitute leadership.

b. eliminate management by objective. Eliminate management by numbers, numerical goals. Substitute leadership.

12. a. remove barriers that rob the hourly worker of his right to pride of workmanship. The responsibility of supervisors must be changed from sheer numbers to quality.

b. remove barriers that rob people in management and in engineering of their right to pride of workmanship. This means, *inter alia*, abolishment of the annual or merit rating and of management by objective.

13. Institute a vigorous program of education and self improvement.

14. Put everybody in the company to work to accomplish the transformation. The transformation is everybody's job.

The fourteen points express familiar ideas and concepts. Deming disciples would argue that this is because Deming's management philosophy has been widely accepted, but Duncan and Van Matre (1990) and Vastag (2000), among others, have noted that little in Deming's philosophy is really new. Gabor relates that ISHIKAWA Kaoru, a leader in the Japanese total quality control (TQC) movement, asserted that Deming had borrowed many of the ideas for his fourteen points from Japanese TQC and from Juran (Gabor 1990: 98). Duncan and Van Matre (1990: 5) point out that the only one of the fourteen points that is at odds with traditional management prescriptions is Deming's hostility to quantitative goal-setting. This is ironic, because an important difference between Deming's management philosophy and Japanese TQC is that in Japanese TQC managers set all manner of numeric targets, including targets that serve a motivational function only (Gitlow 1994: 202).

Whether or not Deming's philosophy was original, what impact did it have on contemporary American management? Extensive descriptions of Deming's work with American companies may be found in Gabor (1990, 2000a). She has characterized Deming's legacy at Ford as 'complicated' (Gabor 2000a: 195). This characterization is appropriate in describing the difficulty in specifying Deming's influence at companies where he worked. At Ford, he is credited with helping direct the company's focus towards customer satisfaction, and in influencing changes in Ford's goals and values, but he was unsuccessful in getting the company to abandon pay-for-performance reward systems (Gabor 2000a: 195–6). Nashua Corporation subsequently suffered serious financial problems through unsuccessful diversification, and chose not to replace the executive in charge of quality, a Deming disciple,

when he retired. Florida Power and Light, the first American company to win the Deming Prize, thereafter changed its emphasis on quality when it changed CEOs (Main 1994: 198–209). An intensive survey of TQM deployment at forty-four leading US companies, including Ford and General Motors, disclosed that Crosby was more influential than either Deming or Juran, and that those companies that claimed to be following Deming's teachings adopted an approach to quality that emphasized SQC (Easton and Jarrell 2000: 102–107). Another study found Crosby, Deming and Juran to have largely similar approaches, and that companies often combined elements of all three to meet company-specific needs (Snyder *et al.* 1994: 46–7). But if Deming's impact on management practice was limited, this would appear to have been, at least partially, a self-imposed limitation. As Gabor observed, Deming created a personality cult, demanding absolute loyalty from his followers and taking on as clients only those companies in which top management showed itself willing to adopt his philosophy; a philosophy that required unquestioned acceptance of all of its tenets (Gabor 1990: 14, 186–7).

By the time of his death, Deming had attained a public status that transcended celebrity. He was lionized by the American media; an American magazine article that listed nine people or events that had changed the world began with the Apostle Paul and ended with Deming (Crainer 2000). One element of the Deming legend credited him with Japan's extraordinary industrial resurgence following the Second World War. The title of his biography hailed him as 'the man who discovered quality' (Gabor 1990). His accomplishments in research, teaching and popularization of SQC are significant. He wrote several major books and hundreds of articles on statistical theory and practice. His influence in raising awareness of the importance of quality in business was considerable; an estimated 50,000 people attended his four-day seminars on quality

(Boardman 1994: 181). However, his actual accomplishments have become overshadowed by others' versions of those accomplishments. Despite his claim to have developed a profound system of knowledge that would remain useful for 100 years, his original contributions to management theory and practice remain difficult to identify.

In an article published on the hundredth anniversary of Deming's birth, Gabor observed that Deming's name has been all but forgotten in management but that the quality movement he helped inspire is very much alive. This is both a fitting and accurate epitaph (Gabor 2000b).

BIBLIOGRAPHY

Boardman, T.J. (1994) 'W. Edwards Deming, 1990–93', *The American Statistician* 48(3): 179–87.

Butman, J. (1997) *Juran, A Lifetime of Influence*, New York: John Wiley.

Crainer, S. (2000) *The Management Century*, San Francisco: Jossey-Bass.

Crosby, P. (1979) *Quality is Free*, New York: McGraw-Hill.

Deming, W.E. (1986) *Out of the Crisis*, Cambridge, MA: MIT Center for Advanced Engineering Study.

—— (1993) *The New Economics for Industry, Government, Education*, Cambridge, MA: MIT Center for Advanced Engineering Study.

Duncan, W.J. and Van Matre, J.G. (1990) 'The Gospel According to Deming: Is It Really New?', *Business Horizons* (July–August): 3–9.

Easton, G.S. and Jarrell, S.L. (2000) 'Patterns in the Deployment of Total Quality Management', in R.E. Cole and W.R. Scott (eds), *The Quality Movement and Organization Theory*, Thousand Oaks, CA: Sage, 89–130.

Feigenbaum, A. (1950) *Total Quality Control*, 3rd edn, New York: McGraw-Hill, 1991.

Gabor, A. (1990) *The Man Who Discovered*

Quality, New York: Times Books.

—— (2000a) *The Capitalist Philosophers*, New York: Times Books.

—— (2000b) 'He Made America Think About Quality', *Fortune* (30 October): 292–3.

Gitlow, H.S. (1994) 'A Comparison of Japanese Total Quality Control and Deming's Theory of Management', *The American Statistician* 48(3): 197–203.

Green, C. (1992) *The Quality Imperative: A Business Week Guide*, New York: McGraw-Hill.

Kilian, C.S. (1994) *The World of W. Edwards Deming*, 2nd edn, Knoxville, TN: SPC Press.

Main, J. (1994) *Quality Wars: A Juran Institute Report*, New York: The Free Press.

Noguchi J. (1995) 'The Legacy of W. Edwards Deming', *Quality Progress* 28(12): 35–43.

Snyder, N.H., Dowd, J.J, Jr and Houghton, D.M. (1994) *Vision, Values and Courage: Leadership for Quality Management*, New York: The Free Press.

Tsutsui, W.M. (1996) 'W. Edwards Deming and the Origins of Quality Control in Japan', *Journal of Japanese Studies* 22(2): 295–325.

Vastag, G. (2000) 'W. Edwards Deming', in M.M. Helms (ed.), *The Encyclopedia of Management*, 4th edn, Detroit: Gale, 191–6.

Wren, D.A. and Greenwood, R.G. (1998) *Management Innovators*, New York: Oxford University Press.

STR

DEMOSTHENES of Athens (384 BC–322 BC)

The story of Demosthenes' life was set down by the writer Plutarch around AD 75. Modern historians consider Plutarch's account often inaccurate, but nevertheless it does relate some basic facts. Demosthenes was the son of an Athenian merchant by the same name who operated a sword factory. In 377 BC, his father died, and the young Demosthenes was swindled out of his inheritance by his guardians.

One day the guardians brought the boy Demosthenes to a public trial. When Demosthenes heard the orator Callistratus speak, he was, records Plutarch, inspired to become an orator himself, despite his lack of formal schooling. When he first spoke in the Assembly, he was derided for his lack of confidence, but eventually he became the most powerful orator in Athens and many of his speeches have been preserved. Being what one would today describe as a nationalist, Demosthenes turned his rhetoric against the commercial ethic which he saw as corrupting Athens and weakening her in the impending struggle with Philip of Macedon (359 BC–336 BC).

Demosthenes was one of the earliest critics of a market mentality not yet codified into an ideology. Many Athenians no longer farmed but made their living by trading in pottery, metals and other goods. Witnessing the everyday hagglings and deals in the central market-place, Demosthenes denounced a society in which politics and justice were reduced to commerce and commerce was reduced to war. He was one of the first explicitly to compare business with warfare. In his oration 'Against the Crown', Demosthenes described how the buyer defeated the seller whenever he bought something, but the seller who refused a bribe was a winner over the buyer. Demosthenes' metaphors worked on the assumption that 'in commercial exchange there were winners and losers, just as in battles and bribery' (Reden 1995: 120).

The anger of Demosthenes highlighted the unravelling of the consensus that made history's first free market society work so admirably in the fifth century BC. Victor Davis Hanson (1995) described Greece as a society of egalitarian farmers who adapted themselves to a business economy filled with immigrants and slaves. Money could now be made in banking, trading, mining and manufacturing. Athens became democratized, turning to trade and empire for subsistence. In the new money economy, the rich tended to become richer and the poor poorer, but these disparities were mitigated in the fifth century BC by a social safety net and a maritime economy. The defeat of Athens in the terrible Peloponnesian War with Sparta and the loss of empire produced a leaner and harsher market society and a decline in civic patriotism not unlike that found in Britain or America in the 1990s.

BIBLIOGRAPHY

Davies, J.K. (1993) *Democracy and Classical Greece*, 2nd edn, Cambridge, MA: Harvard University Press.

Hanson, V.D. (1995) *The Other Greeks: The Family Farm and the Agrarian Roots of Western Civilization*, New York: The Free Press.

Moore, K. and Lewis, D. (1999) *Birth of the Multinational: 2000 Years of Ancient Business History from Ashur to Augustus*, Copenhagen: Copenhagen Business School Press.

Plutarch (1985) *Plutarch's Lives: Demosthenes and Cicero, Alexander and Caesar*, trans. B. Perrin, Cambridge, MA: Harvard University Press.

Reden, S. von (1995) *Exchange in Ancient Greece*, London: Duckworth.

DCL

DENG Xiaopeng (1904–97)

Deng Xiaopeng was born Deng Xixian, the son of a minor local official, on 12 July 1904 in the village of Baifang, in the southwest of Sichuan province in Western China. He died in Beijing on 19 February 1997, of a combination of respiratory problems and Parkinson's disease. In 1920, at the age of sixteen, Deng travelled to France to study. He lived in France for most of the next six years, working as a labourer to support himself while studying. In 1922 he joined the Communist Party of China, which had been founded the previous year in Shanghai. In 1926 he travelled briefly to Moscow before returning to China, changing his name to Deng Xiaopeng. He married three times; his first wife died in childbirth, and his second deserted him following an ideological dispute within the party. His third and lasting marriage was to Zhuo Lin in 1939; they had five children.

Deng was a prominent supporter of MAO Zedong during the Long March of 1934–5 and the years of resistance to Japanese and Nationalist troops. From 1945 to 1949 he was a senior officer in the Communist army that drove the Nationalists out of mainland China; in 1950 he led the Chinese invasion of Tibet. In 1952 he was promoted to vice-premier, and in 1956 to deputy premier and secretary general of the Communist Party. His first break with Mao came during the Great Leap Forward (1958–62) when Mao's economic policies collapsed and China experienced mass famine. Supporting President Liu Shaoqi against Mao, Deng argued that ideologically pure policies were of no use if they did not work in practice, and that the party's first task was to feed its people: his pragmatism found utterance in the famous saying, 'It doesn't matter if a cat is black or white, so long as it catches mice.'

In 1966 the Cultural Revolution began and Deng was disgraced, stripped of all powers and sent to do forced labour in the countryside. Hounded by the Red Guards, his brother com-

mitted suicide and his eldest son was crippled and left confined to a wheelchair. Hatred of the anarchy and chaos of the Cultural Revolution was a main motive factor in Deng's later actions. In 1973, needing someone to restore order, Mao was forced to rehabilitate him, but in 1976 he was disgraced again, being saved this time only by Mao's death later in the year. In 1977 Deng was rehabilitated once more, this time with the backing of most of the party to carry out his economic reforms. His goal was to achieve rapid modernization of the economy, including an improvement in personal living standards. At the same time, he wished to ensure that the reform process was carefully controlled; economic overheating could be even more dangerous than continued stagnation. He foresaw correctly that too rapid a pace of reform could lead to the breakdown of social and political order, as indeed happened in many of the countries of the former Soviet bloc a decade later. To many Chinese, the present plight of Russia vindicates Deng's policy of strictly controlled reform.

In 1978 the party formally adopted Deng's programme of economic reform and opening up to the outside world. Put simply, the programme had two elements: (1) the introduction of a limited version of the market economy and a reduction in the role of the state, and (2) the open-door policy whereby Western businesses were allowed to enter China on a supervised basis. At first these reforms were restricted to experimental Special Economic Zones (SEZs) in coastal regions, but through the 1980s and 1990s more and more of the country was opened up for market reforms. Throughout the late 1980s and most of the 1990s China enjoyed very rapid growth in both gross domestic product and personal incomes and living standards. China seemed at last to have joined the family of nations, and in 1985 *Time* magazine made Deng its man of the year.

In 1990, an initially small protest by students commemorating the anniversary of the May Fourth Movement, a liberal protest group which had flourished briefly in 1919, escalated rapidly into a mass rally and occupation of Tiananmen Square in Beijing. The protestors called for more rapid political and social reforms, exactly the kind of changes that Deng saw as dangerous. When labour unions began joining the protestors Deng feared the worst, and authorized the use of armed force to crush the protest. The operation was bungled, and resulted in around 1,000 deaths, including those of some soldiers. Deng was vilified in the West, while simultaneously conservative elements in China tried to push back his reforms. Deng fought back against these, undertaking a successful tour of the SEZs in 1992, but by now he was increasingly ill. His last public appearance was in 1994.

Not himself a business manager, Deng understood fully the important role that professional management plays, and his reforms were the first step in building, or at least rebuilding, a Chinese management culture in mainland China. One of the key goals of his reform programme was to encourage the professionalization of management. To this end he reduced the role of the state and the Communist Party in the workplace, promoting the actual business managers to positions of full responsibility. His reform programme encouraged the establishment of Western-style management education, and even more importantly, encouraged young Chinese with talent to study abroad – as he himself had done – and learn from Western culture. His aim was not to adopt Western culture wholesale – far from it – but to study that culture, 'cherrypick' the best elements, and adapt them to Chinese ways. He encouraged a synthesis, a business culture which would be essentially Chinese but would have Western elements. His own writings (Deng 1987; Wu 1996) are full of this idea of synthesis.

Deng argued against the orthodox communist view – and indeed the orthodox capitalist view – that the free market was a capitalist creation. Free markets, he observed, had existed in feudal societies, and had been

adapted for use in capitalist societies. Why could they not then be adapted to socialist societies? Thus he argued for the creation of a 'socialist market economy', one which would use the essential features of the free market, including professional management, to achieve the goals of socialism.

Four years after his death, it is difficult to see whether Deng's experiment has worked as he intended. Some observers deride the idea of a 'socialist market economy' and believe China is now embarked on the road to Western-style capitalism. Others believe that Chinese cultural characteristics such as Confucianism (see CONFUCIUS) will limit the journey in that direction, and that ultimately there will be a reaction that will lead to a more Chinese, and possibly even a more socialist, emphasis in Chinese economy and society. Despite large US and European business presences in China, by far the largest foreign presence in the country has taken the form of overseas Chinese investment by men such as LI Ka-sheng or Robert KWOK. Few doubt, however, that professional management has arrived in China to stay. It may even be that a 'Chinese model' of management is beginning to emerge, one with notably different features to the management models of the West (Ambler and Witzel 2000).

At the time of writing, Deng is still identified by most people in the West with the deaths in Tiananmen Square. Against this tragedy, however, should be set Deng's achievements; under his leadership, half a billion people were lifted out of poverty. Considerable time may have to pass before his legacy can be fully and fairly evaluated.

BIBLIOGRAPHY
Ambler, T. and Witzel, M. (2000) *Doing Business in China*, London: Routledge.
Deng X. (1987) *Fundamental Issues in Present-day China*, Beijing: Foreign Languages Press.
'The Last Emperor' (1997) *Time*,
www.time.com/time/deng/home.html.
Wu J. (1996) *On Deng Xiaopeng Thought*, Beijing: Foreign Languages Press.

MLW

DENNISON, Henry Sturgis (1877–1952)

Henry Sturgis Dennison was born on 4 March 1877 in Boston, Massachusetts, the son of Henry Beals Dennison and Emma Stanley Dennison. He died in Framingham, Massachusetts on 29 February 1952. Henry Beals Dennison was president of the Dennison Manufacturing Company, founded in 1844 by his own father, Andrew Dennison, when the competition in the New England shoe industry forced Andrew to seek new business opportunities. Andrew's eldest son was a Boston jeweller, and suggested that his father transfer his skill from cutting leather to cutting paper, and that his two sisters then take the paper and cover jewellery boxes that could be sold in the jewellery store (Hayes 1929). This modest cottage industry eventually grew and diversified into a company selling a complete line of stationary items including labels, tickets, adhesives, paper decorations and shipping tags.

Henry Dennison attended the Roxbury Latin School and graduated from Harvard College in 1899. He was an accomplished violinist at the age of nine, and tuned his own piano. He was a naturalist and inventor, and was curious about psychiatry and public affairs (Galbraith 1981). Upon graduation from college he joined the family business and married Mary Tyler Thurber in 1901. The couple had four children. His first wife died in 1936, and in 1944 he married Gertrude B. Petri. Dennison worked in various positions with the family company before being elected a director in 1909.

John Kenneth GALBRAITH met Dennison in 1936 and stated that he was 'arguably the most interesting businessman in the United States at the time' (Galbraith 1981: 61). According to Galbraith, Dennison was a small man with a bald head whose 'need to attend to numerous interests caused him to dart rather than walk and to begin all sentences in the middle. It was only after considerable practice that it was possible to make sense out of what he was saying' (Galbraith 1981: 61). Feldman (1922) described him in terms routinely ascribed to modern leaders. He was certainly more than a manager. He was a man of broad vision who did not need to dominate because he could win by time and reason. He was a person of good cheer, poise and patience. To him, nothing was ever a failure if it served as an experiment. He did, however, hold many of his business associates in disdain, and a few of them reciprocated by boycotting Dennison products because of his radical tendencies (Galbraith 1981).

In 1917 Dennison succeeded his grandfather and father as president of the Dennison Manufacturing Company and built a reputation as author, industrialist, social reformer and public servant (Nelson 1999). Under Dennison's leadership, the company remained a *de facto* family business for more than a hundred years. In 1967 the Dennison Manufacturing Company merged with the National Blank Book Company, and in 1990 it became a subsidiary of Avery-Dennison Incorporated.

As an author, Dennison's most important contribution was *Organization Engineering* (1931), a pioneering work on the human factor in business. In this book, Dennison discussed a broad range of topics of contemporary interest including teamwork, leadership and the need for continuous reorganization in light of an ever-changing business environment. Other writings as a sole author and with other industrialists covered a variety of topics including monetary and fiscal policy, international trade, taxation and education (Leeds *et al.* 1938).

As an industrialist, Dennison implemented revolutionary reforms for workers. He made the Dennison Manufacturing Company his private laboratory for testing theories of social reform. The company had a clinic, library, cafeteria and savings bank. In 1913 he created a personnel department, and in 1916 he boldly introduced unemployment insurance for his employees. Dennison believed that unemployment could be prevented by good management, and considered benefit payments the penalty a company had to pay for failing to prevent unemployment. He was convinced that careful planning could buffer business organizations from the inevitable ups and downs of the business cycle. (Unfortunately, his company like many others suffered greatly during the Great Depression.) As President of the Taylor Society, he openly welcomed innovative executives and made the society a forum for industrial reform issues. He supported the International Management Institute, the National Bureau of Economic Research and the Social Science Research Council (Earl 1955).

In the early 1920s, the Dennison Manufacturing Company, along with other major United States corporations such as Standard Oil of New Jersey, Goodyear, Westinghouse, International Harvester and American Telephone and Telegraph, implemented employee representation plans to provide avenues for employees to make suggestions for improved practices and for handling grievances (Gullett and Duncan 1976). The Dennison plan, however, was unique in the manner in which it allowed employee involvement in its design and implementation. The works committee at the company was instrumental in improving physical working conditions, facilitating two-way vertical communication, instituting an employee profit-sharing plan and establishing a housing fund from which employees could borrow at lower than market interest rates (Meine 1924).

As a social reformer, Dennison devoted a great deal of attention to his distrust of the corporate form of organization. His concern was more practical than academic, as demonstrated by the changes he made in his own company. His most ambitious and innovative undertaking was a plan to transfer the control of the company from outside stockholders to managers and employees.

In 1878 the Dennison Manufacturing Company incorporated and distributed voting stock to its owner-managers. However, by 1910 substantial blocks of the company's stock were held by outsiders. Henry Dennison, who was works manager at the time, and Charles Dennison, the president of the company, worried that outsiders would exercise too much control over operations (Vollmers 1997). With the aid of Mrs James Peter Warbasse, the company's largest stockholder, Dennison was able to accomplish an innovative reorganization that provided safeguards against excessive external control (Nelson 1999).

The impetus for Dennison's plan was the dysfunctional affects caused by absentee stockholders. In the typical corporation then, as today, most owners did not work for or manage the organization. The stockholder's concern was for the return they could make on their investment and little more. If they could make a higher return by selling their interest in one corporation and purchasing shares in another, the transfer costs were minimal. While absentee investors made a one-time contribution in the form of their investment, managers and workers had an ongoing personal stake in the success of the company.

Dennison believed that a new concept of corporate control was needed. His new concept was based on two principles of efficiency engineering and common sense: (1) responsibility must be closely related to ability, and (2) reward must be closely related to service. This required that businesses assure that voting control was retained by individuals familiar with and directly involved in the success of the firm, and that profits were

shared with those who directly influenced productivity (Duncan and Gullett 1974). According to Dennison, once wages increased to the point of providing for essential needs, the distribution of profits became an important determinant of the energy expended towards greater production. It was his contention that the normal human being, in spite of the possibility of increasing his or her own earnings would reduce effort if it was known that increasing productivity would increase the returns of absentee stockholders (Dennison 1920: 159).

To prevent such a reduction in effort, Dennison devised a corporate structure whereby investors received a priority return for their act of investment and managers and workers received returns based on the company's performance. Prior to 1924, managers and employees of the Dennison Manufacturing Company were made partners in the business and participated in sharing the profits of the firm. This structure was developed in such a way that investors held either first or second preferred stock. First and second preferred paid fixed returns and were cumulative: all present and past earnings on preferred stock had to be paid in full before any payments could be made to holders of common stock.

The company directors declared a dividend on partnership stocks each year, and any amount remaining after the preferred stockholders were paid went to managers and employees. The management partners received two-thirds of the residual, and the employee partners received one-third. Payments to the management and employee partners were made in the form of stock, which was non-transferable. If a manager or employee left the firm, the stock was converted to second preferred. If the Company failed to produce the full amount of preferred dividends, control reverted to the holders of first preferred stock (Gorton 1926).

Dennison, although a reformer, was realistic about the likelihood of corporations will-

ingly following his lead in the transfer of industrial control from investors to managers and workers (McQuaid 1977). In a book written with John Kenneth Galbraith (Dennison and Galbraith 1938), he therefore endorsed a number of reforms resulting from the Securities Exchange Act of 1934. The authors argued for the simplification of the corporate form of organization, separation of stockholder ownership and control of corporations, board of director responsibility and restriction on the number of board memberships, and government supervision of securities markets.

As a public servant, Dennison held numerous appointed positions. To illustrate only a few of the more important, he was adviser to the chairman of the War Industries Board and Assistant Director of the Central Bureau of Planning and Statistics from 1917 to 1918, a member of President Wilson's Industrial Conference in 1919 and a member of President Harding's Unemployment Conference in 1921. He was a director of the US Post Office Department's Service Relations Division 1922–8, chaired the Industrial Advisory Board of the US Department of Commerce in 1934, and was a director of the Federal Reserve Bank of Boston 1937–45.

BIBLIOGRAPHY

Dennison, H.S. (1920) 'Production and Profits', *Annals of the American Academy of Political and Social Sciences* 66(3): 159–61.

——— (1931) *Organization Engineering*, New York: McGraw-Hill.

Dennison, H.S. and Galbraith, J.K. (1938) *Modern Competition and Business Policy*, New York: Oxford University Press.

Duncan, W.J. and Gullett, C.R. (1974) 'Henry Sturgis Dennison: The Manager and the Social Critic', *Journal of Business Research* 2(2): 133–46.

Earl, P.A. (1955) 'Henry Sturgis Dennison', in J.A. Garraty (ed.), *Directory of American Biography*, New York: Charles Scribner's Sons, suppl. 5 (1951–5), 164–5.

Feldman, H. (1922) 'The Outstanding Features of the Dennison Management', *Industrial Management* 65(2): 67–73.

Galbraith, J.K. (1981) *A Life in Our Times: Memoirs*, Boston: Houghton Mifflin.

Gorton, J. (1926) *Profit Sharing and Stock Ownership for Employees*, New York: Harper and Brothers (see chapter on Dennison Manufacturing Company, 259–68).

Gullett, C.R. and Duncan, W.J. (1976) 'Employee Representation Reappraised', *Conference Board Record* 13(6): 32–6.

Hayes, E.P. (1929) 'History of the Dennison Manufacturing Company', *Journal of Economic and Business History* 1(4): 467–502.

Health, C. (1929) 'History of the Dennison Manufacturing Company II', *Journal of Economic and Business History* 2(1): 163–202.

Leeds, M.E., Flanders, R.E., Filene, L. and Dennison, H.S. (1938) *Toward Full Employment*, New York: McGraw-Hill.

McQuaid, K. (1977) 'Henry S. Dennison and the Science of Industrial Reform 1900–1950', *American Journal of Ethics and Sociology* 36(4): 79–98.

Meine, F.J. (1924) 'The Introduction and Development of the Works Committee in the Dennison Manufacturing Company', *Journal of Personnel Research* 3(8): 130–41.

Nelson, D. (1999) 'Henry Sturgis Dennison', in J.A. Garraty and M.C. Carnes (eds), *American National Biography*, New York: Oxford University Press, 445–6.

Vollmers, G. (1997) 'Industrial Home Work of the Dennison Manufacturing Company of Framingham, Massachusetts, 1912–1935', *Business History Review* 71(3): 444–70.

WJD

DETERDING, Henri Wilhelm August
(1866–1939)

Henri Wilhelm August Deterding was born in Amsterdam on 19 April 1866 and died at St Moritz, Switzerland on 4 February 1939. He was the son of a merchant marine captain, who died when Deterding was five years old. He moved to east Asia as a young man, finding employment as a bookkeeper with a bank in the Dutch East Indies. In 1896 he joined the Royal Dutch petroleum company, charged with reorganizing sales first in Sumatra and subsequently throughout the entire region. He had a formidable talent for accounts and finances, 'a lynx-eye for balance sheets' (Howarth 1997: 54), which enabled him to rise quickly within the company. In 1900 he became managing director upon the death of J.B.A. Kessler.

At the time, Royal Dutch was involved in tough three-way competition with Standard Oil and the Shell Transport and Trading Company. Deterding moved quickly to exploit the potential for sales of Indonesian oil in European markets. After delivery, profits were enhanced by filling empty Royal Dutch tankers with Russian kerosene for sale in Asian markets (Sampson 1975: 48). Such was the success of Royal Dutch that Shell was put under intense pressure. After some joint activities, the two companies formally merged in 1907, creating the Royal Dutch/Shell Group. However, it was not a merger of equals, and although it was the smaller of the two, Royal Dutch became the dominant partner, holding 60 per cent of the joint assets. Deterding subsequently became group managing director and Marcus SAMUEL became the chairman.

Under Deterding's leadership the group diversified throughout world markets. Deterding was instrumental in making Royal Dutch/Shell more international in scope than any of its rivals. As well as its East Indies properties, the company opened new oil fields in Romania, Russia, Latin America and the United States. Sales massively increased, in part because of the British Navy's decision to convert from coal- to oil-powered ships, but more so as a result of the burgeoning increase in the numbers of petrol-engine automobiles.

At the same time, the character of the Royal Dutch/Shell Group changed. Despite the fact that Dutch interests predominated, Deterding saw the advantages of cultivating a British culture. He moved his offices from The Hague to London and the group was soon generally perceived as a British enterprise. Indeed, in gratitude for his wartime services helping to organize British petroleum resources, Deterding was knighted in 1921 (Howarth 1997: 116).

After the war, Deterding tried to replace industry competition with cooperation. However, his efforts were initially thwarted by developments in the Soviet Union. There the group's considerable assets had been expropriated by the new Soviet government. In response, an outraged Deterding organized a boycott of Russian oil. When an American company broke the boycott and sold Russian oil in British India, Royal Dutch/Shell retaliated and a severe price war erupted, which also dragged in several other companies (Jones 1981: 209).

The price war ended in 1928 as a result of the so-called 'Pool Agreement' reached at Achnacarry castle in Scotland during a meeting arranged by Deterding that included Sir John Cadman of Anglo-Persian, Walter C. TEAGLE of Standard Oil of New Jersey and William Mellon of Gulf. This agreement, made in secret, was in essence a price-fixing arrangement that would last for years.

During the early 1930s Deterding became increasingly 'autocratic with signs of incipient megalomania' (Sampson 1975: 80). These tendencies were highlighted by his autobiography, which has been described as a 'masterpiece of vanity and egocentricity' (Howarth 1997: 187). Furthermore, his political views changed from simple anti-communism to open admiration for fascism generally and Nazi Germany in particular. This alarmed his fellow

directors sufficiently for them to ease him out of the managing director's chair in November 1936. Thereafter he left Britain to live on an estate in Germany.

BIBLIOGRAPHY

Deterding, H. and Naylor, S. (1934) *An International Oilman*, London: Harper and Brothers.

Henriques, R. (1960) *Marcus Samuel*, London: Barrie and Rockcliff.

Howarth, S. (1997) *A Century in Oil: The 'Shell' Transport and Trading Company, 1897–1997*, London: Weidenfeld and Nicolson.

Jones, G. (1981) *The State and the Emergence of the British Oil Industry*, London: Macmillan.

Roberts, G. (1976) *The Most Powerful Man in the World*, Westport, CT: Hyperion Press.

Sampson, A. (1975) *The Seven Sisters. The Great Oil Companies and the World they Made*, London: Hodder and Stoughton.

SK

DEUTSCH, Oscar (1893–1941)

Oscar Deutsch was born in Birmingham on 12 August 1893, the son of Leopold and Leah Deutsch Jewish immigrants from central Europe. He died of cancer on 5 December 1941, also in Birmingham. His father owned a scrap metal business. He was educated at King Edward's Grammar School in Birmingham, and then joined the family firm. Deutsch married Lily Tanchan in 1918, and the couple had three sons.

Around 1920, Deutsch and two school friends, Michael Balcon and Victor Saville, set up a small motion picture distribution company, Victory Motion Pictures. Balcon and Saville later moved on to producing films, with Deutsch as an occasional investor. Deutsch himself was more attracted to the cinema business, and in 1925 joined a partnership owning a small group of cinemas in the Coventry area. He seems to have quickly realized the drawbacks of existing cinemas: 'The cinema, in its early days, did not consider beauty of interior necessary to an entertainment seen by its patrons in the dark. Any bare, unbeautiful barn with glaring colours and grotesque ornaments became a picture palace. Good taste and cinemas had not met' (Bruce 1937: 20). Seating and projection equipment were often also of poor quality. In 1928 he built his new cinema at Brierley Hill; in 1930 the first Odeon cinema was built at Perry Barr. By 1933 Deutsch and Odeon had twenty-six cinemas; by 1936 the total had risen to 142 and Deutsch was challenging the established firms, Gaumont British and Associated British. He served as chairman of Odeon until his death, when he was succeeded by J. Arthur RANK.

Much appraisal of Odeon has centred on the strong brand image built by Deutsch, in particular in the design and decor of his cinemas. Here, much of the credit must go to Lily Deutsch, the director in charge of design who oversaw the Odeon visual image. Distinctive buildings, often purpose-designed by leading architects, were decorated in a clean, streamlined, modern fashion, quite unlike the baroque fantasies of the older picture palaces. A further key factor, however, was location. Because he was for the most part building new cinemas rather than renovating older buildings, Deutsch could pick and choose his locations. In many cities he chose sites where rapid population growth could be expected nearby, thus ensuring a captive audience; he was one of the first to build cinemas in the suburbs. In other areas he chose sites convenient for public transport; in London, Odeons were often located near Underground stations. A further factor was Deutsch's early alliance with United Artists, the Hollywood film-maker established

by Mary Pickford and her partners. United had a reputation for producing quality pictures, and Deutsch's cinemas could trade on that reputation.

Bruce (1937) says that Odeon was run on a decentralized basis, with local managers having some input into what films were shown; managers could also pass information about local tastes and conditions to head office, enabling decisions to be influenced in this way as well. The head office was small and tightly run, with many departments consisting of only a few people. Deutsch himself worked long hours, usually until well after midnight even when his cancer was in its final stages, and was noted as a master of detail.

BIBLIOGRAPHY

Bruce, M. (1937) *The History of Odeon Theatres*, London: Odeon.
Chanan, M. (1983) 'The Emergence of an Industry', in J. Curran and V. Porter (eds), *British Cinema History*, London: Weidenfeld and Nicolson, 39–56.
Murphy, R. (1984) 'Deutsch, Oscar', in D.J. Jeremy (ed.), *Dictionary of Business Biography*, London: Butterworths, vol. 2, 89–93.

MLW

DICKSEE, Lawrence Robert (1864–1932)

Lawrence Robert Dicksee was born in London on 1 May 1864 and died there on 14 February 1932. His father, J.R. Dicksee, was a successful businessman. Lawrence was educated at the City of London School, and then went into practice as a chartered accountant in 1886, becoming a partner in Sellars, Dicksee and Company in London. He married Nora Beatrice in 1894; there is no record of any children.

From 1902 Dicksee held a number of academic posts. In that year he began lecturing on accounting at the London School of Economics (LSE), in which capacity he continued until his retirement in 1927. He was professor of accounting at the University of Birmingham from 1902 to 1906. In 1919 he was appointed Sir Ernest Cassel Profesor of Accountancy and Business Methods at the University of London, serving until 1926; he was also dean of the faculty of economics at London from 1925 to 1926.

An early pioneer of management education in the UK, Dicksee wrote a large number of books, mostly textbooks based on his lectures at the LSE, and mostly focused on accounting practice. He did have broader interests, however, and his book *Business Organization* (1910) is an early attempt at sythesizing economic theory with business practice. This work, again intended for students, is a textbook showing how to order and structure a business. It is of particular interest for its chapters on responsibility and control. Here, Dicksee offers an early version of the view later to become popular in the United States, namely that employers exercised great care in the tending and maintenance of their machinery, which often represented a considerable capital investment; why, therefore, should they not exercise similar care for their employees, who often represent a similar investment? Dicksee contrasts labour management unfavourably with the management of plant, and stresses the importance of training, good employee relations, and proper pay and working conditions.

Later work shows Dicksee to have been influenced by the efficiency movement. His *The True Basis of Efficiency* (1922) suggests that management should be educative rather than directional; leadership, not direction, is what is required. To achieve this, managers need to build links of trust with staff, involve them in the business, and pay attention to their needs. The essential elements for business success, he believes, are training, equipment,

leadership and morale, and it is up to managers to see that all four of these are attended to. His view that efficiency in administration has two aspects, the material and the spiritual, is reminiscent of the earlier views of CASSON and EMERSON.

BIBLIOGRAPHY
Dicksee, L.R. (1910) *Business Organisation*, London: Longmans, Green and Co.
—— (1922) *The True Basis of Efficiency*, London: Gee and Co.
Kitchen, J. and Parker, R.H. (1980) *Accounting Thought and Education: Six English Pioneers*, London: Institute of Chartered Accountants.

MLW

DISNEY, Walter Elias (1901–66)

Walt Disney was born in Chicago on 5 December 1901 to Elias and Flora Disney, and died in Tulsa, Oklahoma on 15 December 1966. He was a product of the American Midwest. His childhood was spent on a farm in rural Missouri among dogs, ducks, cattle, pigs, cats and other animals, creatures that would one day inspire and populate his feature films and cartoons. From a very early age he had a love of drawing. Following service in the First World War, the largely self-educated Disney worked as a commercial artist in Kansas City and then ventured into the new realm of animation. The 1920s were a time of struggle for the start-up animator. His first business in Missouri failed, and in 1923, he moved to California and went into business with his brother Roy, whose business acumen meshed well with his own imagination.

Disney's first character, Oswald the Rabbit, was misappropriated by his distributor, who also enticed away most of his staff. Disney was determined never again to lose control of any of his characters and went about creating a new one, inspired by the mice that used to crawl through his Kansas City studio. His wife Lillian Bounds, whom he had married in 1925, suggested the name Mickey Mouse. Mickey's first feature, *Steamboat Willie*, premiered in November 1928 and he immediately won the hearts of millions, becoming a superstar of the 1920s. His antics and mannerisms were supposedly based on those of Charlie Chaplin.

Disney combined creative eccentricity and marketing genius, and knew cinema goers wanted escape in place of heavy social commentary. However, the Disney pictures unintentionally offered a form of social commentary all the same. Disney expressed a kind of populism, in which the mistreated underdog turned the tables on the villain trying to eat or defraud him. *The Three Little Pigs* (1933) was taken by many as a parable of the times, with the wolf symbolizing the Great Depression. Throughout the 1930s the Disney enterprise grew enormously. By the early 1940s Disney was creating animated feature films such as *Snow White*, *Pinocchio*, *Dumbo* and *Bambi*. The *New York Times* praised him as the 'Horatio Alger of the cinema', and many saw him as an entrepreneurial hero in the new field of entertainment.

Disney's business philosophy involved finding his niche, which was animation, and pursuing it with single-minded determination: 'Invent your own job; take such an interest in it that you eat, sleep, dream, walk, talk, and live nothing but your work until you succeed' (Brands 1999: 188). During the 1930s Disney films netted some $20,000 per picture.

Disney was also a marketing genius. He gave Disney a brand name. Mickey Mouse toys, lunchboxes, caps, shirts, watches and a multitude of other products with the Disney brand earned him millions. Disney also knew how to be on the leading edge of entertainment technology. He was a pioneer in sound and in Technicolor animation, and leaped quickly

into the new media of television. The weekly *Disneyland* television show (1954) and the *Mickey Mouse Club* (1955) attracted 19 million viewers for each show. Also in 1955 Disneyland opened in Anaheim, California, where it became one of the biggest tourist attractions in the world. The tremendous synergy between the television, movie, theme park and other promotions created a marketing revolution, as each element in turn promoted the other.

By the late 1950s and early 1960s Disney's enormous enterprise was earning over $100 million a year and defined not only American marketing but American culture. Disney had set an example for other media producers to follow. His ideology remained a populist one, but one that had shifted more to the right. Once a New Dealer, Disney in 1964 supported the Republican candidacy of conservative Arizona senator, Barry Goldwater (1909–98). His entertainment was middlebrow and not targeted at elites. He promoted American heroes such as Davy Crockett and Francis Marion, and ridiculed big government and big business when they trampled upon the average American. There was a subtle pro-nature message and a belief that Americans could do anything they set their minds to.

By the time of his death in 1966, Disney had not only shaped the American and world entertainment of the twentieth century, but both reflected and defined much of what was quintessential in American popular culture. The inability of his successors to copy his genius and a changing cultural environment almost marginalized the Disney enterprise until Michael EISNER reinvented the Disney tradition in the mid-1980s.

BIBLIOGRAPHY

Brands, H.W. (1999) *Masters of Enterprise: Giants of American Business from John Jacob Astor and J.P. Morgan to Bill Gates and Oprah Winfrey*, New York: Free Press.
'Walter Elias Disney' (1999) *McGraw-Hill Encyclopedia of World Biography*, Detroit, MI: Gale Research, Inc., vol. 5, 26–7.
Watts, S. (1997) *The Magic Kingdom: Walt Disney and the American Way of Life*, Boston: Houghton Mifflin.

DCL

DREW, Daniel (1797–1879)

Daniel Drew was born on his family's farm near Carmel, New York, on 29 July 1797 and died in New York on 18 September 1879. Raised on a small farm in New York state, Drew was forced to quit school at an early age to help run the struggling enterprise. In his late teens he held a number of jobs as a cattle drover. An incurable schemer, he developed a technique of feeding his herd salt and allowing them to drink large quantities of water the night before a sale, thereby adding some fifty pounds to each head of cattle. He sold such 'watered stock' to Henry Astor, a prosperous New York City butcher and brother of fur and real estate tycoon John Jacob ASTOR, who subsequently and inexplicably had partnerships with Drew in other business dealings.

Later Drew entered the steamboat business, challenging Cornelius 'Commodore' VANDERBILT for control of the Hudson River traffic between Albany and New York City. As his empire expanded, Drew founded the Wall Street brokerage firm of Drew, Robinson and Company to finance his ventures. It quickly became his base of operations, as Drew discovered he could make more money through speculation than operating steamboat companies.

Consequently, in the 1850s he followed his long-time rival and sometime partner Vanderbilt into the burgeoning railroad industry. Drew then devoted nearly all his

energy to stock manipulations, particularly on shares of the Erie Railroad. During that phase of his career he continued to tilt with Vanderbilt, who had forged the powerful New York Central railroad system; this originally stretched from New York City to Albany and, after the Civil War, to the fast growing metropolis of Chicago. As president of the Erie, 'Uncle Daniel', as Drew was often called, infuriated Vanderbilt by launching a rate war, whereupon the 'Commodore' launched a campaign to obtain control of the Erie. Drew retaliated, enlisting new and powerful allies Jay GOULD and 'Jubilee' Jim Fisk. The trio moved the line's headquarters to New Jersey and, in a complex series of manoeuvres that included the issue of phoney common stock and the bribery of various public officials, fended off the Vanderbilt challenge. Their unethical business practices gave rise to the term 'watered stock'.

In the end, however, the allies fell out, and Drew resigned from the presidency, leaving Gould in control. His losses during the battle combined with further setbacks in the Panic of 1873 to ruin Drew. In 1876 he filed for bankruptcy and was forced to live on the charity of his family. He died three years later.

BIBLIOGRAPHY

Adams, C.F., Jr, and Adams, H. (1886) *Chapters of Erie and Other Essays*, New York: Henry Holt.

Browder, C. (1986) *The Money Game in Old New York: Daniel Drew and His Times*, Lexington, KY: University Press of Kentucky.

Klein, M. (1986) *The Life and Legend of Jay Gould*, Baltimore: Johns Hopkins University Press.

Mott, E.H. (1899) *Between the Ocean and the Lakes: The Story of Erie*, New York: John S. Collins.

White, B. (1910) *The Book of Daniel Drew*, New York: Doubleday, Page.

WTW

DRUCKER, Peter Ferdinand (1909–)

Peter Drucker was born on 19 November 1909 in Vienna. His father, Adolph Drucker, was a prominent lawyer and senior civil servant. His mother, Caroline Bond, had an English father, who had been a banker; she was one of the first women in Austria to study medicine, and attended lectures by Sigmund Freud. Both parents were high achievers. The household is described as being Lutheran and comfortable middle class, with a flow of visitors who were politicians, academics or from the arts.

By the middle of 1917, however, life in Austria was changing for all, as the effects of being on the losing side of the First World War took hold. Rampant inflation gripped the country, with the Austrian krone falling to one 75,000th of its value in the four years after 1917. It was in this rapidly changing world that Drucker grew up. Influences outside home also had an effect. His two junior schoolteachers set the basic template for his learning: one taught him to concentrate upon his strengths, and the other to learn by objective examination. After junior school Drucker was educated at the classics-based Vienna Gymnasium, but his interest in learning was also stimulated outside school at several Viennese intellectual salons, where he was treated as an adult, and where he had to learn to research and then have his work critically examined.

A week short of his fourteenth birthday Drucker, as the youngest and newest 'comrade', was honoured by being appointed a banner carrier at a Young Socialist rally. Partway through the walk he abandoned the march and the banner. He later said: 'I only found out I didn't belong. But of course I only found out that I was a bystander on that cold and blustery November day. Bystanders are born rather than made' (Drucker 1979: 4).

At seventeen, Drucker left school and Vienna and became an apprentice clerk in a small business in Hamburg that exported

hardware to India. Despite his full-time job he enrolled as a part-time student in the law faculty at Hamburg University. Weekday evenings were spent in the library: 'I read and read and read everything in German, English and French' (Beatty 1998: 12). He learned that Verdi wrote his most difficult opera, *Falstaff*, when he was eighty, and this made an indelible impression on him: he resolved that he would use Verdi's principles as a life model in trying for perfection and not giving up in advanced age (Beatty 1998: 12).

While still in Hamburg Drucker had an experience, which would rank among the most fundamental of his life. Reading Søren Kierkegaard's *Fear and Trembling* reinforced his Christian beliefs and his commitment to the Protestant work ethic, emphasizing morality and integrity, and adding a spiritual need to the secular nature of his work and teaching. After fifteen months Drucker transferred to Frankfurt University, adding statistics to his subjects. Part of the general syllabus was admiralty law, which Drucker told Beatty was 'a microcosm of Western History, society, technology, legal thought and economy' (Beatty 1998: 14), which Drucker would later use as a template to teach management.

His fluency in English enabled his appointment as a securities analyst at an old merchant bank that had been taken over by a Wall Street brokerage business. One of his first published works celebrated the health of the stock market. The forecast proved wrong, as his job ended with the crash of the New York Stock Exchange in the autumn of 1929, but not before he had started to write articles for a learned econometric journal. Now twenty years of age, he was appointed a financial writer on Frankfurt's leading newspaper, *Frankfurt General Anzeiger*. Within two years he had become senior editor of foreign and economic news. By 1931, at the age of twenty-two, Drucker had obtained his doctorate in public and international law, adding lecturing at the university to his activities. With the completion of his doctorate and what was forecast

to be a promising career, he became eligible to be appointed *dozent*, a university lecturer post which was conditional on his becoming a German national.

Drucker's rejection of this condition, and of the Nazis, came in the publication of a small monograph, *Fr J Stahl: Konservative Staatslehre & Geschichtliche Entwiclung Motrtueringan* (Fr J Stahl: Conservative Philosophy and Historical Continuity). Stahl was an obscure and difficult German philosopher from the first half of the nineteenth century, who believed that even in periods of political and economic change, conservatism based upon Protestant principles could continue, with a place for a constitutional monarch. Shortly before this work's publication in 1933, Drucker left Germany for Vienna. The work was recognized by the Nazis, as intended, as a rejection of their ideas. This, coupled with the Christian convert Stahl's Jewish blood, was sufficient for the work to be banned and burnt. Stahl's significance to Drucker was related to Drucker's acceptance that the old Cartesian world of everything having its place was over; but that order was still possible, with Stahl's philosophy, in what Drucker perceived to be a world of discontinuities. Berthold Freyberg, who claimed to be Drucker's oldest friend, having met him while they were clerk colleagues in Hamburg, wrote of Stahl: 'the work ... foreshadowed his entire subsequent development' (Freyberg 1970: 18).

After a short stay in Vienna, Drucker left for England to find work. His first job was as a trainee securities analyst in an insurance organization, and lasted a few months. Next he worked with a small London merchant bank, Freedberg and Company, as economic report writer and executive secretary to the partners. Subsequently he became a partner, learning about mergers and acquisitions, and how his clients' businesses worked. He stayed with the company until he moved to New York in 1937. While in England he continued his education by attending John Maynard KEYNES's

lectures at Cambridge University. Drucker said that while he could have been an economist, he realized that economists were only interested in inanimate items such as commodities, trade and finance, whereas his interest was in people. He also contributed to a book that disputed the Nazi version of the German economy, *Germany, The Last Four Years* (Germanicus 1937) By 1935 he had recommenced his work in journalism, writing for American magazines and newspapers.

Before leaving for New York, Drucker married Doris Schmitz, a physicist and writer from Mainz, Germany on 16 January 1937. They have four children and six grandchildren. Drucker felt on arriving in America in 1937 that he had escaped the Old World. It was this promise to escape that he had made to himself at the youth rally as a teenager.

Drucker arrived in New York with commissions to write for two London newspapers including the *Financial News*, forerunner to the *Financial Times*, and other newspapers in Glasgow and Sheffield. He was also retained as a financial adviser and economist to a group of British investors for his previous merchant bank, Freedberg and Company. Drucker quickly added to his journalist commissions *The Virginian Quarterly Review*, *The Washington Post*, *Harpers Magazine*, *Asia*, *New Republic* and *Philadelphia Saturday Evening Post*. *Reader's Digest* and *The Review of Politics* were later added, as his range of topics extended from European history, economics, politics and foreign affairs to philosophy, education, religion and the arts.

Drucker's first book, *The End of Economic Man* (1939), a study of the new totalitarianism, was conceived in Europe but published in America. The first sentence, 'This book is a political book', sets out his purpose. The book tracks the breakdown of the events that caused the break-up of European society between the world wars. With the political, economic and spiritual world bankrupt, people had lost the will for freedom and had capitulated. The totalitarianism of Italy, Germany, Austria and

Russia had filled the gap. Drucker suggested an alternative which would give freedom, status and function, one that was influenced by Stahl's discontinuities, Kierkegaard's existentialism and RATHENAU's social and industrial order. Although this is not a management book, Drucker describes Hitler's denationalization of the German banks; this would later develop into Drucker's concept of reprivatization, which the Thatcher government in the UK credited as the inspiration for its privatization policy. The book had a considerable impact; notably, communists attacked the suggestion that Hitler and Stalin would agree on a pact, but subsequent events proved this forecast correct. Others praised it, including Winston Churchill, who instructed that it should be essential reading for British military officer candidates.

In 1940 Drucker set up an independent consultancy as an adviser on the German economy and politics. His clients included the American government. His return to teaching began at Sarah Lawrence College in Bronxville, New York in 1941, teaching economics and statistics one day a week. In late 1941 he moved to Bennington College, Vermont on a weekly basis and also lectured to small colleges throughout America, having visited over fifty by the time the United States went to war in 1941. By the summer of 1942 Drucker had taken up a full-time appointment at Bennington, which was described as a highly visible woman's college because of its progressive teaching formats. During his stay there he became a US citizen. He remained at Bennington until 1949, as professor of politics and philosophy. Drucker said that he knew that he wanted to keep on teaching, and was given the freedom to teach whatever subject needed teaching. He taught philosophy, political theory, economic history, American government, American history, literature and religion.

The End of Economic Man signalled the end of the Old World order. His next book, *The Future of Industrial Man* (1942), started

to look forward to the new. The book has just one topic: 'How can an industrial society be built on a free society' (Drucker 1942: 7). The first task was to make the power of the management of business legitimate. After examination, Drucker agreed with BERLE and MEANS that the divorce of ownership of business from control by independent management is not legitimate power, as in practice it is power without responsibility. For Drucker, authority and responsibility are partners that should be indivisible. Power without responsibility is corruption. While accepting that the basis for business was legal, he could not agree that it was constitutionally legitimate. Management's first responsibility was to produce economic results as profits; the second responsibility was to work in a manner that is for the good of society while never attempting to take over the work of society. He warned that lack of responsible behaviour would result in hostility from society at large and interference from the government in particular. The major idea of the book was that the corporation, the big industrial business, should encourage a self-governing plant community, in which the worker would find his place in changing society. The influence was that of Rathenau, but Drucker's ideas were that people must have status and freedom of choice with responsibility, whereas Rathenau's ideas were more prescriptive. Both, however, agreed that the 'demon' was 'unemployment' and advocated social benefits such as economic support and training to provide opportunities. Drucker regards what was to become his 'autonomous' self-governing plant community as one of his best ideas. But it was never fulfilled, as workers became more affluent and thus more independent of the workplace. Drucker's interest in management also emerges further in this work, which makes reference to FORD and TAYLOR, and also SCHUMPETER, to whom he attributed the most consistent and effective contemporary theory of capitalism.

Drucker had concluded while in Nazi Germany that totalitarianism was not the way for the world. His identification of American free market capitalism as an alternative was now emerging. What he had discovered was a dynamic force that drives capitalism. That force is management, which had received considerable attention from writers during the late nineteenth century and the preceding part of the twentieth century. By 1943 Drucker had decided that he wanted to make a study of contemporary management practices. He received an invitation from General Motors, then the largest corporation in the world with 500,000 employees, to conduct a study 'on the governance of the big organization, its structure and constitution, on the place of big business in society, and on the principle of industrial order' (Drucker 1979: 258). The results of this study were published as his first management book, *Concept of the Corporation* (1946), published in the UK as *Big Business* (1947), as the publishers believed that the American title would be meaningless in Britain. The book was the first ever about an industrial enterprise as a social organization. It put people at the centre of management activities. It reflects and acknowledges Mooney and Reiley's *Onward Industry!* (1931), which identified the organization as a social entity (later Drucker credited Rathenau with an earlier expression of this) and also that the life-giving element of an organization is management as the 'vital spark'.

Drucker describes Alfred P. SLOAN's structure of organization, federal decentralization and its components. The list is comprehensive, missing only Sloan's obsession with safety at work. What Drucker displayed is an ability to identify the essentials. All of the activities described would receive full treatment by Drucker in his later work. The needs of society, the worker and the enterprise are discussed, along with the essentiality of balancing their mutual interests. The job of top management is identified as being the setting of objectives (policies), the agreeing of targets and the measurement of the results. In addition, top management must plan for succession and obtain

sufficient profit for the enterprise to continue and succeed in the future. This is the start of Drucker's thorough examination of the meaning of profit. Identified is General Motors' policy of making character loans to dealers who do not have normal asset collateral, this being today's 'venture capital'. Drucker commends its invention and advocates it as a general commercial policy. The power of the market is recognized, along with the essential need to satisfy the customer's wants, which may be 'economically irrational' (Drucker 1946: 248). The book is a mixture of advice, understanding, encouragement, criticism and required discoveries. What is emerging is a workable world, never perfect but dependent on everybody taking responsibility and performing their tasks. The manager, who must manage, will only be judged by results, which must always be obtained by acting ethically. Criticized are the labour unions, which have still to find a contributory role but never do. Also criticized is personnel management for failing to manage people by motivation, which is the key to people management. Personnel management, despite name changes to human relations and human resources, never escapes Drucker's criticism because in his view it concentrates on what people cannot do rather than what they can do. This is also at the root of his criticism of psychological tests as a human resources gadget. In later work, Drucker concludes that only a third of appointments succeed: a third fail from the employer's point of view, and the remaining third from the employee's point of view. Drucker later advised people to assess where they fitted in the new era of the knowledge worker, and to make quality decisions about their lives and families. He recommends proven psychological tests as a tool for individuals to determine their aptitude for their career.

The third area for criticism is traditional accounting methods, which are designed for an age of trading commerce rather than a processing one. General Motors, at the time of Drucker's research, had evolved what was the most appropriate cost accounts system. It replaced previous systems of control only, with control and measurement. What Drucker realized was that the method needed developing. Drucker's contribution in pioneering work on transactional analysis as a building block of activity accounting was acknowledged by specialists such as Robert Kaplan and N. Thomas Johnson. His view was that few, if any, systems are ever complete; they need refinement and complementing with alternative methodology.

Concept of the Corporation was an enormous success, and like many of Drucker's books has been in continual print since its launch. However, General Motors thought the book critical of the corporation and sympathetic to the unions, as the book's publication coincided with the unions calling a damaging 113-day strike. Sloan thought that Drucker was wrong, but was entitled to his opinion. The book launched Drucker's career as a management writer, but it also posed questions, not about his academic ability *per se*, but about his academic judgement in mixing economic and social sciences. He was not invited to continue his membership of the American Political Science Association.

Drucker's next book, *The New Society* (1949), was a development and tidying of his previous ideas. Its publication preceded his moving back to New York in 1950 as professor of management at the graduate business school of New York University, where he remained until 1971. His management consulting business was now becoming well established, with clients including Sears Roebuck, General Motors, ITT and major railroads. He was now further developing and refining his management ideas by practising with top corporations while researching and considering the work of others.

The Practice of Management (1954) is regarded by many as Drucker's seminal work. Together with his four preceding books, it is the foundation of his philosophy. *The Practice of Management* was written as a handbook

for consultancy clients. Drucker accepted that management was older than the pyramids, but a book was needed to enable people to be able to learn it. The book is a guide rather than an orthodox textbook. While containing some checklists, it offers a more flexible approach than other management writings, and contains a mixture of the definitive and the exploratory. Managers, he says, must learn to think. In a world that is rapidly and unpredictably changing, the manager must be adaptable. He must shape the future to create opportunities rather than wait for the problems. The manager of the future will have to learn to look beyond his own speciality, even beyond his own organization and its industry. What is happening beyond will affect the future for the manager. The book introduced to the world 'Management by Objectives and Self-control' (MBO), which can be regarded as a 'philosophy of management' (Drucker 1954: 134). This enabled managers to help or set objectives, take responsibility and measure their own performance. It makes delegation a meaningful practice. It also makes possible a move away from command and control management.

The book has some very clear messages, some of which are drawn from his previous works. The first duty of a business is to survive: 'The guiding principles of business economics ... [are] the avoidance of loss' (Drucker 1954: 44). Drucker describes what objectives are and how the managers will set them. Central to the manager's role is the treatment of workers: they are not a commodity but a unique resource which, when properly motivated by being given opportunities and training, will contribute to and develop managerial vision, and take responsibility. The book recognizes that federal decentralization is the preferred organizational structure, but there are others as well. The first task is not to choose the structure but to ask, 'what is our business' and 'what should it be'? (Drucker 1954, chap. 6) Once these questions have been answered, then the structure can be chosen.

Drucker is fully aware that the organization has to perform economically, and confirms profit as an essential feature. However, his view is that its traditional definition is too narrow. The profit of the enterprise must provide, as its social responsibility, for yesterday's costs, today's and the future's needs, and pay taxes to fund government services. Very clearly described is how managers manage by objectives; what the objectives are; and how they must be set. The management function of the board of directors is defined as being policies, performance and results. The operations managers' function is to perform within the policies and produce their part of the results by applying Drucker's development of Henri FAYOL's five basic functions – setting objectives, organizing, motivation, measuring and communicating – not in a 'top-down' or 'bottom-up' sense, but in a multi-directional fashion. Drucker then adds a sixth basic function: the development of people; including oneself.

Drucker attributes Henry Ford's near failure at the end of the Second World War, after his incredibly successful empire-building in earlier decades, to his having not managers but only assistants. He feels that the way that work is carried out is changing. The growth of manual workers has peaked. The growing sector is now that of the knowledge worker and the professional. Most of these are not managers, but they make a managerial contribution. Drucker points out that Taylor's theories about productivity and the separation of work and planning are not applicable to knowledge workers, who must take responsibility for planning their own work, as they cannot be controlled as a manual worker might be. The problem of Taylor's separation of work and planning exercised Drucker's mind for several decades. He ultimately resolved this by arguing that Taylor did not say that work and planning had to be performed by different people. Once it was accepted that the same person could perform both tasks, then Taylor was appropriate for knowledge work. In fact, the only

practical way that the new breed of worker, the knowledge technologist, could work was in this manner.

A working example of the integration of work and planning, albeit for manual workers, is Drucker's description of what Thomas J. WATSON's IBM had been practising since the 1930s. The workers' tasks are engineered to be as simple as possible. Then, with training, other skills are developed. The workers are then encouraged to contribute to the policy of continual improvements, resulting in increased productivity. The improvements are reflected in product improvement, which creates more sales, securing jobs and establishing attitudes of acceptance of the necessity to change. IBM managers are seen as assistants to their workers. What Drucker identified here is what would be later termed 're-engineering'; he gives credit to IBM executives, Charles R. Walker and E.L.W. Richardson for developing the method (Drucker 1954: 252). Influence from this book can also be found in MCGREGOR's 'Theory Y' and HERZBERG's concept of 'hygiene factors'.

But arguably the most permanent impact of the book was encapsulated in the Drucker epigram: 'There is only one valid definition of business purpose: *to create a customer*' (Drucker 1954: 35; he later added, 'and get paid'). Because its purpose is to create a customer, any business enterprise has two and only these two basic functions: marketing and innovation. These are what Drucker calls the 'entrepreneurial functions'. As he goes on to say, 'The economic revolution of the American economy since 1900 has in large part been a marketing revolution ...' (Drucker 1954: 35–6). Theodore LEVITT later highlighted Drucker's contribution to this field: 'Peter Drucker created and publicised the marketing concept and nobody had ever really acknowledged it' (Levitt 1970: 8). A similar comment comes from George S. Day: 'Compelling visions are best nourished in market-driven organizations. While there are many views on what this means, all start with Drucker's original formulation' (Day 1999: 18).

Drucker went on to develop these ideas in *Managing for Results* (1964), a book that he claims was the first written on strategy but that is also very much a marketing book. He divides an enterprise's products into eleven groups, including 'yesterday's breadwinners', 'management's egos' and 'failures', all of which need to be disposed of. Today's and yesterday's breadwinners give large volumes and low margins. Tomorrow's breadwinners are 'what everybody hopes all products are', but are 'not as common as company press releases ... assume'; 'a company had better have at least one of them around' (Drucker 1964: 48–50). Drucker poses the question of whether Prince Charming will come before Cinderella gets old. The marketing concept was still further refined and developed in Drucker's later work. After initially identifying marketing and innovation as the two basic functions of the entrepreneurial function, by 1985 Drucker had developed a working discipline of innovation, 'the specific tool of the entrepreneur', 'which was capable of being learned, capable of being practised' (Drucker 1985: 17). The inspiration here was the Austrian economist Joseph SCHUMPETER, who had developed a theory of economics that incorporated the entrepreneurial function, and the French economist J.B. SAY, who had identified the entrepreneur's function in the early nineteenth century. Drucker now added the entrepreneurial function to the practice of management.

In *The Practice of Management*, Drucker identifies the need for more leaders, as the few natural geniuses available will not meet the demand. In later work, he decided that leadership is a skill that can be learnt but not taught. Learning is made possible by developing and applying managerial skills. Drucker rejected the vogue of participation management of the 1980s as nonsense, because someone always had to make the final and often painful decision. Among leadership skills was the ability to be prepared for trouble, as it always arrives in all organizations sooner or later.

The Practice of Management was not only an immediate success but also, in common with many of his books, became a permanent classic, being awarded the 1998 Financial Times/Booz Allen Global Business Books award as a book which had stood the test of time as an important contribution to business thinking. The impact of the publication of *The Practice of Management* on management was considerable. Management by objective became the best-known practice in management for at least the next two decades. Although it is now considered by many a concept of the past, it is still practised today under various names. The book gave Drucker international recognition and made him perhaps the most sought-after practising management consultant in the world. He began his long association with Japan and was among the first Westerners to write knowledgeably and extensively about Japanese management and the influences upon it of Japanese culture. In addition, he continued to write books and articles, and to teach and undertake research. With an established readership for his articles and books, he was able to introduce managers to many new ideas. For example, he introduced demographics as a forecasting tool. He once commented that 'The major events that determine the future have already happened – irrevocably' (Drucker 1957: 2), showing how the manager must operate simultaneously in two time scales, the present and the future.

Drucker was also one of the first writers to recognize that the impact of computers would be in data processing rather than in decision making. While others were forecasting redundancies, he was forecasting that computers would create work for thousands of clerks. However, the demands of business for knowledge workers would absorb the potential for increased leisure time by expanding the need for education. Knowledge was likened to electricity at the turn of the nineteenth and twentieth centuries, as the new 'energy'. Increased leisure time would do little to help the manager who spends most of his time attending to non-managerial priorities, resulting in a constant shortage of time. The solution for the manager was to recognize the difference between efficiency and effectiveness. Efficiency was getting things done right; but this poses a problem, as it may not be the right task. Effectiveness is 'to get the right things done' (Drucker 1966: 1).

The Age of Discontinuity: Guidelines to our Changing Society was published in 1969. In this work, Drucker wrote that 'we are disenchanted with government because it ... does not perform' (Drucker 1969: 226), and recommended for the first time that government required 'reprivatization' to shed some of its activities (Drucker 1969: 218). Drucker also forecast that the world was becoming 'the global shopping centre' (Drucker 1969: 71).

In 1970 Drucker moved to the Claremont Graduate School in California, where he was appointed Clarke Professor of Social Science and Management at the Graduate Management Centre (this was renamed after him in 1987, the first public management school to be named after a serving professor). His landmark book *Management: Tasks, Responsibilities, Practices* (1974), along with *The Practice of Management*, is considered a seminal work. It collects Drucker's ideas to date, with some additions. Whereas *The Practice of Management* was centred on management by objectives as part of a decentralized structure, *Management* identifies that while MBO is the practice, the structures of organizations are having to become more adaptable in a world that has changed (and is changing) since decentralization was the ideal. Various team structures are becoming appropriate. However, this is not the same as empowerment, which Drucker rejects as merely moving responsibility from the top of the organization to the bottom; which is still power. The total responsibility of every individual in MBO has been tempered. Drucker has accepted that Abraham MASLOW is correct and that he and Douglas McGregor are wrong. Maslow, while a supporter of Theory Y, that people want sat-

isfaction from work, could not accept that all must and can take responsibility, or even that all will work: 'The world is not, Maslow concluded, peopled by adults. It has its full share of permanently immature' (Drucker 1974: 233).

It is the new knowledge industries that have changed the world. Managers who have never done the job themselves are supervising workers for the first time; layers of management are being stripped away as organizations become 'lean'. Structures are now compared to 'jazz combos', where each players knows what to do without being told, or to 'a symphony orchestra', where the conductor understands the score but expects players to perform their tasks. Regardless of the structure, the organization will have to produce results. This will still be the object of the structure, as it was and is with all other forms. Eventually, as knowledge work gathers momentum in all organizations, all will be both workers and managers, as all will have to manage their own contribution. Management has now become established as multi-organizational; it has extended its confines from business management to include organizations in the non-profit sector. However, the warning that the latter will have to be managed differently from organizations that have profit as their goal is notably absent.

Drucker followed *Management* with *The Unseen Revolution* (1976), which he regarded as one of his best books. Its thesis was that American pensions and mutual funds were increasingly the major shareholders in big business, and that the workers were the investors in the funds. It followed that the funds, although not nationalized, were being socialized. Although the change is fundamental, it still does not make management power constitutional.

Since *The Unseen Revolution*, Drucker's books have continued in a regular pattern. He has continued to give advice, highlight problems and set new tasks for managers. In the 1980s he warned that management had moved from being non-controversial to being attacked. He also condemned the grey (black) economy as destructive. By the 1990s the future of the corporation was in doubt; the future seemed to lie with smaller entrepreneurial businesses. While organizations were collecting more and more information about their existing customers, Drucker warned that few knew much about their potential customers. He cited the mighty Wal-Mart, which while having 14 per cent of the American consumer market, needed to know about the 86 per cent who were not customers (Drucker 1995: 30). Despite Wal-Mart not knowing about their non-customers, however, they were obviously satisfying their customers. Not so Drucker's long-admired British firm, Marks and Spencer. He wrote about them first in *Managing for Results*, and continued to do so for the next three decades. The firm's recent failures suggest that they have forgotten advice from one of Drucker's many unique practical guides. Referring to an old retailer known as 'Uncle Henry', Drucker records his criticism of the new owners of what had been his 'retail chain'. 'I listened to a dozen buyers for the chain. They're very bright. But they're not buying bargains for the customers; they're buying bargains for the store. That's the wrong thing to do.' 'Uncle Henry' sold his shares. Within two years his forecast came true and the business began to decline (Drucker 1979: 201).

Drucker continues to desribe himself as a writer, teacher and consultant. He has published thirty-five books, which have sold millions of copies and which have been translated into over thirty languages. His works cover aspects of management, society, economics and politics, and also include 102 essays, some of which have been individually published, spread over three decades. Subjects of essays include Alfred P. Sloan, John Maynard Keynes, Joseph Schumpeter, Søren Kierkegaard, the need for lifestyle planning and extensive writings on Japan, including its art. He has written an autobiography and two novels, which also have management content. Many of his books have been continuously in

print since their publication and have been prize-winners. Arrangements have been made with Harvard University Books to keep in print all of his books for seventeen years after his death. He has written for *Harvard Business Review* since 1950, the longest ever contributor. He has written for the *Wall Street Journal*, *Forbes*, *The Economist*, *Atlantic Monthly* and many other quality publications. Assessments of his written output confirm that his books contain three and a half million words and his other writing a similar amount.

While living in London Drucker became interested in Japanese painting of the fourteenth to nineteenth centuries, and has since become an expert, advising collectors and museums, including some in Japan. He is co-author of an exhibition catalogue, *Adventures of the Brush*, and from 1979 to 1985 was a professorial lecturer in Oriental history. The development of a network theory in higher mathematics is a further addition to his achievements.

Drucker's consultancy work has specialized in strategy and policy for businesses and non-profit organizations. His clients include many of the world's largest corporations as well as small and entrepreneurial companies; non-profit clients include universities, hospitals and community services together with international agencies and governments. He has numerous honorary doctorates and other awards reflecting his national and international standing. To mark his ninetieth birthday, his native Austria awarded him the Cross of Honour for Science and Art.

Drucker sees himself as an intellectual rather than an academic. His method is that of 1890s 'Gestalt psychology (German word for structure or configuration) in which we don't see lines and points but we see configurations as a whole' (Drucker 1970: 61). From this flows his holistic approach, which gives his work its unique character by joining together activities, disciplines and events that previously had not identified relationships with each other. As regards his view of the future, he told the guests at his ninetieth birthday party in Los Angeles in 1999 that big corporations did not seem to be able to survive for more than thirty years. The corporation, the unique invention of the twentieth century, is not going to be able to survive into the twenty-first century. Much of this is to do with management having lost its challenge, because we know much more about management, we know the routine. People will still work for a living, but the opportunities for the twenty-first century are going to be in the non-profit area, the social sector, as they were in business during the twentieth century. In anticipation of this change, Drucker has been spending more of his time in the non-profit sector. He is involved with charity work, and is the chairman of the Peter F. Drucker Foundation for Non Profit Management, the mission of which is to help the social sectors achieve excellence in performance and build responsible citizenship. There is also a Peter F Drucker Canadian Foundation.

A few days before Joseph Schumpeter died in 1950, he told Drucker's father: 'you know, Adolphe, I have now reached the age where I know its not enough to be remembered for books or theories. One does not make a difference unless it is a difference to people's lives'. Drucker says he has never forgotten that conversation; it gave him the measure of his achievement (Beatty 1998: 187–8). Drucker also wrote of a further Schumpeterian influence: for Schumpeter, what was important was not the answer but the right question.

Drucker is today the most quoted writer on management. He has been the subject of four full biographies and one guide. In compilations on management writers, it is almost impossible to find one that excludes him. Regularly in these compilations, his work is used to explain the ideas of others. He has more books in print than any other management writer. It is fair to mention, however, that he also has his critics. Some academics have criticized his writings for lacking academic rigour, as his collections of essays contain much journalistic work. Yet, none of Drucker's critics

have sold a fraction of the numbers of books that he has, nor have any had his extensive influence. When Drucker writes that 'the purpose of a business is to create a customer', his book sales confirm that he is capable of practising his own philosophy. He writes for the market of businessmen and responsibly intelligent people. When asked who had directly influenced them, Bill GATES of Microsoft and Jack WELCH of General Electric, America's top businessmen, said: 'Drucker'. Among many other achievements in Drucker's career is the total adulation of one Korean businessman, who changed his name to Peter Drucker.

BIBLIOGRAPHY

Beatty, J. (1998) *The World According to Drucker*, London: Orion Business Books.

Day, G.S. (1999) *Market Driven Strategy*, New York and London: Free Press.

Drucker, P.F. (1939) *The End of Economic Man*, London: William Heinemann.

—— (1942) *The Future of Industrial Man*, New York: The John Day Co.

—— (1946) *Concept of the Corporation*, New York: The John Day Co.

—— (1949) *The New Society*, London: William Heinemann.

—— (1954) *The Practice of Management*, London: Heron Books.

—— (1957) *America's Next Twenty Years*, New York: Harper and Brothers.

—— (1964) *Managing for Results*, London: William Heinemann.

—— (1966) *The Effective Executive*, New York: Harper and Row.

—— (1969) *The Age of Discontinuity*, London: William Heinemann.

—— (1970) *Technology Management and Society*, London: William Heinemann.

—— (1974) *Management: Tasks, Responsibilities, Practices*, London: William Heinemann.

—— (1976) *The Unseen Revolution*, London: William Heinemann.

—— (1979) *Adventures of a Bystander*, New York: Harper and Row.

—— (1985) *Innovation and Entrepreneurship*, London: William Heinemann.

—— (1995) *Managing in a Time of Great Change*, Oxford: Butterworth-Heinemann.

—— (1999) *Management Challenges for the 21st Century*, Oxford: Butterworth-Heinemann.

Freyberg, B. (1970) 'The Genesis of Peter Drucker's Thought', in T.H. Bonaparte and J.E. Flaherty (eds), *Peter Drucker: Contributions to Business Enterprise*, New York: New York University Press, 17–22.

'Germanicus' (1937) *Germany: The Last Four Years*, London: Eyre and Spottiswoode.

Kantrow, A. (1980) 'Why Read Peter Drucker?', *Harvard Business Review*, January–February.

Kennedy, C. (1991) *Guide to the Management Gurus*, London: Century Business Books.

Levitt, T. (1970) 'The Living Legacy of Peter Drucker', in T.H. Bonaparte and J.E. Flaherty (eds), *Peter Drucker: Contributions to Business Enterprise*, New York: New York University Press, 5–16.

Wren, D.A. (1994) *The Evolution of Management Thought*, New York: John Wiley and Sons.

HPS

DU PONT, Pierre Samuel (1870–1954)

Pierre Samuel du Pont was born in Wilmington, Delaware on 15 January 1870, to Lammot and Mary du Pont, and died there on 5 April 1954. His father was president of the old established firm of Du Pont, which is

almost as old as the United States itself (Perrett 1989). In 1802 Robert Fulton, inventor of the steamboat, had persuaded Eleuthére Irénée du Pont de Nemours, a French chemist and gunpowder-maker, to come to America. Du Pont, who had been taught by the great French chemist Antoine Lavoisier, set up the first Du Pont factory in Wilmington, Delaware. Du Pont's gunpowder was both cheap and reliable, and it helped the US Army, his chief customer, to fight Britain to a draw in the war of 1812.

Du Pont became the quintessential American family enterprise. In 1837 Eleuthére du Pont passed the firm to his son Alfred, and in 1850 to Alfred's younger brother Henry. Henry and his nephew Lammot presided over the firm during the Civil War, earning over $1 million in profits. In 1872 Lammot was elected president of the Du Pont firm. He died in 1884, as did Henry du Pont in 1889, allowing a younger generation of the family to rise to power.

Pierre du Pont, along with his ten brothers and sisters, grew up in Philadelphia away from the family firm in Delaware. His father's death, however, made him the head of the family. In spite of this he was able to attend the Massachusetts Institute of Technology (MIT), whence he graduated with a degree in chemistry in 1890. Returning to the family firm in Delaware, he soon discovered that the Du Pont enterprise was hopelessly outdated in both its management and its technical expertise. At this time he was experimenting with smokeless gunpowder, but found little encouragement from the more conservative members of his family who still ran Du Pont.

Between 1899 and 1902 du Pont obtained valuable experience managing the Johnson Company in Lorain, Ohio, where he worked with his cousin, T. Coleman du Pont. He would also become acquainted with another manager, John J. Raskob. The Johnson Company was eventually liquidated, with its assets sold to J.P. MORGAN's Federal Steel Company. Pierre, Coleman, and Raskob then used the proceeds to invest in the streetcar system of Dallas, Texas. From managing these operations, du Pont emerged with both considerable management expertise and the nucleus of a management team.

In 1902 a quiet generational coup took place at Du Pont. In February, following the death of senior partner Eugene du Pont, the other partners planned to sell Du Pont to a competitor, Laflin and Rand. One of the youngest of the partners, Alfred du Pont, together with Pierre and Coleman, saved the firm, buying it outright for $12 million. Coleman was installed as president, Alfred as general manager and Pierre as treasurer. Pierre du Pont was now able to set about his plan for modernizing Du Pont. The E.I. du Pont de Nemours Powder Company was incorporated in May 1903. With Pierre negotiating the contracts, the new company expanded rapidly, buying Laflin and Rand and other competitors so that by 1904 it controlled 70 per cent of the gunpowder industry.

In the early 1900s Pierre and Coleman du Pont created the management structure of the twentieth-century corporation, described by Chandler and Salsbury (1971). Du Pont production was decentralized and organized into divisions for black powder, smokeless powder and dynamite. A central sales department and a purchasing organization were set up. The latter had its own nitrate mines and railway in Chile, as well as laboratories for research and development. Department managers, the most important of which served on the executive committee of the board of directors, were directly accountable to Coleman du Pont.

One of Pierre du Pont's most important contributions lay in the revolution in managerial accounting created by himself and Raskob. Du Pont was now a huge, vertically integrated multinational company, which needed to keep track of the profit and loss of all its divisions and subsidiaries. Pierre needed to know which was making money – and which was not – at any given time. He explored new methods of asset accounting and financial forecasting to

determine what the rate of return on every investment would be. His accountants, using the new techniques of control accounting, were able to estimate income and expenditures for future years, making possible long-term planning.

In 1909 Pierre du Pont became acting president of the corporation. Like Standard Oil, Du Pont became a prime target of the anti-trust policies of both the Theodore Roosevelt and William Howard Taft administrations. In response, Pierre du Pont set up the Atlas and the Hercules companies to circumvent the anti-trust legislation.

No other American company stood to be more directly affected by the coming of the First World War than Du Pont. While the United States was not formally involved until 1917, from 1914 Du Pont struggled to fill huge contracts for both Britain and France. Du Pont knew he had to expand. In 1913 the corporation made 8,400,000 tons of smokeless powder; by 1916 it was producing 200 million tons, rising to 455 million tons by the time the United States entered the war in 1917. Du Pont's accounting enabled him to project the potential losses if the war ended suddenly, so in the early stages he charged his customers high prices so as to pay for the building of new factories to expand production.

During the war du Pont married his first cousin, Alice Belin, in 1915. He also antagonized Alfred and much of his family during a dispute over some stock sold by Coleman du Pont, who was now personally investing in insurance and hotels. After the war Pierre du Pont resigned as chairman of the board. By the end of 1920, however, he was serving as president of the General Motors Corporation. The fortunes of General Motors (GM) and Du Pont had been linked since 1915. When William C. DURANT temporarily lost control of GM to a consortium of bankers, du Pont served as the temporary chairman of GM's board. Durant recaptured his company and asked du Pont to remain. Due to the war and unwise postwar expansion, Durant became heavily indebted to Pierre du Pont and the Du Pont company. When GM's stock collapsed in the autumn of 1920, a consortium of Du Pont and Morgan partners saved the auto-maker, but at the cost of Durant's resignation. Du Pont now owned 36 per cent of GM, and Pierre du Pont now ran it.

Pierre du Pont's brief reign at GM, described by SLOAN in his memoirs (1990), laid the groundwork for the auto-maker's future triumph over Henry FORD. More importantly, the Du Pont methods of control accounting and decentralization spread from GM to many large American corporations in the 1930s and 1940s, a process described by Alfred CHANDLER in his *Strategy and Structure* (1962). Du Pont did not reorganize GM alone, but worked with parts and accessories manager Alfred P. Sloan, Jr. He brought in experienced Du Pont managers who placed GM on the same systematic accounting basis they had implemented in Delaware. The operations of Chevrolet, Cadillac and other divisions were decentralized, while a central office maintained overall direction and control just as it did in Delaware. In 1923 du Pont turned the company over to Sloan, remaining as chairman of the board until 1929.

Du Pont was active in civic society as well as the business world. Most notable was his interest in furthering public education. In 1918 he had helped form and fund the Service Citizens of Delaware. The following year he co-authored a report documenting the serious deficiencies in Delaware education. Becoming president of the Delaware school board, he worked to promote teacher training, school sanitation and improved attendance. By 1925 Delaware school attendance had doubled. Du Pont then served as school tax commissioner, securing funding for more schools and even contributing his own money to the cause. He helped fund the entire African-American educational system in Delaware. He also served as Delaware Tax Commissioner from 1929 to 1937 and from 1944 to 1949.

Du Pont's main political cause, besides education, was the repeal of the Eighteenth Amendment mandating prohibition of alcoholic beverages. Pierre saw prohibition as an unenforceable interference against personal rights, a major incentive to organized crime, and costly in terms of lost revenues and higher taxes. Traditionally a Republican, he supported the Democrats in 1928 when Raskob became Governor Alfred E. Smith's campaign manager. When the Great Depression came, Pierre served on a local unemployment relief commission, and supported Franklin Roosevelt for President in 1932. At first he took part in the New Deal, serving as an adviser to both the federal Commerce Department and the Industrial Advisory Committee of the National Recovery Administration (NRA), as well as the National Labor Board. By 1934, however, Pierre had broken with the New Deal and had returned his support to the Republican Party. He contributed financially to the conservative Liberty League, which opposed Roosevelt and his policies as 'socialist' and anti-business.

In the last twenty years of his life du Pont largely withdrew from business and public life. His legacy was the creation of the giant firms of Du Pont and GM, which served as the model for much of American management from the 1940s through to the 1960s. He was nothing less than the architect of the twentieth-century corporation:

During that generation, the coming of the modern corporation was one of the most important developments in the American economy. And of that generation few men were more involved than Pierre du Pont in the shaping of this powerful economic institution.

(Chandler and Salsbury 1971: 592)

BIBLIOGRAPHY
Chandler, A.D., Jr (1962) *Strategy and Structure: Chapters in the History of American Industrial Enterprise,* Cambridge, MA: MIT Press.
——— (1999) 'du Pont, Pierre Samuel', in J.A. Garraty and M.C. Carnes (eds), *American National Biography*, Oxford: Oxford University Press, vol. 7, 127–9.
Chandler, A.D. Jr and Salsbury, S. (1971) *Pierre S. du Pont and the Making of the Modern Corporation*, New York: Harper and Row.
Perrett, G. (1989) *A Country Made by War: From the Revolution to Vietnam – The Story of America's Rise to Power*, New York, Random House.
Sloan, A.P., Jr (1990) *My Years with General Motors*, ed. J.D. McDonald and C. Stevens, New York: Currency Doubleday.
Zilg, G.C. (1971) *Du Pont: Behind the Nylon Curtain*, Englewood Cliffs, NJ: Prentice-Hall.

DCL

DUNLOP, John Thomas (1914–)

John Thomas Dunlop was born in Placerville, California on 15 July 1914. He attended the University of California, Berkeley (1933–6), Stanford University (1936–7), Cambridge University (1937–8) and, following John Kenneth GALBRAITH's suggestion, Harvard University from 1938. He began at Harvard as a teaching fellow, and spent most of the rest of his academic career there, although this career was frequently interspersed with periods of full-time and part-time practical and policy work in industrial relations. Dunlop is a distinguished labour economist, but is best known as a pre-eminent post Second World War scholar of industrial relations, helping establish it as a distinctive academic subject, and with widespread and continuing influence on its scope, content and theory. He is also a long-

standing public policy contributor in the United States; he served as secretary of labor in President Gerald Ford's administration, and has advised on labour law reform and arbitration, and chaired the Dunlop Commission. Thus, for over sixty years Dunlop has cast a long shadow over industrial relations academia, practice and policy.

For many participants in the field of industrial relations in the United States, as well as the public in general, Dunlop is best known for his practical involvement in the area. His contributions include the following: (1) work with stabilization agencies concerned with dispute settlement, including the War Labor Board (1943–5), Wage Stabilization Board (1950–53) and Construction Industry Stabilization Commission (1971–4), which he chaired; (2) stabilization agencies concerned with informal dispute settlement, include the Cost of Living Council (1973–4) and the Tripartite Pay Advisory Committee (1979–80); (3) boards of enquiry under the Taft-Hartley Act; (4) resolution of disputes at critical installations, such as the President's Commission on Labor Relations in the Atomic Energy Installations (1948–9), the Missile Sites Labor Commissions (1961–7) and the Nevada Test Site Committee (1965–7); (5) railways and airlines, including the Presidential Railroad Commission (1960–62), the Emergency Board of 167 American Airlines and the Transport Workers Union of America; (6) the construction industry, including the Wage Adjustment Board (1943–7), Construction Industry Joint Conference (1958–68), Appeals Board (Jurisdictional Disputes) (1965–8) and work as arbitrator on jurisdictional issues; (7) private umpire arbitration, for example for the Pittsburgh Plate Glass Company and Eastern Airlines; (8) private labour–management committees (as neutral member or umpire) such as at Kaiser Steel Company (1959–67) and Tailored Clothing Companies (1977–); and (9) public sector committees, including the Governor's Committee on Public Employee Relations, New York State (1965–9), Joint Labor–Management Committee for Municipal Police and Fire, Commonwealth of Massachusetts (1977–) and the Task Force in Public Pensions and Disability, Commonwealth of Massachusetts (1982) (Poole 1988).

Along with this wealth of policy-based and more practical involvement in industrial relations, Dunlop also theorized and wrote on the subject. Running through much of both practical and written work was a dual focus: first, on labour peace, and a preference for jointly negotiated regulations, and second, a general endorsement of trade unions and long-standing interest in labour issues, such as in society, public image, practices and future roles (Bok and Dunlop 1970).

Dunlop (1944) produced an early and influential book with his major theory of wage determination under trade unions. It is this work for which he is best known in the academic sphere in the United States. The book covered a variety of themes, including the development of an economic model of trade unions, patterns of wage variation etc., and especially union wage policy and 'bargaining power'. He argued that the non-income objectives of union wage policy included membership promotion, work allocation, leisure, the introduction of technical changes, working conditions and trade entry. His interpretation of 'bargaining power' was grounded in the recognition of the inequalities between 'buyers' and 'sellers' in the market-place and rooted in economic analysis. This was an important work not only in its own right, but also as a spur to stimulating much further analysis on trade union wage policies and so on.

Dunlop (1984) also developed theoretically the key areas of negotiation and collective bargaining. He emphasized the importance of these and mediation as a means of dispute settlement rather than relying on markets or governmental direction. This work developed abstract as well as practical approaches to negotiations, outlining key 'principles' to the process and the characteristics of labour–management negotiations, with their great com-

plexity and diversity of interests. Importantly, he reminded readers that groups expected to continue to be engaged and interact in the future, that parties to the negotiations were not monolithic, and that negotiators were concerned with more than a single issue. These key points, caveats and nuances need to be remembered, for example by many 'macho mangers' and by MBA students involved in negotiations and simulations.

More recently, Dunlop (1992) emphasized the importance of human resource development for international competitiveness. This was in the context of poor US productivity performance. For Dunlop, improvements in this area required a more skilled work force, which in turn depended on aspects such as the education system, health care, training, family policy, labour–management policies and public services. He added his substantial influence and credibility to the debates and ideas concerning the development of trained and adaptable human resources as not just important to, but at the very heart of, competitive advantage. This key argument is of relevance to policy makers, governments, management and trade unions across many economies.

In Britain and in many other countries, Dunlop continues to be most known and noted for his seminal work applying the systems approach to industrial relations and holistic explanation (Dunlop 1958). This work helped in establishing the contours of the subject and influenced British approaches to the discipline, and created an influential, if not dominant, paradigm. While there had been many earlier writings in the field of labour, Dunlop's critical contribution was to forge the core elements of a subject area and its distinctiveness from other social sciences. Dunlop himself was influenced by Talcott Parsons, an eminent sociologist, whose functionalism and work used the analogy of systems thinking, with its antecedence in biology, as a framework for accounting for the nature and direction of society. The attractions of systems theory were numerous and included its seeming ability to make sense of a disparate set of phenomena in a period of rapid postwar growth in the United States, create an orderly description of its object and study, and provide an account of the variety of parts and connect them together through the logic of the function each appeared to play in sustaining the whole system. Such views usefully recognized that patterns of relationships have continually to adapt and are linked. There are interrelationships between the parts, and a tendency for changes in one part to have implications in another.

Furthermore, Dunlop wanted to generate a 'general' theory of industrial relations for at least two reasons. First, he saw an avalanche of facts outrunning any theory within which they could be located. Importantly, the contemporary American spatial and temporal context, such as the dynamic and diverse labour force, was also influential. Second, he wanted to give industrial relations a similar status to that which economics was seen to enjoy. He therefore set himself the task of creating the means to enable analysis and interpretation of a wide range of facts and practices, facilitate comparative analysis and link experience with ideas. His landmark book detailing his famous 'industrial relations system' was the result. He produced a broad-based integrative framework as he sought 'to provide tools of analysis to interpret and gain understanding of the widest possible range of industrial relations facts and practices', and 'to explain why particular rules are established in particular industrial relations systems and how and why they change in response to changes affecting the system' (Dunlop 1958: vi, ix). A pluralist perspective and lens in this work were obvious.

For Dunlop, the industrial relations system was a separate but related and overlapping subsystem of society. It was composed of four interrelated elements: (1) 'actors' (hierarchies of managers, workers and government agencies), who operate within (2) 'contexts' (technological characteristics of workplaces and work communities; market/budgetary

constraints; locus and distribution of power), which established (3) 'rules' for the workplace (regulatory frameworks, developed by a range of processes and presented in a variety of forms which expressed the terms and nature of the employment relationship), with (4) an 'ideology' (set of ideas and beliefs commonly held within the system which not only define the role of each actor, but also their views of each other) binding the system together. Thus, actors made rules within the constraints imposed by the contexts and their ideology. Dunlop went on to examine the substantive and procedural rules of industrial relations in coal mining and construction in a number of countries to show that the similarity of many of the rules could be explained by technologies and market conditions which transcended national boundaries, and that dissimilarities of rules on other matters were due to 'special features' of the national industrial relations system. In this way, he developed a 'systematic body of ideas for arranging and interpreting the known facts of worker–management–government interactions' (Dunlop 1958: 380).

Over the years, Dunlop and his industrial relations system have been subject to a variety of interpretations, modifications and criticisms, including some from supporters (Hyman 1975; Salamon 1998). These revolve around the system's problematical and debatable assumptions, which can be condensed into critiques that it was: (1) not really a testable 'theory'; (2) ahistorical, static and focused on formality; and (3) riven by universalistic, consensual and conservative presumptions and value-laden terms. For many the 'system' was more a 'model' or even a 'description'. It reduced industrial relations to the maintenance of stability and regularity, and failed to give enough emphasis to history, diversity in management and trade unions, informal organizations and the unequal power between actors. Neither did it recognize that a variety of ideologies can exist, and that these may clash and produce not consensus but conflict, which can be an output of industrial relations and not just some

sort of aberration in the rule production process. Indeed, the opposite can be argued, that rules may be more required if there is no consensus to regulate disagreement, with less need for rules if there is consensus. Its restrictive views on how conflict was controlled underplayed the processes through which it was generated, and its general assumption that the status quo was unproblematic reinforced views that this was legitimate, inevitable and unchangeable. Furthermore, it emphasized 'roles' rather than 'people' and so ignored behavioural traits and variables, did not reflect the real nature of wider society and was ambiguous as to whether the location of the contexts was part of the system or external constraints.

Critically, Dunlop's very terms were seen as problematic. For instance, 'system', which implied a set of rules and functional integration of component institutions, something that is orderly and capable of description, displayed a common set of values that binds it together and makes a system. An equilibrium is achieved with an emphasis on stability maintenance. Thus, the industrial relations system reaches a point of balance within itself and its internal constituencies, while at the same time reflecting the needs of the wider society of which it is part. Yet, what constitutes order is not absolute, but a matter of perception, belief and degree.

Even British pluralists of friendly persuasion made criticisms. Hugh CLEGG (1979: 449) noted that because of 'catch-all' expressions and failure to pick out relevant elements in the locus and distribution of power and relationships with patterns of employment rules, Dunlop's claim to have established a general theory was not established. Furthermore, modifications occurred, such as those based on differences of opinion on the purpose and objectives of the industrial relations system (Wood et al. 1975), with less emphasis on Dunlopian stability and survival, and more on the social control needs of management. These criticisms and changes also partly led to the development

of the area of strategy in the field, which went on to emerge as an important development from the 1980s onwards (Kochan *et al.* 1984).

Despite these diverse and weighty punches, the industrial relations system has survived the bombardment, and has left a deep and important legacy for the academic community. First, it helped in the establishment of a distinctive subject and its core elements and differences from other social sciences. Second, it bequeathed a set of terms that have remained embedded in the area's lexicon. Indeed, the influence of Dunlop's systems analysis (and focus on stability and order in industrial relations) was also clearly evident in the work of prominent British industrial relations academics such as Clegg, FLANDERS and FOX, as well as the 'Oxford School of Industrial Relations' they forged and public policy prescriptions they influenced. Thus, the contours and content of British industrial relations academia and public policy analysis and prescription were heavily influenced by such Dunlopian views. Even after forty years, Dunlop's industrial relations system is covered in most related courses, as well as in introductory chapters and teaching texts in the area, as an important starting point and building block.

In sum, Dunlop remains an important figure in industrial relations, and management practice and thought. Throughout much of the second half of the twentieth century his 'footprints' were deep and long lasting. Much of his work has had a long 'shelf life' in the orthodoxy of the discipline, and has also generated a plethora of work by others, while his public policy output, profile and stature remain impressive, solid and unalloyed. We can rightly state that so much after Dunlop was built 'on the shoulders of giants'. We could well go further and consider giving him the sobriquet of key 'founder' of the area of industrial relations.

Acknowledgements
Thanks to Michael Poole for earlier comments.

BIBLIOGRAPHY
Bok, D. and Dunlop, J. (1970) *Labor and the American Community*, New York: Simon and Schuster.
Clegg, H. (1979) *The Changing System of Industrial Relations*, Oxford: Blackwell.
Dunlop, J. (1944) *Wage Determination under Trade Unions*, New York: Macmillan.
—— (1958) *Industrial Relations Systems*, New York: Holt, Reinhart and Winston.
—— (1984) *Dispute Resolution: Negotiation and Consensus Building*, Dover, MA: Auburn House.
—— (1992) 'The Challenge of Human Resources Development', *Industrial Relations* 31(1): 50–55.
Dunlop, J. and Galenson, W. (eds) (1978) *Labor in the Twentieth Century*, New York: Academic Press.
Hyman, R. (1975) *Industrial Relations: A Marxist Introduction*, London: Macmillan.
Kaufman, B. (ed.) (1988) *How Labor Markets Work*, Lexington, MA: D.C. Heath and Co.
Kochan, T. (1995) 'Using the Dunlop Report to Achieve Mutual Gains', *Industrial Relations* 34(3): 350–66.
Kochan, T., Katz, H. and McKersie, A. (1984) *The Transformation of American Industrial Relations*, New York: Basic Books.
Poole, M. (1988) 'Dunlop, John Thomas', in M. Warner (ed.), *IEBM Handbook of Management Thinking*, London: International Thomson Business Press, 166–72.
Salamon, M. (1998) *Industrial Relations Theory and Practice*, London: Prentice-Hall.
Wood, S. *et al.* (1979) 'The "Industrial Relations System" Concept as a Basis for Theory in Industrial Relations', *British Journal of Industrial Relations* 13(33): 295.

CR

DUNNING, John H. (1927–)

John Dunning was born in Sandy, Bedfordshire on 26 June 1927. He was educated at the Forest School (Waltham Forest) and John Syons School, Harrow. After a brief period working in the City of London, first in an insurance broker's office and then in a bank, he joined the Royal Naval Volunteer Reserve (RNVR) and was commissioned as an officer in 1946. Leaving the navy in 1948, Dunning read for a BSc in economics at the City of London College and University College in London, and graduated with a first class honours degree in 1951. Following a period of research at University College, he was appointed lecturer and then senior lecturer at the University of Southampton, where he also earned his Ph.D. Beyond his earned degrees he also has honorary degrees from the University of Uppsala, the Autonomous University of Madrid and the University of Antwerp. In 1964 he was appointed foundation professor of economics at the University of Reading, where he continued until his retirement in 1992. He also held a joint appointment at Rutgers University in New Jersey from 1988 to 1992.

Called the doyen of international business researchers, Dunning has researched the economics of foreign direct investment (FDI) and the activities of multinationals enterprises (MNEs). One of the first to focus on MNEs, he has been followed in the field by three generations of international business scholars. In a globalizing world, Dunning's focus on MNEs has been seminal to our unfolding understanding of this important part of the world economy. His main influence on academic study has come through more than forty books, dozens of articles in academic journals and service on numerous editorial boards. During the 1990s Dunning was the most cited author in international business studies. His most influential works include his first book, *American Investment in British Manufacturing Industry*, first published in 1958 and recently reissued in an updated edition; *Multinationals Enterprises and the Global Economy* (1993); and an article in the *Journal of International Business*, 'Toward an Eclectic Theory of International Production: Some Empirical Tests' (1980). This pivotal article introduced his idea of the eclectic paradigm to the world: it was followed by numerous articles and books by Dunning and others which together have helped promote the paradigm as one of the key theoretical foundations of the study of international business.

Dunning has been a fixture at international business conferences for over forty years, not only presenting papers but also serving as the president of both the Academy of International Business and the International Trade and Finance Association. He has been a visiting professor at numerous universities including the Stockholm School of Economics, the University of California at Berkeley, HEC in Montreal, Boston University, the University of Hawaii and the University of International Business and Economics in Beijing. He has given courses of lectures at many other universities.

Beyond his influence on the academic study of MNEs and FDI, Dunning has also had influence on government policy and business practice. His influence on government thinking has been especially felt through his work as senior economic adviser to the Division on Transnational Corporations and Investment of UNCTAD (United Nations Commission on Trade and Development) in Geneva. He has for many years been a great influence on UNCTAD's annual report on MNEs and FDI, the World Investment Report. He has also been a frequent adviser to the British and American governments. His most direct influence on business has been as the chairman of a London-based economic and management consultant, Economists Advisory Group, which he co-founded in 1965.

In his seventies, Dunning continues to contribute to the debate on globalization, most recently in his book *Global Capitalism at Bay*

(2000), the title recalling Raymond Vernon's famous book from the 1960s, *Sovereignty at Bay*. In the autumn of 2001 Dunning is planning a major conference in Italy on the Moral Imperatives of Global Capitalism. A man of many parts, Dunning has also served as a Baptist lay preacher and president elect of the Southern Baptist Association.

BIBLIOGRAPHY
Dunning, J.H. (1958) *American Investment in British Manufacturing Industry*, London: George Allen and Unwin.
—— (1980) 'Toward an Eclectic Theory of International Production: Some Empirical Tests', *Journal of International Business*, 11(1): 9–31.
—— (1993) *Multinationals Enterprises and the Global Economy*, Wokingham: Addison-Wesley.
—— (2000) *Global Capitalism at Bay*, Wokingham: Addison-Wesley.

KJM

DURANT, William Crapo (1861–1947)

William Crapo Durant was born on 8 December 1861 in Boston to William Clark Durant, a businessman, and his wife Rebecca Crapo Durant. He died in New York City on 18 March 1947. His father soon deserted the family, but the Durants were spared the ordeal of poverty by an inheritance from Rebecca's father, a successful investor and former governor of Michigan. In 1872 Durant moved with his family to Flint, Michigan. His numerous relatives were fairly well off. After attending high school and working in a family sawmill, he decided to become an entrepreneur on his own. He was a born salesman, and started with medicine, cigars and insurance. In 1885 he married Clara Pitt and eventually

fathered two children. He and Clara divorced in 1908, and Durant then married Catherine Lederer; there were no children from this marriage.

Together with a friend, Durant bought a small cartage company in 1886, which they rechristened the Flint Road Cart Company. In the following fifteen years he turned this small firm into the Durant-Dort Carriage Company, the biggest carriage-maker in the United States. According to historian Richard Crabb, 'The Durant-Dort Carriage Company, with its coast-to-coast business and its component and assembly plants across the country, was the General Motors of the buggy industry' (Crabb 1969: 235). The company made wagons, carriages, buggies and carts. Durant-Dort had its local showrooms and service centres, and it purchased subsidiaries to make its wheels, axles and other parts. Durant became a millionaire and in the process laid the pattern that all future car manufacturers would follow.

In 1904 Durant made the leap from carriages to cars. Flint was also the home of the Buick Motor Company, one of a number of fledgling companies making 'horseless carriages' run by internal combustion engines, and these companies were already beginning to feel the pressure of a saturated market. The car in 1904 was still a luxury item which few could afford. There were few paved roads to drive it on. Durant, however, quickly saw the potential of the motor car, and acquired Buick. He began to run it like his carriage firm. He acquired supply companies, internalized his operations and set up his sales and service divisions. By 1907 Buick had the biggest car factory in the world and was marketing several models. Competition in this new world was already ruinous and Durant, like John D. ROCKEFELLER in petroleum, Andrew CARNEGIE in steel and John Pierpoint MORGAN in regards to railways, wanted to 'rationalize' the young auto market. He offered to merge with Ford, Oldsmobile and others, but they refused.

Henry FORD was by now mass producing the immensely popular Model T. Durant set

out to become his chief rival, and on 28 September 1908 incorporated the General Motors Company in New Jersey. General Motors (GM) was in the beginning a holding company designed to allow Buick to circumvent anti-trust laws. This was but the first step in an expansion by which Durant acquired Oldsmobile, Cadillac and a score of other companies. According to Crabb, for Durant, 'building General Motors was simply an extension of his earlier career in horse-drawn vehicles' (Crabb 1969: 235). The acquisition of the highly profitable Cadillac Motor Car Company in 1909 for $4,500,000 'served notice on everyone that General Motors was a new force with which to reckon in the motorcar business of the United States' (Crabb 1969: 239).

Durant's philosophy of car-making was very different from that of Ford. While 'Ford was completely dedicated to the concept of building a single car capable of meeting a wide range of needs so that high volume could reduce production costs and, ultimately, the price of the car', Durant 'believed that the future would belong to the organization that produced a line of motorcars ranging from light, inexpensive vehicles to large, expensive automobiles' (Crabb 1969: 235).

Durant was a bold visionary, but hardly a systematic administrator, according to Lee Dunlap, his Oakland-Pontiac manager:

When Mr. Durant visited one of his plants it was like a visitation of a cyclone. He would lead his staff in, take off his coat, begin issuing orders, dictating letters and calling the ends of the continent on the telephone: talking in his easy way to New York, Chicago, San Francisco ... Only a phenomenal memory could keep his deals straight; he worked so fast that the records were always behind.

(Crabb 1969: 244)

GM made a profit of $9 million in 1908 and over $10 million in 1909. Few investors in 1910, however, believed that the car would actually replace the buggy. Durant meanwhile acquired the unprofitable Heany Lamp Company in 1910, paying for it with huge amounts of GM stock. This expansion took up so much capital that GM went heavily into debt in 1910 and had to be rescued by a consortium of bankers. Durant lost control of GM for the next five years, remaining a stockholder and director.

The low-priced Chevrolet was Durant's child not by birth but by adoption (Edsforth 1999). The real father was Louis Chevrolet, a Buick racing-car driver. Durant financed the car as well as two other smaller Flint companies that were buying up the dying carriage companies and converting them to making cars. In 1913 Durant had folded these firms into Chevrolet's Flint operation. Chevrolet continued buying up other small companies as the car market further began to shake out. Chevrolet was rechartered in Delaware, and Durant set up Chevrolet plants near New York, in St Louis, inFort Worth and in the San Francisco Bay area, and a Canadian subsidiary in Oshawa, Ontario. By 1915 only the Model T was selling more units than Chevrolet.

The growing success of the Chevrolet helped Durant regain control of GM. Under the bankers, GM had paid off its debts but had little to show in profits. Durant bought up GM stock in exchange for Chevrolet stock, permitting him to become president of the company once more in June 1916. He then reincorporated GM as a Delaware company including Chevrolet and the parts conglomerate United Motors; he went on to acquire Fisher Body and Frigidaire. In this new attempt to expand, Durant was dependent upon the capital of Pierre DU PONT. Durant and Du Pont, however, had a severe temperamental clash; du Pont was a systematic, procedure-driven manager who perfected the art of control accounting, while Durant was an entrepreneur who often went with his feelings, juggled his options and took risks, often in

secret. Durant's dependency upon the du Ponts and weaknesses in his management once gain cost him ownership of GM, this time for good. Only Buick and Chevrolet were really making money; the rest of the group was far less profitable. The company was too disorganized and overcommitted in the stock market. In the downturn of 1920, the price of GM shares plummeted and du Pont took over the company.

For the remainder of his life, Durant went from one failed venture to another. He first tried to start his own car company, which struggled on through the 1920s and then was wiped out during the Great Depression. Other ventures met with even less success. Durant died in 1947. He lived long enough, nonetheless, to see GM transformed by his successor Alfred P. SLOAN into the most successful company in the world. Much of the solid GM edifice would be built by managers upon the foundation laid by Durant the entrepreneur.

BIBLIOGRAPHY

Crabb, R. (1969) *Birth of a Giant: The Men and Incidents that Gave America the Motorcar*, Philadelphia, PA: Chilton Book Company.

Edsforth, R. (1999) 'Durant, William Crapo', in J.A. Garraty and M. Carnes (eds), *American National Biography*, New York: Oxford University Press, vol. 27, 148–51.

Langworth, R.M. and Norbye, J.P. (1986) *The Complete History of General Motors, 1908–1986*, New York: Beekman House.

'William Crapo Durant' (1999) *The McGraw-Hill Encyclopedia of World Biography*, Detroit, MI: Gale Research, Inc., vol. 5, 158.

DCL

DUTIES OF THE VIZIER (*c.*1520 BC)

The name of the author of *Duties of the Vizier*, an ancient Egyptian manual of administration, is unknown, but he was probably a high court official writing in the second half of the reign of the Pharaoh Ahmose (*c.*1539 BC–1514 BC), founder of the Eighteenth Dynasty (Van den Boorn 1988: 344; other authors have assigned earlier dates). Four copies of the text have been discovered, all in tombs dating from the Eighteenth and Nineteenth Dynasties. The first published edition of *Duties of the Vizier* was that of Philippe Virey in 1889, but this editor, failing to understand the nature of Egyptian writing, managed somehow to translate the text backwards. The best modern edition is that of Van den Boorn (1988).

The text itself, the earliest manual of management and administration yet discovered, sets out the duties of the important royal official known as the *t3ty*, a title usually translated as 'vizier'. It is divided into nineteen short sections, each of which defines some aspect of the vizier's managerial role. These in turn can be classed into three groups: (1) those relating to the management of the royal household itself, the *pr-nsw*; (2) those relating to the command and control of the centralized civil administration; and (3) a more general category concerning powers delegated to the vizier by the pharaoh. Procedures are laid down for internal communication (daily reports were required from key departments), security, the appointment and management of key subordinate personnel, and operational control over the departments of the civil service. Mention is also made of the vizier's own department, the *h3 n t3ty*, consisting of support staff who helped him to carry out these functions.

The overall picture describes an authoritarian, top-down but minutely detailed system of management and administration. *Duties of the Vizier* was written at a time when Egypt had only recently been reunited after a period of fragmentation and foreign occupation.

Ahmose, the reunifier of Egypt, aimed 'to reinstal proper government and effective administration throughout the country' (Van den Boorn 1988: 345). In doing so, he sought to establish a strong centralized system of reporting and control, coupled with an efficient central management of the kingdom's resources. The relationship between the pharaoh and his vizier was not unlike that between a chairman of the board and his managing director.

The extent to which the *Duties of the Vizier* reflects the actual views of Pharaoh Ahmose is not clear, and he is highly unlikely to have written the work himself. Van den Boorn suggests that the impetus may have come from Ahmose's mother, Ahhotep, who remained in charge of the civil administration of Egypt during the long periods when the pharaoh was absent in the field with his armies. It was Ahhotep who was responsible for many of the administrative reforms of this period, and the *Duties of the Vizier* may represent attempts by her and her officials to codify those reforms.

BIBLIOGRAPHY
Martin-Pardey, E. (1999) 'Administrative Bureaucracy', in K.A. Bard (ed.), *Encyclopedia of the Archaeology of Ancient Egypt*, London: Routledge, 115–18.
Van den Boorn, G.P.F. (1988) *The Duties of the Vizier*, London: Kegan Paul International.

MLW

E

EASTMAN, George (1854–1932)

George Eastman was born in Waterville, New York on 12 July 1854 and died by his own hand at Rochester, New York on 14 March 1932. Eastman's father, a teacher of penmanship, founded Rochester's first commercial college. Eastman started work at the age of thirteen, working in an insurance office for three dollars a week. He later moved to the Rochester Savings Bank, where he advanced rapidly, earning $1,400 a year by the age of twenty-two. At this time he began experimenting with photography, first as a hobby and later with the idea of commercially manufacturing photographic plates. He was attracted to the possibility of developing a 'dry-plate' emulsion as an alternative to the cumbersome and difficult coating and developing of wet plates. He hoped his dry-plate emulsion would drastically reduce the size and weight of photographic equipment. By 1879 he was ready to patent his dry-plate process, and in 1880 he entered into a partnership with Henry A. Strong, quit his bank job, and devoted himself full-time to his small photographic business.

In 1884 he began searching for a transparent and flexible film and achieved his first breakthrough, preparing a paper-backed film. By 1888 he had expanded from dry plates and film to cameras, marketing the first Kodak. The Kodak (the name was invented by Eastman and chosen for its unique nature) was priced at twenty-five dollars and held film containing 100 exposures. The camera had to be mailed back to the factory, where the exposures were developed and the camera reloaded and returned to the customer. Despite this cumbersome process, it was a huge success. By 1889, largely due to the work of his chemist Henry M. Reichenbach, Eastman had patented a transparent film. This film proved crucial in the advancement of motion pictures.

By the end of the 1880s Eastman had emerged as a major figure in the plate, film, camera and motion picture industries. By the end of the 1890s, he dominated each of these fields. The company increased rapidly in size and capitalization, and continued to offer important innovations and improvements in its products. In short order Eastman introduced daylight loading film, a pocket Kodak, a five-dollar camera and stronger motion picture film. To manage the necessary production and expansion Eastman adhered to four key principles, all relatively new to American business: mass production, low unit cost, extensive advertising, and international distribution. In 1891 Eastman opened his Kodak Park plant. Sitting on 230 acres, with over 7,000 employees, Kodak was, in the words of historian Sanford Jacoby, a 'behemoth of capital-intensive mass production' (Jacoby 1997: 59). At Kodak Park, Eastman perfected the techniques of mass production long before Henry FORD brought them to the automobile industry. The resulting low costs were a necessary step in reaching Eastman's goal of bringing photography within the reach of most Americans.

With production increasing, Eastman's early and innovative use of advertising played an important role in helping to stimulate the necessary demand. The name Kodak joined the small list of brand names which came to be identified as their product, and Kodak's early slogan, 'You press the button. We do the rest,' was so successful Gilbert and Sullivan wrote it into the lyrics for their 1893 operetta *Utopia, Limited*. Kodak's targeted advertising especially sought to reach women, moving the camera from a predominantly male hobby to a family necessity. Finally, Kodak's early expansion overseas allowed it to rapidly consolidate control of the international market for film.

In addition, Eastman recognized the importance of scientific research and was a pioneer in the creation of corporate research and development facilities. He actively recruited scientists of international reputation and devoted a substantial sum to building research laboratories in Rochester. Utilizing its strong vertical, horizontal and spatial integration, and adhering to its core principles of low-cost production, effective advertising, international sales, and continual technical improvement and innovation enabled Eastman Kodak to dominate the film and camera markets.

Control of between 75 and 80 per cent of the American film market combined with massive profits at a time of heightened anti-trust concern, however, brought the attention of the Justice Department. Anti-trust investigations were begun in 1911. A prospective amicable settlement was abandoned by the government after the election of Woodrow Wilson in 1912, and in 1915 the Eastman Kodak Company of New Jersey (organized in 1901 to take advantage of the state's notoriously lax tax laws) was found to be in violation of the Sherman Anti-trust Act. The case was ultimately dismissed on appeal after Eastman signed a consent decree agreeing to sell some subsidiaries and change certain business practices. Thereafter, Eastman continued to fear government involvement in his business. This fear led him to cooperate with the government whenever possible to forestall scrutiny. During the First World War Kodak produced photographic materials for the army and navy, trained the US signal corps in photography, and manufactured numerous synthetic chemicals in an attempt to make the USA more economically independent. After the war Eastman made a point of cancelling government bills and refusing what he decided were excessive profits on war work.

As suggested by his war work, Eastman shared with many progressive-era industrialists the belief that corporations had a responsibility to serve the public good. Eastman was a pioneer in employee welfare programmes whose complicated origins can partially be explained by his paternalist belief that corporations could and should take over many of the functions that families and local communities seemed unable to discharge. But Eastman was aware of the resentment such paternalism could cause (he changed the name of the governing department from the Welfare Fund to the Kodak Employees' Association) and designed his programmes to provide more tangible benefits. As Eastman said, 'You can talk about cooperation and good feeling and friendliness from morn to midnight, but the thing the worker appreciates is the same thing the man at the helm appreciates – dollars and cents' (Jacoby 1997: 64).

To that end, Kodak's employee benefits were heavily economic. Kodak offered a share in the profits for executives, accident and sickness insurance for all employees, a building and loan association, a pension system and a stock purchase programme, along with the more common and less substantial corporate culture building events such as company picnics, dances, sports leagues and amateur theatricals. On three occasions Eastman distributed substantial amounts of his personal wealth to employees, either directly or by endowing various welfare programmes. Perhaps most unusual among the list of Kodak benefits was the wage dividend, instituted in

1912. As originally constituted, it paid employees a 2 per cent bonus on their wages for the previous five years. Kodak's pension, established in 1929, was also an important innovation. In an era when the few existing company pensions were discretionary and unfunded, the Kodak pension fund was the first in the nation, among major employers, to be contractual, non-discretionary and fully insured.

These programmes also originated in less idealistic and more practical concerns. Prominent among these was the desire to prevent the spread of unionization, something the deeply conservative and staunchly Republican Eastman adamantly opposed. Eastman was also continually concerned with the public reputation of his company, fearing more anti-monopoly proceedings and greater government regulation. All of Eastman's large stock gifts were bestowed during periods when Eastman perceived unionization as a threat, and his announcement of the wage dividend came the same year as the government's anti-trust case. A related motivation for corporate welfare work was Eastman's recognition that employee loyalty was a crucial component of his company's success and must be assiduously cultivated. Eastman recognized that his plants were unusually dependent on the disposition of their labour forces; sabotage was easy in a work environment where direct supervision was almost impossible, and the extreme spatial concentration of Kodak plants meant a strike could prove disastrous. Whatever the precise nature of their origins, Eastman Kodak provided one of the most expansive of benefit and welfare programmes during the heyday of welfare capitalism, and unlike many of the programmes founded concurrently, most of Kodak's programmes survived the Depression intact. Kodak's particular brand of welfare capitalism, with its emphasis on financial benefits and retaining its workers, was distinctive in its ability to last into the 1960s, long after most of industrial America had moved to collective bargaining as the basis for labour relations.

By the 1920s, with his company's dominant position consolidated and his edifice of welfare programmes constructed, Eastman decreased his involvement in Eastman Kodak and began to expand his philanthropic activities. His charitable giving had begun with a gift of $200,000 to the Rochester Mechanics Institute in 1899 and a later smaller gift to the University of Rochester. As he expanded the scale of his gifts, the majority were to institutions in his local community and to universities and colleges. Here again his motivation was both civic and practical. As he said, 'From the Kodak point of view I consider it a very highly desirable thing to have a good college here, not only to help train good men but also to make Rochester an attractive place for Kodak men to live and bring up their families' (Jacoby 1997: 60).

Eastman had a lifelong dislike of publicity and attention, and his early gifts to a favourite institution, the Massachusetts Institute of Technology (MIT), were presented on the behalf of 'Mr. Smith'. It was not until 1920, when Eastman, seeking to break up his large holdings of Kodak stock, gave MIT a large stock gift, that his identity was revealed. By then he had donated $20 million to the university. All told, he also donated more than $35 million to the University of Rochester, $2.5 million to create and fund a Rochester dental dispensary, $5 million to international dental clinics, and more than $2 million each to the Hampton (Virginia) and Tuskegee (Alabama) Negro Institutes.

Eastman had no wife or children. Living alone in the mammoth house he built in Rochester, he cultivated his interests in big game hunting, flowers and music. By nature an ascetic, taciturn and reticent man, he had never become much involved in the civic life of Rochester, despite his many donations. Most of his social life was with the people with whom he worked. By the early 1930s he was no longer directly involved either at the plant or at the office and rarely visited either. His health was deteriorating. On 14 March 1932,

immediately after the signing of his last will, Eastman shot himself in the heart, leaving the note 'To my friends; my work is done. Why wait?' His work had included pioneering photographic innovations, the creation of a modern industrial giant built on principles of industrial organization and management that would be widely emulated, the innovative use of industrial research laboratories staffed by scientists of international repute, a humane and generous system of employee relations, and a key financial role in the development of educational institutions such as the University of Rochester. Eastman was a model of what the progressive businessmen could accomplish during an era when businessmen enjoyed both enormous prestige and power.

BIBLIOGRAPHY

Ackerman, C.W. (1930) *George Eastman*, Boston and New York: Houghton Mifflin.

Brayer, E. (1996) *George Eastman: A Biography*, Baltimore and London: The Johns Hopkins University Press.

Butterfield, R. (1954) 'The Prodigious Life of George Eastman', *Life*, 26 April.

Jacoby, S.M. (1997) *Modern Manors: Welfare Capitalism Since the New Deal*, Princeton, NJ: Princeton University Press.

RV

EBTEHAJ, Abol Hassan (1899–1999)

Abol Hassan Ebtehaj was born in Rasht, capital of Gilan province in northern Iran, on 29 November 1899. He died, probably in London, on 24 February 1999. He was the second child of Ephraim Ebtehaj al-Molk, a member of the Persian civil service, and his wife Fatima Khanoum. At the age of eleven he was sent with his brother to be educated at the Lycée Montaigne in Paris and then at the Syrian Protestant College in Beirut, where he learned fluent French and English. His father was murdered by bandits during the chaos at the end of the First World War, and the family fled to Tehran. Family connections arranged for a job for Ebtehaj at the Ministry of War, but he then decided to go into banking and joined the British-owned Imperial Bank of Persia. Over the next ten years he rose to the rank of assistant to the chief inspector, one of the senior British officials of the bank. He married Mariam Nabavi, daughter of a diplomat.

The Imperial Bank had at this time many of the functions of a state bank. In 1928 the reforming shah Reza Pehlavi established the Bank Melli Iran with a view to removing control of central banking from foreign hands. Ebtehaj played an invaluable role for the Imperial Bank in the negotiations that followed, and secured a number of important concessions. However, according to Bostock and Jones (1989), authors of the definitive English-language study of Ebtehaj, he learned that despite his abilities he could not be promoted to a senior position in the bank, as these were all reserved for Britons.

Ebtehaj resigned from the Imperial Bank in 1936 and immediately found a senior post in the ministry of finance, where his experience and talents ensured his rapid rise. By 1938 he was vice-governor of Bank Melli, and in 1940 was made chairman of the state mortgage bank, Bank Rahni. In 1942 he was made governor of Bank Melli: 'a mere six years after leaving the British bank he was in a position to dictate policy and terms to the institution which had turned a deaf ear to his requests for equal opportunity and treatment' (Bostock and Jones 1989: 28). He reformed the corrupt administration at Bank Melli and made it the country's leading bank. His independence and obvious lack of political ambition made him a man the government could trust; and trust was the value which Ebtehaj prized most of all. He offered his employees good wages and working conditions in exchange for high standards:

No law or Government decision could compel people to place their money and their confidence in a bank they could not trust and whose services they did not find satisfactory. I said I demanded from them absolute integrity and honesty, accuracy and attention and courtesy to the customers ... always remembering that we were their servants and not their masters.

(Bostock and Jones 1989: 39)

Ebtehaj introduced profit sharing, and in wartime provided basic rations to staff; other benefits included a subsidized restaurant, health-care services, a swimming pool and gymnasium; security guards were instructed to use the latter regularly, 'with notable results' (Bostock and Jones 1989: 40). In the broader world of banking, he took control of foreign credit operations and many other central banking functions, to the fury of rivals such as the Imperial Bank.

Not only did Ebtehaj reform and strengthen Bank Melli and provide a model for employee relations, he also greatly enhanced Iran's reputation abroad. With him at the helm, Bank Melli and Iran were increasingly treated like equal partners in world financial affairs. When Ebtehaj later led the Iranian delegation to the Bretton Woods conference, he won the respect of all there, including John Maynard KEYNES.

Political manoeuvrings by rivals led to his dismissal in 1950. He served as ambassador to Paris 1950–52, and from 1952 to 1954 worked with the International Monetary Fund in Washington. Returning to Iran, he was invited by the shah to head Plan Organization, a body which was to coordinate economic planning in the country. He managed this with considerable success, but resigned in 1959 after failing to persuade the shah to devote the country's vast oil revenues to funding development rather than arms. In 1961 he gave a speech at an International Industrial Conference in San Francisco criticizing bilateral aid, especially between the United States and Iran; in 1962 he was arrested in Iran and

imprisoned for almost a year. An international press campaign led by Henry LUCE and supported by John F. Kennedy secured his release, and he left public life and went into private banking and insurance. All his property in Iran was confiscated during the 1979 revolution and he and his wife settled in the south of France, later moving to London. He remains an exemplar of financial management in the modern age, particularly in his understanding of the role of trust and integrity in financial relationships.

BIBLIOGRAPHY
Bostock, F. and Jones, G. (1989) *Planning and Power in Iran: Ebtehaj and Economic Development Under the Shah*, London: Frank Cass.

MLW

EDISON, Thomas Alva (1847–1931)

Thomas Alva Edison was born in Milan, Ohio on 11 February 1847, the son of Samuel and Nancy Edison. He died at home in Orange, New Jersey on 18 October 1931, a few days after collapsing at a celebration dinner marking the fiftieth anniversary of his invention of the light bulb. His father, a storekeeper, was one of the followers of the Canadian rebel William Lyon Mackenzie, and fled to the United States after the abortive revolt of 1837. Edison himself was educated largely at home, in a household that Israel (1998) describes as radical and free-thinking; Thomas Paine was one of Samuel Edison's favourite authors. His upbringing explains much of Edison's attitude to life and to science: challenging, innovative and unwilling to accept limits.

An entrepreneurial spirit was also revealed at an early age. By the age of twelve, Edison was selling newspapers and food to passengers

on the local railway, and while in his middle teens he edited and published a local newspaper. He was fascinated by news of the invention of the telegraph, and received free tuition as a telegraph operator after he saved the life of the operator's son. From the age of sixteen he was working as a telegraph operator by day and experimenting with improvements to the apparatus by night. Despite a serious hearing problem, he worked his way to the top of his profession and was hired as a wire service operator by the Western Union. In 1867 he patented his first major invention, an improved duplex telegraph. In 1868 he moved to Boston, and then in 1869 to New York, where he became a full-time inventor. In 1870 he moved to New Jersey, finally settling at Menlo Park in 1876, the site of his most famous work.

The story of Edison's inventions is too complex to tell in a short space, and has been well described by Israel (1998) and Clark (1997). Edison took out 1,093 patents, more than any other person; the first was granted when he was twenty, the last was taken out a few days before his death. His attitude to invention was pragmatic, and he always sought a practical use, usually in business, for his inventions; if this failed to materialize, he quickly moved on to the next idea. The perfect research and development executive, Edison was a never-failing fund of ideas on which business could draw. The electric light bulb and the phonograph are his most famous work, but his experimentation in the field of electricity seemingly knew no bounds; he was even involved in early designs for an electric chair, and was involved in an actual execution in an attempt to prove the superiority of his direct current (DC) system over that of the rival alternating current (AC) developed by George WESTINGHOUSE.

Edison's influence on management is debatable. Many of his inventions, particularly in the communications field, such as improvements to the telegraph and the telephone (the latter invented by Alexander Graham BELL just ahead of Edison), were important in increasing the scale and scope of managerial work; faster communications meant improved coordination over distance. At a time when American companies were moving towards large-scale operations, this was very important. Personally, he is usually described as an inventor rather than a businessman; Herbert CASSON, who knew him well, dismissed his managerial abilities on the grounds that Edison seldom exploited his own inventions. Yet as Davis (1987) points out, Edison did exploit the electric light very successfully, raising funds from backers such as J.P. MORGAN to set up the Edison Electric Illuminating Company in New York.

Testimony to his greatest influence, though, comes from Henry FORD, who knew Edison well (the two used to go on camping trips together, along with Harvey FIRESTONE). Edison, says Ford, changed Americans' attitudes to science and how it could be used to solve basic problems, including in management; Edison's true achievement was in 'linking science with our everyday life and demonstrating that, through patient, unremitting testing and trying, any problem may eventually be solved' (Ford and Crowther 1930: 26). Edison, says Ford, showed how scientific methods could be used in industry in a wide variety of ways, not just in technology and machinery. Ford's final tribute is worth quoting:

> he is the founder of modern industry in this country. He has formed for us a new kind of declaration of independence ... in the nature of a kit of tools, by the use of which each and every person among us has gained a larger measure of economic liberty than had ever previously been thought possible.
>
> (Ford and Crowther 1930: 25)

BIBLIOGRAPHY

Clark, R.W. (1997) *Edison: The Man Who Made the Future*, London: Macdonald and Jane's.

Davis, W. (1987) *The Innovators: The*

Essential Guide to Business Thinkers, London: Ebury Press.

Ford, H. and Crowther, S. (1930) *My Friend Mr Edison*, London: Ernest Benn.

Israel, P. (1998) *Edison: A Life of Invention*, New York: John Wiley and Sons.

Wachhorst, W. (1981) *Thomas Alva Edison: An American Myth*, Cambridge, MA: MIT Press.

MLW

EISNER, Michael Dammann (1942–)

Michael Eisner, current chairman and CEO of the Walt Disney Company, was born in Mount Kisco, New York on 7 March 1942, to J. Lester and Margaret Eisner. He was educated at prep school in Lawrenceville, New Jersey before going to Denison University in Granville, Ohio in 1961. He realized that a country's most lasting legacy is not political but artistic. Majoring in theatre, he began writing plays. Eisner soon displayed his lifelong talent for imagination and creativity, as well as his people and business skills. From 1963–7 he worked in entry level jobs at the National Broadcasting Corporation (NBC) and later at the Columbia Broadcasting Corporation (CBS).

In 1967 Eisner began a nine-year sojourn with the American Broadcasting Corporation (ABC). ABC, fascinated with his 'simplicity, charm, enthusiasm, and lack of corporate polish', put him in charge of programme development (Flower 1991: 43). Soon, his popular shows such as *Happy Days*, a nostalgic romantic comedy set in an idealized 1950s, showed his intuition for what Americans wanted to watch. His flair at promoting the 'Fonz' and other loveable, eccentric characters helped the struggling ABC to overtake

both NBC and CBS. In 1976 Eisner became President of Paramount film studios, where his popular films, including *Saturday Night Fever, Grease, Heaven Can Wait, Raiders of the Lost Ark, Airplane!*, the *Star Trek* series and *Flashdance*, helped Paramount's profits triple from $39 million in 1973 to $140 million in 1983.

In 1984 Eisner took over the troubled Walt Disney Productions. Once the giant of Hollywood family entertainment, the studio had produced only two successful films from 1969 to 1984. The studio was $900 million in debt, and desperately trying to fend off attacks by corporate raiders who wanted to dismantle it.

Eisner worked a managerial and marketing revolution. Walt Disney Productions became the Walt Disney Company. Working eighteen-hour days, he and his staff brought about one of the most remarkable turnarounds in business history. To do so, he had to transform Disney's culture without destroying it. Eisner had to deal with the question of, in his own words, 'whether or not we can evolve into a giant company without losing that family feeling' (Flower 1991: 197). That culture, however, was so entrenched that Eisner felt it could only be changed from the top down. Eisner brought in sixty new executives and let go 1,000 employees. He also set up a strategic planning department. While promoting classic Disney features such as *Pinocchio* on video, he began to rework Disney's image by making more adult films such as *Down and Out in Beverly Hills, Ruthless People* and *Good Morning, Vietnam* on the Touchstone label.

Eisner was not interested in short-term profits alone. The essence of Disney culture was safeguarding the reputation of a Disney brand name that was the key to far greater long-term profits. According to Disney executive Frank Wells, 'you really do have a larger responsibility when you carry that name around' (Flower 1991: 181).

Eisner reinvented Disney in a world being remade by globalization, high technology and

demographics. The world of the 1980s craved American entertainment, and many could now afford to enjoy it on video recorders and cable television. People demanded more sophisticated films than those of the 1950s. Through aggressive marketing of the old and the new, Eisner transformed Disney from a faltering firm servicing a dwindling market to a formidable global competitor. Revenues grew from $98 million to almost $3 billion between 1984 and 1987 (Flower 1991). By 1990 Eisner had tripled Disney's assets and increased its stock value twelvefold.

BIBILOGRAPHY

Flower, J. (1991) *Prince of the Magic Kingdom: Michael Eisner and the Re-Making of Disney*, New York: John Wiley and Sons.

DCL

ELBOURNE, Edward Tregaskis
(1875–1935)

Edward Tregaskis Elbourne was born in Birmingham on 12 June 1875 and died in London on 18 October 1935. He was educated at King Edward's School, Birmingham, and then undertook technical and engineering training in Birmingham and in Barrow-in-Furness. Completing his training in 1896, he first found work as a draughtsman. He seems to have had a lively curiosity about work and management methods, and in 1900 visited the United States to study machine tools and factory organization. He learned a great deal from this visit (Urwick and Brech 1957: 148–9), and on returning to Britain took up his first management position, as works organizer and accountant at John Thornycroft and Company. Over the next few years he advanced rapidly. By 1914 he was factory

works accountant for Vickers Sons and Maxim's plant at Erith, south east of London. He later went on to be departmental works manager for Birmingham Small Arms, and assistant general manager of the Ponders End Shell Works. Here he worked with Henry (later Sir Henry) Brindley, who, like Elbourne, had a considerable interest in the problems of industrial administration and efficiency. At the end of the First World War, after a highly successful career in industry, Elbourne joined Brindley in setting up the engineering consultancy business Brindley and Elbourne. Brindley died soon after, in 1920, and Elbourne continued on alone. In 1926 he was appointed director of marketing investigation at Shaw, Wardlow and Company in London. He continued to work as an organization consultant until his death.

Elbourne's major achievements were in the field of management education. He believed strongly in the importance of education for managers, and was the moving spirit behind the establishment of the Institute for Industrial Administration in 1920. He was also the Institute's honorary director of education, and continually pressed for the establishment of courses in industrial administration in Britain. The first such was finally offered by the Regent Street Polytechnic in London in 1927, with Elbourne and B.C. Adams as joint directors of the programme. Elbourne continued to play an important role in the affairs of the Institute, and meanwhile persuaded two of the major professional associations, the Institute of Electrical Engineers and the Institute of Mechanical Engineers, to include industrial administration as a subject within their examination scheme. He was also an important influence on the establishment of the Department of Business Administration at the London School of Economics, where he lectured on costing, and he served as an examiner for the commerce degree at the University of London.

Elbourne's final initiative in the field of education was aimed at providing an equivalent of

the army's staff colleges for industry, an institution where managers could take a break in mid-career, update and improve their knowledge and skills, and prepare for positions of leadership. In effect, Elbourne was envisioning a prototype of executive education of the type offered today by many business schools. However, he was only able to bring about an experimental series of courses at Loughborough College in November 1934 before his own untimely death the following year.

Elbourne wrote several books, in which the focus was largely on the practical issues of day-to-day management. *Factory Administration and Accounts* (1914), his first book, was not written specifically as a textbook, but nonetheless came to be accepted as one. Urwick and Brech (1957: 149) note that the book came to the attention of Sir John Mann, a senior civil servant in the Ministry of Munitions, who encouraged managers in firms engaged on government work to buy it. Largely as a result of Mann's endorsement, the book sold some 10,000 copies, a phenomenal figure for a book on management in Britain at that time. The bulk of *Factory Administration and Accounts* is in fact about accounting, and Elbourne is here attempting to bring accounting into the mainstream of management thinking, to make it a fundamental part of management rather than a specialist or ancillary activity. The book's primary goal is to make accounting methods and measures understandable to and usable by non-accounting specialists. Despite the title, Elbourne considers issues such as design and administration only briefly and in not much detail. He does, however, define management as consisting of three related sets of tasks: works administration, sales administration and financial administration (Elbourne 1914: 21).

Two further of Elbourne's books deserve note. His interest in marketing research led him to write *The Marketing Problem* (1926), which looked at US advances in marketing and suggested how these could be applied in Britain. This is one of the first detailed examinations by

a British writer of the new developments in marketing being pioneered by US managers and academics. Much of the book is devoted to summarizing the writings of American thinkers and practitioners, including L.D.H. WELD among others. Elbourne recommends the adoption of many American practices such as market research and analysis, supported by the work of independent marketing consultants, or 'counsels', and also the use of new techniques in advertising and promotion; he also looks at advances in distribution. The book includes a twenty-five page list of books on marketing published up to 1925, by authorities such as Weld, Percival White, Paul CHERINGTON, Melvin COPELAND, Fred CLARK, J.O. McKINSEY and Walter Lippincott. Despite its obvious value, the book apparently was not a commercial success.

Fundamentals of Industrial Administration (1934), his final book, was intended as a syllabus for new programmes of training and education such as the one he was then helping to set up at Loughborough (Urwick and Brech 1957). Unusually for a business text, the book starts with a detailed historical synopsis, attempting to explain how the growth of industrial organization, and especially organizational forms, led in turn to the growth of management. This is a fairly standard general textbook on management, interesting in that it was the first such work written in Britain which was intended to accompany a course of study. Interesting too are the final chapters on the general principles of management, in which Elbourne shows that for all his study of American scientific management, he remains at heart a follower of the British cultural tradition in which management is seen as an art, not a science. Like Oliver SHELDON before him, he believes that scientific management is an important tool and should be adopted by British firms, but that it is not all there is to management. He quotes Sheldon at length, along with other authorities, on the importance of the human factor: a manager's job is not just to manage systems and machines, but

also to manage people. He finishes off with his own set of 'principles', which, taken together, make up management: these are investigation, goal-setting ('objective' in Elbourne's term), organization, direction, experiment and control. 'Experiment' is one of the most interesting of these, referring to the need for continuous improvement: 'If the principles of continuity and mobility are to be observed it is necessary to make arrangement for constant experiment with a view to improving features of the organization or system' (Elbourne 1934: 575).

Urwick and Brech (1957) cite Elbourne as one of the major forces in the development of management education and training in Britain following the First World War. Some of his writings were more successful than others, but at the very least they are an important testimony to the growing awareness of the issues involved in professional management in Britain in the 1920s and 1930s. If few of Elbourne's works were original in themselves, he was an important and able disseminator, one who did much to popularize the new techniques among the British managerial classes.

BIBLIOGRAPHY
Elbourne, E.T. (1914) *Factory Administration and Accounts*, London: Longmans, Green and Co.
—— (1919) *The Costing Problem*, London: The Library Press.
—— (1926) *The Marketing Problem: How it is Being Tackled in the USA*, London: Longmans, Green and Co.; repr. Bristol: Thoemmes Press, 2000.
—— (1934) *Fundamentals of Industrial Administration: An Introduction to Industrial Organization, Management and Economics*, London: Macdonald and Evans.
Sears, J.E. (ed.) (1922) *Who's Who in Engineering*, London: The Compendium Publishing Company.
Urwick, L.F. and Brech, E.F.L. (1957) *The Making of Scientific Management*, vol. 1, *Thirteen Pioneers*, London: 1949; repr. Bristol: Thoemmes Press, 1994.

MLW

ELLISON, Lawrence Joseph (1944–)

Lawrence Joseph Ellison was born in New York on 17 August 1944. His mother was unmarried, and Ellison was adopted while still a baby by his aunt and uncle in Chicago. He has married three times, to Adda Quinn in 1967, Nancy Wheeler in 1977 and Barbara Boothe in 1983; all three marriages have ended in divorce. Ellison graduated from South Shore High School in Chicago in 1962 and entered the University of Illinois, but left after two years without taking a degree. He moved to California in 1966, apparently with the idea of studying medicine at the University of California, but he was already becoming fascinated with computers and had developed his skills as a programmer. From 1967 to 1971 he worked as a programmer and systems architect with Amdahl Corporation, a high-tech start-up near Santa Clara, California. He became particularly interested in relational databases, a new type of software program that began development around 1970.

In 1972, seeing only limited prospects, Ellison left Amdahl and joined Precision Instrument Company (later Omex) as vice-president in charge of systems development. In 1977 he and two partners, Bob Miner and Ed Oates founded the Oracle Company in Redwood, California, initially as a maker and supplier of relational databases. Ellison was chairman and chief executive officer of the new firm and, as rapidly became clear, the business brains behind it.

Ellison's strategy was simple: to grow the firm as quickly as possible. He believed that

there would ultimately be a shake-out in the computer and software industries, as too many firms were chasing too small a market and many of these firms were not ultimately sound; when the crash came, only the strong would survive. To this end he pushed his product engineers and his sales staff relentlessly. His strategy has, to date, paid off: Oracle has climbed into the ranks of the world's most powerful high-tech firms alongside the likes of IBM, Microsoft, Sun Microsystems and Netscape.

Ellison achieved his goal by creating an atmosphere of relentless pressure within the firm (Wilson 1997). His sales force became notorious for their aggression. One member of the sales management team once suggested a simple strategy for dealing with competition: 'Cut off the oxygen' (Wilson 1997: 158). In a highly controversial move, which appears to have shocked even Ellison, the company sales director authorized sales staff to be paid, quite literally, in bags of gold.

Wilson, in his biography of Ellison, takes a highly critical view of his subject, but even this critique cannot obscure a picture of what is obviously a considerable managerial talent. Ellison's sense of strategic vision, of the necessity of growth in order to create bulwarks against future downturns, stands head and shoulders above the hit-and-miss approach of many of his competitors. Of all the high-tech entrepreneurs of the late twentieth century, only Andrew GROVE is his match in terms of management skill and perceptiveness. In the coming century, it is leaders such as Grove and Ellison who are likely to be the most reliable role models for managers in newly evolved business sectors.

BIBLIOGRAPHY
Wilson, M. (1997) *The Difference Between God and Larry Ellison*, New York: Morrow.

MLW

ELLISON, William (1790–1861)

William Ellison was born in 1790 (exact date unknown) on a plantation near Winnsboro, South Carolina. He died at his home near Stateburg, South Carolina on 5 December 1861. Originally christened April Ellison, he was born a slave, the son of a black slave woman and a white man; Johnson and Roark (1984) believe his father was the plantation's owner, himself called William Ellison. Most such children were sent to work as field slaves on the plantations, but Ellison received special treatment. At age eight he was apprenticed to a cotton gin maker in Winnsboro, learning the trade and also learning to read and write and some elementary accounting skills. In January 1811 he had a daughter by a slave woman named Matilda. He was emancipated in 1816; Johnson and Roark (1984) suggest that April Ellison purchased his freedom from his former master. He later purchased the freedom of Matilda and his daughter, and the couple married; they went on to have three sons. April Ellison changed his given name to William in 1820, on the grounds that 'April' was a slave's name, unsuitable for a man of business.

Following emancipation, Ellison set up his own business as a cotton gin maker in the town of Stateburg. This was a shrewd business move, as the cotton industry was growing rapidly and demand for gins was increasing. Ellison's industry and skill was such that he not only won an important share of the market in South Carolina but began exporting to other cotton-growing states. In order to expand, Ellison needed labour, and to acquire labour he did what any white businessman in the area would have done: he bought slaves. He purchased his first two slaves in 1820, and by 1840 he owned thirty adult slaves. Ellison's business boomed and he branched out into carpentry and blacksmithing, and by 1835 had begun to invest in land. He bought the former estate of the governor of South Carolina near Stateburg, and eventually acquired over 300 acres of cotton-growing land. By 1850 he was

a very rich man, the value of his land and slaves putting him in the top 5 per cent of South Carolina's population in terms of wealth.

Ingham and Feldman (1994) note that because of his wealth and status, Ellison came to be held in high regard by the white elite in South Carolina. Close study of his career, however, suggests that the acquisition of wealth and status was itself a key element in Ellison's continued success. He had to tread a very fine line: too little ostentation would mark him down as nothing more than an ex-slave, while too much would arouse the envy of his white neighbours. Ellison chose an approach which ensured that the white planters could feel comfortable dealing with him, and allowed him to build close relationships with customers in the white community.

Ellison's career was remarkable in many ways. A highly able manager, he was entirely self-taught as a businessman and learned his way into management. His near-unique status as a wealthy black businessman in the white-dominated society of pre-Civil War South Carolina offers undoubted lessons for cross-cultural management. Modern historians have condemned Ellison for his part in enslaving his own people, but his management abilities continue to command respect. Those abilities not only made him wealthy, but they also allowed him to transcend his status and move across cultures.

BIBLIOGRAPHY

Ingham, J.N. and Feldman, L.B. (1994) *African-American Business Leaders: A Biographical Dictionary*, Westport, CT: Greenwood Press.

Johnson, M.P. and Roark, J.L. (1984) *Black Masters: A Free Family of Color in the Old South*, New York: W.W. Norton

MLW

EMERSON, Harrington (1853–1931)

Harrington Emerson was born at Trenton, New Jersey on 2 August 1853, the son of Edwin and Mary Louise Emerson. He died in New York on 23 May 1931. Emerson's father was a professor of political economy who taught at several European universities, and Emerson himself was educated at a variety of schools in Paris, Munich, Siena and Athens. While in his late teens he saw at first hand the Franco-Prussian War of 1870–71, an event which made a deep impression on him. He was subsequently to say that a combination of French character and German military efficiency helped form his later ideas on management. Among other influences, he cited studies under a European music teacher, observing the results obtained by breeders of racehorses, and ideas passed on by a leading railway surveyor, A.B. Smith (Drury 1915: 113).

Emerson took a degree in engineering from the Royal Polytechnic in Munich. Returning to the United States, he took up a post as professor of modern languages at the State University of Nebraska, where he remained from 1876 to 1882. He married Florence Brooks in 1879, and the couple had three children; after her death he married again, to Mary Suplee in 1895, and they had three or four children (sources disagree on the number). Emerson left academia in 1883 and embarked on an entrepreneurial career, investing in finance and real estate but also returning to engineering. As a contractor for the US government he undertook a number of important surveys, notably of submarine cable routes to Alaska and Asia for the War Department, and later of West Coast coalfields. There are also references to his involvement in prospecting for gold in the Yukon, although this presumably was before the Klondike gold rush of 1898.

In the 1890s Emerson began a series of private consultancies with railway firms, particularly 'in the field of systematizing management in railway shops' (Drury 1915: 113). How he became involved in this field is not

clear, but it seems that a combination of this practical experience with his engineering training and earlier exposure to European culture and science began to come together at this point. In 1895, Emerson told Drury, he began a series of surveys of American industrial plants, comparing their actual production costs with optimum costs. In 1900 he established his consulting firm, the Emerson Company, and began advising a variety of clients, primarily mining and railway firms; at this point he was still specializing in cost reduction, primarily through the elimination of wastes. However, Emerson's ideas were evolving all the time, and in 1902 he undertook his first full-scale reorganization of a factory. What Emerson was doing here was effectively process engineering; he worked his way through the processes of planning, scheduling and production, aiming to treat the firm as a harmonious whole, not a series of independent functions.

In 1904 Emerson took on the job that would make his reputation, the reorganization of the maintenance shops of the Santa Fe Railroad (as described in more detail in Emerson 1911; Drury 1915: 126–9). His task was to reorganize the motive power department, which handled the repair and maintenance of locomotives and which had been plagued with labour problems. The job took Emerson some three years, during which he employed thirty-one expert assistants to go through the department from top to bottom. The programme of improvements, known as 'betterment works', had two goals: (1) to restore labour peace, and (2) to improve workplace efficiency. Emerson saw these two goals as being linked; indeed, the first goal was contingent on the second. Reforms to the system of supervision and labour management could not proceed until the workers' own tasks and tools had been standardized. Emerson's team focused on the routing and scheduling of work, ensuring that jobs were carried out according to standard procedures: 'All the work in the machine shop was arranged so that it could be controlled from dispatch-boards located in a central office; likewise on a bulletin-board was indicated the progress of repair of each locomotive' (Drury 1915: 127). Once tasks and duties were standardized, everyone in the shop, workers, foremen and supervisors alike, knew what was expected of them and according to what schedule, and a major source of workplace friction was removed. The second half of Emerson's task was the introduction of a bonus system which rewarded those workers who performed efficiently and well. This system was not simply imposed on the workers; although Emerson insisted that the standardized times which formed the basis of work schedules were ones which any worker could achieve, nonetheless 'the schedule is a moral contract or agreement with the men as to a particular machine operation, rate of wages and time'. Gaining the informed consent of the workers to the new system was vital, and 'extreme emphasis was laid on the individual character of the relations of men and management' (Drury 1915: 127).

By 1906, says Drury (1915: 128), the Santa Fe had achieved cost savings on the order of $1.25 million. (During successive reorganizations part of Emerson's system was dismantled, but Drury concludes that the main part of the system remained intact even under new ownership and management.) The work attracted enormous interest, and Emerson became one of the most sought after consultants in the country. By 1915 he had introduced his efficiency methods into more than 200 firms, including many railways and mining firms but also a number of manufacturers. He continued to develop his system, producing his famous twelve principles of efficiency (Emerson 1913). In 1908 he approached Herbert CASSON, then enjoying considerable fame as a writer and speaker on business methods, and offered him a partnership. A year with the mercurial Casson seems to have been enough for both men; Casson departed to apply the techniques of efficiency to advertising and public relations, while Emerson continued to devote

himself to production and labour issues. In 1921 he served as a member of Herbert Hoover's Commission on the Elimination of Waste in Industry, and published his final book, *The Science of Human Engineering*, a home-study course for managers that combined the features of efficiency with those of psychology. Little is heard of him after this, and he seems to have retired in the mid-1920s.

Following his success with the Santa Fe, Emerson published a series of articles in *The Engineering Magazine* in 1908–1909. Those articles were collected in one volume, *Efficiency as a Basis for Operations and Wages*, originally published by John Dunlap in 1909 and later republished by *The Engineering Magazine*. Publication of the articles together seems to have slightly dissatisfied Emerson, and he resolved to develop his system into a fuller scheme. The result was *The Twelve Principles of Efficiency*, which first appeared in 1911, appeared in revised form in 1913 and then went through several editions, remaining in print until after Emerson's death.

Emerson was one of the leading figures of the scientific management movement. A contemporary, H.B. Drury, noted that 'Emerson has done more than any other single man to popularize the subject of scientific management' (1915: 117). Herbert Casson, his friend, admirer and sometime business partner, also described him as the leading exponent of scientific management. Emerson himself, however, rarely used the term 'scientific management' in connection with his own work, preferring instead 'efficiency'.

Although his work has much in common with that of the gurus of scientific management such as Frederick W. TAYLOR, Henry GANTT and Frank and Lillian GILBRETH, there are also significant divergences. Notably, Emerson rejected the functional system of organization espoused by Taylor and Gantt, preferring instead the line and staff system. Credit for the adaptation of this system from military thinking and its subsequent dissemination in management thinking and practice belongs largely to Emerson, whose ideas were later taken up by writers as varied as Casson, Lyndall URWICK, Luther GULICK, Joseph JURAN and Philip Sargant FLORENCE.

Emerson was largely responsible for introducing the word 'efficiency' into the language of business; today, it is a concept to which common reference is made. However, its meaning has evolved somewhat since Emerson's day. In particular, Emerson saw efficiency as based on natural principles; nature, he believed, was ultimately efficient, and there were plenty of examples in the natural world to prove this. Achieving efficiency, then, was not so much about *imposing* an efficiency system as it was about structuring an organization so that efficiency would be achieved naturally – the best way to achieve efficiency is to eliminate inefficiency. This theme is returned to several times in the course of *Efficiency as a Basis for Operations and Wages*, which, as noted, was closely based on his work with the Santa Fe railway.

Inefficiencies, says Emerson, come in two forms: there are inefficiencies in processes and materials, and there are inefficiencies in people, societies and nations. Of the two, the first type of inefficiency is in many ways least harmful. If inefficient materials are used, they simply give way; if inefficient processes are in place, when the limits of their efficiency are reached they simply stop working. The second is much more serious in that 'to the inefficiency of an individual or a nation there is no predeterminable limitation' (Emerson 1909: 23). Human inefficiency is constant, especially when it is embedded in a society or culture. Yet, despite the importance of human inefficiency, Emerson notes that the attention of science is largely focused elsewhere: 'In the passion for modern scientific accuracy it has proved more interesting, and more has been done to solve the lesser problem of efficiency in process or material, almost wholly ignoring the larger problem of individual or national efficiency' (1909: 23).

Two conditions are necessary, says Emerson, for achieving human efficiency: (1) the right

standards, and (2) the right organization. Of these, it is clear that the organization must come first. In *Efficiency as a Basis for Operations and Wages*, he devotes three full chapters to the line and staff method of organization. The line and staff model is in practice made up of a blend of two organizational submodels, the line organization and the staff organization. The line organization is hierarchical and functional; each member knows his or her place and carries out allotted tasks on a procedural basis. The staff organization is organic and interdependent, with members relying on each other to carry out their work. A crucial distinction between the two is the role of knowledge. In the line organization, 'one man knows much more than any other' (1909: 55) and that person guides the organization; so, if the leader loses direction, the organization is lost as well. All the other members of the organization depend on the leader, not on each other. In the staff organization, knowledge is held in common: 'The strength of the staff organization lies in its ability to multiply many-fold the effectiveness of other staff members, all co-operating to make possible such a wonderful thing as a man, a humming-bird, a midge, or a yellow-fever microbe' (1909: 56).

In fact, many organizations combine the line and staff principles, creating a mix of organism and construct. At a simple level, Emerson uses the example of a baseball team (1909: 58–9). The batting side uses the line principle: each player comes to the plate in turn in pre-arranged order and bats without any dependence on his team-mates. The fielding side use the staff principle: pitcher, catcher and fielders work together as a unit, all depending on each other to some degree. The two sides alternate these functions as the game progresses from innings to innings.

The greatest exponent of the line and staff principle in management, says Emerson, was not a businessman at all but a military commander, the Prussian Field-Marshal Helmuth von MOLTKE. As a young man, Emerson had witnessed at first hand Moltke's astonishing victory over the French army in the Franco-Prussian War. He says he saw the course of the war from both sides (intriguingly, he does not say how he managed this), and his conclusion was that the critical factor in the Prussian victory was the line and staff organization. The well-drilled line performed on the battlefield exactly as it ought, guided by the seemingly omnipresent and omniscient staff. The French, relying almost exclusively on the line principle, could not respond effectively and were defeated. Moltke's great achievement, Emerson concludes (1913: 14–18), was to make rapid, decisive and relatively bloodless wars possible; long, bloody and inefficient conflicts such as the American Civil War were now a thing of the past.

There is irony here, in that Emerson was writing on the eve of one of the most bloody and inefficient conflicts of all time, the First World War – a conflict, moreover, in which most of the combatants had adopted the line and staff principle. With hindsight, the weakness in Emerson's proposition shows through. Moltke's victory was in large part due to his own brilliant leadership and planning, qualities conspicuously absent from most of the high commands in the First World War. The same defects must from time to time occur in business, and Emerson notes this when he describes the staff as being present to assist and support the leader. Ultimately, it would seem, no matter how good the staff work, if leadership is lacking, the enterprise will fail (1913: 401–403).

Emerson links the need for standards to the adoption of the staff principle. Line organization, he says dismissively, 'needs few standards, usually crude and often fictitious. Seniority or precedence is one of its standards, and closely interwoven is the fundamental standard of immediate and unquestioning obedience almost as automatic as the obedience of sheep to the leader' (1909: 96). Staff, on the other hand, has 'an unlimited multiplicity of scientific standards, higher than all personality

... The staff expert receives from his chief principles which are higher than the chief, since they are part of the eternal laws of the universe' (1909: 97). It is here that Emerson has most in common with the other proponents of scientific management: he believes that adherence to standards of measurement and process that are based on science will eliminate inefficiencies, and thus lead perforce to efficiency. He also believes in a process of continuous improvement, with standards constantly being revised in the light of new knowledge: 'Staff standards are based on specific human authority only until new facts substitute better authority' (1909: 98). Likewise, Emerson is clear that standards do not exist for their own sake:

Staff standards are not theoretical abstractions but scientific approximations, and are evolved for the use of the line, the sole justification of standards being that they will make line work more efficient. Staff standards, being for the benefit of the line and often entrusted to line officials, must be put in the form of permanent instructions so that all may understand what is being aimed at, and deviations by the line be noted and reprimanded

(Emerson 1909: 98)

Chapter 6 of *Efficiency as a Basis for Operations and Wages* offers the most detailed account of how standards are actually achieved in practice. The first stage consists of five detailed surveys of (1) methods of materials handling; (2) condition of machines and tools; (3) labour audits, noting discrepancies between what workers were supposed to be doing and what they were actually doing; (4) relationships between current costs and standard costs; and (5) the speed of movement of work through the shop (1909: 125). Each of these five lines of investigation is then developed as a field of measurement and control, in the charge of experts; the building up of this pool of experts in effect creates the staff. The experts devise and institute standardized systems for materials handling to eliminate wastage; maintenance to keep machines in good repair; wages to ensure workers are motivated and rewarded; costings to ensure that profit and loss can be measured accurately; and task and process times to ensure that work moves through the plant or shop at a natural rate, unencumbered by delays.

Working on and developing these concepts still further led Emerson to his famous twelve principles of efficiency (Emerson 1913). These are, in summary form:

1. Clearly defined ideals: the organization must know what its goals are, what it stands for, and its relationship with society.

2. Common sense: the organization must be practical in its methods and outlook.

3. Competent counsel: the organization should seek wise advice, turning to external experts if it lacks the necessary staff expertise.

4. Discipline: not so much top-down discipline as internal discipline and self-discipline, with workers conforming willingly and readily to the systems in place.

5. The fair deal: workers should be treated fairly at all times, to encourage their participation in the efficiency movement.

6. Reliable, immediate and adequate records: measurement over time is important in determining if efficiency has been achieved.

7. Despatching: workflow must be scheduled in such a way that processes move smoothly.

8. Standards and schedules: the establishment of these is, as discussed above, fundamental to the achievement of efficiency.

9. Standardized conditions: workplace conditions should be standardized according to natural scientific precepts, and should evolve as new knowledge becomes available.

10. Standardized operations: likewise, operations should follow scientific principles, particularly in terms of planning and work methods.

11. Written instructions: all standards should be recorded in the form of written instructions to workers and foremen, which detail not only the standards themselves but the methods of compliance.

12. Efficiency reward: if workers achieve efficiency, then they should be duly rewarded.

One of the truly modern aspects of Emerson's views is that he sees organizational efficiency as being achieved from the bottom up. The staff is there to serve the line, not the other way around; even if the staff have controlling positions, with powers of reprimand and discipline over the line, these functions are ultimately about moving the line to greater efficiency. The worker is there to assist his machine to run efficiently, not to exercise dominion over it; the foreman is there to help his workers achieve their targets, not to control them on behalf of the superintendent; and so on up the line to the chief executive who is ultimately the servant of the organization, not its master. Thus Emerson believes in basic principles such as full reward for efficient workers (he favours Taylor and Gantt's bonus system, and argues at one point in favour of a minimum wage).

Emerson also extends these principles beyond the organization, seeing businesses in the context of broader society and arguing that more efficient businesses will make for more efficient societies. He is highly critical of American society at the beginning of the twentieth century, which he sees as riddled with inefficiencies and ill-equipped to compete with either the established powers of Europe or the rising power of Japan. In part he blames this situation on the European heritage; an admirer of European culture, he feels nonetheless that this culture has been adapted too uncritically in the United States, without proper regard for the actual pragmatic needs of the new American society. By adopting efficiency methods such as the line and staff principle (itself, of course, a product of Europe), he believes the USA can eliminate waste and become efficient and competitive:

> We have not put our trust in kings; let us not put it in natural resources, but grasp the truth that exhaustless wealth lies in the latent and as yet undeveloped capacities of individuals, of corporations, of states. Instead of oppression from the top, engendering antagonisms and strife, ambitious pressure should come from the bottom, guidance and assistance from the top.
>
> (Emerson 1909: 242)

These two books mark out Emerson as an original thinker of some note. His relationship to the other figures of the scientific management movement is difficult to assess. He knew of Taylor's work, and Drury says he was among the audience when Taylor read his famous paper on shop management before the American Society of Mechanical Engineers in 1903. Drury says further that Emerson sometimes referred to Taylor as the source of his ideas (Drury 1915: 116). On the other hand, Emerson also believed that many of Taylor's ideas were overambitious and unlikely to succeed. The two men were never close; they met first in 1900 and seldom thereafter. Indeed, it is hard to imagine two men more unalike than Emerson, well-travelled and brought up in an academic milieu, erudite, cultured and cultivated, and Taylor, the ex-shop foreman, an engineer's engineer, pragmatic and somewhat puritanical. Whereas Taylor's ideas stemmed from intensive study and practice, Emerson's influences were more eclectic.

Emerson's influence on others is equally difficult to determine. He is credited as the great popularizer of scientific management, but there is little hard evidence to show how far

Emerson was personally responsible for the take-up of scientific management by firms; in terms of method, it is the techniques pioneered by Taylor, Gantt and the Gilbreths that are more frequently observable. Emerson's influence was more general. He did not so much provide a toolkit – although he did try to provide concrete examples of how standardization could be achieved – as create the awareness that change was necessary and stimulate managers and industrialists to look at new ways of thinking and practice. For such a highly successful communicator, he seems to have been unable – or perhaps unwilling – to explain in detail his equally successful consultancy techniques.

In part, this lack may be due to the fact that Emerson did not use or recommend standardized systems, only standard tools; he tended rather to argue for organizational flexibility. In the words of Drury, 'Emerson's methods are flexible, rather than stereotyped; his time studies and standards are approximate rather than exhaustively exact; and he relies much on the self-direction of his subordinates' (Drury 1915: 116). This is apparent in his espousal of the line and staff principle, his one undeniably influential concept; it is much more important to get the organization right than it is to set exact measurements. Efficiency, in the final analysis, is about eliminating waste, not creating systems.

Though he is called a prophet of scientific management, Emerson's work is closer to a philosophy than a science. In the final analysis, for all his devotion to New-World-style organization and principle, Emerson was at least as much a product of Europe as of America, and science and art would always be co-equal; management was not only about results, but about higher things as well. He rejects the idea that business is about 'supernal men working through principles to realize supernal ideals' (Emerson 1913: 423), but he believes that what is good for business is also good for society. As he concludes in *The Twelve Principles of Efficiency*: 'It is impossible that righteousness married to wisdom should rule without immensely benefitting humanity' (Emerson 1913: 423).

BIBLIOGRAPHY

Casson, H.N. (1931) *The Story of My Life*, London: Efficiency Magazine.

Drury, H.B. (1915) *Scientific Management: A History and Criticism*, New York: Columbia University Press.

Emerson, H. (1909) *Efficiency as a Basis for Operations and Wages*, New York: John R. Dunlap.

—— (1911) 'How Railroad Efficiency Can Be Managed', *Engineering Magazine* 42(October): 10–16.

—— (1913) *The Twelve Principles of Efficiency*, New York: The Engineering Magazine Company.

—— (1921) *The Science of Human Engineering*, New York: The Man Message Corporation.

MLW

EMERY, Frederick Edmund (1925–97)

Frederick Edmund Emery was born in Narrogin, a country town in Western Australia, on 31 August 1925, and died in Canberra on 10 April 1997. Fred's father was a cattle drover and sheep shearer, who used to tell Fred stories about his work along the Canning Track in Western Australia (WA). In the late 1930s his father went into business, but was bankrupted by his dishonest partner. Fred's mother worked at cleaning houses. Fred was dux of Fremantle Boys' High School (1939) and began working as a draughtsman in the WA Mines Department, (1939–43) until his high intelligence was recognized and he was advised to study at the University of Western Australia. The professor of education

helped him prepare for university entry, and Fred Emery graduated with honours in 1946, having studied science in the psychology department.

As an undergraduate Emery became much interested in politics, and like many young intellectuals he was drawn to social democracy. He decided to join the Communist Party of Australia, hoping that the world could be made a better place under communist ideas than those offered by capitalism in the 1930s. At the same time he was attracted to the ideas of the social psychologist Kurt LEWIN and his views of group dynamics. After graduation, when Emery was teaching in the psychology department at his university, he introduced Lewin's concepts to his class and colleagues (Trahair 1988).

After two years teaching at the University of Western Australia, Emery was invited to be a lecturer in the department of psychology at the University of Melbourne. In Melbourne, Emery married his undergraduate sweetheart from Perth, raised a family, and lectured in collective behaviour and family studies with a strong Lewinian emphasis. In 1951–2 he sailed to Europe as a UNESCO Fellow in Paris, and briefly visited the Tavistock Institute of Human Relations, London, where he became aware of Eric TRIST's work in the coal-mining industry and his early formulation of socio-technical systems theory.

In Melbourne, Emery's research centred on the UNESCO study of social structure and personality in a rural community in Victoria, and in 1953 he was awarded a Ph.D. The research was published a year later (Oeser and Emery 1954). He followed this with a study of how information about the new agricultural technology reached farmers in Victoria (Emery 1959).

During the early 1950s Emery learned enough about communism in Russia to see that its totalitarian state was anathema to what he hoped for. He set about teaching those who would listen to him in Melbourne that support for the Communist Party was no way to a social democracy. This made him many enemies, and did not alter the way he was seen by the Australian Security and Intelligence Organization. Not until the last few years of his academic life was he allowed to spend more than a very short time, sometimes only hours, in the United States. For many years he believed that American officialdom suspected him of being a communist sleeper.

In 1957 Emery became a senior lecturer in charge of a mass communication project in the Department of Audio-Visual Aids at the University of Melbourne, and published one of the first systematic studies on the psychological impact of television (Emery 1959). The following year he accepted an appointment as Senior Fellow at the Tavistock Institute of Human Relations, where he worked until his return to Australia in 1969. While at the Tavistock Institute he spent a sabbatical leave as a Fellow of the Center for Advanced Studies in the Behavioral Sciences at Palo Alto (1967–8), chaired the Human Resources Centre at the Tavistock (1968–9) and edited *Human Relations*. His wife Francis became ill and died shortly after their return to Australia.

Emery was a Senior Research Fellow in Sociology at the Australian National University (1969–74), and later joined the Centre for Continuing Education (1974–80). For two years he researched psychological aspects of policy making, before becoming Busch Professor of Social Systems Science at the University of Pennsylvania (1982–4). In the late 1980s and early 1990s he was an independent scholar, and his home office in Canberra was an international centre of open systems thinkers, specialists who worked in socio-technical systems, and workplace reformers.

While at the Tavistock Institute in the early 1960s, Emery worked closely with Eric Trist using action research in organizations in Britain and Scandinavia, establishing the value of self-managing work teams, and refining and extending open system theory for modern organizations. With Trist, he devised the

Search Conference in 1959–60. They also published on the four environments of modern organizations in which the 'turbulent' environment was introduced (Emery and Trist 1965). Like Trist, Emery was a prolific writer, publishing on socio-technical systems and securing a reputation as an outstanding social scientist in systems thinking, organizational theory, communications, penology, education, political science, strategic thinking, policy sciences, marketing, defence studies, military strategy, addiction, learning and perception. Much of his work appears in the Tavistock Anthology (Trist and Murray 1990, 1993; Trist *et al.* 1997). With his second wife, Merrelyn Emery, he developed participative design workshops to help ordinary people choose realizable, realistic futures, and organize themselves in self-managed work groups. As well as helping individuals, he contributed to a worldwide trend of organizations to rebuild themselves around self-management teams of multiskilled workers.

At present, Merrelyn Emery is carrying forward her late husband's work on the Search Conferences in many countries. The Search Conference is a participative method for human organizations to achieve desirable futures, and is an alternative to the conventional uses of elite groups, expert staff and external consultants to impose directives from above. This is done by assembling people who normally work together to establish plans for the workplace they share. The Search Conference assumes its participants are purposive, are able to seek ideals together, are powerfully moved by a sense of common purpose, and can shift from points of conflict to common ground. In three days, the Search Conference decides on a long-term plan of achievable aims with explicit procedures to achieve them.

The first Search Conference was held from 10 to 16 July 1960 at Barford House, Warwick, UK by London's Tavistock Institute of Human Relations. It was planned and conducted by Emery and Trist. The problem was to help change two large organizations. The senior executives of the Bristol and Siddley aero-engine companies had been directed by the British government to create a single operating firm. Over the next ten years, eleven more Search Conferences were held, involving organizations such as the National Farmers' Association in England and diplomats in an international conflict in South East Asia. Thereafter the Search Conference technique was developed further in Canberra (1970–82), and used in Holland, Norway, France and Canada. It is well established in North America, and is now recognized as a valuable alternative for achieving a better future for communities, regions, industrial organizations, private companies and government agencies. The theory of the Search Conference is a direct result of Emery's lifetime of action research, his use of Lewinian ideas, and his own principles of participative design, industrial democracy and open system thinking (Emery 1996; Emery and Purser 1996; Weisbord 1992).

Internationally, Emery was widely respected, but in Australia he endured many attacks from leaders in large private and public organizations who assumed bureaucracy was the most suitable form of domination for work. Emery was one of entrenched bureaucracy's major critics, and published frequently on the design of organizations for participative democracy (Emery 1993). Except for the degree of doctor of science *honoris causa* (1992) from Macquarie University in Sydney, and the inaugural Elton Mayo Award (1988) from the Australian Psychological Society, Emery received little formal recognition within Australian academic circles (Gloster 1997). The faculty of business and economics at Monash University, Melbourne, published the first collection of Emery's work (Barton and Selsky 1999).

BIBLIOGRAPHY

Barton, J. and Selsky, J. (eds) (1999) *The Emery Archives: A Content Analysis*, Caulfield East, Victoria: Faculty of

Business and Economics, Monash University.

Emery, F.E. (1959) 'Psychological Effects of the Western Film: A Study in Television Viewing I and II', *Human Relations* 12: 195–213, 215–32.

Emery, F.E. and Oeser, O.A. (1958) *Information, Decision and Action*, Melbourne: Melbourne University Press.

Emery, F.E. and Trist, E.L. (1965) 'The Causal Texture of Organizational Environments', *Human Relations* 13: 21–32.

Emery, M. (ed.) (1993) *Participative Design for Participative Democracy*, Canberra: Centre for Continuing Education, Australian National University.

—— (1996) 'The Search Conference: Design and Management of Learning with a Solution to the Pairing Puzzle', in E.L. Trist, F.E. Emery and H. Murray (eds), *The Social Engagement of Social Science: A Tavistock Anthology Volume III: The Socio-ecological Perspective*, Philadelphia: University of Pennsylvania Press, 389–411.

Emery, M. and Purser, R.E. (1996) *The Search Conference: A Powerful Method for Planning Organizational Change and Community Action*, San Francisco: Jossey-Bass.

Gloster, M. (1997) 'Obituary: Frederick Edmund Emery: A Pioneer in Self-Management', *The Age*, 2 June, C2.

Oeser, O.A. and Emery, F.E. (1954) *Social Structure and Personality in a Rural Community*, London: Routledge and Kegan Paul.

Trahair, R.C.S. (1988) personal communication, November 1988.

Trist, E.L. and Murray, H. (eds) (1990) *The Social Engagement of Social Science: A Tavistock Anthology: Volume I: The Socio-psychological Perspective*, Philadelphia: University of Pennsylvania Press.

—— (1993) *The Social Engagement of Social Science: A Tavistock Anthology: Volume II: The Socio-technical Perspective*, Philadelphia: University of Pennsylvania Press.

Trist, E.L., Emery, F.E. and Murray, H. (eds) (1997) *The Social Engagement of Social Science: A Tavistock Anthology: Volume III: The Socio-ecological Perspective*, Philadelphia: University of Pennsylvania Press.

Weisbord, M.R. (1992) *Discovering Common Ground: How Future Search Conferences Bring People Together to Achieve Breakthrough Innovation, Empowerment, Shared Vision and Collaborative Action*, San Francisco: Berrett-Koehler Publishers.

RT

ENGELS, Friedrich (1820–95)

Friedrich Engels was born in Barmen, in the Prussian Rhineland, on 28 November 1820 to Friedrich and Elisabeth Engels. He died in London on 5 August 1895. According to David Riazanov's biography, first published in 1927 (Riazanov 1996), the senior Friedrich Engels was a textile merchant who operated factories not only in the German states but also in Manchester, UK. Being an evangelical pietist, the senior Engels embodied a Protestant work ethic not unlike that described by the German sociologist Max WEBER, in which striving for business success was enjoined as a religious duty.

The younger Engels grew up alienated by his father's harshness. It is not improbable to speculate that Engels' angry rejection of both religion and capitalism came in reaction to his harsh upbringing and his father's mixture of extremely strict religiosity and acquisitiveness. The younger Engels was raised to be a busi-

nessman and an evangelical. In 1837 his father sent him to work in an office in Bremen, which he did until 1840. Engels did not enjoy business; he wanted to be a writer. Away from his father, he cast off all religion and embraced the democratic and rationalist ideals of the European left. By 1841 Engels was serving in the Prussian artillery in Berlin. Here he encountered not only the Young Hegelians, a group of radicals led by Bruno Bauer and his brother Edgar, who adhered to the philosophy of Georg Wilhelm Friedrich Hegel, but also a bright young philosophy student named Karl MARX. They first met in the autumn of 1842.

Beginning in different places, Marx and Engels in the early 1840s arrived at the same destination: revolutionary socialism. Marx, sinking into poverty, encountered communism from the French revolutionary tradition; Engels, much more well off, was moved by his personal encounters with early industrialism. The latter went to Manchester in 1842 to work in his father's textile factory. Here he received an education in *laissez-faire* capitalism in the very city that was its moral and economic home. As he worked in his father's plant, Engels read Adam SMITH, Thomas MALTHUS, David Ricardo and other classical economists, as well as socialists such as Charles Fourier and Pierre-Joseph Proudhon. From the English writers he learned of the doctrines of the free market, and from Fourier and Proudhon he learned some of the earliest critiques of capitalism. Engels also recorded his descriptions of the workings of the economy in Manchester in a book, *The Condition of the Working Class in England in 1844*, published in German in 1845 (Engels 1986).

The Condition of the Working Class in England in 1844 presented an appalling portrait of industrial Manchester. Decrepit and crumbling dwellings blackened with soot barely fit for human habitation were jammed together as closely as possible with no semblance of planning. Dirt and filth were everywhere; the River Irk was coal-black and filled with rubbish and slime from the sewage

dumped by tanneries, dye works and gas works. Upstream, conditions were even worse: half-ruined dwellings with dirt floors and broken doors and windows, heaps of rubbish and an unbearable stench. Engels compared the homes of Manchester workers to rabbit warrens and cattle pens. He blamed the greed of the new industrial class and its new market ideology for having 'increased the tendency towards selfishness' and promoting 'greed to the position of a guiding principle in the conduct of affairs. For the bourgeoisie, love of money has become the ruling passion of life' (Engels 1986: 24).

Engels saw in the growing labour unrest the reality that class war had already been declared. This first manifested itself in the form of crime, followed by anti-factory protests and then by strikes and the formation of trade unions. While unions could sometimes raise wages, Engels saw their weakness in times of economic depression. Nonetheless, their rise stimulated his belief that a new proletarian class was emerging.

In the summer of 1844 Engels left Manchester for Paris and later for Brussels. Here he and Marx became closely acquainted, their worldviews now identical. Marx provided Engels with a vast theoretical framework for communism; Engels provided Marx with hard economic data and experience to bolster his theory, fully expressed for the first time in the 1848 *Manifesto of the Communist Party*. Both Marx and Engels greeted the continental revolutions of 1848 with the expectation that the crisis of capitalism had come. While the revolution in France was more proletarian, that in Germany was still middle class but was supported by Marx and Engels as a necessary step along the road. When the revolutions failed Engels returned to England, where the now stateless Marx joined him.

From 1849 to 1869 Engels worked in his father's Manchester factory to support not only himself and his two mistresses, Lydia and Mary Burns, but the unemployable Marx and his large family. The senior Engels died in

1860, and by 1864 Friedrich Engels, revolutionary communist, was also a reluctant capitalist, being a full partner in the firm and manager of the Manchester branch. He owned two homes, belonged to the local stock exchange and went fox-hunting with the local gentry. Engels compromised with the business world, says Riazanov, only out of necessity, for the sake of Marx as well as himself. To him, business management was 'a dog's trade' (Riazanov 1996), and he when he was able to retire in 1869 with enough money to support both himself and Marx, he did so gleefully.

Engels moved to London and spent the rest of his life writing, taking care of Marx, who died in 1883, and corresponding with a rising socialist movement. Without Engels, Marx could never have completed even the first volume of Das Kapital. He wrote to Engels: 'I owe it only to you, that this has been possible' (Riazanov 1996). One of Engels' duties now became handling Marx's correspondence with the growing labour movement, which was organized into the First International. Engels was able to apply his managerial and organizational skills as a business person to the work of the International, but his middle-class manners and formality never engendered the love and trust among socialists that Marx, in spite of his contentious personality, inspired. Socialist workers saw the impoverished Marx as one of their own; Engels, says Riazanov, at first seemed too 'bourgeois', too fastidious, too orderly.

As Marx's health faded, Engels moved more and more to the fore. As industrialism grew, and along with it the European working class, and as economic depressions recurred in the 1870s, 1880s and 1890s, Marxist ideas became a force to be reckoned with. Even then, labour movements often applied them in a manner displeasing to both Marx and Engels. When Eugen Dühring criticized Marx for being insufficiently revolutionary, Engels wrote a book against him, later translated as *Socialism, Utopian and Scientific* (1882).

Socialism, Utopian and Scientific demonstrated that 'Engels ... knew the significance of advertising' even in selling communism (Riazanov 1996). Marx was often hard to comprehend, but Engels could address workers in more readable language. *Socialism, Utopian and Scientific* likely made more converts to the Marxist cause than did *Das Kapital*. French Marxists were strongly inspired by it, as were those of other countries when Engels, fluent in a number of languages, translated it for them. Marx may have formulated modern communism, but Engels marketed it to thousands, including the Russian Georgi Plekhanov, the mentor of Vladimir Lenin and Leon Trotsky.

More comprehensive than the *Manifesto* and more readable than *Das Kapital*, *Socialism, Utopian and Scientific* outlined the Marxist conception of history and economics updated for the 1880s. With Marx in great pain from his boils and unable to concentrate upon much writing, Engels now became the chief communist theoretician. He applied Marxist theory to the new emerging managerial capitalism of the late nineteenth century, with its large-scale monopolistic control, trust organization, state ownership and growth of a white-collar salaried class. Engels observed that free competition was now insufficient, and that firms in a given industry were now uniting in trusts. Because this open 'exploitation of the community by a small band of dividend-mongers' was so intolerable, Engels predicted the rise of a mixed economy and public ownership even under capitalism, where 'the state will ultimately have to undertake the direction of production ... first in the great institutions for intercourse and communication – the post office, the telegraphs, the railways' (Engels 1882: 102–3). He then went on to describe the rise of a salaried managerial class, the rise of investor capitalism, and even a vision of a white-collar depression:

All the social functions of the capitalist are now performed by salaried employees. The capitalist has no further social function

than that of pocketing dividends, tearing off coupons, and gambling on the Stock Exchange, where the different capitalists despoil one another of their capital. At first, the capitalistic mode of production forces out the workers. Now, it forces out the capitalists, and reduces them, just as it reduced the workers, to the ranks of the surplus-population, although not immediately into those of the industrial reserve army.

(Engels 1882: 103)

Engels, of course, saw this as a prelude to the proletarian revolution he envisioned in 1848, and history has not validated his predictions as a whole. Nonetheless, he was partially correct in his predictions about the development of capitalism in the twentieth century. Marx had expounded the theory of communism; Engels marketed it for a mass audience and sought to apply it to a coming new century. According to Riazanov, his intellectual influence upon the rising generation of socialists of the 1880s and 1890s who now composed the Second International was that of being Marx's chief interpreter, bringing in science and history to bolster communist theory. Engels himself, shortly before his death, even suggested that socialism might come to Britain by peaceful means.

BIBLIOGRAPHY

Carver, T. (1989) *Friedrich Engels: His Life and Thought*, London: Macmillan.
Engels, F. (1986) 'Manchester in 1844', from F. Engels, *The Condition of the Working Class in England in 1844*, in I. Howe (ed.), *Essential Works of Socialism*, New Haven, CT: Yale University Press, 18–31.
—— (1882) *Socialism, Utopian and Scientific*, trans. E. Aveling, in L.S. Feuer, *Marx and Engels, Basic Writings on Politics and Philosophy*, New York: Anchor Books, 1989, 68–111.
'Engels, Friedrich' (1999) *McGraw-Hill Encyclopedia of World Biography*, Detroit, MI: Gale Research, Inc., vol. 5, 286–8.
Lenin, V.I. (1896) 'Biographical Article on Friedrich Engels', *Rabotnik* 1–2, Marxists Internet Archive, http://www.ex.ac.uk/Projects/meia/Bio/Marx-Karl/fe1895.htm, 29 October 2000.
McClellan, D. (1978) *Friedrich Engels*, London: Penguin.
Riazanov, D. (1996) *Karl Marx and Friedrich Engels: An Introduction to their Lives and Work*, trans. J. Kunitz, http://www.ex.ac.uk/Projects/meia/Riazanov/Archive/1927-Marx, 29 October 2000.
Rubel, M. (1980) *Marx: Life and Works*, trans. M. Bottomore, New York: Facts on File, Inc.
Wheen, F. (2000) *Karl Marx: A Life*, New York: W.W. Norton and Co.

DCL

ETZIONI, Amitai (1929–)

Amitai Etzioni was born in Cologne, Germany on 4 January 1929 to the German Jewish family of Willi and Gertrude Falk. Fleeing Hitler, the family settled in Palestine in 1938, where they changed their name to Etzioni. Etzioni took part in Israel's war of independence in 1948, and then earned his bachelor's degree in 1954 and his masters in 1956, both from Jerusalem's Hebrew University.

Etzioni entered the University of California at Berkeley in 1957, studying under the distinguished sociologist Seymour Martin Lipset. After earning his Ph.D., Etzioni began teaching at Columbia University in 1958. His major works centred around the realms of community and society. In 1961 he wrote *A Comparative Analysis of Complex Organizations*, in which

he developed a common framework for comparing the organization of institutions such as a corporation or church with those of an army, a firm or a government.

In 1964 Etzioni went on to publish *Modern Organizations*. The first part of this work examined the goals of organizations, which he saw as serving many functions. A goal could often depict a future state of affairs or set down guidelines for activity, or become a source of legitimacy and standards. Organizations, however, could often acquire their own needs. A charitable fundraiser might begin spending more on its own buildings and staff than those it was set up to help.

Etzioni next looked at organizational structures. The classical scientific management approach pioneered by the disciples of Frederick W. TAYLOR saw workers as motivated by economic rewards. The system it recommended was hierarchical, tightly controlled and procedure-driven, and it divided labour into specific tasks. A second approach, based on human relations theory, arose in reaction to Taylorism. Founded on a series of experiments undertaken at the Western Electric plant in Hawthorne, Illinois between 1927 and 1932, human relations theory assumed workers had other goals besides money and preferred to labour in an environment that was less structured and based upon informal, emotional relationships (see MAYO and ROETHLISBERGER). Such a model might be found in Latin or Asian cultures.

Etzioni, drawing upon the work of Max WEBER, argued for a third model of organization that he saw as more accurate than the other two. The scientific model assumed no conflict between the interests of labour and management in an organization. That workers might find repetitively turning the same screws on an assembly line mind-numbing or alienating was often ignored. The human relations model assumed that everyone in an organization operated like part of a harmonious family rather than an efficient machine. There were, however, tensions – group versus personal needs, discipline versus autonomy, rank versus division – that belied these neat models.

Looking at hospitals, prisons, churches, schools, social-work agencies and other organizations, Etzioni formulated a structural approach to organization theory. Organizations were large complex social units in which all kinds of groups interacted. Some might share an interest in making profits but not in how they were distributed. Frustration and tensions on the job were real, and there were limits to how far these could be reduced, for they were built into the very nature of the organization. The human relations approach argued that most labour/management problems might be solved through better communications. A rumour of mass layoffs demoralizes work on the shop floor until it is dispelled. What, asked Etzioni, happens if the rumour is true? Conflicting interests in the workplace were a reality, and recognizing them was the key to resolving them, or at least mitigating their effects. These themes also appear in *The Active Society*, published in 1968, which called for studying society as an organic whole, instead of a mere collection of groups or individuals.

While Etzioni was becoming conscious of the importance of community during the 1960s, he was and remains a strong believer in both the individual and democracy. He aligned himself with the left wing of the Democratic Party, championed arms control, and opposed both the Moon race and US participation in the Vietnam War. He also married Minerva Morales in 1965; the couple had five sons.

In the early 1970s, Etzioni focused upon the moral and social implications of genetic engineering and the new biotechnologies, expressing his concern over their effects on human liberty and morality. How would society be affected, he asked, if parents could choose the sex of their children? Throughout the remainder of the decade, he continued to teach sociology at Columbia and wrote numerous articles on social issues. From 1978 to 1979 Etzioni worked at the Brookings Institution, and he served as an adviser to Richard Harden,

Special Assistant to US President Jimmy Carter from 1979 to 1980.

As Etzioni established his reputation as one of the United States' brightest sociologists, he was also becoming aware of the impact of the upheavals of the 1960s and early 1970s upon the nation's culture and society. Vietnam and Watergate undermined faith in government; the research of Ralph NADER undermined faith in business; inflation and recession undermined faith in prosperity. Under Presidents Lyndon B. Johnson and even Richard Nixon, welfare programmes had expanded enormously and were seen by many as entitlements. The success of the African-American Civil Rights Movement inspired feminists and other groups to assert their rights, while many former activists turned inward to pursue personal fulfilment. The new climate of cynicism, when combined with the slowing of economic growth in the later 1970s, spurred the popularity of individualistic and libertarian thought which helped secure the election of Ronald Reagan in 1980.

By the early 1980s, Etzioni saw that something was terribly wrong, and in 1983 attempted to offer a diagnosis in the form of *An Immodest Agenda: Rebuilding America before the 21st Century*. This was a landmark work, setting the agenda for his later works and growing out of Etzioni's earlier concerns with viewing society as a community. That community, he argued, was now in grave danger, from the new pandemic of individualism. 'Many Americans', he lamented, '... are no longer willing or able to take care of themselves and each other' (Etzioni 1983: 3). While himself a Democrat, Etzioni blamed both 'ego-centered individualism' and big government for undermining the families, schools and neighbourhoods upon which communities depended. In this 'hollowing of America', family responsibilities declined at the same time that more was demanded of government in taking care of the children of working mothers and the elderly. People demanded more police while being less willing to help the victims of crime, and demanded more enforcement of ethical conduct while being less willing to practice it themselves. Admitting that bigger government 'lessens the individual and diminished individuals foster more government', Etzioni rejected the Reagan administration's belief that dismantling big government would automatically restore a moral society: 'Reducing the government does not by itself secure reconstruction of individuals. And without such reconstruction a vacuum will be created, leaving a viable community and a strong economy unprovided for' (Etzioni 1983: 4). The result would be either a backlash return to statism or a society so polarized that it would undergo a social catastrophe.

Etzioni sharply criticized the ideology of the individualist Reagan/Thatcher conservatives as it was represented by their chief economists, Milton FRIEDMAN and Friedrich von HAYEK. Friedman contrasted market freedom with government coercion. In response to this debate between market individualism and state collectivism, Etzioni offered a communitarian alternative: 'People do not relate to one another only as participants in economic transactions or as subjects of a government' (Etzioni 1983: 9), but as parents, children, brothers, sisters, neighbours, friends and citizens. Such relationships of mutual respect, duty and concern pointed 'to the existence and significance of a third realm between government and market, the realm of community' (Etzioni 1983: 9).

To Etzioni, the authoritarianism of many religious fundamentalists, whom he called New Tories, was as repellent as libertarianism. Here the government was given the role of legislating morality, banning abortion and mandating the teaching of creationism in schools. According to Etzioni, this would do little good. Outlawing abortion would not save families; making children pray in school would not make them more righteous; imposing the death penalty would, he felt, deter few crimes. Community had to come from within, through the consent of free and committed individuals.

An Immodest Agenda symbolized the first important systematic attack by a major social

philosopher upon the libertarianism of Friedman, Hayek and others, including Ayn RAND and David Stockman. To Etzioni, the libertarian creed was now far more influential than the handful of votes garnered by the US Libertarian Party. Market libertarians saw, he said, only the state versus the individual. Libertarians felt consumers could always tell a good product from a bad. People, they argued, deserved the right to smoke, kill themselves, use harmful drugs, not use helmets or seat belts. Libertarians also believed that accidents and sickness were the fault of individuals who made wrong choices, not manufacturers who made unsafe products and polluted the environment, or health organizations that provided inadequate care. To this, Etzioni replied that personal lifestyles are shaped by communities. A careful driver can be killed in a community that tolerates drunken drivers.

Etzioni criticized libertarians, whom he dubbed the New Whigs, be they academic like Gary S. Becker, or popular, like Robert Ringer, for picturing 'the whole social world was dominated by the market, or the society itself as a market of sorts' (Etzioni 1983: 13). This led, he felt, to very destructive thinking. Marriage became a transaction in which benefits had to exceed costs, as did respect for the law. People were assumed to be cool and calculating instead of being emotionally tied to one another. People married for status, and performed acts of kindness on a value-for-value basis, expecting compensation in the marketplace of life.

Etzioni continued to develop this theme during the administrations of Ronald Reagan (1981–9), George Bush (1989–93) and Bill Clinton (1993–2001). As market-oriented thinking became more and more the prevailing orthodoxy, Etzioni intensified his intellectual counterattack. In 1991 he founded a quarterly journal, *The Responsive Community*, with the slogan 'Rights and Responsibilities'. *The Responsive Community* has served for a decade as the major intellectual organ for a growing communitarian movement which

attracted both Democrats such as Senator Bill Bradley and Republicans such as Jack Kemp and William Bennett. By 1993 Etzioni had organized a citizen lobby known as the Communitarian Network. The organization's goals revolved around the rebuilding of family and local communities.

In 1993 Etzioni published *The Spirit of Community*, which defined the goals of the communitarian movement and reiterated his themes of 1983. In an age of a surging bull market, in which shareholder capitalism began to sweep all before it, he decried the practices of insider trading, churning accounts and cornering the market. The fruits of the new seemingly amoral business culture of downsizing and globalization were not good: 'Too many businesspeople', he said, 'no longer accept the responsibility of stewardship' or the duty 'to reach beyond furthering self or corporate advancement or to serve as trustees of a special undertaking'. Airlines and health care were less safe as:

Speculation, cronyism, bribery, and raiding corporate coffers have left numerous savings and loans, banks, insurance companies, and pension funds teetering on the brink of insolvency and have shattered public confidence, which in turn damages the country's economic performance
(Etzioni 1993: 28–9)

In the later 1990s, as the stock market rose ever higher, Etzioni published two more books, *The New Golden Rule: Community and Morality in a Democratic Society* (1997) and *The Limits of Privacy* (1999). In the latter book, Etzioni upheld his commitment to individual personal freedom and privacy while insisting that sometimes it would have to be subordinated, like all personal rights, to the public good.

Etzioni continues to be a prolific writer and a vocal critic of both libertarianism and conservative authoritarianism. No lover of big government, disliking the sense of rights

without responsibilities he felt it bred, he nevertheless revived the old notion of the Greek city-state in which community and citizenship balanced the need for market freedom. Just as there could be no personal freedom without personal responsibility, there could be no market freedom without business ethics or responsibility.

BIBLIOGRAPHY

Etzioni, A. (1961) *A Comparative Analysis of Complex Organizations*, Glencoe, IL: The Free Press.

—— (1964) *Modern Organizations*, Englewood Cliffs, NJ: Prentice-Hall.

—— (1983) *An Immodest Agenda: Rebuilding America Before the 21st Century*, New York: McGraw-Hill.

—— (1988) *The Moral Dimension: Towards a New Economics*, New York: The Free Press.

—— (1993) *The Spirit of Community, The Reinvention of American Society*, New York: Simon and Schuster.

—— (1997) *The New Golden Rule: Community and Morality in a Democratic Society*, New York: Basic Books.

—— (1999) *The Limits of Privacy*, New York: Basic Books.

'Etzioni, Amitai [Werner]' (1980) in C. Moritz (ed.), *Current Biography Yearbook*, New York: The H.W. Wilson Company, 101–4.

DCL

F

FAYOL, Jules Henri (1841–1925)

Henri Fayol was born in Galata, a suburb of Constantinople on 29 July 1841, the son of an engineer, André Fayol, and his wife Eugénie. He died in Paris of complications following an operation on a stomach ulcer on 19 November 1925. The family came originally from Le Veurdre in the prefecture of Allier in central France, where Fayol's grandfather was a weaver. His father had trained as an architectural engineer, and was sent to Constantinople to set up a factory for casting cannon barrels; in 1845 he was appointed superintendent of a project to build a bridge across the Golden Horn from Constantinople to Galata, the project being financed by the French government. When this project was complete the family returned to France and settled in La Voulte-sur-Rhone, where Henri Fayol received his primary education; later he attended a technical art school in Valence, followed by the Lycée Imperial in Lyon and the Saint-Étienne Mining School.

Boigues Rambourg, later the Comambault Company, had been established in 1853 through the merger of seven companies. Its head office was in Paris, but much management responsibility was delegated to mine managers, in this case to Stephane Mony, general manager of the Commentry mine. In 1860 the most urgent managerial problem for the Commentry mine was fires in the mine and subsidence of the ground at both the Commentry and Montvicq pits. To solve this problem, Mony decided to hire mining engineers with outstanding ability from the Saint-Etienne Mining School. Fayol was among those recruited, and joined the firm as a mining engineer and management trainee in October 1860, aged nineteen. Mony became his mentor, and Fayol later succeeded Mony as manager of the Commentry mine when the latter went on to become senior partner. In 1875 he married Adelade Celeste Marie Saule and settled his residence in Saint-Front, where his company was located. The couple went on to have two daughters and a son.

Mony led Boigues Rambourg through a period of sound development, and provided firm leadership. Under his guidance, in 1874 the partnership decided to convert to a joint-stock company, renamed the Commentry-Fourchambault Company, Ltd. Mony continued to lead the company for some years until his death in 1884. Anatole le Brun Sessevale, one of the senior owners of the company, assumed the vacant presidency but was not competent enough to take effective countermeasures to deal with the depression in the iron and steel industry which had been going on since 1882. Differences over management strategy led to antagonism between Sessevale and the other directors, and he was obliged to resign in 1888. The board of directors of Comambault then appointed Henri Fayol as president on 8 March 1888, even though he was not yet a director; he served as a salaried president for twelve years from 1888 to 1900, until an assembly of shareholders finally nominated him to the board.

The depression in the iron and steel industry, which lasted from 1882 to 1887, had a particular impact on companies in central France, already weakened since the 1860s by competition from producers in the north and east. In this crisis, Commentry-Fourchambault was forced to change its business strategy and consider merging with other firms in order to survive. Fayol, after taking over the presidency, pursued this policy energetically. In 1892 negotiations for the amalgamation of the company with a mining and iron manufacturing company located in Decazeville, Aveyron prefecture were finalized, and the merger was approved at the assembly of the shareholders in July of that year; in 1899 shareholders voted to change the company name to Commentry-Fourchambault et Decazeville Company, Ltd.

Fayol went on to direct the management of the company for thirty years. As a manager, he pursued a fourfold strategy: audacious expansion of scrap and build, pursuit of further opportunities for mergers, growing investment in research and development, and continued diversification. An excellent engineer, he also proved himself to be a talented and successful manager and leader, and Commentry-Fourchambault became a model of a successful mining enterprise.

Fayol resigned from the presidency in May 1918, and the post was taken over by Claude Mugnet, the husband of his niece. Although Fayol remained a director, he went on to devote himself to work with professional societies and the development and diffusion of his own theories on management, which later became known as Fayolism. Among other efforts he founded the Centre d'Études Administratives in Paris in 1920, one of the leading centres of the study and professionalization of management in France. His ideas had many converts and won him an enthusiastic following. Although initially there was some friction between his followers and those of Henri LE CHATELIER, who espoused a kind of scientific management more directly connected to the ideas of Frederick W. TAYLOR,

both Fayol and Le Chatelier moved to dissipate this rivalry in the early 1920s, believing that for the good of management all the various schools should collaborate. Fayol himself continued to live in his apartment in the 7th arrondissement of Paris, working on despite growing ill-health. He died in 1925.

Fayol's concept of management was firmly rooted in the management practices he had developed at Commentry-Fourchambault over the course of many years, but his work was also based on the positive philosophy of Auguste Comte and the experimental method developed by Claude Bernard in accordance with the positivist philosophy oriented method, in which inference is directly and accurately applied to a variety of facts gathered through observation and experiments. These methods were applied by Fayol to the theory of administration.

In all business enterprises of whatever type and field of activity, he believed, there exist six types of activity. These are production, commerce, finance, security, accounting and management. However, as business organizations become larger in scale, becoming more strongly organized and hierarchical, the importance of the last function, management, is enhanced. This implies the necessity of business management being based on objective and scientific foundations. Fayol was firmly of the view that managers' abilities should be enhanced by providing them with management education. Such education should aim to teach general principles of management to managers. Since no such general principles of management then existed, Fayol set out to develop principles which would be applicable to all types of organization. These are described in his major work, *Administration industrielle et générale* (General and Industrial Management), published in 1917.

According to Fayol, the purpose of administration in a business organization is to unify the six types of activity mentioned above, all of which are indispensable if the organization is to meet its goals and realize its purpose.

Management, as the most important of these functions, has the following tasks: (1) to predict the future and make plans; (2) to construct organizational mechanisms; (3) to issue orders; (4) to coordinate various types of activity; and (5) to control activity to ensure that all work conforms to the previously established plans. He goes on to present fourteen management rules or principles which are an important part of the execution of the manager's function. These, summarized briefly, are:

1. Division of labour, so as to achieve the maximum efficiency from labour.

2. The establishment of authority.

3. The enforcement of discipline.

4. Unified command, so that no employee reports to more than one supervisor.

5. Unity of direction, with all control emanating from one source.

6. Subordination of individual interests to the interest of the organization.

7. Fair remuneration for all (although Fayol was not in favour of profit sharing).

8. Centralization of control and authority.

9. A scalar hierarchy, in which each employee is aware of his or her place and duties.

10. A sense of order and purpose.

11. Equity and fairness in dealings between staff and managers.

12. Stability of jobs and positions, with a view to ensuring low turnover of staff and managers.

13. Development of individual initiative on the part of managers.

14. *Esprit de corps* and the maintenance of staff and management morale.

Fayol's approach to management became very popular, and was later commented on by writers such as Lyndall URWICK and Luther GULICK. In later years he came to be seen as a figure of equal stature to Frederick W. Taylor; while the latter was known as the father of the science of management, Fayol, in recognition of his broader and more holistic approach, became known as the father of the science of administration. From his work developed a school of thinking that studied the problems of management in terms of management process, and this management process school remained important and influential until after the Second World War, when its work was largely supplanted by modern organization theory, as developed by Chester I. BARNARD.

BIBLIOGRAPHY

Fayol, J.H. (1917) *Administration industrielle et générale* (General and Industrial Management), Paris: Dunod et Pinat; trans. I. Gray, New York: David S. Lake, 1984.

—— (1918) *L'éveil de l'esprit public* (Waking up the Public Spirit), Paris: Dunod et Pinat.

—— (1921) *L'incapacité industrielle de l'État: P.T.T.* (Industrial Incapability of the State: The Ministry of Posts and Telecommunications), Paris: Dunod.

Sasaki, T. (1999) 'The Comambault Company Revisited', *Journal of Economics* 68(4): 113–28.

Wren, D.A. (ed.) (1995) 'Henri Fayol and the Emergence of General Management Theory', *Journal of Management History* 1(3): 5–12.

ST

FIEDLER, Fred Edward (1922–)

Fred Edward Fiedler was born in Vienna, Austria on 13 July 1922. His parents, Victor and Helga Schallinger Fiedler, owned a textile

and tailoring supply store prior to 1938. Fred was their only child. After completing secondary school, he served a brief apprenticeship in his father's textile business before emigrating to the United States in 1938 and settling in South Bend, Indiana. After his high school graduation in 1940, Fiedler held a variety of low-level jobs in Indiana, Michigan and California, before returning to Indiana and a job at the Indiana and Michigan Electric Company. Following the German invasion of Austria, meanwhile, Fiedler's parents moved first to Shanghai and then to the United States in 1946.

In the summer of 1942, Fiedler enrolled in engineering courses at Western Michigan College of Education (now Western Michigan University, in Kalamazoo), but quickly decided engineering was not his field. He also applied to and was accepted by the University of Chicago. He served in the US Army from 1942 to 1945. Following basic training and a brief assignment in a medical battalion, he was sent to Indiana University for training in the Turkish Area and Language Studies programme. Later he served in an infantry battalion, military civilian affairs and the military government. During tours of duty in England and Germany, Fiedler was involved in training, interpreting, telephone communications and public safety. Fiedler had met Judith M. Joseph at the University of Chicago before entering the army, and they married shortly after his discharge on 14 April 1946. They have collaborated on research and writing over the years, and have four children.

Fiedler developed an interest in psychology in his early teens from reading his father's books on the topic. He took several extension courses in psychology while serving in the army. After his discharge from the army in November 1945, Fiedler was readmitted to the University of Chicago and resumed his study of psychology in January 1946. He received a master's degree in industrial and organizational psychology in 1947 and his Ph.D. in clinical psychology in 1949.

During his years at the University of Chicago, Fiedler was actively involved in research under some of the most prominent names in the field, such as Lee Cronbach and Donald Campbell. Among the university's professors were L.L. Thurstone and Thelma G. Thurstone, Donald Fiske, Carl Rogers and William Foote Whyte. Fiedler's master's thesis was on 'The Efficacy of Preventive Psychotherapy for Alleviating Examination Anxiety', and his dissertation, entitled 'A Comparative Investigation of the Therapeutic Relationships Created by Experts and Non-experts of the Psychoanalytic, Non-directive, and Adlerian Schools', is one of his most frequently cited works.

While at the University of Chicago he was a trainee and then a research assistant with the Veterans Administration (VA), and continued working for a year after his graduation as a research associate and instructor for the VA in Chicago. Following a summer in the Combat Crew Research Laboratory at Randolph Field, he became associate director on a naval research contract at the University of Illinois' College of Education. His work during this period with Donald Fiske and Lee Cronbach sparked his lifelong interest in leadership.

From 1950 until 1969, Fiedler was on the faculty of the University of Illinois, where he initiated and directed the Group Effectiveness Research Laboratory (GERL). Harry Triandis and Joseph McGrath were associate directors. Research associates included Martin Chemers, Peter Dachler, David DeVries, Jack Feldman, Richard Hackman, J.G. Hunt, Edwin Hutchins, Daniel Ilgen and Terence Mitchell. While at the University of Illinois, Fiedler was appointed head of the social, differential, personality and industrial psychology divisions. His wife worked as a research sociologist in the university's Survey Research Center.

In 1969 Fiedler moved to the University of Washington where he remained on the faculty until his retirement in 1993. There he established the Organizational Research Group and directed the Group Effectiveness Research

Laboratory. His wife became assistant director of the University of Washington's Educational Assessment Center. Among his associates were Gary Latham, Terence Mitchell, Lee Beach, Martin Chemers, James G. Hunt, Richard Hackman and Daniel Ilgen.

In the late 1940s the emphasis in leadership research shifted from traits and the personal characteristics of leaders to leadership styles and behaviours. From the late 1960s through the 1980s, leadership interests turned to contingency models of leadership. One of the earliest and best known is Fiedler's contingency model of leadership effectiveness. Published in 1967 as *A Theory of Leadership Effectiveness*, the model immediately drew attention as the first leadership theory operationally to measure the interaction between leadership personality and the leader's situational control in predicting leadership performance.

While many scholars assumed that there was one best style of leadership, Fiedler's contingency model postulates that the leader's effectiveness is based on 'situational contingency', or a match between the leader's style and situational favourableness, later called situational control. More than 400 studies have since investigated this relationship.

A key component in Fiedler's contingency theory is the least preferred co-worker (LPC) scale, an instrument for measuring an individual's leadership orientation using eighteen to twenty-five pairs of adjectives and an eight-point bipolar scale between each pair. Respondents are asked to consider the person they liked working with the least, either presently or in the past, and rate that co-worker on each pair of adjectives. High-LPC or relationship-motivated leaders describe their least preferred co-worker in more positive terms and are concerned with maintaining good interpersonal relations. Low-LPC or task-motivated leaders describe their least preferred co-worker in rejecting and negative terms, and give higher priority to the task than to interpersonal relations.

According to Fiedler, there is no ideal leader. Both low-LPC (task-oriented) and high-LPC (relationship-oriented) leaders can be effective, if their leadership orientation fits the situation. The contingency theory allows for predicting the characteristics of the appropriate situations for effectiveness. Three situational components determine the favourableness or situational control: leader–member relations, task structure and position power. Fiedler found that low-LPC leaders are more effective in extremely favourable or unfavourable situations, whereas high-LPC leaders perform best in situations with intermediate favourability.

Since personality is relatively stable, the contingency model suggests that improving effectiveness requires changing the situation to fit the leader. The organization or the leader may increase or decrease task structure and position power, and training and group development may improve leader–member relations. Leader-Match is a self paced leadership training programme designed to help leaders alter the favourableness of the situation, or situational control. The 1976 book describing Leader-Match was co-authored by Martin Chemers and Linda Mahar.

Fiedler's contingency theory has drawn criticism because it implies that the only alternative for an unalterable mismatch between leader orientation and an unfavourable situation is changing the leader. The model's validity has also been disputed, despite many supportive tests (Bass 1990). Other criticisms concern the methodology of measuring leadership style through the LPC inventory and the nature of the supporting evidence (Ashour 1973; Schriesheim and Kerr 1977a, 1977b; Vecchio 1977, 1983). Fiedler and his associates have provided decades of research to support and refine the contingency theory. Cognitive resource theory (CRT) modifies Fiedler's basic contingency model by adding traits of the leader (Fiedler and Garcia 1987). CRT tries to identify the conditions under which leaders and group members will use their intellectual

resources, skills and knowledge effectively. While it has been generally assumed that more intelligent and more experienced leaders will perform better than those with less intelligence and experience, this assumption is not supported by Fiedler's research.

To Fiedler, stress is a key determinant of leader effectiveness (Fiedler and Garcia 1987; Fiedler *et al.* 1993), and a distinction is made between stress related to the leader's superior, and stress related to subordinates or the situation itself. In stressful situations, leaders dwell on the stressful relations with others and cannot focus their intellectual abilities on the job. Thus, intelligence is more effective and used more often in stress-free situations. Fiedler has found that experience impairs performance in low-stress conditions but contributes to performance under high-stress conditions. As with other situational factors, for stressful situations Fiedler recommends altering or engineering the leadership situation to capitalize on the leader's strengths.

Fiedler is known around the world for his writing, lectures and consulting work. Throughout his career, Fiedler has received research grants and contracts from many government agencies and private foundations. He held research fellowships at the University of Amsterdam from 1957 to 1958, at the University of Louvain in Belgium from 1963 to 1964, and at Templeton College, Oxford from 1986 to 1987. He has served as a consultant for various federal and local government agencies and private industries in the United States and abroad.

Fiedler was recognized by the American Psychological Association for counselling research in 1971 and for his contributions to military psychology in 1979. He received the Stogdill Award for Distinguished Contributions to Leadership in 1978. The American Academy of Management honoured Fiedler as a Distinguished Educator in Management in 1993, and the Society for Industrial and Organizational Psychology recognized his outstanding scientific contribu-

tions in 1996. In 1999 the American Psychological Society presented Fiedler with its James McKeen Cattell Award. Fiedler is a member of the International Association of Applied Psychology and a past president of that organization's Division of Organizational Psychology. He is a fellow of the American Psychological Association and a member of the Society for Experimental Social Psychology and the Midwestern Psychological Association. He has authored or co-authored more than 200 scientific papers and several books. His articles are frequently cited by others and have been published by the most respected journals in the fields of psychology, leadership and management.

Fiedler's career spans more than fifty years. Even in retirement, he continues to inspire and encourage research on leadership and other related topics. He proposed the contingency theory of leadership very early in his career, and has spent years since then testing its assumptions and making revisions. He has willingly debated his critics, offering additional research and alternative explanations based on his own investigations and the growing body of knowledge in the field. Fiedler and his contingency theory of leadership deserve a prominent place in the history of management thought. He was one of the first to recognize and produce a leadership model that combines personality traits and contextual factors. The more recent cognitive resource theory promises to extend his influence many years into the future.

BIBLIOGRAPHY

Ashour, A.S. (1973) 'The Contingency Model of Leadership Effectiveness: An Evaluation', *Organizational Behavior and Human Decision Processes*, 9(3): 339–55.

Bass, B.M. (1990) 'Leader March', in *Handbook of Leadership*, New York: The Free Press, 494–510, 651–2, 840–41.

Fiedler, F.E. (1958) *Leader Attitudes and Group Effectiveness*, Urbana, IL:

University of Illinois Press.
—— (1967) *A Theory of Leadership Effectiveness*, New York: McGraw-Hill.
—— (1971) *Leadership*, New York: General Learning Press.
—— (1981) *Leader Attitudes and Group Effectiveness*, Westport, CT: Greenwood Publishing Group.
—— (1992) 'Life in a Pretzel-shaped Universe', in A.G. Bedeian (ed.), *Management Laureates: A Collection of Autobiographical Essays*, Greenwich, CT: JAI Press, vol. 1, 301–34.
—— (1994) *Leadership Experience and Leadership Performance*, Alexandria, VA: US Army Research Institute for the Behavioral and Social Sciences.
—— (1997) *Directory of the American Psychological Association*, Chicago: St James Press, 419.
Fiedler, F.E. and Chemers, M.M. (1974) *Leadership and Effective Management*, Glenview, IL: Scott, Foresman and Co.
Fiedler, F.E. and Garcia, J.E. (1987) *New Approaches to Leadership, Cognitive Resources and Organizational Performance*, New York: John Wiley and Sons.
Fiedler, F.E., Chemers, M.M. and Mahar, L. (1976) *Improving Leadership Effectiveness: The Leader Match Concept*, New York: John Wiley and Sons.
Fiedler, F.E., Garcia, J.E. and Lewis, C.T. (1986) *People Management, and Productivity*, Boston: Allyn and Bacon.
Fiedler, F.E., Gibson, F.W. and Barrett, K.M. (1993) 'Stress, Babble, and the Utilization of the Leader's Intellectual Abilities', *Leadership Quarterly* 4(2): 189–208.
Fiedler, F.E., Godfrey, E.P. and Hall, D.M. (1959) *Boards, Management and Company Success*, Danville, IL: Interstate Publishers.
Hooijberg, R. and Choi, J. (1999) 'From Austria to the United States and from

Evaluating Therapists to Developing Cognitive Resources Theory: An Interview with Fred Fiedler', *Leadership Quarterly* 10(4): 653–66.
King, B., Streufert, S. and Fiedler, F.E. (1978) *Managerial Control and Organizational Democracy*, Washington, DC: V.H. Winston and Sons.
Schriesheim, C.A. and Kerr, S. (1977a) 'Theories and Measures of Leadership', in J.G. Hunt, and L.L. Larson (eds), *Leadership: The Cutting Edge*, Carbondale, IL: Southern Illinois University Press, 9–45.
—— (1977b) 'R.I.P LPC: A Response to Fiedler', in J.G. Hunt, and L.L. Larson (eds), *Leadership: The Cutting Edge*, Carbondale, IL: Southern Illinois University Press, 51–6.
Vecchio, R.P. (1977) 'An Empirical Examination of the Validity of Fiedler's Model of Leadership Effectiveness', *Organizational Behavior and Human Performance* 19: 180–206.
—— (1983) 'Assessing the Validity of Fiedler's Contingency Model of Leadership Effectiveness: A Closer look at Strube and Garcia', *Psychological Bulletin* 93: 404–8.

JAEB

FILENE, Edward Albert (1860–1937)

Edward Albert Filene was born in Salem, Massachusetts on 3 September 1860 and died in Paris on 26 September 1937. His father, William Filene, was an immigrant from Eastern Europe who had settled in Boston and built up a small but prosperous retail business. After finishing high school, Filene had planned to attend Harvard University, but his father's ill health required that he take

over the family business instead; he became president of William Filene's Sons in 1879, at the age of nineteen. Over the next thirty years he built up Filene's business, establishing one of the largest and most successful department stores in the country. He became a noted philanthropist and had some importance as a social commentator. Never married, he was reportedly a man of difficult temper who made few close friends, and his abrasive personality may have prevented his ideas from becoming more widely disseminated (Urwick 1956).

Filene's principles of marketing for retail operations were publicized in several books, notably *More Profits from Merchandizing* (1925) and *The Model Stock Plan* (1930), and were of considerable influence in the development of retailing in the United States. He believed that the primary purpose of marketing is not to make a profit, but to satisfy customer needs; if this is done successfully, then profits will follow. He was one of the first to use the slogan, 'The customer is always right'. He competed successfully with his rivals on cost, aiming for low margins and rapid turnover of stock, the ancestor of the 'pile it high and sell it cheap' philosophy used by later retailers such as Sam WALTON. This philosophy was backed up with detailed accounting and inventory control systems. Urwick (1956) credits him with being the first to apply the principles of scientific management to retailing in the United States.

Filene was also noted for maintaining good relations with this staff, and was an early proponent of industrial democracy; major decisions affecting the running of the store were sometimes put to a vote. He paid well and reduced working hours. In the wider community, he was one of the early organizers of the credit union movement in the United States, and in 1920 used some of his wealth to found the Twentieth Century Fund, an institution conducting research into economic and social issues. In 1927, through the fund, he established the International Management Institute in Geneva, a permanent international body coordinating research and development in management.

In *Successful Living in this Machine Age* (1932), Filene pondered on the social changes that mass production and the rise of large corporations had wrought on America. He linked the rise of mass production to the rise of what VEBLEN had called 'the leisure classes', pointing out that many of the goods being produced and sold *en masse* were being purchased by those who had time and money to spare; thus mass production both led to greater consumer demand and was itself a product of greater consumer affluence. He believed that business owners and managers had a twofold responsibility to society: first, to provide employment which made affluence possible, and second, to provide goods which satisfied the needs of the newly affluent.

BIBLIOGRAPHY
Filene, E.A. (1925) *More Profits from Merchandizing*, Chicago: A.W. Shaw.
—— (1930) *The Model Stock Plan*, New York: McGraw-Hill.
—— (1932) *Successful Living in this Machine Age*, London: Jonathan Cape.
Urwick, L.F. (1956) *The Golden Book of Management*, London: Newman Neame.

MLW

FIRESTONE, Harvey (1868–1938)

Harvey Firestone was born in Columbiana County, Ohio on 20 December 1868 and died in Miami Beach, Florida on 7 February 1938. He was the founder and chief executive of the Firestone Tire and Rubber Company, which he led to become the second largest company in its industry. Firestone entered the

tyre business through the buggy industry, which used solid rubber tyres. By 1900 he was based in Akron, Ohio, a centre of rubber manufacturing, with his own Firestone Tire and Rubber Company. The goal of the new firm was to produce tyres at lower prices, which it succeeded in doing in part by avoiding established patents and royalty charges. The future business strategy of the Firestone Tire and Rubber Company was set: the aim was to be a low-cost producer, with aggressive pricing and growth policies. Firestone refused to enter into agreements designed to maintain prices. He entered the tyre-manufacturing (as opposed to tyre-mounting) business in 1902. His firm was, however, rooted in the older solid tyre technology of the buggy business, not the newer pneumatic technology used by the rapidly growing automobile industry. Thus Firestone faced the major challenge of a declining market for solid tyres, although he continued to earn profits from solid tyres; pneumatic technology was too new and unreliable for fire engines, a tyre market that Firestone dominated.

Firestone met the automobile tyre challenge with characteristic aggressiveness, again with regard to patents. Pneumatic tyres were at the time attached to wheels using patents for a clincher system, by which the hard rubber bead on a tyre was forced inside the narrower rim of a wheel. The association controlling the patents for the clincher tyre, seeking to restrict entry into the field and thereby maintain high prices, refused Firestone a licence to use the technology. Firestone's response was to devise a cheaper means of mounting pneumatic tyres while avoiding the clincher tyre patents, and to reinvest the profits from the solid tyre business in the new pneumatic field. When Henry FORD, then a small automobile manufacturer near Detroit, asked for bids on a contract for his new Model N car, Firestone substantially undercut the price of a clincher tyre and won the business.

This deal began a lifelong personal friendship and business relationship, which lasted for the rest of the century, between Ford, Firestone and their firms. Eventually, the two entrepreneurs were able to break patent associations that restricted growth in their respective industries. Within a few years Ford had become the world's largest automobile manufacturer, and Ford favoured Firestone in tyre purchases.

Important as supplying tyres for new vehicles was to Firestone and his competitors, the more lucrative business was in replacement tyres. Firestone succeeded in this market by maintaining low prices and by using innovative and aggressive marketing techniques. Firestone practised vertical integration, complete with investments in a rubber plantation in Liberia and a chain of retail and repair shops.

By the 1930s Firestone was withdrawing from the day-to-day affairs of his firm. Firestone Tire nevertheless retained the strategy of its founder. After the Second World War the firm expanded aggressively and continued its reputation in the industry of being a low-cost and able manufacturer. In 1988, after the firm had suffered serious losses from the sales of defective radial tyres a decade earlier, it was purchased by the Japanese Bridgestone Company. This merger was part of a worldwide trend of consolidation in the tyre manufacturing business.

BIBLIOGRAPHY

Firestone, H. with Crowther, S. (1926) *Men and Rubber: The Story of Business*, Garden City, NY: Doubleday, Page.

French, M.J. (1991) *The U.S. Tire Industry*, Boston: Twayne.

Lief, A. (1951) *Harvey Firestone: Free Man of Enterprise*, New York: McGraw-Hill.

KAK

FITZ NEAL, Richard (or Fitz Nigel: c.1130–98)

Richard Fitz Neal (or Fitz Nigel) was born c.1130, the possibly illegitimate son of Nigel, bishop of Ely and treasurer of England under Henry I and Henry II. He died on 10 September 1198. Richard's great uncle was Roger le Poer, chancellor, chief justiciar and Bishop of Salisbury under Henry I and Stephen. His mother's identity is unknown, although she was probably of English rather than Norman descent. During the war between Stephen and his half-sister Matilda, the young Richard was twice sent as a hostage to Stephen, first for two years from 1141 to 1143, and again in the autumn of 1144. Between such unusual interruptions, his education continued at the monastery in Ely, and upon the accession of Henry II in 1154 and his father's return to government service, Richard's civil service career began. He was probably a chief writing clerk in the exchequer before his father purchased the position of treasurer for him in the late 1150s. The position of treasurer was a senior one within the exchequer, but still subordinate to both the chief justiciar and the barons of the exchequer. His father paid £400 for Richard's advancement.

Shortly after this advance in his secular career, his parallel clerical career also moved forward. He was appointed as archdeacon of Ely in 1160 (enabling him to manage the diocese while his father, the bishop, was ill). In the 1170s he was made a canon of St Paul's and archdeacon of Colchester, and in 1184 he became dean of Lincoln, all of which provided him with an income. After missing out on the appointment to the bishopric of Lincoln in 1186, he was elevated to the see of London in 1189. He remained in government service as treasurer of the exchequer until his death.

Fitz Neal's secular activities were not confined to the exchequer, for he also acted as an itinerant justice of the eyre in the south-west counties in 1179 and in East Anglia in 1194. He also acted as a judge in the Court of Common Pleas at Westminster and as a judge in the Exchequer Court. He was selected to help in the reorganization of the Normandy exchequer in the 1170s. His political activities during the upheavals of Richard I's reign were minimal, although he was involved in negotiations between Richard's chancellor, William Longchamp, and Prince John in 1191.

Fitz Neal's term of office as treasurer was over forty years, and as such he was in a unique position to write about the workings of that institution. He had an intimate knowledge of the day-to-day workings of the exchequer, allied with the experience of other administrative and legal activities, to look at it as part of a larger governmental structure. This in-depth knowledge informs what is Fitz Neal's primary claim to fame, the *Diologus de Scaccario* or The Course of the Exchequer. This book is a mixture of personnel manual, description of the jobs of each member of the exchequer staff, and procedural guide to the creation of the exchequer's most important financial record, the Pipe Roll, which recorded royal income and expenditure. The *Diologus*, as one commentator points out, is not a complete guide to all the workings of the exchequer and there is some evidence that a more complete work was envisaged by the author. The existing work is nevertheless a 'severely practical treatise' (Fitz Neal 1950: xviii) on the workings of a key government department. The surviving text seems to have been a first edition dating to c.1177, partially reworked by Fitz Neal a decade or so later. Some idea of his motivation for writing such a book is contained in the prologue to the book, wherein the 'pupil' asks the 'Master' 'to leave a record of his knowledge of the exchequer for others to follow' (Fitz Neal 1950: 5). The 'pupil' also asked that any such book must be written in commonplace language and need not be subject to the rhetorical devices of philosophy and the liberal arts. The language and terms used should be those which could be understood by clerks and others concerned with the procedures and structures of the exchequer.

This extraordinary book contains a detailed discussion of all the relevant staff functions of the exchequer and is a unique manual both for contemporaries, who could use it as an everyday guide, and for later students of administration who seek to understand the workings of the medieval civil services and the financial administration of England. Even though it occasionally describes the theory of the organization rather than its actual day-to-day working, as its twentieth-century editor concludes, 'its lucidity and exactness are more suggestive of the nineteenth century than of the twelfth' (Fitz Neal 1950: xxii). Fitz Neal's writing was based on decades of continual attendance at Exchequer proceedings, since, as treasurer, it was his job to oversee the compilation of the annual Pipe Roll and it was his dictation which the clerks transcribed to make up that roll.

BIBLIOGRAPHY

Clanchy, M.T. (1993) *From Memory to Written Record, England 1066–1307*, 2nd edn, Oxford: Blackwell.

Fitz Neal, R. (1950) *Diologus de Scaccario & Constitutio Domus Regis*, ed. C. Johnson, London: Thomas Nelson and Sons.

'Fitz Neal, Richard' (1885) in L. Stephen and S. Lee (eds), *Dictionary of National Biography*, London: Small, Elder and Co., vol. 19, 186–8.

Richardson, H.G. and Sayles, G.O. (1963) *The Governance of Mediaeval England from the Conquest to the Magna Carta*, Edinburgh: Edinburgh University Press, 245–50.

ML

FLAGLER, Henry Morrison (1830–1913)

Henry Morrison Flagler was born in Hopewell, New York on 2 January 1830, the son of a Presbyterian minister. He died in Palm Beach, Florida on 20 May 1913. After leaving home at the age of fourteen Flagler worked at a variety of jobs, eventually becoming a grain merchant in the area around Sandusky, Ohio in 1850. Among his contacts was John D. ROCKEFELLER, then in the grain business in Cleveland. In the 1860s he relocated to Michigan, dealing in grain and also in salt; he prospered during the American Civil War, but went into debt in the postwar slump. Moving to Cleveland in 1865, he set up a general merchandise firm, and also renewed his contact with Rockefeller.

Rockefeller was at this point just entering the oil business, and in 1866 he invited Flagler to join him in the partnership Rockefeller, Andrews and Flagler. Energetic and decisive, Flagler used his experience and contacts as a merchant to organize the efficient shipment of oil by rail. He became second only to Rockefeller in the hierarchy of the rapidly growing organiztion, and in 1870 was named secretary and treasurer of the newly founded Standard Oil. Having moved to New York in 1877, in 1882 he became president of Standard Oil Company of New Jersey, remaining as a vice-president until 1908, and as a director until 1911.

Flagler had married Mary Harkness in 1853, and they had three children. After her death in 1881, Flagler married her nurse, Ida Shourds, in 1883. While honeymooning on the then undeveloped east coast of Florida, Flagler was captivated by the beauty of the area's natural surroundings. He wondered if rich Americans who habitually wintered on the French Riviera could be attracted here instead, and set out to answer his own question. Neither his own career nor Florida would ever be quite the same.

Florida at that point was rural and undeveloped, with less than 800 kilometres (500 miles) of railroad and virtually no infrastruc-

ture. Undeterred, Flagler built the $1 million luxury Ponce de Leon hotel in St Augustine in 1885–8, at the same time upgrading the railways so tourists could travel in comfort. When the venture proved to be an almost immediate success, more hotels followed. The railway began not only carrying tourists in but also hauling fruit out, bringing a boom to the Florida citrus fruit industry. When the severe winter of 1894–5 killed many fruit trees, Flagler gave the farmers free seed and made personal loans to those who were destitute.

In 1896 Flagler extended his Florida East Coast Railway south to Miami, where he built not only more hotels but all the infrastructure needed to support the town, including a power plant, street lights, sewerage works and even churches. Like Henry HUNTINGTON in California, Flagler found that to reach his own goals he had not only to manage his core business but also to serve in effect as planner and developer of the entire region. This activity he carried out with great skill. His final achievement was the bridging of the Florida Keys, linking Key West to Miami by rail in 1912.

In 1899 Ida Flagler was declared insane. Flagler was finally able to divorce her in 1901 and was married for the third time, to Mary Kenan, with whom he lived in the Miami suburb of Palm Beach, the object of some cynosure for having more or less abandoned his previous wife. Opinions of Flagler were generally mixed: some believed he exploited and ruined Florida for his own profit, but others hailed him as the builder and even saviour of the state.

BIBLIOGRAPHY
Akin, E.N. (1988) *Flagler: Rockefeller Partner and Florida Baron*, Kent, OH: Kent State University Press.

MLW

FLANDERS, Allan (1910–73)

Allan Flanders was born in London on 27 July 1910 and died in Kenilworth, Warwickshire on 29 September 1973. He was educated at Latymer Upper School, then the at adult school run by the International Socialist Camp fund in Germany. This shaped his ideas of ethical socialism, which remained his compass. Following the rise of the Nazis, Flanders returned to Britain, sustaining his views on ethical socialism via the Socialist Vanguard/Union group and its *Socialist Commentary*. He worked as a draughtsman and research assistant at the Trade Union Congress (1943), helping prepare its 'Report on Postwar Reconstruction'. As head of the Political Branch, part of the Control Commission, he returned to Germany (1946), and played a key role in reconstructing industrial trade unionism, a central feature of its political economy.

Flanders' academic career was spent predominantly at the University of Oxford as senior lecturer in industrial relations (1949–69) and faculty fellow, Nuffield College (1964–9). He moved to the University of Warwick's Industrial Relations Research Unit as reader in industrial relations (1971–3). He interspersed this with employment and public policy involvement. This included membership of the Secretary of State's Colonial Advisory Committee (1954–62), a role as adviser to the National Board for Prices and Incomes (1965–8) and full-time membership of the Commission on Industrial Relations (1969–71), as well as influence on the most famous of reports in the field, the Donovan report (Turner 1968). He was awarded a CBE in 1971.

Much of Flanders' work is collected in *Management and Unions* (1970). This displays his ideas on the changing roles and responsibilities of unions, management and government, and analysis of industrial relations and collective bargaining in terms of job regulation and social partnership. His seminal work on productivity bargaining (Flanders 1964) also

helped establish his reputation, being revisited almost a quarter of a century later (Ahlstrand 1990). He also wrote books on trade unions (Flanders 1952) and industrial democracy (Flanders *et al.* 1968), along with WOODWARD. He co-edited the path-breaking and founding text of the 'Oxford School of Industrial Relations' (Flanders and Clegg 1954), of which he was a central member along with his friends Hugh CLEGG and Alan FOX. This group was influential in policy terms and also colonized academia.

Flanders famously defined industrial relations as 'a system of rules' and 'the study of the institutions of job regulation' (Flanders 1965: 10). Even critics conceded that this was a pioneering, influential and significant attempt to give theoretical unity, precision and meaning to industrial relations (Hyman 1975). Flanders then went on to analyse trade unions. They had 'two faces' ('sword of justice' and 'vested interest'), participated in job regulation for worker development and were attached to 'voluntarism'. Furthermore, he developed 'explanatory dimensions' (see Poole 1981), was working on a theory of union growth as a first step to a general theory, and was critical to others' theoretical work (Clegg 1976). His earlier unpublished work contain fairly elaborate union theorizing (Kelly 1998). Flanders also developed an understanding of collective bargaining. Contrasting with more classical conceptions, collective bargaining was seen as a more political and rule-making process by joint regulation, a participative form of decision making, enhancing self-respect and dignity, and an expression of industrial and pluralist democracy. Similarly, productivity bargaining could reconstruct and democratize workplace relations via negotiation and joint agreement and responsibility, extending collective bargaining and integrating shop stewards into the managerial process, while producing respect for workplace democracy in management (Ahlstrand 1990).

Flanders wrote about issues that are now highly topical and contentious. For instance, he argued that management and business needed accepted standards of conduct to define 'moral' and 'social' responsibilities. Lack of management training and development was identified. Similarly, Flanderite echoes can be heard in employee involvement and social partnership debates. Even a quarter of a century after his death, Flanders' relevance to industrial relations and management remains.

Acknowledgements
Thanks to John Kelly, Rod Martin and Pat McGovern for earlier comments.

BIBLIOGRAPHY
Ahlstrand, B. (1990) *The Quest for Productivity: A Case Study of Fawley after Flanders*, Cambridge: Cambridge University Press.
Clegg, H. (1976) *Trade Unionism Under Collective Bargaining: A Theory Based on Comparisons of Six Countries*, Oxford: Blackwell.
—— (1990) 'The Oxford School of Industrial Relations', *Warwick Papers in Industrial Relations*, IRRU, University of Warwick, 31.
Flanders, A. (1952) *Trade Unions*, London: Hutchinson's University Library.
—— (1964) *The Fawley Productivity Agreements: A Case Study of Management and Collective Bargaining*, London: Faber and Faber.
—— (1965) *Industrial Relations: What is Wrong with the System?*, London: Faber.
—— (1970) *Management and Unions: The Theory and Reform of Industrial Relations*, London: Faber and Faber.
—— (1974) 'The Tradition of Voluntarism', *British Journal of Industrial Relations* 12(3): 352–70.
Flanders, A. and Clegg, H. (eds) (1954) *The System of Industrial Relations in Great Britain: Its History, Law and Institutions*, Oxford: Blackwell.
Flanders, A., Pomeranz, R. and Woodward, J. (1968) *Experiment in Industrial*

Democracy: A Case Study of the John Lewis Partnership, London: Faber and Faber.

Fox, A. (1975) 'Collective Bargaining, Flanders and the Webbs', *British Journal of Industrial Relations* 13(2): 151–74.

Kelly, J. (1998) *Rethinking Industrial Relations: Mobilization, Collectivism and Long Waves*, London: Routledge.

Hyman, R. (1975) *Industrial Relations: A Marxist Introduction*, London: Macmillan.

Poole, M. (1981) *Theories of Trade Unionism: A Sociology of Industrial Relations*, London: Routledge and Kegan Paul.

Turner, H.A. (1968) 'The Royal Commission's Research Papers', *British Journal of Industrial Relations* 6(3): 346–59.

CR

FLORENCE, Philip Sargant (1890–1982)

Philip Sargant Florence was born in London on 25 June 1890, the son of the musician Henry Smythe Florence and the artist and writer Mary Sargant Florence. He died on 29 January 1982 in Birmingham. After education at Rugby School and Caius College, Cambridge, where he took an MA, he went to New York to study for his Ph.D. at Columbia University. From 1917 to 1921 he was lecturer at the Bureau of Industrial Research and Bureau of Personnel Administration in New York. He married Lella Faye Secor in 1917, and the couple had two sons.

Returning to Britain, Florence held a variety of posts at Cambridge, mainly at Magdalene College and in the department of economics. He then moved to the University of Birmingham, where he remained for the rest of his career; he was professor of commerce from 1929 to 1955, and dean of faculty from 1947 to 1950. Florence was awarded the CBE in 1952.

Florence is best known as an industrial economist, focusing on theories of the firm and the impacts of human behaviour on economics and organizations. His early work on fatigue and industrial unrest (Florence 1918, 1924) convinced him that many of the problems faced by industry were not economic at all, but rather human in origin. That conviction comes through strongly in his principal work, *The Logic of Industrial Organization* (1933) and its two follow-up studies, *Investment, Location, and Size of Plant* (1948) and *The Logic of British and American Industry* (1953). Political science and psychology, he says, are at least as important in the study of organization as is economics, and he is highly critical of the growing trend towards abstract analysis which leaves the human factor out of the equation (Florence 1953: 1–2).

Florence begins with an apparent paradox. The logic of organizations, he says, seems to suggest that big is best. 'Big' here means both large-scale production and large-scale organization (he makes the valuable point that many large organizations actually undertake production on a fairly small scale) (Florence 1933: 1–2). Combining both would make for optimum efficiency, which he defines as 'maximum return physical, pecuniary or psychological at minimum physical, pecuniary or psychological cost' (1933: 260). Throughout his work, Florence is careful to stress that efficiency is not solely about profit and cost; other human factors are at play as well, and the most efficient factory is not necessarily the one with the best cost ratios.

Yet, despite this supposed logic, and despite numerous individual examples to the contrary, industry as a whole has not moved towards large-scale production and organization. In both Britain and the United States, small firms continue to outnumber large ones, and continue to account for the majority of pro-

duction and employment. Whence, then, is the source of this 'illogic'? Florence identifies three principal factors: (1) the individual and 'illogical' nature of human demand; (2) the burdens which large-scale organization places on management in terms of control; and (3) the tendency of people to feel less involved in and committed to larger organizations than smaller ones. All three of these are social and psychological factors which are often omitted by analysts who see the firm, and particularly its management, as primarily rational in national: 'men engaged in business as administrators and investors are, no less than the labourers they employ, human beings, not, as is often assumed, hundred per cent efficiency experts' (1933: 263). Large-scale operation, then, does not necessarily result in efficiency.

As marketing writers such as CHERINGTON had been pointing out for at least a decade before Florence, there is a fundamental mismatch between consumer buying patterns and large-scale production, in that consumers tend to buy on a small scale, at uncertain times and places. This poses a problem for distribution and production planning. Consumers also vary not only their rate of consumption, but also the type of consumption, by demanding new or seasonal products; Florence points to the Christmas gift market as the prime example of this (1933: 60–64). Competitors complicate the picture by introducing their own new products and stimulating demand in different ways, so that the market as a whole is constantly evolving.

The question of the span of control is still more difficult. There is, Florence says, 'great difficulty in adjustment of employment, investment and management relations into the frame of large-scale organization' (1933: 263). The problems are both technical and human. Large-scale organization perforce means specialization and localization, with concentration of different types or stages of production in different places; this leads to problems of coordination, and also in knowledge dissemination. Further to this, managers themselves, being human,

tend not to come in standard forms, which efficiency would seem to require; they have different motivations, different needs, and different styles and habits of working. To illustrate this, Florence uses a series of management archetypes – the head of a family business, the entrepreneur, the ex-professional man, the ex-foreman, the ex-technician and so on – all of whom react to issues and solve problems in different ways (1933: 204–20, 265–6). This can be a source of great creativity, but it can also be a barrier to efficiency.

The question of human relations in large organizations is the most important of all: 'there is a specific loss of stimulus to the human factor psychologically connected with large-scale organization, and since scale of operation is partly dependent on scale of organizations, this offsets the physical advantages of large-scale operation' (1933: 264). Paradoxically, large-scale organization creates individual inefficiency; workers identify less with the firm and more with their own interests. Again, this is a human problem, not an economic one.

These three factors, then, tend to limit the size of firms, which grow to the limits imposed by their ability to meet customer demand, the ability of top management to exercise control, and by labour's apparent law of diminishing returns. The theoretical efficiencies of large-scale organization are thwarted by the practical inefficiencies or 'illogicalities' which occur during growth.

All three problems, Florence believes, are capable of partial solution. Firms need to give attention to forecasting and analysis of market demand, in order to reduce risk and uncertainty where consumers and competitors are concerned. The fluid, constantly changing nature of consumer demand means that these risks can never be entirely eliminated, but they can be minimized (1933: 260). The question of the span of control requires attention to organizational principles. Florence is critical of old-fashioned hierarchical management, based largely on military organization, which he sees as placing too much responsibility on those at

the top of the pyramid; only an exceptionally gifted manager can govern a large firm directly (1933: 119–22). He also sees the functional system, based on Taylorism (see TAYLOR), as inefficient as it involves unnecessary duplication and organization (1933: 127ff.). In common with other British writers of the period such as URWICK, he believes that the best principle for organizing large-scale businesses is the line and staff principle, with line management functions delegated down to the lowest possible level, and staff functions concentrated at headquarters. He believes too that this principle, by allowing for maximum decentralization, helps solve the problem of labour inefficiency; workers will be more committed to their own unit than they will to the larger firm. The firm, he says, can be compared to the church, while the individual plant can be compared to the congregation; people feel themselves members of the first, but the truly important social relationships which lead to efficiency are constructed within the second. Florence mentions in this context the methods of the Czech entrepreneur Tomas BAT'A, who broke his large operation up into semi-autonomous subunits of no more than 200 workers, and believes that this may be a model to follow (1933: 163–4).

Yet although these measures can break down some of the barriers to large-scale organization, they cannot remove them all. What, then, is the optimum scale for organizations in order to achieve maximum efficiency? Florence is undecided on this, and even doubts whether it is possible to reach such a measure; the conditions for optimum efficiency vary greatly from industry to industry, and the constantly evolving nature of competition and consumer demand mean that even the very measures of optimality tend to change. This, he points out, is the key problem with planned economies. It is not possible to plan production for optimum efficiency unless one can also plan *consumption*; and this, given the illogicality and irrationality of consumer demand, cannot be done (1933: 8). Far better to let the free market

have its way, and ensure that companies are flexible and able to change and adapt their own organizations to meet the challenges of the market.

Florence does not develop a 'system' as such, and flexibility is not a word he uses frequently, but the thrust of his arguments is that firms need to develop flexible systems, especially human systems. He calls for firms to be viewed as political entities, and his discussions of political relations within the firm may be influenced by MACHIAVELLI (1933: 118–9). More commonly, he speaks of the need to examine the firm's social systems; the powerful metaphor of the firm as church is used repeatedly. In *Investment, Location, and Size of Plant* (1948) he seems to move away from any idea of optimality at all, and instead argues that investment decisions need to be made on the basis of specific conditions at the time and place of operation.

Florence made a number of other useful contributions as well. His work on labour inefficiency was very important in its day, as he showed for the first time how it was possible to measure the impacts of factors such as fatigue, illness, accidents and labour turnover on efficiency and profitability; he may have been the first writer to work out the actual financial costs of labour turnover (his methods of measurement remain broadly accurate) (Florence 1924). His later work on labour looks at labour as a process, with various inputs – the workplace (including type and hours of work, physical conditions and social relationships), the wage (including amount and method of payment) and the worker (his or her personality, skills and training) – combining to produce what he calls the 'human factor'. The human factor is defined as a combination of the worker's *capacity* to work (how much he or she can do) and the worker's *willingness* to work (how much he or she will do). Inefficiencies in labour nearly always stem from a deficiency in one or the other aspect of the human factor. Such inefficiencies can be measured, Florence says, not only in the form

of the quantity and quality of output, but also in areas such as accidents, absenteeism, strikes and industrial disputes, and labour turnover (Florence 1949).

Florence sums up the nature of management as 'the ability and will to control large organizations', combined with the older but still vitally important requisite for entrepreneurship. The two together represent the powers of coordination and the powers of initiative, a blend of which is required in every successful manager (Florence 1933: 241). Along with many writers of the 1930s and 1950s, he calls for the recognition of management as a profession, and for more and better education for managers.

Florence's work is now largely obscure, and he is not frequently cited even by industrial economists. He nonetheless made an important contribution with his views on the importance of the human factor, and these views, unfashionable in the 1960s and 1970s, are very much in line with the mainstream of thinking today.

BIBLIOGRAPHY
Florence, P.S. (1918) *Use of Factory Statistics in the Investigation of Industrial Fatigue*, New York: Columbia University Press.
—— (1924) *Economics of Fatigue and Unrest*, London: George Allen and Unwin.
—— (1933) *The Logic of Industrial Organization*, London: Kegan, Paul, Trench, Trubner.
—— (1948) *Investment, Location, and Size of Plant*, Cambridge: Cambridge University Press.
—— (1949) *Labour*, London: Hutchinson.
—— (1953) *The Logic of British and American Industry*, London: Routledge and Kegan Paul.
—— (1957) *Industry and the State*, London: Hutchinson.
—— (1964) *Economics and Sociology of Industry*, London: C.A. Watts.

MLW

FOLLETT, Mary Parker (1868–1933)

Mary Parker Follett was born in Quincy, Massachusetts on 3 September 1868, into an old New England family, and died in Boston on 18 December 1933. She was educated at the Thayer Academy in Boston, and then attended Radcliffe College, where she took a mixed degree in philosophy, law, history and political science. She spent a year studying at Newnham College, Cambridge and also spent some time in Paris before returning to finish her degree, graduating *summa cum laude* in 1898. Settling in Boston with her friend Isobel Briggs, Follett became involved in social work in the city, organizing centres to provide educational and social services in working-class districts; these centres later developed into placement bureaux and vocational training establishments.

Although the main focus of her education had been on politics (she had published her first book, *The Speaker of the House of Representatives*, in 1896 while still at Radcliffe), her experiences in Boston opened her up to a broader perspective in which political, social and economic issues were intertwined. Her next book, *The New State–Group Organization* (1918), was a consideration of the relationship between the individual and society, and on the role that relationship plays in the maintenance of democracy. By now Follett was also beginning to consider the workings of the human mind, looking at the role that personal desires, needs and wants play in the individual's relations with society; psychology and the role of knowledge were added to the mix. The result of her deliberations on these themes was *Creative Experience* (1924), Follett's best book and the one which has had the most impact.

Creative Experience was widely read and reviewed on publication. In particular, the book was taken up by academics studying business administration, and even by many managers. Henry Metcalf, director of the Bureau of Personnel Administration in New

York, saw the potential of Follett's work for management, and invited her to give a course of lectures. Across the Atlantic, Benjamin Seebohm ROWNTREE read the book and asked Follett to lecture at one of his annual conferences in Oxford; she went on to become a fixture at these events. At one conference she met Lyndall URWICK, who became a great supporter of her work and arranged for her to give further lectures in Britain, notably at the London School of Economics. In 1928, after the death of Isobel Briggs, Follett decided to settle in Britain and moved to London, where she lived in Chelsea with another friend, Dame Katherine Furze. In 1933 she returned briefly to Boston to settle some financial affairs, but fell ill and died there.

The popularity of *Creative Experience* should perhaps be understood against its background. By the mid-1920s, the scientific management movement dominated management thinking in both the United States and many parts of Europe. However, scientific management was not regarded with universal enthusiasm. In its extreme forms, such as that advocated with great success by Charles BEDAUX, scientific management could be technocratic and bureaucratic – it emphasized the role of the technical expert, and appeared (and in many cases actually did) downgrade the roles not only of the worker on the shop floor but also of senior managers, who often felt that the technical and efficiency experts were taking control of the business out of their hands (this situation had arisen at least in part because top managers themselves rarely had much technical training). The time was ripe for a theory of administration which would provide a more humanistic approach to the subject, and Follett's *Creative Experience* fit the bill.

That is not to deny the power of the book itself, which is justly seen as one of the most influential management texts of the twentieth century; but the book most certainly arrived at the right moment. Follett opens the book by questioning the whole concept of what she calls 'vicarious experience', that is relying on

the experience and skills of others rather than acquiring knowledge for ourselves. She questions whether experts can be regarded as custodians of truth, in the same way that it is questionable whether the law is really the guardian of truth. She does not dismiss experts out of hand, and acknowledges that their own experience and knowledge means that they *do* have access to truth, or at least part of it; what is dangerous, she feels, is the way in which others rely unquestioningly on experts to do their thinking for them.

Follett's view of society, and of organizations is one where people at all levels are motivated to work and participate. They should gather their own information, make their own decisions, define their own roles and shape their own lives. She also rejects empiricism: experience should not be used to create theories and concepts, but to inform the mind and liberate the spirit in a process which she calls 'evocation'. In this way, experience can become truly creative, a powerful force that creates advancement and progress. As she sums up:

> We seek reality in experience. Let us reject the realm of the compensatory; it is fair, but a prison. Experience may be hard but we claim its gifts because they are real, even though our feet bleed on its stones. We seek progressive advancement through the transformation of daily experience. Into what, conceptual pictures? No, daily experience must be translated not into conceptual pictures but into spiritual conviction. Experience can both guide and guard us. Foolish indeed are those who do not bring oil to its burning.
>
> (Follett 1924: 302)

The importance of psychological theory is evident throughout *Creative Experience*, and Follett makes reference to concepts such as Gestalt. Ultimately, however, this is not a book about psychology any more than it is about any other branch of knowledge. Follett

believed in the unity of knowledge, and she draws on political, social, economic and legal theory as well as psychology and biology to construct a holistic picture of how we think, feel and experience, not only as individuals but as individuals-in-groups. Urwick and Brech (1949) argued what Follett was aiming for was nothing less than an overarching philosophy of groups and organizations. *Creative Experience* did not provide a complete philosophy, but it set Follett and others – notably Metcalf, Urwick and the Australian psychologist Elton MAYO – down the road towards one.

The interest in Follett's work coming from the field of management and administration studies may have taken Follett somewhat by surprise; she had never written on this area before. But if so, she took this in her stride. As Urwick and Brech (1949) comment, she did not so much change direction to study business and management as incorporate these fields into her already broad area of interest. Her collected lectures at the Bureau of Public Administration, the Rowntree conferences and the London School of Economics (Metcalf and Urwick 1941; Urwick 1949) show how she applied a wide range of theory from many disciplines to the problems of management. She spoke constantly of the need for personal growth and development as a key to management success; the gathering of experience and knowledge broadened the person and made the manager more effective and better able to maintain and coordinate relationships, which she saw as all-important to both business and social effectiveness.

This emphasis on relationships and coordination is at the heart of what may be her best-known later work, her lectures on managerial control. One of these lectures, 'The Process of Control', delivered at the London School of Economics and reprinted after her death by Urwick and Luther GULICK in their landmark *Papers on the Science of Administration* (1937), sums up her thinking on this subject.

The purpose of control, says Follett at the start of the lecture, is not to control people but to control *facts*; in other words, the real control that matters is the control of information. Second, effective control of this sort cannot stem from one source; to be effective, control has to be 'the correlation of many controls rather than a superimposed control' (Follett 1937: 161). She goes on:

The ramifications of modern industry are too wide-spread, its organization too complex, its problems too intricate for it to be possible for industry to be managed by commands from the top alone. This being so, we find that when central control is spoken of, that does not mean a point of radiation, but the gathering of many controls existing throughout the enterprise.
(Follett 1937: 161)

What we mean by 'control', then, is really 'coordination'. In a famous and often cited passage, she goes on to offer four fundamental principles of coordination (Follett 1937: 161):

1. Coordination as the reciprocal relating of all the factors in a situation.

2. Coordination by direct contact of the responsible people concerned.

3. Coordination in the early stages.

4. Coordination as a continuing process.

The first of these is the most complex, and it takes us back to the heart of Follett's philosophy as spelled out in *Creative Experience*. When two or more people work together, she says, they combine their thinking through a process she calls 'adjustment'. In a game of doubles tennis, for example, each player has to adjust their thinking to take account of the movements and actions of their partner. In a large business organization the heads of each department constantly 'adjust' their thinking to reflect the actions and activities of their col-

leagues and their departments; this adjustment is reflected in the way in which each head controls their own department. At the same time, of course, they are *also* adjusting their thinking to a whole host of other factors going on in the environment around them. All these different sets of thinking interpenetrate each other, and the activities of any one department reflect this combined thinking set which governs its coordination. Thus no department exists in isolation, nor is the organization merely a set of departments set side by side; rather, it is a unified whole bound together by this set of thinking relationships. This affects everything the organization does. Follett gives an example: merchandising (or marketing) 'is not merely a bringing together of designing, engineering, manufacturing and sales departments, it is these in their total relativity' (Follett 1937: 162).

It is not enough to be able to view and see all the factors in a situation; we have also to be able to understand how each factor affects every other factor in that situation, and then view the outcome as a single yet complex and dynamic situation. Here Follett is influenced by biological science, and she may be the first management writer to speak of an 'environmental complex' in which a business exists and both affects and is affected by its environment (though very similar ideas had been advocated twenty years earlier by Thorstein VEBLEN). The principle of reciprocal relationship, which can be roughly summed up as everything in a given environment both affects and is affected by everything else in that environment is a core principle of Follett's work; it was a major influence on the development of human relations theory by the likes of Mayo, ROETHLISBERGER and WHITEHEAD, and its influence can be seen in a variety of versions of interdependence theory in the 1950s through to the 1970s, and wherever holistic thinking about management is found.

The remaining three principles are less complex. Follett advocates that coordination should be handled directly by the responsible managers, not from unseen figures on high; where spans of control are insufficiently large, lateral coordination between heads of department is preferable to vertical coordination from the top down. Generally, however, it is preferable that coordination should be undertaken by managers who are in direct contact with the workers.

By coordination at the early stages Follett means that coordination should be built into a system from its inception. Policy formulation should be coordinated from the outset, as in this way the interplay of ideas, the reciprocal relationship described above, makes itself felt early on and both smoothes coordination and adds value to the thinking and planning processes. By contrast, in systems where policy is developed in isolation and different elements are brought in afterwards to coordinate the execution of that policy, relationships are rougher, and coordinated thinking has less of a chance to make an impact. Finally, Follett views coordination as a continuous process, one which must happen as a natural part of the management of the business organization. She advocates continuous coordination on the grounds that it leads both to easier problem solving and to the generation of knowledge which can improve working methods in the future. In a prefiguring of later work on strategy and planning, she also argues that continuous coordination creates what later became known as feedback loops, whereby plans and policies can be easily adjusted in the light of fresh information.

In all this it is clear that Follett rejects the mechanistic view of the organization, and opts instead for a social and biological one. This is most clear when she discusses the nature of control. She argues that 'organization *is* control' – organizations in effect have no other purpose – but goes on to state that the real nature of control is about coordinating the parts:

Biologists tell us that the organizing activity of the organism is the directing activity,

that the organism gets its power of self-direction through being an organism, that is, through the functional relating of the parts.

On the physiological level, controls means co-ordination. I can't get up in the morning, I can't walk downstairs without that co-ordination of muscles which is control. The athlete has more of that co-ordination than I have and therefore has more control ...

This is just what we have found in business.
(Follett 1937: 166–7)

Control by attempting to force one element to perform an action alone, says Follett, is not control at all. In the reality of business life, even the most autocratic of board of directors does not have sole control; as soon as lower layers of management are added, responsibility is delegated and control is shared, and from that moment on coordination becomes a necessity.

The most important control of all, Follett concludes, is self-control. In a passage which is a direct appeal to greater democracy in industrial organizations, she argues that a form of collective control which coordinates the actions of all members of the organization by allowing them participation in the control process is the right way forward for industry:

If you accept my definition of control as a self-generating process, as the interweaving experience of all those who are performing a functional part of the activity under consideration, does not that constitute an imperative? Are we not every one of us bound to take some part consciously in this process? Today we are slaves to chaos in which we are living. To get our affairs in hand, to feel a grip on them, to become free, we must learn, and practice, I am sure, the methods of collective control. To this task we can all devote ourselves. At the same time that we are selling goods or making goods, or whatever we are doing, we can be working in harmony with this fundamental law of lie. We can be assured that by this method, control is in our power.
(Follett 1937: 169)

An important thinker who brought her formidable intellect to bear on many aspects of organizational life, Mary Parker Follett remains one of the seminal figures in management thinking in the twentieth century. Her work had a direct impact on the formation of the human relations school, and indirectly influences management thinking today. Her work can be criticized on the grounds that it is over-philosophical and lacks attention to key principles, but such criticisms are perhaps unfair; Follett never sought to provide managers with tools for their hand, but urged instead that they should alter their ways of thinking. Hers is a philosophical approach, and none the less valid for that. In the early twenty-first century, Follett's approach to the problems of coordination and control still provides food for thought for management practitioners.

BIBLIOGRAPHY
Follett, M.P. (1896) *The Speaker of the House of Representatives*, New York: Longmans Green.
——— (1918) *The New State–Group Organization: The Solution for Popular Government*, New York: Longmans Green.
——— (1924) *Creative Experience*, New York: Longmans Green.
——— (1937) 'The Process of Control', in L. Gulick and L.F. Urwick (eds), *Papers on the Science of Administration*, New York: Institute of Public Administration, 159–69.
Graham, P. (ed.) *Mary Parker Follett: Prophet of Management*, Boston, MA: Harvard Business School Press.
Metcalf, H.C. and Urwick, L.F. (eds) (1941) *Dynamic Administration: The*

Collected Papers of Mary Parker Follett, Bath: Management Publications Trust.

Urwick, L.F. (ed.) (1949) *Freedom and Coordination*, London: Management Publications Trust.

—— (1956) *The Golden Book of Management*, London: Newman Neame.

Urwick, L.F. and Brech, E.F.L. (1949) *The Making of Scientific Management*, vol. 1, *Management in British Industry*, London: Management Publications Trust; repr. Bristol: Thoemmes Press, 1994.

MLW

FORD, Edsel (1893–1943)

Edsel Ford was born in Detroit, Michigan on 6 November 1893, the only son of Henry FORD and his wife Clara. He died of stomach cancer at his home in Grosse Pointe, Michigan on 26 May 1943. He married Eleanor Clay in 1916; they had four children. He was educated at Detroit University School but did not attend university, and in 1912 joined Ford Motor Company. At his father's instruction, he apprenticed in a number of different departments of the company, learning the details of the business. This apprenticeship was short; when James COUZENS resigned from the board in 1915, Edsel Ford, then aged twenty-two, was promoted into his place as company secretary. In 1919 he became president of the company, and held this position until his death.

Edsel Ford was the temperamental opposite of his father. He appreciated the arts and design, becoming a notable collector and patronizing leading artists such as the Mexican muralist Diego Rivera; from a design perspective, he pressed repeatedly and without success for Ford's cars to become more 'stylish' and better able to compete with the products of General Motors. He opposed the latter's increasingly autocratic and heavy-handed management methods; his own views of labour relations were enlightened, and he did not oppose trade unions. However, Henry Ford continued to dominate both the company and his son, and Edsel Ford's views were seldom if ever allowed to prevail. Through the 1930s the two were on increasingly bad terms personally, with the autocratic Ford bullying and hectoring his son, who in turn became more and more withdrawn. Edsel Ford did have a few successes: in 1927, after a long struggle, he finally persuaded his father to drop the outmoded Model T and replace it with the more up-to-date Model A, and in 1940 he overcame Henry Ford's reluctance to convert part of Ford's production facilities to military aircraft manufacture.

In 1922 Ford acquired the Lincoln Motor Company, which became Edsel Ford's personal fief. Free of the interference of his father, he was able to put into practice his own views on labour management and design. Hiring in top designers, he helped Lincoln produce some of the most stylish and attractive cars yet built, including the famous Lincoln Continental, which appeared just before the Second World War. Although Edsel Ford's influence on the Ford Motor Company was minimal, many of his ideas were picked up after the war by his son and successor, Henry FORD II, who helped turn Ford's fortunes around.

BIBLIOGRAPHY
Nevins, A. and Hill, F.E. (1957) *Ford: Expansion and Challenge*, New York: Scribner.

—— (1962) *Ford: Decline and Rebirth*, New York: Scribner.

MLW

FORD, Henry (1863–1947)

Henry Ford was born on a farm near Dearborn, Michigan on 30 July 1863, one of eight children of William and Mary Ford. He died at his Detroit home, Fair Lane on 7 April 1947. He was educated in the local public school, where he learned mathematics and also a little reading and writing. Barely literate when he finished school in 1879, he was fascinated by machinery and determined to find work as a mechanic. At the age of sixteen he apprenticed at Flower Brothers Machine Shop in Detroit, and later at the Detroit Drydock Company; he also took a part-time job as a watch repairman. The three years he spent in Detroit gave Ford considerable practical experience in various aspects of engineering. He himself was particularly interested in watches and gears, and seems at one time to have considered going into watchmaking as a business.

Returning home in 1882, Ford first set up a small machine shop and carried out work for neighbouring farmers, and later took a job with Westinghouse as a district engineer, travelling and servicing steam engines. In 1888 he married Clara Bryant; they had one son, Edsel Bryant FORD, in 1893. Now determined to make a career in engineering, Ford moved his family back to Detroit that same year and he found a job with the Edison Illuminating Company; he was promoted rapidly, and by 1893 was chief engineer for the Chicago area.

By the 1890s invention fever was sweeping the United States. Inspired by the examples of Thomas EDISON and Alexander Graham BELL, whose work was already changing the nature of American life and culture, thousands of amateur engineers built workshops and tried to invent working examples of new devices such as aeroplanes and motor cars. Ford was one of these. What exactly directed his attention to cars is not known, but his early experience with watches and gears helped him solve one of the major problems: how to convert the motive power provided by a steam or internal combustion engine into drive through the

wheels. His simple design for a transmission led to his development of a working automobile in 1896. The car, which he called a quadricycle, ran on bicycle wheels and weighed just 227 kilograms (500 pounds) in total. Ford promptly sold it to raise capital for further experiments, and continued to make and sell experimental prototypes in this fashion for some years. He later recalled a chance meeting with Thomas Edison at which the latter quizzed him about his designs and encouraged him to carry on; the meeting, Ford said, was a great inspiration to him. Later he and Edison became close friends, and they and Harvey FIRESTONE used to go on 'boy's own' camping expeditions into the Michigan wilderness; a rare form of relaxation for this driven man.

In 1899, with capital provided by a Detroit lumber dealer, William Murphy, Ford established the Detroit Automobile Company and resigned from Edison to become the new firm's superintendent in charge of production. This first attempt by Ford at producing motor cars on a commercial basis was a total failure, largely because Ford knew nothing about production and managed to make only a handful of cars. Undeterred, Ford and his backers tried again, setting up the Henry Ford Company in 1900. Again, few cars were actually built, but one of these proved to be a successful racing car. Ford became suddenly enthusiastic about motor racing and neglected his business, and accordingly was fired from the Henry Ford Company in 1902 (the company went on to become the Cadillac Motor Car Company and eventually became part of General Motors). Ford joined the former racing car driver Tom Cooper in a partnership which built the 999, a car which set a world land speed record and also made its driver Barney Oldfield a national hero. Among Cooper's associates was the young draughtsman Charles SORENSON, who was talent-spotted by Ford and rose to become one of his most trusted and effective managers.

His racing car triumphs under his belt, Ford seems to have come to his senses and gone back to his original plan, which was to build

cheap, efficient cars which could be widely sold on an affordable basis. With fresh backing, this time from the Detroit coal dealer Alexander Malcolmson, and with more engineering talent in the person of Childe Harold Willis, Ford established the Ford Motor Company in Detroit in June 1903. Partners included John and Horace Dodge, who supplied Ford's original engines, and James COUZENS, a Malcolmson employee who acted as treasurer. Ford provided the engineering and production knowledge, and was appointed vice-president and general manager. The new company was almost immediately embroiled in a patent suit with the Association of Licensed Automobile Manufacturers (ALAM), backed by rivals such as Packard and Olds Motor Company, which claimed to have sole rights to manufacture gasoline-powered automobiles. Ford, who had earlier applied to join ALAM and been turned down, decided to fight the suit. He eventually won his case in 1911; in the meantime, typically, Ford continued on with his own plans as though the problem did not exist. These plans, for the production of small, cheap cars that could be sold to ordinary people, led to yet another problem, this time with his chief backer Malcolmson, who advocated the strategy adopted by most other carmakers, producing expensive luxury models for the high end of the market. Ford bought out Malcolmson in 1906 and went ahead with the development of the Model N, a cheap runabout that went on sale later that year for $600.

To cut costs, Ford began a policy of vertical integration by taking over some of his main suppliers, beginning with the John R. Keim steelworks in Buffalo, New York. With Keim, Ford acquired the services of yet another talented manager, William KNUDSEN. Together, Knudsen, Sorenson and Couzens formed one of the greatest management teams the world has yet seen; with Ford, they made the mass production of motor cars happen and propelled Ford into a position of utter dominance in the industry, far outstripping rivals such as the fledgling General Motors (GM) of William C. DURANT; for the next decade, only John North WILLYS at Overland ever seriously threatened Ford's dominance.

That dominance was founded on two factors: the Model T, launched in 1908, and the building of the assembly line production plant at Highland Park, Michigan, which began production in 1910. Designed by Ford and Wills, the Model T, or 'Tin Lizzie' as it was nicknamed by affectionate drivers, first went on sale for $825, but Ford constantly sought to drag the price down, trading volume of sales for unit profits; in the mid-1920s prices fell as low as $275 for a new Model T. With a twenty-two-horsepower engine and advanced chassis and steering design, the car was technologically advanced when first launched, yet its design was so simple that interchangeable parts could be easily mass produced and then assembled. Between 1908 and 1927, seventeen million Model Ts were sold, more than all other models of car put together at the time.

Designed by architect Albert Kahn and purpose-built for the production of the Model T, the Highland Park plant covered sixty-two acres. It featured the largest assembly line yet seen in the world, and had been carefully engineered to increase car production to speeds beyond anything yet attempted; instead of twelve to fourteen hours to assemble a finished car, the previous norm, Model Ts could now be assembled from stocks of finished parts in an hour and a half.

The opening of Highland Park sent a shock through the US business world. Visitors from other companies and even other countries flocked to see it; among those who learned from Ford's production methods was the Czech shoemaker Tomas BAT'A, who would later establish his own revolutionary approach to management in Europe. Ford won plaudits not only for his mechanical engineering but for his attention to detail and carefully engineered production system, which was based in large part on the methods of scientific management

advocated by Frederick W. TAYLOR, but also owed much to earlier mass production systems such as that developed by Cyrus Hall MCCORMACK. In terms of worker relations, too, Ford was seen as a visionary. In 1914 he cut the working day to eight hours, believing this to be the optimum working day for worker efficiency, and also initiated the famous $5 daily wage, nearly double the going rate in the industry.

The period 1910–20 was Ford's heyday. He was feted as a hero in the United States, where his goal of bringing cheap motoring to the masses had brought about a transport revolution in society, in which even clerks and manual workers could afford a car. Ford had democratized transport, and changed the face of America in the process; the country's long love affair with the automobile had begun. Overseas he became an almost mythical figure. Strangely, Communist Russia was full of admiration for Ford – Lenin and Trotsky admired his methods, *Pravda* serialized his books and delegations of Soviet officials and factory managers came to Detroit to study 'Fordism' in action, and the philosophies of both Ford and Taylor were transplanted into Soviet industry. In Britain, on the other hand, attitudes were more ambivalent: by the 1920s Ford's public image and egotism were beginning to attract more attention than his cars, and Aldous Huxley went on to satirize Ford in *Brave New World*, where the deity is known as 'Our Ford' rather than 'Our Lord'.

Cracks had already begun to appear during the First World War. Ford was a convinced pacifist, and in 1915 chartered a 'Peace Ship' to sail to Europe to try to resolve the war by negotiation; he also attempted to hand out pacifist literature with each car he sold. This led to a break with James Couzens, the talented administrator and salesman in charge of Ford's marketing effort, who left in 1915 to take up a career in politics. Knudsen was the next to go, resigning in 1921 over Ford's refusal to countenance a replacement for the ageing Model T; he joined Ford's rival General Motors, now being capably run by Pierre DU PONT and Alfred SLOAN, and played a key role in developing the Chevrolet, the low-priced competitor that ultimately drove the Model T out of the market. Sorenson and Edsel Ford, who had succeeded Couzens, were unable to make much headway against Ford's growing autocracy.

By 1920 the pace of innovation at Ford was slowing. Convinced that his original recipe for success was the correct one, Ford failed to see that times had moved on; indeed, he himself had been responsible for much of the change. The novelty of car travel was wearing off; now people wanted more features from their cars and, indeed, were developing different sets of needs and motivations for buying cars. GM was willing to cater to these different needs; Ford was not. His famous remark, 'a customer can have a car of any colour he wants, so long as it is black', may be apocryphal but is indicative of a mindset. When Chevrolet began cutting into Ford's market, Ford's only method of fighting back was to cut prices still further, which meant that Charlie Sorenson, now in sole charge of production, had to find new ways of cutting costs. The atmosphere in Ford factories changed, too. Wages were cut by nearly half; worker education and many other benefits were done away with; Ford's famous sociological department which had studied worker motivation was closed down; strict discipline was enforced which prevented workers from whistling or even talking during shifts.

In the mid-1920s Ford showed signs of change once more. Sorenson and Edsel Ford finally persuaded Ford to drop the now almost moribund Model T and bring out a new model, the Model A. Ford plants shut down production while the new car was quickly designed and marketed (400,000 advance orders were received before the first car was ever produced). The Model A was nothing like as revolutionary as the Model T, but it showed some response to consumer needs and was successful; and it helped keep Ford in business,

though now lagging third in numbers of cars sold behind GM and Chrysler. The opening of the great River Rouge plant in 1927 to produce the Model A also had favourable results in terms of impact and profitability. Diversification began for the first time. The development of an aircraft industry was a limited success, although the Ford Trimotor was a very advanced and efficient design, but production ceased in the 1930s. The acquisition of Lincoln Motor Company was more successful; under the direct guidance of Edsel Ford, Lincoln became the maker of the USA's most luxurious cars.

The 1930s saw continued decline. Edsel Ford, bullied by his father and increasingly ill, had lost all influence. Even Sorenson could do little to reason with the old man. Ford's new confidante was Harry Bennett, a former prizefighter who was connected to the Mafia in Chicago, and who now ran the Ford Service Department, a group of informers and thugs who enforced discipline among the work force with an iron hand. The workers, tried beyond any reasonable limits of loyalty, finally rebelled and tried to unionize; when Bennett's men beat up several union organizers, the workers struck in 1941 and compelled recognition of the United Auto Workers. Ford suffered a stroke in 1938, and from then on was both physically and mentally ill, paranoid and, in the words of the normally loyal Sorenson, suffering from hallucinations. In 1940 Ford refused to participate in the government's aircraft manufacturing programme largely because of a paranoid delusion that President Franklin D. Roosevelt was out to destroy him (the fact that William Knudsen was in charge of the programme probably did not help to allay Ford's suspicions). Edsel Ford and Sorenson finally persuaded him to take part, and the Willow Run production plant was established near Ypsilanti, Michigan to make heavy bombers; even so, Ford would never go near the plant, convinced he would be assassinated by government spies. Harry Bennett was now virtually in control of both the company and

Ford himself; Charlie Sorenson recalls the sight of Clara Ford in tears at the thought of what 'that monster' was doing to her husband.

Edsel Ford's death in 1943 brought about a crisis, as Ford insisted on resuming the presidency of the firm. Clara Ford and her widowed daughter-in-law now staged a rebellion of their own, threatening to sell their shares to outsiders unless the octogenarian leader stood down. He finally gave way; intervention at the top levels of government secured the release of Edsel's son, Henry FORD II, from military service and he returned home to take up the presidency. Despite no management training or background whatever, Ford proved adept at his job, and in the immediate postwar years assembled a team which included future senior Ford executives Ernest R. Breech, Lee IACOCCA and Robert McNAMARA, and began turning the beleaguered company around.

Ford has assumed an almost mythical status in the history of American business and in the national epic more generally. The two images, however, are sharply at variance. In US history, he is the man who democratized the automobile; he played a key role in the concept of 'freedom' in American society, in which freedom of mobility granted through the car plays a large part. He is a folk hero on a par with Edison or COLT. In business history, however, it has become fashionable to compare Ford unfavourably with his rivals at GM, notably Alfred Sloan. GM was progressive and innovative, Ford was conservative and unreceptive to change; GM was focused on the market, Ford was focused on production; GM was divisionalized and efficient, Ford was centralized and inefficient; and most of all, GM was managed by professionals with a separation of ownership and control, while Ford was managed by its family owners.

All of these theses are challengeable, of course, especially the last. GM initially had little separation of ownership and control, especially under Durant and du Pont, while Ford, in the early stages at least, had a number of brilliant managers on his senior staff. The

problem, as Nevins and Hill (1957) point out in the second of their highly detailed studies of Ford, is that most comparisons are valid depending when they are made. The Ford of 1934 is by no means the same as the Ford of 1914. That Ford himself went on too long is undeniable; equally, it is hard to deny his successes in his early years, or his impact on management both in the car industry and more generally.

Nevins and Hill describe Ford's basic managerial insight as being based on five related facts:

that the American people needed cars in millions; that a single durable inexpensive model could meet that demand; that when new technological elements were woven together to create mass production, they could furnish millions of cheap vehicles; that price reduction meant market expansion; and that high wages meant high buying power. This was as obvious, when demonstrated, as Columbus's art of standing an egg on its end. Until then it was so far from clear that Ford had to battle his principal partner and the current manufacturing trend to prove it. A special kind of genius lies in seeing what everybody admits to be obvious – after the exceptional mind thinks of it; and Ford had that genius. It changed the world.

(Nevins and Hill 1957: 614)

He was also a brilliant engineer, one who was probably at his happiest when designing. Dearborn Engineering, the corporate research and development group centred around Ford himself was, in the years before 1920 at least, was a hive of activity and ideas. These ideas concerned process as well as product. Highland Park was every bit as revolutionary as the car it created; River Rouge, though more control-oriented, still contained its share of technological and engineering wizardry; Willow Run, though plagued with initial problems, later achieved the unheard of feat of

producing one four-engined B-24 bomber every hour. To the end of his days, Ford possessed an almost intuitive understanding of production engineering and process flows. Virtually every mass production system ever developed in the world since owes at least something to Ford and his ideas.

That Ford himself gave much thought to both what he was doing and his purpose in doing it is clear from his writings. Although these must be used with care, as their primary purpose was often self-aggrandisement, there are frequent passages where he muses to his co-author Samuel Crowther on his purpose and goals. The following, from *Moving Forward* (1931) is interesting on a number of levels:

Through all the years that I have been in business I have never yet found our business bad as a result of any outside force. It has always been due to some defect in our own company, and whenever we located and repaired that defect our business became good again – regardless of what anyone else might be doing. And it will always be found that this country has nationally bad business when business men are drifting, and that business is good when men take hold of their own affairs, put leadership into them, and push forward in spite of obstacles. Only disaster can result when the fundamental principles of business are disregarded and what looks like the easiest way is taken. These fundamentals, as I see them, are:

(1) To make an ever-increasingly large quantity of goods of the best possible quality, to make them in the best and most economical fashion, and to force them out onto the market.

(2) To strive always for higher quality and lower prices as well as lower costs.

(3) To raise wages gradually but continuously – and never to cut them.

(4) To get the goods to the consumer in the most economical manner so that the benefits of low-cost production may reach him.

These fundamentals are all summed up in the single word 'service' ... The service starts with discovering what people need and then supplying that need according to the principles that have just been given.
(Ford and Crowther 1931: 2–3).

As a statement of philosophy, this shows both the strengths and weaknesses of Henry Ford's approach to management. On the one hand there is the attention to quality, to the product and, despite his critics, to the needs of the market. On the other hand, there is the ignoring of competition and the centring of responsibility on the manager himself. Part Frederick Winslow Taylor, part Friedrich Wilhelm Nietschze, here is a portrait of the executive as superman, capable of solving all problems through authority and control. It is a philosophy which, like the man himself, is full of contrary aspects and is not capable of being sustained for long.

Certainly at the time these words were written, Ford had abandoned large parts of this philosophy in practice. He became increasingly autocratic in manner, driving away most members of his brilliant management team and losing access to the talent pool that had made the early company successful. His bullying and humiliation of his son scandalized all around him; the normally loyal Sorenson is highly critical of Ford on this point and calls Ford's handling of his son his greatest failure. His paranoia and suspicion of all around him changed his relationship with his work force from one of happy cooperation to one of fear. There are two faces to Fordism, just as there were two faces to Ford himself. Sorenson commented that Ford feared and shunned ostentation, and never seemed at home in the luxurious mansion he had built for himself at Fair Lane, yet that paradoxically he craved the limelight and did all he could to stimulate the growth of the Ford myth. By 1920, if not earlier, he had begun to believe his own mythologizing. Like Napoleon, he went on too long.

BIBLIOGRAPHY
Burlinghame, R. (1949) *Backgrounds of Power: The Human Story of Mass Production*, New York: Charles Scribner's Sons.
Ford, H. (1929) *My Philosophy of Industry*, London: Harrap.
Ford, H. and Crowther, S. (1922) *My Life and Work*, New York: Doubleday.
—— (1926) *Today and Tomorrow*, New York: Garden City.
—— (1930) *My Friend Mr Edison*, London: Ernest Benn.
—— (1931) *Moving Forward*, New York: Garden City.
Nevins, A.N. and Hill, F.E. (1954) *Ford: The Times, the Man, the Company*, New York: Charles Scribner's Sons.
—— (1957) *Ford: Expansion and Challenge, 1915–1933*, New York: Charles Scribner's Sons.
—— (1962) *Ford: Decline and Rebirth*, New York: Charles Scribner's Sons.
Sorenson, C. and Williamson, S.T. (1957) *Forty Years with Ford*, London: Jonathan Cape.
Sward, K. (1948) *The Legend of Henry Ford*, New York: Rinehart.

MLW

FORD, Henry, II (1917–87)

Henry Ford II was born on 4 September 1917 in Detroit, Michigan, the son of Edsel FORD and his wife, Eleanor Clay, and the grandson of Henry FORD. He died in Detroit of legion-

naire's disease on 29 September 1987. He married three times: to Anne McDonnell in 1940, to Maria Austin in 1965 and to Kathleen Duross in 1980; there were three children from the first marriage. After schooling, he attended Yale University but did not take a degree. He joined the US Navy in 1941 and served with the rank of ensign, though did not go overseas. In 1943, following the death of his father, Ford received his discharge from Secretary of the Navy Frank Knox to enable him to return to Detroit and assist his ageing grandfather in the management of Ford Motor Company, which was playing a critical role in the war effort. Ford became a vice-president in 1943, and president of the company in 1949.

Ford took over the company at a time when labour relations were poor, productivity was low and the company was losing $9 million a month. He shook up Ford's moribund management team, dismissing many of the older men who had served under his grandfather, promoting new talent such as Lee IACOCCA and hiring in outsiders such as Ernest R. Breech from General Motors, and also Charles Thornton and Robert MCNAMARA. He overhauled Ford's design and marketing programme, encouraging his executives to become market-oriented; the company was not in the business of selling cars, he said, but in the business of selling 'personal mobility'. Not all the new designs were successful – the Edsel, in particular, was an over-engineered and costly failure – but the company was able to compete successfully against General Motors and the Japanese auto-makers through the 1950s and 1960s.

Perhaps Ford's most important management initiative was to encourage the company to become more international. Before 1945, Ford presence outside the United States had been limited to Britain and one or two other countries; Henry Ford II gave the company a global presence and re-established its worldwide brand identity. He looked abroad for alliances and investments; in the 1970s he came close to

merging Ford with Giovanni AGNELLI's Fiat, and later in the decade he bought a stake in the Japanese car-maker Mazda. This international presence helped saved the company when the domestic car market collapsed in the 1970s.

Ford began withdrawing from active management in the late 1970s. His later years were unhappy; two marriages had failed and he suffered from problems with alcohol. An autocrat by nature, he quarrelled with Iacocca and others, who then departed to work for his competitors. Nonetheless, he had achieved what many had believed to be impossible: with virtually no management experience or training, he had rescued the failing Ford Motor Company from almost certain bankruptcy and had restored it to a position as one of the top three car-makers in the United States. How much this achievement was due to Ford himself and how much depended on talented juniors such as Iacocca and McNamara is difficult to say; but team-building is generally agreed to be an important aspect of management, and in this respect, in his early years at least, Ford was highly successful.

BIBLIOGRAPHY
Hayes, W. (1990) *Henry: A Life of Henry Ford II*, New York: Grove Weidenfeld.

MLW

FORRESTER, Jay Wright (1918–)

Jay Wright Forrester was born in Arnold, Nebraska on 14 July 1918 and spent his early life on his family's cattle ranch. He studied electrical engineering at the University of Nebraska, and became a research assistant at the Massachusetts Institute of Technology (MIT) in 1939, where he began his career as an electrical engineer working on servo mechanisms for radar and weapons. He was awarded

his masters degree from MIT in 1945, and shortly after was made director of MIT's digital computer laboratory, where from 1946 to 1951 he was responsible for the design and construction of one of the first high-speed digital computers. He rapidly became one of the nation's leading engineers in the design and applications of computers. He was made head of the digital computer division at MIT's Lincoln Laboratory in 1952, where he developed his patent for magnetic core memory. Believing that computers would have significant benefits in a number of applications, he began to use his computing expertise to address the problems of corporate industry.

Forrester was made professor of management of the Sloan School at MIT in 1956, and there spent the next thirty-three years of his career exploring the dynamic structures of social systems. Beginning in 1957 he developed methods of industrial dynamics as a way to understand and design corporate policy. His engineering expertise led him to identify the concept of feedback in industrial systems and to study their subsequent dynamic behaviour. While working with General Electric, he discovered that managers' interventions in inventory control and staffing levels were producing counter-intuitive effects, due precisely to the combination of feedback loops in operation. He used his experience with modelling systems and building simulations to develop an approach to managing the behaviour of social systems. Forrester proposed that 'feedback concepts can provide a sound theoretical foundation and integrating framework for diverse observations on the behaviour of social systems' (Forrester 1961).

Forrester brought together ideas from control engineering (including concepts of feedback and system self-regulation) with cybernetics (the nature of information and its role in control systems) and organizational theory (the structure of human organizations and the mechanisms of human decision making) to build the field of system dynamics. He used these concepts to develop techniques for representing and simulating complex, non-linear, multi-loop feedback systems. This work found a broad range of real-world applications. In 1961 he published *Industrial Dynamics*, in which he put forward his new approach to systems analysis which later became known as system dynamics. This became immediately controversial, receiving both enthusiastic praise and vicious condemnation. The three main features of the system dynamics approach are (1) feedback loops operating in the system; (2) computer simulation that could map out the changing behaviour of the interaction of multiple feedbacks; and (3) an engagement with people's mental models. Forrester held that the most important information about social systems is people's assumptions about what causes what. This was an unusual contribution for a systems engineer, and the emphasis he placed on mental models undoubtedly contributed to the wide uptake of his approach to dealing with systems.

In 1968 Forrester extended the approach with colleagues to study the growth and stagnation of urban areas, producing his book *Urban Dynamics* (1969), in which he demonstrates how different parts of the system become dominant at different times and, again, the counter-intuitive behaviour of social systems. His subsequent major books expanded on the scope of system dynamics from the analysis of an industrial firm to an unlimited field of application, including specifically the entire world. He called for the development of a new profession, that of social dynamics, with structures of training and theory, experiments and principles. He used his vantage point to highlight the need for the exploration of alternative political and economic rationales that would be compatible with a finite world. He asserted that only by discovering how the ethical, political, physical, technical, economic and social forces of society interact with one another can we understand the alternative patterns of future development. This thinking was a clear forerunner to the

more recent work on sustainable development. It was his hope that system dynamics could be the unifying framework and vehicle for interdisciplinary communication in finding the alternatives to growth: 'Not only is system dynamics capable of accepting the descriptive knowledge from diverse fields but it also shows how present policies lead to future consequences' (Forrester 1975). His concern was to find a path for both industrial and underdeveloped nations through the transition from growth to 'viable equilibrium'.

Forrester was a member of the Club of Rome, a private group of members meeting to find ways to better understand the changes occurring in the world, now understood as the *global problematique*. The renowned *Limits to Growth* study grew out of the club's planned programme to explore the alternatives to the *problematique* driven by manifestations of stress in the world system such as excessive population, rising pollution and increasing inequality in standards of living. This study was based on Forrester's system dynamics approach. The publication of this work in *World Dynamics* (1971) received much attention in the press, principally attracting support from environmentalists who shared similar concerns, and from engineers who understood the methods and approach. The work made explicit Forrester's belief that forces within the world system must and will rise far enough to suppress the power of growth. It also attracted significant criticism from economists, who believed variously that the model was incomplete and were concerned about the costs and feasibility of halting economic growth, although Forrester notes that the debate shifted soon after to what strategy should be used to slow economic growth rather than whether it should be slowed.

His model of the world as a system paid particular attention to the interrelationships between parts of the system in an attempt to avoid undesirable and unintended consequences of our actions. It was a dynamic model of population, capital investment, geographical space, natural resources, pollution and food production. Forrester emphasized that as with other models, important variables had to be omitted, that aggregation lost distinctions between developed and underdeveloped countries, and that the concepts were rooted in the attitudes and concerns of the time. However, he defended the use of models (even though they are poor representations) with reference to the fact that humans act at all times on the models and mental images they have formed personally. In striving to ensure that the most acceptable model was also the best model, he urged that the best existing model should be identified at each point in time, that it should be used in preference to traditional models, and that there should be continual effort to improve available world models. This call was answered by a growing field of researchers working in the field of global modelling.

Forrester noted that 'all systems seem to have sensitive influence points through which the behaviour of the system can be improved ... however these influence points are usually not in the locations where most people expect them to be' (Forrester 1975), and understood that simple direct actions would not result in a desired outcome, whereas acting upon feedback loops may be more effective. His thinking was an early foreshadow of contemporary complexity theory and its understanding of 'control parameters'.

Forrester's significant contribution to systems thinking and to management practice has been acknowledged with many awards and honours. In 1968 he received the Inventor of the Year Award from George Washington University, and in 1969 the Valdmer Poulsen Gold Medal from the Danish Academy of Technical Sciences; in 1972 the IEEE awarded him both the medal of honour and the Systems, Man and Cybernetics Society Award for outstanding accomplishment. He was inducted into the US National Inventors Hall of Fame in 1979. Later in his career, having retired from the Sloan School in 1989, Forrester was able to pursue his long-time

interest in the application of system dynamics to learning, and worked to create learning materials to help teachers and students from kindergarten age upwards to adopt 'learner-directed learning' across the curriculum.

Essentially a man of action and practicality, Forrester was anti-utopian in his approach to the future. He was prepared to work with pragmatic, imperfect tools in order to get a job done. He was also of the conviction, however, that the traditions of civilization could be altered to become compatible with global equilibrium. His work in combining computer simulation with feedback thinking was a major advance in the field, and had a wide application from adverting strategy to managing the growth of start-up companies and the US national economy. His work underpins much of the current work done on modelling social systems.

BIBLIOGRAPHY

Forrester, J.W. (1961) *Industrial Dynamics*, Portland, OR: Productivity Press, 215–19.
—— (1969) *Urban Dynamics*, Portland, OR: Productivity Press.
—— (1973) *World Dynamics*, 2nd edn, Cambridge, MA: Wright-Allen Press.
—— (1975) *Collected Papers of Jay W Forrester*, Cambridge, MA: Wright-Allen Press.
Lane, D. (1998) 'Forrester, Jay Wright', in M. Warner (ed.), *IEBM Handbook of Management Thinking*, London: International Thomson Business Press, 215–19.
Legasto, A.A., Forrrester, J.W. and Lyneis, J.M. (eds) (1980) *System Dynamics*, Amsterdam: North Holland.
Meadows, D.H. and Robinson, J.M. (1985) *The Electronic Oracle*, New York: John Wiley and Sons.

AJ

FOUCAULT, Michel (1926–84)

The French philosopher Michel Foucault was born in Poitiers on 15 October 1926. He died in Paris on 25 June 1984. After the Second World War, Foucault moved to Paris and studied at the Ecole Normale Supérieure. Having received his *agrégation* (degree) in philosophy in 1952, he taught for three years at the University of Lille. His subsequent research at the University of Uppsala later led to his first major book, *Madness and Civilization* (1961; the English translation appeared in 1965). After research in Warsaw and Hamburg, Foucault returned to France in 1960, obtained a doctorate and taught at Clermont-Ferrand for six years.

During this, perhaps the most productive period of his life, he established himself as an idiosyncratic thinker with an ingenious ability to blend philosophy and history. His method of 'archaeology of knowledge', further developed in *The Birth of the Clinic* (1963) and *The Order of Things* (1966), investigated the formation and transformation of modern systems of knowledge ('discursive practices') through definition and marginalization of some groups and features of life. After two years in Tunisia, Foucault moved back to France following the social upheaval of 1968. He became head of the philosophy department at the newly created University of Paris VIII at Vincennes and published a major book on his methodology, *The Archaeology of Knowledge* (1969).

In 1970 Foucault was appointed to a chair in the 'history of the systems of thought' at the College de France. After receiving a tenure for life at the most renowned academic institution in France, Foucault somewhat neglected academic activities in favour of explicitly political work such as campaigning against police brutality or prison conditions. He also lectured widely, steadily building his reputation and influence in Europe, the United States and Japan. Over time, his political concerns turned to human rights and the critique of totalitari-

anism. In his last books, *Discipline and Punish* (1975) and *The History of Sexuality, Volumes I–III* (1976–84), Foucault arguably reached the culmination of his thought.

Although Foucault has not explicitly applied his concepts to business organizations, his writings have inspired management scholars engaged in criticisms of dominant ideologies, concepts and practices of management. Their main inspiration is Foucault's discussion of power. According to Foucault, power is a central and ubiquitous feature in social life, rather than a product of social hierarchy possessed by dominant individuals or groups. Power stems from the regimes of truth and practices of ordinary life. Foucault focuses on discursive practices that define knowledge, the norms of acceptable behaviour, and various social identities that reproduce those norms. In modern times, the difference between normal and abnormal has been developed by scientific disciplines (medicine, psychiatry, penology) and social institutions (hospitals, asylums, prisons and so on). Disciplinary practices and institutionalized power have spread throughout social life. Not surprisingly, Foucault argues that all organizations resemble prisons. This observation seems to be implicit in most of Foucauldian writings that deal with organizations and management.

BIBLIOGRAPHY

Bullock, A. and Woodings, R.B. (eds) (1983) *The Fontana Dictionary of Modern Thinkers*, London: Fontana Press.

Eribon, D. (1991) *Michel Foucault*, trans. B. Wing, Cambridge, MA: Harvard University Press.

Foucault, M. (1961) *Madness and Civilization*, trans. R. Howard, New York: Pantheon, 1965.

—— (1963) *The Birth of the Clinic*, trans. A.M. Sheridan Smith, New York: Pantheon, 1973.

—— (1966) *The Order of Things*, trans. A. Sheridan, New York: Vintage, 1970.

—— (1969) *The Archaeology of Knowledge*, trans. A. Sheridan, New York: Pantheon, 1972.

—— (1975) *Discipline and Punish*, trans. A. Sheridan, New York: Pantheon, 1977.

—— (1978) *The History of Sexuality, Volume 1: An Introduction*, trans. R. Hurley, New York: Pantheon.

Miller, J. (1993) *The Passion of Michel Foucault*, New York: Simon and Schuster.

DR

FOX, Alan (1920–)

Alan Fox was born in London on 23 January 1920. After leaving school at fourteen, he spent six years (1934–40) as an office clerk and semi-skilled factory worker (producing photographic film). This was followed by six years (1940–46) with the RAF and operational flying in photographic reconnaissance during the Second World War, with seventy-five combat missions in the Far East, where he won the Distinguished Flying Medal. This wartime experience had a great influence on Fox.

During his next job, as a forestry labourer, Fox saw an advertisement urging working people to study. He attended Ruskin College, Oxford (1946–8), followed by Exeter College (1948–50) and Nuffield College (1950–51). He then became lecturer in industrial relations and economic organization at Ruskin College (1951–7), research fellow at Nuffield College (1957–63) and lecturer in industrial sociology (1963–79) in the department of social and administrative studies, combined for a period with a fellowship at the Oxford Centre for Management Studies (now Templeton College). He deliberately chose not to apply for professorships (Fox 1990) and took early retirement at sixty.

Fox (1990: 210–11) was 'marked' by his past and Oxford, which changed the structure of his thinking and feeling. He became interested in patterns of industrial relations (in nineteenth-century Birmingham and the Black Country) and the industrial and social structure creating them, while his earlier experiences had aroused a general interest in power relationships within organizations. He was also influenced by FLANDERS' conceptual thinking (Fox 1990), by WOODWARD, and by his collaborations with mentors and friends including CLEGG. He was a member of the 'Oxford School of Industrial Relations', a group which had a considerable impact on the field.

Fox started with trade union history, working with Clegg and Thompson for six years, but developed his more analytical concerns. He was interested in a theoretical framework of concepts and motivations which made sense of facts and problems and related them to wider society, becoming 'hooked on an intellectual search for a theoretical analysis' (Fox 1990: 224). Much of his thought and inquiry then focused on organizational structure and behaviour, 'in an attempt to understand why individuals and groups at their place of work believed and behaved as they did in their relationships with each other in their reactions to authority and status, and in their responses to the wider society' (Fox 1990: 228).

Fox wrote on numerous areas, from union history to management strategies to secure compliance and industrial sociology. He developed an analysis of society that was radical but non-Marxist, shifting from a pluralist perspective, even if a breach with erstwhile colleagues and friends resulted. Fox's work and analysis continue to be relevant and are frequently referred to. For example, his seminal work on 'perspectives' (unitary, pluralist, radical) in employment relations included two key points (Fox 1966:1). First, the 'frame of reference' which people use shapes how they expect people to behave and think they ought

to behave, react to people's actual behaviour and choose methods to change their behaviour. Second, people's behaviour, and the 'pattern' and 'temper' of industrial relations, is determined by 'structural determinants and 'social organisation', and so we can expect only limited success if we try to modify behaviour solely by external sanctions brought to bear from outside the industry. Similarly, Fox's work on the underpinnings and evolution of industrial relations systems and social forces that shaped them (Fox 1985a) and on 'trust' (Fox 1974a, 1974b) retains its freshness. Indeed, his conception of high trust and discretion in work relations and organizations has been proselytized in a variety of business areas including contemporary models of human resource management and empowerment, although without the radical situational changes he recommended. His probe into society's characteristics and attitudes, and his questioning of 'easy' solutions (which were naive, as problems were so deep-seated they often needed major reappraisal and reconsideration of attitudes towards authority, power and equality) remain valid and should be read by the area's more simplistic gurus.

Fox remained a working-class outsider in favour of radical Fabian-style change from a leftist political party. Fox (1990: v) 'contributed notably to our understanding of the peculiarities of a most peculiar nation' with work 'of both sociological imagination and passionate personal testimony'. In short, 'Foxite' views on equality, social justice and reform to produce prosperity and fairness via 'high trust' bargaining, collaboration and relations remain as powerful and relevant today as in his own time.

Acknowledgements
Thanks to Paul Edwards, Rod Martin and Pat McGovern for earlier comments.

BIBLIOGRAPHY
Clegg, H.A., Fox, A. and Thompson, A.F. (1964) *A History of British Trade*

Unions, vol. 1, Oxford: Oxford University Press.

Fox, A. (1958) *A History of the National Union of Boot and Shoe Operatives, 1874–1957*, Oxford: Blackwell.

—— (1966) *Industrial Sociology and Industrial Relations*, Research Paper 3, Royal Commission on Trade Unions and Employers Associations, London: HMSO.

—— (1971) *A Sociology of Work in Industry*, London: Macmillan.

—— (1973) 'Industrial Relations: A Social Critique of Pluralist Ideology', in J. Chile (ed.), *Man and Organisation*, London: Allen and Unwin.

—— (1974a) *Man Mismanagement*, London: Hutchinson.

—— (1974b) *Beyond Contract: Work, Power and Trust Relations*, London: Faber.

—— (1975) 'Collective Bargaining, Flanders and the Webbs', *British Journal of Industrial Relations* 13(2): 151–74.

—— (1985a) *History and Heritage: The Social Origins of the British Industrial Relations System*, London: Allen and Unwin.

—— (1985b) *Man Mismanagement*, London: Hutchinson.

—— (1990) *A Very Late Development: An Autobiography*, Coventry: IRRU.

CR

FREDERICK II, King of Prussia (1712–86)

Frederick II was born in Berlin on 24 January 1712, the son of King Frederick William I of Prussia. He died at the palace of Sans Souci, near Potsdam on 17 August 1786. He succeeded his father as king of Prussia on 31 May 1740, and fought a successful war with the Holy Roman Empire (the War of the Austrian Succession, 1740–44). From 1756–62 (the Seven Years War) Prussia fought against a powerful alliance of the Empire, France, Sweden and Russia. Despite being overwhelmingly outnumbered, Frederick fought his opponents to a stalemate and concluded a successful peace treaty in 1763. So well organized was his Prussian army and state that at the conclusion of hostilities the Prussian treasury was not only in credit, but actually had a larger balance than at the start of the war.

Frederick was the most admired military leader of his age, and his battles and campaigns were analysed by later writers such as BÜLOW, JOMINI and CLAUSEWITZ. He thus exercised a considerable influence over the development of concepts such as strategy and logistics. Frederick was greatly influenced by the ideas of the Enlightenment, particularly on science. Witzel (1999) notes that Frederick applied scientific principles to warfare in much the same way as the proponents of scientific management. His strategic principles, particularly concerning the concentration and application of force, were also admired by later writers on economics and management.

Though he was a tactical genius and a master of improvisation, Frederick disliked battles, seeing them as too subject to the laws of chance. He preferred the methodical science of manoeuvre, by which he hoped to defeat his opponents without fighting. In his *Instruction of Frederick the Great for His Generals* (1747), he emphasizes sound organization and planning. His success was due to three managerial fundamentals: effective tools, good communication and strong leadership. The Prussian state, including its economy, was structured so as to support the war effort. An efficient system of reserves meant his regiments could be brought up to strength after each battle, and the state arsenals and factories ensured Prussia was self-sufficient in all but a few commodities. Although the Prussian army was famous for

its strict discipline, it was also highly trained and efficient. Frederick emphasized the concept of *Korpsgeist*, the ability of members of an organization (such as an army regiment) to identify with the organization and put its interests over their own.

Communications were vital to the Prussian military system, and Frederick's staff included a small corps of aides-de-camp who were both his messenger service and his eyes and ears on the battlefield; thanks to good information flows, the fast-marching Prussian infantry could usually outmanoeuvre their opponents. Leadership was provided by Frederick himself, ably supported by a small, well-trained staff of officers. His style was highly personal and familiar; he knew many of his officers and men by name. Recognizing that the army regarded his presence as a kind of guarantor of victory, he would not leave a battlefield, even if wounded, until that victory had been assured. However, when fighting a war on several fronts, Frederick often had to depend on less capable subordinate generals, and he never entirely solved the problem of how to control his military machine from a distance.

BIBLIOGRAPHY

Asprey, R.B. (1986) *Frederick the Great: The Magnificent Enigma*, New York: Ticknor and Fields.

Duffy, C. (1985) *Frederick the Great: A Military Life*, London: Routledge and Kegan Paul.

Fraser, D. (2000) *Frederick the Great, King of Prussia*, London: Allen Lane.

Witzel, M. (1999) 'Martial Management', *Financial Times Mastering Management Review* 20: 16–19.

MLW

FRÉMINVILLE, Charles-Clément de la Poix de (1856–1936)

Charles de la Poix de Fréminville was born in Lorient, France on 16 August 1856 and died in Paris on 3 June 1936. His family were of the minor aristocracy, though not well-to-do. Fréminville received a technical education, taking a degree in engineering from the École Centrale. He joined the equipment section of the Paris-Orleans Railway, rising to the rank of chief engineer. He went on to have a highly successful managerial career. He joined the motor vehicle maker Panhard & Levasseur in 1899, rising to the post of assistant managing director. During the First World War he served as chief engineer at the shipbuilders Chantiers de Penhoët in St Nazaire. In 1919 he was a member of the French government economic mission to the United States. Finally, he was appointed chief engineer with the great steel and manufacturing firm of Schneider, which post he held until his death.

Fréminville had early exposure to American business methods in the course of two visits to the United States in the 1880s. He became aware of developments in scientific management, most probably through his contacts with Henri LE CHATELIER, who first popularized scientific management in France in his journal, *Revue de Métallurgie*, for which Fréminville began writing around 1907. However, according to Urwick and Brech (1949), it was not until 1912, when he first met Frederick Winslow TAYLOR, that Fréminville became a real enthusiast for the system. During the First World War, as well as working at Penhoët, Fréminville served as a consulting engineer in a number of naval yards and armaments factories, helping to improve efficiency. Before the war, scientific management had something of a bad name in France, being equated with a mechanistic approach and the exploitation of labour; Fréminville's wartime efforts seem to have done much to dispel this view.

After the war Fréminville continued to work closely with Le Chatelier, and was involved

with him in the foundation of the Conférence de l'Organisation Française (COF: French Conference on Scientific Management, in 1920. The previous year, Henri FAYOL and his colleagues had established the Centre d'Études Administratives (CEA: Centre of Administrative Studies) as a means for disseminating Fayol's theories on administration. Followers of the COF and CEA soon entered into rivalry, each claiming the supremacy of their system of management over the other. Deeply concerned at the divisive effect this trend might have on the growth and professionalization of management in France, Fréminville and Le Chatelier began working to bring the two schools together. In 1925 at the Second International Management Congress in Brussels, Fayol announced that in his view there was no essential conflict between his own work and that of Taylor, and that the two schools of thought should be seen as complementary. In the words of Urwick and Brech:

> it fell to de Fréminville ... to grasp the hand thus extended warmly and gladly and to symbolise in the body that arose from that union – the Comité de l'Organisation Française – fusion of two complementary pioneer lines in the evolution of management thought.
>
> (Urwick and Brech 1949: 108)

Fréminville served as president of the new body for some years, and was also president of the Fourth International Management Congress in Paris in 1929.

Like Le Chatelier, Fréminville was an interpreter and translator rather than a deeply original thinker, but his work in demonstrating how scientific management could be used effectively had a considerable impact on French industry, especially in steel and engineering. His persuasiveness as an apostle of the scientific management movement may have been due to the fact that he did not regard scientific management as being especially American. Rather, he believed it to be merely a logical continuation of universal scientific principles that could be traced back to René Descartes in the seventeenth century. By placing scientific management into a larger – and European – tradition of scientific endeavour, Fréminville made it seem both less alien and more natural to European minds. His work was widely read not just in France but all over continental Europe.

BIBLIOGRAPHY
Fréminville, C. de (1918) *Quelques aperçus sur la système Taylor* (The Fundamental Principles of the Taylor Method), Paris: A. Maréchal.
Humphreys, G.G. (1986) *Taylorism in France, 1904–1920: The Impact of Scientific Management on Factory Relations and Society*, New York: Garland.
Urwick, L.F. and Brech, E.F.L. (1949) *The Making of Scientific Management*, vol. 2, *Management in British Industry*, London: Management Publications Trust; repr. Bristol: Thoemmes Press, 1994.

MLW

FRIEDMAN, Milton (1912–)

Milton Friedman was born in Brooklyn, New York on 31 July 1912. He was the son of Jeno Saul Friedman and Sarah Ethel Friedman, Jewish immigrants from the western Ukraine. In 1925 the family moved to Rahway, New Jersey, not far from New Brunswick, the site of what was then Princeton College. In 1928 Milton Friedman began to attend Rutgers, obtaining his BA in economics in 1932. At Rutgers, he was a pupil of Arthur Burns, the future Chairman of the Federal Reserve and an influence in shaping Friedman's own economic views.

Friedman entered the University of Chicago, from which he obtained his MA in 1933. After writing a master's thesis on railway stock prices, he soon began to publish pieces in the *Quarterly Journal of Economics* and other journals. Between his masters degree and doctorate he worked in Washington as an economist, where he contributed to a 1939 government study of consumer expenditures in the United States. By 1941 he was working as a tax economist with the United States Treasury. Friedman began his Ph.D. work at Columbia University in 1943, graduating in 1946 after completing a dissertation on income from independent professional practice. By 1946 Friedman was teaching economics at the University of Chicago, where he remained until 1980.

At Chicago, Friedman established a friendship with the noted Austrian economist Friedrich von HAYEK. More than anyone else, Hayek's free market views shaped Friedman's own. By the end of the 1950s, Friedman had become the best known member of an emergent Chicago School of economics, which challenged the Keynesian orthodoxy dominant in most university faculties. During the 1950s Friedman turned the University of Chicago into a renowned bastion of market-oriented thinking. Not all of the Chicago faculty, however, were as libertarian in their thinking as Friedman or Hayek: Paul Douglas was a Democrat, Oskar Lange a market-oriented socialist.

The Nixon administration very much disappointed Friedman. He considered Nixon to be a most intelligent man in his grasp of economics, but one too willing to compromise his principles. The wage and price controls which Nixon imposed to protect the US dollar in August 1971 appalled him. Ronald Reagan, whom Friedman served as a policy adviser, impressed him far more as one who stuck to his market principles, deregulating prices of oil and gas.

By the middle of the 1970s, events were beginning to discredit the economics of John Maynard KEYNES. In the aftermath of the Yom Kippur War of 1973, the oil-producing countries began to raise prices. The traditional Keynesian remedies no longer seemed to be working. According to Keynesian logic, governments should not have to face inflation and unemployment at the same time. Attempts by both the Nixon administration and the British government of Edward Heath to control inflation via a price and incomes policy were failing. In Chile, the policies of a Marxist government brought the country to the point of economic disaster, leading to a rightist military coup. By 1975 New York City hovered on the verge of bankruptcy, for which many blamed its social welfare policies.

According to Yergin and Stanislaw (1999), Friedman offered alternative policies to those of Keynesianism, and it seemed that many were now willing to consider them. His credibility was further enhanced when his mentor Hayek was a joint winner of the Nobel Prize for Economics in 1974. By 1975 Margaret Thatcher was leader of the British Conservative party, which she transformed according to monetarist principles, employing Friedman as her adviser. In Chile, the regime of General Augusto Pinochet turned to some of Friedman's followers from the University of Chicago to restructure the Chilean economy on free market lines.

Friedman's ideas received wide exposure in a television mini-series aired in 1976 entitled *Free to Choose*, which was turned into Friedman's most popular book (Friedman and Friedman 1980). *Free to Choose* signalled that free market economics had rapidly entered the mainstream and was becoming the new economic orthodoxy. It taught Friedman's monetarist and libertarian economics in a persuasive popular form, using everyday examples. The book was an instant success.

In *Free to Choose*, Friedman, a practical libertarian, nonetheless expressed his ideal concept of the role of government. Citing Adam SMITH, he insisted that government had four legitimate functions:

1. Protecting life and property from violence, including national defence.

2. Setting forth laws and administering justice through the court system.

3. Providing for public works such as transportation and communication.

4. In a limited manner, taking care of those not able or responsible enough to care for themselves.

Friedman traced American success to the minimal government devised by Jefferson and the free market economics of Smith. The source of many problems, he argued, was the attempt to move from equality of opportunity to equality of outcome.

Friedman looked upon the history of the nineteenth century in a very positive light. In Britain between 1846 and 1897, living standards improved dramatically for all classes while the level of government spending fell from 25 per cent to 10 per cent of GDP. After the turn of the century, however, many were seduced into embracing the notion that big government, in the right hands, would make life much better. Nineteenth-century America, for Friedman, was not a gilded age of 'robber barons' but a time of golden opportunity in which farmers and workers, as well as immigrants, steadily improved their lot. Government spending did not exceed 12 per cent of national income before 1929, and only 3 per cent of this was federal spending. Private charities such as the Salvation Army flourished. Internationally, the century from 1815 to 1914 was the most peaceful and prosperous in human history, said Friedman, largely due to free trade and free world markets, which also provided a counter to domestic monopolies.

As an individualist, Friedman insisted that market and fairness were often mutually exclusive: 'Life is not fair. It is tempting to believe that government can rectify what nature has spurned. But it is also important to recognize how much we benefit from the very unfairness we deplore' (Friedman and Friedman 1980: 137). Should government spend billions to give every one boxing lessons to make them the equal of Muhammad Ali? What if at the end of an evening in a casino the winners had to pay the losers? If individuals bore the consequences, they should make the decisions. One could not rely upon the price mechanism without accepting unequal income as the result: 'If what a person gets does not depend on the price he receives ... what incentive does he have to seek out information on prices or to act on the basis of that information?' (Friedman and Friedman 1980: 23). Why work hard, accumulate capital, or seek the best bargain if the result was all the same in the end? The system of personal risk and responsibility created Ford and Standard Oil. Friedman was certainly not against philanthropy, so long as it was voluntary, but utterly rejected any efforts to equalize outcome. He believed that academics and bureaucrats who preached egalitarianism were living a double standard, as they were highly paid.

As far as Friedman was concerned, collectivist and redistributionist economics was morally corrupting as well. When a society such as Britain taxed earned income at over 80 per cent in the top bracket and unearned income at 98 per cent, this encouraged tax evasion, which in turn undermined lack of respect for law, and resulted in higher crime and fraud everywhere. In contrast, the more free the market, the more equality would result.

Friedman also stirred controversy with his views on business ethics. He rejected not only government intervention, but also the concept that business had social responsibilities that were not dictated by the market. In an article written for the *New York Times Magazine* of 13 September 1970 he criticized executives who felt they had a social duty to provide jobs, end discrimination or avoid pollution. To Friedman, this concept was 'pure and unadulterated socialism' disguised as free enterprise (Friedman 1970).

Friedman insisted that only individuals had responsibilities, not companies. An executive was responsible to his directors and shareholders. Spending money on anti-pollution equipment or training the hardcore unemployed would mean higher prices to consumers, lower dividends for shareholders and lower wages for employees, which Friedman saw as an onerous form of taxation without representation. In effect, it reduced the executive to the role of public employee. Adam Smith had condemned the notion of 'trading for the public good' and so did Friedman, who felt that morally this would bolster the view that profits were immoral:

> But the doctrine of 'social responsibility' taken seriously would extend the scope of the political mechanism to every human activity. It does not differ in philosophy from the most explicitly collectivist doctrine. It differs only by professing to believe that collectivist ends can be attained without collectivist means. That is why, in my book 'Capitalism and Freedom,' I have called it a 'fundamentally subversive doctrine' in a free society, and have said that in such a society, 'there is one and only one social responsibility of business – to use its resources and engage in activities designed to increase its profits so long as it stays within the rules of the game, which is to say, engages in open and free competition without deception or fraud.
>
> (Friedman 1970)

During the 1980s Friedman's policies appeared to be meeting with success, further enhancing his reputation. The Thatcher government effected a social revolution in Britain, curbing both inflation and the power of the militant unions by controlling the money supply and deregulating markets. Despite the harshness of its regime, Chile slowly began to move back to economic prosperity. In the United States, the monetarist policies of the Federal Reserve under Paul Volcker and Alan Greenspan helped end inflation and pave the way for a major economic boom.

Friedman, still articulate and writing, lives near San Francisco. According to an interview with the American C-Span network in September 2000, he remains the chief free market economist in the world. He declares that he is not a conservative, but 'a small-l libertarian' who supports the Republicans rather than the Libertarian Party as the more appropriate vehicle for his views. His libertarianism is tempered, however, by a strong sense of the practical. In his ideal state, the role of government would be sharply pruned back from taking 40 per cent of Americans' earnings to a mere 10 per cent. He would fully privatize social security, allowing people to decide what fraction of their income they would devote to their own retirement. Friedman would provide a basic safety of food and shelter for the very poor through a negative income tax. A gold standard is not realistic, he says, when the state controls such a large part of the economy. Any government surplus would be used to reduce taxes.

While he admired the libertarian Austrian economists, he considered Friedman Hayek's mentor Ludwig von MISES a bit too doctrinaire for his liking. Though he regarded Mises, as he did Ayn RAND, as a remarkable free market thinker, he considered him and many other libertarians to be too 'intolerant'. Friedman felt and still feels that free market thinkers needed to be learners, not rigid disciples of a frozen creed. He admires those such as Federal Reserve Chairman Alan Greenspan, a former disciple of Ayn Rand, whom he considers to be the most outstanding Federal Reserve Chairman in the bank's history.

BIBLIOGRAPHY

'Friedman, Milton' (1969) in C. Moritz (ed.), *Current Biography*, New York: H.W. Wilson Company, 151–4.

Friedman, Milton (1957) *A Theory of the Consumptive Function*, Princeton, NJ: Princeton University Press.

—— (1962) *Capitalism and Freedom*, Chicago: University of Chicago Press.

—— (1970) 'The Social Responsibility of Business Is to Increase Its Profits', *The New York Times Magazine*, 13 September; text in Free University of Berlin, 'Warum Neoliberalismus?' (Why Neoliberalism?), http://userpage.fu-berlin.de/~comtess/neolib/corp-resp.html, 17 May 2001.

—— (2000) 'In Depth', *C-SPAN2 Booknotes*, televised interview aired on Sunday 3 September.

Friedman, M. and Friedman, R. (1980) *Free to Choose: A Personal Statement*, New York: Harcourt, Brace, Jovanovich.

Yergin, D. and Stanislaw, J. (1999) *The Commanding Heights: The Battle between Government and the Marketplace that is Remaking the Modern World*, New York: Simon and Schuster.

DCL

FUGGER, Jakob (1459–1526)

Jakob Fugger was born in Augsburg, Germany on 6 March 1459 and died there on 30 January 1526. His grandfather had founded a small cloth-weaving business; his father, Jakob Fugger, expanded into general trade and managed a mint in the mining district of the Tyrol, establishing several branches in south Germany and northern Italy. Jakob the younger had originally been destined for a career in the church but, on the death of an older brother, was taken into the business instead. He became a partner in 1473, aged just fourteen, but does not seem to have handled business until 1478, when he joined the family's agency at the Fondaco dei Tedeschi in Venice. Here he studied bookkeeping and probably received some basic management training. In 1485 he was put in charge of the Fugger agency at Innsbruck, where he made investments in the copper and silver mines of the Tyrol, and also began loaning money to Maximilian I, the future Holy Roman Emperor. In 1495 Fugger began developing a series of copper mines in Hungary and Silesia, in which he invested heavily; by 1500 he controlled most of the European copper trade and was the dominant partner in the family business.

The trade in copper and silver, the supply of which he controlled, led Fugger naturally into minting and banking; quite literally, he made money. Like many other late medieval merchant princes, notably Cosimo dei MEDICI, Fugger's banking capital was derived from profits made in other industries, usually manufacturing, mining or trade. From 1507 onwards Fugger lent increasingly large sums to the Emperor Maximilian; many of these loans were mortgages on crown lands, and as many of these were never redeemed, Fugger also acquired extensive landholdings. The emperor, beleaguered by enemies at home and abroad, relied on Fugger almost exclusively for financial assistance; records speak of some transactions as large as 300,000 guilders (over £35 million in today's money) to fight foreign wars, and others of as little as 1,000 guilders to pay the royal household's most pressing debts. In return, Maximilian ennobled Fugger as a count in 1514. In 1518 Fugger and his agents set up a massive loan syndicate, with investors in Spain, Italy, Germany and Eastern Europe, which raised around 550,000 guilders (around £60 million) to finance the election of the Holy Roman Emperor Charles V.

The relationship with Maximilian and then with Charles was the key to Fugger's greatest successes. Like Cosimo dei Medici when lending to the popes, Fugger knew that many of the loans he made to the emperors would never be recovered; some were secured on property, but few to the full value of the loan. However, so long as the loans to the emperors could be covered by profits gained in other

fields, the cost was well worth it. The imperial connection gave Fugger privileged access to other, more profitable customers. Even more importantly, in an age of political uncertainty and constant change, having a grateful emperor on his books as a client meant that Fugger could enjoy a measure of security and protection afforded to few of his rivals; put simply, if he was threatened either financially or physically, Fugger could call in powerful favours.

Known in Augsburg simply as 'Fugger the Rich', Jakob Fugger dominated the European financial world for two decades. A man of fixed purpose and great determination, he tended to set his sights on a goal, develop a strategy and then pursue that strategy unswervingly to its end. The business, like most banks of its day, operated on a network basis with agents in all the major financial centres of Europe; sometimes these agents were directly employed, sometimes they were employed by partnerships established with other banks. As well as transacting business, these agents gathered information. At the headquarters in Augsburg, Jakob Fugger himself kept the firm's master accounts and collated information received from agents abroad; both these things were done on a daily basis. Fugger once wrote that he could not go soundly to sleep at night without knowing that somewhere that day he had made a profit, however small it might be. This combination of tight monitoring of information and a flexible, far-flung network gave Fugger the ability to respond quickly to crises. Like most successful business leaders of his day he was also a considerable philanthropist, and modern Augsburg still has many buildings built by him and his descendants.

By the time of his death, Fugger's importance rivalled that of kings and emperors. An Augsburg chronicler wrote:

The names of Jakob Fugger and his nephews are known in all kingdoms and lands; yea, and among the heathen also ... All the merchants of the world have called him an enlightened man, and all the heathen have wondered at him. He is the glory of all Germany.

(Quoted in Ehrenberg 1928: 83)

(The 'heathen' probably refers to Fugger's business contacts in Asia, where he had established a number of silk factories, adding to his manufacturing portfolio.) He had married, but unhappily, and had no children. On his death he bequeathed to his nephew, Anton Fugger, a fortune worth over 2 million guilders (over £280 million in today's money).

Anton Fugger was also a talented manager, and despite increasing political turmoil in Germany and abroad, expanded the firm's operations to include cattle ranches in Hungary, the spice trade with the East Indies, and mining in Chile and Peru. By the time of his death in 1546 he had increased the company's capital to over 5 million guilders. However, the firm had also taken on debts, something which Jakob Fugger had rarely done; he far preferred expansion to be financed from retained earnings. After Anton's death the bank's fortunes declined. In the 1560s there was a short but disastrous period of management by Anton's nephew, Hans Jakob Fugger; he was succeeded by Anton's eldest son, Marx Fugger, who was capable but helpless to prevent catastrophes such as the Spanish state bankruptcy of 1575, which cost the bank heavily. Many of its manufacturing assets had to be sold to recoup the losses. By 1600 the firm was in irrecoverable decline. Jakob Fugger had made getting close to the centre of power a priority in ensuring the security of his business; his successors had failed to continue this policy, and paid the price.

BIBLIOGRAPHY
Ehrenberg, R. (1928) *Capital and Finance in the Age of the Renaissance: A Study of the Fuggers and Their Connections*, trans. H.M. Lucas, London: Jonathan Cape.

MLW

FUGGER, Philip Eduard (1546–1618)

Philip Eduard Fugger was born in Augsburg, Germany on 11 February 1546 and died there on 14 August 1618. His father, Count George Fugger, was a nephew of Anton Fugger and great-nephew of Jakob FUGGER, 'the Rich', who had established the family's banking fortunes. Philip Fugger had little do with the family business in the disastrous second half of the sixteenth century; his private fortune already assured, he devoted himself to collecting works of art and books.

Among his other activities, Fugger was the compiler of the collection of correspondence now known as the 'Fugger Newsletters'. This correspondence, which amounts to about 35,000 pages and is now held in the Vienna National Library, consists of political and economic news and facts gathered from all over Europe. Much of the material is in the form of letters written to Philip Fugger himself, but he also collected many *Neue Zeitungen* (newsletters), popular printed sheets which circulated around southern Germany describing important political and social events.

It was once thought that this material had been gathered deliberately as a commercial service, and that the Fuggers ran a business information service, selling news and market information to customers (the collection also continues, mistakenly, to be associated with Jakob Fugger). In fact, it is unlikely that the Fuggers would have shared such valuable information with anyone else, and Philip Fugger's efforts, insofar as they were commercial at all, would have been directed at assisting the fortunes of his own house. The business importance of the Fugger Newsletters is not so great as was once thought; but they remain a testament to how business leaders and managers could and did raise and manage information in the age before wireless technology.

BIBLIOGRAPHY
Klarwill, V. von (ed.) (1925) *The Fugger Newsletters*, London: Bodley Head.

FUJISAWA Takeo (1910–88)

Fujisawa Takeo was born in Tokyo, the son of a poor trader, on 10 November 1910 and died there on 30 December 1988. His father worked for a time as a painter, and on another occasion was the owner of a shabby cinema. Because of the family's poverty, Fujisawa had to look for a job as soon as he graduated from middle school, taking a place in an address-writing workshop. He was then employed by an iron materials dealer, Mitsuwa Shokai, and was soon entrusted with the management of Mitsuwa's shop, with chief responsibility for sales. Thanks to the opportunities that came his way while trading in this small shop, Fujisawa became familiar with the tool-selling business. In 1939, at the age of twenty-nine, he established his own business, Nihon Kiko Kenkyusho. Shortly before Japan's defeat in the Second World War, however, Fujisawa closed this company and moved to Fukushima prefecture to avoid the air raids of the US bombers that were targeting Tokyo.

In the summer of 1949 Fujisawa met HONDA Soichiro in Tokyo for the first time. Since Honda was anxious to devote himself exclusively to technological development, he was looking for a capable manager to take charge of finance, accounting and general management, which he himself had always found difficult to deal with. Honda and Fujisawa found their views and opinions to be entirely in accord, and decided to go into business together, with Honda as president and Fujisawa as vice-president of Honda Motors.

In the early 1950s Honda Motor Company, Ltd grew its business rapidly thanks to its strong sales of motorcycles. However, this growth brought cash-flow problems for the company. Fujisawa attempted to solve the problem by collecting cash from customers as rapidly as possible, while at the same time delaying payment to suppliers. However, this procedure is a risky one, and becomes dangerous when the company fails to maintain its rapid growth. In the case of Honda, the

company planned to develop a version of its popular Dream motorcycle with a larger engine, but the project developed an unexpected problem in that the engine tended to overheat, which in turn melted some of its plastic components. The result was a financial crisis from 1954 to 1956. Both Honda and Fujisawa worked to solve the problem, Honda by making improvements in the technology and Fujisawa by restructuring the management system in the company.

In 1956 Fujisawa began studying the Italian Mopetto, a small motorcycle with an engine of less than 50cc, and believed he could use a similar product as a lever to expand the motorcycle market in Japan. In response to this idea, Honda Soichiro developed the Super-Cab of 1958. The Super-Cab marketed at 55,000 yen, about one-quarter the price of other makers' products. More than one million were eventually produced.

Fujisawa's business philosophy consisted of expanding consumption and growing the market, mainly through the introduction of smaller, cheaper products. In September 1956 Honda USA was established in Los Angeles, the beginning of Honda's full participation in overseas markets. The company believed that, given the United States' dominance, success in this market would be replicated throughout the world – therefore the United States had to be the main target market. At this time, only large motorcycles were on the market in the USA. Honda succeeded in changing the image of the motorcycle in America, and the Super-Cab became the mainstay of a booming small motorcycle market which had never existed before. The management philosophy of introducing small, inexpensive vehicles was carried through into the development of automobiles as well.

Although Fujisawa was ostensibly only the vice-president of Honda Motors, the company could not have accomplished its many successes, particularly in international markets, without him. It was Fujisawa who was really responsible for the management of the company, and it was to his great managerial talents that it owed its recovery and growth during the 1950s and 1960s.

After the business crisis of 1954, the biggest problem in management facing Fujisawa was the development of a system which would allow Honda Motors to expand its activity as a company, systematically and in a coordinated form, but without being dependent on a specific personality such as himself or Honda Soichiro. In 1960 he separated the technological development division from Honda Motors. He abolished the system of individual directors' offices in 1964, and introduced a 'leaders' office' that required all the directors and managers to work together in a single large room. He intended that the role of the directors should be to consider and discuss the administrative problems concerning the future of the company, and also to plan for successors to positions in top management. In August 1973 Fujisawa and Honda both retired from their posts and entrusted the company administration to their appointed successors.

BIBLIOGRAPHY

Fujisawa T. (1984) *Taimatsu wa Jibun no Te de* (Bear Your Torch in Your Own Hand), Tokyo: Sangyo Noritsu Junior College Press.
——— (1986) *Keiei ni Owari wa Nai* (No End Can Be Found With Management), Tokyo: Nesco.
Yamamoto Y. (1992) *Fujisawa Takeo no Kenkyu* (Fujisawa Takeo Unmasked), Tokyo: Kanoh Shobo.

ST

FUKUZAWA Yukichi (1835–1901)

Fukuzawa Yukichi was born on 10 January 1835 in Osaka, Japan, the second son of

Fukuzawa Hyakusuke, a low-ranking warrior of the fief of Nakatsu in the state of Buzen. He died in Tokyo on 3 February 1901. His father, who had a talent for learning, often had difficulties in performing his services for the fief and suffered much misery, and throughout his life Fukuzawa was severely critical of feudal systems which caused much hardship.

In 1854 Fukuzawa went to Nagasaki to study. For a long time Nagasaki had been the sole outlet through which the Japanese came into contact with foreign countries, as Japan was then sealed off by the policy of seclusion which had been adopted by the Tokugawa Shogunate. In 1855 Fukuzawa joined Ogata Kouan's *teki juku* (private school for young people of ability), where he studied the Dutch language, the human sciences and the culture of the Western world. In 1858 he moved to Edo (Tokyo), where he established a small school teaching the Dutch language and Western sciences. In 1859 he visited the port of Yokohama, which had just been opened up to British and American traders, and this visit convinced him of the necessity to learn English in order to study Western science and culture more widely; he then began to teach himself English.

In 1860 Fukuzawa was a member of the Shogunate delegation that travelled to the United States aboard the warship *Kanrin Maru*. While in the USA he greatly enriched his experience and knowledge of overseas affairs. Returning to Japan, he was employed by the Shogunate as a translator. In 1861 he spent a year in Europe, again as a member of a Shogunate delegation, visiting a number of European countries. In 1867 he travelled overseas for a third time, and collected a warship which the Shogunate had ordered from an American shipyard. After the Meiji Restoration of 1868, however, he assumed no further official posts, and devoted himself as a private individual to furthering the spread of education for the remainder of his life.

Based on the experiences acquired while travelling in the countries of Europe and in the United States, Fukuzawa became an enthusiastic educator and enlightened thinker. His first small school, established in 1858, was renamed Keio Gijuku in 1868 and was relocated to Mita, Tokyo in 1871; the school today is known as Keio Gijuku University, and is one of the leading private universities in Japan. Fukuzawa is honoured as the founder of Keio University.

In his book *Seiyo Jijo* (Western Affairs) (1866–72), Fukuzawa introduced to Japan the political systems and cultures he had experienced in Europe and the United States. This work exercised great influence on the political thought of Japan, then in the midst of a dramatic conversion from a state of seclusion to an open nation. In his later *Gakumon no Susume* (Recommendations for Learning) (1872–6), Fukuzawa explained the dignity of human independence based on the theory of natural rights advocated by Western thinkers such as Jean-Jacques Rousseau, which stated that human beings are inherently equal and free and are in possession of the right to pursue individual happiness, which is a heaven-endowed human right. Fukuzawa went on to argue that practical learning should be highly valued. In 1873 Fukuzawa and his colleagues founded an association named Meiroku-sha, followed by the publication of the journal *Meiroku Zasshi*, and embarked on the spread of their enlightenment. In the book *Bunmei-ron no Gairyaku* (An Outline of the Theory of Civilization) (1875), Fukuzawa spoke of the importance of practical learning based on the thought of British utilitarianism, which he believed to be important in the search for national independence. Consequently, he severely criticized feudal ethics and doctrine. He had long been aware of the importance of economics in social science, and studied the doctrines of the economic liberalism of Adam SMITH and Francis Wayland. In connection with trade policies, however, his ideas were subject to fluctuation between liberalism and protectionism according to the situation from year to year. In 1867 he translated Wayland's

The Elements of Political Economy (1837), which was later published as *Seiyo Jijou Gairon* (Another Version of Western Affairs). Fukuzawa's enlightenment thinking culminated in his *Fukuo Jiden* (Fukuzawa's Autobiography) (1899), respected as a masterpiece of biographical literature.

From the standpoint of his political liberal thought, Fukuzawa had long insisted on the necessity for a national assembly in Japan. However, he did not take part in the so-called liberal civil rights campaign, and also emphasized the development of the state's power in accordance with harmony between the state and the people. He founded the newspaper *Jiji Shinpo* (Bulletin on Current Topics) which, though strictly non-partisan, promoted his own principles of politics. In his book *Fujin-ron* (Women's Status) (1885), he launched a fierce criticism of Japan's age-old feudal family system together with the problems of monogamy and equality of the sexes.

After the inter-party strife of 1882 and 1884, Fukuzawa began to give priority to state power over civil rights. His thinking became more conservative, and finally right wing. With regard to the Sino-Japanese War of 1894–5, in which Japan launched an aggressive expansion into Korea and contested suzerainty of the country with the empire of China, he supported the war, believing that it was a struggle to protect 'civilization against barbarism'. He also proposed a truce between the political parties in order to facilitate Japanese expansion overseas, and taxes to raise funds for that purpose. In his book *Datsu-a-ron* (Evasion from Asia) (1885) he emphasized Japan's strength and potential leadership role in Asia.

Fukuzawa's legacy was the introduction and application of Western ideas and concepts to many areas of activity, not the least of which was business management. He played in important role in improving education in Japan, which in turn has had important consequences for the development of

Japanese management. More directly, he encouraged the development of strong business and management in Japan as a way of helping to ensure strong national growth and development, a theme which has continued to the present day.

BIBLIOGRAPHY

Fukuzawa, Y. (1866–72) *Seijyo Jiyo* (Western Affairs), Tokyo: Shokodo.
—— (1872–6) *Gakumon no Susume* (Recommendations for Learning), Tokyo: Iwanami Shoten, 1942.
—— (1875) *Bunmeiron no Gairyaku* (An Outline of the Theory of Civilization), Tokyo: Iwanami Shoten, 1962.
—— (1958–64) *Fukuzawa Yukichi Zenshu* (A Complete Edition of Fukuzawa Yukichi), 21 vols, Tokyo: Iwanami Shoten.

ST

FURNESS, Christopher (1852–1912)

Christopher Furness was born in West Hartlepool, County Durham on 23 April 1852, the son of John and Averill Furness. He died at his home, Grantley Hall, on 11 November 1912. Furness's father had established a small grocery business in West Hartlepool, taking his sons into partnership; under John Furness's management the firm prospered and moved into grocery wholesaling, import and export in the 1860s. Christopher Furness joined the firm in 1870 and quickly showed his ability, cornering the Swedish grain market during the Franco-Prussian War of 1870 and netting the company a profit of over £50,000 (Boyce 1986). He joined the firm as a partner in 1872, becoming involved in the family's initial moves into ship-owning. When his brothers saw ship-

owning as too risky and decided to pull out, Furness bought the ships and went into business for himself in 1882.

His expansion, in the difficult and highly competitive world of shipbuilding, was breathtakingly swift. From the beginning he adopted a strategy of vertical integration, purchasing the West Hartlepool shipyard Edward Withy and Comapny in 1883, and merging the two firms as Furness, Withy and Company in 1891. Beginning in the mid-1890s he bought marine engineering firms, steel mills, coal mines and steel plate makers, creating a complete vertically integrated shipbuilding and ship-owning structure. The engineering, shipbuilding and ship-owning businesses were closely integrated under the direct control of Furness, Withy, the group's central holding company; the steel and coal businesses were more loosely integrated and pursued business interests elsewhere, as well as supplying the group. As well as establishing new enterprises, Furness frequently bought up poorly performing firms at bargain prices, injected new capital and technology, and integrated them into his existing businesses.

At the same time, Furness continued to expand his ship-owning interests. In the 1890s he moved into the Transatlantic trade, initially in partnership with J.P. MORGAN. Like many ship-owners of the period, Furness used short-term partnerships to break into new markets, then consolidated his own control over certain lines. In 1902, when Morgan attempted to establish an Atlantic shipping monopoly, the International Mercantile Marine (IMM), Furness allied with the Cunard and Elder Dempster lines to fight him off. By the end of 1912, according to Pollard and Robinson (1979), Furness owned or controlled 307 ships of 1.4 million gross tonnage.

A political liberal, Furness served as MP for Hartlepool from 1891 to 1896 and from 1900 to 1910; knighted in 1895, he was raised to the peerage in 1910. He was an economic nationalist, and his book *The American Invasion* (1902) is a call to British management and workers to respond to the competitive challenge posed by the United States. He believed more and better education for managers is necessary, and that British managers should become more entrepreneurial and more adaptable. He also recommended a less adversarial approach to the problems of labour. This theme is taken up in more detail in *Industrial Peace and Industrial Efficiency* (1908), in which he calls for a partnership between capital and labour; both, he says, 'came together at the summons of enterprise' (Furness 1908: 12), and so both have the same goal. His calls for co-partnership between management and labour fell on deaf ears in his own firm, however, and a co-partnership scheme at Furness, Withy was abandoned after less than a year.

BIBLIOGRAPHY
Boyce, G. (1984) 'Furness, Christopher', in D.J. Jeremy (ed.), *Dictionary of Business Biography*, London: Butterworths, vol. 2, 443–9.

Furness, C. (1902) *The American Invasion*, London: Simpkin, Marshall, Hamilton, Kent and Co.

—— (1908) *Industrial Peace and Industrial Efficiency*, West Hartlepool: Alexander Salton.

Pollard, S. and Robinson, P. (1979) *The British Shipbuilding Industry 1870–1914*, Cambridge, MA: Harvard University Press.

MLW

G

GALBRAITH, John Kenneth (1908–)

John Kenneth Galbraith was born in the town of Iona Station, Ontario on 15 October 1908, the son of a farmer who had also been a teacher and worked as an insurance salesman. Originally intending to be a farmer and husbandman, Galbraith entered the Ontario Agricultural College in Guelph, Ontario in 1930, just as the Great Depression descended upon Canada. Canadians suffered severely as their country was highly dependent on exports. Galbraith was drawn to the study of economics by the realization that he could learn to be the best farmer in the world, but it would avail him nothing if he could not sell his crops or his hogs (Galbraith 1994). In 1934 Galbraith was awarded a scholarship in agricultural economy to attend the University of California at Berkeley. He graduated in 1937, and was teaching at Berkeley when he was offered a position at Harvard University. The salary was substantially more than he was earning at Berkeley, and he accepted.

In his study of economics Galbraith had read *The Wealth of Nations* by Adam SMITH, whom he admired, and was taught, as was every other student of economics, from the *Principles of Economics* (1890) of Alfred MARSHALL. In the 1930s and 1940s Galbraith broadly accepted the standard classical model of market competition in which all firms were subject to market forces regardless of their size, derived from Smith and Marshall.

Another economist who profoundly affected Galbraith's thought was John Maynard KEYNES, whose *General Theory of Employment, Interest and Money* (1936) helped Galbraith understand the Great Depression of the 1930s. He became a Keynesian and New Dealer. In 1937 Galbraith went to study at Cambridge University, hoping to learn from Keynes, but was unable to do so as his mentor had suffered a heart attack. Later, during the Second World War, Keynes paid Galbraith a surprise visit, but the two men did not become close.

During the war Galbraith, now a US citizen, worked with the National Defense Advisory Commission and then became deputy administrator for the Office of Price Administration. After the war, in 1946 he served as director of the Strategic Bombing Survey and the Office of Economic Security. He had also served as editor of *Fortune* magazine from 1943 to 1948. In 1949 he resumed teaching at Harvard as a full professor of economics. He was already well known as a writer. In his earliest works, *Modern Competition and Business Policy* (1938), *A Theory of Price Control* (1952) and *American Capitalism* (1952), he was already questioning Marshall's textbook models of free competition. In *American Capitalism*, he contended that big corporations could be balanced by other big corporations and above all by Big Labour. In *The Great Crash: 1929* (1955), Galbraith attributed the disaster of the Wall Street Crash of 1929 to reckless speculation.

Galbraith's visit to India in 1955 also affected his thinking. Working as an adviser to the Indian Statistical Institute, he developed a strong love and affinity for the peoples of India and their cultures. Returning to Harvard, Galbraith concluded that the economics he was teaching needed also to be adapted for students from the developing world. The contrast between the poverty of India and the affluence of 1950s America helped inspire one of Galbraith's most controversial books. In *The Affluent Society* (1958), he sought to shift the economic debate from issues of poverty to those relating to a country in which a majority of the population were middle-class consumers and in which the poor were a minority. In India the relationship between increased production and happiness was never in doubt, but in the United States that relationship could be questioned. Galbraith was increasingly critical of a society in which gross national product was being treated as an end in itself. Billions of dollars were now being spent upon wants and luxuries, encouraged by advertising, in the private sector, while important public concerns such as education, welfare, urban renewal and transportation were starved for funds. Galbraith described the discrepancy between private consumption and public expenditure as the 'social balance'. He was also one of the first American writers to express concern over what economic growth might do to the environment. *The Affluent Society* was not well received by a generation that had endured the Great Depression, enjoyed the stability of suburbia and did not mind having secure jobs. Nonetheless, the book helped focus attention on the persistence of poverty in urban ghettos, the Deep South and West Virginia, particularly after the Democratic Party came to power in 1961.

Galbraith had been a personal friend of Senator John F. Kennedy, who sometimes phoned him for advice. When Kennedy became president, he appointed Galbraith ambassador to India at the latter's request. Galbraith served in India from 1961 to 1963,

returning to Harvard after Kennedy's death. The new administration of Lyndon B. Johnson sought to address Galbraith's concerns over poverty, but Galbraith himself became further disillusioned by the Vietnam War. During this period he completed what is probably his most important book, *The New Industrial State* (1967).

Building upon *American Capitalism*, *The New Industrial State* called for a reconsideration of traditional theories of market competition. In an age of giant corporations and economic concentration, the traditional formulas of supply and demand did not apply as they once did. True, there were still hundreds of thousands of small entrepreneurs whose prices, wages and profits fluctuated according to the laws of supply and demand as Adam Smith and Alfred Marshall taught that they had. Companies like General Motors, American Telephone and Telegraph, IBM or General Electric, on the other hand, operated by a different set of rules. One had to qualify the notion of free enterprise when a thousand corporations accounted for half of all American goods and services. Instead of being subject to market forces, the big corporations were powerful enough to dictate them. They could organize preferential markets through defence contracts, collude to fix prices and create their own demand through advertising. Suppose Ford or Chrysler wanted to market a new car: Galbraith argued that they would do so knowing what the price would be in five years, what the demand would be and what the costs would be. This ability to plan meant the elimination of uncertainty and the supercession of the market; corporations control the market, not the consumer. The corporations are run by managers, who create and occupy the technostructure which controls planning; the managers do not directly reap profits, which go instead to distant shareholders. Some of the arguments in *The New Industrial State* had to some extent been heard before, notably in BURNHAM's *The Managerial Revolution* in

the 1940s, and concerns about vertical integration and excessive control had been voiced by Lewis HANEY in the 1920s. Galbraith, however, pulls these various strands of thought together in a powerful critique of corporate culture.

Further books such as *Economics and the Public Purpose* (1973), *Money* (1975) and *The Age of Uncertainty* (1977) reinforced Galbraith's reputation as the major economist of the American left and the chief academic opponent of Milton FRIEDMAN. The intellectual tide, however, was beginning to run strongly in Friedman's direction by the mid-1970s as the Keynesian remedies preached by Galbraith seemed unable to distribute shares of what seemed to be a shrinking pie. In spite of the neoclassical revival, Galbraith remained a Keynesian throughout the 1980s and 1990s. In an interview in 1994 he reiterated his belief that economies did not automatically operate on their own but needed some governmental direction (Galbraith 1994). In hard times, government should stimulate demand, and should restrain it during boom times. Underneath the new vogue of conservatism, Galbraith insisted that most American presidents, including Ronald Reagan, were still Keynesians even if they would not admit it.

In the 1990s Galbraith was still proud to call himself a 'liberal' at a time when even Democratic candidates shunned the label (in the United States the term 'liberal' connotes not a free market individualist as it sometimes does in Britain but rather a mildly collectivist position akin to that of New Labour or the Liberal Democrats). For Galbraith, the term connoted someone who supported the market where it worked and called for government action where it was needed, without being bound by any fixed ideology. When asked in 1994 what contribution he most wished to be remembered for, Galbraith replied that it would be his theory on how the corporate economy often operated in defiance of the laws of the market.

BIBLIOGRAPHY

Galbraith, John Kenneth (1938) *Modern Competition and Business Policy*, Cambridge, MA: Harvard University Press.

—— (1952) *A Theory of Price Control*, Cambridge, MA: Harvard University Press.

—— (1952) *American Capitalism*, Boston: Houghton Mifflin.

—— (1955) *The Great Crash: 1929*, Boston: Houghton Mifflin.

—— (1958) *The Affluent Society*, Boston: Houghton Mifflin.

—— (1967) *The New Industrial State*, Boston: Houghton Mifflin.

—— (1973) *Economics and the Public Purpose*, Boston: Houghton Mifflin.

—— (1975) *Money*, Boston: Houghton Mifflin.

—— (1977) *The Age of Uncertainty*, Boston: Houghton Mifflin.

—— (1981) *A Life in Our Times: Memoirs*, Boston: Houghton Mifflin.

—— (1992) *The Culture of Contentment*, Boston: Houghton Mifflin.

—— (1994) interview with Brian Lamb, C-Span, Booknotes, 13 November 1994, http://www.booknotes.org/transcripts/10076.htm, 13 December 2000.

Hession, C.H. (1972) *John Kenneth Galbraith and His Critics*, New York: W.W. Norton and Co.

Lamson, P. (1991) *Speaking of Galbraith: A Personal Portrait*, New York: Ticknor and Fields.

Rutherford, D. (1998) 'Galbraith, John Kenneth', in M. Warner (ed.), *Handbook of Management Thinking*, London: International Thomson Business Press, 238–42.

DCL

GALVIN, Robert William (1922–)

Robert William Galvin was born on 9 October 1922 in Marshfield, Wisconsin, into a devoted family of modest means which later became one of the wealthiest in the United States. Paul Galvin, Robert's father, suffered bankruptcy shortly after the birth of his only child. The family then moved to Chicago where, after experiencing another bankruptcy, Paul Galvin founded the Galvin Manufacturing Corporation in 1928 to manufacture battery eliminators. Located at 847 West Harrison Street, the concern employed only five workers upon opening. Within months, however, Galvin's new enterprise appeared doomed, as the market for battery eliminators evaporated. The older Galvin then astutely moved the company into an entirely new product line, the car radio. What was an unheard of and high-risk innovation in 1930 soon became commonplace in the expanding automobile culture which was sweeping the car-crazed United States. Galvin's first commercial automobile radio was dubbed the 'Motorola', a name signifying both motion and the radio. The product's popularity ultimately convinced Paul Galvin to rename the company Motorola in 1947.

Robert Galvin grew up in the Rogers Park neighbourhood on the north side of Chicago and Evanston, a suburb just north of the city. From the age of seven, he accompanied his father to company meetings and business trips across the country, which proved to be informal training for his eventual succession as head of Motorola. He attended Notre Dame University for two years before joining the US Army Signal Corps in 1942. At the end of the Second World War he returned to his father's company, working first as a stockboy and eventually as a production-line troubleshooter. By then Galvin Manufacturing was located on the west side of Chicago at 4545 West Augusta Boulevard. Galvin quickly advanced within the ranks before being promoted to executive vice-president

in 1948, and to president in 1956, only three years before his father died.

When Robert Galvin assumed the presidency of Motorola, the firm was earning $227 million a year manufacturing car radios, walkie-talkies, solid-state colour televisions and phonographs. Over the ensuing three decades, Galvin transformed Motorola into an $11 billion per year electronics colossus, employing over 100,000 people. As the president or chairman of Motorola, Inc. from 1956 to 1990, Galvin was the leading electronics executive in the United States. He was an advocate of 'virtual perfection', a manufacturing and production theory emphasizing 'total quality' for the final product. Proponents sometimes referred to this as the 'six sigma' philosophy. As a manufacturing strategy, virtual perfection marked a dramatic departure from the scientific management techniques developed by Frederick Winslow TAYLOR early in the twentieth century.

Motorola's success and longevity rested, in part, on Galvin's ability to adapt to changing conditions in the American economy. Like his father more than half a century earlier, Galvin completely abandoned historically successful but declining product lines for newer, high-risk commodities. In the mid-1980s, he led Motorola's move into miniaturizing pagers and cellular phones, just before those markets took off. By 1990 Motorola had jettisoned television production and was the leading manufacturer of two-way radios, cellular phones, pagers and advanced dispatch systems for commercial automobile fleets. The company was the fourth largest maker of semiconductors in the United States. Unlike International Business Machines (IBM), which faltered upon entering a new technological phase (moving from mainframe computers to personal computers), Motorola nimbly moved from conventional two-way radios and televisions to cellular radios and pagers.

In the second half of the twentieth century, Galvin was the foremost proponent of virtual perfection. In 1978, after a Motorola general

sales manager pointed out numerous poor features in Motorola's product line, Galvin began emphasizing 'total quality'. Galvin sought to create a corporate and production culture that did as much as possible to please the customer. In the 'six sigma' philosophy, Galvin sought a production goal in which all variations remained within six standard deviations from norm, or achieving a quality level of 3.4 defects per million; hence the label 'virtual perfection'. Galvin was influenced by the ideas of Joseph JURAN and other postwar industrial theorists, but in the end insisted that Motorola developed its own production philosophy and system.

Virtual perfection departed dramatically from the scientific management techniques developed by Taylor. Galvin believed the Taylor approach was outdated and a top-down phenomenon, evaluating and measuring factory-floor production at the level of the individual worker. By contrast, Motorola organized workers into independent, self-directed teams with no formal supervisor. Galvin sought 'to determine from the bottom up' what were the needs for production. He believed that virtual perfection ultimately saved immense amounts of time while producing a better quality product. Characteristically, there was never a single time-clock in any Motorola plant.

In the latter years of his career, Galvin became a proponent of new and innovative forms of industrial and business education. Beginning with the Motorola Training and Education Center, a corporate training department which opened in 1981, Galvin was one of the first to introduce continuous training programmes for employees in his American factories. Along with Motorola University and the Galvin Center for Continuing Education (1986), Motorola employed new delivery technologies such as computer-based training, electronic publishing, satellite communications and other interactive training systems to serve as both classroom facilities and electronic distribution points. Galvin envisioned Motorola University supplementing the existing system of higher education and enabling Motorola employees to attend in-depth seminars without leaving their work locations. Satellite-transmitted seminars soon replaced business trips. By 1985 Motorola devoted over one million hours to training 25,000 of its 90,000 employees worldwide, an investment of $44 million.

Motorola's success generated political appointments for Galvin. In 1970 he served on the US President's Commission for International Trade and Investment. From 1982 to 1985 Galvin chaired the Industry Policy Advisory Committee to the US Special Representative to the Multilateral Trade Negotiations. Galvin was also active in the Republican Party, serving as the finance chairman in several electoral campaigns of US Senator Charles Percy of Illinois.

By the 1980s Galvin was a leading advocate increasing trade relationships with Asian nations. During that time, Motorola attacked Japanese producers for 'dumping' cellular phones in the United States, a charge later upheld by the International Trade Commission, while restricting access to United States corporations in Japan. Galvin was later identified as a key architect in opening up the Japanese semiconductor market in 1986, and in leading Motorola's expansion elsewhere in Asia. In 2000 Motorola received permission to construct two additional large factories in China valued at $1.9 billion, making the firm the largest private corporation in China.

In 1990 Galvin retired as Motorola's chairman and was later succeeded by his son Christopher. Robert Galvin remained involved in long-term corporate planning as the head of Motorola's executive committee. He was inducted into the National Business Hall of Fame (1991) and received the National Medal of Technology (1991) and the Marshall Field Making History Award of the Chicago Historical Society (1995). Just prior to his retirement as chairman, Galvin was named one of the first recipients of the Malcolm Baldrige National Quality Award from the

Department of Commerce (1988). He is described by business reporters as 'the elder statesman of Chicago business' (*Chicago Sun-Times*, 9 July 2000).

BIBLIOGRAPHY

Galvin, R.W. (1991) *The Idea of Ideas*, Schaumberg, IL: Motorola University Press.

McKenna, J.F. (1991) 'Bob Galvin Predicts Life After Perfection', *Industry Week* 240, 21 January: 12–15.

Petrakis, H.M. (1965) *The Founder's Touch*, New York: McGraw-Hill.

Thompson, K.R. (1992) 'A Conversation with Robert W. Galvin', *Organizational Dynamics* 20(Spring): 56–9.

TG

GANDHI, Mohandas Karamchand
(1869–1948)

Mohandas Karamchand Gandhi was born in Porbandar, India on 2 October 1869, the son of a politician, Karamchand Uttamchand, and his wife Putalibai. He was assassinated by a Hindu zealot on 30 January 1948, in the garden of a house in Delhi belonging to the industrialist G.D. BIRLA. After education in India, he studied law in London and then returned briefly to India. In 1893 he moved to South Africa, where he practised law and helped to organize protest movements against the increasingly racist government. Returning to India in 1915, he became involved in the growing movement for Indian self-rule, particularly after the Amritsar massacre of 1919. With Birla's support he launched the 'Quit India' movement and was in time acknowledged by most Indians as the leader of the independence struggle. He won the respect of both Indian and British political leaders, and played a central role in making India an independent nation in 1948. Rabindranath Tagore dubbed him Mahatma, or 'Great Soul', a nickname still used by many to identify Gandhi today.

While in South Africa Gandhi had become involved with the labour movement, which was attempting to organize resistance to racism. On his return to India he also worked with labour movements, especially the textile workers union in Ahmedabad; here for many years he served as a conciliator, helping to work out problems between management and employees. Bose (1956) provides an overview of Gandhi's views on labour–management relations. To understand these fully, it is necessary to appreciate the nature of Gandhi's own thinking. Gandhi developed a political-religious philosophy drawing on Hindu and Jain thought, but also influenced by Islamic and Christian sources, including the writings of John Ruskin and Leo Tolstoy (Bose 1956; Hoffman 1998). Central to his doctrine were the concept of holding fast to truth (*satyagraha*), the idea of non-violent resistance to oppression, and the need for peaceful co-existence and mutual cooperation.

It is these three points – and especially the latter – which formed the foundation for his views on industrial relations. Gandhi absolutely eschewed a confrontational approach; he felt that the way forward was to persuade capital and labour that they shared common interests and a common goal, namely prosperity. For the one to achieve prosperity at the expense of the other, he felt, would be a violation of ethical principles and would contradict *satyagraha*: hence he was equally opposed to the oppression of workers and forced nationalization of industry. Only with great reluctance, as in Ahmedabad in 1918, would he advise workers to strike (on this occasion, he also undertook to fast until the strike ended; it was over in three days). His usual method was conciliation and negotiation, always with a view to finding common ground and persuading the parties towards it.

He advocated profit sharing, and encouraged enlightened employers such as Birla and TATA to provide more educational and health-care facilities for employees. At the same time, he stressed to workers the need for discipline and harmony, and advocated self-discipline or *sanyyam* ('blossoming when there is inner harmony as a result of inner strength', Bose 1956: 68).

The idea of mutual cooperation and the harmonization of the interests of workers and management has been advocated by many others, notably Robert OWEN and many of the later Victorian industrialists. Most took this position for reasons of either moral duty as employers or enlightened self-interest. Gandhi's system, however, stresses the essential equality of both parties, and thus that they have equal responsibilities in achieving and maintaining harmony. Although the elimination of confrontation is easier said than done, the possibilities inherent in Gandhi's system remain worth exploring.

BIBLIOGRAPHY

Bose, R.N. (1956) *Gandhian Technique and Tradition in Industrial Relations*, Calcutta: All-India Institute of Social Welfare and Business Management.
Hoffman, F.J. (1998) 'Gandhi, Mohandas Karamchand', in E. Craig (ed.), *Routledge Encyclopedia of Philosophy*, London: Routledge, vol. 3, 842–3.

MLW

GANTT, Henry Laurence (1861–1919)

Henry Laurence Gantt was born on a plantation in the state of Maryland on 18 May 1861, not long after the outbreak of the American Civil War. He died at his home in New York on 23 November 1919. The family home was several times in the path of one of the warring armies which fought across Maryland and northern Virginia from 1861 to 1865, and much of their farm was ruined; Gantt, indeed, grew up in an atmosphere of some hardship. The family fortunes later recovered somewhat and Gantt was educated at the McDonagh School, going on to Johns Hopkins University in Baltimore, where he received his AB degree in 1880. He returned to the McDonagh School and taught natural science and mechanics there for three years. In 1884 he secured a job as a draughtsman with an iron foundry and also attended the Stevens Institute of Technology, graduating in 1884 with a degree in mechanical engineering, a year after Frederick Winslow TAYLOR graduated with the same degree.

In 1887 Gantt joined the Midvale Steel Company in Philadelphia as an assistant in the engineering department. He then served for a little under two years as assistant to Taylor, then chief engineer, and worked with Taylor on the early development of the latter's famous system of management. Gantt was then promoted to superintendent of the casting department, and in 1893 left Midvale to take up a variety of technical and consulting positions around Philadelphia; his contact with Taylor became infrequent. In 1899, however, Taylor was called in to undertake his now famous consultancy project at Bethlehem Steel, and sent at once for Gantt. From 1899 to 1902 Gantt worked closely with Taylor and Carl BARTH on the consultancy. He remained at the plant for some months after the dismissal of Taylor and the subsequent purchase of Bethlehem by Charles M. SCHWAB, finally resigning in late 1902.

From 1902 to 1919 Gantt engaged in private consultancy work, initially in association with Taylor or one of the other members of his circle. His consultancy clients included Westinghouse, Canadian Pacific Railways, Union Typewriter, American Locomotive Company and a number of textile mills. Gantt also became friendly with Frank GILBRETH and his wife Lillian GILBRETH, and was particu-

larly interested in their work on motion study. He played a leading role in the promotion of scientific management; indeed, it was at his New York apartment in 1913 that supporters of the movement agreed to adopt the term to cover all their work. Significantly, Taylor was not present at the meeting, and relations between him and Gantt worsened as the latter grew closer to the Gilbreths. Gantt was also increasingly unwell, but this did not prevent him from undertaking war work in 1917, working with Frankford Arsenal and the Emergency Fleet Corporation.

Gantt's best-known work was undertaken at Bethlehem in partnership with Taylor. He is most known for two achievements: the development of the 'task and bonus' system and the invention of graphic charts for production control, the famous 'Gantt charts'. The task and bonus system actually has its origins in Taylor and Gantt's work at Midvale, and has been described as an improvement on Taylor's differential rate system. Under Gantt's system, the worker was given a specific stated reward if he or she could perform a task within the time allotted, and then a further bonus if he or she could significantly better that time. Like Taylor's system, the task and bonus system depended on management's first making an accurate study of the time required to perform a task. However, it was much simpler to administer and was perceived to be more equitable; Drury (1915) comments that by 1915 his wage system had largely replaced that of Taylor.

The first Gantt chart, known as a 'daily balance chart', was developed at Bethlehem for the purpose of describing the process of work. Updated daily, the chart showed how work was progressing and, says URWICK, facilitated 'continuous pre-planning of production' (Urwick 1956: 90). Gantt went on to develop other charts to depict costs and expenses graphically. 'The final evolution, the bar-chart which bears his name, made the important change of planning production programmes in terms of *time* instead of quantities. Nothing could be simpler than the Gantt Chart, yet

nothing could at the time have been more revolutionary' (Urwick 1956: 90).

Because Gantt worked so closely with Taylor, he is often overshadowed by the latter and his work is frequently seen as just another form of Taylorism. In fact, Gantt had important views on industrial relations that were recognized by Robert HOXIE, who treated Gantt's approach to labour as partially independent of that of Taylor, particularly with respect to the concept of justice for workers (Hoxie 1916). Gantt is now widely considered to be one of the founding fathers of the American industrial democracy movement. His own best-known book, *Work, Wages and Profits* (1910), takes as its theme the utilization of scientific management for the common good of both worker and employer:

Those who have given even superficial study to the subject are beginning to realize the enormous gain that can be made in the efficiency of workmen, if they are properly directed and provided with proper appliances. Few, however, have realized another fact of equal importance, namely, that to maintain *permanently* this increase of efficiency, the workman must be allowed a portion of the benefit derived from it.

(Gantt 1910: 23)

He goes on:

To obtain this high degree of efficiency successfully, however, the same careful scientific analysis and investigation must be applied to every labor detail as the chemist or biologist applies to his work. Wherever this has been done, it has been found possible to reduce expenses, and, at the same time, to increase wages, producing a condition satisfactory to both employer and employee.

(Gantt 1910: 23)

Gantt's thesis is simple: a properly conducted scientific investigation into the nature of work

at each plant will inevitably establish facts concerning the nature and value of the labour required to carry out those tasks. Once these facts have been established, labour and management can come to an easy agreement on the best form of remuneration. There will no longer be any need for a confrontational approach by labour to management, and vice versa, as the main sources of disagreement will have been removed.

For all his emphasis on science, Gantt's is not a rigid mind. He is opposed to cross-industry standards for judging work, and believes that each factory is an individual environment with its own standards and needs; investigations should not be applied generally, but should be conducted in each workplace separately. He is particularly adamant that scientific management is about principles, not rules:

The man who undertakes to introduce scientific management and pins his faith to rules, and the use of forms and blanks, without thoroughly comprehending the principles upon which it is based, will fail. Forms and blanks are simply the means to an end. If the end is not kept clearly in mind, the use of these forms and blanks is apt to be detrimental rather than beneficial.

(Gantt 1910: 8)

This may seem ironic coming from the inventor of the most famous process chart of all time, but Gantt was always adamant that the purpose of his charts was to provide information on which managers could make decisions, not to make the decisions for them. Even by 1910 he was aware of the potential straitjacketing effect which the use of charts and forms could have on less sophisticated managerial minds. Much of his later work argues for greater sophistication, creativity and training in management.

Personally, Gantt was a likeable man, much more successful as an apostle of scientific management than his dour colleague Taylor. Observers spoke of his flexible mind and adaptable outlook; a mutual friend commented that whereas Taylor would simply bore through an obstacle, Gantt would find a way around it, or even change goals altogether (Drury 1915). His work and writing both betray a strong concern for the human element in both work force and management. In 1929 the American Society of Mechanical Engineers and the Institute of Management jointly established the annual award of the Henry Laurence Gantt Gold Medal for distinguished achievement in industrial management as a service to the community. The first award was made, posthumously, to Gantt himself.

BIBLIOGRAPHY

Drury, H.B. (1915) *Scientific Management*, New York: Longmans Green.

Gantt, H.L. (1910) *Work, Wages and Profits*, New York: Engineering Magazine Co.; 2nd edn, 1913.

—— (1916) *Industrial Leadership*, New Haven, CT: Yale University Press.

—— (1919) *Organizing for Work*, New York: Harcourt, Brace.

Hoxie, R.F. (1916) *Scientific Management and Labor*, New York: D. Appleton and Co.

Urwick, L.F. (1956) *The Golden Book of Management*, London: Newman Neame.

MLW

GARNSEY, Gilbert Francis (1883–1932)

Gilbert Franics Garnsey was born in Wellington, Somerset on 21 March 1883, the son of William and Emily Garnsey. He died suddenly in London on 16 June 1932. Educated at Wellington School, he began his articles as an accountant in 1900, completing his final examinations in 1905. As a young man he was a keen footballer, playing on

several occasions with Aston Villa's second team. He joined the London office of Price Waterhouse and became a partner in 1913. Ill health prevented him from being accepted for military service, and he worked instead with the Ministry of Munitions throughout the war as an auditor and controller of accounts; he was knighted for his service in 1918. After the First World War he continued to serve in a number of public capacities. His work with Price Waterhouse involved him in several large-scale reconstructions and reorganizations, in which Garnsey branched out from simple accounting to more general consultancy and work as a 'company doctor', foreshadowing the work of today's corporate restructuring specialists. He came to public attention for his role in uncovering a massive fraud at the Royal Mail in the 1920s.

Garnsey was also a strong advocate of the need for more and better international accounting standards. His book *Limitations of a Balance Sheet* (1929) looks at criticisms of balance sheets as not providing enough information to investors. He refutes this charge up to a point, saying that balance sheets do what they set out to do, but investors need much more information than the balance sheet provides, and should look more broadly at the firm and at other aspects of its management beyond the financial basics. Companies should also address this issue and provide more and better information, particularly in areas such as earning capacity. The problem goes far beyond mere accounting: 'the problem would appear to be one of social philosophy rather than accountancy' (Garnsey 1929: 40). He finishes this passage with a caustic comment on the fecklessness of investors:

At the same time, it is desirable to point out that much valuable information which could be extracted from published accounts is frequently lost owing to the apathy of shareholders in general. When disaster comes, it is often those who were too apathetic to study the accounts in times of prosperity who are loudest in their denunciations.

(Garnsey 1929: 41)

Garnsey also became something of a specialist on consolidations and the development of holding companies. *Holding Companies and their Published Accounts* (1923) discusses some of the financial and accounting implications of holding companies. He describes how holding companies developed out of the general philosophy of consolidation, and his belief that combination is better than 'ruinous' competition. Combinations, he says, lead to low costs, the pooling of resources, expertise and knowledge, the reduction of duplication and so on. They also lead to many problems, not least of which is 'complexity of company organization and, consequently, a tendency to obscure results and thus deceive shareholders as to the real value of their holdings' (Garnsey 1923: 4). The book then goes on to set out best practice for holding company accounts. Again, the emphasis is on transparency; although Garnsey does not use this term directly, the concept is implicit. Garnsey's work helped pave the way for much work on accounting standardization worldwide later in the century.

BIBLIOGRAPHY
Edwards, J.R. (1984) 'Garnsey, Sir Gilbert Francis', in D.J. Jeremy (ed.), *Dictionary of Business Biography*, London: Butterworths, vol. 2, 487–90.

Garnsey, G. (1923) *Holding Companies and their Published Accounts*, London: · Gee and Co.

—— (1929) *Limitations of a Balance Sheet*, London: Gee and Co.

Garnsey, G. and Haydon, T.E. (1925) *The Secretary's Manual on the Law and Practice of Joint Stock Companies*, 19th edn, London: Jordan and Sons.

MLW

GATES, William Henry, III (1955–)

Bill Gates was born in Seattle, Washington on 28 October 1955 to William Henry Gates, Jr and Mary Gates. As home of the Boeing Corporation (see BOEING), Seattle in the early 1960s was already a city of the future. The Seattle World's Fair of 1962, with its Space Needle, took the theme of technology of the twenty-first century. The exhibits of the fair made a strong impression upon six-year-old Bill Gates. There he saw giant IBM main-frames, and an exhibit on the World of Tomorrow in which a futuristic office forecast inventions that could send electronic mail and machines that could talk to one another. The General Electric pavilion envisioned wall-sized television screens, videocassette recorders and personal home computers.

As a youth, Bill Gates was small and thin. Younger than his classmates, he still stood out in terms of mathematic and general intellectual ability. He had an IQ of 160–70 and a competitive, nonconformist manner that later helped to make him a successful entrepreneur. In 1967 Gates entered the all-male Seattle Lakeside School. Students here formed their own cliques, and Gates was remembered as a serious but talkative member of the maths and science clique. Maths and science students such as Gates tended to keep to themselves at Lakeside, but in the autumn of 1968 Gates made a discovery that would ultimately change the world for ever. In the maths and science building, Gates discovered an old teletype machine. With its keyboard, printer and telephone modem, it resembled the personal computer of the future.

When Gates first encountered computers, they had been in existence for thirty years without playing a dominant role in the economy. The first commercial computer of the early 1950s, the Universal Automatic Computer (UNIVAC) of Remington Rand, used vacuum tubes and was affordable only by the federal government and a few big firms such as General Electric. Transistors made it possible for IBM, Honeywell and a few others to build smaller machines in the late 1950s, but these were still cumbersome. Their application in business was limited until new computer languages such as COBOL (Common Business-Oriented Language) and FORTRAN (Formula Translator) let computers operate not just with binary digits but words and formulae. By the time Bill Gates was in secondary school, computers were using printed circuits, running several programs at the same time, and being used by companies in systems analysis. Gates joined the computer revolution when it was still in its infancy. Even though renting time on the teletype was expensive, its availability gave him the opportunity to pursue what soon became his overwhelming passion: writing programs.

While still a teenager, Bill Gates was already entering the world of business. At Lakeside he had made friends with another young computer enthusiast, Paul Allen. Both were very good at creating programs in a simple language called BASIC, and were hired to work for the school's Computer Centre Corporation, or C-Cubed. By 1971 Allen and Gates, both still in their teens, had set up their own company, Traf-O-Data. According to his own account in his book *The Road Ahead* (1995), Gates already had both a love for computers and a belief that they would one day become small, economical and powerful.

Gates entered Harvard in 1973, and, after completing his first year, went to work for Honeywell in the summer of 1974. By this time the world was on the verge of the personal computer revolution. By 1964 a new generation of computer hardware included the integrated circuit and with it, by the end of the 1960s, the silicon computer chip. The first Intel microchips were produced in 1971. As early as 1972 Gates was experimenting with the Intel 8008 microchip to see if it could be made to run BASIC programs. The 8008 was too small, but the 8080, introduced in the spring of 1974, had ten times its power. While still not powerful enough, it enabled Gates to

envision a different kind of computer that would be affordable and that would give himself and Allen a whole new marketing niche:

> Computer hardware, which had once been scarce, would soon be readily available, and access to computers would no longer be charged for at a high hourly rate. It seemed to us people would find all kinds of new uses for computing if it was cheap. Then, software would be the key to delivering the full potential of these machines. Paul and I speculated that Japanese companies and IBM would likely produce most of the hardware. And why not? The microprocessor would change the structure of the industry. Maybe there was a place for the two of us.
>
> (Gates 1995: 15)

From his Harvard dormitory, Gates sent letters to the major computer firms, offering to write them a version of BASIC for the new Intel chip. No one responded to his offer.

Bill Gates's genius was not so much in making his own inventions, however, as in bringing together the technology of others. He invented neither the microchip nor the desktop computer, but in 1975 he and Paul Allen married them for life in a way that would change the world. In January 1975 *Popular Electronics* magazine announced that a company called Model – later Micro, Instrumentation and Telemetry Systems (MITS) – had invented a small computer called the Altair 8080.

The Altair had no monitor or keyboard, and operated by flipping switches and flashing lights. Gates noted its limitations, for it lacked software, could not be programmed and was more a novelty than a tool. But he also sensed its potential, and the danger of not acting on that potential. His reaction was 'Oh no! It's happening without us! People are going to go write real software for this chip.' Although this 'would happen

sooner rather than later', Gates wanted to be involved from the start: 'The chance to get in on the first stages of the PC revolution seemed the opportunity of a lifetime, and I seized it' (Gates 1995: 16).

Gates and Allen set to work without either an Altair or an 8080 chip, but in the winter of 1975 they were able to write a BASIC program for the Altair within five weeks. The result was the birth of a company which Gates and Allen first called Micro-Soft, and eventually Microsoft. First based in Albuquerque, New Mexico, the firm soon relocated to Seattle. To make it work, both took risks: Allen left his programming job at Honeywell and Gates dropped out of Harvard in 1976. He felt it was worth the risk, for 'the window of opportunity to start a software company might not open again' (Gates 1995: 18).

In the beginning, Microsoft was a barebones operation in which Gates and Allen financed everything themselves. According to Gates, the key to Microsoft's success lay in their vision that there would soon be cheap computers everywhere, and that they would be in the right place at the right time to write the software for them:

> We got there first and our early success gave us the chance to hire many smart people. We built a worldwide sales force and used the revenue it generated to fund new products. From the beginning we set off down a road that was headed in the right direction.
>
> (Gates 1995: 18)

MITS was soon receiving many orders for its Altair computer. BASIC software began to spread, sometimes through pirated versions. By the end of 1976 Microsoft had contracts with several firms, including General Electric, and was grossing $100,000 a year. By 1977 and 1978 Microsoft was beginning to diversify, writing programs in COBOL and FORTRAN for microcomputers produced by Tandy, Commodore and others.

Gates advanced on the broadest of fronts, signing licensing agreements for his software with a number of computer companies in the late 1970s. His next client was Steve JOBS, who had founded Apple Computers in 1976. In April 1977 Jobs brought out his Apple II, which contained a spreadsheet called VisCalc and a word-processing program called WordStar. Gates recognized that people's decisions to buy computers were often based on the applications that came with them.

With Microsoft grossing $4 million per year by 1979, Gates now entered the applications market. The computer industry was beginning to standardize, and small businesses were now beginning to buy personal computers on a large scale in a market dominated at first by Radio Shack and Apple. According to Michael Flint (2000), the windfall for Gates and Microsoft came in 1980 when John Opel of International Business Machines (IBM) determined to enter the personal computer market. While utterly dominating the market in mainframes, IBM's executives recognized the threat of the microcomputer. Traditionally internalizing research, marketing and sales, IBM, in a race against time, was compelled to outsource its development of software.

The coming of the IBM personal computer would accelerate the standardization of the industry exponentially. IBM's team built its hardware from existing components that were readily available, permitting other companies to 'clone' the IBM technology. IBM used microchips from Intel, and licensed the operating system and applications from Microsoft. Gates worked closely with IBM technicians to produce the Microsoft Disk Operating System, or MS-DOS.

In August 1981 the IBM personal computer, backed by the giant's brand name, went on sale. Microsoft granted, for a one-time fee, the right to MS-DOS for IBM as its standard operating system. IBM sold DOS with its IBM 360 and later computers for only $60. This was smart marketing on the part of Gates, who saw far more long-term gains in defining the technical rules of the software market:

> Our goal was not to make money directly from IBM, but to profit from licensing MS-DOS to computer companies that wanted to offer machines more or less compatible with the IBM PC. IBM could use our software for free, but it did not have any exclusive license or control of future enhancements. This put Microsoft in the business of licensing software platform to the personal-computer industry.
>
> (Gates 1995: 49)

The IBM personal computer quickly began to capture the microcomputer market. By 1982 software companies were writing all sorts of applications compatible with it. Not only Microsoft Word and Excel, but Lotus Development's Lotus 1-2-3 were now written for both IBM and DOS. Any computer firm not compatible with this software began to go out of business. By 1984 DEC, Texas Instruments, Xerox and all others save Apple and the IBM clones had fled the personal computer market. The number of personal computers rose from two million to five million. By 1985 Microsoft was earning $150 million annually and employing 1,000 people.

Although Microsoft and IBM now dominated the market, Gates was never one for complacency. Apple, IBM's sole serious competitor, was creating a market for its popular Macintosh computers. The 'Mac', as it is known, was an extremely user-friendly machine. When one logged on to an IBM computer, one had to access files and applications via a cumbersome DOS code that used a confusing array of letters, numbers and punctuation marks. A Mac user turned on his machine and slid a device called a graphic user interface – or more popularly, a 'mouse' – across his or her desk. The mouse was connected to a pointer on the screen. Files were listed on the screen by pictures called icons. To

open a file, all one had to do was move the pointer over the icon and click on it. The file opened up as a window, several of which could be open at the same time. Gates knew by 1983 that both Microsoft and IBM would have to replace DOS with a similar type of operating system. By 1984 Microsoft Windows 1.0 was on the market and an instant success, preserving the dominance of the IBM-compatible computer.

By 1990 Microsoft was the world's largest software firm, a $1-billion corporation with offices in Britain, France, Germany, Ireland, Australia, Singapore, Indonesia and Malaysia. Windows 3.0, released in 1990, became standard software on most IBM-compatible computers, of which there were now at least fifty million. During the 1990s Microsoft earnings reached almost $6 billion in 1995, and $14 billion in 1998, by which time Microsoft was the most admired company in the United States, employed over 28,000 people, and had entered the entertainment industry through its merger with Dreamworks SICG and the creation of the MSNBC online news network. When Windows 95 was released in 1995, it was a major media and news event.

The next major challenge facing Microsoft was the coming of the Internet. This created an even more explosive revolution than the personal computer. From half a million online users in 1991 the number of had grown tenfold by the middle of the decade, when private providers began to take over the World Wide Web. This number grew tenfold again, to over forty million by 1998. Once again Gates faced a new challenge with the marketing by Netscape of Netscape Navigator, a browser software allowing users to connect with the World Wide Web. In August 1995 Microsoft released its own Internet Explorer 1.0, following it with Internet Explorer 2.0 in November 1995 and version 3.0 in August 1996. During 1997 Gates made an agreement with Apple in which the latter would install Internet Explorer as its default browser.

While Microsoft was the most admired corporation, and was surpassed in market value in 1997 only by General Electric and Coca-Cola, many compared it to the Morgan Bank or Standard Oil. Chief among these was the US Department of Justice, which in 1994 began investigating Microsoft for alleged monopolistic practices. On 21 May 1998 the federal government and twenty state governments filed an anti-trust action against Microsoft. The Department of Justice's Anti-trust Division argued that Microsoft was a clear monopoly that controlled 90 per cent of the software market. In November 1999 Federal Judge Penfield Jackson ruled that 'Microsoft engaged in a concerted series of actions designed to protect its monopoly power' (Cohen 1999: 63). The government alleged that the firm bound its browser into its Windows 98 operating system to shut out Netscape, pressured Intel out of the software market, and also sought to use its market advantage to coerce IBM, Compaq, Apple and others. The judge insisted that Microsoft, in its zeal to suppress its competitors, was depriving consumers of the new innovations a more open market would have brought.

In their defence, Gates and his attorneys argued that they had broken no law and acted only because they saw the new technologies of Netscape, Intel, Upstart Linux and Java as a potential threat in a highly competitive business in which today's software giant may be tomorrow's dinosaur. If Washington resorted to draconian anti-trust actions, no company would be able to protect its trade secrets from its rivals or itself from government regulation. The situation has not been fully resolved at time of writing.

In 1999 Gates published a second book, *Business @ the Speed of Thought: Using a Digital Nervous System*, in which he outlined his management philosophy. Business, he predicted, would change more in the next decade than in the last fifty years. The key issue in the 2000s would be about *velocity*, about how quickly the nature of business itself would

change. A company will have to adjust to market shifts in a matter of hours, not weeks. Gates argued that those business leaders who are able to react most quickly to rapid change and can empower their units and line employees to do the same will survive and prosper. Many decisions will no longer be made at the centre. Workers will need access to smart machines at their desks. Everything in a company will be put into digital form, for now, business decisions have to move at the pace of electronic markets' (Gates 1999: 412).

Regardless of the outcome of the government's anti-trust action, Bill Gates in the year 2001 remained in a position to shape if not dominate the course of the age of e-commerce. The richest and most influential business figure in the world in the 1990s, he is the unquestioned leader of the digital revolution.

BIBLIOGRAPHY

Cohen, A. (1999) 'Bill Gates' Monopoly: The Findings of Fact', *Time* 154(20): 60–69.

Flint, M. (2000) 'Microsoft History', in 'Microsoft and the Freedom to Subjugate', http://www.geocities.com/free2 subj/mshist.html, 28 November 2000.

Gates, B. (1995) *The Road Ahead*, with N. Myhrvold and P. Rinearson, New York: Viking Penguin.

——— (1999) *Business @ the Speed of Thought: Using a Digital Nervous System*, with C. Hemingway, NewYork: Warner Books.

Manes, S. and Andrews, P. (1994) *Gates: How Microsoft's Mogul Reinvented an Industry and Made Himself the Richest Man in America*, NewYork: Touchstone.

DCL

GAY, Edwin Francis (1867–1946)

Edwin Francis Gay was born in Detroit, Michigan on 27 October 1867, the son of Aaron and Mary Gay. He died at Pasadena, California on 8 February 1946. His father was a prosperous timber merchant. Gay was educated at schools in Michigan and in Europe before taking an AB in philosophy and history from the University of Michigan in 1890. He then went to the University of Berlin for graduate study in medieval history. Becoming attracted to the scholar's life, he remained in Europe for the next twelve years, studying at various universities including Leipzig, Zurich and Florence, and finally completing his Ph.D. at Berlin in 1902. He had married his university classmate Louise Randolph in 1892; a notable scholar herself, she accompanied Gay to Europe and worked with him. Both the Gays would later recall this as an idyllic time in which they were able completely to immerse themselves in their passion for study.

In 1902 Gay returned to the United States and took up a post as instructor in economics at Harvard University. Both his intellectual power and hitherto undiscovered administrative talents marked him out as a rising star, and he was made professor and chairman of the department of economics in 1906. When Harvard's president, Charles Eliot, began developing his plan for a business school, Gay was one of his key advisers in the run-up to the school's establishment in 1908.

Eliot's first choice for dean of the new school was William Lyon Mackenzie King, formerly an instructor in economics at Harvard and now deputy minister of labour in the Canadian government. King turned the post down (he went on to become Canada's longest serving prime minister), and in February 1908 the post was offered to Gay, who accepted with reluctance. Once having taken up the post, however, he worked indefatigably to make Harvard Business School a success, winning the admiration of the school's supporters and opponents alike. After his initial reluctance

was overcome, Gay came to see the School as a chance to combine scholarship and action:

> To fashion, build, and manage a school which would train men for business as a profession; to bring his wide range of knowledge to bear on planning and guiding that training; to inculcate an awareness of the social obligations and consquences of business enterprise; and to do this for a country that was travelling fast toward economic maturity and preeminence – here indeed was a call to active service that could not be declined.
>
> (Heaton 1952: 69)

His commitment to Harvard Business School was total; as Charles Eliot later said, 'he transferred himself body and soul to the new School, put all his time and strength into it' (Heaton 1952: 74).

Gay was working with no models to guide him; only the universities of Pennsylvania and Dartmouth had previously established graduate schools of business (the Wharton and Tuck schools, respectively). No matter how much managerial and academic talent he was able to recruit to the school, the blueprint for it had to be his own. It was Gay who determined the guiding philosophy of the school, which he saw as resting on two key ideas. First, he defined the task of the business manager as 'making things to sell at a profit (decently)'. Second, he defined the school's own task as 'to experiment and to learn what the *content* and *form* should be for the training of mature students primarily for "making" or "selling"' (Heaton 1952: 76). The key qualities necessary in a successful manager were courage, judgement and sympathy, and it was the school's role to inculcate and strengthen these in students through education.

It was Gay who determined that the degree offered by the school would be called 'Master of Business Administration', a title which became adopted around the world. It was Gay too who adapted the case system pioneered

by Harvard Law School to the study of management. This proved to be a difficult task, as there was no pre-existing body of case material. A key ally here was the publisher and writer Arch W. SHAW, an early and enthusiastic supporter, who was tasked by Gay with building up a bank of case studies. Innovatively, Shaw began developing 'living' case studies as well as written ones, giving students a chance to study 'live action' problems. Shaw was also a moving force behind the establishment of the Bureau of Business Research, one the initial functions of which was to supply case study material.

Most important of all, Gay sought to move away from the traditional format of classroom lectures, towards teaching methods that would involve and challenge students and stimulate their imaginations. Melvin COPELAND, who was recruited by Gay in 1909 and asked to begin teaching a marketing course at thirty-six hours notice, later recalled encountering Gay a couple of weeks after teaching had begun. When the dean asked how the course was going, Copeland replied, 'I have found enough to talk about so far.' 'That is not the question,' replied Gay. 'Have you found enough to keep the students talking?' Copeland, taking the broad hint, abandoned his lecturing style for one of classroom discussion, and followed this through the rest of his career. Much later, he realized that Gay had selected him as a 'guinea pig' for introduction of classroom discussion and the case method in marketing (Copeland 1958: 59–60).

By his own admission, Gay had no business or management experience. He proved adept, however, at finding people who had such experience and winning them over to his cause. This was not altogether easy: many of the captains of industry approached proved to be inadequate teachers, while others lacked the time to commit to the venture. Gay several times approached Frederick W. TAYLOR, the founding father of scientific management, but was repeatedly rebuffed; he then turned his attention to Taylor's associate Carl BARTH,

and by dint of persistence eventually persuaded Barth to give a course of lectures. Barth was won over, and so too was Taylor, who taught occasionally at the school until his death. Gay also recruited the important academic figures who would be the cornerstone of Harvard Business School in its early years, such as W.J. Cunningham and especially Paul CHERINGTON, the school's first professor of marketing. Realizing early on that established academics would have difficulty adapting to his methods, he also sought out new talent, recruiting men such as Melvin Copeland and inculcating them with his vision. Other important figures like Arch Shaw, T.W. Lamont and the economist Wesley Clair MITCHELL became key supporters.

By 1917 the school was beginning to prosper and Gay, exhausted, resigned as dean. He served as adviser to the US Shipping Board during the First World War. In 1919, deciding not to return to Harvard, he accepted an offer from Lamont to take over the editorship of the New York *Evening Post*, which the latter owned. This move was not a success, and in 1924 the newspaper went bankrupt. Gay then returned to Harvard as a professor of economic history, where he remained until he retired in 1936. Moving to California, he served on the research staff of the Huntingdon Library until stricken with pneumonia in January 1946. He died the following month.

Gay's achievements at Harvard Business School were considerable. The pedagogic methods he developed there were widely imitated: the case method remains standard at most business schools today. Gay's philosophy of business education likewise remains at the heart of most thinking on the subject. His personal managerial accomplishment in getting the school off the ground should not be overrated; the progenitor of the case study could himself be regarded as a useful case example of developing and carrying through a highly successful innovation. Heaton's tribute to him is by and large an accurate assessment of his character and methods:

The early history of the School had something of the flavour of a cause, a crusade, or a movement beyond the frontier of educational settlement, with Gay as leader, inspirer, and challenger. He never told his colleagues what to do, for he would not have known what instructions to give. Instead he sent them off to explore, with a double piece of advice: to remember that there were no experts in this new field and that the printing of a statement did not make it authentic. His own faith, resourcefulness, and expenditure of energy impelled them to give the best that was in them, so that each man made his full contribution to the policies and programs that were a team product rather than the achievement of any one person.

(Heaton 1952: 81)

Yet Gay himself, in his later years, regarded his own career as a failure. In 1908 he had departed from the historical and economic research that he loved, and was never able to recapture the passion for his work that he had felt in his youth. He wrote to a friend in 1935: 'It is one of my serious regrets that I ever undertook the deanship of the Business School' (Heaton 1952: 6).

BIBLIOGRAPHY
Copeland, M. (1958) *And Mark the Era: The Story of Harvard Business School*, Boston: Little, Brown.
Heaton, H.K. (1952) *A Scholar in Action: Edwin F. Gay*, Cambridge, MA: Harvard University Press.

MLW

GEDDES, Eric Campbell (1875–1937)

Eric Geddes was born in Agra, India on 26 September 1875, the son of Acland Geddes

and his wife Christina. He died suddenly on 22 June 1937 at his home in Sussex. His father was a civil engineer; his mother was notable for her organization of the School of Medicine for Women at the University of Edinburgh, and was the sister-in-law of Elizabeth Garrett Anderson, Britain's first practising female doctor. He married Alice Stokes in 1900. Geddes was educated in Britain, although with mixed results; he developed a rebellious streak and was expelled from four different schools, and later confessed that he did not find much of interest to him at school (Grieves 1985). In 1893 he went to the United States, where he worked at a variety of jobs including labouring in one of Andrew CARNEGIE's steel mills, selling typewriters and working in a lumber yard. He also worked as a brakeman on freight trains and as an assistant yard master on the Baltimore and Ohio railway, experience that he was later able to turn to useful account. However, he returned to Edinburgh in 1895 with less money than when he had set out.

Family connections enabled him to get a job in India with a timber firm. He proved a success at this, managing his timber yard competently and also extending the company's light railway which hauled timber out of the Himalaya foothills. In 1899 the agent for an Indian railway, the Rohilkund and Kumaon, saw the line and was impressed enough to offer Geddes a job; by 1901 he was the railway's traffic superintendent. In 1904 he supervised the movement of troops on the Northwest Frontier during a Russian invasion scare, and won the congratulations of the commanding general, Lord Kitchener, for his efficiency. At the end of the year Geddes was offered job in Britain with Great North-Eastern Railways, as claims agent, and thereafter rose rapidly through the ranks of the company's management; by 1911 he was deputy general manager, with the promise of the top job when the incumbent, Sir Alexander Butterworth, retired a few year later.

The outbreak of the First World War led to a decisive break in Geddes's career. In late

1914 he once again met Lord Kitchener, who also introduced him to the then minister of munitions, David Lloyd George. Recalling Geddes's services in India, Kitchener asked Geddes to go to France to study the railway system used by the British Expeditionary Force for supplying troops at the front. This study was never actually conducted, but Lloyd George, impressed by Geddes's energy, asked him to take up a post in the Ministry of Munitions; by early 1915 Geddes was deputy director-general of munitions supply, responsible for running the national arsenals and for supplying arms and ammunition to the front. In early 1916, when a serious shortage of artillery shells developed, Geddes took personal charge of the manufacturing effort, introduced effective production planning and control, and helped create the huge flow of munitions which enabled the British to fight the Battle of the Somme that summer. For this effort, Geddes was knighted in 1916.

In September 1916 the government at last succeeded in finding a role for Geddes in managing the military railways in France. He was appointed director-general of transportation, and was assigned to the staff of Field Marshal Sir Douglas Haig in France, with the rank of major-general. He got on well with Haig, who placed great trust in him and gave him carte blanche to shake up the army transport system. By 1917, again through the application of systematic planning, scheduling and control, Geddes had greatly improved the army's transport, and the flow of supplies and troops to the front.

By now Geddes was being regarded as something of a miracle worker. In April 1917 Britain was facing defeat thanks to the efforts of the German U-boats, which were crippling Allied merchant shipping. The admiralty, under First Sea Lord Sir John Jellicoe, the victor of Jutland, appeared to be unable to organize a response. In May 1917 Geddes was appointed to the admiralty as a controller, with a seat on the admiralty board and the rank of vice-admiral (uniquely, for a few

months he held this rank along with his earlier rank of major-general). His brief was to increase the flow of naval supplies and make the navy more effective. He met with obstruction and obfuscation at every turn; the senior naval officers bitterly resented the intrusion of a civilian into their affairs, and Geddes did not have the authority to compel them to provide him with the information he needed. Accordingly, in July 1917 Geddes was made First Lord of the Admiralty, the civilian equivalent of the First Sea Lord, and given full powers to reform the navy. After insisting on the dismissal of the obstructive Jellicoe, Geddes was able to introduce a number of administrative reforms which made the navy more efficient and played a small but significant role in the defeat of the U-boats.

After the war Geddes was due to return to Great North-Eastern Railways, but none of the parties involved seem to have been keen to see him return to civilian life. He was released from his contract with the railway and remained in government. He was already active in politics, having resigned his military commissions and having served as MP for Cambridge since 1918; Grieves (1985) credits Geddes with the famous phrase coined during the election campaign that year, that when exacting war reparations from defeated Germany, the latter should be 'squeezed until the pips squeak'.

Geddes helped organize the new Ministry of Transport, taking over as minister on the department's foundation in 1919. In 1921, at Lloyd George's request, he chaired the Committee on National Expenditure, which recommended and oversaw the swingeing cuts in government expenditure in 1922 that came to be known as the 'Geddes Axe'. But by then, says Grieves, Geddes was already becoming disillusioned with politics; the challenges of wartime achievement had been replaced by penny-pinching and petty bickering, and Geddes looked in vain for some task to accomplish. Not finding it, in 1922 he resigned his cabinet post and his seat, and left politics.

Employment for a manager of his talents was not long in coming. Dunlop Rubber Company, one of the first companies to produce pneumatic rubber tyres for bicycles and automobiles, had been founded in 1888 by a Belfast veterinarian, John Dunlop, who had patented the original pneumatic tyre. Dunlop had for some time been one of the largest and richest of British companies, but by the early 1920s it had run into trouble, thanks to feckless management by its then chairman, Sir Arthur du Cros, and was losing money. When du Cros resigned as chairman in 1922, Geddes was invited to take his place. He threw himself into the job with his customary energy. Getting rid of a number of inefficient managers and reassuring the company's bankers, he then embarked on a strategy of acquisitions which both broadened the manufacturing base and diversified its product line. Geddes also emphasized product quality, and secured a number of endorsements from celebrity users of Dunlop tyres, including Captain Malcolm Campbell, holder of the world land speed record (in a car using Dunlop tyres), which raised brand profile and assisted advertising. He also implemented accounting and cost control procedures, and shook out the company's organization with a view to improving efficiency at all levels. Finally, he invested heavily in research and development with a view to bringing new products onto the market that would put Dunlop ahead of its competitors.

As if chairing one large international company was not enough, Geddes in 1924 also accepted the chairmanship of the recently formed Imperial Airways. This was quite a different affair from the private sector, highly competitive and market-oriented Dunlop; Imperial Airways was a state company and subject to some extent to the Ministry of Transport and the Air Ministry. Geddes's dual strategy was to protect the fledgling airline from excessive interference by ministry officials (of which he had of course recently been one) and to grow its business, expanding routes and fighting off competition from the Dutch

airline KLM. Imperial Airways grew steadily under Geddes's tenure; after his death he was succeeded as chairman by John REITH, who oversaw its transformation into British Overseas Airways Corporation (BOAC); today it is known as British Airways.

Geddes found time in his career to write one book, *Mass Production: The Revolution which Changes Everything* (1931), which remains of some interest to the historian. Geddes saw in mass production a revolution as powerful as those in politics and science. Mass production, he says, does not mean merely producing goods in large quantities; it also includes specialization and division of labour with machinery, with the double aim of improving quality and decreasing waste. It means a rise in the number of 'mental' as opposed to purely manual workers, with consequences for society. He had by 1931 an ambivalent view of the role of the state; he was against free trade and in favour of protectionism, but largely, it seems, because all of Britain's competitors were also protectionist. He was opposed to state ownership of industry, but he believed that the state could play an important role in supporting industry.

The manager's manager, Geddes was a success at virtually every task he undertook, seemingly proving the view that the main ingredient in successful management is the application of principle. Geddes's approach to management, in the civil service, the military or the commercial world, would have gladdened the heart of any proponent of scientific management. His first step was always to gather information, and armies of assistants and researchers would spend weeks collecting data and analysing it into a series of reports which gave a clear picture of the present situation. Then Geddes would act decisively, allocating resources and setting up organizations and schedules, and all the while monitoring the progress of each project through accounts and reports. As Grieves says:

Geddes employed an analytical method to the formulation of problem-solving techniques which was based on a quantitative evaluation of the relevant section of the organisation. His approach valued teamwork, and his staff were recruited for the purpose of collecting data and providing information to assess the effectiveness of managerial intervention. It was a practical approach of measurement and reorganisation to promote frameworks of efficiency without too much regard for the political context or ideological assumptions.

(Grieves 1985: xi)

A tall man with a sometimes ebullient personality, he did not suffer fools gladly, but could be endlessly patient and charming when necessary. His own worst enemy appears to have been boredom; as at school so in later life, when Geddes found he was being insufficiently challenged he would look around for something else to do. He remains one of the most professional and successful men to occupy a position of managerial responsibility in Britain in the twentieth century.

BIBLIOGRAPHY
Bagwell, P.S. (1974) *The Transport Revolution*, London: B.T. Batsford.
Geddes, E. (1931) *Mass Production: The Revolution which Changes Everything*, London: Dunlop Rubber Co. Ltd.
Grieves, K. (1985) *Sir Eric Geddes: Business and Government in War and Peace*, Manchester: Manchester University Press.

MLW

GENEEN, Harold Sydney (1910–97)

Harold Sydney Geneen was born in Bournemouth, England on 22 January 1910 to

Samuel and Aida Geneen. He died in New York on 25 November 1997. His father, a merchant, was of Portuguese Jewish ancestry, his mother was Italian. Harold himself was raised as a Catholic. In December 1910 the Geneens emigrated to the United States. By 1915 they had separated, with Samuel pursuing a business career, Aida a singing career, and Harold placed in a boarding school.

According to biographer Robert Schoenberg (1985), Geneen had a relatively happy youth in spite of his broken home, although he found it hard to trust others as he felt deserted by both parents. Attending the Suffield School near Hartford, Connecticut from 1917 to 1926, he excelled in mathematics. He could not at first afford to enter college, so he began working as a page on the New York Stock Exchange. During the 1920s the work was profitable, but Geneen saw little future in it for himself. He wanted something more steady.

Between 1928 and 1934 Geneen put himself through night school at New York University, majoring in accounting. By 1932 he was working for the Mayflower Associates, landing a job even at the worst of the Great Depression. His degree helped him find work, and in 1934 he moved on to Lybrand, Ross Brothers, and Montgomery, where he worked until 1942. Geneen distinguished himself from the others around him by his single-minded dedication to his work. He loved figures for their own sake, for they told him the whole story of a company. He took the profit and loss of his clients, says Schoenberg, personally and seriously.

By the time the United States entered the Second World War in December 1941, Harold Geneen was bored with his job and sought a more challenging position with a producing industry. He found it in January 1942 with Amertorp, a subsidiary of the American Can Company. By May he was hard at work designing an accounting system for the firm's plant in Forest Park, Illinois. His next task was setting up a cost control system at the firm's St Louis plant. This system had to track the cost of every component in every torpedo. Geneen's system sent an envelope with every part and punched a ticket at every operation. The system made it possible to pinpoint any production defect, slowdown or problem.

When Geneen really wanted more than all else, according to Schoenberg (1985), was a career in which he would have complete control and responsibility. He achieved this dream in stages. His next career move was to Bell and Howell in 1946, but within a year he had moved to the steel firm of Jones and Laughlin, where he remained for twelve years. Here Geneen further developed his accounting methods, partly inspired by those of Alfred P. SLOAN of General Motors, for turning around a struggling firm. Geneen wanted to know the profit on each product line, and organized accounting as far down as he could in the production chain. Steel production was a volatile business, and managers would often lay off workers at random, or whole departments, during a downturn. Geneen had a much more practical approach: every division should have a downsizing plan for every 10 per cent of lost returns. These plans would involve more than layoffs, and include shift reductions and other economies.

A bigger challenge waited Geneen when he was hired by the Boston technological firm of Raytheon in June of 1956. Managed by Charles Francis Adams, Jr, Raytheon was a company in trouble. Even though it had $175 millon in revenues, its stock had recently plummeted to one-quarter of its former value. Raytheon, a firm of brilliant scientists and unprofitable managers, managed to stay afloat thanks to its military contracts for the Hawk and Sparrow tactical missiles.

Geneen discovered that the non-military sector of the company was losing money badly. The management was rigidly centralized and had little idea how each of the divisions were doing. The key to Geneen's approach was improving the ratio between returns and expenses, and eliminating any calculation not

concerned with profit. He met with the firm's engineers in order to explain to them that greater profits meant more resources for their research. Geneen worked systematically to slash inventory costs by requesting the armed forces pay more in advance. By subcontracting, he passed fully 50 per cent of Raytheon's inventory costs on to the subcontractors.

As he had done before, Geneen set up profit and loss accounting in the smallest divisions possible. The company was to be run systematically on the basis of what Geneen called *competitive ratios*. Geneen calculated the ratio of sales/personnel and sales/profit, and applied these ratios throughout all Raytheon operations. He then set the goal of 3 per cent net profit on sales, 10 per cent on civilian contracts, and 18 per cent on shareholder investment.

One of Geneen's most unique innovations was the monthly financial and operating meeting. Here he would scrutinize closely the detailed reports of his managers. These reports were not mere ledgers, but contained explanations of the figures. A management policy group met once a month, where full reports from every unit were submitted. Every division knew what was going on in every other division. Geneen would pick up details from these memos that no one else could. He wanted all management problems to be aired in the open. Norman Krim, a Raytheon manager, quotes Geneen:

Above all it is important that there be no 'covering up' of our problems at any management level ... If I were to look for any single indication of management's strength *or ability in any company* ... the degree of 'openness and objectivity' in appraising its own performance would be the single most important index of management's strength.
(Schoenberg 1985: 89)

According to Schoenberg (1985) and Sampson (1974, 1996), Geneen was seen as intrusive and heavy-handed by many in the firm, who resented his tampering with Raytheon's paternalistic culture which seemingly minimized the importance of profit. He pressured employees to work nights, and to put the firm above even their families. But the figures spoke for themselves. Geneen's techniques freed over $30 million in money for profitable investment. Sales rose from $175 million to $375 million between 1956 and 1958. Raytheon became the top employer in Massachusetts.

Geneen's controversial but remarkable success finally enabled him to acquire a presidency of his own, in a firm much bigger than Raytheon. On 10 June 1959, Harold Geneen became president of International Telephone and Telegraph, better known as ITT. On the surface, says Anthony Sampson in his *Sovereign State of ITT* (1974), ITT looked formidable, a giant conglomerate with 116 plants in over twenty countries and sales of almost $766 million. Geneen's keen eye nonetheless saw the clay feet of the giant. ITT's management structure was very loose. It was more a loose collection of uncoordinated companies than a single firm. The European companies were totally separate from the North American and Latin American branches. The United States accounted for only one-fifth of ITT's $29 million profits; politically volatile Latin America accounted for one-third of all ITT earnings. No one knew what ITT earned in profits until the end of a business year.

Wherever he looked, Geneen found lack of organization, duplication of effort and many unprofitable contracts. The European ITT firms basically depended upon servicing the government telephone monopolies of their various countries, which kept rates down while preventing investment in new systems. In Latin America, ITT monopolized the telephone systems in Brazil, Chile and Peru, as well as Puerto Rico and the Virgin Islands.

Geneen's maxim was that managers ought to *manage*. He fired many of the unprofitable managers and brought in some of his associates from Raytheon. Managers, he felt, ought to lead instead of merely reacting to problems.

They needed a conscious long-term strategy as to what their firm should achieve, and where it ought to be one, two or five years in the future. Unlike his predecessor, Sosthenes Behn, who ran ITT from his home, Geneen moved the firm's headquarters into a tall office tower on New York's Park Avenue. Here he set up what Anthony Sampson described as 'the most intricate and rigorous system of financial control that the world has ever seen' (Sampson 1974: 70). The Raytheon system of regular meetings, systematic reports, ratios, targets, five-year plans and close oversight by Geneen was applied to ITT on a much bigger scale.

In March of 1963 Geneen prepared a memo in which he was quite pessimistic about the investment climate in Europe. He saw the governments there becoming more hostile to the United States and more nationalistic. With over 80 per cent of its trade and investments overseas, Geneen wanted ITT to be more American. The large amount of investment in Latin America was a cause of concern to him, especially when Fidel Castro expropriated the ITT phone company in Cuba. Geneen proposed that ITT begin to acquire American firms, so that by 1970 a majority of its earnings would come from domestic, not foreign sources. He began to buy companies in many diverse fields which he thought would be profitable. Geneen, however, had a particular interest in service companies with transferable technology.

During the 1960s, according to Sampson, the multinational enterprise truly came into its own, as did the conglomerate form of business organization in which totally unrelated companies were joined together in a single corporate organization. ITT was the prime example of this trend. Geneen first made an alliance with the Lazard Frères investment bank, whose capital it used to acquire a number of companies. First, there was the car rental firm Avis, followed by Sheraton Hotels, Continental Insurance, the publisher Howard Sams, William Levitt's housing firm, Pennsylvania Glass Sand, Continental Baking and many others.

Under Geneen, ITT's revenues grew from $765 million in 1959 to a gargantuan $22 billion in 1978. The conglomerate operated 400 companies in seventy countries and employed 425,000 people by 1974. Not everyone was happy with Geneen's formula for success. Robert Townsend of Avis, bought out by ITT, lamented what he saw as the rigidity of Geneen's business culture and its detrimental impact upon small, creative individualistic firms. When ITT tried to acquire the American Broadcasting Corporation in 1966, it was blocked from doing so by the United States Justice Department.

When the Justice Department also sought to prevent ITT from acquiring Hartford Insurance, the company lobbied against it and gave the Republican Party $400,000 for it 1972 campaign. This revelation, published in early 1972, tarnished ITT's image. The revelations regarding ITT activity in Chile were even more damaging. Geneen, conscious of the fact that 12 per cent of ITT's profits came from its Chilean telephone company, offered the Central Intelligence Agency $1 million to prevent the Marxist government of Salvador Allende from expropriating ITT's holdings. Allegations of similar activities in Indonesia, Iran, Mexico and other countries eventually surfaced as well, further undermining ITT's reputation (Sampson 1996).

The Chile revelations of 1973 were the beginning of the end of Geneen's career with ITT (Schoenberg 1985). The conglomerate's stock plunged from sixty dollars to twelve. The United States Internal Revenue Service ruled that ITT's acquisition of Hartford Insurance was not tax free, and that it owed the agency $100 million. Mergers no longer granted ITT the huge growth they had in the 1960s. While the company was still making money, the rate of profit began to decline. Avis and Levitt began to lose money, and Europe entered a long period of economic stagnation. ITT's image was now tarnished, its meetings

picketed and its offices bombed on several occasions.

Geneen remained a brilliant manager to the end, but as he faced the possibility of a perjury indictment (which was never filed), ITT's board of directors decided not to renew his contract, and, aged sixty-seven, on 1 January 1978, he surrendered the presidency to Lyman Hamilton. His own health failing due to palsy, Geneen nevertheless worked as an independent investor until his death.

Shortly before his death in late 1997 Geneen, at the age of eight-seven, published *The Synergy Myth, and Other Ailments of Business Today*. In this work, he summarized his lifelong management philosophy. As in his 1984 book *Managing*, he reiterated that there was 'no secret, no magic formula' to business success save 'the old-fashioned virtues of hard work, honesty, and risk taking' (Geneen 1997: xii). Management fads such as Theory Z and Total Quality Management were in his mind 'baloney'. The biggest flaw in managers was the unwillingness to take risks. This, in Geneen's mind, was as bad for business as laziness and dishonesty. He felt particular disdain for the term 'synergy', which he felt was nothing but hope that somehow a merger would be greater than the sum of its parts.

Geneen continued to defend the usefulness of the conglomerate, in spite of the fact that only ITT, General Electric and two others were now listed by the *Wall Street Journal* as being such. Reflecting upon ITT, he made the point that its very diversity gave it choices which more focused companies lacked. General Motors lives and dies by cars, but ITT could sell both telephone service and bread: 'The conglomerate is the ideal vehicle for exploiting the rich possibilities of risk taking without jeopardizing the corporation's survival.' If risk was like a bucking bronco, 'a conglomerate is the vest way to enjoy the ride' (Geneen 1997: xvi).

One of the most effective managers in history, Harold Geneen contributed to the art of management the ability to coordinate and operate a huge multinational with many component firms and effectively integrate the smallest part with the whole. He was the epitome of scientific management and control accounting carried to its logical extent. After Geneen, even though the large centralized conglomerate form began to lose its appeal, the science of detailed budgeting and planning would be regarded as an absolute necessity for a competitive firm (Schoenberg 1985).

BIBLIOGRAPHY
Barnet, R.J. and Müller, R.E. (1974) *Global Reach, The Power of the Multinational Corporations*, New York: Simon and Schuster.
Geneen, H. with Moscow, A. (1984) *Managing*, Garden City, NY: Doubleday.
────── (1997) *The Synergy Myth, and Other Ailments of Business Today*, with B. Bowers, New York: St Martin's Press.
Sampson, A. (1974) *The Sovereign State of ITT*, Greenwich, CT: Fawcett Publications.
────── (1996) *Company Man, The Rise and Fall of Corporate Life*, London: HarperCollins Business.
Schoenberg, R.J. (1985) *Geneen*, New York: W.W. Norton and Company, Inc.

DCL

GESTETNER, David (1854–1939)

David Gestetner was born in Csorna, Hungary in March 1854 and died in Nice on 8 March 1939. He married Sophie Lazarus in 1885, and they had seven children. Leaving school at the age of thirteen, he worked at a variety of jobs in Vienna before emigrating to the United States in 1873, where he sold paper kites and helped run a laundry. Returning to Vienna in 1876 he joined an uncle's glue and gelatine

manufacturing business where, as a spin-off from the main business, he began making equipment for hectographs (a copying process which used gelatine pads to create an impression). In 1879 he left this business and moved to London, where he went to work for the stationers Fairholme and Company in Shoe Lane. Here he patented a new copying process, the cyclostyle, which used perforated stencils and ink pads; with this machine, once the stencil had been prepared, a skilled operator could make a copy every ten seconds. For the first time, offices had access to a cheap and efficient duplicating machine.

With the support of Fairholme, Gestetner set up a small workshop and began making and selling cyclostyles, and appointed an agent to sell for him in the United States. He also continued to make and patent improvements to the original cyclostyle design. The relationships with both Fairholme and the American agent were uneven, with a number of disputes over patents and rights, and eventually Gestetner took over sole rights to the patents and began developing his own factory. In 1909 he built a factory in Tottenham, North London, which was extended in 1919. He also organized his own in-house sales force and set up branches around the UK. Overseas expansion followed, and in the 1920s subsidiary companies were established in Europe, North America and India.

Much of the overseas expansion following the First World War was driven by Gestetner's son Sigismund, who took over as chairman of the firm in 1922. Whereas David Gestetner was at heart an inventor, albeit one with a shrewd grasp of the market and its needs, Sigismund was an organizer and better all-round manager. Both father and son shared a number of common traits, however. Both were strong believers in training, and Gestetner was a pioneer in in-house sales and sales management training. Both also believed strongly in maintaining good relations with employees, and placed a strong emphasis on teamwork.

Gestetner understood early that one of the keys to successful office management is the transmission of information. By developing machinery to enable documents to be duplicated quickly and cheaply, he helped businesses to speed up their information flows and become more efficient. Duplicating machines have since been supplanted by other forms of technology, but the basic principle behind their use remains the same. Along with Samuel MORSE, Thomas EDISON and other inventor-entrepreneurs of the late nineteenth century, Gestetner helped lay the groundwork for the information revolution.

BIBLIOGRAPHY

Shaw, C. (1984) 'Gestetner, David', in D. Jeremy (ed.), *Dictionary of Business Biography*, London: Butterworths, vol. 2, 519–25.

MLW

GETTY, Jean Paul (1892–1976)

Jean Paul Getty was born on 15 December 1892 in Minneapolis, Minnesota and died of a heart attack, while suffering from prostate cancer, at Sutton Place in Surrey on 6 June 1976. He was the son and sole surviving child of George Franklin Getty, an insurance attorney and oil investor, and Sarah Catherine McPherson Risher. In 1903 his father purchased 1,100 acres near Bartlesville, Indian Territory (now Oklahoma) and, after striking oil on this land in 1904, moved his family to the town of Bartlesville. Despite his youth, Getty quickly displayed an astute sense of business enterprise, and developed a keen interest in the oil industry and in his father's oil-prospecting firm, which had been incorporated as the Minnehoma Oil Company. George Getty decided in 1906 for personal reasons to relocate

his family from the Indiana Territory to southern California, but Jean Paul Getty spent time each summer as a teenager working in his father's oil fields around Tulsa. After graduating from high school in 1909, he took a job with his father's oil-prospecting firm.

Getty briefly attended the University of Southern California before transferring to the University of California at Berkeley in 1911, but later withdrew and enrolled at Oxford University. In 1913 he sat for and earned a noncollegiate diploma in economics and political science, and then embarked on a tour of Europe before returning to the oil fields of Oklahoma. As a student, he had a reputation for being less interested in study than in travel and in achieving the means that would permit him to pursue the life he imagined for himself.

In September 1914 Getty was surveying oil fields and, with his father's backing, started buying up low-priced oil leases in the so-called red-beds area of Oklahoma. Contrary to prevailing wisdom, these leases proved to be rich in oil deposits, and by buying and selling these oil leases and drilling wildcat oil wells in Oklahoma, Getty made his first million dollars by June 1916. After achieving economic success, including being named a director in his father's oil company, he left Tulsa for Los Angeles. He remained in southern California for two years, where it was presumably much easier to pursue another of his life's interests – women. In 1918 Getty returned to the family's Oklahoma-based oil business, but encouraged his father to enlarge the firm's oil business to the new oil fields in California. By 1922 the Gettys' Californian oilfields were a significant part of the family business. In March 1923 his father suffered a heart attack and during his absence, Jean Paul assumed the role of supervisor at George F. Getty, Inc. It was also during this period that the tensions between father, mother and son became more strained and more public.

Upon his father's death in 1930, Getty assumed the presidency and became general manager of George F. Getty, Inc. In 1933 he acquired complete control when he purchased 18,000 shares of stock from his mother. Getty pursued an expansionary strategy throughout the 1930s and acquired a majority interest in Pacific Western, California's largest oil company at the time. The economic crisis of the Great Depression in the United States provided Getty with the opportunity to buy up the stock of rival oil companies at depressed prices. He embarked on a campaign to acquire Tidewater Associated Oil Company, but was opposed by Standard Oil. Since Standard Oil controlled Tidewater through the Mission Company, Getty began buying stock in Mission and had purchased 40 per cent of Mission's stock by 1936. Getty would ultimately acquire Tidewater, but did not achieve that control until 1951.

In 1937 Getty acquired Skelly Oil. One of the subsidiaries that Getty acquired with Skelly was Spartan Aircraft. After the United States entered the Second World War, Getty telegraphed the under-secretary of the navy, James V. Forrestal, to offer his services. The navy declined his offer for active duty but did encourage Getty to gear up his industrial capacity for the war effort. During the war, Spartan Aircraft manufactured spare parts and trainers for the military. Getty personally supervised this wartime production, and boasted of Spartan's reputation and record of wartime production. In the years after the war, Spartan converted its manufacturing capacity and profitably produced mobile homes.

Like other aspects of his life, there are alternative interpretations of Getty's motives. Since he had toured Europe widely throughout the 1930s and had developed friendships with some officials in Nazi Germany, there were those who questioned his loyalties and judgement. Accordingly, his commitment to the American war effort was interpreted by some as evidence of his patriotism, while others cynically dismissed his efforts as an attempt to rehabilitate a damaged reputation.

In 1949 Getty, through Pacific Western, moved to expand his oil business into the

Middle East by obtaining a sixty-year lease from King Saud of Saudi Arabia for a concession in the lands, known as the Neutral Zone, between Saudi Arabia and Kuwait. Getty was assuming significant risk since oil had not yet been discovered in this particular region. Getty agreed to a compensation scheme that required sizeable payments even if oil remained undiscovered. After a number of initial dry wells and an investment of some $30 million, a substantial oil reserve was discovered in February 1953, and Getty's fortune went from millions to billions.

After having finally gained control of the Mission Company and having become its president, Getty renamed Pacific Western the Getty Oil Company in 1956. Getty also purchased the first supertankers to transport oil, increased the number of retail gas stations and built a new refinery in Delaware. As well as his holdings in oil, real estate and manufacturing made Jean Paul Getty one of the world's richest men. Getty's holdings would ultimately include some 200 companies, with around 12,000 employees. *Fortune* magazine's 1957 pronouncement that Getty was the world's richest man brought him a level of celebrity that drew attention to his life and personality. Admired by some for his relentless and even ruthless business practices, and detested by others for these same practices, as a celebrity Getty became an icon of what was either good or bad about American business. For example, there is the often repeated story of the billionaire Getty installing pay phones in his country mansion. Getty claimed he did this so that his guests would not feel they were imposing on him; others interpreted it as a miserly act worthy of a character similar to Charles Dickens's Scrooge.

Beginning in the 1930s, Getty was a celebrated collector of fine art, including paintings, sculpture, carpets, tapestries, eighteenth-century French furniture and English silverware, and rare and first-edition books. He founded the J. Paul Getty Museum in Malibu, California in 1953. In 1970 construction began on a new structure for the museum, which was completed in 1974 at a total cost of around $1 billion. After his death in 1976, Getty's will endowed it with an additional $1.2 billion after probate, making it one of the world's richest museums. His country estate, where he lived for the last twenty-five years of his life, became the Getty Arts Centre.

Despite his many business achievements and the accumulation of vast personal wealth, Getty's personal life was marked by few enduring relationships and hardship. He was married and divorced five times and had five sons, one of whom died in adolescence and another of whom committed suicide as an adult. In July 1973 Getty's seventeen-year-old grandson J. Paul Getty III was kidnapped in Italy and held for ransom for five months before he was released, minus his right ear. The celebrity of the Getty name helped make this one of the world's most infamous kidnapping cases. Getty had initially rejected the kidnappers' demand, insisting that any payment would create an incentive to harm his other fourteen grandchildren. Ultimately he loaned his son, Eugene Paul, enough money to pay the kidnappers.

In the years after the Second World War Getty spent little time in the United States, living and controlling many of his businesses from hotel suites in Paris and London. In 1959 he moved to Sutton Place, a sixteenth-century Tudor mansion in Surrey, so as to remain close to his lucrative Middle Eastern oil interests. As he grew older, Getty became increasingly reclusive and dysfunctional, and misery seemed to haunt his descendants. When asked about his legacy, Getty quipped, 'money doesn't necessarily have any connection with happiness. Maybe with unhappiness.' At the time of his death, Getty's personal wealth was estimated at $2–4 billion.

BIBLIOGRAPHY
Getty, J.P. (1965) *How to be Rich*, New York: Jove.
——— (1976) *As I See It: The*

Autobiography of J. Paul Getty, Englewood Cliffs, NJ: Prentice-Hall.

Lenzner, R. (1985) *The Great Getty: The Life and Loves of J. Paul Getty, Richest Man in the World*, New York: Crown Publishers.

Miller, R. (1985) *The House of Getty*, New York: Henry Holt.

TES

GHOSHAL, Sumantra (1948–)

Sumantra Ghoshal was born in Calcutta on 26 September 1948. He was educated in the United States – he holds Ph.D. degrees in management from both Massachusetts Institute of Technology (MIT) and Harvard Business School. He is presently Robert P. Bauman Professor in Strategic Leadership at the London Business School, where he is a member of the strategy and international management faculty. Prior to joining the London Business School he taught at INSEAD in Fontainebleu, France and at MIT's Sloan School of Management in the United States. Ghoshal serves on the editorial boards of several academic and professional journals, and speaks frequently at top management conferences in Europe, North America and Asia on topics related to strategy and organization of transnational companies, the changing roles and tasks of corporate leaders, and the challenges of managing radical change. He maintains teaching and consulting relations with several companies around the world, and serves as the chairman of the supervisory board of Duncan-Goenka, a large diversified business group in India.

Described by the *Economist* as a 'Euroguru', Ghoshal's research focuses on strategic, organizational and managerial issues confronting large, global companies. He first came to prominence with the book *Managing Across Borders: The Transnational Solution* (1989), co-authored with Christopher Bartlett. It has been listed in the *Financial Times* as one of the fifty most influential management books of the twentieth century, and has been translated into nine languages. *The Differentiated Network: Organizing the Multinational Corporation for Value Creation*, co-authored with Nitin Nohria, won the George Terry Book Award in 1997. Another work, *The Individualized Corporation*, also co-authored with Christopher Bartlett, won the Igor Ansoff Award for strategy in 1997, and has been translated into seven languages. In all, Ghoshal has published ten books, over forty-five articles and several award-winning case studies.

Apart from coining the much-used word 'transnational', *Managing Across Borders* became one of the boldest and most accurate pronouncements of the arrival of a new era of global competition and truly global organizations. *The Individualized Corporation* marked a further step forward in the thinking of Ghoshal and Bartlett; here they show how new, revitalizing organizational forms are continuously emerging.

In the 1980s, Ghoshal started by categorizing existing firms into three forms:

1. The multinational or multi-domestic enterprise, as exemplified by Unilever or Philips, whose strength lies in a high degree of local responsiveness. It is a decentralized federation of local firms linked together by a web of personal controls (expatriates from the home country firm who occupy key positions abroad).

2. The global enterprise, such as Ford and Matsushita, whose strengths are scale efficiencies and cost advantages. Global scale facilities, often centralized in the home country, produce standardized products, while overseas operations are considered as delivery pipelines to tap into global market opportunities. There is tight control

of strategic decisions, resources and information by the global hub.

3. The international enterprise whose strength is its ability to transfer knowledge and expertise to overseas environments that are less advanced. It is a co-coordinated federation of local firms, controlled by sophisticated management systems and corporate staffs. The attitude of the parent company tends to be parochial, fostered by the superior know-how at the centre.

Ghoshal and Bartlett then suggest that global competition is forcing many of these firms to shift to a fourth model, which they call the transnational (as typified by Percy BARNEVIK's ABB). This firm has to combine local responsiveness with global efficiency and the ability to transfer know-how better, cheaper and faster: 'a company that is big and small, global and local, decentralized but with central control'. The transnational firm is a network of specialized or differentiated units, with attention paid to managing integrative linkages between local firms as well as with the centre. The subsidiary becomes a distinctive asset rather than simply an arm of the parent company. Manufacturing and technology development are located wherever it makes sense, but there is an explicit focus on leveraging local know-how in order to exploit worldwide opportunities.

The demise of the divisionalized corporation – as illustrated by Alfred SLOAN's General Motors – lies at the heart of Ghoshal and Bartlett's work in the 1990s. They point to the difficulties of managing growth through acquisitions; and the dangerously high level of diversity in businesses which have acquired companies indiscriminately in the quest for growth. They have also declared as obsolete the assumption of independence among different businesses, technologies and geographic markets which is central to the design of most divisionalized corporations. Such independence, they say, actively works against the prime need: integration and the creation of 'a coherent system for value delivery'.

Pointing out the difficulties of 'implementing third-generation strategies through second-generation organizations run by first-generation managers', Ghoshal mapped and recorded the death of a variety of corporate truisms (for example, William Whyte's *Organization Man*). 'Third generation strategies are sophisticated and multi-dimensional. The real problem lies in managers themselves and the real challenge is how to develop and maintain managers to operate in the new type of organization,' he says.

Using a purpose–people process model, Ghoshal exhorts companies to develop self-renewal abilities. 'You cannot renew a company without revitalizing its people. Yet you cannot teach an old dog new tricks. But what you can do, is to change the smell of the place.' Adults do not change their basic attitudes unless they encounter personal tragedy. Events at work rarely make such an impact. If organizations are to revitalize people, they must change the context of what they create around people. 'The oppressive atmosphere in most large companies resembles downtown Calcutta in summer', says Ghoshal. 'We intellectualize a lot in management. But if you walk into a factory or a unit, within the first 15 minutes you get a smell of the place.' Vague and elusive though 'smell' sounds, Ghoshal believes that it can be nurtured. 'Smell can be created and maintained – look at 3M in the US or HDFC in India. Ultimately the job of the manager is to get ordinary people to create extra ordinary results.'

To do so requires stretch and discipline, a concept illustrated by Intel as led by Andrew GROVE. Ghoshal explains:

At Intel there is constructive confrontation. It is demanded that you explain your point of view. The flip side is that at the end of a meeting a decision is made and you have to commit to it. Stretch and discipline are the yin and yang of business.

The need to revitalize is often overlooked by successful enterprises. 'Satisfactory under-performance is a far greater problem than a crisis', he says, pointing to the example of Westinghouse which is now one-seventh the size of General Electric in revenue terms.

Over 20 years, three generations of top management have presided over the massive decline of a top US corporation yet 80% of the time the company thought it was doing well. Westinghouse CEOs were very competent and committed. They'd risen through the ranks and did the right things. Yet they presided over massive decline.

Companies blazing trails today are those who have moved beyond strategy-structure systems to purpose ('the company as a social institution held together by shared values'); people ('helping individuals to become the best they can be'); and process ('primary organizing devices'). Three core processes enable companies to switch from the vicious cycle of unprofitable growth into a virtuous one of profitable growth: an *entrepreneurial* process to drive the externally oriented opportunity-seeking behaviour of their companies; an *integration* process to link and leverage their diverse resources and competencies lodged in different business, regional or functional areas; and a *renewal* process constantly to challenge the existing ways, to prevent past success formulae from ossifying into a recipe for future disaster. No doubt these factors are less hard and robust than the three Ss, but Ghoshal, believes they are the way forward.

BIBLIOGRAPHY

Bartlett, C.A. and Ghoshal, S. (1989) *Managing Across Borders: The Transnational Solution*, Boston, MA: Harvard Business School Press.
—— (1992) *Transnational Management: Text, Cases and Readings*, New York: Richard D. Irwin.

Ghoshal, S. and Bartlett, C.A. (1997) *The Individualized Corporation*, New York: HarperCollins.
Ghoshal, S. and Westney, D.E. (eds) (1993) *Organizing Theory and the Multinational Corporation*, London: Macmillan and New York: St Martin's Press.
Goshal, S., Piramal, G. and Bartlett, C.A. (2000) *Managing Radical Change: What Indian Companies Must Do To Become World-class*, New Delhi: Penguin Books.
Hendry, J., Eccles, T., Ghoshal, S. and Williamson, P. (1992) *European Cases in Strategic Management*, London: Chapman and Hall.
Lorange, P., Scott Morton, M. and Ghoshal, S. (1986) *Strategic Control*, St Paul, MN: West Publishing Co.
Mintzberg, H., Quinn, J.B. and Ghoshal, S. (1995) *The Strategy Process: European Perspective*, London: Prentice-Hall.
Nohria, N. and Ghoshal, S. (1997) *The Differentiated Network: Organizing Multinational Coporations for Value Creation*, San Francisco: Jossey-Bass.

GP

GIANNINI, Amadeo Peter (1870–1949)

Amadeo Peter Giannini was born in San Jose, California on 6 May 1870 and died in San Mateo, California on 3 June 1949. Giannini was the son of Italian immigrants. He attended school through the eighth grade, and then began working for his stepfather's wholesale produce company. Giannini was so successful in this business that he became a partner by the age of nineteen. In 1901 Giannini sold his interest in the firm to his employees and retired. A year later, however, he was asked to manage his recently deceased father-in-law's large estate, which included a seat on a bank

board in San Francisco's North Beach area. This experience gave Giannini insight into the business potential of meeting the financing needs of small borrowers, and in 1904 he organized the Bank of Italy to meet this goal. Initially, the bank made small loans mostly to Italian merchants, farmers and labourers, and his direct contact with customers and then unconventional promotions expanded the bank to nearly $1 million in assets within two years.

The banking crisis caused by the Panic of 1907 convinced Giannini that only large banks were truly safe, but most large banks of the day did not attend to the needs of small customers. To make his bank bigger in a way that would still serve small borrowers, he successfully pushed for state banking laws to permit branch banking. During the 1910s he acquired several small banks and made them into branches of the Bank of Italy. In 1928 Giannini took advantage of liberalized banking regulations created by the McFadden Act of 1927 to expand and reorganize his banking interests. He formed a holding company, Transamerica Corporation, and converted Bank of Italy to a national charter. This conversion allowed Giannini to buy banks with strong branch networks in other states, and within a year his banking operations stretched from California to New York, as well as Italy. In 1930 he reorganized his bank holdings into two firms, the nationally chartered Bank of America National Trust and Savings Association, and the state-chartered Bank of America for his California operations. In 1933 changes in the law allowed Bank of America National Trust and Savings Association to absorb the state-chartered bank as well. The Bank of America built its business primarily by serving small businesses and individuals. It was also the first to create an extensive branch banking system. It was one of the largest and most innovative banking firms in the world, and its work helped transform modern banking practices.

Giannini left Transamerica shortly after this reorganization, but soon returned to help guide the firm through the banking crises of 1932–3. His leadership helped the company weather the Great Depression, and by 1939 the total assets of the bank had doubled to $1.6 billion. The growth of Giannini's banking business, however, drew increased criticism from competitors, and in 1949 the Federal Reserve Board held anti-trust hearings that eventually forced Transamerica to sell all its banking stock except that of Bank of America.

Giannini did not live to see the partial dismantling of his banking empire, but at the time of his death Bank of America was the world's largest commercial bank, with over 500 branches in California, and offices worldwide. Transamerica Corporation was also a large diversified conglomerate controlling banks, financial institutions, real estate and industrial companies. Although it never reached his goal of a worldwide network of branch banks, Giannini's bank was important in the economic growth of California and the Pacific coast region.

BIBLIOGRAPHY
Bonadio, F.A. (1994) A.P. Giannini: Banker of America, Berkeley, CA: University of California Press.
Nash, G.D. (1992) A.P. Giannini and the Bank of America, Norman, OK: University of Oklahoma Press.

DM

GIBBS, Antony (1756–1815)

Antony Gibbs was born in Exeter, Devon, one of eleven children of George Gibbs, a surgeon, and Anne Vickery Gibbs. He died in London on 10 December 1815. After an education at Exeter Grammar School, Gibbs served an apprenticeship with Brook, a cloth exporter trading with Spain. Gathering knowledge of

the Spanish market, Gibbs set up his own business as an exporter to Spain and Italy in 1778, and also joined his brother Abraham as part-owner of a woollen mill. In 1784 he married Dorothea Hucks, daughter of a Yorkshire wine merchant; they had seven children.

In 1789 Gibbs ran into financial troubles and went bankrupt. The reasons for this failure are unclear, but they may relate to the worsening political situation in Europe, which was having an effect on trade. The next two decades saw Gibbs involved in a desperate struggle to keep his business ventures alive through a series of continental wars; only his own tenacity and ingenuity allowed him to succeed.

Determined to repair his fortunes and repay his debts, Gibbs moved his young family to Madrid in 1789. He first worked as an agent for English exporters to Spain, then moved to Malaga and invested his meagre capital in a business exporting Spanish produce to England. He nearly went bankrupt again when Spain went to war with England in 1797, and was forced to relocate to neutral Portugal; here, however, he developed a profitable business smuggling English cloth into Spain via Lisbon. When peace came in 1801 he established a merchant house in Cadiz, the principal Spanish port trading with Latin America, and was able to develop his first tentative contacts with Mexico and Peru. The Cadiz house was forced to close when war again intervened in 1805, and Gibbs fell back on his business interests in Portugal once more. However, when Spain joined the anti-French coalition in 1808, Gibbs was finally able to put the Cadiz business on a firm footing. After re-establishing the business there he returned to England, where he proceeded to develop the firm's growing trade with Spain, Portugal, Gibraltar and Latin America. The firm, now called Antony Gibbs and Son, finally managed to clear its debts and entered a period of great prosperity.

As a manager, Gibbs was primarily a builder. Circumstances required this; only in the last seven years of his life did the political situation allow him to expand the business as he might have done had times been more peaceful. But the business structure he had laid was strong and enduring; it was based on a network of contacts in three countries, and the beginnings of a further network in the New World. Under his son and successor, Henry Gibbs, permanent establishments were opened in Lima in 1822, Guyaquil in 1823 and Valparaiso in 1826. In the 1850s and 1860s, the Spanish and Latin American contacts paid off with the granting to the firm of a monopoly in the shipment of guano from Peru. This highly lucrative trade resulted in huge profits, which the firm used to develop its banking operations; by the 1870s, Gibbs was the largest merchant bank in the City of London. Histories of the House of Gibbs universally pay tribute to its founder, whose career demonstrates how firmness of purpose is one of the central management virtues.

BIBLIOGRAPHY
Gibbs, J.A. (1922) *The History of Antony and Dorothea Gibbs*, London: Saint Catherine Press.
Mathew, W.M. (1981) *The House of Gibbs and the Peruvian Guano Monopoly*, London: Royal Historical Society.
Maude, W. (1958) *Merchants and Bankers*, London: Antony Gibbs and Sons Ltd.

MLW

GILBRETH, Frank Bunker (1868–1924)

Frank Bunker Gilbreth was born in Freeport, Maine on 7 July 1868 to Hiram and Martha Gilbreth. He died in Montclair, New Jersey, on 14 June 1924. Gilbreth attended Boston English High School. While he was an average student, he had a mechanically adept mind

and passed his entrance examinations for the Massachusetts Institute of Technology. However, he chose instead to go to work for Whidden and Company Construction, where he was hired in a quasi-management training position. Later, from 1895 through 1911, he was president of Frank Gilbreth Construction, and, starting in 1912, he and his wife formed Gilbreth Consulting, Incorporated. In February 1921 he was honoured by being asked to display his motion study work at the Olympic Exposition in London. He also received an honorary LLD from the University of Maine in 1920.

At Whidden Construction, his first assignment was as a bricklayer's apprentice, but he was not satisfied with merely learning a skill. He wanted to know why his instructors laid a brick using one set of motions when working on their own, and different motions when they were teaching him. These observations were the beginning of Gilbreth's pioneering work in motion study and ergonomics, and led to his first invention. At the age of twenty-four, he was granted the first of many patents for what he called his 'non-stooping scaffold'. This scaffold was designed to improve the rate at which bricks were laid. However, the truly significant fact was that the design intentionally reduced the amount of stress and fatigue on the workers' backs. Prior to his invention, bricklayers spent most of their time bending over to pick up bricks and then mortar, both of which were kept beside the worker's feet. With Gilbreth's scaffold, a second level was added, at the worker's waist height, for the storage of materials. The scaffold would be raised so that the top of the wall, being built, was always even with the worker's torso. In this way, the worker could lay more brick in a day and would be less fatigued, particularly in terms of back strain.

In 1895 Frank Gilbreth formed his own construction company, which built projects all over the United States. With little in the way of formal management training, the success of his company was the result of a growing system of acquired knowledge, which Gilbreth called his 'field system'. He was once advised that he did not have a system unless it was written down, and he took this advice to heart. The field system was a written set of rules and standards. These standards were based on past experience of what methods worked and what did not. His long-standing rule was that anyone could make an alternative suggestion, but this change would have to be evaluated and found to be more efficient before it was adopted. If the new rule was accepted, the developer was paid for the suggestion and a new standard established.

The summer of 1903 marked two important events in the history of business management. Frederick W. TAYLOR presented his paper called 'Shop Management' before the American Society of Mechanical Engineers, and Frank Gilbreth first met his future wife and business partner, Lillian Moller (see Lillian GILBRETH). These two events led to the later formation of Gilbreth Consulting Engineers. During their courtship, Frank told Lillian that he wanted two things from their marriage. First, he wanted her to be not only his wife but also his business partner. He needed someone who could learn the business and help him with improvements. His second desire was that they should have twelve children, and more specifically six boys and six girls. The often comical aspects of the Gilbreth 'dozen' were made famous by the books *Cheaper by the Dozen* and *Belles on Their Toes* written by two of their children.

Gilbreth later read Taylor's paper on shop management. In this paper, he thought he found the epitome of his own efforts to systematize the operation of his construction company. This inspired the Gilbreths to write their first books: *Field System* (1908a) and *Concrete System* (1908b) and later, *Bricklaying System* (1909). Frank Gilbreth became almost obsessed with Taylor and his system, which later came to be known as scientific management. Taylor in turn became interested in Gilbreth's work in bricklaying

improvements, where the output of bricklayers had been increased from an average of 125 bricks per hour to 350. Taylor later included a chapter on Gilbreth's work in his book *Principles of Scientific Management*, first published in 1911.

While he was an ardent supporter of Taylor and his system, Frank Gilbreth believed that he and Lillian, who was then studying for her doctorate in psychology, could help to improve the Taylor system, using their motion study work and by developing a greater emphasis on the human factor, an element largely absent from Taylor's system. Unknown to Gilbreth, the last thing Taylor wanted was what he called 'those damned improvements'. Taylor felt that his system, as written, was perfect and should not be tinkered with. Indeed, Taylor and his disciples on several occasions did everything they could to squelch the Gilbreths' consulting practice.

Ironically, after Taylor's death, these same disciples (notably Sanford Thompson and Horace Hathaway) then tried to take credit for many of the Gilbreths' innovations and even claimed that Taylor first came up with the idea of motion study. This notion is negated by two letters exchanged between Frank Gilbreth and Frederick Taylor, in 1913. In a letter to Taylor, Gilbreth, who had just patented his micromotion study apparatus, offered to give the system to Taylor. Taylor, who felt the system was no more than a gadget, replied that Gilbreth was the better man to develop the system.

In modern parlance, people talk about 'time and motion studies' as if they were somehow linked as a system. However, the two systems were never used together until more than twenty-five years after Frank Gilbreth's death (Jaffe 1984). Taylor's time study was a part of a system to optimize the output of workers. He would study the basic tasks performed, using a stopwatch to measure the times of the best workers. These times would then be used to formulate piecework pay to reward workers able to meet the new standard. In contrast, the Gilbreths' system of motion study did not establish time standards, but instead established standards for how materials and tools could best be designed and arranged to fit the abilities of the human worker. In his free moments Gilbreth championed causes ranging from the rights of the disabled to the Simplified Spelling movement.

As with his early experiences in bricklaying, Frank Gilbreth believed that there was One Best Way to perform a task, not one best time, as Taylor's system promoted. The Gilbreths later would call their system 'The One Best Way To Do Work'. Their book, *Motion Study* (1911), was significant in that it contained detailed lists of various physical, mental and sociological attributes of the individual. This study drew two important conclusions: (1) that with the wide variety of attributes and exponential combinations of these attributes, there was no such thing as an average worker, but (2) there were some commonalties which could be addressed. The first of these common aspects the tackled by the Gilbreths was fatigue.

Studies and papers examining fatigue were numerous during Gilbreth's lifetime. However, these studies either focused on measuring the worker's physical endurance or called for reducing the length of work days (which in this era ranged from twelve to sixteen hours per day). In their book *Fatigue Study* (1916), the Gilbreths asked, why should we measure the limits of fatigue (which they knew would vary from person to person); why not simply eliminate *all unnecessary fatigue* by eliminating wasted motions and make the remaining work as simple as possible? In this way, a business would provide optimum conditions, which would allow each worker to perform at their best.

A prime example of their fatigue work involved modifying chairs and workbenches to meet the individual statures of the workers. They recognized that excessive reaches for tools and parts caused unnecessary fatigue, and they designed many simple appliances to

reduce this overexertion. Recognizing that fatigue was also caused by remaining in one position all day, they invented the concept of the 'sit-stand' workstation.

The final piece of the motion study system developed when the Gilbreths became interested in ways to employ disabled workers. They found that by analysing the essential elements of a task, and with minor design accommodations, the majority of jobs could be performed by people with almost any type or combination of disabilities. Not only was this ground-breaking work in the movement to employ the disabled, it drove home the point that, no matter the condition or need, the workplace could and should accommodate the physical needs of the worker.

Frank Gilbreth developed numerous methods for studying the motions of workers. He first employed the fledgling field of motion pictures, where films of work tasks were studied frame by frame. Owing to the great expense of this method, he invented the cyclegraph and chronocyclegraph. These methods used time-exposed photographs in combination with flashing lights attached to the workers' hands or head. The results showed not only the path of travel of the motion, but the time it took to complete. Charts and other analysis methods were also developed to track unnecessary or overly fatiguing motions. In order to set standards in the study of motions, the Gilbreths identified seventeen different motions, which they called *Therbligs* (the name derived from rearranging the letters of Gilbreth). By charting the Therbligs of each hand, they could identify long reaches, unnecessary pauses or redundant motions. From these studies, the Gilbreths developed numerous devices which today are considered mainstays of ergonomic design. For example, in their typing studies, they were the first to propose a redesign of the keyboard (later developed by August Dvorak), the wrist rest, the shift-lock key and the copy holder. With no modern test instruments or detailed ergonomics studies, the Gilbreths were able to identify the best biomechanical abilities of the human form, and design tools and work to fit them.

Frank Gilbreth also invented the process chart, a form of 'macro-motion study', whereby the manufacturing process was traced from raw materials to finished product. The process chart used symbols to characterize types of work activities, so that redundant or unnecessary steps could be discovered and eliminated. Not only has the process chart, with minor variations and improvements, remained an important tool in business efficiency, it has also given birth to other applications. Remarkable similarities can be found in methods such as fault tree analysis as well as systems safety techniques.

One important legacy of Frank Gilbreth's work can be found in modern hospital operating theatres. Then, as now, it was recognized that the shorter the duration of an operation, the better were the chances for the patient's recovery. Using motion study, Gilbreth found that contemporary operations were grossly inefficient, in that the doctor spent half of the operating time looking for the next instrument he needed. Frank felt that a superior method would be to have the doctor signal or call for his next instrument and to have the nurse place it in his hand. While we easily recognize this technique as common practice today, Gilbreth had to fight long and hard for its acceptance. Many of his other methods of reducing motions and achieving greater speed were also adopted. Just a few examples include using the *Therblig* of 'prepositioning' a tool, whereby the nurse would place the instrument in the doctor's hand in the position in which it would be used. Gilbreth's packet principle, was also developed, according to which nurses arranged instruments on a tray in the order in which they would be used, thus saving further time. Today, hospital emergency rooms are stocked with prearranged instrument trays, each designated to perform specific procedures.

The successes of Frank and Lillian Gilbreth received sporadic recognition while Frank was

alive, but he did not receive proper recognition for much of his pioneering work until many years after his death. Recognition was further muddled by some of Taylor's followers, who were quick to condemn Gilbreth's methods and equally quick to take credit for his accomplishments. However, thanks to the efforts of Lillian Gilbreth, the pioneering work of Gilbreth, Incorporated was not forgotten. Next to raising and educating her family, her main objective was to see that Frank received proper credit for his work. She also ensured that their papers were preserved at Purdue University.

Despite the many Gilbreth innovations already in use, there are many more yet to be adopted. A large portion of the business community is still opposed to ergonomics as being too costly, despite the proof that the Gilbreths offered of dramatic increases in production. Businesses whose workers put in long hours are just now recognizing the benefits of providing these employees with places to take short naps to improve their alertness, a proposal made by the Gilbreths in 1911. And most of all, the Gilbreths' call for inclusion of the 'human factor' into the way employers deal with employees remains a challenge for managers everywhere.

BIBLIOGRAPHY
Note: the first four works listed below were published under Frank Gilbreth's name alone, but were in fact co-authored with Lillian Gilbreth. Her name began appearing on the covers from 1912 on.
Gilbreth, F. (1908a) *Field System*, New York: Myron C. Clark.
—— (1908a) *Concrete System*, New York: The Engineering News Publishing Company.
—— (1909) *Bricklaying System*, New York: Myron C. Clark.
—— (1911) *Motion Study*, New York: Van Nostrand Company.
Gilbreth, F. and Gilbreth L. (1912) *Primer of Scientific Management*, New York: Van Nostrand Company.
—— (1916) *Fatigue Study*, New York: Sturgis and Walton.
—— (1917) *Applied Motion Study*, New York: Sturgis and Walton.
—— (1920) *Motion Study for the Handicapped*, New York: Macmillan.
Gilbreth, F.B., Jr and Carey, E.G. (1949) *Cheaper by the Dozen*, London: William Heinemann.
—— (1950) *Belles on the Their Toes*, London: William Heinemann.
Jaffe, W. (1984) 'Standardisation and Scientific Management', *Mechanical Engineering* (April): 56–9.
Yost, E. (1949) *Frank and Lillian Gilbreth: Partners for Life*, New Brunswick, NJ: Rutgers University Press.

DF

GILBRETH, Lillian Evelyn Moller (1878–1972)

Lillian Evelyn Moller was born on 24 May 1878 in Oakland, California, where her German-American parents owned a hardware and plumbing supply business. She died on 2 January 1972, in Phoenix, Arizona. During her childhood, in her own words, she was 'an introvert by inclination ... she lived most happily in her books' (Gilbreth 1998: 57). Her love of reading led her to enter the University of California at Berkeley, against some opposition from her parents, who felt that young ladies had no need of college. She received her BA in 1900 and her master's degree in 1903, both in literature, hoping for a future in teaching or college administration. Upon completion of her undergraduate degree, Lillian was chosen as the first woman to deliver a commencement address at Berkeley. This period was also one of her first experiences

with blatant gender discrimination: when she achieved the same score as a young man in competition for the Phi Beta Kappa Key, she was told that the man would in fact receive the award because he had more use for it (Gilbreth 1998: 72)

In 1903 she met Frank Bunker GILBRETH, then the president of his own construction company. They married in October 1904, with a plan to raise twelve children and to be full partners both at home and in Frank's business. Together the Gilbreths developed techniques for finding the one best way to do work, starting with the various tasks of building construction. By 1911 Lillian was already establishing herself as a leading advocate of applying psychology to the job of management; she took a Ph.D. in psychology from Brown University in 1915. Upon their two specialities – motion study and the psychology of management – the Gilbreths built a distinctive management system which they offered to businesses from 1912 to 1924 as an alternative to Frederick TAYLOR's more famous system. Although they started out as allies of Taylor, differences arose and by 1921 they were arguing that their industrial management system was both more scientific and more humane than Taylor's time study system.

In 1924 Frank Gilbreth was invited to Europe to help launch the First International Management Congress, but he died of a heart attack a few days before they were due to sail. Lillian Gilbreth found herself on her own with eleven children to raise. She set about achieving two major goals. First, she had to generate a living that would not only keep the family together, but also see to it that all the children were able to attend university. Second, she wanted to see that her husband received proper credit for his work and that this work was carried on. Her first step in this latter venture was to attend the International Management Congress in Frank's place and to deliver his speech.

Upon returning home, she found that almost all of their clients had either cancelled or failed to renew their contracts. Even though she had been an equal working partner in Gilbreth, Inc., most of the firm's clients had little faith that she could undertake consulting work alone. Some businessmen still sought her counsel but, in order to avoid ridicule, they consulted with her by phone or mail rather than in person. Nonetheless, Gilbreth was able to keep the family afloat financially by starting, in late 1925, to teach a motion study course in her home to representatives from various businesses. At the same time, she pursued consulting contracts with firms employing women such as a secretarial training school, a sandwich-making company and department stores such as Macys, where she worked without pay or even a signed contract (this work ultimately did lead to paying contracts with other retailers, however).

Gilbreth soon began to recognize that she would need to reinvent Gilbreth, Inc. in such a way that a woman management expert would be considered acceptable, even preferable. As a person, Lillian Gilbreth tried to avoid confrontation. In the partnership, she had always been the quiet peacemaker who countered Frank's sometimes less than diplomatic approach. It is no surprise, then, that she chose not to take up the battle for women's rights. Instead, she took a pragmatic approach to improving women's lives. With recent advances in both household technology and child development research, she thought she could offer useful advice to American homemakers. In two household advice books in the mid-1920s, *The Homemaker and Her Job* (1927) and *Living With Our Children* (1928), she brought the ideas and methods of scientific management to bear on homemaking. Even though these books were not the first to extend business management methods to homemaking, Gilbreth's writings were the first to show homemakers how to conduct their own motion studies, and psychological studies of themselves and their children.

These books helped to establish Gilbreth as a homemaking expert, drawing on her increas-

ingly public persona as a domestic whiz/mother of eleven. This led to contracts with utility companies and women's magazines designing efficiency kitchens. For example, she designed 'The Kitchen Practical' for the Brooklyn Borough Gas Company in 1929 and several other efficiency kitchens for the *New York Herald Tribune Magazine* in 1930. Efficiency kitchens promoted Gilbreth's engineering methods and expertise, applying motion study and psychology, to homemaking, but they also promoted the latest kitchen appliances and the utilities that powered these appliances. Thus, these projects brought Lillian into a commercial realm during a period when middle- and upper-class kitchens changed from large rooms accommodating several servants to small, technologically up-to-date workspaces perfect for the solitary homemaker. She emphasized correct heights of work surfaces and a circular workspace that would minimize reaching, walking, bending and lifting. In effect, the principles of Gilbreth-style scientific management were made operational in the kitchen. Lillian's personal story as a struggling, widowed mother of eleven added a fascinating backdrop to the spectacle offered by these kitchens and attracted consumers to the philosophy, as well as the appliances on display. These kitchens were toured by thousands of women and publicized in women's magazines. By 1930 the income she was earning from these commercial projects allowed her to stop teaching her motion study courses.

In 1929, at the onset of the Great Depression, her friend and fellow engineer President Herbert Hoover called her to Washington to head up the women's division of his Emergency Committee on Unemployment. She was by that time a recognized spokesperson on women and work, and, thanks to opinion research she carried out for such firms as Johnson and Johnson, she was also considered capable of doing sophisticated research on the needs and desires of women nationwide. American women became better understood by government and private companies thanks to her efforts.

In the early 1930s she was offered a part-time professorship at Purdue University, where first her husband and then she had given annual lectures for many years. There she founded the 'work simplification' curriculum in the school of home economics, and established a motion study laboratory in the school of management. She commuted by train from her home in New Jersey to Purdue (in West Lafayette, Indiana), staying about a month at a time and living in a girl's dormitory. Her children were all of school age by that time, but she still worried about them constantly and sometimes requested the advice of her college-age dorm-mates when one of her children was having a problem.

The 1940s, 1950s and 1960s saw Gilbreth pursue a variety of research topics and speaking engagements, often on the topic of household scientific management. Home economics departments, such as the one at the University of Connecticut in Storrs, borrowed her services to set up their practice kitchens and work simplification courses. Companies such as Maytag invited her as special guest and speaker at their annual banquets. Engineering professor Alan Mogenson invited her to do a series of annual talks on this subject to his students in Lake Placid, New York. She travelled around the world studying management advances and delivering speeches on the pioneers of scientific management and what their historical legacy can offer the contemporary world; a gifted speaker, she became an unofficial ambassador to the world's business community, promoting the exchange of management knowledge. During the New Deal era and the Second World War, Gilbreth remained on call to the Women's Bureau of the Department of Labour. Her success in mobilizing women's clubs during the Depression stood as evidence of her insight into the needs of women and their social groups. In all, she served in posts for six consecutive US presidents, beginning with Herbert Hoover in 1929.

Gilbreth considered her greatest achievement to be her efforts to design kitchens and other accommodations for disabled homemakers. This was an extension of her work with Frank in designing workspaces for disabled war veterans. It attracted the interest of such organizations as the American Heart Association, which called upon her to design a 'Heart of the Home Kitchen' for homemakers with heart conditions. Mothers who had suffered from polio required specially engineered clothes for themselves and their small children, and she contributed to these advances behind the scenes. Looking back at these efforts from the present era with the Americans With Disabilities Act becoming part of the business mindset, her efforts might seem minute; but for individuals with disabilities in the 1940s and 1950s, her work was probably viewed as a godsend that male engineers might never have provided.

From a management historian's point of view, perhaps Gilbreth's greatest historical contribution was to the human factors approach in modern management. To the new field of personnel management, she offered pioneering words on the subject of individual differences as well as practical methods for ascertaining, measuring and adjusting placement of workers in ways that capitalized on these differences. In the 1930s, for example, she often wrote on the topic of job satisfaction, arguing that different types of work can be found satisfying to different types of individuals. The key was to match individuals to the type of work that fit their natural attributes. This was a far more advanced image of the worker than that espoused by Frederick Taylor and his associates in the early days of management; and it was a view that recognized the need to improve the work experience in many jobs so that no worker was expected to waste his or her special talents and skills.

Lillian Gilbreth's legacy to women worldwide is not limited to her professional contributions. Over the course of her life, and especially after the publication of the famous books about her family (*Cheaper By the Dozen* and *Belles On Their Toes*), she provided a role model that inspired thousands of women to hold onto the dream of having a career and a family in spite of the obstacles that persist in a patriarchal society. She had a remarkable and distinguished career as 'America's First Lady of Engineering', along with a large, well-adjusted and successful family. Her marriage to Frank Gilbreth set high standards for modern couples, long before the two-earner family became the norm. Then, from 1924 onward, she did it all without the help of a husband, and with only a handyman and occasional secretary in her employ. Women of today, with comparatively normal careers and small, manageable families, still stand in awe of this woman. She was a prototype of the modern superwoman, balancing family and career, and somehow remaining humble and personable in the process. Many women in science, engineering and management today cite Lillian Gilbreth as an influence on their own decision to have a career.

As to her pledge to see that Frank Gilbreth received credit for his work and that that work was carried on, she kept her promise. In the 1930s she began to prepare her own and Frank's papers for donation to Purdue University. The Gilbreth Collection is an important historical record which can still provide ideas and inspiration. As to Frank's favourite invention, motion study, she continued to teach the techniques in her early classes in Montclair and later at Purdue. She also played a major role in later work in motion study by the likes of Anne Shaw (in England), Ralph Barnes and Alan Mogenson. It is through her students and colleagues that her intellectual legacy continues to shape managerial practice and the work experience around the world.

Aside from her doctorate in industrial psychology, she received twenty-three honorary degrees and twenty-six awards in her lifetime.

BIBLIOGRAPHY

Gilbreth, F.B, Jr (1994) *Ancestors of the Dozen*, private printing.

Gilbreth, F. and Gilbreth, L. (1912) *Primer of Scientific Management*, New York: Van Nostrand Co.

—— (1916) *Fatigue Study*, New York: Sturgis and Walton.

—— (1917) *Applied Motion Study*, New York: Sturgis and Walton.

—— (1920) *Motion Study for the Handicapped*, New York: Macmillan.

Gilbreth, L.M. (1914) *The Psychology of Management*, New York: Sturgis and Wilton.

—— (1924) *Quest for the One Best Way*, Chicago: Chicago Society of Industrial Engineers.

—— (1927) *The Homemaker and Her Job*, New York: D. Appleton.

—— (1928) *Living With Our Children*, New York: W.W. Norton.

—— (1998) *As I Remember*, Norcross, GA: Engineering and Management Press

Gilbreth, L.M. and Cook, A.R. (1947) *The Forman and Manpower Management*, New York: McGraw Hill.

Gilbreth, L.M. and Yost, E. (1944) *Normal Lives for the Disabled*, New York: Macmillan.

Gilbreth, L.M., Thomas, O.M. and Clymer, E. (1954) *Management in the Home*, New York: Dodd, Mead and Co.

LG
DF

GIRARD, Stephen (1750–1831)

Stephen Girard was born in Bordeaux, France on 20 May 1750, the son of a French naval officer. He died near Philadelphia on 26 December 1831. Though blind in one eye from birth, he resolved on a career at sea. At the age of fourteen he sailed as a cabin boy on a trading ship to the West Indies. Remaining in the West Indies for some years, he became involved in trade and was appointed a ship's captain in 1773, aged twenty-three. On a visit to New York in 1774, however, he decided to give up the sea and became instead a partner in a merchant business. He moved to Philadelphia in 1776, just before the outbreak of the American Revolution. He married Mary Lum in 1777. The couple had no children; she later became mentally ill and was institutionalized until her death in 1815.

Girard seems to have prospered despite the conflict, and after the end of the war began engaging in foreign trade and buying ships. He quickly amassed a fortune, and, like many rich traders before him, invested some of his capital in banking. The private Bank of Stephen Girard, established in Philadelphia in 1810, quickly became one of the more important financial institutions in Pennsylvania, even (illegally) issuing its own bank notes. Now one of the most important financiers in the country, in 1812 Girard entered a syndicate along with John Jacob ASTOR to sell government bonds to finance the war of 1812. After the war he was a founder director of the Bank of the United States, but resigned after disagreement with the bank's president. A philanthropist, he established Girard College, a large private school near Philadelphia.

One of the most successful bankers in US history, Girard is the outstanding example of the early nineteenth-century accumulator of capital who prospered, largely through trade, and did much to lay the foundations on which the first large American corporations were built later in the century. The astonishing successes of the American financial community in the nineteenth century have often been overlooked, but it seems clear that this success was critical to the later rapid growth of industry. The railways and other large firms which emerged after the American Civil War could not have done so without capital, and it was

men like Girard who launched the financial institutions which provided that capital.

BIBLIOGRAPHY
Macmaster, J.B. (1918) *The Life and Times of Stephen Girard*, 2 vols, Philadelphia: J.B. Lippincott.

MLW

GODAI Tomoatsu (1835–85)

Godai Tomoatsu was born into a warrior family in the fief of Satsuma (Kagoshima prefecture) on 26 December 1835 and died on 25 September 1885. He became an official of the fief, and from a young age showed an interest in Western learning and knowledge. In 1857 he went to Nagasaki, where he learned from Dutch naval officers various types of technology and the arts of navigation, gunnery, and measurement and survey. In 1859 he went to Shanghai to improve his knowledge of overseas affairs. In 1863 there occurred the Namamugi Incident, when several Englishman who had disturbed a procession of Shimazu Hisamitsu, a half-brother of Shimazu Nariakira, the lord of the Satsuma clan, were killed by sword-wielding *samurai*. This led to the Satsu-Ei War (Anglo-Satsuma War) in 1864. During the war Godai was captured, and he took the opportunity to learn English from his British captors.

In 1865, following his lord's orders, he went to Europe as director of exchange students from the fief of Satsuma, and while there made a study of European affairs. Returning home, he endeavoured to transplant the methods of modern industry from Europe to Japan. He helped introduce a joint stock ownership system, and advised on the purchase of spinning machines and the construction of Nagasaki Ship Repairing Station (later Mitsubishi Dockyard). After the Meiji Restoration, Godai became a foreign bureau official undertaking negotiations with foreign countries. He went on to become both Osaka prefecture judge and accounting authority judge, and then retired from his official posts in 1869 to go into business.

His first venture, a gold/silver analysis centre, made him very wealthy. He went on to purchase collieries in various parts of Japan. As an agency to unify these businesses, he established Kosei-kan in 1873. The systems and management rules adopted here came to be regarded as a model of colliery management. In 1876 Godai built a modern indigo manufacturing factory called Choyo-kan. In 1878 he established Osaka Association of Rice Dealers and the Stock Exchange, Chamber of Commerce, and Commercial Law Teaching Institution, thus establishing the basic institutions and foundations of the Osaka financial circle. Starting Kansai Trading Company in 1881, Godai embarked on trade in Hokkaido.

In the early period of Japanese capitalism, Godai Tomoatsu was a leader powerful and competent enough to be regarded as an opponent of SHIBUSAWA Eiichi, the other great entrepreneur of the period. However, most of the enterprises Godai established were designed to respond to national needs, and suffered from financial problems. When he died in 1885, he left huge debts behind him.

BIBLIOGRAPHY
Godai R. (ed.) (1933) *Godai Tomoatsu Den* (Godai Tomoatsu's Biography), Osaka: Godai Ryusaku.
Nihon Keieishi Kenkyusho (ed.) *Godai Tomoatsu Denki Shiryo* (Godai Tomoatsu's Chronological Records), 4 vols, Tokyo: Toyo Keizai Shinpou Sha.

ST

GODO Takuo (1877–1956)

Godo Takuo was born in Tokyo on 23 September 1877 and died there on 7 April 1956. After graduation from the department of engineering of Tokyo Imperial University in 1901, Godo started his career as an engineer in the navy. In 1905 he was posted to Sir W.G. Armstrong, Whitworth and Company, Ltd, from which the Japanese navy ordered its warships, and acquired experience in the study of technology and in techniques for shipbuilding and factory management. Through his stay in the United States in 1917–18 and in Europe in 1919–20, he gained an understanding of the First World War as a total war between the economic and industrial powers. In his view, the fundamental three conditions of efficiency were personnel, equipment and organization.

As chief of the artillery department at Kure Naval Arsenal, Godo introduced the 'limit gauge' system from May 1921 in response to the mass production of artillery accelerated by the expansion plan for the combined fleet. 'Godo's system called for a revolution in the production process, with provision for accelerated division of labor, centralized planning, stopwatch time study, cost accounting, Gantt chart tracking, and instruction card procedures' (Tsutsui 1998: 32). Although the execution of the limit gauge system at Kure Naval Arsenal was short-lived, as the Washington Treaty brought to an end the conditions for mass production of artillery, the limit gauge system model introduced by Godo continued to attract the attention of engineers and managers in the interwar period.

After retirement from the navy, Godo was installed in 1929 as president of Showa Steel Company, Ltd in northeastern China, where he set up a section for efficiency for the first time in the firm's history. He invited a production engineer from Deutsche Maschinenfabrik AG, who directed the section and introduced the techniques of scientific and production management into the company. Godo was appointed a minister of commerce and industry, and of railways, in 1937, a member of the House of Peers also in 1937, president of the Japan Chamber of Commerce and Industry in 1938, and again minister of commerce and industry along with agriculture and forestry in 1939. In 1942 he took up the post of the first president of the Japan Management Association, which had been established through the amalgamation of the Japan Efficiency Federation and the Japan Industrial Association, two vital organizations for the promotion of the scientific management movement in Japan. After the Second World War, the General Headquarters of the Supreme Commander for the Allied Powers purged him from public service, due to his former service at cabinet-level positions. In 1952, however, he became the third president of the Japan Management Association, taking the helm of that organization once again.

BIBLIOGRAPHY
Godo T. (1931) 'On Some Experiences in the Scientific Management of Machine Shops', in World Engineering Congress (ed.), *World Engineering Congress Tokyo 1929 Proceedings*, vol. 38, Scientific Management, Tokyo: World Engineering Congress.
Namiki T. *et al.* (eds) (1993) *Monodukuri wo Ichiryu Nishita Otokotachi* (The Men Who Upgraded Manufacturing to be First Class), Tokyo: Nikkan Kogyo Shinbunsha.
Sasaki S. (1998), *Kagakuteki Kanriho no Nihonteki Tenkai* (Japanese-style Development of Scientific Management), Tokyo: Yuhikaku.
Takahashi M. (1994) *'Kagakuteki Kanriho' to Nihon Kigyo* ('Scientific Management' and Japanese Firms), Tokyo: Ochanomizu Shobo.
Tsutsui, W. M. (1998), *Manufacturing Ideology: Scientific Management in Twentieth-century Japan*, Princeton, NJ: Princeton University Press.

SM

GOIZUETA, Roberto Crispulo (1931–97)

Roberto Crispulo Goizueta was born in Havana, Cuba on 18 November 1931 to a relatively wealthy family. He died on 18 October 1997 in Atlanta, Georgia. Goizueta grew up in one of the nicest neighbourhoods in the capital city. He attended Belen Academy, a Jesuit institution that has been called 'a veritable fortress of wealth and power for the aristocratic class of prerevolutionary Cuba' (Greising 1998: 8). While a student he visited the United States for summer camps, and then spent a year in prep school at Cheshire Academy in Connecticut. Accepted by several elite universities, Goizueta chose Yale and majored in chemical engineering. Soon after graduation in 1953 he married Olguita Casteleiro, whom he had begun dating while at Belen.

After graduating from Yale, Goizueta spent about a year working for his father in the family firm which dealt in architecture, real estate and sugar refining. Soon, however, he decided that he wanted to prove himself outside the family's business. In mid-1954 Goizueta spotted a classified advertisement for an unnamed company seeking a recently graduated chemical engineer with good English skills – precisely his qualifications. The employer was Coca-Cola, and he got the job. Believing that the young man should have a personal stake in the company, Goizueta's father loaned him $8,000 to buy 100 shares of the Atlanta-based soft drink giant. Fortuitously, the shares were placed in a custodial account in New York City.

The young engineer quickly became a key figure in technical matters such as quality control for the five Coke bottling plants in Cuba. He made several trips to Atlanta and even met Robert W. Woodruff, the president and personification of Coca-Cola. When Fidel Castro, also a Belen Academy graduate, took control of the country in 1959, Goizueta, like many among Cuba's elite, left for the United States. By mid-1960 nationalization of Coke's plants seemed imminent, and the Castro government was restricting the export of money and technical information. In order not to reveal that the family intended to emigrate, Roberto and Olguita departed in early October 1960 with only a couple of hundred dollars and clothes suitable for a vacation. Like most early Cuban émigrés, Goizueta assumed that he would some day return when the Castro regime collapsed. He even compiled from memory an inventory of the physical assets of Coca-Cola's Cuban plants to use as evidence in future claims proceedings.

Goizueta had established himself well enough in the company that he had a new job assignment as soon as he reached Miami, an advantage that most fellow Cubans in the United States did not have. At first, the Goizueta family lived in a modest Miami apartment, but soon their fortunes began to rise. Attached to Latin American technical operations and working out of an office in Nassau, Goizueta travelled throughout the region. Spurning offers from other companies, he made important contacts that would serve him well as he climbed Coke's corporate ladder.

In 1964, new Coke president Paul Austin brought Goizueta to Atlanta to work at company headquarters. Austin had met Goizueta in pre-Castro Havana, and the Cuban fit with Austin's plans to emphasize international operations. Austin put the engineer to work analysing the structure of company decision making, first in technical operations and then in other fields. The early confidence that Austin placed in 33-year-old Goizueta was the career turning point that moved him from purely engineering concerns to broader management issues. Goizueta was the first immigrant to be given such a critical headquarters task. His supreme confidence, impeccable grooming and gentlemanly, even aristocratic, demeanour helped Goizueta move comfortably among executives much his senior.

Goizueta's first major report on management restructuring called for a more central-

ized approach to formulating technical standards and providing expertise, while still allowing for decentralized decision making consistent with those standards. Greising (1998: 36) believed that this approach 'would become a hallmark of Goizueta's approach to broader management and strategic challenges as chief executive of the company'. On the basis of this work Goizueta was promoted to vice-president of technical research and development, becoming at the age of thirty-five the youngest vice-president in company history. Already closely linked to the rising Austin, Goizueta now had opportunity for occasional visits with Woodruff, still known as 'the Boss', and learned to flatter Woodruff as a key means to further advancement.

Goizueta's career took a leap forward in 1974, when a senior executive suffered a debilitating heart attack. Goizueta moved into the gap, and Austin made him senior vice-president of the technical division. Importantly, Goizueta now became one of only two executives who knew the secret formula for concocting Coca-Cola syrup. At this time the relationship between Austin and Woodruff was becoming strained, primarily over Austin's efforts to diversify through corporate acquisitions. Although 'the Boss' was no longer president or chairman, he remained the most influential force in the company through his domination of the finance committee and by virtue of the fact that he remained the single largest stockholder. Goizueta had to negotiate a fine line between loyalty to Austin, his mentor, and courting the favour of Woodruff. He proved especially adept at the latter.

By the end of 1979 there was intense competition among top executives to succeed the ageing Austin. Most outside observers did not see Goizueta as a leading candidate to move up, but his competitors inside were well aware that the Cuban was an astute corporate politician. The leading candidates for the top job appeared to be Ian R. Wilson, a South African who was then heading Far East operations, and Donald R. Keough, who was in charge of US operations. Wilson was cosier with Woodruff even than Goizueta, and he was also Austin's choice as successor. His abrasive style, his principally international emphasis, his status as a white South African, and perhaps most of all, Robert Woodruff's and the board's growing disenchantment with Austin all worked against Wilson. In early 1980 Keough and Goizueta formed an alliance, each agreeing to appoint the other as number two if he should win the top spot.

In May 1980 Woodruff, still in control of a majority of the board despite his ninety years and failing health, informed Austin that he had decided that Goizueta would be the successor. Goizueta quickly assumed the position of president while Austin, for the time being, remained CEO and chairman of the board. In twenty-six years, the supremely self-confident Cuban engineer had gone from answering a blind 'help wanted' ad in a Havana newspaper to the presidency of one of the world's best-known companies. But his ascendancy to the chairmanship and full control was not yet complete.

The key to Coca-Cola's operations in the United States and abroad was the independent bottler system. These companies bought Coke syrup, mixed it with carbonated water and distributed the finished product. Many of the US bottlers were not pleased with the choice of Goizueta. They tended to prefer Keough, who was more attuned to the marketing than the technical side of operations. Even Woodruff was not sure that he wanted Goizueta to have full control. Goizueta realized this weakness, and he quickly set out to ingratiate himself with the bottlers, especially with the financially stronger ones that could be expected to absorb smaller, poorer performing firms. This strategy, along with strong support from key members of the board of Atlanta's Trust Company Bank, worked. The untimely death of a potential Woodruff-backed figurehead chairman sealed the contest. Only 100 days after they had named him president, the Coca-Cola board designated Roberto Goizueta as

chairman and chief executive officer, to be effective from early 1981. The new CEO stood by his agreement to make Donald Keough the clear second in command as president and chief operating officer.

Goizueta moved quickly to put his mark on Coke's elderly and conservative board of directors. He pushed through age and term restrictions that would eventually move Woodruff's old cronies aside. More importantly, he wrested control of the all-important finance committee from 'the Boss'. Goizueta still courted Woodruff's blessings for major moves such as borrowing money to buy out bottlers, but no one doubted any longer that the Cuban was firmly in charge.

The new chairman faced several challenges, the most troubling of which was that his flagship brand was losing domestic market share to arch-rival Pepsi-Cola. Also needing attention were inefficiencies in overseas operations and a generally unprofitable collection of diversified subsidiaries. Coke's stock value had seriously lagged, and many of company's biggest investors, including Trust Company Bank, had backed Goizueta in the hopes that he was the leader who could restore shareholder value. The chairman understood that challenge at the most basic level because he still held the original 100 shares that he obtained in 1954 when he first went to work for Coke in Havana in 1954. Although technically a hired hand, Goizueta thought and acted like an owner.

Goizueta made it clear to bottlers and executives that he held no reverence for 'sacred cows', not even the secret formula. As a chemical engineer, he regarded the formula as a chemical compound that could be altered and improved. As a corporate engineer of sorts, he regarded the 'Coke' name as an asset that could be leveraged for greater profit. These two assumptions led him to one of his greatest triumphs and to his most public disaster.

The triumph was Diet Coke. The company's diet cola Tab sold well, but its once rapid growth rate had flattened by the early 1980s. Tradition and fear of legal technicalities had kept the company from using the 'Coke' name on any product save the original concoction. In fact, Goizueta had looked favourably on the Diet Coke project in the 1970s, but he chose not to champion it while he was jockeying for executive leadership. Paul Austin, in one of his last major decisions as CEO, pulled the plug on Diet Coke, but now that he was in charge Goizueta quickly revived the effort. Tradition did not concern Goizueta, and the legal fears proved to be considerably overstated. Confident that the Coke brand would make the product a success, and assured that company chemists had formulated a beverage that tasted better than other diet drinks, including Tab, Goizueta was ready to move. Again using his charm to bring Woodruff over to his side, Goizueta released Diet Coke in the summer of 1982. It was an immediate success: by the end of 1983 it was the nation's fourth most popular soft drink behind only Coke, Pepsi and 7-Up. Diet Coke's slogan 'just for the taste of it' symbolized a whole new market for low-calorie sodas.

In his next assault on a sacred cow, Goizueta learned that taste was not enough. Pepsi mounted an advertising campaign based on taste tests that showed their product winning in head-to-head consumer comparisons. Coke's secret replications of the tests showed Pepsi to be right. And sales figures showed Pepsi gaining, more from minor brands than from Coke, but gaining nonetheless. Executives were worried, and rightly so.

As in the case of Diet Coke, Goizueta had encouraged laboratory work on the formula while he was head of the technical division, but he had not pushed for implementation while he worked at that level. The laboratories and test marketers worked feverishly, and secretly, to find a formula that consumers would prefer. It was not an easy task. Everyone knew that Pepsi tasted sweeter, but simply adding more sugar to Coca-Cola would not do the trick. Ironically, in the meantime Pepsi had quit

using taste tests in its advertising because the campaign was getting old and the 'Cola War' was costing too much in price cuts.

Coca-Cola market researchers were aware that loyal Coke drinkers might resist a new formula for reasons of emotion as much as palate. But, as it turned out, they underestimated the depth of those feelings. Clinical taste tests were not enough because, as Frederick Allen, author of the company history *Secret Formula*, later wrote: 'taste buds would always be compromised by the thoughts and emotions and associations that the name of the product conjured up in their minds. Knowing what they were drinking would always affect the taste' (Allen 1994: 401). Goizueta knew that no one was more emotionally attached to Coca-Cola than Robert Woodruff. According to Allen, the CEO gently hinted to 'the Boss' about the possible need to tinker with the formula but never told him point blank that a change was in the works because Woodruff would have 'hit me over the head' (Allen 1994: 408).

While the new Coke project was brewing, Goizueta was making other moves that, coupled with Diet Coke's success, enhanced corporate profits and substantially raised stock prices. In early 1982 he purchased Columbia Pictures. The Hollywood diversification quickly turned a profit with some box office successes, and Coke was able to divest itself of Columbia for a sizeable capital gain. The Columbia deal, at first widely criticized, helped give Goizueta a reputation for financial as well as technical brilliance. In the meantime, Goizueta also jettisoned Coke's wine and coffee lines and other subsidiaries.

By 1984 Coke's chemists and marketers were convinced that they had a product that would consistently beat Pepsi, and original Coke itself, in head-to-head taste tests. For a combination of legal, ethical and marketing reasons, Goizueta and his team rejected the idea of just quietly making the change and not announcing it. Also, there was a vigorous internal debate about whether to retire original

Coke or to market both a new and regular product. The main problem with the two-brand strategy was that it would likely divide market share and assure first place for Pepsi even if the two products combined outsold the rival. According to Allen, Goizueta had to be convinced to add the word 'new' to the actual name of the beverage and he had to be persuaded not to mention explicitly the Pepsi challenge in the initial press conference and early promotion of the change. In retrospect, the CEO would have been better off to have gone with his initial approach.

Despite the Herculean efforts at secrecy, word had leaked out, and Pepsi was ready with a vigorous, and effective, response to the announcement of New Coke in April 1985. Pepsi simply declared that they had won the 'Cola War'. In Pepsi's view, Coca-Cola was not just introducing a reformulated product, they were admitting that they had been beaten. Much of the press accepted this explanation, and a surprisingly inept initial press conference by Goizueta and Keough probably made matters worse rather than better. As Allen succinctly put it, 'Long before they had ever tasted a sip of it, millions of Americans decided they *hated* New Coke ... Many people didn't *want* to like New Coke. The were unable to give it a fair chance' (Allen 1994: 413–14). Editorial cartoonists, late night comedians and even the respected conservative radio commentator Paul Harvey ridiculed the change. The public outcry was nearly unanimous.

As an engineer who believed in facts and figures, Goizueta had a difficult time comprehending that consumers would make such a non-rational decision. But as an executive, Goizueta could recognize a mistake, and he was not afraid to admit it and fix it. In mid-summer, less than three months after the introduction of New Coke, Goizueta bowed to public pressure and announced that 'Classic Coke' was back. Personally, Goizueta preferred New Coke and continued to drink it even after Coke Classic returned, but he was the exception. For a brief few months Pepsi

gained sales leadership, but by early 1986 Coca-Cola Classic was back on top. Meanwhile, Diet Coke passed 7-Up to capture third place. Pepsi had won a battle but not the war. As CEO, Goizueta shouldered blame for the initial decision, and it would stay with him for the rest of his career; but all was forgiven by Coca-Cola stockholders as their net worth climbed sky high in the late 1980s and 1990s. Goizueta knew that competition was the driving force of the free market system. 'If Pepsi-Cola didn't exist,' he told a reporter years after the New Coke episode, 'I would try to invent it. It keeps us, and them, on our toes and keeps us lean' (Roush 1996).

In fact, increasing stockholder value was Goizueta's primary goal to which all other goals were subordinated. Unlike during Paul Austin's leadership, Coca-Cola under Goizueta carefully cultivated Wall Street. Along with Keough, he met often with financial executives and portfolio managers. One of the tactics for increased value was to increase per capita consumption in global markets where Coca-Cola was one of the world's two or three best-known brand names. International sales expanded rapidly, especially in newly opened Eastern Europe and in Japan. In a highly publicized coup, Goizueta convinced Venezuela's leading bottling company to switch from Pepsi to Coke. Wall Street responded very positively, and values soared. Among the major investors showing confidence in Coke was financial genius Warren Buffet, whose stake grew about fourfold in only three years from 1989 to 1992. Goizueta himself became famously rich thanks to generous stock options that the board granted him. The size of his compensation package attracted the attention of the business press, but few stockholders complained because he had made them rich too. The market value of Coke when he took the reins was just over $4 billion; the value at his death stood around $150 billion. Goizueta had engineered a thirty-fourfold increase in sixteen years. He died as the wealthiest Hispanic in the United States with a personal worth of $1.3 billion in Coca-Cola stock, $3 million of which came from the original $8,000 worth of shares he bought in 1954 (*Los Angeles Times*, 19 October 1997; *Fortune*, 13 October 1997).

Even though the Coca-Cola board had induced Goizueta to serve past the normal retirement age of sixty-five, he knew that he needed to prepare the next generation of leadership. About a year before his death the veteran chairman told an *Atlanta Constitution* writer,

My No. 1 task right now, as opposed to 1980 and 1981 when I kind of cleaned house, is to acquire and identify talented people and ensue they are developed and to have the systems in place to move this company to a higher plateau of achievement.

(Roush 1996)

The Cuban CEO who had succeeded native Georgian Paul Austin spent several years grooming another native Georgian, M. Douglas Ivester, to be his successor. Shortly before Goizueta's death *Fortune* magazine described their relationship as 'an almost perfect partnership – Ivester managing the business ... and Goizueta managing big-picture strategy and Coke's marvelous relationship with the Street'. A stock analyst was quoted as predicting that 'the transition will be seamless' (Sellers 1997). Only days after this article appeared, Goizueta died of cancer, and the analyst's prediction proved accurate.

Following his death, former President Jimmy Carter declared, 'perhaps no other corporate leader in modern times has so beautifully exemplified the American dream' (Associated Press, 19 October 1997). Indeed, Goizueta lived a twentieth-century version of the Gilded Age rags-to-riches stories of 'robber barons' such as Andrew CARNEGIE. A young, nearly penniless immigrant, a refugee from Castro's Cuba, he rose to the zenith of American business.

BIBLIOGRAPHY

Allen, F. (1994) *Secret Formula: How Brilliant Marketing and Relentless Salesmanship Made Coda-Cola the Best-known Product in the World*, New York: HarperBusiness.

Barry, T. (1998) 'Georgia's Most Respected CEO for 1998', *Georgia Trend* (May): 18ff.

Cline, K. (1989) 'Roberto Goizueta and the Cola Revolution', *Atlanta Business Chronicle* (10 April): 1ff.

Greising, D. (1998) *I'd Like the World to Buy a Coke: The Life and Leadership of Roberto Goizueta*, New York, John Wiley and Sons.

Huey, J. (1997) 'In Search of Roberto's Secret Formula', *Fortune* (29 December): 230ff.

Morris, B. (1995) 'Roberto Goizueta and Jack Welch: The Wealth Builders', *Fortune* (11 December): 80ff.

Oliver, T. (1986) *The Real Coke, the Real Story*, New York: Random House.

Roush, C. (1996) 'Coca-Cola's Guiding Light', *Atlanta Constitution* (24 November): H1, H3.

Sellers, P. (1997) 'Where Coke goes from Here', *Fortune* (13 October): 88–91.

BR

GOLDWYN, Samuel (1882–1974)

Samuel Goldwyn was born Schmuel Gelbfisz (altered to Samuel Goldfish) on 27 August 1882 – the date is also quoted as 1884 and as possibly July 1879 (Gomery 1999: 216; Berg 1989: 5) – in Warsaw to Aaron David Gelbfisz, a peddler, and Hannah Reban Jarecka (other sources give his parents' names as Abraham and Hannah Goldfish). He died on 31 January 1974 in Los Angeles. He emigrated to Gloversville, New York as a teenager. He had some orthodox Jewish education in Poland, and one year of night school at the Gloversville Business College. He married Blanche Lasky in 1910, and the couple had one daughter; he later married Frances Howard in 1925, and they had one son.

Goldwyn started working in a glove factory and rapidly rose to become a partner in the firm. He was a highly successful glove salesman. Through his marriage to Blanche Lasky, he met Jesse Lasky, a vaudeville producer. The two men formed the Jesse L. Lasky Feature Picture Play Company in 1913, and produced the first American-made feature-length film, *The Squaw Man*, which was directed by Cecil B. DeMille in his directorial debut. Goldwyn and Lasky merged their company with Adolph Zukor's Famous Players, and Goldwyn eventually sold out for $900,000. In 1917 Goldwyn joined with the Selwyn brothers, who were Broadway producers. They dubbed their new venture Goldwyn Pictures Company. Goldwyn liked the name (a combination of Goldfish and Selwyn) so much that he adopted it as his legal name. Eventually their company merged with Metro pictures and became Metro-Goldwyn-Mayer (MGM). Goldwyn became an independent producer in 1922, although he temporarily aligned his efforts with United Artists.

Goldwyn's management style included tolerance of 'yes men': as he admitted, 'I'll take 50 per cent efficiency to get 100 per cent loyalty' (Krebs 1974: 34). As a producer, he 'coddled actors, writers, and directors, but when he felt they were not producing what he had expected of them, he switched tactics and heaped invective upon them' (Krebs 1974: 34). One writer, Ben Hecht, found that Goldwyn's treatment of him was similar to 'an irritated man shaking a slot machine' (Krebs 1974: 34). Goldwyn was known for seeking strong scripts, refusing to use outside funding and making high-quality films. He refused to underestimate his audience: 'Entertainment ... does not automatically exclude thought. The minds of an

intelligent audience do not stop working even when they are most relaxed' ('Goldwyn, Samuel' 1944: 248). His films were popular, including *The Best Years of Our Lives* and *Wuthering Heights*, and during a twenty-year period his films drew more than 200 million customers. Unfortunately, his last film, *Porgy and Bess*, flopped amidst criticism of its portrayal of blacks. He also had difficulty with the changing mores of Hollywood films, being disgusted with the free-wheeling depictions of sex in the 1960s.

Goldwyn had an ability to discover stars, including Tallulah Bankhead, Robert Montgomery, Gary Cooper, Teresa Wright, Ronald Colman, Rudolph Valentino and Eddie Cantor. Unfortunately, he let Cooper go from his studio and later had to pay large sums to get him back. He also misjudged the potential of actress Anna Sten, whom he first characterized as having 'the face of a sphinx', but saying later: 'She's colossal in a small way' (Krebs 1974: 34).

As Goldwyn once described himself: I was a rebel, a lone wolf. My pictures were my own; I financed them myself and answered solely to myself. My mistakes and my successes were my own. My one rule was to please myself, and if I did that, there was a good chance I would please others.

(Krebs 1974: 34)

BIBLIOGRAPHY
Berg, A. (1989) *Goldwyn: A Biography*, New York: Alfred A. Knopf.
'Goldwyn, Samuel' (1944) *Current Biography, Who's Who and Why*, New York: H.W. Wilson and Co., vol. 5: 246–9.
Gomery, D. (1999) 'Goldwyn, Samuel', in J.A. Garraty and M. Carnes (eds), *American National Biography*, New York: Oxford University Press, vol. 9, 214–16.
Krebs, A. (1974) 'Samuel Goldwyn Dies at 91', *New York Times* 123(42,377), sect. 1: 1, 34.

DS

GOLLANCZ, Victor (1893–1967)

Victor Gollancz was born in London on 9 April 1893, the son of a jeweller. He died on 8 February 1967, having suffered a stroke the previous autumn. Educated at St Paul's School, he took a degree in classics from New College, Oxford, where he also began his lifelong attraction to socialism. He served in the British Army in the First World War. In 1919 he married Ruth Löwy, the daughter of a stockbroker; they had five children.

In 1921 Gollancz joined the publishing company Benn Brothers. He showed an immediate affinity for publishing and his talents were recognized by Sir Ernest Benn, who asked Gollancz to become managing director of a new venture, Ernest Benn Ltd, in 1923. Under Gollancz's direction, Ernest Benn Ltd became the first British publishing company to undertake large-scale advertising, shaking up a hitherto moribund market.

In 1927 a personality clash with Sir Ernest Benn led to Gollancz's departure. He then established his own firm, Victor Gollancz Ltd. With a reputation as a brilliant publisher, he was able to attract the necessary investment without difficulty. He retained a controlling interest in the firm for himself, and the other directors gave Gollancz near total authority, relying on his genius. They were not mistaken; Victor Gollancz Ltd became one of the most profitable and successful firms in British publishing history.

Gollancz's success was based on two complementary factors: his attention to the product and his instinctive flair for marketing. He was well aware that the success of the firm

depended on his being able to recruit, and keep, best-selling authors. He devoted much of his time to maintaining good relations with authors, cultivating the best and discarding the rest. He was choosy about which books he published – Edwards (1987: 177) comments that he was 'always prepared to suffer financially rather than dilute the quality of his list' – but once he had decided accept a book, he did his utmost to make that book a success.

Gollancz knew that the book market could be stimulated, and, to the outrage of his rivals, undertook large-scale advertising campaigns; on some occasions he took out full-page newspaper advertisements in the *Observer* (Hodges 1978), a step of hitherto undreamed of boldness. Gollancz also revolutionized the design of books, employing the brilliant typographer Stanley Morrison and a number of artists (including his wife Ruth) to produce innovative typefaces and cover designs. Hodges (1978: 30) calls Gollancz's and Morrison's designs 'one of the most brilliant and successful innovations in publishing this century'.

Gollancz knew how to find and employ talent, but his autocratic methods made him difficult to work with. Edwards quotes a colleague:

Gollancz saw himself as the conductor of the orchestra, determining the time and tempo. When a book he did not like made money, he had a feeling of resentment. Even where he liked a book, he was indifferent to its success if he had not himself planned it.

(Edwards 1987: 148)

Many called him a genius, but the same people might also call him a bully (Edwards 1987: 150).

A lifelong socialist, despite his knighthood of 1955, Gollancz was a prolific writer. Most of his books are on socialist political issues or, from the 1940s onward, on the Holocaust in Nazi Germany and the moral issues it raised.

Industrial Ideals (1920) is his only book which touches on management. He comments in detail on profit sharing and joint control, both of which he sees as socialist methods being adopted into the capitalist system. The ultimate aim should be industrial peace. Socialists attack both these methods, however, as distractions from the real aim of socialism; both leave ultimate control in the hands of a few (workers and managers), instead of the whole community. Gollancz does not say whether he believes this to be a good thing.

BIBLIOGRAPHY

Edwards, R.D. (1987) *Victor Gollancz: A Biography*, London: Victor Gollancz.
Gollancz, V. (1920) *Industrial Ideals*, Oxford: Oxford University Press.
Hodges, S. (1978) *Gollancz: The Story of a Publishing House*, London: Victor Gollancz.

MLW

GOODRICH, Benjamin Franklin (1841–88)

Benjamin Franklin Goodrich was born in Ripley, New York on 4 November 1841 and died in Manitou Springs, Colorado on 3 August 1888. Goodrich was an ambitious man who came into the business world following a brief career as a physician. He graduated from the Cleveland Medical College in 1860, and served in the Union army as a surgeon during the American Civil War. After the war, Goodrich tried establishing a medical practice in several locations. These efforts were apparently not successful, for Goodrich sought a personal fortune in the burgeoning postwar economy. His restless ambition led him to leave the medical field in favour of a business position in New York City, where he worked

briefly in the shipping department of an oil firm.

While in New York, Goodrich became involved in several real estate ventures with some success. Intrigued by the possibilities of rubber manufacturing, Goodrich and a friend, John Morris, invested $10,000 in the Hudson River Rubber Company in 1869. This firm, however, proved burdened by debt, worn-out machinery and intense competition. Soon these problems led Goodrich to look for a western location that might allow him to escape the intense competition of New York, while satisfying newer customers in the expanding economy. His travels took him to Akron, Ohio, where local business and civic leaders were willing to help Goodrich establish a new firm. They pledged an investment of $15,000 to help the young manufacturer relocate to Akron. The Goodrich, Tew Company began in 1870 as an Akron partnership, the first rubber manufacturing firm west of the Appalachian mountains. (In 1880 the firm became the B.F. Goodrich Company.) Akron proved to be a good location, with canal and rail connections to raw material supplies and, in particular, the markets of growing Midwestern industries. Eventually other entrepreneurs invested in Akron rubber manufacturing establishments, and the city became known as the world's rubber capital.

As an entrepreneur, Goodrich established a diversified strategy, one that continued to characterize his firm long after his death. The firm's principal products were fire hoses and machinery belts, but it also manufactured rubber goods ranging from jar rings to washing-machine rollers. (Goodrich avoided rubber shoe manufacturing, however, as this was an intensely competitive business.) Hoses and belts were especially profitable products in the Midwestern markets of growing cities and expanding railroads, mines and factories. In 1881, after its first full year of operation as a corporation, the B.F. Goodrich Company made profits of $69,000 on sales of $319,000; its assets were only $233,000. Shortly before Goodrich's death in 1888, the firm had assets of $564,000, earning an annual profit of $107,000.

Goodrich was also personally involved in the business. He worked in a small laboratory on the compounding of rubber, trying various formulae – and keeping them secret and proprietary – in an effort to improve rubber products. In fact, science was an important part of successful rubber manufacturing, and the B.F. Goodrich Company, shortly after the founder's premature death from tuberculosis, established one of the nations first industrial laboratories.

Goodrich's personal legacy was a business strategy of diversified manufacturing aimed at a variety of industrial and consumer markets supported by careful scientific development of rubber compounds. The B.F. Goodrich Company continued as a diversified manufacturer for a century following its founder's death. It also was known as a scientifically innovative firm, pioneering new plastics and rubbers.

BIBLIOGRAPHY
Blackford, M.G. and Kerr, K.A. (1996) B.F. Goodrich: Tradition and Transformation, 1870–1995, Columbus: Ohio State University Press.

KAK

GORDY, Berry, Jr (1929–)

Berry Gordy Jr was born on 28 November 1929 in Detroit, Michigan. Born and raised in a ghetto area of Detroit, Gordy tried his hand at professional boxing before deciding – after ten wins and four losses – that the ring was too tough and the featherweight class was not profitable enough. He tried running a jazz specialty record store, but went bankrupt. He then

directed his attention towards the emerging field of R&B, promoting his talents as a songwriter and record producer. In 1957 Gordy scored his first commercial breakthrough when R&B star Jackie Wilson turned his song *Reet Petite* into a minor pop hit for Brunswick Records. Follow-up hits for Wilson and Brunswick consolidated Gordy's reputation as Detroit's leading song-writer.

In 1959 Gordy founded Motown Records as a vehicle for independently producing and mar-keting his own music, and also for marketing the songwriting and performing talents of Detroit's bright young black singers and musi-cians. He chose the name in acknowledgement of Detroit's popularly designated status as 'Motor Town', home of the Ford Motor Company and other major car manufacturers.

In 1960 Gordy signed to his label a teenage quintet, Smokey Robinson and the Miracles, who produced two major hits, 'Way Over There' and 'Shop Around'. With the ensuing profits, Gordy expanded his label's talent roster. His ability to spot a commercial prospect never failed; over the next two years he signed such promising newcomers as Mary Wells, the Supremes, the Marvelettes, Martha and the Vandellas, the Temptations, Marvin Gaye and the hit-oriented songwriting team of Lamont Dozier, Eddie Holland and Brian Holland. In the years following, Gordy added such talents as Stevie Wonder, the Four Tops, and Jr Walker and the All Stars. Diana Ross, who graduated from lead singer of the Supremes to solo stardom, became known as Motown's first all-around entertainer.

The result was huge success, artistic and financial, for Motown Records. which grew to become the United States' largest black-owned entertainment conglomerate. In the process, Gordy moved black 'rhythm and blues' music (R&B) into the popular mainstream and rendered obsolete the old US *Billboard* magazine practice of listing R&B and 'Top 100' as separate, race-segregated pop music cate-gories. A key factor in this success was Gordy's insistence on taking personal responsibility for what he called 'quality control'. This meant that songs could not emerge from the recording studio as finished product until they were up to what he considered 'Motown standards'.

For much of the 1960s, the number of records Motown released, relative to the company's size, was one of the lowest in the music industry. However, the percentage of these that became hits was one of the highest. In 1966 alone, it was estimated that fully 75 per cent of Motown releases made the US pop charts.

In 1971 Gordy moved Motown to Hollywood and diversified into motion pictures, television programmes and theatrical productions. During the 1970s many of Motown's top artists defected to other labels, but the company retained its position as an important independent label with the record-ings of Stevie Wonder, the Commodores and Rick James. In the 1980s, however, Motown Records struggled. Ross signed with RCA and Gaye with Columbia. Some disenchanted former employees sued Motown, alleging failure to pay royalties. Gordy by this time was more interested in producing television programmes such as *Lonesome Dove* than in making hit records. In July 1988 he sold Motown Records to MCA and Boston Ventures for $61 million. In 1990 he was inducted into America's Rock and Roll Hall of Fame. Joe McEwen and Jim Miller wrote in *Rolling Stone* magazine that 'through a com-bination of pugnacious panache, shrewd judge-ment and good taste, Gordy became the mogul of the most profitable black music concern in the world' (Miller 1980: 235).

BIBLIOGRAPHY

Miller, J. (ed.) (1980) *The Rolling Stone Illustrated History of Rock & Roll*, New York: Random House.

Stambler, I. (1977) *Encyclopedia of Pop, Rock and Soul,* New York: St Martin's Press.

BB

GOULD, Jay (1836–92)

Jason Gould was born on 27 May 1836 and died in New York on 2 December 1892. Born to John and Mary Gould, poor farmers in Roxbury, New York, Gould's youth was very much shaped by his poverty as well as his poor health His mother died when he was four, and Gould himself almost died from pneumonia and typhus. His unhappy youth helped, according to O'Connor (1962), to condition his Darwinian outlook on life. In Gould's mind there was no excuse for being poor, for poverty meant sickness, starvation and death. Gould, however, had all the attributes of a future entrepreneur: he was bright, quick-witted, a self-starter and persistent. He would stop at nothing to become rich. He taught himself accounting and surveying, then went into business as a tanner. But by the time Gould was twenty, around 1857, he had found his life's calling as a Wall Street financier. Gould quickly mastered the new art of finance capital, becoming one of the most successful brokers in history.

On Wall Street, Gould's strategy was to take over ailing businesses and make them profitable. In 1874 he bought the Pacific Mail Steamship Company and then the Union Pacific Railroad, which was poorly managed and tarnished by political scandal. Gould was not able to fix the Union Pacific, however, and sold his holdings in the railway. He then set out to create his own railway by merging part of the Kansas Pacific, the Missouri Pacific, the Wabash, and the Denver and Rio Grande between 1879 and 1881. He extended this system into parts of the Midwest, New York and New England, so that by 1881 Gould controlled 21,000 kilometres (13,000 miles) of track, more than the New York Central or the Pennsylvania. That same year, Gould also bought the Western Union telegraph network.

In control of both the giant Missouri Pacific and Western Union, Gould was now as powerful, if not more so, than Standard Oil, Carnegie Steel or the New York Central. His effort to corner the gold market in 1884 trig-gered a panic which endangered his empire, but it survived. His health began to fail, but he continued to be active, even repurchasing the Union Pacific in 1890.

When he died in 1892 Gould left behind both a successful empire in transportation and communication, and a reputation for questionable dealings that would, more than anything else, help to shape the image of Gould as a Robber Baron. Historians have not been kind to Jay Gould. To Josephson (1962) among many others, he was an unscrupulous manipulator who ran the Erie Railroad, watered stock and bribed state legislators. But in the 1990s, an age of corporate restructuring and shareholder value, Gould came to be seen in a more favourable light (see for example Klein 1999) as a master financier and successful business leader who could turn around ailing corporations.

BIBLIOGRAPHY

Josephson, M. (1962) *The Robber Barons: The Great American Capitalists, 1861–1901*, New York: Harcourt, Brace, Jovanovich.

Klein, M. (1986) *The Life and Legend of Jay Gould*, Baltimore, MD: Johns Hopkins University Press.

——— (1999) 'Gould, Jay', *American National Biography*, ed. J.A. Garraty and M.C. Carnes, New York: Oxford University Press, vol. 9, 344–7.

O'Connor, R. (1962) *Gould's Millions*, Garden City, NY: Doubleday.

DCL

GRAHAM, Katharine (1917–)

Katharine Meyer was born in New York City on 16 June 1917, the fourth of five children born to Eugene Meyer, a wealthy Wall Street businessman, and Agnes Elizabeth (Ernst)

Meyer, an author and philanthropist. Growing up in Washington, DC, Katharine Meyer showed an early interest in journalism. She wrote for the school magazine while attending Madeira, a private boarding school in Virginia. After her father purchased the moribund *Washington Post* for $825,000 at a bankruptcy auction in 1933, Katharine held occasional summer jobs at the paper while completing a BA in history at the University of Chicago. She spent a year working as a labour reporter for the *San Francisco News* after graduating from university. She then accepted her father's invitation to join the *Washington Post*. Because as publisher's daughter she would have felt awkward working as a reporter, she opted to write editorials instead.

In June 1940 she married Philip Graham, a Harvard Law School graduate who worked as a clerk for two Supreme Court justices and dreamed of entering politics. After serving in the US Army Air Corps during the Second World War he abandoned his political ambitions and – at his father-in-law's request – accepted the position of associate publisher at the *Washington Post*. At that point Katharine stopped working at the *Post* and devoted herself to raising her daughter and three sons.

Philip Graham found the *Post* to be a struggling paper that barely broke even, and helped put it on a firmer financial footing after becoming publisher in 1948. He merged the *Post* with one of its rivals, the money-losing *Washington Times-Herald*, and added *Newsweek* magazine to the company's growing stable of holdings. He also expanded radio and television holdings and helped establish an international news service.

In August 1963 Philip Graham – who suffered from manic depression – committed suicide. Katharine Graham became president of the Washington Post Company, and later publisher of the newspaper. At first awkward and insecure in her role as principal owner of the company, she publicly asserted herself as a strong newspaper executive in 1971, when she decided that the *Post* should defy a US court

order and publish excerpts from a classified Pentagon study of US military involvement in Vietnam. The following year, she supported her editor, Benjamin C. Bradlee, in his position that the *Post* should investigate a seemingly innocuous burglary at the Democratic National Committee headquarters at Washington's Watergate apartment complex. The investigation, conducted by *Post* reporters Bob Woodward and Carl Bernstein, ultimately led to the indictment of several White House officials and to the resignation of President Richard Nixon in August 1974.

Graham held the title of publisher until 1979, and was generally considered the most powerful woman in US newspaper publishing. The *Post* grew in influence and stature under her leadership until it joined the elite, along with the *New York Times* and *Los Angeles Times*. It was read and consulted by presidents and prime ministers, and exerted a powerful influence on American political life. In 1979 Graham turned the title of publisher over to her son Donald, but as chairman of the Washington Post Company until 1991 she remained active in all areas of the business, from advising on editorial policy to devising strategies for diversifying the company's holdings. In 1988 *Business Month* magazine listed the Washington Post Company as one of the 'five best managed companies' in America. Two years later, Graham received *Fortune* magazine's Business Hall of Fame award, having proven herself to be a stronger corporate head than either of the two men who influenced her earlier life, her father and her husband.

Graham retired in 1991, and published her memoirs in 1997. Known as a forceful and courageous publisher, she knew when to rely on the expertise of her editors and when to assume responsibility for decisions. Mike Wallace, a reporter for the US public affairs television programme *60 Minutes*, told the *Post* on the occasion of her seventieth birthday in 1987 that 'she is a woman who in effect, I suppose, came to the job unprepared and

turned out to be one of the giants of journalism in the last quarter century' (*Dictionary of Literary Biography* 1993: 110).

BIBLIOGRAPHY

Davis, D. (1979) *Katharine the Great: Katharine Graham and the Washington Post*, New York: Harcourt Brace Jovanovich.

Dictionary of Literary Biography (1993) Volume 127: American Newspaper Publishers, 1950–1990, Detroit: Gale Research.

Felsenthal, C. (1993) *Power, Privilege and the Post: The Katharine Graham Story*, New York: Putnam's.

Graham, K. (1997) *Personal History*, New York: Random House.

BB

GRESHAM, Thomas (*c.*1519–1579)

Thomas Gresham was born in London around 1519, and died there on 21 November 1579, probably of a stroke. His father was Sir Richard Gresham, a prosperous mercer and sometime Lord Mayor of London, who also, according to de Roover (1949: 18), enriched himself during the dissolution of the monasteries in the 1530s. He was educated at St Paul's school and Gonville Hall, Cambridge, and then was eight years an apprentice mercer to his uncle, Sir John Gresham. He married Anne Ferneley, widow of another mercer, in 1543 and was admitted to the livery of his company in 1544.

Gresham owed his early advancement to his father Sir Richard, an adroit trimmer who shifted his allegiance variously from Cardinal Wolsey to Thomas Cromwell, from the Duke of Somerset to the Duke of Northumberland, as the political fortunes of each rose and fell.

Thomas Gresham was given preferred positions, and in 1552 was sent to Antwerp to act as the royal agent. This was a vitally important post, as the primary task of the office holder was to manage the huge royal debt run up by King Henry VIII. Antwerp was then the preeminent money market in Europe, and Gresham's job was to negotiate the renewal of each loan when it came due, paying off high-interest loans where possible by negotiating further borrowing at lower rates.

Quite how he managed this daunting task remains obscure; as de Roover comments, Gresham 'was one whom Nature had endowed with a practical flair but with no matching gift of explaining it' (de Roover 1949: 16). He continued to hold the post until 1574, but the importance of the role declined after about 1560, largely because Gresham had done his job well and the debt had been reduced to a manageable size. He broke his leg in a fall from his horse in 1560 and was thereafter permanently lame, which made him less willing to travel. He had also become rich through his own business dealings and money market speculation in Antwerp, and, spending more time in London, began investing in profitable ventures in the iron industry; in addition, he took an interest in education and made provision in his will for the founding of Gresham College. He founded a small banking business, the Grasshopper, which in the eighteenth century came into the hands of Thomas MARTIN and his descendants and was transformed into Martin's Bank, and which in the twentieth century produced one of the great governors of the Bank of England, Montagu NORMAN. He wrote a paper, *Memorandum on the Understanding of Exchange*, which remains a useful document for the study of money markets of the time, and to him is attributed the adage 'bad money drives out good', which later became known as Gresham's Law. Gresham's own later years were unhappy: his son and heir, his only legitimate child, died in an accident in 1563, and he and his wife separated.

Gresham's permanent memorial was the establishment of the Royal Exchange, which he built with his own money (although, as de Roover notes, the City of London provided the land, and Gresham also built a row of shops beside the exchange from which he drew rents). The purpose of the Exchange was to provide a market for trading in bills of exchange. A patriot, he had an early vision of London as an international financial centre, and wanted to set up a money market to rival that of Antwerp. This did not happen, but, as de Roover says, what the Exchange did do 'was to provide an overwhelmingly native body with facilities not readily accessible before. Easily first among these was insurance, which settled in from the outset and has become identified – one might almost say synonymous – with the Royal Exchange ever since' (de Roover 1948: 19). Thus, although Gresham's vision did not come true in his own lifetime, he did found the first great financial institution of the City of London. Bindoff (1973: 6) notes how in the nineteenth century, when London was the world's undisputed financial capital, the Victorians revived his reputation and adopted him as a kind of 'tribal hero' of the City of London.

BIBLIOGRAPHY
Bindoff, S.T. (1973) *The Fame of Sir Thomas Gresham*, London: Jonathan Cape.
Burgon, J.W. (1832) *The Life and Times of Sir Thomas Gresham*, 2 vols, London: Robert Jennings.
Chandler, G. (1964) *Four Centuries of Banking*, London: B.T. Batsford.
de Roover, R. (1949) *Gresham on Foreign Exchange*, Cambridge, MA: Harvard University Press.

MLW

GROVE, Andrew Stephen (1936–)

Andrew Stephen Grove was born Andras Grof in Budapest on 2 September 1936, the son of George Grof, a businessman, and his wife Maria, a bookkeeper. He grew up in a Hungary during the Second World War and under the postwar communist regime, and left the country after the abortive Hungarian Revolution of 1956, arriving in the United States in 1957. He became a US citizen in 1962. Grove's higher education was all undertaken in the United States; he took a BA from City College, New York in 1960, and a Ph.D. in chemical engineering from the University of California at Berkeley in 1963. He married Eva Kastan in 1958; they have two children.

Following his Ph.D., Grove joined the Fairchild Semiconductor Research Laboratory in San Jose, California, where he was a member of technical staff from 1963 to 1966, section head in surface and device physics from 1966 to 1967, and assistant director of research and development from 1967 to 1968. Here he worked under Gordon Moore and Robert NOYCE, who had been the first to discover how effectively to use silicon chips in making semiconductors. When Moore and Noyce left Fairchild to set up Intel in 1968, they invited Grove to join them. Here he served as vice-president and director of operations from 1968 to 1975, executive vice-president from 1975 to 1979, and chief operating officer from 1976 to 1987; he became president in 1979 and chief executive officer in 1987. A man of great energy, he also lectured at Berkeley from 1966 to 1972, and for many years he wrote a newspaper column for the San Jose *Mercury*.

Although Noyce and Moore had founded Intel, it was under Grove's leadership that the company rose to occupy a position of dominance in its industry. Jackson describes how Grove has transformed the company:

From being an innovator, it became a company whose objective was to deliver –

to make sure its good ideas were turned into practical products that customers could use, products that arrived on schedule and at prices that fell consistently year by year. This transformation was no mean feat. It forced Intel to become rigorously organized and focussed, and to find a balance that allowed it to keep firm control over its operations without jeopardizing the creativity of the scientists who were its greatest assets. The result of this transformation was that Intel rose to domination of its industry.

(Jackson 1998: xiii)

Intel chips are now used in the vast majority of PCs made around the world. Grove himself believes in technology as a kind of unstoppable force: in technology, he says, 'what can be done will be done' (Grove 1996: 5). Like Noyce, he links technological development with social progress.

Grove has a strong management philosophy, which he has set out in several books. He sees information as being at the heart of the management process. In his own working life, he constantly collects and filters information, and he encourages all his employees to do the same. He believes too in the need for emotion and belief in work – intuition is as important as analysis. He does not believe in continuous hands-on management, although he is less *laissez-faire* in this regard than was Robert Noyce; but he argues that as managers have limited time and energy, they should concentrate on doing those things that will have the maximum impact, moving to the point where their leverage will be greatest.

High Output Management (1983) is aimed at middle managers, whom Grove sees as 'the muscle and bone of every sizeable organization', but often ignored by theorists (1983: ix). The book, which is amusingly written in a light tone, sets out to define what it is that managers *do*. In one metaphor, he compares the doing of management to a waiter serving breakfast: both have the same basics of pro-

duction, 'to build and deliver products in response to the demands of the customer at a *scheduled* delivery time, at an *acceptable* quality level, and at the *lowest* possible cost (1983: 3). He argues that managerial activity should not be confused with output. Planning, negotiation, allocating resources and training are things that managers *do*; the output is what they actually *produce*. At Intel, he says, the managerial output is not ideas, it is silicon wafers; the outputs of high-school principals are students, the outputs of surgeons are healed patients, and so on. A manager's output is the output of his own organization (1983: 38). This means that management is a team activity, and so 'the single most important task of a manager is to elicit peak performance from his subordinates' (1983: 145). Managers need to know what motivates their employees; here Grove refers specifically to MASLOW's hierarchy of needs, and argues that managers need to be aware of how these needs motivate employees and subordinates.

Only the Paranoid Survive (1996) is both sharper and more thoughtful. Writing in the aftermath of a disastrous incident in which half a billion dollars worth of defective Pentium chips had to be recalled and replaced, Grove warns against managerial complacency:

I believe in the value of paranoia. Business success contains the seeds of its own destruction. The more successful you are, the more people want a chunk of your business and then another chunk and then another until there is nothing left. I believe that the prime responsibility of a manager is to guard constantly against other people's attacks and to inculcate this guardian attitude in the people under his or her management.

(Grove 1996: 3)

He conceptualizes change in the business environment not as a continuous process but as a series of flash points or 'strategic inflection points', times when the fundamentals by

which a business has existed and operated suddenly change. These strategic inflection points have some similarity to the paradigm shifts described by T.S. KUHN. The appearance of one of these points can mean new opportunities, or it can mean the beginning of the end, depending on how the business responds. Formal planning cannot anticipate these kinds of change, and therefore manages have to be able to respond to the unanticipated.

One of the difficulties in dealing with strategic inflection points is recognizing them when they arrive: how can the manager distinguish signals from noise (1996: 101)? The answer, says Grove, is for managers to engage in vigorous debate, sharing information and generating new ideas. Always challenge the data, he says; ask what it is really telling to you; listen to everyone around you. Everyone must be encouraged to speak; fear of punishment, in many organizations, is the great inhibitor of discussion, and this in turn leads to signals being missed. He recognizes that many managers will not find this easy: 'With all the rhetoric about how management is about change, the fact is that we managers loathe change, especially when it involves us. Getting through a strategic inflection point involves confusion, uncertainty and disorder' (1996: 123).

Getting through a strategic inflection point is tense and chaotic; there are no rules here, precisely because the ground rules themselves are changing. But, says Grove,

at some point you, the leader, begin to sense a vague outline of the new direction. By this time, however, your company is dispirited, demoralized or just plain tired. Getting this far took a lot of energy from you; you must now reach into whatever reservoir of energy you have left to motivate yourself and, most importantly, the people who depend on you so you can become healthy again.

(Grove 1996: 139)

Change is almost like a sickness, and companies need strength and stamina to recover. Now is the time to make sense of the picture, to rein in chaos, and proceed towards goals. In another metaphor, Grove describes passing a strategic inflection point as like crossing the Valley of Death.

BIBLIOGRAPHY
Grove, A.S. (1967) *The Physics and Technology of Semiconductor Devices*, New York: Wiley.
—— (1983) *High Output Management*, New York: Random House.
—— (1996) *Only the Paranoid Survive: How to Exploit the Crisis Points that Challenge Every Company and Career*, New York: HarperCollins.
Jackson, T. (1998) *Inside Intel: Andy Grove and the Rise of the World's Most Powerful Chip Company*, London: Penguin.

MLW

GUANZI (7th century BC)

Guanzi or 'Master Guan' has been tentatively identified with Guan Zhong, the prime minister of the north Chinese state of Qi, who, in the 7th century BC, built up that state's economy and made it into an agricultural and trading power. The book known as the *Guanzi*, named in his honour, encapsulates his thought and was probably compiled initially at the Jixia Academy in Qi in the fourth century BC, but was also – like most Chinese classics – added to and amended over succeeding centuries, notably during the Han dynasty. The modern version was probably compiled by the scholar Liu Xiang in the first century BC (Robinet 1998) and has accretions of Legalist, Confucian and Daoist ideas.

To Guanzi himself can probably be ascribed the book's chapters on economics, which describe the circulation of goods and money within an economy. The book, which purports to be a handbook of statecraft, urges princes to monitor this circulation closely, with two objectives in mind: first, they should guard against excessive accumulation of goods by a small minority, which would result in poverty for the majority; and second, they should encourage productivity so as to grow the stock of goods in circulation. Robinet notes that the work appears to favour agriculture over craft and trading businesses, but this is likely to be a reflection of the need to ensure an adequate supply of food at a time when China's population was growing rapidly; the importance of the crafts and of commerce as wealth creators is recognized. The chapters on agriculture go into some detail on agricultural management, providing information on sowing and harvest times for important crops; there is also a chapter on the importance of recording land distribution using maps, an early example of the importance of record-keeping and data-gathering. These chapters of the *Guanzi* give an interesting insight into the management of economic systems in early China.

The political chapters are largely of later origin, and are largely a synthesis of Legalist and Confucian ideas about the nature of rule and control (see HAN FEIZI; CONFUCIUS). The *Guanzi* organizes society in a strong hierarchy, with the prince at the top of the pyramid and others owing duty and loyalty to him; unlike earlier Confucian writings, the *Guanzi* plays down the duties the prince owes to his subjects, and stresses a more formal and less familial form of control and governance. It does, however, lay down that princes must follow the *dao* or 'moral path', laying down ethical standards for rule. The *Guanzi* had some influence in the Han dynasty period, an influence that can often be detected in later Chinese works on administration and business.

BIBLIOGRAPHY

Rickett, W.A. (1985) *Guanzi: Political, Economic, and Philosophical Essays from Early China*, Princeton, NJ: Princeton University Press.

Robinet, I. (1998) 'Guanzi', in E. Craig (ed.), *Routledge Encyclopedia of Philosophy*, London: Routledge, vol. 4, 186–7.

MLW

GUGGENHEIM, Daniel (1856–1930)

Daniel Guggenheim was born in Philadelphia on 9 July 1856, the son of Meyer and Barbara Guggenheim. He died at his home on Long Island, New York on 28 September 1930. Guggenheim's father had emigrated from Switzerland and set up a lace-importing business in the United States; Guggenheim joined the family firm at the age of eighteen and then went himself to Switzerland, where he worked as a lace buyer for the next eleven years. The family business prospered during those years, and M. Guggenheim and Sons became involved in silver and lead mining in the American West. Returning from Switzerland, Daniel Guggenheim pushed for the firm to focus on refining and smelting rather than ore extraction, seeing the former as more profitable and less risky. He also pressed for the adoption of new technologies to achieve greater cost savings and efficiency. Taking over the firm when his father retired, Guggenheim ploughed much of his profits back into the firm and expanded rapidly. In 1890 he moved into Mexico, negotiating concessions from Mexican president Porfirio Diaz and establishing smelters and a highly profitable copper mine.

During the 1890s firms in many industries moved to consolidate and form combines. Smelting firms merged into the American Smelting and Refining Company (ASARCO) in

1899, and pressure was placed on Guggenheim to join the combine. He resisted, however, until he could secure terms favourable to himself and his business; when ASARCO finally bought out Guggenheim in 1901, he became the combine's chairman. More rapid expansion followed, with mines and smelters all over North America as well as in Chile and the Belgian Congo. Guggenheim turned to J.P. MORGAN for fresh supplies of capital, which was then invested in new technologies on a continuous basis. Under Guggenheim, ASARCO became the world's largest, most technologically advanced and most efficient mining corporation.

The transformation from labour-intensive work to highly skilled and mechanized processes in mining and smelting led to labour unrest. Initially confrontational, Guggenheim, like other mine-owners, advocated breaking strikes by force. Around 1910, however, he seems to have had a change of heart. Hoyt (1967) suggests that there was something of a conversion on the road to Damascus, with Guggenheim, having achieved great wealth, now beginning to consider his social responsibilities. Impetus may have come from his wife Florence, whom he had married in 1884; a noted philanthropist, Florence Guggenheim saw to it that much of the Guggenheim fortune was spent on good causes. However, a wave of violent strikes which swept the mining industry from 1911 to 1913 certainly had a strong impact. With miners and security men fighting and killing each other, Guggenheim believed that the only way to avoid anarchy was to achieve labour peace. He began trying to set an example, reducing working hours and providing housing and medical benefits for workers. He also began making direct contacts with the leaders of the labour movement. With John D. ROCKEFELLER, Jr, Guggenheim arranged a meeting with Samuel Gompers at which a plan for labour peace, at least for the duration of the First World War, was worked out. The plan appears to have been only partially successful, with some of Guggenheim's subordinates preferring confrontation to cooperation, and the violence continued.

Whatever his initial motives, Guggenheim became deeply interested in the sociological and psychological aspects of labour relations, and in his later years he seems to have made a real attempt to understand worker motivation, in particular the motivation to strike or create unrest. In 1915 he stunned the United States Industrial Relations Commission, before which he was testifying, when he said that employees were justified in organizing, as many capitalists were too arbitrary in their treatment of their workers:

There is today too great a difference between the rich man and the poor man. To remedy this is too big a job for the state or the employer to tackle single-handed. There should be a combination in this work between the Federal government, the state, the employer and the employee. The men want more comforts – more of the luxuries of life. They are entitled to them. I say this because humanity owes it to them.

(Hoyt 1967: 236)

In an article published that same year, Guggenheim openly called for state intervention in the labour market to protect workers. Among the measures he advocated were minimum wages and working conditions, compulsory profit sharing and compulsory measures to promote industrial democracy. He did not believe that corporations – including, it seems, his own – could undertake such reforms unaided, and that only the government could achieve lasting labour peace. The necessity for such measures, he believed, was clear:

I think the difference between the rich man and the poor man is very much too great, and it is only by taking steps to bridge the gulf between them that we shall be able to get away from the unrest now prevailing among the working classes.

(Guggenheim 1915: 210).

Guggenheim also continued to be interested in new technology. He was an early backer of the aircraft industry, and funded the first American school of aeronautics. In the 1920s he became involved in nitrate mining in Chile, in a joint venture with Chilean government, but this went badly wrong when nitrate prices collapsed in 1929; at the time of Guggenheim's death, the company was suffering heavy losses. The Chilean government dissolved the joint venture in 1933. The company survived, but lost its world pre-eminence.

BIBLIOGRAPHY

Guggenheim, D. (1915) 'Some Thoughts on Industrial Unrest', *Annals of the American Academy of Political and Social Science* 59(May): 209–11.
Hoyt, E.P. (1967) *The Guggenheims and the American Dream*, New York: Funk and Wagnalls.

MLW

GULICK, Luther Halsey, III (1892–1993)

Luther Halsey Gulick III was born in Osaka, Japan on 17 January 1892 and died in New York on 10 January 1993, a week short of his 101st birthday. His family background was remarkable. His grandparents, Luther and Louisa Gulick, were among the first missionaries to Hawaii and Micronesia; they later worked in China and Japan, where Dr Gulick translated the Bible into Japanese. Their son, Luther Halsey Gulick, Jr, became one of the founders of the modern physical education movement; he served as secretary of the physical training department of the Young Men's Christian Association (YMCA) from 1887 to 1903, during which time he devised the YMCA's famous triangular emblem, worked tirelessly to promote the organization

and, along with James Naismith, developed and promoted the game of basketball. He and his wife, Charlotte Vetter Gulick, travelled widely in the course of these and other activities, and it was on one such trip to Japan that Luther Halsey Gulick III was born.

Like his father, Gulick attended Oberlin College, graduating with an AB in 1914. His father, after leaving the YMCA, had served as an adviser to a number of public health departments, and it may have been this that prompted Gulick towards a career in public administration. In 1916 he joined the research staff of the Bureau of Municipal Research in New York. This organization had been established in 1906 to provide staff support for the New York City municipal government and had been immediately recognized as a success; it was imitated in many other large American cities. In 1911 the New York bureau had added a training school for public servants to its facilities, and in 1914 the economic historian Charles Beard, then a professor at Columbia University, was appointed as the training school's director. Beard, one of the most respected intellectuals of his day, seems to have been a considerable influence on Gulick, although he was far from sharing the former's pacifist views.

In 1917, when the United States entered the First World War, Gulick joined the US Army while Beard resigned from the faculty of Columbia in protest at the university's decision to support the war and suppress dissent. This divergence seems not to have harmed the two men's working relationship, however; Beard was named director of the bureau in 1918, and he appointed the returning Gulick to succeed him as head of the training school in 1919. Beard's tenure as director does not seem to have been a success, in part because of the cloud of suspicion that hung over his pacifist activities; in 1919, in a minor precursor of the McCarthy anti-communist campaign of the 1950s, Beard was one of several intellectuals named by US military intelligence as a suspected foreign agent. He was forced to resign

in 1921 and Gulick, just twenty-nine years old, was his chosen successor.

Over the course of the next decade, Gulick oversaw the transformation of the bureau from an urban to a global organization. Immediately after his appointment, he completed the bureau's reorganization under its new name, the National Institute for Public Administration (NIPA). The training school was hived off to Syracuse University in 1924, and under Gulick's leadership NIPA began focusing on national and, increasingly, international problems of administration. At home, clients included the federal government and several state and city governments; overseas, Gulick followed in his family's footsteps in Japan, advising on the establishment of the Institute of Municipal Research in Tokyo – which was modelled on NIPA – and conducting a study of the reconstruction of Tokyo following the 1923 Kanto earthquake. In 1927–8 NIPA carried out studies for the government of Yugoslavia, and from 1929 to 1930 it advised the Chinese government of Chiang Kai-shek on fiscal reform (though without much effect). In recognition of its increasing international role, NIPA dropped the word 'National' from its title and became simply the Institute for Public Administration (IPA).

By the 1930s Gulick was probably the world's leading authority on public administration. US and foreign governments consulted him frequently. In 1931 he was named Eaton Professor of Municipal Science and Administration at Columbia University, a post which he held until 1942. He was a prime mover in the establishment of the Public Administration Clearinghouse. He was invited to serve on the Brownlow Committee, chaired by Louis F. Brownlow and charged by President Franklin D. Roosevelt with reorganizing the office of the president. After the Second World War he was active in further national and international work, including consultations with the city of Calcutta on developing a new water supply, and with President Nasser on a new constitution for Egypt. He retired in 1961, but continued to write and lecture. Over the course of his career he wrote or co-authored some fifteen books and more than 200 articles; the first of these was published in 1920 and the last seventy years later, when Gulick was ninety-seven.

Most of Gulick's works are practical and focused on particular issues; they include an astonishing number of reports of commissions and committees of inquiry which he chaired. In three particular works, however, Gulick sets out his philosophy of administration clearly. The first of these is his introduction to *Papers on the Science of Administration* (1937), edited by himself and Lyndall URWICK. This book, a management classic, was conceived of by Gulick and published by the IPA in New York; as well as essays by Gulick and Urwick, it contains contributions by such notables as Henri FAYOL, Mary Parker FOLLETT and James MOONEY. The second book, *Administrative Reflections from World War II* (1948), is a thought-provoking attempt to apply some of the lessons learned during the war to peacetime administrative practices. The third, *The Metropolitan Problem and American Ideas* (1962), is based on a series of lectures on government and administration which Gulick gave at the University of Michigan the year he retired; it is largely based on the other two works, but does contain some new insights.

Like his contemporaries in the scientific management movement, Gulick believed that public administration could be made more effective if it were practised according to a set of guiding principles. He saw no essential difference between public sector administration and private sector business management, believing that the processes and practices involved were identical: both had strategic goals and targets, both sought greater efficiency and both developed organizations as a method of reaching their goals. This last point is particularly important. Gulick believed that organizations were tools, means of achieving an end. Rather than building an organization and guiding it towards a goal, the goal should

be firmly fixed in the first instance and the organization then configured to meet that goal. Gulick can here be seen as occupying a middle point between Fayol's earlier 'top down' concept of organizations being designed and guided according to grand principles, and, later, CHANDLER's famous dictum that 'structure follows strategy'. Systematic purpose and clear policy, said Gulick, would always achieve desired ends, so long as the organization was technically capable of reaching those ends.

Thus while scientific management's focus, initially at least, was on the task and the worker, Gulick's primary concern was the organization as a whole. His choice of collaborators for *Papers on the Science of Administration* shows clearly his interests and influences: they include Mooney's investigations into the roots of organization, Follett's work on the social nature of organizations, Fayol's grand principles and Urwick's development of the line and staff concept.

Gulick's own contribution is a conceptualization of organization that is both simple and dynamic. All organizations, he says, are characterized by a tension between the need for division and the need for coordination. The 'division' to which Gulick refers is the classical concept of the division of labour as described by PETTY and Adam SMITH, among others, and which Gulick now sees as the root of all organizations: 'Work division is the foundation of organization; indeed, the reason for organization' (Gulick and Urwick 1937: 3). The classical economic – and scientific management – view that efficiency is achieved through the division of labour is one with which Gulick agrees. However, he says, it is important to recognize that there are limits beyond which labour cannot usefully be divided. Technology and custom provide some limits, although there may be ways of overcoming these. Nor does it make sense to divide labour to the point where defined tasks require the labour of less than one person; this would mean less, rather than more, efficiency. There are also organic limitations to the division of labour. It might,

says Gulick, be more efficient to have the front half of the cow in the pasture grazing while the rear half is in the barn being milked, but any attempt to divide the cow in this fashion would, for obvious reasons, fail.

Divided labour makes for efficiency, but only if the labour and its outputs are harmonized with the organization's goals. This is achieved, says Gulick, through a seemingly opposed process, that of coordination. In any system or organization which relies on the division of labour, there must be some person or persons whose primary function is to ensure the coordination of all the organization's component parts. That role Gulick assigns to the organization's leaders (there are clear reflections here of the line and staff principle). The leader should also be the organizational architect: to him or her falls responsibility for both designing the system by which labour is divided – that is, the structure and organization of the various work units, together with the assignation of tasks to each – and for the ongoing coordination of these units.

Work units can be coordinated in four ways: by purpose (that is, the aims of the work unit), by process (what the unit actually does, such as engineering or accounting), by persons or things dealt with or served (products made, customers served and so on) and by geographical place or location (Gulick and Urwick 1937: 33–4). Each of these four methods requires a different form of coordinating activity:

If all the departments are set up on the basis of purpose, then the task of the chief executive will be to see that the major purposes are not in conflict and that the various processes which are used are consistent ... If all the departments are set up on the basis of process, the work methods will be well standardized on professional lines, and the chief executive will have to see that these are coordinated and timed to produce the results and render the services ... If place be the basis of departmentalization, that is, if the

services be decentralized, then the task of the chief executive is ... to see that each of these services makes use of standard techniques and that the work in each area is part of a general programme and policy.

(Gulick and Urwick 1937: 33–4)

In fact, it is seldom that departments are defined according to one of these four criteria alone. Frequently, two, three or all four criteria will apply. This of course renders the task of the chief executive still more complex. Departments may overlap in one or more of these areas; work units which can be neatly segregated by process may overlap in geographical terms, or vice versa. A critical task of the chief executive is to reduce as far as possible the friction that such overlaps may cause.

To reduce friction, the chief executive has a further weapon at his disposal. As well as coordinating the organization through purpose, process, product/service and place, he or she can also coordinate the organization through ideas. It is this method, says Gulick, that allows the frictions and conflicts between work units to be smoothed out and the whole organization to be brought to bear on a consistent course towards its goals. Indeed, *without* coordination by ideas, the organization will fail:

Any large and complicated enterprise would be incapable of effective organization if reliance for co-ordination were placed in organization alone. Organization is necessary; in a large enterprise it is essential, but it does not take the place of a dominant central idea as the foundation of action and self-co-ordination in the daily operation of all parts of the enterprise. Accordingly, the most difficult task of the chief executive is not command, it is leadership, that is, the development of the desire and will to work together for a purpose in the minds of those who are associated in any activity.

(Gulick and Urwick 1937: 37)

Ideally, each organization should have a single guiding idea, one which is universally understood throughout the organization; it was this sense of a single uniting purpose, more than any other single factor, which led to US and Allied victory in the Second World War (Gulick 1948). In the end, it could be argued that Gulick sees ideas as more potent and more powerful than organizations. People need ideas, to motivate them and to give them purpose; their performance will improve and they will make greater sacrifices if their minds as well as their physical labour is committed to the task in hand. One of top management's key jobs, then, is the dissemination and diffusion of this idea, 'the translation from purpose to programme' (Gulick 1948: 78). Summing up the lessons of the US war effort, he argues that:

Organizations and the men who direct them are expendable. In a world of unprecedented emergencies and uncharted experiences, many things must be tried. When some fail to meet the situation, or when they have served their immediate purpose, they must be superseded. They are casualties, sacrificed in the process of institutional running.

(Gulick 1948: 31).

Ultimately, however, just as there are limits to the division of labour, so also there are limits to coordination. Five factors, says Gulick, combine to limit the ability of leaders to achieve full coordination. These are (1) uncertainty concerning the future; (2) lack of knowledge on the part the leaders; (3) lack of administrative or management skills on the part of the leaders; (4) a general lack of knowledge and skills on the part of other members of the organization; and (5) what Gulick calls 'the vast number of variables involved and the incompleteness of human knowledge, particularly with regard to man and life' (Gulick and Urwick 1937: 40). It is noteworthy that all five of Gulick's limits to coordination revolve around some form of knowledge, or rather, the

lack of some of these forms of knowledge. If division is limited by organic and technical constraints, then coordination is limited in large part by lack of knowledge.

The need, then, is to get a balance between division and coordination. Excessive division will pull the organization apart centrifugally; excessive coordination will result in compression and concentration, and a corresponding loss of efficiency. Coordination, says Gulick, must be managed with a delicate hand; he is strongly in favour of decentralization and of allowing work units to work with minimal control, preferring coordination by 'guiding ideas' to that by command and constraint.

So powerful should these guiding ideas be, says Gulick, that individual members of the organization should be prepared to sacrifice themselves for the greater good; even, if necessary, serving as scapegoats. In a controversial passage written after the Second World War, he says:

the prestige of top management must be maintained even though this involves a certain shifting of responsibility for individual failures and successes to subordinate organizations and men. This is cruel to those organizations and men, but it preserves the integrity of total management in a world of trial and error. In administration, as in baseball, it is the batting average that counts, not the occasional strikeout. Top management must be held accountable for the total record, not each segment. (Gulick 1948: 32)

This is a sentiment with which many in top management might agree, but the statement opens something of a gap in Gulick's thinking where human motivations are concerned. What sort of motivation is required for people to sacrifice their own careers and livelihoods in this fashion? In wartime, where survival is at stake, such selflessness occurs. In the peacetime world of business, the stakes are lower and such selflessness is correspondingly more

rare. Just as there are limits to the leader's span of control, so too are there limits to employees' willingness to become totally involved with their organization.

Yet it is this mix of attitudes, part authoritarian and part humanist, part American and part European, which makes Gulick as a thinker so fascinating. He did not fully resolve the conflicts inherent in his own ideas, but we can see in him the beginnings of a global thinker, drawing his influences not only from the recent American past but from the broader and older context of Europe; and influenced too, even if only in subtle ways through his family connections, by the thought of the Far East. Unlike many of his American contemporaries, he did not believe there was one best way to manage organizations; there were universal principles of organization, but it was up to each group and its leaders to chart their own strategy towards their own goals.

One of the outstanding figures in the history of public administration, Gulick guided what was essentially a new discipline through its formative years in the 1920s, and gave it a philosophy and a framework in the 1930s and 1940s. He was one of the first to realize that public administration could – and indeed must – learn from new developments in business management, especially new systems of thought such as scientific management and the human relations school. But for Gulick, the link between private sector and public sector management was a two-way street; each could contribute to the other. His collaboration with Lyndall Urwick resulted in a management classic; his own work is often strictly practical, but he never lost sight of the ultimate goals and aims of management in either sphere.

BIBLIOGRAPHY
Fitch, L.C. (1997) *Make Democracy Work: The Life and Letters of Luther Halsey Gulick, 1892–1993*, Berkeley, CA: Institute of Government Studies.
Gulick, L.H. (1948) *Administrative*

Reflections from World War II,
University, AL: University of Alabama
Press.

—— (1962) *The Metropolitan Problem
and American Ideas*, New York: Alfred
A. Knopf.

Gulick, L.H. and Urwick, L.F. (eds) (1937)
Papers on the Science of Administration,
New York: Institute of Public
Administration.

Institute of Public Administration (2000)
'Timeline of Events in IPA's History',
http://www.theipa.org, 19 April 2001.

MLW

GUTENBERG, Erich (1897–1984)

Erich Gutenberg was born in Erfort,
Germany on 13 September 1897 and died in
Cologne on 22 August 1984. He studied
physics at Hanover University but later
switched to economics; he studied economics and philosophy at Halle University, and
obtained his doctorate in 1921. Gutenberg
later studied the economics of business
administration under the guidance of Julius
August F. Schmidt and W. Kalveram to
obtain his professor's qualification at
Munster University. From 1929 to 1938 he
worked as a management auditor in the
industrial world. He then became a professor
at Kraustal Mining University in 1938, and
at the University of Jena in 1940. In 1947 he
was invited to join Frankfurt University, after
Schmidt's retirement. In 1951 he moved to
Cologne University to take over the professorship vacated by the retirement of
SCHMALENBACH. Gutenberg made great contributions to the theoretical deepening of the
economics of business administration, and
trained many researchers. In 1966 he retired
from his official post, and died in 1984.

After the Second World War, in 1949,
Germany was divided into East and West.
Despite the disadvantages engendered by the
Cold War, the government of Konrad
Adenauer managed to achieve rapid economic
recovery in accordance with economic policies
based on the new liberalism referred to by F.A.
von HAYEK as the social market principle. This
principle relied on competition to maintain
order in the market, without state interference. Gutenberg, who supported the social
market principle, distinguished forms of
business administration based on *regime-free
factors* and *regime-related factors*. The three
regime-free factors – the system of production
elements and their linkage process, the principle of economic performance, and financial
equilibrium – are required for any kind of
political and economic regime: in order to
maintain financial equilibrium, business
administration links the production elements in
a rational and economic manner. However,
at this stage is added the influence of the three
regime-related factors, those which depend on
the political and economical regime to which
the individual business administration belongs.
The first of these factors is the method of har-
monizing demand and supply, which is conducted according to either a principle of
autonomy (free market) or a principle of
organs (command economy). The second is
the leading principle of individual business
administration, which can be either a profit-
seeking economic principle or a principle of
planned benefits production. The third principle concerns decision making in business
administration, and can result in either independent decision making or co-decision
making.

The final form of business administration is
determined by the combination of the three
regime-related factors superimposed on the
structure of the three regime-free factors. A
capitalist form of business administration is
determined by the combination of the
autonomous principle, the profit-seeking
economic principle and the independent

decision principle. On the other hand, the communist form of business administration is determined by the combination of the organs principle, the planned benefits production principle and the co-decision principle.

The capitalist form of business administration as defined by Gutenberg is a process of linkage between production elements, such as the labourers' contribution, administrative means, materials and so on. He believed that the major problem confronting capitalist business enterprises concerns productivity as a quantitative relation between the supply of the individual production *elements* and the results created by the linkage or production *process*. He approached this problem by introducing a deductive and numerical method of microeconomics. In particular, he emphasized the importance of the executive functions in linking the fundamental production elements, describing them as the 'fourth production element'. From Gutenberg's theory of the importance of administrative functions carried out by executives came an economics of business administration based on decision theory.

When the problem of the productivity of business administration is discussed, a theory of cost becomes indispensable. Traditional cost theory was first systematized by Eugen Schmalenbach, and was further developed by Konrad MELLEROWICZ. According to this theory, the total cost process of business administration is seen as having an S-shaped curve. Gutenberg sought the basis of this theory in a law of profits. According to this law, when the supply amount of a certain production element is increased, with the other production elements remaining constant at a certain level, then the volume of production will increase exponentially up to a certain point, an exponential increase in yield. When the increase in the amount of supply exceeds this point, however, the increase in the amount of the product is converted into an exponential *decrease* in yield. Gutenberg called this law an A-type production function, and declared that

the process of the yield and the process of the total cost were in a relation of inverse functions. He then rejected the total cost theory based on the S-shaped curve due to the fact that, in industrial administration, very little interchangeability of production elements is available, and additional supply of production elements will be valueless unless the operating speed or operating method of the production facilities themselves is changed to handle the increase in volume.

Additionally, Gutenberg argued that any measurement of marginal production force is likewise impossible. Here he presented what he called the B-type production function, in which the ability to replace production elements is not admitted. Whereas traditional cost theory traces an S-shaped curve when looking at the relationship between operating degree and total cost, in the B-type production function the process is traced in a linear manner to the extent of the maximum operation degree, showing an exponential decrease when the maximum value is exceeded. However, since business administrators are always reluctant to allow costs to be exponentially increased, Gutenberg assumed that total cost follows the process in a linear manner. A bitter controversy arose over cost theory, between the followers of traditional theory, which saw the economics of business administration as applied science, and those who followed Gutenberg's theory, which viewed administration as theoretical science. Gutenberg's scholastic concern was to elevate the economics of business administration to the level of theoretical science, and to explain the subject systematically and theoretically. His efforts have brought about a fruitful outcome in the form of an attempt at numerical systematization of the economic theory of business administration.

BIBLIOGRAPHY

Gutenberg, E. (1929) *Die Unternehmung als Gegenstand betriebswirtschaftlicher Theorie* (Enterprise as an Object for the

Science of Business Administration),
Berlin/Vienna.
———— (1951–69) *Grundlagen der
Betriebswirtschaftslehre* (Fundamentals
of the Science of Business
Administration), 3 vols, Berlin: Springer
Verlag.
———— (1958) *Einfurung in die
Betriebswirtschaftslehre* (Introduction to
the Science of Business Administration),
Wiesbaden: Gabler.

Hirata, M. (1971) *Gutenberg no
Keieikeizaigaku* (Gutenberg's Theory of
Business Administration), Tokyo:
Moriyama Shoten.

ST

H

HAAS, Robert Douglas (1942–)

Robert Douglas Haas was born in San Francisco on 3 April 1942, the son of Walter and Evelyn Haas; his family are descended from a nephew of Levi STRAUSS, founder of the clothing manufacturer of that name. He married Colleen Gershon in 1974; they have one daughter. Haas took his BA at the University of California in 1964, and then served as a volunteer with the Peace Corps in the Ivory Coast (1964–6). Returning home, he took his MBA from Harvard Business School in 1968, and was then a fellow at the White House from 1968 to 1969, before joining McKinsey and Company from 1969 to 1972. He then joined Levi Strauss in 1973. He was the company vice-president for corporate planning and policy from 1978 to 1980, chief operating officer from 1981 to 1984, president and chief executive officer from 1985 to 1990, and has been chairman since 1990, stepping down as chief executive officer in 1999. He has held a number of other posts including trustee of the Brookings Institution and member of the Trilateral Commission.

During his tenure at the top of Levi Strauss, Haas led a turnaround of the once moribund company. Sales and profit grew rapidly, especially in the 1980s, on the back of new brands such as Dockers and Slates, whose creation Haas had closely managed. He also greatly developed Levi Strauss's overseas markets, turning the company into a global business and giving its brands international status. In 1985 he made the company private through a leveraged buyout, one of the largest such buyouts attempted up to that time. Haas has provided strong leadership coupled with a clear global vision. His career to date shows how the application of strong management can turn around ageing companies and give them a new lease of life, apparently in defiance of corporate life-cycle theory.

HALSEY, Frederick A. (1856–1935)

Frederick A. Halsey was born in Unadilla, New York on 12 July 1856, the son of a doctor. He died on 20 October 1935 in New York City. After receiving a bachelor's degree in mechanical engineering from Cornell University in 1878, Halsey took a job as an engineer with the Rand Drill Company, where he worked from 1880 to 1990. He married Stella Spencer in 1885, and the couple had two daughters. Halsey was promoted to the position of engineer and general manager of Canadian Rand Drill Company in 1890. In 1894 he joined the staff of *American Machinist* as associate editor; he was promoted to editor in 1907, and became editor emeritus in 1911.

Halsey's most notable achievement was the development of the wages and efficiency system known as the premium plan, first presented in a paper to the American Society of

Mechanical Engineers in 1891 (see Drury 1915: 41–50 for a detailed summary). Halsey, like many of his fellow engineers, saw wage systems as a way of increasing industrial efficiency. The best way of achieving efficiency, it was felt, was to provide incentives for employees to work more efficiently, and the best way of doing this was to link wages with output.

Prefacing his description of the premium plan, Halsey noted that the two most common incentive systems then in use, piecework and profit sharing, were both flawed. Profit sharing tended to reward all workers equally, so that the idle benefited at the expense of the industrious; also, profits could arise from causes other than increased efficiency. For both these reasons, profit sharing did not always provide a strong incentive. In piecework systems, the problem was rather the opposite: as soon as workers increased output, employers tended to cut the piece rate, so that the workers ended up doing more for the same wage. Again, there was no lasting incentive.

Halsey's premium plan was a revised version of the piece-rate system which was intended to solve the problem of rate-cutting. It consisted of paying, in addition to a basic day wage, a premium based on time saved per task. Each task had a standard benchmark in terms of time required to complete it; if the worker could complete the task more quickly, he or she would then earn the premium rate on top of the day rate. The premium rate itself was usually fixed at about one-third the day rate; Halsey was emphatic that the premium rate should never go as high as the day rate. The one-third figure, says Halsey, is generally ideal in that it provides sufficient incentive for the workers without tempting employers into cutting rates. If they were to do so, the workers could simply reduce their rate of output and fall back on their basic day rates, rather than being trapped into working harder as they would be in a piece-rate system.

There is evidence that, nonetheless, employers did sometimes try to cut premium rates. A modified form of the premium plan called the Rowan plan, developed by the marine engine-maker David Rowan and Company in Glasgow around 1900, attempted to counter this by introducing a slightly more complicated scheme in which day rates as well as premium rates could be raised to reward increased output. Thus even if premium rates were cut, a higher day rate would still obtain.

Although Halsey developed the premium plan while working for Rand Drill Company, curiously, the system appears to have been first tried out in another firm, the Springer Torsion Balance Company, in 1888 (Drury 1915: 48). The plan proved to be very effective, with studies showing that the time to complete standard tasks was often reduced by as much as 30–40 per cent. By 1902 the premium plan was in use in factories all over North America and in several European countries, including Britain and Germany. The premium plan was just one of several such systems developed in the 1880s, the other notable example being the gain-sharing plan of Henry R. TOWNE. Both were an influence on Frederick Winslow TAYLOR, as he makes clear in his early papers on his differential rate system (itself a modified piecework system). Generously, Halsey later commented that Taylor's system was superior to his own and recommended that employers should use the Taylor system.

From 1900 onward Halsey was increasingly preoccupied with campaigning against the metric system. He became one of metrification's most impassioned opponents, arguing that (1) the metric system was no more efficient than the present system; (2) the introduction of the metric system would mean great costs for no discernible gain in efficiency; and (3) governments were behaving immorally in compelling adoption of the metric system. His efforts were a major factor in the rejection of the metric system by the US Congress in 1906. Halsey wrote nine books and a large number of articles on various subjects to do with engineering and management, and few miss the chance to attack the metric system still further. One quote will give an idea of his views:

Nowhere has the system made material progress in industry except when backed by the policeman's club ...With their system of weights and measures as a foundation, the English-speaking peoples have built up the greatest commercial and industrial structure the world has known. This system they are asked to abandon for the benefit of others at a cost that is beyond estimate, and for compensating advantages that to themselves are wholly trivial and imaginary. They are asked to enter the slough of despond in which metric Europe wallows in order to help metric Europe out.

(Halsey 1904: 12)

BIBLIOGRAPHY

Drury, H.B. (1915) *Scientific Management*, New York: Columbia University Press.

Halsey, F.A. (1904) *The Metric Fallacy*, New York: D. Van Nostrand and Co.

—— (1905) 'The Premium Plan of Paying for Labour', in J.R. Commons (ed.), *Trade Unionism and Labour Problems*, Boston: Ginn and Co.

—— (1914) *Methods of Machine Shop Work*, New York: McGraw-Hill.

MLW

HAMEL, Gary (1954–)

Gary Hamel attended Andrews University in Michigan, taking a BSc in 1975, and then University of Michigan, where he received an MBA in 1976; he later received a Ph.D. in business from Michigan in 1990. While still working on his thesis, Hamel joined the faculty of the London Business School, where he remains visiting professor of strategy and international management. With C.K. PRAHALAD, with whom he has collaborated professionally for many years, he founded the management consultancy group Strategos. The two authors have collaborated on seven articles for *Harvard Business Review*, two of which won the McKinsey prize for best article to be published in the journal that year, and a best-selling book, *Competing for the Future* (1994). Hamel remains one of the most popular management gurus in the world, and is widely sought after as a speaker.

Hamel is probably most famous for his work with Prahalad on strategy, and in particular on the concept of 'core competencies'. The latter are often defined as being simply 'what a company is good at', but in reality, Hamel and Prahalad say, there is much more to it. Core competencies are not what the corporation values about itself; they are what customers value about the corporation. The define a core competency as a unique skill or attribute which customers value highly, which cannot be easily transferred out of the corporation, but which can be replicated across a range of products/services/markets with which the company is engaged. Any definition of core competences must begin with the customer's point of view; any attribute which cannot be seen to be desired by the customer is *ipso facto* not a core competence.

This is a deceptively simple concept, but one which has great importance for strategy and strategic development. In *Competing for the Future*, Hamel and Prahalad develop on this basic premise to explain what companies and managers should be doing today if they are to win out over their competitors in the future. They believe that companies should always be trying to go a step beyond their rivals, seeking revolutionary rather than evolutionary advances. Hamel has returned to this last theme in his most recent book, *Leading the Revolution* (2001).

BIBLIOGRAPHY

Hamel, G. (2001) *Leading the Revolution*, New York: McGraw-Hill.

Hamel, G. and Prahalad, C.K. (1989)

Competing for the Future: Breakthrough Strategies, Boston, MA: Harvard Business School Press.

MLW

HAMILTON, Alexander (1757–1804)

Alexander Hamilton was born on the Caribbean island of Nevis on 11 January 1757, the illegitimate son of James Hamilton, a Scottish merchant, and Rachel Lavien, a Huguenot shopkeeper. He was mortally wounded in a duel with Republican politician Aaron Burr at Weehawken, New Jersey on 11 July 1804, and died in New York the following day.

His father deserted the family shortly before his mother died in 1368. A local Presbyterian minister raised funds to send Hamilton to school in New York, where he attended King's College (now Columbia University) in 1774. On the outbreak of the American Revolution, Hamilton joined the rebels, fighting with distinction at the battles of White Plains and Trenton. He was rewarded with an appointment as aide-de-camp to General George Washington, an event which marked the beginning of his political career. After the war Hamilton became a member of Congress and was instrumental in drafting the Constitution of the United States; under Washington's presidency, he was appointed the first US Secretary of the Treasury in 1789, and was instrumental in establishing the administrative machinery of government in the USA. He married Elizabeth Schuyler in 1780; the marriage produced eight children.

During his time as Secretary of Treasury, Hamilton developed plans for reviving the United States economy. He saw the national economy and national security as strongly linked. Unlike many writers then and since, Hamilton believed that commercial growth and prosperity made war more likely, not less; commerce did not inevitably lead to peace. The commercial interests of the United States thus had to support its military interests, and vice versa. To this end, Hamilton was a strong believer in an integrated economy with a diverse industrial portfolio. A protectionist, he particularly favoured government support for small but strategically important industrial sectors which would enable them to grow rapidly (what is now known as the 'infant industry' concept).

Hamilton's vision of the growth of the US economy was largely adopted by political and business leaders throughout the nineteenth century, although the pendulum of fashion oscillated (then as now) between protectionism and free trade. His economic approach can be summed up as viewing what is good for business as good for the nation, and vice versa. This outlook shaped the views of American managers and business leaders for generations, and was particularly well suited to the polyethnic character of American business, leading to a sense of corporate solidarity and a view that personal enrichment was a social and moral good (in contrast with the paternalist ethos prevalent in most European societies). It also led to the close relations between big business and government in the USA, sometimes verging on corporatism, which persisted at least into the 1960s. Not himself a businessman, Hamilton was both a talented administrator and a powerful influence on the shaping of managerial culture in the United States.

BIBLIOGRAPHY
Frisch, M.J. (1991) *Alexander Hamilton and the Political Order*, Lanham, MD: University Press of America.
McKee, S. (ed.) (1934) *Papers on Public Credit, Commerce and Finance by Alexander Hamilton*, New York: Columbia University Press.

Mitchell, B. (1976) *Alexander Hamilton: A Concise Biography*, New York: Oxford University Press.

MLW

HAMMER, Armand (1898–1990)

Armand Hammer was born in New York City on 21 May 1898, the son of Julius Hammer, a Russian immigrant, and his wife Rose. He died in Los Angeles on 10 December 1990. He married three times: to Olga von Root in 1925, to Angela Zevely in 1943, and to Frances Tilman Barrett in 1956; the first two marriages ended in divorce, and there was one son from the first marriage. After high school in New York, Hammer studied medicine, graduating from the Columbia College of Physicians and Surgeons in 1921. However, he had concurrently been working as a manager in his father's pharmaceutical business, and was already a millionaire by the age of twenty. He abandoned medicine for a career in business.

Hammer's opportunity came in the 1920s, in the newly established USSR. While Western governments and companies ostracized the communist government, Hammer used family connections in Russia to get into Moscow and meet top officials, eventually securing a meeting with Lenin. He settled in Moscow for a time and became an important East–West business conduit, exporting Russian products such as asbestos, and importing foodstuffs and machinery. The rise of Stalin meant the end of his business in Russia, however, and he returned to New York, where for a time he ran a successful business dealing in art and artefacts; he also became a noted collector of artworks, and founded a major gallery in New York. After the repeal of prohibition he also invested in a number of distilleries, and then after the Second World War he moved into cattle ranching.

In 1957 Hammer changed direction yet again, acquiring a controlling interest in the financially troubled Occidental Petroleum Company. Rebuilding the company and putting it on a sound financial footing required some years, but in 1966 Occidental struck a very large oil field in the deserts of central Libya, propelling the company into the ranks of major oil producers. When the government of Colonel Moammar al-Qadafi came to power in 1969, threatening nationalization of the oil industry, Hammer struck a bargain which allowed the government a majority share in the profits and gave Occidental a virtual monopoly on oil production. As he had done with Lenin fifty years earlier, Hammer now became a window on the world for the otherwise isolated Libya, facilitating imports and exports and sometimes assisting in negotiations with other powers. Hammer had also maintained his contacts with Russia over the decades, again helping to facilitate East–West negotiations on a number of occasions; he became a personal friend of the last communist leader, Mikhail Gorbachev, and one of Hammer's last public acts was to fly medical teams to the Ukraine to assist in the aftermath of the Chernobyl nuclear disaster.

Hammer was a master of relationship management. He understand better than most twentieth-century business leaders the relationship between politics and business; his talent was to be able to persuade political leaders of all persuasions, ranging from Western liberals to Soviet communists to Islamic revolutionaries, of his views and to gain their trust. This ability to make and maintain relationships at the highest level – often in the face of his home country's public opinion – marks Hammer out as an intelligent and courageous manager and business leader.

BIBLIOGRAPHY
Hammer, A. and Lyndon, N. (1987)
Hammer, New York: Putnam.
Weinberg, S. (1989) *Armand Hammer: The Untold Story*, Boston: Little, Brown and Co.

MLW

HAMMER, Michael (1948–)

After taking his bachelor's, master's and Ph.D. degrees at Massachusetts Institute of Technology (MIT), Michael Hammer joined IBM as a software engineer before returning to MIT as a professor of computer science. In the late 1980s he participated, with Thomas Davenport, in the PRISM research project run by the Index consulting group, which developed the concepts that were to launch him as one of the most influential management 'gurus' of the early 1990s. In articles published in the 1990 volumes of the *Sloan Management Review* and *Harvard Business Review* respectively, Davenport and Hammer discussed their findings in terms of a new approach to management that they called business process redesign, or reengineering. This proclaimed that the power of modern information technology provided an opportunity for corporations to reinvent themselves around business processes and achieve dramatic performance improvements. Hammer's article, characteristically entitled 'Reengineering Work: Don't Automate, Obliterate', achieved rapid recognition and his subsequent book (*Reengineering the Corporation: A Manifesto for Business Revolution*) with James Champy of CSC Index topped the best-seller lists on its publication in 1993.

Hammer's definition of reengineering is 'the fundamental rethinking and radical redesign of business processes to achieve dramatic improvements in contemporary measures of business performance', of which the key words are seen to be 'radical', 'dramatic' and 'process'. 'Radical' is taken to indicate that redesign should start with a blank slate: throw out all the old processes and assumptions and start again. Reengineering is a new beginning. 'Dramatic' refers to reengineering's performance improvement targets. In contrast to the incremental approach of total quality management, reengineering aims for step changes rather than marginal improvement. Finally, 'process' indicates that businesses should be organized around horizontal processes, 'collections of activities that take various kinds of input and create an output that is of value to a customer' (Hammer and Champy 1993: 35), rather than on traditional, vertical functional lines.

Hammer's claims for reengineering in these works were nothing if not bold. Reengineering was described as the biggest breakthrough in management thinking since Adam SMITH, and readers were assured that performance improvements such as 'taking 78 days out of an 80-day turnaround time, cutting 75% of overhead and eliminating 80% of errors' (Hammer 1990: 112) could be achieved by any organization following its precepts. Reengineering was also seen to create a 'new world of work' involving shifts: from functional departments to process teams; from simple tasks to multidimensional work; from control to empowerment; from training to education; from payment for activity to compensation by results; from promotion by performance to advancement based on ability; from protective to productive values; from managers as supervisors to managers as coaches; from hierarchical to flat organizational structures; and from executives as scorekeepers to executive leadership.

If, as critics such as Grint (1994) argued, few, if any, of these ideas were quite as novel or radical as Hammer suggested, they certainly seemed to have remarkable appeal to managers at the time. Thus in his second book (*The*

Reengineering Revolution, with Steve Stanton), published in 1996, Hammer reported that more than three-quarters of America's largest companies were said to be undertaking reengineering projects in 1994, while Davenport (1995) estimated the size of the market for reengineering consultancy and related services to be $51 billion in 1995.

Perhaps because of this remarkable success, reengineering also attracted its fair share of critics. While some, such as Grint (1994), focused on accounting for the concept's exceptional popularity (given its unexceptional content), others questioned its efficacy, noting that, as with PETERS and Waterman's *In Search of Excellence* (1982), many of Hammer's reengineering exemplars had subsequently fallen on hard times. In this they were assisted by a (later much regretted) statement in 'Reengineering the Corporation', that 50 to 70 per cent of organizations undertaking reengineering failed to achieve the dramatic results they intended. Although Hammer sought to dismiss this 'myth' in *The Reengineering Revolution*, arguing that reengineering was not inherently risky – indeed, success was 'guaranteed' for those who followed its principles correctly – doubts about reengineering's effectiveness continued to grow.

A more substantive concern was raised by writers such as Davenport (1995), Hammer's erstwhile colleague on the PRISM project, who argued that reengineering's treatment of the human side of organizations was seriously deficient. Having himself likened reengineering to a neutron bomb that destroys people and leaves structures standing, and having advocated an aggressive top-down approach to reengineering implementation, sweeping away old practices and eliminating many jobs, Hammer was forced to concede that reengineering might have been 'insufficiently appreciative of the human dimension', a fault that he attributed to his engineering background (White 1996). He continued to resist, however, suggestions that reengineering was simply a euphemism for mindless downsizing.

In retrospect, it would seem that 1995 marked the turning point in the fortunes of reengineering. Although Hammer continued to promote reengineering (Hammer 1996; Hammer and Stanton 1999), albeit emphasizing the enduring contribution of its process orientation in an age of enterprise systems and e-commerce rather than the more extravagant claims of its unique solution to the problems of modern management, the concept seems to be popularly viewed as having been a passing fad. Indeed, Hammer's 1996 book was entitled *Beyond Reengineering*.

Hammer's achievement, therefore, is that of having captured, for a period in the early 1990s at least, the popular imagination with a simple, but arguably derivative, message about how companies should, and could, organize themselves around processes rather than functions. As Jones (1994) notes, this has been attributable in no small measure to his effectiveness as a writer and speaker. Citing business leaders, American cultural, sporting and political figures as well as classic writers to support and illuminate the ideas, his writing is studded with catch phrases such as 'paving the cowpaths', 'rearranging the deckchairs on the Titanic', or 'dusting the furniture at Pompeii', and supported by alliterative lists and enumerated 'principles'. The language is simple, direct and supremely self-confident. As a speaker, his evangelical style of delivery is also frequently remarked upon. Indeed, he has himself described reengineering as a theology. It is unclear, therefore, whether in the longer term reengineering will be seen as a phenomenon of primarily historical and sociological interest, or as having made a significant contribution to management. Hammer's role in promoting the concept and thereby perhaps providing the rationale for significant programmes of organizational restructuring in the early 1990s, however, would seem undeniable.

BIBLIOGRAPHY
Davenport, T.H. (1995) 'The Fad that Forgot People', *Fast Company*

(November): 70–74.

Grint, K. (1994) 'Reengineering History: Social Resonances and Business Process Reengineering', *Organization* 1(1): 179–201.

Hammer, M. (1990) 'Reengineering Work: Don't Automate, Obliterate', *Harvard Business Review* (July–August): 104–12.

—— (1996) *Beyond Reengineering*, London: HarperCollins.

Hammer, M. and Champy, J. (1993) *Reengineering the Corporation: A Manifesto for Business Revolution*, London: Nicholas Brealey.

Hammer, M. and Stanton, S. (1996) *The Reengineering Revolution*, London: HarperCollins.

—— (1999) 'How Process Enterprises Really Work', *Harvard Business Review* (November–December): 108–18.

Jones, M.R. (1994) 'Don't Emancipate, Exaggerate: Rhetoric, "Reality" and Reengineering', in R. Baskerville, S. Smithson and J. DeGross (eds), *Information Technology and New Emergent Forms of Organizations*, Amsterdam: North-Holland, 357–78.

White, J.B. (1996) 'Reengineering Gurus take Steps to Remodel their Stalling Vehicles', *Wall Street Journal*, 26 November: A1.

MJ

HAN FEIZI (*c.*280 BC–233 BC)

Han Feizi was born in north China in the state of Han around 280 BC, a member of that state's ruling family. He committed suicide in 233 BC probably in Xian, then the capital of the state of Qin. Originally a Confucian, he had studied under the great Confucian philosopher Xunzi (298 BC–238 BC), but was later attracted to the school of philosophy known later as legalism, whose foremost exponent had been Shang Yang (d. 338 BC). Legalism as proposed by Shang Yang laid out a strict hierarchical order for society, with firmly defined duties for everyone from ministers of the king down to the merchants and peasants. Harsh punishments were decreed for those who failed in their duty, for whatever reason. As the minister of the king of Qin, Shang Yang put these principles into practice and created a well-organized if despotic state. Han Feizi attempted to persuade his kinsman, the ruler of Han, to adopt a similar system, but was rebuffed. Instead, he committed his thoughts on legalism to writing, creating a highly systematic and philosophical version of legalism which won him a considerable following, including King Zheng of Qin.

In 233 BC Han Feizi was sent by the court of Han as an emissary to King Zheng; the two men met, and Zheng was so impressed by the philosopher that he offered him a post in his own country. However, the first minister of Qin at the time was Li Si, who had been a fellow student with Han Feizi at the academy of Xunzi, and he now feared that Han Feizi would become his rival at court. He arranged for the latter's arrest on trumped-up charges and then forced him to commit suicide while in prison. Nevertheless, Zheng had been converted to Han Feizi's brand of legalism. By 221 BC Zheng had conquered the other warring kingdoms of China, unified the country for the first time, and took the throne as first emperor of China under the title Qin Shi Huangdi. Among his many achievements (including the building of the Great Wall and the Grand Canal) was the creation of the imperial bureaucracy, which was modelled on legalist lines. When the Qin dynasty fell in 206 BC, its successors discarded most of the legalist aspects of the state but kept the bureaucracy.

Han Feizi rejected the Confucian notion that most people tend towards the good and can be relied upon to behave ethically through a social system which exerts pressure on people to conform. To him, the only way to achieve con-

formity was through the rule of law. His system of thought was based on three important principles. The first of these was *fa*, meaning roughly 'prescriptive standards', but also with connotations of law and punishment. People should comply with *fa* so that their behaviour conforms with the public good, or be punished as a result. The second was *shi*, meaning 'authority' or 'power'. The exercise of *shi* is necessary to ensure compliance with *fa*; but conversely, *shi* should also be governed by the dictates of *fa* to prevent abuses of power. The third was *shu*, the technique of controlling the bureaucracy by comparing 'word' with 'deed' (or more generally, potential performance with the actuality).

Taken together, the three principles of *fa*, *shi* and *shu* provided a system of management which was the guiding force for Chinese administration for the next two millennia, at least until the fall of the empire in 1911 (and Westerners travelling in China may still detect their influences today). Han Feizi's views of administration are harsh and bureaucratic by today's standards, but it is worth noting that this, the world's first formal system of administration, is also its longest lasting.

BIBLIOGRAPHY

Chang L.S. (1999) 'Han Feizi', in E. Craig (ed.), *Routledge Encyclopedia of Philosophy*, London: Routledge, vol. 4, 219–20.

Watson, B. (1964) *Han Fei Tzu: Basic Writings*, New York: Columbia University Press.

MLW

HANAWA Yoshikazu (1935?–)

Hanawa Yoshikazu graduated from Tokyo University and began work at Nissan in 1957. His rise has paralleled that of Nissan itself. By 1989 he was president of Nissan North America, and in 1991 he was made executive vice-president; he became president of Nissan in 1996.

Having grown from a small Japanese auto firm in 1945, by 1985 Nissan was a force to be reckoned with. Writers such as Halberstam (1986) praised it as the embodiment of Japan's *keiretsu* system of lifetime employment and honour-bound company networks. But Nissan's weaknesses and those of the *keiretsu* system came to the fore after the Japanese economy crashed in 1989. By 1993 Nissan was losing money, and when Hanawa became president he took over the helm of a much weakened company.

After taking over as president, Hanawa attempted to resuscitate the ailing company with traditional Japanese remedies, borrowing money from banks and the government, cutting inventories and closing down Nissan's lavish Tokyo headquarters. It was soon apparent that much stronger measures would be needed, as Nissan continued to post ever heavier losses. Larimer (1999) commented that Nissan's difficulties were a microcosm of Japanese management itself:

In recent years, Japanese companies have repeatedly opted to shield one another from the need to change. The *keiretsu* tend to protect their money-losing businesses. Nissan is a good example. It has been using barely half of its manufacturing capacity and yet supporting a large network of suppliers that have little incentive to offer competitive prices. Despite declining market share and sales, nobody dared tinker with the system, despite its stunning inefficiencies. *Keiretsu* ties are extensive and touch every part of the lives of a group's employees. At Sumitomo Bank, for example, staff are encouraged to drink only Asahi beer because the brewery is in its *keiretsu*. Some business groups even have marriage counselors who help young employees find mates from within the *keiretsu*.

(Larimer 1999)*

By 1998, with Nissan deeply in debt and in very real danger of bankruptcy, Hanawa embarked upon a revolution in Japanese management not unlike that of Daimler-Benz's Jürgen SCHREMPP in Germany. He recognized that Nissan could not survive as it was, with unimaginative bureaucratic management and unpopular products. In mid-1998 Hanawa began negotiations with Renault, which resulted in the formation of an intercontinental Nissan/Renault business alliance. The French semi-public firm obtained a one-third stake in Nissan and ownership of its European financial branches. The alliance was designed to save Nissan over $3 billion in long-term production costs. The new alliance was now the world's fourth largest auto maker, behind General Motors, DaimlerChrysler and Toyota.

Hanawa then embarked upon his most controversial step, a drastic restructuring, unprecedented in Japanese business history, under the direction of a new operations officer, Renault's Carlos Ghosn. According to *The New York Times* (19 October 1999), Nissan would shut down three of its plants and eliminate 21,000 out of 148,000 jobs, mostly by attrition and early retirement. One-half of Nissan's suppliers would be cut and one-tenth of its showrooms closed. Larimer described the drastic restructuring of 1999:

In February, after Nissan Motor took the radical step of putting itself up for sale, chief executive Yoshikazu Hanawa was asked whether he would consider breaking Japan Inc.'s long-standing taboo and fire workers to cut costs. His answer to Time: 'We'll handle the employment issue carefully.' Last week, the country's second-largest carmaker announced that it would shut five plants, cut ties to hundreds of suppliers and – gasp! – let go of 21,000 workers. Hanawa's explanation: 'We don't have other alternatives. To survive, we must do this.'

(Larimer 1999)*

Hanawa's restructuring plan met with an outcry of protests from many who feared that it signified the beginning of the end for the Japanese system of lifetime employment. According to Larimer, who cited University of Tokyo economist Noguchi Yukio, analysts are waiting to see if the restructring is 'the real thing'. If Hanawa is successful, some believe, there could well be a kind of domino effect, with banks consolidating and the *keiretsu* in turn beginning to disintegrate: 'Stronger companies will no longer need to rely on allied banks for capital; weaker firms will find themselves without banks to depend on' (Larimer 1999).

If that scenario pans out, it will mean an end to ways of doing business that date back to the early part of this century, when Japanese companies were grouped as *zaibatsu* (the precursors of today's *keiretsu*) and backed by the government. These powerful business alliances supplied Japan's war machine, and survived attempts to dismantle them during the post-Second World War US occupation. As Noguchi comments: 'We used it [the *keirestsu* system] to our advantage then, with every worker cooperating and getting together for a single-minded purpose ... The problem is, the technology changed but our system didn't' (Larimer 1999).* The *keiretsu* also face an increasing threat from the Internet, which is changing the relationship between manufacturers and suppliers. Whether or not this threat materializes in strength, Hanawa's management has symbolized Japan's need and efforts to adapt to the global economy and form new global business alliances. His strength of purpose and creativity in finding solutions make him a role model for modern managers to follow.

BIBLIOGRAPHY

Halberstam, D. (1986) *The Reckoning*, New York: Avon Books.

Larimer, T. (1999) 'Great News: No More Jobs for Life', *Time*, 1 November, http://www.cnn.com /ASIANOW/time/

magazine/99/1101/japan.nissan.html, 6 September 2000.

Strom, S. (1999) 'Cuts by Nissan Are Deeper Than Foreseen', *New York Times*, 19 October.

DCL

HANDY, Charles Brian (1932–)

Charles Brian Handy was born in County Kildare, Ireland on 25 July 1932, the son of Archdeacon Brian Handy and his wife Joan. After schooling in Ireland, he took a BA in Greats at Oriel College, Oxford in 1956, and in 1967 an MBA from the Sloan School of Management at Massachusetts Institute of Technology. His managerial career included posts with Shell International and the Anglo-American Corporation. In 1967 he moved into academia, joining the faculty of London Business School; he was made a full professor in 1972, and joined the board of governors in 1974. He was visiting professor from 1977 to 1994, and is now a fellow of the school. Handy played an important role in the revival of British management education and thought that took place in the 1970s. His first book, *Understanding Organizations* (1976), was an international best-seller. From 1977 to 1981 he served as Warden of St George's House, Windsor, a private study and conference centre, and he was chairman of the Royal Society for the Encouragement of Arts, Manufacture and Commerce from 1987 to 1989.

Already a highly respected scholar and thinker, Handy's reputation as a guru was established by two important works, *The Age of Unreason* (1989) and *The Empty Raincoat* (1994), both of which have remained in print continuously since publication. During the 1990s, while remaining a visiting professor at London Business School, Handy concentrated on writing and broadcasting, producing several more books and becoming a regular contributor to *Thought for the Day*, a religious-philosophical opinion programme broadcast by the BBC. In 2000 an opinion poll conducted over the Internet named Handy the second most influential management thinker of all time, outranked only by Peter DRUCKER (FT Dynamo 2001). Handy and his wife Elizabeth have two children; they currently live near Diss, Norfolk.

For the purposes of analysis, Handy's thought can be divided into three stages, although it should be emphasized from the outset that strong common themes run through all three. In the first stage Handy developed his theories of organization behaviour, first outlined in *Understanding Organizations* and developed further in *The Gods of Management* (1979b). In the second he focused on the management of paradox, the central theme of both *The Age of Unreason* and *The Empty Raincoat*. The third stage moves beyond the study of paradox *per se* to a search for personal values and meaning in an increasingly paradoxical world; this is the central focus of works such as *Beyond Certainty* (1996) and *The Hungry Spirit* (1997a). Over the course of more than twenty years, Handy's thought has progressed from more or less conventional – though highly original – conceptualizations of organizations and culture to an intense concern for the plight of the individual and his or her social, psychological and spiritual welfare in an organizational environment of constant flux and change.

In many ways, *Understanding Organizations* is the most powerful of Handy's books, even if it lacks the appeal of his later works; it lays down solid principles which, as noted, permeate Handy's later and more personal writings. The most important of these, perhaps, is his conceptualization of organiza-

tion culture. Cultures, he says, can be distinguished by certain features, notably the roles and functions of the individuals within them and the power that those individuals have. Analysing these features, he creates a fourfold classification of organization cultures: *power cultures, role cultures, task cultures* and *person cultures* (Handy 1976, 1979a).

Power cultures, which Handy also refers to as 'club cultures', are those where power is concentrated in the hands of a single dominant individual, such as the founding entrepreneur. All power flows from one central source in the organization through a web-like network of influence and communication. Control is exercised on a personal level rather than through rules or procedures. Note that these cultures are not necessarily strongly hierarchical; indeed, as the metaphor of the web indicates, they often substitute formal hierarchy for close personal bonds. These cultures, if embedded in an organization, can make that organization very flexible, powerful and quick to respond. Their great weakness is their dependence on the dominant individual at the centre; human nature is capricious, and the leader cannot be expected to be right all the time. But when he or she makes a mistake, the entire organization suffers.

Role cultures, in contrast, are hierarchical and bureaucratic. Organizations with a strong role culture tend to place a premium on functional specialization: finance, marketing, production and other tasks are assigned to specific departments, often with some separation between the departments. Jobs and authority are strongly defined; reporting is vertical, with coordination taking place among a fairly narrow band of senior managers at the top of the organization. Handy likens this structure to a Greek temple, with the departments serving as the supporting pillars and the upper tier of coordinating managers functioning as a kind of roof. These organizations, like buildings, tend to be strong and efficient, but rigid.

In task cultures, the primary orientation is on the job or project. Organizations which are based on this culture tend to be very flexible and adaptive; people are used to moving between groups and teams, which are formed and reformed as needed to undertake specific projects. Their major weakness is the lack of a leading or coordinating points. In power cultures direction and control emanate from the centre, and in role cultures they come down from the top. In task cultures, there is no obvious focal point; with lack of directed power may also come lack of responsibility. Despite the fashion for such cultures even in the 1970s, Handy advises caution:

It [the task culture] is the culture most in tune with current ideologies of change and adaptation, individual freedom and low status differentials. But ... it is not always the appropriate culture for the climate and technology. If organizations do not all embrace this culture, it may be that they are not just out-of-date and old-fashioned – but right.

(Handy 1976: 189)

Person cultures, says Handy, exist only to assist and serve their members. Person cultures can also be thought of as clusters, with members drawn together almost at random on the basis of self-interest, and no other common bond. Organizations based on the person culture are rare: the examples Handy gives are barristers' chambers and hippie communes.

Although he describes these cultures in detail, Handy does not assert the primacy of any one of them over the others. Indeed, his ideal organization would have room for all four somewhere within it. In *Gods of Organization*, Handy develops these cultures further, using as metaphor the pantheon of Greek gods. Just as Greek society had room for many gods, he says, so organizations should have room for many cultures. He goes on to assign a particular Greek god to each of his four cultures: Zeus is the god of the power culture, powerful but capricious and unpre-

dictable; Apollo, god of logic, is assigned to the role culture; Athena the war goddess is assigned to the task culture (although her role as weaver and patron of craft-workers might seem equally appropriate); and the self-interested and sometimes chaotic Dionysos is assigned to the person culture. Given that, in the view of most modern scholars, the Greek gods were in large part personifications of human psychological traits, the metaphor seems an apt one. The use of metaphor can be a powerful descriptive tool when thinking about organizations, and has been used to great effect by Gareth MORGAN and Max BOISOT. The fourfold classification, too, is strongly reminiscent of Boisot's typology of markets, bureaucracies, fiefs and clans, and of Geert HOFSTEDE's four features of organization culture (power distance, individualism–collectivism, masculinity–femininity and uncertainty avoidance). Whether this resemblance is more than superficial has yet to be established, but there is clearly room for further work in this field.

As noted, Handy does not believe that organizations are, or should be, homogeneous. All organizations, he says, have a tendency to subdivide themselves into groups, either formally or informally. Groups have many names and functions, and organizations rely on them for a variety of purposes: to distribute, manage and control work, to solve problems and take decisions, to collect and process information and ideas, to coordinate activities within the organization, to increase commitment and involvement, and to negotiate and resolve conflicts. Likewise, individuals also use groups for purposes of their own: as a means of satisfying social or affiliation needs, as a means of defining a concept of self, as a means of acquiring support for their own personal objectives, and as a means for sharing or taking part in a common purpose. All of these are important human needs, and Handy returns to these in many of his later works.

It is one thing to create groups, but quite another to make them effective. Group effec-

tiveness, says Handy, depends on three sets of factors. The first set, which he labels 'givens', include the size and composition of the group, the environment in which it works and the nature of its tasks. The second set consists of 'intervening factors', which include the style of leadership, the processes by which the group carries out its work and, most importantly, the motivation of its members. The third set are the 'outcomes', including the group's productivity and the resulting satisfaction of its members.

Motivation is only one of the many variables which affect how organizations function – Handy lists over sixty (1976: 219), but it is one to which he gives considerable time. In a long passage in *Understanding Organizations* (1976: 29–59), he discusses what he calls the 'motivation calculus'. Each individual, in the context of his or her needs and in the context of the likely result of any action calculates how much effort he or she will have to expend in order to achieve this result. This calculation is not made in isolation: we are not so self-interested as all that. All of us also have a psychological contract with the organization(s) to which we belong, and the nature of this contract affects our calculus. These contracts can come in one of three types: (1) coercive, where we have no choice but to perform the duties required of us; (2) calculative, where our primary consideration is personal gain or reward; and (3) cooperative, where we identify with the organization's goals and make them our own, so that the maximum reward to the organization is also the maximum reward to ourselves. Again, real-life situations are rarely so simple; most psychological contracts contain elements of two or all three of these types, and it is rare to find 'pure' types.

In Handy's view, then, organizations are social organisms, not mechanical constructs. In his next major work, *The Age of Unreason*, Handy turns his attention to the social aspects of organizational culture. Diversity within organizations is a positive force; he sees this diversity as an essential prerequisite for orga-

nizational flexibility, itself a necessity when managing in an age of paradox, change and flux. Yet diversity can lead to conflicts in organizations where there is tight central control. Handy's solution is decentralization, or 'federalism' as he calls it in *The Gods of Management* and *The Empty Raincoat*, in which subgroups work semi-independently, grouped in what he calls 'organizational villages'. These small subunits could then work relatively free from central interference, and could develop the cultures that best suited their own group and individual needs.

It is interesting to compare the 'organizational village' with some earlier attempts at decentralization, such as that developed by BAT'A in the 1930s. In *The Age of Unreason*, however, Handy takes the concept further. Here he describes what he calls the 'shamrock organization', essentially a model for organizational decentralization. This is essentially a tripartite structure. The first leaf of the shamrock is composed of core workers, such as professionals and technicians, whose work is essential to the organization. They are the prime repositories of organizational knowledge, and it is they who give the organization its goals and direction. Core workers are well remunerated and receive many benefits, but in return are expected to work long hours and give high levels of commitment to the organization.

The second leaf of the shamrock consists of contract workers, doing non-vital but still essential jobs whose nature is often tangential to the organization's main purpose. These contract workers are specialists in their own fields, and can often earn more money and/or get more satisfaction by working freelance or for specialist organizations. The third leaf consists of part-time and temporary workers who are hired as and when they are needed in order to meet peaks of labour demand. This third group, less well paid and less motivated, are obviously vulnerable, and organizations should resist the temptation to squeeze the maximum labour from them in exchange for the minimum reward; only good wages and rewards will ensure a good quality of output.

The problem of managing these different cultures is one which Handy addresses at some length. His concern is not just for managerial adaptability and flexibility in terms of group effectiveness, but for managers themselves, who find the conflicts inherent in diverse groups are placing them under increasing levels of stress. Forced to manage conflicts between different cultures over time, often without clear objectives, managers are caught between the need to generate trust and the need to exercise control. Traditional forms of organization may have been inflexible, but they provided at least short-term security. In these new patterns of organization, how will people develop their careers, provide for their families and their own old age? Who will train them and educate them? What other aspects of life and society can give them security?

The Age of Unreason was an international best-seller, but some critics accused Handy of trying to provide overly deterministic solutions: the shamrock organization was seen as an organizational blueprint rather than as a metaphor for the management of diversity. His response in his next major work, *The Empty Raincoat*, was to focus on one of the core psychological and social aspects of management: the management of paradox. The problem of paradox had already surfaced in his earlier work, but here Handy makes a determined effort to show how paradox can be understood and managed. As in his writings on organization, the first step to managing paradox is to classify it: he opens the book by listing nine forms of paradox which confront us in our professional lives. These are, briefly:

1. The paradox of intelligence: intelligence is the greatest single source of wealth but it is also the most difficult to own and control.

2. The paradox of work: as our society becomes more efficient, there is less work

to do and consequently more 'enforced idleness'.

3. The paradox of productivity: greater productivity has been achieved by fewer people working longer hours, with a consequent increase in unemployment and underemployment.

4. The paradox of time: greater efficiency has in theory led to more leisure time, yet the pressures on our time are greater than ever.

5. The paradox of riches: the increasing concentration of wealth in the hands of fewer people is actually leading to a slackening of demand.

6. The paradox of organizations: new business organizations have to be structured yet flexible, global yet local.

7. The paradox of age: every generation believes itself to be different from its predecessor, but assumes the next generation will be the same as itself.

8. The paradox of the individual: we seek to be individuals, yet we identify – and are identified by others – with the groups and organizations to which we belong.

9. The principle of fairness: justice demands that all should be treated equally, yet our system of distribution makes it inevitable that some will achieve and earn more than others.

Paradox confuses, says Handy, 'because things don't behave in the way we instinctively expect them to behave. What worked so well last time around is not guaranteed to work as well next time' (Handy 1994: 47). Although *The Empty Raincoat* was hailed as a statement of the postmodern business dilemma, of the problems of management in an age of change and flux, Handy makes it clear that paradox is not new; indeed, it is a problem as old as society. To deal with it, he reinvokes two old concepts, reinvented, as he says, for the modern world: these are *twin citizenship* and

subsidiarity. Twin citizenship is simply the assuming of multiple loyalties to different identity groups; thus one can be both a Texan and an American, a Bavarian and a German. In the same way, within organizations a climate can be created that allows people to feel loyalty both to their own group(s) and to the organization as a whole, without a conflict necessarily being created. Subsidiarity consists of the delegation of responsibility from the centre to the constituent parts. As a political principle, this resembles the federalism discussed in his earlier work, but here Handy maintains that subsidiarity is also a moral principle, a duty laid on those in power; although he does not say so explicitly, he appears to argue that the delegation of responsibility is concurrent with individuals' rights.

The Empty Raincoat, then, is not a prescription for management but an introduction to a 'new' way of thinking, one in which variables are taken for granted and in which diversity, change, flux and paradox are assumed and understood. Paradox need not be seen as a barrier; it can even be an asset. To reach this point, however, we need to adopt a less mechanistic, scientific approach to management, and pick up one that is more philosophical and humanistic, one in which a corporate scorecard includes assets such as the intelligence and knowledge of employees, levels of customer satisfaction, and contributions to social environmental well-being. The ethics of business which Handy introduces here is one which focuses on personal welfare over profit (this point is later driven home with emphasis in *The Hungry Spirit*). Near the end of *The Empty Raincoat* he launches a vigorous attack on the Cartesian values which have pervaded management up to this point. Kant, not Descartes, is Handy's intellectual hero here, as he attacks the view that the only true knowledge is science: 'That way lies a moral vacuum, where nothing is right and nothing really wrong. That way also lies inertia ...' (1994: 238). He goes on to summarize the argument of *The Critique of Pure Reason*:

It is God in the human soul, Kant said, not God the architect of the scientific universe, who makes sense of who we are. 'How do you know this?' he was asked. 'Because of the moral force within me', he replied.

It is as good an answer as I know. Faith has no reasons. If there were reasons, or logic, there would be no need of faith. I cannot prove there is a point to our existence ... Even if there is no point, even if it is all a game of science, we must still believe that there is a point. If we don't believe that, there will be no reason to do anything, believe anything, change anything. The world would then be at the mercy of all those who did believe that they could change things. It is a risk we cannot run.
(Handy 1994: 238–9)

Ultimately, managers are not technicians; they are *moral beings*. Without that sense of ethics, and indeed of faith, which Handy describes, they become no more than automaton servants of their organization, doomed to run down and die once the organization itself runs out of energy to propel them. With the right inspiration, however, they can transcend the limits of organization and reach out to touch the future. In doing so, they re-energize their organizations and propel them forward. People die, says Handy, but organizations can live forever (Handy 1997b).

Somewhere in the 1990s, almost imperceptibly, Handy crossed over the borderline between management thinking and philosophy. His books no longer speak to the manager alone, but to all people; his search for deeper meaning in an age of paradox relates more to human existence than to economic behaviour. Yet he continues to see the two as inseparable: our economic well-being both depends on and contributes to our spiritual well-being. In his purely management writings, he drew upon a wide variety of sources for inspiration: myths and legends, works of art and nature, and not least his own faith. Today, he takes his understanding of our socioeconomic relationships back into his considerations of broader meaning.

BIBLIOGRAPHY
FT Dynamo (2001) 'Thinkers 50 Survey', in association with Suntop Media, http://www.ftdynamo.com, 15 January 2001.
Handy, C. (1976) *Understanding Organizations*, London: Penguin.
—— (1979a) *Gods of Organization*, London: Arrow.
—— (1979b) *The Gods of Management*, London: Arrow.
—— (1984) *The Future of Work*, Oxford: Blackwell.
—— (1989) *The Age of Unreason*, London: Business Books.
—— (1994) *The Empty Raincoat*, London: Hutchinson.
—— (1995) 'Trust and the Virtual Organization', *Harvard Business Review* (May–June): 40–50; repr. in D. Pugh (ed.), *Organization Theory: Selected Readings*, 4th edn, London: Penguin, 83–95.
—— (1996) *Beyond Certainty*, London: Arrow.
—— (1997a) *The Hungry Spirit*, London: Random House.
—— (1997b) 'The Search for Meaning', The Peter F. Drucker Foundation for Nonprofit Management, http://www.pfdf.org/leaderbooks/121/summer97/handy.html, 5 Febuary 2001.
Kennedy, C. (1994) *Managing With the Gurus*, London: Century.
Kurtzmann, J. (1995) 'An Interview with Charles Handy', *Strategy and Business*, 4th quarter, http://www.strategy-business.com/thoughtleaders/95405, 5 Febuary 2001.

MLW

HANEY, Lewis Henry (b. 1882)

Lewis Henry Haney was born in Eureka, Illinois on 30 March 1882. He took his AB in economics at Dartmouth College in 1903, and his Ph.D. at the University of Wisconsin in 1906. He taught economics at the University of Iowa from 1906 to 1908, then was assistant professor at the University of Michigan from 1908 to 1910 and professor at the University of Texas from 1910 to 1916. He was a member of the Economic Advisory Board of the Federal Trade Commission (1916–20) and was then briefly director of research for the South Wholesale Grocers Association (1920) before taking up a post as chief of the cost marketing division of the US Department of Agriculture in 1921. He also returned to academia, taking up an appointment as professor of economics at New York University in 1921 and director of business research at the university from 1921 to 1930.

Haney's economics, which show strongly the emphasis of Alfred MARSHALL, led him to a consideration of the role of human agency rather than a strict mechanical approach to the market. His *History of Economic Thought* (1911) was a highly influential work and was widely cited by business economists of the day. Haney traces the development of economic ideas and systems as far back as Mosaic and Vedic law, and examines their development through classical Greek and Roman philosophy, through the Middle Ages, and so on up to his own time. The thrust of his work was to show that economics is an evolutionary rather than a revolutionary process, and that forms of economic behaviour change only slowly.

Business Organization and Combination (1913) applied economic analysis to activities of the business corporation. Particularly noteworthy is a chapter which examines the internal workings of organizations, especially the role, nature and function of management. Haney develops what he calls an 'hourglass' model of the large corporation, in which the interests of large and diverse groups of share-holders and employees are funnelled together in the space occupied by a comparatively small group, the corporation's executives and managers. Management exists to serve the interests of both these groups, but divergences in their interests can lead to conflicting loyalties. In terms of organization, Haney was a functionalist and a supporter of the line and staff principle; he argued that management, like labour, needed to be divided to achieve maximum efficiency.

A largely conservative thinker, Haney was opposed to 'integrated marketing', the growing trend in the early twentieth century among large corporations to integrate downstream and manage their own distribution networks. He saw this trend as tending to increase producer power over both retailers and consumers, leading to abuses such as 'excessive' advertising and price fixing. He was vigorously opposed in this view by his fellow economist L.D.H. WELD, then serving as director of research for the meat-packing firm of Swift; their debate was played out in the pages of *American Economic Review* over the course of 1920–21. The issues raised during the debate remain live ones in terms of both business ethics and the economics of the market-place.

BIBLIOGRAPHY
Cattell, J.M., Cattell, J. and Ross, E.E. (1941) *Leaders in Education*, 2nd edn, Lancaster, PA: The Science Press.
Haney, L.H. (1911) *History of Economic Thought*, New York: Macmillan; revised edn 1922.
––––– (1913) *Business Organization and Combination*, New York: Macmillan.
––––– (1920) 'Integration in Marketing', *American Economic Review* 10: 528–40.
––––– (1921) 'Integration in Marketing: Reply to L.D.H. Weld', *American Economic Review* 11: 487–9.
Weld, L.D.H, Haney, L.H. and Gray, L.C. (1921) 'Is Large-scale Centralized Organization of Marketing in the Interest of the Public? Roundtable Discussion',

American Economic Review 10(suppl.): 215–24.

MLW

HARLAND, Edward James (1831–95)

Edward James Harland was born in Scarborough on 15 May 1831. He died at his home in County Leitrim, Ireland on 24 December 1895. His father, Dr William Harland, was a medical practitioner who also had a passionate interest in engineering and science, and who experimented with both steam engines and electricity; among his friends was the engineer George STEPHENSON. Harland was educated first at a grammar school and then at the Edinburgh Academy. Originally intending to become a barrister, he inherited his father's interest in science and decided instead to become an engineer. At the age of fifteen he was apprenticed at the engineering works of Robert Stephenson and Company in Newcastle, a firm which was then pioneering the techniques of iron-hulled ship construction. Harland was thus able to take his technical training in one of the most technologically advanced workshops in the world.

Another family friend, the Hamburg and Liverpool merchant Gustav Christian Schwabe, helped Harland get his first job as a journeyman, at the Clydebank engine-maker J. and G. Thomson. Schwabe was a major shareholder in the Liverpool shipping firm John Bibby and Sons, which at Schwabe's instigation was converting from wooden sailing vessels to iron-hulled steamers, engines for which were made by Thomson. When Thomson expanded into shipbuilding, Harland was promoted to lead draughtsman. In 1853, however, he was head-hunted back to Tyneside, as manager of Thomas Toward's yard in Newcastle. At twenty-two, Harland had already mastered the essentials of management, as he describes his work at Toward's:

> I found the work, as practised there, rough and ready; but by steady attention to all the details, and by careful inspection when passing the 'piece work' ... I contrived to raise the standard of excellence, without a corresponding increase in price ... I observed that quality was a very important element in all commercial success.
>
> (Moss and Hume 1986: 15)

After a year with Toward, Harland went to Belfast, where he was appointed manager at Robert Hickson's yard. Again, his energy and drive made an impact. He instilled firm discipline among the workforce, which responded by striking. Partly as a result of the strike, the firm experienced severe financial difficulties, but Harland was nevertheless able to complete several major orders. In 1858 he bought out the struggling Hickson, taking over the yard.

Belfast was not then a major centre for shipbuilding; there were only a few small yards, no supporting infrastructure and no pool of expertise. Harland saw this as an advantage: to him, Belfast was a blank sheet on which he could write his own design for a modern, high-technology shipyard without having to adapt to or overcome previous traditions and working practices. Belfast also had an immense pool of cheap, if unskilled, labour; trained technicians and foremen could be recruited individually from Tyneside and the Clyde. By 1859 Harland was already expanding, taking over a neighbouring shipyard and merging it with his own, and working on new and innovative ship designs.

Harland's personal networks played an important role in his success. The connection with Gustav Schwabe was crucial in the early years. In 1861 Schwabe's nephew Gustav Wolff, already employed at the yard, became a partner, and the business was renamed

Harland and Wolff. In 1858, John Bibby and Sons placed an order for three iron steamships, followed by six more in 1860. Other clients followed Bibby; between 1861 and 1864, despite a severe economic slump caused by the American Civil War, Harland and Wolff launched sixteen ships. Most of the earnings were ploughed back into the firm, which invested continuously in new capacity and new technology even in times of economic depression.

The shipbuilding industry was very recession-prone, and over-capacity was a constant threat. Harland's strategic response to this problem was twofold. At the high-technology end of the market he was constantly pushing the envelope, adopting new building technologies, new deck and hull structures, new engines and so on; there were always premium customers demanding these high-cost and high-priced ships. At the same time he continued to build wooden sailing vessels into the 1880s, knowing that these small, cheap ships always had a market, even if the profits were lower than for the big iron ships. Through this dual marketing strategy, Harland and Wolff launched over 100 ships in their first twenty years, and grew to be one of the largest shipyards in the world.

In 1869 Schwabe brought Harland together with Thomas ISMAY, then in the process of establishing the White Star Line of passenger vessels. Ismay promptly placed an order with Harland for five large passenger steamers. Harland agreed to build these on the basis of cost plus 4 per cent commission on the first cost of the ship; cost included materials and labour, but not overheads. This imaginative arrangement was repeated with other clients, and again allowed Harland and Wolff to attract premium business. Harland and Wolff continued to build ever larger and grander ships for White Star; other passenger lines, seeing the success of White Star, then came to Harland with orders for similar ships.

In 1860 Harland married Rosa Wann, the daughter of a Belfast stockbroker. This gave him an entry into local society, and he adopted Ulster as his home. (In return, Belfast city council built much of the necessary infrastructure to support the shipyard, which had become the city's largest employer.) He served as mayor of Belfast from 1885 to 1887 and was a strong Unionist; during the Home Rule debate of the mid-1880s he considered withdrawing from Belfast and relocating to mainland Britain. On the other side of the coin, Harland was highly protective of his Catholic workers and tried in both his commercial and civic capacities to calm the considerable tensions between the Catholic and Protestant communities. However, he could not prevent the departure of most of the Catholic workmen during the riots which followed defeat of the Home Rule Bill in Parliament in 1886. Following his election as a Unionist MP in 1887 he moved to London, handing over nearly all responsibility for management to William PIRRIE, who had joined the firm in 1862 and become a partner in 1874. Harland was knighted in 1885, and received a baronetcy the following year.

Harland combined technical knowledge and attention to detail with imagination and an ability to innovate in both technology and managerial practice. He became one of the most important figures in world shipping, revolutionized shipbuilding design and practice, and founded a firm which continues to survive and remains an important part of the Northern Ireland economy to this day.

BIBLIOGRAPHY
Moss, M. and Hume, J.R. (1986) *Shipbuilders to the World: 125 Years of Harland and Wolff, Belfast, 1861–1986*, Belfast: The Blackstaff Press.

MLW

HARMAN, Willis Walter (1918–97)

Willis Walter Harman was born in Seattle, Washington on 16 August 1918, the son of Fred Harman, an engineer, and his wife Marguerite. He died in Stanford, California on 30 January 1997. His formal education and early career were technical. He received a BS in electrical engineering in 1939 from the University of Washington. After the Second World War, during which he was on active service for five years as a naval reserve officer, he gained an MS in Physics and a Ph.D. in electrical engineering, both from Stanford University in 1948. He married Charlene Reamer in 1941, and they had four children.

Harman began his academic career at Stanford University as assistant professor in electrical engineering in 1948. After three years as associate professor at the University of Florida, he returned to Stanford as a professor in 1952, teaching electronics, communication theory and systems analysis. During his time there as professor of engineering–economy systems, he became interested in the 'sensitivity training' and 'human potential' movement. This convinced him of the importance of the task of self-discovery, and he consequently developed his teaching around this philosophy. Shortly after, in 1958, he received the George Washington Award for his outstanding contribution to engineering education from the Society for Engineering Education.

Harman was greatly influenced by the work of Alfred M. Hubbard, Humphry Osmond, Aldous Huxley and others in their attempts to build a systematic study of consciousness. They believed that this new understanding could play an important role in the steering of society. These influences are evident in his *An Incomplete Guide to the Future* (1976), in which Harman explores new images of the human, and makes challenges to definitions of knowledge governed by scientific orthodoxy. The book is an eloquent call to futures studies at a deeply human level, while at the same time setting out much of the pioneering thinking of futures studies. Harman succinctly illustrates some of the key dilemmas facing the transforming of industrial society, including the growth dilemma, the distribution dilemma, and what he describes as the work-roles dilemma – the inability of industrialized societies to provide enough satisfying work roles to meet the needs and expectations of their citizens. Drawing on a wide range of philosophy, images and poetry, the book is an exemplar of the multidisciplinary approach Harman advocates.

As he became more involved and interested in social questions, Harman moved into social policy analysis and in 1966 joined the Stanford Research Institute (SRI). The following year he became director of the Educational Policy Research Center at SRI. The centre was asked to investigate alternative future possibilities for the society and their implications for educational policy as part of a US government programme in 1968. Under Harman's direction the centre developed a new, multidisciplinary approach to identify and assess the plausibility of a vast number of future possibilities for society. Part of the approach was to construct sequences of these possible futures, which came to be known as 'future histories'. The policy implications they explored revealed that only a handful of possible futures were at all desirable. Furthermore, due to the interrelatedness of the *problematique*, the desirable futures required fundamental changes in the industrial culture.

SRI developed a Center for the Study of Social Policy to continue the work, of which Harman became director. He went on to assess the conceptual foundation of thinking and doing that might support a benign transition to such a future, choosing to focus on images of the nature of people in relationship with the universe. One of the most important projects was published as *Changing Images of Man* (1982). During the fourteen years of the work of the futures research group at SRI, Harman played a central role in the evolution of the group's ideas and approaches.

Harman also developed, with Joe Armstrong, a functional strategy and framework for conducting technology assessments (TA). TA are generally described as a type of policy studies which examines the widest possible scope of impacts and consequences in society of the introduction of new technologies. Harman's was a significant early contribution to the development of the field.

Harman's *Global Mind Change* (1988) penetrated to the heart of the global predicament and moved it forward to a transformed world. Slaughter sums up the character of this book: 'His treatment of three metaphysical perspectives is exemplary in its understated economy, and the book opens out the prospect of cultural recovery on a global scale' (Slaughter 1995: 192). In general, Harman's work was clear-sighted, persuasive and accessible. His contribution to addressing complex social problems and to studying the future should be more widely acknowledged.

BIBLIOGRAPHY
Harman, W.W. (1976) *An Incomplete Guide to the Future*, Stanford, CA: Stanford University Press.
—— (1988) *Global Mind Change*, Indianapolis, IN: Knowledge Systems, Inc.
Markley, O. and Harman, W.W. (1982) *Changing Images of Man*, Oxford: Pergamon Press.
Slaughter, R.A. (1995) *The Foresight Principle*, Twickenham: Adamantine Press.

AJ

HASTINGS, Warren (1732–1818)

Warren Hastings was born at Churchill, Oxfordshire on 6 December 1732, the son of Pynaston and Hester Hastings. He died at home at Daylesford, Worcestershire on 22 August 1818. His family were of aristocratic origins but had become impoverished and lost their estates; his father was a penniless rector who married three times, finally dying in Barbados in 1744. His mother died giving birth to him. Hastings was brought up first by an uncle and then by a guardian, who saw him well educated; he attended Westminster School, where he was a scholar of some distinction. His guardian found a place for him with the East India Company and in 1750, at the age of eighteen, Hastings arrived at Calcutta, where he was employed by the Company as a commercial agent. In 1753 he was sent to the Company's post at Kasimbazar, the commercial district of Murshidabad, the capital of Bengal. Here he quickly established good relations with important Indian officials and merchants; notably, he admired and respected Indian culture and made some attempts to learn the local language.

More generally, however, relations between the nawabs of Bengal and the East India Company were worsening, despite the efforts of both Hastings and Indian businessmen such as at the banking house of Jagat Seth (see CHAND, FATEH). In 1756 when the new nawab, Siraj-ad-Daula, attacked and destroyed the Company's post at Calcutta, Hastings was briefly imprisoned at Murshidabad, but was soon set free. He joined the survivors from Calcutta at Falta, where they had taken refuge, and used his Indian connections to procure food supplies to stop the refugees from starving. Among the survivors was Mary Elliott, widow of an army officer who had died in the Black Hole of Calcutta; Hastings married her in early 1757 before joining Robert Clive's East India Company army which was marching to retake Calcutta. During the period around the Battle of Plassey, in which Clive defeated and overthrew Siraj-ad-Daula, Hastings was Clive's contact with the Indian princes and merchants who supported the Company, including Jagat Seth. Hastings also provided valuable information

about the movement of Siraj-ad-Daula's forces before Plassey.

In 1757, aged twenty-four, Hastings became the Company's chief agent at Kasimbazar. Four years later he was recalled to Calcutta, where he joined the council of the Company's government of Bengal (the Bengal presidency). Now in a position of some power and authority, he attempted to solve some of the administrative and legal problems that had arisen between the Company and the new nawab, Kasim Ali. He drafted a treaty, which was approved by Kasim Ali but repudiated by the Company's council, whose members accused him of being too pro-Indian. Kasim Ali then accused Hastings of treachery and war broke out, during which a number of Company officials were murdered by Kasim Ali's troops; so too was Mahatab Chand, the second Jagat Seth, and his brother. Troops under Clive moved in to overthrow Kasim Ali and restore order. This time, rather than supporting a new native ruler, the Company assumed direct government of a large part of the province. Hastings was bitterly opposed to this measure, thus gaining the enmity of Clive, whose idea it had been. But Hastings's own strategy in Bengal had been a failure, and in 1764 he returned to London. His wife had died a year earlier.

Hastings spent the next five years in London, effectively unemployed. He used the time well; he became a minor member of London literary society, making the acquaintance of Samuel Johnson (the two continued to correspond after Hastings returned to India). He also promoted a scheme for educating and training recruits to the East India Company, emphasizing the need to learn about Eastern languages and culture before taking up a post. This plan was ultimately adopted as the basis of the Company's training college at Hayleybury (see MALTHUS). Unlike many of his colleagues, Hastings had not profited personally from his time in India; when, in 1769, he was recalled to serve on the council of the Madras presidency, he had to borrow his passage money from friends. His fellow passengers on the voyage included a German nobleman, Baron von Imhoff, and his wife. Hastings and Marian von Imhoff began a love affair; they married in 1777 following the Imhoffs' divorce, but had no children.

In 1771 Hastings was appointed governor of the Bengal presidency. He immediately set about reforming the administration in the lands now held by the Company, replacing corrupt British tax collectors with efficient Indian ones, and returning control of most local lawcourts to Indian judges; he began the codifying and translating into English of the various complex statutes of Hindu law. He also reformed the Company's finances, cutting back expenditures and reducing debt accumulated during the 1760s, so that the Bengal trade began to show a profit once more (one of his devices for increasing revenue was to encourage the development of the opium trade with China). He lent troops to the Mogul emperor during the Rohilla War of 1774, but by now was increasingly convinced that the empire was doomed and that the Company was the only force that could stop India from sliding into anarchy, with consequences for the Company's trade. He also argued that the clumsy system of administration by three separate presidencies needed to be made more efficient, and further that all the Company's Indian lands and trade should be controlled by a single governor-general.

The Regulating Act of 1774 allowed the Company to appoint its first governor-general, and Hastings was chosen for the post. Like earlier trading ventures such as the Dutch East India Company (see COEN), the Company had ostensibly learned that, given the vast distances involved, control had to be localized (in fact, the directors in London continued to meddle). It had also learned that, in a time of political turmoil, it could not safeguard its own business without becoming involved in politics. Hastings seems to have been a reluctant convert to this point of view, but once he adopted it he implemented his policies with his

customary efficiency. He intended, he informed the Company's directors in London, to make the Company a power in India to rival that of the Moghuls.

In 1775 activists in Boston, Massachusetts dumped a cargo of East India Company tea into the harbour, triggering off the American Revolution. France entered the war on the side of the colonies, and French colonial officials in India began intriguing with local powers such as the nizam of Hyderabad and the Mahratta princes against the Company. Hastings proved himself as good a soldier as he was a businessman and adminstrator, and in a series of short sharp wars defeated the Indian princes and the French. By 1780 the Company was indeed the major power in India and its profits were rising fast.

Yet Hastings's position was never secure. As noted, the directors in London interfered constantly in his affairs, even promoting factionalism against him within his own council of advisers in India. Several bitter opponents of Hastings, and in particular of his treatment of Indian officials and princes, which was considered 'soft', had been appointed to the council against Hastings's wishes, and these blocked him at every turn. Hastings himself made a number of serious mistakes, notably his complicity in the execution of Nand Kumar, a former raja of Bengal. In 1784 he was finally forced to resign and returned home. In 1787 the House of Commons impeached him for corruption; the trial dragged on for seven years. Finally acquitted, Hastings was not recognized for his achievements until long after; he never received a knighthood or peerage, uniquely among governor-generals of India. Ironically, those who pilloried him most vigorously were liberals like Lord Macaulay and James Mill, who argued that he should have done more to eradicate the 'backward' Indian culture and introduce British civilization. In India he was remembered more fondly, and after his death Indian and British residents alike subscribed to a statue in his memory at Calcutta.

When Hastings first arrived in India, his ostensible task was to manage the Company's lucrative trade with Bengal. In fact, it was impossible to avoid becoming further entangled in Bengal politics. There was no free market; licences to trade were issued by the nawabs and other princes, and could be revoked at will. In the turbulent political climate following the breakup of the Mogul empire, many parties were scrambling for power, and the granting and revoking of trade licences was a key weapon in the struggle. The Company and its agents could submit meekly to the vicissitudes of fortune, or they could get involved in the struggle and try to exert influence over the political rulers to maintain their own position. Ultimately, it proved impossible to exert power at arm's length; as first Clive and then Hastings learned, in the end the Company would have to join the scramble for power and become, in effect, an Indian ruler. By the time Hastings went to Madras and, later, took over the governor-generalship, he had learned this lesson well. His later career was largely taken up with the use of force and diplomacy to protect trade. The East India Company had crossed the line between commercial and political power, and it would never go back.

Viewed from a modern perspective, it is easy to condemn Hastings as the architect of a colonial system which reduced India to a period of subservience for two centuries. Without denying this, we should also look at Hastings's methods; he was one of the most successful business leaders and administrators of his day. He was a believer in what we would today call localization and devolved power; this is seen most notably in his system of administration, which was lean and simple with relatively few layers of hierarchy, and Indian rather than British officials in place except at the very top levels. Peter DRUCKER has pointed out that the Company administered India with a civil service of around 1,000; today it employs 22 million (Drucker 1989: 205). Hastings reduced corruption,

which he saw as clogging up the administrative system and making it less efficient. Hastings believed in co-opting people rather than controlling them, and far preferred coming to terms with Indian leaders than fighting them; war was used only when the Company's security was seriously threatened. That security, and in particular the security of trade and commerce, was his ultimate and only goal.

BIBLIOGRAPHY

Drucker, P. (1989) *The New Realities*, Oxford: Heinemann.

Edwardes, M. (1976) *Warren Hastings: King of the Nabobs*, London: Hart-Davis, MacGibbon.

Feiling, K. (1954) *Warren Hastings*, London: Macmillan.

Woodruff, P. (1953) *The Men Who Ruled India*, London: Jonathan Cape.

MLW

HATHAWAY, Horace King (1878–1944)

Horace King Hathaway was born in San Francisco on 9 April 1878, and died in Palo Alto, California on 12 June 1944. Trained at the Drexel Institute in Philadelphia, he worked with Midvale Steel Company from 1896 to 1902, working his way up from apprentice to foreman. From 1902 to 1904 he was superintendent of the Payne Engine Company at Elmira, New York. He then joined the Link-Belt Company in Philadelphia, where he worked with Carl BARTH and Frederick W. TAYLOR to bring in a production system based on scientific management. In 1905 Hathaway and Barth performed a similar task at the Tabor Manufacturing Company in Philadelphia with great success: by 1910 the failing company had been turned around and output had more than trebled. Hathaway ultimately became vice-president of the company.

In 1907 Hathaway joined Taylor's consulting practice in Philadelphia, where – apart from a period of service with the US Army from 1917 to 1919 – he remained until 1923. He also lectured at Harvard Business School, the Massachusetts Institute of Technology and the Wharton School at the University of Pennsylvania. In 1923 Hathaway returned to the West Coast for several years, working as a consulting engineer; in 1927 he joined the Mallinckrodt Chemical Works in St Louis, where he remained until 1941, when he returned to San Francisco and set up a consulting practice. From 1937 until his death he was a lecturer at the School of Business at Stanford University.

The youngest of the Taylor team, Hathaway was also one of the most active of its members in terms of teaching and writing. He published a number of important articles describing the Taylor system.

BIBLIOGRAPHY

Drury, H.B. (1915) *Scientific Management*, New York: Columbia University Press.

Hathaway, H. (1911) 'Prerequisites to the Introduction of Scientific Management', *Engineering Magazine* 41; repr. in C.B. Thompson (ed.), *Scientific Management*, Cambridge, MA: Harvard University Press, 1914.

—— (1912) 'The Planning Department: Its Organization and Function', *Industrial Engineering* 12; repr. in C.B. Thompson (ed.), *Scientific Management*, Cambridge, MA: Harvard University Press, 1914.

Urwick, L.F. (ed.) (1956) *The Golden Book of Management*, London: Newman Neame.

HAYEK, Friedrich Auguste von
(1899–1992)

Friedrich Auguste von Hayek was born in Vienna on 8 May 1899, the son of Professor Auguste von Hayek, and died in Freiburg, Germany on 23 March 1992. He was very much a product of Austrian life both under the Habsburg dominion and the first interwar Republic; he was old enough to have known turn of the century Vienna economists Carl Menger and Eugene von Böhm-Bawerk, and came from the same intellectual milieu that shaped both Joseph SCHUMPETER and Peter DRUCKER. In his early years Hayek attended the University of Vienna. In the beginning he had no desire to be an economist. His family, who were mainly civil servants and scientists, inspired him to want to be a botanist. When the First World War broke out, Hayek served in the army as a non-commissioned officer, and was shaken by the traumatic dissolution of the Austro-Hungarian state in 1918–19.

Hayek now felt a need to change society for the better. Like many Austrians, he first flirted with socialism. Instead of becoming a botanist, he chose a career in economics and law. In 1921 he went to work for the civil service of the greatly reduced Austrian state. He studied first at New York University until he could not afford to continue, and then returned to Vienna. Here, in 1922–3, he studied under the man who would influence his thinking more than anyone else: Ludwig von MISES.

Intellectually brilliant and highly persuasive, Mises was single-handedly responsible for the revival of the Austrian tradition in economics. He was also the most thoroughgoing free market economist in history. His 1922 work, *Socialism*, radically transformed the thinking of many of his pupils, including Hayek. At the time, living in inflation-racked 'Red Vienna' under socialist rule, Hayek saw his monthly stipend of 500 kronen swell to one million within a year, with no gain in his purchasing power. Mises provided a convincing explanation for hyperinflation: socialism, or indeed any form of interventionism, simply did not work. Without a price system, said Mises, to send constant signals of supply and demand to producers and consumers, government planners were incapable of rational decisions or any perception of economic reality.

Hayek was now an ardent free marketer and a disciple of Mises. From 1924 to 1926 he worked in the civil service. He married Helen von Fritsch in 1926. He became director of the Austrian Institute of Economic Research in 1927, and an economics lecturer at the University of Vienna in 1929.

In 1931 Hayek left Austria to join the faculty of the London School of Economics. Under Lionel Robbins, the institution at that time was still the bastion of resistance to the new economic thought represented by John Maynard KEYNES. As early as the 1930s Hayek was formulating his attack on Keynes's interventionist approach to economics. According to Hayek, attempts by governments to manage economies by taxation and deficit spending would only lead to permanent inflation.

Hayek began to publish in the late 1920s and early 1930s, but, during the Depression, his ideas had little appeal as economists and eventually politicians turned to the interventionism of Keynes. By the middle of the 1940s socialism in either its Marxist or Fabian forms seemed triumphant, and Hayek was a voice in the wilderness. Undeterred, in 1944 he published his *magnum opus*, *The Road to Serfdom*. Here he reiterated his major theme that socialist planning was not only impractical but also an impossible dream, because sound investments could only be made by price-conscious individuals:

The marvel is that in a case like that of a scarcity of one raw material, without an order being issued, without more than perhaps a handful of people knowing the cause, tens of thousands of people whose

identity could not be ascertained by months of investigation, are made to use the material or its products more sparingly, that is, they move in the right direction.
(Yergin and Stanislaw 1999: 143)

Hayek felt that a little bit of socialism would eventually lead to more and more socialism. A young Oxford undergraduate from Grantham, Margaret Roberts (later Thatcher), found *The Road to Serfdom* highly convincing. The book was also published by the University of Chicago, where Hayek in turn exerted a strong influence upon the young Milton FRIEDMAN. By 1950 Hayek himself was teaching at Chicago. Here, from 1950 to 1962, he continued to crusade for a libertarian economics that was still quite unpopular in the age of the Cold War and the mixed economy. With plenty of cheap energy, no depression and expanding economies, the Keynesian model seemed at first unquestioned.

Hayek, however, believed that eventually the internal flaws he saw in planned and even mixed economies would become apparent. Reality, he felt, would eventually convince multitudes of the rationality of the free market. In the meantime, Hayek organized an international think-tank, known as the Mont Pèlerin Society, in 1947 to help promote his market ideas. One of the economists who belonged to this group was Friedman.

Hayek remained a European at heart, returning to take up a position at the University of Freiburg in 1962. Though he shared much with Mises, including a common faith in a gold standard, non-intervention in the market and planning by individuals, Hayek was less of a free enterprise purist than his mentor. Mises saw the world almost totally in terms of economics, while Hayek's 1960 *Constitution of Liberty* insisted that government had a limited role in preserving the laws and rules that would ensure a competitive economy. For Hayek, the market alone was not enough. Libertarian as it was, 'Austrian' economics needed to be adapted to the real world.

By 1974 it appeared that Hayek's time had finally come. The oil crisis erupting in the wake of the Yom Kippur War (1973) compounded the inflation unleashed by the growth of welfare states and the Vietnam War. Suddenly the old Keynesian medicines no longer seemed to work, as both inflation and unemployment grew, while most world economies shrank. Hayek provided many with an explanation as to why. At the same time, his views on competition and the mechanics of markets began to cast an influence on the area where management theory overlaps with economics, and Hayek, like others such as Herbert SIMON and Oliver WILLIAMSON, provided explanations as to how markets worked and why.

The joint award of the 1974 Nobel Prize for Economics to Gunnar Myrdal, a socialist, and the libertarian Hayek symbolized that market ideas were no longer seen as reactionary or extremist. The era of Margaret Thatcher and Ronald Reagan was soon to follow, as governments adopted Hayek's analysis and Friedman's proposals. Hayek thus lived long enough to see his worldview become an important force in shaping the new orthodoxy.

BIBLIOGRAPHY

Hayek, F.A. von (1931) *Prices and Production*, London: Routledge.
——— (1937) *Monetary Nationalism and International Stability*, London: Longmans Green.
——— (1944) *The Road to Serfdom*, London: Routledge and Kegan Paul.
——— (1949) *Individualism and Economic Order*, London: Routledge and Kegan Paul.
——— (1960) *The Constitution of Liberty*, London: Routledge and Kegan Paul.
'Hayek, Friedrich A(ugust von)' (1945) *Current Biography, Who's Who and Why*, ed. A. Rothe, New York: H.W. Wilson, 271–3.
Yergin, D. and Stanislaw, J. (1999) *The Commanding Heights, The Battle*

between Government and the Marketplace that is Remaking the Modern World, New York: Simon and Schuster.

DCL

HEARST, William Randolph (1863–1951)

William Randolph Hearst was born on 29 April 1863 in San Francisco, California and died at his estate San Simeon, California on 14 August 1951. He was the son of George Hearst, a mine developer and US senator, and Phoebe Apperson. He first became involved in journalism while attending Harvard College during the 1880s, working for the *Harvard Lampoon* and Joseph PULITZER's New York *World*. In 1886 he took charge of the *San Francisco Examiner*, a weak paper owned by his father, and made it a commercial success. Nine years later he acquired the New York *Morning Journal*, which placed him in direct competition with Pulitzer.

Hearst's main contribution to newspaper publishing was his willingness to invest money in the media, and his was the first fortune based on newspapers and magazines. Using his father's wealth, Hearst spared no expense to buy newspapers and hire journalists from competitors. By 1913 Hearst owned seven daily newspapers, five magazines, two news services and a film company. One reason for Hearst's success was that his publications appealed to people across class and ethnic lines by extensive use of pictures and an eclectic mix of articles.

Hearst was best known for his use of emotionally charged stories to attract readers. Dubbed by the press as 'yellow journalism', after the Yellow Kid cartoon figure created by Richard Outcault, these stories not only boosted circulation but also shaped public opinion. The most famous use of this writing style occurred in 1898 when Hearst whipped up public hatred of Spain and support for Cuban rebels. The sinking of the battleship USS *Maine* was sensationalized to such an extent that President McKinley was essentially forced to declare war on Spain, and Hearst publicly took credit for this decision.

Hearst was also involved in Democratic Party politics, and actively supported the causes of organized labour, the urban working class and Progressive Era reformers. Although he served from 1903 to 1907 in the US House of Representatives as a Democrat from New York, Hearst lost several other attempts to hold office, including mayor of New York City in 1905 and 1909, lieutenant governor of New York in 1906, and the Democratic presidential nomination in 1904. Hearst's private life was also complex. He married several times, and used his vast personal fortune to build his palatial mansion at San Simeon, and assemble one of the largest private art collections in the country. In 1937 Hearst was the subject of Orson Welles's movie *Citizen Kane*.

By the 1920s Hearst's business acumen was failing, as evidenced by his decision to pursue market share for his publications at the expense of profitability. Although his papers accounted for 14 per cent of all daily circulation and nearly a quarter of the Sunday papers sold in the 1930s, he was so deeply in debt that he was forced to give up control of his holdings. New professional managers sold unprofitable media and real estate, and by 1940 only seventeen of the forty-two papers Hearst had bought or established remained. At the end of his life, Hearst still headed the largest news conglomerate in the USA with sixteen dailies, two Sunday papers and nine magazines. He controlled 10 per cent of daily circulation after the Second World War.

BIBLIOGRAPHY
Nasaw, D. (2000) *The Chief: The Life of William Randolph Hearst*, Boston: Houghton Mifflin.

Swanberg, W.A. (1961) *Citizen Hearst: A Biography of William Randolph Hearst*, New York: Scribner.

DM

HEFNER, Hugh Marston (1926–)

Hugh Hefner was born in Chicago on 9 April 1926, the son of Glenn and Grace Hefner. Graduating from high school in 1944 he joined the US Army, where he served as a clerk and also drew cartoons for an army newspaper. Discharged in 1946, he attended the Chicago Art Institute, then enrolled in the University of Illinois, where he graduated with a BA in well under the normal time through enrolling in extra classes; he largely paid his way through university by work as a cartoonist, and also found time to edit the university's student newspaper, where one of the features he introduced was 'Co-ed of the Month'.

Graduating in 1949, Hefner worked briefly as an assistant personnel manager and an advertising copywriter. In 1951 he took a job as a copywriter with *Esquire* magazine, but promptly lost it when the magazine relocated its head office to New York. Hefner now resolved to start a magazine of his own. He correctly forecast that the economic boom of the 1950s would lead in time to a social revolution, and that prewar trends towards more relaxed social mores and a freer attitude to sex would continue, and it was in this direction that he decided to fashion his market niche. The result was *Playboy*, the first issue of which was laid out on Hefner's kitchen table and which went on sale in December 1953; he did not commission a subsequent issue because he had no money to pay for it. The magazine sold 50,000 copies within days, making Hefner's fortune.

Apart from its obvious features – the first issue featured the famous centrefold picture of the then model Marilyn Monroe, who went on to Hollywood stardom and notoriety of her own – the magazine also developed a reputation for incisive, sometimes cutting-edge journalism. During the 1950s and 1960s it became a 'must read' for American men, despite violent opposition in the Bible Belt states and by conservatives everywhere. Its radical edge dulled in the 1970s, but by then it had established a place in American folklore. Hefner used his profits to diversify into other ventures such as music promotion and nightclubs, and to fashion a playboy lifestyle for himself. He remains an outstanding example of how marketing success can be ensured simply by being in the right place at the right time.

HEINEN, Edmund (1919–96)

Edmund Heinen was born in Eschlingen, Germany on 18 May 1919 and died in Munich on 22 June 1996. He studied at Frankfurt University before obtaining his doctorate at Saarbrücken University, and received his professor's qualification from the same university in 1951. From 1952 to 1954 he was a lecturer at Saarbrücken University, and he held the post of professor from 1954 to 1957. In the latter year he took up a professorship at Munich University.

Heinen's early interest was directed towards a cost theory of the economics of business administration. In his major book, *Betriebswirtschaftliche Kostenlehre* (Cost Theory of Business Administration), published in 1959, he observed that, contrary to traditional cost theory which analyses a single element of production capability as a theoretical model, modern cost theory as formulated by Erich GUTENBERG is reliable enough to be used as a basis for a production theory which

uses the whole complex of production capabilities as a theoretical model. Furthermore, by introducing decision-making theory to cost theory, Heinen proposed a C-type production function which expanded Gutenberg's B-type.

Heinen accepted Gutenberg's theory where importance was attached to the problem of decision making or management planning, but expanded this theory by attempting to systematize the economics of business administration from a decision-making perspective. He saw decision making as a human activity, though without linking it to personality or spirit as in the theory of Heinrich NICKLISCH. Human activity conceived of in such a manner might be explained as a relationship between the end and the means. Provided that this relationship is the optimum, then that human activity is a rational one.

Heinen accepts Gutenberg's definition of business administration which sees it as a linking process between the elements of production, but he further defines business administration as a complex socio-technical open system which has a number of functional subsystems. The components of this system are decision makers placed in a variety of mutual relationships, and therefore business administration is a decision-making system which includes an information system, object system and social system as subsystems. In his decision-making-oriented economics of business administration, the purposes of the enterprise account for a large proportion of business endeavours. He describes enterprise purposes as multidimensional practice, and believes that these purposes form a purpose system where they have mutual concerns.

In expanding on Gutenberg's ideas, Heinen offered both an explanation of business administration from a decision-making perspective and also a method of problem solving. This theory of organization and management based on both system theory and decision-making theory has produced a new economics of business administration in Germany.

BIBLIOGRAPHY
Heinen, E. (1956) *Die Kosten, ihr Begriff und ihr Wesen* (Cost, Its Concept and System), Saarbrucken.
—— (1957) *Anpassungsprosse und ihre Kostenmassigen Konsequenzen* (Adaptive Process and Its Cost Saving), Cologne: Opladen.
—— (1959) *Betriebswirtschaftliche Kostenlehre* (Cost Theory of Business Administration), Wiesbaden: Gabler.
—— (1966) *Das Zielsystem der Unternehmung* (Object System of Business Enterprise), Wiesbaden: Gabler.

ST

HEINZ, Henry John (1844–1919)

Henry John Heinz was born in Pittsburgh, Pennsylvania on 11 October 1844, the eldest of eight children of German immigrants, Henry and Margaretha Heinz. He died at his mansion, Greenlawn, in Pittsburgh on 14 May 1919. He grew up in Sharpsburg, Pennsylvania, where his father owned a small brickworks. From an early age he displayed an entrepreneurial bent, and from the age of eight began selling surplus vegetables from the family garden. Finding he was making a profit, he embarked on the business more seriously, setting up hothouses and acquiring more land. By the time he was sixteen, Heinz was employing local women to sell for him and was also supplying vegetables on contract to greengrocers in Pittsburgh.

In 1859 Heinz took a course at Duff's Business College in Pittsburgh, one of a number of small business training colleges which had sprung up around the United States in the 1840s and 1850s; they taught accounting and bookkeeping and also some rudimentary management skills, and were in many

ways the forerunners of today's business schools. Armed with these skills, in 1865 Heinz used his profits from the grocery business to buy a half share in his father's brickyard. Here he made some minor adjustments to the kilns and drying apparatus which improved the quality and output of bricks. Alberts (1973) notes that Heinz maintained a lifelong interest in bricks, and in later years visitors to his office were sometimes surprised to see piles of brick samples stacked on his desk.

In the meantime his developing food business continued. He became a specialist in the production of horseradish, and in the first of many marketing innovations, began packaging and selling horseradish in clear glass bottles so that consumers could see both the quantity and quality of the product they were getting. In 1869 he and a friend, L.C. Noble, set up a partnership to produce and sell horseradish and other food products in Pittsburgh. In the same year he married Sarah Sloan Young, an Irishwoman whose family had emigrated to the United States from County Down; they went on to have five children. Heinz and Noble expanded quickly into other products such as vinegar, pickles and sauerkraut, and branched out as far afield as Chicago and St Louis. However, although Heinz was a capable financial manager, he was unable to cope with the combination of falling agricultural prices and tight credit in the summer of 1875, and by the end of the year, Heinz, Noble and Company had been forced into bankruptcy. Heinz later paid his share of the firm's debts in full.

Despite the financial problems, Heinz knew he was onto a winning business formula. He formed a new partnership in 1876 with his brother John and cousin Frederick Heinz, and himself became general manager of the new firm F. and J. Heinz Company. Investing heavily in food preparation equipment, Heinz specialized in the production of pickles and produced a range of products that began winning awards for quality. By 1879 he had paid off the company's debts. Heinz was one of the first to realize the vast potential of the newly invented process for preserving food in tinned metal containers, and in 1881 made further investments in this technology. Throughout the 1880s he launched range after range of canned foods, including such modern staples as canned vegetables, canned spaghetti and canned beans.

In 1888 Heinz bought out the shares of his partners and re-established the business as H.J. Heinz and Company. His was now one of the leading food-processing businesses in the United States. He built a vast new factory on the banks of the Allegheny River, designed in what Alberts (1973: 91) describes as 'solid Pittsburgh Romanesque'. Other factories followed as the company expanded; by the middle 1890s it was the largest canning and pickling business in the world. By 1900 Heinz was making 200 products in nine factories, and had a branch house in London and agencies worldwide. Highly vertically integrated, the business made its own bottles and cans, owned its own railway cars and had 16,000 acres of directly owned land, as well as importing agricultural produce from all around the world.

In 1905 the company incorporated, with Heinz and the other managing partners, including his son Howard, becoming the sole shareholders. He continued to be actively involved in the management of the firm until the last years of his life. In the early 1890s he built a mansion in Pittsburgh, which he called Greenlawn, and became friendly with others of the Pittsburgh millionaires' set including Henry Clay Frick and George WESTINGHOUSE. Heinz's wife died in 1894; he himself died in 1919.

Heinz's early management training at Duff's Business College, slight though it was by today's standards, was of some importance in shaping his management outlook. From Duff's he gained an appreciation of the importance of financial management skills; in the early stages of his businesses, Heinz often served as bookkeeper and accountant himself, and later continued to monitor closely the basic financial

indicators. Yet Heinz was not a cost-cutting manager; he balanced financial requirements with the other needs of his business, and used accounting information to help determine where the most profitable opportunities lay. Heinz was one of those rare and imaginative managers who used accounting and financial data to explore opportunities for growth. He always had a strict regard for business fundamentals; as McCafferty, for many years his private secretary, said: 'He was not a dreamer or a visionary, who went into business and by chance made a success. He was a businessman by origin, by preference, and by training' (McCafferty 1923: 137).

One of Heinz's most imaginative arrangements was related to the maintenance of product quality standards. He appreciated from the beginning that his products would be successful if he could maintain high and consistent quality. In the 1880s Heinz began developing purchasing arrangements with farmer, especially growers of cucumbers and cabbage used in making pickles and sauerkraut. By these arrangements, Heinz would agree to purchase the farmer's entire output of a given crop at a previously agreed price, usually well above the average market rate; for their part, the farmers had to allow inspection of crops by Heinz technicians and to plant and harvest specific crops at specific times to ensure the best quality of output. Heinz got the quality he needed, the farmers were well paid, and the agricultural community of the Midwest learned more about scientific farming methods (Heinz's farming technicians were hired from the country's leading agricultural colleges). Heinz and his managers were constant advocates of higher standards in the food industry; he supported the Pure Food Crusade of the 1890s and the Pure Food and Drug Act of 1906, a position which brought him into conflict with other food producers.

It is for his advances in marketing and branding, however, that Heinz is best remembered, and here it seems that his own intuition rather than training was his chief guide.

McCafferty tells the story of how Heinz 57 varieties, one of the most famous brands in American history, was conceived:

Its origin was in 1896. Mr Heinz, while in an elevated railroad train in New York, saw among the car-advertising cards one about shoes with the expression: '21 Styles'. It set him to thinking, and as he told it: 'I said to myself, "we do not have styles of products, but we do have varieties of products." Counting up how many we had, I counted well beyond 57, but "57" kept coming back into my mind. "Seven, seven" – there are so many illustrations of the psychological influence of that figure and of its alluring significance to people of all ages and races that "58 Varieties" or "59 Varieties" did not appeal at all to me as being equally strong. I got off the train immediately, went down to the lithographers, where I designed a street-car card and had it distributed throughout the United States. I myself did not realize how highly successful a slogan it was going to be.'

(McCafferty 1923: 147)

Previously, in heavily branded industries such as soap, the practice had been to brand each product or product line separately. In Heinz's case this would have been so expensive as to be impracticable. His inspiration was to create a single corporate brand that could be applied across all products.

Even before the development of this famous brand, however, Heinz had shown himself to be an innovative marketer. His sales staff used then untried methods such as product demonstrations and free samples given away at public events; these methods were expensive, but they were also highly effective. At the Chicago World's Fair in 1893, Heinz hit on another give-away: setting up a Heinz pavilion, he gave each visitor a free 'pickle pin' as a memento. Alberts calls this 'one of the most famous give-aways in merchandising history', and notes

that so many people crowded into the pavilion that the floors began to sag and had to be reinforced (Alberts 1973: 123). He opened the Allegheny works to visitors and set up guided tours; at the height of the tourist season, the works saw as many as 20,000 visitors a year.

In 1900 Heinz sponsored the first advertising billboard lit by electric light bulbs; the sign featured 1,200 light bulbs, 'at a time when a single bulb was a curiosity' (Alberts 1973: 128). The *New York Times* called it a 'work of advertising genius', and the billboard itself became an important tourist attraction until its demolition a few years later to make way for the construction of the Flatiron Building.

Perhaps the most splendid of all Heinz's promotional efforts was the Heinz Ocean Pier in Atlantic City, New Jersey, sometimes called the 'Crystal Palace by the Sea' and sometimes, less reverently, 'The Sea Shore Home of the 57 Varieties'. Nine hundred feet in length, the pier featured a glass pavilion with a sun room and reading room, and of course a kitchen giving out free samples of Heinz products. At the height of its popularity before the First World War, the pier was attracting over 20,000 people a year. Its popularity declined in the 1930s, however, and the pier was finally abandoned after being badly damaged by a hurricane in the autumn of 1944. The pier, splendid though it was, never really paid back its cost to the company, and is the one aberration in Heinz's otherwise shrewd career of cost-effective marketing.

Heinz's enlightened approach to business extended also to his relationships with his employees. Strongly paternalistic in approach, he believed in hiring employees young, training them in his business methods and promoting on merit; he believed that all employees ought to feel part of the Heinz family. McCafferty, who knew him well (although he is obviously biased in his favour), writes of how Heinz's business philosophy was a comingling of ethics and sound business principles, and of how he sought to infuse this personal view into the organization:

A cardinal article of his faith was that men can be trusted, that most men would rather do right than wrong. He perceived that the reason they did not adhere to their best inclinations was that they were afraid they could not succeed that way in business. His big deed of human leadership was to show men that they did not need to be afraid.

(McCafferty 1923: 127)

Heinz, says McCafferty, emphasized welfare work not to head off industrial unrest, but because he thought it was right. His was one of the first companies in the United States to introduce free life insurance for employees.

Robert Alberts, author of what remains the best study of Heinz to date, summarizes Heinz's philosophy of business in what he calls the eight 'Important Ideas'. These ideas are a balanced mix of sound business principles, an approach to the market based on a mixture of intuition and common sense, and an ethical view which is embedded at the heart of his approach. The eight principles are summarized as follows:

1. Housewives are willing to pay someone else to take over a share of their more tedious kitchen work (Alberts 1973: 7).

2. A pure article of superior quality will find a ready market through its own intrinsic merit – if it is properly packaged and promoted (1973: 7).

3. To improve the finished product that comes out of the bottle, can or crock, you must improve it in the ground, when and where it is grown (1973: 47).

4. Our Market is the World (1973: 79).

5. Humanize the business system of today and you will have the remedy for the present discontent that characterizes the commercial world and fosters a spirit of enmity between capital and labour (1973: 90).

6. Let the public assist you in advertising

your products and promoting your name (1973: 123).

7. Good foods, properly processed, will keep without the addition of preservatives (1973: 171).

8. If people could work together in religion, then lasting peace might be found (1973: 191).

Like many of the great business leaders of his day, Heinz had strong social principles. He was deeply religious, although his faith had different varieties, and he seems at times to have been a Lutheran, an Episcopalian, a Methodist Episcopalian and a Presbyterian, to the baffled amusement of his Ulster Protestant wife. He was for twenty-five years a Sunday school superintendent, and later served on the executive council of both the International Sunday School Association and the World Sunday School Association. He took his Christian values into both civic and business life. He served as vice-president of the Pittsburgh Chamber of Commerce and on a number of other civic bodies. He was also a noted art collector and philanthropist; among his many civic roles in later life was the presidency of the Pittsburgh branch of the Egyptian Exploration Fund.

Heinz left behind him a solid business and an enduring brand name. A marketing innovator, he was also a very able all-round manager, able to balance commercial needs with ethical behaviour, financial controls with marketing costs in a way that led to a high degree of both efficiency and effectiveness. He remains one of the outstanding managerial figures of his generation.

BIBLIOGRAPHY
Alberts, R.C. (1973) *The Good Provider: H.J. Heinz and His 57 Varieties*, London: Arthur Barker.
McCafferty, E.D. (1923) *Henry J. Heinz: A Biography*, New York: Bartlett Orr Press.

MLW

HERZBERG, Frederick Irving (1923–2000)

Frederick Irving Herzberg was born in Lynn, Massachusetts on 18 April 1923, the son of Lithuanian immigrants Lewis and Gertrude Herzberg. He died in Salt Lake City, Utah on 19 January 2000. He married Shirley Bedell in 1944; they had one son. Herzberg grew up in New York City and was educated at City College New York. His studies were interrupted by the Second World War, where he served as a noncommissioned officer in the US Army, winning the Bronze Star for valour; he was also one of the first Allied soldiers to enter Dachau concentration camp, and was assigned the task of providing food and medical care to the survivors immediately after the liberation. Returning to academic life, Herzberg completed his BS degree in 1946 and went on to take an MS and Ph.D. in psychology at the University of Pittsburgh. He was research director of psychological services at Pittsburgh from 1951 to 1957, and professor of psychology at Case Western Reserve University in Cleveland from 1957 to 1972. In 1972 he was appointed professor of management at the College of Business, University of Utah, where he remained until his retirement in 1995.

Herzberg's reputation is built upon a theory of motivation at work in organizations, also known as 'actualization-atmosphere' factors, based upon the hierarchical human needs approach and on the great biblical myths of Adam and Abraham. The actualization factors are the work itself and all forms of acknowledgement of work done. Acting upon these factors enables an individual's behaviour at work to be shaped over the long term. Atmosphere factors include remuneration, job security, management policy in the company and relations between colleagues. Acting on these leads to short-term satisfaction. The implicit hypothesis in this theory is that the individual should grow through their work. His research as applied to company organization had considerable success in the 1970s. He led management policy towards job enrich-

ment and enlargement of tasks, of multi-tasking and of job rotation, and was critical of TAYLOR's view of the individual at work.

According to the so-called theory of 'needs', human beings are comparable to animals in that they are governed by needs. For humans there is a hierarchy of needs, with that of self-accomplishment made possible through work at the top. Moreover, the great Judaeo-Christian myths express motivations shared by all humanity. The story of Adam teaches us that the first man was created perfect in all aspects, but that God drove him out of earthly Paradise once he ate the fruit from the tree of knowledge. From there comes the notion of guilt and of humans having to pay the penalty, leading him to try to escape from uncomfortable situations in his environment. In the world of work, individual strives to improve his or her working conditions; however, this improvement does not permit the individual at work to satisfy his or her need for self-fulfilment. It is therefore necessary to search elsewhere. The other story which gives an alternative picture of mankind is that of Abraham. Abraham was assured by God of attaining the Promised Land, provided he obeyed God, got up and followed. This vision signified that humans are resourceful beings as they have been given innate positive attributes. It is a dynamic perspective in which humans are seen as being full of potential but in need of guidance to demonstrate it.

These two natures of being human equate to two outlooks on humanity. One falls within a pessimistic tradition of human nature, in which humans, pinioned by the consequences of original sin, must be supervised and guided. The other outlook, this time optimistic, sees humans as beings full of positive attributes provided that their environment enables them to unlock and activate them.

Herzberg finds confirmation of this dual theory of motivation in the empirical research he has led. He maintains it has enabled him to discover and define factors of satisfaction or discontent at work. The first of these, the actu-

alization factors, which emanate from Abraham's nature and lead to satisfaction at work, are achievement, recognition for achievement, work itself, responsibility and the possibility for development or growth. Factors of discontent, or atmosphere factors, arising from Adam's nature, are management policy in the company, management (its qualities and failings), remuneration, work conditions, relations between people (management, employees, equals), prestige, job security and personal factors (where work affects personal life, such as in the case of relocation).

Actualization factors provide a sense of lasting satisfaction. Having a fulfilling job (not routine or lacking interest), receiving recognition for work done, being given responsibility are all actions leading to lasting changes in attitude. Actions such as increase in salary, change of manager, alteration in human resource management, improvement of working conditions, provision of a job guarantee and intervention in workplace relations all tend only towards a lowering of tension, albeit a noticeable one, but they do not alter behaviour deep down.

In his empirical research, carried out in organizations across the world and in all professional fields, Herzberg has shown that individuals always recall positively actions relating to actualization factors ('I had a more interesting job', or 'my boss congratulated me on this job') whereas they always recall negatively actions relating to atmosphere factors ('I had a rise in salary; it's better, but it doesn't equate to what the company should have done', etc).

Amongst the examples put forward by Herzberg, that of the work organization of the secretaries at the Bell Telephone Company has become famous. These secretaries had to answer letters from shareholders of the company. The standardized replies were checked by supervisors. The secretaries' morale was low, absenteeism high and errors numerous. Several atmosphere factors (increase in salary, changes to and development of the hierarchy and planning of the

work environment) failed to change anything. It was decided to change the way the work was organized. Each secretary was put in charge of a specific area, in which she became an expert, able to advise her colleagues. Supervision was reduced. Each wrote and signed letters herself. They themselves organized the day's workload. The result was a significant rise in productivity and a quality of response never before achieved.

Managerial policy on task enrichment and enlargement and job rotation from 1960 to 1970 owe much to the theories of Herzberg. Until that time the dominant ideas had been those of Taylor, namely that the individuals at work essentially demanded high salaries, thereby acknowledging more or less openly that they could work without necessarily being interested in the work they were doing. In this vision, the nature of the work and that of the tasks took second place. The period from 1960 to 1980 was a time when disaffection with work and the rejection of unskilled work (the absenteeism record of unskilled workers, disregard for quality almost to the extent of sabotage, rejection of work through lack of interest) became important concerns for managers and politicians in charge. Movements such as those of the hippies on the west coast of the United States, or the student movements of 1968 in Europe appeared to threaten a society built upon industrial order and seemed to be signs of rejection of a society that was supposed to confer well-being but alienated those who served it.

One response to these threats from within Herzberg's body of work was an explanation of the crisis being due to the failure to take the fundamental needs of human nature into consideration. Many managers, politicians and trade union leaders accepted this explanation. Policies to improve working conditions, above all for unskilled workers in large organizations, arose out of Herzberg's work. In order to make the work more attractive and to motivate operators and employees, new tasks

were added to repetitive tasks (minor adjustments, maintenance, cleaning, customer despatch, rotation of jobs between operators, etc.). Workstations were re-examined in order to give more responsibility to salaried employees, responsibility that the Taylor division of work had removed.

The success of Herzberg's motivational theory is linked to the contribution of the sociocultural movement from the psychologically, even psychoanalytically orientated work of the Tavistock Institute in London. The central idea is that in order to alter an individual's behaviour, one must act on the group. When members of a small work group are given autonomy and when confidence is shown in them (semi-autonomous groups), they will behave much more productively than under the old system. The concept of the semi-autonomous group was a great success, just when Herzberg's ideas were becoming well known. The two movements combined to exert their influence. In the 1970s, changes in the enrichment and enlargement of tasks were combined with semi-autonomous groups.

Various celebrated reforms were put into place in line with Herzberg's theories. The first was undoubtedly that of the Volvo factories in Kalmar, Sweden at the beginning of the 1970s. A poor social climate had developed (very high absenteeism rate, lack of quality) so management decided to do away with the car assembly line and to replace it with production organized by units. Car parts brought to the reduced workshops were assembled by a team of workers who themselves organized how the work was shared out, ensured it was done in the given time and controlled quality. The tasks were therefore enlarged and enriched, and the workers gained versatility. The results were wholly positive: improved social climate, sharp decline in the absenteeism rate, spectacular rise in quality. Observers from around the world came to visit the factory where the management had dared to do away with the traditional assembly line.

Many other measures were put into effect over the same period in other European countries, often by government bodies. In Germany, the 'Humanisierung der Arbeit' (Work Humanizing) programme, launched by the Social Democrat government (at the beginning of the 1970s), was at the forefront of important research and measures centred on the reorganization of the workplace. In France, in 1974, the government created l'Agence Nationale pour l'Amelioration des Conditions de Travail (National Agency for the Improvement of Work Conditions) in order to encourage social innovation and to launch research programmes. Many innovations aimed at improving conditions and the organization of work were aided and followed through by the agency, and used as an example in its publications.

In Britain, even if the movement has been less important (the country has a long history of industrialization, with greater emphasis given to professional abilities, and a higher degree of autonomy and control in the workshops), many new work systems (enriched and enlarged work, autonomous groups) have been introduced in organizations. In the United States, even though the movement has been reined in by the tradition of collective bargaining, whose rules, such as the seniority rule and job description, are extremely difficult to change, numerous projects connected with the quality of workplace life have been carried out. New systems for the organization of work have been introduced by management, not without great resistance from the trade unions. Herzberg's ideas have contributed towards launching an important movement of work reorganization and change within companies and in industrial relations.

Herzberg has greatly contributed towards rejection of the ideas of Taylor and FORD on human nature. He reminds us strongly that the workers are motivated by their interest in what they do, that they can buy into and interest themselves in their work. He contributed to reducing excess division of labour, gave autonomy to the least qualified workers, and saw beyond work conditions, bringing to the fore the organization of work itself, in the sense of lessening its traditional division. In this sense, he was an instigator of more flexible, supple organizations, of networked companies as we now know them.

Despite this, Herzberg's theses have aged a lot. There is a theoretical weakness in the theory of needs and their formation into a hierarchy – needs defined independently of the workplace situation and without considering the actual individual. There is a real behavioural determinism operating here. No one has since proved that fulfilment at work should be a universal and permanent motivation. Each individual chooses the way in which he or she will achieve fulfilment, and that way can undergo change. There are thousands of ways of fulfilling oneself at work: strikes, sabotage, industrial action, absenteeism, retirement, etc. In its universal attempt to explain behaviour and to do this away from where the action is taking place, the theory of needs is self-limiting. The advice given by Herzberg has above all consisted of proposing an improved organization. However, the central assertion of his theory, that of people's need for fulfilment in work, is false.

BIBLIOGRAPHY

Bernoux, P. (1998) 'Herzberg, Frederick', in M. Warner (ed.), *IEBM Handbook of Management Thinking*, London: International Thomson Business Press, 294–300.

Herzberg, F. (1959) *Managerial Choice: To Be Efficient and To Be Human*, New York: Dow-Jones Irwin.

—— (1966) *Work and the Nature of Man*, Cleveland, OH: The World Publishing Company.

'Obituary: Frederick Irving Herzberg' (2000) *Salt Lake City Tribune*, 23 January; http://www.siop.org/tip/

backissues/TipApril00/31Obituaries.html,
16 April 2001.

PB (trans. Susan Nevard)

HEWLETT, William (1913–2001)

William Hewlett was born in Ann Arbor, Michigan on 20 May 1913. He died at his home in Palo Alto, California on 12 January 2001. The son of a doctor who taught medicine at the University of Michigan, Hewlett grew up in San Francisco after his father became a professor at the Stanford Medical School. He described his childhood as 'busy and happy', and fondly recalled family vacations spent in the Sierra Nevada, where he developed a love for the outdoors that he retained for the rest of his life (Packard 1995: 19).

Hewlett revealed an early curiosity about the way things worked, and often conducted home-made experiments to find out. Some involved explosives, and Hewlett later counted himself lucky not to have killed himself. While science came easy to him at school, he had great difficulty reading and writing, and that hampered him in other subjects. He overcame his dyslexia by developing the ability to listen carefully and memorize his schoolwork.

When Hewlett was twelve years old, his father died of a brain tumour. He said later that if his father had survived, he might have chosen a career in medicine. Instead, he chose electrical engineering.

Because he did so poorly in almost all high school subjects except the sciences, Hewlett had difficulty gaining admission to Stanford. He believed he was accepted only because his father had taught there. He met David PACKARD in his freshman year, and the two had become close friends by the time they were seniors. Both were influenced by their engineering professor, Frederick Terman, who promoted a relationship between the scientific and engineering community of Stanford and the emerging high-tech industries of what eventually became California's Silicon Valley. Terman advised Hewlett and Packard to gain experience and knowledge before taking steps to start their own business.

Both travelled eastward after graduation. Packard worked at General Electric in Schenectady, New York, and Hewlett continued his studies at the Massachusetts Institute of Technology (MIT). He received his master's degree in electrical engineering from MIT in 1936. Hewlett then returned to Stanford, where Terman helped him win a contract to construct an electronic device for recording brainwaves. When Packard opted to leave General Electric and return to California in 1938, Terman arranged a research fellowship for him at Stanford and encouraged the two engineers to open their own business. He suggested that Hewlett's invention of a resistance-capacity audio oscillator for testing sound equipment should be the kernel of the business.

The garage of the house that Hewlett and Packard were renting in Palo Alto, California became their first business address. In 1939 Hewlett received an engineering degree from Stanford and the partners made their first commercial sale to the Walt Disney Studios, which purchased eight of Hewlett's oscillators for use in making the animated film *Fantasia*. The two entrepreneurs moved from their garage to a rented building in Palo Alto, where they swept the floors, kept the books and took the inventory themselves, as their product line of electronic measuring and testing instruments expanded.

During the Second World War, the company developed products for military applications that were important enough to earn Packard a draft exemption. He ran the company by himself while Hewlett served in the US armed forces, first as a signal officer and then as head of the electronics division of

the War Department's special staff. Hewlett was discharged in 1945 and returned to Hewlett-Packard to lead its research and development efforts, while Packard retained responsibility for the company's business. By the time Hewlett-Packard incorporated in 1947, the company had 111 employees on its payroll and was reporting annual sales of $679,000.

With Hewlett serving as engineering team leader, the company became a mecca for America's bright young scientists and engineers. The best talent at such eastern US institutions as MIT and Bell Labs took notice, and the western migration of America's technological community began. At Hewlett-Packard they found an environment conducive to encouraging technological innovation. 'There is a feeling that everyone is part of a team, and that team is H-P,' said Hewlett. 'It is an idea based on the individual. It exists because people have seen that it works, and they believe that this feeling makes H-P what it is' (Peters and Waterman 1982: 233).

Within the business, David Packard was the management strategist who devised ways to keep their company functioning like a small, close-knit family as it expanded internationally. Hewlett was the technological guru who believed that employees with innovative engineering and scientific ideas should be front and centre in the operation of the company as it adapted to meet changing market demands. With Hewlett motivating and encouraging them, the scientists and engineers kept Hewlett-Packard at the forefront of technological development in the United States. When he challenged them to develop a computer that would fit in his desk drawer, they invented the HP 9100 calculator, the first computer of its type to be as small as a typewriter. Hewlett then challenged them to go one step further, asking them to make a calculator that would fit in his pocket. They responded with the HP 35, a hand-held calculator that turned out to be the company's first real consumer product, selling well to the general public. Prior to its introduction in 1972, Hewlett-Packard had marketed its products solely to the scientific and engineering communities.

Hewlett spent forty years with Hewlett-Packard. In accordance with the company's plan for management succession, he retired as chief executive officer in 1978, when the company had 57,000 employees and was producing annual revenues of $3 billion. But he still retained an active interest in the company. That became clear to the American business community in 1990, when he and Packard, then both in their late seventies, reasserted themselves in Hewlett-Packard's operations. They used their influence to revamp the company's management structure, which they viewed as having become too bureaucratic and too centralized, and succeeded in arresting the downward movement of the company's profits.

Along with his continuing interest in the business operations of Hewlett-Packard, Hewlett maintained his interest in technological advancements. In 1985 he was awarded America's highest scientific honour, the National Medal of Science. In 1991 he received the Silicon Valley Engineering Hall of Fame Award, and the following year he received the National Inventors Hall of Fame Award.

A series of strokes in the late 1990s slowed Hewlett's movements and limited his ability to participate in the business culture he had created. However, even from his hospital bed he continued to demonstrate his prowess as a mathematician. When a female friend, by way of small talk during a visit to his hospital bedside, told Hewlett about her concern that her high heels might leave marks on a parquet floor, Hewlett responded by asking her how much she weighed. He then proceeded to calculate – one day after suffering a stroke – whether the pounds per square inch she exerted on the floor would be enough to make an impression. The 'garage genius' still had a problem to solve.

BIBLIOGRAPHY

Packard, D. (1995) *The HP Way: How Bill Hewlett and I Built Our Company*, New York: HarperCollins.

Peters, T.J. and Waterman, R.H. (1982) *In Search of Excellence*, New York: Warner Books.

BB

HIBI Osuke (1860–1931)

Hibi Osuke was born on 26 June 1860, the second son of Takeda Yasudayu, a warrior of the fief of Kurume in Kushihara, Mitsui District, Kurume City. He was adopted by the Hibi family in March 1879. He married Hibi Haruno in 1882. After he finished his studies in Keio Gijyuku in 1884, he was employed at the Azabu Astronomical Observatory. At the invitation of NAKAMIGAWA Hikojiro, he joined Mitsui Bank, taking up the post of vice-manager of the head office in 1896. In 1904 Mitsui separated its dry goods division, which had been suffering from bad management, from the main Mitsui business. Hibi was transferred to the deficit-ridden dry goods store, where he developed his talent for business reorganization. He became known as an entrepreneur and was a key figure in establishing the Mitsukoshi Dry Goods Store Company, Ltd, where he was appointed to the post of executive director. From this position, modernizing and enhancing the social status of retail business, he worked towards establishing Japan's first fully fledged department store, taking Britain's Harrods department store as a model. Thus the prototype of contemporary department store management in Japan was created.

BIBLIOGRAPHY

Hoshino K. (1951) *Hibi Ohsuke*, Tokyo: Soubun Sha.

Takahashi J. (1972) *Mitsukoshi Depa-to no 300 Nen* (The Management Strategy of Mitsukoshi Department Store for 300 Years), Tokyo: Sankei Shinbun Sha.

ST

HILL, James Jerome (1838–1916)

James Jerome Hill was born in Rockwood, Eramosa Township, Ontario on 16 September 1838 and died of peritonitis in St Paul, Minnesota on 29 May 1916. One of three surviving children, he was fourteen when his father died, and he was forced to quit school for work in a country store. While still a teenager, he left Canada for the United States, where he took up residence in Saint Paul in Minnesota Territory. There he soon became an integral figure in the transformation of Minnesota from a raw frontier to an economically diverse region. Active in the steamboat trade on the Mississippi and Red rivers, he expanded into warehousing and the fuel business, and later invested heavily in Minnesota's Iron Range and the mining industries of Iowa, Montana and Washington state.

Approaching middle age, he entered into the railroad business, in 1877 joining with Norman Kittson, John S. Kennedy, and Canadians Donald SMITH and George Stephen to complete the St Paul and Pacific railway from Minneapolis–St Paul to the Canadian border. Subsequently he built to the west, finally completing what became the Great Northern Railway from St Paul to Seattle in 1893. Alone among US transcontinental lines, the Great Northern remained solvent and avoided bankruptcy in the hard times of the 1890s.

Through his founding and leadership of the Great Northern Railway, Hill dominated rail transportation and played a significant role in

the economic development of the American Northwest during the late nineteenth and early twentieth centuries. Allying himself with the nation's preeminent investment banking firm, the house of J.P. MORGAN, Hill obtained control of the Northern Pacific and Chicago, Burlington and Quincy railroads. He became one of the leading figures in the rise of 'big business' in the United States. Following a dramatic conflict with Edward H. Harriman, Hill presided over the Northern Securities holding company (1901–1904), the largest railroad organization of its day, which included the 'Hill Lines' controlled by himself and Morgan. Although the US Supreme Court ordered the dissolution of Northern Securities under provisions of the Sherman Anti-trust Act, the same railroads merged again in 1970 to become the Burlington Northern (now Burlington Northern Santa Fe) system.

After 1900 Hill involved himself in a wide variety of other pursuits. He delivered countless public addresses on a broad range of topics, including international trade, agronomy, finance and the environment. He remained an important adviser to US presidents from the 1880s until his death. He ran model experimental farms in Minnesota to develop superior livestock and crop yields for settlers locating near his railroads. His philanthropic interests were wide-ranging and included significant support for educational, religious and charitable organizations throughout Minnesota, the Northwest and the nation. In his adopted home town, he constructed the James J. Hill Reference Library, which houses his personal papers, to encourage individual self-improvement. When he died suddenly in 1916, James J. Hill was still at work, penning his thoughts on the wisdom of the nation's military 'preparedness' in light of the First World War.

BIBLIOGRAPHY

Hidy, R.W., Hidy, M.E., Scott, R.V. and Hofsommer, D.L. (1988) *The Great Northern Railway: A History*, Boston: Harvard Business School Press.

Hill, J.J. (1910) *Highways of Progress*, New York: Doubleday and Page.

Malone, M.P. (1996) *James J. Hill: Empire Builder of the Northwest*, Norman, OK: University of Oklahoma Press.

Martin, A. (1976) *James J. Hill and the Opening of the Northwest*, New York: Oxford University Press.

Pyle, J.G. (1916-1917) *The Life of James J. Hill*, 2 vols, Garden City, NY: Doubleday and Page.

WTW

HILL, Philip Ernest (1873–1944)

Philip Ernest Hill was born in Torquay, Devon on 11 April 1873, the son of Philip Hill, a cab driver, and his wife Mary, who kept a lodging house. He died in Windlesham, Surrey on 15 August 1944. He married four times: to Katherine Evans (died 1903), the actress Jessica Fitzwilliam (divorced 1921), the actress Vera Graves (divorced 1930) and finally in 1934 to Phyllis Partington, with whom he 'lived happily ever after' (Corley 1984: 238). Hill was educated at Taunton Independent College, where, according to Corley (1984), he received some commercial education, and then found employment in the offices of an estate agent in Newton Abbot, Devon, later serving for a short time in the Fourth Dragoon Guards. He then settled in Cardiff, where he worked as an estate agent and married his first wife. After the deaths of his wife and their only child in 1903, Hill moved to London, again setting up as an estate agent and valuer.

In 1923 a chance meeting brought Hill into contact with the conductor Sir Thomas Beecham, son of the late pharmaceuticals manufacturer Sir Joseph BEECHAM. At the time of his death in 1916 Beecham senior had been in

the process of buying the Covent Garden estate in central London from the Duke of Bedford. Beecham's death and the war had greatly complicated the sale, which had been handed over to the notoriously labyrinthine Court of Chancery. Hill applied himself to sorting out the problem, and in less than a year had secured clear title to the property and helped set up a new company, Beecham's Estates and Pills, to manage it, being appointed a director of the new firm.

Hill's next step was to separate the incompatible commercial property and pharmaceuticals businesses, which he managed with great delicacy and skill. Beecham's Pills was incorporated in 1928 and, through several successful mergers, became Britain's largest pharmaceuticals company. Hill served as its first chairman and, through the 1930s, guided it through several other major acquisitions and also invested heavily in research and development. By the end of the 1940s, says Corley (1984), Beechams was one of the country's leading science-based organizations, and dominated the pharmaceuticals industry.

The estate arm of the business, meanwhile, became the Covent Garden Property Company and went public in 1933, with Hill once again serving as chairman. This company expanded aggressively into the retail chemists market, buying up several leading national chains. In 1933 Hill only just missed a chance to buy the Boots chain of retail chemists, which had been sold by its founder, Jesse BOOT, in 1920; control of this company would have given him the majority of the British market.

Hill also invested in the leisure industry; he was an early backer of J. Arthur RANK, and helped the latter take a share of Oscar DEUTSCH's very successful Odeon cinema chain. Perhaps most significantly in terms of British history, in 1935 he provided the financial muscle that amalgamated a number of aircraft firms into the Hawker Siddeley Corporation; he remained on the board as a financial adviser to the new chairman, T.O.M. SOPWITH, and helped the company raise the capital to finance the development and construction of the Hurricane fighter, which later helped the Royal Air Force win the Battle of Britain.

Hill is often dismissed as a mere property speculator. He was that, of course, although 'mere' is hardly the term for a man who was worth over £3 million at the time of his death. But he was also a gifted financier, one who helped the companies he governed chart a course through the economically troubled period of the Great Depression and, in most cases, grow and prosper. Not a technical man himself, he was able to develop effective partnerships with technicians and engineers at Beecham and later at Hawker Siddeley. Corley (1984) notes that he rarely interfered in the day-to-day running of his companies, preferring to delegate where possible to experts in their given fields, and to concentrate on strategy and finance. Like Eric GEDDES, another great British business leader of the interwar period, Hill showed that the managerial spirit was alive and well in at least some quarters of the British economy.

BIBLIOGRAPHY
Corley, T.A.B. (1984) 'Hill, Philip Ernest', in D.J. Jeremy (ed.), *Dictionary of Business Biography*, London: Butterworths, vol. 2, 235–9.

MLW

HILL, Rowland (1795–1879)

Rowland Hill was born in Kidderminster, Worcestershire on 3 December 1795, the third son of Thomas Hill, a schoolteacher, and his wife Sarah. He died in London on 27 August 1879. In 1802 the family moved to Birmingham, where Hill's father had purchased a school; Hill was educated there and

later joined his father as a teacher. As a boy, says Hey (1976), he had a broad range of interests but showed a particular aptitude for science and engineering. He tried to apply the principles of his scientific knowledge to the solution of everyday problems. The Hill family was a close one, and Hill and his brothers frequently worked together and set up joint ventures; for a time, the family even held all their property in common, and even after this arrangement ended the brothers contributed to a joint insurance scheme which benefited any family member who was having financial problems.

In 1819, in partnership with his brother Matthew, Hill opened the Hazelwood School in Birmingham. The school, which was designed and built by him, was also a radical experiment in educational reform. Among other features, the school was run on a democratic basis, with a code of rules laid down by Hill but implemented by the pupils themselves through a system of 'magistrates' and 'courts'. The school was hailed by Jeremy Bentham and other reformers as a great advance in education, and the Hill principles were widely copied, particularly in Sweden. In 1827 a second school was opened in London. In 1833, however, Hill was forced to retire on grounds of ill health, leaving two of his brothers in charge of the school.

Looking for other occupations, Hill became interested in a variety of projects, including the colonization of New South Wales and the design of a rotary printing press, which he patented in 1835. His chief project, however, became the reform of the postal system. In Britain in the 1830s, postal rates were very high (rates also varied by the distance the letter was travelling) and letters were almost never prepaid, with the result that only the wealthy tended to use the postal system. Although some cities and areas had introduced reforms, these had never caught on nationwide, thanks to entrenched opposition from the treasury. Hill calculated that by using prepaid post either by means of franked letters or stamps and by

reducing the rates to a modest amount – he ultimately settled on 1p per half-ounce – charged uniformly no matter what distance the letter was travelling, the postal system could generate a much greater volume of traffic – a volume that would, moreover, increase the revenues coming into the treasury.

These proposals were published in his pamphlet *Post Office Reform* in 1837, and immediately won widespread public approval. The Penny Postage Act was passed in 1839, and Hill was sent to the treasury to implement the new system. Despite entrenched opposition from treasury civil servants, the uniform penny postage system was introduced on 10 January 1840. The famous Penny Black postage stamp, designed by Hill's brother Edwin, was also introduced. As Hill had foreseen, the volume of post rose immediately and treasury revenues rose as well. However, he had made too many enemies, and in 1842 he was dismissed from his post. He served as chairman of the London and Brighton Railway from 1843 to 1846, where again his organizational abilities made their mark and resulted in the railway's profits increasing. In 1846 a new government recalled him to the Post Office, where he continued to struggle with bureaucrats (despite his opponents threatening him with assassination on several occasions) and improve the efficiency of the service until ill health finally forced his retirement in 1864. By the time of his death, the British postal service had been copied in more than sixty countries around the world; in the words of William Ewart Gladstone, his reforms 'had run like wildfire throughout the civilized world'. Hill was knighted in 1860; when he died he was given a state funeral and burial in Westminster Abbey.

Hill was more than just an innovator; he was also a superb organizer and manager who fully understood the principles of organization. Among his most bitterly opposed reforms at the Post Office were his moves to shorten hours of work and raise wages. He also understood the basic market principle that cutting prices would grow the volume of the business,

and increase revenues and profits. Above all, in his practical application of scientific principles to running a business, Hill foreshadowed the coming revolution of scientific management. At the same time, he had given the world of business one of its most valuable tools: although the telegraph and the telephone would reduce dependence on the postal system to a degree, until very near our own time the postal service remained the primary conduit by which businesses transmitted information. In the early twentieth century, a new form of business, mail-order retailing, began using the postal system to deliver goods to customers. Hill's Post Office was a major step forward in the growth of modern management.

BIBLIOGRAPHY

Hey, C.G. (1976) *Rowland Hill: Victorian Genius and Benefactor*, London: Quiller Press.

MLW

HILL, William (1903–71)

William Hill was born in Birmingham on 16 July 1903, one of eleven children of William and Lavinia Hill. He died in London on 15 October 1971. Initially following his father's trade as a coach painter, he became interested in horse racing while in his teens. He seems to have realized early the truism that the only people consistently to make money out of horse racing are bookmakers and, raising a small amount of capital, established himself at racecourses around the Midlands. An early bankruptcy seems to have affected him only insofar as it taught him caution, and he was back in business within a few months. In 1929 he relocated to London, where he established himself at the local horse and greyhound racing tracks and opened an office in Jermyn Street.

By 1939 the organization had grown substantially, with Hill diversifying into football coupons and postal betting, and a new headquarters was opened on Park Lane.

Following the Second World War the steady course of expansion continued. In 1954 Hill moved to a simplified multidivisional form of organization, with his racecourse betting, football and postal betting operations established as separate companies owned by a holding company. The reorganization was largely completed by 1956. In the 1960s Hill initially opposed the introduction of licensed betting shops, but when it became clear that these were proving successful he moved into the field, purchasing several existing chains and quickly establishing the William Hill group as the largest betting shop chain in Britain. Hill retired in 1969 and died two years later, a highly respected and, indeed, respectable businessman.

Hill's career serves as an example of how applying management principles can lead to business success even in the most unconventional of industries. In a trade full of individualists and entrepreneurs, Hill carved out a major business organization, the first time such large-scale organization had been applied (legitimately) to the bookmaking business. He backed his organizational skills with a strong attention to detail and sound knowledge of his business; he was an excellent judge of horses, becoming an important breeder and owner in his own right, and knew better than most how to lay odds. He was also a shrewd and instinctive marketer: 'he believed that all his customers should receive the most courteous service, no matter how small their bet, and backed this with integrity and the initiative to know what the public wanted and to give it to them in full value' (Abbey 1985: 241). His approach to the public meant that inexperienced racegoers and gamblers could be made to feel welcome and would be more likely to indulge in their hobby, at the same ensuring Hill a flow of loyal customers.

BIBLIOGRAPHY
Abbey, H.W. (1985) 'Hill, William', in D.J. Jeremy (ed.), *Dictionary of Business Biography*, London: Butterworths, vol. 3, 239–42.

MLW

HILTON, Conrad Nicholson (1887–1979)

Conrad Nicholson Hilton was born in San Antonio, New Mexico on 25 December 1887, the son of Augustus and Mary Hilton. He died in Santa Monica, California on 3 January 1979. He married three times: to Mary Barron in 1925 (divorced 1934), to actress Zsa Zsa Gabor in 1942 (divorced 1946) and to Mary Frances in 1976; these marriage produced four children. He attended military schools in Albuquerque and Roswell, New Mexico and later St Michael's College in Santa Fe and the New Mexico Institute of Mining. He joined his father, a general storekeeper, as a partner in business, served in the New Mexico state legislature from 1912, and was an officer in the US Army quartermaster corps in France in 1917–18. He helped to found the New Mexico State Bank in 1913. After the death of his father in 1918 he took over the business with the intention of moving into banking, but instead saw a business opportunity in the run-down Mobley Hotel in Cisco, Texas. Finding the hotel business profitable, Hilton began to expand. Lacking capital, his initial strategy was to buy run-down hotels and renovate them. As the business grew, however, he began building new hotels on leased land, starting in Dallas and gradually expanding across Texas and the Southwest. By 1930 he owned eight hotels.

The operation remained under-capitalized, and the Depression forced Hilton close to bankruptcy, but he managed to put together a partnership with two other hoteliers that kept them all afloat. In 1934 the merger failed, and Hilton went his own way again with five hotels. This time he had access to sufficient capital and resumed his expansion. He began buying prestige hotels such as the Waldorf in New York, and then moved on to purchasing existing chains. In 1948 he moved overseas to Puerto Rico, establishing Hilton International Corporation. He also diversified into related businesses, setting up the Carte Blanche credit-card company and a car rental chain. By the time of his death there were 260 Hilton hotels around the world, either directly owned or franchised, and Hilton himself was worth half a billion dollars. He retired in 1966, handing over control to his son Barron Hilton.

Hilton's success was founded on several key factors. First, he had a strong sense for the best strategic locations, and knew where to place or buy hotels to attract the maximum number of travellers. Second, he built a strong brand identity for Hilton, with large advertising campaigns and standardized service offerings that guaranteed quality and consistency. Third, he worked to build up staff morale, encouraging them to feel involved in the business and to treat customers as guests. His autobiography *Be My Guest* (1957) was for many years distributed free to customers.

BIBLIOGRAPHY
Hilton, C. (1957) *Be My Guest*, Englewood Cliffs, NJ: Prentice-Hall.

HIRAI Yasutaro (1896–1970)

Hirai Yasutaro was born in Kobe on 10 October 1896 and died there on 2 July 1970. After graduating from Kobe Higher Commercial School (Kobe University), he entered the professional faculty at Tokyo Higher Commercial School. Graduating from

this school, he was immediately invited to assume a post as lecturer at Kobe Higher Commercial School, his *alma mater*. He developed the course of lectures on the science of business administration to be taught in Japan. In 1923 he was appointed professor. From 1921 to 1925 he studied abroad in Britain, Germany, the United States and Italy. In 1924 he attended the meeting of the German Society of Business Administration in Jena, the only foreigner to do so. In 1925 he published a guidebook on the economics of business administration while lecturing at Frankfurt University in cooperation with Alfred Isaac, assistant professor at Frankfurt.

Hirai saw the science of business administration as another type of science, different from economics. He took it for granted that the study of economic activity based on plans under a unified concept was the science of business administration. He was of the view that all activities associated with business administration were appropriate subjects for this science. Features of Hirai's theory include the need to understand the organization from a viewpoint similar to that of modern systems theory. Problems of business administration should always be seen in association with the economic activity of whole business entities, and administration should be seen as action based on concepts and plans formulated by individual economic subjects. Hirai rejects the older 'economic man' model of economics. He posits the figure of the human being as central to the understanding of management. His management theory, although never completed, has a theoretical structure which has much in common with modern organization theory.

Although he was still a young scholar, Hirai participated in the establishment of the Japan Society of Business Administration, and made great contributions to the development of the study of business administration for many years after. He was engaged in the study and teaching of business administration at Kobe University. From Hirai's seminars there thirty-one researchers on business administration and accounting were produced. He was also active in university administration, and established the new department for business administration at Kobe Economic University (now Kobe University) in 1944. In 1949 he established the first faculty of business administration at a Japanese university; in 1973 he established a postgraduate section within the faculty, offering first master's degrees and later doctoral programmes. Hirai himself was granted the first doctorate in business administration in Japan. He also edited Japan's first glossary of business administration, published in 1952.

Hirai introduced Japan to the German Society of Business Administration at an early date, and worked hard to develop reciprocal relationships between the two bodies. In 1968 he was designated an honorary member of the German Society of Business Administration, the first Japanese to be so honoured. In 1952 he played a role as a promoter to allow Japan to participate in the Congrès International du Organisation Scientifique (CIOS). In 1961 he was nominated a fellow of CIOS, again the first Japanese to be so honoured. He was also nominated to the US Academy of Management. Hirai was thus the first Japanese scholar of business administration to become prominent on the international scene.

As a disciple of UEDA Teijiro, Hirai Yasutaro not only constructed his own theory of business administration, but also made great contributions to the development of the study of this science in Japan. Descriptions of his career almost always include adjectival words or phrases such as 'the first' or 'for the first time in Japan'. He made the reputation of Japanese business scholarship, both inside the country and internationally.

BIBLIOGRAPHY
Hirai Y. (1932) *Keiei Keizaigaku Nyumon* (Introduction to the Science of Business Administration), Tokyo: Chikura Shoten.
—— (1952) (ed.) *Keieigaku Jiten*

(Dictionary of Business Administration), Tokyo: Diamond Sha.

Hirai Y. and Deutsch, P. (1938) *Neuest Betriebswirtschaftliches Quellenbuch* (Newest Sourcebook for Industrial Management Studies), Leipzig: Felix Meine.

Hirai Y. and Isaac, A. (1925) *Quellenbuch der Betriebswirtschaftslehre* (Sourcebook for Industrial Management Studies), Berlin: Spaeth and Linde.

Mano Osamu (1996) 'Hirai Yasutaro no Kobetsu Keizaigaku' (Hirai Yasutaro's Individual Economics), in Japan Society for the History of Management Theories (ed.), *Nihon no Keieigaku wo Kizuita Hitotachi* (The People Who Built Up the Science of Business Administration in Japan), Annual Report, vol. 3, 27–37.

ST

HIROSE Saihei (1828–1914)

Hirose Saihei was born in Yabu Village, Yasu County, Ohmi State (Yasu City, Shiga prefecture) in May 1828 and died in Osaka. In 1839 he served as an apprentice in the accounting office of the Besshi Copper Mine, owned by Sumitomo. By nature fond of learning, he began to study *Shisho* (four books consisting of the *Daigaku*, *Chuyo*, *Rongo*, and *Moshi*, fundamental texts of Confucianism) while he was working for the accounting office. He married in 1856, and shortly after he and his wife were concurrently accepted as an adopted couple by Hirose Giemon, one of the Hirose family's kinsmen. In 1857 Hirose Saihei was promoted to the post of general manager of the Besshi Copper Mine. He later became chairman of the entire Sumitomo *zaibatsu* (group of businesses).

In the turbulent period of the Meiji Restoration in the 1860s, one of Hirose's most important achievements was preventing the Besshi Copper Mine from being confiscated by the army, which was attempting to topple the Tokugawa shogunate. Hirose opened negotiations with high-ranking government officials including Iwakura Tomomi, and persuaded them to allow Sumitomo to keep the mine. At the time, Sumitomo was suffering from acute financial difficulties, and was even considering the sale of Besshi Copper Mine in order to secure capital funds. However Hirose, who opposed this idea, was able to rationalize the administration of the mining firm and to introduce overseas technology. The introduction of steam-hoisting machines was completed in 1890, and rock drills were used to construct a railroad for conveying copper ore in 1891. This resulted in a great increase in output in the production of copper: from 360 to 420 tons a year immediately after the Meiji Restoration to 2,022 tons a year in 1890.

The founder of the Sumitomo family was Shibata Masatomo, the second son of Shibata Masayuki and grandson of Shibata Katsuie, well-known warlord and vassal of Oda Nobunaga, one of the great military leaders of sixteenth-century Japan. However, Sumitomo's business ancestor is Sumitomo Rizaemon, who developed a new method of refining copper called *nanban-buki* (southern barbarians' blowing) at the end of the sixteenth century. Ribei, Rizaemon's son, who married Masatomo's daughter, developed the business of mining copper ore and refining and selling the metal product. The Sumitomos moved from Kyoto to Osaka in the 1620s, and established *nanban-buki* technology there. Combining the mining and refining of copper with the money exchange business, the Sumitomo business saw an age of prosperity. However, profits declined sharply at the end of the Edo period, and the family business was driven into a deep depression. Thanks to the rationalization and modernization of the administration of the copper mine undertaken

by Hirose Saihei, however, the business recovered. As well as improving the administration of the copper-mining business, Hirose worked to reform the family constitution or family laws of the Sumitomo.

With Sumitomo Financial Combine's power as background, Hirose took part in the establishment of the Osaka Chamber of Commerce and Industry, Osaka Stock Transaction Office, Osaka Mercantile Ship Company and many other ventures. Thus he became a prominent member of the Kansai financial circle. However, the Sumitomo family gradually came to oppose Hirose's dictatorial policies and methods of administration, and he was forced to resign from the post of chairman of Sumitomo. He also retired from the financial circle.

BIBLIOGRAPHY
'Hirose Saihei Hansei Monogatari' (Hirose Saihei's Life) (1965) in Choh Sachio (ed.), *Gendai Nihon Kiroku Zenshu* (The Complete Edition of Modern Japan's Records), 8 vols, Tokyo: Chikuma Shobo.

ST

HOFSTEDE, Gerard Hendrik (1928–)

Gerard Hendrik (Geert) Hofstede was born at Haarlem, the Netherlands on 2 October 1928. During his early years he attended Gymnasium B (grammar school), receiving a diploma in 1945. This was followed by two years of vocational training in mechanical engineering at HTS (technical college), which included a trip to Indonesia as a ship's engineer. He attended Delft Technical University and obtained an MSc in mechanical engineering in 1953.

Upon graduation, Hofstede began his professional career in the Dutch army as a tech-

nical officer from 1953 to 1955. In 1955 he married Maaike van den Hoek, who holds an MA in French from the University of Amsterdam and an MA in Islamic languages and civilization from the Free University of Brussels. They have since had four sons. From the military, Hofstede moved into industry, where he held a variety of positions including worker, foreman, engineer and plant manager until 1965. During the latter position at N.J. Menko, a textiles mill, he embarked on part-time doctoral studies, and in 1967 was awarded a Ph.D. in social sciences from the University of Groningen. His doctoral thesis, entitled 'The Game of Budget Control', was supervised by Professor Herman A. Hutte. Perhaps it was these early experiences and travel far afield that set the stage for his later work.

In 1965 Hofstede joined IBM Europe's Executive Development Department and eventually became manager of personnel research from 1968 to 1971. Following his time at IBM, Hofstede held a number of successive positions, including visiting lecturer in organizational behaviour at IMEDE, Switzerland, professor of organizational behaviour at the European Institute for Advanced Studies in Management, Belgium, visiting professor of organizational behaviour at INSEAD, France, director of human resources for Fasson Europe and Dean of SEMAFOR Management College, the Netherlands. In 1980 he co-founded the Institute for Research on Intercultural Cooperation (IRIC) in the Netherlands, and has since taken on the roles of professor of organizational anthropology and international management at the University of Maastricht and professor emeritus at the University of Hong Kong. At the time of writing he is a senior fellow of the IRIC and a fellow of the Centre for Economic Research at Tilburg University. He has written six books and more than 170 journal articles. His most significant works are *Culture's Consequences* (1980a) and *Cultures and Organizations* (1991). Hofstede has also held

a variety of visitorships in Austria, Hawaii, Hong Kong and Australia, among others.

The conceptualization of culture is not new, and owes much of its heritage to anthropology, the study of primitive civilizations, ways of life and customs. Hofstede (1980a, 1984b) developed a new typology by which national cultures can be distinguished along four bipolar dimensions: (1) power distance, (2) individualism–collectivism, (3) masculinity–femininity and (4) uncertainty avoidance. Although numerous definitions of culture exist, Hofstede's is perhaps the most widely employed: 'the collective programming of the mind which distinguishes the members of one human group from another ... Culture, in this sense, includes systems of values; and values are among the building blocks of culture' (1984a: 21).

To construct his model, Hofstede applied a wide variety of disciplines, including psychology, sociology, history, political science, economics and anthropology, and he also utilized data collected from 116,000 responses to a standardized questionnaire delivered in forty countries. The survey itself was undertaken at two different time intervals between 1967 and 1973, and participants were drawn from a variety of levels within a single company code-named HERMES, later to be revealed as IBM. Interestingly enough much of the fruits of this research were accidental, as the original purpose of the survey was to evaluate employee attitudes, not dimensions of national culture. However, in reviewing the results, Hofstede soon recognized the opportunity to explore culture and its consequences.

The results obtained for each country were rated by dimension, and placed on an index to differentiate visually the uniqueness of a national culture. Essentially, Hofstede created a multi-country map or international landscape of national culture distinctiveness. Power distance scores the extent to which members in a society accept an unequal distribution of power: 'Inequality can occur in areas such as prestige, wealth, and power; and different societies put different weights on status consistency among these areas' (Hofstede 1980a: 92). The willingness to tolerate inequalities in power distribution is readily observable in superior–subordinate relationships. In high power-distance countries, such as the Philippines, India, Yugoslavia or France, subordinates rarely deviate from an organization's hierarchy or reporting structure, irrespective of the circumstances. The opposite is true in nations with low-power distance scores, typified by Austria and Israel. In these nations, it is commonplace for subordinates to bypass their supervisor to seek a higher authority.

Individualism–collectivism distinguishes between individual self-interest and a group's collective interests. Individualism implies a loose social integration in which individuals primarily focus on their own personal interests and those of their immediate families. In contrast, collectivists associate themselves with the group's common goals and objectives. The United States, Australia and Britain scored the highest on individualism, and highly regard values such as free will and self-determination. At the opposite end of the spectrum, Columbia, Venezuela and Pakistan are characterized by loyalty to the group and the promotion of harmony.

Masculinity–femininity measures nations according to the division of roles and values between sexes. For instance, the dominant values in a masculine society (Japan and Austria) emphasize assertiveness, achievement and material success, whereas feminine cultures (Sweden and Norway) emphasize human relationships, concern for others and the quality of life.

Finally, uncertainty avoidance is defined as the extent to which individuals accept uncertainty and ambiguity in various situations. Hofstede's research suggests that British culture, which scores low on this dimension, appears to be far more tolerant of uncertainty than many other high-scoring societies, most

notably Greece, Portugal, Japan and France. Lifetime-oriented employment is relatively common in high-scoring countries; however, low-scoring countries (Hong Kong and Singapore) tend to have higher job mobility rates.

In later work, Hofstede and Bond (1988) added a fifth dimension, labelled 'Confucian dynamism' or 'short-term versus long-term orientation'. Confucian dynamism or time-orientation measures the degree to which people have a future-oriented (long-term orientation) or a present/past-oriented perspective (short-term orientation) (see CONFUCIUS). A high score represents an 'employee's devotion to the work ethic and their respect for tradition' (Adler 1997: 58).

Hofstede's work (1980a) has been widely cited, with some 1,036 quotations in the Social Science Citation Index (SSCI) during the period from 1980 to 1993 alone (Sondergaard 1994), making him one of the most influential authors on the subject of international business and national culture (Chandy and Williams 1994). His model has also been extensively adopted and applied to the study of cultural differences in a variety of other disciplines, such as accounting, sales and marketing (Murphy 1999), decision making (Vitell et al. 1993) and strategy formulation (Schneider 1989), to name but a few. Hofstede's model has important implications for motivation in the workplace (Hofstede 1980b) and the adoption of various management initiatives, namely leadership styles (Adler 1997), compensation practices, budgeting, conflict resolution (Adler 1997; Tse et al. 1994), innovation (Shane 1995) and the like.

Despite its popularity, however, Hofstede's thesis is the subject of intense scrutiny and criticism. Legions of researchers and practitioners have identified constraints, as summarized by Sondergaard (1994) and Westwood and Everett (1987). These, for the most part, focus on methodological, theoretical and implementation concerns. Some

researchers have suggested that additional dimensions should be added, such as, 'shame and guilt' (Hunt 1981), paternalism (Dorfman and Howell 1988) or Triandis's twenty dimensions (1982). Others have attempted to create their own typologies. For instance, Kluckhohn and Strodtbeck's value orientations (1961) describe culture in terms of various sets of value orientations towards the world and humankind. Likewise, Hampden-Turner and Trompenaars (1993) have listed seven different cultures of capitalism, but unlike Hofstede, their model is not prescriptive in nature; they define culture as the 'way in which people solve problems', implying shared meaning and cultural cohesion, and they demonstrate that different cultures have different ways of solving common problems or dilemmas. This approach lends support to the idea that cross-cultural management can generate more strategic options (Darlington 1996).

Another consideration advanced by researchers, such as Roberts and Boyacigiller (1984) and Sondergaard (1994), is whether Hofstede's model can be used to reflect the present day. They claim that Hofstede's work is out of date. However, for the time being, this view has been invalidated by substantial recent research which generated similar results to Hofstede. A similar argument suggests that cultural values are becoming more similar (converging) as a result of increased contact and integration of nations, thus eroding cultural distinctiveness (Ohmae 1990). However, Child (1981) concludes, that although macro policies, procedures and other features are becoming more similar on an international level, the micro factors, behaviours and values shared by members of a culture remain intact.

Lastly, the applicability and implementation of Hofstede's model is perhaps the most controversial subject of them all. The proposition that human behaviour is conditioned solely by national culture is too simplistic, and ignores the influence of a variety of other

environmental factors, personal differences, and situational contingencies (political, legal, religious, technological, economic, etc.), especially in international business. Therefore, any framework adopted for analysing or enhancing our understanding of different cultures or societies must also include and strike a balance between a host of other competing claims.

The debate relating to Hofstede's thesis continues to run, and it is evident that some problems remain. However, Hofstede (1980a) himself recognizes these limitations and rightly challenges others to employ additional research techniques. Perhaps Westwood and Everett (1987: 199) sum up best when they state that 'we are expecting too much of Hofstede within the context of one study ... Hofstede cannot be criticized for not being God'. What is evident from a critical examination of Hofstede's work is that further research is warranted and that any limitations should be considered when utilizing his framework as a basis of analysis.

To conclude, Hofstede's thesis is certainly one of the most significant and popular contributions in the cultural arena. His pioneering study and subsequent research draw our attention to the importance of understanding differences in national cultural more fully, and ultimately underscore its highly pervasive and complex nature. His work also alerts us to the need for greater cultural sensitivity, and warns of the dangers of attempting unilaterally to apply 'Western' management practices to other countries and cultures without the necessary adaptation. There are also strong implications for managing diversity in the workplace. No doubt the importance of his model will continue to grow as world trade expands and as people and businesses cross borders.

BIBLIOGRAPHY

Adler, N.J. (1997) *International Dimensions of Organizational Behavior*, 3rd edn, London: International Thomson Publishing.

Chandy, P.R. and Williams, T. (1994) 'The Impact of Journals and Authors on International Business Research: A Citational Analysis of JIBS Articles', *Journal of International Business Studies* 25(4): 715–28.

Child, J. (1981) 'Culture, Contingency and Capitalism in the Cross-national Study of Organisations', *Research in Organizational Behavior* 3: 303–56.

Darlington, G. (1996) 'Culture: A Theoretical Review', in P. Joynt and M. Warner (eds), *Managing Across Cultures: Issues and Perspectives*, London: International Thomson Publishing.

Dorfman, P. and Howell, J.P. (1988) 'Dimensions of National Culture and Effective Leadership Patterns: Hofstede Revisited', *Advances in International Comparative Management* 3: 127–50.

Hampden-Turner, C. and Trompenaars, F. (1993) *The Seven Cultures of Capitalism*, Garden City, NY: Doubleday.

Hofstede, G. (1980a) *Culture's Consequences: International Differences in Work-related Values*, Beverly Hills, CA: Sage.

—— (1980b) 'Motivation, Leadership, and Organization: Do American Theories Apply Abroad?', *Organization Dynamics* (Summer): 42–63.

—— (1984a) 'National Cultures Revisited', *Asia Pacific Journal of Management* 1: 22–8.

—— (1984b) 'Cultural Dimensions in Management and Planning', *Asia Pacific Journal of Management* 1: 81–99.

—— (1991) *Cultures and Organizations: Software of the Mind*, London: McGraw-Hill.

Hofstede, G. and Bond, M.H. (1988) 'The Confucius Connection: From Cultural Roots to Economic Growth', *Organizational Dynamics* 16: 5–21.

Hunt, J.W. (1981) 'Applying American Behavioural Science: Some Cross-cultural Problems', *Organizational Dynamics* (Summer): 55–62.

Kluckhohn, F.R. and Strodtbeck, F.L. (1961) *Variations in Value Orientations*, Evanston, IL: Row, Peterson and Co.

Murphy, W.H. (1999) 'Hofstede's National Culture as a Guide for Sales Practices Across Countries: The Case of a MNC's Sales Practices in Australia and New Zealand', *Australian Journal of Management* 24(1): 37–58.

Ohmae, K. (1990) *The Borderless World: Power and Strategy in the Interlinked Economy*, New York: Harper Business.

Roberts, K.H. and Boyacigiller, N.A. (1984) 'Cross-national Organisational Research: The Grasp of the Blinded Men', *Research in Organizational Behavior* 6: 423–75.

Schneider, S.C. (1989) 'Strategy Formulation: The Impact of National Culture', *Organization Studies* 10(2): 149–68.

Shane, S. (1995) 'Uncertainty Avoidance and the Preference for Innovation Championing Roles', *Journal of International Business Studies* 26(1): 47–68.

Sondergaard, M. (1994) 'Hofstede's Consequences: A Study of Reviews, Citations and Replications', *Organization Studies* 15: 447–56.

Triandis, H.C. (1982) 'Review of Culture's Consequence: International Differences in Work-related Values', *Human Organization* 41: 86–90.

Tse, D.K., Francis, J. and Walls, J. (1994) 'Cultural Differences in Conducting Intra- and Inter-cultural Negotiations: A Sino-Canadian Comparison', *Journal of International Business Studies* 25(3): 537–55.

Vitell, S.J., Nwachukwu, S. and Barnes, J.H. (1993) 'The Effects of Culture on Ethical Decision-making: An Application of Hofstede's Typology', *Journal of Business Studies* 12: 753–60.

Westwood, R.G. and Everett, J.E. (1987) 'Culture's Consequences: A Methodology for Comparative Management Studies in Southeast Asia?' *Asia Pacific Journal of Management* 4(3): 187–202.

Yeh, R. (1988) 'On Hofstede's Treatment of Chinese and Japanese Values', *Asia Pacific Journal of Management* 6(1): 149–60.

FC-B

HOLDEN, Edward Hopkinson (1848–1919)

Edward Hopkinson Holden was born in Tottington, Lancashire on 11 May 1848, the son of Henry and Anne Holden. He died of heart disease in Chertsey, Surrey on 23 July 1919. He married Anne Cassie in 1877, and they had three children. After completing elementary school, Holden worked as a shop clerk and then, at the age of sixteen, became an apprentice at the Manchester and County Bank, a small regional bank in the northwest of England. While an apprentice and later a cashier at the bank, Holden attended evening classes and studied a number of subjects, including law. In 1881 he moved to the Birmingham and Midland Bank (more usually known as the Midland Bank) as an accountant. He quickly came to the notice of the directors, who promoted him to secretary of the bank in 1883. Working with J.A. Christie, the bank's sub-manager, Holden managed a series of acquisitions beginning with the Union Bank of Birmingham in 1883, which made the Midland the largest bank in its region by 1890. In that year Holden was appointed general manager of the bank, and he and Christie were given free rein to pursue their expansion plans; three London banks were purchased in 1891, giving Midland access to the City of London and a seat on the London Clearing House. The bank was renamed the London and Midland, and transferred its headquarters to

458

London in 1891. Further growth and amalgamation followed in the 1890s, by the end of which decade Midland had shot to a position as one of the leading banks in the country, and Holden was one of the most respected bankers.

In 1898 Holden was promoted to managing director with an annual salary of £5,000, sixteen times his starting salary as an accountant seventeen years earlier. He now began a period of consolidation, streamlining the group's administrative structure and centralizing authority in the bank's Threadneedle Street headquarters. Although Green (1985) comments that Holden was an authoritarian who preferred to exercise direct control over the bank, by 1898 the organization had grown to such a size that this was no longer possible. Much of the day-to-day running of operations was delegated to three general managers, freeing up Holden to manage strategy and policy, including further expansion and yet more mergers. The general impression is that Holden was initially reluctant to delegate, but became more used to doing so with the passage of time as he grew to trust his subordinate, and the system could be plainly seen to be working. In 1904 he made the first of several extended visits to North America, establishing reciprocal working arrangements with a number of banks there.

In 1908 Holden was appointed chairman of the London and Midland Bank. This led him to still further delegation of responsibility to his managers, although he continued to handle the business of particularly important clients, such as the department store owner Gordon SELFRIDGE or the shipbuilder William PIRRIE, on a personal basis. A tough banker who insisted on strict financial accountability from his clients, he nonetheless supported many through times of crisis; he prevented other banks from taking advantage of Pirrie's occasional financial problems at Harland and Wolff, and he supported Herbert AUSTIN through the periodic downturns in the fledgling motor industry. In 1911 Holden led a consortium of other banks to rescue the Yorkshire Penny Bank, which was on the verge of collapse. This effort more than any other marked Holden out as the unacknowledged leader of the London banking community. During the First World War he led the commission that negotiated fixed exchange rates between the Allies for the duration of the war, and undertook many other public services; he had also served as a Liberal MP from 1906 to 1910. He received a baronetcy in 1909, but twice declined a peerage.

Holden was a tireless worker and had a good eye for detail. Even his few recreations, such as cycling, were suspiciously like work, and it was rumoured at the Midland that the chairman's cycling tours nearly always resulted in the opening of new branches in towns and villages through which he had passed. In the earlier stages of his career he pursued banking amalgamation almost as an article of faith, arguing that banks had to grow in size in order to survive in an increasingly uncertain and international financial market. Later, as chairman of the Midland, he devoted himself not only to securing the future of his own bank but also that of London as a financial centre. His legacy was the Midland Bank, one of the four largest banks in the UK until the early 1990s, when it merged with the Hongkong and Shanghai Bank.

BIBLIOGRAPHY
Green, E. (1985) 'Holden, Sir Edward Hopkinson', in D.J. Jeremy (ed.), *Dictionary of Business Biography*, London: Butterworths, vol. 3, 290–98.
Kynaston, D. (1995) *The City of London*, vol. 2, *The Golden Years, 1890–1914*, London: Chatto and Windus.

MLW

HOLLERITH, Herman (1860–1929)

Herman Hollerith was born in Buffalo, New York on 29 February 1860 and died in Washington, DC on 17 November 1929. He was educated in New York and attended the Columbia School of Mines, from which he graduated with a distinction at the age of nineteen. In 1879 he became a special agent for the industrial census with the Census Bureau in Washington, DC. During his tenure, the Census Bureau undertook the 1880 US population census. The monumental task of tabulating the census made a deep impression on Hollerith; a peak work force of nearly 1,500 clerks required seven years to complete the task, almost entirely without benefit of office machinery.

In 1882 Hollerith became an instructor in mechanical engineering at Massachusetts Institute of Technology, where he began, in his own time, to develop a machine for census tabulation. He returned to Washington after a year to become a patent agent. In 1888, in preparation for the upcoming decennial population census, the Census Bureau held a competition for an improved system to expedite the tabulation. Following a number of trials, Hollerith won the competition with his Electrical Tabulating System. In the Hollerith system, the schedule for each individual in the census was transcribed onto a card as a set of set of punched holes. Once punched, the cards could be automatically sorted and tabulated by the census machinery. Altogether, some 62 million cards were punched for the census, which took two and one-half years to complete. Although the cost of tabulating the 1890 census was higher than in the previous census, the greater volume of useful tabulations and the speed with which they were produced meant that there would never be a return to manual methods.

In 1896 Hollerith incorporated the Tabulating Machine Company (TMC) to supply the census system to other nations, and to develop machines for commercial use. The Hollerith machines were rented, providing a constant income stream, while the cards were sold, providing a second very lucrative source of income. (This basic revenue model was to sustained TMC, and later IBM, until the latter's 1956 anti-trust consent decree, when it agreed either to sell or to lease its machines and to permit the use of non-IBM cards.)

In 1905 the Census Bureau decided to develop its own tabulating system, rather than pay what it considered to be the extortionate prices demanded by Hollerith. From this point on, Hollerith put all his energies into developing the commercial market, creating a range of fully automatic equipment. The tabulating system consisted of three basic machines: a card punch for recording data onto cards, a sorting machine for arranging cards into numerical sequence, and the tabulator for totalling the data on the cards. The new equipment facilitated full-scale commercial accounting operations as well as statistical tabulations. By 1911 TMC was supplying data-processing systems to a hundred of the largest firms in the United States.

In 1911, while Hollerith was in ill health, TMC was sold for $2.3 million in a merger organized by the trust builder Charles R. Flint. TMC thus became the principal constituent of the Computing-Tabulating-Recording Company (C-T-R). Hollerith personally received $1.2 million from the sale, which allowed him to retire in considerable luxury. He continued to serve as a technical consultant to C-T-R, but after a few years his contributions were taken over by the experimental department created within the company to improve and develop the machines. C-T-R was renamed International Business Machines (IBM) in 1924, and its subsequent rise to become the leading global supplier of data-processing equipment was largely due to its president, Thomas J. WATSON, Sr. Hollerith's achievement was essentially that of an inventor-entrepreneur, creating the technology and establishing it in the market-place.

BIBLIOGRAPHY

Austrian, G.D. (1982) *Herman Hollerith: Forgotten Giant of Information Processing*, New York: Columbia University Press.

Pugh, E.W. (1995) *Building IBM: Shaping an Industry and Its Technology*, Cambridge, MA: MIT Press.

MC-K

HONDA Soichiro (1906–91)

Honda Soichiro was born into the family of a poor blacksmith in Komyo-mura (Tenryu City) in the suburbs of Hamamatsu City, Shizuoka prefecture on 17 November 1906. He died in Tokyo on 5 August 1991. After completing elementary school in his village, he was employed by Art Shokai, an automobile repair business, in Hongo, Tokyo in April 1922, where he learned about automobile mechanics. In April 1928 Honda opened a branch shop of Art Shokai in Hamamatsu, and his business grew quickly. Later, however, he closed the shop, because he detested having to compete with his own former employees, whom he had trained in repair work.

In 1934 Honda established a company called Tokai Seiki, manufacturing piston rings, but everything went wrong thanks to the poor quality of metal-casting technology. Under the guidance of Professor Tashiro of Hamamatsu Higher Engineering School, Honda was able to improve the quality of his materials. The experience also made him strongly aware of his need for more professional knowledge, and he attended evening courses at the Machine Engineering Department of the Higher School for the next two years, acquiring fundamental knowledge of engineering. Tokai Seiki's products were used for army trucks during the Second World War, and the company became a very large enterprise. Honda invited Ishida Taizo, a former director of Toyota, to teach him how to conduct management.

After Japan's defeat in the war, Honda sold Tokai Seiki to Toyota. He used the profits to establish Honda Technology Research Institute in Hamamatsu City in January 1946, where he engaged in the manufacture of a table salt making machine, frosted glass machines and similar equipment. He also bought the former Japanese army's small-size engines for communication equipment at low prices, and remodelled them so that they could be attached to bicycles. These powered bicycles were marketed and sold very rapidly. With this as momentum, Honda went on to build his own engines to be attached to bicycles.

Honda established Honda Motor Company, Ltd, with twenty employees and a capital stock of 2 million yen, in September 1948, and started production of motorcycles. Through an introduction by a friend in the summer of the following year, Honda met FUJISAWA Takeo. The two men got along at once, and agreed to run Honda Motor Company jointly. Fujisawa was entrusted with sales, finance and management, which Honda always found difficult to manage, whereas Honda himself remained in charge of technological development.

Honda developed a motorcycle with a two-cycle engine named 'Dream' in 1948. In 1951 the company developed Japan's first four-cycle engine motorcycles, followed by the development of scooters. In June 1954 Honda went abroad to inspect the TT Race on the Isle of Man in Britain and the motorcycle industry in Europe. In 1958 the company developed the Super Cub, a midget motorbike. Honda Motor Company went on to develop successively a number of new products, and began to build up a monopolistic position in the Japanese motorcycle industry. In 1961 Honda's motorcycles secured a clean sweep in the Isle of Man TT Race, taking the first six positions. Almost in parallel with the estab-

lishment of Honda Motors USA in Los Angeles on June 1959, Honda embarked on a full-fledged export drive into the international market.

In 1962 Honda made its first entry into the four-wheel vehicle industry, and in 1964 a mass-production car factory was established. The first product was a sports car with a 500cc engine. A light passenger car called N360 marketed in 1967 was evaluated in its performance and design; this car went on to account for the greatest proportion of light motor car production in Japan within just three months from the outset of marketing.

Honda Motor Company spun off its technological development division to form Honda Technology Research Institute Company, Ltd in 1960, and Honda Soichiro himself assumed the presidency of the new company, taking the leadership in its technological development. Environmental pollution was coming to be a worldwide problem in the 1960s, and the emphasis in technological development moved from efficient engine production to countermeasures against public hazards. Honda Soichiro, who had already expended much effort on the development of air-cooled engines, issued a command to study the development of water-cooled engines in 1969. This policy change made it possible to develop the clean combustion engine. In January 1973 Honda Motor became the first car-maker in the world to produce an engine which met the standards of the US Air Pollution Prevention Law (Muskie Law). In December of the same year, automobiles with this engine were marketed for the first time. Concurrently, Honda allowed the patent for the technology to be opened with a view to diffusing the production of low-pollution cars and other vehicles. In August 1973, two months before the first oil crisis assaulted the world economy, both Honda Soichiro and Fujisawa Takeo retired from the presidency and vice-presidency of the Honda Motor Company.

Honda Soichiro was an engineer who always cherished his own unique philosophy.

Based on his idea that one's work should always seek to meet the demands of others, he engaged in the constant technological development of cars and vehicles that would meet the demands of the market. Furthermore, based on his ideology that no progress can be expected where technology does not meet with philosophy, he always encouraged his workers to exhibit originality and creativity. He insisted that all installations and facilities be developed within the company. The technological development based on Honda's unique management philosophy was linked with the excellent management skills of Fujisawa Takeo, co-leader in business, which has made it possible for Honda Motor to accomplish its astonishing growth.

BIBLIOGRAPHY
Honda S. (1982) *Watakushi no Te ga Kataru* (My Hand Talks), Tokyo: Kodan Sha.
—— (1983) *Omoshiroi kara Yaru* (I'll Do That Because It Is Interesting), Tokyo: Yomiuri Shinbun Sha.
Nishida M. (1983) *Katari Tsugu Keiei: Honda to tomoni 30 Nen* (Thirty Years with Honda: Management To Be Successively Learned), Tokyo: Kodan Sha.
Honda no Ayumi Committee (1984) *Honda no Ayumi 1973–83* (Honda's Journey 1973–83), Tokyo: Honda Motor Co., Ltd.

ST

HOPWOOD, Anthony G. (1944–)

Anthony Hopwood was born in Stoke-on-Trent, Staffordshire on 18 May 1944. His decision to seek a career in accounting was made while still at grammar school. He

attended the London School of Economics, where he took a degree in economics and accounting in 1965; later education included an MBA from the University of Chicago in 1967 and a Ph.D. (while recipient of a Fulbright Scholarship) from Chicago in 1971. He subsequently taught at Manchester Business School (1971–3), Henley Management College (1973–5), the Oxford Centre for Management Studies (1976–8), London Business School (1978–85) and the London School of Economics (1985–95). He later returned to Oxford, where he has been deputy director of the School of Management Studies, and is now professor of operations management.

As well as his teaching work, Hopwood has conducted a body of original research which has done much to change the image and indeed the nature of accounting within business organizations. His prime interest has been to study 'accounting in action' within organizations, and to break down the functional walls that surrounded accounting and integrate it more fully into everyday business activities. As well as the author of several important books, he is the founder editor of the journal *Accounting, Organization and Society*, established in 1976, in the pages of which much of this research by Hopwood and colleagues has been published. Under Hopwood's influence, management accounting, not only in Britain but also in mainland Europe and increasingly in the United States, has been changing its profile and is now becoming an accepted part of every manager's basic skills set. In the process, Hopwood has helped to re-establish the link between strategy and the bottom line which had for some time been de-emphasized in management textbooks and training.

BIBLIOGRAPHY
Hopwood, A.G. (1974) *Accounting and Human Behaviour*, London: Accountancy Age Books.
——— (1988) *Accounting from the Outside*, New York: Garland.

HOXIE, Robert Franklin (1868–1916)

Robert Franklin Hoxie was born in Edmeston, New York on 29 April 1868, the son of Solomon and Lucy Hoxie. He committed suicide in Chicago on 22 June 1916. He married Lucy Bennett in 1898; they had no children. Hoxie took his bachelor's degree from Cornell University in 1893, and then served as an instructor in economics, first at Cornell College, Iowa and then at Washington University in St Louis, before returning to teach at Cornell University in 1903. He took a Ph.D. from the University of Chicago in 1905, where one of his professors was Thorstein VEBLEN. In 1906 he was appointed associate professor of political economy at Chicago, a post which he held until his death. In 1914 he was appointed special investigator to the US Commission on Industrial Relations, and it was in this capacity that he produced his most important works, the books *Scientific Management and Labor* (1915) and *Scientific Management and Social Welfare* (1916). In later life Hoxie suffered from severe depression, and this illness led to his suicide.

Hoxie's work on scientific management arose out of an increasing concern that the techniques of scientific management, particularly as expounded and practised by Frederick W. TAYLOR and his associates, although designed to make the life of the worker easier, were actually leading to labour unrest. A strike at the Watertown Arsenal following the introduction of the Taylor system led some congressmen to call for the use of the stopwatch (used in time studies) to be banned in factories. Faced with a growing labour and political problem, the government set up the Commission on Industrial Relations and invited Hoxie to conduct an investigation into the problem.

Scientific Management and Labor is a remarkable book, not least in that it is one of the few fair and impartial works on scientific management to have been written contemporary with the movement itself. Hoxie's report

follows two themes: (1) the claims of scientific management relative to labour, and (2) the objections raised by trades unions to scientific management. He discusses both these themes through a detailed and critical look at the nature and practices of scientific management in the workplace. In terms of the claims of scientific management, he makes a critical distinction between the systems espoused by Taylor, Henry GANTT and Harrington EMERSON (appendices spell out the differing views of each man in full). He notes Taylor's claims that scientific management leads to both greater efficiency and greater democracy, and then sums up the claims by trade unions to the opposite effect, namely that scientific management is undemocratic, inefficient and not even particularly scientific; and moreover, that the tight controls required to make the system work lead to higher levels of labour unrest.

After analysing these claims, Hoxie concludes that both have some merit. In defence of scientific management, he accepts that some of its measures and practices are crude, but that the discipline is still young and refinement is ongoing. The impact of scientific management in terms of eliminating waste and improving business efficiency is undoubted, and on this merit alone the system should be considered and adopted. However, Hoxie finds that scientific management does not *per se* provide any greater protection for the worker, nor that there is any inbuilt tendency towards industrial democracy. Workers under scientific management, he concludes, are at the mercy of employers who are guided variously by their 'ideals, personal views, humanitarianism or sordid desire for immediate profit with slight regard for labor's welfare' (Hoxie 1915: 138). It follows, therefore, that labour must organize in order to counterbalance the power of management. To the tension this would cause in the workplace Hoxie saw no immediate solution; he regarded that tension as the price that would have to be paid for industrial progress.

BIBLIOGRAPHY

Hoxie, R.F. (1915) *Scientific Management and Labor*, New York: D. Appleton and Co.

——— (1916) *Scientific Management and Social Welfare*, New York: Survey Books.

MLW

HUNTINGTON, Henry Edwards (1850–1927)

Henry Edwards Huntington was born in Oneonta, New York on 27 February 1850 and died in Philadelphia on 23 May 1927. He was the son of Solon Huntington, a merchant, land speculator and farmer, and Harriet Saunders, but his business career developed through his close relationship with his uncle, railway magnate Collis Huntington. In 1871, Huntington began working for Collis at a variety of positions primarily with his eastern railroads. In 1892 Huntington moved to San Francisco, where Collis was president of the Southern Pacific Railroad, and advanced within the company so that by 1900 he appeared ready to succeed his uncle. When Collis died that year, however, the majority stockholders blocked his election. Although Huntington was already wealthy enough to retire, he instead moved to Southern California where he controlled the Los Angeles Railway, and focused on real estate development.

Huntington realized that to build a real estate empire in and around Los Angeles he needed to accomplish two basic objectives. First, to add value to the agricultural land in Southern California, he had to build a comprehensive rail system that would connect it to businesses in Los Angeles. Second, he wanted to develop this land as suburban communities and build utilities to attract home-

buyers. In 1901 Huntington and several investors formed the interurban Pacific Electric Railway, that would connect small outlying communities to downtown Los Angeles and his Los Angeles Railway. A year later, he formed the Huntington Land and Improvement Company to purchase, subdivide and sell land for residential use, as well as the Pacific Light and Power Company to supply electricity for his trolley system, with excess power sold to other consumers.

Huntington's strategy for developing Southern California proved very successful and profitable. By 1910 his railroads consisted of over 1,900 kilometres (1,200 miles) of track that blanketed the region, while his power company supplied nearly 20 per cent of the electricity in the city of Los Angeles. More importantly, as one of the largest landowners in Los Angeles County, Huntington played a critical role in the geographic, social and economic development of this metropolitan area. Based on this work and skilful promotions, Los Angeles grew from a population from 50,395 in 1890 to more than 576,000 thirty years later.

In 1910 Huntington began to disengage himself from his business concerns and became a serious collector of rare books and paintings. Huntington purchased several individual collections, and to preserve them and promote their use, in 1919 he endowed a trust that established the Huntington Library, Art Collections and Botanical Gardens, all at his estate in San Marino, California. Henry Huntington's name remains prominent throughout Southern California, as evidenced by Huntington Beach, Huntington Park, Huntington Drive, the Huntington Hospital and the Huntington Hotel.

BIBLIOGRAPHY
Friedricks, W.B. (1992) *Henry E. Huntington and the Creation of Southern California*, Columbus, OH: Ohio State University Press.
Thorpe, J. (1994) *Henry Edwards Huntington: A Biography*, Berkeley, CA: University of California Press.

DM

I

IACOCCA, Lee (1924–)

Lee Iacocca was born as Lido Anthony Iacocca in Allentown, Pennsylvania on 15 October 1924. His parents, Nicola and Antoinette Iacocca, had immigrated from Italy. They were a family of entrepreneurs who lost almost everything during the Great Depression. By the time Iacocca had graduated from high school in Allentown in 1942, he had determined to become an auto company manager. His health exempting him from military service (he had suffered from rheumatic fever), Iacocca entered Lehigh University in Bethlehem, Pennsylvania. Doing poorly in physics, he switched from mechanical to industrial engineering. He nevertheless graduated with high grades in 1945, earned a master's in mechanical engineering from Princeton in 1946, and went to work for the Ford Motor Company in August 1946.

Iacocca began as an engineer but soon moved to a role which better fit his personality: sales. Over the following decade Iacocca worked his way up through the ranks of Ford sales in Pennsylvania. During 1956 he turned the sales figures in the Philadelphia district from the lowest in the nation to the best. From there his rise as Ford's top salesman was meteoric. By 1960 he was in charge of marketing all Ford cars and trucks, and in that year succeeded Robert MCNAMARA as vice-president of the Ford division.

One of Iacocca's greatest talents was his almost intuitive ability to know what the public wanted to buy. As the boom generation entered their teens, he knew Ford needed a stylish car that would appeal to them. The Ford Mustang, unveiled in March 1964, was a triumph of both design and brilliant marketing. It sold 400,000 in one year and earned Iacocca promotion to vice-president of all North American auto operations in 1967. The same genius that produced the sporty Mustang now created the Mercury Cougar for the sports car market, the Mercury Marquis for the medium price market, and the Lincoln Mark III for the luxury market.

Iacocca's progressive management philosophy stressed intuition and initiative as well as careful accounting. One could spend a lot of time, he said, gathering facts on markets, but one could listen too much to the accountants, who by their very nature 'tend to be defensive, conservative, and pessimistic' while salesmen like himself were 'aggressive, speculative, and optimistic'. Both were necessary: 'If the bean counters are too weak, the company will spend itself into bankruptcy. But if they're too strong, the company won't meet the market or stay competitive' (Iacocca and Novak 1986: 46). It was important, moreover, that a manager set the tone for his firm: 'Business, after all, is nothing more than a bunch of human relationships.' One needed to 'start with good people, lay out the rules, communicate with your employees, motivate them, and reward them if they perform' (Iacocca and Kleinfeld 1988: 74).

In December 1970 Iacocca was named sole president of the entire Ford Motor Company by Henry FORD II. His first act was to embark

on a programme of cost-cutting measures and downsizing of non-automotive lines. Iacocca's successes, however, made him appear a threat to Henry Ford II, who harassed and eventually fired him in July 1978.

Iacocca lost no time in finding a new job as president and chief executive officer of Chrysler Corporation. By the late 1970s, the smallest of the Big Three was in very serious trouble. Rising oil prices, federal anti-pollution regulations and intense Japanese competition, when combined with deficient management, threatened to doom the company. In the third quarter of 1978 Chrysler lost $158 million. Iacocca faced a seemingly impossible task. Chrysler's accounting system had no financial controls, rewarded overproduction, and its Plymouths and Dodges were poorly engineered. The first thing Chrysler needed was money, so Iacocca sold off its non-automotive properties and all operations outside North America. Japanese inventory techniques were also introduced.

Chrysler's situation became even more desperate in the wake of the Iranian Revolution of 1979. As gasoline became scarce, sales of trucks and 'gas-guzzling' cars which used large amounts of fuel plummeted. Iacocca turned to Washington, obtaining a $1.5 billion loan from Congress. He then applied all his management and public relations skills to rescuing the valuable corporation. It is likely that no one but Lee Iacocca could have inspired Chrysler's employees and shareholders to accept the drastic measures he took. Almost 60,000 of Chrysler's 130,000 workers were laid off, twenty out of sixty plants were eliminated, salaries and wages were cut (including that of Iacocca himself, who set an example). Union leader Douglas Fraser of the United Auto Workers was appointed to the board of directors.

Iacocca went on television with a series of commercials urging consumers, 'If you can find a better car [than Chrysler's], buy it.' New models were introduced – the Dodge Aries and the Plymouth Reliant, frontwheel-drive

K-Cars which were economical but roomy. By 1981 they had captured a fifth of the compact auto market and were praised by *Motor Trend* magazine as cars of the year. Under Iacocca, Chrysler not only recovered but triumphed in the 1980s. In 1983 Chrysler paid back the federal loan in full. The introduction of the minivan guaranteed Chrysler's success in a vast new niche. In 1984 Chrysler posted a profit of $2.4 billion and, by 1988, a healthy US market share of almost 15 per cent.

In his later years Iacocca continued to innovate, creating the Dodge Viper and restructuring Chrysler's vehicle manufacturing procedures on the basis of Swedish-style platform teams in which each division had considerable autonomy. He even hinted at what his successor – Robert Eaton, who took over in December 1993 – would accomplish: a global business alliance with a major German or Japanese auto-maker. It is as the creator of the Mustang and the saviour of Chrysler, however, that Iacocca will be most remembered.

BIBLIOGRAPHY

Iacocca, L. and Kleinfeld, S. (1988) *Talking Straight*, New York: Bantam Books.

Iacocca, L. and Novak, W. (1986) *Iacocca: An Autobiography*, New York: Bantam Books.

DCL

IBUKA Masaru (1908–97)

Ibuka Masaru was born in Nikko, Japan on 11 April 1908 and died in Tokyo on 19 December 1997. He was the son of a mining engineer employed by Furukawa Mining at the Nikko Copper Works; he died when Ibuka was two years old. In 1921 he entered Kobe First Middle School. While still a schoolboy, he

became interested in amateur radio. In 1930 he entered the electrical engineering department of Waseda University as a student. While still an undergraduate, Ibuka invented luminous neon. At the Paris Exhibition, Ibuka received a price for excellence in invention, and also applied for a patent for his invention. Graduating from university in 1933, he took a job with the Photo Chemical Laboratory, but there were difficulties in finding him a suitable post with this company. He then moved to Nihon Ko-on Kogyo (Japan Light and Sound Industry Company, Ltd), which was established in 1936, and joined the radio technology division. The products of this division became the company's major commodities. Ibuka then decided to set up an independent business, and established the Japan Metrology Equipment Company, Ltd. This company developed and produced a variety of equipment and apparatus, including tuning-fork oscillators and frequency relays required by the army.

In October 1945, immediately after the defeat of Japan in the Second World War, when Tokyo had been reduced to ruins that extended as far as the eye could see, Ibuka rented a small console room in the third floor of Shiroki-ya (Tokyo Department Store), which had by chance not been damaged by the US Air Force's bombardment, with a view to establishing a small institute called Tokyo Communications Laboratory, with just ten employees. High-quality engineers with whom Ibuka was acquainted joined the company one by one; they included MORITA Akio, Yasuda Jun'ichi, Iwama Kazuo, Tsukamoto Tetsuo, Kihara Nobutoshi and others. With these as a pivotal research group, a company was established which later took the name Sony. Originally this was a 'guinea pig' enterprise which specialized in the development of new technology by any means, and which gradually developed successful new products. In 1946 the Tokyo Communications Laboratory incorporated itself into a joint-stock company, Tokyo Communications Industry Ltd, with

Ibuka taking the post of executive director. In establishing this company, as he said in the initial prospectus, he wanted to build an ideal factory with an atmosphere of freedom in research and broadmindedness in management. In 1950 he was appointed president. In 1958 the company formally changed its name to Sony Corporation.

The principal products of the company in its early years were short-wave radio converters and vacuum tube voltmeters. Ibuka specialized in the production of converters for radios instead of radio sets. He then set out to develop and manufacture magnetic recorders. The prototype of a magnetic tape recorder was tested successfully in August 1949, and work focused on the development of this project. Ibuka also took out a patent, a successful strategy which meant high barriers for other companies seeking to enter this market. In March 1952 Ibuka went to the United States with a view to inspecting both ways of using tape recorders and means of producing them. While there, he learned that a transistor had been successfully developed by the Bell Institute and patented in 1948; accordingly, in October 1953 Ibuka signed a contract with Western Electric for technical support in the production of transistors for use in radio sets. In August 1955 the first transistor radios were marketed. This initial marketing effort was a failure, as the products suffered from poor quality and high prices. Ibuka then adopted an opposite strategy to that which he had used with tape recorders; he offered to open up the patent to other companies so as to allow in other producers and expand the market.

From the second half of the 1950s the Japanese television set market began to grow rapidly. The number of companies mass producing televisions in Japan was about twenty-five in 1955, but this had declined to ten in 1958, and the process appeared to be leading towards monopolization. It was under these conditions that Ibuka chose to enter the television market in 1957. He set out first to develop transistor-based black and white tele-

vision sets. In 1957 silicon transistors were developed, and this led to the marketing of the first transistor televisions in 1960. Around this time, in the late 1950s competition began to develop in the tape recorder market in Japan, and this spurred Sony to establish its first US subsidiary to market tape recorders.

In 1975 Sony began marketing its newly developed cassette videotape recorders in the domestic market, the system being known as Betamax. In the following year Japan Victor launched its rival VHS system, and cut-throat competition between Betamax and VHS ensued. Japan Victor formed a VHS family group, and successfully achieved the establishment of VHS as a *de facto* industry standard. Sony, which had led the technological development, was defeated by VHS in market competition.

One of Ibuka's characteristic attitudes was 'to get to new things no one else is willing to do', and his market development and technology strategy focused on ideas such as the making of portable electronics products, the development of high-quality advanced technology products and entry into new export markets. In order to secure competitive domination, he stressed not only the need for advanced technology in terms of product development but also a discriminating approach which focused on reducing the size of products.

Ibuka, as an engineer, had long been keenly interested in children's education, and he established an elementary school science education promotion fund in 1959. From that time on he remained an ardent promoter of education for young children and infants. In 1968 he established a young children's enlightenment society, with himself as a director.

For his many great achievements over the years, in both developing new technology and entrepreneurship, Ibuka received many prizes in Japan and overseas. In 1986 he was invested with the First Order of Merit with the Grand Cordon of the Rising Sun. In 1989 he was nominated as a person of cultural merit, and

was invested with the Order of Cultural Merit in 1992. At his death in 1997, he left behind Sony, one of the representative business enterprises of the modern age in Japan. Ibuka, the founder of this corporation, was at heart an engineer but one with excellent management sense, who converted a love of technological development into a modern world enterprise.

BIBLIOGRAPHY

Ibuka M. (1971) *Yoichen dewa Ososugiru* (Too Late in Starting from Kindergarten), Tokyo: Goma Shobu.

—— (1985) *Sozo eno Tabi* (A Journey to Creation), Tokyo: Kosei Shuppan Sha.

Sony Corporation (ed.) *Sony Soritsu 40 Shunen Kinenshi: Genryu* (The Source: The Fortieth Anniversary of the Establishment of the Sony Corporation), Tokyo: Sony Corporation.

ST

IDEMITSU Sazoh (1895–1981)

Idemitsu Sazoh was born in Akama-machi, Munakata-gun, Fukuoka prefecture on 22 August 1895, the second son of an indigo wholesaler. He died in Osaka on 7 March 1981. After graduating from Fukuoka Commercial School in 1905 he entered Kobe Higher Commercial School (a forerunner of Kobe University). While at this school he was impressed by Professor Uchiike Renkichi's lectures referring to the social function of commerce as the distributor linking production with consumption. Immediately after graduation in 1909, Idemitsu joined Sakai and Company, a small company dealing in wheat flour and machine oil, with only six employees.

Thanks to various problems in his own family's business, including bad management and the increasing importation of German

dyestuffs, Idemitsu was compelled to leave Sakai and Company in 1911, and established his own business house, Idemitsu and Company, in Moji City. This company, which sold petroleum, developed smoothly and extended its business activities to China. Idemitsu always attached importance to a management attitude which gave priority to the customer and followed a policy of 'retailing in wide regions'. That is, Idemitsu sold petroleum by expanding his retail activities into a wide range of regions. Corresponding to the development of Japan's sphere of military influence in East Asia, the Idemitsu company emphasized the development of business activities throughout the East Asian region, and Idemitsu became the principal petroleum seller in East Asia. He became president of the Moji Chamber of Commerce and Industry, and was elected a member of the House of Peers.

After Japan's defeat in 1945 Idemitsu's company, Idemitsu Kosan, lost all of its overseas offices and assets, the pivot of the company's business. However, Idemitsu believed he could recover his company's business by relying on its human assets. He never dismissed a single one of his 800 employees, who were gradually being sent back to Japan from overseas. He diversified into unfamiliar businesses, such as agriculture and fishing, printing, brewing, repair and sale of radios, the recovery of fuel tank oils from the former Imperial Army, and so on. In this manner, Idemitsu did his utmost to keep the business going and enable his employees at least to eat. Here a decisive difference can be seen between irresponsible salaried managers in the contemporary business world who attach importance to their own self-protection and maximization of their own utility, and the inaugurater of an enterprise who believes firmly and foremost in the development of that enterprise.

After Japan's defeat, the large American and British oil companies that sent representatives to the oil advisory group at the General Headquarters of the US Occupation Force changed their policy to one of developing local petroleum refineries across Japan. These major companies strengthened their influence by linking up with local Japanese petroleum companies and employing the latter as sub-contractors. In 1947 Idemitsu Kosan was refounded as Shin-Idemitsu Kosan, and began to trace its own path to becoming a major national petroleum company without reliance on foreign capital. The company became a wholesale petroleum dealer, importing not only crude petroleum but also petroleum products; for example, Idemitsu imported and sold high-octane fuel from the United States after the conclusion of the San Francisco Peace Treaty in 1951 opened this market. Shin-Idemitsu Kosan then built a state of the art 18,774-ton ocean-going tanker, the *Nissho Maru II*, taking the initiative in Japanese ownership of ocean-going tankers. On 10 April 1953 the *Nissho Maru II* arrived at the port of Abadan in the Persian Gulf, in the midst of a controversy between Iran and Britain over the proposed nationalization of the Anglo-Iranian Petroleum Company, and loaded 24,000 kilolitres of Iranian oil. The ship then returned to Japan with its cargo, attracting international attention. In 1960, during the Cold War, the company generated further controversy by importing oil from the Soviet Union.

Idemitsu Kosan was a company which developed with the support of its founder's strong personality and unique philosophy. The management approach of 'retail in wide regions' showed the attachment of importance to customers. This was matched with a management policy which emphasized human resources policy and the enterprise's self-dependence and self-reliance. Although Idemitsu Kosan is a leading company in the petroleum industry, it has only a small amount of stock, and none of its stock is issued on the open market. The company has no labour union. A unique approach to personnel control, free of both an attendance book method and a mandatory retirement system, has been adopted within the company. The company

owner is not called 'president'; rather he is the 'store master'.

Other business leaders in Japan have adopted Idemitsu Sazoh's management philosophy. The company itself remains the leader of the Japanese petroleum industry, and is continuing to grow. Idemitsu himself retired from the presidency in 1966 to become chairman of the board of directors.

BIBLIOGRAPHY

Idemitsu S. (1962) *Ningen Soncho 50 Nen* (Respectful of People for Fifty Years), Tokyo: Shunju Sha.

Idemitsu Kosan Company (ed.) (1970) *Idemitsu 50 Nen Shi* (Idemitsu's 50-year History), Osaka: Idemitsu Kosan Co., Ltd.

ST

IKEDA Toshio (1923–74)

Ikeda Toshio was born in Ryogoku, Tokyo on 7 August 1923. He died in November 1974. Endowed with a talent for mathematics from infancy, he graduated from the electrical engineering department of the Tokyo Institute of Technology, the most prestigious educational organization for technology and science in Japan, in 1946. In December of that year he joined the Fuji Tsushinki Seizo Company, Ltd. He was placed in a development section of the company and worked on computer development. The relay computer FACOM (Fujitsu Automatic Computer) 100 was completed in 1954 by the development team of which Ikeda was the chief engineer. Although it was never marketed, it attracted much attention thanks to its high level of technology. Under the leadership of Okada Kanjiro, who took over as company president in 1959, Fujitsu embarked on a strategy of developing reliable computers

based on Ikeda's original concept, with a view to making computers the company's core business.

In the 1960s Japanese computer-makers gradually developed tie-ups with US enterprises. However, Ikeda was against this trend. On 7 May 1964 IBM publicized the development of a hybrid integrated circuit SLT (solid logic technology) based on a new concept. Fujitsu, which had followed its own development route, completed the FACOM 230 series in September 1965, but Fujitsu's computers were not compatible with IBM models and could not meet users' expectations. The result was a market failure.

Ikeda was promoted to the post of executive manager on 1 November 1964. He was sent periodically on trips overseas, and became well acquainted with developments in the computer industry around the world. He was aware that IBM's computer architecture was already regarded as the global standard, and IBM-compatible software was in use by a very large number of users, and he realized that, realistically, these users had to continue using IBM-compatible products. The completion of the compatible FACOM 230-60 in March 1968 was a great success. Ikeda now adopted a managerial policy of aiming for products which were compatible with IBM systems.

In November 1970 Ikeda was appointed executive director of Fujitsu. On 11 September 1969 he had met with G.M. Amdahl, general manager of the IBM Advanced Computer Institute. These two distinguished computer technologists immediately found themselves in agreement. Amdahl had been the chief engineer of the IBM 360 series, and more recently had developed the family concept where the same kinds of software could be used on computers of many different types, large and small. He then left IBM in 1970 to establish the Amdahl Corporation, with the goal of developing a computer which could outperform the IBM 370, using large-size integrated circuits (LSIs) as basic components. Cooperation with Amdahl helped further

Ikeda's anti-IBM strategy. In order to procure the vast funds needed for LSI computer development, the six Japanese computer-makers were classed into three groups by the Ministry of International Trade and Industry (MITI). Fujitsu was paired with Hitachi, which had experience of manufacturing IBM-compatible devices.

Further developing his world strategy which aimed to encircle IBM, Ikeda also began developing reciprocal relationships with computer companies in other countries. In the middle of this effort he became ill suddenly at Haneda Airport on 11 November 1974, and died very shortly thereafter. His strategic concept was later, ironically, realized by young US ventures such as Microsoft and Compaq, not in the world of large-scale business computers, but in the sphere of the personal computer.

In a period when IBM held hegemony over the computer industry in the rest of the world, it was never able to account for more than 50 per cent of the Japanese market. Japan never succumbed to IBM's hegemony. Ikeda Toshio, an entrepreneur and leader in the development of Japan's own computer technology at Fujitsu, was perhaps the greatest moving force in the development of the computer industry in Japan and in resisting the encroachments of IBM.

BIBLIOGRAPHY

Company History Editing Group of Fuji Tsushinki Seizo Company (ed.) (1976–86) *Fujitsu Shashi* (History of Fujitsu Limited), Tokyo: Fuji Tsushinki Seizo Co., Ltd.
Company History Group of Fuji Tsushinki Seizo Company (ed.) (1964) *Fujitsu Shashi* (History of Fujitsu Limited), Tokyo: Fuji Tsushinki Seizo Co., Ltd.
Ikeda Kinen Ronbun-Shu Editing Committee (1978) *Ikeda Kinen Ronbun-Shu* (Ikeda's Memorial Papers), Tokyo: Fujitsu Co., Ltd.

ST

INAMORI Kazuo (1932–)

Inamori Kazuo was born the second son of a family of seven children in a residential town called Shimazu Estate in Yakushi-machi, Kagoshima City on 30 January 1932. His father, who once followed barely profitable occupations such as errand boy for a printing house, name-card printing assistant and so on, later became a printer himself, but always suffered from chronic poverty. In 1944 Inamori took the entrance examination for the noted Kagoshima First Middle School, but failed. To make matters worse, he then contracted tuberculosis. Supported by his family's financial aid, he made up his mind to go to university in 1951. He took the entrance examination for Osaka University, but again failed. Finally he was successful in the entrance examination for applied chemistry, at the faculty of engineering of Kagoshima Prefectural University, and went on to study organic chemistry. After graduating in 1955, he wanted to join a company working in organic synthesis chemistry and dealing with petrochemical technology. However, every leading company was reluctant to hire students other than those who had graduated from prestigious universities, and Inamori was at a loss as to where to find a position. Eventually he was employed by Shofu Industry Company, Ltd, an insulator-maker in Kyoto. He was obliged to change the subject of his graduation thesis on organic chemistry to one on inorganic chemistry.

Shofu Industry, although an insulator-maker, had plans to diversify into other types of products, and Inamori, employed by the company as a researcher, was asked to work on the development of manufacturing technology for making specific magnetic parts for cathode ray tubes, which were ordered by the Matsushita Denki Kogyo Company. The focal points in the production of ceramic products is to make the raw material combination homogeneous and to control baking temperature. At first, no method could be found to deal with

these difficulties. A ceramic material called forsterite was ultimately developed, which solved the problem. Inamori moved to the specific magnetic technology section, and began to work on developing the mass production of this part. Next he was engaged in the development of ceramic vacuum tubes, ordered by Hitachi Ltd. During the process of the development of these tubes he had a falling out with his supervisors, and determined to leave the company and establish his own company. On 13 December 1958 Inamori retired from Shofu Industry.

In April 1959 a small company with just twenty employees was established by Inamori and a circle of eight close colleagues. The company was called Kyoto Ceramic, Ltd; its sponsors including Miyamoto Otoya, President of Miyamoto Electric, Ltd, who was sympathetic to Inamori and invested 2 million yen; a further million yen was invested by Inamori and his young engineers. Inamori became director and manager of technology; later he became successively executive director, managing director and then president in 1966. In 1985 he was appointed president and chairman of the board of directors. The company was renamed Kyocera in 1982.

Kyoto Ceramic started its operation in an old wooden building which Miyamoto Electric had been using as a warehouse. At first Kyoto Ceramic was engaged in the production of ceramic parts and components for the installation of cathode ray tubes. Later the company began to expand its business by accepting the orders which had been rejected by other companies because they were unable to develop the required products. In 1965 Texas Instruments of the United States used Kyoto Ceramic's products for the Apollo Project. In 1966, when Inamori assumed the presidency, Kyoto Ceramic received a large order for ceramic substrates from IBM. The order required strict accuracy of a level that had never been attained by any other maker in the world. But the company believes that if no other company in the world can do a

thing, then it will have to do that thing itself; to the surprise of its competitors, Kyoto Ceramic succeeded in meeting IBM's requirements.

The momentum for Kyoto Ceramic to make its next great stride was the development of ceramic-laminated packages for semiconductor-integrated circuits. In 1969 the US Fairchild Corporation placed an order with the company for high-density packages. However, the order required the development of these products to be attained within three months. The company's package-making team members devoted themselves to its development day and night, resulting in the successful accomplishment of the work of creating multi-layered IC (integrated circuit) packages. In 1970 production of laminated packages was started. The development of these products brought about rapid growth.

Despite the fact that Kyocera has nothing that can be called core technology, the company has expanded quickly. This is because it has been successful in the development of various types of technology associated with ceramics as pivotal products by systematizing this technology. In 1984 under joint management with Sony, Secom, Ushio Electric and others, the company established the Second Denden Project (DDI), with Inamori as chairman. The company's advance into the fields of information and communication as core industries in the twenty-first century is under way. In 1987 Kansai Cellular Phone was established, and its mobile communication business is being developed.

When Inamori was young, he was frustrated because he was very sick with tuberculosis, then believed to be an incurable disease, and also because he failed in his entrance examinations. Seeking a method to cure the disease and to dispel the agony of his setbacks in life, he read Taniguchi Masaharu's *Seimei no Jisso* (The Real Aspect of Life), and was strongly influenced by it. The book is the holy writ of a new religion, Seicho-no-Ie (House of Life Elongation)

established by Taniguchi. Inamori agreed with Taniguchi that, to achieve success, both enthusiasm to accomplish something and strenuous effort are required. Through a succession of setbacks at the start of his career, continuing in the struggle experienced research and development, Inamori came to cherish his own philosophical view that the factor that moves people is not money but the linking of human minds in comradeship and unity; and that the outcomes of the human life or work are dependent on 'the product of a way to think and enthusiasm or effort'. In other words, infiltration into the subconsciousness of the desire to accomplish something is a decisive factor for success. Since 1978 Kyocera has adopted its own management system called 'amoeba management' along the lines of Inamori's unique management philosophy.

Inamori established the Inamori Fund using his private property, and also founded the Kyoto Prize. In 1995 he assumed the presidency of the Kyoto Chamber of Commerce and Industry. For his contributions as an engineer and business leader, he has received many prizes from both inside and outside Japan. In September 1996 he declared that he would retire from the business world and embraced the Buddhist faith; he took the tonsure in the Enfukuji Temple in Kyoto in September 1997.

BIBLIOGRAPHY
Inamori K. (1996) *Seiko eno Jyonetsu* (Passion for Success), Osaka: PHP Research Institute.
———— (1997) *Keiten Aijin: Watashi no Keiei wo Sasaeta Mono* (Respectful to the Heaven and Affectionate to People: The Factors that Supported Me), Osaka: PHP Research Institute.

ST

INGHERAMI, Giovanni di Baldino
(*c*.1412–54)

Giovanni di Baldino Ingherami was born in Florence, probably in 1412, and died there some time in 1454. His family were probably clients of the Medici. After training, Ingherami joined the Medici Bank around 1430, and by 1435 was a factor in the Rome office, working as a business agent of the Medici at the papal court. He was a valued employee and his salary was steadily increased; by 1439 he was earning 80 ducats a year (de Roover 1963: 234), compared to an apprentice's starting salary of 5 ducats a year. In 1440 he was called back to Florence and handpicked by Cosimo dei MEDICI to take over the management of the Tavola, the Medici's banking and foreign exchange division. Evidence of the trust and esteem in which he was held is found in an instruction of 1440 which grants to Ingherami the power to make out bills of exchange in the name of the Tavola, a power until then held only by Cosimo and his general manager, Giovanni d'Amerigo BENCI.

Ingherami proved his worth in his new role, and in 1445 Cosimo rewarded him by taking him into partnership; an agreement was drawn up whereby Ingherami would receive one-eighth of the profits of the Tavola. No details are recorded, but this must have made him a very wealthy man. This partnership or profit-sharing device was commonly used by the Medici for securing the services of talented managers. Partnerships were usually of only two or three years, allowing the arrangement to be broken off relatively easily if either side was dissatisfied; they do not appear to have functioned as 'golden handcuffs', but the incentive they provided must have been considerable.

Ingherami continued in his post until his death of unknown causes in 1454. He was succeeded by his brother Francesco, born in 1414, who had joined the Tavola as a bookkeeper in the early 1440s and similarly proven his worth; he was granted a partnership in

1447. He continued in his post until his death in 1470. The Ingherami brothers are good examples of a type; educated men who found positions in the lower ranks of the Medici hierarchy and, through their own efforts, rose to senior positions and were finally rewarded with a share of the profits.

BIBLIOGRAPHY

de Roover, R. (1963) *The Rise and Decline of the Medici Bank*, Cambridge, MA: Harvard University Press.

MLW

ISHIBASHI Shojiro (1889–1976)

Ishibashi Shojiro was born in Fukuoka prefecture in Japan in 1889 and graduated from Kurume Shogyo Gakko (Kurume Commercial School) in 1906. Although he was willing to go to university, he decided to work for his father's small tailoring business, or *shimaya*, which produced and sold shirts, gaiters, cloth footwear (*tabi*) and so on. Soon after joining the family business, his father was stricken with heart disease and his elder bother was called up for service in the army. Under difficult circumstances, Ishibashi soon distinguished himself. He recognized that many small items were produced and sold in his small business, and this led to higher running costs. He decided to concentrate on producing and selling a single item: *tabi*. In 1908 he purchased automatic sewing machines and cutters from abroad, and set them up to increase productivity in his factory.

Ishibashi was a man of innovative and challenging spirit. As a *tabi* producer, he created a succession of successful products under the Asahi brand. First, he established a uniform price covering various types and sizes of *tabi*. At that time, prices varied with style and size.

The uniform pricing strategy met with approval, and his products were popular. They were called '20 Sen Kinitsu Asahi Tabi', meaning that they were uniformly priced at 0.2 yen. His company, Nippon Tabi Kabusikigaisha (Nippon Footwear Company, Ltd) suffered losses during the severe recession in 1920. Nevertheless Ishibashi, who now had 1,000 workers, tried to develop a new product, *jikatabi*. This was made by pasting the rubber sole to the cloth uppers, instead of sewing them, making the *tabi* stronger. In 1922 Ishibashi also started to produce rubber soles in-house to reduce production costs. His new model, called *Asahi Jikatabi*, became another big hit item, selling 1.5 million units in 1923.

Ishibashi did not overlook changes in Japanese lifestyle. When his elder brother bought a pair of American-made tennis shoes from Mitsukoshi, he decided to produce sneakers, or shoes with rubber soles. He expected that the demand would increase as more people wore Western clothes. His factory was destroyed by fire in 1924, but Shojiro regarded this accident as a good opportunity to modernize his factory by setting up a mass-production system to produce sneakers. At the same time, he raised his capital from 1 million yen in 1925 to 5 million yen in 1928.

After this success, Ishibashi turned to producing tyres, expecting that the demand for these would increase as the number of cars increased. In 1928 the domestic market for tyres was worth 10.75 million yen. Far East Dunlop and Yokohama Gomu Seizo (a joint venture between Yokohama Densen and B.F. GOODRICH) were the main producers. Ishibashi worried that foreign tyre-makers would come to dominate the growing market completely, and decided to produce tyres on behalf of Japan. In 1931 he established Bridgestone Tire Company, Ltd. The reason for using a Western-like brand name was based on his belief that foreign brand names created a positive image, and also that it could be useful

in selling his products abroad in future. The brand name 'Bridgestone' came from his surname, *Ishi-bashi*: *ishi* means 'stone', and *bashi* means 'bridge'. In the beginning, 25 per cent of his products were defective, but he managed to improve quality. In 1932 Bridgestone Tire received an award for high quality from the Ministry of Commerce and Industry. In 1935–6, its market share measured by the yen base became 30.9 per cent, second behind Far East Dunlop in Japan (42.5 per cent).

Aside from his business, Ishibashi donated money for education, welfare and cultural activities. He built the Bridgestone Art Museum and the Ishibashi Bunka (Culture) Center. His motto was: 'I for Bridgestone, Bridgestone for Japan's prosperity, and all for people's joy and happiness.' He was a man of innovative and challenging spirit.

BIBLIOGRAPHY

Shinomiya M. (1999) 'Ishibashi Shojiro: A Founder of Bridgestone', in Udagawa M. (ed.), *The Case Book on Japan's Entrepreneurs*, Tokyo: Yuhikaku, 211–21.

ShM

ISHIDA Baigan (1685–1744)

Ishida Baigan was born the second son of Ishida Gon'emon, a farmer, in Tohge Village, Kuwata County, Tanba State in 1685. He died in September 1744 at his home in Kyoto. Baigan's real name was Okinaga, but he was usually called by his infant name, Kanpei. Baigan is Ishida Okinaga's scholastic name.

When Baigan was eleven years of age he went to Kyoto, then the capital of Japan, where he was employed by a business house as a boy apprentice. However, the business went into bankruptcy when he was fifteen, and the poor apprentice was compelled to return home. In 1707, at the age of twenty-three, he again went to Kyoto to serve the Kuroyanagi family, a business house in Kyoto, as an apprentice. In the meantime, he had come to be keenly interested in Shinto, and studied the religion along with other scholastic subjects. When he was about thirty-five, he placed himself under a regime of penance and self-mortification with a view to acquiring ideal concepts in his own thought. He later made the acquaintance of Oguri Ryoun, and developed thought and practices concerning a variety of scholastic subjects under Oguri's guidance. He became thoroughly enlightened thanks to a kind of spiritual experience of his own, which he called 'Invention'. He went on from this enlightenment experience to develop his own system of thought.

In 1729, now aged forty-five, Baigan began holding open seminar classes, free of tuition, in his house in Kyoto, endeavouring thus to spread his ideas. Before long, disciples including Tejima Toan also began disseminating Baigan's ideas, and his thought gradually spread not only to commoners but also to the warriors of the upper classes. Eventually Baigan's ideas were taken up by the Tokugawa Shogunate, and his thought thus spread throughout the nation. In 1739 Baigan published a book entitled *Tohi Mondo* (Controversy on Urbanology and Country Problems). This was followed in 1744 by a second work, *Ken'yaku Saika-Ron* (Problems on Frugality and Maintenance of Home Finance).

Tohi Mondo, consisting of four volumes, describes the principles of Sekimon Shingaku (Baigan School's Spiritual Ethics). The term *shingaku* implies features of 'Ryochi Shingaku', a system of thought advocating unification of knowledge and action which was initiated by Won Yomei, one of the great thinkers of the Ming Dynasty in China. The *shingaku* of Ishida Baigan consists of the learning of an ethical self-consciousness

through the study of three types of religious and philosophical concept – Shinto, Confucianism and Buddhism – but based on the everyday life experiences of ordinary people. Sekimon Shingaku is thus a highly practical philosophy. Baigan's doctrine of self-reliance is drawn in part from Zhu Xi, and partly also from the thought of Mencius.

According to Sekimon Shingaku, all things under the sun are produced based on heavenly intention and are nurtured, and humans also can be aware of heaven's intention. Keeping such insistence in mind, the social roles of the merchants who desire to make profits were evaluated. Emphasis was placed on honesty and frugality as required rules of behaviour for merchants; honesty and frugality are virtues required for all human beings, and frugality results in the proper use of all things, including humans, in accordance with heavenly intention. Through honesty and frugality, the way of the merchants, the human way and the heavenly way were unified. Through introspection, people could become aware of honesty and frugality as ways of living as merchants and town traders. No gain or profit could be consistent with heavenly principles until such retrospection or awareness was achieved.

In the Edo Age (1604–1868), people were grouped according to social status in one of four classes: the warrior class, the farmer class, the manufacturer class and the trader class. It was believed that merchants were ignoble people and belonged to the lowest class. Baigan attempted to clarify merchants' social roles and make plain the meaning of their existence. At the same time, he emphasized to the merchants the ethical issues surrounding their profit-making. His doctrine became widespread and was highly regarded.

BIBLIOGRAPHY

Furuta S. and Imai J. (eds) (1979) *Ishida Baigan no Shisou* (Ishida Baigan's Philosophy), Tokyo: Pelican Sha.
Ishida B. (1739) *Tohi Mondo* (Controversy on Urbanology and Country Problems).
—— (1744) *Ken'yaku Saika-Ron* (Problems on Frugality and Maintenance of Home Finance).
Ishikawa K. (1968) *Ishida Baigan to Tohi Mondo* (Ishida Baigan and Controversy on Urbanology and Country Problems), Tokyo: Iwanami Shoten.
Takemura E. (1997) *The Perception of Work in Tokugawa Japan: A Study of Ishida Baigan and Ninomiya Sontoku*, Lanham, MD: University Press of America.
Takenaka S. (1977) *Nihonteki Keiei no Genryu: Shingaku no Keieirinen wo Megutte* (A Source of Japanese-style Management: Around the Management Theory Dependent on Theology), Kyoto: Minerva Shoten.

ST

ISHIKAWA Kaoru (1915–89)

Ishikawa Kaoru was born in Nishigawara, Takinogawa Ward, Tokyo City on 13 July 1915, the eldest son of nine children of Ishikawa Ichiro and his wife Tomiko. He died in Tokyo on 16 April 1989. In April 1923 he entered the elementary school associated with Tokyo Higher Normal School, and in April 1928 he entered the middle school associated with the same establishment. In April 1933 he entered Tokyo High School. In April 1936 he entered the applied chemistry department, faculty of engineering, Imperial University of Tokyo, graduating in March 1939. He then worked for Nissan Chemical Industries, Ltd. At that time, in accordance with national policy, the company was engaged in the introduction of technology from Germany for the purpose of manufacturing artificial petroleum by means of the liquefaction of oil. Ishikawa

was posted to a research institute in Ohji, Tokyo. In May 1939 he was mobilized by the navy as technology lieutenant. In May 1940 he was placed on the reserve list. In June of the same year, he was employed by Nissan Liquid Fuel Company, Ltd. In February 1942 he married Ujiie Keiko.

In 1924, dissatisfied with traditional quality control methods which removed inferior goods by inspecting the final product piece by piece, Dr Walter Shewhart of the Bell Research Institute developed a new statistical method for quality control. According to this method, control charts were applied to engineering. During the Second World War the United States needed to develop better quality control in the production of munitions, and for this purpose the Wartime Standards Z1 was promulgated. In 1946 the American Standards of Quality Control (ASQC) were established. In Britain, E.S. Pearson's book *The Application of Statistical Methods to Industrial Standardization and Quality Control* had been published in 1935, and the British standards system had been introduced in Japan before the war, but because of the numerical and mathematical difficulty of applying them to practical use, there was little diffusion of these standards.

In Japan after the defeat in 1945 the US Occupation Force was troubled by malfunctions and disconnections in telephone communication. The military authorities asked Japan to adopt new methods for quality control in electrical communications equipment, and instruction for that purpose were begun. In 1945 the Japan Industrial Standard Association was established, and the Industrial Standard Survey Conference was set up in 1946. In addition, in 1949 the Industrial Standardization Law was enacted, resulting in the inauguration of the JIS indication system. In 1950 the Agricultural Resource Standard Law was also promulgated, to be followed by the quality indication system of JAS marks.

In May 1946 the Japan Union of Science and Engineering (JUSE), later to be a centre of the study and practice of quality control in Japan, was established, and Ishikawa Kaoru's father Ichiro was appointed chairman. In the autumn of 1948, a quality control study circle was established within JUSE. Ishikawa, who was appointed assistant professor at the faculty of engineering at the Imperial University of Tokyo in January 1947 (he was promoted to professor in 1960), became involved in the study of the statistical method of quality control. Based on the output of the quality control study circle, JUSE held Japan's first course of lectures under the title 'Quality Control Seminar Basic Course' in September 1949. Ishikawa was asked to be a lecturer. He became a member of the study circle, called the Quality Control Research Group, and became more fully engaged in the study of quality control.

In regard to the introduction of quality control to vertically controlled and hierarchical Japanese companies, Ishikawa was of the opinion that merely introducing quality control to the workplace was not sufficient, and that no fruitful outcome would result unless quality control was introduced across the hierarchy and in all divisions. He also believed that in introducing total quality control, quality control education at the level of top management was the most important factor of all. He proposed that JUSE should hold various types of quality control seminars for executives, division managers, engineers, forepeople, sales representatives and purchasers. He himself taught on such seminars, running a total quality control education programme through radio and television. In the 1960s he began developing programmes of quality control education for the workers on the shop floor. He also proposed the formation of quality control circles as a means of diffusing quality control, on the grounds that best outcomes would not be realized if workers were left to study quality control on their own. Enabling all workers to study quality control might result in an increase in efficiency. Ishikawa also became editor in

chief of *The Site and QC*, a magazine specifically devoted to quality control, first published in 1962.

Ishikawa became a member of the Association for Statistical Quality Control (ASQC) in 1951, and was appointed the general manager of the Japan branch of the society; he was later elected fellow of ASQC. In 1972 he was invested with the Grant Prize of the ASQC. In 1971 the Japan Academy of Quality Control was founded, with Ishikawa as one of its promoters; he was vice-president from 1971 to 1974 and president from 1974 to 1975. From the late 1960s Ishikawa frequently visited developing countries to conduct classes on quality control in order to diffuse the subject more widely.

In 1976 Ishikawa retired from Tokyo University, following the institution's mandatory retirement policy, and took up a professorship at Tokyo Rika Daigaku. In April 1978 he became president of Musashi Institute of Technology. In 1980, when the Japanese economy was in the midst of its prosperity, the American television company NBC broadcast a special programme entitled 'If Japan can, why can't we?' Spurred on by this, TQC inspection delegations from abroad rushed to Japan, resulting in a rapid diffusion of the quality control circle campaign to foreign countries. In 1986 Ishikawa delivered a lecture to the US House of Representatives Members' Delegation to Japan in connection with quality control circles, one result of which was the founding of the Malcolm Baldridge State Quality Control Prize. That year Ishikawa was recommended as an honorary member of ASQC. In 1988 he was invested by the Japanese Government with the Second Class Order of the Sacred Treasure.

Ishikawa made a great contribution to the competitiveness of Japanese exports after the Second World War by spreading the techniques of total quality control (TQC) among Japanese companies, resulting in an enhancement in the quality of Japan's industrial products. Before the war, Japanese goods were so notorious for their poor quality that foreign consumers associated 'inferior quality and cheap prices' with the brand 'Made in Japan'. Ishikawa developed and diffused techniques such as the quality control circle, where all the personnel of the company from the president to the workers were asked to participate in a campaign to express their ideas on the enhancement of product quality. One of the results was Japanese economic success.

BIBLIOGRAPHY

Editorial Committee of Dr Ishikawa's Memories (1993) *Ishikawa Kaoru: the Man and Quality Control*, Tokyo: privately published by his wife.
Ishikawa K. (1954) *Hinshitsu Kanri Nyumon* (A Guide to Quality Control), Tokyo: Nihon Kagaku Gijyutsu Renmei (JUSE) Shuppan Sha.
—— (1968) *Genba no QC Shuhou* (QC Method on the Spot), Tokyo: JUSE.
—— (1981) *Nihonteki Hinshitsu Kanri* (Japanese Quality Control), Tokyo: JUSE.
—— (1985) *How to Operate QC Circle Activity*, Tokyo: JUSE.

ST

ISMAY, Thomas (1837–99)

Thomas Ismay was born in Maryport, Cumberland on 7 January 1837, the son of Joseph and Margaret Ismay. He died at his home, Dawpool in Cheshire, on 23 February 1899 after a series of heart attacks. He married Margaret Bruce in 1859; they had three children. Ismay was educated at Croft House School, where he studied science and navigation. In 1853 he apprenticed with the Liverpool shipbroking firm Imrie, Tomlinson and Company, and in 1856 spent a year at sea.

In 1857 he set up a shipbroking partnership with Philip Nelson and bought his first ship. Ismay traded as a shipbroker and ship owner for the next few years, and by 1865 owned or part owned about a dozen vessels. In 1866 he bought the bankrupt White Star line for £1,000 and began working his own ships on White Star's routes to Australia and New Zealand.

Opportunity knocked for Ismay in 1869, when a chance meeting brought him into contact with Gustav Schwabe, uncle of G.C. Wolff, who in turn was partner to the shipbuilder Edward HARLAND. Schwabe was anxious to invest in shipping, and brought Ismay and Harland together. The result was the founding of the Ocean Steam Navigation Company, in which Schwabe and Harland were both investors; the *quid pro quo* was that Harland and Wolff would be the exclusive builders for White Star.

Throughout the 1870s White Star steadily expanded, taking advantage of Harland and Wolff's advanced new designs to provide both speed and comfort for passengers. The builders were commissioned on a cost-plus basis, and given a free hand to build the best ships possible. This arrangement worked because Ismay worked very closely with both Harland and his successor William PIRRIE – in fact, the three men became close personal friends – and developed strong bonds of trust. By the time of Ismay's death, White Star was operating twenty-one liners, all built by Harland and Wolff, at a gross tonnage of around 160,000 tons. Only Cunard had a larger share of the Transatlantic market.

A cautious man, Ismay ordered his captains to avoid risks at all costs, even if this meant delays; this was contrary to practice with many lines, but Ismay was well aware of the bad publicity that could result from accidents. Although his ships regularly held the Blue Riband for the fastest Atlantic crossing, this honour meant little to Ismay, who was much more interested in the safety and comfort of his passengers. To achieve this, he was willing to spend almost any amount; he was rewarded with full ships and high profits. In his later years he was a noted philanthropist and served on many government committees concerned with the maritime trades. He was offered a baronetcy in 1897 but declined it. On his death, telegrams of condolence were received by his family from all over the world, including one from Kaiser Wilhelm of Germany, whose U-boats would later sink a large portion of the White Star fleet. Ismay was succeeded as chairman by his son Joseph Bruce Ismay, who continued the long relationship with Harland and Wolff; he was among the survivors of the sinking of the *Titanic* in 1912.

BIBLIOGRAPHY

Moss, M. and Hume, J.R. (1986) *Shipbuilders to the World: 125 Years of Harland and Wolff, Belfast, 1861–1986*, Belfast: The Blackstaff Press.

Oldham, W.J. (1961) *The Ismay Line*, London: The Journal of Commerce.

MLW

ITOBAAL of Tyre (*fl.* 891 BC–859 BC)

Itobaal, priest of the sun god Melqart, seized the throne of Tyre in 891 BC (Moscati 1968). Tyre at the time was the leading commercial city of the eastern Mediterranean. Ambitious and ruthless, Itobaal, mentioned in 1 Kings 16: 31 as Ethbaal, was an early exponent of cross-border investment strategy.

Tyre was challenged in the early ninth century BC by the advance of the armies of Assyria led by Ashurnasirpal II (883 BC–859 BC) and Shalmaneser III (859 BC–824 BC). In order to resist this force, Itobaal sought to create a unified state and economy embracing not only all Phoenician cities but the Kingdom of Israel, then ruled by the chariot general

Omri (885 BC–874 BC) and his son Ahab (874 BC–853 BC), to whom Itobaal had married his daughter, Jezebel.

Tyrian business was tightly integrated. Royal enterprises, private merchants, guilds of traders and craftsman and the navy interlocked in a *keiretsu*-like alliance system. Copper from Cyprus was turned into goods in Tyre, then exported to Israel in return for the wheat of Galilee and Samaria. Archaeology shows evidence of a Tyrian commercial presence in Samaria and in other cities such as Megiddo, where guilds of Tyrian craftsmen also operated.

According to Silver (1995), the temple priesthood played an important role in Phoenician business culture. Temples acted as banks and multinational distribution networks for Tyrian goods. The priests of Melqart notarized and regulated commerce. Near Eastern merchants also embraced new gods and goddesses when they made alliances or traded goods. Any nation doing business with Tyre incorporated Melqart alongside their own gods such as Hadad, Ra, Chemosh, Ashur or Marduk.

So long as most cultures were polytheistic, the practice of swapping deities worked successfully, but not in Israel. Under the House of Ahab, the worship of Melqart became the state religion in a kingdom in which the God of Abraham and Moses was still acknowledged in theory as the only true deity. The feudal business practices of Tyre clashed sharply with the 'Jeffersonian' tradition of independent yeoman farmers found in Israel. Economic legislation became weighted in favour of creditors instead of debtors. The notion underlying the Melqart business ethic in Israel was that a few efficient landowners could generate far more capital than a multitude of smallholders. The ministry of the prophet Eliyahu (Elijah) exposed a growing discontent which generated a nationalist anti-Tyrian military coup in 841 BC, led by the chariot general Jehu.

Itobaal met with more success in Syria and even south-eastern Anatolia, where he planted other colonies. These colonies became part of an internalized trading network based on the temples which encompassed the entire Levant. This network, according to Aubet (1996), extended to the western Mediterranean in the reigns of his successors. Itobaal, despite his failure to understand Israel's unique business culture, thus helped establish the foundation for the first internalized intercontinental trading network.

BIBLIOGRAPHY

Aubet, M.E. (1996) *The Phoenicians and the West: Politics, Colonies and Trade*, trans. M. Turton, Cambridge: Cambridge University Press.

Harden, D.B. (1962) *The Phoenicians*, New York: Frederick A. Praeger.

Moore, K. and Lewis, D. (1999) *Birth of the Multinational: 2000 Years of Ancient Business History from Ashur to Augustus*, Copenhagen: Copenhagen Business School Press.

—— (2000) *The Foundations of Corporate Empire*, London: Financial Times Books.

Moscati, S. (1968) *The World of the Phoenicians*, trans. A. Hamilton, New York: Praeger.

Silver, M. (1995) *Economic Structures of Antiquity*, Westport, CT: Greenwood Press.

DCL

IWASAKI Koyata (1879–1945)

Iwasaki Koyata was born on 3 August 1879, the eldest son of Iwasaki Yanosuke (1851–1908), himself the younger brother of IWASAKI Yataro. He died on 2 December 1945. He attended the faculty of law at the Imperial University of Tokyo, but left without completing a degree. He went then to Britain for a

course of study, and in 1905 took a degree from Cambridge University. Returning to Japan in 1906 he was appointed vice-president of the Mitsubishi Limited Partnership. In 1916 he succeeded as president of the company, becoming the fourth leader of Mitsubishi. As president, he ordered the company's subordinate firms to become independent, and converted the main Mitsubishi company into a holding company, thus establishing the combine system known as the Mitsubishi *zaibatsu*. He made strong investments in new fields of business such as iron manufacturing, electrical machinery, aircraft manufacturing and oil refining, all these serving to solidify the foundations of the *zaibatsu* in the Japanese economic world.

Iwasaki's management philosophy rested on 'the formation of a public-oriented Mitsubishi'. He decided to make public offerings of stock in companies under Mitsubishi's umbrella after 1920, with a view to raising funds to back further expansion of the business. He offered still more shares in 1940, increasing the capital of Mitsubishi Corporation, the reorganized form of the old Mitsubishi Limited Partnership. The business creed of Iwasaki as an entrepreneur rested on the concepts, 'accomplishment of service for intended projects', and 'clarifying everything'. With service for national interests as the target of Mitsubishi's management, and with full transparency, he went on to promote his business. During the Second World War he continuously ordered employees throughout the Mitsubishi combine to exert themselves towards increasing military production. At the war's end, he rejected the order issued by the general headquarters of the US Occupation Forces to liquidate all *zaibatsus*, declaring there were no adequate grounds for such a move.

Iwasaki founded both the Mitsubishi Economic Research Institute, one of the most prominent think-tanks in Japan, and Seikei Gakuen, a prestigious private school in Tokyo.

BIBLIOGRAPHY

Iwasaki Koyata Den Editing Committee (ed.) (1979) *Iwasaki Koyata Den* (Iwasaki Koyata's Biography), Tokyo: Iwasaki Koyata Den Editing Committee.

Noda K. (1970) 'Keiei Kanri Kan' (Management Philosophy), in Noda Kazuo (ed.), *Zaikaijin Shiso Zenshu* (Collection of Business Leaders' Philosophies), 3 vols, Tokyo: Diamond Sha.

ST

IWASAKI Yataro (1834–85)

Iwasaki Yataro was born on 11 December 1834, the first son of Iwasaki Yajiro, a masterless *samurai* who resided in Inokuchi-mura, Aki county, Tosa state (Aki City, Kochi prefecture). He died in Tokyo of stomach cancer on 2 July 1885. In 1865 he became an employee of Kaisei-kan, a business house run by the lordship of Tosa. In 1867, working as a caretaker and security guard, Iwasaki joined Kaien-tai, a military unit for coastal defence formed by Goto Shokiro, Sakamoto Ryoma and their associates. During the Toba-Fushimi conflict, Iwasaki worked for Tosa Shokai (Tosa Commercial Firm) and was sent to Nagasaki, where he was in charge of logistic supply for the Tosa Clan army which was fighting to topple the Tokugawa Shogunate.

In 1870 Iwasaki, who was allowed to take over the management of Nishi-Nagahori Shokai, another business run by the Tosa lordship, established the Tosa Kaisei-Sha with the purpose of engaging in maritime business. The business, renamed Tsukumo Shokai in 1871, came into the possession of Iwasaki in accordance with the policy of the abolition of clans and settlement of prefectures. The

business was renamed Mitsukawa Shokai in January 1872, and finally became Mitsubishi Shokai in March 1873. The new commercial firm's head office was located in Tokyo.

In February 1874 the former *samurai* of Saga, who were opposed to the Meiji government's newly inaugurated policy of assimilating European culture, revolted in what became known as the *Saga no Ran* (Saga Incident). In the same year, some Japanese fishermen were killed by some inhabitants of Taiwan; taking advantage of this incident, Japan dispatched troops to Taiwan. In both these incidents, Iwasaki asked the government to entrust him with the exclusive transportation of military forces and munitions. To compensate Iwasaki for this work, the government allowed him to take control of government-owned ships free of charge. Mitsubishi Shokai, which was renamed Mitsubishi Kisen in 1875, became a powerful force in Japanese merchant shipping, buying up the American-owned Pacific Ocean Liner Corporation and driving the British P&O Steam Navigation Company out of the market. Mitsubishi eventually established a monopoly in Japanese coastal shipping.

During the anti-government rebellion begun by former Kyushu *samurai* families led by Saigo Takamori, the *Seinan no Eki* (Incident in South-eastern Japan), Iwasaki and Mitsubishi earned huge profits. In addition to maritime business, he expanded into related activities such as marine insurance, money exchanging and warehouse holding, together with other transportation-related businesses. He also became involved in mining. In 1883 the Mitsui company, which was favoured by prominent new government officials, entered the maritime cargo-carrying business by establishing a transportation company supported by government investment. This caused cut-throat business competition between Mitsui and Mitsubishi. Through mediation by the government, which was afraid that both companies would collapse, Mitsui and Mitsubishi jointly established the Nihon Yusen Company, Ltd in 1885. Iwasaki had also by this time established the Mitsubishi Money Exchange Store and the Mitsubishi Iron Manufacturing Plant, and had taken over Takashima Colliery and the Nagasaki Shipbuilding Plant from government ownership, further expanding his business into what later became known as the Mitsubishi *zaibatsu*.

BIBLIOGRAPHY
Irimajiri Y. (1960) *Iwasaki Yataro*, Tokyo: Yoshikawa Kohbunkan.
Tanaka S. (1955) *Iwasaki Yataro Den* (Iwasaki Yataro's Biography), Tokyo: Toyo Shokan.

ST

J

JACKSON, Thomas (1841–1915)

Thomas Jackson was born in Crossmaglen, County Armagh, the son of a farmer. After a private education he became a clerk in the Bank of Ireland in Belfast in 1860. In 1864 he joined the Agra Bank and was sent to the Far East; when the bank ran into problems in 1866 Jackson was released from his contract and joined the Hongkong and Shanghai Bank. Here he rose rapidly, partly through his own abilities and partly, as King (1987) says, because there was a shortage of qualified staff in the region. Jackson became in quick succession chief accountant in Shanghai, agent in Hangzhou and manager in Yokohama, where he married Amelia Dare in 1871. In 1872 he was invited to take over the important post of manager in Shanghai, but declined, preferring to concentrate on growing the bank's business in Japan.

In 1874–5 the bank ran into serious problems due to a combination of bad investments and bad loans. Several senior staff in the Far East were dismissed, and in 1876 Jackson was appointed chief manager with instructions to sort out the problems. His energy and skills at once made an impact: he reorganized the moribund Shanghai office, instituted new controls to prevent further bad loans, and began developing new relationships and agencies. Largely at his urging, the bank opened offices in New York and Hamburg, establishing links with foreign competitors operating in China, and in the process becoming a truly global bank. In 1888 Jackson returned to Britain, where he was knighted for his services (he was later made a baronet) and made managing director of the bank. However, in 1892 his successor in the Far East ran into problems, and the directors asked Jackson to return to Shanghai. From then until 1902 the head office of the bank was *de facto* in Shanghai; Jackson ran the bank almost independently of the directors and was the dominant leader and managerial force. In 1902 he returned to England and retired, but continued to serve as a director until his death in London in 1915.

Jackson's greatest impact lay in his development of relationships with the Chinese government. In the 1870s and 1880s China's leaders, or at least some individuals such as Lı Hongzhang, were taking tentative steps towards modernization. Under Jackson's management, the Hongkong and Shanghai Bank became the leading lender to the Chinese government, pushing aside not only other foreign competitors but domestic Chinese banks. Despite its problems, China was still a rich country, the banking opportunities were many, and profits soared. Much of the bank's business was in foreign exchange, and Jackson also had a talent for spotting market trends and knowing where to shift his money; foreign exchange profits were a mainstay of the bank under his management. Many other foreign banks, lacking his skills, went bankrupt or were forced to close, giving Jackson a still greater share of the market.

Jackson was adept at managing in an environment of change and flux; he regarded the rapid market fluctuations of the Far East as opportunities, not as threats. He was not a gambler; he managed his finances prudently and according to strict controls, and the risks he ran were always calculated ones. His contemporaries regarded him as lucky ('Lucky Jackson' was his nickname from early on), but observers such as King concluded that much of his 'luck' was in fact the result of his own talents and skills. He made the Hongkong and Shanghai Bank pre-eminent in the world of Far Eastern finance, a position it still occupies today.

BIBLIOGRAPHY
King, F.H.H. (1987) *The History of the Hongkong and Shanghai Banking Corporation*, vol. 1, *The Hongkong Bank in Late Imperial China, 1864–1902*, Cambridge: Cambridge University Press.

MLW

JAGAN SETH, *see* Chand

JAQUES, Elliott (1917–)

Elliott Jaques was born in Toronto on 18 January 1917. He studied at the University of Toronto, obtaining a BA and an MA before going on to Johns Hopkins Medical School. He served as a major in the Royal Canadian Army Medical Corps in the Second World War, and completed a Ph.D. at Harvard before moving to Britain and becoming a founding member of the Tavistock Institute of Human Relations in London. He became a psychoanalyst in 1951, and set up the Brunel Institute of Organisation and Social Studies (BIOSS) at Brunel University in Britain in 1970. Since 1985 he has lived in the United States, where he is visiting research professor in management studies at George Washington University, Washington, DC.

Jaques's understanding of human nature, his highly empirical approach and his wish to put social science on a proper scientific footing are grounded in medicine, psychiatry and psychoanalysis. Soon after the war he and his colleagues began what was to become a thirty-year project with the Glacier Metal Company in Britain. He has worked extensively in the United States, Australia and Canada, and his work has had a significant impact on the US military. Jaques's models were further codified with his colleagues in BIOSS, and his ideas continue to be elaborated and applied through its work in private, public, religious and military organizations across the world.

Jaques is a prolific writer of books and articles about his key concept of 'requisite organization' – an organization in which people can work and be together in ways that all feel to be fair. The title of his first book, *The Changing Culture of a Factory* (1951), was one of the earliest uses of 'culture' in reference to the workplace. The essence of his early thinking was distilled in *Measurement of Responsibility* (1956), and the profound insights of this early work were elaborated into a system for designing, managing and leading 'felt-fair' organizations, for example, in *Requisite Organization* (1988).

In collaboration with colleagues at the Tavistock Institute, Jaques developed 'social analysis', an approach to understanding the life of an organization through attentive listening and analytical feedback. Consultants offered analyses, but made no recommendations and never arrogated to themselves the responsibilities of the people in the organization who had initiated the study. At the heart of the process

lay 'listening to the music behind the words', with acute sensitivity to every aspect of what each person said and to every hint of what could, with encouragement, be articulated (Rowbottom 1977).

This attentive listening created a climate in which people could voice the subtleties of experience they lived but had not articulated; the tacit knowledge of which Michel Polanyi speaks. They found themselves able to say how they felt about the process of their work, about the decisions they were called upon to make and the anxiety of waiting to see how they turned out, about the reward they felt would be fair for the level of responsibility they were asked to carry, about their working relationships with others and how they felt about the fairness of their working conditions.

Jaques's approach to people, work and the design of organizations is best understood in the light of his belief that people working together should be treated as people. From this it follows that organizations should be designed in such a way as to provide conditions that induce confidence, trust and competence, and to remove those that produce anxiety, confusion and incompetence. In a requisite organization, people work together in ways that strengthen bonds of mutual trust and fairness, enhance imagination and innovation, and reduce suspicion and mistrust; the organization achieves its purposes and contributes to the health of the wider society. 'Anti-requisite' organizations support autocratic coercion and destructive anxiety, and thus inhibit creativity. Although they may appear to be effective for some years, they eventually flounder.

When Jaques originally communicated his ideas about the nature of work and of people, they were not fully heard. Fifty years later, changes in the environment and in society have created a more receptive climate. In particular, globalization and the growth of knowledge work have helped to focus attention on the economic value of what people treated as individuals bring to work, and on the conditions that encourage them and make the most of their contribution.

A key idea is Jaques's 1956 definition of work as 'the exercise of discretion within prescribed limits to reach a goal within a stated completion time'. The contemporary phrase for 'exercising discretion' is to 'make the call' – to choose a course of action when one does not emerge from analysis. From his attentive listening and his psychoanalytic understanding, Jaques came to see that the discretionary content of work has a special feel for people because it is about the fine judgements they make when they do not and cannot know what to do. As Jaques put it, this is a

> sphere of psychological activity which, although extremely familiar, remains ... ill-defined. There is no satisfactory ... language for it. We speak about judgement, intuition, nous ... We cannot put into words what it is that we are taking into account in doing what we are doing, and in that sense we do not know that what we are doing will get us where we want to go, will achieve the result we want to achieve. We judge that it will, we think it will, but we are not sure *and only time will tell*.
>
> (Jaques 1988: 156)

If this discretionary content is not bounded, there can be no coherence in the work people do together, and an individual could be completely overwhelmed by expectations. It is the manager's responsibility to 'prescribe' limits, to set rules objectively in the form of policies (written and unwritten), procedures and physical controls which must be obeyed. By defining the field, these limits free the person to use his or her discretion in coping with uncertainties, vicissitudes and unknowns as they feel towards the wisest way of forwarding the work for which they are responsible (Jaques 1956; Evans 1979).

Characteristic of Jaques is his sensitivity to how it *feels* to adhere to prescribed limits: the person is responding to choices someone else

has made, and can assess and control his or her contribution by reference to objective standards. Appraisal and control of how we exercise our discretion has no immediate reference external to ourselves; we can evaluate it only through reference to intuitively sensed internal standards until completion time, when the effect of our decisions can be externally reviewed.

Completion time, when the quality of decisions is revealed, is an important aspect of Jaques's thinking. Throughout his writing (especially *The Form of Time*, 1982) he has drawn attention to the significance of time and uncertainty for human behaviour, and to the anxiety of waiting to see the fruits of one's decision making. The external corollary of this individual anxiety is the manager waiting for sufficient feedback to be confident that each of the people working for him or her is making decisions that are robust over time. In some projects this reassurance is forthcoming in weeks, in others it may be five years before the quality of the decision making can be evaluated. As Jaques gathered more and more evidence of the span of time that had to elapse before the quality of decisions could be seen, he realized that there was a consistent pattern. Decisions about some kinds of work could be evaluated in three months; decisions about other kinds needed a year; some – especially when improvement was involved – could not be evaluated before two years had passed; and others – where completely new ways of approaching production, customers, a market had to be developed – required five years to completion time. Still others – where a new combination of product, process, research, technology, markets had to come into being – could not be evaluated for ten years. Beyond that, global institutions made decisions about changes, critical masses of capital, people and positioning, where fruits could not be seen for twenty or more years.

Jaques used this evidence to construct a framework of levels of complexity of work in which authority is distributed and managers

can be held to account in ways they feel to be fair. Despite the pace of change and decisions fifty years later and the pressure for quick completion, these time-scales remain robust as measures of the evolving life and complexity of an organization.

Another significant contribution to the requisite organization in which people are more likely to be creative and responsible is Jaques's hypothesis that the capacity in each individual to use their judgement to make decisions grows over time at broadly predictable rates. This hypothesis arose from extensive studies of earning progression of individuals that yielded an array of curves similar in structure to the curves generated by mathematical studies of growing organisms.

As Jaques realized that people made consistent links between their earnings, their responsibilities and exercising discretion, it occurred to him that the progression curves might also reflect a consistent pattern of growth in the capacity to exercise discretion: 'capability'. This hypothesis has been systematically tested over twenty five-years in longitudinal studies of 'capability' in a wide range of organizations and cultures in developed and developing economies. These studies demonstrate that capability does grow at broadly predictable rates and that, if each individual is to use it to the full, this growth must be paced with growth in responsibility. To be prevented from working at full capacity by being asked to carry too much or too little responsibility is constricting, degrading and finally persecuting. The studies make it clear that there are no differences in distribution of capability with regard to gender, race or educational opportunity (Stamp 1986).

Much of Jaques's thinking has become common currency in organizations: 'discretion', 'judgement calls' and 'time-horizons' are widely used. 'Flattening' of organizations more often than not leads to a pattern of levels as defined by him, and when 'downsizing' removes a level of work that is necessary, it soon creeps back in. Interest in 'empowering'

people at work is an attempt to gain access to the discretionary energy of people. In a requisite organization, each person will be 'empowered' to use their discretion within a framework of prescribed limits; one of the fundamental tenets of such an organization being that each person is able to use his or her capability to exercise discretion to the full, both as it is and as it grows.

Research into the cognitive unconscious (Reber 1993) provides support for Jaques's emphasis on the direct connection between the processes involved in work and unconscious mental activity:

> Industrial society ... has overvalued ... the critical, the conscious, the verbal, the brain ... everything to do with knowledge ... It has lost its ability sufficiently to value and to feel secure in relying upon the other side of the human equation – the side that contains intuition, judgement, flowing unverbalised sense, the feel of the situation, the deeper sense of simply understanding what is right and wrong or fair or just, the sense of the reasonable, the ability to sit back and reflect and remember and to feel a part of one's past and present, and to identify with other human beings, to feel empathy and sensitivity ... what Keats has called 'negative capability' ... being in uncertainties, mysteries, doubts without any irritable reaching after facts and reason.
>
> (Jaques 1982: 221)

BIBLIOGRAPHY

Evans, J. (1979) *The Management of Human Capacity*, London: MCB Publications.

Jaques, E. (1951) *The Changing Culture of a Factory*, London: Tavistock Publications.

—— (1956) *Measurement of Responsibility*, London: Tavistock Publications.

—— (1961) *Equitable Payment*, London: Heinemann Educational Books.

—— (1976) *A General Theory of Bureaucracy*, London: Heinemann.

—— (1982) *The Form of Time*, London: Heinemann Educational Books.

—— (1988) *Requisite Organization*, Falls Church, VA: Cason Hall and Co; 2nd edn, *Requisite Organization: A Total System for Effective Managerial Organization and Managerial Leadership for the 21st Century*, 1997.

—— (1990) *Creativity and Work*, Madison, CT: International Universities Press.

Jaques, E. and Brown W. (1965) *Glacier Project Papers*, London: Heinemann.

Jaques, E. and Cason K. (1994) *Human Capability*, Falls Church, VA: Cason Hall and Co.

Jaques, E. and Clement, S. (1991) *Executive Leadership*, Falls Church, VA: Cason Hall and Co.

Jaques, E., Gibson, R. and Isaac, J. (1978) *Levels of Abstraction in Logic and Human Action: A Theory of Discontinuity in the Structure of Mathematical Logic, Psychological Behaviour and Social Organization*, London: Heinemann.

Reber, A. (1993) *Implicit Learning and Tacit Knowledge: An Essay on the Cognitive Unconscious*, Oxford: Oxford University Press.

Rowbottom, R. (1977) *Social Analysis*, London: Heinemann.

Stamp, G. (1986) 'Some Observations on the Career Paths of Women', *Journal of Applied Behavioural Science* 22(4): 385–96.

—— (1992) *Day of Judgment: In Festschrift for Elliott Jaques*, Falls Church, VA: Cason Hall and Co.

Stamp, G. and Stamp, C. (1993) 'Well-being at Work: Aligning Purposes, People, Strategies and Structures', *The International Journal of Career Management* 5(3).

GS

JARDINE, William (1784–1843)

William Jardine was born in Lochmaben, Scotland in 1784, and died in London in 1842. In 1802, aged eighteen, he joined the East India Company's merchant fleet as a surgeon's mate and, on his first voyage, sailed to Canton (Guangzhou) in south China. Over the next fourteen years he travelled frequently to China, coming to know the people and its markets well. He was promoted to surgeon and styled himself Dr Jardine, although it is difficult to know exactly what his medical qualifications were.

Since the 1770s the East India Company had been shipping opium to Whampoa, the Western trading station just outside Canton, and selling it to local merchants who in turn sold it (illegally) into China. The Company, which had a legal monopoly on trade between China and Britain, used the profits of opium sales to purchase tea, silks and porcelain for sale in its home market, leading to a triangular trade between China, London and India. In 1816 Jardine, aware of the huge profits which could be made by selling opium, left the sea and went to work as an agent for the house of Magniac and Company in Whampoa. He was so successful as an opium seller that he was made a full partner in 1825. However, Magniac, like most of the Western agencies at Canton was unstable and chronically badly managed. In 1832 Jardine and James Matheson left to set up their own firm, Jardine Matheson.

Although opium could be profitable, like all illicit trades it was also a highly risky one. Jardine was determined to break the monopoly held by the East India Company on more conventional goods, and was aware that sentiment in Britain favoured him. In 1832 he began openly exporting tea from Canton to London. Not only was no legal move made to stop him, but two years later the Company's monopoly on China trade was ended. The five years that followed were, however, even more unstable and chaotic than before. With all restrictions ended, private traders in opium rushed to China and the volume of the drug passing through Canton rose sharply. In 1839 the Chinese authorities clamped down on the trade and seized hundreds of thousands of pounds worth of opium. The traders, led by Jardine Matheson, demanded the support of their government; the result was the First Opium War (1840–42), which led to the establishment of Hong Kong.

Jardine, like the East India Company before him, established a triangular trade. His system was to persuade British investors to put up funds by purchasing bills of exchange in London, which were sent out to be negotiated in Calcutta or Bombay. The funds were used to purchase opium, which was shipped to China; the profits from this transaction were returned to Britain in the form of goods, usually tea or silks. Agents in London and Calcutta handled two corners of the transactions, while Jardine and Matheson handled the third in China. As Cheong (1979: 166) says, 'Prices and rates of negotiation and commission were left to the agents in China to determine', meaning that Jardine and Matheson in effect had a licence to print money. The main activity in China was networking, preserving good relations with the Chinese *hongs* or merchant houses in Canton who bought the smuggled opium from Jardine Matheson.

Jardine's reputation today is an unsavoury one, and Western as well as Chinese historians have compared him to a Columbian drug baron. The defence, that opium was legal in Britain and its trade considered legitimate, is a poor one, given that trade was obviously illegal in China. Setting ethical issues aside, however, as Cheong comments, likeable or unlikeable, 'this was the stuff of which the most successful China houses were made, and these were the men, and these were their methods' (1979: 270). Jardine and Matheson were not only highly successful businessmen who built a lasting business organization, they also helped pave the way – however inadvertently – for the future prosperity of south China.

BIBLIOGRAPHY

Blake, R. (1999) *Jardine Matheson: Traders of the Far East*, London: Weidenfeld and Nicolson.

Cheong, W.B. (1979) *Mandarins and Merchants: Jardine Matheson & Co., A China Agency of the Early Nineteenth Century*, London: Curzon.

MLW

JOBS, Steve (1955–)

Steve Jobs was born in San Francisco, California on 24 February 1955. The adopted son of machine-shop technician Paul Jobs and his wife Clara, he grew up in the working-class communities of Mountain View and adjoining Los Altos, which are located in the area of northern California that came to be known as Silicon Valley when the original American developers of the miniature transistor turned the area into a centre for high-technology research and manufacture. An early interest in electronic gadgets prompted Steve Jobs to attend after-school lectures by engineers and scientists at the Hewlett-Packard electronics firm, where, at the age of thirteen, he landed his first summer job, working on an assembly line. Demonstrating the brashness that would become the hallmark of his character, Jobs phoned company co-founder Bill HEWLETT at home to ask for electronic parts. A bemused Hewlett acquired the parts for him and offered him a summer internship.

Also employed at Hewlett-Packard at that time was Steve Wozniak, five years Jobs's senior. Despite the age difference, the two became friends. They also became partners in crime when, as a prank, they designed and marketed for profit a 'blue box' system for making long-distance phone calls without payment. In 1972 Jobs finished high school and enrolled in Reed College, a liberal arts junior college in Portland, Oregon. He grew his hair long, experimented with psychedelic drugs, embraced Zen Buddhism, became a vegetarian, and lived in a rural commune, where he subsisted on a diet of apples, pears and other fruit. In early 1974 he returned to California and worked as an electronics technician for Atari, a company that manufactured shopping-arcade video games. He left after three months to visit India in search of spiritual enlightenment. When he returned, he resumed employment with Atari.

In January 1975 *Popular Electronics* magazine in the United States ran a cover story on a newly developed computer kit for hobbyists called the Altair, and announced that the era of personal computing was at hand. Jobs and Wozniak joined a local computer hobbyists' club and started talking about ways to turn this emerging technology into a product with mass appeal. They formed a partnership, calling themselves Apple Computer after Jobs's favourite fruit. Working in the garage of Jobs's parents' home, Wozniak and Jobs designed and built a prototype of the Apple I, a preassembled computer circuit board. A local electronics equipment retailer ordered fifty of the boards, and sold them at $666.66 apiece, more than twice what it cost the two young entrepreneurs to build them.

Because the Apple I came without a keyboard, monitor, power supply or case, it appealed only to hobbyists and electronics enthusiasts. The Apple II followed, with features more suited to the general user. Microcomputers from other manufacturers appeared on the market at the same time, but the Apple II quickly outpaced its competitors. The marketing drive and missionary zeal of Steve Jobs, coupled with his ability to attract media attention, became key factors in the early success of his company. At the age of twenty-one, invariably dressed in shorts, T-shirt and sandals, the bearded Jobs was hailed

by the media as something of a prophet: a technological visionary who stood as a symbol of something larger. As Young notes,

> his youth and good looks, his ability to say the quotable thing ... and an American public looking for a hero ... combined to make this one slender, intense young man a mythic figure amid the revitalized economy of post-Vietnam America.
>
> (Young 1988: 128)

At the age of twenty-three, Jobs was a millionaire. At twenty-four, he was worth $10 million; by the age of twenty-five his net worth was over $100 million. He was the youngest person ever to make the *Forbes* magazine list of America's richest people, and one of only a handful to have done so without inherited wealth.

But not everything he touched turned to gold. The Apple III had to be withdrawn because of design flaws. Another failure was the Lisa, a $10,000 computer aimed at the small business market, which Jobs named after his daughter. Jobs eventually cancelled the Lisa project when it took longer than projected to succeed. He did bounce back with the Macintosh, a machine that simplified computing for the ordinary consumer because it used the graphics-based, 'point and click' technology of a hand-held 'mouse' for its various functions, rather than relying on cumbersome, text-based keyboard commands. However, because the Macintosh was considerably more expensive than the lines of personal computers being developed by other manufacturers – particularly those using 'clones' of an operating system developed by Bill GATES's Microsoft software company for the giant International Business Machines (IBM) corporation – the Apple machine soon acquired the image of an elitist product, not one developed for the mass consumer market. The cheaper machines lacked the sophisticated 'user-friendly' features of the Macintosh, yet they flourished in the market-place while Apple faltered.

In 1985 continuing poor sales and internal problems at Apple Computer led to a restructuring of the company and the forced resignation of Jobs. He started a new company called NeXT, and spent the next four years developing a home computer for scholars and scientists that proved to be elegant, innovative and powerful but – with a price tag of $10,000 – so expensive that it had to be repositioned as a business computer. NeXT struggled until Jobs closed the hardware division and turned the company into a software firm. He purchased the digital animation division of Lucasfilm Ltd – a small motion picture studio owned by the film director George Lucas – to create Pixar Animation Studios.

By 1995 Jobs's star was on the rise again. Pixar, in conjunction with the Disney Corporation, released *Toy Story*, the first computer-generated feature film, and it became a box office hit. Apple Computer, meanwhile, was losing money and market share following the release of Microsoft's popular Windows 95, an operating system with a graphics-based interface technology similar to that of the Macintosh. Eager to develop a new operating-system strategy, Apple bought NeXT for $400 million in late 1996 and made Jobs a consultant to the company he had co-founded. Six months later, the executive board of Apple ousted the company's chief executive officer (CEO) Gil Amelio and appointed Jobs as 'interim' CEO.

In 1998 Jobs re-emerged publicly as a computer visionary, and Apple regained its reputation as a profitable trend-setter with the introduction of the iMac, a stylish, candy-coloured, one-piece computer that boosted Apple's share of the American home computer market from 6 to 12 per cent. In early 2000 Jobs agreed to drop the word 'interim' from his title and resume the role of permanent CEO. He received a salary of only $1 a year but was awarded options on ten million shares of Apple stock and a Gulfstream V jet plane for his personal use. Twenty-five years after starting his quest to change the fabric of

American life with his consumer-oriented computing machines, Jobs was still pursuing his dream of building computers for people, not for corporations. More than just marketing hardware and software, he was marketing a symbol: an image of American life in which the computer becomes an empowering cultural force.

BIBLIOGRAPHY
Butcher, L. (1988) *Accidental Millionaire: The Rise and Fall of Steve Jobs at Apple Computer*, New York: Paragon House.
Deutschman, A. (2000) *The Second Coming of Steve Jobs*, New York: Broadway Books.
Young, J.S. (1988) *Steve Jobs: The Journey is the Reward*, Glenview, Illinois: Scott, Foresman and Co.

BB

JOHN OF SALISBURY (*c.*1115–80)

John of Salisbury was born probably in or near Salisbury, Wiltshire around 1115. He died in Chartres sometime in 1180. He his known to have studied in Paris in the mid-1130s at one of the liberal arts schools on Mont Sainte-Geneviève; among his masters there were the most noted philosophers of the day, including Peter Abelard and the Platonist scholars Thierry of Chartres, William of Conches and Gilbert de la Porée. In 1147 he joined the personal staff of Theobald, Archbishop of Canterbury. As an intelligent and well-educated assistant, he was used by Theobald for a variety of tasks, including as manager of his own household, and as an emissary or negotiator. He also became friendly with another rising star on Theobald's staff, Thomas à Becket. John became a strong defender of the rights and political power of the church against the crown, and supported Becket after the latter became archbishop; as a result he was several times forced into exile. After Becket's murder in 1170, John returned to England and was given several ecclesiastical offices, and in 1176 he returned to France, where he was appointed bishop of Chartres.

In addition to his active political and administrative career, John was also a scholar and writer of note. Trained by some of the best and most forward-thinking minds of the day, he himself continued to have an innovative approach to problems of theology and philosophy, although this approach was usually tempered with a strong dose of pragmatism. He produced several works of note, including the educational treatise *Metalogicon* and, in particular, the *Policraticus*, a work of proto-political philosophy. The main thrust of the *Policraticus* is an attack on those princes and political leaders who allow themselves to be governed by worldly excess rather than philosophy. Government, says John, should be conducted according to philosophical principles, not the whims of princes; these principles are larger than any individual, and in fact govern our worldly activity, whether we recognize them or not. Government and administration could only be successful if they were carried out according to the dictates of higher principles.

John is the first to conceive of an administrative body (in this case, the state) as being similar to a living organism. He uses the metaphor of the human body to describe how the state is governed: the prince is the head of the state, the senate is its heart, the agricultural workers and soldiers are equivalent to its limbs and so on. This metaphor would later be used by early twentieth-century writers on organization, most notably Charles KNOEPPEL, although it is not certain that these writers were familiar with John's work.

BIBLIOGRAPHY
John of Salisbury (1159) *Policraticus*, trans. J. Dickinson, *Policraticus: The*

Statesman's Book, New York: Knopf, 1927.

Jordan, M.D. (1998) 'John of Salisbury', in E. Craig (ed.), *Routledge Encyclopedia of Philosophy*, London: Routledge, vol. 5, 115–17.

MLW

JOHNSON, Howard Dearing (1896–1972)

Howard Dearing Johnson was born in Boston, Massachusetts on 2 February 1896 (some sources indicate that he was born in 1897 or 1898, although the day and month are not in dispute), the son of John Hayes Johnson and Olive Bell Wright. He died on 20 June 1972 in New York City. Johnson's family lived and worked in the greater Boston area, where his father was a cigar merchant. John Johnson was of Swedish descent and Olive Johnson was of Scottish and Irish heritage. Howard's parents lived in Boston for the first several years of marriage before moving to Wollaston, a suburb of the city, in 1902. Howard was an only son but had three sisters, and early accounts suggest that John Johnson tried to assure that his son would be raised as a 'man' amidst a family dominated by females. Boxing matches, sledding incidents, name calling and the accompanying bruises and scars were not uncommon in the Johnson household. Speculation is that these early traumas contributed to the young Howard's independence, cockiness and resilience.

After leaving school at a young age (following yet another disagreement with his father), Johnson went to work for his father in his tobacco business. Records indicate that he helped build the business through the introduction of new products and time spent on the road as a travelling salesman. The First World War interrupted his tobacco career and

Johnson entered the military, where he provided medical operations with supplies. Upon his return, he rejoined his father in the family business. His father's premature death less than two years later would have an impact on his career direction. He sold the store after reducing its debt, and moved on to other things.

Howard Johnson's early entry into the food service industry is well documented. He began with the purchase of the Walker-Barlow's drug store in Wollaston. The store came complete with a soda fountain from which ice cream was sold. Following his initial disappointment with the quality of the ice cream, he made some adjustments to the recipe and was eventually satisfied. He soon recognized the popularity and profitability of the ice cream compared to the other product lines, and, upon the advice of his accountant, promoted this particular aspect of his business. Expanding, he opened a series of ice-cream stands on the beach, for which he recruited youngsters to sell the product. These satellite operations generated over $200,000 in one summer of operation. Beginning with only chocolate and vanilla ice cream, he continued to add new flavours until he reached the then famous twenty-eight varieties. Again recognizing opportunity when it presented itself, he expanded his offerings to include frankfurters and other sundries. Having grown his beach food-service operation, his next step was to open a full-fledged restaurant.

Johnson's first restaurant was located in Quincy, Massachusetts, south of Boston. He opened it in 1928 in an office building. The restaurant had a typically 'down-east' menu which included Boston baked beans, frankfurters, clam chowder and fried clams. These were to become, along with his premium ice cream, the restaurant's signature items that helped to establish the restaurant company as an integral part of the American landscape. Eventually the Howard Johnson menus would grow to some 700 items, most of which were supplied by a central commissary, also owned

by the company. Simply prepared food, value, firm standards and vision allowed his business to grow. He was a stickler for quality; this attention to quality is attributed to his days as a tobacconist, when he had more than one encounter with suppliers who tried to provide him with substandard product.

Perhaps one of Johnson's greatest contributions to the international hospitality industry came with his decision to franchise his operation (after opening only one store). While not the first in the industry to franchise, he approached the notion of franchising with a formalized plan, one that encompassed standards for the entire restaurant operation from the menu to the architecture. His first franchise was opened in Orleans on Cape Cod in 1935, and within a year he had opened a total of seventeen restaurants.

From the beginning, Howard Johnson's vision was founded on a belief that the automobile would rule, a belief reflected in the growth of the company in eastern Massachusetts to his dominance of the American turnpikes in the second half of the century. His seventeen restaurants had grown to 200 by the coming of the Second World War. Johnson then had to re-evaluate his strategy: 90 per cent of his restaurants closed as a direct result of the war and subsequent rationing. This, ironically, led to other opportunities for the entrepreneur. His business acumen allowed him to survive the war by a variety of means: continuing to make ice cream for other retail operations, and becoming the food-service provider for colleges and military operations.

Following the war, Johnson picked up where he had left off. He grew the chain from twelve units in wartime to 200 once again in a few short years. By the 1950s he had opened 400 restaurants. He then decided to diversify and enter the lodging business. He opened his first hotel in Savannah, Georgia in 1954, and grew this chain as well. The company expanded over the next two decades to 1,000 restaurants by its peak in the mid-1970s; and in addition to the signature restaurant chain, the company also controlled over 500 motor lodges and two smaller food-service chains: Red Coach Grill and Ground Round. Until at least 1958 (a year before he stepped down as president of the company) Johnson maintained the company's corporate offices in Wollaston, Massachusetts, where it all began. In 1959 he turned the company over to his son, who eventually took it public and then sold it. Johnson remained for some time as treasurer and chairman of the company he built. He had married, to Bernice Manley, and they had one son and one daughter.

Howard Johnson has been characterized as hard-working, independent and a stickler for detail, although he was known to label himself as a promoter and nothing else. Various quotations attributed to him portray a man who was no-nonsense, detail-oriented and introspective. He will best be remembered for building a business (several times over); helping to develop the franchise restaurant system as we know it today; creating the concept of the 'turnpike' restaurant; and perfecting a frozen-food distribution system (through which he supplied all of his restaurants). In short, he changed the way that the restaurant and lodging industries were operated as well as the way in which they were perceived by the public.

Most Americans born prior to 1970 are familiar with the name of Howard Johnson and the famous orange roofs that sit atop his restaurants. He has been referred to as 'probably the best known name to ever appear in the restaurant business' (Lundberg 1976). At the very least, Howard Johnson was an innovator, entrepreneur and pioneer in the hospitality industry. From humble beginnings, he made his mark on the hospitality industry in a variety of ways.

BIBLIOGRAPHY
Alexander, J. (1958) 'Host of the Highways', *Saturday Evening Post*, 19 July.

Baird, C. (2000) Personal communication with director and archivist, Conrad Hilton College, University of Houston, 19 September.

Clark, W.H. and Moynahan, J.H.S. (1955) 'Howard Dearing Johnson: The Roadside Host', in *Famous Leaders of Industry*, Boston: L.C. Page and Co.

Howard Johnson Hotels and Inns, *Brand History*, www.hojo.com/ctg/cgi-bin/HowardJohnson/brand_history, 15 May 2001.

Howard Johnson International (2000) Personal communication with Andrew Miller, Public Relations, Cendant Corporation, 8 September.

Lundberg, D.E. (1976) *The Hotel and Restaurant Business*, Boston: Cahners Books International.

'Obituary: Howard D. Johnson' (1972) *New York Times*, 21 June, 46.

CB

JOHNSON, John Harold (1918–)

John Harold Johnson was born in Arkansas City, Arkansas on 19 January 1918, the son of Leroy Johnson, a mill worker, and Gertrude Jenkins. His father was killed in a mill accident when Johnson was six, and although his mother remarried, the family lived in considerable poverty. In 1933 Johnson and his mother moved to Chicago hoping to find a better life. A bright student, Johnson was educated at Du Sable High School in Chicago's South Side; fellow pupils included Harold Washington, later mayor of Chicago, and the future jazz musician Nat 'King' Cole.

In 1936 Johnson enrolled at the University of Chicago, financing his studies through part-time work at Supreme Liberty Life Insurance, the largest black-owned insurance company in the United States. Supreme Life's president, Harry H. Pace, was Johnson's early mentor, and while at Supreme Life Johnson learned how black businessmen like Pace were able to capture the increasingly affluent black market – not because of their colour but because they understood the needs of the market better than did their white counterparts. He also became friendly with Earl Dickerson, another Supreme Life executive who was also active in Chicago politics. In 1941 Johnson married Eunice Walker; they had two children.

In the late 1930s Johnson had become interested in publishing, and was appointed assistant editor of Supreme Life's monthly newsletter. It was while working on this project that Johnson conceived of the idea of a black equivalent to *Reader's Digest*. Raising a loan of $500 with his mother's furniture as collateral, Johnson launched his first magazine, *Negro Digest*, in 1942. Ingham and Feldman (1994) note that the take-up was slow at first, until Johnson hit on an idea for a series, 'If I Were a Negro', in which prominent white people were invited to contribute articles. One of the first contributors was Eleanor Roosevelt, wife of President Franklin D. Roosevelt. This coup resulted in a trebling of the journal's circulation almost overnight.

In 1943 Johnson quit Supreme Life to devote himself full-time to publishing. In 1945 he launched his second journal, this one based on the very successful picture journal *Life*, published by Henry LUCE. Johnson's version of *Life* was *Ebony*, a glossy magazine which aimed to 'mirror the happier side of life – the positive, everyday achievements from Harlem to Hollywood' (Ingham and Feldman 1994: 372). The portrayal of a positive image had an immediate impact on its black audience, and *Ebony* quickly reached a circulation of 400,000. The next step was to gather advertising; in the early years *Ebony* lost money despite its massive circulation, and had to be supported by its sister publication the *Negro Digest*. Johnson's breakthrough came when he persuaded radio-maker Zenith to advertise

in *Ebony*; Zenith's president, Eugene McDonald, not only remained a steady advertiser but persuaded other big names to advertise as well. *Ebony* was now in profit.

More journals followed, including *Jet*, a weekly news magazine, and *Tan*, a 'true confessions' type magazine. Johnson also branched out into book publishing and other ventures, of which easily the most successful was Fashion Fair Cosmetics, which produced a range of cosmetics and skincare products for black women. By the end of the 1980s Fashion Fair products were being sold in more than 1,500 stores across the country (Ingham and Feldman 1994: 374). Johnson also owns radio and television stations, and later bought his old employer, Supreme Life.

It has been estimated that Johnson's publications reach 60 per cent of the black adult market in the United States (Davis 1987). *Ebony* now has a circulation of over 1.5 million. Johnson himself has his critics: civil rights leaders have attacked him for not taking a harder line over racist issues, and closer to home he has been described by employees as an autocrat and a hard taskmaster. Johnson rebuts these criticisms, particularly the former. But there is little denying that he has a genius for finding and exploiting market niches. His understanding of the cultural needs of African-Americans has been matched by his ability to design and bring to market products to meet those needs. He is one of the outstanding entrepreneurs of twentieth-century America.

BIBLIOGRAPHY
Davis, W. (1987) *The Innovators: The Essential Guide to Business Thinkers*, London: Ebury Press.
Ingham, J.N. and Feldman, L.B. (1994) *African-American Business Leaders: A Biographical Dictionary*, Westport, CT: Greenwood Press.

MLW

JOMINI, Antoine-Henri (1779–1869)

Antoine-Henri Jomini was born in Payerne, Switzerland on 6 March 1779 and died, aged ninety, at Passy in France on 24 March 1869. While still in his teens, working as an apprentice banker, he became involved in revolutionary politics and supported the pro-French republican movement in Switzerland. In 1803, greatly influenced by the career of Napoleon, he published his first work on military strategy. In 1805 he joined the staff of General (later Marshal) Ney, one of Napoleon's most prominent commanders. He served with great distinction in the French army, but during the summer of 1813 Jomini quarrelled with Napoleon's chief of staff, Marshal Berthier, and defected to the Russians. During more than forty years in Russian service, he served as aide-de-camp to Tsars Alexander I and Nicholas I, organized the Russian military academy and served in the Crimean War of 1854–5. After returning to France, he was military adviser to Emperor Napoleon III.

A prolific writer, Jomini was known for two works in particular. The first, *Traité des grandes opérations militaires*, was published in 1805. A study of the campaigns of Frederick the Great (see FREDERICK II), this work made his reputation as a military theorist. The second, *Précis de l'art de la guerre*, appeared in 1838 and is Jomini's most profound and enduring work, which influenced writers on both military and business strategy until well into the twentieth century.

Early in his career, Jomini became convinced that warfare, seemingly chaotic, was in fact governed by enduring principles. In particular he believed, like CLAUSEWITZ, that strategy should be formulated and carried out according to universal scientific precepts (Jomini 1805). Earlier writers had expressed similar views, but it was Jomini who most fully developed the idea of applying scientific principles to warfare.

Jomini's idea of strategy, in the words of Shy (1986: 168), consisted of 'bringing

superior force to bear on a point where the enemy is both weaker and liable to crippling damage'. The issue that preoccupied much of his later work was how this could be done. He was the first to develop the concept of logistics, 'the practical art of moving armies', which included a whole variety of subdisciplines such as planning, supply management, movement, intelligence, communications and record keeping (Jomini 1838). Jomini saw logistics as a staff function, or, in modern terms, as a managerial task; the commander-in-chief had an oversight or general management role, while individual staff officers looked after specialist functions. Careful management of the organization and logistics of an organization was seen as a prerequisite to the achievement of strategic goals. In a similar vein, Jomini also wrote extensively on the nature of organization.

Jomini has been called the 'father of modern strategy' (Shy 1986), and his influence on strategic thinking permeated the development of business strategy in the early twentieth century during the heyday of scientific management (which owes much to Jomini's view that efficiency could be achieved through the application of scientific principles). Of still greater importance, however, may be his definition and development of the idea of logistics.

BIBLIOGRAPHY

Handel, M.I. (1992) *Masters of War: Sun Tzu, Clausewitz and Jomini*, London: Frank Cass.

Jomini, A.-H. (1805) *Traité des grandes opérations militaires, contenant l'histoire des campagnes de Frédéric II* ... , 5 vols, Paris, full edition published 1811; trans. S.B. Holabird, *Treatise on Grand Military Operations*, New York, 1865.

—— (1838) *Précis de l'art de la guerre*, Paris; trans. G.H. Mendel and W.P. Craighill, *The Art of War*, Philadelphia: Lippincott, 1862.

Shy, J. (1986) 'Jomini', in P. Paret (ed.), *Makers of Modern Strategy*, Princeton, NJ: Princeton University Press, 143–85.

MLW

JOUVENEL, Bertrand de (1903–87)

Bertrand de Jouvenel was born in Paris into an influential family, the son of Henry de Jouvenel, a statesman, senator and editor of Paris' *Le Matin*. He died in France. Married, he had two children, one of whom, Hugues de Jouvenel, has carried on his father's work at the Futuribles Institute. His best education, he claimed was spending happy summers in his childhood reading the wide range of books in his mother's house. His mother, Claire Boas, was also a notable figure, the creator of La Bienvenue Française, an institution to promote communication and contact between diplomats; through this organization she facilitated the negotiations on the formation of an independent Czechoslovakia. His childhood and early adolescence were spent immersed in an artistic and journalistic milieu, giving him a taste for polemic and illustrating the attraction of power. All his life he was surrounded by decision makers who were engaged in matters relating to directing society for the public good.

De Jouvenel became a journalist, specializing in economic questions and international relations. He published his first book, *L'Economie dirigée* (The Directed Economy), at the age of twenty-five. His early thinking drew on the work of ENGELS, and was much influenced by his stepmother, Colette. He became a leading thinker and idealist, following the thinking of Rousseau, and wrote on a wide range of social and political issues with an ethical perspective. An opponent of the Vichy government established in 1940, he was forced to leave France in 1943 and settled for a time in Switzerland, where he produced his renowned work *Power:*

Its Nature and the History of its Growth, in 1945. His work became famous, and he was invited to lecture at universities all over the world. His work was characterized by scholarship, clarity and reasoned argument. His contributions to thinking on the fundamentals of economics and politics were substantial, but they were matched by his contribution to establishing the field of futures studies.

A later book, *The Pure Theory of Politics* (1963), shows de Jouvenel's characteristic breadth and insight. He links the affective nature of humans with the power of politics, at the same time linking the need for affinity, human ego, with the handicap that modern society provides weak affinity between people. In truth, as well as with apposite wit, he asserts that, 'the development of the child should receive a great deal of attention from students of Politics – the form of adult activity wherein the traits of childish behaviour are best preserved' (de Jouvenel 1963).

De Jouvenel was one of the leading pioneers of futures thinking – what he termed *la prospective*. He saw forecasts as a necessity of modern society, declaring, 'We have to make wagers about the future; we have no choice in the matter' (de Jouvenel 1967: 277). He attached great hope to the study of the future, saying that, 'It is because we think that the fate of Troy could have been changed if Cassandra had been heard, that foresight seems useful, in a word, because we are free from denial' (Roussel 1993).

With funding from the Ford Foundation, de Jouvenel founded the Futuribles research institute in France with the aim of stimulating efforts in social and political forecasting. The name reflects his conviction that study of the future must involve free choice and people's determination; it combines the word 'future' with 'possibilities'. He and his colleagues believed the consideration of the future to be a social duty, and that there was a need to stimulate the orientation of the social sciences towards the future. In attempting to draw together work done on different aspects of the future, and to provoke discussions about the intellectual manoeuvres used in predicting, the work of the Futuribles team was presented at seminars in the early 1960s.

De Jouvenel's principal work on forecasting and prevision, *The Art of Conjecture* (1967), sets out much of the early groundwork of futures thinking, and is still regarded as an important, classic text. His drive to improve the methodology of futures studies and forecasting is summed up at the end of the book: 'We are forever making forecasts – with scanty data, no awareness of method, no criticism and no cooperation. It is urgent that we make this ... a co-operative and organic endeavour, subject to greater exigencies of intellectual rigour' (de Jouvenel 1967: 277). He neatly summarized the underlying dilemma of futures studies, saying that there can be no knowledge of the future, but on the other hand the only 'useful knowledge' we have relates to the future. He declared: 'The real reason we study the future is so that we can find ways of trying to bend the course of events in a way which will bring the probable closer to the desirable' (de Jouvenel 1967). His hope with this work was that it would serve to eliminate prejudices against what he describes as a useful activity, and the development of a natural activity: 'prejudices for which justification is found every time, which is too often, that a conjecture is disguised as prophecy' (de Jouvenel 1967: ix).

De Jouvenel clearly set boundaries around the expectations from futures studies, with a reasoned use of terminology that highlighted the danger of perceived certainty in forecasts. He warned that the forecaster should fear credulity far more than scepticism in his audience. Ever a champion of the cause of futures, he was most effective through his contributions to, and emphasis on the importance of, the study of futures methodology. He was a writer and thinker of considerable insight, concerned with the fundamental issues of society, particularly power, politics and the future.

BIBLIOGRAPHY

Jouvenel, B. de (1945) *Power: Its Nature and the History of its Growth*, Boston: Beacon Press.

—— (1951) *The Ethics of Redistribution*, Cambridge: Cambridge University Press.

—— (1963) *The Pure Theory of Politics*, Cambridge: Cambridge University Press.

—— (1967) *The Art of Conjecture*, London: Weidenfeld and Nicolson, New York: Basic Books.

Roussel, E. (1993) *Bertrand de Jouvenel: Itineraire 1928–1976*, Paris: Plon.

AJ

JUNGK, Robert (1913–94)

Robert Jungk was born Robert Baum in Berlin on 5 November 1913, the son of a writer. He died in Salzburg, Austria on 14 July 1994. A Jewish student at the University of Berlin when Hitler came to power, he was arrested soon after the Reichstag fire for anti-Nazi activities, and had his citizenship revoked. Thanks to the intervention of his friends he was released shortly after, and went on to continue his degree studies at the Sorbonne in Paris. Two years later he returned to Germany to work illegally for a subversive press service, but again had to flee, this time to Czechoslovakia in 1933, where he set up another anti-Nazi agency. When Prague fell in 1939 he transferred his activities to Paris, and when Paris fell he moved to Switzerland. Even there he was arrested and jailed, as his anti-Nazi writings were not tolerable to the neutral state. He was released thanks to a powerful American friend, and became the Central European correspondent for the London *Observer* from 1944 to 1945, in which capacity he covered the Nuremberg Trials. He completed his education, taking his Ph.D. in Zurich with a thesis on the resistance of the Swiss press to censorship. In 1945 he returned to Germany and worked as a correspondent in Yugoslavia and Hungary, later moving to the United States as correspondent for Swiss newspapers. He became a US citizen, but later moved back to Europe and settled in Salzburg. He married Ruth Suschizky in 1948, and had two sons.

Jungk's experiences and observations of persecution left him feeling deeply powerless about the Holocaust, particularly when he was unable to persuade other journalists to write about it. This frustration became the source of his lifelong drive to devise ways in which ordinary people can participate, fight back and influence the course of events. He demonstrated a long resistance to tyranny, and was sensitive to oppression in all its forms. He was a renowned and passionate humanist, and wrote compelling accounts of the impacts of nuclear holocaust. He was a long-time opposer of nuclear arms, lecturing and demonstrating all over the world. This work against the nuclear threat was an important part of his life's work, dedicated to the future and to peace.

Jungk's early experiences forged the major themes of his work: the power and potential destructiveness of modern technologies, the corresponding need for careful foresight and the struggle to preserve human qualities in the changing postwar world. He was awarded numerous prizes, including the Prix de la Resistance in 1960, the International Peace Prize in 1961 and the German Conservation Prize in 1978.

His book *Tomorrow is Already Here* (1954) attacked the materialism of the Western world. He challenged the prevalent view that the future was the promise of a world of technological achievement, 'where research and development would constantly increase humanity's feelings of omnipotence'. A later book, *The Everyman Project* (1976) provided constructive responses to what he saw as the deepening dilemmas of the West. Jungk believed passionately that we should not go blindly into the

future, and actively called for citizen imagination and involvement in the invention of new social institutions; the invention of nonviolent methods of bring about social, political and economic change; the inventions of alternative occupations; new goals and values; and the creation of a creative society. This urging became the inspiration for the development of the Institute for Social Inventions based in London, of which he later became president. He became a pioneer in the field of futures studies as a means of responding to these challenges. In 1953 he founded the first Institute for Research into the Future; later, with Johan Galtung, he co-founded the International Conference on Futurism in 1967, out of which emerged the World Futures Studies Federation. In 1987 he established the Robert Jungk International Futures Library with the support of the city of Salzburg.

Jungk made significant and practical contributions to the development of the humanist and ecological perspective, in futures studies particularly, but also management. His principal contribution to management thinking was his development of a democratic (participatory) approach to enable people to become involved in developing creative ideas and projects to shape their own futures, 'the futures workshop'. Jungk was driven by the ideal of real participation in decisions. He challenged the common practice of inadequate consultation and participation where it came too late to have any impact. It was the initial stages of problem definition which he identified as the most important for people to participate in.

His approach was eminently practical and lively, and was built upon a strong philosophy of openness and inclusivity. He describes the workshop as having three phases after the preparation phase. The first is a critique phase to bring out all the grievances and negative experiences relating to the topic. This is followed by a fantasy phase, in which ideas, desires and fantasies, and alternative views are expressed. The ideas are developed by working groups into solutions and brought into the implementation phase, where the present constraints and power structures are examined. Imaginative solutions are sought to get around these and to develop a plan of action. He drew on the creative thinking techniques of DE BONO, amongst others, for this part of the process.

Jungk's techniques have become widely used in Europe (particularly in Austria, Denmark and Switzerland) and had particular success in influencing social and political change in particular regions, as well as exploring the future of particular industries. This has impacted on the philosophy of public sector decision-making processes and planning, and community development. He saw his future workshop techniques being used to solve problems in businesses, schools and voluntary organizations, in designing individual and community development plans, and for enlivening meetings and seminars. Jungk's work brought together the work and philosophies of de JOUVENEL, Kenneth and Elise BOULDING, Galtung and McHALE, and it continues to hold a significant place in the field of futures studies. His methods continue to be developed and applied by futurists throughout the world.

Jungk's aim was to capture what he believed was the most neglected and most important of all resources: people's imaginations. In 1962 he was among the first to organize methods of drawing on imagination as a means to solve problems and specifically to focus on bringing about desirable change. His success was partly due to his insight into psychology and the realization that much of people's passivity is to be explained by the hostility of our social environment to anything from the realms of our imagination. He gave future workshops the task of righting the damage done by what he called the 'mass suppression of the imagination', noting that negative future expectations more often end up as self-fulfilling prophecies, while positive images of a future bring better prospects of its attainment.

Jungk was driven by the conviction that the future was colonized by a tiny group of people,

and that citizens were too often moving into a future shaped by this elite. He equally believed, however, that it was possible for small groups to bring about significant change. He was committed to activism, although he noted that it was 'just as essential for people to know what they were fighting for, not just what they were fighting against'. He was awarded a Right Livelihood Award ('the alternative Nobel Prize') in 1986 for his work on future workshops, and for fighting for sane alternatives and ecological awareness.

BIBLIOGRAPHY
Jungk, R. (1954) *Tomorrow is Already Here*, trans. M. Waldman, London: Hart-Davis.
—— (1976) *The Everyman Project: Resources for a Humane Future*, London: Thames and Hudson.
Jungk, R. and Mullert, N. (1987) *Future Workshops: How to Create Desirable Futures*, London: Institute for Social Inventions.
Right Livelihood Awards (2001) *Robert Jungk – 1986*, http://www. rightlivelihood.se, 15 March 2001.
Slaughter, R.A. (1994) *Robert Jungk, Futurist and Social Inventor*, Brisbane: World Futures Studies Federation.

AJ

JURAN, Joseph Moses (1904–)

Joseph Moses Juran was born in Braila, Romania on 24 December 1904. When he was five his father departed for America, seeking a better life for the family. Three years later, in 1912, the rest of the family joined his father in Minnesota. Growing up in Minnesota, Joseph Juran helped his family make ends meet by doing whatever jobs he could find: 'Joe drove a team of horses, he worked as a laborer, a shoe salesman, bootblack, grocery clerk and as a bookkeeper for the local icehouse' (Butman and Roessner 1995: xxvi). He excelled in school and advanced three years ahead of boys his age. Having a sharp tongue and being the youngest in his class, he often became the prey for classroom bullies. 'The grind of school, poverty, never-ending jobs and chores at home' (Butman and Roessner 1995: xxvi) were challenges that helped toughen this very young high school graduate. At the time, his self-esteem was not particularly high; however, this would change thanks to a favourable change in his environment.

Enrolling at the University of Minnesota in 1920, he became the first member of his family to attend college. Becoming a good chess player, Juran found an activity that challenged his analytical mind. In time he became the University of Minnesota chess champion and also performed well in state-wide competitions. His success at chess enabled him to improve his self-esteem. 'Gradually, he shed the image of the skinny misfit and outsider; now he knew that his difference was in the nature of a gift, rather than a curse' (Butman and Roessner 1995: xxvi).

In 1924 Juran completed his studies at the University of Minnesota, graduating with a BS in electrical engineering. Finding employment at Western Electric, he was assigned to the Inspection Department of the Hawthorne Plant near Chicago. At that time the Hawthorne Plant employed about 40,000 workers, with approximately 5,000 of them devoted to inspection. Working on the function of inspection, Joseph Juran enthusiastically began his lifelong quest for quality products, and advanced through a series of management and staff positions. He eventually became a key member of the newly formed Inspection Statistical Department: 'It was one of the first such departments established in industry in this country. In retrospect, the greatest significance of this department may have been that it set Juran firmly on the path

toward his life's work' (Butman and Roessner 1995: xxviii).

In 1928 Joseph Juran wrote his first work about quality. Entitled *Statistical Methods Applied to Manufacturing Problems*, it discussed the role of sampling in analysing and controlling the quality of manufactured products. Later it became part of the *AT&T Statistical Quality Control Handbook*, still in use today. As might be expected, the number of managers, administrators and line workers at the Hawthorne Plant decreased substantially during the Great Depression. While many were let go, others who had proven themselves to be particularly able were relocated to other necessary positions within Western Electric. Juran had not only proven himself, but he also had the ability to improve quality and productivity at Western Electric at a time when any gains in efficiency were critical. Because of these talents, Juran was relocated to New York City in 1937, where he assumed an enviable position as head of Industrial Engineering at Western Electric's corporate headquarters. In this capacity, he exchanged ideas about industrial engineering with many other companies. While visiting General Motors in Detroit, he got the idea for the now famous concept known as the 'Pareto Principle'.

While quality managers today teach and use Pareto analysis, many of them are unaware that Juran conceptualized this approach and that Pareto had little to do with it. Essentially, when Juran worked with company-wide quality committees, his approach was to work on the most critical problems first. Indeed, he encouraged focusing on what he called the 'vital few' before attempting to solve many other trivial problems. Years later, Juran acknowledged that this was an improper attribution to Vilfredo Pareto, an Italian economist of the late 1800s and early 1900s: 'Proper attribution would be to Max Otto Lorenz, who developed the "Lorenze Curve", which displays the deviation of a sample from the standard' (Wren and Greenwood 1998: 215–6).

The Pareto principle is widely used now in the quality management field and is sometimes described as the 80/20 rule. In this case, it is thought that 80 per cent of the problems are caused by 20 per cent of operations. The application of this concept places a high priority on solving the vital few problems without diverting attention unnecessarily towards trivial problems. Another application of Juran's Pareto principle (often referred to as Pareto analysis) is that customers in a sales effort, for example, can be categorized into vital few customers and useful many customers. Although both of these categories of customers are important, they may need to be treated differently. In this regard, Pareto analysis helps identify and focus attention on the needs of different groups. Graphic presentation of this analysis is often presented with Pareto charts: 'Pareto charts are useful after brainstorming and then constructing a cause-effect diagram to identify those items that could be responsible for the most impact' (Brocka and Brocka 1992: 299).

At the start of the Second World War, Juran departed from Western Electric to serve as an assistant administrator with the Lend-Lease Administration in Washington, DC. This organization managed the shipment of material to friendly nations at the beginning of the war . 'Here, Juran became enmeshed in managing governmental processes, including a massive problem in what today might be called "renumerating government", or "business process engineering"' (Butman and Roessner 1995: xxx). As this organization expanded, Juran led a multi-agency team that cut government red tape and paper log-jams that bogged down important shipments that were stranded on the docks. As the war progressed, Juran's team redesigned far-reaching shipping processes that sped up the movement of essential lend-lease war materials to the United States' allies.

At the conclusion of the Second World War, Juran decided to forgo working for corporate America and government, and instead launched his own efforts as an independent

person. His intentions at the time were to use the balance of his life to philosophize, research, write, lecture and consult on management. Initially, he served as chair of the Department of Administrative Engineering at New York University. In time he built a consulting practice, wrote books and developed quality management lectures for the American Management Association. In 1951 the publication of his *Quality Control Handbook* helped establish Juran's reputation as an authority on quality and, because of this reputation, he received numerous requests to lecture and consult. This book, now known as *Juran's Quality Control Handbook*, is in its fourth edition. The first three editions sold in excess of 350,000 copies, cumulatively.

During the last two decades of the twentieth century, W. Edwards DEMING was often considered the primary expert on quality management, while Joseph Juran was never considered less than second in an array of countless champions of the quality movement. Although Deming worked with large groups of executives in Japan starting in the summer of 1950, Juran joined the effort in 1954. It should be emphasized that both men respected each other and got along very well; however, Deming claimed that 'Juran tended to issue "far-out statements and platitudes" about management. Juran thought Deming was wrong, for instance, to tell management to "drive out fear." Juran believes "fear can bring out the best in people"' (Cortada and Woods 1998: 33–4). 'Juran [also] felt that Deming was basically a statistician who had spent much of his life without direct corporate experience and responsibilities, while Juran had more of a managerial viewpoint' (Wren and Greenwood 1998: 217).

Both Deming and Juran played a major role in helping the Japanese overcome their reputation as a producer of poor quality products. Japan had a period of rapid economic growth from the mid-1950s through the 1960s. This was also a time of significant progress in the effectiveness of Japan's quality control efforts.

In the normal course of events, Juran's reputation from of his *Quality Control Handbook* came to the attention of Ken-ichi Koyanagi, then managing director of the Union of Japanese Scientists and Engineers (JUSE). In 1952 Deming arranged for Ken-ichi to meet Juran at an American Society for Quality Control meeting held in Syracuse, New York. Two years later, Juran accepted JUSE's invitation and made his first visit to Japan from 4 July to 17 August 1954. Although some of Juran's material was not new to the Japanese, many of his ideas and approaches were both needed and fresh. For example, Juran's Pareto principle of the vital few and useful many was well received. During his factory visits in Japan during 1954, Juran noticed what seemed to be an overemphasis on statistical tools and a corresponding shortage of the application of managerial tools. 'It is important to emphasize that the content of Juran's lectures differed from that of the lectures given by Deming. In particular, it should be remembered that while Deming's field was statistics, Juran's field was management' (Nonaka 1995: 540). Consequently, Juran's visits were significant in changing Japan's emphasis from statistical quality control to the management of quality and company-wide quality control.

When Juran visited Japan for the second time in November and December 1960, he conducted courses for top executives and chiefs of divisions and sections in Tokyo and Osaka. Returning to Japan on numerous occasions after 1960, Juran continued to make a substantial contribution to Japan's industrial renaissance. In reflecting on the assistance that he and Deming had given to the Japanese, Juran seemed to minimize its importance and related 'if Deming and I had never gone there, the Japanese quality revolution would have taken place without us' (Juran 1994: 10). Deming had similar thoughts when he considered his own efforts in helping the Japanese; he felt 'that he did not cause the great transformation that occurred in Japanese management and manufacturing. Rather, the Japanese

caused these changes themselves' (Petersen 1987: 136). Beyond the modesty of both Juran and Deming, we find that these men were very instrumental in helping the Japanese achieve their own industrial renaissance. In fact, the Japanese appreciate the splendid efforts of both. In the years to follow, the emperor of Japan awarded each of them the Second Order Medal of the Sacred Treasure, the nation's highest award presented to foreigners.

Back in the United States during the 1980s, many leaders had difficulty in defining quality. Some confused quality with luxury and wondered if it was really critical. Juran defined quality as 'fitness for use' (Juran 1989: 15). It should be recognized that Juran emphasized 'that it is the user who is really the concern, not some abstract ideal of quality' (Sashkin and Kiser 1993: 55). In this instance consumers, for example, receive what they expect. This is the opposite of what marketers sometimes call 'bait and switch'. A suitable example of not being fit for use are the poor quality Firestone tyres that caused serious automobile accidents at the start of the twenty-first century. These consumers did not expect luxury tyres, but they did expect tyres that were 'fit for use'. Unfortunately for Firestone, this was not the case. Had Juran's approach to quality management been followed, Firestone and Ford could have saved themselves a considerable loss in time, money and reputation.

Throughout his efforts to improve quality, Juran criticized two mistaken opinions that have prevented many American managers from producing quality products and services. The first is that many managers 'have not yet accepted the fact that they, not the workers, must shoulder most of the responsibility for the performance of their companies' (Hunt 1992: 66). Another mistaken opinion is that managers 'fail to realize the great financial gains to be made once quality becomes their top priority' (Hunt 1992: 66).

As Juran's philosophy about quality management evolved further, many of his earlier concepts developed into additional practical approaches suitable for the workplace. Juran defined quality management as 'the process of identifying and administering the activities needed to achieve the quality objectives of an organization' (Juran and Gryna 1993: 7). It became obvious to Juran that individual piece-meal efforts would accomplish little in attempting to improve the quality of an organization's output. Instead, he insisted on a company-wide quality effort. This systematic approach used throughout a company would be 'quite similar to the method long used to set and meet financial goals' (Juran 1988a: 244–5). Getting more specific, Juran urged that quality operations 'require some form of coordination that has enough force to put company performance ahead of departmental goals' (248). This level of company-wide quality management would be necessary for effective joint planning, project teams, early warning systems and genuine employee participation.

One of Juran's first steps for achieving quality is to conduct a company-wide assessment of quality. According to Juran, this assessment furnishes a starting point for understanding the size of the quality issue, and the specific areas requiring attention. This assessment consists of four elements:

1. Cost of poor quality.

2. Standing in the marketplace.

3. Quality culture in the organization.

4. Operation of the company quality system.
(Juran and Gryna 1993: 15)

In organizing for quality, Juran visualizes that coordination of quality activities requires coordination for control and coordination for creating change. In addition, 'to achieve quality excellence, upper management must lead the quality effort' (Juran and Gryna 1993: 155). Further, a quality council consisting of upper managers should develop a quality strategy and guide its implementation. In addition, 'middle management executes the quality strategy through a variety of roles [and] inputs

from the work force' (Juran and Gryna 1993: 155). Quality teams create change; however, the implementation of the quality strategy occurs through the chain of command in the line organization instead of a staff quality department. Throughout this overall effort is an emphasis on company-wide quality control.

Juran's method for the management of quality consists of three processes. They are quality planning, quality control and quality improvement. These three processes, taken together are referred to as the Juran trilogy, and are shown in more detail below:

Steps in Juran's quality planning process

1. Determine quality goals.

2. Develop plans to meet these goals.

3. Identify the resources to meet these goals.

4. Translate the goals into quality.

5. Summarize 1 to 4 into a quality plan.
(Flood 1993: 18–19)

Steps in Juran's quality control process

1. Evaluate performance.

2. Compare performance with set goals.

3. Take action on the difference.
(Flood 1993: 19)

Steps in Juran's quality improvement process

1. Establish the infrastructure needed to secure annual quality improvement.

2. Identify the specific needs for improvement – the improvement *projects*.

3. For each project, establish a project team with clear responsibilities for bringing the project to a successful conclusion.

4. Provide the resources, motivation, and training needed by the teams to (a) diagnose the causes, (b) stimulate establishment of a remedy, and (c) establish controls to hold the gains.
(Cortada and Woods 1995: 195)

After the Second World War, when Juran decided to work on his own he intended to philosophize, research, write, lecture, and consult about management. Juran not only developed theory about quality management, but was also able to teach how to apply this theory.

Like others who made significant contributions to business and society, Juran is not without critics. The critics tend to dwell on issues one would expect to be directed towards someone born about ninety-five years ago; that is that he is old-fashioned, lacks an understanding of modern human relations, and does not understand bottom-up leadership and motivation. Robert Flood's remarks are typical; he considers that Juran's emphasis on management's responsibility 'fails to get to grips with the literature on motivation and leadership' (Flood 1993: 21). In addition, 'the contribution that the worker can make is undervalued, rejecting in principle bottom-up initiatives in the west' (Flood 1993: 22). In discussing the human dimensions further, Flood adds that Juran's methods 'in many ways are traditional and old fashioned' (Flood 1993: 22). Counter to the views of Flood, one could argue that Juran *does* recognize the human element. Indeed, according to Juran, 'An understanding of the human situations associated with the job will go far to solve the technical ones; in fact, such understanding may be a prerequisite of a solution' (Brelin *et al.* 1995: 183). Based on his work, Juran should also be credited with being a flexible and capable change agent. With regards to his outlook on adapting to change, Juran furnished his thoughts about being stuck in a traditional routine: 'by dozing on our habitual square we can lose touch with reality and the changing environment. Norms and standards are helpful, but inadequate if they fail to adapt or follow requirements' (Teboul 1991: 32). He added: 'Nothing can be justified by the mere fact of its existence' (Teboul 1991: 32).

It would be difficult to state where Juran made his most significant contribution. An observation by Warren Schmidt and Jerome

Finnigan credits Juran for his significant work with the Japanese, but in commenting on his work in the United States they add that 'his work was better received in Japan' (Schmidt and Finnigan 1993: 174). Schmidt and Finnigan are probably correct in terms of Juran's current notoriety, but one could also argue that the long-term effect of Juran's philosophy in the United States is more profound. In spite of the collapse of the fad connected with total quality management, Juran's ideas and approaches for quality management are still alive in some segments of business and industry. The Juran Institute is also keeping alive Juran's philosophy and the application of his ideas. He founded the Juran Institute in 1979 to pursue his quality management goals: 'The Institute offers consulting and management training in quality management' (Mitra 1993: 57). Located in Wilton, Connecticut, it 'offers a video-based training program which is a structured project-by-project process designed to produce an improvement in quality and reduction in quality-related costs' (Evans and Lindsay 1989: 454).

In 1987 Juran relinquished his leadership of the Juran Institute and is now chairman emeritus. After his last series of lectures in 1993–4, entitled 'The Last Word', he stopped all public appearances to devote time to writing and his family. Time will give the definitive assessment of Juran's long-term impact.

BIBLIOGRAPHY

Brelin, H.K., Davenport, K.S., Jennings, L.P. and Murphy, P.F. (1995) *Focused Quality: Managing for Results*, New York: John Wiley and Sons.

Brocka, B. and Brocka, M.S. (1992) *Quality Management: Implementing the Best Ideas of the Masters*, Homewood, IL: Business One Irwin.

Butman, J. and Roessner, J. (1995) 'Foreword', in J.M. Juran (ed.), *Managerial Breakthrough: The Classic Book on Improving Management Performance*, New York: McGraw-Hill.

Cortada, J.W. and Woods, J.A. (1995) *The McGraw-Hill Encyclopedia of Quality Terms and Concepts*, New York: McGraw-Hill.

—— (1998) *The Quality Yearbook*, New York: McGraw-Hill.

Evans, J.R. and Lindsay, W.M. (1989) *The Management and Control of Quality*, St Paul, MN: West Publishing Company.

Flood, R.L. (1993) *Beyond T.Q.M.*, New York: John Wiley and Sons.

Hunt, V.D. (1992) *Quality in America: How to Implement a Competitive Quality Program*, Homewood, IL: Business One Irwin.

Juran, J.M. (1988a) *Juran on Planning for Quality*, New York: The Free Press.

—— (1988b) *Juran's Quality Control Handbook*, 4th edn, New York: McGraw-Hill.

—— (1989) *Juran on Leadership for Quality: An Executive Handbook*, New York: The Free Press.

—— (1994) 'Quality Advisor: A Century of Quality', *Manufacturing Engineering* (September): 10–11.

Juran, J.M. and Gryna, F.M. (1993) *Quality Planning and Analysis*, New York: McGraw-Hill.

Mitra, A. (1993) *Fundamentals of Quality Control and Improvement*, New York: Macmillan.

Nonaka I. (1995) 'The Recent History of Managing for Quality in Japan', in J.M. Juran (ed.), *A History of Managing for Quality: The Evolution, Trends, and Future Directions of Managing for Quality*, Milwaukee, WI: ASQC Press, 517–52.

Petersen, P.B. (1987) 'The Contribution of W. Edwards Deming to Japanese Management Theory and Practice', *Academy of Management Best Paper Proceedings 1987* (11 August): 133–7.

Rao, A. *et al.* (1996) *Total Quality*

Management: A Cross-Functional Perspective, New York: John Wiley and Sons.

Sashkin, M. and Kiser, K.J. (1993) *Putting Total Quality Management to Work*, San Francisco: Berrett-Koehler.

Schmidt, W. and Finnigan, J.P. (1993) *TQ Manager: A Practical Guide for Managing in a Total Quality Organization*, San Francisco: Jossey-Bass.

Teboul, J. (1991) *Managing Quality Dynamics*, New York: Prentice Hall.

Wren, D.A. and Greenwood, R.G. (1998) *Management Innovators: The People and Ideas that have Shaped Modern Business*, New York: Oxford University Press.

PP